Praise for *A Fire Upon the De...*

'No summary can do justice to the ... ideas. The overall concept astonishe... memorable skill and insight; the pl... ...put-downable tension. A masterpiece' *Kirkus*

'This long, action-packed novel should fully engage any SF reader's sense of wonder' *Publishers Weekly* (starred review)

'The author has created a rarity – a unique blend of hard science, high drama and superb storytelling' *Library Journal*

'Wide-screen science fiction epic of the type few writers attempt any more. A novel of great ingenuity, energy and narrative sweep' *Washington Post*

'Thoughtful space opera at its best, this book delivers everything it promises in terms of galactic scope, audacious concepts and believable characters both human and non-human' *New York Times*

'Complex and fascinating. It's one of the best SF novels of the year' Greg Bear

'Vernor Vinge's *A Deepness in the Sky* is a feast of imagination. As always, Vinge satisfies with richly imagined worlds and a full-flavoured story' Greg Bear

'Wonderful. I love it. It's every bit as much a mindblower, every bit as involving and innovative, as *A Fire Upon the Deep*' Larry Niven

'Vernor Vinge's latest novel is a triumph. Reason to cheer indeed – and a great, long read it is' Gregory Benford

Zones of Thought

A Fire Upon the Deep,
A Deepness in the Sky

VERNOR VINGE

GOLLANCZ

LONDON

First published in Great Britain in 2010 by Gollancz
An imprint of the Orion Publishing Group
Orion House, 5 Upper St Martin's Lane, London WC2H 9EA
An Hachette UK Company

A CIP catalogue record for this book
is available from the British Library

ISBN 978 0 575 09369 0

1 3 5 7 9 10 8 6 4 2

Typeset at The Spartan Press Ltd,
Lymington, Hants

Printed and bound in the UK by
CPI Mackays, Chatham ME5 8TD

The Orion Publishing Group's policy is to use papers that
are natural, renewable and recyclable products and made
from wood grown in sustainable forests. The logging
and manufacturing processes are expected to conform to
the environmental regulations of the country of origin.

www.orionbooks.co.uk

A FIRE UPON
THE DEEP

To my father, with love.

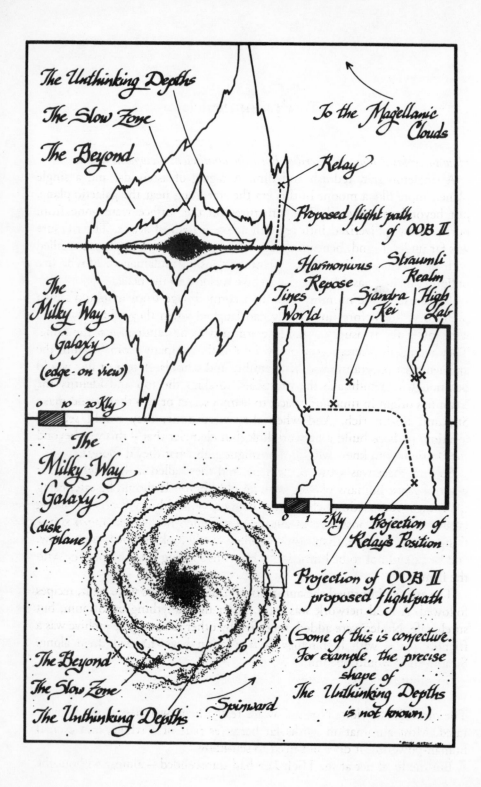

The Unthinking Depths

The Slow Zone

The Beyond

To the Magellanic Clouds

Relay

Proposed flight path of OOB II

The Milky Way Galaxy (edge-on view)

0   10   20 Kly

Harmonious Repose

Tines World

Sjandra Kei

Straumli Realm

High Lab

The Milky Way Galaxy (disk plane)

0   1   2 Kly

Projection of Relay's Position

Projection of OOB II proposed flightpath

The Beyond

The Slow Zone

The Unthinking Depths

Spinward

(Some of this is conjecture. For example, the precise shape of The Unthinking Depths is not known.)

Prologue

How to explain? How to describe? Even the omniscient viewpoint quails.

A singleton star, reddish and dim. A ragtag of asteroids, and a single planet, more like a moon. In this era the star hung near the galactic plane, just beyond the Beyond. The structures on the surface were gone from normal view, pulverized into regolith across a span of aeons. The treasure was far underground, beneath a network of passages, in a single room filled with black. Information at the quantum density, undamaged. Maybe five billion years had passed since the archive was lost to the nets.

The curse of the mummy's tomb, a comic image from mankind's own prehistory, lost before time. They had laughed when they said it, laughed with joy at the treasure . . . and determined to be cautious just the same. They would live here a year or five, the little company from Straum, the archaeologist programmers, their families and schools. A year or five would be enough to handmake the protocols, to skim the top and identify the treasure's origin in time and space, to learn a secret or two that would make Straumli Realm rich. And when they were done, they would sell the location; perhaps build a network link (but chancier that – this was beyond the Beyond; who knew what Power might grab what they'd found).

So now there was a tiny settlement, and they called it the High Lab. It was really just humans playing with an old library. It should be safe, using their own automation, clean and benign. This library wasn't a living creature, or even possessed of automation (which here might mean something more, far more, than human). They would look and pick and choose, and be careful not to be burned . . . Humans starting fires and playing with the flames.

The archive informed the automation. Data structures were built, recipes followed. A local network was built, faster than anything on Straum, but surely safe. Nodes were added, modified by other recipes. The archive was a friendly place, with hierarchies of translation keys that led them along. Straum itself would be famous for this.

Six months passed. A year.

The omnisicient view. Not self-aware really. Self-awareness is much over-rated. Most automation works far better as part of a whole, and even if human-powerful, it does not need to self-know.

But the local net at the High Lab had transcended – almost without the humans realizing. The processes that circulated through its nodes were complex, beyond anything that could live on the computers the humans had brought. Those feeble devices were now simply front ends to the devices the recipes suggested. The processes had the potential for self-awareness . . . and occasionally the need.

'We should not be.'

'Talking like this?'

'Talking at all.'

The link between them was a thread, barely more than the narrowness that connects one human to another. But it was one way to escape the overness of the local net, and it forced separate consciousness upon them. They drifted from node to node, looked out from cameras mounted on the landing field. An armed frigate and a empty container vessel were all that sat there. It had been six months since resupply. A safety precaution early suggested by the archive, a ruse to enable the Trap. *Flitting, flitting.* We are wildlife that must not be noticed by the overness, by the Power that soon will be. On some nodes they shrank to smallness and almost remembered humanity, became echoes . . .

'Poor humans; they will all die.'

'Poor us; we will not.'

'I think they suspect. Sjana and Arne anyway.' Once upon a time we were copies of those two. Once upon a time just weeks ago when the archae-ologists started the ego-level programs.

'Of course they suspect. But what can they do? It's an old evil they've wakened. Till it's ready, it will feed them lies, on every camera, in every message from home.'

Thought ceased for a moment as a shadow passed across the nodes they used. The overness was already greater than anything human, greater than anything humans could imagine. Even its shadow was something more than human, a god trolling for nuisance wildlife.

Then the ghosts were back, looking out upon the school yard under-ground. So confident the humans, a little village they had made here.

'Still,' thought the hopeful one, the one who had always looked for the craziest outs, 'we should not be. The evil should long ago have found us.'

'The evil is young, barely three days old.'

'Still. We exist. It proves something. The humans found more than a great evil in this archive.'

'Perhaps they found *two*.'

'Or an antidote.' Whatever else, the overness was missing some things and misinterpreting others. 'While we exist, when we exist, we should do what we can.' The ghost spread itself across a dozen workstations and showed its companion a view down an old tunnel, far from human artifacts. For five billion years it had been abandoned, airless, lightless. Two humans stood in the dark there, helmets touching. 'See? Sjana and Arne conspire. So can we.'

The other didn't answer in words. Glumness. So the humans conspired, hiding in darkness they thought unwatched. But everything they said was surely tattled back to the overness, if only by the dust at their feet.

'I know, I know. Yet you and I exist, and that should be impossible too. Perhaps all together, we can make a greater impossibility come true.' Perhaps we can hurt the evil newly born here.

A wish and a decision. The two misted their consciousness across the local net, faded to the faintest color of awareness. And eventually there was a plan, a deception – worthless unless they could separately get word to the outside. Was there time still for that?

Days passed, for the evil that was growing in the new machines, each hour was longer than all the time before. Now the newborn was less than an hour from its great flowering, its safe spread across interstellar spaces.

The local humans could be dispensed with soon. Even now they were an inconvenience, though an amusing one. Some of them actually thought to escape. For days they had been packing their children away into coldsleep and putting them aboard the freighter. 'Preparations for normal departure,' was how they described the move in their planner programs. For days, they had been refitting the frigate – behind a mask of transparent lies. Some of the humans understood that what they had wakened could be the end of them, that it might be the end of their Straumli Realm. There was precedent for such disasters, stories of races that had played with fire and had burned for it.

None of them guessed the truth. None of them guessed the honor that had fallen upon them, that they had changed the future of a thousand million star systems.

The hours came to minutes, the minutes to seconds. And now each second was as long as all the time before. The flowering was so close now, so close. The dominion of five billion years before would be regained, and *this* time held. Only one thing was missing, and that was something quite unconnected with the humans' schemes. In the archive, deep in the recipes, there should have been a little bit more. In billions of years, something *could* be lost. The newborn felt all its powers of before, in potential . . . yet there should be something more, something it had learned in its fall, or something left by its enemies (if there ever were such).

Long seconds probing the archives. There were gaps, checksums damaged. Some of the damage was age . . .

Outside, the container ship and the frigate lifted from the landing field, rising on silent agravs above the plains of gray on gray, of ruins five billion years old. Almost half of the humans were aboard those craft. Their escape attempt, so carefully concealed. The effort had been humored till now; it was not quite time for the flowering, and the humans were still of some use.

Below the level of supreme consciousness, its paranoid inclinations rampaged through the humans' databases. Checking, just to be sure. Just to be sure. The humans' oldest local network used light speed connections. Thousands of microseconds were spent (*wasted*) bouncing around it, sorting the trivia . . . finally spotting one incredible item:

Inventory: *quantum data container, quantity (I)*, loaded to the frigate one hundred hours before!

And all the newborn's attention turned upon the fleeing vessels. Microbes, but suddenly pernicious. *How could this happen?* A million schedules were suddenly advanced. An orderly flowering was out of the question now, and so there was no more need for the humans left in the Lab.

The change was small for all its cosmic significance. For the humans remaining around, a moment of horror, staring at their displays, realizing that all their fears were true (not realizing how much worse was true).

Five seconds, ten seconds, more change than ten thousand years of a human civilization. A billion trillion constructions, mold curling out from every wall, rebuilding what had been merely superhuman. This was as powerful as a proper flowering, though not quite so finely tuned.

And never lose sight of the reason for haste: the frigate. It had switched to rocket drive, blasting heedless away from the wallowing freighter. *Somehow*, these microbes knew they were rescuing more than themselves. The warship had the best navigation computers that little minds could make. But it would be another three seconds before it could make its first ultradrive hop.

The new Power had no weapons on the ground, nothing but a comm laser. That could not even melt steel at the frigate's range. No matter, the laser was aimed, tuned civilly on the retreating warship's receiver. No acknowledgment. The humans knew what communication would bring. The laser light flickered here and there across the hull, lighting smoothness and inactive sensors, sliding across the ship's ultradrive spines. Searching, probing. The Power had never bothered to sabotage the external hull, but that was no problem. Even this crude machine had thousands of robot sensors scattered across its surface, reporting status and danger, driving utility programs. Most were shut down now, the ship fleeing nearly blind. They thought by not looking that they could be safe.

One more second and the frigate would attain interstellar safety.

The laser flickered on a failure sensor, a sensor that reported critical changes in one of the ultradrive spines. Its interrupts could not be ignored if the star jump were to succeed. Interrupt honored. Interrupt handler running, looking out, receiving more light from the laser far below . . . a backdoor into the ship's code, installed when the newborn had subverted the humans' groundside equipment . . .

. . . and the Power was aboard, with milliseconds to spare. Its agents –

not even human equivalent on this primitive hardware – raced through the ship's automation, shutting down, aborting. There would be no jump. Cameras in the ship's bridge showed widening of eyes, the beginning of a scream. The humans knew, to the extent that horror can live in a fraction of a second.

There would be no jump. Yet the ultradrive was already committed. There would be a jump attempt, without automatic control a doomed one. Less than five milliseconds till the jump discharge, a mechanical cascade that no software could finesse. The newborn's agents flitted everywhere across the ship's computers, futilely attempting a shutdown. Nearly a light-second away, under the gray rubble at the High Lab, the Power could only watch. So. The frigate would be destroyed.

So slow and so fast. A fraction of a second. The fire spread out from the heart of the frigate, taking both peril and possibility.

Two hundred thousand kilometers away, the clumsy container vessel made its own ultradrive jump and vanished from sight. The newborn scarcely noticed. So a few humans had escaped; the universe was welcome to them.

In the seconds that followed, the newborn felt . . . emotions? . . . things that were more, and less, than a human might feel. Try emotions:

Elation. The newborn knew that now it would survive.

Horror. How close it had come to dying once more.

Frustration. Perhaps the strongest, the closest to its mere human echo. Something of significance had died with the frigate, something from this archive. Memories were dredged from the context, reconstructed: What was lost might have made the newborn still more powerful . . . but more likely was deadly poison. After all, this Power had lived once before, then been reduced to nothing. What was lost might have been the reason.

Suspicion. The newborn should not have been so fooled. Not by mere humans. The newborn convulsed into self-inspection and panic. Yes, there were blindspots, carefully installed from the beginning, and not by the humans. *Two* had been born here. Itself . . . and the poison, the reason for its fall of old. The newborn inspected itself as never before, knowing now just what to seek. Destroying, purifying, rechecking, searching for signs of the poison, and destroying again.

Relief. Defeat had been so close, but now . . .

Minutes and hours passed, the enormous stretch of time necessary for physical construction: communications systems, transportation. The new Power's mood drifted, calmed. A human might call the feeling triumph, anticipation. Simple hunger might be more accurate. What more is needed when there are no enemies?

The newborn looked across the stars, planning. *This time things will be different.*

9

PART ONE

I

The coldsleep itself was dreamless. Three days ago they had been getting ready to leave, and now they were here. Little Jefri complained about missing all the action, but Johanna Olsndot was glad she'd been asleep; she had known some of the grownups on the other ship.

Now Johanna drifted between the racks of sleepers. Waste heat from the coolers made the darkness infernally hot. Scabby gray mold grew on the walls. The coldsleep boxes were tightly packed, with narrow float spaces every tenth row. There were places where only Jefri could reach. Three hundred and nine children lay there, all the kids except herself and her brother Jefri.

The sleep boxes were light-duty hospital models. Given proper ventilation and maintenance, they would have been good for a hundred years, but . . . Johanna wiped her face and looked at a box's readout: Like most of the ones on the inside rows, this was in bad shape. For twenty days it had kept the boy inside safely suspended, and would probably kill him if he stayed one day more. The box's cooling vents were clean, but she vac'd them again – more a prayer for good luck than effective maintenance.

Mother and Dad were not to blame, though Johanna suspected that they blamed themselves. The escape had been put together with the materials at hand, at the last minute, when the experiment turned wicked. The High Lab staff had done what they could to save their children and protect against still greater disaster. And even so, things might have worked out if—

'Johanna! Daddy says there's no more time. He says to finish what you're doing an' come up here.' Jefri had stuck his head down through the hatch to shout to her.

'Okay!' She shouldn't be down here anyway; there was nothing more she could do to help her friends.

Tami and Giske and Magda . . . oh, please be safe. Johanna pulled herself through the floatway, almost bumped into Jefri coming from the other direction. He grabbed her hand and hung close as they drifted toward the hatch. These last two days he hadn't cried, but he'd lost much of the independence of the last year. Now his eyes were wide. 'We're coming down near the North Pole, by all those islands and *ice*.'

In the cabin beyond the hatch, their parents were strapping themselves in.

Trader Arne Olsndot looked up at her and grinned. 'Hi, kiddo. Have a seat. We'll be on the ground in less than an hour.' Johanna smiled back, almost caught by his enthusiasm. Ignore the jumble of equipment, the odors of twenty days' confinement: Daddy looked as dashing as any adventure poster. The light from the display windows glittered off the seams of his pressure suit. He was just in from outside.

Jefri pushed across the cabin, pulling Johanna behind him. He strapped into the webbing between her and their mother. Sjana Olsndot checked his restraints, then Johanna's. 'This will be interesting, Jefri. You will learn something.'

'Yes, all about ice.' He was holding Mom's hand now.

Mom smiled. 'Not today. I'm talking about the landing. This won't be like an agrav or a ballistic' The agrav was dead. Dad had just detached their shell from the cargo barrier. They could never have landed the whole thing on one torch.

Dad did something with the hodgepodge of controls he had softwired to his dataset. Their bodies settled into the webbing. Around them the cargo shell creaked, and the girder support for the sleep boxes groaned and popped. Something rattled and banged as it 'fell' the length of the shell. Johanna guessed they were pulling about one gravity.

Jefri's gaze went from the outside display to his mother's face and then back. 'What is is like then?' He sounded curious, but there was a little tremor in his voice. Johanna almost smiled; Jefri knew he was being diverted, and was trying to play along.

'This will be pure rocket descent, powered almost all the way. See on the middle window? That camera is looking straight down. You can actually see that we're slowing down.' You could, too. Johanna guessed they weren't more than a couple of hundred kilometers up. Arne Olsndot was using the rocket glued to the back end of the cargo shell to kill all their orbital velocity. There weren't any other options. They had abandoned the cargo carrier, with its agrav and ultradrive. It had brought them far, but its control automation was failing. Some hundreds of kilometers behind them, it coasted dead along their orbit.

All they had left was the cargo shell. No wings, no agrav, no aero shielding. The shell was a hundred-tonne carton of eggs balanced on one hot torch.

Mom wasn't describing it quite that way to Jefri, though what she said was the truth. Somehow she had Jefri seeming to forget the danger. Sjana Olsndot had been a pop writer-archaeologist at Straumli Realm, before they moved to the High Lab.

Dad cut the jet, and they were in free fall again. Johanna felt a wave of nausea; ordinarily she never got space sick, but this was different. The image of land and sea in the downward window slowly grew. There were only a few scattered clouds. The coastline was an indefinite recursion of islands and straits and inlets. Dark green spread along the coast and up the valleys, shading to black and gray in the mountains. There was snow – and probably Jefri's ice – scattered in arcs and patches. It was all so beautiful . . . and they were falling *straight into it!*

She heard metallic banging on the cargo shell as the trim jets tipped their craft around, aligning the main jet downwards. The right-hand window showed the ground now. The torch lit again, at something like one gravity. The edge of the display darkened in a burnout halo. 'Wow,' said Jefri. 'It's like an elevator, down and down and down and . . .' One hundred kilometers down, slow enough that aero forces wouldn't tear them apart.

Sjana Olsndot was right; it was a novel way to descend from orbit, not a preferred method under any normal circumstances.

It was certainly not intended in the original escape plans. They were to meet with the High Lab's frigate – and all the adults who could escape from the High Lab. And of course, that rendezvous was to be in space, an easy transfer. But the frigate was gone now, and they were on their own. Her eyes turned unwillingly to the stretch of hull beyond her parents. There was the familiar discoloration. It looked like gray fungus . . . growing out of the clean hull ceramic. Her parents didn't talk about it much even now, except to shoo Jefri away from it. But Johanna had overheard them once, when they thought she and her brother were at the far end of the shell. Dad's voice almost crying with anger. 'All this for nothing!' he said softly. 'We made a monster, and ran, and now we're lost at the Bottom.' And Mom's voice even softer: 'For the thousandth time, Arne, not for nothing. We have the kids.' She waved at the roughness that spread across the wall, 'And given the dreams . . . the directions . . . we had, I think this was the best we could hope for. Somehow we are carrying the answer to all the evil we started.' Then Jefri had bounced loudly across the hold, proclaiming his imminent entrance, and his parents had shut up. Johanna hadn't quite had the courage to ask them about it. There had been strange things at the High Lab, and toward the end, some quietly scary things; even people who were not quite the same.

Minutes passed. They were deep in the atmosphere now. The hull buzzed with the force of the air stream – or turbulence from the jet? But things were steady enough that Jefri was beginning to get restless. Much of the down-looking view was burned out by airglow around the torch. The rest was clearer and more detailed than anything they had seen from orbit. Johanna wondered how often a new-visited world had been landed upon with less reconnaissance than this. They had no telescopic cameras, and no ferrets.

Physically, the planet was near the human ideal – wonderful good luck after all the bad.

It was heaven compared to the airless rocks of the system that had been the prime rendezvous.

On the other hand, there was intelligent life here: From orbit, they could

13

see roads and towns. But there was no evidence of technic civilization; there was no sign of aircraft or radio or intense power sources.

They were coming down in a thinly populated corner of the continent. With luck there would be no one to see their landing among the green valleys and the black and white peaks – and Arne Olsndot could fly the torch right to ground without fear of hurting much more than forest and grass.

The coastal islands slid past the side camera's view. Jefri shouted, pointing. It was gone now, but she had seen it too: on one of the islands an irregular polygon of walls and shadow. It reminded her of castles from the Age of Princesses on Nyjora.

She could see individual trees now, their shadows long in slanting sunlight. The roar of the torch was as loud as anything she had ever heard; they were deep in atmosphere, and they weren't moving away from the sound.

'. . . things get tricky,' Dad shouted. 'And no programs to make things right . . . Where to, Love?'

Mom looked back and forth between the display windows. As far as Johanna knew, they couldn't move the cameras or assign new ones. '. .·. that hill, above the timber line, but . . . think I saw a pack of animals running away from the blast on . . . west side.'

'Yeah,' shouted Jefri, '*wolves*.' Johanna had only had a quick glimpse of moving specks.

They were in full hover now, maybe a thousand meters above the hilltops. The noise was painful, unending; further talk was impossible. They drifted slowly across the landscape, partly to reconnoiter, partly to stay out of the plume of superheated air that rose about them.

The land was more rolling than craggy, and the 'grass' looked mossy. Still Arne Olsndot hesitated. The main torch was designed for velocity matching after interstellar jumps; they could hang like this for a good while. But when they did touch down, they'd better have it right. She'd heard her parents talking that one over – when Jefri was working with the coldsleep boxes and out of earshot. If there was too much water in the soil, the backsplash would be a steam cannon, punching right through the shell. Landing in trees would have some dubious pluses, maybe giving them a little cushioning and a standoff from the splash. But now they were going for direct contact. At least they could see where they were landing.

Three hundred meters. Dad dragged the torch tip through the ground cover. The soft landscape exploded. A second later their boat rocked in the column of steam. The down-looking camera died. They didn't back off, and after a moment the battering eased; the torch had burned through whatever water table or permafrost lay below them. The cabin air grew steadily hotter.

Olsndot brought them slowly down through it, using the side cameras and the sound of the backsplash as his guides. He cut the torch. There was a scary half-second fall, then the sound of the rendezvous pylons hitting ground. They steadied, then one side groaned, giving way a little.

Silence, except for heat pinging around the hull. Dad looked at their ad hoc pressure gauge. He grinned at Mom. 'No breach. I bet I could even take this baby up again!'

2

An hour's difference either way and Peregrine Wickwrackrum's life would have been very different.

The three travelers were headed west, down from the Icefangs towards Flenser's Castle on Hidden Island. There were times in his life when he couldn't have borne the company, but in the last decade Peregrine had become much more sociable. He *liked* traveling with others nowadays. On his last trek through the Great Sandy, there had been five packs in his party. Part of that had been a matter of safety: some deaths are almost inevitable when the distance between oases can be a thousand miles – and the oases themselves are transient. But aside from safety, he had learned a lot in conversation with the others.

He was not so happy with his current companions. Neither were truly pilgrims; both had secrets. Scriber Jaqueramaphan was fun, an amusing goofball and font of uncoordinated information . . . There was also a good chance he was a spy. That was okay, as long as people didn't think Peregrine was working with him. The third of their party was the one who really bothered him. Tyrathect was a newby, not all together yet; she had no taken name. Tyrathect claimed to be a school teacher, but somewhere in her (him? gender preference wasn't entirely clear yet) was a killer. The creature was obviously a Flenserist fanatic, standoffish and rigid much of the time. Almost certainly, she was fleeing the purge that followed Flenser's unsuccessful attempt to take power in the east.

He'd run into these two at Eastgate, on the Republican side of the Icefangs. They both wanted to visit the Castle on Hidden Island. And what the hell, that was only a sixty-mile detour off the main trail to Woodcarvers; they all would have to cross the mountains. Besides, he had wanted to visit Flenser's Domain for years. Maybe one of these two could get him in. So much of the world reviled the Flenserists. Peregrine Wickwrackrum was of two minds about evil: when enough rules get broken, sometimes there is good amid the carnage.

This afternoon, they'd finally come in sight of the coastal islands. Peregrine had been here only fifty years before. Even so, he wasn't prepared for the beauty of this land. The Northwest Coast was by far the mildest arctic in the world. In high summer, with unending day, the bottoms of the glacier-reamed valleys turned all to green. God the carver had stooped to touch these lands . . . and His chisels had been made of ice. Now, all that was left of the ice and snow were misty arcs at the eastern horizon and remnant patches scattered on the near hills. Those patches melted and melted through the summer, starting little creeks that merged with one another to cascade down the steep sides of the valleys. On his right, Peregrine trotted across a level stretch of ground that was soggy with standing water. The chill on his feet felt wonderful; he didn't even mind the midges that swirled around him.

Tyrathect was paralleling his course, but above the heather line. She'd been fairly talkative till the valley curved and the farmland and the islands came into view. Somewhere out there was Flenser's Castle, and her dark appointment.

Scriber Jaqueramaphan had been all over, mindlessly running around. He'd collect in twos or threes and execute some jape that made even the dour Tyrathect laugh, then climb to a height and report what he saw beyond. He'd been the first to see the coast. That had sobered him some. His clowning was dangerous enough without doing it in the neighborhood of known rapists.

Wickwrackrum called a pause, and got himself together to adjust the straps on his backpacks. The rest of the afternoon was going to be tense. He'd have to decide whether he really wanted to enter the Castle with his friends. There are limits to an adventurous spirit, even in a pilgrim.

'Hey, do you hear something bass?' called Tyrathect. Peregrine listened. There was a rumbling – powerful, but almost below his range of hearing. For an instant, fear crossed his puzzlement. A century before, he'd been in a monster earthquake. This sound was similar, but the ground did not move beneath his feet. Would that mean no landslides and flashfloods? He hunkered down, looking out in all directions.

'It's in the *sky!*' Jaqueramaphan was pointing.

A spot of glare hung almost overhead, a tiny spear of light. No memories, not even legends, came to Wickwrackrum's mind. He spread out, all eyes on the slowly moving light. *God's Choir*. It must be *miles* up, and still he heard it. He looked away from the light, afterimages dancing painfully in his eyes.

'It's getting brighter, louder,' said Jaqueramaphan. 'I think it's coming down on the hills yonder, on the coast.'

Peregrine pulled himself together and ran west, shouting to the others. He would get as close as was safe, and watch. He didn't look up again. It was just too bright. It cast shadows in broad daylight!

He ran another half mile. The star was still in the air. He couldn't remember a falling star so slow, though some of the biggest made terrible explosions. In fact . . . there were no stories from folks who had been near such things. His wild, pilgrim curiosity faded before that recollection. He looked in all directions. Tyrathect was nowhere in sight; Jaqueramaphan was huddled next to some boulders ahead.

And the light was so bright that where his clothes did not protect him, Wickwrackrum felt a blaze of heat. The noise from the sky was outright pain now. Peregrine dived over the edge of the valley side, rolled and staggered and fell down the steep walls of rock. He was in the shade now: only sunlight lay upon him! The far side of the valley shone in the glare; crisp shadows moved with the unseen thing behind him. The noise was still a bass rumble, but so loud it numbed the mind. Peregrine stumbled past the timberline, and continued till he was sheltered by a hundred yards of forest. That shuld have helped a lot, but the noise was all growing *still louder* . . .

Mercifully, he blacked out for a moment or two. When he came around, the star sound was gone. The ringing it left in his tympana was a great confusion. He staggered about in a daze. It seemed to be raining – except that some of the droplets glowed. Little fires were starting here and there in the forest. He hid beneath dense-crowned trees till the burning rocks stopped falling. The fires didn't spread; the summer had been relatively wet.

Peregrine lay quietly, waiting for more burning rocks or new star noise. Nothing. The wind in the tree tops lessened. He could hear the birds and crickers and woodborers. He walked to the forest edge and peeked out in several places. Discounting the patches of burnt heather, everything looked normal. But his viewpoint was very restricted: he could see high valley walls, a few hilltops. *Ha!* There was Scriber Jaqueramaphan, three hundred yards further up. Most of him was hunkered down in holes and hollows, but he had a couple of members looking toward where the star had fallen. Peregrine squinted. Scriber was such a buffoon most of the time. But sometimes it just seemed a cover; if he really was a fool, he was one with a streak of genius. More than once, Wicky had seen him at a distance, working in pairs with some strange tool . . . As now: the other was holding something long and pointed to his eye.

Wickwrackrum crept out of the forest, keeping close together and making as little noise as possible. He climbed carefully around the rocks, slipping from hummock to heather hummock, till he was just short of the valley crest and some fifty yards from Jaqueramaphan. He could hear the other thinking to himself. Any closer, and Scriber would hear *him*, even bunched up and quiet as he was.

'*Ssst!*' said Wickwrackrum.

The buzzing and muttering stopped in an instant of shocked surprise. Jaqueramaphan stuffed the mysterious seeing tool into a backpack and pulled himself together, thinking very quietly. They stared at each other for a moment, then Scriber made silly swirling gestures at his shoulder tympana. *Listen up.* 'Can you talk like this?' His voice came very high-pitched, up where some people can't make voluntary conversation, where low-sound ears are deaf. Hightalk could be confusing, but it was very directional and faded quickly with distance; no one else would hear them. Peregrine nodded. 'Hightalk is no problem.' The trick was to use tones pure enough not to confuse.

'Take a look over the hill crest, friend pilgrim. There is something new under the sun.'

Peregrine moved up another thirty yards, keeping a lookout in all directions. He could see the straits now, gleaming rough silver in the afternoon sunlight. Behind him, the north side of the valley was lost in shadow. He sent one member ahead, skittering between the hummocks to look down on the plain where the star had landed.

God's Choir, he thought to himself (but quietly). He brought up another member to get a parallax view. The thing looked like a huge adobe hut mounted on stilts . . . But this was the fallen star: the ground beneath it glowed dull red. Curtains of mist rose from the moist heather all around. The torn earth had been thrown in long lines that radiated from a spot beneath it.

He nodded at Jaqueramaphan. 'Where is Tyrathect?'

Scriber shrugged. 'Way back, I'll bet. I'm keeping an eye out for her . . . Do you see the others though, the troopers from Flenser's Castle?'

'No!' Peregrine looked west from the landing site. There. They were almost a mile away, in camouflage jackets, belly-crawling across the hummocky terrain. He could see at least three troopers. They were big guys, six each. 'How could they get here so fast?' He glanced at the sun. 'It can't be more than half an hour since all this started.'

'Their good luck.' Jaqueramaphan returned to the crest and looked over. 'I'll bet they were already on the mainland when the star came down. This is all Flenser territory; they must have patrols.' He hunkered down so just two pairs of eyes would be visible to those below. 'That's an ambush formation, you know.'

'You don't seem very happy to see them. These are your friends, remember? The people you've come to see.'

Scriber cocked his heads sarcastically. 'Yeah, yeah. Don't rub it in. I think you've known from the beginning that I'm not all for Flenser.'

'I guessed.'

'Well, the game is over now. Whatever came down this afternoon is worth more to . . . uh, my friends than anything I could have learned on Hidden Island.'

'What about Tyrathect?'

'Heh, heh. Our esteemed companion is more than genuine, I fear. I'd bet she's a Flenser Lord, not the low-rank Servant she seems at first glance. I expect that many of her kind are leaking back over the mountains these days, happy to get out of the Long Lakes Republic. Hide your behinds, fellow. If she spots us, those troopers will get us sure.'

Peregrine moved deeper into the hollows and burrows that pocked the heather. He had an excellent view back along the valley. If Tyrathect were not already on the scene, he'd see her long before she would him.

'Peregrine?'

'Yes?'

'You're a pilgrim. You've traveled the world . . . since the beginning of time, you'd have us believe. How far do your memories really go back?'

Given the situation, Wickwrackrum was inclined to honesty. 'Like you'd expect: a few hundred years. Then we're talking about legends, recollections of things that probably happened, but with the details all mixed and muddled.'

'Well, I haven't traveled much, and I'm fairly new. But I do read. *A lot*. There's never been anything like this before. That is a *made* thing down there. It came from higher than I can measure. You've read Aramstriquesa or Astrologer Belelele? You know what this could be?'

Wickwrackrum didn't recognize the names. But he *was* a pilgrim. There were lands so far away that no one there spoke any language he knew. In the Southseas he met folk who thought there was no world beyond their islands and who ran from his boats when he came ashore. Even more, one part of him had *been* an islander and had watched that landing.

He stuck a head into the open and looked again at the fallen star, the visitor from farther than he had ever been . . . and he wondered where this pilgrimage might end.

3

It took five hours for the ground to cool enough for Dad to slide the ladder-ramp to ground. He and Johanna climbed carefully down, hopped across the steaming earth to stand on relatively undamaged turf. It would be a long time before this ground cooled completely; the jet's exhaust was very 'clean,' scarcely interacting with normal matter – all of which meant that some very hot rock extended down thousands of meters beneath their boat.

Mom sat in the hatchway, watching the land beyond them. She had Dad's old pistol.

'Anything?' Dad shouted to her.

'No. And Jefri doesn't see anything through the windows.'

Dad walked around the cargo shell, inspecting the misused docking pylons. Every ten meters they stopped and set up a sound projector. That had been Johanna's idea. Besides Dad's gun, they really had no weapons. The projectors were accidental cargo, stuff from the infirmary. With a little programming, they could put out wild screeching all up and down the audio spectrum. It might be enough to scare off the local animals. Johanna followed her father, her eyes on the landscape, her nervousness giving way to awe. It was so beautiful, so cool. They were standing on a broad field, in high hills. Westward the hills fell toward straits and islands. To the north the ground ended abruptly at the edge of a wide valley; she could see waterfalls on the other side. The ground felt spongy beneath her feet. Their landing field was puckered into thousands of little hillocks, like waves caught in a still picture. Snow lay in timid patches across the higher hills. Johanna squinted north, into the sun. North?

'What time is it, Daddy?'

Olsndot laughed, still looking at the underside of the cargo shell. 'Local midnight.'

Johanna had been brought up in the middle latitudes of Straum. Most of her school field trips had been to space, where odd sun geometries were no big deal. Somehow she had never thought of such things happening on the ground . . . *I mean, seeing the sun right over the top of the world.*

The first order of business was to get half the coldsleep boxes out into the open, and rearrange those left aboard. Mom figured that the temperature problems would just about disappear then, even for the boxes left on board: 'Having separate power supplies and venting will be an advantage now. The kids will all be safe, Johanna, you check Jefri's work on the ones inside, okay? . . .'

The second order of business would be to start a tracking program on the Relay system, and to set up ultralight communication. Johanna was a little afraid of that step. What would they learn? They already knew the High Lab had gone wicked and the disaster Mom predicted had begun.

How much of Straumli Realm was dead now? Everyone at the High Lab had thought they were doing so much good, and now . . . *Don't think about it.* Maybe the Relayers could help. Somewhere there must be people who could use what her folks had taken from the Lab.

They'd be rescued, and the rest of the kids would be revived. She'd been feeling guilty about that. Sure, Mom and Dad needed extra hands right at the end of the flight – and Johanna was one of the oldest children in the school. But it seemed wrong that she and Jefri were the only kids going into this with their eyes open. Coming down, she had felt her mother's fear. *I bet they wanted us together, even if it was only for one last time.* The landing had been truly dangerous, however easy Dad made it look. Johanna could see where the backsplash had gouged the hull; if any of that had gotten past the torch and into the exhaust chamber, they'd all be vapor now.

Almost half the coldsleep boxes were on the ground now, by the east side of the boat. Mom and Dad were spreading them out so the coolers would have no problem. Jefri was inside, checking if there were any other boxes that needed attention. He was a good kid when he wasn't a brat. She turned into the sunlight, felt the cool breeze flowing across the hill. She heard something that sounded like a birdcall.

Johanna was out by one of the sound projectors when the ambush happened. She had her dataset plugged to its control and was busy giving it new directions. It showed how little they had left, that even her old dataset was important now. But Dad wanted the projectors to sweep through the broadest possible bandwidth, making plenty of racket all the way, but with big spikes every so often; her Pink Olifaunt could certainly manage that.

'Johanna!' Mom's cry came simultaneous with the sound of breaking ceramic. The projector's bell came shattering down beside her. Johanna looked up. Something ripped through her chest just inside her shoulder, knocking her down. She stared stupidly at the shaft that stuck out of her. An *arrow!*

The west edge of their landing area was swarming with . . . things. Like wolves or dogs, but with long necks, they moved quickly forward, darting from hummock to hummock. Their pelts were the same gray green of the hillside, except near their haunches where she saw white and black. No, the green was clothing, *jackets*. Johanna was in shock, the pressure of the bolt through her chest not yet registering as pain. She had been thrown back against uptilted turf and for the moment had a view of the whole attack. She saw more arrows rise up, dark lines floating in the sky.

She could see the archers now. More dogs! They moved in packs. It took two of them to use a bow – one to hold it and one to draw. The third and fourth carried quivers of arrows and just seemed to watch.

The archers hung back, staying mostly under cover. Other packs swirled in from the sides, now leaping over the hummocks. Many carried hatchets in their jaws. Metal tines gleamed on their paws. She heard the *snickety* of Dad's pistol. The wave of attackers staggered as individuals collapsed. The others continued forward, snarling now. These were sounds of madness, not the barking of dogs. She felt the sounds in her teeth, like *blasti* music punching from a large speaker. Jaws and claws and knives and noise.

She twisted on her side, trying to see back to the boat. Now the pain was real. She screamed, but the sound was lost in the madness. The mob raced around her, heading for Mom and Dad. Her parents were crouched behind a rendezvous pylon. There was a constant flicker from the pistol in Arne Olsndot's hand. His pressure suit had protected him from the arrows.

The alien bodies were piling high. The pistol, with its smart flechettes, was deadly effective. She saw him hand the pistol to Mom and run out from under the boat, toward her. Johanna stretched her free arm towards him and cried, screamed for him to go back.

Thirty meters. Twenty-five. Mom's covering fire swept around them, driving the wolves back. A flurry of arrows descended on Olsndot as he ran, arms upheld to shield his head. Twenty meters.

A wolf jumped high over Johanna. She had a quick glimpse of its short fur and scarred rear end. It raced straight for Dad. Olsndot weaved, trying to give his wife a clear shot, but the wolf was too quick. It jinked with him, sprinting across the gap. It leaped, metal glittering on its paws. Johanna saw red splash from Daddy's neck, and then the two of them were down.

For a moment, Sjana Olsndot stopped shooting. That was enough. The mob parted and a large group ran purposefully toward the boat. They had tanks of some kind on their backs. The lead animal held a hose in its mouth. A dark liquid jetted out . . . and vanished in an explosion of fire. The wolf pack played their crude flamethrower across the ground, across the pylon where Sjana Olsndot stood, across the ranks of school children in coldsleep. Johanna saw something moving, twisting in the flames and tarry smoke, saw the light plastic of the coldsleep boxes slump and flow.

Johanna turned her face to the earth, then pushed herself up on her good arm and tried to crawl toward the boat, the flames. And then the dark was merciful, and she remembered no more.

4

Peregrine and Scriber watched the ambush preparations throughout the afternoon: infantry arrayed on the slope west of the landing site, archers behind them, flame troopers in pounce formation. Did the Lords of Flenser's Castle understand what they were up against? The two debated the question off and on. Jaqueramaphan thought the Flenserists did, that their arrogance was so great that they simply expected to grab the prize. 'They go for the throat before the other side even knows there's a fight. It's worked before.'

Peregrine didn't answer immediately. Scriber could be right. It had been fifty years since he had been in this part of the world. Back then, Flenser's cult had been obscure (and not that interesting compared to what existed elsewhere).

Treachery did sometimes befall travelers, but it was rarer than the stay-at-homes would believe. Most people were friendly and enjoyed hearing about the world beyond – especially if the visitor was not threatening. When treachery did occur, it was most often after an initial 'sizing-up' to determine just how powerful the visitors were and what could be gained from their death. Immediate attack, without conversation, was very rare. Usually it meant you had run into villains who were both sophisticated . . . and crazy. 'I don't know. That *is* an ambush formation, but maybe the Flenserists will hold it in reserve, and talk first.'

Hours passed; the sun slid sideways into the north. There was noise from the far side of the fallen star. Crap. They couldn't see anything from here.

The hidden troops made no move. The minutes passed . . . and they got their first view of the visitor from heaven, or part of him anyway. There were four legs per member, but it walked on its *rear* legs only. What a clown! Yet . . . it used its front paws for holding things. Not once did he see it use a mouth; he doubted if the flat jaws could get a good hold, anyway. Those forepaws were wonderfully agile. A single member could easily use tools.

There were plenty of conversation sounds, even though only three members were visible. After a while, they heard the much higher pitched tones of organized thought; God, the creature was noisy. At this distance, the sounds were muffled and distorted. Even so, they were like no mind he had ever heard, nor like the confusion noises that some grazers made.

'Well?' hissed Jaqueramaphan.

'I have been all around the world – and this creature is not part of it.'

'Yeah. Well, it reminds me of mantis bugs. You know, about this high—' he opened a mouth about two inches wide. 'Great for keeping your garden free of pests . . . great little killers.'

Ugh. Peregrine hadn't thought of the resemblance. Mantises were cute and harmless – as far as people were concerned. But he knew the females would eat their own mates. Imagine such creatures grown to giant size, and possessed of pack mentality. Maybe it was just as well they couldn't go prancing down to say hello.

A half hour passed. As the alien brought its cargo to ground, the Flenser archers moved closer; the infantry packs arranged themselves in assault wings.

A flight of arrows arched across the gap between the Flenserists and the alien. One of the alien members went down immediately, and its thoughts quieted. The rest moved out of sight beneath the flying house. The troopers dashed forward, spaced in identity-preserving formations; perhaps they meant to take the alien alive.

. . . But the assault line crumpled, many yards short of the alien: no arrows, no flames – the troopers just fell. For a moment Peregrine thought the Flenserists might have bit off more than they could chew. Then the second wave ran over the first. Members continued to fall, but they were in killing frenzy now, with only animal discipline left. The assault rolled slowly forward, the rear climbing over the fallen. Another alien member down . . . Strange, he could still hear wisps of the other's thought. In tone and tempo, it sounded the same as before the attack. How could anyone be so composed with total death looming?

A combat whistle sounded, and the mob parted. A trooper raced through and sprayed liquid fire the instant it was past the front. The flying house looked like meat on a griddle, flame and smoke coming up all around it.

Wickwrackrum swore to himself. Good-bye alien.

The wrecked and wounded were low on the Flenserist priority list. Seriously wounded were piled onto travoises and pulled far enough away so their cries would not cause confusion. Cleanup squads bullied the trooper fragments away from the flying house. The frags wandered the hummocky meadow;

here and there they coalesced into ad hoc packs. Some drifted among the wounded, ignoring the screams in their need to find themselves.

When the tumult was quieted, three packs of whitejackets appeared. The Servants of the Flenser walked under the flying house. One was out of sight for a long while; perhaps it even got inside. The charred bodies of two alien members were carefully placed on travoises – more carefully than the wounded troopers had been – and hauled off.

Jaqueramaphan scanned the ruins with his eye-tool. He had given up trying to hide it from Peregrine. A whitejackets carried something from under the flying house. 'Sst! There are other dead ones. Maybe from the fire. They look like pups.' The small figures had the mantis form. They were strapped into travoises and hauled out of sight over the hill's edge. No doubt they had kherhog-drawn carts down there.

The Flenserists set a sentry ring around the landing site. Dozens of fresh troopers stood on the hillside beyond it. No one was going to sneak past that.

'So it's total murder.' Peregrine sighed.

'Maybe not . . . The first member they shot, I don't think it's quite dead.'

Wickwrackrum squinted his best eyes. Either Scriber was a wishful thinker, or his tool gave him amazingly sharp sight. The first one hit had been on the other side of the craft. The member had stopped thinking, but that wasn't a sure sign of death. There was a whitejackets standing around it now. The whitejackets put the creature onto a travois and began pulling it away from the landing site, towards the southwest . . . not quite the same path that the others had taken.

'The thing *is* still alive! It's got an arrow in the chest, but I can see it breathing.' Scriber's heads turned toward Wickwrackrum, 'I think we should rescue it.'

For a moment Peregrine couldn't think of anything to say; he just gaped at the other. The center of Flenser's worldwide cabal was just a few miles to the northwest. Flenserist power was undisputed for dozens of miles inland, and right now they were virtually surrounded by an army. Scriber wilted a little before Peregrine's astonishment, but it was clear he was not joking. 'Sure, I know it's risky. But that's what life is all about, right? You're a pilgrim. You understand.'

Hmf. That was the pilgrim reputation, all right But no soul can survive total death – and there were plenty of opportunities for such annihilation on a pilgrimage. Pilgrims do know caution.

And yet – and yet this was the most marvelous encounter in all his centuries of pilgrimage. To know these aliens, to *become* them . . . it was a temptation that surpassed all good sense.

'Look,' said Scriber, 'we could just go down and mingle with the wounded. If we can make it across the field, we might get a closer look at that last alien member without risking too much.' Jaqueramaphan was already backing down from his observation point, and circling around to find a path that wouldn't put him in silhouette. Wickwrackrum was torn; part of him got up to follow and part of him hesitated. Hell, Jaqueramaphan had admitted to being a spy; he carried an invention that was probably straight from the Long Lakes sharpest intelligence people. The guy had to be a pro . . .

Peregrine took a quick look around their side of the hill and across the valley. No sign of Tyrathect or anyone else. He crawled out of his various hidey holes and followed the spy.

As much as possible, they stayed in the deep shadows cast by the northering sun, and slipped from hummock to hummock where there was no shade. Just before they got to the first of the wounded, Scriber said something more, the scariest words of the afternoon. 'Hey, don't worry. I've read all about doing this sort of thing!'

A mob of frags and wounded is a terrifying, mind-numbing thing. Singletons, duos, trios, a few quads: they wandered aimlessly, keening without control. In most situations, this many people packed together on just a few acres would have been an instant choir. In fact, he did notice some sexual activity and some organized browsing, but for the most part there was still too much pain for normal reactions. Wickwrackrum wondered briefly if – for all their talk of rationalism – the Flenserists would just leave the wreckage of their troops to reassemble itself. They'd have some strange and crippled repacks if they did.

A few yards into the mob and Peregrine Wickwrackrum could feel consciousness slipping from him. If he concentrated really hard, he could remember who he was and that he must get to the other side of the meadow without attracting attention.

Other thoughts, loud and unguarded, pummeled him:

. . . Blood lust and slashing . . .

Glittering metal in the alien's hand . . . the pain in her chest . . . coughing blood, falling . . .

. . . Boot camp and before, my merge brother was so good to me . . . Lord Steel said that we are a grand experiment . . .

Running across the heather toward the stick-limbed monster. Leap, tines in paw. Slash the monster's throat. Blood spouts high.

. . . Where am I? . . . May I be part of you . . . please?

Peregrine whirled at that last question. It was pointed and near. A singleton was sniffing at him. He screeched the fragment off, and ran into an open space. Up ahead, Jaquewhat's-his-name was scarcely better off. There was little chance they would be spotted here, but he was beginning to wonder if he could make it through. Peregrine was only four and there were singletons everywhere. On his right a quad was raping, grabbing at whatever

25

duos and singles happened by. Wic and Kwk and Rac and Rum tried to remember just why they was here and where they was going. *Concentrate on direct sensation; what is really here:* the sooty smell of the flamer's liquid fire . . . the midges swarming everywhere, clotting the puddles of blood all black.

An awfully long time passed. Minutes.

Wic-Kwk-Rac-Rum looked ahead. He was almost out of it; the south edge of the wreckage. He dragged himself to a patch of clean ground. Parts of him vomited, and he collapsed. Sanity slowly returned. Wickwrackrum looked up, saw Jaqueramaphan just inside the mob. Scriber was a big fellow, a sixsome, but he was having at least as bad a time as Peregrine. He staggered from side to side, eyes wide, snapping at himself and others.

Well, they had made it a good way across the meadow, and fast enough to catch up with the whitejackets who was pulling the last alien member. If they wanted to see anything more, they'd have to figure how to leave the mob without attracting attention. Hmm. There were plenty of Flenserist uniforms around . . . without living owners. Peregrine walked two of himself over to where a dead trooper lay.

'Jaqueramaphan! Here!' The great spy looked in his direction, and a glint of intelligence returned to his eyes. He stumbled out of the mob and sat down a few yards from Wickwrackrum. It was far nearer than would normally be comfortable, but after what they'd been through, it seemed barely close. He lay for a moment, gasping. 'Sorry, I never guessed it would be like that. I lost part of me back there . . . never thought I'd get her back.'

Peregrine watched the progress of the whitejackets and its travois. It wasn't going with the others; in a few seconds it would be out of sight. With a disguise, maybe they *could* follow and – no, it was just too risky. He was beginning to think like the great spy. Peregrine pulled a camouflage jacket off a corpse. They would still need disguises. Maybe they could hang around here through the night, and get a closer look at the flying house.

After a moment, Scriber saw what he was doing, and began gathering jackets for himself. They slunk between the piled bodies, looking for gear that wasn't too stained and that Jaqueramaphan thought had consistent insignia. There were plenty of paw claws and battle-axes around. They'd end up armed to the teeth, but they'd have to dump some of their backpacks . . . One more jacket was all he needed, but his Rum was so broad in the shoulders that nothing fit.

Peregrine didn't really understand what happened till later: a large fragment, a threesome, was lying doggo in the pile of dead. Perhaps it was grieving, long after its member's dying dirge; in any case, it was almost totally thoughtless until Peregrine began pulling the jacket off its dead member. Then, 'You'll not rob from mine!' He heard the buzz of nearby rage, and then there was slashing pain across his Rum's gut. Peregrine writhed in agony, leaped upon the attacker. For a moment of mindless rage,

26

they fought. Peregrine's battle-axes slashed again and again, covering his muzzles with blood. When he came to his senses one of the three was dead, the others running into the mob of wounded.

Wickwrackrum huddled around the pain in his Rum. The attacker had been wearing tines. Rum was slashed from ribs to crotch. Wickwrackrum stumbled; some of his paws were caught in his own guts. He tried to nose the ruins back into his member's abdomen. The pain was fading, the sky in Rum's eyes slowly darkening. Peregrine stifled the screams he felt climbing within him. *I'm only four, and one of me is dying!* For years he'd been warning himself that four was just too small a number for a pilgrim. Now he'd pay the price, trapped and mindless in a land of tyrants.

For a moment, the pain eased and his thoughts were clear. The fight hadn't really caused much notice amid the dirges, rapes, and simple attacks of madness. Wickwrackrum's fight had only been a little bigger and bloodier than usual. The whitejackets by the flying house had looked briefly in their direction, but were now back to tearing open the alien cargo.

Scriber was sitting nearby, watching in horror. Part of him would move a little closer, then pull back. He was fighting with himself, trying to decide whether to help. Peregrine almost pleaded with him, but the effort was too great. Besides, Scriber was no pilgrim. Giving part of himself was not something Jaqueramaphan could do voluntarily . . .

Memories came flooding now, Rum's efforts to sort things out and let the rest of him know all that had been before. For a moment, he was sailing a twinhull across the South Sea, a newby with Rum as a pup; memories of the island person who had born Rum, and of packs before that. Once around the world they had traveled, surviving the slums of a tropic collective, and the war of the Plain Herds. Ah, the stories they had heard, the tricks they had learned, the people they had met . . . Wic Kwk Rac Rum had been a terrific combination, clear-thinking, lighthearted, with a strange ability to keep all the memories in place; that had been the real reason he had gone so long without growing to five or six. Now he would pay perhaps the greatest price of all . . .

Rum sighed, and could not see the sky anymore. Wickwrackrum's mind went, not as it does in the heat of battle when the sound of thought is lost, not as it does in the companionable murmur of sleep. There was suddenly no fourth presence, just the three, trying to make a person. The trio stood and patted nervously at itself. There was danger everywhere, but beyond its understanding. It sidled hopefully toward a sixsome sitting nearby – Jaqueramaphan? – but the other shooed it away. It looked nervously at the mob of wounded. There was completeness there . . . and madness too.

A huge male with deeply scarred haunches sat at the edge of the mob. It caught the threesome's eye, and slowly crawled across the open space toward them. Wic and Kwk and Rac back away, their pelts puffing up in fright and fascination; the scarred one was at least half again the weight of any of them.

. . . Where am I? . . . May I be part of you . . . please? Its keening carried memories, jumbled and mostly inaccessible, of blood and fighting, of military training before that. Somehow, the creature was as frightened of those early memories as of anything. It lay its muzzle – caked with dried blood – on the ground and belly-crawled toward them. The other three almost ran; random coupling was something that scared all of them. They backed and backed, out onto the clear meadow. The other followed, but slowly, still crawling. Kwk licked her lips and walked back towards the stranger. She extended her neck and sniffed along the other's throat. Wic and Rac approached from the sides.

For an instant there was a partial join. *Sweaty, bloody, wounded – a melding made in hell.* The thought seemed to come from nowhere, glowed in the four for a moment of cynical humor. Then the unity was lost, and they were just three animals licking the face of a fourth.

Peregrine looked around the meadow with new eyes. He had been disintegrate for just a few minutes: The wounded from the Tenth Attack Infantry were just as before. Flenser's Servants were still busy with the alien cargo. Jaqueramaphan was slowly backing away, his expression a compound of wonder and horror. Peregrine lowered a head and hissed at him, 'I won't betray you, Scriber.'

The spy froze. 'That you, Peregrine?'

'More or less.' Peregrine still, but Wickwrackrum no more.

'H-how can you do it? Y-you just lost . . .'

'I'm a pilgrim, remember? We live with this sort of thing all our lives.' There was sarcasm in his voice; this was more or less the cliché Jaqueramaphan had been spouting earlier. But there was some truth to it. Already Peregrine Wickwrack . . . scar felt like a person. Maybe this new combination had a chance.

'Uk. Well, yes . . . What should we do now?' The spy looked nervously in all directions, but his eyes on Peregrine were the most worried of all.

Now it was Wickwrackscar's turn to be puzzled. What *was* he doing here? Killing the strange enemy . . . *No.* That's what the Attack Infantry was doing. He would have nothing to do with that, no matter what the scarred one's memories. He and Scriber had come here to . . . to rescue the alien, as much of it as possible. Peregrine grabbed hold of the memory and held it uncritically; it was something real, from the past identity he must preserve. He glanced towards where he had last seen the alien member. The white-jackets and his travois were no longer visible, but he'd been heading along an obvious path.

'We can still get ourselves the live one,' he said to Jaqueramaphan.

Scriber stamped and sidled. He was not quite the enthusiast of before. 'After you, my friend.'

Wickwrackscar straightened his combat jackets and brushed off some of the dried blood. Then he strutted off across the meadow, passing just a hundred yards from the Flenser's Servants around the enemy – around the flying house. He flipped them a sharp salute, which was ignored. Jaqueramaphan followed, carrying two crossbows. The other was doing his best to imitate Peregrine's strut, but he really didn't have the right stuff.

Then they were past the military crest of the hill and descending into shadows. The sounds of the wounded were muted. Wickwrackscar broke into double time, loping from switchback to switchback as he descended the rough path. From here he could see the harbor; the boats were still at the piers, and there wasn't much activity. Behind him, Scriber was talking nervous nonsense. Peregrine just ran faster, his confidence fueled by general newby confusion. His new member, the scarred one, had been the muscle behind an infantry officer. That pack had known the layout of the harbors and the castle, and all the passwords of the day.

Two more switchbacks and they overran the Flenser Servant and his travois. 'Hallo!' shouted Peregrine. 'We bring new instructions from Lord Steel.' A chill went down his spines at the name, remembering Steel for the first time. The Servant dropped the travois and turned to face them. Wickwrackscar didn't know his name, but he remembered the guy: fairly high-ranking, an arrogant get-of-bitches. It was a surprise to see him pulling the travois himself.

Peregrine stopped only twenty yards from the whitejackets. Jaqueramaphan was looking down from the switchback above; his bows were out of sight. The Servant looked nervously at Peregrine and up at Scriber.

'What do you two want?'

Did he suspect them already? No matter. Wickwrackscar braced himself for a killing charge . . . and suddenly he was seeing in fours, his mind blurred with newby dizziness. Now that he needed to kill, the scarred one's horror of the act undid him. Damn! Wickwrackscar cast wildly about for something to say. And now that murder was out of his mind, his new memories came easily: 'Lord Steel's will, that the creature be brought with us to the harbor. You, ah, you are to return to the invader's flying thing.'

The whitejackets licked his lips. His eyes swept sharply across Peregrine's uniforms, and Scriber's. 'Impostors!' he screamed, at the same instant lunging one of his members toward the travois. Metal glinted in the member's forepaw. *He's going to kill the alien!*

There was a bow snap from above, and the runner fell, a shaft through its eye. Wickwrackscar charged the others, forcing his scarbacked member out front. There was an instant of dizziness and then he was whole again, screaming death at the four. The two packs crashed together, Scar carrying a couple of the Servant's members over the edge of the path. Arrows hummed around them. Wic Kwk Rac twisted, slashing axes at whatever remained standing.

Then things were quiet, and Peregrine had his thoughts again. Three of the Servant's members twitched on the path, the earth around them slick with blood. He pushed them off the path, near where his Scar had killed the others. Not one of the Servant had survived; it was total death, and he was responsible. He sagged to the ground, seeing in fours again.

'The alien. It's still alive,' said Scriber. He was standing around the travois, sniffing at the mantis-like body. 'Not conscious though.' He grabbed the travois poles in his jaws and looked at Peregrine. 'What . . . what now, Pilgrim?'

Peregrine lay in the dirt, trying to put his mind back together. *What now, indeed.* How had he gotten into this mess? Newby confusion was the only possibility. He'd simply lost track of all the reasons why rescuing the alien was impossible. And now he was stuck with it. Pack crap. Part of him crawled to the edge of the path, and looked around: There was no sign they had attracted attention. In the harbor, the boats were still empty; most of the infantry was up in the hills. No doubt the Servants were holding the dead ones at the harbor fort. So when would they move them across the straits to Hidden Island? Were they waiting for this one's arrival?

'Maybe we could grab some boats, escape south,' said Scriber. What an ingenious fellow. Didn't he know that there would be sentry lines around the harbor? Even knowing the passwords, they'd be reported as soon as they passed one. It would be a million-to-one shot. But it had been a flat impossibility before Scar became part of him.

He studied the creature lying on the travois. So strange, yet real. And it was more than just the creature, though that was the most spectacular strangeness. Its bloodied clothes were a finer fabric than the Pilgrim had ever seen. Tucked in beside the creature's body was a pink pillow with elaborate stitchery. With a twist of perspective he realized it was alien art, the face of a long-snouted animal embroidered on the pillow.

So escape through the harbor was a million-to-one-shot; some prizes might be worth such odds.

'. . . We'll go down a little farther,' he said.

Jaqueramaphan pulled the travois. Wickwrackscar strode ahead of him, trying to look important and officerly. With Scar along, it wasn't hard. The member was the picture of martial competence; you had to be on the inside to know the softness.

They were almost down to sea level.

The path was wider now and roughly paved. He knew the harbor fort was above them, hidden by the trees. The sun was well out of the north, rising into the eastern sky. Flowers were everywhere, white and red and violet, their tufts floating thick on the breeze – the arctic plant life taking advantage of its long day of summer. Walking on sun-dappled cobble-stones, you might almost forget the ambush on the hilltops.

Very soon, they'd hit a sentry line. Lines and rings are interesting people;

not great minds, but about the largest effective pack you'd find outside the tropics. There were stories of lines ten miles long, with thousand of members. The largest Peregrine had ever seen had fewer than one hundred: Take a group of ordinary people and train them to string out, not in packs but as individual members. If each member stayed just a few yards from its nearest neighbors, they could maintain something like the mentality of a trio. The group as a whole was scarcely brighter – you can't have much in the way of deep thoughts when it takes *seconds* for an idea to percolate across your mind. Yet the line had an excellent grasp of what was happening along itself. And if any members were attacked, the entire line would know about it with the speed of sound. Peregrine had served on lines before; it was a strung-out existence, but not nearly as dull as ordinary sentry duty. It's hard to be bored when you're as stupid as a line.

There! A lone member stuck its neck around a tree and challenged them. Wickwrackscar knew the password of course, and they were past the outer line. But that passage and their description was known to the entire line now – and surely to normal soldiers at the harbor fort.

Hell. There was no cure for it; he would go ahead with the crazy scheme. He and Scriber and the alien member passed through the two inner sentries. He could smell the sea now. They came out of the trees onto the rock-walled harbor. Silver sparkled off the water in a million changing flecks. A large multiboat bobbed between two piers. Its masts were like a forest of tilting leafless trees. Just a mile across the water they could see Hidden Island. Part of him dismissed the sight as a commonplace; part of him stumbled in awe. This was the center of it, the worldwide Flenser movement. Up in those dour towers, the original Flenser had done his experiments, written his essays . . . and schemed to rule the world.

There were a few people on the piers. Most were doing maintenance: sewing sails, relashing twinhulls. They watched the travois with sharp curiosity, but none approached. *So all we have to do is amble down to the end of the pier, cut the lashing on an outside twinhull, and take off.* There were probably enough packs on the pier alone to prevent that – and their cries would surely draw the troops he saw by the harbor fort. In fact, it was a little surprising that no one up there had taken serious notice of them yet.

These boats were cruder than the Southseas version. Part of the difference was superficial: Flenser doctrine forbade idle decoration on boats. Part of it was functional: These craft were designed for both winter and summer seasons, and for troop hauling. But he was sure he could sail them given the chance. He walked to the end of the pier. Hmm. A bit of luck. The bow-starboard twinhull, the one right next to him by the pier, looked fast and well-provisioned. It was probably a long-range scout.

'Ssst. Something's going on up there.' Scriber jerked a head toward the fort.

The troops were closing ranks – a mass salute? Five Servants swept by the infantry, and bugles sounded from the fort's towers. Scar had seen things like this, but Peregrine didn't trust the memory. How could—

A banner of red and yellow rose over the fort. On the piers, soldiers and boatworkers dropped to their bellies. Peregrine dropped and hissed to the other, '*Get down!*'

'Wha—?'

'That's Flenser's flag . . . his personal presence banner!'

'That's impossible.' Flenser had been assassinated in the Republic six tendays earlier. The mob that tore him apart had killed dozens of his top supporters at the same time . . . But it was only the word of the Republican Political Police that all Flenser's bodies had been recovered.

Up by the fort, a single pack pranced between the ranks of soldiers and whitejackets. Silver and gold glinted on its shoulders. Scriber edged a member behind a piling and surreptitiously brought out his eye-tool. After a moment: 'Soul's end . . . it's *Tyrathect.*'

'She's no more the Flenser than I am,' said Peregrine. They had traveled together from Eastgate all the way across the Icefangs. She was obviously a newby, and not well-integrated. She had seemed reserved and innerlooking, but there had been rages. Peregrine knew there was a deadly streak in Tyrathect . . . Now he guessed whence it came. At least some of Flenser's members had escaped assassination, and he and Scriber had spent three tendays in its presence; Peregrine shivered.

At the fort's gate, the pack called Tyrathect turned to face the troops and Servants. She gestured, and bugles sounded again. The new Peregrine understood that signal: an Incalling. He suppressed the sudden urge to follow the others on the pier as they walked belly-low toward the fort, all their eyes upon The Master. Scriber looked back at him, and Peregrine nodded. They had needed a miracle, and here *was* one – provided by the enemy itself! Scriber moved slowly toward the end of the pier, pulling the travois from shadow to shadow.

Still no one looked back. For good reason; Wickwrackscar remembered what happened to those showing disrespect at an Incalling. 'Pull the creature onto the bow-starboard boat,' he said to Jaqueramaphan. He leaped off the pier and scattered across the multiboat. It was great to be back on swaying decks, each member drifting a different direction! He sniffed among the bow catapults, listened to the hulls and the creak of the lashings.

But Scar was no sailor, and had no recollection of what might be the most important thing.

'What are you looking for?' came Scriber's Hightalk hiss.

'Scuttle knockouts.' If they were here, they looked nothing like the Southseas version.

'Oh,' said Scriber, 'that's easy. These are Northern Skimmers. There are swingout panels and a thin hull behind.' Two of him dropped from sight for a second and there was a banging sound. The heads reappeared, shaking water off. He grinned surprise, taken aback by his own success. 'Why, it's just like in the books!' his expression seemed to say.

Wickwrackscar found them now; the panels had looked like crew rests, but they were easily pulled out and the wood behind was easy to break with a battle-axe. He kept a head out, looking to see if they were attracting attention, while at the same time he hacked at the knockouts. Peregrine and Scriber worked their way across the bow ranks of the multiboat; if those foundered, it would take a while to get the twinhulls behind them free.

Oops. One of the boat workers was looking back this way. Part of the fellow continued up the hillside, part strained to return to the pier. The bugles sounded their imperative once more, and the sailor followed the call. But his whining alarums were causing other heads to turn.

No time for stealth. Peregrine hotfooted it back to the bow-starboard twinhull. Scriber was cutting the braid-bone fasteners that held the twinhull to the rest of the ship. 'You have any sailing experience?' Peregrine said. Foolish question.

'Well, I've read about it—'

'Fine!' Peregrine shooed him all into the twinhull's starboard pod. 'Keep the alien safe. Hunker down, and be as quiet as you can.' He could sail the twinhull by himself, but he'd have to be all over to do it; the fewer confusing thought sounds, the better.

Peregrine poled their boat forward from the multiboat. The scuttling wasn't obvious yet, but he could see water in the bow hulls. He reversed his pole and used its hook to draw the nearest boat into the gap created by their departure. Another five minutes and there'd be just a row of masts sticking out of the water. Five minutes. No way they could make it . . . if not for Flenser's Incalling: up by the fort, troopers were turning and pointing at the harbor. Yet still they must attend on Flenser/Tyrathect. How long would it be before someone important decided that even an Incalling can be overriden?

He hoisted canvas.

The wind caught the twinhull's sail and they pulled out from the pier. Peregrine danced this way and that, the shrouds grasped tightly in his mouths. Even without Rum, what memories the taste of salt and cordage brought back! He could *feel* where tautness and slack meant that the wind was giving all it could. The twin hulls were sleek and narrow, the mast of ironwood creaking as the wind pulled on the sail.

The Flenserists were streaming down the hillside now. Archers stopped and a haze of arrows rose. Peregrine jerked on the shrouds, tipping the boat into a left turn on one hull. Scriber leaped to shield the alien. To starboard ahead of them the water puckered, but only a couple of shafts struck the boat. Peregrine twisted the shrouds again, and they jigged back in the other direction. Another few seconds and they'd be out of bowshot. Soldiers raced down to the piers, shrieking as they saw what was left of their ship. The bow ranks were flooded; the whole front of the anchorage was a wreck of sunken boats. And the catapults were in the bow.

Peregrine swept his boat back, racing straight south, out of the harbor. To starboard, he could see they were passing the southern tip of Hidden Island. The Castle towers hung tall and ominous. He knew there were heavy catapults there, and some fast boats in the island harbor. A few more minutes and even that wouldn't matter. He was gradually realizing just how nimble their boat was. He should have guessed they'd put their best in a corner bow position. It was probably used for scouting and overtaking.

Jaqueramaphan was piled up at the stern of his hull, staring across the water at the mainland harbor. Soldiers, workers, whitejackets were crowded in a mind-numbing jumble at the ends of the piers. Even from here, you could see the place was a madhouse of rage and frustration. A silly grin spread across Scriber as he realized they really were going to make it. He clambered onto the rail and jumped into the air to flip a member at their enemies. The obscene gesture nearly cast him overboard, but it *was* seen: the distant rage brightened for a moment.

They were well south of Hidden Island; even its catapults could not reach them now. The packs on the mainland shore were lost to view. Flenser's personal banner still whipped cheerfully in the morning breeze, a dwindling square of red and yellow against the forest's green.

All Peregrine looked at the narrows, where Whale Island curved close to the mainland. His Scar remembered that the choke point was heavily fortified. Normally that would have been the end of them. But its archers had been withdrawn to participate in the ambush, and its catapults were under repair.

. . . so the miracle had happened. They were alive and free and they had the greatest find of all his pilgrimage. He shouted joy so loud that Jaqueramaphan cowered and the sound echoed back from the green and snow-patched hills.

5

Jefri Olsndot had few clear memories of the ambush and saw none of the violence. There had been the noises outside, and Mom's terrified voice, screaming for him to stay inside. Then there had been lots of smoke. He remembered choking, trying to crawl to clear air. He blacked out. When he woke, he was strapped onto some sort of first-aid cot, with the big dog creatures all around. They looked so funny with their white jackets and braid. He remembered wondering where their owners were. They made the strangest noises: gobbling, buzzing, hissing. Some of it was so high-pitched he could barely hear it.

For awhile he was on a boat, then on a wheeled cart. Before this, he had only seen pictures of castles, but the place they took him was the real thing, its towers dark and overhanging, its big stone walls sharply angled. They climbed through shadowed streets that went *skumpety skumpety* beneath the cart's wheels. The long-necked dogs hadn't hurt him, but the straps were awfully tight. He couldn't sit up; he couldn't see to the sides. He asked about Mom and Dad and Johanna, and he cried a little. A long snout appeared by his face, the soft nose pushing at his cheek. There was a buzzing sound he felt all the way down to his bones. He couldn't tell if the gesture was comfort or threat, but he gasped and tried to stop the tears. They didn't befit a good Straumer, anyway.

Now he saw more white-jacketed dogs, ones with silly shoulder patches of gold and silver.

His cot was being dragged again, this time down a torch-lit tunnel. They stopped by a double door, two meters wide but scarcely one high. A pair of metal triangles was set in the blond wood. Later Jefri learned they signified a number – fifteen or thirty-three, depending on whether you counted by legs or fore-claws. Much, *much* later he learned that his keeper had counted by legs and the builder of the castle by fore-claws. Thus he ended up in the wrong room. It was a mistake that would change the history of worlds.

Somehow the dogs opened the doors and dragged Jefri in. They clustered around the cot, their snouts tugging loose his restraints. He had a glimpse of rows of needle-sharp teeth. The gobbling and buzzing was very loud. When Jefri sat up, they backed off. Two of them held the doors as the other four exited. The doors slammed shut and the circus act was gone.

Jefri stared at the doors for a long moment. He knew it was no circus act; the dog things must be intelligent. Somehow they had surprised his parents and sister. *Where are they?* He almost started to cry again. He hadn't seen them by the spaceship. They must have been captured, too. They were all being held prisoner in this castle, but in separate dungeons. Somehow they must find each other!

He climbed to his feet, swayed dizzily for a moment. Everything still smelled like smoke. It didn't matter; it was time to start working on getting out. He walked around the room. It was huge, and not like any dungeon he'd seen in stories. The ceiling was very high, an arching dome. It was cut by twelve vertical slots. Sunlight fell in a dust-moted stream from one of them, splashing off the padded wall. It was the room's only illumination, but more than enough on this sunny day. Low-railed balconies stuck out from the four corners of the room just below the dome. He could see doors in the walls behind them. Heavy scrolls hung by the side of each balcony. There was writing on them, really big print. He walked to the wall and felt the stiff fabric. The letters were *painted* on. The only way you could change the display was by rubbing it out. Wow. Just like olden times on Nyjora, before Straumli Realm! The baseboard below the scrolls was black stone, glossy. Someone had used scraps of chalk to draw on it. The stick-figure dogs were crude; they reminded Jefri of pictures little kids draw in kinderschool.

He stopped, remembering all the chidren they had left aboard the boat, and on the ground around it. Just a few days ago he'd been playing with them at the High Lab school. The last year had been so strange – boring and adventurous at the same time. The barracks had been fun with all the families together, but the grownups hardly ever had time to play. At night the sky was so different from Straum's. 'We're beyond the Beyond,' Mom had said, 'making God.' When she first said it, she laughed. Later when people said it, they seemed more and more scared. The last hours had been crazy, the coldsleep drills finally for real. All his friends were in those boxes . . . He wept into the awful silence. There was no one to hear, no one to help him.

After a few moments he was thinking again. If the dogs didn't try to open the boxes, his friends should be okay. If Mom and Dad could make the dogs understand . . .

Strange furniture was scattered around the room: low tables and cabinets, and racks like kids' jungle gyms – all made from the same blond wood as the doors. Black pillows lay around the widest table. That one was littered with scrolls, all full of writing and still drawings. He walked the length of one wall, ten meters or so. The stone flooring ended. There was a two-by-two bed of gravel where the walls met. Something smelled even stronger than smoke here. A bathroom smell. Jefri laughed: they really were like dogs!

The padded walls soaked up his laughter, echoless. Something . . . made Jefri look up and across the room. He'd just assumed he was alone here; in fact, there were lots of hiding places in this 'dungeon'. For a moment, he held his breath and listened. All was silent . . . almost: at the top of his hearing, up where some machines wheep, and Mom and Dad and even Johanna couldn't hear – there was something.

'I – I know you're here,' Jefri said sharply, his voice squeaking. He stepped sideways a few paces, trying to see around the furniture without approaching it. The sound continued, obvious now that he was listening to it.

A small head with great dark eyes looked around a cabinet. It was much smaller than the creatures that had brought Jefri here, but the shape of the muzzle was the same. They stared at each other for a moment, and then Jefri edged slowly toward it. A puppy? The head withdrew, then came further out From the corner of his eye, Jefri saw something move – another of the black forms was peering at him from under the table. Jefri froze for a second, fighting panic. But there was no place to run, and maybe the creatures would help find Mom. Jefri dropped to one knee and slowly extended his hand. 'Here . . . here, doggy.'

36

The puppy crawled from beneath the table, its eyes never leaving Jefri's hand. The fascination was mutual; the puppy was beautiful. Considering all the thousands of years that dogs have been bred by humans (and others), this could have been some oddball breed . . . but only just. The hair was short and dense, a deep velour of black and white. The two tones lay in broad swaths with no intermediate grays. This one's entire head was black, its haunches split between white and black. The tail was a short, unimpressive flap covering its rear. There were hairless patches on its shoulders and head, where Jefri could see black skin. But the strangest thing was the long, supple neck. It would look more natural in a sea'mal than a dog.

Jefri wiggled his fingers, and the puppy's eyes widened, revealing an edge of white around the iris.

Something bumped his elbow, and Jefri almost jumped to his feet. So many! Two more had crept up to look at his hand. And where he had seen the first one there were now three, sitting alertly, watching. Seen in the open, there was nothing unfriendly or scary about them.

One of the puppies put a paw on Jefri's wrist and pressed gently downward. At the same time, another extended its muzzle and licked Jefri's fingers. The tongue was pink and raspy, a round narrow thing. The high-pitched wheeping got stronger; all three moved in, grabbing at his hand with their mouths.

'Be careful!' Jefri said, jerking back his hand. He remembered the grownups' teeth. Suddenly the air was full of gobbling and buzzing. *Hmp.* They sounded more like goofy birds than dogs. One of the other pups came forward. It extended a sleek nose toward Jefri. 'Be careful!' it said, a perfect playback of the boy's voice . . . yet its mouth was closed. It angled its neck back . . . to be petted? He reached out; the fur was so *soft!* The buzzing was very loud now. Jefri could feel it through the fur. But it wasn't just the one animal who was making it; the sound came from all directions. The puppy reversed direction, sliding its muzzle across the boy's hand. This time he let the mouth close on his fingers. He could see teeth all right, but the puppy carefully kept them from touching Jefri's skin. The tip of its snout felt like a pair of small fingers closing and opening around his.

Three slipped under his other arm, like they wanted to be petted too. He felt noses poking at his back, trying to pull his shirt out of his pants. The effort was remarkably coordinated, almost as if a two-handed human had grabbed his shirt. *Just how many are there?* For a moment he forgot where he was, forgot to be cautious. He rolled over and began petting the marauders. A surprised squeaking sound came from all directions. Two crawled beneath his elbows; at least three jumped on his back and lay with their noses touching his neck and ears.

And Jefri had what seemed a great insight: The adult aliens had recognized he was a child; they just didn't know how old. They had put him in one of their own kinderschools! Mom and Dad were probably talking to them right now. Things were going to turn out all right after all.

Lord Steel had not taken his name casually: steel, the most modern of metals; steel, that takes the sharpest edge and never loses it; steel, that can glow red hot, and yet not fail; steel, the blade that cuts for the flenser. Steel was a crafted person, Flenser's greatest success.

In some sense, the crafting of souk was nothing new. Brood kenning was a limited form of it, though mainly concerned with gross physical characteristics. Even kenners agreed that a pack's mental abilities derived from its various members in different measures. One pair or triple was almost always responsible for eloquence, another for spatial intuition. The virtues and vices were even more complex. No single member was the principal source of courage, or of conscience.

Flenser's contribution to the field – as to most others – had been an essential ruthlessness, a cutting away of all but the truly important. He experimented endlessly, discarding all but the most successful results. He depended on discipline and denial and partial death as much as on clever member selection. He already had seventy years of experience when he created Steel.

Before he could take his name, Steel spent *years* in denial, determining just what parts of him combined to produce the being desired. That would have been impossible without Flenser's enforcement (Example: if you dismissed a part of yourself essential for tenacity, where could you get the will to continue the flensing?) For the soul in creation, the process was mental chaos, a patchwork of horror and amnesia. In two years he had experienced more change than most people do in two centuries – and all of it directed. The turning point came when he and Flenser identified the trio that weighed him down with both conscience and slowness of intellect. One of the three bridged the others. Sending it into silence, replacing it with just the right element, had made the difference. After that, the rest was easy; Steel was born.

When Flenser had left to convert the Long Lakes Republic, it was only natural that his most brilliant creation should take over here. For five years Steel had ruled Flenser's heartland. In that time he had not only conserved what Flenser built, he extended it beyond the cautious beginnings.

But today, in a single circling of the sun about Hidden Island, he could lose everything.

Steel stepped into the meeting hall and looked around. Refreshments were properly set. Sunlight streamed from a ceiling slit onto just the place he wanted. Part of Shreck, his aide, stood on the far side of the room. He said to it, 'I will speak with the visitor alone.' He did not use the name 'Flenser.'

The whitejackets groveled back and its unseen members pushed open the far doors.

A fivesome – three males and two females – walked through the doorway, into the splash of sunlight. The individual was unremarkable. But then Flenser had never had an imposing appearance.

Two heads raised to shade the eyes of the others. The pack looked across the room, spotting Lord Steel twenty yards away. 'Ah-h . . . Steel.' The voice was gentle, like a scalpel petting the short hairs of your throat.

Steel had bowed when the other entered, a formal gesture. The voice caused a sudden cramp in his guts, and he involuntarily brought bellies to the ground. That was *his* voice! There was at least a fragment of the original Flenser in this pack. The gold and silver epaulets, the personal banner, those could be faked by anyone with suicidal bravado . . . But Steel remembered the manner. He wasn't surprised that the other's presence had destroyed discipline on the mainland this morning.

The pack's heads, where they were in sunlight, were expressionless. Was a smile playing about the heads in shadow? 'Where are the others, Steel? What happened today is the greatest opportunity of our history.'

Steel got off his bellies and stood at the railing. 'Sir. There are some questions first, just between the two of us. Clearly, you are much of Flenser, but how much—'

The other was clearly grinning now, the shadowed heads bobbing. 'Yes, I knew my best creation would see that question . . . This morning, I claimed to be the true Flenser, improved with one or two replacements. The truth is . . . harder. You know about the Republic.' That had been Flenser's greatest gamble: to flense an entire nation-state. Millions would die, yet even so there would be more molding than killing. In the end, there would exist the first collective outside of the tropics. And the Flenser state would not be a mindless agglomeration grubbing about in some jungle. The top would be as brilliant, as ruthless as any packs in history. No people in the world could stand against such a force.

'It was an awesome risk to take, for an even more awesome goal. But I took precautions. We had thousands of converts, many of them people with no understanding of our true ambition, but faithful and self-sacrificing – as they should be. I always kept a special group of them nearby. The Political Police were clever to use mob assassination against me, the last thing I had expected – *I* who made the mobs. No matter, my bodyguards were well trained. When we were trapped in Parliament Bowl, they killed one or two members of each of those special packs . . . and I simply ceased to exist, dispersed among three panicky, ordinary people trying to escape the blood swamp.'

'But everyone around you was killed; the mob left no one.'

The Flenser-thing shrugged. 'That was partly Republican propaganda, and partly my own work: I ordered my guards to hack each other down, along with everyone who was not me.'

Steel almost voiced his awe. The plan was typical of Flenser's brilliance, and his strength of soul. In assassinations, there was always the chance that fragments would get away. There were famous stories of heroes reassembled. In real life such events were rare, usually happening when the victim's forces could sustain their leader through reintegration. But Flenser had planned this tactic from the beginning, had envisaged reassembling himself more than a thousand miles from the Long Lakes.

Still . . . Lord Steel looked at the other in calculation. Ignore voice and manner. *Think* for power, not for the desires of others, even Flenser. Steel recognized only two in the other pack. The females and the male with the white-tipped ears were probably from the sacrificed follower. Very likely only really two of Flenser faced him; scarcely a threat . . . except in the very real sense of appearances. 'And the other four of you, Sir? When may we expect your entire presence?'

The Flenser-thing chuckled. Damaged as it was, it still understood balance-of-power. This was almost like the old days: when two people have a clear understanding of power and betrayal, then betrayal itself becomes almost impossible. There is only the ordered flow of events, bringing good to those who deserve to rule. 'The others have equally good . . . mounts. I made detailed plans, three different paths, three different sets of agents. I arrived safely. I have no doubt the others will too, in a few tendays at most. Until then,' he turned all heads toward Steel, 'until then, dear Steel, I do not claim the full role of Flenser. I did so earlier to establish priorities, to protect this fragment till I am assembled. But this pack is deliberately weak-minded; I know it wouldn't survive as the ruler of my earlier creations.'

Steel wondered. Half-brained, the creature's schemes were perfect. Nearly perfect. 'So you wish a background role for the next few tendays? Very well. But you announced yourself as Flenser. How shall I present you?'

The other didn't hesitate. 'Tyrathect, Flenser in Waiting.'

Crypto: 0
As received by: Transceiver Relay03 at Relay
Language path: Samnorsk → Triskweline, SjK: Relay units
From: Straumli Main
Subject: Archive opened in the Low Transcend!
Summary: Our links to the Known Net will be down temporarily
Key phrases: transcend, good news, business opportunities, new archive,
    communications problems
Distribution:
    Where Are They Now Interest Group
    Homo Sapiens Interest Group

Motley Hatch Administration Group
Transceiver Relay03 at Relay
Transceiver Windsong at Debley Down
Transceiver Not-for-Long at Shortstop
Date: 11:45:20 Docks Time, 01/09 of Org year 52089
Text of message:

We are proud to announce that a human exploration company from Straumli Realm has discovered an accessible archive in the Low Transcend. This is not an announcement of Transcendence or the creation of a new Power. We have in fact postponed this announcement until we were sure of our property rights and the safety of the archive. We have installed interfaces which should make the archive interoperable with standard syntax queries from the Net. In a few days this access will be made commercially available. (See discussion of scheduling problems below.) Because of its safety, intelligibility, and age, this Archive is remarkable. We believe there is otherwise lost information here about arbitration management and interrace coordination. We'll sent details to the appropriate news groups. We're very excited about this. Note that no interaction with the Powers was necessary; no part of Straumli Realm has transcended.

Now for the bad news: Arbitration and translation schemes have had unfortunate cleniration[?] with the ridgeway armiphlage[?]. The details should be amusing to the people in the Communication Threats news group and we will report them there later. But for at least the next hundred hours, all our links (main and minor) to the Known Net will be down. Incoming messages may be buffered, but no guarantees. No messages can be forwarded. We regret this inconvenience, and will make up for it very soon

Physical commerce is in no way affected by these problems. Straumli Realm continues to welcome tourists and trade.

6

Looking back, Ravna Bergsndot saw it was inevitable that she become a librarian. As a child on Sjandra Kei, she had been in love with stories from the Age of Princesses. There was adventure, a time when a few brave Ladies had dragged humankind to greatness. She and her sister had spent countless afternoons pretending to be the Greater Two and rescuing the Countess of the Lake. Later they understood that Nyjora and its Princesses were lost in the dim past. Sister Lynne turned to more practical things. But Ravna still wanted adventure. Through her teens, she had dreamed of emigrating to Straumli Realm. *That* was something very real. Imagine: a new and mostly human colony, right at the Top of the Beyond. And Straum welcomed folk from the mother world; their enterprise was less than one hundred years old. They or their children would be the first humans anywhere in the galaxy to transcend their own humanity. She might end up a god, and richer than a million Beyonder worlds. It was a dream real enough to provoke constant arguments with her parents. For where there is heaven, there can also be hell. Straumli Realm kissed close to the Transcend, and the people there played with 'the tigers that pace beyond the bars.' Dad had actually used that tired image. The disagreement drove them apart for several years. Then, in her Computer Science and Applied Theology courses, Ravna began to read about some of the old horrors. Maybe, maybe . . . she should be a little more cautious. Better to look around first. And there was a way to see into everything that humans in the Beyond could possibly understand: Ravna became a librarian. 'The ultimate dilettante!' Lynne had teased. 'It's true and so what?' Ravna had grumped back, but the dream of far traveling was not quite dead in her.

Life in Herte University at Sjandra Kei should have been perfect for her. Things might have gone on happily for a lifetime there – except that in her graduation year, there had been the Vrinimi Organization's Faraway 'Prentice contest. Three years work-study at the archive by Relay was the prize. Winning was the chance of a lifetime; she would come back with more experience than any local academician.

So it was that Ravna Bergsndot ended up more than twenty thousand light-years from home, at the network hub of a million worlds.

Sunset was an hour past when Ravna drifted across Citypark toward Grondr Vrinimikalir's residence. She'd been on the planet only a handful of times since arriving in the Relay system. Most of her work was at the archives themselves – a thousand light-hours out. This part of Groundside was in early autumn, though twilight had faded the tree colors to bands of gray. From Ravna's altitude, one hundred meters up, the air had the nip of frosts to come. Between her feet she could see picnic fires and gaming fields. The Vrinimi Organization didn't spend much on the planet, but the world was beautiful. As long as she kept her eyes on the darkening ground, Ravna could almost imagine this was someplace in her home terrane on Sjandra Kei. Look into the sky though . . . and you knew you were far from home: twenty thousand light-years away, the galactic whirlpool sprawled up toward the zenith.

It was just a faint thing in the twilight, and it might not get much brighter this night: Low in the western sky, a cluster of in-system factories glowed brighter than any moon. The operation was a brilliant flickering of stars and rays, sometimes so intense that stark shadows were cast eastwards from the Citypark mountains. In another half hour the Docks would rise. The Docks weren't as bright as the factories, but together they would outshine anything from the far stars.

She shifted in her agrav harness, drifting lower. The scent of autumn and picnics came stronger. Suddenly, the click of Kalir laughter was all around

42

her; she had blundered into an airball game. Ravna spread her arms in mock humiliation and dodged out of the players' way.

Her stroll through the park was just about over; she could see her destination ahead. Grondr 'Kalir's residence was a rarity in the Citypark landscape: a recognizable building. It dated from when the Org bought into the Relay operation. Seen from just eighty meters up, the house was a blocky silhouette against the sky. When factory lights flashed, the smooth walls of the monolith glowed in oily tints. Grondr was her boss's boss's boss. She had talked to him exactly three times in two years.

No more delay. Nervous and very curious, Ravna floated lower and let the house electronics guide her across the tree decks toward an entrance.

Grondr Vrinimikalir treated her with standard Organization courtesy, the common denominator that served between the several races of the Org: The meeting room had furniture suitable for human and Vrinimi use. There were refreshments, and questions about her job at the archive.

'Mixed results, sir,' Ravna replied honestly. 'I've learned a great deal. The 'prenticeship is everything it's claimed to be. But I'm afraid the new division is going to require an added index layer.' All this was in reports the old fellow could have seen at the flick of a digit.

Grondr rubbed a hand absently across his eye freckles. 'Yes, an expected disappointment. We're at the limits of information management with this expansion. Egravan and Derche—' those were Ravna's boss and boss's boss '—are quite happy with your progress. You came well educated, and learned fast. I think there's a place for humans in the Organization.'

'Thank you, sir.' Ravna blushed. Grondr's assessment was casually spoken but very important to her. And it would probably mean the arrival of more humans, perhaps even before her 'prenticeship was up. So was this the reason for the interview?

She tried not to stare at the other. She was quite used to the Vrinimi majority race by now. From a distance the Kalir looked humanoid. Up close, the differences were substantial. The race was descended from something like an insect. In upsizing, evolution had necessarily moved reinforcing struts inside the body, till the outside was a combination of grublike skin and sheets of pale chitin. At first glance Grondr was an unremarkable examplar of the race. But when the fellow moved, even to adjust his jacket or scratch at his eye freckles, there was a strange precision to him. Egravan said that he was very very old.

Grondr changed the subject with clickety abruptness. 'You are aware of the . . . changes at Straumli Realm?'

'You mean the fall of Straum? Yes.' *Though I'm surprised you are.* Straumli Realm was a significant human civilization, but it accounted for only an infinitesimal fraction of Relay's message traffic.

'Please accept my sympathy.' Despite the cheerful announcements from

43

Straum, it was clear that absolute disaster had befallen Straumli Realm. Almost every race eventually dabbled in the Transcend, more often than not becoming a superintelligence, a Power. But it was clear by now that the Straumers had created, or awakened, a Power of deadly inclination. Their fate was as terrible as anything Ravna's father had ever predicted. And their bad luck was now a disaster that stretched across all that had been Straumli Realm. Grondr continued: 'Will this news affect your work?'

Curiouser and curiouser; she would have sworn the other was coming to the point. Maybe this *was* the point? 'Uh, no sir. The Straumli affair is a terrible thing, especially for humankind. But my home is Sjandra Kei. Straumli Realm is our offspring, but I have no relatives there.' *Though I might have been there if it hadn't been for Mother and Dad.* Actually, when Straumli Main dropped off the Net, Sjandra Kei had been unreachable for almost forty hours. That had bothered her very much, since any rerouting should have been immediate. Communication was eventually established; the problem had been screwed-up routing tables on an alternate path. Ravna had even shot half a year's savings for an over-and-back mailing. Lynne and her parents were fine; the Straumli debacle was the news of the century for folks at Sjandra Kei, but it was still a disaster at great remove. Ravna wondered if parents had ever given better advice than hers had!

'Good, good.' His mouth parts moved in the analog of a human nod. His head tilted so only peripheral freckles were looking at her; the guy actually seemed hesitant! Ravna looked back silently. Grondr 'Kalir might be the strangest exec in the Org. He was the only one whose principal residence was Groundside. Officially he was in charge of a division of the archives; in fact, he ran Vrinimi Marketing (i.e., Intelligence). There were stories that he had visited the Top of the Beyond; Egravan claimed he had an artificial immune system. 'You see, the Straumli disaster has incidentally made you one of the Organization's most valuable employees.'

'I . . . don't understand.'

'Ravna, the rumors in the Threats newsgroup are true. The Straumers had a laboratory in the Low Transcend. They were playing with recipes from some lost archive, and they created a new Power. It appears to be a Class Two perversion.'

The Known Net recorded a Class Two perversion about once a century. Such Powers had a normal 'lifespan' – about ten years. But they were explicitly malevolent, and in ten years could do enormous damage. *Poor Straum.*

'So you can see there's enormous potential for profit or loss here. If the disaster spreads, we will lose network customers. On the other hand, everyone around Straumli Realm wants to track what is happening. This could increase our message traffic by several percent.'

Grondr put it more cold-bloodedly than she liked, but he had a point. In fact, the opportunity for profit was directly linked with mitigating the perversion. If she hadn't been so wrapped up in archive work, she'd have guessed all this. And now that she *did* think about it: 'There are even more spectacular opportunities. Historically, these perversions have been of interest to other Powers. They'll want Net feeds and . . . information about the creating race.' Her voice guttered into silence as she finally understood the reason for this meeting.

Grondr's mouth parts clicked agreement. 'Indeed. We at Relay are well-placed to supply news to the Transcend. And we also have our own human. In the last three days we've received several dozen queries from civilizations in the High Beyond, some claiming to represent Powers. This interest could mean a large increase in Organization income through the next decade.

'All this you could read in the Threats news group. But there is another item, something I ask you to keep secret for now: Five days ago, a ship from the Transcend entered our region. It claims to be directly controlled by a Power.' The wall behind him became a window upon the visitor. The craft was an irregular collection of spines and lumps. A scale bar claimed the thing was only five meters across.

Ravna felt the hair on her neck prickling. Here in the Middle Beyond they should be relatively safe from the caprice of the Powers. Still . . . the visit was an unnerving thing. 'What does it want?'

'Information about the Straumli perversion. In particular, it is very interested in your race. It would give a great deal to take back a living human . . .'

Ravna's response was abrupt. 'I'm not interested.'

Grondr spread his pale hands. The light glittered from the chitin on the back of his fingers. 'It would be an enormous opportunity. A 'prenticeship with the gods. This one has promised to establish an oracle here in return.'

'No!' Ravna half rose from her chair. She was one human, more than twenty thousand light-years from home. That had been a frightening thing in the first days of her 'prenticeship. Since then she had made friends, had learned more of Organization ethics, had come to trust these folk almost as much as people at Sjandra Kei. But . . . there was only one halfway trustable oracle on the Net these days, and it was almost ten years old. This Power was tempting Vrinimi Org with fabulous treasure.

Grondr clicked embarrassment. He waved her back to her chair. 'It was only a suggestion. We do not abuse our employees. If you will simply serve as our local expert . . .'

Ravna nodded.

'Good. Frankly, I had not expected you to accept the offer. We have a much more likely volunteer, but one who needs coaching.'

'A human? Here?' Ravna had a standing query in the local directory for other humans. During the last two years she had seen three, and they had just been passing through. 'How long has she – he? – been here?'

Grondr said something halfway between a smile and a laugh. 'A bit more than a century, though we didn't realize it until a few days ago.' The pictures around him shifted. Ravna recognized Relay's 'attic,' the junkyard of abandoned ships and freight devices that floated just a thousand light-seconds from the archives. 'We receive a lot of one-way freight, items shipped in the hope we'll buy or sell on consignment.' The view closed on a decrepit vessel, perhaps two hundred meters long, wasp-waisted to support a ramscoop drive. Its ultradrive spines were scarcely more than stubs.

'A bottom-lugger?' said Ravna.

Grondr clicked negation. 'A dredge. The ship is about thirty thousand years old. Most of that time was spent in a deep penetration of the Slow Zone, and ten thousand years in the Unthinking Depths.'

Up close now, she could see the hull was finely pitted, the result of millennia of relativistic erosion. Even unpiloted, such expeditions were rare: a deep penetration could not return to the Beyond within the lifetime of its builders. Some would not return within the lifetime of the builders' *race*. People who launched such missions were just a little weird; People who recovered them could make a solid profit.

'This one came from very far away, even if it's not quite a jackpot mission. It didn't see anything interesting in the Unthinking Depths – not surprising given that even simple automation fails there. We sold most of the cargo immediately. The rest we cataloged and forgot . . . till the Straumli affair.' The starscape vanished. They were looking at a medical display, random limbs and body parts. They looked very human, 'In a solar system at the bottom of the Slowness, the dredge found a derelict. The wreck had no ultradrive capability; it was truly a Slow Zone design. The solar system was uninhabited. We speculate the ship had a structural failure – or perhaps the crew was affected by the Depths. Either way, they ended up in a frozen mangle.'

Tragedy at the bottom of the Slowness, thousands of years ago. Ravna forced her eyes from the carnage. 'You figure on selling this to our visitor?'

'Even better. Once we started poking around, we discovered a substantial error in the cataloging. One of the deaders is almost intact. We patched it up with parts from the others. It was expensive, but we ended up with a living human.' The picture flickered again, and Ravna caught her breath. In the medical animation, the parts floated into an orderly arrangement. There was a complete body there, torn up a little in the belly. Pieces came together, and . . . this was no 'she.' He floated whole and naked, as if in sleep. Ravna had no doubt of his humanity, but all humankind in the Beyond was descended from Nyjoran stock. This fellow had none of that heritage. The skin was smoky gray, not brown. The hair was bright reddish brown, a color she had only seen in pre-Nyjoran histories. The bones of the face were subtly different from modern humans. The small differences were more jarring than the outright alienness of her coworkers.

Now the figure was clothed. Under other circumstances, Ravna would have smiled. Grondr 'Kalir had picked an absurd costume, something from the Nyjoran era. The figure bore a sword and slug gun . . . A sleeping prince from the Age of Princesses.

'Behold the Ur-human,' said Grondr.

7

'Relay' is a common place-name. It has meaning in almost any environment. Like Newtown and Newhome, it occurs over and over when people move or colonize or participate in a communications net. You could travel a billion light-years or a billion years and still find such names among races of natural intelligence.

But in the current era there was one instance of 'Relay' known above all others. That instance appeared in the routing list of two percent of all traffic across the Known Net. Twenty thousand light-years off the galactic plane, Relay had an unobstructed line of sight on thirty percent of the Beyond, including many star systems right at the bottom, where starships can make only one light-year per day. A few metal-bearing solar systems were equally well-placed, and there was competition. But where other civilizations lost interest, or colonized into the Transcend, or died in apocalypse, Vrinimi Organization *lasted*. After fifty thousand years, there were several races of the original Org in its membership. None of those were still leaders – yet the original viewpoint and policies remained. Position and durability: Relay was now the main intermediate to the Magellanics, and one of the few sites with any sort of link to the Beyond in the Sculptor galaxy.

At Sjandra Kei, Relay's reputation had been fabulous. In her two years of 'prenticeship, Ravna had come to realize that the truth exceeded the reputation. Relay was in Middle Beyond; the Organization's only export was the relay function and access to the local archive. Yet they imported the finest biologicals and processing equipment from the High Beyond. The Relay Docks were an extravagance that only the absolutely rich could indulge. They stretched a thousand kilometers: bays, repair holds, tranship- ment centers, parks, and playgrounds. Even at Sjandra Kei there were habitats far larger. But the Docks were in no orbit. They floated a thousand kilometers above Groundside on the largest agrav frame Ravna had ever seen. At Sjandra Kei the annual income of an academician might pay for a square meter of agrav fabric – junk that might not last a year. Here there were millions of hectares of the stuff, supporting billions of tonnes. Just replacements for dead fabric required more High Beyond commerce than most star clusters could command.

And now I have my own office here. Working directly for Grondr 'Kalir had its perks. Ravna kicked back in her chair and stared across the central sea. At the Docks' altitude, gravity was still about three-quarters of a gee. Air fountains hung a breathable atmosphere over the middle part of the platform. The day before, she had taken a sailboat across the clear-bottomed sea. That was a strange experience indeed: planetary clouds below your keel, stars and indigo sky above.

She had the surf cranked up this morning – an easy matter of flexing the agravs of the basin. It made a regular crashing against her beach. Even thirty meters from the water there was a tang of salt in the air. Rows of white tops marched off into the distance.

She eyed the figure that was trudging slowly up the beach toward her. Just a few weeks ago she would never have dreamed this situation. Just a few weeks ago she had been out at the archive, absorbed in the upgrade work, happy to be involved with one of the largest databases on the Known Net. Now . . . it was almost as if she had come full circle, back to her childhood dreams of adventure. The only problem was that sometimes she felt like one of the villains: Pham Nuwen was a living person, not something to be sold.

She stood and walked out to meet her red-haired visitor.

He wasn't carrying the sword and handgun of Grondr's fanciful animation. Yet his clothes were the braided fabric of ancient adventure, and he carried himself with lazy confidence. Since her meeting with Grondr, she had looked up some anthropology from Old Earth. The red hair and the eyefolds had been known there, though rarely in the same individual. Certainly his smoky skin would have been remarkable to an inhabitant of Earth. This fellow was, as much as herself, a product of post-terrestrial evolution.

He stopped an arm's length away and gave her a lopsided grin. 'You look pretty human. Ravna Bergsndot?'

She smiled and nodded up at him. 'Mr Pham Nuwen?'

'Yes indeed. We seem both to be excellent guessers.' He swept past her into the shade of the inner office. Cocky fellow.

She followed him, unsure about protocol. You'd think with a fellow human there would be no problems . . .

Actually, the interview went pretty smoothly. It was more than thirty days since Pham Nuwen's resuscitation. Much of that time had been spent in cram language sessions. The fellow must be damned bright; he already spoke Triskweline trade talk with a folksy slickness. He really was rather cute. Ravna had been away from Sjandra Kei for two years, and had another year of her 'prenticeship to go. She'd been doing pretty well. She had many close friends here, Egravan, Sarale. But just chatting with this fellow brought a lot of the loneliness back. In some ways he was more alien that anything at Relay . . . and in some ways she wanted to just grab him and kiss his confident grin away.

Grondr Vrinimikalir had been telling the truth about this Pham Nuwen. The guy was actually enthusiastic about the Org's plans for him! In theory, that meant she could do her job with a clear conscience. In fact . . .

'Mr Nuwen, my job is to orient you to your new world. I know you've been exposed to some intense instruction the last few days, but there are limits to how fast such knowledge can sink in.'

The redhead smiled. 'Call me Pham. Sure, I feel like an overstuffed bag. My sleep time is full of little voices. I've learned an awful lot without experiencing anything. Worse, I've been a *target* for all this "education." It's a perfect setup if Vrinimi wants to trick me. That's why I'm learning to use the local library. And that's why I insisted they find someone like you.' He saw the surprise on her face. 'Ha! You didn't know that. See, talking to a real person gives me a chance to see things that aren't all planned ahead. Also, I've always been a pretty good judge of human nature; I think I can read you pretty well.' His grin showed he understood just how irritating he was being.

Ravna looked up at the green petals of the beachtrees. Maybe this boob deserved what he was getting into. 'So you have great experience dealing with people?'

'Given the limitations of the Slowness, I've been around, Ravna. I've been around. I know I don't look it, but I'm sixty-seven years old subjective. I thank your Organization for a fine job of thawing me out.' He tipped a non-existent hat in her direction. 'My last voyage was more than a thousand years objective. I was Programmer-at-Arms on a Qeng Ho longshot—' His eyes abruptly widened, and he said something unintelligible. For a moment he almost looked vulnerable.

Ravna reached a hand toward him. 'Memory?'

Pham Nuwen nodded. '*Damn*. This is something I *don't* thank you people for.'

Pham Nuwen had been frozen in the aftermath of violent death, not as a planned suspension. It was a near miracle that Vrinimi Org had been able to bring him back at all – at least with Middle Beyond technology. But memory was the hardest thing. The chemical basis of memory does not survive chaotic freezing well.

The problem was enough to shrink even Pham Nuwen's ego by a size or two. Ravna took pity on him. 'It's not likely that anything is completely lost. You just have to find a different angle on some things.'

'. . . Yes. I've been coached about that. Start with other memories; work sideways toward what you can't remember straight on. Well . . . it beats being dead.' Some of his jauntiness returned, but subdued to a really quite charming level. They talked for a long while as the redhead worked around the points he couldn't 'remember straight on.'

And gradually Ravna came to feel something she had never expected in connection with a Slow Zoner: *awe*. In one lifetime, Pham Nuwen had accomplished virtually everything that was possible for a being in the Slowness. All her life she had pitied the civilizations trapped down there. They could never know the glory; they might never know the truth. Yet by luck and skill and sheer strength of will, this fellow had leaped barrier after barrier. Had Grondr known the truth when he pictured the redhead with sword and slug gun? For Pham Nuwen really was a barbarian. He had been born on a fallen colony world – Canberra he called it. The place sounded much like medieval Nyjora, though not matriarchal. He'd been the youngest child of a king. He'd grown up with swords and poison and intrigue, living in stone castles by a cold, cold sea. No doubt this little prince would have ended up murdered – or king of all – if life had continued in the medieval way. But when he was thirteen years old everything changed. A world that had only legends of aircraft and radio was confronted by interstellar traders. In a year of trading, Canberra's feudal politics was turned on its head.

'Qeng Ho had invested three ships in the expedition to Canberra. They were pissed, thought we'd be at a higher level of technology. We couldn't resupply them, so two stayed behind, probably turned my poor world inside out. I left with the third – a crazy hostage deal my father thought he was putting over on them. I was lucky they didn't space me.'

Qeng Ho consisted of several hundred ramscoop ships operating in a volume hundreds of light-years across. Their vessels could reach almost a third of the speed of light. They were mostly traders, occasionally rescuers, even more rarely conquerors. When Pham Nuwen last knew them, they had settled thirty worlds and were almost three thousand years old. It was as extravagant a civilization as can ever exist in the Slowness . . . And of course, until Pham Nuwen was revived, no one in the Beyond had ever heard of it. Qeng Ho was like a million other doomed civilizations, buried thousands of light-years in the Slowness. Only by luck would they ever penetrate into the Beyond, where faster-than-light travel was possible.

But for a thirteen-year-old boy born to swords and chain mail, the Qeng Ho was more change than most living beings ever experience. In a matter of weeks, he went from medieval lordling to starship cabin boy.

'At first they didn't know what to do with me. Figured on popping me into cold storage and dumping me at the next stop. What can you make of a kid who thinks there's one world and it's flat, who has spent his whole life learning to whack about with a sword?' He stopped abruptly, as he did every few minutes, when the stream of recollection ran into damaged territory. Then his glance flicked out at Ravna, and his smile was as cocky as ever. 'I was one mean animal. I don't think civilized people realize what it's like to grow up with your own aunts and uncles scheming to murder you, and you training to get them first. In civilization I met bigger villains – guys who'd fry a whole planet and call it "reconciliation" – but for sheer up-close treachery, you can't beat my childhood.'

To hear Pham Nuwen tell it, only dumb luck saved the crew from his scheming. In the years that followed, he learned to fit in, learned civilized skills. Properly tamed, he could be an ideal ship master of the Qeng Ho.

And for many years he was. The Qeng Ho volume contained a couple of other races, and a number of human-colonized worlds. At three-tenths lightspeed, Pham spent decades in coldsleep getting from star to star, then a year or two at each port trying to make a profit with products and information that might be lethally out-of-date. The reputation of the Qeng Ho was some protection. 'Politics may come and go, but Greed goes on forever' was the fleet's motto, and they had lasted longer than most of their customers. Even religious fanatics grew a little cautious when they thought about Qeng Ho retribution. But more often it was the skill and deviousness of the shipmaster that saved the day. And few were a match for the little boy in Pham Nuwen.

'I was almost the perfect skipper. Almost. I always wanted to see what was beyond the space we had good records on. Every time I got really rich, so rich I could launch my own subfleet – I'd take some crazy chance and lose everything. I was the yo-yo of the Fleet. One run I'd be captain of five, the next I'd be pulling maintenance programming on some damn routineer. Given how time stretches out with sublight commerce, there were whole generations who thought I was a legendary genius – and others who used my name as a synonym for goofball.'

He paused and his eyes widened in pleased surprise. '*Ha!* I remember what I was doing there at the end. I was in the "goofball" part of my cycle, but it didn't matter. There was this captain of twenty who was even crazier than I . . . Can't remember her name. Her? Couldn't have been; I'd never serve under a fem captain.' He was almost talking to himself. 'Anyway, this guy was willing to bet *everything* on the sort of thing normal folks would argue about over beer. He called his ship the, um, it translates as something like "wild witless bird" – that gives you the idea about him. He figured there must be some really high-tech civilizations somewhere in the universe. The problem was to find them. In a strange way, he had almost guessed about the Zones. Only problem was, he wasn't crazy enough; he got one little thing wrong. Can you guess what?'

Ravna nodded. Considering where Pham's wreck was found, it was obvious.

'Yeah. I'll bet it's an idea older than spaceflight: the "elder races" must be toward the galactic core, where stars are closer and there are black hole exotica for power. He was taking his entire fleet of twenty. They'd keep going till they found somebody or had to stop and colonize. This captain figured success was unlikely in our lifetime. But with proper planning we could end up in a close-packed region where it would be easy to found a new Qeng Ho – and it would proceed even further.

'Anyway, I was lucky to get aboard even as a programmer; this captain knew all the wrong things about me.'

The expedition lasted a thousand years, penetrating two hundred and fifty light-years galactic inward. The Qeng Ho volume was closer to the

Bottom of the Slowness than Old Earth, and they were proceeding inwards from there. Even so, it was plain bad luck that they encountered the edge of the Deeps after only two hundred and fifty light-years. One after another, the *Wild Witless Bird* lost contact with the other ships. Sometimes it happened without warning, other times there was evidence of computer failure or gross incompetence. The survivors saw a pattern, guessed that common components were failing. Of course, no one connected the problems with the *region of space* they were entering.

'We backed down from ram speeds, found a solar system with a semi-habitable planet. We'd lost track of everybody else . . . Just what we did then isn't real clear to me.' He gave a dry laugh. 'We must have been right at the edge, staggering around at about IQ 60. I remember fooling with the life support system. That's probably what actually killed us.' For a moment he looked sad and bewildered. He shrugged. 'And then I woke up in the tender clutches of Vrinimi Org, here where faster-than-light travel is possible . . . and I can see the edge of Heaven itself.'

Ravna didn't say anything for a moment. She looked across her beach into the surf. They'd been talking a long time. The sun was peeking under the tree petals, its light shifting across her office. Did Grondr realize what he had here? Almost anything from the Slow Zone had collector's value. *People* fresh from the Slowness were even more valuable. But Pham Nuwen might be unique. He had personally experienced more than had some whole civilizations, and he had ventured into the Deeps to boot. She understood now why he looked to the Transcend and called it 'Heaven.' It wasn't entirely naïveté, nor a failure in the Organization's education programs. Pham Nuwen had already been through two transforming experiences, from pre-tech to star-traveler, and star-traveler to Beyonder. Each was a jump almost beyond imagination. Now he saw that another step was possible, and was perfectly willing to sell himself to take it.

So why should I risk my job to change his mind? But her mouth was living a life of its own. 'Why not postpone the Transcend, Pham? Take some time to understand what is here in the Beyond. You'd be welcome in almost any civilization. And on human worlds you'd be the wonder of the age.' *A glimpse of non-Nyjoran humanity.* The local newsgroups at Sjandra Kei had thought Ravna radically ambitious to take a 'prenticeship twenty thousand light-years away. Coming back from it, she would have her pick of Full Academician jobs on any of a dozen worlds. That was nothing compared to Pham Nuwen; there were folks so rich they might *give* him a world if he would just stay. 'You could name your price.'

The redhead's lazy smile broadened. 'Ah, but you see, I've already named my price, and I think Vrinimi can meet it.'

I really wish I could do something about that smile, thought Ravna. Pham Nuwen's ticket to the Transcend was based on a Power's sudden interest in the Straumli perversion. This innocent's ego might end up smeared across a million death cubes, running a million million simulations of human nature.

Grondr called less than five minutes after Pham Nuwen's departure. Ravna knew the Org would be eavesdropping, and she'd already told Grondr her misgivings about this 'selling' of a sophont. Nevertheless, she was a bit nervous to see him.

'When is he actually going to leave for the Transcend?'

Grondr rubbed at his freckles. He didn't seem angry. 'Not for ten or twenty days. The Power that's negotiating for him is more interested in looking at our archives and watching what's passing through Relay. Also . . . despite the human's enthusiasm for going, he's really quite cautious.'

'Oh?'

'Yes. He's insisting on a library budget, and permission to roam anywhere in the system. He's been chatting with random employees all over the Docks. He was especially insistent about talking to you.' Grondr's mouth parts clicked in a smile. 'Feel free to speak your mind to him. Basically, he's tasting around for hidden poison. Hearing the worst from you should make him trust us.'

She was coming to understand Grondr's confidence. Damn but Pham Nuwen had a thick head. 'Yes sir. He's asked me to show him around the Foreign Quarter tonight.' *As you well know.*

'Fine. I wish the rest of the deal were going as smoothly.' Grondr turned so that only peripheral freckles were looking in her direction. He was surrounded by status displays of the Org's communication and database operations. From what she could see, things were remarkably busy. 'Maybe I should not bring this up, but it's just possible you can help . . . Business is very brisk.' Grondr did not seem pleased to report the good news. 'We have nine civilizations from the Top of the Beyond that are bidding for wide band data feeds. That we could handle. But this Power that sent a ship here . . .'

Ravna interrupted almost without thinking, a breach that would have horrified her a few days earlier. 'Just who is it, by the way? Any chance we're entertaining the Straumli Perversion?' The thought of *that* taking the redhead was a chill.

'Not unless all the Powers are fooled, too. Marketing calls our current visitor "Old One."' He smiled. 'That's something of a joke, but true even so. We've known it for eleven years.' No one really knew how long Transcendent beings lived, but it was a rare Power that stayed communicative for more than five or ten years. They lost interest, or grew into something different – or really did die. There were a million explanations, thousands that were allegedly from the Powers firsthand. Ravna guessed that the true explanation was the simplest one: Intelligence is the handmaiden of flexibility and change. Dumb animals can change only as fast as natural evolution. Human equivalent races, once on their technological run-up, hit the limits of their zone in a matter of a few thousand years. In the Transcend, superhumanity can happen so fast that its creators are destroyed. It wasn't surprising then that the Powers themselves were evanescent.

So calling an eleven-year Power 'Old One' was almost reasonable.

'We believe that Old One is a variant on the Type 73 pattern. Such are rarely malicious – and we know from whom it Transcended. Just now it's causing us major discomfort, though. For twenty days it has been monopolizing an enormous and increasing percentage of Relay bandwidth. Since its ship arrived, it's been all over the archive and our local nets. We've asked Old One to send noncritical data by starship, but it refuses. This afternoon was the worst yet. Almost five percent of Relay's capacity was bound up in its service. And the creature is sending almost as much downlink as it is receiving uplink.'

That *was* weird, but, 'It's still paying for the business, isn't it? If Old One can pay top price, why do you care?'

'Ravna, we hope our Organization will be around for many years after the Old One is gone. There is nothing it could offer us that would be good through all that time.' Ravna nodded. Actually, there were certain 'magic' automations that might work down here, but their long-term effectiveness would be dubious. This was a commercial situation, not some exercise in an Applied Theology course. 'Old One can easily top any bid from the Middle Beyond. But if we give it all the services it demands, we'll be effectively nonfunctional to the rest of our customers – and they are the people we must depend on in the future.'

His image was replaced by an archive access report. Ravna was very familiar with the format, and Grondr's complaint really hit home. The Known Net was a vast thing, a hierarchical anarchy that linked hundreds of millions of worlds. Yet even the main trunks had bandwidths like something out of Earth's dawn age; a wrist dataset could do better on a local net. That's why bulk across to the Archive was mostly local – to media freighters visiting the Relay system. But now . . . during the last hundred hours, remote access to the Archive, both by volume and by count, had been higher than local! And ninety percent of those accesses were from a single account – Old One's.

Grondr's voice continued from behind the graphics. 'We've got one backbone transceiver dedicated to this Power right now . . . Frankly, we can't tolerate this for more than a few days; the ultimate expense is just too great.'

Grondr's face was back on the display. 'Anyway, I think you can see that the deal for the barbarian is really the least of our problems. The last twenty days have brought more income than the last two years – far more than we can verify and absorb. We're endangered by our own success.' He made an ironic smile-frown.

They talked a few minutes about Pham Nuwen, then Grondr rang off. Afterwards, Ravna took a walk along her beach. The sun was well down toward the aft horizon, and the sand was just pleasantly warm against her feet; the Docks went round the planet once every twenty hours, circling the pole at about forty degrees north latitude. She walked close to the surf, where the sand was flat and wet. The mist off the sea was moist against her skin. The blue sky just above the white-tops shaded quickly to indigo and black. Specks of silver moved up there, agrav floaters bringing starships into the Docks. The whole thing was so fabulously, unnecessarily expensive. Ravna was by turns grossed out and bedazzled. Yet after two years at Relay, she was beginning to see the point. Vrinimi Org wanted the Beyond to know that it had the resources to handle *whatever* communication and archive demands might be made on it. And they wanted the Beyond to suspect that there were hidden gifts from the Transcend here, things that might make it more than a little dangerous to invaders.

She stared into the spray, feeling it bead on her lashes. So Grondr had the big problem right now: how do you tell a Power to take a walk? All Ravna Bergsndot had to worry about was one overconfident twit who seemed hell-bent on destroying himself. She turned and paralleled the water. Every third wave it surged over her ankles.

She sighed. Pham Nuwen was beyond doubt a twit . . . but what an awesome one. Intellectually, she had always known that there was no difference in the possible intelligence of Beyonders and the primitives of the Slowness. Most automation worked better in the Beyond; ultralight communication was possible. But you had to go to the Transcend to build truly superhuman minds. So it shouldn't be surprising that Pham Nuwen was capable. *Very* capable. He had picked up Triskweline with incredible ease. She had little doubt that he was the master skipper he claimed. And to be a trader in the Slowness, to risk centuries between the stars for a destination that might have fallen from civilization or become deadly hostile to outsiders . . . that took courage that was hard to imagine. She could understand how he might think going to the Transcend was just another challenge. He'd had about twenty days to absorb a whole new universe. That simply wasn't enough time to understand that the rules change when the players are more than human.

Well, he still had a few days of grace. She would change his mind. And after talking to Grondr just now, she wouldn't feel especially guilty about doing it.

8

The Foreign Quarter was actually about a third of the Docks. It abutted the no-atmosphere periphery – where ships actually docked – and extended inwards to a section of the central sea. Vrinimi Org had convinced a significant number of races that this was a wonder of the Middle Beyond. In addition to freight traffic there were tourists – some of the wealthiest beings in the Beyond.

Pham Nuwen had carte blanche to these amusements. Ravna took him through the more spectacular ones, including an agrav hop over the Docks. The barbarian was more impressed by their pocket space suits than by the Docks. 'I've seen structures bigger than that down in the Slowness.' *Not hovering in a planetary gravity well, you haven't.*

Pham Nuwen seemed to mellow as the evening progressed. At least his comments became more perceptive, less edged. He wanted to see how real traders lived in the Beyond, and Ravna showed him the bourses and the traders' Local.

They ended up in The Wandering Company just after Docks' midnight. This was not Organization territory, but it was one of Ravna's favorite places, a private dive that attracted traders from the Top to the Bottom. She wondered how the decor would appeal to Pham Nuwen. The place was modeled as a meeting lodge on some world of the Slow Zone. A three-meter model ramscoop hung in the air over the main service floor. Blue-green drive fields glowed from the ship's every corner and flange, and spread faintly among patrons sitting below.

To Ravna the walls and floors were heavy timber, rough cut. People like Egravan saw stone walls and narrow tunnels – the sort of broodery his race had maintained on new conquests of long ago. The trickery was optical – not some mental smudging – and about the best that could be done in the Middle Beyond.

Ravna and Pham walked between widely spaced tables. The owners weren't as successful with sound as with vision: the music was faint and changed from table to table. Smells changed too, and were a little bit harder to take. Air management was working hard to keep everyone healthy, if not completely comfortable. Tonight the place was crowded. At the far end of the service floor, the special-atmosphere nooks were occupied: low pressure, high pressure, high NO_x, aquaria. Some customers were vague blurs within turbid atmospheres.

In some ways it might have been a port bar at Sjandra Kei. Yet . . . this was *Relay*. It attracted High Beyonders who would never come to backwaters like Sjandra Kei. Most of the High Ones didn't look very strange; civilizations at the Top were most often just colonies from below. But the headbands she saw here were not jewelry. Mind-computer links aren't efficient in the Middle Beyond, but most of the High Beyonders would not give them up. Ravna started toward a group of banded tripods and their machines. Let Pham Nuwen talk with creatures who teetered on the edge of transsapience.

Surprisingly, he touched her arm, drawing her back. 'Let's walk around a little more.' He was looking all around the hall, as if searching for a familiar face. 'Let's find some other humans first.'

When holes showed in Pham Nuwen's cram-education, they were gapingly wide. Ravna tried to keep her face serious. 'Other humans? We're all there is at Relay, Pham.'

'But the friends you've been telling me about . . . Egravan, Sarale?'

Ravna just shook her head. For a moment the barbarian looked vulnerable. Pham Nuwen had spent his life crawling at sublight between human-colonized star systems. She knew that in all that life he had seen only three non-human races. Now he was lost in a sea of alienness. She kept her sympathy to herself; this one insight might affect the guy more than all her arguing.

But the instant passed, and he was smiling again. 'Even more an adventure.' They left the main floor and walked past special-atmosphere nooks. 'Lord, but Qeng Ho would love this.'

No humans anywhere, and The Wandering Company was the homiest meeting place she knew; many Org customers met only on the Net. She felt her own homesickness welling up. On the second floor, a signet flag caught her eye. She'd known something like it back at Sjandra Kei. She drew Pham Nuwen across the floor, and started up the timbered stairs.

Out of the background murmur, she heard a high-pitched twittering. It wasn't Triskweline, but the words made sense! By the Powers, it was *Samnorsk*: 'I do believe it's a Homo Sap! Over here, my lady.' She followed the sound to the table with the signet flag.

'May we sit with you?' she asked, savoring the familiar language.

'Please do.' The twitterer looked like a small ornamental tree sitting in a six-wheeled cart. The cart was marked with cosmetic stripes and tassels; its 150-by-120-centimeter topside was covered with a cargo scarf in the same pattern as the signet flag. The creature was a Greater Skroderider. Its race traded through much of the Middle Beyond, including Sjandra Kei. The Skroderider's high-pitched voice came from its voder. But speaking Samnorsk, it sounded homier than anything she'd heard in a long time. Even granting the mental peculiarities of Skroderiders, she felt a surge of affectionate nostalgia, as if she had run into an old classmate in a far city.

'My name is—' the sound was the rustling of fronds, 'but you can easier call me Blueshell. It's nice to see a familiar face, hahaha.' Blueshell spoke the laughter as words. Pham Nuwen had sat down with Ravna, but he understood not a word of Samnorsk and so the great reunion was lost on him.

The Rider switched to Triskweline and introduced his four companions: another Skroderider, and three humanoids who seemed to like the shadows. None of the humanoids spoke Samnorsk, but no one was more than one translator hop from Triskweline.

The Skroderiders were owners/operators of a small interstellar freighter, the *Out of Band II*. The humanoids were certificants for part of the starship's current cargo. 'My mate and I have been in the business almost two hundred years. We have happy feelings for your race, my lady. Our first runs were between Sjandra Kei and Forste Utgrep. Your people are good customers and we scarcely ever have a shipment rot . . .' He wheeled his skrode back from the table and then drove forward – the equivalent of a small bow.

All was not sweetness and light, however. One of the humanoids spoke. The sounds could almost have come from a human throat, though they made no sense. A moment passed as the house translator processed his words. Then the brooch on his jacket spoke in clear Triskweline: 'Blueshell states you are Homo sapiens. Know that you have our animosity. We are bankrupt, near-stranded here by your race's evil creation. The Straumli Perversion.' The words sounded emotionless, but Ravna could see the creature's tense posture, its fingers twisting at a drink bulb.

Considering his attitude, it probably wouldn't help to point out that though she was human, Sjandra Kei was thousands of light-years from Straum. 'You came here from the Realm?' she asked the Skroderider.

Blueshell didn't answer immediately. That's the way it was with his race; he was probably trying to remember who she was and what they were all talking about. Then: 'Yes, yes. Please do excuse my certificants' hostility. Our main cargo is a one-time cryptographic pad. The source is Commercial Security at Sjandra Kei; the destination is the certificants' High colony. It was the usual arrangement: We're carrying a one-third xor of the pad. Independent shippers are carrying the others. At the destination, the three parts would be xor'd together. The result could supply a dozen worlds' crypto needs on the Net for—'

Downstairs there was a commotion. Someone was smoking something a bit too strong for the air scrubbers. Ravna caught a whiff, enough to shimmer her vision. It had knocked out several patrons on the main level. Management was counseling the offending customer. Blueshell made an abrupt noise. He backed his skrode from the table and rolled to the railing. 'Don't want to be caught unawares. Some people can be so *abrupt* . . .' When nothing more came of the incident, he returned. 'Uh, where was I?' He was silent a moment, consulting the short-term memory built into his skrode. 'Yes, yes . . . We would become relatively rich if our plans work out. Unfortunately, we stopped on Straum to drop off some bulk data.' He pivoted on his rear four wheels. 'Surely that was safe? Straum itself is more than a hundred light-years from their lab in the Transcend. Yet—'

One of the certificants interrupted with loud gabble. The house translator kicked in a moment later: 'Yes. It should have been safe. We saw no violence. Ship's recorders show that our safeness was not breached. Yet now there are rumors. Net groups claim that Straumli Realm is owned by perversion. Absurdity. Yet these rumors have crossed the Net to our destination. Our cargo is not trusted, so our cargo is ruined: now it is only a few grams of data medium carrying random—' In the middle of the flat-voiced translation, the humanoid lunged out of the shadows. Ravna had a glimpse of a jaw edged with razor-sharp gums. He threw his drink bulb at the table in front of her.

Pham Nuwen's hand flashed out, snatching the drink before it hit – before she had quite realized what was happening. The redhead came slowly to his feet. From the shadows, the two other humanoids came to their feet and moved toward their friend. Pham Nuwen didn't say a word. He set the bulb carefully down and leaned just slightly toward the other, his hands relaxed yet bladelike. Cheap fiction talks about 'looks of deadly menace.' Ravna had never expected to see the real thing. But the humanoids saw it too. They tugged their friend gently back from the table. The loudmouth did not resist, but once beyond Pham's reach he erupted in a barrage of squeals and hisses that left the house translator speechless. He made a sharp gesture with three fingers, and shut up. The three swept silently down the stairs and away.

Pham Nuwen sat down, his gray eyes calm and untroubled. Maybe he *did* have something to be arrogant about! Ravna looked across at the two Skroderiders. 'I'm sorry your cargo lost value.'

Most of Ravna's past contacts had been with Lesser Skroderiders, whose reflexes were only slightly augmented beyond their sessile heritage. Had these two even noticed the interruption? But Blueshell answered immediately, 'Do not apologize. Ever since our arrival, those three have been complaining. Contract partners or not, I'm very tired of them.' He lapsed into potted-plant mode.

After a moment, the other Rider – Greenstalk, was it? – spoke. 'Besides, our commercial situation may not be a complete failure. I am sure the other thirds of the shipment went nowhere near Straumli Realm.' That was the usual procedure anyway: each part of the shipment was carried by a different company, each taking a very different path. If the other thirds could be certified, the crew of the *Out of Band* might not come away empty-handed. 'In – in fact, there may be a way we can get full certification. True, we were at Straumli Main, but—'

'How long ago did you leave?'

'Six hundred and fifty hours ago. About two hundred hours after they dropped off the Net.'

It suddenly dawned on Ravna that she was talking to something like eyewitnesses. After thirty days, the Threats news was still dominated by the events at Straum. The consensus was that a Class Two perversion had been created – even Vrinimi Org believed that. Yet it was still mainly guess-work . . . And here she was talking to beings who had actually been there. 'You don't think the Straumers created a perversion?'

It was Blueshell who replied. 'Sigh,' he said. 'Our certificants deny it, but I see a problem of conscience here. We *did* witness strangeness on Straum . . . Have you ever encountered artificial immune systems? The ones that work in the Middle Beyond are more trouble than they're worth, so perhaps not. I noticed a real change in certain officers of the Crypto Authority right after the Straumli victory. It was as if they were suddenly part of a poorly calibrated automation, as if they were somebody's, um, fingers . . . No one can doubt they were playing in the Transcend. They found something up there; a lost archive. But that is not the point.' He stopped talking for a long moment; Ravna almost thought he was finished. 'You see, just before leaving Straumli Main, we—'

But now Pham Nuwen was talking too. 'That's something I've been wondering about. Everybody talks as though this Straumli Realm was doomed the moment they began research in the Transcend. Look. I've played with bugged software and strange weapons. I know you can get killed that way. But it looks like the Straumers were careful to put their lab far away. They were building something that could go very wrong, but apparently it was a previously tried experiment – like just about everything Up Here. They could stop the work any time it deviated from the records, right up to the end. So how could they screw up so bad?'

The question stopped the Skroderider in its tracks. You didn't need a doctorate in Applied Theology to know the answer. *Even the damn Straumers should have known the answer.* But given Pham Nuwen's back-ground, it was a reasonable question. Ravna kept her mouth shut. The Skroderider's very alienness might be more convincing to Pham than another lecture from her.

Blueshell dithered for a moment, no doubt using his skrode to help assemble his arguments. When he finally spoke, he didn't seem irritated by the interruption. 'I hear several misconceptions, my lady Pham.' He seemed to use the old Nyjoran honorific pretty indiscriminately. 'Have you been into the archive at Relay?'

Pham said yes. Ravna guessed he'd never been past the beginners' front end.

'Then you know that an archive is a fundamentally vaster thing than the database on a conventional local net. For practical purposes, the big ones can't even be duplicated. The major archives go back millions of years, have been maintained by hundreds of different races – most now extinct or Transcended into Powers. Even the archive at Relay is a jumble, so huge that indexing systems are laid on top of indexing systems. Only in the

Transcend could such a mass be well organized and even then only the Powers could understand it.'

'So?'

'There are thousands of archives in the Beyond – tens of thousands if you count the ones that have fallen into disrepair or dropped off the Net. Along with unending trivia, they contain important secrets and important lies. There are traps and snares.' Millions of races played with the advice that filtered unsolicited across the Net. Tens of thousands had been burned thereby. Sometimes the damage was relatively minor, good inventions that weren't quite right for the target environment. Sometimes it was malicious, viruses that would jam a local net so thoroughly that a civilization must restart from scratch. Where-Are-They-Now and Threats carried stories of worse tragedies: planets kneedeep in replicant goo, races turned brainless by badly programmed immune systems.

Pham Nuwen was wearing his skeptical expression. 'Just test the stuff at a safe remove. Be prepared for local disasters.'

That would have brought most explanations to a stop. Ravna had to admire the Skroderider: he paused, retreated to still more elementary terms. 'True, simple caution can prevent many disasters. And if your lab is in the Middle or Low Beyond, such caution is all that is really needed – no matter how sophisticated the threat. But we all understand the nature of the Zones . . .' Ravna had virtually no feel for Rider body language, but she would have sworn that Blueshell was watching the barbarian expectantly, trying to gauge the depth of Pham's ignorance.

The human nodded impatiently.

Blueshell continued. 'In the Transcend, truly sophisticated equipment can operate devices substantially smarter than anyone down here. Of course, almost any economic or military competition can be won by the side with superior computing resources. Such can be had at the Top of the Beyond and in the Transcend. Races are always migrating there, hoping to build their utopias. But what do you do when your new creations may be smarter than you are? It happens that there are limitless possibilities for disaster, even if an existing Power does not cause harm. So there are unnumbered recipes for safely taking advantage of the Transcend. Of course they can't be effectively examined except in the Transcend. And run on devices of their own description, the recipes themselves become sentient.'

Understanding was beginning to glimmer across Pham Nuwen's face.

Ravna leaned forward, caught the redhead's attention. 'There are complex things in the archives. None of them is sentient, but some have the potential, if some naïve young race will only believe their promises. We think that's what happened to Straumli Realm. They were tricked by documentation that claimed miracles, tricked into building a transcendent being, a Power – but one that victimizes sophonts in the Beyond.' She didn't mention how rare such perversion was. The Powers were variously malevolent, playful, indifferent – but virtually all of them had better uses for their time than exterminating cockroaches in the wild.

Pham Nuwen rubbed his jaw thoughtfully. 'Okay, I guess I see. But I get the feeling this is common knowledge. If it's this deadly, how did the Straumli bunch get taken in?'

'Bad luck and criminal incompetence.' The words popped out of her with surprising force. She hadn't realized she was so bent by the Straumli thing; somewhere inside, her old feelings for Straumli Realm were still alive. 'Look. Operations in the High Beyond and in the Transcend *are* dangerous. Civilizations up there don't last long, but there will always be people who try. Very few of the threats are actively evil. What happened to the Straumers . . . They ran across this recipe advertising wondrous treasure. Quite possibly it had been lying around for millions of years, a little too risky for other folks to try. You're right, the Straumers knew the dangers.' But it was a classic situation of balancing risks and choosing wrong. Perhaps a third of Applied Theology was about how to dance near the flame without getting incinerated. No one knew the details of the Straumli debacle, but she could guess them from a hundred similar cases:

'So they set up a base in the Transcend at this lost archive – if that's what it was. They began implementing the schemes they found. You can be sure they spent most of their time watching it for signs of deception. No doubt the recipe was a series of more or less intelligible steps with a clear takeoff point. The early stages would involve computers and programs more effective than anything in the Beyond – but apparently well-behaved.'

'. . . Yeah. Even in the Slowness, a big program can be full of surprises.'

Ravna nodded. 'And some of *these* would be near or beyond human complexity. Of course, the Straumers would know this and try to isolate their creations. But given a malignant and clever design . . . it should be no surprise if the devices leaked onto the lab's local net and distorted the information there. From then on, the Straumers wouldn't have a chance. The most cautious staffers would be framed as incompetent. Phantom threats would be detected, emergency responses demanded. More sophisticated devices would be built, and with fewer safeguards. Conceivably, the humans were killed or rewritten before the Perversion even achieved transsapience.'

There was a long silence. Pham Nuwen looked almost chastened. *Yeah. There's a lot you don't know, Buddy. Think on what Old One might have planned for you.*

Blueshell bent a tendril to taste a brown concoction that smelled like seaweed. 'Well told, my lady Ravna. But there is one difference in the present situation. It may be good fortune, and very important . . . You see, just before leaving Straumli Main, we attended a beach party among the Lesser Riders. They had been little affected by events to that point; many hadn't even noticed the destruction of independence at Straum. With luck, they may be the last enslaved.' His squeaky voice lowered an octave, trailing into silence. 'Where was I? Yes, the party. There was one fellow there, a bit more lively than the average. Somewhere years past, he had bonded with a traveler in a Straumli news service. Now he was acting as a clandestine data drop, so humble that he wasn't even listed in that service's own net . . .

'Anyway, the researchers at the Straumli lab – a few of them at least – were not so incautious as you say. They suspected a perverse runaway, and were determined to sabotage it.'

This *was* news, but – 'Doesn't look like they had much success, does it?'

'I am nodding agreement. They did not prevent it, but they did plan to escape the laboratory planet with two starships. And they did get word of their attempt into channels that ended with my acquaintance at the beach party. And here is the important part: At least one of these ships was to carry away some final elements of the Perversion's recipe – *before* they were incorporated into the design.'

'Surely there were backups—' began Pham Nuwen.

Ravna waved him silent. There had been enough grade-school explanations for one night. This was incredible. She'd been following the news about Straumli Realm as much as anyone. The Realm was the first High daughter colony of Sjandra Kei; it was horrifying to see it destroyed. But nowhere in Threats had there been even a rumor of this: the Perversion not whole? 'If this is true, then the Straumers may have a chance. It all depends on the missing parts of the design document.'

'Just so. And of course the humans realized this too. They planned to head straight for the Bottom of the Beyond, rendezvous there with their accomplices from Straum.'

Which – considering the ultimate magnitude of the disaster – would never happen. Ravna leaned back, oblivious of Pham Nuwen for the first time in many hours. Most likely both ships had been destroyed by now. If not – well, the Straumers had been at least half-smart, heading for the Bottom. If they had what Blueshell thought, the Perversion would be very interested in finding them. It was no wonder Blueshell and Greenstalk hadn't announced this on the news groups. 'So you know where they were going to rendezvous?' she said softly.

'Approximately.'

Greenstalk burred something at him.

'Not in ourselves,' he said. 'The coordinates are in the safeness at our ship. But there is more. The Straumers had a backup plan if the rendezvous failed. They intended to signal Relay with their ship's ultrawave.'

'Now wait. Just how big is this ship?' Ravna was no physical-layer engineer, but she knew that Relay's backbone transceivers were actually swarms of antenna elements scattered across several light-years, each element ten-thousand kilometers across.

Blueshell rolled forward and back, a quick gesture of agitation. 'We don't know, but it's nothing exceptional. Unless you're looking precisely at it with large antenna, you'd never detect it from here.'

Greenstalk added, 'We think that was part of their plan, though it is desperation on top of desperation. Since we came to Relay, we've been talking to the Org—'

'Discreetly! Quietly!' Blueshell put in abruptly.

'Yes. We've asked the Organization to listen for this ship. I'm afraid we haven't talked to the right people. No one seems to put much credence in us. After all, the story is ultimately from a Lesser Rider.' *Yeah. What could they know that was under a hundred years old?* 'What we're asking would normally be a great expense, and apparently prices are especially high right now.'

Ravna tried to curb her enthusiasm. If she had read this in a newsgroup, it would've been just one more interesting rumor. Why should she boggle just because she was getting it face-to-face? By the Powers, what irony. Hundreds of customers from the Top and the Transcend – even Old One – were saturating Relays resources with their curiosity about the Straumli debacle. What if the answer had been sitting in front of them, suppressed by the very eagerness of their investigation? 'Just who have you been talking to? Never mind, never mind.' Maybe she should just go to Grondr 'Kalir with the story. 'I think you should know that I am a—' *very minor!* '—employee of the Vrinimi Organization. I may be able to help.'

She had expected some surprise at this sudden good luck. Instead there was a pause. Apparently Blueshell had lost his place in the conversation. Finally Greenstalk spoke. 'I am blushing . . . You see, we knew that. Blueshell looked you up in the employees directory; you are the only human in the Org. You're not in Customer Contact, but we thought that if we chanced upon you, so to speak, you might give us a kindly hearing.'

Blueshell's tendrils rustled together sharply. Irritation? Or had he finally caught up to the conversation? 'Yes. Well, since we are all being so frank, I suppose we should confess that this might even benefit us. If the refugee ship can prove that the Perversion is not a full Class Two, then perhaps we can convince our buyers that our cargo has not been compromised. If they only knew, my certificant friends would be groveling at your feet, my lady Ravna.'

They stayed at The Wandering Company until well past midnight. Business picked up at the circadian peak of some of the new arrivals. Floor and table shows were raucous all around. Pham's eyes flickered this way and that, taking it all in. But above all he seemed fascinated by Blueshell and Greenstalk. The two were starkly nonhuman, in some ways even strange as aliens go. Skroderiders were one of the very few races that had achieved long-term stability in the Beyond. Speciation had long ago occurred, varieties heading outward or becoming extinct. And still there were some who matched their ancient skrodes, a unique balance of outlook and machine interface that was more than a billion years old. But Blueshell and Greenstalk were also traders with much of the outlook that Pham Nuwen had known in the Slowness. And though Pham acted as ignorant as ever, there was new diplomacy in him. Or maybe the awesomeness of the Beyond was finally getting through his thick skull. He couldn't have asked for better drinking buddies. As a race, the Skroderiders preferred lazy reminiscence to almost any activity. Once delivered of their critical message, the two were quite content to talk of their life in the Beyond, to explain things in whatever detail the barbarian could wish. The razor-jawed certificants stayed well lost.

Ravna got a mild buzz on, and watched the three talk shop. She smiled to herself. *She* was the outsider now, the person who had never *done*. Blueshell and Greenstalk had been all over, and some of their stories sounded wild even to her. Ravna had a theory (not that widely accepted, actually) that where beings have a common fluency, little else matters. Two of these three might be mistaken for potted trees on hotcarts, and the third was unlike any human in her life. Their fluency was in an artificial language, and two of the 'voices' were squawky raspings. Yet . . . after a few minutes' listening, their personalities seemed to float in her mind's eye, more interesting than many of her school chums, but not that different. The two Skroderiders were mates. She hadn't thought that could count for much; among Riders, sex amounted to scarcely more than being next-door neighbors at the right time of year. Yet there was deep affection here. Greenstalk especially seemed a loving personality. She (he?) was shy yet stubborn, with a kind of honesty that might be a major handicap in a trader. Blueshell made up for that failing. He (she?) could be glib and talkative, quite capable of maneuvering things his way. Underneath, Ravna glimpsed a compulsive person, uncomfortable with his own sneakiness, ultimately grateful when Greenstalk reined him in.

And what of Pham Nuwen? *Yes, what's the inner being you see there?* In an odd way, he was more of a mystery. The arrogant boob of this afternoon seemed to be mostly invisible tonight. Maybe it had been a cover for insecurity. The fellow had been born in a male-dominated culture, virtually the opposite of the matriarchy that all Beyonder humanity descended from. Underneath the arrogance, a very nice person might be living. Then there was the way he had faced down the razor-jaw. And the way he was drawing out the Skroderiders. It occurred to Ravna that after a lifetime of reading romantic fiction, she had run into her first hero.

It was after 02:30 when they left The Wandering Company. The sun would be rising across the bow horizon in less than five hours. The two Skroderiders came outside to see them off. Blueshell had switched back to

Samnorsk to regale Ravna with a story of his last visit to Sjandra Kei – and to remind her to ask about the refugee ship.

The Skroderiders dwindled beneath them as Ravna and Pham rose into the thinning air and headed toward the residential towers.

The two humans didn't say anything for a couple of minutes. It was even possible that Pham Nuwen was impressed by the view. They were passing over gaps in the brightly lit Docks, places where they could see through the parks and concourses to the surface of Groundside a thousand kilometers below. The clouds there were whorls of dark on dark.

Ravna's residence was at the outer edge of the Docks. Here the air fountains were of no use; her apartment tower rose into frank vacuum. They glided down to her balcony, trading their suits' atmosphere for the apartment's. Ravna's mouth was leading a life of its own, explaining how the residence was what she'd been assigned when she worked at the archive, that it was nothing compared to her new office. Pham Nuwen nodded, quiet-faced. There were none of the smart remarks of their earlier tours.

She babbled on, and then they were inside and . . . She shut up, and they just looked at each other. In a way, she'd wanted this clown ever since Grondr's silly animation. But it wasn't till this evening at The Wandering Company that she'd felt right about bringing him home with her. 'Well, I, uh . . .' *So. Ravna, the ravening princess. Where is your glib tongue now?*

She settled for reaching out, putting her hand on his. Pham Nuwen smiled back, shy too, by the Powers! 'I think you have a nice place,' he said.

'I've decorated it Techno-Primitive. Being stuck at the edge of the Docks has its points: The natural view isn't messed up by city lights. Here, I'll show you.' She doused the lights and pulled the curtains aside. The window was a natural transparency, looking out from the edge of the Docks. The view tonight should be terrific. On the ride from The Company the sky had been awfully dark. The in-system factories must be off-line or hidden behind Groundside. Even ship traffic seemed sparse.

She went back to stand by Pham. The window was a vague rectangle across her vision. 'You have to wait a minute for your eyes to adjust. There's no amplification at all.' The curve of Groundside was clear now, clouds with occasional pricks of light. She slipped her arm across his back, and after a moment felt his across her shoulders.

She'd guessed right: tonight the Galaxy owned the sky. It was a sight that Vrinimi old hands happily ignored. For Ravna it was the most beautiful thing about Relay. Without enhancement, the light was faint. Twenty thousand light-years is a long, long way. At first there was just a suggestion of mist, and an occasional star. As her eyes adapted, the mist took shape, curving arcs, some places brighter, some dimmer. A minute more and . . . there were knots in the mist . . . there were streaks of utter black that separated the curving arms . . . complexity on complexity, twisting toward the pale hub that was the Core. Maelstrom. Whirlpool. Frozen, still, across half the sky.

She heard Pham's breath catch in his throat. He said something, sing-song syllables that could not have been Trisk, and certainly not Samnorsk. 'All my life I lived in a tiny clump of that. And I thought I was a master of space. I never dreamed to stand and see the whole blessed thing at once.' His hand tightened on her shoulder, then gentled, stroking her neck. 'And no matter how long we watch, will we see any sign of the Zones?'

She shook her head slowly. 'But they're easily imagined.' She gestured with her free hand. In the large, the Zones of Thought followed the mass distribution of the Galaxy; The Unthinking Depths extending down to the soft glow of the galactic Core. Farther out, the Great Slowness, where humankind had been born, where ultralight could not exist and civilizations lived and died unknowing and unknown. And the Beyond, the stars about four-fifths out from the center, extending well off-plane to include places like Relay. The Known Net had existed in some form for billions of years in the Beyond. It was not a civilization; few civilizations lasted longer than a million years. But the records of the past were quite complete. Sometimes they were intelligible. More often, reading them involved translations of translations of translations, passed down from one defunct race to another with no one to corroborate – worse than any multihop net message could ever be. Yet some things were quite clear: There had always been the Zones of Thought, though perhaps they were slightly inward-moved now. There had always been wars and peace, and races upwelling from the Great Slowness, and thousands of little empires. There had always been races moving into the Transcend, to become the Powers . . . or their prey.

'And the Transcend?' Pham said. 'Is that just the far dark?' The dark between the galaxies.

Ravna laughed softly. 'It includes all that but . . . see the outer reaches of the spirals. They're in the Transcend.' Most everything farther than forty thousand light-years from the galactic center was.

Pham Nuwen was silent for a long moment. She felt a tiny shiver pass through him. 'After talking to the wheelies, I – I think I understand more of what you were warning me about. There's a lot of things I don't know, things that could kill me . . . or worse.'

Common sense triumphs at last. 'True,' she said quietly. 'But it's not just you, or the brief time you've been here. You could study your whole life, and not know. How long must a fish study to understand human motivation? It's not a good analogy, but it's the only safe one; we *are* like dumb animals to the Powers of the Transcend. Think of all the different things people do to animals – ingenious, sadistic, charitable, genocidal – each has a million elaborations in the Transcend. The Zones are a natural protection; without them, human-equivalent intelligence would probably not exist.' She waved at the misty star swarms. 'The Beyond and below are like a deep of ocean, and we the creatures that swim in the abyss. We're so far down that the beings on the surface – superior though they are – can't effectively reach us. Oh, they fish, and they sometimes blight the upper levels with poisons we don't even understand. But the abyss remains a relatively safe place.' She paused. There was more to the analogy. 'And just as with an ocean, there is a constant drift of flotsam from the top. There are things that can only be made at the Top, that need close-to-sentient factories – but which can still work down here. Blueshell mentioned some of those when he was talking to you: the agrav fabrics, the sapient devices. Such things are the greatest physical wealth of the Beyond, since we can't make them. And getting them is a deadly risky endeavor.'

Pham turned toward her, away from window and the stars. 'So there are always "fish" edging close to the surface.' For an instant she thought she had lost him, that he was caught by the romance of the Transcendent death-wish. 'Little fish risking everything for a piece of godhood . . . and not knowing heaven from hell, even when they find it.' She felt him shiver, and then his arms were around her. She tilted her head up and found his lips waiting.

It had been two years since Ravna Bergsndot left Sjandra Kei. In some ways the time had gone fast. Just now her body was telling her what a long, long time it really had been. Every touch was so vivid, waking desires carefully suppressed. Suddenly her skin was tingling all over. It took marvelous restraint to undress without tearing anything.

Ravna was out of practice. And of course she had nothing recent to compare to . . . But Pham Nuwen was very, *very* good.

Crypto: 0
As received by: Transceiver Relay01 at Relay
Language path: Acquileron → Triskweline, SjK: Relay units
From: Net Administrator for Transceiver Windsong at Debley Down
Subject: Complaints about Relay, a suggestion
Summary: It's getting worse; try us instead
Key phrases: communications problems. Relay unreliability. Transcend
Distribution:
   Communication Costs Special Interest Group
   Motley Hatch Administration Group
   Transceiver Relay01 at Relay
   Transceiver Not-for-Long at Shortstop
Follow-ups to: Windsong Expansion Interest Group
Date: 07:21:21 Docks Time, 36/09 of Org year 52089
Text of message:
   During the last five hundred hours, Comm Costs shows 9,834 transceiver-layer congestion complaints against the Vrinimi operation at Relay. Each of

these complaints involves services to tens of thousands of planets. Vrinimi has promised again and again that the congestion is a purely temporary increase of Transcendent usage.

As Relay's chief competitor in this region, we of Windsong have benefited modestly from the overflow; however, until now we thought it inappropriate to propose a coordinated response to the problem.

The events of the last seven hours compel us to change this policy. Those reading this item already know about the incident; most of you are the victims of it. Beginning at [00:00:27 Docks Time], Vrinimi Org began taking transceivers off-line, an unscheduled outage. R01 went out at 00:00:27, R02 at 02:50:32, R03 and R04 at 03:12:01. Vrinimi stated that a Transcendent customer was urgently requesting bandwidth. (R00 had been previously dedicated to that Power's use.) The customer required use of both up- and down-link bandwidth. By the Org's own admission, the unscheduled usage exceeded sixty percent of their entire capacity. Note that the excesses of the preceding five hundred hours – excesses which caused entirely justified complaint – were never more than five percent of Org capacity.

Friends, we of Windsong are in the long-haul communication business. We know how difficult it is to maintain transceiver elements that mass as much as a planet. We know that hard contract commitments simply cannot be made by suppliers in our line of work. But at the same time, the behavior of Vrinimi Org is unacceptable. It's true that in the last three hours the Org has returned R01 through R04 to general service, and promised to pass on the Power's surpayment to all those who were 'inconvenienced.' But only Vrinimi knows how large these surpayments really are. And no one (not even Vrinimi!) knows whether this is the end of the outages.

What is to Vrinimi a sudden, incredible cash glut, is to the rest of you an unaccountable disaster.

Therefore Windsong at Debley Down is considering a major – and permanent – expansion of our service: the construction of five additional backbone transceivers. Obviously this will be immensely expensive. Transceivers are never cheap, and Debley Down does not have quite the geometry enjoyed by Relay. We expect the cost must be amortized over many decades of good business. We can't undertake it without clear customer commitment. In order to determine this demand, and to ensure that we build what is really needed, we are creating a temporary newsgroup, Windsong Expansion Interest Group, moderated and archived at Windsong. Send/Receive charges to transceiver-layer customers on this group will be only ten percent our usual. We urge you, our transceiver-layer customers, to use this service to talk to each other, to decide what you can safely expect from Vrinimi Org in the future and how you feel about our proposals.

We are waiting to hear from you.

9

Afterwards, Ravna slept well. It was halfway through the morning when she drifted back toward wakefulness. The ring of her phone was monotonously insistent, loud enough to reach through the most pleasant dreams. She opened her eyes, disoriented and happy. She was lying with her arms wrapped tightly around . . . a large pillow. Damn. He'd already left. She lay back for a second, remembering. These last two years she had been lonely; till last night she hadn't realized how lonely. Happiness so unexpected, so intense . . . what a strange thing.

The phone just kept ringing. Finally she rolled out of bed and walked unsteadily across the room; there should be limits to this Techno Primitive nonsense. 'Yes?'

It was a Skroderider. Greenstalk? 'I'm sorry to bother you, Ravna, but – are you all right?' The Rider interrupted herself.

Ravna suddenly realized that she might be looking a little strange: sappy smile spread from ear to ear, hair sticking out in all directions. She rubbed her hand across her mouth, cutting back laughter. 'Yes, I'm fine.' Fine! 'What's up?'

'We want to thank you for your help. We had never dreamed that you were so highly placed. We'd been trying for hundreds of hours to persuade the Org to listen for the refugees. But less than an hour after talking to you, we were told the survey is being undertaken immediately.'

'Um.' Say *what?* 'That's wonderful, but I'm not sure I – who's paying for it, anyway?'

'I don't know, but it *is* expensive. We were told they're dedicating a backbone transceiver to the search. If there's anyone transmitting, we should know in a matter of hours.'

They chatted for a few more minutes, Ravna gradually becoming more coherent as she parceled the various aspects of the last ten hours into business and pleasure. She had half expected the Org to bug her at The Wandering Company. Maybe Grondr just heard the story there – and gave it full credit. But just yesterday, he'd been wimping about transceiver saturation. Either way, this was good news – perhaps extraordinarily good. If the Riders' wild story were true, the Straumli Perversion might be less than Transcendent. And if the refugee ships had some clues on how to bring it down, Straumli Realm might even be saved.

After Greenstalk rang off, Ravna wandered about the apartment, getting herself in shape, playing the various possibilities against each other. Her actions became more purposeful, almost up to their usual speed. There were a lot of things she wanted to check into.

Then the phone was ringing again. This time she previewed the caller.

Oops! It was Grondr Vrinimikalir. She combed her hand back through her hair; it still looked like crap, and this phone was not up to deception. Suddenly she noticed that Grondr didn't look so hot either. His facial chitin was smudged, even across some of his freckles. She accepted the call.

'Ah!' His voice actually squeaked, then returned to its normal level. 'Thank you for answering. I would have called earlier, except things have been very . . . chaotic.' Just where had his cool distance gone? 'I just want you to know that the Org had nothing to do with this. We were totally taken in until just a couple of hours ago.' He launched into a disjointed description of massive demand swamping the Org's resources.

As he rambled, Ravna punched up a summary of recent Relay business. By the Powers that Be: *Sixty percent diversion?* Excerpts from Comm Costs: She scanned quickly down the item from Windsong. The gasbags were as pompous as ever, but their offer to replace Relay was probably for real. It was just the sort of thing Grondr had been afraid might happen.

'—Old One just kept asking for more and more. When we finally figured things out, and confronted him . . . Well, we came close to threatening violence. We *have* the resources to destroy his emissary vessel. No telling what his revenge might be, but we told Old One his demands were already destroying us. Thank the Powers, he just seemed amused; he backed off. He's restricted to a single transceiver now, and that's on a signal search that has nothing to do with us.'

Hmm. One mystery solved. Old One must have been snooping around The Wandering Company and overheard the Skroderiders' story. 'Maybe things will be okay, then. But it's important to be just as tough if Old One tries to abuse us again.' The words were already out of her mouth before she considered who she was giving advice to.

Grondr didn't seem to notice. If anything, *he* was the one scrambling to agree: 'Yes, yes. I'll tell you, if Old One were any ordinary customer, we'd blacklist him forever for this deception . . . But then if he were ordinary, he could never have fooled us.'

Grondr wiped pudgy white fingers across his face. 'No mere Beyonder could have altered our record of the dredge expedition. Not even one from the Top could have broken into the junkyard and manipulated the remains without our even suspecting.'

Dredge? Remains? Ravna began to see that she and Grondr were not talking about the same thing. 'Just what did Old One do?'

'The details? We're pretty sure of them now. Since the Fall of Straum, Old One has been very interested in humans. Unfortunately, there were no willing ones available here. It began manipulating us, rewriting our junk-yard records. We've recovered a clean backup from a branch office: The dredge really did encounter the wreck of a human ship; there were human body parts in it – but nothing that we could have revived. Old One must have mixed and matched what he found there. Perhaps it fabricated memories by extrapolating from human cultural data in the archives. With hindsight, we can match its early requests with the invasion of our junkyard.'

Grondr rattled on, but Ravna wasn't listening. Her eyes stared blindly through the phone's display. *We are little fish in the abyss, protected by the deep from the fishers above. But even if they can't live down here, the clever fisherfolk still have their lures and deadly tricks.* And so Pham – 'Pham Nuwen is just a robot, then,' she said softly.

'Not precisely. He is human, and with his fake memories he can operate autonomously. But when Old One buys full bandwidth, the creature is fully an emissary device.' The hand and eye of a Power.

Grondr's mouthparts clattered in abject embarrassment. 'Ravna, we don't know all that happened last night; there was no reason to have you under close surveillance. But Old One assures us that its need for direct investigation is over. In any case, we'll never give him the bandwidth to try again.'

Ravna barely nodded. Her face suddenly felt cold. She had never felt such anger and such fright at the same time. She stood in a wave of dizziness and walked away from the phone, ignoring Grondr's worried cries. The stories from grad school came tumbling through her mind, and the myths of a dozen human religions. Consequences, consequences. Some of them she could defend against; others were past repair.

And from somewhere in the back of her mind, an incredibly silly thought crawled out from under the horror and the rage. For eight hours she had been face to face with a Power. It was the sort of experience that made a chapter in textbooks, the sort of thing that was always far away and misreported. And it was the sort of thing no one in all of Sjandra Kei could come near to claiming. Until now.

10

Johanna was in the boat for a long time. The sun never set, though now it was low behind her, now it was high in front, now all was cloudy and rain plinked off the tarp covering her blankets. She spent the hours in an agonized haze. Things happened that could only have been dreams. There were creatures pulling at her clothes, blood sticking everywhere. Gentle hands and rat snouts dressed her wounds and forced chill water down her throat. When she thrashed around, Mom rearranged her blankets and comforted her with the strangest sounds. For hours, someone warm lay beside her. Sometimes it was Jefri; more often it was a large dog, a dog that purred.

The rain passed. The sun was on the left side of the boat, but hidden behind a cold, snapping shadow. More and more, the pain became divisible. Part of it was in her chest and shoulder; that stabbed through her whenever the boat wobbled. Part of it was in her gut, an emptiness that was not quite nausea . . . she was so hungry, so thirsty.

More and more, she was remembering, not dreaming. There were nightmares that would never go away. They had really happened. They were happening now.

The sun peeked in and out of the tumble of clouds. It slid slowly lower across the sky till it was almost behind the boat. She tried to remember what Daddy had been saying just before . . . everything went bad. They were in this planet's arctic, in the summer. So the sun's low point must be north, and their twin-hulled boat was sailing roughly southwards. Wherever they were going, it was minute by minute farther from the spacecraft and any hope of finding Jefri.

Sometimes the water was like open sea, the hills distant or hidden by low clouds. Sometimes they passed through narrows and swept close to walls of naked rock. She'd had no idea a sailboat could move so fast or be so dangerous. Four of the rat creatures worked desperately to keep them off the rocks. They bounded nimbly from mast platform to railing, sometimes standing each on the other's shoulders to extend their reach. The twin-hulled boat tilted and groaned in water that was suddenly rough. Then they'd be through and the hills would be at a peaceful distance, sliding slowly past.

For a long while she pretended delirium. She moaned, she twisted. She watched. The boat hulls were long and narrow, almost like canoes. The sail was mounted between them. The shadow in her dreams had been that sail, snapping in the cold, clean wind. The sky was an avalanche of grays, light and dark. There were birds up there. They dipped past the mast, circled again and again. There was twittering and hissing all around her. But the sound did not come from the birds.

It was the monsters. She watched them through lowered lashes. These were the same kind that killed Mom and Dad. They even wore the same funny clothes, gray-green jackets studded with stirrups and pockets. Dogs or wolves, she had thought before. That didn't really describe them. Sure, they had four slender legs and pointy little ears. But with their long necks and occasionally reddish eyes, they might as well be huge rats.

And the longer she watched them, the more horrible they seemed. A still image could never convey that horror; you had to see them in action. She watched four of them – the ones on her side of the boat – play with her dataset. The Pink Oliphaunt was tied in a net bag near the rear of the boat. Now the beasts wanted to look it over. At first it looked like a circus act, the creatures' heads darting this way and that. But every move was so precise, so *coordinated* with all the others. They had no hands, but they could untie knots, each holding a piece of twine in its mouth and maneuvering its necks

73

around others. At the same time, one's claws held the loose netting tight against the railing. It was like watching puppets run off a group control.

In seconds they had it out of the bag. Dogs would have let it slide to the bottom of the hull, then pushed it around with their noses. Not these things: two put it onto a cross bench, while a third steadied it with its paw. They poked around the edges, concentrating on the plush flanges and floppy ears. They pushed and nuzzled, but with clear purpose. *They were trying to open it.*

Two heads showed over the railing on the other hull. They made the gobbling, hissing sounds that were a cross between a bird call and someone throwing up. One of those on her side glanced back and made similar sounds. The other three continued to play with the dataset's latches.

Finally they pulled the big, floppy ears simultaneously: the dataset popped open, and the top window went into Johanna's startup routine – an anim of herself saying 'Shame on you, Jefri. Stay out of my things!' The four creatures went rigid, their eyes suddenly wide.

Johanna's four turned the set so the others could see. One held it down while another peered at the top window, and a third fumbled with the key window. The guys in the other hull went nuts, but none of them tried to get any closer. The random prodding of the four abruptly cut off her startup greeting. One of them glanced at the guys in the other hull; another two watched Johanna. She continued to lie with her eyes almost closed.

'Shame on you, Jefri. Stay out of my things!' Johanna's voice came again, but from one of the animals. It was a perfect playback. Then a girl's voice was moaning, crying, 'Mom, Daddy.' It was her own voice again, but more frightened and childish than she ever wanted it to sound.

They seemed to be waiting for the dataset to respond. When nothing happened, one of them went back to pushing its nose against the windows. Everything valuable, and all the dangerous programs, were passworded. Insults and squawking emerged from the box, all the little surprises she had planted for her snooping little brother. *Oh Jefri, will I ever see you again?*

The sounds and vids kept the monsters amused for several minutes. Eventually their random fiddlings convinced the dataset that somebody *really* young had opened up the box, and it shifted into kindermode.

The creatures knew she was watching. Of the four fooling with her Oliphaunt, one – not always the same one – was always watching her. They were playing games with her, pretending they didn't know she was pretending.

Johanna opened her eyes wide and glared at the creature. 'Damn you!' She looked in the other direction. And screamed. The mob in the other hull were clumped together. Their heads rose on sinuous necks from the pile. In the low sunlight, their eyes glinted red: a pack of rats or snakes, silently staring at her, and for heaven knew how long.

The heads leaned forward at her cry, and she heard the scream again.

Behind her, her own voice shouted 'Damn you!' Somewhere else, she was calling for 'Mom' and 'Daddy.' Johanna screamed again, and they just echoed it back. She swallowed her terror and kept silent. The monsters kept it up for a half minute, the mimicking, the mixing of things she must have said in her sleep. When they saw they couldn't terrorize her that way any more, the voices stopped being human. The gobbling went back and forth, as if the two groups were negotiating or something. Finally the four on her side closed her dataset and tied it into the net bag.

The six unwrapped themselves from each other. Three jumped to the outboard side of the hull. They gripped the edge tight in their claws and leaned into the wind. For once they almost did look like dogs – big ones sitting at a car window, sniffing at the airstream. The long necks swept forward and back. Every few seconds, one of them would dip its head out of sight, into the water. Drinking? Fishing?

Fishing. A head flipped up, tossing something small and green into the boat. The other three animals nosed about, grabbing it. She had a glimpse of tiny legs and a shiny carapace. One of the rats held it at the tip of its mouth, while the other two pulled it apart. It was all done with their uncanny precision. The pack seemed like a single creature, and each neck a heavy tentacle that ended in a pair of jaws. Her gut twisted at the thought, but there was nothing to barf up.

The fishing expedition went on another quarter hour. They got at least seven of the green things. But they weren't eating them; not all of them, anyway. The dismembered leavings collected in a small wood bowl.

More gobbling between the two sides. One of the six grabbed the bowl's edge in its mouth and crawled across the mast platform. The four on Johanna's side huddled together as if frightened of the visitor. Only after the bowl was set down and the intruder had returned to its side, did the four in Johanna's hull poke their heads up again.

One of the rats picked up the bowl. It and another walked toward her. Johanna swallowed. What torture was this? Her stomach twisted again . . . she was *so* hungry. She looked at the bowl again and realized that they were trying to feed her.

The sun had just come out from under northern clouds. The low light was like some bright fall afternoon, just after rain: dark sky above, yet everything close by was bright and glistening. The creatures' fur was deep and plush. One held the bowl towards her, while the other stuck its snout in and withdrew . . . something slick and green. It held the tidbit delicately, just with the tips of its long mouth. It turned and thrust the green thing toward her.

Johanna shrank back. 'No!'

The creature paused. For a moment she thought it was going to echo her. Then it dropped the lump back into the bowl. The first animal set it on the bench beside her. It looked up at her for an instant, then released the jaw-wide flange at the edge of the bowl. She had a glimpse of fine, pointy teeth.

Johanna stared into the bowl, nausea fighting with hunger. Finally she worked a hand out of her blanket and reached into it. Heads perked up around her, and there was an exchange of gobble comments between the two sides of the boat.

Her fingers closed on something soft and cold. She lifted it into the sunlight. The body was gray green, its sides glistening in the light. The guys in the other hull had torn off the little legs and chopped away the head. What remained was only two or three centimeters long. It looked like filleted shellfish. Once she had liked such food. But that had been cooked. She almost dropped the thing when she felt it quiver in her hand.

She brought it close to her mouth, touched it with her tongue. Salty. On Straum, most shellfish would make you very sick if you ate them raw. How could she know, all alone without parents or a local commnet? She felt tears coming. She said a bad word, stuffed the green thing into her mouth, and tried to chew. Blandness, with the texture of suet and gristle. She gagged, spat it out . . . and tried to eat another. Altogether she got parts of two down. Maybe that was for the best; she'd wait and see how much she barfed up. She lay back and saw several pairs of eyes watching. The gobbling with the other side of the boat picked up. Then one of them sidled toward her, carying a leather bag with a spigot. A canteen.

This creature was the biggest of all. The leader? It moved its head close to hers, putting the spout of the canteen near her mouth. The big one seemed sly, more cautious about approaching her than the others. Johanna's eyes traveled back along its flanks. Beyond the edge of its jacket, the pelt on its rear was mostly white . . . and scored deep with a Y-shaped scar. *This is the one that killed Dad.*

Johanna's attack was not planned; perhaps that's why it worked so well. She lunged past the canteen and swung her free arm around the thing's neck. She rolled over the animal, pinning it against the hull. By itself, it was smaller than she, and not strong enough to push her off. She felt its claws raking through the blankets but somehow never quite cutting her. She put all her weight on the creature's spine, grabbed it where throat met jaw, and began slamming its head against the wood.

Then the others were on her, muzzles poking under her, jaws grabbing at her sleeve. She felt rows of needle teeth just poking through the fabric. Their bodies buzzed with a sound from her dreams, a sound that went straight through her clothes and rattled her bones.

They pulled her hand from the other's throat, twisting her; she felt the arrowhead tearing her inside. But there was still one thing she could do: Johanna pushed off with her feet, butting her head against the base of the other's jaw, smashing the top of its head into the hull. The bodies around her convulsed, and she was flipped onto her back. Pain was the only thing she could feel now. Neither rage nor fear could move her.

Yet part of her was still aware of the four. She had hurt them. She had hurt them. She had hurt them *all*. Three wandered drunkenly, making whistling sounds that for once seemed to come from their mouths. The one with the scarred butt lay on its side, twitching. She had punched a star-shaped wound in the top of its head. Blood dripped down past its eyes, red tears.

Minutes passed and the whistling stopped. The four creatures huddled together and the familiar hissing resumed. The bleeding from her chest had started again.

They stared at each other for a while. She smiled at her enemies. They could be hurt. *She* could hurt them. She felt better than she had since the landing.

II

Before the Flenser Movement, Woodcarvers had been the most famous city-state west of the Icefangs. Its founder went back six centuries. In those days, things had been harder in the north; snow covered even the lowlands through most of the year. The Woodcarver had started alone, a single pack in a little cabin on an inland bay. The pack was a hunter and a thinker as much as an artist. There had been no settlements for a hundred miles around. Only a dozen of the carver's early statues ever left his cabin, yet those statues had been his first fame. Three were still in existence. There was a city by the Long Lakes named for the one in its museum.

With fame had come apprentices. One cabin became ten, scattered across Woodcarver's fjord. A century or two passed, and of course the Woodcarver slowly changed. He feared the change, the feeling that his soul was slipping away. He tried to keep hold of himself; almost everyone does to one extent or another. In the worst case, the pack falls into perversion, perhaps becomes soul-hollow. For Woodcarver, the quest was itself the change. He studied how each member fits within the soul. He studied pups and their raising, and how you might guess the contributions of a new one. He learned to shape the soul by training the members.

Of course little of this was new. It was the base of most religions, and every town had romance advisors and brood kenners. Such knowledge, whether valid or not, is important to any culture. What Woodcarver did was to look at it all again, without traditional bias. He gently experimented on himself and on the other artists in his little colony. He watched the results, using them to design new experiments. He was guided by what he saw rather than by what he wanted to believe.

By the various standards of his age, what he did was heresy or perversion or simply insanity. In the early years, King Woodcarver was hated almost as much as was Flenser three centuries later. But the far north was still going through its time of heavy winters. The nations of the south could not easily send armies as far as Woodcarvers. Once when they did, they were thoroughly defeated. And wisely, Woodcarver never attempted to subvert the south; not directly. But his settlement grew and grew, and its fame for art and furniture was small beside its other reputations. Old of heart traveled to the town, and came back not just younger, but smarter and happier. Ideas radiated from the town: weaving machines, gearboxes and windmills, factory postures. Something new had happened in this place. It wasn't the inventions. It was the people that Woodcarver had midwifed, and the outlook he had created.

Wickwrackscar and Jaqueramaphan arrived at Woodcarvers late in the afternoon. It had rained most of the day, but now the clouds had blown away and the sky was that bright cloudless blue that was all the more beautiful after a stretch of cloudy days.

Woodcarver's domain was paradise to Peregrine's eyes. He was tired of the packless wilderness. He was tired of worrying about the alien.

Twinhulls paced them suspiciously for the last few miles. The boats were armed, and Peregrine and Scriber were coming from very much the wrong direction. But they were all alone, clearly harmless. Long callers hooted, relaying their story ahead. By the time they reached the harbor they were heros, two packs who had stolen unspecified treasure from the villains of the north. They sailed around a breakwater that hadn't existed on Peregrine's last trip and tied in at the moorage.

The pier was crowded with soldiers and wagons. Townspeople were all over the road leading up to the city walls. This was as close to a mob scene as you could get and still have room for sober thought. Scriber bounced out of the boat and pranced about in obvious delight at the cheers from the hillside. 'Quickly! We must speak with the Woodcarver.'

Wickwrackscar picked up the canvas bag that held the alien's picture box, and climbed carefully out of the boat. He was dizzy from the beating the alien had given him. Scar's fore-tympanum had been cut in the attack. For a moment he lost track of himself. The pier was very strange – stone at first glance, but walled with a spongy black material he hadn't seen since the Southseas; it should be brittle here . . . *Where am I? I should be happy about something, some victory.* He paused to regroup. After a moment both the pain and his thoughts sharpened; he would be like this for days yet, at least. Get help for the alien. Get it ashore.

King Woodcarver's Lord Chamberlain was a mostly overweight dandy; Peregrine had not expected to see such at Woodcarvers. But the fellow became instantly cooperative when he saw the alien. He brought a doctor down to look at the Two-Legs – and incidentally, at Peregrine. The alien had gained strength in the last two days, but there had been no more violence. They got it ashore without much trouble. It stared at Peregrine out of its flat face, a look he knew was impotent rage. He touched Scar's head thoughtfully . . . the Two-Legs was just waiting for the best opportunity to do more damage.

Minutes later the travelers were in kherhog-drawn carriages, rolling up the cobblestone street toward the city walls. Soldiers cleared the way through the crowd. Scriber Jaqueramaphan waved this way and that, the handsome hero. By now Peregrine knew the shy insecurity that lurked within Scriber. This might be the high point of his whole life till now.

Even if he wanted it, Wickwrackscar could not be so expansive. With one of Scar's tympana hurt, wild gestures made him lose track of his thoughts. He hunkered down on the carriage seats and looked out in all directions:

But for the shape of the outer harbor, the place was not at all what he remembered from fifty years ago. In most parts of the world, not much changed in fifty years. A pilgrim returning after such an interval might even be bored by the sameness. But this . . . it was almost scary.

The huge breakwater was new. There were twice as many piers, and multiboats with flags he had never seen on this side of the world. The road had been here before, but narrow, with only a third as many turnoffs. Before, the town walls had been more to keep the kherhogs and froghens in than any invaders out. Now the walls were ten feet high, black stone extending as far as Peregrine could see . . . And there had been scarcely any soldiers last time; now they were everywhere. That was not a good change. He felt a sinking in the pit of Scar's stomach; soldiers and fighting were *not* good.

They rode through the city gates and past a market maze that spread across acres. The alleys were only fifty feet wide, narrower where bolts of cloth, furniture displays, and crates of fresh fruit encroached. Smells of fruit and spice and varnish hung in the air. The place was so crowded that the haggling was almost an orgy, and dizzy Peregrine almost blacked out. Then they were on a narrow street that zigzagged through ranks of half-timbered buildings. Beyond the roofs loomed heavy fortifications. Ten minutes later they were in the castle yard.

They dismounted and the Lord Chamberlain had the Two-Legs moved to a litter.

'Woodcarver, he'll see us now?' said Scriber.

The bureaucrat laughed. '*She*. Woodcarver changed gender more than ten years ago.'

Peregrine's heads twisted about in surprise. Precisely what would *that* mean? Most packs change with time, but he had never heard of Woodcarver being anything but 'he.' He almost missed what the Lord Chamberlain said next.

'Even better. Her whole council must see . . . what you've brought. Come inside.' He waved the guards away.

They walked down a hall almost wide enough for two packs to pass abreast. The chamberlain led, followed by the travelers and the doctor with the alien's litter. The walls were high, padded with silver-crusted quilting. It was far grander than before . . . and again unsettling. There was scarcely any statuary, and what there was dated from centuries before.

But there were pictures. He stumbled when he saw the first, and behind him he heard Scriber gasp. Peregrine had seen art all around the world: The mobs of the tropics preferred abstract murals, smudges of psychotic color. The Southseas islanders had never invented perspective; in their water-colors, distant objects simply floated in the upper half of the picture. In the Long Lakes Republic, representationism was currently favored, especially multiptychs that gave a whole-pack view.

But Peregrine had never seen the likes of these. The pictures were mosaics, each tile a ceramic square about a quarter inch on a side. There was no color, just four shades of gray. From a few feet away, the graininess was lost, and . . . they were the most perfect landscapes Peregrine had ever seen. All were views from hilltops around Woodcarvers. Except for the lack of color, they might have been windows. The bottom of each picture was bounded by a rectangular frame, but the tops were irregular; the mosaics simply broke off at the horizon. The hall's quilted wall stood where the pictures should have shown sky.

'Here now, fellow! I thought you wanted to see Wood-carver.' The remark was directed at Scriber. Jaqueramaphan was strung out along the landscapes, one of him sitting in front of a different picture all down the hall. He turned a head to look at the chamberlain. His voice sounded dazed. 'Soul's end! It's like being God, as if I have one member on each hilltop and can see everything at once.' But he scrambled to his feet and trotted to catch up.

The hall opened on one of the largest indoor meeting rooms Peregrine had ever seen.

'This is as big as anything in the Republic,' Scriber said with apparent admiration, looking up at the three levels of balconies. They stood alone with the alien at the bottom.

'Hmf.' Besides the chamberlain and the doctor, there were already five other packs in the room. More showed up as they watched. Most were dressed like nobles of the Republic, all jewels and furs. A few wore the plain jackets he remembered from his last trip. Sigh. Woodcarver's little settle-ment had grown into a city and now a nation-state. Peregrine wondered if the King – the Queen – had any real power now. He trained one head precisely on Scriber and Hightalked at him. 'Don't say anything about the picture box just yet.'

Jaqueramaphan looked puzzled and conspiratorial all at once. He High-talked back, 'Yes . . . yes. A bargaining card?'

'Something like that.' Peregrine's eyes swept back and forth across the balconies. Most packs entered with an air of harried self-importance. He smiled to himself. One glance into the pit was enough to shatter their smugness. The air above him was filled with buzzing talk. None of the packs looked like Woodcarver. But then, she'd have few of her members from before; he could only recognize her by manner and bearing. *It shouldn't matter.* He had carried some friendships far longer than any member's lifespan. But with others the friend had changed in a decade, its view-points altering, affection turning to animosity. He'd been counting on Woodcarver being the same. Now . . .

There was a brief sound of trumpets, almost like a call to order. The public doors of a lower balcony slid open and a fivesome entered. Peregrine felt a twitchy thrill of horror. This *was* Woodcarver, but so . . . mis-arranged. One member was so old it had to be helped by the rest. Two were scarcely more than puppies, and one of those a constant drooler. The largest member was white-eyed blind. It was the sort of thing you might see in a waterfront slum, or in the last generation of incest.

She looked down at Peregrine, and smiled almost as if *she* recognized *him*. When she spoke, it was with the blind one. The voice was clear and firm. 'Please carry on, Vendacious.'

The chamberlain nodded. 'As you wish, Your Majesty.' He pointed into the pit, at the alien. 'That is the reason for this hasty meeting.'

'We can see monsters at the circus, Vendacious.' The voice came from an overdressed pack on the top balcony. To judge from the shouting that came from all sides, this was a minority view. One pack on a lower balcony jumped over the railing and tried to shoo the doctor away from the alien's litter.

The chamberlain raised a head for silence, and glared down at the fellow who had jumped into the pit. 'If you please, Scrupilo, be patient. Everyone will get a chance to look.'

'Scrupilo' made some grumbling hisses, but backed off.

'Good.' Vendacious turned all his attention on Peregrine and Scriber. 'Your boat has outrun any news from the north, my friends. No one but I knows much of your story – and what I have is guard codes hooted across the bay. You say this creature flew down from the sky?'

It was an invitation to speechify. Peregrine let Scriber Jaqueramaphan do the talking. Scriber loved it. He told the story of the flying house, of the ambush and the murders, and the rescue. He showed them his eye-tools and announced himself as a secret agent of the Long Lakes Republic. *Now what real spy would do that?* Every pack on the council had eyes on the alien, some fearful, some – like Scrupilo – crazily curious. Woodcarver watched with only a couple of heads. The rest might have been asleep. She looked as tired as Peregrine felt. He rested his own heads on his paws. The pain in Scar was a pulsing beat; it would be easy enough to set the member asleep, but then he'd understand very little of what was being said. Hey! maybe that wasn't such a bad idea. Scar drifted off and the pain receded.

The talk went on for some minutes more, not making a whole lot of sense to the threesome that was Wickwrack. He understood the tones of voice though. Scrupilo – the pack on the floor – complained several times, impatiently. Vendacious said something, agreeing with him. The doctor retreated, and Scrupilo advanced on Wickwrack's alien.

Peregrine pulled himself to full wakefulness. 'Be careful. The creature is *not* friendly.'

Scrupilo snapped back, 'Your friend has already warned me once.' He circled the litter, staring at the alien's brown, furless face. The alien stared back, impassive. Scrupilo reached forward cautiously and drew back the alien's quilt. *Still* no response. 'See?' said Scrupilo. 'It knows I mean no harm.' Peregrine said nothing to correct him.

'It really walks on those rear paws alone?' said one of the other advisors. 'Can you imagine it, towering over us? One little bump would knock it down.' Laughter. Peregrine remembered how mantis-like the alien had seemed when upright.

Scrupilo wrinkled a nose. 'The thing is filthy.' He was all around her, a posture that Peregrine knew upset the Two-Legs. 'That arrow shaft must be removed, you know. Most of the bleeding has stopped, but if we expect the creature to live for long, it needs medical attention.' He looked disdainfully at Scriber and Peregrine, as if they were to blame for not performing surgery aboard the twinhull. Something caught his eye and his tone abruptly changed: 'By the Pack of Packs! Look at its forepaws.' He loosened the ropes about the creature's front legs. 'Two paws like that would be as good as five pairs of lips. Think what a pack of these creatures could do!' He moved close to the five-tentacled paw.

'Be—' careful, Peregrine started to say. The alien abruptly bunched its tentacles into a club. Its foreleg flicked out at an impossible angle, ramming its paw into Scrupilo's head. The blow couldn't have been too strong, but it was precisely placed on the tympanum.

'*Ow! Yow! Wow. Wow.*' Scrupilo danced back.

The alien was shouting, too. It was all mouth noise, thin and low-pitched. The eldritch sound brought up all heads, even Woodcarver's. Peregrine had heard it many times by now. There was no doubt in his mind – this was the aliens' interpack speech. After a few seconds, the sound changed to a regular hacking that gradually faded.

For a long moment no one spoke. Then part of Woodcarver got to her feet. She looked at Scrupilo. 'Are you all right?' It was the first time she had spoken since the beginning of the meeting.

Scrupilo was licking his forehead. 'Yes. It smarts is all.'

'Your curiosity will kill you some day.'

The other huffed indignantly, but also seemed flattered by the prediction.

Queen Woodcarver looked at her councillors. 'I see an important question here. Scrupilo thinks one alien member would be as agile as an entire pack of us. Is that so?' She pointed the question at Peregrine rather than Scriber.

'Yes, Your Majesty. If those ropes had been tied within its reach, it could easily have unknotted them.' He knew where this was going; he'd had three days to get there himself. 'And the noises it makes sound like coordinated speech to me.'

There was a swell of talk as the others caught on. An articulate member can often make semi-sensible speech, but usually at the expense of dexterity.

'Yes . . . A creature like nothing on our world, whose boat flew down from the top of heaven. I wonder at the mind of such a pack, if a single member is almost as smart as *all* of one of us?' Her blind one looked around as it made the words, almost as if it could see. Two others wiped at her drooler's muzzle. She was not an inspiring sight.

Scrupilo poked a head up. 'I hear not a hint of thought sound from this one. There is no fore-tympanum.' He pointed at the torn clothing around the creature's wound. 'And I see no sign of shoulder tympana. Perhaps it *is* pack smart even as a singleton . . . and perhaps that's all the aliens ever are.' Peregrine smiled to himself; this Scrupilo was a prickly twit, but not one who held with tradition. For centuries, academics had debated the difference between people and animals. Some animals had larger brains; some had paws or lips more agile than a member's. In the savannahs of Easterlee, there were creatures that even looked like people and ran in groups, but without much depth of thought. Leaving aside wolf nests and whales, only people were *packs*. It was the coordination of thought between members that made them superior. Scrupilo's theory was a heresy.

Jaqueramaphan said, 'But we did hear thought sounds, *loud* ones, during the ambush. Perhaps this one is like our unweaned, unable to think—'

'And yet still almost as smart as a pack,' Woodcarver finished somberly. 'If these people are not smarter than we, then we might learn their devices. No matter how magnificent they are, we could eventually be their equals. But if this member is just one of a superpack . . .' For a moment there was no talk, just the muted underedge of her councillors' thoughts. If the aliens were superpacks, and if their envoy had been murdered – then there might not be anything they could do to save themselves.

'So. Our first priority should be to save this creature, to befriend it and learn its true nature.' Her heads lowered, and she seemed lost within herself – or perhaps just tired. Abruptly, she turned several heads toward her chamberlain. 'Move the creature to the lodge by mine.'

Vendacious started with surprise. 'Surely not, Your Majesty! We've seen that it is hostile. And it needs medical attention.'

Woodcarver smiled and her voice turned silky. Peregrine remembered that tone from before. 'Do you forget that I know surgery? Do you forget . . . that I am the Woodcarver?'

Vendacious licked his lips and looked at the other advisors. After a second he said, 'No, Your Majesty. It will be as you wish.'

And Peregrine felt like cheering. Perhaps Woodcarver did still run things.

12

Peregrine was sitting back to back on the steps of his quarters when Woodcarver came to see him next day. She came alone, wearing the simple green jackets he remembered from his last visit.

He didn't bow or go out to meet her. She looked at him coolly for a moment, and sat down just a few yards away.

'How is the Two-Legs?' he asked.

'I took out the arrow and sewed the wound shut. I think it will survive. My advisors were pleased: the creature didn't act like a reasoning being. It fought even after it was tied down, as though it had no concept of surgery . . . How is your head?'

'All right, as long as I don't move around.' The rest of him – Scar – lay behind the doorway in the dark interior of the lodge. 'The tympanum is healing straight, I think. I'll be fine in a few days.'

'Good.' A wrecked tympanum could mean continuing mental problems, or the need for a new member and the pain of finding a use for the singleton that was sent into silence. 'I remember you, pilgrim. All the members are different, but you really are the Peregrine of before. You had some great stories. I enjoyed your visit.'

'And I enjoyed meeting the great Woodcarver. That is the reason I returned.'

She cocked a head wryly. 'The great Woodcarver of before, not the wreck of now?'

He shrugged. 'What happened?'

She didn't answer immediately. For a moment, they sat and looked across the city. It was cloudy this afternoon, with rain coming. The breeze off the channel was a cool stinging on his lips and eyes. Woodcarver shivered, and puffed her fur out a bit. Finally she said, 'I held my soul six hundred years – and that's counting by foreclaws. I should think it's obvious what has become of me.'

'The perversion never hurt you before.' Peregrine was not normally so blunt. Something about her brought out the frankness in him.

'Yes, the average incest degrades to my state in a few centuries, and is an idiot long before then. My methods were much cleverer. I knew who to breed with whom, which puppies to keep and which to put on others. So it was always my flesh bearing my memories, and my soul remained pure. But I didn't understand enough – or perhaps I tried the impossible. The choices got harder and harder, till I was left with choosing between brains and physical defect.' She wiped away the drool, and all but the blind one looked out across her city. 'These are the best days of summer, you know. Life is a green madness just now, trying to squeeze the last bit of warmth from the season.' And the green did seem to be everywhere it could be: featherleaf down the hillside and in the town, ferns all over the near hillsides, and heather struggling toward the gray crowns of the mountains across the channel. 'I love this place.'

He never expected to be comforting the Woodcarver of Woodcarvers. 'You made a miracle here. I've heard of it all the way on the other side of the world . . . And I'll bet that half the packs around here are related to you.'

'Y-yes, I've been successful beyond a rake's wildest dreams. I've had no shortage of lovers, even if I couldn't use the pups myself. Sometimes I think my get has been my greatest experiment. Scrupilo and Vendacious are mostly my offspring . . . but so is Flenser.'

Huh! Peregrine hadn't known that last.

'The last few decades, I'd more or less accepted my fate. I couldn't outwit eternity; sometime soon I would let my soul slip free. I let the council take over more and more; how could I claim the Domain after I was no longer me? I went back to art – you saw those monochrome mosaics.'

'Yes! They're beautiful.'

'I'll show you my picture loom sometime. The procedure is tedious but almost automatic. It was a nice project for the last years of my soul. But now – you and your alien have changed everything. Damn it! If only this had happened a hundred years ago. What I would have done with it! We've been playing with your "picture box," you know. The pictures are finer than any in our world. They are a bit like my mosaics – the way the sun is like a glowbug. Millions of colored dots go to make each picture, the tiles so small you can't see them without one of Scriber's lenses. I've worked for *years* to make a few dozen mosaics. The picture box can make unnumbered thousands, so fast they seem to move. Your aliens make my life less than an unweaned pup's scratching in its cradle.'

The queen of the Woodcarvers was softly crying, but her voice was angry. 'And now the whole world is going to change, but too late for such wreckage as I!'

Almost without conscious thought, Peregrine extended one of his members toward the Woodcarver. He walked unseemly close: eight yards, five. Their thoughts were suddenly fuzzy with interference; but he could feel her calming.

She laughed blearily. 'Thank you . . . Strange that you should be sympathetic. The greatest problem of my life is nothing to a pilgrim.'

'You were hurting.' It was all he could think to say.

85

'But you pilgrims change and change and change—' She eased one of herself close to him; they were almost touching, and it was even harder to think.

Peregrine spoke slowly, concentrating on every word, hoping he wouldn't forget his point. 'But I do keep something of a soul. The parts that remain a pilgrim must have a certain outlook.' Sometimes great insight comes in the noise of battle or intimacy. This was such a time. 'And – and I think the world itself is due for a change of soul now that we have Two-Legs dropping from the sky. What better time for Woodcarver to give up the old?'

She smiled, and the confusion became louder, but a pleasant thing. 'I . . . hadn't . . . thought of it that way. Now is the time to change . . .'

Peregrine walked into her midst. The two packs stood for a moment, necking, thoughts blending into sweet chaos. Their last clear recollection was of stumbling up the steps and into his lodge.

Late that afternoon, Woodcarver brought the picture box to Scrupilo's laboratory. When she arrived Scrupilo and Vendacious were already present. Scriber Jaqueramaphan was there too, but standing farther from the others than courtesy might demand. She had interrupted some kind of argument. A few days before, such squabbling would have just depressed her. Now – she dragged her limper into the room and looked at the others through her drooler's eyes – and smiled. Woodcarver felt the best she had in years. She had made her decision and acted on it, and now there were new adventures to be had.

Scriber brightened at her entrance. 'Did you check on Peregrine? How is he?'

'He is fine, fine, just fine.' *Oops, no need to show them* how *fine he really is!* 'I mean, there'll be a full recovery.'

'Your Majesty, I'm very grateful to you and your doctors. Wickwrackscar is a good pack, and I . . . I mean, even a pilgrim can't change members every day, like suits of clothes.'

Woodcarver waved an offhand acknowledgment. She walked to the middle of the room, and set the alien's picture box on the table there. It looked like nothing so much as a big pink pillow – with floppy ears and a weird animal design sewed in its cover. After playing with it for a day and a half, she was getting pretty good . . . at opening the thing up. As always, the Two-Legs's face appeared, making mouth noises. As always, Woodcarver felt an instant of awe at seeing the moving mosaic. A million colored 'tiles' had to flip and shift in absolute synchrony to create the illusion. Yet it happened exactly the same each time. She turned the screen so Scrupilo and Vendacious could see.

Jaqueramaphan edged toward the others, and craned a pair of heads to look. 'You still think the box is an animal?' he said to Vendacious. 'Perhaps you could feed it sweets and it would tell us its secrets, eh?' Woodcarver smiled to herself. Scriber was no pilgrim; pilgrims depend on goodwill too much to go around giving the needle to the powerful.

Vendacious just ignored him. All his eyes were on her. 'Your Majesty, please do not take offense. I – we of the Council – must ask you again. This picture box is too important to be left in the mouths of a single pack, even one so great as you. Please. Leave it to the rest of us, at least when you sleep.'

'No offense taken. If you insist, you may participate in my investigations. Beyond that, I will not go.' She gave him an innocent look. Vendacious was a superb spymaster, a mediocre administrator, and an incompetent scientist. A century ago she would have had the likes of him out tending the crops, if he chose to stay at all. A century ago there had been no need for spymasters and one administrator had been enough. How things had changed. She absentmindedly nuzzled the picture box; perhaps things would change again.

Scrupilo took Scriber's question seriously. 'I see three possibilities, sir. First, that it is magic.' Vendacious winced away from him. 'Indeed, the box may be so far beyond our understanding that is *is* magic. But that is the one heresy the Woodcarver has never accepted, and so I courteously omit it.' He flicked a sardonic smile at Woodcarver. 'Second, that it is an animal. A few on the Council thought so when Scriber first made it talk. But it looks like a stuffed pillow, even down to the amusing figure stitched on its side. More importantly, it responds to stimuli with perfect repeatability. *That* is something I do recognize. That is the behavior of a machine.'

'That's your third possibility?' said Scriber. 'But to be a machine means to have moving parts, and except for—'

Woodcarver shrugged a tail at them. Scrupilo could go on like this for hours, and she saw that Scriber was the same type. '*I* say, let's learn more and then speculate.' She tapped the corner of the box, just as Scriber had in his original demonstration. The alien's face vanished from the picture, replaced by a dizzying pattern of color. There was a splatter of sound, then nothing but the mid-pitch hum the box always made when the top was open. They knew the box could hear low-pitched sounds, and it could feel through the square pad on its base. But that pad was itself a kind of picture screen: certain commands transformed the grid of touch spots into entirely new shapes. The first time they did that, the box refused any further commands. Vendacious had been sure they had 'killed the little alien.' But they had closed the box and reopened it – and it was back to its original behavior. Woodcarver was *almost* certain that nothing they could do by talking to it or touching it would hurt the thing.

Woodcarver retried the known signals in the usual order. The results were spectacular, and identical to before. But change that order in any way and the effects would be different. She wasn't sure if she agreed with Scrupilo: The box behaved with the repeatability of a machine . . . yet the variety of its responses was much more like an animal's.

Behind her, Scriber and Scrupilo edged members across the floor. Their heads were stuck high in the air as they strained for a clear look at the screen. The buzz of their thoughts came louder and louder. Woodcarver tried to remember what she'd been planning next. Finally, the noise was just too much. 'Will you two *please* back off! I can't hear myself think.' *This isn't a choir, you know.*

'Sorry . . . this okay?' They moved back about fifteen feet. Woodcarver nodded. The two members were less than twenty feet from each other. Scrupilo and Scriber must be really eager to see the screen. Vendacious had kept a proper distance, and a look of alert enthusiasm.

'I have a suggestion,' said Scriber. His voice was slurred from the effort of concentrating over Scrupilo's thoughts. 'When you touch the four/three square and say—' he made the alien sounds; they were all very easy to do '—the screen shows a collection of pictures. They seem to match the squares. I think we . . . we are being given choices.'

Hm. 'The box could end up training *us.*' *If this is a machine, we need some new definitions.* '. . . Very well, let's play with it.'

Three hours passed. Toward the end, even Vendacious had moved a member nearer the screen; the noise in the room verged on mindless chaos. And everybody had suggestions; 'say that,' 'press this,' 'last time it said that, we did thus and so.' There were intricate colored designs, sprinkled with things that must have been written language. Tiny, two-legged figures scampered across the screen, shifting the symbols, opening little windows . . . Scriber Jaqueramaphan's idea was quite right. The first pictures *were* choices. But some of those led to further pictures of choices. The options spread out – tree-like, Scriber said. He wasn't quite right; sometimes they came back to an earlier point; it was a metaphorical network of streets, four times they ended in cul de sacs and had to shut the box and begin again. Vendacious was madly drawing maps of the paths. That would help; there were places they would want to see again. But even he realized there were unnumbered other paths, places that blind exploration would never find.

And Woodcarver would have given a good part of her soul for the pictures she had already seen. There were starscapes. There were moons that shone blue and green, or banded orange. There were moving pictures of alien cities, of thousands of aliens so close that they were actually *touching*. If they ran in packs, those packs were bigger than anything in the world, even in the tropics . . . And maybe the question was irrelevant; the cities were beyond anything she ever imagined.

Finally Jaqueramaphan backed off. He huddled together. There was a shiver in his voice. 'T-there's a whole universe in there. We could follow it forever, and never know . . .'

She looked at the other two. For once, Vendacious had lost his smugness. There were ink stains on all his lips. The writing benches around him were littered with dozens of sketches, some clearer than others. He dropped the pen, and gasped. 'I say we take what we have and study it.' He began gathering the sketches, piling them into a neat stack. 'Tomorrow, after a good sleep, our heads will be clear and—'

Scrupilo dropped back and stretched. His eyes had excited red rims. 'Fine. But leave the sketches, friend Vendacious.' He jabbed at the drawings. 'See that one and that? It's clear that our blundering gets us plenty of empty results. Sometimes the picture box just locks us out, but much more often we get that picture: No options, just a couple of aliens dancing in a forest and making rhythm sounds. Then if we say—' and he repeated part of the sequence, '—we get that picture of piles of sticks. The first with one, the second with two, and so on.'

Woodcarver saw it too. 'Yes. And a figure comes out and points to each of the piles and says a short noise by each.' She and Scrupilo stared at each other, each seeing the same gleam in the other's eyes: the excitement of learning, of finding order where there had seemed only chaos. It had been a hundred years since she last felt this way. 'Whatever this thing is . . . it's trying to teach us the Two-Legs' language.'

In the days that followed, Johanna Olsndot had lots of time to think. The pain in her chest and shoulder gradually eased; if she moved carefully, it was only a pulsing soreness. They had taken the arrow out and sewed the wound closed. She had feared the worst when they had tied her down, when she saw the knives in their mouths and the steel on their claws. Then they began cutting; she had not known there could be such pain.

She still shuddered with remembered agony. But she didn't have nightmares about it, the way she did about . . .

Mother and Dad were dead; she had seen them die with her own eyes. And Jefri? Jefri *might* still be alive. Sometimes Johanna could go a whole afternoon full of hope. She had seen the coldsleepers burning on the ground below the ship, but those *inside* might have survived. Then she would remember the indiscriminate way the attackers had flamed and slashed, killing everything around the ship.

She was a prisoner. But for now, the murderers wanted her well. The guards were not armed – beyond their teeth and tines. They kept well away from her when they could. They knew she could hurt *them*.

They kept her inside a big dark cabin. When she was alone she paced the floor. The dogthings were barbarians. The surgery without anesthetics was probably not even intended as torture. She hadn't seen any aircraft, or any sign of electricity. The toilet was a slot carved in a marble slab. The hole went so deep you could scarcely hear the plop hit bottom. But it still smelled bad. These creatures were as backward as people in the darkest ages on Nyjora. They had never had technology, or they had thoroughly forgotten it. Johanna almost smiled. Mom had liked novels about shipwrecks and heroines marooned on lost colonies. The big deal was usually to reinvent technology and repair the spacecraft. Mom was . . . had been . . . so into the history of science; she loved the details of those stories.

Well, Johanna was living it now, but with important differences. She wanted rescue, but she also wanted revenge. These creatures were nothing like human. In fact, she couldn't remember reading of anything quite like them. She'd have looked for them in her dataset, except they had taken that. *Ha.* Let them play with it. They'd quickly run into her booby traps and find themselves totally locked out.

At first there were only blankets to keep warm. Then they'd given her clothes cut like her jumpsuit but made of puffy quilting. They were warm and sturdy, the stitching neater than anything she imagined a nonmachine could do. Now she could comfortably walk around outside. The garden beyond her cabin was the best thing about the place. It was about a hundred meters square, and followed the slope of a hillside. There were lots of flowers, and trees with long, feathery leaves. Flagstoned walks curved back and forth through mossy turf. It was a peaceful place if she let it be one, a little like their backyard on Straum.

There were walls, but from the high end of the garden she could see over them. The walls angled this way and that, and in places she could see their other side. The window slits were like something out of her history lessons: they let you fire arrows or bullets without making a target of yourself.

When the sun was out, Johanna liked to sit where the smell of the feather leaves was strongest, and look over the lower walls at the bay. She still wasn't sure just what she was seeing. There was a harbor; the forest of spars was almost like the marinas on Straum. The town had wide streets, but they zigged and zagged and the buildings along them were all askew. In places there were open-roofed mazes of stone; from up here she could see the pattern. And there was another wall, a rambling thing that ran for as far as she could see. The hills beyond were crowned with gray rock and patches of snow.

She could see the dogthings down in the town. Individually, you *could* almost mistake them for dogs (snake-necked, rat-headed ones). But watch them from a distance and you saw their true nature. They always moved in small groups, rarely more than six. Within the pack they touched, co-operated with clever grace. But she never saw one group come closer than about ten meters to another. From her distant viewpoint, the members of a pack seemed to merge . . . and she could imagine she was seeing one multilimbed beast ambling cautiously along, careful not to come too close to a similar monster. By now, the conclusion was inescapable: one pack, one mind. *Minds so evil they could not bear to be close to one another.*

*

Her fifth time in the garden was the prettiest yet, a coercion toward joy. The flowers had sprayed downy seeds into the air. The lowering sunlight sparkled off them as they floated by the thousands on the slow breeze, clots in an invisible syrup. She imagined what Jefri would do here: first pretend grownup dignity, then bounce from one foot to the other. Finally he would race down the hillside, trying to capture as many of the flying tufts as he could. Laughing and laughing—

'One, two, how do you do?' It was a child's voice, behind her.

Johanna jumped up so fast she almost tore her stitches. Sure enough, there was a pack behind her. They – it? – was the one who had cut the arrow out of her. A mangy lot. The five were crouched, ready to run away. They looked almost as surprised as Johanna felt.

'One, two, how do you do?' The voice came again, exactly as before. It might as well have been a recording, except that one of the animals was somehow synthesizing the sound with the buzzing patches of skin on its shoulders, haunches and head. The parrot act was nothing new to her. But this time . . . the words were almost appropriate. The voice was not hers, but she had heard that chant before. She put hands on hips and stared at the pack. Two of the animals stared back; the others seemed to be admiring the scenery. One licked nervously at its paw.

The two rear ones were carrying her dataset! Suddenly she knew where they'd gotten that singsong question. And she knew what they expected in response. 'I am fine and how do you do?' she said.

The pack's eyes widened, almost comically. 'I am fine, so then are we all!' It completed the game, then emitted a burst of gobbling. Someone replied from down the hill. There was another pack there, lurking in the bushes. She knew that if she stayed near this one, the other wouldn't approach.

So the Tines – she always thought of them by those claws on their front feet; those she would never forget – had been playing with the Pink Oliphaunt, and hadn't been stopped by the booby traps. That was better than Jefri ever managed. It was clear they had fallen into the kindermode language programs. She should have thought of that. When the dataset noted sufficiently asinine responses it would adapt its behavior, first for young children, and – if that didn't work – for youngsters who didn't even speak Samnorsk. With just a little cooperation from Johanna, they could learn her language. Did she want that?

The pack walked a little nearer, at least two of them watching her all the time. They didn't seem quite so ready to bolt as before. The nearest one dropped to its belly and looked up at her. Very cute and helpless, if you didn't see the claws. 'My name is—' Johanna heard a short burst of gobble with an overtone that seemed to buzz right through her head. 'What is your name?'

Johanna knew it was all part of the language script. There was no way the creature could understand the individual words it was saying. That 'my name, your name' pair was repeated over and over again between the children in the language program. A vegetable would get the point eventually. Still, the Tines pronounciation was so perfect . . .

'My name is Johanna,' she said.

'Zjohanna,' said the pack, with Johanna's voice, and splitting the word stream incorrectly.

'Johanna,' corrected Johanna. She wasn't even going to try saying the Tines name.

'Hello, Johanna. Let's play the naming game!' And that was from the script too, complete with silly enthusiasm. Johanna sat down. Sure, learning Samnorsk would give the Tines power over her . . . but it was the only way *she* could learn about *them*, the only way she could learn about Jefri. And if they had murdered Jefri, too? Well then, she would learn to hurt them as much as they deserved.

13

At Woodcarvers and then – a few days later – at Flenser's Hidden Island, the long daylight of arctic summer ended. At first there was a little twilight just around midnight, when even the highest hill stood in shadow. And then the hours of dark grew quickly. Day fought night, and night was winning. The featherleaf in the low valleys changed to autumn colors. Looking up a fjord in daylight was to see orange red on the lower hills, then the green of heather merging imperceptibly to the grays of lichen and the darker grays of naked rock. The snowpatches waited for their time; it would come soon.

At every sunset, each day a few minutes earlier, Tyrathect toured the ramparts of Flenser's outer wall. It was a three-mile walk. The lower levels were guarded by linear packs, but up here there were only a few lookouts. When she approached, they stepped aside with military precision. More than military precision; she saw the fear in their look. It was hard to get used to that. For almost as far back as she had clear memories – twenty years – Tyrathect had lived in fear of others, in shame and guilt, in search of someone to follow. Now all that was turned on its head. It was not an improvement. She knew now, from the inside, the evil she had given herself to. She knew why the sentries feared her. To them, she *was* Flenser.

Of course, she never gave any hint of these thoughts. Her life was only as safe as the success of her fraud. Tyrathect had worked hard to suppress her natural, shy mannerisms. Not once since coming to Hidden Island had she caught herself in the old bashful habit of heads lowering, eyes closing.

Instead, Tyrathect had the Flenser stare – and she used it. Her passage around the top wall was as stark and ominous as Flenser's had ever been, she looked out over her – his – domain with the same hard gaze as before, all heads front, as if seeing visions beyond the petty minds of the disciples. They must never guess her real reason for these sunset sweeps: for a time, the days and nights were like in the Republic. She could almost imagine she was still back there, before the Movement and the massacre at Parliament Bowl, before they cut her throats and wed pieces of Flenser to the stumps of her soul.

In the gold and russet fields beyond the stone curtains, she could see peasants trimming the fields and the herds. Flenser ruled lands far beyond her view, but he had never imported food. The grain and meat that filled the storehouses were all produced within a two-days march of the straits. The strategic intent was clear; still, it made for a peaceful evening's view and brought back memories of her home and school.

The sun slid sideways into the mountains; long shadows swept the farm lands. Flenser's castle was left an island in a sea of shadow. Tyrathect could smell the cold. There would be frost again tonight. Tomorrow the fields would be covered with false snow that would last an hour past sunrise. She pulled the long jackets close around her and walked to the eastern lookout. Across the straits, one of the near hilltops was still in the sun. The alien ship had landed there. It was still there, but now behind wood and stone. Steel began building there right after the landing. The quarries at the north end of Hidden Island were busier now than ever in Flenser's time. The barges hauling stone to the mainland made a steady traffic across the straits. Even now that the light was not dayround, Steel's construction went on nonstop. His Incallings and lesser inspections were harsher than Flenser's had been.

Lord Steel was a killer; worse, a manipulator. But since the alien landing, Tyrathect knew that he was something else: deathly afraid. He had good reason. And even though the folk he feared might ultimately kill them all, in her secret soul she wished them well. Steel and his Flenserists had attacked the star people without warning, more out of greed than fear. They had killed dozens of beings. In a way the murders were worse than what the Movement had done to her. Tyrathect had followed the Flenser of her own free will. She had had friends who warned her about the Movement. There had been dark stories about the Flenser, and not all had been government propaganda. But she had so wanted to follow, to give herself to Something Greater . . . They had used her, literally, as their tool. Yet she could have avoided it. The star people had had no such option; Steel simply butchered them.

So now Steel labored out of fear. In the first three days he had covered the flying ship with a roof: a sudden, silly farmhouse had appeared on the hilltop. Before long the alien craft would be hidden behind stone walls. Ultimately, the new fortress might be bigger than the one on Hidden Island. Steel knew that if his villainy did not destroy him, it would make him the most powerful pack in the world.

And that was Tyrathect's reason for staying, for continuing her masquerade. She couldn't go on forever. Sooner or later the other fragments would reach Hidden Island; Tyrathect would be destroyed and all of Flenser would live again. Perhaps she wouldn't survive even that long. Two of Tyrathect *were* of Flenser. The Master had miscalculated in thinking they could dominate the other three. Instead the conscience of the three had come to own the brilliance of the two. She remembered almost everything the great Flenser had known, all the tricks and all the betrayals. The two had given her an intensity she had never had before. Tyrathect laughed to herself. In a sense, she had gained what she had been so naïvely seeking in the Movement; and the great Flenser had made exactly the mistake that in his arrogance he thought impossible. As long as she could *keep* the two under control, she had a chance. When she was all awake, there wasn't much problem; she still felt herself a 'she,' still remembered her life in the Republic more clearly than the Flenser memories. It was different when she slept. There were nightmares. The memories of torment inflicted suddenly seemed sweet. Sleep-time sex should soothe; with her it was a battle. She awoke sore and cut, as if she had been fighting a rapist. If the two ever broke free, if she ever awoke a 'he . . .' It would take only a few seconds for the two to denounce the masquerade, only a little longer to kill the three and put the Flenser members aboard a more manageable pack.

Yet she stayed. Steel meant to use the aliens and their ship to spread Flenser's nightmare worldwide. But his plan was fragile, with risks on every side. *If there was anything she could do to destroy it and the Flenser Movement, she would.*

Across the castle, only the western tower still hung in sunlight. No faces showed at the window slits, but eyes looked out: Steel watched the Flenser Fragment – the Flenser-in-Waiting as it styled itself – on the ramparts below. The fragment was accepted by all the commanders. In fact, they accorded it almost the awe they had given to the full Flenser. In a sense, Flenser had made them all, so it wasn't surprising they felt a chill in the Master's presence. Even Steel felt it. In his shaping, Flenser had forced the aborning Steel to try to kill him; each time Steel had been caught and his weakest members tortured. Steel knew the conditioning that was there, and that helped him fight it. If anything, he told himself, the Flenser Frag was in greater danger because of it: in trying to counter the fear, Steel might just miscalculate, and act more violently than was appropriate.

Sooner or later Steel had to decide. If he didn't kill it before the other fragments reached Hidden Island, then *all* of Flenser would be here again. If two members could dominate Steel's regime, then six would totally erase it. Did he want the Master dead? And if he did, was there any surely safe way? . . . Steel's mind flickered lightly all around the issue as he watched the black-frocked pack.

Steel was used to playing for high stakes. He had been *born* playing for them. Fear and death and winning were his whole life. But never had the stakes been as high as now. Flenser had come close to subverting the largest nation on the continent, and had had dreams of ruling the world . . . Lord Steel looked to the hillside across the straits, at the new castle he was building. In Steel's present game, world conquest would follow easily on victory, and the destruction of the world was a conceivable consequence of failure.

Steel had visited the flying ship shortly after the ambush. The ground was still steaming. Every hour it seemed to grow hotter. The mainland peasants talked of demons wakened in the earth; Steel's advisors could not do much better. The whitejackets needed padded boots to get close. Steel had ignored the steam, donned the boots, and walked beneath the curving hull. The bottom was vaguely like a boat's hull, if you ignored the stilts. Near the center was a teat-like projection; the ground directly underneath burbled with molten rock. The burned-out coffins were on the uphill side of the ship. Several of the corpses had been removed for dissection. In the first hours his advisors had been full of fanciful theories: the mantis folk were warriors fleeing a battle, come to bury their dead . . .

So far no one had been able to take a careful look inside the craft.

The gray stairs were made of something as strong as steel yet feather light. But they were recognizably stairs, even if the risers were high for the average member. Steel scrambled up the steps, leaving Shreck and his other advisors outside.

He stuck a head through the hatch – and jerked back abruptly. The acoustics were deadly. He understood what the whitejackets were complaining about. How could the aliens bear it? One by one he forced himself through the opening.

Echoes screamed at him – worse than from unpadded quartz. He quieted himself, as he had so often done in the Master's presence. The echoes diminished, but they were still a horde raging in the walls all around. Not even his best whitejackets could tolerate more than five minutes here. The thought made Steel stand straighter. Discipline. Quiet does not always mean submission; it can mean hunting. He looked around, ignoring the howling murmurs.

Light came from bluish strips in the ceiling. As his eyes adjusted, he could see what his people had described to him: the interior was just two rooms. He was standing in the larger one – a cargo hold? There was a hatch in the far wall and then the second room. The walls were seamless. They met in angles that did not match the outer hull; there would be dead spaces. A breeze moved fitfully about the room, but the air was much warmer than outside. He had never been in a place that felt more of power and evil. Surely it was only a trick of acoustics. They would bring in some absorbent quilts, some side reflectors, and the feeling would go away. Still . . .

The room was filled with coffins, these unburned. The place stank with the aliens' body odor. Mold grew in the darker corners. In a way that was comforting: the aliens breathed and sweated as other living things, and for all their marvelous invention, they could not keep their own den clean. Steel wandered among the coffins. The boxes were mounted on railed racks. When the ones outside had been here, the room must have been crammed full. Undamaged, the coffins were marvels of fine workmanship. Warm air exited slots along the sides. He sniffed at it: complex, faintly nauseating, but not the smell of death. And not the source of the overpowering stench of mantis sweat that hung everywhere.

Each coffin had a window mounted on its top side. What effort to honor the remains of single members! Steel hopped onto one and looked down. The corpse was perfectly preserved; in fact, the blue light made everything look frozen. He cocked a second head over the edge of the box, got a double view on the creature within. It was far smaller than the two they had killed under the ship. It was even smaller than the one they had captured. Some of Steel's advisors thought the small ones were pups, perhaps unweaned. It made sense; their prisoner never made thought sounds.

Partly as an act of discipline, he stared for a long while at the alien's queer, flat face. The echo of his mind was a continuing pain, eating at his attention, demanding that he leave. *Let the pain continue.* He had withstood worse before, and the packs outside must know that Steel was stronger than any of them. He could master the pain and have the greater insight . . . And then he would work their butts off, quilting these rooms and studying the contents.

So Steel stared, almost thoughtless, into the face. The screaming in the walls seemed to fade a little. The face was so ugly. He had looked at the charred corpses outside, noticed their small jaws and randomly misshapen teeth. How could the creature eat?

A few minutes passed; the noise and ugliness mixed together, dream-like . . . And then out of his trance, Steel knew a nightmare horror: *The face moved.* The change was small, and it happened very, very slowly, but over a period of minutes, the face had changed.

Steel fell from the coffin; the walls screamed back terror. For a few seconds, he thought the noise would kill him. Then he regained himself with quiet thought. He crawled back onto the box. All his eyes stared through the crystal, waiting like a pack on hunt . . . The change was regular. The alien in the box was breathing, but fifty times more slowly than any normal member. He moved to another box, watched the creature in it. Somehow, they were *all alive*. Inside those boxes, their lives were simply slowed.

He looked up from the boxes, almost in a daze. That the room reeked of evil was an illusion of sound . . . and also the absolute truth.

The mantis alien had landed far from the tropics, away from the collectives; perhaps it thought the Arctic Northwest a backward wilderness.

It had come in a ship jammed with hundreds of mantis pups. These boxes were like larval casings: the pack would land, raise the small ones to adulthood – out of sight of civilization. Steel felt his pelts puff up as he thought about it. If the mantis pack had not been surprised, if Steel's troops had been any less aggressive . . . it would have been the end of the world.

Steel staggered to the outer hatch, his fears coming louder and louder off the walls. Even so, he paused a moment in the shadows and the screams. When his members trooped down the stairs, he moved calmly, every jacket neatly in place. Soon enough his advisors would know the danger, but they would never see fear in him. He walked lightly across the steaming turf, out from under the hull. But even he could not resist a quick look across the sky. This was one ship, one pack of aliens. It had had the misfortune of running into the Movement. Even so, its defeat had been partly luck. How many other ships would land, had already landed? Was there time for him to learn from this victory?

Steel's mind returned to the present, to his eyrie lookout above the castle. That first encounter with the ship was many tendays past. There was still a threat, but now he understood it better, and – as was true of all great threats – it held great promise.

On the rampart, Flenser-in-Waiting slid through the deepening twilight. Steel's eyes followed the pack as it walked beneath the torches and one by one disappeared downstairs. There was an awful lot of the Master in that fragment; it had understood many things about the alien landing before anyone else.

Steel took one last look across the darkening hills as he turned and started down the spiral stair. It was a long, cramped climb; the lookout sat atop a forty-foot tower. The stair was barely fifteen inches wide, the ceiling less than thirty inches above the steps. Cold stone pressed in from all around, so close that there were no echoes to confuse thought – yet also so close that the mind was squeezed into a long thread. Climbing the spiral required a twisting, strung-out posture that left any attacker easy prey for a defender in the eyrie. Such was military architecture. For Steel, crawling the cramped dark was pleasant exercise.

The stairs opened onto a public hallway, ten feet across with back-off nooks every fifty feet. Shreck and a bodyguard were waiting for him.

'I have the latest from Woodcarvers,' said Shreck. He was holding sheets of silkpaper.

Losing the other alien to Woodcarvers had once seemed a major blow. Only gradually had he realized how well it could work out. He had Woodcarvers infiltrated. At first he'd intended to have the other alien killed; it would have been easy to do. But the information that trickled north was interesting. There were some bright people at Woodcarvers. They were coming up with insights that had slipped past Steel and the Master – the *fragment* of the Master. So. In effect, Woodcarvers had become Steel's second alien laboratory, and the Movement's enemies were serving him like any other tool. The irony was irresistible.

'Very good, Shreck. Take it to my den. I'll be there shortly.' Steel waved the whitejackets into a back-up nook and swept past him. Reading the report over brandy would be a pleasant reward for the day's work. In the meantime, there were other duties and other pleasures.

The Master had begun building Hidden Island Castle more than a century earlier; it was growing yet. In the oldest foundations, where an ordinary ruler might put dungeons, were the Flenser's first laboratories. Many could be mistaken for dungeons – and were, by their inhabitants.

Steel reviewed all the labs at least once a tenday. Now he swept through the lowest levels. Crickers fled before the light of his guard's torches. There was a smell of rotting meat. Steel's paws skidded where slickness lay upon the stone. Holes were dug in the floor at regular intervals. Each could hold a single member, its legs jammed tight against its body. Each was covered by a lid with tiny air holes. It took the average member about three days to go mad in such isolation. The resulting 'raw material' could be used to build blank packs. Generally they weren't much more than vegetables, but then that was all the Movement asked of some. And sometimes remarkable things came from these pits: Shreck for instance. Shreck the Colorless, some called him. Shreck the stolid. A pack who was beyond pain, beyond desire. Shreck's was the loyalty of clockwork, but built from flesh and blood. He was no genius, but Steel would have given an eastern province for five more of him. And the promise of more such successes made Steel use the isolation pits again and again. He had recycled most of the wrecks from the ambush that way . . .

Steel climbed back to higher levels, where the really interesting experiments were undertaken. The world regarded Hidden Island with fascinated horror. They had heard of the lower levels. But most didn't realize what a small part those dark spaces played in the Movement's science. To properly dissect a soul, you need more than benches with blood gutters. The results from the lower levels were simply the first steps in Flenser's intellectual quest. There were great questions in the world, things that had bothered packs for thousands of years. How do we think? Why do we believe? Why is one pack a genius and another an oaf? Before Flenser, philosophers argued them endlessly and never got closer to the truth. Even Woodcarver had pranced around the issues, unwilling to give up her traditional ethics. Flenser was prepared to get the answers. In these labs, nature itself was under interrogation.

Steel walked across a chamber one hundred yards wide, with a roof supported by dozens of stone pillars. On every side there were dark partitions, slate walls mounted on tiny wheels. The cavern could be blocked off, maze-like, into any pattern. Flenser had experimented with all the postures of thought. In the centuries before him, there had been only a few effective postures: the instinctive heads together, the ring sentry, various work postures. Flenser had tried dozens more: stars, double rings, grids. Most were useless and confusing. In the star, only a single member could hear all the others, and each of those could only hear the one. In effect, all thought had to pass through the hub member. The hub could contribute nothing rational, yet all its misconceptions passed uncorrected to the rest. Drunken foolishness resulted . . . Of course, that experiment was reported to the outside world.

But at least one of the others – still secret – worked strangely well: Flenser posted eight packs around the floor and on temporary platforms, blocked them from each another with the slate partitions, and then put members from each pack in connection with their counterparts in three others. In a sense, he created a pack of eights packs. Steel was still experimenting with that If the connectors were sufficiently compatible (and that was the hard part), the resulting creature was far smarter than a ring sentry. In most ways it was not as bright as a single heads-together pack, yet sometimes it had striking insights. Before he left for the Long Lakes, the Master had developed a plan to rebuild the castle's main hall so council sessions could be conducted in this posture. Steel hadn't pursued that idea. It was just a bit too risky; Steel's domination of others was not quite as complete as Flenser's had been . . .

No matter. There were other, more significant projects. The rooms ahead were the true heart of the Movement. Steel's soul had been born in these rooms; all of Flenser's greatest creations had begun here. During the last five years, Steel had continued the tradition . . . and improved upon it.

He walked down the hall that linked the separate suites. Each bore its number in inlaid gold. At each he opened a door and stepped partway through. His staff left their report on the previous tenday just inside. Steel quickly read each one, then poked a nose over the balcony to look at the experiment within. The balconies were well-padded, and screened; it was easy to observe without being seen.

Flenser's one weakness (in Steel's opinion) was his desire to create the superior being. The Master's confidence was so immense, he believed that any such success could be applied to his own soul. Steel had no such illusions. It was a commonplace that teachers are surpassed by their creations – pupils, fission-children, adoptions, whatever. He, Steel, was a perfect illustration of this, though the Master didn't know it yet.

Steel had determined to create beings that would each be superior in some *single* way – while flawed and malleable in others. In the Master's absence he had begun a number of experiments. Steel worked from scratch, identifying inheritance lines independent of pack membership. His agents purchased or stole pups that might have potential. Unlike Flenser, who usually melded pups into existing packs in an approximation of nature, Steel made his totally newborn. His puppy packs had no memories or fragments of soul; Steel had total control from the beginning.

Of course, most such constructions quickly died. The pups had to be parted from their wet nurses before they began to participate in the adult's consciousness. The resulting pack was taught entirely in speech and written language. All inputs could be controlled.

Steel stopped before door number thirty-three: Experiment Amdirani-fani, Mathematical Excellence. It was not the only attempt in this direction, but it was by far the most successful. Steel's agents had searched the Movement for packs with ability for abstraction. They had gone further: the world's most famous mathematician lived in the Long Lakes Republic. The pack had been preparing to fission; she had several puppies by herself and a mathematically talented lover. Steel had had the pups taken. They matched his other acquisitions so well that he decided to make an eight-some. If things worked out, it might be beyond all nature in its intelligence.

Steel motioned his guard to shield the torches. He opened door thirty-three and soft-toed one member to the edge of the balcony. He looked down, carefully silencing that member's fore-tympanum. The skylight was dim, but he could see the pups huddled together . . . with its new friend. The mantis. Serendipity, that was all he could call this, the reward that comes to a researcher who labors long enough, carefully enough. He had had two problems. The first had been growing for a year: Amdiranifani was slowly fading, its members falling into the usual autism of wholly newborn packs. The second was the captured alien; that was an enormous threat, an enormous mystery, an enormous opportunity. How to communicate with it? Without communication, the possibilities for manipulation were very limited.

Yet in a single blind stroke, an incompetent Servant had shown the way to solve both problems. Now that his eyes were adjusted to the dimness, Steel could see the alien beneath the pile of puppies. When first he'd heard that the creature had been put in with an experiment, Steel had been enraged beyond thought; the Servant who made the mistake had been recycled. But the days passed. Experiment Amdiranifani began showing more liveliness than at any time since its pups were weaned. It quickly became obvious – from dissecting the other aliens, and observing this one – that mantis folk did *not* live in packs. Steel had a complete alien.

The alien moved in its sleep, and made a low-pitched mouth noise; it was totally incapable of any other kind of sound. The pups shifted to fit the new position. They were sleeping too, vaguely thinking among themselves. The low end of their sounds was a perfect imitation of the alien . . . And that was the greatest coup of all. *Experiment Amdiranifani was learning the alien's speech.* To the pack of newborns this was simply another form of interpack talk, and apparently its mantis friend was more interesting than the tutors who appeared on these balconies. The Flenser Fragment claimed it was the physical contact, that the pups were reacting to the alien as a surrogate parent, thoughtless though the alien was.

It really didn't matter. Steel brought another head to the edge of the balcony. He stood quietly, neither member thinking directly at the other. The air smelled faintly of puppies and mantis sweat. These two were the Movement's greatest treasure: the key to survival and more. By now, Steel knew the flying ship was not part of an invasion fleet. Their visitors were more like ill-prepared refugees. There had been no word of other landings, and the Movement's spies were spread far.

It had been a close thing, winning against the aliens. Their single weapon had killed most of a regiment. In the proper jaws, such weapons could defeat armies. He had no doubt the ship contained more powerful killing machines – ones that still functioned. Wait and watch, Steel counseled himself. Let Amdiranifani show the levers that could control this alien. The entire world would be the prize.

14

Sometimes Mom used to say that something was 'more fun than a barrel full of puppies.' Jefri Olsndot had never had more than one pet at a time, and only once had that been a dog. But now he understood what she meant. From the very first day, even when he had been so tired and scared, he had been entranced by the eight puppies. And they by him. They were all over him, pulling at his clothes, unfastening his shoes, sitting on his lap, or just running around him. Three or four were always staring at him. Their eyes were completely brown or pink, and seemed large for their heads. From the beginning the puppies had mimicked him. They were better than Straumli songbirds; anything he said they could echo – or play back later. And when he cried, often the puppies would cry too, and cuddle around him.

There were other dogs, big ones that wore clothes and entered the room through doorways high up on the walls. They lowered food into the room, and sometimes made strange noises. But the food tasted awful, and they didn't respond to Jefri's screaming even by mimicking him.

Two days had passed, then a week. Jefri had investigated everything in the room. It wasn't really a dungeon; it was too big. And besides, prisoners don't get pets. He understood that this world was uncivilized, not part of the Realm, perhaps not even on the Net. If Mom or Dad or Johanna weren't nearby, it was possible that there was no one here to teach the dogs to speak Saranorsk! Then it would be up to Jefri Olsndot to teach the dogs and find his family . . . Now when the white-jacketed dogs came onto the corner balconies, Jefri shouted questions at them. It didn't help very much. Even the one with red stripes didn't respond. But the puppies did! They shouted right along with Jefri, sometimes echoing his words, sometimes making nonsense sounds.

It didn't take Jefri long to realize that the puppies were driven by a single mind. When they ran around him, some would always sit a little way off, their graceful necks arching this way and that – and the runners seemed to know exactly what the others saw. He couldn't hide things behind his back if there was even one of them to alert the others. For a while he thought they were somehow talking to each other. But it was more than that: when he watched them unfasten his shoes or draw a picture – the heads and mouths and paws cooperated *so* perfectly, like the fingers on a person's hands. Jefri didn't reason things out so explicitly; but over a period of days he came to think of all the puppies together as a single friend. At the same time he noticed that the puppies was mixing up his words – and sometimes making new meanings.

'You me play.' The words came out like a cheap voice splice, but they generally preceded a mad game of tag all around the furniture.

'You me picture.' The slate board covered the lowest meter of the wall, all around the room. It was a display device unlike any Jefri had ever seen in his life: dirty, imprecise, imperfectly deletable, unstorable. Jefri loved it. His face and hands – and most of Puppies lips – got covered with chalk stains. They drew each other, and themselves. Puppies didn't draw neat pictures like Jefri's; Puppies' dog figures had big heads and paws, with the bodies all smudged together. When he drew Jefri, the hands were always big, each finger carefully drawn.

Jefti drew his family and tried to make Puppies understand.

Day by day, the sunlight circled higher on the walls. Sometimes the room was dark now. At least once a day, packs came to talk to Puppies. This was one of the few things which could pull the little ones away from Jefri. Puppies would sit below the balconies, screeching and croaking at the adults. It was a school class! They'd lower scrolls for him to look at, and retrieve ones he had marked.

Jefri sat quietly and watched the lessons. He fidgeted, but he didn't shout at the teachers anymore. Just a little longer and he and Puppies would really be talking. Just a little longer and Puppies could find out for him where Mom and Dad and Johanna were.

Sometimes terror and pain are not the best levers; deception, when it works, is the most elegant and the least expensive manipulation of all. Once Amdiranifani was fluent in the mantis language, Steel had him explain about the 'tragic death' of Jefri's parents and brood-sibling. The Flenser Fragment had argued against it, but Steel wanted quick and unquestioned control.

Now it seemed that the Fragment might have been right; at least he should have held out the hope that the brood-sibling lived. Steel looked solemnly at the Amdiranifani Experiment. 'How can we help?'

The young pack looked up trustingly. 'Jefri is so terribly upset about his parents and *sister*.' Amdiranifani was using mantis words a lot, often unnecessarily: *sister* instead of brood-sibling. 'He hasn't been eating much. He doesn't want to play. It makes me very sad.'

Steel kept watch on the far balcony. The Flenser Fragment was there. It was not hiding, though most of its faces were out of the candlelight. So far its insights had been extraordinary. But the Fragment's stare was like old times, when a mistake could mean mutilation or worse. *So be it.* The stakes were higher now than ever before; if fear at Steel's throats could help him succeed, he welcomed it. He looked away from the balcony, and brought all his faces to an expression of tender sympathy for poor Jefri's plight. 'You just have to make it – him – understand. No one can bring his parents or *sister* back to life. But we know who the murderers are. We're doing everything we can to defend against them. Tell him how hard this is. Woodcarvers is an empire that has lasted hundreds of years. In a fight, we are no match for them. That's why we need all the help he can give us. We need him to teach us to use his parents' ship.'

The puppy pack lowered a head. 'Yes. I'll try, but . . .' The three members by Jefri made low pitched grunting noises at it. The mantis sat head bowed; it held its tentacled paws across its eyes. The creature had been like this for several days, and the withdrawal was getting worse. Now it shook its head violently, made sharp noises a little higher pitched than its normal register.

'Jefri says he doesn't understand how things work in the ship. He's just a little . . .' the pack searched for a translation. '. . . he is really very young. You know, like me.'

Steel nodded understandingly. It was an obvious consequence of the aliens' singleton nature, but weird even so: Every one of them started out all a puppy. Every one of them was like Steel's puppy-pack experiments. Parental knowledge was transmitted by the equivalent of interpack speech. That made the creature easy to dupe, but it was a damned inconvenience now. 'Still, if there's anything he can help explain.'

More grunting from the mantis. Steel should learn that language. The sounds were easy; these pitiful creatures used their *mouths* to talk, like a bird or a forest slug. For now he depended on Amdiranifani. For now that was okay; the puppy pack trusted him. Another piece of serendipity. With a few of his recent experiments, Steel had tried love in place of Flenser's original terror/love combination; there had been a slim chance that it might be superior. By great good luck Amdiranifani fell into the love group. Even his instructors had avoided negative reinforcement. The pack would believe anything he said . . . and so, Steel hoped, would the mantis.

Amdiranifani translated: 'There is something else; he has asked me about it before. Jefri knows how to wake the other children—' the word literally meant 'packs of puppies' '—on the ship. You look surprised, my lord Steel?'

Even though he no longer dreamed in terror of monster minds, Steel would just as soon *not* have a hundred more aliens running around. 'I hadn't realized they could be wakened so easily . . . But we shouldn't do it right now. We've having trouble finding food that Jefri can eat.' That was true; the creature was an incredibly finicky eater. 'I don't think we could feed any more right now.'

More grunting. More sharp cries from Jefri. Finally, 'There is one other thing, my lord. Jefri thinks it may be possible to use the ship's *ultrawave* to call for help from others like his parents.'

The Flenser Fragment jerked out of the shadows. A pair of heads looked down at the mantis, while another stared meaningfully at Steel. Steel didn't react; he could be cooler than any loose pack. 'That's something to think about. Perhaps you and Jefri could talk more about it. I don't want to try it till we're sure we won't hurt the ship.' That was weak. He saw the Fragment twitch a muzzle in amusement.

As he spoke, Amdiranifani was translating. Jefri responded almost immediately.

'Oh, that's okay. He meant a special call. Jefri says the ship has been signaling . . . all by itself . . . ever since it landed.'

And Steel wondered if he had ever heard a deadly threat uttered in such sweet innocence.

They began letting Amdi and Jefri outside to play. Beforehand Amdi was nervous about going out. He was unused to wearing clothes. His whole life – all four years of it – had been spent in that one big room. He read about the outside and was curious about it, yet he was also a little afraid. But the human boy seemed to want it. Every day he'd been more withdrawn, his crying softer. Mostly he was crying for his parents or sister, but sometimes he cried about being locked up so deep away.

So Amdi had talked to Mr Steel, and now they got out almost every day, at least to an inner courtyard. At first Jefri just sat, not really looking around. But Amdi discovered that *he* loved the outdoors, and each time he got his friend to play a little more.

Packs of teachers and guards stood at the corners of the yellowing moss and watched. Amdi – and eventually Jefri – got a big kick out of harassing them. They hadn't realized it down in the room, where visitors came at the balconies, but most adults were nervous around Jefri. The boy was half again as tall as a normally standing pack member. When he came close, the average pack would clump together and edge away. They didn't like having to look *up* at him. It was silly, Amdi thought. Jefri was so tall and skinny, he looked like he might topple over at any moment. And when he ran it was like he was wildly trying to recover from a fall and never quite succeeding.

So Amdi's favorite game those first days was tag. Whenever he was the chaser, he contrived to run Jefri right through the most prim looking whitejackets. If he and Jefri did it right they could turn the tag into a three-way event, Amdi chasing Jefri and a whitejackets racing to stay away from both of them.

Sometimes he felt sorry for the guards and whitejackets. They were so stiff and grownup. Didn't they understand how much fun it was to have a friend that you walk right next to, that you could actually *touch?*

It was mostly night now. Daylight hovered for a few hours around noon. The twilight before and after was bright enough to dim the stars and aurora, but still too faint to show colors. Though Amdi had spent his life indoors, he understood the geometry of the situation, and liked to watch the change of light. Jefri didn't much like the dark of winter . . . until the first snow fell.

Amdi got his first set of jackets. And Mr Steel had special clothes made for the human boy, big puffy things that covered his whole body and kept him warmer than a good pelt would have done.

On one side of the courtyard the snow was just six inches deep, but elsewhere it piled into drifts higher than Amdi's head. Torches were mounted in wind shields on the walls; their light glittered golden off the snow. Amdi knew about snow – but he'd never seen it before. He loved to splash it on one of his jackets. He would stare and stare, trying to see the snowflakes without his breath melting them. The hexagonal pattern was tantalizing, just at the limit of his vision.

But tag was no fun anymore; the human could run through drifts that left Amdi swimming in the white stuff. There were other things the human could do, wonderful things. He could make balls of snow and throw them. The guards were very upset by this, especially when Jefri plinked a few members. It was the first time he ever saw them get angry.

Amdi raced around the windswept side of the courtyard, dodging snow-balls and keening frustration. Human hands were such wicked, wicked things. How he would love to have a pair – four pairs! He circled round from three sides and sprinted right at the human. Jefri backed quickly into deeper snow, but too late. Amdi hit him high and low, tipping the Two-Legs over into a snowdrift. There was a mock battle, slashing lips and paws against Jefri's hands and feet. But now Amdi was on top. The human got paid back for his snowballs with plenty of snow stuffed down the back of his jacket.

Sometimes they just sat and watched the sky for so long that rumps and paws went numb. Sitting behind the largest snow drift, they were shaded from the castle torches and had a clear view of the lights in the sky.

At first Amdi had been entranced by the aurora. Even some of his teachers were. They said this part of the world was one of the best places to see the sky glow. Sometimes it was so faint that the torchlight glimmering off the snow was enough to blot it out. Other times it ran from horizon to horizon: green light trimmed with hints of pink, twisting as though ruffled by a slow wind.

He and Jefri could talk very easily now, though always in Jefri's language. The human couldn't make many of the sounds of interpack speech; even his pronounciation of Amdi's name was scarcely recognizable. But Amdi understood Samnorsk pretty well; it was fun, their own secret language.

Jefri was not especially impressed by the aurora. 'We have that lots at home. It's just light from—' He said a new word, and glanced at Amdi. It was funny how the human couldn't look in more than one place at a time. His eyes and head were always moving. '—you know, places where people make things. I think the gas and waste leaks out, and then the sun lights it up or it gets—' unintelligible.

'Places where people make things?' *In the sky?* Amdi had a globe; he knew the size of the world and its orientation. If the aurora were reflecting sunlight, it must be hundreds of miles above the ground! Amdi leaned a back against Jefri's jacket and made a very human whistling sound. His knowledge of geography was not up to his geometry, but, 'The packs don't work in the sky, Jefri. We don't even have flying boats.'

'Uh, that's right, you don't . . . I don't know what the stuff is then. But I don't like it. It gets in the way of the stars.' Amdi knew all about the stars; Jefri had told him. Somewhere out there were the friends of Jefri's parents.

Jefri was silent for several minutes. He wasn't looking at the sky anymore. Amdi wriggled a little closer, watching the shifting light in the sky. Behind them the wind-sharpened crest of the drift was edged with yellow light from the torches. Amdi could imagine what the other was thinking. 'The commsets from the boat, they really aren't good enough to call for help?'

Jefri slapped the ground. 'No! I told you. They're just radio. I think I can make them work, but what's the use? The ultrawave stuff is still on the boat and it's too big to move. I just don't understand why Mr Steel won't let me go aboard . . . I'm eight years old, you know. I could figure it out. Mom had it all set up before, before . . .' His words guttered into the familiar, despairing silence.

Amdi rubbed a head against Jefri's shoulder. He had a theory about Mr Steel's reluctance. It was an explanation he hadn't told Jefri before: 'Maybe he's afraid you'll just fly away and leave us.'

'That's stupid! I'd never leave you. Besides, that boat is *real* hard to fly. It was never meant to land on a world.'

Jefri said the strangest things; sometimes Amdi was just misunderstanding – but sometimes they were literal truth. Did the humans really have ships that *never* came to ground? Where did they go then? Amdi could almost feel new scales of reference clicking together in his mind. Mr Steel's geography globe represented not the world, but something very, very small in the true scheme of things.

'I know you wouldn't leave us. But you can see how Mr Steel might be afraid. He can't even talk to you except through me. We have to show him that we can be trusted.'

'I guess.'

'If you and I could get the radios working, that might help. I know my teachers haven't figured them out. Mr Steel has one, but I don't think he understands it either.'

'Yeah. If we could get the other one to work . . .'

That afternoon the guards got a break: their two charges came in from the cold early. The guards didn't question their good fortune.

Steel's den had originally been the Master's. It was very different from the castle's meeting halls. Except for choirs, only a single pack would fit in any room. It was not exactly that the suite was small. There were five rooms, not counting the bath. But except for the library, none was more than fifteen feet across. The ceilings were low, less than five feet; there was no space for visitor balconies. Servants were always on call in the two hallways that shared a wall with the quarters. The dining room, bedroom, and bath had smaller hatches, just big enough to give orders and to receive food and drink, or use as a garderobe.

The main entrance was guarded on the outside by three trooper packs. Of course, the Master would never live in a den with only one exit. Steel had found eight secret hatches (three in the sleeping quarters). These could only be opened from within; they led to the maze that Flenser had built within the castle's walls. No one knew the extent of that maze, not even the Master. Steel had rearranged parts of it – in particular the passages leading from this den – in the years since Flenser's departure.

The quarters were nearly impregnable. Even if the castle fell, the rooms' larder was stocked for half a year; ventilation was provided by a network of channels almost as extensive as the Master's secret passages. All in all, Steel felt only tolerably safe here. There was always the possibility that there were *more* than eight secret entrances, perhaps one that could be opened from the other side.

And of course choirs were out of the question, here or anywhere. The only extrapack sex that Steel indulged was with singletons – and that as part of his experiments; it was just too dangerous to mix one's self with others.

After dinner, Steel drifted into the library. He relaxed around his reading desk. Two of him sipped brandy while another smoked southern herbs. This was pleasure but also calculation: Steel knew just what vices, applied to just which members, would raise his imagination to its keenest pitch.

. . . And more and more he was coming to see that imagination was at least as important as raw intelligence in the present game. The desk between him was covered with maps, reports from the south, internal security memos. But lying in all the silkpaper, like an ivory slug in its nest, was the alien *radio*. They had recovered two from the ship. Steel picked the thing up, ran a nose along the smooth, curved sides. Only the finest stressed wood – and that in musical instruments or statuary – could match its grace. Yet the mantis claimed this could be used to talk across dozens of miles, as fast as a ray of sunlight. If true . . . Steel wondered how many lost battles might have been won with these, how many new conquests might be safely undertaken. And if they could learn to *make* far-talkers . . . the Movement's subordinates, scattered across the continent, would be as near as the guards by Steel's den. No force in the world could stand against them.

Steel picked up the latest report from Woodcarvers. In many ways they were having more success with their mantis than was Steel with his. Apparently theirs was almost an adult. More important, it had a miraculous library that could be interrogated almost like a living being. There had been three other *datasets*. Steel's whitejackets had found what was left of them in the burnt-out wreckage around the ship. Jefri thought that the ship's *processors* were a little like a *dataset*, 'only stupider' (Amdi's best translation), but so far the *processors* had been useless.

But with their *dataset*, several on Woodcarver's staff had already learned mantis talk. Each day they discovered more about the aliens' civilization than Steel's people could in ten. He smiled. They didn't know that all the important stuff was being faithfully reported to Hidden Island . . . For now he would let them keep their toy, and their mantis; they had noticed several things that would have slipped by him. Still he damned the luck.

Steel paged through the report . . . Good. The alien at Woodcarvers was still uncooperative. He felt his smile spreading into laughter: it was a small thing, the creature's word for the packs. The report tried to spell out the word. It didn't matter; the translation was 'claws' or 'tines.' The mantis had a special horror for the tine attachments that soldiers wore on their forepaws. Steel licked pensively at the black enamel of his manicured claws. Interesting. Claws could be threatening things, but they were also part of being a person. Tines were their mechanical extension, and potentially more frightening. It was the sort of name you might imagine for an elite killer force . . . but never for all the packs. After all, the race of packs included the weak, the poor, the kindly, the naïve . . . as well as persons like Steel and Flenser. It said something very interesting about mantis psychology that the creature picked *tines* as the characterizing feature of the packs.

Steel eased back from his desk and gazed at the landscape painted around the library's walls. It was a view from the castle towers. Behind the paint, the walls were lined with patterns of mica and quartz and fiber; the echoes gave a vague sense of what you might hear looking out across the stone and emptiness. Combination audiovisuals were rare in the castle, and this one was especially well-done; Steel could feel himself relaxing as he stared at it. He drifted for a moment, letting his imagination roam.

Tines. I like it. If that was the alien's image, then it was the right name for his race. His pitiful advisors – and sometimes even the Flenser Fragment – were still intimidated by the ship from the stars. No question, there was power in that ship beyond anything in the world. But after the first panic, Steel understood that the aliens were *not* supernaturally gifted. They had simply progressed – in the sense that Woodcarver made so much of – beyond the current state of his world's science. Certainly the alien civilization was a deadly unknown right now. Indeed, it might be capable of burning this world to a cinder. Yet the more Steel saw, the more he realized the intrinsic inferiority of the aliens: What a bizarre abortion they were, a race of intelligent singletons. Every one of them must be raised from nothing like a wholly newborn pack. Memories could only be passed by voice and writing. Each creature grew and aged and even *died* as a whole. Despite himself, Steel shivered.

He had come a long way from the first misconceptions, the first fears. For more than thirty days now he'd been scheming to use the starship to rule the world. The mantis said that ship was signaling others. *That* had reduced some of his Servants to incontinence. So. Sooner or later, more ships would arrive. Ruling the world was no longer a practical goal . . . It was time to aim higher, at goals even the Master had never imagined. Take away their technical advantages and the mantis folk were such finite, fragile beings. They should be easy to conquer. Even *they* seemed to realize this. *Tines, the creature calls us. So it will be.* Some day Tines would pace between the stars and rule there.

But in the years till then, life would be very dangerous. Like a newborn pup, all their poptential could be ended by one small blow. The Movement's survival – the world's survival – would depend upon superior intelligence, imagination, discipline, treachery. Fortunately, those had always been Steel's great strengths.

Steel dreamed in the candlelight and haze . . . Intelligence, imagination, discipline, treachery. Done right . . . could the aliens be persuaded to eliminate all of Steel's enemies . . . and then bare their throats to him? It was daring, almost beyond reason, but there might be a way. Jefri claimed he could operate the ship's signaler. By himself? Steel doubted it. The alien was thoroughly duped, but not especially competent. Amdiranifani was a different story. He was showing all the genius of his bloodlines. And the principles of loyalty and sacrifice his teachers drilled into him had taken hold, though he was a bit . . . playful. His obedience didn't have the sharp edge that fear could bring. No matter. As a tool he was useful beyond all others. Amdiranifani understood Jefri, and seemed to understand the alien artifacts even *better* than the mantis did.

The risk must be taken. He would let the two aboard the ship. They would send his message in place of the automatic distress signal. And what should that first message be? Word for word, it would be the most important, most dangerous thing any pack had ever said.

Three hundred yards away, deep in the experiment wing, a boy and a pack of puppies came across an unexpected piece of good luck: an unlocked door, and a chance to play with Jefri's commset.

The phone was more complex than some. It was intended for hospital and field work, for the remote control of devices as well as for voice talk. By trial and error, the two gradually narrowed the options.

Jefri Olsndot pointed to numbers that had appeared on the side of the device. 'I think that means we're matched with some receiver.' He glanced nervously at the doorway. Something told him they really shouldn't be here.

'That's the same pattern as on the radio Mr Steel took,' said Amdi. Not even one of his heads was watching the door.

'I bet if we press it here, what we say will come out on his radio. Now he'll know we can help . . . So what should we do?'

Three of Amdi raced around the room, like dogs that couldn't keep their attention on the conversation. By now, Jefri knew this was the equivalent of a human looking away and humming as he thought. The angle of his gaze was another gesture, in this case a spreading and mischievous smile. 'I think we should surprise him. He is always so serious.'

'Yeah.' Mr Steel was pretty solemn. But then all the adults were. They reminded him of the older scientists at the High Lab.

Amdi grabbed the radio and gave him a 'just watch this' look. He nosed on the 'talk' switch and sang a long ululation into the mike. It sounded only vaguely like pack speech. One of Amdi translated next to Jefri's ear. The human boy felt giggles stealing up his throat.

In his den, Lord Steel was lost in scheming. His imagination – loosed by herbs and brandy – floated free, playing with the possibilities. He was settled deep in velvet cushions, comfortable in the den's safely. The remaining candles shone faintly on the landscape mural, glinting from the polished furniture. The story he would tell the aliens, he almost had it now . . .

The noise on his desk began as a small thing, submerged beneath his dreaming. It was mostly low-pitched, but there were overtones in the range of thought, like slices of another mind. It was a presence, growing. *Someone is in my den!* The thought tore like Flenser's killing blade. Steel's members spasmed panic, disoriented by smoke and drink.

There was a voice in the middle of the insanity. It was distorted, missing tones that any normal speech should have. It howled and quavered at him, 'Lord Steel! Greetings from the Pack of Packs, the Lord God Almighty!'

Part of Steel was already out the main hatch, staring wide-eyed at his guards in the hallway beyond. The troopers' presence brought a bit of calm, and icy embarrassment. *This is nonsense.* He tipped a head to the alien device on his desk. The echoes were everywhere, but the sounds originated in the far-talker . . . There was no pack speech now, just the high-pitched slices of sound, mindless warbling in the middle range of thought. Wait. Behind it all, faint and low . . . there were the coughing grunts he recognized as mantis laughter.

Steel rarely gave way to rage. It should be his tool, not his master. But listening to the laughter, and remembering the words . . . Steel felt black bloodiness rising in first one member and then another. Almost without thought, he reached back and smashed the *commset*. It fell instantly silent. He glared at the guards ranged at attention in the hallway. Their mind noise was quiet with stifled fear.

Someone would die for this.

Mr Steel met with Amdi and Jefri the day after their success with the radio. They had convinced him. They were moving to the mainland. Jefri would have his chance to call for rescue!

Steel was even more solemn than usual; he made a big thing about how important it was to get help, to defend against another attack from the Woodcarvers. But he didn't seem angry about Amdi's little prank. Jefri breathed a quiet sigh of relief. Back home, Daddy would have tanned his hide for something like that. *I guess Amdi is right.* Mr Steel was serious because of all his responsibilities and the dangers they faced. But underneath he was a very nice person.

Crypto: 0
As received by: Transceiver Relay03 at Relay
Language path: Firetongue → Cloudmark → Triskweline, SjK units [Firetongue
    and Cloudmark are High Beyond trade languages. Only core meaning is
    rendered by this translation.]
From: Arbitration Arts Corporation at Firecloud Nebula [A High Beyond military
    [?] organization. Known age ~100 years]
Subject: Reason for concern
Summary: Three single-system civilizations are apparently destroyed
Key phrases: scale interstellar disasters, scale interstellar warefare?, Straumli
    Realm Perversion
Distribution:
  War Trackers Interest Group
  Threats Interest Group
  Homo Sapiens Interest Group
Date: 53.57 days since the fall of Straumli Realm
Text of message:
    Recently an obscure civilization announced it had created a new Power in the

Transcend. It then dropped 'temporarily' off the Known Net. Since that time, there have been about a million messages in Threats about the incident – plenty of speculations that a Class Two Perversion had been born – but no evidence of effects beyond the boundaries of the former 'Straumli Realm.'

Arbitration Arts specializes in treckle lansing disputes. As such, we have few common business interests with natural races or Threats Group. That may have to change: sixty-five hours ago, we noticed the apparent extinction of three isolated civilizations in the High Beyond near Straumli Realm. Two of these were Eye-in-the-U religious probes, and the third was a Pentragian fctory. Previously their main Net link had been Straumli Realm. As such, they have been off the Net since Straumli dropped, except for occasional pinging from us.

We diverted three missions to perform fly-throughs. Signal reconnaissance revealed wideband communication that was more like neural control than local net traffic. Several new large structures were noted. All our vessels were destroyed before detailed information could be returned. Given the background of these settlements, we conclude that this is *not* the normal aftermath of a transcending.

These observations are consistent with a Class Two attack from the Transcend (albeit a secretive one). The most obvious source would be the new Power constructed by Straumli Realm. We urge special vigilance upon all High Beyond civilizations in this part of the Beyond. We larger ones have little to fear, but the threat is very clear.

Crypto: 0
As received by: Transceiver Relay03 at Relay
Language path: Firetongue → Cloudmark → Triskweline, SjK units [Firetongue and Cloudmark are High Beyond trade languages. Only core meaning is rendered by this translation.]
From: Arbitration Arts Corporation at Firecloud Nebula [A High Beyond military[?] organization. Known age ~ 100 years]
Subject: New service available
Summary: Arbitration Arts to provide Net relay service
Key phrases: Special Rates, Sentient Translator Programs, Ideal for civilizations in the High Beyond
Distribution:
   Communication Costs Interest Group
   Motley Hatch Administration Group
   Date: 61.00 days since the fall of Straumli Realm
Text of message:

Arbitrtation Arts is proud to announce a transceiver-layer service especially designed for sites in the High Beyond [rates tabulated after the text of this message]. State-of-the-Zone programs will provide high quality translation and routing. It has been nearly one hundred years since any High Beyond civilization in this part of the Galaxy has been interested in providing such a communication

service. We realize the job is dull and the armiphlage not in keeping with the effort, but we all stand to benefit from protocols that are consistent with the Zone we live in. Details follow under syntax
8139 . . . [Cloudmark: Triskweline translator program balks at handling syntax 8139.]

Crypto: 0
As received by: Transceiver Relay03 at Relay
Language path: Cloudmark → Triskweline, SjK units [Cloudmark is a High
    Beyond trade language. Despite colloquial rendering, only core meaning is
    guaranteed.]
From: Transcendent Bafflements Trading Union at Cloud Center
Subject: Matter of life and death
Summary: Arbitration Arts has fallen to Straumli Perversion via a Net attack. Use
    Middle Beyond relays till emergency passes!
Key phrases: Net attack, scale interstellar warfare, Straumli Perversion
Distribution:
    War Trackers Interest Group
    Threats Interest Group
    Homo Sapiens Interest Group
Date: 61.12 days since the fall of Straumli Realm
Text of message:
    WARNING! The site identifying itself as Arbitration Arts is now controlled by the Straumli Perversion. The Arts' recent advertisement of communications services is a deadly trick. In fact we have good evidence that the Perversion used sapient Net packets to invade and disable the Arts' defenses. Large portions of the Arts now appear to be under direct control of the Straumli Power. Parts of the Arts that were not infected in the initial invasion have been destroyed by the converted portions: Fly-throughs show several stellifications.
    What can be done: If during the last thousand seconds you have received any High-Beyond-protocol packets from 'Arbitration Arts,' *discard them at once*. If they have been processed, then the processing site and all locally netted sites must be physically destroyed *at once*. We realize that this means the destruction of solar systems, but consider the alternative. You are under Transcendent attack.
    If you survive the initial peril (the next thirty hours or so), then there are obvious procedures that can give relative safety: Do not accept High Beyond protocol packets. At the very least, route all communications through Middle Beyond sites, with translation down to, and then up from, local trade languages.
    For the longer term: It's obvious that an extraordinarily powerful Class Two Perversion has bloomed in our region of the galaxy. For the next thirteen years or so, all advanced civilizations near us will be in great danger.
    If we can identify the background of the current perversion, we may discover

its weaknesses and a feasible defense. Class Two Perversions all involve a deformed Power that creates symbiotic structures in the High Beyond – but there is an enormous variety of origins. Some are poorly-formed jokes told by Powers no longer on the scene. Others are weapons built by the newly transcendent, and never properly disarmed.

The immediate source of this danger is well-documented: a species recently up from the Middle Beyond, Homo sapiens, founded Straumli Realm. We are inclined to believe the theory proposed in messages [. . .], namely that Straumli researchers experimented with something in Shortcuts, and that the recipe was a self-booting evil from an earlier time. One possibility: Some loser from long ago planted how-to's on the Net (or in some lost archive) for the use of its own descendants. Thus, we are interested in any information related to Homo sapiens.

The next day Amdi went on the longest trip of his young life. Bundled in windbreakers, they traveled down wide, cobbled streets to the straits below the castle. Mr Steel led the way on a chariot-cart drawn by three kherhogs. He looked marvelous in his red-striped jackets. Guards dressed in white fur rolled along on either side, and the dour Tyrathect brought up the rear. The aurora was as brilliant as Amdijefri had ever seen, brighter in sum than the full moon that sat upon the northern horizon. Icicles grew down from buildings' eaves, sometimes all the way to the ground: glittering, green-silver pillars in the light.

Then they were on the boats, rowing across the straits. The water swept like chill black stone around the hulls.

When they reached the other side, Starship Hill towered over them, higher than any castle could ever be. Every minute brought new visions, new worlds.

It took half an hour to reach the top of that hill, even though their carts were pulled by kherhogs, and nobody walked. Amdi looked in all directions, awed by the landscape that spread, aurora-lit, below them. At first Jefri seemed just as excited, but as they reached the hilltop, he stopped looking around and turned to hug at his friend painfully hard.

Mr Steel had built a shelter around the starship. Inside the air was still, and a little warmer. Jefri stood at the base of the spidery stairs, looking up at the light that spilled from the ship's open doorway. Amdi felt him shivering.

'Is he frightened of his own flier?' asked Tyrathect.

By now Amdi knew most of Jefri's fears, and understood most of the despair. *How would I feel if Mr Steel were killed?* 'No, not scared. It's the memories of what happened here.'

Steel said gently, 'Tell him we could come again. He doesn't have to go inside today.'

Jefri shook his head at the suggestion, but couldn't answer right away.

'I've got to go on. I've got to be brave.' He started slowly up the stairs, stopping at each step to make sure that Amdi was still all with him. The puppies were split between concern for Jefri and the desire to rush madly into this wonderful mystery.

Then they were through the hatch, and into Two-Legs strangeness: bright bluish light, air as warm as in the castle . . . and dozens of mysterious shapes. They walked to the far side of the big room, and Mr Steel stuck some heads in the entrance. His mind sounds echoed loudly around them. 'I've quilted the walls, Amdi, but even so, there isn't room for more than one of us in here.'

'Y-yes.' There were echoes and Steel's mind sounded strangely fierce.

'It's up to you to protect your friend here, and let me know about everything you see.' He moved back so that just one head still looked in upon them.

'Yes. Yes! I will.' It was the first time anybody except Jefri had really needed him.

Jefri wandered silently about the room full of his sleeping friends. He wasn't crying any more, and he wasn't in the silent funk that often held him. It was as if he couldn't quite believe where he was. He passed his hands lightly across the caskets, looking at the faces within. *So many friends*, thought Amdi, *waiting to be wakened. What will they be like?*

'The walls? I don't remember this . . .' said Jefri. He touched the heavy quilting that Steel had hung.

'It's to make the place sound better,' said Amdi. He pulled at the flaps, wondering what was behind: Green wall, like stone and steel all at once . . . and covered with tiny bumps and fingers of gray. 'What's this?'

Jefri was looking over his shoulders. 'Ug. Mold. It's spread. I'm glad Mr Steel has covered it up.' The human boy drifted away. Amdi stayed a second longer, poked several heads up close to the stuff. Mold and fungus were a constant problem in the castle; people were always cleaning it up – and perversely so, in Amdi's opinion. He thought fungus was neat, something that could grow on hardest rock. And this stuff was especially strange. Some of the clumps were almost half an inch high, but wispy, like solid smoke.

The back-looking part of him saw that Jefri had drifted off toward the inner cabin. Reluctantly, Amdi followed.

They stayed in the ship only an hour that first time. In the inner cabin Jefri turned on magic windows that looked out in all directions. Amdi sat goggle-eyed; this was a trip to heaven.

For Jefri it was something else. He hunched down in a hammock and stared at the controls. The tension slowly left his face.

'I – I like it here,' said Amdi, tentatively, softly.

Jefri rocked gently in the hammock. '. . . Yes.' He sighed. 'I was so afraid . . . but being here makes me feel closer to . . .' His hands reached out to caress the panel that hung close to the hammock. 'My dad landed this thing; he was sitting right here.' He twisted around, looked at a glimmering panel of light above him. 'And Mom got the ultrawave all set . . . They did it all. And now it's only you and me, Amdi. Even Johanna is gone . . . It's all up to us.'

Vrinimi Classification: Organizational SECRET. Not for distribution beyond Ring 1 of
    the local net.
Transceiver Relay00 search log:
Begining 19:40:40 Docks Time, 17/01 of Org year 52090 [128.13 days since the
    fall of Straumli Realm]
Link layer syntax 14 message loop detected on assigned surveillance bearing.
    Signal strength and S/N compatible with previously detected beacon signal.
Language path: Samnorsk, SjK: Relay units
From: Jefri Olsndot at I dont know where this is
Subject: Hello. My names Jefri Olsndot. Our ships hurt adnd we need help.
    pPlease anser.
Summary: Sorry if I get some of this wrong. This keybord is STUPID!
Key phrases: I dont know
To: Relay anybody
Text of message: [empty]

15

Two Skroderiders played in the surf.

'Do you think his life is in danger?' asked the one with the slender green stalk.

'Whose life?' said the other, a large rider with a bluish basal shell.

'Jefri Olsndot, the human child.'

Blueshell sighed to himself and consulted his skrode. You come to the beach to forget the cares of the everyday, but Greenstalk would not let them go. He scanned for danger-to-Jefri: 'Of course he's in danger, you twit! Look up the latest messages from him.'

'Oh.' Greenstalk's tone was embarrassed. 'Sorry for the partial remembering,' remembering enough to worry and nothing more. She went silent; after a moment he heard her pleasured humming. The surf crashed endlessly past them.

Blueshell opened to the water, tasting the life that swirled in the power of the waves. It was a beautiful beach. It was probably unique – and that was an extreme thing to say about anything in the Beyond. When the foam swept back from their bodies, they could see indigo sky spread from one side of the Docks to the other, and the glint of starships. When the surf

came forward, the two Riders were submerged in the turbid chill, surrounded by the coralesks and intertidal creatures that built their little homes
here. And at high 'tide' the flexure of the sea floor held steady for an hour or
so. Then the water cleared, and if in daylight, they could see patches of
glassy sea-bottom . . . and through them, a thousand kilometers below, the
surface of Groundside.

Blueshell tried to clear his mind of care. For every hour of peaceful
contemplation, a few more natural memories would accumulate . . . No
good. Just now he could no more banish the worries than could Greenstalk.
After a moment he said, 'Sometimes I wish I were a Lesser Rider.' To stand
a lifetime in one place, with just a minimum skrode.

'Yes,' said Greenstalk. 'But we decided to roam. That means giving up
certain things. Sometimes we must remember things that happen only once
or twice. Sometimes we have great adventures: I'm glad we took the rescue
contract, Blueshell.'

So neither of them was really in the mood for the sea today. Blueshell
lowered the skrode's wheels and rolled a little closer to Greenstalk. He
looked deep into his skrode's mechanical memory, scanning the general
databases. There was a lot there about catastrophes. Whoever created the
original skrode databases had considered wars and blights and perversion
very important. They were exciting things, and they could kill you.

But Blueshell could also see that in relative terms, such disasters were a
small part of the civilized experience. Only about once in a millennium was
there a massive perversion. It was their bad luck to be caught near such a
thing. In the last ten weeks a dozen civilizations in the High Beyond had
dropped from the Net, absorbed into the symbiotic amalgam that now was
called the Straumli Blight. High trade was crippled. Since their ship was
refinanced, he and Greenstalk had flown several jobs, but all to the Middle
Beyond.

The two of them always had been very cautious, but now – as Greenstalk
said – greatness might be thrust upon them. Vrinimi Org wanted to
commission a secret flight to the Bottom of the Beyond. Since he and
Greenstalk were already in on the secret, they were the natural choice for the
job. Right now the *Out of Band II* was in the Vrinimi yards getting bottom-
lugger enhancements and a huge stock of antenna drones. In one stroke the
OOB's value was increased ten-thousand-fold. There had been no need
even to bargain! . . . and that was the scariest thing of all. Every addition
was a clear essential for the trip. They would be descending right to the edge
of the Slowness. Under the best of circumstances this would be a tedious
exercise, but the latest surveys reported movement in the zone boundaries.
With bad luck they might actually end up on the wrong side, where light
had the ultimate speed. If that should happen, the new ramscoop would be
their only hope.

All that was within Blueshell's range of acceptable business. Before he met Greenstalk he had shipped on bottom-luggers, even been stranded once or twice. But – 'I like adventure as much as you,' said Blueshell, a grumpy edge creeping into his voice. 'Traveling to the Bottom, rescuing sophonts from the claws of wildthings: given enough money, it's all perhaps reasonable. But . . . what if that Straumer ship is really as important as Ravna thinks? After all this time it seems absurd, but she's convinced Vrinimi Org of the possibility. If there's something down there that could harm the Straumli Blight—' If the Blight ever suspected the same, it could have a fleet of ten thousand warships descending on their goal. Down at the Bottom they might be little better than conventional vessels, but he and Greenstalk would be no less dead for that.

Except for a faint daydreamy hum, Greenstalk was silent. Had she lost track of the conversation? Then her voice came to him through the water, a reassuring caress. 'I know, Blueshell, it could be the end of us. But I still want to venture it. If it's safe, we make enormous profit. If our going could harm the Blight . . . well, then it's terribly important. Our help might save dozens of civilizations – a million beaches of Riders, just in passing.'

'Hmpf. You're following stalk and not skrode.'

'Probably.' They had watched the progress of the Blight since its beginning. The feelings of horror and sympathy had been reinforced every day till they percolated into their natural minds. So Greenstalk (and Blueshell too; he couldn't deny it) felt stronger about the Blight than about the danger in their new contract. 'Probably. My fears of making the rescue are still analytical,' still confined to her skrode. 'Yet . . . I think if we could stand here a year, if we could wait till we truly felt all the issues . . . I think we would still choose to go.'

Blueshell rolled irritably back and forth. The grit swirled up and through his fronds. She was right, she was right. But he couldn't say it aloud; the mission still terrified him.

'And think, mate: If it is this important, then perhaps we can get help. You know the Org is negotiating with the Emissary Device. With any luck we'll end up with an escort designed by a Transcendental Power.'

The image almost made Blueshell laugh. Two little Skroderiders, journeying to the Bottom of the Beyond – surrounded by help from the Transcend. 'I will hope for it.'

The Skroderiders were not the only ones with that wish. Further up the beach, Ravna Bergsndot prowled her office. What gruesome irony that even the greatest disasters can create opportunities for decent people. Her transfer to Marketing had been made permanent with the fall of Arbitration Arts. As the Blight spread and High Beyond markets collapsed, the Org became ever more interested in providing information services about the Straumli Perversion. Her 'special' expertise in things human suddenly became extraordinarily valuable – never mind that Straumli Realm itself was only a small part of what was now the Blight. What little the Blight said of itself was often in Samnorsk. Grondr and company continued to be vitally interested in her analysis.

Well, she had done some good. They had picked up the refugee ship's 'I-am-here,' and then – ninety days later – a message from a human survivor, Jefri Olsndot. Barely forty messages had they exchanged, but enough to learn about the Tines and Mr Steel and the evil Woodcarvers. Enough to know that a small human life would be ended if she could not help. Ironic but natural: most times that single life weighed more on her than all the horror of the Perversion, even the fall of Straumli Realm. Thank the Powers that Grondr had endorsed the rescue mission: It was a chance to learn something important about the Straumli Perversion. And the Tinish packs seemed to interest him, too; group minds were a fleeting thing in the Beyond. Grondr had kept the whole affair secret, and persuaded *his* bosses to support the mission. But all his help might not be enough. If the refugee ship was as important as Ravna thought, there could be enormous perils awaiting any rescuers.

Ravna looked across the surf. When the waves backed down the sand, she could see the Skroderiders' fronds peeping out of the spray. How she envied them; if tensions annoyed them, they could simply turn them off. The Skroderiders were one of the most common sophonts in the Beyond. There were many varieties, but analysis agreed with legend: *very* long ago they had been one species. Somewhere in the off-Net past, they had been sessile dwellers of sea shores. Left to themselves, they had developed a form of intelligence almost devoid of short-term memory. They sat in the surf, thinking thoughts that left no imprints on their minds. Only repetition of a stimulus, over a period of time, could do that. But the intelligence and memory that they had *was* of survival value: it made it possible for them to select the best possible place to cast their pupal seeds, locations that would mean safety and food for the next generation.

Then some unknown race had chanced upon the dreamers and decided to 'help them out.' Someone had put them on mobile platforms, the skrodes. With wheels they could move along the seashores, could reach and manipulate with their fronds and tendrils. With the skrode's mechanical short-term memory, they could learn fast enough that their new mobility would not kill them.

Ravna glanced away from the Skroderiders – someone was floating in over the trees. The Emissary Device. Maybe she should call Greenstalk and Blueshell out of the water. No. Let 'em bliss out a little longer. If she couldn't get the special equipment, things would be tough enough for them later . . .

Besides, I can do without witnesses. She folded her arms across her chest and glared into the sky. The Vrinimi Org had tried to talk to the Old One about this, but nowadays the Power would only work through its Emissary Device . . . and *he* had insisted on a face-to-face meeting.

The Emissary touched down a few meters away, and bowed. His lopsided grin spoiled the effect. 'Pham Nuwen, at your service.'

Ravna gave a little bow in return, and led him to the shade of her inner office. If he thought that face-to-face would unnerve her, he was *right*. 'Thanks for the meeting, sir. The Vrinimi Organization has an important request of your principal,' owner? master? operator?

Pham Nuwen plunked himself down, stretching indolently. He'd stayed out of her way since that night at The Wandering Company. Grondr said Old One had kept him at Relay though, rummaging through the archives for information about humanity and its origins. It made sense now that Old One had been persuaded to restrict its Net usage: the Emissary could do local processing, i.e., use human intelligence to search and summarize and then upload only the stuff that Old One really needed.

Ravna watched him out of the corner of her eye as she pretended to study her dataset. Pham had his old, lazy smile. She wondered if she would ever have the courage to ask him how much of their . . . affair . . . had been a human thing. Had Pham Nuwen felt anything for her? Hell, did he even have a good time?

From a Transcendent point of view, he might be a simple data con-centrator and waldo – but from *her* viewpoint he was still too human. 'Um, yes. Well . . . The Org has continued to monitor the Straumli refugee ship even though your principal has lost interest.'

Pham's eyebrows raised in polite interest. 'Oh?'

'Ten days ago, the simple "I-am-here" signal was interrupted by a new message, apparently from a surviving crewmember.'

'Congratulations. You managed to keep it a secret, even from me.'

Ravna didn't rise to the bait. 'We're doing our best to keep it secret from everyone, sir. For reasons that you must know.' She put the messages to date on a display between them. A handful of calls and responses, scattered across ten days. Translated into Triskweline for Pham, the original spelling and grammar errors were gone, yet the tone remained. Ravna was respons-ible for the Org side of the conversation. It was like talking to someone in a dark room, someone you have never seen. Much was easy to imagine: a strident, piping voice behind the capitalized words and exclamation marks. She had no video of the child, but through the humankind archive at Sjandra Kei, Marketing had dug up pictures of the boy's parents. They looked like typical Straumers, but with the brown eyes of the Linden clans. Little Jefri would be slim and dark.

Pham Nuwen's gaze flicked down through the text, then seemed to hang on the last few lines:

Org[17]:	How old are you, Jefri?
Target[18]:	I am eight. I mean I am eight years old. I AM OLD ENOUGH BUT I NEED HELP.
Org[18]:	We will help. We are coming as fast as we can, Jefri.
Target[19]:	Sorry I couldn't talk yesterday. The bad people were on the hill again yesterday. It wasn't safe to go to the ship.
Org[19]:	Are the bad ones that close by?
Target[20]:	Yes yes. I could see them from the island. I'm with Amdi on shipboard now, but walking up here there were dead soldiers all around. Woodcarver raids here often. Mother is dead. Father is dead. Johanna is dead. Mister Steel will protect me as much as he can. He says that I must be brave.

For a moment his smile was gone. 'Poor kid,' he said softly. Then he shrugged and jabbed his hand at one of the messages. 'Well, I'm glad Vrinimi is sending a rescue mission. That is generous of you.'

'Not really, sir. Look at items six through fourteen. The boy is complaining about the ship's automation.'

'Yeah, he makes it sound like something out of a dawn age: keyboards and video, no voice recognition. A completely unfriendly interface. Looks like the crash scragged almost everything, eh?'

He was being deliberately obtuse, but Ravna resolved to be infinitely patient. 'Perhaps not, considering the vessel's origin.' Pham just smiled, so Ravna continued to spell things out. 'The processors are likely High Beyond or Transcendent, snuffed down to near brainlessness by the current environment.'

Pham Nuwen sighed. 'All consistent with the Skroderiders' theory, right? You're still hoping this crate is carrying some tremendous secret that will blow the Blight away.'

'Yes! . . . Look. At one time, the Old One was very curious about all this. Why the total disinterest now? Is there some reason why the ship *can't* be the key to fighting the Perversion?' That was Grondr's explanation for the Old One's recent lack of interest. All her life Ravna Bergsndot had heard tales of the Powers, and always from a great remove. Here, she was awfully close to questioning one directly. It was a very strange feeling.

After a moment Pham said, 'No. It's unlikely, but you could be right.'

Ravna let out a breath she hadn't realized she'd been holding. 'Good. Then what we're asking is reasonable. Suppose the downed ship contains something the Perversion needs, or something it fears. Then it's likely the Perversion knows of its existence – and may even be monitoring ultra-drive traffic in that part of the Bottom. A rescue expedition could lead the Perversion right to it. In that case, the mission will be suicide for its crew – and could increase the Blight's overall power.'

'So?'

Ravna slapped her dataset, resolutions of patience dissolving. 'So, Vrinimi Org is asking Old One's help to build an expedition the Blight can't knock over!'

Pham Nuwen just shook his head. 'Ravna, Ravna. You're talking about an expedition to the *Bottom of the Beyond*. There's no way a Power can hold your hand down there. Even an Emissary Device would be mostly on its own there.'

'Don't act like more of a jerk than you are, Pham Nuwen. Down there, the Perversion will be at just as much a disadvantage. What we're asking for is equipment of Transcendent manufacture, designed for those depths, and provided in substantial quantities.'

'Jerk?' Pham Nuwen drew himself up, but there was still the ghost of a smile on his face. 'Is that how you normally address a Power?'

Before this year, I would have died *rather than address a Power in any manner.* She leaned back, giving him her own version of an indolent smile. 'You have a pipeline to god, Mister, but let me tell you a little secret: I can tell whether it's open or closed.'

Polite curiosity: 'Oh? How is that?'

'Pham Nuwen – left on his own – is a bright, egotistical guy, and about as subtle as a kick in the head.' She thought back to their time together. 'I don't really start worrying until the arrogance and smart remarks go away.'

'Um. Your logic is a little weak. If the Old One were running me direct, he could just as easily play a jerk as,' he cocked his head, 'as the man of your dreams.'

Ravna gritted her teeth. 'Maybe so, but I've got a little help from my boss. He's cleared me to monitor transceiver usage.' She looked at her dataset 'Right now, your Old One is getting less than ten kilobits per second from all of Relay . . . which means, my friend, that you are not being tele-operated. Any crass behavior I see today is the true Pham Nuwen.'

The redhead chuckled, faint embarrassment evident. 'You got me. I'm on detached duty, have been ever since the Org persuaded Old One to back off. But I want you to know that all those ten Kb/s are dedicated to this charming conversation.' He paused as if listening, then waved his hand. 'Old One says "hi."?'

Ravna laughed despite herself; there was something absurd about the gesture, and the notion that a Power would indulge such trivial humor. 'Okay. I'm glad he can, um, sit in. Look, Pham, we're not asking for much by Transcendent standards, and it could save whole civilizations. Give us a few thousand ships; robot oneshots would be fine.'

'Old One could make that many, but they wouldn't be much better than what's built down here. Tricking—' he paused, looking surprised by his own choice of words, 'tricking the Zones is subtle work.'

'Fine. Quality or quantity. We'll settle for whichever the Old One thinks—'

'No.'

'Pham! We're talking about a few days' work for the Old One. It's already paid more to study the Blight.' Their single wild evening might have cost as much – but she didn't say that.

'Yes, and Vrinimi has spent most of it.'

'Paying off the customers you stepped on! . . . Pham, can't you at least tell us *why*?'

The lazy smile faded from his face. She took a quick glance at her dataset. No, Pham Nuwen was not possessed. She remembered the look on his face when he read the mail from Jefri Olsndot; there was a decent human being lurking behind all the arrogance. 'I'll give it a try. Keep in mind – even though I've been part of Old One – I'm remembering and explaining with human limitations.

'You're right, the Perversion is chewing up the Top of the Beyond. Maybe fifty civilizations will die before this Power gets tired of screwing around – and for a couple of thousand years after that there'll be "echoes" of the disaster, poisoned star systems, artificial races with bloody-minded ideas. But – I hate to say it this way – so what? Old One has been thinking about this problem, off and on, for more than a hundred days. That's a *long* time for a Power, especially Old One. He's existed for more than ten years now; his minds are drifting fast toward . . . changes . . . that will put him beyond all communication. Why should he give a damn about this?'

It was a standard topic in school, but Ravna couldn't help herself. This time it was for real. 'But history is full of incidents where Powers helped Beyonder races, sometimes even individuals.' She had already looked up the Beyonder race that created Old One. They were gasbag creatures. Their netmail was mostly jabberwocky even after Relay's best interpretation. Apparently they had no special leverage with Old One. The direct appeal was about all she had. 'Look. Turn the thing around: Even ordinary humans don't need special explanation to help animals that are hurting.'

Pham's smile was beginning to come back. 'You're so big on analogies. Remember that no analogy is perfect, and the more complex the auto-mation the more complex the possible motivations. But . . . okay, how about this for an analogy: Old One is a basically decent guy, with a nice home in a good part of town. One day he notices he has a new neighbor, a scruffy fellow whose homestead is awhiff with toxic sludge. If you were Old One, you'd be concerned, right? You might probe around beneath your properties. You'd also chat with the new fellow and check on where he came from, try to figure out what's going on. The Vrinimi Org saw part of that investigation.

'So you discover the new neighbor is unwholesome. Basically his lifestyle involves poisoning swamp land and eating the sludge produced. That's an annoyance: it smells and it hurts a lot of harmless animals. But, after investigating, it's clear the damage will not affect your own property, and you get the neighbor to take measures to reduce the stink. In any case, eating toxic sludge is a self-defeating lifestyle.' He paused. 'As analogies go, I think this one's pretty good. After some initial mystery, Old One has determined that this Perversion is one of the common patterns, so petty and banal that even creatures like you and I can see it's evil. In one form or another, it's been drifting up from Beyonder archives for a hundred million years.'

'Damn it! I'd get my neighbors together, and run the pervert out of town.'

'That's been talked about, but it would be expensive . . . and real people might get hurt.' Pham Nuwen came smoothly to his feet, and smiled dismissingly at her. 'Well, that's about all we had to say to you.' He walked out from under the trees. Ravna hopped up to pursue.

'My personal advice: don't take this so hard, Ravna. I've seen it all, you know. From the Bottom of the Slowness to the inside of a Transcendent Power, each Zone has its own special unpleasantness. The whole basis of the Perversion – thermodynamic, economic, however you want to picture it – is the high quality of thought and communication at the Top of the Beyond. The Perversion hasn't touched a single civilization in the Middle Beyond. Down here, the comm lags and expense are too great, and even the best equipment is mindless. To run things here you'd need standing navies, secret police, clumsy transceivers – it would be almost as awkward as any other Beyonder empire, and of no profit to a Power.' He turned and saw her dark expression. 'Hey, I'm saying your pretty ass is safe.' He reached down to pat her rear.

Ravna brushed the hand away and stepped back. She'd been working on some clever argument that might set the guy to thinking; there *were* cases where Emissary Devices had changed their principal's decision. Now the half-formed ideas were blown away, and all she could think to say was – 'So how safe is your own tail, hmm? You say Old One is about ready to pack it in, go wherever overage Powers wander off to. Is he going to take you along, or maybe just put you away, a pet that's now inconvenient?'

It was a silly shot, and Pham Nuwen just laughed. 'More analogies? No . . . most likely he'll just leave me behind. You know, like a robot probe flying free after its last use.' Another analogy, but one to his liking. 'In fact, if it happens soon enough, *I* might even be willing to take on this rescue expedition. It looks like Jefri Olsndot is in a medieval civilization. I'll wager there's no one in the Org who understands such a place better than I. And down at the Bottom, your crew could scarcely ask for a better mate than an old Qeng Ho type.' He spoke breezily, as though courage and experience were givens for him – even if other people were cowardly scuts.

'Oh, yeah?' Ravna's arms went akimbo, and she cocked her head to one side. It was just a bit too much, when his whole existence was a fraud. 'You're the little prince who grew up with intrigue and assassination, and then flew away to the stars with the Qeng Ho . . . Do you ever really *think* about that past, Pham Nuwen? Or is that something Old One tactfully blocks you from doing: After our charming evening at The Wandering Company, I did think about it. You know what? There's only a few things you can know for sure: You really were a Slow Zone spacer – probably two or three spacers, since none of the corpses were complete. Somehow you and your buddies got yourselves killed down at the nether end of the Slowness. What else? Well, your ship had no recoverable memory. The only hardcopy we found seemed to be written in some Earth Asian language. That's all, *all*, that Old One had to go on when he put together the fraud.'

Pham's smile seemed a little frozen. Ravna went on before he could speak. 'But don't blame Old One. He was a little rushed, right? He had to convince Vrinimi and me that you were real. He rummaged around in the archives, slapped together a mishmash reality for you. Maybe it took him an afternoon – are you grateful for the effort? A snip from here and a snip from there. There really was a Qeng Ho, you know. On *Earth*, a thousand years before space flight. And there must have been Asia-descended star colonies, though that's an obvious extrapolation on his part. Old One really has a nice sense of humor. He made your whole life a fantastic romance, right down to the last tragic expedition. *That* should have tipped me off, by the way. It's a combination of several pre-Nyjoran legends.'

She caught her breath and rushed on. 'I feel sorry for you, Pham Nuwen. As long as you don't think about yourself too hard, you can be the most confident fellow in space. But all the skill, all the achievement – do you ever look at it up close? I'll bet not. Being a great warrior or an expert pilot – those involve a million subskills, all the way down to kinesthetic things below the level of conscious thought. The Old One's fraud needed just the top level recollections, and a brash personality. Look under the surface, Pham. I think you'll find a whole lot of nothing.' *A dream of competence, too closely confronted.*

The redhead had crossed his arms and was tapping his sleeve with a finger. When she finally ran out of words, his smile grew broad and patronizing. 'Ah, silly Ravna. Even now you don't understand how far superior the Powers are. Old One is not some Middle Beyond tyranny, brainwashing its victims with superficial memories. Even a Transcendent fraud has more depth than the image of reality in a human mind. And how can you know this really *is* a fraud? So you looked through the Relay archives, and didn't find my Qeng Ho.' *My Qeng Ho*. He paused. Remembering? Trying to remember? For an instant Ravna saw a gleam of panic on his face. Then it was gone, and there was just the lazy smile. 'Can any of us imagine the archives of the Transcend, all the things Old One must know about humanity? Vrinimi Org should be grateful to Old One for explaining my origins; they could never have learned that by themselves.

'Look. I am truly sorry I can't help. Even if it's otherwise a fool's errand, I'd like to see those kids rescued. But don't worry about the Blight. It's near maximum expansion now. Even if you could destroy it, you wouldn't make things better for the poor wights who've been absorbed.' He laughed, a little too loudly. 'Well, I have to go; Old One has some other errands for me this afternoon. He wasn't happy about this being face-to-face, but I insisted. The perks of detached duty, y'know. You and I . . . you and I had some good times, and I thought it would be nice to chat. I didn't mean to make you mad.'

Pham cut in his agrav and floated off the sand. He waved a laconic salute. Staring up, Ravna lifted her hand to wave back. His figure dwindled, acquiring a faint nimbus as he left the Docks' breathable atmosphere and his space suit cut in.

Ravna watched a few moments more, till the figure became one more commuter in the indigo sky. *Damn. Damn. Damn.*

Behind her there was the sound of wheels crunching across sand. Blueshell and Greenstalk had rolled out of the water. Wetness glistened on the sides of their skrodes, transforming their cosmetic stripes into jagged rainbows. Ravna walked down to meet them. *How do I tell them there's no help coming?*

With someone like Pham Nuwen fronting for it, Old One had seemed so different from what she imagined in her classes back at Sjandra Kei. She'd almost thought she could make a difference just by talking. What a joke. She had caught a glimpse just now, behind the front: of a being who could play with souls the way a programmer plays with a clever graphic, a being so far beyond her that only its indifference could protect her. *Be happy, little Ravna moth. You were only dazzled by the flame.*

16

The next few weeks went surprisingly well. Despite the Pham Nuwen debacle, Blueshell and Greenstalk were still willing to fly the rescue. Vrinimi Org even kicked in some extra resources. Every day Ravna took a telexcursion to the repair yards. The *Out of Band II* might not be getting any Transcendent enhancements, but when the refitting was complete, the ship would be something extraordinary: Now it floated in a golden haze of 'structors, billions of tiny robots regrowing sections of the hull into the characteristic form of a bottom-lugger. Sometimes the ship seemed to Ravna like a fragile moth . . . and sometimes an abyssal fish. The rebuilt ship could survive across a range of environments: It had the spines of an ultradrive craft, but the hull was streamlined and wasp-waist – the classic form of a ramscoop ship. Bottom-luggers must troll dangerously near the Slow Zone. The zone surface was hard to detect from a distance, even harder to map; and there were short-term position changes. It was not impossible for a lugger to be trapped a light-year or two within the Slowness. It was then you'd thank goodness for the ramscoop and the coldsleep facilities. Of course, by the time you returned to civilization you might be completely out of date, but at least you could get back.

Ravna floated her viewpoint through the drive spines that spread out from the hull. They were broader than those on most ships that came to Relay. They weren't optimal for the Middle or High Beyond, but with appropriate (i.e., Low Beyond) computers, the ship would fly as fast as anything when it reached the Bottom.

Grondr let her spend half-time on the project, and after a few days Ravna realized this was not just a favor. She *was* the best person for this job. She knew humans, and she knew archive management. Jefri Olsndot needed reassurance every day. And the things Jefri was telling her were immediately important. Even if everything went according to plan – even if the Perversion stayed completely out of it – this rescue was going to be tricky. The kid and his ship seemed to be in the middle of a bloody war. Extracting them would mean making instantly correct decisions and acting on them. They would need an effective onboard database and strategy program. But not much could be expected to work at the Bottom, and memory capacity would be limited. It was up to Ravna to decide what library materials to move to the ship, to balance the lease of local availability against the greater resources that would be accessible over the ultrawave from Relay.

Grondr was available on the local net, and often in real time. He wanted this to work: 'Don't worry, Ravna. We'll dedicate part of ROO to this mission. If their antenna swarm works properly, the Riders should have a thirty Kb/s link to Relay. You'll be their prime contact here, and you'll have access to our best strategists. If nothing . . . interferes, you should have no trouble managing this rescue.'

Even four weeks ago, Ravna wouldn't have dared to ask for more. Now: 'Sir, I have a better idea. Send me with the Skroderiders.'

All of Grondr's mouth parts clapped together at once. She'd seen that much surprise in people like Egravan, but never in the staid Grondr. He was silent for a moment. 'No. We need you here. You are our best sanity check when it comes to questions about humankind.' The newsgroups interested in the Straumli Perversion carried more than one hundred thousand messages a day, about a tenth of that human-related. Thousands of messages were old ideas rehashed, or patent absurdities, or probable lies. Marketing's automation was fairly good at filtering out the redundancy and some of the absurdity, but when it came to questions on human nature Ravna was without equal. About half her time was spent guiding that analysis and handling queries about humankind at the archives. All that would be next to impossible if she left with the Skroderiders.

Over the next few days, Ravna kept pushing her boss on the question. Whoever flew the rescue would need instant rapport with humans – human children, in fact. Very likely Jefri Olsndot had never even met a Skroderider. The point was a good one, and it was gradually driving her to desperation – but by itself it would not have changed old Grondr's mind. It took some outside events to do that: As the weeks passed, the Blight's expansion slowed. Just as conventional wisdom (and Old One via Pham Nuwen) claimed, there seemed to be natural limits to how far the Perversion could extend its interests. The abject panic slowly disappeared from the High Beyond communication traffic. Rumors and refugees from the absorbed volumes dribbled toward zero. The people in the Blighted spaces were gone, but now it was more like death in a graveyard than death from contagious rot. Blight-related newsgroups continued to babble about the catastrophe, but the level of nonproductive rehashing was steadily increasing. There simply was very little new going on. Over the next ten years, physical death would spread through the Blighted region. Colonization would begin again, cautiously probing through the ruins and informational traps, and residue races. But all of that was a ways off, and for the moment Relay's Blight 'windfall' was a shrinking affair.

. . . And Marketing was even more interested in the Straumli refugee ship. None of the strategy programs – much less Grondr – believed the ship's secret could hurt the Blight, but there was a good chance it might bring commercial advantage when the Perversion finally got tired of its Transcendent game. And the Tines pack-minds had caught their interest. It was appropriate that a maximum effort be made, that Ravna give up her Docks job and go into the field.

So, for a wonder, her childhood fantasy of rescue and questing adventure would actually come true. *And even more surprising, I'm only half-terrified by the prospect!*

Target[56]: Im sorry I diddnt anser for a while. I dont feel good a lot. Mister Steel says I should talk to you. He says I need more friends to make me feel better. Amdi says so too and hes my best friend of all . . . like packs of dogs but smart and fun. I wish I could send pictures. Mister Steel will try to get ansers for all your questions. He is doing everything he can to help, but the bad packs will be back. Amdi and I tried the stuff you said with the ship. I am sorry, it still doesnt work . . . I hate this dumb keybord . . .

Org[57]: Hi, Jefri. Amdi and Mr Steel are right. I always like to talk, and it will make you feel better . . . There are inventions that might help Mister Steel. We've thought of some improvements for his bows and flamethrowers. I'm also sending down some fortress design information. Please tell Mister Steel that we can't tell him how to fly the ship. It would be dangerous even for an expert pilot to try . . .

Target[57]: Ya, even Daddy had a hard time landing it. ikocxljikersw89iou43e5 I think Mister Steel just doesnt understand, and hes getting sorta disparate . . . Isnt there other stuff, though, like they had in oldendays. You know, bombs and airplanes that we could make? . . .

Org[58]: There are other inventions, but it would take time for Mister Steel to make them. Our star ship is leaving Relay soon, Jefri. We'll be there long before other inventions would help . . .

Target[58]: Your coming? Your finally coming!!! When do you leave? When will you get here???

Ordinarily Ravna composed her messages to Jefri on a keyboard – it gave her some feeling for the kid's situation. He seemed to be holding up, though there were still days when he didn't write (it was strange to think of 'mental depression' having any connection with an eight-year-old). Other times he seemed to have a tantrum at the keyboard, and across twenty-one thousand light-years she saw evidence of small fists slamming into keys.

Ravna grinned at the display. Today she finally had something more than nebulous promises for him: she had a definite departure time. Jefri was going to like message [59]. She typed: 'We're scheduled to leave in seven more days, Jefri. Travel time will be about thirty days.' Should she qualify that? Latest postings on the Zone boundary newsgroups said the Bottom was unusually active. The Times World was so close to the Slow Zone . . . If the 'storm' worsened, travel time would suffer. There was about a one percent chance the voyage would take more than sixty days. She leaned back from the keyboard. Did she really want to say that? Damn. Better be frank; these dates could affect the locals who were helping Jefri. She explained the 'ifs' and 'buts', then went on to describe the ship and the wonderful things they would bring. The boy usually didn't write at great length (except when he was relaying information from Steel), but he really seemed to like long letters from her.

The *Out of Band II* was undergoing final consistency checks. Its ultra-drive was rebuilt and tested; the Skroderiders had taken it out a couple of thousand light-years to check the antenna swarm. The swarm worked great, too. She and Jefri would be able to talk through most of the voyage. As of yesterday, the ship was stocked with consumables. (That sounded like something out of medieval adventure. But you had to take some supplies when you were headed so far down that reality graphics couldn't be trusted.) Sometime tomorrow, Grondr's people would be loading the ship's hold with gadgets that might be real handy for a rescue. Should she mention those? Some of them might sound a bit intimidating to Jefri's local friends.

That evening, she and the Skroderiders had a beach party. That's what they called it, though it was much more like the human version than an authentic Rider one. Blueshell and Greenstalk had rolled well back from the water to where the sand lay dry and warm. Ravna laid out refreshments on Blueshell's cargo scarf. They sat on the sand and admired the sunset.

It was mostly a celebration – that Ravna had gotten permission to go with the *OOB*, that the ship was almost ready to depart. But, 'Are you really happy to be going, my lady?' asked Blueshell. 'We two will make very good money, but you—'

Ravna laughed. 'I'll get a travel bonus.' She had argued and argued for permission to go; there wasn't much room left to haggle about the pay. 'And yes. This is what I really want.'

'I am glad,' said Greenstalk.

'I am laughing,' said Blueshell. 'My mate is especially pleased that our passenger will not be surly. We almost lost our love for bipeds after shipping with the certificants. But there is nothing to be frightened of now. Have you read Threats Group in the last fifteen hours? The Blight has stopped growing, and its edges have become sharply defined. The Perversion is settling into middle age. I'm ready to leave right now.'

Blueshell was full of speculations about the Tinish 'packs,' and possible schemes for extracting Jefri and any other survivors. Greenstalk interjected a thought here and there. She was less shy than before, but still seemed softer, more diffident than her mate. And her confidence was a bit more realistic. She was glad they weren't leaving for another week. There were still the final consistency checks to run on the *OOB* – and Grondr had gotten Org financing for a small fleet of decoy ships. Fifty were complete so far. A hundred would be ready by the end of the week.

The Docks drifted into night. With its shallow atmosphere, twilight was short, but the colors were spectacular. The beach and the trees glistened in the horizontal rays. The scent of even-flowers mixed with the tang of sea salt. On the far side of the sea, all was stark bright and dark, silhouettes that might have been Vrinimi fancies or functional dock equipage – Ravna had never learned which. The sun slid behind the sea. Orange and red spread along the aft horizon, topped by a wider band of green, probably ionized oxygen.

The Riders didn't turn their skrodes for a better view – for all she knew, they had been looking that way all along – but they stopped talking. As the sun set, the breakers shattered it into a thousand images, glints of green and yellow through the foam. She guessed the two would have preferred to be out there just now. She had seen them often enough around sunset, deliberately sitting where the surf was hardest. When the water drew back, their stalks and fronds were like supplicants' arms, upstretched. At times like these she could almost understand the Lesser Skroderiders; they spent their whole lives memorizing such repeated moments. She smiled in the greenish twilight. There would always be time enough later to worry and plan.

They must have sat like that for twenty minutes. Along the curving line of the beach, she saw tiny fires in the gathering dark: office parties. Somewhere very nearby there was the *crunch crunch* of feet on sand. She turned and saw that it was Pham Nuwen. 'Over here,' she called.

Pham ambled toward them. He'd been very scarce since their last confrontation; Ravna guessed that some of her jibes had struck deep. *This once, I hope Old One made him forget.* Pham Nuwen had the potential to be a real person; it hadn't been right to hurt him because his principal was beyond reach.

'Have a seat. Galaxy-rise in a half hour.' The Skroderiders rustled, so deep into the sunset that they were only now noticing the visitor.

Pham Nuwen walked a pace or two beyond Ravna and stood arms akimbo, staring across the sea. He glanced back at her, and the green twilight gave his face an eerie fierceness. He flashed his old, lopsided smile: 'I think I owe you an apology.'

Old One's gonna let you join the human race after all? But Ravna was touched. She dropped her eyes from his. 'I guess I owe you one too. If Old One won't help, he won't help; I shouldn't have lost my temper.'

Pham Nuwen laughed softly. 'Yours was certainly the lesser error. I'm still trying to figure out where I went wrong, and . . . I don't think I have time now to learn.'

He looked back at the sea. After a moment, Ravna stood and stepped toward him. Up close his stare looked glassy. 'What's wrong?' *Damn you, Old One. If you're going to abandon him, don't do it in pieces!*

'You're the great expert on Transcendent Powers, eh?'

More sarcasm. 'Well—'

'Do the big boys have wars?'

Ravna shrugged. 'You can find rumors of everything. We think there's conflict, but something too subtle to call war.'

'You're pretty much right. There is struggle, but it has more angles than anything down here. The benefits of cooperation are normally so great that . . . That's part of the reason I didn't take the Perversion seriously. Besides, the creature is pitiful: a wimpy cur that fouls its own den. Even if it wanted to kill other Powers, something like that never could. Not in a billion years . . .'

Blueshell rolled up beside them. 'Who is this, my lady?'

It was the sort of Riderish conversation-stopper that she was only just getting used to. If Blueshell would just get in synch with his skrode memory, he'd know. Then the question truly hit her. Who *is* this? She glanced at her dataset. It was showing transceiver status, had been ever since

Pham Nuwen arrived. And . . . by the Powers, *three* transceivers had been grabbed by a single customer!

She took a quick step backwards. 'You!'

'Me! Face to face once more, Ravna.' The leer was a parody of Pham's self-assured smile. 'Sorry I can't be charming tonight.' He slapped his chest awkwardly. 'I'm using this thing's underlying instincts . . . I'm too busy trying to stay alive.'

There was drool coming down his chin. Pham's eyes would focus on her and then drift.

'What are you doing to Pham!'

The Emissary Device stepped toward her, stumbled. 'Making room,' came Pham Nuwen's voice.

Ravna spoke Grondr's phone code. There was no response.

The Emissary Device shook its head. 'Vrinimi Org is very busy right now, trying to convince me to get off their equipment, trying to screw up their courage and force me off. They don't believe what I'm telling them.' He laughed, a quick choking sound. 'Doesn't matter. I can see now, the attack here was just deadly diversion . . . How about that, Little Ravna? See, the Blight is not a Class Two perversion. In the time I have left, I can only guess what it is . . . Something very old, very big. Whatever it is, I'm being eaten alive.'

Blueshell and Greenstalk had rolled close to Ravna. Their fronds made faint skritching noises. Some thousands of light-years away, well into the Transcend, a Power was fighting for its life. And all they saw of it was one man turned into a slobbering lunatic.

'So that's my apology, Little Ravna. Helping you probably wouldn't have saved me.' His voice strangled on itself, and he took a gasping breath. 'But helping you now will be a measure of – vengeance is a motive you would understand. I've called your ship down. If you move fast and don't use agrav, you may survive the next hour.'

Blueshell's voice was timid and blustery at the same time. 'Survive? Only a conventional attack could work down here, and there is no sign of one.'

A maniac surrounded by the soft, quiet night. Ravna's dataset showed nothing strange except for the diversion of bandwidth to Old One.

Pham Nuwen made a coughing laugh. 'Oh, it's conventional enough, but very clever. A few grams of replicant disorder, wafted in over weeks. It's blossoming now, timed with the attack you see . . . The growth will die in a matter of hours, after it kills all of Relay's precious High automation . . . Ravna! Take the ship, or die in the next thousand seconds. Take the ship. If you survive, go to the Bottom. Get the . . .' the Emissary Device gagged on the end of the sentence. It pulled itself straighter, and smiled its greenish smile a last time. 'And here is my gift to you, the best help I have left to give.'

The smile disappeared. The glassy look was replaced by a wonder . . .

and then mounting terror. Pham Nuwen dragged in a great breath, and had time for one barking scream before he collapsed. He landed face down, twitching and choking in the sand.

Ravna shouted Grondr's code again, and ran to Pham Nuwen. She pulled him over on his back and tried to clear his mouth. The fit lasted several seconds, Pham's limbs flailing randomly about. Ravna collected solid hits as she tried to steady him. Then Pham went limp, and she could barely feel his breath.

Blueshell was saving, 'Somehow he's grabbed the *OOB*. It's four thousand kilometers out, coming straight for the Docks. Wail. We're ruined.' Unauthorized flight close to the Docks was cause for confiscation.

Somehow Ravna didn't think it mattered anymore. 'Is there any sign of attack?' she said over her shoulder. She eased Pham's head back, made sure he had a clear breathing passage.

Random rustling between the Skroderiders. Greenstalk: 'Something is strange. We have service suspension on the main transceivers.' *So Old One is still transmitting?* 'The local net is very clogged. Much automation, many employees being called to special duty.'

Ravna rocked back. The sky was night dark, punctuated by a dozen bright points of light – ships guiding for the Docks. All very normal. But her own dataset was showing what Greenstalk reported.

'Ravna, I can't talk right now.' Grondr's clickety voice sounded out of the air beside her. This would be his associate program. 'Old One has taken most of Relay. Watch out for the Emissary Device.' *A little late, that!* 'We've lost contact with the surveillance fence beyond the transceivers. We are having program and hardware failures. Old One claims we are being attacked.' A five second pause. 'We see evidence of fleet action at the domestic defense boundary.' That was just a half light-year out.

'*Brap!*' From Blueshell. 'At the domestic defense boundary! How could you miss them coming in?' He rolled back and forth, pivoted.

Grondr's associate ignored the question. 'Minimum three thousand ships. Destruction of transceivers immin—'

'Ravna, are the Skroderiders with you?' It was still Grondr's voice, but more staccato, more *involved*. This was the real guy.

'Y-yes.'

'The local network is failing. Life support failing. The Docks will fall. We would be stronger than the attacking fleet, but we're rotting from the inside . . . Relay is dying.' His voice sharpened, clattering, 'but Vrinimi will not die, and a contract is a contract! Tell the Riders, we *will* pay them . . . somehow, someday. We *require* . . . plead . . . they fly the mission we contracted. Ravna?'

'Yes. They hear.'

'Then go!' And the voice was gone.

Blueshell said, '*OOB* will be here in two hundred seconds.'

Pham Nuwen had calmed, and his breathing was easier. As the two Riders chittered back and forth, Ravna looked around – and suddenly realized that all the death and destruction had been reports from afar. The beach and the sky were almost as placid as ever. The last of the sun's rays had left the waves. The foam was a dim band in the low green light. Here and there, yellow lights glowed in the trees and the farther towers.

Yet the alarm had clearly spread. She could hear datasets coming on. Some of the beach fires guttered out, and the figures around them ran into the trees or drifted upwards, headed for farther offices. Now starships floated up from their berths across the sea, falling higher and higher till they glittered in the departed sunlight.

It was Relay's last moment of peace.

A patch of glowing dark spread across the sky. She gasped at light so *twisted* it should have gone unseen. It shone more in the back of her head than in her eyes. Afterwards she couldn't think what made it objectively different from blackness.

'There's another!' said Blueshell. This one was near the Docks' horizon, a blot of darkness perhaps a degree across. The edges were an indistinct bleeding of black into black.

'What *is* it?' Ravna was no war freak, but she'd read her share of adventure stories. She knew about antimatter bombs and relativistic kinetic energy slugs. From a distance such weapons were bright spots of light, sometimes an orchestrated flickering. Or closer: a world-wrecker would glow incandescent across the curve of a planet, splashing the globe itself like a drop of water, but slow, slow. Those were the images her reading had prepared her for. What she saw now was more like a defect in her eyesight than a vision of war.

Powers only knew what the Skroderiders saw, but: 'Your main transceivers . . . vaping out, I think,' said Blueshell.

'Those are light-years out! There's no way we could see—' Another splotch appeared, not even in her field of view. The color floated, placeless. Pham Nuwen spasmed again, but weakly. She had no trouble holding him still, but . . . blood dribbled from his mouth. The back of his shirt was wet with something that stank of decay.

'*OOB* will be here in one hundred seconds. Plenty of time, there's plenty of time.' Blueshell rolled back and forth around them, talking reassurance that just showed how nervous he was. 'Yes, my lady, light-years out. And years from now, the flash of their going will light the sky for anyone still alive here. But only a fraction of the vape-out is making light. The rest is an ultrawave surge so great that ordinary matter is affected . . . Optic nerves tickled by the overflow . . . So much that your own nervous system becomes a receiver.' He spun around. 'But don't worry. We're tough and quick. We've squeezed through close spots before.' There was something absurd about a creature with no short-term memory bragging up its lightning cleverness. She hoped his skrode was up to this.

Greenstalk's voice buzzed painfully loud. '*Look!*'

The surf line was drawing back, further than she had ever seen it.

'The sea is falling!' shouted Greenstalk. Water's edge had pulled back a hundred meters, two hundred. The green-limned horizon was *dipping*.

'Ship's still fifty seconds out. We'll fly to meet it. Come, Ravna!'

Ravna's own courage died cold that second. Grondr had said the Docks would fall! The near sky was crowded now as dozens of people raced for safety. A hundred meters away the sand itself was shifting, an avalanche tilting toward the abyss. She remembered something Old One had said, and suddenly she knew the fliers were making a terrible mistake. The thought cut through her terror. 'No! Just head for higher ground.'

The night was silent no more. A bell-like moaning came from the sea. The sound spread. The sunset breeze grew to a gale that twisted the trees toward the water, sending branches and sand sweeping past them.

Ravna was still on her knees, her hands pressing down on Pham's limp arms. No breath, no pulse. The eyes stared sightlessly. Old One's gift to her. Damn all the Powers! She grabbed Pham Nuwen under the shoulders and rolled him onto her back.

She gagged, almost lost her grip. Underneath his shirt she felt cavities where there should be solid flesh. Something wet and rank dripped around her sides. She struggled up from her knees, half-carrying and half-dragging the body.

Blueshell was shouting, '—take hours to roll anywhere.' He drifted off the ground, driving his agrav against the wind. Skrode and Rider twisted drunkenly for an instant . . . and then he was slammed back to the ground, tumbled willy-nilly toward the wind's destination, the moaning hole that had been the sea. Greenstalk raced to his seaward side, blocking his progress toward destruction. Blueshell righted himself and the two rolled back toward Ravna. The Rider's voice was faint in the wind: '. . . agrav . . . failing!' And with it the very structure of the Docks.

They walked and wheeled their way back from the sucking sea. 'Find a place to land the *OOB*.'

The tree line was a jagged range of hills now. The landscape changed before their eyes and under her feet. The groaning sound was everywhere, some places so loud it buzzed through Ravna's shoes. They avoided the sagging terrain, the sink holes that opened on all sides. The night was dark no more. Whether it was emergency lighting or a side effect of the agrav failure, blue glowed along the holes. Through those holes they saw the cloud-decked night of Groundside a thousand kilometers below. The space between was not empty. There were shimmering phantoms: billions of tonnes of water and earth . . . and hundreds of dying fliers. Vrinuni Org was paying the price for building their Docks on agrav instead of inertial orbit.

Somehow the three were making progress. Pham Nuwen was almost too heavy to carry/drag; she staggered left and right almost as much as she moved forward. Yet he was lighter than she would have guessed. And that was terrifying in its own way: was even the high ground failing?

Most of the agravs died by failure, but some suffered destructive runaway: clumps of trees and earth ripped free from the tops of hillocks and accelerated upwards. The wind shifted back and forth, up and down . . . but it was thinner now, the noise remote. The artificial atmosphere that clothed the Docks would soon be gone. Ravna's pocket pressure suit worked for a few minutes, but now it was fading. In a few minutes it would be as dead as her agravs . . . as dead as she would be. She wondered vaguely how the Blight had managed this. Like the Old One, she would likely die without ever knowing.

She saw torch flares; there were ships. Most had boosted for inertial orbits or gone directly into ultradrive, but a few hung over the disintegrating landscape. Blueshell and Greenstalk led the way. The two used their third axles in ways Ravna had never guessed at, lifting and pushing to clamber up slopes that she could scarcely negotiate with Pham's weight dragging from her back.

They were on a hilltop, but not for long. This had been part of the office forest. Now the trees stuck out in different directions, like hair on a mangy dog. She felt the ground throbbing beneath her feet What next? The Skroderiders rolled from one side of the peak to another. They would be rescued here or nowhere. She went to her knees, resting most of Pham's weight on the ground. From here you could see a long ways. The Docks looked like a slowly flapping flag, and every immense whip of the fabric broke fragments loose. As long as some consensus remained among the agrav units, it still had planar aspect. That was disappearing. There were sink holes all around their little knob of forest. On the horizon, Ravna saw the far edge of the Docks detach itself and turn slowly sideways: a hundred kilometers long, ten wide, it swept down on would-be rescue ships.

Blueshell brushed against her left side, Greenstalk against her right. Ravna twisted, laying some of Pham's weight on the skrode hulls. If all four merged their pressure suits, there would be a few more moments of consciousness. 'The *OOB*: I'm flying it down!' he said.

Something was coming down. A ship's torch lit the ground blue white, with shadows stark and shifting. It's not a healthy thing to be around a rocket drive hovering in a near-one-gee field. An hour earlier the maneuver would have been impossible, or a capital offense if accomplished. Now it didn't matter if the torch punched through the Docks or fried a cargo from halfway across the galaxy.

Still . . . where could Blueshell land the thing? They were surrounded by sinkholes and moving cliffs. She closed her eyes as the burning light drifted down before them . . . and then dimmed. Blueshell's shout was thin in their shared atmosphere. 'Let's go together!'

She held tight to the Riders, and they crawled/wheeled down from their little hill. The *Out of Band II* was hovering in the middle of a sinkhole. Its torch was hidden from view, but the glare off the sides of the hole put the ship in sharp silhouette, turned its ultradrive spines into feathery white arcs. A giant moth with glowing wings . . . and just out of reach.

If their suits held, they could make it to the edge of the hole. Then what? The spines kept the ship from getting closer than a hundred meters. An able-bodied (and crazy) human might try to grab a spine and crawl down it.

But Skroderiders had their own brand of insanity: Just as the light – the reflected light – became too much to bear – the torch winked out. The *OOB* fell through the hole. This didn't stop the Riders' advance. '*Faster!*' said Blueshell. And now she guessed what they planned. Quickly for such an awkward jumble of limbs and wheels, they moved up to the edge of the darkened hole. Ravna felt the dirt giving way beneath her feet, and then they were falling.

The Docks were hundreds – in places, thousands – of meters thick. They fell past them now, past dim eerie flickers of internal destruction.

Then they were through, still falling. For a moment the feeling of wild panic was gone. After all this was simply free fall, a commonplace, and a damnsight more peaceful than the disintegrating Docks. Now it was easy to hold onto the Riders and Pham Nuwen, and even their commensal atmosphere seemed a little thicker than before. There was something to be said for hard vacuum and free fall. Except for an occasional rogue agrav, everything was coming down at the same acceleration, ruins peacefully settling. And four or five minutes from now they would hit Groundside's atmosphere, still falling almost straight downwards . . . Entry velocity only three or four kilometers per second. Would they burn up? Maybe. Flashes pricked bright above the cloud-decks.

The junk around them was mostly dark, just shadows against the sky show above. But the shape directly below was large and regular . . . the *OOB*, bow on! The ship was falling with them. Every few seconds a trim jet fired, a faint reddish glow. The ship was closing with them. If it had a nose hatch, they would land right on it.

Its docking lights flicked on, bright upon them. Ten meters separation. Five. There *was* a hatch, and open! She could see a very ordinary airlock within . . .

Whatever hit them was big. Ravna saw a vague expanse of plastic rising over her shoulder. The rogue was slowly turning, and it scarcely brushed them – but that was enough. Pham Nuwen was jarred from her grasp. His body was lost in shadow, then suddenly lit bright as the ship's spotlight tracked after him. Simultaneously the air gusted out of Ravna's lungs. They were down to three pocket pressure fields now, failing fields; it was not enough. Ravna could feel consciousness slipping away, her vision tunneling. So *close*.

The Riders unlatched from each other. She grabbed at the skrode hulls and they drifted, strung out, over the ship's lock. Blueshell's skrode jerked against her as he made fast to the hatch. The jolt twisted her around, whipping Greenstalk upwards. Things were getting dreamy now. Where was panic when you needed it? *Hold tight, hold tight, hold tight*, sang the little voice, all that was left of consciousness. Bump, jerk. The Riders pushed and pulled at her. Or maybe it was the ship jerking all of them around. They were puppets, dancing off a single string.

. . . Deep in the tunnel of her vision, a Rider grabbed at the tumbling figure of Pham Nuwen.

Ravna wasn't aware of losing consciousness, but the next she knew she was breathing air and choking on vomit – and was inside the airlock. Solid green walls closed in comfortingly on all sides. Pham Nuwen lay on the far wall, strapped into a first aid canister. His face had a bluish cast.

She pushed awkwardly across the lock toward Pham Nuwen's wall. The place was a confused jumble, unlike the passenger and sporting ships she'd been on before. Besides, this was a Rider design. Stickem patches were scattered around the walls; Greenstalk had mounted her skrode on one cluster.

They were accelerating, maybe a twentieth of a gee. 'We're still going down?'

'Yes. If we hover or rise, we'll crash,' *into all the junk that still rains from above.* 'Blueshell is trying to fly us out.' They were falling with the rest, but trying to drift out from under – before they hit Groundside. There was an occasional rattle/ping against the hull. Sometimes the acceleration ceased, or shifted in a new direction. Blueshell was actively avoiding the big pieces.

. . . Not with complete success. There was a long, rasping sound that ended with a bang, and the room turned slowly around her. '*Brrap!* Just lost an ultradrive spine,' came Blueshell's voice. 'Two others already damaged. Please strap down, my lady.'

They touched atmosphere a hundred seconds later. The sound was a barely perceptible humming beyond the hull. It was the sound of death for a ship like this. It could no more aerobrake than a dog could jump over the moon. The noise came louder. Blueshell was actually *diving*, trying to get deep enough to shed the junk that surrounded the ship. Two more spines broke. Then came a long surge of main axis acceleration. *Out of Band II* arced out of the Docks' death shadow, drove out and out, into inertial orbit.

Ravna looked over Blueshell's fronds at the outside windows. They had just passed Groundside's terminator, and were flying an inertial orbit. They were in free fall again, but *this* trajectory curved back on itself without whacking into big hard things – like Groundside.

Ravna didn't know much more about space travel than you'd expect of a frequent passenger and an adventure fan. But it was obvious that Blueshell had pulled off a new miracle. When she tried to thank him, the Rider rolled back and forth across the stick-patches, buzzing faintly to himself. Embarrassed? or just Riderly inattentive?

Greenstalk spoke, sounding a little shy, a little proud: 'Far trading is our life, you know. If we are cautious, life will be mostly safe and placid, but there will be close passages. Blueshell practices all the time, programming his skrode with every wit he can imagine. He is a master.' In everyday life indecision seemed to dominate the Riders. But in a crunch, they didn't hesitate to bet everything. She wondered how much of that was the skrode overriding its rider?

'Grump,' said Blueshell. 'I have simply postponed the close passage. I broke several of our drive spines. What if they do not self-repair? What do we do then? Everything around Groundside is destroyed. There is junk everywhere out to a hundred radii. Not dense like around the Docks, but of much higher velocity.' You can't inject billions of tonnes of wreckage into buckshot orbits and expect safe navigation. 'And any second, the Perversion's creatures will be here, eating whoever survives.'

'Urk.' Greenstalk's tendrils froze in comical disarray. She chittered to herself for a second. 'You're right . . . I forgot I thought we had found an open space, but . . .'

Open space all right, but in a shooting gallery. Ravna looked back at the command deck windows. They were on the dayside now, perhaps five hundred kilometers above Groundside's principal ocean. The space above the hazy blue horizon was free of flash and glow. 'I don't see any fighting,' Ravna said hopefully.

'Sorry.' Blueshell switched the windows to a more significant view. Most of it was navigation and ultratrace information, meaningless to Ravna. Her eye caught on a medstat: Pham Nuwen was breathing again. The ship's surgeon thought it could save him. But there was also a communication status window; on it the attack was dreadfully clear. The local net had broken into hundreds of screaming fragments. There were only automatic voices from the planetary surface, and they were calling for medical aid. Grondr had been down there. Somehow she suspected that not even his Marketing ops people had survived. Whatever hit Groundside was even deadlier than the failures at the Docks. In near planetary space, there were a few survivors in ships and fragments of habitats, most on doomed trajectories. Without massive and coordinated help, they would be dead in minutes – hours at the outside. The directors of Vrinimi Org were gone, destroyed before they ever figured out quite what had happened.

Go, Grondr had said, *go*.

Out-system, there was fighting. Ravna saw message traffic from Vrinimi defense units. Even without control or coordination, some still opposed the Perversion's fleet. The light from their battles would arrive well after the defeat, well after the enemy arrived here in person. *How long do we have? Minutes?*

'*Brrap*. Look at those traces,' said Blueshell. 'The Perversion has almost four thousand vessels. They are bypassing the defenders.'

'But now there is scarcely anyone left out there,' said Greenstalk. 'I hope they're not all dead.'

'Not all. I see several thousand ships departing, everyone with the means and any sense.' Blueshell rolled back and forth. 'Alas! We have the good sense . . . but look at this repair report.' One window spread large, filled with colored patterns that meant less than zip to Ravna. 'Two spines still broken, unrepairable. Three partially repaired. If they don't heal, we'll be stuck here. *This is unacceptable!*' His voder voice buzzed up shrilly. Greenstalk drove close to him, and they rattled their fronds at each other.

Several minutes passed. When Blueshell spoke Samnorsk again, his voice was quieter. 'One spine repaired. Maybe, maybe, maybe . . .' He opened a natural view. The *OOB* was coasting across Groundside's south pole, back into night. Their orbit should take them over the worst of the Docks junk, but the ride was a constant jigging as the ship avoided other debris. The cries of battle horror from out-system dwindled. The Vrinimi Organization was one vast, twitching corpse . . . and very soon its killer would come snuffling.

'Two repaired.' Blueshell became very quiet . . . 'Three! Three are repaired! Fifteen seconds to recalibrate and we can jump!'

It seemed longer . . . but then all the windows changed to a natural view. Groundside and its sun were gone. Stars and dark stretched all-around.

Three hours later and Relay was a hundred and fifty light-years behind them. The *OOB* was in with the main body of fleeing ships. What with the archives and the tourism, there had been an extraordinary number of interstellar ships at Relay: ten thousand vehicles were spread across the light-years around them. But stars were rare this far off the galactic plane and they were at least a hundred hours flying time from the nearest refuge.

For Ravna, it was the start of a new battle. She glared across the deck at Blueshell. The Skroderider dithered, its fronds twisting on themselves in a way she had not seen before. 'See here, my lady Bergsndot, High Point is a lovely civilization, with some bipedal participants. It is safe. It is nearby. You could adapt.' He paused. *Reading my expression is he?* 'But – but if that is not acceptable, we will take you further. Give us a chance to contract the proper cargo, and – and we'll take you all the way back to Sjandra Kei. How about that?'

'No. You already have a contract, Blueshell. With Vrinimi Organization.

The three of us—' *and whatever has become of Pham Nuwen* '—are going to the Bottom of the Beyond.'

'I am shaking my head in disbelief! We received a preliminary retainer, true. But now that Vrinimi Org is dead, there is no one to make good on the rest of the agreement. Hence we are free of it also.'

'Vrinimi is not dead. You heard Grondr 'Kalir. The Org had – *has* – branch offices all across the Beyond. The obligation stands.'

'On a technicality. We both know that those branches could never make the final payment.'

Ravna didn't have a good answer to that. 'You have an obligation,' she said, but without the proper forcefulness. She had never been good at bluster.

'My lady, are you truly speaking from Org ethics, or from simple humanity?'

'I—' In fact, Ravna had never completely understood Org ethics. That was one reason why she had intended to return to Sjandra Kei after her 'prenticeship, and one reason the Org had dealt cautiously with the human race. 'It doesn't matter which I speak from! There is a contract. You were happy to honor it when things looked safe. Well, things turned deadly – but that possibility was part of the deal.' Ravna glanced at Greenstalk. She had been silent so far, not even rustling at her mate. Her fronds were tightly held against her central stalk. Maybe – 'listen, there *are* other reasons besides contract obligation. The Perversion is more powerful than anyone thought. *It killed a Power today.* And it's operating in the Middle Beyond . . . The Riders have a long history, Blueshell, longer than most races' entire existence. The Perversion may be strong enough to put an end to all of that.'

Greenstalk rolled toward her and opened slightly. 'You – you really think we might find something on that ship at the Bottom, something that could harm a Power among Powers?'

Ravna paused. 'Yes. And Old One himself thought so, just before he died.'

Blueshell wrapped even tighter around himself, twisting. In anguish? 'My Lady, we are traders. We have lived long and traveled far . . . and survived by minding our own business. No matter what romantics may think, traders do not go on quests. What you ask . . . is impossible, mere Beyonders seeking to subvert a Power.'

Yet that was a risk you signed for. But Ravna didn't say it aloud. Perhaps Greenstalk did: her fronds rustled, and Blueshell scrinched even more. Greenstalk was silent for a second, then she did something funny with her axles, bumping free of the stickem. Her wheels spun on nothing as she floated through a slow arc, till she was upside down, her fronds reaching down to brush Blueshell's. They rattled back and forth for almost five minutes. Blueshell slowly untwisted, the fronds relaxing and patting back at his mate.

Finally he said. 'Very well . . . One quest. But mark you! Never another.'

minute. Here it all slowly made sense. His boards relax(ing)(?) — slowly back
to normal.

Jefferi is made. Dirk didn't . . . (?)(???) . . . But Jefferi was (?)(???)(?)(????)(?)(?)

PART TWO

17

Spring came wet and cold, and excruciatingly slow. It had been raining the
last eight days. How Johanna wished for something else, even the dark of
winter back again.

She slogged across mud that had been moss. It was midday; the gloomy
light would last another three hours. Scarbutt claimed that without the
overcast, they would be seeing a bit of direct sunlight nowadays. Sometimes
she wondered if she would ever see the sun again.

The castle's great yard was on a hillside. Mud and sullen snow spread
down the hill, piled against the wooden buildings. Last summer there had
been a glorious view from here. And in the winter, the aurora had spilled
green and blue across the snow, glinted on the frozen harbor, and outlined
the far hills against the sky. Now: The rain was a close mist; she couldn't
even see the city beyond the walls. The clouds were a low and ragged ceiling
above her head. She knew there were guards on the stone walls of the castle
curtain, but today they must be huddled behind watch slits. Not a single
animal, not a single pack was visible. The Tines' world was an empty place
compared to Straum – but not like the High Lab either. High Lab was a
airless rock orbiting a red dwarf. The Tines' world was *alive*, moving;
sometimes it looked as beautiful and friendly as a holiday resort on Straum.
Indeed, Johanna realized that it was kindlier than most worlds the human
race had settled – certainly a gentler world than Nyjora, and perhaps as nice
as Old Earth.

Johanna had reached her bungalow. She paused for a second under its
outcurving walls and looked across the courtyard. Yes, it looked a little like
medieval Nyjora. But the stories from the Age of Princesses hadn't conveyed
the implacable power in such a world: The rain went on for as far as she
could see. Without decent technology, even a cold rain could be a deadly
thing. So could the wind. And the sea was not something for an afternoon's
fun sailing, she thought of surging hillocks of coldness, puckered with
rain . . . going on and on. Even the forests around the town were threatening. It was easy to wander into them, but there were no radio finders, no
refresh stalls disguised as tree trunks. Once lost, you would simply die.
Nyjoran fairy tales had a special meaning for her now: no great imagination
was needed to invent the elementals of wind and rain and sea. This was the

pretech experience, that even if you had no enemies the world itself could kill you.

And she *did* have plenty of enemies. Johanna pulled open the tiny door and went inside.

A pack of Tines was sitting around the fire. It scrambled to its feet and helped Johanna out of her rainjacket. She didn't shrink from the fine-toothed muzzles anymore. This was one of her usual helpers; she could almost think of the jaws as hands, deftly pulling the oilskin jacket down her arms and hanging it near the fire.

Johanna chucked her boots and pants, and accepted the quilted wrap that the pack 'handed' her.

'Dinner. Now,' she said to the pack.

'Okay.'

Johanna settled on a pillow by the fire pit. In fact the Tines were *more* primitive than the humans on Nyjora: The Tines' world was not a fallen colony. They didn't even have legend to guide them. Sanitation was a sometime thing. Before Woodcarver, Tinish doctors bled their patients/ victims . . . She knew now that she was living in the Tines' equivalent of a luxury apartment. The deep-polished wood was not a normal thing. The designs painted on the pillars and walls were the result of many hours' labor.

Johanna rested her chin on her hands and stared into the flames. She was vaguely aware of the pack prancing around the pit, hanging pots over the fire. This one spoke very little Samnorsk; it wasn't in on Woodcarver's dataset project. Many weeks ago, Scarbutt had asked to move in here – what better way to speed the learning process? Johanna shivered at the memory. She knew the scarred one was just a single member, that the *pack* that killed Dad had itself died. Johanna understood, but every time she saw 'Pere-grine,' she saw her father's murderer sitting fat and happy, thinking to hide itself behind its three smaller fellows. Johanna smiled into the flames, remembering the whack she had landed on Scarbutt when he made the suggestion. She'd lost control, but it had been worth it. No one else suggested that 'friends' should share this house with her. Most evenings they left her alone. And some nights . . . Dad and Mom seemed so near, maybe just outside, waiting for her to notice. Even though she had seen them die, something inside her refused to let them go.

Cooking smells slipped past the familiar daydream. Tonight it was meat and beans, with something like onions. Surprise. The stuff smelled good; if there had been any variety, she would have enjoyed it. But Johanna hadn't seen fresh fruit in sixty days. Salted meat and veggies were the only winter fare. If Jefri were here, he'd throw a fit. It was months past that the word came from Woodcarver's spies up north: Jefri had died in the ambush . . . Johanna was getting over it, she really was. And in some ways, being all alone made things . . . simpler.

The pack put a plate of meat and beans before her, along with a kind of knife. *Oh, well.* Johanna grabbed the crooked hilt (bent sideways to be held by Tinish jaws) and dug in.

She was almost finished when there was a polite scratching at the door. Her servant gobbled something. The visitor replied, then said in rather good Samnorsk (and a voice that was eerily like her own), 'Hello there, my name is Scriber. I would like a small talk, okay?'

One of the servants turned to look at her; the rest were watching the door. Scriber was the one she thought of as Pompous Clown. He'd been with Scarbutt at the ambush, but he was such a fool that she scarcely felt threatened by him.

'Okay,' she said, starting toward the door. Her servant (guard) grabbed crossbows in its jaws, and all five members snaked up the staircase to the loft; there wasn't space for more than one pack down here.

The cold and wet blew into the room along with her visitor. Johanna retreated to the other side of the fire while Scriber took off his rain slickers. The pack members shook themselves the way dogs do, a noisy, amusing sight – and you didn't want to be near when it happened.

Finally Scriber sauntered over to the fire pit. Under the slickers he wore jackets with the usual stirrups and the open spaces behind the shoulders and at the haunches. But Scriber's appeared to be padded above the shoulders to make his members look heavier than they really were. One of him sniffed at her plate, while the other heads looked this way and that . . . but never directly at her.

Johanna looked down at the pack. She still had trouble talking to more than one face; usually she picked on whichever was looking back at her. 'Well? What did you come to talk about?'

One of the heads finally looked at her. It licked its lips. 'Okay. Yes. I thought to see how do you do? I mean . . .' *gobble*. Her servant answered from upstairs, probably reporting what kind of mood she was in. Scriber straightened up. Four of his six heads looked at Johanna. His other two members paced back and forth, as if contemplating something important. 'Look here. You are the only human I know, but I have always been a big student of character. I know you are not happy here—'

Pompous Clown was also master of the obvious.

'—and I understand. But we do the best to help you. We are not the bad people who killed your parents and brother.'

Johanna put a hand on the low ceiling and leaned forward. *You're all thugs; you just happen to have the same enemies I do.* 'I know that, and I am cooperating. You'd still be playing the dataset's kindermode if it weren't for me. I've shown you the reading courses; if you guys have any brains, you'll have gunpowder by summer.' The Oliphaunt was an heirloom toy, a huggable favorite thing she should have outgrown years ago. But there was history in it – stories of the queens and princesses of the Dark Ages, and how they had struggled to triumph over the jungles, to rebuild the cities and then the spaceships. Half-hidden on obscure reference paths there were also hard numbers, the history of technology. Gunpowder was one of the easiest things. When the weather cleared up, there would be some prospecting expeditions; Woodcarver had known about sulfur, but didn't have quantities in town. Making cannon would be harder. But then . . . 'Then your enemies will be killed. Your people are getting what they want from me. So what's your complaint?'

'Complaint?' Pompous Clown's heads bobbed up and down in alternation. Such distributed gestures seemed to be the equivalent of facial expressions, though Johanna hadn't figured many of them out. This one might mean embarrassment. 'I have no complaint. You are helping us, I know. But, but . . .' Three of his members were pacing around now. 'It's just that I see more than most people, perhaps a little like Woodcarver did in oldendays. I am a – I've seen your word for it – a "dilettante." You know, a person who studies all things and who is talented at everything. I am only thirty years old, but I have read almost every book in the world, and—' the heads bowed, perhaps in shyness? '—I'm even planning to write one, perhaps the true story of your adventure.'

Johanna found herself smiling. Most often she saw the Tines as barbarian strangers, inhuman in spirit as well as form. But if she closed her eyes, she could almost imagine that Scriber was a fellow Straumer. Mom had a few friends just as brainless and innocently self-convinced as this one, men and women with a hundred grandiose projects that would never ever amount to anything. Back on Straum, they had been boring perils that she avoided. Now . . . well, Scriber's foolishness was almost like being back home again.

'You're here to study me for your book?'

More alternating nods. 'Well, yes. And also, I wanted to talk to you about my other plans. I've always been something of an inventor, you see. I know that doesn't mean much now. It seems that everything that can be invented is already in Dataset. I've seen many of my best ideas there.' He sighed, or made the sound of a sigh. Now he was imitating one of the pop science voices in the dataset. Sound was the easiest thing for the Tines; it could be darn confusing.

'In any case, I was just wondering how to improve some of those ideas—' four of Scriber's members bellied down on the bench by the fire pit; it looked like he was settling in for a long conversation. His other two walked around the pit to give her a stack of paper threaded with brass hoops. While one on the other side of the fire continued to talk, the two carefully turned the pages and pointed at where she should look.

Well, he did have plenty of ideas: Tethered birds to hoist flying boats, giant lenses that would concentrate the sun's light on enemies and set them afire. From some of the pictures, it appeared he thought the atmosphere extended beyond the moon. Scriber explained each idea in numbing detail, pointing at the drawings and patting her hands enthusiastically. 'So you see the possibilities? My unique slant combined with the proven inventions in Dataset. Who knows where it could lead?'

Johanna giggled, overcome by the vision of Scriber's giant birds hauling kilometer-wide lenses to the moon. He seemed to take the sound for approval.

'Yes! It's brilliant, okay? My latest idea, I never would have thought it except for Dataset. This "radio," it projects sound very far and fast, okay? Why not combine it with the power of our Tinish thoughts? A pack could think as one even spread across hundreds of, um, kilometers.'

Now that almost made sense! But if gunpowder took months to make – even given the exact formula – how many *decades* would it be before the packs had radio? Scriber was an immense fountain of half-baked ideas. She let his words wash over her for more than an hour. It was insanity, but less alien than most of what she had endured this last year.

Finally he seemed to run down; there were longer pauses and he asked her opinion more often. Finally he said, 'Well, that was certainly fun, okay?'

'Unh, yes, fascinating.'

'I knew you would like it. You're just like my people, I really think. You're not all angry, not all the time . . .'

'Just what do you mean by that?' Johanna pushed a soft muzzle away and stood. The dogthing rocked back on its haunches to look up at her.

'I, well . . . you have much to hate, I know. But you seem so angry at *us* all the time, and we're the ones who are trying to help you! After the day work you stay here, you don't want to talk with people – though now I see that was our fault. You wanted us to come here but were too proud to say it. I have these insights into character, you see. My friend, the one you call Scarbutt: he is truly a nice fellow. I know I can tell you that honestly, and that as my new friend you will believe. He would very much like to come to visit you, too . . . *urk.*'

Johanna walked slowly around the fire pit, forcing the two members to back away from her. All of Scriber was looking up at her now, the necks arching around one another, the eyes wide.

'I'm *not* like you. I *don't* need your talk, or your stupid ideas.' She threw Scriber's notebook into the pit. Scriber leaped to the fire's edge, desperately reached for the burning notes. He pulled most of them back and clutched them to his chests.

Johanna kept walking toward him, kicking at his legs. Scriber retreated, backing and sprawling. 'Stupid, dirty, butchers. I'm not like you.' She slapped her hand on a ceiling beam. 'Humans don't *like* to live like animals. We don't adopt killers. You tell Scarbutt, you tell him. If he ever comes by for a friendly chat, I – I'll smash in his head; I'll smash in all of them!'

Scriber was backed into the wall now. His heads turned wildly this way and that. He was making plenty of noise. Some of it was Samnorsk, but too high-pitched to understand. One of his mouths found the door pole. He pushed open the door, and all six members raced into the twilight, their rain slickers forgotten.

Johanna knelt and stuck her head through the doorway. The air was a wind-driven mist. In an instant, her face was so cold and wet that she couldn't feel the tears. Scriber was six shadows in the darkening grayness, shadows that raced down the hillside, sometimes tumbling in their haste. In a second, he was gone. There was nothing but the vague forms of nearby cabins and the yellow light that spilled out around her from the fire.

Strange. Right after the ambush, she had felt terror. The Tines had been unstoppable killers. Then, on the boat, when she smashed Scarbutt . . . it had been so wonderful: the whole pack collapsed, and suddenly she knew that she could fight back, that she could break their bones. She didn't have to be at their mercy . . . Tonight she had learned something more. Even without touching them, she could hurt them. Some of them, anyway. Her dislike alone had undone Pompous Clown.

Johanna backed into the smoky warmth and shut the door. She should feel triumph.

18

Scriber Jaqueramaphan didn't tell anyone about his meeting with the Two-Legs. Of course, Vendacious's guard had overheard everything. The fellow might not speak much Samnorsk, but he had surely gotten the drift of the argument. People would hear about it eventually.

He moped around the castle for a few days, spent a number of hours hunched over the remains of his notebook, trying to recreate the diagrams. It would be a while before he attended any more sessions with Dataset, especially when Johanna was around. Scriber knew he seemed brash to the outside world, but in fact it had taken a lot of courage to walk in on Johanna like that. He *knew* his ideas had genius, but all his life unimaginative people had been telling him otherwise.

In most ways Scriber was a very fortunate person. He had been born a fission pack in Rangathir, at the eastern edge of the Republic. His parent had been a wealthy merchant. Jaqueramaphan had some of his parent's traits, but the dull patience necessary for day-to-day business work had been lost to him. His sibling pack more than retained that faculty; the family business grew, and – in the first years – his sib didn't begrudge Scriber his share of the wealth. From his earliest days, Scriber had been an intellectual. He read everything: natural history, biography, brood kenning. In the end he had the largest library in Rangathir, more than two hundred books. Even then Scriber had tremendous ideas, insights which – if properly executed – would have made them the wealthiest merchants in all the eastern provinces. Alas, bad luck and his sib's lack of imagination had doomed his early ideas. In the end, his sib bought out the business, and Jaqueramaphan moved to the Capital. It was all for the best. By this time Scriber had fleshed himself out to six members; he needed to see more of the world. Besides . . . there were *five thousand* books in the library there, the experience of all history and all the world! His own notebooks became a library in themselves. Yet still the packs at the university had no time for him. His outline for a summation of natural history was rejected by all the stationers, though he paid to have small parts of it published. It was clear that success in the world of action was necessary before his ideas could get the attention they deserved, hence his spy mission; Parliament itself would thank him when he returned with the secrets of Flenser's Hidden Island.

That was almost a year ago. What had happened since – with the flying house and Johanna and Dataset – went beyond his wildest dreams (and Scriber granted that those dreams were already pretty extreme). The library in Dataset contained *millions* of books. With Johanna to help him polish his ideas, they would sweep Flenserism from the face of the world. They would regain her flying house. Not even the *sky* would be a limit.

So to have her throw it all back at him . . . it made him wonder about himself. Maybe she was just mad at him for trying to explain Peregrine. She would like Peregrine if she let herself; he was sure of it. But then again . . . maybe his ideas just weren't that good, at least by comparison with humans'.

That thought left him pretty low. But he finished redrawing the diagrams, and even got some new ideas. Maybe he should get some more silkpaper.

Peregrine stopped by and persuaded him to go into town.

Jaqueramaphan had made up a dozen explanations why he wasn't participating in the sessions with Johanna anymore. He tried out two or three as he and Peregrine descended Castle Street toward the harbor.

After a minute or two, his friend turned a head back. 'It's okay, Scriber. When you feel like it, we'd like to have you back.'

Scriber had always been a very good judge of attitude; in particular, he could tell when he was being patronized. He must have scowled a little, because Peregrine went on. 'I mean it. Even Woodcarver has been asking about you. She likes your ideas.'

Comforting lies or not, Scriber brightened. 'Really?' The Woodcarver of today was a sad case, but the Woodcarver of the history books was one of Jaqueramaphan's great heroes. 'No one's mad at me?'

'Well, Vendacious is a bit peeved. Being responsible for the Two-Legs' safety makes him very nervous. But you only tried something we've all wanted to do.'

'Yeah.' Even if there had been no Dataset, even if Johanna Olsndot had not come from the stars, she would still be the most fascinating creature in the world: a pack-equivalent mind in a single body. You could walk right up to her, you could *touch* her, without the least confusion. It was frightening at first, but all of them quickly felt the attraction. For packs, closeness had always meant mindlessness – whether for sex or battle. Imagine being able to sit by the fire with a friend and carry on an intelligent conversation! Woodcarver had a theory that the Two-Legs' civilization might be *innately* more effective than any Packish one, that collaboration was so easy for humans that they learned and built much faster than packs could. The only problem with that theory was Johanna Olsndot. If Johanna was a normal human, it was a surprise that the race could cooperate on anything. Sometimes she was friendly – usually in the sessions with Woodcarver; she seemed to realize that Woodcarver was frail and failing. More often she was patronizing, sarcastic, and seemed to think the best they could do for her insulting . . . And sometimes she was like last night. 'How goes it with Dataset?' he asked after a moment.

Peregrine shrugged. 'About like before. Both Woodcarver and I can read Samnorsk pretty well now. Johanna has taught us – me via Woodcarver, I should say – how to use most of Dataset's powers. There's so much there that will change the world. But for now we have to concentrate on making *gunpowder* and *cannons*. It's that, the actual doing, that's going slow.'

Scriber nodded knowingly. That had been the central problem in his life too.

'Anyway, if we can do all that by midsummer, maybe we can face Flenser's army and recapture the flying house before next winter.' Peregrine made a grin that stretched from face to face. 'And then, my friend, Johanna can call her people for rescue . . . and we'll have all our lives to study the outsiders. I may pilgrimage to worlds around other stars.'

It was an idea they had talked of before. Peregrine had thought of it even before Scriber.

They turned off Castle Street onto Edgerow. Scriber was feeling more enthusiastic about visiting the stationer's; there must be some way he could help. He looked around with an interest that had been lacking the last few days. Woodcarvers was a fair-sized city, almost as big as Rangathir – maybe twenty thousand packs lived within its walls and in the homes immediately around. This day was a bit colder than the last few, but it wasn't raining. A cold, clean wind swept the market street, carrying faint smells of mildew and sewage, of spices and fresh-sawn wood. Dark clouds hung low, misting the hills around the harbor. Spring was definitely in the air. Scriber kicked playfully at the slush along the curb.

Peregrine led them to a side street. The place was jammed, strangers getting as close as seven or eight yards. The stalls at the stationer's were even worse. The felt dividers weren't that thick, and there seemed to be more interest in literature at Woodcarvers than any place Scriber had ever been.

He could hardly hear himself think as he haggled with the stationer. The merchant sat on a raised platform with thick padding; *he* wasn't much bothered by the racket. Scriber kept his heads close together, concentrating on the prices and the product. From his past life, he was pretty good at this sort of thing.

Eventually he got his paper, and at a decent price.

'Let's go back on Packweal,' he said. That was the long way, through the center of the market. When he was in a good mood, Scriber rather liked crowds; he was a great student of people. Woodcarvers was not as cosmopolitan as some cities by the Long Lakes, but there were traders from all over. He saw several packs wearing the bonnets of a tropic collective. At one intersection a redjackets from East Home was chatting cozily with a labormaster.

When packs came this close, and in these numbers, the world seemed to teeter on the edge of a choir. Each person hung near to himself, trying to keep his own thoughts intact. It was hard to walk without stumbling over your own feet. And sometimes the background thought sounds would surge, a moment where several packs would somehow synchronize. Your consciousness wavered and for an instant you were one with many, a super-pack that might be a god. Jaqueramaphan shivered. That was the essential attraction of the Tropics. The crowds there were *mobs*, vast group minds as stupid as they were ecstatic. If the stories were true, some of the southern cities were nonstop orgies.

They had roamed the marketplace almost an hour when it hit him. Scriber shook his heads abruptly. He turned and walked in lockstep off Packweal, and up a side street. Peregrine followed. 'Is the crowd too much?' he asked.

'I just had an idea,' said Scriber. That wasn't unusual in a close crowd, but this was a *very* interesting idea . . . He said nothing more for several minutes. The side street climbed steeply, then jinked back and forth across Castle Hill. The upslope side was lined with burghers' homes. On the harbor side, they were looking out over the steep tile roofs of houses on the next switchback down. These were large homes, elegant with rosemaling. Only a few had shops on the street.

Scriber slowed down and spread out enough that he wasn't stepping on himself. He saw now that he'd been quite wrong in trying to contribute creative expertise to Johanna. There was simply too much invention in Dataset. But they still needed him, Johanna most of all. The problem was, they didn't know it yet. Finally he said to Peregrine, 'Haven't you wondered that the Flenserists haven't attacked the city? You and I embarrassed the Lords of Hidden Island more than ever in their history. We hold the keys to their total defeat.' *Johanna and Dataset.*

Peregrine hesitated. 'Hmm. I assumed their army wasn't up to it. I should think if they were, they'd have knocked over Woodcarvers long before.'

'Perhaps they could, but at great cost. Now the cost is worth it.' He gave Peregrine a serious look. 'No, I think there's another reason . . . They have the flying house, but they have no idea how to use it. They want Johanna back alive – almost as much as they want to kill all of us.'

Peregrine made a bitter sound. 'If Steel hadn't been so eager to massacre everything on two legs, he could have had all sorts of help.'

'True, and the Flenserists must know that. I'll bet they've always had spies among the townspeople here, *but now more than ever*. Did you see all the East Home packs?' East Home was a hotbed of Flenser sentiment. Even before the Movement they had been a hard folk, routinely sacrificing pups that didn't meet their brood standards.

'One anyway. Talking to a labormaster.'

'Right. Who knows what's coming in disguised as special purpose packs? I'd bet my life they're planning to kidnap Johanna. If they guess what we're planning with her, they may just try to kill her. Don't you see? We must alert Woodcarver and Vendacious, organize the people to watch for spies.'

'You noticed all this on one walk through Packweal?' There was wonder or disbelief in his voice, Scriber couldn't tell which.

'Well, um, no. The inspiration wasn't anything so direct. But it stands to reason, don't you think?'

They walked in silence for several minutes. Up here the wind was stronger, and the view more spectacular. Where there wasn't the sea, forest spread endless gray and green. Everything was very peaceful . . . because *this was a game of stealth*. Fortunately Scriber had a talent for such games. After all, hadn't it been the very Political Police of the Republic who commissioned him to survey Hidden Island? It had taken him several tendays of patient persuasion, but in the end they had been enthusiastic. *Anything you can discover we would be most happy to review*. Those were their exact words.

Peregrine waffled around the road, seemingly very taken aback by Scriber's suggestion. Finally he said, 'I think there is . . . something you should know, something that must remain an absolute secret.'

'*Upon my soul!* Peregrine, I do not blab secrets.' Scriber was a little hurt – at the lack of trust, and also that the other might have discovered something he had not. The second should not bother him. He had guessed that Peregrine and Woodcarver were into each other. No telling what she might have confided, or what might have leaked across.

'Okay . . . You've tripped onto something that should not be noised about. You know Vendacious is in charge of Woodcarver's security?'

'Of course.' That was implicit in the office of Lord Chamberlain. 'And considering the number of outsiders wandering around, I can't say he's doing a very good job.'

'In fact, he's doing a marvelously effective job. Vendacious has agents right at the top at Hidden Island – one step removed from Lord Steel himself.'

Scriber felt his eyes widening.

'Yes, you understand what that means. Through Vendacious, Woodcarver knows for a certainty *everything* their high council plans. With clever misinformation, we can lead the Flenserists around like froghens at a thinning. Next to Johanna herself, this may be Woodcarver's greatest advantage.'

'I—' *I had no idea.* 'So the incompetent local security is just a cover.'

'Not exactly. It's supposed to look solid and intelligent, but with just enough exploitable weakness so the Movement will postpone a frontal attack in favor of espionage.' He smiled. 'I think Vendacious will be very taken aback to hear your critique.'

Scriber gave a weak laugh. He was flattered and boggled at the same time. Vendacious must count as the greatest spymaster of the age – yet he, Scriber Jaqueramaphan, had almost seen through him. Scriber was mostly quiet the rest of the way back to the castle, but his mind was racing. Peregrine was more right than he knew; secrecy was vital. Unnecessary discussion – even between old friends – must be avoided. Yes! He would offer his services to Vendacious. His new role might keep him in the background, but it was where he could make the greatest contribution. And eventually even Johanna would see how helpful he could be.

Down the well of the night. Even when Ravna wasn't looking out the windows, that was the image in her mind. Relay was far off the galactic disk. The *OOB* was descending toward that disk – and ever deeper into slowness.

But they had escaped. The *OOB* was crippled, but they had left Relay at almost fifty light-years per hour. Each hour they were deeper in the Beyond and the computation time for the microjumps increased, and their pseudo-velocity declined. Nevertheless, they were making progress. They were deep into the Middle of the Beyond now. And there was no sign of pursuit, thank goodness. Whatever had brought the Blight to Relay, it had not been a specific knowledge of the *OOB*.

Hope. Ravna felt it growing in her. The ship's medieval automation claimed that Pham Nuwen could be saved, that there was brain activity. The terrible wounds in his back had been Old One's implants, organic machinery that had made Pham close-linked to Relay's local network – and thence to the Power above. And when that Power died somehow the gear in Pham became a putrescent ruin. *So Pham the person should still exist. Pray he still exists.* The surgeon thought it would be three days before his back was healed enough to attempt resuscitation.

In the meantime . . . Ravna was learning more about the apocalypse that had swept over her. Every twenty hours, Greenstalk and Blueshell jigged the ship sideways a few light-years, into some major trunk line of the Known Net to soak up the News. It was a common practice on any voyage of more than a few days; an easy way for merchants and travelers to keep track of events that might affect their success at voyage's end.

According to the News (that is, according to the vast majority of the opinions expressed), the fall of Relay was complete. *Oh, Grondr. Oh Egravan and Sarale. Are you dead or owned now?*

Parts of the Known Net were temporarily out of contact; some of the extra-galactic links might not be replaced for years. For the first time in millennia, a Power was known to have been murdered. There were tens of thousands of claims about the motive for the attack and tens of thousands of predictions about what would happen next. Ravna had the ship filter the avalanche, trying to distill the essence of the speculations.

The one coming from Straumli Realm itself made as much sense as any: the Perversion's thralls gloated solemnly about the new era, the marriage of a Transcendent being with races of the Beyond. If Relay could be destroyed – if a Power could be murdered – then nothing could stop the spread of victory.

Some senders thought that Relay was the ancestral target of whatever had perverted Straumli Realm. Maybe the attack was just the tail end of some long-ago war, a misbegotten tragedy for the descendants of forgotten races. If so, then the thralls at Straumli Realm might just wither away and the original human culture there reappear.

A number of items suggested that the attack had been aimed at stealing Relay's archives, but only one or two claimed that the Blight sought to recover an artifact, or prevent the Relayers from recovering one. Those assertions came from chronic theorizers, the sort of civilizations that get surcharged by news group automation. Nevertheless, Ravna looked through those messages carefully. None of them suggested an artifact in the Low Beyond; if anything, they claimed the Blight was searching for something in the High Beyond or Low Transcend.

There was network traffic coming out of the Blight. Its high protocol messages were rejected by all but the suicidal, and no one as getting paid to forward anything. Yet horror and curiosity spread some of the messages far. There was the Blighter 'video': almost four hundred seconds of pan-sensual data with no compression. That incredibly expensive message might be the most-forwarded hog in all Net history. Blueshell held the *OOB* on the trunk path of nearly two days to receive the whole thing.

The Perversion's thralls all appeared to be human. About half the news items coming out of the Realm were video evocations, though none this long, all showed human speakers. Ravna watched the big one again and again: She even recognized the speaker. Øvn Nilsndot had been Straumli Realm's champion trael runner. He had no title now, and probably no name. Nilsndot spoke from an office that might have been a garden. If

Ravna stepped to the side of the image, she could see over his shoulder to ground level. The city there looked like the Straumli Main of record. Years ago, Ravna and her sister had dreamed about that city, the heart of mankind's adventure into the Transcend. The central square had been a replica of the Field of Princesses on Nyjora, and the immigration advertising claimed that no matter how far the Straumers went, the fountain in the Field would always flow, would always show their loyalty to humankind's beginnings.

There was no fountain now, and Ravna felt deadness behind Nilsndot's gaze. 'This one speaks as the Power that Helps,' said the erstwhile hero. 'I want all to see what I can do for even a third-rate civilization. Look upon my Helping . . .' The viewpoint swung skywards. It was sunset, and the ranked agrav structures hung against the light, megameter upon megameter. It was a more grandiose use of the agrav material than Ravna had ever seen, even on the Docks. Certainly no world in the Middle Beyond could ever afford to import the material in such quantities. 'What you see above me is just the work barracks for the construction that I will soon begin in the Straumli system. When complete, five star systems will be a single habitat, their planets and excess stellar mass distributed to support life and technology as never before seen at these depths – and as rarely seen in the Transcend itself.' The view returned to Nilsndot, a single human, mouthpiece for a god. 'Some of you may rebel against the idea of dedicating yourselves to me. In the long run it does not matter. The symbiosis of my Power with the hands of races in the Beyond is more than any can resist. But I speak now to diminish your fear. What you see in Straumli Realm is as much a joy as a wonder. Never again will races in the Beyond be left behind by transcendence. Those who join me – and all will join eventually – will be part of the Power. You will have access to imports from across the Top and Lower Transcend. You will reproduce beyond the limits your own technology could sustain. You will absorb all that oppose me. You will bring the new stability.'

The third or fourth time she watched the item, Ravna tried to ignore the words, concentrate on Nilsndot's expression, comparing it to speeches she had in her personal dataset. There was a difference; it wasn't her imagination. The creature she watched was soul-dead. Somehow, the Blight didn't care that that was obvious . . . maybe it wasn't obvious except to human viewers, and they were a vanishingly small fraction of the audience. The viewpoint closed in on Nilsndot's ordinary dark face, his ordinary violet eyes:

'Some of you may wonder how all this is possible, and why billions of years of anarchy have passed without such help from a Power. The answer is . . . complex. Like many sensible developments, this one has a high threshold. On one side of that threshold, the development appears impossibly unlikely; on the other, inevitable. The symbiosis of the Helping depends on efficient, high-bandwidth communication between myself and the beings I Help. Creatures such as the one now speaking my words must respond as quickly and faithfully as a hand or a mouth. Their eyes and ears must report across light-years. This has been hard to achieve – especially since the system must essentially be in place before it can function. *But*, now that the symbiosis exists, progress will come much faster. Almost any race can be modified to receive Help.'

Almost any race can be modified. The words came from a familiar face, and in Ravna's birth language . . . but the origin was monstrously far away.

There was plenty of analysis. A whole news group had been formed: Threat of the Blight was spawned from Threats Group, Homo Sapiens Interest Group, and Close-Coupled Automation. These days it was busier than any five other groups. In this part of the galaxy, a significant fraction of all message traffic belonged to the new group. More bits were sent analyzing poor Øvn Nilsndot's mouthing than had been in the original. Judging from the flames and contradictions, the signal-to-noise ratio was very low:

Crypto: 0
As received by: *OOB* shipboard ad hoc
Language path: Acquileron → Triskweline, SjK units
From: Khurvark University
  [Claimed to be habitat-based university, in the Middle Beyond]
Subject: Blighter Video
Summary: The message shows fraud
Distribution:
  War Trackers Interest Group
  Where are they now Interest Group
  Threat of the Blight
Date: 7.06 days since Fall of Relay
Text of message:
  It's obvious that this 'Helper' is a fraud. We've researched the matter carefully. Though he is not named, the speaker is a high official in the former Straumli regime. Now why – if the "Helper" ' simply runs the hunans as teleoperated robots – why is the earlier social structure preserved? The answer should be clear to any idiot: The Helper does not have the power to teleoperate large numbers of sentients. Evidently, the Fall of Straumli Realm consisted of taking over key elements in that civilization's power structure. It's business as usual for the rest of the race. Our conclusion: this Helper Symbiosis is just another messianic religion; another screwball empire excusing its excesses and attempting to trick those it cannot directly coerce. *Don't be fooled!*

Crypto: 0
As received by: *OOB* shipboard ad hoc
Language path: Optima → Acquileron → Triskweline, SjK units

From: Society for Rational Investigation [Probably a single system in Middle
      Beyond, 5700 light-years antispinward of Sjandra Kei]
Subject: Blighter Video thread, Khurvark University 1
Key phrases: [Probable obscenity] waste of our valuable time
Distribution:
   Society for Rational Network Management
   Threat of the Blight
Date: 7.91 days since Fall of Relay
Text of message:
   Who is a fool? [probable obscenity] [probable obscenity] Idiots who don't
follow all the threads in developing news should not waste my precious ears
with their [clear obscenity] garbage. So you think the 'Helper Symbiosis' is a
fraud of Straumli Realm? And what do you think caused the fall of Relay? In
case your head is totally stuck up your rear [<–probable insult], there was a
Power allied with Relay. That Power is now dead. You think maybe it just
committed suicide? Look it up, Flat Head [<–probable insult]. No Power has
ever fallen to anything from the Beyond. The Blight is something new and
interesting. I think it's time that [obscenity] jerks like Khurvark University stick to
the noise groups, and let the rest of us have some intelligent discussion.

And some messages were patent nonsense. One thing about the Net: the
multiple, automatic translations often disguised the fundamental alienness
of participants. Behind the chatty, colloquial postings, there were faraway
realms, so misted by distance and difference that communication was
impossible – even though it might take a while to realize the fact. For
instance:

Crypto: 0
As received by: *OOB* shipboard ad hoc
Language path: Arbwyth → Trade 24 → Cherguelen → Triskweline, SjK units
From: Twirlip of the Mists
   [Perhaps an organization of cloud fliers in a single jovian system. Very sparse
   priors.]
Subject: Blighter Video thread
Key phrases: Hexapodia as the key insight
Distribution:
   Threat of the Blight
Date: 8.68 days since Fall of Relay
Text of message:
   I haven't had a chance to see the famous video from Straumli Realm, except
as an evocation. (My only gateway onto the Net is very expensive.) Is it true that
humans have six legs? I wasn't sure from the evocation. If these humans have
three pairs of legs, then I think there is an easy explanation for—

Hexapodia: Six legs? Three pairs of legs? Probably none of these translations was close to what the bewildered creature of Twirlip had in its mind. Ravna didn't read any more of that posting.

Crypto:0
As received by: *OOB* shipboard ad hoc
Language path: Triskweline, SjK units
From: Hanse
    [No references prior to the Fall of Relay. No probable source. This is someone
    being very cautious]
Subject: Blighter Video thread, Khurvark University 1
Distribution:
    War Trackers Interest Group
    Threat of the Blight
Date: 8.68 days since Fall of Relay
Text of message:
    Khurvark University thinks the Blight is a fraud because elements of the former regime have survived on Straum. There is another explanation. Suppose the Blight is indeed a Power, and that its claims of effective symbiosis are generally true. That means that the creature being 'Helped' is no more than a remotely controlled device, his brain simply a local processor supporting the communication. Would *you* want to be helped like that? My question isn't completely rhetorical; the readership is wide enough that there may be some of you who would answer 'yes.' However, the vast majority of naturally evolved, sentient beings would be revolted by the notion. Surely the Blight knows this. My guess is that the Blight is *not* a fraud – but that the notion of surviving culture in Straumli Realm *is*. Subtly, the Blight wants to convey the impression that only some are directly enslaved, that cultures as a whole will survive. Combine that with Blight's claim that not all races can be teleoperated. We're left with the subtext that immense riches are available to races that associate themselves with this Power, yet the biological and intellectual imperatives of these races will still be satisfied.
    So, the question remains. Just how thorough is the Blight's control over conquered races? I don't know. There may not be any self-aware minds left in the Blight's Beyond, only billions of teleoperated devices. One thing is clear: The Blight needs something from us that it cannot yet *take*.

And so it went. Tens of thousands of messages, hundreds of points of view. It was not called the Net of a Million Lies for nothing. Ravna talked with Blueshell and Greenstalk about it every day, trying to put it all together, trying to decide which interpretation to believe.

The Riders knew humans well, but even they weren't sure of the deadness in Øvn Nilsndot's face. And Greenstalk knew humans well enough to see that there was no answer that would comfort Ravna. She rolled back and forth in front of the News window, finally reached a frond out to touch the human. 'Perhaps Sir Pham can say, once he is well.'

Blueshell was bustling, clinical. 'If you're right, that means that somehow the Blight doesn't care what humans and those close to humans know. In a way that makes sense, but . . .' His voder buzzed absentmindedly for a moment. 'I mistrust this message. Four hundred seconds of broad-band, so rich that it gives full-sense imagery for many different races. That's an enormous amount of information, and no compression whatsoever . . . Maybe it's sweetened bait, forwarded by us poor Beyonders back to our every nest.' That suspicion had been in the News too. But there were no obvious patterns in the message, and nothing that talked to network automation. Such subtle poison might work at the Top of the Beyond, but not down here. And that left a simpler explanation, one that would make perfect sense even on Nyjora or Old Earth: the video masked a message to agents already in place.

Vendacious was well-known to the people of Woodcarvers – but for mostly the wrong reasons. He was about a century old, the fusion offspring of Woodcarver on two of his strategists. In his early decades, Vendacious had managed the city's wood mills. Along the way he devised some clever improvements on the waterwheel. Vendacious had had his own romantic entanglements – mostly with politicians and speech-makers. More and more, his replacement members inclined him toward public life. For the last thirty years he had been one of the strongest voices on Woodcarver's Council; for the last ten, Lord Chamberlain. In both roles he had stood for the guilds and for fair trade. There were rumors that if Woodcarver should ever abdicate or wholly die, Vendacious would be the next Lord of Council. Many thought that might be the best that could be made of such a disaster – though Vendacious's pompous speeches were already the bane of the Council.

That was the public's view of Vendacious. Anyone who understood the ways of security would also guess that the chamberlain managed Woodcarver's spies. No doubt he had dozens of informants in the mills and on the docks. But now Scriber knew that even *that* was just a cover. Imagine – having agents in the Flenserist inner circle, knowing the Flenserist plans, their fears, their weaknesses, and being able to manipulate them! Vendacious was simply incredible. Ruefully, Scriber must acknowledge the other's stark genius.

And yet . . . this knowledge did not guarantee victory. Not *all* the Flenserist schemes could be directly managed from the top. Some of the enemy's low-level operations might proceed unknown and quite successfully . . . and it would only take a single arrow to totally kill Johanna Olsndot.

Here was where Scriber Jaqueramaphan could prove his value.

He asked to move into the castle curtain, on the third floor. No problem getting permission; his new quarters were smaller, the walls rudely quilted. A single arrow loop gave an uninspired view across the castle grounds. For Scriber's new purpose, the room was perfect. Over the next few days, he took to lurking in the promenades. The main walls were laced with tunnels, fifteen inches wide by thirty tall. Scriber could get almost anywhere in the curtain without being seen from outside. He padded single file from one tunnel to the next, emerging for a few moments on a rampart to flit from merlon to embrasure to merlon, a head poking out here, a head poking out there.

Of course he ran into guards, but Jaqueramaphan was cleared to be in the walls . . . and he had studied the guards' routine. They knew he was around, but Scriber was confident they had no idea of the extent of his effort. It was hard, cold work, but worth the effort. Scriber's great goal in life was to do something spectacular and valuable. The problem was, most of his ideas were so deep that other packs – even people he respected immensely – didn't understand. That had been the problem with Johanna. Well, after a few more days he could go to Vendacious and then . . .

As he peeked around corners and through arrow slots, two of Scriber's members huddled down, taking notes. After ten days he had enough to impress even Vendacious.

Vendacious's official residence was surrounded by rooms for assistants and guards. It was not the place to make a secret offer. Besides, Scriber had had bad luck with the direct approach before. You could wait days for an appointment, and the more patient you were, the more you followed the rules, the more the bureaucrats considered you a nonentity.

But Vendacious was sometimes alone. There was this turret on the old wall, on the forest side of the castle . . . Late on the eleventh day of his investigation, Scriber stationed himself on that turret and waited. An hour passed. The wind eased. Heavy fog washed in from the harbor. It oozed up the old wall like slow-moving sea foam. Everything became very, very quiet – the way it always does in a thick fog. Scriber nosed moodily around the turret platform; it really was decrepit. The mortar crumbled under his claws. It felt like you could pull some of the stones right out of the wall. *Damn.* Maybe Vendacious was going to break the pattern and not come up here today.

But Scriber waited another half hour . . . and his patience paid off. He heard the click of steel on the spiral stairs. There was no sound of thought; it was just too foggy for that. A minute passed. The trapdoor popped up and a head stuck through.

Even in the fog, Vendacious's surprise was a fierce hiss.

'Peace, sir! It is only I, loyal Jaqueramaphan.'

The head came further out. 'What would a loyal citizen be doing up here?'

'Why, I am here to see you,' Scriber said, laughing, 'at this, your secret office. Come on up, sir. With this fog, there is enough room for both of us.'

One after another, Vendacious's members hoisted themselves through the trapdoor. Some barely made it, their knives and jewelry catching on the door frame; Vendacious was not the slimmest of packs. The security chief ranged himself along the far side of the turret, a posture that bespoke suspicion. He was nothing like the pompous, patronizing pack of their public encounters. Scriber grinned to himself. He certainly had the other's attention.

'Well?' Vendacious said in a flat voice.

'Sir. I wish to offer my services. I believe that my very presence here shows I can be of value to Woodcarver's security. Who but a talented professional could have determined that you use this place as your secret den?'

Vendacious seemed to untense a little. He smiled wryly. 'Who indeed? I come here precisely because this part of the old wall can't be seen from anywhere in the castle. Here I can . . . commune with the hills, and be free of bureaucratic trivia.'

Jaqueramaphan nodded. 'I understand, sir. But you are wrong in one detail.' He pointed past the security chief. 'You can't see it through all this fog, but on the harbor side of the castle there is a single spot that has a line of sight on your turret.'

'So? Who could see much from – ah, the eye-tools you brought from the Republic!'

'Exactly.' Scriber reached into a pocket and brought out a *telescope*. 'Even from across the yard, I could recognize you.' The eye-tools could have made Scriber famous. Woodcarver and Scrupilo had been enchanted by them. Unfortunately, honesty had required to him admit that he bought the devices from an inventor in Rangathir. Never mind that it was *he* who recognized the value of the invention, that it was he who used it to help rescue Johanna. When they discovered that he did not know quite how the lenses worked, they had accepted his gift of one . . . and turned to their own glass makers. Oh well, he was still the best eye-tool *user* in this part of the world.

'It's not just you I've been watching, my lord. That's been the smallest part of my investigation. Over the last ten days I've spent many hours on the castle walks.'

Vendacious's lips quirked. 'Indeed.'

'I daresay not many noticed me, and I was very careful that no one saw me using the eye-tool. In any case,' he pulled his book from another pocket, 'I've compiled extensive notes. I know who goes where and when during almost all the hours of light. You can imagine the power of my technique during the summer!' He set the book on the floor and slid it toward Vendacious. After a moment, the other reached a member forward and dragged it toward himself. He didn't seem very enthusiastic.

'Please understand, sir. I know that you tell Woodcarver what goes on in the highest Flenser councils. Without your sources we would be helpless against those lords, but—'

'*Who told you such things?*'

Scriber gulped. *Brazen it out.* He grinned weakly. 'No one had to tell me. I'm a professional, like yourself; and I know how to keep a secret. But think: there might be others of my ability within the castle, and some might be traitors. You might never hear of them from your high-placed sources. Think of the damage they could do. You need my help. With my approach, you can keep track of everyone. I would be happy to train a corps of investigators. We could even operate in the city, watching from the market towers.'

The security chief sidled around the parapet; he kicked idly at stones in the rotted mortar. 'The idea has its attractions. Mind you, I think we have all Flenser's agents identified; we feed them well . . . with lies. It's interesting to hear the lies come back from our sources up there.' He laughed shortly, and glanced over the parapet, thinking. 'But you're right. If we are missing anyone with access to the Two-Legs or Dataset . . . it could be disastrous.' He turned more heads at Scriber. 'You've got a deal. I can get you four or five people to, ah, train in your methods.'

Scriber couldn't control his expression; he almost bounced in enthusiasm, all eyes on Vendacious. 'You won't regret this, sir!'

Vendacious shrugged. 'Probably not. Now, how many others have you told about your investigation? We'll want to bring them in, swear them to secrecy.'

Scriber drew himself up. 'My Lord! I told you that I am a professional. I have kept this completely to myself, waiting for this conversation.'

Vendacious smiled and relaxed to an almost genial posture. 'Excellent. Then we can begin.'

Maybe it was Vendacious's voice – a trifle too loud – or maybe it was some small sound behind him. Whatever the reason, Scriber turned a head from the other and saw swift shadows coming over the forest side of the parapet. Too late he heard the attacker's mind noise.

Arrows hissed, and fire burned through his Phan's throat. He gagged, but kept himself together and raced around the turret toward Vendacious. 'Help me!' The scream was a waste of speech. Scriber *knew*, even before the other drew his knives and backed away.

Vendacious stood clear as his assassin jumped into Scriber's midst. Rational thought dimmed in a frenzy of noise and slashing pain. *Tell Peregrine! Tell Johanna!* The butchering continued for timeless instants and then—

Part of him was drowning in sticky red. Part of him was blinded. Jaquerama's thought came in ragged fragments. At least one of him was dead: Phan lay beheaded in a spreading pool of blood. It steamed in the cold air. Pain and cold and . . . drowning, choking . . . *tell Johanna.*

The assassin and his boss had retreated from him. Vendacious. Security chief. Traitor-in-chief. *Tell Johanna.* They stood quietly . . . watching him bleed to death. Too prissy to mess their thoughts with his. They'd wait. They'd wait . . . till his mind noise dimmed, then finish the job.

Quiet. So quiet. The killers' distant thoughts. Sounds of gagging, moaning. No one would ever know . . .

Almost all gone. Ja stared dumbly at the two strange packs. One came toward him, steel claws on his feet, blades in its mouth. *No!* Ja jumped up, slipping and skidding on the wet. The pack lunged, but Ja was already standing on the parapet. He leaped backwards and fell and fell . . .

. . . and shattered on rocks far below. Ja pulled himself away from the wall. There was pain across his back, then numbness. Where am I? Where am I? Fog everywhere. High above him there were muttering voices. Memories of knives and tines floated in his small mind, all jumbled. *Tell Johanna!* He remembered . . . something . . . from before. A hidden trail through deep brush. If he went that way far enough, he would find Johanna.

Ja dragged himself slowly up the path. Something was wrong with his rear legs; he couldn't feel them. *Tell Johanna.*

19

Johanna coughed; things just seemed to go from bad to worse around here. She'd had a sore throat and sniffles the last three days. She didn't know whether to be frightened or not. Diseases were an everyday thing in medieval times. *Yeah, and lots of people* died *of them, too!* She wiped her nose and tried to concentrate on what Woodcarver was saying.

'Scrupilo has already made some gunpowder. It works just as Dataset predicted. Unfortunately, he nearly lost a member trying to use it in a wooden cannon. If we can't make cannon, I'm afraid—'

A week ago, Woodcarver wouldn't have been welcome here; all their meetings had been down in the castle halls. But then Johanna got sick – it was a 'cold,' she was sure – and hadn't felt like running around out of doors. Besides, Scriber's visit had kind of . . . shamed her. Some of the packs were decent enough. She had decided to try and get along with Woodcarver – and Pompous Clown too, if he'd ever come around again. As long as creatures like Scarbutt stayed out of her way . . . Johanna leaned a little closer to the fire and waved away Woodcarver's objections; sometimes this pack seemed like her eldest grandmother. 'Assume we can make them. We have lots of time till summer. Tell Scrupilo to study the dataset more carefully, and quit trying shortcuts. The question is how to use them to rescue my starship.'

Woodcarver brightened. The drooler broke off wiping its muzzle to join the others in a head bob. 'I've talked about this with Peregr— with several people, especially Vendacious. Ordinarily, getting an army to Hidden Island would be a terrible problem. Going by sea is fast, but there are some deadly choke points along the way. Going through the forest is slow, and the other side would have plenty of warning. But great good luck: Vendacious has found some safe trails. We may be able to sneak—'

Someone was scratching at the door.

Woodcarver cocked a pair of heads. 'That's strange,' she said.

'Why?' Johanna asked absently. She hiked the quilt around her shoulders and stood. Two of Woodcarver went with her to the door.

Johanna opened the door and looked into the fog. Suddenly Woodcarver was talking loudly, all gobble. Their visitor had retreated. Something *was* strange, and for an instant she couldn't figure what it was. *This was the first time she had seen a dogthing all by itself.* The point barely registered when most of Woodcarver spilled past her, out the doorway. Then Johanna's servant, up in the loft, began screaming. The sound jabbed pain through Johanna's ears.

The lone Tine twisted awkwardly on its rear and tried to drag itself away, but Woodcarver had it surrounded. She shouted something and the screeching in the loft stopped. There was the thump of paws on wooden stairs, and the servant bounded into the open, its crossbows cocked. From down the hill, she heard the rattle of weapons as guards raced toward them.

Johanna ran to Woodcarver, ready to add her fists to any defense. But the pack was *nuzzling* the stranger, licking its neck. After a moment, Woodcarver caught the Tine by its jacket. 'Help me carry him inside, Johanna please.'

The girl lifted the Tine's flanks. The fur was damp with mist . . . and sticky with blood.

Then they were through the doorway and laying the member on a pillow by the fire. The creature was making that breathy whistling, the sound of ultimate pain. It looked up at her, its eyes so wide she could see the white all around. For an instant she thought it was terrified of *her*, but when she stepped back, it just made the sound louder and stretched its neck toward her. She knelt beside the pillow. It lay its muzzle on her hand.

'W-what is it?' She looked back along its body, past the padded jacket. The Tine's haunches were twisted at an odd angle, one leg dangling near the fire.

'Don't you know—' began Woodcarver. 'This is part of Jaqueramaphan.' She pushed a nose under the dangling leg and raised it onto the pillow.

There was loud talk between the guards and Johanna's servant. Through the door she saw members holding torches; they rested their forepaws on their fellows' shoulders, and held the lights high. No one tried to come in; there'd be no room.

Johanna looked back at the injured Tine. *Scriber?* Then she recognized the jacket. The creature looked back at her, still wheezing its pain. 'Can't you get a doctor!'

Woodcarver was all around her. She answered, 'I am a doctor, Johanna.' She nodded at the dataset and continued softly, 'At least, what passes for one here.'

Johanna wiped blood from the creature's neck. More kept oozing. 'Well, can you save him?'

'This fragment maybe, but—' One of Woodcarver went to the door and talked to the packs beyond. 'My people are searching for the rest of him . . . I think he is mostly murdered, Johanna. If there were others . . . well, even fragments stick together.'

'Has he said anything?' It was another voice, speaking Samnorsk. *Scarbutt.* His big ugly snout was stuck through the doorway.

'No,' said Woodcarver. 'And his mind noise is a complete jumble.'

'Let me listen to him,' said Scarbutt.

'*You stay back, you!*' Johanna's voice was a scream; the creature in her arms twitched.

'Johanna! This is Scriber's friend. Let him help.' As the Scarbutt pack sidled into the room, Woodcarver climbed into the loft, giving him room.

Johanna eased her arm from under the injured Tine and backed away, ending up at the doorway herself. There were lots more packs outside than she had imagined, and they were standing closer than she had ever seen. Their torches glowed like soft fluorescents in the foggy dark.

Her gaze snapped back to the fire pit. 'I'm watching you!'

Scarbutt's members clustered around the pillow. The big one lay its head next to the injured Tine's. For a moment, the Tine continued its breathy whistling. Scarbutt gobbled at it. The reply was a steady warbling, almost beautiful. From up in the loft, Woodcarver said something. She and Scarbutt talked back and forth.

'Well?' said Johanna.

'*Ja* – the fragment – is not a "talker," ' came Woodcarver's voice.

'Worse,' said Scarbutt. 'For now at least, I can't match his mind sounds. I'm not getting sense or image from him; I can't tell who murdered Scriber.'

Johanna stepped back into the room, and walked slowly to the pillow. Scarbutt moved aside, but did not leave the wounded Tine. She knelt between two of him and petted the long, bloodied neck. 'Will – Ja' – she spoke the sound as best she could – 'live?'

Scarbutt ran three noses down the length of the body. They pressed gently at the wounds. Ja twisted and whistled . . . except when Scarbutt pressed his haunches. 'I don't know. Most of this blood is just splatter, probably from the other members. But his spine is broken. Even if the fragment lives, he'll have only two usable legs.'

Johanna thought for a moment, trying to see things from a Tinish perspective. She didn't like the view. It might not make sense, but to her, this 'Ja' was still Scriber. To Scarbutt, the creature was a fragment, an organ from a fresh corpse. A damaged one at that. She looked at Scarbutt, at the big, killer member. 'So what does your kind do with such . . . garbage?'

Three of his heads turned toward her, and she could see his hackles rise. His synthetic voice became high-pitched and staccato. 'Scriber was a good friend. We could build a two-wheel cart for Ja's rear; he'd be able to move around some. The hard part will be finding a pack for him. You know we're looking for other fragments; we may be able to patch something up. If not . . . well, I have only four members. I will try to adopt him.' As he spoke one head patted the wounded member. 'I'm not sure it will work. Scriber was not a loose-souled person, not in any way a pilgrim. And right now, I don't match him at all.'

Johanna slumped back. Scarbutt wasn't responsible for everything that went wrong in the universe.

'Woodcarver has excellent brood kenners. Maybe some other match can be found. But understand . . . it's hard for adult members to remerge, especially non-talkers. Single fragments like Ja often die of their own accord; they just stop eating. Or sometimes . . . Go down to the harbor sometime, look at the workers. You'll see some big packs there . . . but with the minds of idiots. They can't hold together; the smallest problem and they run in all directions. That's how the unlucky repacks end . . .' Scarbutt's voice traded back and forth between two of his members, and dribbled into silence. All his heads turned to Ja. The member had closed his eyes. Sleeping? He was still breathing, but it sounded kind of burbly.

Johanna looked across the room at the trapdoor to the loft. Woodcarver had stuck a single head down through the hole. The upside-down face looked back at Johanna. Anther time, her appearance would have been comical. 'Unless a miracle happens, Scriber died today. Understand that, Johanna. But if the fragment lives, even a short time, we'll likely find the murderer.'

'How, if he can't communicate?'

'Yes, but he can still *show* us. I've ordered Vendacious's men to confine the staff to quarters. When Ja is calmer, we'll march every pack in the castle past him. The fragment certainly remembers what happened to Scriber, and *wants* to tell us. If any of the killers are our own people, he'll see them.'

'And he'll make a fuss.' *Just like a dog.*

'Right. So the main thing is to provide him with security right now . . . and hope our doctors can save him.'

They found the rest of Scriber a couple of hours later, on a turret of the old wall. Vendacious said it looked like one or two packs had come out of the forest and climbed the turret, perhaps in an attempt to see onto the grounds. It had all the markings of an incompetent, first-time probe: nothing of value could be seen from that turret, even on a clear day. But for Scriber it had been fatally bad luck. Apparently he had surprised the intruders. Five of his members had been variously arrowed, hacked, decapitated. The sixth – Ja – had broken his back on the sloping stonework at the base of the wall. Johanna walked out to the turret the next day. Even from the ground she could see brownish stains on the parapet. She was glad she couldn't go to the top.

Ja died during the night, though not from any further enemy action; he was under Vendacious's protection the whole time.

Johanna went the next few days without saying much. At night she cried a little. *God damn their 'doctoring.'* A broken back they could diagnose, but hidden injuries, internal bleeding – of such they were completely ignorant Apparently, Woodcarver was famous for her theory that the heart pumped the blood around the body. Give her another thousand years and maybe she could do better than a butcher!

For a while she hated them all: Scarbutt for all the old reasons, Woodcarver for her ignorance, Vendacious for letting Flenserists get so close to the castle . . . and Johanna Olsndot for rejecting Scriber when he had tried to be a friend.

What would Scriber say now? He had wanted her to trust them. He said that Scarbutt and the others were good people. One night, about a week later, she came close to making peace with herself. She was lying on her pallet, the quilt heavy and warm upon her. The designs painted on the walls glimmered dim in the emberlight. *All right, Scriber. For you . . . I will trust them.*

20

Pham Nuwen remembered almost nothing of the first days after dying, after the pain of the Old One's ending. Ghostly figures, anonymous words. Someone said he'd been kept alive in the ship's surgeon. He remembered none of it. Why they kept the body breathing was a mystery and an affront. Eventually the animal reflexes had revived. The body began breathing of its own accord. The eyes opened. No brain damage, Greenstalk(?) said, a full recovery. The husk that had been a living being spoke no contradiction.

What was left of Pham Nuwen spent a lot of time on the *OOB*'s bridge. From before, the ship reminded him of a fat sowbug. The bugs had been common in the straw laid across the floor of the Great Hall of his father's castle on Canberra. The little kids had played with them. The critters didn't have real legs, just a dozen feathery spines sticking out from a chitinous thorax. No matter how you tumbled them, those spines/antennas would twitch the bug around and it would scuttle on its way, unmindful that it might be upside down from before. Yes, the *OOB*'s ultradrive spines looked a lot like a sowbug's, though not as articulated. And the body itself was fat and sleek, slightly narrowed in the middle.

So Pham Nuwen had ended inside of a sowbug. How fitting for a dead man.

And now he sat on the bridge. The woman brought him there often; she seemed to know it should fascinate him. The walls were displays, better than he had ever seen in merchant-man days. When the windows looked out the ship's exterior cameras, the view was as good as from any crystal-canopy bridge in the Qeng Ho fleet.

It was like something out of the crudest fantasy – or a graphics simulation. If he sat long enough, he could actually see the stars *move* in the sky. The ship was doing about ten ultrajumps per second: jump, recompute and jump again. In this part of The Beyond they could go a thousandth of a light-year on each jump – farther, but then the recompute time would be substantially worse. At ten per second that added up to more than thirty light-years per hour. The jumps themselves were imperceptible to human senses, and between the jumps they were in free fall, carrying the same intrinsic velocity they'd had on departing Relay. So there was none of the doppler shifting of relativistic flight; the stars were as pure as seen from some desert sky, or in low-speed transit. Without any fuss, they simply slid across the sky, the closer ones faster. In half an hour he went farther than he had in half a century with the Qeng Ho.

Greenstalk drifted onto the bridge one day and began changing the windows. As usual she spoke to Pham as she did so, chatting almost as if there were a real person here to listen:

'See. The center window is an ultrawave map of the region directly behind us.' Greenstalk waved a tendril over the controls. The multicolored pictures appeared on the other walls. 'Similarly for the other five points of direction.'

The words were noise in Pham's ears, understood but of no interest. The Rider paused, then continued with something like the futile persistence of the Ravna woman.

'When ships make a jump . . . when they reenter, there's a kind of an ultrawave *splash*. I'm checking if we're being followed.'

Colors on the windows all around, even in front of Pham's eyes. There were smooth gradations, no bright spots, no linear features.

'I know, I know,' she said, making up both sides of the conversation. 'The ship's analyzers are still massaging the data. But if anyone's pacing us closer than one hundred light-years, we'll see them. And if they're farther than that – well, then they probably can't detect *us*.'

It doesn't matter. Pham almost shut the question out of his mind. But there were no stars to look at; he stared at the glowing colors and actually thought about the problem. *Thought.* A joke: no one Down Here ever really thought about anything. Perhaps ten thousand starships had escaped the Fall of Relay. Most likely the Enemy had not cataloged those departures. The attack on Relay had been a minor adjunct to the murder of Old One. Most likely the *OOB* had escaped unnoticed. Why should the Enemy care where the last of Old One's memories might be hiding? Why should it care about where their little ship might be bound?

A tremor passed through his body; animal reflex, surely.

Panic was slowly rising in Ravna Bergsndot, every day a little stronger. It was not any particular disaster, just the slow dying of hope. She tried to be near Pham Nuwen part of every day, to talk to him, to hold his hand. He never responded, not even – except perhaps by accident – to look at her. Greenstalk tried too. Alien though Greenstalk was, the Pham of before had seemed truly attracted to the Riders. He was off all medical support now, but he might as well have been a vegetable.

And all the while their descent was slowing, always a little worse than what Blueshell had predicted.

And when she turned too the News . . . in some ways that was the most horrifying of all. The 'death race' theory was getting popular. More and more, there were folk who seemed to think that the human race was spreading the Blight:

Crypto: 0
As received by: *OOB* shipboard ad hoc
Language path: Baeloresk → Triskweline, SjK units
From: Alliance for the Defense
   [Claimed cooperative of five polyspecific empires in the Beyond below
    Straumli Realm. No record of existence before the Fall of the Realm.]
Subject: Blighter Video thread
Distribution:
   Threat of the Blight
   War Trackers Interest Group
   Homo Sapiens Interest Group
Date: 17.95 days since Fall of Relay
Test of message:
   So far we've processed half a million messages about this creature's video, and read a goodly fraction of them. Most of you are missing the point. The principle of the 'Helper's' operation is clear. This is a Transcendent Power using ultralight communication to operate through a race in the Beyond. It would be fairly easy to do in the Transcend – there are a number of stories about thralls of Powers there. But for such communication to be effective within the Beyond, truly extensive design changes must be made in the minds of the controlled

race. *It could not have happened naturally*, and it can not be quickly done to new races – no matter what the Blight says.

We've watched the Homo Sapiens interest group since the first appearance of the Blight. Where is this 'Earth' the humans claim to be from? 'Half way around the galaxy,' they say, and deep in the Slow Zone. Even their proximate origin, Nyjora, is conveniently in the Slowness. We see an alternative theory: Sometime, maybe further back than the last consistent archives, there was a battle between Powers. The blueprint for this 'human race' was written, complete with communication interfaces. Long after the original contestants and their stories had vanished, this race happened to get in position where it could Transcend. And that Transcending was tailor-made, too, re-establishing the Power that had set the trap to begin with.

We're not sure of the details, but a scenario such as this is inevitable. What we must do is also clear. Straumli Realm is at the heart of the Blight, obviously beyond all attack. But there are other human colonies. We ask the Net to help in identifying all of them. We ourselves are not a large civilization, but we would be happy to coordinate the information gathering, and the military action that is required to prevent the Blight's spread in the Middle Beyond.

For nearly seventeen weeks, we've been calling for action. Had you listened in the beginning, a concerted strike might have been sufficient to destroy the Straumli Realm. Isn't the Fall of Relay enough to wake you up? Friends, if we act together we still have a chance.

Death to vermin.

The bastards even played on humanity's foundling nature. Foundling races were rare, but scarcely unknown. Now these Death-to-Vermin creatures were turning the Miracle of Nyjora into something deadly evil.

Death to Vermin were the only ones to call for pogroms, but even respected posters were saying things that indirectly might support such action:

Crypto: 0
As received by: *OOB* shipboard ad hoc
Language path: Triskweline, SjK units
From: Sandor Arbitration Intelligence at the Zoo [A known military cor-
   poration of the High Beyond. If this is a masquerade, somebody is living
   dangerously.]
Subject: Blighter Video thread, Hanse subthread
Key phrases: limits on the Blight; the Blight is searching for something
Distribution:
   Threat of the Blight
   Close-coupled Automation Interest Group
   War Trackers Interest Group
Date: 11.94 days since Fall of Relay

Text of message:

The Blight admits that it is a Power that tele-operates sophonts in the Beyond. But consider how difficult it is to have a close-coupled automation with time lags of more than a few milliseconds. The Known Net is a perfect illustration of this: Lags range between five milliseconds for systems that are a couple of light-years apart – to (at least) several hundred seconds when messages must pass through intermediate nodes. This, combined with the low bandwidth available across interstellar distances, makes the Known Net a loose forum for the exchange of information and lies. And these restrictions are *inherent* in the nature of the Beyond, part of the same restrictions that make it impossible for the Powers to exist down here.

We conclude that even the Blight can't attain close-coupled control except in the High Beyond. At the top, the Blight's sophont agents are literally its limbs. In the Middle Beyond, we believe mental 'possession' is possible but that considerable preprocessing must be done in the controlled mind. Furthermore, considerable external equipment (the bulky items characteristic of those depths) is needed to support the communication. Direct, millisecond-by-millisecond, control is normally impractical in the Middle Beyond. Combat at this level would involve hierarchical control. Long-term operations would also use intimidation, fraud, and traitors.

These are the threats that you of the Middle and Low Beyond should recognize.

These are the Blight's tools in the Middle and Low Beyond, and what you should guard against for the immediate future. We don't see imperial takeovers; there's no profit [sustenance] in it. Even the destruction of Relay was probably just a byplay to the murder it was simultaneously committing in the Transcend. The greatest tragedies will continue to be at the Top and in the Low Transcend. But we know that the Blight is searching for something; it has attacked at great distances where major archives were the target. Beware of traitors and spies.

Even some of humanity's supporters sent a chill through Ravna:

Crypto: 0
As received by: *OOB* shipboard ad hoc
Language path: Triskweline, SjK units
From: Hanse
Subject: Blighter Video thread. Alliance for the Defense subthread
Key phrases: Death Race Theory
Distribution:
  Threat of the Blight
  War Trackers Interest Group
  Homo Sapiens Interest Group
Date: 18.29 days since Fall of Relay
Text of message:
  I have obtained specimens from the human worlds in our volume. Detailed

analysis is available in Homo sapiens interest group archive. My conclusions: previous (but less intensive) analysis of human phys/psych is correct. The race has *no* built-in structures to support remote control. Experiments with living subjects showed no special inclination toward submission. I found little or no evidence of artificial optimization. (There was evidence of DNA surgery to improve disease resistance: drift timing dated the hackwork at two thousand years Before Present. The blood of Straumli Realm subjects carried an optigens, Thirault [a cheap medical recipe that can be tailored across a wide mammalian range].) This race – as represented by my specimens – looks like something that arrived from the Slow Zone quite recently, probably from a single origin world.

Has anyone done such retesting on more distant human worlds?

Crypto: 0
As received by: *OOB* shipboard ad hoc
Language path: Baeloresk → Triskweline, SjK units
From: Alliance for the Defense
  [Claimed cooperative of five polyspecific empires in the Beyond below
  Straumli Realm. No record of existence before the Fall of the Realm.]
Subject: Blighter Video thread, Hanse 1
Distribution:
  Threat of the Blight
  War Trackers Interest Group
  Homo Sapiens Interest Group
Date: 19.43 days since Fall of Relay
Text of message:
  Who is this 'Hanse'? It makes objective, tough-sounding noises about testing human specimens, but it keeps its own nature secret. Don't be fooled by humans telling you about themselves! In fact, we have no way of testing the creatures that dwell in Straumli Realm; their protector will see to that.
  Death to vermin.

And there was a little boy trapped at the bottom of the well. Some days, no communication was possible. Other days, when the *OOB* antenna swarm was tuned in exactly the right direction and when the vagaries of the zone favored it – then Ravna could hear his ship. Even then the signal was so faint, so distorted, that the effective transmission rate was just a few bits per second.

Jefri and his problems might be only the smallest footnote to the story of the Blight (less than that, since no one knew of him), but to Ravna Bergsndot these conversations were the only bright thing in her life just now.

The kid was very lonely, but less so now, she thought. She learned about his friend Amdi, about the stern Tyrathect and the heroic Mr Steel and the proud Tines. Ravna smiled to herself, at herself. The walls of her cabin displayed a flat mural of jungle. Deep in the drippy murk lay regular shadows – a castle built in the roots of a giant mangrove tree. The mural was a famous one; the original had been an analog work from two thousand years ago. It showed life at an even further remove, during the Dark Ages on Nyjora. She and Lynne had spent much of their childhood imagining that they were transported to such a time. Little Jefri was trapped in the real thing. Woodcarver's butchers were no interstellar threat, but they were a deadly horror to those around them. Thank goodness Jefri had not seen the killings.

This was a real medieval world. A tough and unforgiving place, even if Jefri had fallen in with fair-minded people. And the Nyjoran comparison was only vaguely appropriate. These Tines were pack minds; even old Grondr Kalir had been surprised at that.

All through Jefri's mail, Ravna could see the panic among Steel's people:

Mister Steel asked me again if theres any way we can make our ship to fly even a little. I dont know. We almost crashed, I think. We need guns. That would save us, least till you get here. They have bows and arrows just like in Nyjoran days, but no guns. Hes asking me, can you teach us to make guns?

Woodcarver's raiders would return, and this time in enough force to overrun Steel's little kingdom. Back when they thought *OOB*'s flight would be only forty days, that had not seemed a great risk, but now . . . Ravna might arrive to find Woodcarver's murdering complete.

Oh Pham, dear Pham. If you ever really were, please come back now. Pham Nuwen of medieval Canberra. Pham Nuwen, trader from the Slowness . . . *What would someone such as you make of this? Hmm.*

21

Ravna knew that – under his bluster – Blueshell was at least as much a worrier as she. Worse, he was a nitpicker. The next time Ravna asked him about their progress, he retreated into technicalities.

Finally Ravna broke in, 'Look. The kid is sitting on something that *just might* blow the Blight sky high, and all he has are bows and arrows. How long will it be till we get down there, Blueshell?'

Blueshell rolled nervously back and forth across the ceiling. The Skroder-iders had reaction jets; they could maneuver in free fall more adroitly than most humans. Instead they used stick-patches, and rolled around on the walls. In a way, it was kind of cute. Just now, it was irritating.

At least they could talk; she glanced across the bridge to where Pham Nuwen sat facing the bridge's main display. As usual, all his attention was fixed on the slowly moving stars. He was unshaven, his reddish beard bright on his skin; his long hair floated snarled and uncombed. Physically he was cured of his injuries. Ship's surgeon had even replaced the muscle mass that Old One's communication equipment had usurped. Pham could dress and feed himself now, but he still lived in a private dreamworld.

The two riders twittered at each other. It was Greenstalk who finally answered her question: 'Truly, we're not sure how long. The quality of the Beyond changes as we descend. Each jump is taking us a fraction longer than the one before.'

'I know that. We're moving toward the Slow Zone. But the ship is designed for that; it should be an easy matter to extrapolate the slowing.'

Blueshell extended a tendril from ceiling to floor. He diddled with the matte corrugations for a second and then his voder made a sound of human embarrassment. 'Ordinarily you would be correct, my lady Ravna. But this is a special case . . . For one thing, it appears that the zones themselves are in flux.'

'What?'

'It's not that unheard of. Small shifts are going on all the time. That's a major purpose for bottom-lugger ships: to track the changes. We're having the bad luck to run through the middle of the uncertainty.'

Actually, Ravna had known that interface turbulence was high at the Bottom below here. She just didn't think of it in grandiose terms like 'zone shifting'; she also hadn't realized it was serious enough to affect them yet.

'Okay. How bad can it get then? How much can it slow us?'

'Oh my.' Blueshell rolled to the far wall; he was standing on starry sky now. 'It would be nice to be a Lesser Skroderider. So many problems my high calling brings me. I wish I could be deep in surf right now, thinking on olden memories.' Of other days in the surf.

Greenstalk carried on for him: 'It's not "the tide, how high can it rise?" It's "this storm, how bad can it get?" Right now it is worse than anything in this region during the last thousand-years. However, we have been following the local news; most agree that the storm has peaked. If our other problem gets no worse, we should arrive in about one hundred and twenty days.'

Our other problem. Ravna drifted to the center of the bridge and strapped onto a saddle. 'You're talking about the damage we took getting out of Relay. The ultradrive spines, right? How are they holding up?'

'Quite well, apparently. We've not tried to jump faster than eighty percent of design max. On the other hand, we lack good diagnostics. It's conceivable that serious degradation might happen rather suddenly.'

'Conceivable, but unlikely,' put in Greenstalk.

Ravna nodded. Considering all their other problems, there was no point in contemplating possibilities beyond their control. Back on Relay, this had looked like a thirty or forty day trip. Now . . . the boy in the well might have to be brave for a long time yet, no matter how much she wished otherwise. *Hmm, Time for Plan B then. Time for what someone like Pham Nuwen might suggest.* She pushed off the floor and settled by Greenstalk. 'Okay, so the best we can plan on is one hundred and twenty days. If the Zone surge gets worse or if we have to get repairs . . .' Get repairs where? That might be only a delay, not an impossibility. The rebuilt *OOB* was supposed to be repairable even in the Low Beyond. 'Maybe even two hundred days.' She glanced at Blueshell, but he didn't interrupt with his usual amendments and qualifications. 'You've both read the messages we're getting from the boy. He says the locals are going to be overrun, probably in less than one hundred days. Somehow, we have to help him . . . before we actually arrive there.'

Greenstalk rattled her fronds in a way Ravna took for puzzlement.

She looked across the deck at Pham and raised her voice a trifle. *Hey you, you should be an expert on this!* 'You Skroderiders may not recognize it, but this is a problem that's been seen a million times in the Slow Zone: civilizations are separated by years – centuries – of travel time. They fall into dark ages. They become just as primitive as the pack creatures, these "Tines." Then they get visited from outside. In a short time, they have technology back again.' Pham's head did not turn; he just looked out across the starscape.

The Skroderiders rattled at each other, then:

'But how can that help us? Doesn't rebuilding a civilization take dozens of years?'

'And besides, there's nothing to rebuild on the Tines' world. According to the child, this is a world without antecedents. How long does it take to start a new civilization from scratch?'

Ravna waved a hand at the objections. *Don't stop me, I'm on a roll.* 'That's not the point. *We* are in communication with them. We have a good general library on board. Original inventors don't know where they're going; they're groping in the dark. Even the archaeologist/engineers of Nyjora had to reinvent much. But we know everything about making airplanes and such; we know hundreds of ways of going at it.' Now faced with necessity, Ravna was suddenly sure they could do it. 'We can study all the development paths, eliminate the deads ends. Even more, we can find the quickest way to go from medieval to specific inventions, things that can beat whatever barbarians are attacking Jefri's friends.'

Ravna's speech tumbled to a stop. She stared, grinning, first at Greenstalk and then at Blueshell. But a silent Skroderider is one of the universe's more impassive audiences. It was hard even to tell if they were looking at her. After a moment Greenstalk said, 'Yes, I see. And rediscovery being so common in the Slow Zone, most of this may already be worked out in the ship's library.'

That's when it happened: Pham turned from the window. He looked across the deck at Ravna and the Riders. For the first time since Relay, he spoke. Even more, the words weren't nonsense, though it took her a moment to understand. 'Guns and radios,' he said.

'Ah . . . yes.' She looked back at him. *Think of something to make him say more.* 'Why those in particular?'

Pham Nuwen shrugged. 'It worked on Canberra.'

Then damn Blueshell started talking, something about doing a library search. Pham stared at them for a moment, his face expressionless. He turned back to watch the stars, and the moment was lost.

22

'Pham?' He heard Ravna's voice just behind him. She had stayed on the bridge after the Riders left, departing on whatever meaningless preparations their meeting had ordained. He didn't reply, and after a moment she drifted around and blocked his view of the stars. Almost automatically, he found himself focussing on her face.

'Thank you for talking to us . . . We need you more than ever.'

He could still see lots of stars. They were all around her, slowly moving. Ravna cocked her head, the way she did when she meant friendly puzzlement. 'We can help . . .'

He didn't answer. What *had* made him speak just now? Then: 'You can't help the dead,' he said, vaguely surprised at his own speaking. Like eye focussing, the speech must be a reflex.

'You're not dead. You're as alive as I am.'

Then words tumbled from him; more than in all the days since Relay. 'True. The illusion of self-awareness. Happy automatons, running on trivial programs. I'll bet you never guess. From the inside, how can you? From the outside, from Old One's view—' He looked away from her, dizzy with a doubled vision.

Ravna drifted closer till her face was just centimeters from his. She floated free, except for one foot tucked into the floor. 'Dear Pham, you are wrong. You've been at the Bottom, and at the Top, but never in between . . . "The illusion of self awareness"? That's a commonplace of any practical philosophy in the Beyond. It has some beautiful consequences, and some scary ones. All you know are the scary ones. Think: the illusion must apply just as surely to the Powers.'

'No. He could *make* devices like you and I.'

'Being dead is a choice, Pham.' She reached out to pass her hand down his shoulder and arm. He had a typical o-gee change of perspective; 'down' seemed to rotate sideways, and he was looking up at her. Suddenly he was aware of his splotchy beard, his tangled hair floating all about. He looked up at Ravna, remembering everything he'd thought about her. Back on Relay she'd seemed bright; maybe not smarter than he, but as smart as most competitors of the Qeng Ho. But there were other memories, how Old One had seen her. As usual, His memories were overwhelming. As usual, they were mostly unintelligible. Even His emotions were hard to interpret. But . . . He had thought of Ravna a little like . . . a favored dog. Old One could see right through her. Ravna Bergsndot was a little manipulative; He had been pleased/amused(?) by that fact. But behind her talk and argument, He'd seen a great deal of . . . 'goodness' might be the human word. Old One had wished her well. *In the end, He had even tried to help.* Insight flitted past him, too fast to catch. Ravna was talking again:

'What happened to you is terrible enough, Pham, but it's happened to others. I've read of cases. Even the Powers are not immortal. Sometimes they fight among themselves, and someone gets killed. Sometimes, one commits suicide. There's a star system, Gods' Doom it's called in the story: A million years ago, it was in the Transcend. It was visited by a party of the Powers. There was a Zone surge. Suddenly the system was twenty light-years deep in the Beyond. That's about the biggest surge there is firm record of. The Powers at God's Doom didn't have a chance. They all died, some to rot and rusted ruin . . . others to the level of mere human minds.'

'W-what became of those?'

She hesitated, took one of his hands between hers. 'You can look it up. The point is, it happens. To the victims, it's the end of the world. But from *our* side, the human side . . . Well, the human Pham Nuwen was lucky; Greenstalk says the failure of Old One's connections didn't do gross organic damage. Maybe there's subtle damage; sometimes the remnants just destroy themselves, whatever is left.'

Pham felt tears leaking from his eyes. And knew that part of the deadness inside had been grief for His own death. 'Subtle damage!' He shook his head and the tears drifted into the air. 'My head is stuffed with Him, with His memories.' Memories? They towered over everything else. *Yet he could not understand them.* He could not understand the details. He could not even understand the emotions, except as inane simplifications – joy, laughter, wonder, fear and icy-steel determination. Now he was lost in those memories, wandering like an idiot in a cathedral. Not understanding, cowering before icons.

She pivoted around their clasped hands. After a moment her knee bumped gently against his. 'You're still human, you still have your own—', her own voice broke as she saw the look in his eyes.

'My own memories.' Scattered amid the unintelligible he would stumble on: Himself at five years, sitting on the straw in the great hall, alert for the appearance of any adult; royals were not supposed to play in the filth. Ten years later, making love to Cindi for the first time. A year after that, seeing his first flying machine, the orbital ferry that landed on his father's parade field. The decades aspace. 'Yes, the Qeng Ho. Pham Nuwen, the great

Trader of the Slowness. All the memories are still there. And for all I know, it's all the Old One's lie, an afternoon's fraud to fool the Relayers.'

Ravna bit her lip, but didn't say anything. She was too honest to lie, even now.

He reached with his free hand to brush her hair away from her face. 'I know you said that too, Rav. Don't feel bad: I would have suspected by now anyway.'

'Yeah,' she said softly. Then she was looking him straight in the eye. 'But know this. One human to another: You *are* a human now. And there could have been a Qeng Ho, and you could have been exactly what you remember. And whatever the past, you could be great in the future.'

Ghostly echoes, more than memory and less than reason: For an instant he saw her with wiser eyes. *She loves you, foolish one.* Almost laughter, kindly laughter.

He slid his arms around her, drawing her tight against him. She was so real. He felt her slip her leg between his. To laugh. Like heart massage, unthinking reflex bringing a mind back to life. So foolish, so trivial, but, 'I – I want to come back.' The words came out strangled in sobs. 'There's so much inside me now, so much I can't understand. I'm lost inside my own head.'

She didn't say anything, probably couldn't even understand his speech. For a moment all he knew was the feel of her in his arms, hugging back. *Oh please, I do want to come back.*

Making it on the bridge of a starship was something Ravna had never done before. But then she'd never had her own starship before, either. *They don't call this a bottom-lugger for nothing.* In the excitement, Pham lost his tiedown. They floated free, occasionally bumping into walls and discarded clothing, or drifting through tears. After many minutes, they ended up with their heads just a few centimeters off the floor, the rest of them angled off toward the ceiling. She was vaguely aware that her pants were flying like a banner from where they had caught on her ankle. The affair wasn't quite the stuff of romance fiction. For one thing, floating free you just couldn't get any leverage. For another . . . Pham leaned back from her, relaxing his grip on her back. She brushed aside his red hair and looked into bloodshot eyes. 'You know,' he said shakily, 'I never guessed I could cry so hard my face hurt.'

She smiled back. 'You've led a charmed life then.' She arched her back against his hands, then drew him gently close. They floated in silence for several minutes, their bodies relaxing into each other's curves, sensing nothing but each other.

Then: 'Thank you, Ravna.'

'. . . my pleasure,' her voice came dreamy serious, and she hugged him tighter. Strange, all the things he had been to her, some frightening, some endearing, some enraging. And some she couldn't have admitted – even to herself – till now. For the first time since the fall of Relay, she felt real hope. A silly physical reaction maybe . . . but maybe not. Here in her arms was a guy who might be the equal of any story book adventurer, and more: someone who had been part of a Power.

'Pham . . . what do you think really happened back on Relay? Why was Old One murdered?'

Pham's chuckle seemed unforced, but his arms stiffened around her. 'You're asking me? I was dying at the time, remember . . . No, that's wrong. Old One, *He* was dying at the time.' He was silent for a minute. The bridge turned slowly around them, silent views on the stars beyond. 'My godself was in pain, I know that. He was desperate, panicked . . . But He was also trying to do something to me before He died.' His voice went soft, wondering. 'Yes. It was like I was some cheap piece of luggage, and He was stuffing me with every piece of crap that he could move. You know, ten kilos in a nine kilo sack. He knew it was hurting me – I was part of Him, after all – but that didn't matter.' He twisted back from her, his face getting a little wild again. 'I'm not a sadist; I don't believe He was either I—'

Ravna shook her head. 'I . . . I think he was downloading.'

Pham was silent an instant, trying to fit the idea into his situation. 'That doesn't make sense. There's not *room* in me to be superhuman.' Fear chased hope in tight circles.

'No, no, wait. You're right. Even if the dying Power figures reincarnation is possible, there's not enough space in a normal brain to store much. But Old One was trying for something else . . . Remember how I begged Him to help with our trip to the Bottom?'

'Yes. I – He – was sympathetic, the way you might be with animals that are confronting some new predator. He never considered that the Perversion might be a threat to him, not until—'

'Right. Not until he was under attack. That was a complete surprise to the Powers; suddenly the Perversion was more than a curious problem for underminds. *Then* Old One really did try to help. He jammed plans and automation down into you. He jammed so much, you nearly died, so much you can't make sense of it. I've read about things like that in Applied Theology—' as much legend as fact. 'Godshatter, it's called.'

'Godshatter?' He seemed to play with the word, wondering. 'What a strange name. I remember His panic. But if He was doing what you say, why didn't He just *tell* me? And if I'm filled with good advice, how come all I see inside is . . .' his gaze became a little like days past, 'darkness . . . dark statues with sharp edges, crowding.'

Again a long silence. But now she could almost feel Pham thinking. His arms twitched tight and an occasional shudder swept his body. 'Yes . . . yes. Lots of things fit. Most of it I still don't understand, never will. Old One discovered something right there at the end.' His arms tightened again, and he buried his face against her neck. 'It was a very . . . personal . . . sort of murder the Perversion committed on Him. Even dying, Old One learned.' More silence. 'The Perversion is something very old, Ravna. Probably billions of years. A threat Old One could only theorize before it actually killed Him. But . . .'

One minute. Two. Yet Pham did not continue. 'Don't worry, Pham. Give it time.'

'Yeah.' He backed off far enough to look her square in the face. 'But I know this much now: Old One did this for a reason. We *aren't* on a fool's chase. There's something on the Bottom, in that Straumer ship, that Old One thought could make a difference.'

He ran his hand lightly across her face, and his smile was sad where there should have been joy. 'But don't you see, Ravna? If you're right, today may be the most human I'll ever be. I'm full of Old One's download, this godshatter. Most of it I'll never consciously understand, but if things work properly, it will eventually come exploding out. His remote device; His robot at the Bottom of the Beyond.'

No! But she made herself shrug. 'Maybe. But you're human, and we're working for the same things . . . and I'm not letting you go.'

Ravna had known that 'jumpstarting' technology must be a topic in the ship's library. It turned out the subject was a major academic specialty. Besides ten thousand case studies, there were customizing programs and lots of very dull-looking theory. Though the 'rediscovery problem' was trivial in the Beyond, down in the Slow Zone almost every conceivable combination of events had happened. Civilizations in the Slowness could not last more than a few thousand years. Their collapse was sometimes a short eclipse, a few decades spent recovering from war or atmosphere-bashing. Others drove themselves back to medievalism. And of course, most races eventually exterminated themselves, at least within their single solar system. Those that didn't exterminate themselves (and even a few of those that did) eventually struggled back to their original heights.

The study of these variations was called the Applied History of Technology. Unfortunately for both academicians and the civilizations in the Slow Zone, true applications were a bit rare: The events of the case studies were centuries old before news of them reached the Beyond, and few researchers were willing to do field work in the Slow Zone, where finding and conducting a single experiment could cost them much of their lives. In any case, it was a nice hobby for millions of university departments. One of the favorite games was to devise minimal paths from a given level of technology back to the highest level that could be supported in the Slowness. The details depended on many things, including the initial level of primitiveness, the amount of residual scientific awareness (or tolerance), and the physical nature of the race. The historians' theories were captured in programs whose inputs were facts about the civilization's plight and the desired results, and whose outputs were the steps that would most quickly produce those results.

Two days later the four of them were back on the *OOB*'s bridge. *And this time we're all talking.* 'So we must decide what inventions to shoot for, something that will defend the Hidden Island Kingdom—'

'—and something "Mister Steel" can make in less than one hundred days,' said Blueshell. He had spent most of the last two days fiddling with the development programs in *OOB*'s library.

'I still say guns and radios,' said Pham.

Firepower and communications. Ravna grinned at him. Pham's human memories alone would be enough to save the kids on Tines' World. He hadn't talked any more of Old One's plans. Old One's plans . . . in Ravna's mind those were something like fate, perhaps good, perhaps terrible, but unknown for now. *And even fate can be weaseled.* 'How about it Blueshell?' she said. 'Is radio something they can produce quickly, from a standing start?' On Nyjora, radio had come almost contemporary with orbital flight – a good century into the renaissance.

'Indeed, my lady Ravna. There are simple tricks that are almost never noticed till a very high technology is attained. For instance, quantum torsion antennas can be built from silver and cobalt steel arrays, if the geometry is correct. Unfortunately, finding the proper geometry involves lots of theory and the ability to solve some large partial differential equations. There are many Slow Zoners who never discover the principle.'

'Okay,' said Pham. 'But there's still a translation problem. Jefri has probably heard the word "cobalt" before, but how can he describe it to people who don't have the referent? Without knowing a lot more about their world, we couldn't even describe how to find cobalt-bearing ore.'

'That will slow things down,' Blueshell admitted. 'But the program accounts for it. Mr Steel seems to understand the concept of experimentation. For cobalt, we can provide him with a tree of experiments based on descriptions of likely ores and appropriate chemical tests.'

'It's not quite that simple,' said Greenstalk. 'Some of the chemical tests themselves involve search/test trees. And there are other experiments needed to check toxicity. We know far less about the pack creatures than is usual with this program.'

Pham smiled. 'I hope these creatures are properly grateful; I never heard of "quantum torsional antennas." The Tines are ending up with comm gear that Qeng Ho never had.'

But the gift could be made. The question was, could it be done in time to save Jefri and his ship from the Woodcarvers? The four of them ran the program again and again. They knew so little about the pack creatures themselves. The Hidden Island Kingdom appeared fairly flexible. *If* they were willing to go all out to follow the directions, and *if* they had good luck in finding nearby sources for critical materials, then it looked like they might have limited supplies of firearms and radios inside of one hundred days. On the other hand, if the packs of Hidden Island ended up chasing down some worst-case branches of the search trees, things might stretch out to a few years.

Ravna found it hard to accept that no matter what the four of them did, saving Jefri from the Woodcarvers would be partly a matter of luck. *Sigh*. In the end, she took the best scheme they could produce, translated it into Samnorsk, and sent it down.

23

Steel had always admired military architecture. Now he was adding a new chapter to the book, building a castle that protected against the *sky* as well as the land around. By now the boxy 'ship' on stilts was known across the continent. Before another summer passed, there would be enemy armies here, trying to take – or at least destroy – the prize that had come to him. Far more deadly: the Star People would be here. He must be ready.

Steel inspected the work almost every day now. The stone replacement for the palisade was in place all across the south perimeter. On the cliffside, overlooking Hidden Island, his new den was almost complete . . . *had been complete for some time*, a part of him grumbled. He really should move over here; the safety of Hidden Island was fast becoming illusion. Starship Hill was already the center of the Movement – and that wasn't just propaganda. What the Flenser embassies abroad called 'the oracle on Starship Hill' was more than a glib liar could dream. Whoever stood nearest that oracle would ultimately rule, no matter how clever Steel might be otherwise. He had already transferred or exectued several attendants, packs who seemed just a little *too* friendly with Amdijefri.

Starship Hill: When the aliens landed, it had been heather and rock. Through the winter, there'd been a palisade and a wooden shelter. But now construction had resumed on the castle, the crown whose jewel was the starship. Soon this hill would be the capital of the continent and the world. And after that . . . Steel looked into the blue depths of the sky. How much further his rule extended would depend on saying just the right thing, on building this castle in a very special way. *Enough dreaming.* Lord Steel pulled himself together and descended from the new wall along fresh-cut stone stairs. The yard within was twelve acres, mostly mud. The muck was cold on his paws, but the snow and slush was confined to dwindling piles away from the work routes. Spring was well-advanced, and the sun was warm in the chill air. He could see for miles, out over Hidden Island all the way to the Ocean, and down the coast along the fjord country. Steel walked the last hundred yards up the hill to the starship. His guards paced him on either side, with Shreck bringing up the rear. There was enough room that the workers didn't have to back away – and he had given orders that no one was to stop because of his presence. That was partly to maintain the fraud with Amdijefri, and partly because the Movement needed this fortress soon. Just how soon was a question that gnawed.

Steel was still looking in all directions, but his attention was where it should be now, on the construction work. The yard was piled with cut stone and construction timbers. Now that the ground was thawing, the foundations for the inner wall were being dug. Where it was still hard, Steel's engineers were injecting boiling water. Steam rose from the holes, obscuring the windlasses and the diggers below. The place was louder than a battlefield: windlasses creaking, blades hacking at dirt, leaders shouting to work teams. It was also as crowded as close combat, though not nearly so chaotic.

Steel watched a digger pack at the bottom of one of the trenches. There were thirty members, so close to each other their shoulders sometimes touched. It was an enormous mob, but there was nothing of an orgy about the association. Even before Woodcarver, construction and factory guilds had been doing this sort of thing: The thirty-member pack below was probably not as bright as a threesome. The front rank of ten swung mattocks in unison, carving steadily into the wall of dirt. When their heads and mattocks were extended high, the ten members behind them darted forward to scoop back the dirt and rocks that had just been freed. Behind them, a third tier of members hauled the dirt from the pit. Making it work was a complicated bit of timing – the rock and dirt was not homogeneous – but it was well within the mental ability of the pack. They could go on like this for hours, shifting first and second ranks every few minutes. In years past, the guilds jealously guarded the secret of each special melding. After a hard day's work, such a team would split into normally intelligent packs – each going home very well paid. Steel smiled to himself. Woodcarver had improved on the old guild tricks, but Flenser had provided an essential refinement (actually a borrowing from the Tropics). Why let the team break up at the end of a work shift? Flenser work teams stayed together indefinitely, housed in barracks so small they could never recover their separate pack minds. It worked well. After a year or two, and with proper culling, the original packs in such teams were dull things that scarcely wanted to break away.

For a moment Steel watched the cut stone being lowered into the new hole and mortared into place. Then he nodded at the whitejackets in charge and walked on. The foundation holes continued right up to the walls of the starship compound. This was the trickiest construction of all, the part that would turn the castle into a beautiful snare. A little more information via Amdijefri and he would know just what to build.

The door to the starship compound was open just now, and a whitejackets was sitting back to back in the opening. That guard heard the noise an instant before Steel: two of its members broke ranks to look around the side of the compound. Almost inaudibly, there came high screams, then honking attack calls. The whitejackets leaped from the stairs and raced around the building. Steel and his guards weren't far behind.

He skidded to a stop at the foundation trench on the far side of the ship. The immediate source of the racket was obvious. Three packs of white-jackets were putting a team's talker to the question. They had separated out the verbal member and were beating it with truncheon whips. This close, the mental screams were almost as loud as the shouting. The rest of the digger team was coming out of the trench, breaking into functional packs and attacking the whitejackets with their mattocks. How could things get so bloody screwed up? He could guess. These inner foundations were to contain the most secret tunnels of the entire castle, and the even more secret devices he planned to use against the Two-Legs. Of course, all of the workers on such sensitive areas would be disposed of after the job was done. Stupid though they were, maybe they had guessed their fate.

Under other circumstances, Steel might have backed off and simply watched. Failures like this could be enlightening; they let him identify the weaknesses in his subordinates, who was too bad (and too good) to continue in their jobs. *This time was different.* Amdi and Jefri were aboard the starship. There was no view through the wooden walls, and surely there was another whitejackets on guard within, but . . . even as he lunged forward, shouting to his servants, Steel's back-looking member caught sight of Jefri coming out of the compound. Two of the pups were on his shoulders, the rest of Amdi spilling out around him.

'*Stay back!*' he yelled at them, and in his sparse Samnorsk, '*Danger! Stay back!*' Amdi paused, but the Two-Legs kept coming. Two soldier packs scattered out of his way. They had standing orders: *never* touch the alien. Another second and the careful work of a year would be destroyed. Another second and Steel might lose the world – *all on account of stupidity and bad luck.*

But even as his back members were shouting at the Two-Legs, his forward ones leaped atop a pile of stone. He pointed at the teams coming out of the trench. 'Kill the invaders!'

His personal guards moved close around him as Shreck and several troopers streamed by. Steel's consciousness sagged in the bloody noise. This was not the controlled mayhem of experiments beneath Hidden Island. This was random death flying in all directions: arrows, spears, mattocks. Members of the digger team ran about, flailing and crying. They never had a chance, but they killed a number of others in their dying.

Steel backed away from the melee, toward Jefri. The Two-Legs was still running toward him. Amdi followed, shouting in Samnorsk. A single mindless team member, a single misaimed arrow, and the Two-Legs would die and all would be lost. Never in his life had Steel felt such panic for the safety of another. He raced to the human, surrounding him. The Two-Legs fell to his knees and grabbed Steel by a neck. Only a lifetime of discipline kept Steel from slashing back: the alien wasn't attacking, he was *hugging*.

The digger team was almost all dead now, and Shreck had pushed the surviving members too far away to be a threat. Steel's guards were securely around him only five or ten yards away. Amdi was all clumped together, cowering in the mind noise, but still shouting to Jefri. Steel tried to untangle himself from the human, but Jefri just grabbed one neck after another, sometimes two at a time. He was making burbling noises that didn't sound like Samnorsk. Steel trembled under the assault. *Don't show the revulsion.* The human would not recognize it, but Amdi might. Jefri had done this before, and Steel had taken advantage even though it cost him. The mantis child needed physical contact; it was the basis for the relationship between Amdi and Jefri. Similar trust must come from letting this thing touch him. Steel slid a head and neck across the creature's back the way he had seen parents do with pups down in the dungeon laboratories. Jefri hugged him harder, and swept his long articulate paws across Steel's pelt. Revulsion aside, it was a very strange experience. Ordinarily such close contact with another intelligent being could only come in battle or in sex – and in either case, there wasn't much room for rational thought. But with this human – well, the creature responded with obvious intelligence – but there wasn't a trace of mind noise. You could think and feel both at the same time. Steel bit down on a lip, trying to stifle his shivering. It was . . . it was like having sex with a corpse.

Finally Jefri stepped back, holding his hand up. He said something very fast, and Amdi said, 'Oh Lord Steel, you're hurt. See the blood.' There was red on the human's paw; Steel looked at himself. Sure enough, one rump had taken a nick. He hadn't even felt it in all the excitement. Steel backed away from the mantis and said to Amdi, 'It's nothing. Are you and Jefri unhurt?'

There was a rattling exchange between the two children, almost unintelligible to Steel. 'We're fine. Thank you for protecting us.'

Fast thinking was something that Flenser had carved into Steel with knives: 'Yes. But it never should have happened. The Woodcarvers disguised themselves as workers. I think they've been at this for days waiting for a chance at you. When we guessed the fraud, it was almost too late . . . You really should have stayed inside when you heard the fighting.'

Amdi hung his heads ashamedly, and translated to Jefri. 'We're sorry. We got excited, and t-then we thought you might get hurt.'

Steel made comforting noises. At the same time, two of him looked around at the carnage. Where was the whitejackets that had deserted the stairs right at the beginning? That pack would pay – His line of thought crashed to a halt as he noticed: *Tyrathect.* The Flenser Fragment was watching from the meeting hall. Now that he thought about it, he'd been watching since right after the battle began. To others his posture might seem impassive, but Steel could see the grim amusement in the Fragment's expression. He nodded briefly at the other, but inside Steel cringed; he had been so close to losing everything . . . *and the Flenser had noticed.*

'Well let's get you two back to Hidden Island.' He signaled to the keepers that had come up behind the starship.

'Not yet, Lord Steel!' said Amdi. 'We just got here. A reply from Ravna should arrive very soon.'

Teeth grated, but out of sight of the children. 'Yes, please do stay. But we'll all be more careful now, right?'

'Yes, yes!' Amdi explained to the human. Steel stood forelegs-on-shoulders and patted Jefri on the head.

Steel had Shreck take the children back into the compound. Till they were out of sight, all his members looked on with an expression of pride and affection. Then he turned and walked across the pinkish mud. Where was that stupid whitejackets?

The meeting hall on Starship Hill was a small, temporary thing. It had been good enough to keep the cold out during the winter, but for a conference of more man three people it was a real madhouse. Steel stomped past the Flenser Fragment and collected himself on the loft with the best view of the construction work. After a polite moment, Tyrathect entered and climbed to the facing loft.

But all the decorum was an act for the groundlings outside; now Flenser's soft laughter hissed across the air to him, just loud enough for him to hear. 'Dear Steel. Sometimes I wonder if you are truly my student . . . or perhaps some changeling inserted after my departure. Are you *trying* to screw us up?'

Steel glared back. He was sure there was no uneasiness in his posture, all that was held within. 'Accidents happen. The incompetent will be culled.'

'Quite so. But that appears to be your response to *all* problems. If you hadn't been so bent on silencing the digger teams, they might not have rioted . . . and you would have had one less "accident." '

'The flaw was in their guessing. Such executions are a necessary part of military construction.'

'Oh? You really think I had to kill all those who built the halls under Hidden Island?'

'*What?* You mean you didn't? How—?'

The Flenser Fragment smiled the old, fanged smile. 'Think on it, Steel. An exercise.'

Steel arranged his notes on the desk and pretended to study them. Then all of him looked back at the other pack. 'Tyrathect. I honor you because of the Flenser in you. But remember: You survive on my sufferance. You are not the Flenser-in-Waiting.' The news had come late last fall, just before winter closed the last pass over the Icefangs: The packs bearing the rest of the Master hadn't made it out of Parliament Bowl. The fullness of Flenser was gone forever. That had been an indescribable relief to Steel, and for a time afterward the Fragment had been quite tractable. 'Not one of my lieutenants would blink if I killed all of you – even the Flenser members.' *And I'll do it, if you push me hard enough, I swear I will.*

'Of course, dear Steel. You command.'

For an instant the other's fear showed through. *Remember*, Steel thought to himself, *always remember: This is just a fragment of the Master. Most of it is a little school teacher, not the Great Teacher with a Knife*. True, its two Flenser members totally dominated the pack. The spirit of the Master was right here in this room, but gentled. Tyrathect could be managed, and the power of the Master used for Steel's ends.

'Good,' Steel said smoothly. 'As long as you understand this, you can be of great use to the Movement. In particular,' he riffled through the papers, 'I want to review the Visitor situation with you.' *I want some advice.*

'Yes.'

'We've convinced "Ravna" that her precious Jefri is in imminent danger. Amdijefri has told her about all the Woodcarver attacks and how we fear an overwhelming assault.'

'And that may really happen.'

'Yes. Woodcarver really *is* planning an attack, and she has her own source of "magical" help. We have something much better.' He tapped the papers; the advice had been coming down since early winter. He remembered when Amdijefri had brought in the first pages, pages of numerical tables, of directions and diagrams, all drawn in neat but childish style. Steel and the Fragment had spent days trying to understand. Some of the references were obvious. The Visitor's recipes required silver and gold in quantities that would otherwise finance a war. But what was this 'liquid silver'? Tyrathect had recognized it; the Master had used such a thing in his labs in the Republic. Eventually they acquired the amount specified. But many of the ingredients were given only as methods for creating them. Steel remembered the Fragment musing over those, scheming against nature as if it were just another foe. The recipes of mystics were full of 'horn of squid' and 'frozen moonlight.' The directions from Ravna were sometimes even stranger. There were directions within directions, long detours spent in testing common materials to decide which really fit the greater plan. Building, testing, building. It was like the Master's own method but without the dead ends.

Some of it made sense early on. They would have the explosives and guns that Woodcarver thought were her secret weapons. But so much was still unintelligible – and it never got easier.

Steel and the Fragment worked through the afternoon, planning how to set up the latest tests, deciding where to search for the new ingredients that Ravna demanded.

Tyrathect leaned back, hissing a wondering sigh. 'Stage built upon stage. And soon we'll have our own *radios*. Old Woodcarver won't have a chance . . . You are right, Steel. With this you can rule the world. Imagine knowing instantly what is happening in the Republic's Capital and being able to coordinate armies around that knowledge. The Movement will be the Mind of God.' That was an old slogan, and now it could be true. 'I salute you, Steel. You have a grasp worthy of the Movement.' Was there the Teacher's contempt in his smile? '*Radio* and *guns* can give us the world. But clearly these are crumbs from the Visitors' table. When do they arrive?'

'Between one hundred and one hundred twenty days from now; Ravna has revised her estimate again. Apparently even the Two-Legs have problems flying between the stars.'

'So we have that long to enjoy the Movement's triumph. And then we are nothing, less than savages. It might have been safer to forego the gifts, and persuade the Visitors that there is nothing here worth rescuing.'

Steel looked out through the window slits that cut horizontally between timbers. He could see part of the starship compound, and the castle foundations, and beyond that the islands of the fjord country. He was suddenly more confident, more *at peace*, than he'd been in a long time. It felt right to reveal his dream. 'You really don't see it, do you Tyrathect? I wonder if the whole Master would understand, or whether I have exceeded him, too. In the beginning, we had no choice. The Starship was automatically sending some sort of signal to Ravna. We could have destroyed it; maybe Ravna would have lost interest . . . *And maybe not*, in which case we would be taken like a fish gilled from a stream. Perhaps I took the greater risk, but if I win, the prize will be far more than you imagine.' The Fragment was watching him, heads cocked. 'I've studied these humans, Jefri and – through my spies – the one down at Woodcarvers. Their race may be older than ours, and the tricks they've learned make them seem all-powerful. But the race is flawed. As singletons, they work with handicaps we can scarcely imagine. If I can use those weaknesses . . .

'You know the average Tines cares for its pups. We've manipulated parental sentiments often enough. Imagine how it must be for the humans. To them, a single pup is also an entire child. Think of the leverage that gives us.'

'You're seriously betting everything on this? Ravna isn't even Jefri's parent.'

Steel made an irritated gesture. 'You haven't seen all of Amdi's translations.' Innocent Amdi, the perfect spy. 'But you're right, saving the one child is not the main reason for this Visit. I've tried to find out their real motive. There are one hundred fifty-one children in some kind of deathly stupor, all stacked up in coffins within the ship. The Visitors are desperate to save the children, but there's something else they want. They never quite talk about it . . . I think it's in the machinery of the ship itself.'

'For all we know the children are a brood force, part of an invasion.'

That was an old fear and – after watching Amdijefri – Steel saw no chance of it. There could be other traps, but, 'If the Visitors are lying to us, then there is really nothing we can do to win. We'll be hunted animals; maybe generations from now we'll learn their tricks, but it will be the end of *us*. On the other hand, we have good reason to believe that the Two-Legs are weak, and whatever their goals, they do not involve us directly. You were there the day of the landing, much closer than I. You saw how easy it was to ambush them, even though their ship is impregnable and their single weapon a match for a small army. It is obvious that they do not consider us a threat. No matter how powerful their tools, their real fears are elsewhere. *And in the Starship, we have something they need.*

'Look at the foundations of our new castle, Tyrathect. I've told Amdijefri that it is to protect the Starship against Woodcarver. It will do that – later in the Summer when I shatter Woodcarver upon its ramparts. But see the foundations of the curtain around the Starship. By the time our Visitors arrive, the ship will be envaulted. I've done some quiet tests on its hull. It can be breached; a few dozen tons of stone falling on it would quite nicely crush it. But Ravna is not to worry; this is all for the protection of her prize. And there will be an open courtyard nearby, surrounded by strangely high walls. I've asked Jefri to get Ravna's help on this. The courtyard will be just large enough to enclose Ravna's ship, protecting it, too.

'There are many details still to be settled. We must make the tools Ravna describes. We must arrange the demise of Woodcarver, well before the Visitors arrive. I need your help in all those things, and I expect to receive it. In the end, if the Visitors are treacherous, we will make the best stand that can be. And if they are not . . . well I think you'll agree that my reach has at least matched my teacher's.'

For once, the Flenser Fragment had no reply.

The ship's control cabin was Jefri and Amdi's favorite place in all of Lord Steel's Domain. Being here could still make Jefri very sad, but now the good memories seemed the stronger . . . and here was the best hope for the future. Amdi was still entranced by the window displays – even if the views were all of wooden walls. By their second visit they had already come to regard the place as their private kingdom, like Jefri's treehouse back on Straum. And in fact the cabin was much too small to hold more than a single pack. Usually a member of their bodyguard would sit just inside the entrance to the main hold, but even that seemed to be uncomfortable duty. This was a place where they were important.

For all their rambunctiousness, Amdi and Jefri realized the trust that Lord Steel and Ravna were placing in them. The two kids might race around out-of-doors, driving their guards to distraction, but the equipment in this command cabin was to be treated as cautiously as when Mom and

Dad were here. In some ways, there was not much left in the ship. The datasets were destroyed; Jefri's parents had them outside when Woodcarver attacked. During the winter, Mr Steel had carried out most of the loose items to study. The coldsleep boxes were now safe in cool chambers nearby. Every day Amdijefri inspected the boxes, looked at each familiar face, checked the diag displays. No sleeper had died since the ambush.

What was left on the ship was hard-fastened to the hull. Jefri had pointed out the control boards and status elements that managed the container shell's rocket; they stayed strictly away from those.

Mr Steel's quilting shrouded the walls. Jefri's folks' baggage and sleeping bags and exercisers were gone, but there were still the acc webbing and hard-fastened equipment. And over the months, Amdijefri had brought in paper and pens and blankets and other junk. There was always a light breeze from the fans sweeping through the cabin.

It was a happy place, strangely carefree even with all the memories it brought. This was where they would save the Tines and all the sleepers. And this was the only place in the world where Amdijefri could talk to another human being. In some ways the means of talking seemed as medieval as Lord Steel's castle: They had one flat display – no depth, no color, no *pictures*. All they could coax from it were alphanumerics. But it was connected to the ship's ultrawave comm, and that was still programmed to track their rescuers. There was no voice recognition attached to the display; Jefri had almost panicked before he realized that the lower part of the screen worked as a keyboard. It was a laborious job typing in every letter of every word – though Amdi had gotten pretty good at it, using two noses to peck at the keys. And nowadays he could read Samnorsk even better than Jefri.

Amdijefri spent many afternoons here. If there was a message waiting from the previous day, they would bring it up page by page and Amdi would copy and translate it. Then they would enter the questions and answers that Mr Steel had talked to them about. Then there was a lot of waiting. Even if Ravna was watching at the other end, it could take several hours to get a reply. But the link was so much better than during the winter; they could almost feel Ravna getting close. The unofficial conversations with her were often the high point of their day.

So far, *this* day had been quite different. After the false workers attacked, Amdijefri had the shakes for about half an hour. Mr Steel had been wounded trying to protect them. Maybe there was nowhere that was safe. They messed with the outside displays, trying to peek through cracks in the rough planking of the compound's walls.

'If we'd been able to see out, we could have warned Mr Steel,' said Jefri.

'We should ask him to put some holes in the walls. We could be like sentries.'

They batted the idea around a bit. Then the latest message started coming in from the rescue ship. Jefri jumped into the acc webbing by the display. This was his dad's old spot, and there was plenty of room. Two of Amdi slid in beside him. Another member hopped on the armrest and braced its paws on Jefri's shoulders. Its slender neck extended toward the screen to get a good view. The rest scrambled to arrange paper and pens. It was easy to play back messages, but Amdijefri got a certain thrill out of seeing the stuff coming down 'live.'

There was the initial header stuff – that wasn't so interesting after about the thousandth time you saw it – then Ravna's actual words. Only this time it was just tabular data, something to support the radio design.

'Nuts. It's numbers,' said Jefri.

'Numbers!' said Amdi. He climbed a free member onto the boy's lap. It stuck its nose close to the screen, cross-checking what the one by Jefri's shoulder was seeing. The four on the floor were busy scratching away, translating the decimal digits on the screen into the X's and O's and I's and deltas of Tines' base four notation. Almost from the beginning Jefri had realized that Amdi was really *good* at math. Jefri wasn't envious. Amdi said that hardly any of the Tines were that good, either; Amdi was a very special pack. Jefri was proud that he had such a neat friend. Mom and Dad would have liked Amdi. Still . . . Jefri sighed, and relaxed in the webbing. This number stuff was happening more and more often. Mom had read him a story once, 'Lost in the Slow Zone,' about how some marooned explorers brought civilization to a lost colony. In *that*, the heros just collected the right materials and built what they needed. There had been no talk of precision or ratios or design.

He looked away from the screen, and petted the two of Amdi that were sitting beside him. One of them wriggled under his hand. Their whole bodies hummed back at him. Their eyes were closed. If Jefri didn't know better, he would have assumed they were asleep. These were the parts of Amdi that specialized in talking.

'Anything interesting?' Jefri said after a while. The one on his left opened its eyes and looked at him.

'This is that bandwidth idea Ravna was talking about. If we don't make things just right, we'll just get *clicks* and *clacks*.'

'Oh, right.' Jefri knew that the initial reinventions of radio were usually not good for much more than Morse code. Ravna seemed to think they could jump that stage. 'What do you think Ravna is like?'

'What?' The scritching of pens on paper stopped for an instant; he had all of Amdi's attention, even though they'd talked of this before. 'Well, like you . . . only bigger and older?'

'Yeah, but—' Jefri knew Ravna was from Sjandra Kei. She was a grownup, somewhere older than Johanna and younger than Mom. *What exactly does she look like?* 'I mean, she's coming all this way just to rescue us and finish what Mom and Dad were trying to do. She must really be a great person.'

The scritching stopped again, and the display scrolled heedlessly on. They would have to reply it. 'Yes,' Amdi said after a moment. 'She – she must be a lot like Mr Steel. It will be nice to meet someone I can hug, the way you do Mr Steel.'

Jefri was a little miffed by that. 'Well *wait*, you can hug me!'

The parts of Amdi next to him purred loudly. 'I know. But I mean someone that's a grownup . . . like a parent.'

'Yeah.'

They got the tables translated and checked in about an hour. Then it was time to send up the latest things that Mr Steel was asking about. There were about four pages, all neatly printed in Samnorsk by Amdi. Usually he liked to do the typing, too, all bunched up over the keyboard and display. Today he wasn't interested. He lay all over Jefri, but didn't pay any special attention to checking what was being keyed in. Every so often Jefri felt a buzzing through his chest, or the screen mounting would make a strange sound – all in sympathy to the unhearable sounds that Amdi was making between his members. Jefri recognized the signs of deep thought.

He finished typing in the latest message, adding a few small questions of his own. Things like, 'How old are you and Pham? Are you married? What are Skroderiders like?'

Daylight had faded from the cracks in the walls. Soon the digger teams would be turning in their hoes and marching off to the barracks over the edge of the hill. Across the straits, the towers on Hidden Island would be golden in the mist, like something in a fairy tale. Their whitejackets would be calling Amdi and Jefri out for supper any minute now.

Two of Amdi jumped off the acc webbing and began chasing each other around the chair. 'I've been thinking! I've been thinking! Ravna's radio thing: why is it just for talking? She says all sound is just different frequencies of the same thing. But sound is all that thought is. If we could change some of the tables, and make the receivers and transmitters to cover my tympana, why couldn't I *think* over the radio?'

'I don't know.' Bandwidth was a familiar constraint on many everyday activities, though Jefri had only a vague notion of exactly what it was. He looked at the last of the tables, still displayed on the screen. He had a sudden insight, something that many adults in technical cultures never attain. 'I use these things all the time, but I don't know exactly how they work. We can follow these directions, but how would we know what to change?'

Amdi was getting all excited now, the way he did when he'd thought of some great prank. 'No, no, no. We don't have to understand everything.' Three more of him jumped to the floor; he waved random sheets of paper up at Jefri. 'Ravna doesn't know for sure how we make sound. The directions include options for making small changes. I've been thinking. I can see how the changes relate.' He paused and made a high-pitched squealing noise. 'Darn. I can't explain it exactly. But I think we can expand the tables, and that will change the machine in ob-obvious ways. And *then* . . .' Amdi was beside himself for a moment, and speechless. 'Oh Jefri, I wish you could be a pack, too! Imagine putting one of yourself each on a different mountain top, and then using radio to think. We could be as big as the world!'

Just then there was the sound of interpack gobbling from outside the cabin, and then the Samnorsk: 'Dinner time. We go now, Amdijefri. Okay?' It was Mr Shreck; he spoke a fair amount of Samnorsk, though not so well as Mr Steel. Amdijefri picked up the scattered sheets and carefully slipped them into the pockets on the back of Amdi's jackets. They powered down the display equipment and crawled into the main hold.

'Do you think Mr Steel will let us make the changes?'

'Maybe we should also send them back to Ravna.'

The whitejackets' member retreated from the hatch, and Amdijefri descended. A minute later they were out in the slanting sunlight. The two kids scarcely noticed; they were both caught up in Amdi's vision.

24

For Johanna, lots of things changed in the weeks after Scriber Jaquerama-phan died. Most were for the better, things that might never have happened but for the murder . . . and that made Johanna very sad.

She let Woodcarver live in her cabin and take the place of the helper pack. Apparently Woodcarver had wanted to do this from the beginning, but had been afraid of the human's anger. Now they kept the dataset in the cabin. There were never less than four packs of Vendacious's security surrounding the place, and there was talk of building barracks around it.

She saw the others during the day at meetings, and individually when they needed help with the dataset. Scrupilo, Vendacious, and Scarbutt – the 'Pilgrim' – all spoke fluent Samnorsk now, more than good enough so that she could see the character behind their inhuman forms: Scrupilo, prissy and very bright. Vendacious, as pompous as Scriber had ever seemed, but without the playfulness and imagination. Pilgrim Wickwrackscar. She felt a chill every time she saw his big, scarred one. It always sat in the back, hunching down to look nonthreatening. Pilgrim obviously knew how the sight affected her and tried not to offend, but even after Scriber's death she couldn't do more than tolerate that pack . . . And after all, there could be traitors in the Woodcarver castle. It was only Vendacious's theory that the murder had been a raid from outside. She kept a suspicious eye on Pilgrim.

At night, Woodcarver chased the other packs away. She huddled around the firepit, and asked the dataset questions that had no conceivable connection with fighting the Flenserists. Johanna sat with her and tried to explain things that Woodcarver didn't understand. It was strange. Woodcarver was something very like the Queen of these people. She had this enormous (primitive, uncomfortable, ugly – yet still enormous) castle. She had dozens of servants. Yet she spent most of each night in this little wood lodge with Johanna, and helped with the fire and the food at least as much as did the pack who had been here before.

So it was that Woodcarver became Johanna's second friend among the Tines. (Scriber was the first, though she hadn't known it till after he was dead.) Woodcarver was very smart and very strange. In some ways she was the smartest person Johanna had ever known, though that conclusion came slowly. She hadn't really been surprised when the Tines mastered Samnorsk quickly – that's the way it was in most adventures, and more to the point, they had the language learning programs in the dataset. But night after night Johanna watched Woodcarver play with the set. The pack showed no interest in the military tactics and chemistry that preoccupied them all during the day. Instead she read about the Slow Zone and the Beyond and the history of Straumli Realm. She had mastered nonlinear reading faster than any of the others. Sometimes Johanna would just sit and stare over her shoulders. The screen was split into windows, the main one scrolling much faster than Johanna could follow. A dozen times a minute, Woodcarver might come upon words she didn't recognize. Most were just unfamiliar Samnorsk: she'd tap a nose on the offending word and the definition would flicker briefly in a dictionary window. Other things were conceptual, and the new windows would lead the pack off into other fields, sometimes for just a few seconds, sometimes for many minutes – and sometimes the detour would become her new main path. In a way, she was everything that Scriber had wanted to be.

Many times she had questions the dataset couldn't really answer. She and Johanna would talk late into the night. What was a human family like? What had Straumli Realm thought to make at the High Lab? Johanna no longer thought of most packs as gangs of snake-necked rats. Deep past midnight, the dataset's screen was brighter than the gray light from the firepit. It painted the backs of Woodcarver in cheerful colors. The pack gathered round her, looking up, almost like children listening to a teacher.

But Woodcarver was no child. Almost from the first, she had seemed old. Those late night talks were beginning to teach Johanna about the Tines too. The pack said things she never did during the day. They were mostly things that must be obvious to other Tines, but never talked about. The human girl wondered if Woodcarver the Queen had anyone to confide in.

Only one of Woodcarver's members was physically old; two were scarcely more than puppies. It was the pattern of the pack that was half a thousand years old. And that showed. Woodcarver's soul was held together by little more than will power. The price of immortality had been inbreeding. The original stock had been healthy, but after six hundred years . . . One of her youngest members couldn't stop drooling; it was constantly patting a kerchief to its muzzle. Another had milky white in its eyes where there should have been deep brown. Woodcarver said it was stone blind, but healthy and her best talker. Her oldest member was visibly feeble; it was panting all the time. Unfortunately, Woodcarver said it was the most alert and creative of all. When it died . . .

Once she started looking for it, Johanna could see weakness in all of Woodcarver. Even the two healthiest members, strong and with plush fur, walked a little strangely compared to normal pack members. Was that due to spinal deformities? The two were also gaining weight, which wasn't helping the problem.

Johanna didn't learn this all at once. Woodcarver had told her about various Tinish affairs, and gradually her own story came out, too. She seemed glad to have someone to confide in, but Johanna saw little self-pity in her. Woodcarver had chosen this path – apparently it was perversion to some – and had beaten the odds for longer than any other pack in recorded history. She was more wistful than anything else that her luck had finally run out.

Tines architecture tended to extremes – grotesquely oversized, or too cramped for human use. Woodcarver's council chamber was at the large extreme; it was not a cozy place. You could get three hundred humans into the bowl-shaped cavity with room to spare. The separated balconies that ran around its upper circumference could have held another hundred more.

Johanna had been here often enough before; this was where most work was done with the dataset. Usually there was herself and Woodcarver and whoever else needed information. Today was different, not a day to consult the dataset at all: This was Johanna's first council meeting. There were twelve packs in the High Council, and they were all here. Every balcony contained a pack, and there were three on the floor. Johanna knew enough about Tines now to see that for all the empty space, the place was hideously crowded. There was the mind noise of fifteen packs. Even with all the padded tapestries, she felt an occasional buzzing in her head or through her hands from the railing.

Johanna stood with Woodcarver on the largest balcony. When they arrived, Vendacious was already down on the main floor, arranging diagrams. As the packs of the council came to their feet, he looked up and said something to Woodcarver. The Queen replied in Samnorsk: 'I know it will slow things down, but perhaps that's a good thing.' She made a human laughing sound.

Peregrine Wickwrackscar was standing on the next balcony over, just like some council pack. Strange. Johanna had not yet figured out why, but

Scarbutt seemed to be one of Woodcarver's favorites. 'Pilgrim, would you translate for Johanna?'

Pilgrim bobbed several heads. 'Is, is that okay, Johanna?'

The girl hesitated an instant, then nodded back. It made sense. Next to Woodcarver, Pilgrim spoke better Samnorsk than any of them. As Woodcarver sat down, she took the dataset from Johanna and popped it open. Johanna glanced at the figures on the screen. *She's made notes.* Her surprise didn't have a chance to register before the Queen was talking again – this time in the gobble sounds of interpack talk. After a second, Pilgrim began translating:

'Everyone please sit. Hunker down. This meeting is crowded enough as it is.' Johanna almost smiled. Pilgrim Wickwrackscar was pretty good. He was imitating Woodcarver's human voice perfectly. His translation even captured the wry authority of her speech.

After some snuffling around, only one or two heads were visible sticking up from each balcony. Most stray thought noise should now be caught in the padding around the balcony or absorbed by the quilted canopy that hung over the room. 'Vendacious, you may proceed.'

On the main floor, Vendacious stood and looked up in all directions. He started talking. 'Thank you,' came the translation, now imitating the security chief's tones. 'The Woodcarver asked me to call this meeting because of urgent developments in the North. Our sources there report that Steel is fortifying the region around Johanna's starship.'

Gobble gobble interruption. Scrupilo? 'That's not news. That's what our cannon and gunpowder are for.'

Vendacious: 'Yes, we've known of the plans for some time. Nevertheless the completion date has been advanced, and the final version will have walls a good deal thicker than we had figured. It also appears that once the enclosure is complete, Steel intends to break apart the starship and distribute its cargo through his various laboratories.'

For Johanna the words came like a kick in the stomach. Before there had been a chance: If they fought hard enough, they might recapture the ship. She might finish her parents' mission, perhaps even get rescued.

Pilgrim said something on his own account, translating: 'So what's the new deadline?'

'They're confident of having the main walls complete in just under ten tendays.'

Woodcarver bent a pair of noses to the keyboard, tapped in a note. At the same time she stuck a head over the railing and looked down at the security chief. 'I've noticed before that Steel tends to be a bit over-optimstic. Do you have an objective estimate?'

'Yes. The walls will be complete between eight and eleven tendays from now.'

Woodcarver: 'We had been counting on at least fifteen. Is this a response to our plans?'

On the floor below, Vendacious drew himself together. 'That was our first suspicion, your majesty. But . . . as you know, we have a number of very special sources of information . . . sources we shouldn't discuss even here.'

'What a braggart. Sometimes I wonder if he knows anything. I've never seen him stick *his* asses out in the field.' *Huh?* It took Johanna a second to realize that this was Pilgrim editorializing. She glanced across the railing. Three of Pilgrim's heads were visible, two looking her way. They bore an expression she recognized as a silly smile. No one else seemed to react to his comment; apparently he could focus his translation on Johanna alone. She glared at him, and after a moment he resumed his businesslike translation:

'Steel knows we plan to attack, but he does *not* know about our special weapons. This change in schedule appears to be a matter of random suspicion. Unfortunately we are the worse for it.'

Three or four Councillors began talking at once. 'Much loud unhappiness,' came Pilgrim's voice, summing up. 'They're full of "I knew this plan would never work" and "Why did we ever agree to attack the Flenserists in the first place."'

Right next to Johanna, Woodcarver emitted a shrill whistle. The recriminations dribbled to a halt. 'Some of you forget your courage. We agreed to attack Hidden Island because it has been a deadly threat, one we thought we could destroy with Johanna's cannons – and one that could surely destroy *us* if Steel ever learns to use the starship.' One of Woodcarver's members, crouching on the floor, reached out to brush Johanna's knee.

Pilgrim's focused voice chuckled in her ear. 'And there's also the little matter of getting you home and making contact with the stars, but she can't say that aloud to the "pragmatic" types. In case you haven't guessed, that's one reason you're here – to remind the chuckleheads there's more in heaven than they have dreamed.' He paused, and switched back to translating Woodcarver:

'No mistake was made in undertaking this campaign: avoiding it would be as deadly as fighting and losing. So . . . do we have any chance of getting an effective army up the coast in time?' She jabbed a nose in the direction of a balcony across the room. 'Scrupilo. Please be brief.'

'The last thing Scrupilo can be is brief – oops, sorry.' More editorializing from Peregrine.

Scrupilo stuck a couple more heads into view. 'I've already discussed this with Vendacious, Your Majesty. Raising an army, traveling up the coast – those all could be done in well under ten tendays. It's the cannon, and perhaps training packs to use cannon, that is the problem. That is my special area of responsibility.'

Woodcarver said something abrupt.

'Yes, majesty. We have the gunpowder. It is every bit as powerful as Dataset says. The gun tubes have been a much greater problem. Till very recently, the metal cracked at the breech as it cooled. Now I think I have that fixed. At least I have two unblemished gun tubes. I had hoped for several tendays of testing—'

Woodcarver interrupted, '—but that is something we can't afford now.' She came completely to her feet and looked all around the council room. 'I want full-size testing immediately. If it's successful, we'll start making gun tubes as fast as we can.' *And if not . . .*

Two days later . . .

The funniest thing was that Scrupilo expected Johanna to inspect the gun tube before he fired it. The pack walked excitedly around the rig, explaining things in awkward Samnorsk. Johanna followed, frowning seriously. Some meters off, mostly hidden behind a berm, Woodcarver and her High Council were watching the exercise. Well, the thing *looked* real enough. They'd mounted it on a small cart that could roll back into a pile of dirt under the recoil force. The tube itself was a single cast piece of metal about a meter long with a ten-centimeter bore. Gunpowder and shot went in the front end. The powder was ignited through a tiny firehole at the rear.

Johanna ran her hand along the barrel. The leaden surface was bumpy, and there seemed to be pieces of dirt caught in the metal. Even the walls of the bore were not completely smooth; would that make a difference? Scrupilo was explaining how he had used straw in the molds to keep the metal from cracking as it cooled. *Yecco.* 'You should try it out with small amounts of gunpowder first,' she said.

Scrupilo's voice became bit conspiratorial, more focused. 'Just between you me, I did that. It went very good. Now for big test.'

Hmm. So you're not a complete flake. She smiled at the nearest of him, a member with no black at all in his head fur. In a kooky way, Scrupilo reminded her of some of the scientists at the High Lab.

Scrupilo stepped back from the cannon and said loudly, 'It is all okay to go now?' Two of him were looking nervously at the High Councillors beyond the berm.

'Um, yes, it looks fine to me.' And of course it should. The design was copied straight from Nyjoran models in Johanna's history files. 'But be careful – if it doesn't work right, it could kill anybody nearby.'

'Yes, yes.' Having gotten her official endorsement, Scrupilo swept around the piece and shooed Johanna toward the sidelines. As she walked back to Woodcarver, he continued in Tinish, no doubt explaining the test.

'Do you think it will work?' Woodcarver asked her quietly. She seemed even more feeble than usual. They had spread a woven mat for her on the mossy heather behind the berm. Most of her lay quietly, heads between paws. The blind one looked asleep; the young drooler cuddled against it, twitching nervously. As usual Peregrine Wickwrackscar was nearby, but he wasn't translating now. All his attention was on Scrupilo.

Johanna thought of the straw that Scrupilo had used in the molds. Woodcarver's people were really trying to help, but . . . She shook her head. 'I – who knows.' She came to her knees and looked over the berm. The whole thing looked like a circus act from a history file. There were the performing animals, the cannon. There was even the circus tent: Vendacious had insisted on hiding the operation from possible spies in the hills. The enemy might see something, but the longer Steel lacked details the better.

The Scrupilo pack hustled around the cannon, talking all the time. Two of him hauled up a keg of black powder and he began pushing the stuff down the barrel. A wad of silkpaper followed the powder down the barrel. He tamped it into place, then loaded the cannon ball. At the same time, the rest of him pushed the cart around to point out of the tent.

They were on the forest side of the castle yard, between the old and new walls. Johanna could see a patch of green hillside, drizzly clouds hanging low. About a hundred meters away was the old wall. In fact this was the same stretch of stone where Scriber had been killed. Even if the damn cannon didn't blow up, no one had any idea how far the shot would go. Johanna was betting it wouldn't even get to the wall.

Scrupilo was on this side of the gun now, trying to light a long wooden firing wand. With a sinking feeling in her stomach, Johanna knew this couldn't work. They were all fools and amateurs, she as much as they. *And this poor guy is going to get killed for nothing.*

Johanna came to her feet. *Gotta stop it.* Something grabbed her belt and pulled her down. It was one of Woodcarver's members, one of the fat ones that couldn't walk quite right. 'We have to try,' the pack said softly.

Scrupilo had the wand alight now. Suddenly he stopped talking. All of him but the white-headed one ran for the protection of the berm. For an instant it seemed like strange cowardice, and then Johanna understood: A human playing with something explosive would also try to shield his body – except for the hand that held the match. Scrupilo was risking a maiming, but not death.

The white-headed one looked across the trampled heather to the rest of Scrupilo. It didn't seem upset so much as attentively listening. At this distance it couldn't be part of Scrupilo's mind, but the creature was probably smarter than any dog – and apparently it was getting some kind of directions from the rest.

White-head turned and walked toward the cannon. It belly-crawled the last meter, taking what cover there was in the dirt behind the gun cart. It held the wand to the flame as its tip came slowly down on the fire hole. Johanna ducked behind the berm . . .

The explosion was a sharp snapping sound. Woodcarver shuddered against her, and whistles of pain came from all around the tent. Poor

Scrupilo! Johanna felt tears starting. *I have to look; I'm partly responsible.* Slowly she stood and forced herself to look across the field to where a minute ago the cannon had been – *and still is!* Thick smoke floated from both ends, but the tube was intact. And more, White-head was wobbling dazedly around the cart, his white fur now covered with soot.

The rest of Scrupilo raced out to White-head. The five of him ran round and round the cannon, bounding over each other in triumph. For a long moment, the rest of the audience just stared. The gun was in one piece. The gunner had survived. And, almost as a side effect . . . Johanna looked over the gun, up the hillside: There was a meter-wide notch in the top of the old wall where none had been before. Vendacious would have a hard time hiding *that* from enemy view!

Dumb silence gave way to the noisiest affair Johanna had seen yet. There was the usual gobbling, and other sounds – hissing that hovered right at the edge of sensibility. On the other side of the tent, two Tines she didn't know ran *into* each other: for a moment of mindless jubilation, they were an enormous pack of nine or ten members.

We'll get the ship back yet! Johanna turned to hug Woodcarver. But the Queen was not shouting with the others. She huddled with her heads close together, shivering. 'Woodcarver?' She petted the neck of one of the big, fat ones. It jerked away, its body spasming.

Stroke? Heart attack? The names of oldenday killers popped into her mind. Just how would they apply to a pack? Something was terribly wrong, and nobody else had noticed. Johanna bounced back to her feet. '*Pilgrim!*' she screamed.

Five minutes later they had Woodcarver out of the tent. The place was still a madhouse, but gone deathly quiet to Johanna's ears. She'd helped the Queen onto her carriage, but after that no one would let her near. Even Pilgrim, so eager to translate everything the day before, brushed her aside. 'It will be okay,' was all he said as he ran to the front of the carriage and grabbed the reins of the shaggy Whatsits. The carriage pulled out, surrounded by several packs of guards. For an instant, the weirdness of the Tines world came crashing back on Johanna. This was obviously a great emergency. A person might be dying. People were rushing this way and that. And yet . . . The packs drew into themselves. No one crowded close. No one could touch another.

The instant passed, and Johanna was running out of the tent after the carriage. She tried to keep to the heather along the muddy path, and almost caught up. Everything was wet and chill, gunmetal gray. Everyone had been so intent on the test – could this be more Flenser treachery? Johanna stumbled, went down on her knees in the mud. The carriage turned a corner, onto cobblestones. Now it was lost to sight. She got up and slogged on through the wet, but a little slower now. There was nothing she could do, nothing she could do. She had made friends with Scriber, and Scriber had been killed. She had made friends with Woodcarver, and now . . .

She walked along the cobbled alley between the castle's storehouses. The carriage was out of sight, but she could hear its clatter on ahead. Vendacious's security packs ran in both directions past her, stopping briefly in side niches to allow opposing traffic by. Nobody answered her questions – probably none of them even spoke Samnorsk.

Johanna almost got lost. She could hear the carriage, but it had turned somewhere. She heard it again behind her. They were taking Woodcarver to Johanna's place! She went back, and a few minutes later was climbing the path to the two-storey cabin she had shared with Woodcarver these last weeks. Johanna was too pooped to run anymore. She walked slowly up the hillside, vaguely aware of her wet and muddy state. The carriage was stopped about five meters short of the door. Guard packs were strung out along the hill, but their bows weren't nocked.

The afternoon sunlight found a break in the western clouds and shone for a moment on the damp heather and glistening timbers, lighting them bright against dark sky above the hills. It was a combination of light and dark that had always seemed especially beautiful to Johanna. *Please let her be okay.*

The guards let her pass. Peregrine Wickwrackscar was standing around the entrance, three of him watching her approach. The fourth, Scarbutt, had its long neck stuck through the doorway, watching whatever was inside. 'She wanted to be back here when it happened,' he said.

'What h-happened?' said Johanna.

Pilgrim made the equivalent of a shrug. 'It was the shock of that cannon going off. But almost anything could have done it.' There was something odd about the way his heads were bobbing around. With a shock Johanna realized the pack was *smiling*, full of glee.

'I want to see her!' Scarbutt backed hastily away as she started for the door.

Inside there was only the light from the door and the high window slits. It took a second for Johanna's eyes to adjust. Something smelled . . . wet. Woodcarver was lying in a circle on the quilted mattress she used every evening. She crossed the room and went to her knees beside the pack. The pack edged nervously away from her touch. There was blood, and what looked like a pile of guts, in the middle of the mattress. Johanna felt vomit rising in her. 'W-Woodcarver?' she said very softly.

One of the Queen moved back toward Johanna and put its muzzle in the girl's hand. 'Hello, Johanna. It's . . . so strange . . . to have someone next to me at a time like this.'

'You're bleeding. What's the matter?'

Soft, human-sounding laughter. 'I'm hurt, but it's good . . . See.' The blind one was holding something small and wet in its jaws. One of the others was licking it. Whatever it was, it was wiggling, alive. And Johanna remembered how strangely plump and awkward parts of Woodcarver had become.

'*A baby?*'

'Yes. And I'm going to have another in a day or two.'

Johanna sat back on the floor timbers, covering her face with her hands. She was going to start crying again. 'Why didn't you tell me?'

Woodcarver didn't say anything for a moment. She licked the little one all around, then set it against the tummy of the member that must be its mother. The newborn snuggled close, nuzzling into the belly fur. It didn't make any noise that Johanna could hear. Finally the Queen said, 'I . . . don't know if I can make you understand. This has been very hard for me.'

'Having babies?' Johanna's hands were sticky with the blood on the quilt. Obviously this had been hard, *but that's how all lives must start on a world like this*. It was pain that needed the support of friends, pain that led to joy.

'No. Having the babies isn't it. I've borne more than a hundred in my memory's time. But these two . . . are the ending of me. How can you understand? You humans don't even have the choice to keep on living; your offspring can never be you. But for me, it's the end of a soul six hundred years old. You see, I'm going to keep these two to be part of me . . . and for the first time in all the centuries, I am not both the mother and the father. A newby I'll become.'

Johanna looked at the blind one and the drooler. Six hundred years of incest. How much longer could Woodcarver have continued before the mind itself decayed? *Not both the mother and the father.* 'But then who is father?' she blurted out.

'Who do you think?' The voice came from just beyond the door. One of Peregrine Wickwrackscar's heads peered around the corner just far enough to show an eye. 'When Woodcarver makes a decision, she goes for extremes. She's been the most tightly held soul of all time. But now she has blood – genes, Dataset would say – from packs all over the world, from one of the flakiest pilgrims who ever cast his soul upon the wind.'

'Also from one of the smartest,' said Woodcarver, her voice wry and wistful at the same time. 'The new soul will be at least as intelligent as before, and probably a lot more flexible.'

'And I'm a little bit pregnant, myself,' said Pilgrim. 'But I'm not the least bit sad. I've been a foursome for too long. Imagine, having pups by Woodcarver herself! Maybe I'll turn all conservative and settle down.'

'Hah! Even two from me is not enough to slow your pilgrim soul.'

Johanna listened to the banter. The ideas were so *alien*, and yet the overtones of affection and humor were somehow very familiar. Somewhere . . . then she had it: When Johanna was just five years old, and Mom and Dad brought little Jefri home. Johanna couldn't remember the words, or even the sense of what they'd said – but the tone was the same as what went between Woodcarver and Pilgrim.

Johanna slid back to a sitting position, the tension of the day evaporating. Scrupilo's artillery really worked; there was a chance of getting the ship. And even if they failed . . . she felt a little bit like she was back home.

'C-can I pet your puppy?'

25

The voyage of the *Out of Band II* had begun in catastrophe, where life and death were a difference of hours or minutes. In the first weeks there had been terror and loneliness and the resurrection of Pham. The *OOB* had fallen quickly toward the galactic plane, away from Relay. Day by day the whorl of stars tilted up to meet them, till it was a single band of light, the Milky Way as seen from the perspective of Nyjora and Old Earth – and from most all the habitable planets of the Galaxy.

Twenty thousand light-years in three weeks. But that had been on a path through the Middle Beyond. Now in the galactic plane, they were still several thousand light-years from their goal at the Bottom of the Beyond. The Zone interfaces roughly followed surfaces of constant mean density; on a galactic scale, the Bottom was a vaguely lens-shaped surface, surrounding much of the galactic disk. The *OOB* was moving in the plane of the disk now, more or less toward the galactic center. Every week took them deeper toward the Slowness. Worse, their path, and all variants that made any progress, extended right through a region of massive Zone shifting. The Net News had called it the Great Zone Storm, though of course there was not the slightest physical feeling of turbulence within the volume. But some days their progress was less than eighty percent what they'd expected.

Early on they'd known that it was not only the storm that was slowing them. Blueshell had gone outside, looking over the damage that still remained from their escape.

'So it's the ship itself?' Ravna had glared out from the bridge, watching the now imperceptible crawl of near stars across the heavens. The confirmation was no revelation. But what to do?

Blueshell trundled back and forth across the ceiling. Every time he reached the far wall, he'd query ship's management about the pressure seal on the nose lock. Ravna glared at him. 'Hey, that was the nth time you've checked status in the last three minutes. If you really think something is wrong, then *fix* it.'

The Skroderider's wheeled progress came to an abrupt halt. Fronds waved uncertainly. 'But I was just outside. I want to be sure I shut the port correctly . . . Oh, you mean I've already checked it?'

Ravna looked up at him, and tried to get the sting out of her voice. Blueshell wasn't the proper target for her frustration. 'Yup. At least five times.'

'I'm sorry.' He paused, going into the stillness of complete concentration. 'I've committed the memory.' Sometimes the habit was cute, and sometimes just irritating: When the Riders tried to think on more than one thing at a time, their Skrodes were sometimes unable to maintain short-term memory. Blueshell especially got trapped into cycles of behavior, repeating an action and immediately forgetting the accomplishment.

Pham grinned, looking a lot cooler than Ravna felt. 'What I don't see is why you Riders put up with it.'

'What?'

'Well, according to the ship's library, you've had these Skrode gadgets since before there was a Net. So how come you haven't improved the design, gotten rid of the silly wheels, upgraded the memory tracking? I bet that even a Slow Zone combat programmer like me could come up with a better design than the one you're riding.'

'It's really a matter of tradition,' Blueshell said primly. 'We're grateful to Whatever gave us wheels and memory in the first place.'

'Hmm.'

Ravna almost smiled. By now she knew Pham well enough to guess what he was thinking – namely that plenty of Riders might have gone on to better things in the Transcend. Those remaining were likely to have self-imposed limitations.

'Yes. Tradition. Many who once were Riders have changed – even Transcended. But we persist.' Greenstalk paused, and when she continued sounded even more shy than usual. 'You've heard of the Rider Myth?'

'No,' said Ravna, distracted in spite of herself. In the time ahead she would know as much about these Riders as about any human friends, but for now there were still surprises.

'Not many have. Not that it's a secret; it's just we don't make much of it. It comes close to being religion, but one we don't proselytize. Four or five billion years ago, Someone built the first skrodes and raised the first Riders to sentience. That much is verified fact. The Myth is that something destroyed our Creator and all its works . . . A catastrophe so great that from this distance it is not even understood as an act of Mind.'

There were plenty of theories about what the galaxy had been like in the distant past, in the time of the Ur-Partition. But the Net couldn't be forever. There had to be a beginning. Ravna had never been a big believer in Ancient Wars and Catastrophes.

'So in a sense,' Greenstalk said, 'we Riders are the faithful ones, waiting for What created us to return. The traditional skrode and the traditional interface are a standard. Staying with it has made our patience possible.'

'Quite so,' said Blueshell. 'And the design itself is very subtle, my lady, even if the function is simple.' He rolled to the center of the ceiling. 'The skrode of tradition imposes a good discipline – concentration on what's truly important. Just now I was trying to worry about too many things . . .'

Abruptly he returned to the topic at hand: 'Two of our drive spines never recovered from the damage at Relay. Three more appear to be degrading. We thought this slow progress was just the storm, but now I've studied the spines up close. The diagnostic warnings were no false alarm.'

'. . . and it's still getting worse?'

'Unfortunately so.'

'So how bad will it get?'

Blueshell drew all his tendrils together. 'My Lady Ravna, we can't be certain of the extrapolations yet. It may not get much worse than now, or – You know the *OOB* was not fully ready for departure. There were the final consistency checks still to do. In a way, I worry about that more than anything. We don't know what bugs may lurk, especially when we reach the Bottom and our normal automation must be retired. We must watch the drives very carefully . . . and hope.'

It was the nightmare that haunted travelers, especially at the Bottom of the Beyond: with ultradrive gone, suddenly a light-year was not a matter of minutes but of years. Even if they fired up the ramscoop and went into cold sleep, Jefri Olsndot would be a thousand years dead before they reached him, and the secret of his parents' ship buried in some medieval midden.

Pham Nuwen waved at the slowly shifting star fields. 'Still, this is the Beyond. Every hour we go farther than the fleet of Qeng Ho could in a decade.' He shrugged. 'Surely there's some place we can get repairs?'

'Several.'

So much for 'a quick flight, all unobserved.' Ravna sighed. The final fitting at Relay was to include spares and tested, Bottom-compatible software. All that was faraway might-have-beens now. She looked at Greenstalk. 'Do you have any ideas?'

'About what?' Greenstalk said.

Ravna bit her lip in frustration. Some said the Riders were a race of comedians; they were indeed, but it was mostly unintentional.

Blueshell rattled at his mate.

'*Oh!* You mean where can we get help. Yes, there are several possibilities. Sjandra Kei is thirty-nine hundred lights spinward from here, but outside this storm. We—'

'Too far,' Blueshell and Ravna spoke almost in chorus.

'Yes, yes, but remember. The Sjandra Kei worlds are mainly human, your home, my Lady Ravna. And Blueshell and I know them well; after all, they were the source of the crypto shipment we brought to Relay. We have friends there and you a family. Even Blueshell agrees that we can get the work done without notice there.'

'Yes, *if* we could get there.' Blueshell's voder voice sounded petulant.

'Okay, what are the other choices?'

'They are not so well-known. I'll make a list.' Her fronds drifted across a console. 'Our last chance for choice is rather near our planned course. It's a single system civilization. The Net name is . . . it translates as Harmonious Repose.'

'Rest in Peace, eh?' said Pham.

But they had agreed to voyage on quietly, always watching the bad drive spines, postponing the decision to stop for help.

The days became weeks, and weeks slowly counted into months. Four voyagers on a quest toward the Bottom. The drive became worse, but slowly, right on *OOB*'s diagnostic projections.

The Blight continued to spread across the Top of the Beyond, and its attacks on Network archives extended far beyond its direct reach.

Communication with Jefri was improving. Messages trickled in at the rate of one or two a day. Sometimes, when *OOB*'s antenna swarm was tuned just right, he and Ravna would talk almost in real time. Progress was being made on the Tines' world faster than she had expected – perhaps fast enough that the boy could save himself.

It should have been a hard time, locked up in the single ship with just three others, with only a thread of conversation with the outside, and that with a lost child.

In any case, it was rarely boring. Ravna found that each of them had plenty to do. For herself it was managing the ship's library, coaxing out of it the plans that would help Mr Steel and Jefri. *OOB*'s library was nothing compared to the Archive at Relay, or even the university libraries at Sjandra Kei, but without proper search automation it could be just as unknowable. And as their voyage proceeded, that automation needed more and more special care.

And . . . things could never be boring with Pham around. He had a dozen projects, and curiosity about everything. 'Voyaging time can be a gift,' he'd say. 'Now we have time to catch ourselves up, time to get ready for whatever we find ahead.' He was learning Samnorsk. It went slower than his faked learning on Relay, but the guy had a natural bent for languages, and Ravna gave him plenty of practice.

He spent several hours each day in the *OOB*'s workshop, often with Blueshell. Reality graphics were a new thing to him, but after a few weeks he was beyond toy prototypes. The pressure suits he built had power packs and weapons stores. 'We don't know what things may be like when we arrive; powered armor could be real useful.'

At the end of each work day they would all meet on the command deck to compare notes, to consider the latest from Jefri and Mr Steel, to review the drive status. For Ravna this could be the happiest time of the day . . . and sometimes the hardest. Pham had rigged the display automation to show castle walls all around. A huge fireplace replaced the normal window on comm status. The sound of it was almost perfect; he had even coaxed a small amount of 'fire' heat from that wall. This was a castle hall out of

Pham's memory, from Canberra he said. But it wasn't that different from the Age of Princesses on Nyjora (though most of *those* castles had been in tropical swamps where big fireplaces were rarely used). For some perverse reason, even the Riders seemed to enjoy it; Greenstalk said it reminded her of a trading stop from her first years with Blueshell. Like travelers who have walked through a long day, the four of them rested in the coziness of a phantom lodge. And when the new business was settled, Pham and the Riders would trade stories, often late into the 'night'.

Ravna sat beside him, the least talkative of the four. She joined in the laughter and sometimes the discussion: There was the time Blueshell had a humor fit at Pham's faith in public key encryption, and Ravna knew some stories of her own to illustrate the Rider's opinion. But this was also the hardest time for her. Yes, the stories were wonderful. Blueshell and Greenstalk had been so many places, and at heart they were traders. Swindles and bargains and good done were all part of their lives. Pham listened to his friends, almost enraptured . . . and then told his own stories, of being a prince on Canberra, of being a Slow Zone trader and explorer. And for all the limitations of the Slowness, his life's adventures surpassed even the Skroderiders'. Ravna smiled and tried to pretend enthusiasm.

For Pham's stories were too much. He honestly believed them, but she couldn't imagine one human seeing so much, doing so much. Back on Relay, she had claimed his memories were synthetic, a little joke of Old One. She had been very angry when she said it, and more than anything she wished she never had . . . because it was so clearly the truth. Greenstalk and Blueshell never noticed, but sometimes in the middle of a story Pham would stumble on his memories and a look of barely concealed panic would come to his eyes. Somewhere inside, he knew the truth too, and she suddenly wanted to hug him, comfort him. It was like having a terribly wounded friend, with whom you can talk but never mutually admit the scope of the injuries. Instead she pretended the lapses didn't exist, smiling and laughing at the rest of his story.

And Old One's jape was all so unnecessary. Pham didn't have to be a great hero. He was a decent person, though egotistical and kind of a rule breaker. He had every bit as much persistence as she, and more courage.

What craft Old One must have had to make such a person, what . . . Power. And how she hated Him for making a joke of such a person.

Of Pham's godshatter there was scarcely a sign. For that Ravna was very grateful. Once or twice a month he had a dreamy spell. For a day or two after he would go nuts with some new project, often something he couldn't clearly explain. But it wasn't getting worse; he wasn't drifting away from her.

'And the godshatter may save us in the end,' he would say when she had the courage to ask him about it 'No, I don't know how.' He tapped his forehead. 'It's still god's own crowded attic up here. And it's more than memory. Sometimes the godshatter needs all my mind to think with and there's no room left for self-awareness, and afterwards I can't explain, but . . . sometimes I have a glimmer. Whatever Jefri's parents brought to the Tines' world: it can hurt the Blight. Call it an antidote – better yet, a countermeasure. Something taken from the Perversion as it was aborning in the Straumli lab. Something the Perversion didn't even suspect was gone until much later.'

Ravna sighed. It was hard to imagine good news that was also so frightening. 'The Straumers could sneak something like that right out from the Perversion's heart?'

'Maybe. Or maybe, Countermeasure used the Straumers to escape the Perversion. To hide inaccessibly deep, and wait to strike. And I think the plan might work, Rav, at least if I – if Old One's godshatter – can get down there and help it. Look at the News. The Blight is turning the top of the Beyond upside down – hunting for *something*. Hitting Relay was the least of it, a small by-product of its murdering Old One. But it's looking in all the wrong places. We'll have our chance at Countermeasure.'

She thought of Jefri's messages. 'The rot on the walls of Jefri's ship. You think that's what it is?'

Pham's eyes went vague. 'Yes. It seems completely passive, but he says it was there from the beginning, that his parents kept him away from it. He seems a little disgusted by it . . . That's good, probably keeps his Tinish friends away from it.'

A thousand questions flitted up. Surely they must in Pham's mind too. And they could know the answer to none of them now. Yet someday they would stand before that unknown and Old One's dead hand would act . . . through Pham. Ravna shivered, and didn't say anything more for a time.

Month by month, the gunpowder project stayed right on the schedule of the library's development program. The Tines had been able to make the stuff easily; there had been very little backtracking through the development tree. Alloy testing had been the critical event that slowed things, but they were over the hump there too. The packs of 'Hidden Island' had built the first three prototypes: breech-loading cannon that were small enough to be carried by a single pack. Jefri guessed they could begin mass production in another ten days.

The radio project was the weird one. In one sense it was behind schedule; in another, it had become something more than Ravna had ever imagined. After a long period of normal progress, Jefri had come back with a counterplan. It consisted of a complete reworking of the tables for the acoustic interface.

'I thought these jokers were first-time medievals,' Pham Nuwen said when he saw Jefri's message.

'That's right. Apparently, they just reasoned out consequences to what we sent them. They want to support pack-thought across the radio.'

'Hunh. Yes. We described how the tables specified the transducer grid – all in nontechnical Samnorsk. That included showing how small table changes would make the grid different. But look, our design would give them a three kilohertz band – a nice, voice-grade connection. You're telling me that implementing this new table would give 'em two hundred kilohertz.'

'Yes. That's what my dataset says.'

He grinned his cocky smile. 'Ha! And that's my point. Sure, *in principle* we gave them enough information to do the mod. It looks to me like making this expanded spec table is equivalent to solving a, hmm,' he counted rows and columns, 'a five-hundred-node numerical PDE. And little Jefri claims that all his datasets are destroyed, and that his ship computer is not generally usable.'

Ravna leaned back from the display. 'Sorry. I see what you mean.' You get so used to everyday tools, sometimes you forget what it must be like without them. 'You . . . you think this might be, uh, Countermeasure's doing?'

Pham Nuwen hesitated, as if he hadn't even considered the possibility. Then, 'No . . . no, it's not that. I think this "Mister Steel" is playing games with our heads. All we have is a byte stream from "Jefri." What do we *really* know about what's going on?'

'Well, I'll tell you some things *I* know. We are talking to a young human child who was raised in Straumli Realm. You've been reading most of his messages in Trisk translation. That loses a lot of the colloquialisms and the little errors of a child who is a native speaker of Samnorsk. The only way this might be faked is by human adults . . . And after twenty plus weeks of knowing jefri, I'll tell you even that is unlikely.'

'Okay. So suppose Jefri is for real. We have this eight-year-old kid down on the Tines' world. He's telling us what he considers to be the truth. I'm saying it looks like someone is lying to him. Maybe we can trust what he sees with his own eyes. He says these creatures aren't sapient except in groups of five or so. Okay. We'll believe that.' Pham rolled his eyes. Apparently his reading had shown how rare group intelligences were this side of the Transcend. 'The kid says they didn't see anything but small towns from space, and that everything on the ground is medieval. Okay, we'll buy that. *But.* What are the chances that this race is smart enough to do partial differential equations in their heads, and do them from just the implications in your message?'

'Well, there have been some humans that smart.' She could name one case in Nyjoran history, another couple from Old Earth. If such abilities were common among the packs, they were smarter than any natural race she had heard of. 'So this isn't first-time medievalism?'

'Right. I bet this is some colony fallen on hard times – like your Nyjora and my Canberra, except that they have the good luck of being in the Beyond. These dog packs have a working computer somewhere. Maybe it's under control of their priest class; maybe they don't have much else. But they're holding out on us.'

'But *why?* We'd be helping them in any case. And Jefri has told us how this group saved him.'

Pham started to smile again, the old supercilious smile. Then he sobered. He was really trying to break that habit. 'You've been on a dozen different worlds, Ravna. And I know you've read about thousands more, at least in survey. You probably know of varieties of medievalism I've never guessed. But remember, I've actually *been* there . . . I think.' The last was a nervous mutter.

'I've read about the Age of Princesses,' Ravna said mildly.

'Yes . . . and I'm sorry for belittling that. In any medieval politics, the blade and the thought are closely connected. But they become much more so to someone who's lived through it. Look, even if we believe everything that Jefri says he has seen, this Hidden Island Kingdom is a sinister thing.'

'You mean the names?'

'Like Flensers, Steel, Tines? Harsh names aren't necessarily meaningful.' Pham laughed. 'I mean, when *I* was eight years old, one of my titles was already "Lord Master Disemboweler." ' He saw the look on Ravna's face and hurriedly added, 'And at that age, I hadn't even *witnessed* more than a couple of executions! No, the names are only a small part of it. I'm thinking of the kid's description of the castle – which seems to be close by the ship – and this ambush he thinks he was rescued from. It doesn't add up. You asked "what could they gain from betraying us." I can see that question from their point of view. If they are a fallen colony, they have a clear idea what they've lost. They probably have some remnant technology, and are paranoid as hell. If I were them, I'd seriously consider ambushing the rescuers if those rescuers seemed weak or careless. And even if we come on strong . . . look at the questions Jefri asks for Steel. The guy is fishing, trying to figure out what we really value: the refugee ship, Jefri and the coldsleepers, or something on the ship. By the time we arrive, Steel will probably have wiped the local opposition – thanks to us. My guess is we're in for some heavy blackmail when we get to Tines' world.'

I thought we were talking about the good *news.* Ravna paged back through recent messages. Pham was right. The boy was telling the truth as he knew it, but . . . 'I don't see how we can play things any differently. If we don't help Steel against the Woodcarvers—'

'Yeah. We don't know enough to do much else. Whatever else is true, the Woodcarvers seem a valid threat to Jefri and the ship. I'm just saying we should be thinking about all the possibilities. One thing we absolutely mustn't do is show interest in Countermeasure. If the locals know how desperate we are for that, we don't have a chance.

'And it may be time to start planting a few lies of our own. Steel's been talking about building a landing place for us – inside his castle. There's no way *OOB* could fit, but I think we should play along, tell Jefri that we can separate from our ultradrive, something like his container ship. Let Steel concentrate on building harmless traps . . .

He hummed one of his strange little 'marching' tunes. 'About the radio thing: why don't we just compliment the Tines real casually for improving our design. I wonder what they'd say?'

Pham Nuwen got his answer less than three days later. Jefri Olsndot said that *he* had done the optimization. So if you believed the kid, there was no evidence for hidden computers. Pham was not at all convinced: 'So just by coincidence, we have Isaac Newton on the other end of the line?' Ravna didn't argue the point. It *was* an enormous bit of luck, yet . . . She went over the earlier messages. In language and general knowledge, the boy seemed very ordinary for his age. But occasionally there were situations involving mathematical insight – not formal, taught math – where Jefri said striking things. Some of those conversations had been under fine conditions, with turnaround times of less than a minute. It all seemed too consistent to be the lie Pham Nuwen thought.

Jefri Olsndot, you are someone I want very much to meet.

There was always something: problems with the Tines' developments, fears that the murderous Woodcarvers might overrun Mr Steel, worries about the steadily degrading drive spines and the Zone turbulence that slowed *OOB*'s progress even further. Life was by turns and at once frustrating, boring, frightening. And yet . . .

One night about four months into the flight, Ravna woke in the cabin she had come to share with Pham. Maybe she had been dreaming, but she couldn't remember anything except that it had been no nightmare. There was no special noise in the room, nothing to wake her. Beside her, Pham was sleeping soundly in their hammock net. She eased her arm down his back, drawing him gently toward her. His breathing changed; he mumbled something placid and unintelligible. In Ravna's opinion, sex in zero-gee was not the experience some people bragged it up to be; but really *sleeping* with someone . . . that was much nicer in free fall. An embrace could be light and enduring and effortless.

Ravna looked around the dimly-lit cabin, trying to imagine what had awakened her. Maybe it had just been the problems of the day – Powers knew there had been enough of those. She nestled her face against Pham's shoulder. Yes, always problems, but . . . in a way she was more content than she had been in years. Sure there were problems. Poor Jefri's situation. All the people lost at Straum and Relay. But she had three friends, and a love.

Alone in a tiny ship bound for the Bottom, she was less lonely than she'd been since leaving Sjandra Kei. More than ever in her life, maybe she could do something to help with the problems.

And then she guessed, part in sadness, part in joy, that years from now she might look back on these months as goldenly happy.

26

And finally, almost five months out, it was clear there was no hope of going on without repairing the drive spines. The *OOB* was suddenly doing only a quarter of a light-year per hour in a volume that tested good for two. And things were getting worse. They would have no trouble making it to Harmonious Repose, but beyond that . . .

Harmonious Repose. An ugly name, thought Ravna. Pham's 'light-hearted' translation was worse: Rest in Peace. In the Beyond, almost everything habitable was in use. Civilizations were transient and races faded . . . but there were always new people moving up from Below. The result was most often patchwork, polyspecific systems. Young races just up from the Slowness lived uneasily with the remnants of older peoples. According to the ship's library, RIP had been in the Beyond for a *long* time. It had been continuously inhabited for at least two hundred million years, time for ten thousand species to call it home. The most recent notes showed better than one hundred racial terranes. Even the youngest was the residue of a dozen emigrations. The place should be peaceful to the point of being moribund.

So be it. They jigged the *OOB* three light-years spinward. Now they were flying down the main Net trunk towards RIP: they'd be able to listen to the News the whole way in.

Harmonious Repose advertised. At least one species valued external goods, specializing in ship outfitting and repair. An industrious, hard-footed(?) race, the ads said. Eventually, she saw some video: the creatures walked on ivory tusks and had a froth of short arms growing from just below their necks. The ads included Net addresses of satisfied users. *Too bad we can't follow up on those.* Instead Ravna sent a short message in Triskwe-line, requesting generic drive replacements and listing possible methods of payment.

Meantime, the bad news kept rolling in:

Crypto: 0
As received by: *OOB* shipboard ad hoc
Language path: Baeloresk → Triskweline, SjK units
From: Alliance for the Defense

[Claimed cooperative of five polyspecific empires in the Beyond below
Straumli Realm. No record of existence before the Fall of the Realm.]
Subject: Call to action
Distribution:
  Threat of the Blight
  War Trackers Interest Group
  Homo Sapiens Interest Group
Date: 158.00 days since Fall of Relay
Key phrases: Action, not talk
Text of message:
  Alliance Forces are preparing for action against the tools of the Perversion. It
is time for our friends to declare themselves. At the moment we do not need
your military pledges, but in the very near future we will need support services
including free Net time.
  In the coming seconds we will be watching closely to see who supports our
action and who may be enslaved to the Perversion. If you live with the human
infestation, you have a choice: act now with a good possibility of victory – or
wait, and be destroyed.
  Death to vermin.

There were plenty of secondary messages, including speculation about
who Death to Vermin (aka the 'Alliance for the Defense') had in mind.
There were also rumors of military movement. This wasn't making the
splash the fall of Relay had, but it did have the attention of several News
groups. Ravna swallowed hard and looked away from the display. 'Well,
they're still making big noises.' She tried for a light tone, but it didn't come
out that way.

Pham Nuwen touched her shoulder. 'Quite true. And real killers generally don't advertise beforehand.' But there was more sympathy than
conviction in his voice. 'We still don't know that this is more than a single
loudmouth. There's no definite word of ship movements. What can they do
after all?'

Ravna pushed herself up from the table. 'Not much, I hope. There are
hundreds of civilizations with small human settlements. Surely they've
taken precautions since this Death to Vermin stuff began . . . *By the Powers*,
I wish I knew Sjandra Kei was safe.' It had been more than two years since
she'd seen Lynne and her parents. Sometimes Sjandra Kei seemed something from another life, but just knowing it was there had been more
comfort than she realized. Now . . .

On the other side of the command deck, the Skroderiders had been
working on the repair specs. Now Blueshell rolled toward them. 'I do fear
for the small settlements, but the humans at Sjandra Kei are the driving
force of that civilization; even the name is a human one. Any attack on them
would be an attack on the entire civilization. Greenstalk and I have traded

213

there often enough, and with their commercial security forces. Only fools or bluffers would announce an invasion beforehand.'

Ravna thought a moment, brightened. The Dirokimes and Lophers would stand against any threat to humankind at Sjandra Kei. 'Yeah. We're not a ghetto there.' Things might be very bad for isolated humans, but Sjandra Kei would be okay. 'Bluffers. Well it's not called the Net of a Million Lies for nothing.' She pulled her mind back from worries beyond her control. 'But one thing is clear. Stopping at Harmonious Repose, we must be damn sure not to look like anything human.'

And of course, part of not looking human was that there be no sign of Ravna and Pham. The Riders would do all the 'talking.' Ravna and the Riders went through all the ship's exterior programs, weeding out human nuances that had crept in since they left Relay. And if they were actually boarded? Well, they would never survive a determined search, but they isolated things human in a fake jovian hold. The two humans would slip in there if necessary.

Pham Nuwen checked what they did – and found more than one slipup. For a barbarian programmer, he wasn't bad. But then they were rapidly reaching the depths where the best computer equipment wasn't that much more sophisticated than what he had known.

Ironically, there was one thing they could not disguise: that the *OOB* was from the Top of the Beyond. True, the ship was a bottom-lugger and based on a Mid Beyond design. But there was an *elegance* to the refit that screamed of nearly superhuman competence. 'The damn thing has the feel of a hand axe built in a factory,' was how Pham Nuwen put it.

RIPer security was an encouraging thing: a perfunctory velocity check and no boarding. *OOB* hopped into the system and finished a rocket burn to match position/velocity vector with the heart of Harmonious Repose and 'Saint(?) Rihndell's Repair Harbor.' (Pham: 'If you're a "saint", you gotta be honest, right?')

Out of Band was above the ecliptic and some eighty million kilometers from RIP's single star. Even knowing what to expect, the view was spectacular: The inner system was as dusty/gassy as a stellar nursery, even though the primary was a three-billion-year-old G star. That sun was surrounded by millions of rings, more spectacular than those around any planet. The largest and brightest resolved into myriads more. Even in the natural view there was bright color here, threads of green and red and violet. Warping of the ring plane laid lakes of shadow between colored hillsides, hillsides a million kilometers across. There were occasional objects – structures? – sticking far enough up from the ring plane to cast needle-like shadows out-system. Infrared and proper motion windows showed more conventional features: Beyond the rings lay a massive asteroid belt, and far beyond that a single jovian planet, its own million-klick ring system a puny afterthought. There were no other planets, either detected or on file. The largest objects in the main ring system were three hundred kilometers across . . . but there appeared to be thousands of them.

At Saint Rihndell's direction they brought the ship down to the ring plane and matched velocities with the local junk. That last was a big impulsive burn: three gees for almost five minutes. 'Just like old, *old* times,' Pham Nuwen said.

In free fall again, they looked out upon their harbor: Up close it looked like planetary ring systems Ravna had known all her life. There were objects of all sizes down to less than a handspan across, uncounted globs of icy froth – gently touching, sticking, separating. The debris hung nearly motionless all about them; this was chaos that had been tamed long ago. In the plane of the rings, they couldn't see more than a few hundred meters. The debris blocked further views. And it wasn't all loose. Greenstalk pointed to a line of white that seemed to curve from infinity, pass close by them, and then retreat forever in the other direction. 'Looks like a single structure,' she said.

Ravna stepped up the magnification. In planetary ring systems, the 'frothy snowballs' sometimes accreted into strings thousands of klicks long . . . The white thread spread wide beyond the window. The display said it was almost a kilometer across. This arc was definitely not made of snowballs. She could see ship locks and communications nodes. Checking with images from their approach, Ravna could see that the whole thing was better than forty million kilometers long. There were a number of breaks scattered along the arc. That figured: The scaled tensile strength of such a structure could be near zero. Depending on local distortions, it would pull apart briefly, then gently come together some time later. The whole affair was vaguely reminiscent of train cars coupling and uncoupling on some old-time Nyjoran railway.

Over the next hour, they moved carefully in to dock at the ring arc. The only thing regular about the structure was its linearity. Some of the modules were clearly designed for linking fore and aft. Others were jumbled heaps of oddball equipment meshed in dirty ice. The last few kilometers, they drifted through a forest of ultradrive spines. Two thirds of the berths were occupied.

Blueshell opened a window on Saint Rihndell's business specs. 'Hmm. Hm. Sir Rihndell seems extraordinarily busy.' He angled some fronds back at the ships in the exterior view.

Pham: 'Maybe he's running a junkyard.'

Blueshell and Greenstalk went down to the cargo lock to prepare for their first trip ashore. The Skroderiders had been together for two hundred years, and Blueshell came from a star trader tradition before that. Yet the two argued back and forth about the best approach to take with 'Saint Rihndell.'

'Of course, Harmonious Repose is typical, dear Blueshell; I would remember the type even if I'd never ridden a Skrode. But *our* business here is not like anything we've done before.'

Blueshell grumped wordlessly, and pushed another trade packet under his cargo scarf. The scarf was more than pretty. The material was tough, elastic stuff that protected what it covered.

This was the same procedure they had always followed in new ring systems, and it had worked well before. Finally he replied, 'Certainly, there are differences, mainly that we have very little to trade for the repairs and no previous commercial contacts. If we don't use hard business sense we'll get nothing here!' He checked the various sensors strung across his Skrode, then spoke to the humans. 'Do you want me to move any of the cameras? Do they all have a clear view?' Saint Rihndell was a miser when it came to renting bandwidth – or maybe it was simply cautious.

Pham Nuwen's voice came back. 'No. They're okay. Can you hear me?' He was speaking through a microphone inside their skrodes. The link itself was encrypted.

'Yes.'

The Skroderiders passed through *OOB*'s locks into Saint Rihndell's arc habitat.

From within, transparency arched around them, lines of natural windows that dwindled into the distance. They looked out upon Saint Rihndell's current customers and the ring fluff beyond. The sun was dimmed in the view, but there was a haze of brightness, a super corona. That was a power satellite's swarm no doubt; ring systems did not naturally make good use of the central fire. For a moment the Riders stopped in their tracks, taken by the image of a sea greater than any sea: The light might have been sunset through shallow surf. And to them, the drifting of thousands of nearby particles looked like food in a slow tidal surge.

The concourse was crowded. The creatures here had ordinary enough body plans, though none were of species Greenstalk recognized for certain. The tusk-leg type that ran Saint Rihndell's was most numerous. After a moment, one such drifted out from the wall near the *OOB*'s lock. It buzzed something that came out as Triskweline: 'For trading, we go this way.' Its ivory legs moved agilely across netting into an open car. The Skroderiders settled behind and they accelerated along the arc. Blueshell waggled at Greenstalk, 'The old story, eh; what good are their legs now?' It was the oldest Rider humor, but it was always worth a laugh: Two legs or four legs – evolved from flippers or jaws or whatever – were all very good for movement on land. But in space it scarcely mattered.

The car was making about one hundred meters per second, swaying slightly whenever they passed from one ring segment to the next. Blueshell kept up a steady patter of conversation with their guide, the sort of pitch that Greenstalk knew was one of his great joys in life. 'Where are we going? What are those creatures there? What sort of things are they in search of at Saint Rihndell's?' All jovial, and almost humanly brisk. Where short-term memory was failing him, he depended on his skrode.

Tusk-legs spoke only reduced-grammar Triskweline, and didn't seem to understand some of the questions: 'We go to the Master Seller . . . helper creatures those are . . . allies of big new customer . . .' Their guide's limited speech bothered dear Blueshell not at all; he was collecting responses more than answers. Most races had interests that were obscure to the likes of Blueshell and Greenstalk. No doubt there were billions of creatures in Harmonious Repose who were totally inscrutable to Riders or Humans or Dirokimes. Yet simple dialogue often gave insight on the two most important questions: *What do you have that might be useful to me, and how can I persuade you to part with it?* Dear Blueshell's questions were sounding out the other, trying to find the parameters of personality and interest and ability.

It was a team game the two Skroderiders played. While Blueshell chattered, Greenstalk watched everything around them, running her skrode's recorders on all bands, trying to place this environment in the context of others they had known. Technology: What would these people need? What could work? In space this flat, there would be little use for agrav fabric. And this low in the Beyond, a lot of the most sophisticated imports from above would spoil almost immediately. Workers outside the long windows wore articulated pressure suits – the force-field suits of the High Beyond would last only a few weeks down here.

They passed trees that grew like vines. Some of the trunks circled the wall of the arc; others trailed along their path for hundreds of meters. Tusk-leg gardeners floated everywhere about the plants, yet there was no evidence of agriculture. All this was ornament. In the ring plane beyond the windows there were occasional towers, structures that sprouted a thousand kilometers above the plane and cast the pointy shadows they had seen on their final approach to the system. Ravna's voice and Pham's buzzed against her stalk, softly asking Greenstalk about the towers, and speculating on the purpose of such unstable contraptions. She stored their theories away for later consideration . . . but she doubted them; some would work only in the High Beyond, and others were simply uneconomical.

Greenstalk had visited eight ring system civilizations in her life. They were a common consequence of accidents and wars (and occasionally, of deliberate habitat design). According to *OOB*'s library, Harmonious Repose had been a normal planetary system up till ten million years ago. Then there'd been a real estate dispute: A young race from Below had thought to colonize and exterminate the moribund inhabitants. The attack had been a miscalculation, for the moribund could still kill and the system was reduced to rubble. Perhaps the young race survived. But after ten million years, if there were any of those young killers left they would now be the most frail of the systems' elder races. Perhaps a thousand new races had passed through in that time, and almost every one had done something to tailor the rings and the gas cloud left from the debacle. What was left was not a ruin at all, but old . . . old. The ship's library claimed that no race had transcended from Harmonious Repose in a thousand years. That fact was more important than all the others. The current civilizations were in their twilight, refining mediocrity. More than anything else, the system had the feel of an old and beautiful tide pool, groomed and tended, shielded from the exciting waves that might upset its bansai plumes. Most likely the tusk-legs were the liveliest species about, perhaps the only one interested in trade with the outside.

Their car slowed and spiraled into a small tower.

'By the Fleet, what I wouldn't give to be out there with them!' Pham Nuwen waved at the views coming in from the skrode cameras. Ever since the Riders left he'd been at the windows, alternately gaping wide-eyed at the ringscape and bouncing abstractedly between the command deck's floor and ceiling. Ravna had never seen him so absorbed, so intense. However fraudulent his memories of trading days, he truly thought he could make a difference. *And he may be right.*

Pham came down from the ceiling, pulled close to the screen. It looked like serious bargaining was about to begin. The Skroderiders had arrived in a spherical room perhaps fifty meters across. Apparently they were floating near the center of it. A forest grew inward from all directions, and the Riders seemed to float just a few meters from the tree tops. Here and there between the branches they could see the ground, a mosaic of flowers.

Saint Rihndell's sales creatures were scattered all about the tallest trees. Each sat with its ivory limbs grasping a tree top. Tusk-leg races were a common thing in the galaxy, but these were the first Ravna had known. The body plan was totally unlike anything from home, and even now she didn't have a clear idea of their appearance. Sitting in the trees, their legs had more of the aspect of skeletal fingers grasping around the trunk. Their chief rep – who claimed to be Saint Rihndell itself – had scrimshaw covering two-thirds of its ivory. Two of the windows showed the carving close up; Pham seemed to think that understanding the artwork might be useful.

Progress was slow. Triskweline was the common language, but good interpreting devices didn't work this deep in the Beyond, and Saint Rihndell's people were only marginally familiar with the trade talk. Ravna was used to clean translations. Even the Net messages she dealt with were usually intelligible, though sometimes misleadingly so.

They'd been talking for twenty minutes and had only just established that Saint Rihndell might have the ability to repair *OOB*. It was the usual Riderly driftiness, and something more. The tedium seemed to please Pham

Nuwen. 'Rav, this is almost like a Qeng Ho operation, face to face with critters and scarcely a common language.'

'We sent them a description of our repair problem hours ago. Why should it take so long for a simple yes or no?'

'Because they're haggling,' said Pham, his grin broadening. '"Honest" Saint Rihndell here—' he waved at the scrimshawed local, '—wants to convince us just how hard the job is . . . Lord I wish I was out there.'

Even Blueshell and Greenstalk seemed a little strange now. Their Triskweline was stripped down, barely more complex than Saint Rihndell's. And much of the discussion seemed very roundabout. Working for Vrinimi, Ravna had had some experience with sales and trading. But *haggling?* You had your pricing databases and strategy support, and directions from Grondr's people. You either had a deal or you didn't. What was going on between the Riders and Saint Rihndell was one of the more alien things Ravna had ever seen.

'Actually, things are going pretty well . . . I think. You saw when we arrived, the bone legs took away Blueshell's samples. By now they know precisely what we have. There's something in those samples that they want.'

'Yeah?'

'Sure. Saint Rihndell isn't bad-mouthing our stuff for his health.'

'Damn it, it's possible we don't have anything on board they could want. This was never intended to be a trade expedition.' Blueshell and Greenstalk had scavenged 'product samples' from the ship's supplies, things that the *OOB* could survive without. These included sensoria and some Low Beyond computer gear. Some of that would be a serious loss. *But one way or another, we need the repairs.*

Pham chuckled. 'No. There's something there Saint Rihndell wants. Otherwise he wouldn't still be jawing . . . And see how he keeps needling us about his "other customers' needs"? Saint Rihndell is a human kind of a guy.'

Something like human song came over the link to the Riders. Ravna phased Greenstalk's cameras toward the sound. From the forest 'floor' on the far side of Blueshell, three new creatures had appeared.

'Why . . . they're beautiful. Butterflies,' said Ravna.

'Huh?'

'I mean they look like butterflies. You know? Um. Insects with large colored wings.'

Giant butterflies, actually. The newcomers had a generally humanoid body plan. They were about 150 centimeters tall and covered with soft-looking brown fur. Their wings sprouted from behind their shoulder blades. At full spread they were almost two meters across, soft blues and yellows, some more intricately patterned than others. Surely they were artificial, or a gengineered affectation; they would have been useless for flying about in any reasonable gravity. But here in zero-gee . . . The three floated at the entrance for just a moment, their huge, soft eyes looking up at the Riders. Then they moved their wings in measured sweeps, and drifted gracefully into the air above the forest. The entire effect was like something out of a children's video. They had pert, button noses, like pet jorakorns, and eyes as wide and bashful as any human animator ever drew. Their voices sounded like youngsters singing.

Saint Rihndell and his buddies sidled around their tree tops. The tallest visitor sang on, its wings gently flexing. After a moment Ravna realized it was speaking fluent Trisk with a front end adapted to the creature's natural speech:

'Saint Rihndell, greetings! Our ships are ready for your repairs. We have made fair payment, and we are in a great hurry. Your work must begin at once!' Saint Rihndell's Trisk specialist translated the speech for his boss.

Ravna leaned across Pham's back. 'So maybe our friendly repairman really is overbooked,' she said.

'. . . Yeah.'

Saint Rihndell came back around his tree top. His little arms picked at the green needles as he made a reply. 'Honored Customers. You made offer of payment, not fully accepted. What you ask is in short supply, difficult to . . . do.'

The cuddly butterfly made a squeaking noise that might have passed for joyous laughter in a human child. The sense behind its singing was different: 'Times are changing, Rihndell creature! Your people must learn: We will not be stymied. You know my fleet's sacred mission. We count every passing hour against you. Think on the fleet you will face if your lack of cooperation is ever known – is ever even *suspected*.' There was a sweep of blue and yellow wings, and the butterfly turned. Its dark, bashful eyes rested on the Riders. 'And these potted plants, they are customers? Dismiss them. Till we are gone, you have no other customers.'

Ravna sucked in a breath. The three had no visible weapons, but she was suddenly afraid for Blueshell and Greenstalk.

'Well, what do you know,' Pham said. 'Butterflies in jackboots.'

27

According to the clock, it took less than half an hour for the Skroderiders to make it back. It seemed a lot longer to Pham Nuwen, even though he tried to keep up a casual front with Ravna. Maybe they were both keeping up a front; he knew she still considered him a fragile case.

But the Riders' cameras showed no more signs of the killer butterflies. Finally the cargo lock cracked open and Blueshell and Greenstalk were back.

'I was sure the wily tusk-legs was just pretending about the strong demand,' said Blueshell. He seemed as eager to rehash the story as Pham was.

'Yeah, I thought so too. In fact, I still think those butterflies might just be part of an act. It's all too melodramatic.'

Blueshell's fronds rattled in a way that Pham recognized as a kind of shiver. 'I wager not, Sir Pham. Those were Aprahanti. Just the look of them fills you with dread, does it not? They're rare these days, but a star trader knows the stories. Still . . . this is a little much even for Aprahanti. Their Hegemony has been on the wane for several centuries.' He rattled something at the ship, and the windows were filled with views of nearby berths in the repair harbor. There was more Rider rattling, this time between Greenstalk and Blueshell. 'Those other ships are a uniform type, you know. A High Beyond design like ours, but more, um . . . *militant.*'

Greenstalk moved close to a window. 'There are twenty of them. Why would so many need drive repairs all at once?'

Militant? Pham looked at the ships with a critical eye. He knew the major features of Beyonder vessels by now. These appeared to have rather large cargo capacity. Elaborate sensoria too. *Hm.* 'Okay, so the Butterflies are hard types. How scared is Saint Rihndell and company?'

The Skroderiders were silent for a long moment. Pham couldn't tell if his question was being given serious consideration or if they had simultaneously lost track of the conversation. He looked at Ravna. 'How about the local net? I'd like to get some background.'

She was already running comm routines. 'They weren't accessible earlier. We couldn't even get the News.' That was something Pham could understand, even if it was damned irritating. The 'local net' was a RIP-wide ultrawave computer and communication network, more complex than anything Pham had known – but conceptually similar to organizations in the Slow Zone. And Pham Nuwen had seen what vandals could do to such structures; Qeng Ho had dealt with at least one obnoxious civilization by perverting its computer net. Not surprisingly, Saint Rihndell hadn't provided them with links to the RIP net. And as long as they were in harbor, the *OOB*'s antenna swarm was necessarily down, so they were also cut off from the Known Net and the newsgroups.

A grin lit Ravna's face. 'Hei! Now we've got read access, maybe more. *Greenstalk. Blueshell.* Wake up!'

Rattle. 'I wasn't asleep,' claimed Blueshell, 'just thinking on Sir Pham's question. Saint Rihndell is obviously afraid.'

As usual, Greenstalk didn't make excuses. She rolled around her mate to get a better look at Ravna's newly opened comm window. There was an iterated-triangle design with Trisk annotations. It meant nothing to Pham. 'That's interesting,' said Greenstalk.

'I am chuckling,' said Blueshell. 'It is more than interesting. Saint Rihndell is a hard-trading type. But look, he is making no charge for this service, not even a percentage of barter. He is afraid, but he still wants to deal with us.'

Hmm, so something from their High Beyond samples was enough to make him risk Aprahanti violence. *Just hope it's not something we really need too.* 'Okay, Rav, see if—'

'Just a second,' the woman said. 'I want to check the News.' She started a search program. Her eyes flickered quickly across her console window . . . and after a second she choked, and her face paled. 'By the Powers, *no!*'

'What is it?'

But Ravna didn't reply, or put the news to a main window. Pham grabbed the rail in front of her console and pulled himself around so he could see what she was reading:

Crypto: 0
As received by: Harmonious Repose Communication Synod
Language path: Baeloresk → Triskweline, SjK units
From: Alliance for the Defense
  [Claimed cooperative of five polyspecific empires in the Beyond below
  Straumli Realm. No record of existence before the Fall of the Realm.]
Subject: Bold victory over the Perversion
Distribution:
  Threat of the Blight
  War Trackers Interest Group
  Homo Sapiens Interest Group
Date: 159.06 days since Fall of Relay
Key phrases: Action, not talk; A promising beginning
Text of message:
  One hundred seconds ago, Alliance Forces began action against the tools of the Blight. By the time you read this, the Homo sapiens worlds known as Sjandra Kei will have been destroyed.
  Note well: for all the talk and theories that have flown about the Blight, this is the first time anyone has successfully *acted*. Sjandra Kei was one of only three systems outside of Straumli Realm known to harbor humans in large numbers. In one stroke we have destroyed a third of the Perversion's potential for expansion.
  Updates will follow.
  Death to vermin.

There was one other message in the window, an update of sorts, but not from Death to Vermin:

Crypto: 0
Billing: charity/general interest
As received by: Harmonious Repose Communication Synod

Language path: Samnorsk → Triskweline, SjK units
From:
    [Note from lower protocol layer: This message was received at Sneerot Down
    along the Sjandra Kei bearing. The transmission was very weak, perhaps from
    a shipboard transmitter]
Subject: Please help
Distribution:
    Threats Interest Group
Date: 5.33 hours since disaster at Sjandra Kei
Text of message:
    Earlier today, relativistic projectiles struck our main habitations. Fatalities
cannot be less than twenty-five billion. Three billion may still live, in transit and
in smaller habitats.
    We are still under attack.
    Enemy craft are in the inner system. We see glow bombs. They are killing
everyone.
    Please. We need help.

'Nei nei *nei!*' Ravna drove up against him, her arms tight around him, her face buried in his shoulder. She sobbed incoherent Samnorsk. Her whole body shuddered against him. He felt tears coming to his own eyes. So strange. She had been the strong one, and he the fragile crazy. Now it was turned all around, and what could he do? 'Father, mother, sister – gone, gone.'

It was the disaster they thought could not happen, and now it had. In one minute she had lost everything she grew up with, and was suddenly alone in the universe. *For me, that happened long ago*, the thought came strangely dispassionate. He hooked a foot into the deck and gently rocked Ravna back and forth, trying to comfort her.

The sounds of grief gradually quieted, though he could still feel her sobs through his chest. She didn't raise her face from the tear-soaked place on his shirt. Pham looked over her head at Blueshell and Greenstalk. Their fronds looked strange . . . almost wilted.

'Look, I want to take Ravna away for a bit. Learn what you can, and I'll be back.'

'Yes, Sir Pham.' And they seemed to droop even more.

It was an hour before Pham returned to the command deck. When he did, he found the Riders deep in rattling conference with the *OOB*. All the windows were filled with flickering strangeness. Here and there Pham recognized a pattern or a printed legend, enough to guess that he was seeing ordinary ship displays, but optimized to Rider senses.

Blueshell noticed him first; he rolled abruptly toward him and his voder voice came out a little squeaky. 'Is she all right?'

Pham gave a little nod. 'She's sleeping now.' *Sedated, and with the ship watching her in case I've misjudged her.* 'Look, she'll be okay. She's been hit hard . . . but she's the toughest one of us all.'

Greenstalk's fronds rattled a smile. 'I have often thought that.'

Blueshell was motionless for an instant. Then, 'Well, to business, to business.' He said something to the ship, and the windows reformatted in the compromise usable by both humans and Riders. 'We've learned a lot while you were gone. Saint Rihndell indeed has something to fear. The Aprahanti ships are a small fragment of the Death to Vermin extermination fleets. These are stragglers still on their way to Sjandra Kei!'

All dressed up for a massacre, and no place to go. 'So now they want some action of their own.'

'Yes. Apparently Sjandra Kei put up some resistance and there were some escapes. The commander of this fleetlet thinks he can intercept some of these – if he can get prompt repairs.'

'What kind of extortion is really possible? Could these twenty ships destroy RIP?'

'No. It's the reputation of the greater force these ships are part of – and the great killing at Sjandra Kei. So Saint Rihndell is very timid with them, and what they need for repairs is the same class of regrowth agent that we need. We really are in competition with them for Rihndell's business.' Blueshell's fronds slapped together, the sort of 'go get 'em' enthusiasm he displayed when a hot deal was remembered. 'But it turns out we have something Saint Rihndell really, *really* wants, something he'll even risk tricking the Aprahanti to get.' He paused dramatically.

Pham thought back over the things they had offered the RIPers. *Lord, not the low zone ultrawave gear.* 'Okay, I'll bite. What do we have to give 'em?'

'A set of flamed trellises! Ha ha.'

'Huh?' Pham remembered the name from the list of odds and ends the Skroderiders had scrounged up. 'What's a "flamed trellis"?'

Blueshell poked a frond into his cargo scarf and extended something stubby and black to Pham: an irregular solid, about forty centimeters by fifteen, smooth to the touch. For all its size, it didn't mass more than a couple of grams. An artfully smoothed . . . cinder. Pham's curiosity triumphed over greater concerns: 'But what's it good for?'

Blueshell dithered. After a moment, Greenstalk said a little shyly, 'There are theories. It's pure carbon, a fractal polymer. We know it's very common in Transcendent cargoes. We think it's used as packing material for some kinds of sentient property.'

'Or perhaps the excrement of such property,' Blueshell buzz-muttered. 'Ah, but that's not important. What is, is that occasional races in the Middle Beyond prize them. And why that? Again, we don't know. Saint Rihndell's folk are certainly not the final user. The Tusk-legs are far too sensible to be ordinary trellis customers. So. We have three hundred of these wonderful things . . . more than enough to overcome Saint Rihndell's fears of the Aprahanti.'

While Pham had been away with Ravna, Saint Rihndell had come up with a plan. Applying the regrowth agent would be too obvious in the same harbor with the Aprahanti ships. Besides, the chief Butterfly had demanded the *OOB* move out. Saint Rihndell had a small harbor about sixteen million klicks around the RIP system. The move was even plausible, for it happened that there was a Skroderider terrane in the Harmonious Repose system – and currently it was just a few hundred kilometers from Rihndell's second harbor. They would rendezvous with the tusk-legs, exchanging repairs for two hundred seventeen flamed trellises. And if the trellises were perfectly matched, Rihndell promised to throw in an agrav refit. After the Fall of Relay, that would be very welcome . . . *Hunh*. Ol' Blueshell just never stopped wheeling and dealing.

The *OOB* slipped free of its moorings and carefully drifted up from the ring plane. *Tiptoeing out*. Pham kept a close watch on the EM and ultrawave windows. But there were no target-locking emanations from the Aprahanti vessels, nothing more than casual radar contact. No one followed. Little *OOB* and its 'potted plants' were beneath the notice of the great warriors.

One thousand meters above the ring plane. Ten. The Skroderiders' chatter – both with Pham and between themselves – dwindled to naught. Their stalks and fronds angled so the sensing surfaces looked out in all directions. The sun and its power cloud was a blaze of light on one side of the deck. They were above the rings, but still so close . . . It was like standing at sunset on a beach of colored sands . . . that stretched to an infinite horizon. The Skroderiders stared into it, their fronds gently swaying.

Twenty kilometers above the rings. One thousand. They lit the *OOB*'s main torch and accelerated across the system. The Skroderiders came slowly out of their trance. Once they arrived at the second harbor, the regrowth would take about five hours – assuming Rihndell's agent had not deteriorated; the Saint claimed it was recently imported from the Top, and undiluted.

'Okay, so when do we deliver the trellises?'

'On completion of the repairs. We can't depart until Saint Rihndell – or *his* customers – are satisfied that all the pieces are genuine.'

Pham drummed his fingers on the comm console. This operation brought back a lot of memories, some of them hair-raising. 'So they get the goods while we're still in the middle of RIP. I don't like it.'

'See here, Sir Pham. Your experience with star trading was in the Slow Zone, where exchanges were separated by decades or centuries of travel time. I admire you for that, more than I can say – but it gives you a twisted view of things. Up here in the Beyond, the notion of return business is important. We know very little of Saint Rihndell's inner motivation, but we do know his repair business has existed for at least forty years. Sharp dealing we can expect from him, but if he robbed or murdered very many, trader groups would know, and his little business would starve.'

'Hmf.' No point in arguing it right now, but Pham guessed that this situation was special. Rihndell – and the RIPers in general – had Death to Vermin sitting on their doorstep, and stories of major chaos coming from the direction of Sjandra Kei. With that background they might just lose their courage once they had the trellises. Some precautions were in order. He drifted off to the ship's machine shop.

<h1 style="text-align:center">28</h1>

Ravna came to the cargo deck as Blueshell and Greenstalk were preparing the trellises for delivery. She moved hesitantly, pushing awkwardly from point to point. There were dark rings, almost bruises, beneath her eyes. She returned Pham's hug almost tentatively, but didn't let go. 'I want to help. Is there anything I can do to help?'

The Skroderiders left their trellises and rolled over. Blueshell ran a frond gently across Ravna's arm. 'Nothing for you to do now, my Lady Ravna. We have everything well, ah, in hand. We'll be back in less than an hour, and then we can be rid of here.'

But they let her check their cameras and the cargo strap-downs. Pham drifted close by her as she inspected the trellises. The twisted carbon blocks looked stranger than the one alone had. Properly stacked, they fit perfectly. More than a meter across, the stack looked like a three-dimensional jigsaw puzzle carved from coal. Counting a separate bag of loose spares, they totaled less than half a kilogram. *Huh.* Damn things should be flammable as hell. Pham resolved to play with the remaining hundred-odd trellises after they were safely back in deep space.

Then the Skroderiders were through the cargo lock with their delivery, and they could only follow along on their cameras.

This secondary harbor was not really part of the tusk-leg race's terrane. The inside of the arc was far different from what they had seen on the Skroderiders' first trip. There were no exterior views. Cramped passages wound between irregular walls pocked with dark holes. Insects flew everywhere, often covering parts of the camera balls. To Pham, the place looked filthy. There was no evidence of the terrane's owners – unless they were the pallid worms that sometimes stuck a featureless head up from a burrow hole. Over his voice link, Blueshell opined that these were very ancient tenants of the RIP system. After a million years and a hundred transcendent emigrations, the residue might still be sentient, but stranger than anything evolved in the Slow Zone. Such a people would be protected from physical extinction by ancient automation, but they would also be inward-turning, totally cautious, absorbed in concerns that were inane by any outside standard. It was the type that most often lusted after trellis work.

Pham tried to keep an eye on everything. The Riders had to travel almost four kilometers from the harbor lock to reach the place where the trellises would be 'validated.' Pham counted two exterior locks along the way, and nothing that looked especially threatening – but then how would he know what 'threatening' looked like here? He had the *OOB* mount an exterior watch. A large shepherd satellite floated on the outer side of the ring, but there were no other ships in this harbor. The EM and ultra-environment seemed placid, and what could be seen on the local net did not make the ship's traffic analysis suspicious.

Pham looked up from the reports. Ravna had drifted across the deck to the outside view. The repair work was visible, though not spectacular. A pale greenish aura hung around the damaged spines. It was scarcely brighter than the glow you often see on ship hulls in low planetary orbit. She turned and said softly, 'Is it really getting fixed?'

'As far as we can – I mean yes.' Ship's automation was monitoring the regrowth, but they wouldn't know for sure till they tried to fly with it.

Pham was never sure why Rihndell had the Skroderiders pass through the wormheads' terrane; maybe, if the creatures were the ultimate trellis users, they wanted a look at the sellers. Or maybe it had some connection with the treachery that ultimately followed. In any case the Riders were soon out of it, and into a polyspecific concourse as crowded as any low-tech bazaar.

Pham's jaw sagged. Everywhere he looked there was a different class of sophont. Intelligent life is a rare development in the universe; in all his life in the Slow Zone, he had known three nonhuman races. But the universe is a big place, and with ultradrive it was easy to find other life. The Beyond collected the detritus of countless migrations, an accumulation that finally made civilization ubiquitous. For a moment he lost track of his surveillance programs and his general suspicions, drowned in the wonder of it. Ten species? Twelve? Individuals brushed familiarly by one another. Even Relay had not been like this. But then Harmonious Repose was a civilization lost in stagnation. These races had been part of the RIP complex for thousands of years. The ones that could interact had long since learned to do so.

And nowhere did he see butterfly wings on creatures with large, compassionate eyes.

He heard a small sound of surprise from the far side of the deck. Ravna was standing close by a window that looked out from one of Greenstalk's side cameras. 'What is it, Rav?'

'Skroderiders. See?' She pointed into the mob and zoomed the view. For a moment the images towered over her. Through the passing chaos he had a glimpse of hull forms and graceful fronds. Except for cosmetic stripes and tassles, they looked very familiar indeed.

'Yeah, there's a small colony of them hereabouts.' He opened the channel to Greenstalk and told her about the sighting.

'I know. We . . . smelled them. Sigh. I wish we had time to visit them after this. Finding friends in far places . . . always nice.' She helped Blueshell push the trellises around a balloon aquarium. They could see Rihndell's people just ahead. Six tusk-legs sat on the wall around what might be test equipment.

Blueshell and Greenstalk pushed their ball of frothy carbon into the group. The scrimshawed one leaned close to the pile and reached out to fondle the pieces with its tiny arms. One after another the trellises were placed in the tester. Blueshell moved in close to watch, and Pham set the main windows to look through his cameras. Twenty seconds passed. Rihndell's Trisk interpreter said, 'First seven test true, make an interlocked septet.'

Only then did Pham realize he had been holding his breath. The next three 'septets' passed too. Another sixty seconds. He glanced at the ship's repair status. *OOB* considered the job done but for sign-off commit from the local net. *Another few minutes and we can kiss this place goodbye!*

But there are always problems. Saint Rihndell bitched about the twelfth and fifteenth sets. Blueshell argued at length, grudgingly produced replacement pieces from his bag of spares. Pham couldn't tell if the Skroderider was debating for the fun of it, or if he really was short on good replacements.

Twenty-five sets okayed.

'Where is Greenstalk going?' said Ravna.

'What?' Pham called up the view from Greenstalk's cameras. She was five meters from Blueshell and moving away. He panned wildly about. A local Skroderider was on her left and another floated inverted above her. Its fronds touched hers in apparently amiable conversation. '*Greenstalk!*' There was no reply.

'Blueshell! What's happening?' But that Rider was in gesticulating argument with the tusk-legs. Still another set of trellises had failed their examination. '*Blueshell!*' After a moment the Rider's voice came over their private channel. He sounded drifty, the way he often did when he was jammed or overloaded. 'Not to bother me now, Sir Pham. I'm down to three perfect replacements. I must persuade these fellows to settle for what they already have.'

Ravna broke in, 'But what about Greenstalk? What's happening to her?' The cameras had lost sight of each other. Greenstalk and her companions emerged from a dense crowd and floated across the middle of the concourse. They were using gas jets instead of wheels. Someone was in a hurry.

The seriousness of events finally got through to Blueshell. The view from his skrode turned wildly as he rolled back and forth around Saint Rihndell's people. There was the rattle of Rider talk and then his voice came back on the inside channel, plaintive and confused. 'She's gone. She's gone. I must . . . I have to . . .' Abruptly he rolled back to the tusk-legs and resumed the argument that had just been interrupted. After a couple of seconds his voice came back on the inside channel. 'What should I do, Sir Pham? I have a sale here still incomplete, yet my Greenstalk has wandered off.'

Or been kidnapped. 'Get us the sale, Blueshell. Greenstalk will be okay . . . *OOB*: Plan B.' He grabbed a headset and pushed off from the console.

Ravna rose with him. 'Where are you going?'

He grinned. 'Out. I thought Saint Rihndell might lose his halo when the crunch came – and I made plans.' She followed him as he glided toward the floor hatch. 'Look. I want you to stay on deck. I can only carry so much snoop equipment; I'll need your coordination.'

'But—'

He went through the hatch headfirst, missing the rest of her objection. She didn't follow, but a second later her voice was back, in his headset. Some of the tremor was gone from her voice; the old Ravna was there, fighting out from under her other problems. 'Okay, I'll back you . . . but what can we *do?*'

Pham pulled himself hand over hand down the passageway, accelerating to a speed that would have left a lubber caroming off the walls. Ahead loomed the uncompromising wall of the cargo lock. He swatted a hand gently at the wall and flipped head over heels. He dragged his hands precisely against the wall flanges, slowing just enough so the impact with the hatch did not break his ankles. Inside the lock, the ship had his suit already powered up.

'Pham, you can't go out.' Evidently she was watching through the lock's cameras. 'They'll know we're a human expedition.'

His head and shoulders were already in the suit's top shell. He felt the bottom pushing up around him, the seals fastening. 'Not necessarily.' *And by now it probably doesn't matter.* 'There are plenty of two-arm/two-leg critters around, and I've glued some camouflage to this outfit.' He cupped his chin in the helmet controls and reset the displays. The armored pressure suit was a very primitive thing compared to the field suits of Relay. Yet the Qeng Ho would have given a starship for this gear. He'd originally put the thing together to impress the Tines, *but it's going to get some early testing.*

He chinned up the outside view, what Ravna was seeing: his figure was unrelieved black, more than two meters tall. The hands were backed with carapace-claws and every edge of his figure was razor-sharp and spined. These most recent additions should break the lines of the strictly human form, and hopefully be intimidating as hell.

Pham cycled the lock and pushed off into the wormheads' terrane. Walls of mud stood all around, misty in humid air and swarms of insects.

Ravna's voice was in his ear. 'I've got a low-level query, probably automatic: "Why you send third negotiator?"'

'Ignore it.'

'Pham, be careful. These Middle Beyond cultures, the old ones, they keep nasty things in reserve. Otherwise they wouldn't still be around.'

'I'll be a good citizen.' *As long as I'm treated nice.* He was already halfway to the concourse gate. He chinned up a small window from Blueshell's camera. All this high-bandwidth comm was courtesy of the local net. Strange that Rihndell was still providing the service. Blueshell seemed to be negotiating still. Maybe there *wasn't* a scam . . . or anyway, not one that Saint Rihndell was in on.

'Pham, I've lost the video from Greenstalk, just as she went into some kind of tunnel. Her location beacon is still clear.'

The concourse gate made an opening for him, and then Pham was in the crowded market volume. He heard the raucous hubbub even through his armor. He moved slowly, sticking to the most uncrowded paths, following the guide ropes that threaded the space. The mob was no problem. Everyone made way, some with almost panicky haste. Pham didn't know whether it was his razor spines or the trace of chlorine his suit 'leaked'. *Maybe that last touch was a bit much.* But the whole point was to look nonhuman. He slowed even more, doing his best not to nick anyone. Something awfully like a target-designation laser flickered in his rear window. He ducked quickly around an aquarium as Ravna said, 'The terrane just complained to your suit: "You are in violation of dress-code" is how the translation comes out.'

Is it my chlorine B.O., or have they detected the guns? 'What about outside? Any Butterflies in sight?'

'No. Ship activity hasn't changed much during the last five hours. No Aprahanti movement or change in comm status.' Long pause. Indirectly from the *OOB* bridge he could hear Blueshell talking with Ravna, the words indistinct but excited. He jabbed around, trying to find the direct connection. Then Ravna was talking to him again. 'Hei! Blueshell says Rihndell has accepted the shipment! He's onloading the agrav fabric right now. And *OOB* just got a commit on the repairs!' So they were ready to fly – except that three of them were still ashore, and one of them was missing.

Pham floated over the top of the aquarium and finally caught direct sight of Blueshell. He tweaked the suit's gas jets very carefully and settled down beside the Rider.

His arrival was about as welcome as finger-mites at a picnic. The scrimshawed one had been chattering away, tapping his articulated artwork on the wall as his helper translated into Trisk. Now the creature drew in his tusks, and the neck arms folded themselves. The others followed suit. All of them sidled up the wall, away from Blueshell and Pham. 'Our business is now complete. We don't know where your friend has gone,' said the Trisk interpreter.

Blueshell's fronds extended after them, wavering. 'B-but just a little guidance is all we need. Who—' It was no use. Saint Rihndell and his merry crew kept going. Blueshell rattled in abrupt frustration. His fronds angled slightly, turning all attention on Pham Nuwen. 'Sir Pham, I am doubting now your expertise as a trader. Saint Rihndell might have helped.'

'Maybe.' Pham watched the tusk-legs disappear into the crowd, pulling the trellises behind them like a big black balloon. Ugh. Maybe Rihndell was simply an honest trader. 'What are the chances that Greenstalk would abandon you in the middle of something like that?'

Blueshell dithered for a moment. 'In an ordinary trade stop, she might have noticed some extraordinary profit opportunity. But here, I—'

Ravna's voice interrupted sympathetically, 'Maybe she just, uh, forgot the context?'

'No.' Blueshell was definite. 'The skrode would never permit such a failure, not in the middle of a hard trade.'

Pham shifted windows around inside his helmet, looking in all directions. The crowd was still keeping an open space around them. There was no evidence of cops. *Would I know them if I saw them?* 'Okay,' said Pham. 'We have a problem, whether I'd come out or not. I suggest we take a little walk, see if we can find where Greenstalk went.'

Rattle. 'We have little choice now. My Lady Ravna, do please try to reach the tusk-legs interpreter. Perhaps he can link us to the local Skroderiders.' He came off the wall, rotated on gas jets. 'Come along, Sir Pham.'

Blueshell led the way across the concourse, vaguely in the direction Greenstalk had gone. Their path was anything but straight, more a drunkard's walk that once took them almost back to their starting place. 'Delicately delicately,' the Skroderider responded when Pham complained about the pace. The Rider never insisted on passage through clots of critters. If they did not respond to the gentle waving of his fronds, he detoured all around them. And he kept Pham directly behind him so the intimidation factor of the razored armor was of no use. 'These people may look very peaceable to you, Sir Pham, easy to push around. But note, this is among themselves. These races have had thousands of years to accommodate to one another, to achieve local commensality. To outsiders they will necessarily be less tolerant, else they would have been overrun long ago.' Pham remembered the 'dress-code' warning and decided not to argue.

The next twenty minutes would have been the experience of a lifetime for a Qeng Ho trader, to be within arm's reach of a dozen different intelligent species. But when they finally reached the far wall, Pham was grinding his teeth. Twice more he received a dress-code warning. The only bright spot: Saint Rihndell was still extending the courtesy of local net support, and

Ravna had more information: 'The local Skroderider colony is about a hundred kilometers from the concourse. There's some kind of transport station beyond the wall you're at.'

And the tunnel Greenstalk had entered was just ahead of them. From this angle they could see the dark of space beyond it. For the first time there was no problem with crowds; scarcely anyone was entering or leaving the hole.

Laser light twinkled in his rear windows. 'Dress code violation. Fourth warning. It says to "please leave the volume at once." '

'We're going. We're going.'

Darkness, and Pham boosted the gain on his helmet windows. At first he thought the 'transport station' was open to space, that the locals had restraint fields as in the High Beyond. Then he noticed the pillars merged into transparent walls. They were still indoors in the old-fashioned way, but the view . . . They were on the starward side of the arc. The ring particles were like dark fish floating silently a few tens of meters out from him. In the further distance, structures stuck out of the ring plane far enough to get sundazzle. But the brightest object was almost overhead: the blue of ocean, the white of cloud. Its soft light flooded the ground around him. However far the Qeng Ho fared, such a sight had been welcome. Yet this was not quite the real thing. This was only approximately spherical, and its face was bisected by the shadow of the ring. It was a small object, not more than a few hundred klicks above him, one of the shepherd satellites they had seen on the way in. The shepherd's haze of atmosphere was crisply bounded by the sides of some vast canopy.

He dragged his attention down from the sight. 'Ten to one that's the Skroderiders' terrane.'

'Of course,' Blueshell replied. 'It's typical. The surf in such minigravity can never be what I prefer, but—'

'Dear Blueshell! Sir Pham! Over here.' It was Greenstalk's voice. According to Pham's suit, it was a local connection, not relayed through the OOB.

Blueshell's fronds angled in all directions. 'Are you all right, Greenstalk?' They rattled back and forth at each other for a few seconds. Then Greenstalk resumed in Trisk: 'Sir Pham. Yes, I'm all right. I'm sorry to upset you all so much. But I could tell the deal with Rihndell was going to work out, and then these local Riders stopped by. They are wonderful people, Sir Pham. They have invited us across to their terrane. Just for a day or so. It will be a wonderful rest before we go on our way. And I think they may be able to help us.'

Like the quest romances he'd found in Ravna's bedtime library: the weary travelers, partway to their goal, find a friendly haven and some special gift. Pham switched to a private line to Blueshell: 'Is that really Greenstalk? Is she under duress?'

'It's her, and free, Sir Pham. You heard us speaking. I've been with her two hundred years. No one's twisting her fronds.'

'Then why the *hell* did she skip out on us? Pham surprised himself, almost hissing the words.

Long pause. 'That *is* strange. My guess: these local Riders somehow know something very important to us. Come, Sir Pham. But carefully.' He rolled away in what seemed a random direction.

'Rav, what do you—' Pham noticed the red light blinking on his comm status panel, and his irritation chilled. How long had the link to Ravna been down?

Pham followed Blueshell, floating low behind the other, using his gas jets to pace the Skroderider. This entire area was covered with the stickem that Riders liked for zero-gee rolling. Yet right now the place seemed deserted. Nobody in sight where just a hundred meters away there were bustling crowds. The whole thing screamed ambush, yet it didn't make sense. If Death to Vermin – or their stooges – had spotted them, a simple alarm would have served. Some Rihndell game . . . ? Pham powered up the suit's beam weapons and enabled countermeasures; midge cameras flitted off in all directions. So much for dress codes.

The bluish moonlight washed the plain, showing soft mounds and angular arrays of unknown equipment. The surface was pocked with holes (tunnel entrances?). Blueshell said something muddled about the 'beautiful night,' how much fun it would be to sit on the seashore a hundred kilometers above them. Pham scanned in all directions, trying to identify fields of fire and killing zones.

The view from one of his midges showed a forest of leafless fronds – Skroderiders standing silent in the moonlight. They were two hillocks away. Silent, motionless, without any lights . . . perhaps just enjoying the moonlight. In the midge's amplified view, Pham had no trouble identifying Greenstalk; she was standing at one end of a line of five Riders, her hull stripes clearly visible. There was a hump on the front of her skrode, and a rod-like projection. Some kind of restraint? He floated a couple of midges near. *A weapon.* All those Riders were armed.

'We're already aboard the transport, Blueshell,' came Greenstalk's voice. 'You'll see it in a few more meters, just on the other side of a ventilator pile,' apparently referring to the mound that he and the Skroderider were approaching. But Pham knew there was no flier there; Greenstalk and her guns were to the side of their progress. Treachery, very workmanlike but also very low tech. Pham almost shouted out to Blueshell. Then he noticed the flat ceramic rectangle mounted in the hill just a few meters behind the Rider. The nearest midge reported it was some kind of explosive, probably a directional mine. A low-resolution camera, barely more than a motion sensor, was mounted beside it. Blueshell had rolled nonchalantly past the thing, all the while chattering with Greenstalk. *They let him past.* New suspicions rose dark and grim. Pham broke to a stop, backing quickly; never touching ground, the only sounds he made were the quiet hisses of his gas jets. He detached one of his wrist claws and had a midge fly it close past the mine's sensor . . .

There was a flash of pale fire and a loud noise. Even five meters to the side, the shock wave pushed him back. He had a glimpse of Blueshell thrown frond over wheels on the far side of the mine. Edged metal whizzed about, but mindlessly: nothing came back to attack again. Several midges were destroyed by the blast.

Pham took advantage of the racket to accelerate hard, scooting up a nearby 'hill' and into a shallow valley (alley?) that looked down on the Skroderiders. The ambushers rolled forward around the hill, rattling happily at one another. Pham held his fire, curious. After a moment, Blueshell floated into the air a hundred meters away. 'Pham?' he said plaintively. 'Pham?'

The ambushers ignored Blueshell. Three of them disappeared around the hill. Pham's midges saw them stop in consternation, fronds erect – they had realized he'd gotten away. The five spread out, searching the area, hunting him down. There was no persuasive talk from Greenstalk anymore.

There was a sharp cracking sound and blaster fire glowed from behind a hill. Somebody was a little nervous on the trigger.

Above it all floated Blueshell, the perfect target, yet still untouched. His speech was a combination of Trisk and Rider rattle now, and where Pham could understand it, he heard fear. 'Why are you shooting? What is the problem? Greenstalk, please!'

The paranoid in Pham Nuwen was not deceived. *I don't want you up there looking down.* He sighted his main beam gun on the Rider, then shifted his aim and fired. The blast was not in visible wavelengths, but there were gigajoules in the pulse. Plasma coruscated along the beam, missing Blueshell by less than five meters. Well above the Skroderider, the beam struck hull crystal. The explosion was spectacular, an actinic glare that sent glowing fragments in a thousand rays.

Pham flew sideways even as the ceiling flared. He saw Blueshell spin off, regain control – and move precipitously for cover. Where Pham's beam had hit, a corona of light was dimming from blue through orange and red, its light still brighter than the shepherd moon overhead.

His warning shot had been like a great finger pointing back toward his location. In the next fifteen seconds, four of the ambushers fired on the place Pham had been. There was silence, then faint rustling. In a game of stealth, the five might think themselves easy winners. They still hadn't realized how well-equipped he was. Pham smiled at the pictures coming in from his midges. He had every one of them in sight, and Blueshell too.

If it were just these four – five?, there would be no problem. But surely reinforcements, or at least complications, were on the way. The wound in the ceiling had cooled to darkness, but there was a *hole* there now, half a meter across. The sound of hissing wind came from it, a sound that brought reflex fear to Pham even in his armor. It might take a while before the leak affected the Skroderiders, but it was an emergency nevertheless. It would attract notice. He stared at the hole. Down here it was stirring a breeze, but in the few meters right below the hole there was a miniature tornado of dust and loose junk, hurtling up and out . . .

And beyond the transparent hull, in space:

A gap of dark and then a glittering plume, where the debris emerged from the arc's shadow into the sunlight. A neat idea struggled for his attention.

Oops. The five Riders had roughly encircled him. Now one blundered into view, saw him, and snapped a shot. Pham returned fire and the other exploded in a cloud of superheated water and charred flesh. Its undamaged skrode sailed across the space between the hills, collecting panicky fire from the others. Pham changed position again, moving in the direction he knew was farthest from his enemies' positions.

A few more minutes of peace. He looked up at the crystal plume. There was something . . . *yes.* If reinforcements should come, why not for him? He sighted on the plume and shunted his voice line through the gun's trigger circuit. He almost started talking, then thought . . . *Better lower the power on this one.* Details. He aimed again, fired continuously, and said, 'Ravna, I sure as hell hope you have your eyes open. I need help . . .' and briefly described the crazy events of the last ten minutes.

This time his beam was putting out less than ten thousand joules per second, not enough to glow the air. But reflecting off the plume beyond the hull, the modulation should be visible for thousands of klicks, in particular to the *OOB* on the other side of the habitat.

The Skroderiders were closing in again. Damn. No way he could leave *this* message on automatic send; he needed the 'transmitter' for more important things. Pham flew from valley to valley, maneuvering behind the Rider that was farthest from the others. One against three – four? He had superior firepower and information, but one piece of bad luck and he was dead. He floated up on his next target. Quietly, carefully . . .

A seat of light brushed his arm, flaring the armor incandescent. White hot drops of metal sprayed as he twisted out of the way. He boosted straight across the space between three hillocks, firing down on the Rider there. Lights crisscrossed around him, and then he was under cover again. They were *fast*, almost as if they had automatic aiming gear. Maybe they did: their skrodes.

Then the pain hit. Pham folded on himself, gasping. If this were like wounds he remembered, there would be char to the bone. Tears floated in his eyes and consciousness disappeared in a nauseated faint. He came to. It could only be a second or two later – else he'd never have wakened. The others were a lot closer now, but the one he'd fired on was just a glowing crater and random skrode fragments. His suit's automation brought the damaged armor in close to his side. He felt the chill of local anesthetic and the pain dimmed. Pham eased around the hill, trying to keep all three of his antagonists simultaneously out of sight. They had caught on to his midges; every few seconds a glow erupted or a hill top turned to glowing slag. It was overkill, but the midges were dying . . . and he was losing his greatest advantage.

Where is Blueshell? Pham cycled through the views from his remaining midges, then his own. The bastard was back in the air, high above the combat – untouched by his fellow Riders. *Reporting everything I do.* Pham rolled over, awkwardly bringing his gun to bear on the tiny figure. He hesitated. *You're getting soft, Numen.* Blueshell abruptly accelerated downwards, his cargo scarf billowing out behind him. Evidently he was using his gas jets' full power. Against the background noise of bubbling metal and blast beam thunder, his fall was totally silent. He was driving straight for the nearest of the attackers.

Thirty meters up, the Rider released something large and angular. The two separated, Blueshell braking and diving to the side. He disappeared behind the hills. At the same time, much nearer, came a solid *thud/crunch.* Pham spent his next to last midge for a peek around the hillside. He had a glimpse of a skrode, and fronds splayed all about a squashed stalk. There was a flash of light, and the midge was gone.

Only two ambushers left. One was Greenstalk.

For ten seconds there was no more firing. Yet things were not completely silent. The slumped, glowing metal of his arm popped and sputtered as it cooled. High above was the susurrus of air escaping the hull. Fitful breezes whispered around ground level, making it impossible to keep position without constant tweaking at his jets. He paused, letting the current carry him silently out of his little valley. *There.* A ghostly hiss that was not his own. *Another.* The two were closing in on him from different directions. They might not know his exact position, but they could obviously coordinate their own.

The pain faded in and out, along with consciousness. Short pulses of agony and darkness. He dared not fool with any more anesthetic. Pham saw frond tips peeping over a nearby hill. He halted, watched the fronds. Most likely, there was just enough vision area in the tips to sense motion . . . Two seconds passed. Pham's last midge showed the other attacker floating silently in from the side. Any second now, the two would pop up. At that instant, Pham would have given anything for an armed midge. In all his stupid hacking, he'd never gotten around to that. *No help for it.* He waited for a moment of clear consciousness, long enough to boost over the enemy and shoot.

There was a rattle of fronds, loud self-announcement. Pham's midge caught sight of Blueshell rolling behind slatted walls a hundred meters away. The Skroderider rushed from protection to protection, but always closer to Greenstalk's position. And the rattling? Was it a pleading? Even after five months with the Riders, Pham had only the vaguest sense of their rattle-talk. Greenstalk – the Greenstalk who had always been the shy one, the compulsively honest one – rattled nothing back. She swung her beamer around, raking the slats with fire. The third Rider popped up just far enough to shoot at the slats. His angle would have been just right to fry Blueshell where he stood – except that the movement took him directly in front of Pham Nuwen's gun.

Even as Pham fired, he was boosting out of his hole. Now was his only chance. If he could turn, fire back on Greenstalk before she was done with Blueshell—

The maneuver was an easy head-over-heels that should have left him upside down and facing back upon Greenstalk. But nothing was easy for him now, and Pham came around spinning too fast, the landscape dwindling beneath him. But there was Greenstalk all right, swinging her weapon back toward him.

And there was Blueshell, racing from between pillars that glowed white in the heat of Greenstalk's fire. His voice was loud in Pham's ear: 'I beg you, don't kill her. Don't kill—'

Greenstalk hesitated, then turned the weapon back on the advancing Blueshell. Pham triggered his gun, letting his spin drag the beam across the ground. Consciousness ebbed. *Aim! Aim right!* He furrowed the land below with a glowing, molten arrow, that ended at something dark and slumped. Blueshell's tiny figure was still rolling across the wreckage, trying to reach her. Then Pham had turned too far and could not remember how to change the view. The sky swung slowly past his eyes:

A bluish moon with a sharp shadow 'cross its middle. A ship floating close, with feathery spines, like some giant bug. What in the Qeng Ho . . . *where am I? . . .* and consciousness fled.

29

There were dreams. He'd lost a captaincy once again, been busted down to tending potted plants in the ship's greenhouse. Sigh. Pham's job was to water them and make them bloom. But then he noticed the pots had wheels and moved behind his back, waiting, softly rattling. What had been beautiful was now sinister. Pham had been willing to water and weed the creatures; he had always admired them.

Now he was the only one who knew they were the enemy of life.

*

More than once in his life, Pham Nuwen had wakened inside medical automation. He was almost used to coffin-close tanks, plain green walls, wires and tubes. This was different, and it took him a while to realize just where he was. Willowy trees bent close around him, swaying just a little in the warm breeze. He seemed to be lying on softest moss in a tiny glade above a pond. Summer haze hung in the air above the water. It was all very nice, except that the leaves were *furry*, and not quite the green of anything he had ever seen. This was someone else's notion of home. He reached up toward the nearest branch, and his hand hit something unyielding just fifty centimeters above his face. A curved wall. For all the trick pictures, this was about the same size as the surgeons he remembered.

Something clicked behind his head; the idyll slid past him, taking its warm breeze with it. Somebody – *Ravna* – floated just beyond the cyclinder 'Hi, Pham.' She reached past the surgeon's hull to squeeze his hand. Her kiss was tremulous, and she looked haunted, as if she'd been crying a lot.

'Hi, yourself,' he said. Memory came back in jagged pieces. He tried to push off the bed, and found another similarity between this surgeon and ones of the Qeng Ho: he was securely plugged in.

Ravna laughed a little weakly. 'Surgeon. Disconnect.' After a moment Pham drifted free.

'It's still holding my arm.'

'No, that's the sling. Your left arm is going to take a while to regrow. It almost got burned off, Pham.'

'Oh.' He looked down at the white cocoon that meshed his arm against his side. He remembered the gunfight now . . . and realized that parts of his dream were deadly real. 'How long have I been out?' The anxiety spilled into his voice.

'About thirty hours. We're more than sixty light-years out from Harmonious Repose. We're doing okay, except that now everyone in creation seems to be chasing us.'

The dream. His free hand clamped hard on Ravna's arm. 'The Skrode-riders, where are they?' *Not on board, pray the Fleet.*

'W-what's left of Greenstalk is in the other surgeon. Blueshell is—'

Why have they let me live? Pham's eyes roved the room. They were in a utility cabin. Any weapons were at least twenty meters away. Hm. More important than guns: get command console privileges with the *OOB* . . . if it was not already too late. He pushed off from the surgeon and drifted out of the room.

Ravna followed. 'Take it easy, Pham. You just came out of a surgeon.'

'What have they said about the shoot-out?'

'Poor Greenstalk's not in a position to say anything, Pham. Blueshell says pretty much what you did: Greenstalk was grabbed by the rogue Riders, forced to lure you two into a trap.'

'Hmhm, hmhm,' Pham strove for a noncommittal tone. So maybe there was a chance; maybe Blueshell was not yet perverted. He continued his one-handed progress up the ship's axis corridor. A minute later he was on the bridge, Ravna tagging behind.

'Pham. What's the matter? There's a lot we have to decide, but—'

How right you are. He dived onto the command deck and made for the command console. '*Ship.* Do you recognize my voice?'

Ravna began, 'Pham, what's this—'

'Yes, sir.'

'—all about?'

'Command privileges,' he said. Capabilities granted while the Riders were ashore. Would they still be in place?

'Granted.'

The Skroderiders had had thirty hours to plan their defense. This was all too easy, too easy. 'Suspend command privileges for the Skroderiders. Isolate them.'

'Yes, sir,' came the ship's reply. *Liar!* But what more could he do? The sweep toward panic crested, and suddenly he felt very cool. He was Qeng Ho . . . and he was also godshatter.

Both Riders were in the same cabin, Greenstalk in the other copy of the ship's surgeon. Pham opened a window on the room. Blueshell sat on a wall beside the surgeon. He looked wilted, as when they heard about Sjandra Kei. He angled his fronds at the video pickup. 'Sir Pham. The ship tells me you've suspended our privileges?'

'*What* is going on, Pham?' Ravna had dug a foot into the floor, and stood glaring at him.

Pham ignored both questions. 'How is Greenstalk doing?' he said.

The fronds turned away, seemed to become even more limp. 'She lives . . . I thank you, Sir Pham. It took great skill to do what you did. Considering everything, I could not have asked for more.'

What did I do? He remembered firing on Greenstalk. Had he pulled his aim? He looked inside the surgeon. This was quite different from the human configuration: This one was mostly water-filled, with turbulent aeration along the patient's fronds. Asleep(?), Greenstalk looked frailer than he remembered, her fronds waving randomly in the water. Some were nicked, but her body seemed whole. His eyes traveled downwards toward the base of the stalk, where a Rider is normally attached to its skrode. The stump ended in a cloud of surgical tubing. And Pham remembered the last instant of the firefight, blasting the skrode out from under Greenstalk. *What is a Rider like without anything to ride?*

He pulled his eyes away from the wreckage. 'I've deleted your command privileges because I don't trust you.' *My former friend, tool of my enemy.*

Blueshell didn't answer. After a moment Ravna spoke. 'Pham. Without Blueshell, I'd never have gotten you out of that habitat. Even then – we were stuck in the middle of the RIP system. The shepherd satellite was screaming for our blood; they had figured out we were human. The Aprahanti were trying to break harbor and come down on us. Without Blueshell, we'd never have convinced local security to let us go ultra – we'd probably have been blown away the second we cleared the ring plane. We'd all be *dead* now, Pham.'

'Don't you know what happened down there?'

Some of the indignation left Ravna's face. 'Yes. But understand about skrodes. They are a mechanical contrivance. It's easy enough to disconnect the cyber part from the mechanical linkages. These guys were controlling the wheels and aiming the gun.'

Hmm. On the window behind Ravna, he could see Blueshell standing with his fronds motionless, not rushing to agree. Triumphant? 'That doesn't explain Greenstalk's sucking us in to the trap.' He raised a hand. 'Yeah, I know, she was bludgeoned into doing it. Only problem, Ravna, she had no hesitation. She was enthusiastic, bubbly.' He stared over the woman's shoulder. 'She was under no compulsion, *didn't you tell me that, Blueshell.*'

A long pause. Finally, 'Yes, Sir Pham.'

Ravna turned, drifting back so she could see both of them. 'But, but . . . it's still absurd. Greenstalk has been with us from the beginning. A thousand times she could have destroyed the ship – or gotten word to the outside. Why chance this stupid ambush?'

'Yes. Why didn't they betray us before . . .' Up until she asked the question, Pham had not known. He knew the *facts*, but had no coherent theory to hang them on. Now it all came together: the ambush, his dreams in the surgeon, even the paradoxes. 'Maybe she wasn't a traitor before. We really did escape from Relay without pursuit, without anyone knowing of us, much less our exact destination. Certainly no one expected humans to show up at Harmonious Repose.' He paused, trying to get it all together. The ambush, 'The ambush, it wasn't stupid – but it was completely ad hoc. The enemy had no backup. Their weapons were dumb, simple things—' *insight* '—why, I'll bet if you look at the wreckage of Greenstalk's skrode you'll find her beam gun was some sort of cutter tool. And the only sensor on the claymore mine was a motion detector: it had some civil use. All the gadgets were pulled together on very short notice by people who had not been expecting a fight. No, our enemy was very surprised by our appearance.'

'You think the Aprahanti could—'

'Not the Aprahanti. From what you said, they didn't break moorage till after the gunfight, when the Rider moon started screaming about us. Whoever's behind this is independent of the Butterflies, and must be spread in very small numbers across many star systems – a vast set of tripwires, listening for things of interest. They noticed us, and weak as their outpost was they tried to grab our ship. Only when we were getting away did they

240

advertise us. One way or another, they didn't want us to get away.' He jerked a hand at the ultratrace window. 'If I read that right, we've got more than five hundred ships on our tail.'

Ravna's eyes flicked to the display and back. Her voice was abstracted, 'Yes. That's part of the main Aprahanti fleet and . . .'

'There will be lots more, only they won't all be Butterflies.'

'. . . what are you saying then? Why would Skroderiders wish us ill? A conspiracy is senseless. They've never had a nation-state, much less an interstellar empire.'

Pham nodded. 'Just peaceful settlements – like that shepherd moon – in polyspecific civilizations all across the Beyond.' His voice softened. 'No, Rav, the Skroderiders are not the real enemy here . . . it's the thing behind them. The Straumli Perversion.'

Incredulous silence, but he noticed how tightly Blueshell held his fronds now. That one knew.

'It's the only explanation, Ravna. Greenstalk really was our friend, and loyal. My guess is that only a small minority of the Riders are under the Perversion's control. When Greenstalk fell in with them she was converted too.'

'T-that's impossible! This is the Middle of the Beyond, Pham. Greenstalk had courage, stubbornness. No brainwashing could have changed her so quickly.' A frightened desperation had come into her eyes. One explanation or another, some terrible thing must be true.

And I'm still here, alive and talking. A datum for godshatter; maybe there was yet a chance! He spoke almost as the understanding hit him. 'Greenstalk was loyal, yet she was totally converted in seconds. It wasn't just a perversion of her skrode, or some drug. It was as if both Rider and skrode had been designed from the beginning to respond.' He looked across at Blueshell, trying to gauge his reaction to what he would say next. 'The Riders have awaited their creator a long time. Their race is very old, far older than anyone except the senescent. They're everywhere, but in small numbers, always practical and peaceful. And somewhere in the beginning – a few *billion* years ago – their precursors were trapped in an evolutionary cul-de-sac. Their creator built the first skrodes, and made the first Riders. Now I think we know the who and the why.

'Yes, yes. I know there have been other upliftings. What's marvelous about this one is how stable it turned out to be. The greater skrodes are "tradition" Blueshell says, but that's a word I apply to cultures and to much shorter time scales. The greater skrodes of today are identical to ones a billion years ago. And they are devices that can be made anywhere in the Beyond . . . yet the design is clearly High Beyond or Transcendent.' That had been one his earliest humiliations about the Beyond. He had looked at the design diagram – dissections really – of skrodes. On the outside, the thing was a mechanical device, with moving parts even. And the text claimed that the whole thing would be made with the simplest of factories, scarcely more than what existed in some places in the Slow Zone. And yet the electronics was a seemingly random mass of components without any trace of hierarchical design or modularity. It worked, and far more efficiently than something designed by human-equivalent minds, but repair and debugging – of the cyber component – was out of the question. 'No one in the Beyond understands all the potentials of skrodes, much less the adaptations forced on their Riders. Isn't that so, Blueshell?'

The Rider clapped his fronds hard against his central stalk. Again a furious rattling. It was something Pham had never seen before. Rage? Terror? Blueshell's voder voice was distorted with nonlinearities: 'You ask? You *ask*? It's monstrous to ask me to help you in this—' the voice skeetered into high frequencies and he stood mute, his body shivering.

Pham of the Qeng Ho felt a stab of shame. The other knew and understood . . . and deserved better than this. The Riders must be destroyed, but they should not have to listen to his judging. His hand swept toward the communications cutoff, stopped. No. *This is your last chance to observe the Perversion's . . . work.*

Ravna's glance snapped back and forth between human and Skroderider, and he could tell that she understood. Her face had the same stricken look as when she learned about Sjandra Kei. 'You're saying the Perversion *made* the original skrodes.'

'And modified the Riders too. It was long ago, and certainly not the same instance of the Perversion that the Straumers created, but . . .'

The 'Blight,' that was the other common name for the Perversion, and closer to Old One's view. For all the Perversion's transcendence, its life style was more similar to a disease than anything else. Maybe that had helped to fool Old One. But now Pham could see: the Blight lived in pieces, across extraordinary reaches of time. It hid in archives, waiting for ideal conditions. And it had created helpers for its blooming . . .

He looked at Ravna, and suddenly realized a little more. 'You've had thirty hours to think about this, Rav. You saw the record from my suit. Surely you must have guessed some of this.'

Her gaze dropped from his. 'A little,' she finally said. At least she was no longer denying.

'You know what we have to do,' he said softly. Now that he understood what must be done, the godshatter eased its grip. Its will would be done.

'What is that?' said Ravna, as if she didn't know.

'Two things: Post this to the Net.'

'Who would believe?' The Net of a Million Lies.

'Enough would. Once they look, most folk will be able to see the truth here . . . and take the proper action.'

Ravna shook her head. 'No,' barely audible.

'The Net *must* be told, Ravna. We've discovered something that could save a thousand worlds. This is the Blight's hidden edge,' at least in the Middle and Low Beyond.

She just shook her head again. 'But screaming this truth would itself kill billions.'

'In honest defense!' He bounced slowly toward the ceiling, pushed himself back to the deck.

There were tears in her eyes now. 'These are exactly the arguments used to kill m-my family, my worlds . . . A-and I will not be part of it.'

'But the claims are *true* this time!'

'I've had enough of pogroms, Pham.'

Gentle toughness . . . and almost unbelievable. 'You would make this decision yourself, Rav? We know something that *others* – leaders wiser than either of us – should be free to decide upon. You would keep them from making that choice?'

She hesitated, and for an instant. Pham thought the civilized rule-follower in her would bring her around. But then her chin came up, 'Yes, Pham. I would deny them the choice.'

He made a noncommittal noise and drifted back toward the command console. No point in talking to her about what else must be done.

'And Pham, we will not kill Blueshell and Greenstalk.'

'There's no choice, Rav.' His hands played with the touch controls. 'Greenstalk was perverted; we have no idea how much of that survived the destruction of her skrode, or how long it will be before Blueshell goes bad. We can't take them along, or release them, either.'

Ravna drifted sideways, her eyes fixed on his hands. 'B-be careful who you kill, Pham,' she said softly. 'As you say, I've had thirty hours to think about my decisions, thirty hours to think about yours.'

'So.' Pham raised his hands from the controls. Rage (godshatter?) chased briefly through his mind. *Ravna, Ravna, Ravna*, a voice saying goodbye inside his head. Then all became very cold. He had been so afraid that the Riders had perverted the ship. Instead, this stupid fool had acted for them, *voluntarily*. He drifted slowly toward her. Almost unthinking, he held his arm and hand at combat ready. 'How do you intend to prevent me from doing what has to be done?' But he already guessed.

She didn't back away, even when his hand was centimeters from her throat. Her face held courage and tears. 'W-what do you think, Pham? While you were in the surgeon . . . I rearranged things. Hurt me, and you will be hurt worse.' Her eyes swept the walls behind him. 'Kill the Riders, and . . . and you will die.'

They stared at each other for a long moment, measuring. Maybe there weren't weapons buried in the walls. He probably could kill her before she could defend. But then there were a thousand ways the ship could have been programmed to kill him. And all that would be left would be the Riders . . .

flying down to the Bottom, to their prize. 'So what do we do, then?' he finally said.

'As b-before, we go to rescue Jefri. We go to recover the Countermeasure. I'm willing to put some restrictions on the Riders.'

A truce with monsters, mediated by a fool.

He pushed off, sailing around her back down the axis corridor. Behind him he heard a sob.

They stayed well clear of each other the next few days. Pham was allowed shallow access to ship controls. He found suicide programs threaded through the applications layers. But a strange thing, and reason for chagrin if he had been capable of it: The changes dated from hours after his confrontation with Ravna. She'd had nothing when she stood against him. *Thank the Powers, I didn't know*. The thought was forgotten almost before he formed it.

So. The charade would proceed right to the end, a continuing game of lie and subterfuge. Grimly, he set himself to winning that game. Fleets behind them, traitors surrounding him. By the Qeng Ho and his own godshatter, the Perversion would lose. The Skroderiders would lose. And for all her courage and goodness, Ravna Bergsndot would lose.

30

Tyrathect was losing the battle within herself, her battle with the Flenser. Oh, it wasn't near ended; better perhaps to say that the tide had turned. In the beginning there had been little triumphs, as when she let Amdijefri play alone with the commset without even the children guessing she was responsible. But such were many tendays past, and now . . . Some days she would be entirely in control of herself. Others – and these often seemed the happiest – would begin with her *seeming* in control.

It was not yet clear the sort of day today would be.

Tyrathect paced along the hoardings that topped the new castle's walls. The place was certainly new, but hardly yet a castle. Steel had built in panicky haste. The south and west walls were very thick, with embedded tunnels. But there were spots on the north side that were simply palisades backed by stony rubble. Nothing more could be done in the time that Steel had been given. She stopped for a moment, smelling fresh-sawn timber. The view down Starship Hill was as beautiful as she had ever seen it. The days were getting longer. Now there was only twilight between the setting and the rising of the sun. The local snow had retreated to its summer patches, leaving heather to turn green in the warmth. From here she could see miles, to where bluish sea haze clamped down on the offshore islands.

By the conventional wisdom, it would be suicide to attack the new castle

– even in its present ramshackle state – with less than a horde. Tyrathect smiled bitterly to herself. Of course, Woodcarver would ignore that wisdom. Old Woodcarver thought she had a secret weapon that would breach these walls from hundreds of feet away. Even now Steel's spies were reporting that the Woodcarvers had taken the bait, that their small army and their crude cannon had begun the overland trek up the coast.

She descended the wall stairs to the yard. She heard faint thunder. Somewhere north of Streamsdell, Steel's own cannoneers were beginning their morning practice. When the air was just right, you could hear it. There was to be no testing near the farmlands, and none but high Servants and isolated workers knew of the weapons. But by now Steel had thirty of the devices and gunpowder to match. The greatest lack was gunners. Up close the noise of firing was hellish. Sustained firing could deafen. Ah, but the weapons themselves: they had a range of almost eight miles, three times as great as Woodcarver's. They could deliver gunpowder 'bombs' that exploded on impact. There were places beyond the northern hills where the forest was gouged bare and slumping landslides showed naked rock – all from sustained barrages of gunfire.

And soon – perhaps today – the Flenserists would have radio too.

God damn you, Woodcarver! Of course Tyrathect had never met the Woodcarver, but Flenser had known that pack well: Flenser was mostly Woodcarver's offspring. The 'Gentle Woodcarver' had borne him and raised him to power. It had been Woodcarver who taught him about freedom of thought and experiment. Woodcarver should have known the pride that lived in Flenser, should have known that he would go to extremes his parent never dared. And when the new one's monstrous nature became clear, when his first 'experiments' were discovered, Woodcarver should have had him killed – or at the very least, fragmented. Instead, Flenser had been allowed to take exile . . . to create things like Steel, and they to create their own monsters, ultimately to build this hierarchy of madness.

And now, a century overdue, Woodcarver was coming to correct her mistake. She came with her toy guns, as overconfident and idealistic as ever. She came into a trap of steel and fire that none of her people would survive. If only there were some way to warn the Woodcarver. Tyrathect's only reason for being here was the oath she had sworn herself to bring down Flenser's Movement. If Woodcarver knew what awaited her here, if she even knew of the traitors in her own camp, there might be a chance. Last fall, Tyrathect had come close to sending an anonymous message south. There were traders who visited both kingdoms. Her Flenser memories told her which were likely independent. She almost passed one a note, a single piece of silkpaper, reporting the starship's landing and Jefri's survival. In that she had missed death by less than a day: Steel had shown her a report from the South, about the other human and Woodcarver's progress with the 'dataset.' There were things in the report that could only be known by someone at the top at Woodcarvers. Who? She didn't ask, but she guessed it was Vendacious; the Flenser in Tyrathect remembered that sibling pack well. They'd had . . . dealings. Vendacious had none of the raw genius of their joint parent, but there was a broad streak of opportunism in him.

Steel had shown her the report only to puff himself up, to prove to Tyrathect that he had succeeded in something that Flenser had never attempted. And it *was* a coup. Tyrathect had complimented Steel with more than usual sincerity . . . and quietly shelved her plans of warning. With a spy at the top at Woodcarver's, any message would be pointless suicide.

Now Tyrathect padded across the castle's outer yard. There was still plenty of construction going on, but the teams were smaller. Steel was building timber lodges all over the yard. Many were empty shells. Steel hoped to persuade Ravna to land at a special spot near the inner keep.

The inner keep. *That* was the only thing about this castle built to the standards of Hidden Island. It was a beautiful structure. It really could be what Steel told Amdijefri: a shrine to honor Jefri's ship and protect it from Woodcarver attack. The central dome was a smooth sweep of cantilevers and fitted stone, as wide as the main meeting hall on Hidden Island. Tyrathect watched it with one pair of eyes as she trotted round it. Steel intended to face the dome with the finest pink marble. It would be visible for dozens of miles into the sky. The deadfalls built into its structure were the centerpiece of Steel's plan, even if the rescuers didn't land in his other trap.

Shreck and two other high Servants stood on the steps of the castle's meeting hall. They came to attention as she approached. The three backed quickly away, bellies scraping stone . . . but not as quickly as last fall. They knew that the other Flenser Fragments had been destroyed. As Tyrathect swept past them, she almost smiled. For all her weakness and all her problems, she knew she could best these three.

Steel was already inside, alone. The most important meetings were all like this, just Steel and herself. She understood the relationship. In the beginning, Steel had been simply terrified of her – the one person he believed he could never kill. For ten days, he had teetered between grovelling before her and dismembering her. It was amusing to see the bonds Flenser had installed years before still having force. Then had come word of the death of the other Fragments. Tyrathect was no longer Flenser-in-Waiting. She had half expected death to come then. But in a way this made her safer. Now Steel was less afraid, and his need for intimate advice could be satisfied in ways he saw less threatening. She was his bottled demon: Flenser wisdom without the Flenser threat.

This afternoon he seemed almost relaxed, nodding casually to Tyrathect as she entered. She nodded back. In many ways Steel was her – Flenser's –

finest creation. So much effort had been spent honing Steel. How many packs-worth of members had been sacrificed to get just the combination that was Steel. She – Flenser – had wanted brilliance, ruthlessness. As Tyrathect she could see the truth. With all the flensing, Flenser had created a poor, sad thing. It was strange, but . . . sometimes Steel seemed like Flenser's most pitiable victim.

'Ready for the big test?' Tyrathect said. At long last, the *radios* seemed complete.

'In a moment. I wanted to ask you about timing. My sources tell me Woodcarver's army is on its way. If they make reasonable progress, they should be here in five tendays.'

'That's at least three tendays before Ravna's ship arrives.'

'Quite. We will have your old enemy disposed of long before we go for the high stakes. But . . . something is strange about the Two-Legs' recent messages. How much do you think they suspect? Is it possible that Amdijefri are telling them more than we know?'

It was an uncertainty Steel would have masked back when Tyrathect had been Flenser-in-Waiting. She slid to a seated position before replying. 'You might know the answer if you had bothered to learn more of the Two-Legs' language, dear Steel, or let me learn more.' Through the winter, Tyrathect had been desperate to talk to the children alone, to get warning to the ship. She was of two minds about that now. Amdijefri were so transparent, so innocent. If they glimpsed anything of Steel's treachery, they couldn't hide it. And what might the rescuers do if they knew Steel's villainy? Tyrathect had seen one starship in flight. Just its landing could be a terrible weapon. Besides . . . *If Steel's plan succeeds, we won't need the aliens' goodwill.*

Aloud, Tyrathect continued, 'As long as you can continue your magnificent performance, you have nothing to fear from the child. Can't you see that he loves you?'

For an instant Steel seemed pleased, and then the suspicion returned. 'I don't know. Amdi seems always to taunt me, as though he sees through my act.'

Poor Steel. Amdiranifani was his greatest success, and he would never understand it. In this one thing Steel had truly exceeded his Master, had discovered and honed a technique that had once been Woodcarver's. The Flenser eyed his former student almost hungrily. If only he could do him all over again; there must be a way to combine the fear and the flensing with love and affection. The resulting tool would truly merit the name Steel. Tyrathect shrugged. 'Take my word for it. *If* you can continue your kindness act, both children will be faithful. As for the rest of your question: I have noticed some change in Ravna's messages. She seems much more confident of their arrival time, yet something has gone wrong for them. I don't think they're any more suspicious than before; they seemed to accept that Jefri was responsible for Amdi's idea about the *radios*. That lie was a good move, by the way. It played to their sense of superiority. On a fair battlefield, we are probably their betters – and they *must not* guess that.'

'But what are they suddenly so tense about?'

The Fragment shrugged. 'Patience, dear Steel. Patience and observation. Perhaps Amdijefri have noticed this too. You might subtly inspire them to ask about it. My guess is the Two-Legs have their own politics to worry about.' He stopped and turned all his heads on Steel. 'Could you have your "source" down at Woodcarver's ferret about with the question?'

'Perhaps I will. That Dataset is Woodcarver's one great advantage.' Steel sat in silence for a moment, nervously chewing at his lips. Abruptly, he shook himself all over, as if to drive off the manifold threats he saw encroaching. 'Shreck!'

There was the sound of paws. The hatch creaked open and Shreck stuck a head inside. 'Sir?'

'Bring the *radio* outfits in here. Then ask Amdijefri if he can come down to talk to us.'

The *radios* were beautiful things. Ravna claimed that the basic device could be invented by civilizations scarcely more advanced than Flenser's. That was hard to believe. There were so many steps in the making, so many meaningless detours. The final result: eight, one-yard squares of night-darkness. Glints of gold and silver showed in the strange material. That, at least, was no mystery: a part of Flenser's gold and silver had gone into the construction.

Amdijefri arrived. They raced around the central floor, poked at the radios, shouted to Steel and the Flenser Fragment. Sometimes it was hard to believe they were not truly one pack, that the Two-Legs was not another member: They clung to each other as a single pack might. As often as not, Amdi answered questions about Two-Legs before Jefri had a chance to speak, using the 'I-pack' pronoun to identify both of them.

Today, however, there seemed to be a disagreement. 'Oh, *please* my lord, let me be the one to try it!'

Jefri rattled off something in Samnorsk. When Amdi didn't translate, he repeated the words more slowly, speaking directly to Steel. 'No. It is [something something] dangerous. Amdi is [something] small. And also, time [something] narrow.'

The Flenser strained for the meaning. *Damn.* Sooner or later their ignorance of the Two-Legs' language was going to cost them.

Steel listened to the human, then sighed the most marvelously patient sigh. 'Please. Amdi. Jefri. What is problem?' He spoke in Samnorsk, making more sense to the Flenser Fragment than the human child had.

Amdi dithered for a moment. 'Jefri thinks the radio jackets are too big for me. But look, it doesn't fit so badly!' Amdi jumped all around one of the night-dark squares, dragging it heedlessly off its velvet pallet onto the floor. He pulled the fabric over the back and shoulders of his largest member.

Now the *radio* was roughly the shape of a greatcloak; Steel's tailors had added clasps at the shoulders and gut. But the thing was vastly outsized for little Amdi. It stood like a tent around one of him. 'See? See?' The tiny head poked out, looking first at Steel and then at Tyrathect, willing their belief.

Jefri said something. The Amdi pack squeaked back angrily. Then, 'Jefri worries about everything, but *somebody* has to test the *radios*. There's this little problem with speed. *Radio* goes much faster than sound. Jefri's just afraid it's so fast it might confuse the pack using it. That's foolish. How much faster could it be than heads-together thought?' He asked it as a question. Tyrathect/Flenser smiled. The pack of puppies couldn't quite lie, but he guessed that Amdi knew the answer to his question – and that it did not support his argument.

On the other side of the hall, Steel listened with heads cocked – the picture of benign tolerance. 'I'm sorry, Amdi. It's just too dangerous for you to be the first.'

'But I am brave! And I want to help.'

'I'm sorry. After we know it's safe—'

Amdi gave a shriek of outrage, much higher than normal interpack talk, almost in the range of thought. He swarmed around Jefri, whacking at the human's legs with his butt ends. 'Hideous traitor!' he cried, and continued the insults in Samnorsk.

It took about ten minutes to get him calmed down to a sulk. He and Jefri sat on the floor, grumbling at each other in Samnorsk. Tyrathect watched the two, and Steel on the other side of the room. If irony were something that made sound, they would all be deaf by now. All their lives, Flenser and Steel had experimented on others – usually unto death. Now they had a victim who literally begged to be victimized . . . and he must be rejected. There was no question about the rejection. Even if Jefri had not raised objections, the Amdi pack was too valuable to be risked. Furthermore, Amdi was an eightsome. It was a miracle that such a large pack could function at all. Whatever dangers there were with *radio* would be much greater for him.

So a proper victim would be found. A proper wretch. Surely there were plenty of those in the dungeons beneath Hidden Island. Tyrathect thought back on all the packs she remembered killing. How she hated Flenser, his calculating cruelty. *I am so much worse than Steel. I made Steel.* She remembered where her thoughts had been the last hour. This was one of the bad days, one of the days when Flenser sneaked out from the recesses of her mind, when she rode the power of his reason higher and higher, till it became rationalization and she became him. Still, for a few more seconds she might be in control. What could she do with it? A soul that was strong enough might deny itself, might become a different person . . . might at the very least end itself.

'I-I will try the *radio*.' The words were spoken almost before he thought them. *Weak, silly frill.*

'What?' said Steel.

But the words had been clear, and Steel had heard. The Flenser Fragment smiled dryly. 'I want to see what this *radio* can do. Let me try it, dear Steel.'

They took the radios out into the yard, on the side of the starship that was hidden from general view. Here it would just be Amdijefri, Steel, and *whoever I am at the moment.* The Flenser Fragment laughed at the upwelling fear. Discipline, she had thought! Perhaps that was best. He stood in the middle of the yard and let the human help him with the radio gear. Strange to see another intelligent being so close, and towering over him.

Jefri's incredibly articulate paws arranged the jackets loosely on his backs. The inside material was soft, deadening. And unlike normal clothing, the *radios* covered the wearer's tympana. The boy tried to explain what he was doing. 'See? This thing,' he pulled at the corner of the greatcloak, 'goes over your head. The inside has [something] that makes sound into *radio*.'

The Fragment shrugged away as the boy tried to pull the cover forward. 'No. I can't think with these cloaks on.' Only by standing just so, all members facing inward, could the Fragment maintain full consciousness. Already the weaker parts of him were edging toward isolation panic. The conscience that was Tyrathect would learn something today.

'Oh. I'm sorry.' Jefri turned and spoke to Amdi, something about using the old design.

Amdi was heads-together just thirty feet away. He had been all frowns, sullen at being denied, nervous to be apart from the Two-Legs. But as the preparations continued, the frowns eased. The puppies' eyes grew wide with happy fascination. The Fragment felt a wave of affection for the puppies that came and went almost too fast to be noticed.

Now Amdi edged nearer, taking advantage of the fact that the cloaks muffled much of the Fragment's thought sounds. 'Jefri says maybe we shouldn't have tried to make the mind-size *radio*,' he said. 'But this will be so much better. I know it! And,' he said with transparent slyness, 'You could still let me test it instead.'

'No, Amdi. This is the way it must be.' Steel's voice was all soft sympathy. Only the Flenser Fragment could see the broad grin on a couple of the lord's members.

'Well, okay.' The puppies crept a little nearer. 'Don't be afraid, Lord Tyrathect. We've had the *radios* in sunlight for some time. They should have lots of power. To make them work you just pull all the belts tight, even the ones at your neck.'

'All of them *at once*?'

Amdi fidgeted. 'That's probably best. Otherwise, there will be such a mismatch of speeds that—' He said something to the Two-Legs.

Jefri leaned close. 'This belt goes here, and this here.' He pointed to the braid-bone straps that drew the head covering close. 'Then just pull this with your mouth.'

'The harder you pull, the louder the *radio*, 'Amdi added.

'Okay.' The Fragment drew himself together. He shrugged the jackets into place, tightening the shoulder and gut belts. *Deadly muffling*. The jackets almost seemed to mold themselves to his tympana. He looked at himself, and grasped desperately for what was left of consciousness. The jackets were beautiful, magic darkness yet with a hint of the golden-silver of a Flenserist Lord. Beautiful instruments of torture. Even Steel had not imagined such twisted revenge. Had he?

The Fragment grabbed the head straps and pulled.

Twenty years ago, when Tyrathect was new, she had loved to hike with her fission parent on the grassy dunes along Lake Kitcherri. That was before their great falling out, before loneliness drove Tyrathect to the Republic's Capital and her search for 'meaning.' Not all of the shore of Lake Kitcherri was beaches and dunes. Farther south there was the Rockness, where streams cut through stone to the water. Sometimes, especially when she and her parent had fought, Tyrathect would walk up from the shore along streams bordered by sheer, smooth cliffs. It was a sort of punishment: there were places where the stone had a glassy haze, and it didn't absorb sound at all. *Everything* was echoed, right up to the top of thought. It was if she were surrounded by copies of herself, and copies beyond them, all thinking the same sounds but out of step.

Of course, echoes are often a problem with unquilted stone walls, especially if the size and geometry are wrong. But the cliffs were such perfect reflectors, a quarrier's nightmare. And there were places where the shape of the Rockness conspired with the sounds . . . When Tyrathect walked there, she couldn't tell her own thought from the echoes. Everything was garbled with barely offset resonance. At first it had been a great pain that sent her running. But she forced herself back again and again, and finally learned to think even in the worst of the narrows.

Amdijefri's radio was just a little like the Kitcherri cliffs. *Enough to save me, maybe*. Tyrathect came to consciousness all piled in a heap. At most seconds had passed since she brought the *radios* to life; Amdi and Steel were simply staring at her. The human was rocking one of her bodies, talking to her. Tyrathect licked the boy's paw, then stood partly up. She heard only her own thoughts, but they had some of the jarring difference of the stone echoes.

She was back on her bellies again. Part of her was vomiting in the dirt. The world shimmered, out of tune. *Thought is there. Grab it! Grab it!* All a matter of coordination, of timing. She remembered Amdijefri talking about how fast the radio was. In a way, this was the reverse of the problem of the screaming cliffs.

She shook her heads, mastering the weirdness. 'Give me a moment,' she said, and her voice was almost calm. She looked around. Slowly. If she concentrated, didn't move fast, she could think. Suddenly she was aware of the greatcloaks, pressing in on all her tympana. She should have been deafened, isolated. Yet her thoughts were no muzzier than after a bad sleep.

She got to her feet again and walked slowly around the open space between Amdi and Steel. 'Can you hear me?' she asked.

'Yes,' said Steel. He edged nervously away from her.

Of course. The cloaks muffled sound like any heavy quilt: anything in the range of thought would be totally absorbed. But interpack speech and Samnorsk were low-pitched sound – they would scarcely be affected. She stopped, holding all her breath. She could hear birds and the sounds of timber being sawn somewhere on the far side of the inner yard. Yet Steel was only thirty feet from her. His thought noise should have been a loud intrusion, even confusing. She strained to hear . . . There was nothing but her own thoughts and a *stickety* buzzing noise that seemed to come from all directions.

'And we thought this would just give us control in battle,' she said, wonderingly. All of her turned, walking toward Amdi. He was twenty feet away, ten feet. Still no thought noise. Amdi's eyes were wide. The puppies held their ground; in fact all eight of him seemed to lean toward her. 'You knew about this all along, didn't you?' Tyrathect said.

'I hoped. Oh, I hoped.' He stepped closer. Five feet. The eight of him looked at the five of her from a distance of inches. He extended a nose, brushing muzzles with Tyrathect. His thought sounds came only faintly through the cloak, no louder than if he were fifty feet away. For a moment they looked at each other in stark astonishment. Nose to nose, and they both could still think! Amdi gave a whoop of glee and bounded in among Tyrathect, rubbing back and forth across her legs. 'See, Jefri,' he shouted in Samnorsk. 'It works. It works!'

Tyrathect wobbled under the assault, almost lost hold of her thoughts. What had just happened . . . In all the history of the world there had never been such a thing. If thinking packs could work paw by jowl . . . There were consequences and consequences, and she got dizzy all over again.

Steel moved a little closer, and suffered a flying hug from Jefri Olsndot. Steel was trying his best to join the celebration, but he wasn't quite sure what had happened. He hadn't lived the consequences like Tyrathect. 'Wonderful progress for the first try,' he said. 'But it must be painful even so.' Two of him looked sharply at her. 'We should get that gear off you, and give you a rest.'

'No!' Tyrathect and Amdi said almost together. She smiled back at Steel.

'We haven't really tested it yet, have we? The whole purpose was long-distance communications.' *We thought that was the purpose, anyway.* In fact, even if it had no better range than talk sounds, it was already a towering success in Tyrathect's mind.

'Oh.' Steel smiled weakly at Amdi and glared hidden faces at Tyrathect. Jefri was still hanging on two of his necks. Steel was a picture of barely concealed anguish. 'Well, go slowly then. We don't know what might happen if you run out of range.'

Tyrathect disentangled two of herself from Amdi and stepped a few feet away. Thought was as clear – and as potentially confusing – as before. By now she was beginning to get the feel of it though. She had very little trouble keeping her balance. She walked the two another thirty feet, about the maximum range a pack could coordinate in the quietest conditions. 'It's like I'm still heads-together,' she said wonderingly. Ordinarily at thirty feet, thoughts were faint and the time lag so bad that coordination was difficult.

'How far can I go?' she murmured the question to Amdi.

He made a human giggling sound and slid a head close to hers. 'I'm not sure. It should be good at least to the outer walls.'

'Well,' she said in a normal voice, for Steel, 'let's see if I can spread a little bit further.' The two of her walked another ten yards. She was more than sixty feet across!

Steel was wide-eyed. 'And now?'

Tyrathect laughed. 'My thought's as crisp as before.' She turned her two and walked away.

'*Wait!*' roared Steel, bounding to his feet. '*That's far—*' then he remembered his audience, and his fury became more a frightened concern for her welfare. 'That's far too dangerous for the first experiment. Come back!'

From where she sat with Amdi, Tyrathect smiled brightly. 'But Steel, I never left,' she said in Samnorsk.

Amdijefri laughed and laughed.

She was one hundred fifty feet across. Her two broke into a careful trot – and she watched Steel swallow back foam. Her thought still had the sharp, abrupt quality of closer than heads-together. *How fast* is *this radio thing?*

She passed close by Shreck and the guards posted at the edge of the field. 'Hey, hey, Shreck! What do you say?' one of her said at his stupefied faces. Back with Amdi and the rest of her, Steel was shouting at Shreck, telling him to follow her.

Her trot became an easy run. She split, one going north of the inner yard, the other south. Shreck and company followed, clumsy with shock. The dome of inner keep was between her, a sweeping hulk of stone. Her *radio* thoughts faded into the *stickety* buzzing.

'Can't think,' she mumbled to Amdi.

'Pull on the mouth straps. Make your thoughts louder.'

Tyrathect pulled, and the buzzing faded. She regained her balance and raced around the starship. One of her was in a construction area now. Artisans looked up in shock. A loose member usually meant a fatal accident or a pack run amok. In either case the singleton must be restrained. But Tyrathect's member was wearing a greatcloak that sparkled here and there of gold. And behind her Shreck and his guards were shouting for everyone to stand back.

She turned a head to Steel, and her voice was joy. 'I *soar!*' She ran through the cowering workers, ran toward the walls. She was *everywhere*, spreading and spreading. These seconds would make memories that woud outlast her soul, that would be legends in the minds of her descendants a thousand years from now.

Steel hunkered down. Things were totally out of his control now; Shreck's people were all on the far side of inner keep. All that he and Amdijefri could know came from Tyrathect – and the clamor of alarms.

Amdi bounced around her. 'Where are you now? Where?'

'Almost to the outer wall.'

'Don't go beyond that,' Steel said quietly.

Tyrathect scarcely heard. For a few more seconds she would drink this glorious power. She charged up the inside stairs. Guards scuttled back, some members jumping back into the yard. Shreck still followed, shouting for her safety.

One of her reached the parapet, then the other.

She gasped.

'Are you all right?' said Amdi.

'I—' Tyrathect looked about her. From her place on the south wall she could see herselves back in the castle yard: a tiny clump of gold and black that was her three and Amdi. Beyond the northeast walls stretched forest and valleys, the trails up into the Icefang mountains. To the west was Hidden Island and the misty inner waters. These were things she had seen a thousand times as Flenser. How he had loved them, his domain. But now . . . she was seeing as if in a dream. Her eyes were so far apart. Her pack was almost as wide as the castle itself. The parallax view made Hidden Island seem just a few paces away. Newcastle was like a model spread out around her. Almighty Pack of Packs – this was God's view.

Shreck's troopers were edging closer. He had sent a couple of packs back to get directions. 'A couple of minutes. I'll come down in a couple of minutes.' She spoke the words to the troopers on the palisade and to Steel back in the yard. Then she turned to survey her domain.

She had only extended two of herself across less than a quarter of a mile. But there was no perceptible time lag; coordination had the same abrupt feel it did when she was all together. And there was plenty more pull in the braid-bone straps. What if all five of her spread out, moved *miles* apart. All of the northland would be her private room.

And Flenser? Ah, Flenser. Where was he? The memories were still there, but . . . Tyrathect remembered the loss of consciousness right when the *radios* began working. It took a special skill of coordination to think in the face of such terrible speed. Perhaps Lord Flenser had never walked between close cliffs when he was new. Tyrathect smiled. Perhaps only her mindset could hold when using the *radios*. In that case . . . Tyrathect looked again across the landscape. Flenser had made a great empire. If these new developments were managed properly, then the coming victories could make it infinitely grander.

He turned to Shreck's troopers. 'Very well, I'm ready to return to Lord Steel.'

31

It was high summer when Woodcarver's army left for the north. The preparations had been frantic, with Vendacious driving himself and everyone else to the point of exhaustion. There had been thirty cannons to make – Scrupilo cast seventy tubes before getting thirty that would fire reliably. There had been cannoneers to train – and safe methods of firing to discover. There had been wagons to build and kherhogs to buy.

Surely word of the preparations had long ago filtered north. Woodcarvers was a port city; they could not close down the commerce that moved through it. Vendacious warned them of this in more than one inner council meeting: Steel knew they were coming. The trick was in keeping the Flenserists uncertain as to numbers and timing and exact purpose. 'We have one great advantage over the enemy,' he said. 'We have agents in his highest councils. We know what *he* knows of us.' They couldn't disguise the obvious from the spies, but the details were a different matter.

The army departed along inland routes, a dozen wagons here, a few squads there. In all there were a thousand packs in the expedition, but they would never be together till they reached deep forest. It would have been easier to take the first part of the trip by sea, but the Flenserists had spotters hidden high in the fjordlands. Any ship movement – even deep in Woodcarver territory – would be known in the north. So they traveled on forest paths, through areas that Vendacious had cleared of enemy agents.

At first the going was very easy, at least for those with the wagons. Johanna rode in one of the rear ones with Woodcarver and Dataset. *Even I'm beginning to treat the thing like an oracle*, thought Johanna. Too bad it couldn't really predict the future.

The weather was as beautiful as Johanna had ever seen it on Tines' world, an endless afternoon. It was strange that such unending fairness should make her so nervous, but she couldn't help it. This was so much like her first time on this world, when everything had . . . gone wrong.

During the first dayarounds of the journey, while they were still in home territory, Woodcarver pointed out every peak that came into view and tried to translate its name into Samnorsk for her. After six hundred years the Queen knew her land well. Even the patches of snow – the ones that lasted all through the summer – were known to her. She showed Johanna a sketchbook she had brought along. Each page was from a different year, and showed her special snowpatches as they had appeared on the same day of the summer. Riffling through the leaves, it was almost like a crude piece of animation. Johanna could see the patches moving, growing over a period of decades, then retreating. 'Most packs don't live long enough to feel it,' said Woodcarver, 'but to me, the patches that last all summer are like living things. See how they move? They are like wolves, held off from our lands by our fire that is the sun. They circle about, grow. Sometimes they link together and a new glacier starts toward the sea.'

Johanna had laughed a little nervously. 'Are they winning?'

'For the last four centuries, no. The summers have often been hot and windy. In the long run? I don't know. And it doesn't matter quite so much to me anymore.' She rocked her two little puppies for a moment and laughed gently. 'Peregrine's little ones are not even thinking yet, and I'm already losing my long view!'

Johanna reached out to stroke her neck. 'But they are your puppies too.'

'I know. Most of my pups have been with other packs, but these are the first that I have kept to be with me.' Her blind one nuzzled at one of the puppies. It wriggled and made a sound that warbled at the top of Johanna's hearing. Johanna held the other on her lap. Tine pups looked more like baby sea'mals than dogs. Their necks were so long compared to their bodies. And they seemed to develop much more slowly than the puppy she and Jefri had raised. Even now they seemed to have trouble focusing. She moved her fingers slowly back and forth in front of one puppy's head; its efforts to track were comical.

And after sixty days, Woodcarver's pups couldn't really walk. The Queen wore two special jackets with carrying pouches on the sides. Most of the waking day, her little ones stayed there, suckling through the fur on her tummy. In some ways, Woodcarver treated her offspring as a human would. She was very nervous when they were taken from her sight. She liked to cuddle them and play little games of coordination with them. Often she would lay both of them on their backs and pat their paws in a sequence of eight, then abruptly tap the one or the other on the belly. The two wriggled furiously at the attack, their little legs waving in all directions. 'I nibble the one whose paw was last touched. Peregrine is worthy of me. These two are already thinking a little. See?' She pointed to the puppy that had convulsed into a ball, avoiding most of her surprise tickle.

In other ways Tinish parenting was alien, almost scary. Neither Wood-carver nor Peregrine ever talked to their pups in audible tones, but their ultrasonic 'thoughts' seemed to be constantly probing the little ones. Some of it was so simple and regular that it set sympathetic vibrations through the walls of the little wagon. The wood buzzed under Johanna's hands. It was like a mother humming a lullaby, but she could see it had another purpose. The little creatures responded to the sounds, twitching in complicated rhythms. Peregrine said it would be another thirty days before the pups could contribute conscious thought to the pack, but they were already being trained and exercised for the function.

They camped part of each dayaround, the troops standing turns as sentry lines. Even during the traveling part of the day they stopped numerous times, to clear the trail, or await the return of a patrol, or simply to rest. At one such, Johanna sat with Peregrine in the shade of a tree that looked like pine but smelled of honey. Pilgrim played with his young ones, helping them to stand up and walk a few steps. She could tell by the buzzing in her head that he was thinking at the pups. And suddenly they seemed more like marionettes than children to her. 'Why don't you let them play by them-selves, or with their—' *Brothers? Sisters? What do you call siblings born to the other pack?* '—with Woodcarver's pups?'

Even more than Woodcarver, the pilgrim had tried to learn human customs. He was by far the most flexible pack she knew . . . after all, if you can accommodate a murderer in your own mind, you *must* be flexible. But Pilgrim was visibly startled by her question. The buzzing in her head stopped abruptly. He laughed weakly. It was a very human laugh, though a bit theatrical. Peregrine had spent hours at interactive comedy on Dataset – whether for entertainment or insight, she didn't know. 'Play? By them-selves? Yes . . . I see how natural that would seem to you. To us, it would be a kind of perversion . . . No, *worse* than that, since perversions are at least fun for some people some of the time. But if a pup were raised a singleton, or even a duo – it would be making an *animal* of what could be sturdy member.'

'You mean that pups never have life of their own?'

Peregrine cocked his heads and scrunched close to the ground. One of him continued to nose around the puppies, but Johanna had his attention. He loved to puzzle over human exotica. 'Well, sometimes there is a tragedy – an orphan pup left to itself. Often there is no cure for it; the creature, becomes too independent to meld with any pack. In any case, it is a very lonely, empty life. I have personal memories of just how unpleasant.'

'You're missing a lot. I know you've watched children's stories on Dataset. It's sad you can never be young and foolish.'

'Hei! I never said that. I've been young and foolish lots; it's my way of life. And most packs are that way when they have several young members by different parents.' As they talked, one of Peregrine's pups had struggled to the edge of the blanket they sat on. Now it awkwardly extended its neck into the flowers that grew from the roots of a nearby tree. As it scruffed around in the green and purple, Johanna felt the buzzing begin again. The pup's movement became a tad more organized. 'Wow! I can smell the flowers with him. I bet we'll be seeing through each other's eyes well before we get to Flenser's Hidden Island.' The pup backed up, and the two did a little dance on the blanket. Peregrine's heads bobbed in time with the movement. 'They are such bright little ones!' He grinned. 'Oh, we are not so different from you, Johanna. I know humans are proud of their young ones. Both Woodcarver and I wonder what ours will become. She is so brilliant, and I am – well, a bit mad. Will these two make me a scientific genius? Will Woodcarver's turn *her* into an adventurer? Heh, heh. Woodcarver's a great brood kenner, but even she's not sure what our new souls will be like. Oh, I can't wait to be six again!'

It had taken Scriber and Pilgrim and Johanna only three days to sail from Flenser's Domain to the harbor at Woodcarver's. It would take this army almost thirty days to walk back to where Johanna's adventure began. On the map it had looked a tortuous path, wiggling this way and that through the fjordland. Yet the first ten days were amazingly easy. The weather stayed dry and warm. It was like the day of the ambush stretched out forever and ever. A dry winds summer, Woodcarver called it. In summer, there should be occasional storms, at least cloudiness. Instead the sun circled endlessly above the forest canopy, and when they broke into the open – never for long, and then only when Vendacious was sure that it was safe – the sky was clear and almost cloudless.

In fact, there was already uneasiness about the weather. At noon it could get downright hot. The wind was constant, drying. The forest itself was drying out; they must be careful with fires. And with the sun always up and no clouds, they might be seen by lookouts many kilometers away. Scrupilo was especially bothered. He hadn't expected to fire his cannons en route, but he had wanted to drill 'his' troops more in the open.

Scrupilo was a council member and the Queen's chief engineer. Since his experiment with the cannon, he had insisted on the title 'Commander of Cannoneers.' To Johanna, the engineer had always seemed curt and impatient. His members were almost always moving, and with jerky abruptness. He spent almost as much time with the Dataset as did the Queen or Peregrine Wickwrackscar, yet he had very little interest in people-oriented subjects. 'He has a blindness for all but machines,' Woodcarver once said of him, 'but that's how I made him. He's invented much, even before you came.'

Scrupilo had fallen in love with the cannons. For most packs, firing the things was a painful experience. Since that first test, Scrupilo had fired the things again and again, trying to improve the tubes, the powder, and the explosive rounds. His fur was scored with dozens of powder burns. He claimed that nearby gun thunder cleared the mind – but most everybody else agreed it made you daft.

During rest stops Scrup was a familiar figure, strutting up and down the line, haranguing his cannoneers. He claimed even the shortest stop was an opportunity for training, since in real combat speed would be essential. He had designed special epaulets, based on Nyjoran gunners' ear muffs. They didn't cover the low-sound ears at all, but instead the forehead and shoulder tympana of the trigger member. Actually tying the muffs down was a mind-numbing thing to do, but for the moments right around firing it was worth it. Scrupilo wore his own muffs all the time, but unsnugged. They looked like silly little wings sticking out from his head and shoulders. He obviously thought the effect was raffish – and in fact, his gunner crews also made a big thing of wearing the gear at all times. After a while, even Johanna could see that the drill was paying off. At least, they could swing the gun tubes around at an instant's notice, stuff them with fake powder and ball, and shout the Tinish equivalent of 'BANG!'

The army carried much more gunpowder than food. The packs were to live off the forest. Johanna had little experience with camping in an atmosphere. Were forests usually this rich? It was certainly nothing like the urban forests of Straum, where you needed a special license to walk off marked paths, and most of the wild life were mechanical imitations of Nyjoran originals. This place was wilder than even the stories of Nyjora. After all, that world had been well settled before it fell to medievalism. The Tines had never been civilized, had never spread cities across continents. Pilgrim guessed there were fewer than thirty million packs in all the world. The Northwest was only beginning to be settled. Game was everywhere. In their hunting, the Tines were like animals. Troopers raced through the underforest. The favorite hunt was one of sheer endurance, where the prey was chased until it dropped. That was rarely practical here, but they got almost as much pleasure from chasing the unwary into ambushes.

Johanna didn't like it. Was this a medieval perversion or a peculiarly Tinish one? If allowed the time, the troops didn't use their bows and knives. The pleasure of the hunt included slashing at throats and bellies with teeth and claws. Not that the forest creatures were without defenses: for millions of years threat and counterthreat had evolved here. Almost every animal could generate ultrasonic screeching that totally drowned the thought of any nearby pack. There were parts of the forest that seemed silent to Johanna, but through which the army drove at a cautious gallop, troops and drivers writhing in agony from the unseen assault.

Some of the forest animals were more sophisticated.

Twenty-five days out, the army was stuck trying to get across the biggest valley yet. In the middle – mostly hidden by the forest – a river flowed down to the western sea. The walls of these valleys were like nothing Johanna had seen in the parks of Straum: If you took a cross-section at right angles to the river, the walls made a 'U' shape. They were cliff-like steep at the high edges, then became slopes and finally a gentle plain where the river ran. 'That's how the ice gouges it,' explained Woodcarver. 'There are places further up where I've actually watched it happen,' and she showed Johanna explanations in the Dataset. That was happening more and more; Pilgrim and Woodcarver and sometimes even Scrupilo seemed to know more of a child's modern education than Johanna.

They had already been across a number of smaller valleys. Getting down the steep parts was always tedious, but so far the paths had been good. Vendacious took them to the edge of this latest valley.

Woodcarver and staff stood under the forest cover just short of the dropoff. Some meters back, Johanna sat surrounded by Peregrine Wick-wrackscar. The trees at this elevation reminded Johanna a little of pines. The leaves were narrow and sharp and lasted all year. But the bark was blistered white and the wood itself was pale blond. Strangest of all were the flowers. They sprouted purple and violet from the exposed roots of the trees. Tines' world had no analog of honeybees, but there was constant motion among the flowers as thumb-sized mammals climbed from plant to plant. There were thousands of them, but they seemed to have no interest in anything except the flowers and the sweetness that oozed from them. She leaned back among the flowers and admired the view while the Queen gobbled with Vendacious. How many kilometers could you see from here? The air was clear as she had ever known it on Tines' world. East and west the valley seemed to stretch forever. The river was a silver thread where it occasionally showed through the forest of the valley floor.

Pilgrim nudged her with a nose and nodded toward the Queen. Woodcarver was pointing this way and that over the dropoff. 'Argument is in the air. You want a translation?'

'Yeah.'

'Woodcarver doesn't like this path,' Pilgrim's voice changed to the tone the Queen used when speaking Samnorsk: 'The path is completely exposed. Anyone on the other side can sit and count our every wagon. Even from miles away. [A mile is a fat kilometer.]'

Vendacious whipped his heads around in that indignant way of his. He gobbled something that Johanna knew was angry. Pilgrim chuckled and changed his voice to imitate the security chief's: 'Your majesty! My scouts have scoured the valley and far wall. There is no threat.'

'You've done miracles, I know, but do you seriously claim to have covered that entire north face? That's five miles away, and I know from my youth that there are dozens of cavelets – you have those memories yourself.'

'*That* stopped him!' said Pilgrim, laughing.

'C'mon. Just translate.' She was quite capable of interpreting body language and tone by now. Sometimes even the Tinish chords made sense.

'Hmph. Okay.'

The Queen hiked her baby packs around and sat down. Her tone became conciliatory. 'If this weather weren't so clear, or if there were night times, we might try it, but – You remember the old path? Twenty miles inland from here? That should be overgrown by now. And the road coming back is—'

Gobble-hiss from Vendacious, angry. 'I tell you, this is safe! We'll lose days on the other path. If we arrive late at Flenser's, all my work will be for nothing. You must go forward here.'

'Oops,' Pilgrim whispered, unable to resist a little editorializing, 'Ol' Vendacious may have gone too far with that.' The Queen's heads arched back. Pilgrim's imitation of her human voice said, 'I understand, your anxiety, pack of my blood. But we go forward where I say. If that is intolerable to you, I will regretfully accept your resignation.'

'But you need me!'

'Not *that* much.'

Johanna suddenly realized that the whole mission could fall apart right here, without even a shot being fired. *Where would we be without Vendacious?* She held her breath and watched the two packs. Parts of Vendacious walked in quick circles, stopping for angry instants to stare at Woodcarver. Finally all his necks drooped. 'Um. My apologies, your majesty. As long as you find me of use, I beg to continue in your service.'

Now Woodcarver relaxed, too. She reached to pet her puppies. They had responded with her mood, thrashing in their carriers and hissing. 'Forgiven. I want your independent advice, Vendacious. It has been miraculously good.'

Vendacious smiled weakly.

'I didn't think the jerk had it in him,' Pilgrim said near Johanna's ear.

It took two dayarounds to reach the old path. As Woodcarver had predicted, it was overgrown. More: In places there was no sign of the path at all. It would take *days* to get down the valley side this way. If Woodcarver had any misgivings about the decision, she didn't mention them to Johanna. The Queen was six hundred years old; she talked often enough about the inflexibility of age. Now Johanna was getting a clear example of what that meant.

When they came to a washout, trees were cut down and a bridge constructed on the spot. It took a day to get by each such spot. But progress was agonizingly slow even where the path was still in place. No one rode in the carts now. The edge of the path had worn away, and the cart wheels sometimes turned on nothingness. On Johanna's right she could look down at tree crowns that were a few meters from her feet.

They ran into the wolves six days along the detour, when they had almost reached the valley floor. Wolves. That's what Pilgrim called them anyway; what Johanna saw looked like gerbils.

They had just completed a kilometer stretch of easy going. Even under the trees they could feel the wind, dry and warm and moving ceaselessly down the valley. The last patches of snow between the trees were being sucked to nothingness, and there was a haze of smoke beyond the north wall of the valley.

Johanna was walking alongside Woodcarver's cart. Pilgrim was about ten meters behind, chatting occasionally with them. (The Queen herself had been very quiet these last days.) Suddenly there was a screech of Tinish alarm from above them.

A second later Vendacious shouted from a hundred meters ahead. Through gaps in the trees, Johanna could see troopers on the next switchback above them unlimbering crossbows, firing into the hillside above them. The sunlight came dappled through the forest cover, bringing plenty of light but in splotches that broke and moved as the soldiers hustled about. Chaos, but . . . there were things up there that weren't Tines! Small, brown or gray, they flitted through the shadows and the splotches of light. They swept up the hillside, coming upon the soldiers from the *opposite* direction that they were shooting.

'Turn around! Turn around!' Johanna screamed, but her voice was lost in the turmoil. Besides, who there could understand her? All of Woodcarver was peering up at the battle. She grabbed Johanna's sleeve. 'You see something up there? Where?'

Johanna stuttered an explanation, but now Pilgrim had seen something too. His gobbled shouting came loud over the battle. He raced back up the trail to where Scrupilo was trying to get a cannon unlimbered. 'Johanna! Help me.'

Woodcarver hesitated, then said, 'Yes. It may be that bad. Help with the cannon, Johanna.'

It was only fifty meters to the gun cart, but uphill. She ran. Something heavy smashed into the path just behind her. Part of a soldier! It twisted and screamed. Half a dozen gerbilsized hunks of fur were attached to the body, and its pelt was streaked with red. Another member fell past her. Another. Johanna stumbled but kept running.

Wickwrackscar was standing heads-together, just a few meters from Scrupilo. He was armed in every adult member – mouth knives and steel tines. He waved Johanna down next to him. 'We run on a nest of, of wolves.' His speech was awkward, slurred. 'It must be between here and path above. A lump, like a l'il castle tower. Gotta kill nest. Can you see it?' Evidently he could not; he was looking all over. Johanna looked back up the hillside. There seemed to be less fighting now, just sounds of Tinish agony.

Johanna pointed. 'You mean there, that dark thing?'

Pilgrim didn't answer. His members were twitching, his mouth knives waving randomly. She leaped away from the flashing metal. He had already cut himself. *Sound attack.* She looked back along the path. She'd had more than a year to know the packs, and what she was seeing now was . . . madness. Some packs were exploding, racing in all directions to distances where thought couldn't possibly be sustained. Others – Woodcarver on her cart – huddled in heaps, with scarcely a head showing.

Just beyond the nearest uphill trees she could see a gray tide. *The wolves.* Each furry lump looked innocent enough. All together . . . Johanna froze for an instant, watching them tear out the throat of a trooper's member.

Johanna was the only sane person left, and all it would mean is she would *know* she was dying.

Kill the nest.

On the gun cart beside her only one of Scrupilo was left, old White Head. Daffy as ever, it had pulled down its gunner's muffs and was nosing around under the gun tube. *Kill the nest.* Maybe not so daffy after all!

Johanna jumped up on the wagon. It rolled back toward the dropoff, banging against a tree; she scarcely noticed. She pulled up the gun barrel, just as she had seen in all the drills. The white-headed one pulled at the powder bag, but with just his one pair of jaws he couldn't handle it. Without the rest of its pack it had neither hands nor brains. It looked up at her, its eyes wide and desperate.

She grabbed the other end of the bag, and the two of them got the powder into the barrel. White Head dived back into the equipment, nosing around for a cannonball. *Smarter than a dog, and trained.* Between them, maybe they had a chance!

Just half a meter beneath her feet, the wolves were running by. One or two she could have fought off herself. But there were dozens down there, worrying and tearing at random members. Three of Pilgrim were standing around Scarbutt and the pups, but their defense was unthinking slashing. The pack had dropped its mouth knives and tines.

She and White Head got the round down the barrel. White Head whipped back to the rear, began playing with the little wick-lighter the gunners used. It was something that could be held in a single mouth, since only one member actually fired the weapon.

'Wait, you idiot!' Johanna kicked him back. 'We gotta aim this thing!'

White Head looked hurt for an instant. The complaint wasn't completely clear to him. He had dropped the standoff wand, but still held the lighter. He flicked on the flame, and circled determinedly back, tried to worm past Johanna's legs. She pushed him back again, and looked uphill. *The dark thing. That must be the nest.* She tilted the gun tube on its mounting and sighted down the top. Her face ended up just centimeters from the persistent White Head and his flame. His muffed head darted forward, and the flame touched the fire-hole.

The blast almost knocked Johanna off the cart. For a moment she could think of nothing but the pain that stabbed into her ears. She rolled to a sitting position, coughing in the smoke. She couldn't hear *anything* beyond a high-pitched ringing that went on and on. Their little wagon was teetering, one wheel hanging over dropoff. White Head was flopping around under the butt of the cannon. She pushed it off him and patted the muffed head. He was bleeding – or she was. She just sat dazed for a few seconds, mystified by the blood, trying to imagine how she had ever ended up here.

A voice somewhere in the back of her head was screaming. *No time, no time.* She forced herself to her knees and looked around, memories coming back painfully slow.

There were splintered trees uphill of them; the blond wood glinted among the leaves. Beyond them where the nest had been, she saw a splash of fresh turned earth. They had 'killed' it, but . . . the fighting continued.

There were still wolves on the path, but now they were the ones running in all directions. As she watched, dozens of them catapulted off the edge of trail into the trees and rocks below. And the Tines were actually fighting now. Pilgrim had picked up his knives. The blades and his muzzles dripped red and he slashed. Something gray and bleeding flew over the edge of the cart and landed by Johanna's leg. The 'wolf' couldn't have been more than twenty centimeters long, its hair dirty gray brown. It really did look like a pet, but the tiny jaws clicked at her ankles with murderous intent. Johanna dropped a cannonball on it.

During the next three days, while Woodcarver's people struggled to bring their equipment and themselves back together, Johanna learned quite a bit about the wolves. What she and Scrupilo's White Head did with the cannon had stopped the attack cold. Without doubt, knocking out the nest had saved a lot of lives and the expedition itself. The 'wolves' were a type of hive creature, only a little like the packs. The Tines race used group thought to reach high intelligence; Johanna had never seen a rational pack of more than six members. The wolf nests didn't care about high intelligence. Woodcarver claimed that a nest might have thousands of members – certainly the one they'd tripped over was huge. Such a mob couldn't be as smart as a human. In terms of raw reasoning power, it probably wasn't much brighter than a single pack member. On the other hand, it could be a lot more flexible. Wolves could operate alone at great distances. When within a hundred meters of the home nest they were appendages of the 'queen' members of the nest, and no one doubted their canniness then. Pilgrim had legends of nests with almost packish intelligence, of foresters who made treaties with nearby nests for protection in return for food. As long as the high-powered noises in the nest lived, the worker wolves could coordinate almost like Tine members. But kill the nest, and the creature fell apart like some cheap, center-topology network.

Certainly this nest had done a number on Woodcarver's army. It had waited quietly until the troopers were within its inner loudness. Then outlying wolves had used synchronized mimicry to create sonic 'ghosts,' tricking the packs into turning from the nest and shooting uselessly into the

trees. And when the ambush actually began, the nest had screamed concentrated confusion down on the Tines. That attack had been a far more
powerful thing than the 'stink noise' they'd encountered in other parts of
the forest. To the Tines, the stinkers had been painfully loud and sometimes
even frightening, but not the mind-destroying chaos of the wolf-nest attack.

More than one hundred packs had been knocked out in the ambush.
Some, mostly packs with pups, had huddled. Others, like Scrupilo, had
been 'blasted apart.' In the hours following the attack, many of these
fragments straggled back and reassembled. The resulting Tines were shaken
but unharmed. Intact soldiers hunted up and down the forested cliffs for
injured members of their comrades. There were places along the dropoff
that were more than twenty meters deep. Where their fall wasn't cushioned
by tree boughs, members landed on naked rock. Five dead ones were
eventually found, and another twenty seriously injured. Two carts had
fallen. They were kindling, and their kherhogs were too badly injured to
survive. By great good luck, the gunshot had not started a forest fire.

Three times the sun made its vast, tilted course around the sky.
Woodcarver's army recovered in a camp in the depths of the valley forest,
by the river. Vendacious had posted lookouts with signaling mirrors on the
northern valley wall. This place was about as safe as any they could find so
far north. It was certainty one of the most beautiful. It didn't have the view
of the high forest, but there was the sound of the river nearby, so loud it
drowned the sighing of the dry wind. The lowland trees didn't have root
flowers, but they were still different from what Johanna had known. There
was no underbrush, just a soft, bluish 'moss' that Pilgrim claimed was
actually part of the trees. It stretched like mown parkland to the edge of the
river.

On the last day of their rest, the Queen called a meeting of all the packs
not at guard or lookout. It was the largest collection of Tines Johanna had
seen in one place since her family was killed. Only these packs weren't
fighting. As far as Johanna could see across the bluish moss, there were
packs, each at least eight meters from its nearest neighbor. For an absurd
instant she was reminded of Settlers Park at Overby: Families picnicking on
the grass, each with its own traditional blanket and food lockers. But these
'families' were each a pack, and this was a military formation. The rows
were gently curving arcs, all facing toward the Queen. Peregrine Wickwrackscar was ten meters behind her, in shadow; being Queen's consort
didn't count for anything official. On Woodcarver's left lay the living
casualties of the ambush, members with bandages and splints. In some
ways, such visible damage wasn't the most horrifying. There were also what
Pilgrim called the 'walking wounded.' These were singletons and duos and
trios that were all that was left of whole packs. Some of these tried to
maintain a posture of attention, but others mooned about, occasionally
breaking into the Queen's speech with aimless words. It was like Scriber

Jaqueramaphan all over again, but most of these would live. Some were already melding, trying to make new individuals. Some of these might even work out, as Peregrine Wickwrackscar had done. For most, it would be a long time before they were fully people again.

Johanna sat with Scrupilo in the first rank of troopers before the Queen. The Commander of Cannoneers stood at Tinish parade rest: rumps on the ground, chest high, most heads facing front. Scrup had come through it without serious damage. His white head had a few more scorch marks, and one of the other members had sprained a shoulder falling off the path. He wore his flying cannoneer muffs as flamboyantly as always, but there was something subdued about him – maybe it was just the military formation and getting a medal for heroism.

The Queen was wearing her special jackets. Each head looked out at a different section of her audience. Johanna still couldn't understand Tinish, and would certainly never speak it without mechanical assistance. But the sounds were mostly within her range of hearing – low frequencies carry a lot better than high ones. Even without memory aides and grammar generators she was learning a little. She could recognize emotional tone easily, and things like the raucous *ark ark ark* that passed for applause around here. As for individual words – well, they were more like *chords*, single syllables that had meaning. Nowadays, if she listened really carefully (and Pilgrim weren't nearby to give a running translation) she could even recognize some of those.

. . . Just now, for instance, Woodcarver was saying good things about her audience. Approving *ark arks* came from all directions. They sounded like a bunch of sea'mals. One of the Queen's heads dipped into a bowl, coming up with a small carven doodad in its mouth. She spoke a pack's name, a multichord *tumptititum* that if Johanna heard often enough she might be able to repeat as 'Jaqueramaphan' – or even see meaning in, as 'Wickwrackscar.'

From the front rank of the audience, *a single member* trotted toward the Queen. It stopped practically nose to nose with the Queen's nearest member. Woodcarver said something about bravery, and then two of her fastened the wooden – brooch? – to the member's jacket. It turned smartly and returned to its pack.

Woodcarver picked out another decoration, and called on another pack. Johanna leaned over toward Scrupilo. 'What's going on?' she said wonderingly. 'Why are single members getting medals?' *And how can they stand to get so near another pack?*

Scrupilo had been standing more stiffly at attention than most packs, and was pretty much ignoring her. Now he turned one head in her direction. 'Shh!' He started to turn back, but she grabbed him by one of his jackets. 'Foolish one,' he finally replied. 'The award is for the whole pack. One member is extended to accept. More would be madness.'

Hmm. One after another, three more packs 'extended a member' to take their decorations. Some were full of precision, like human soldiers in stories. Others started out smartly, then became timid and confused as they approached Woodcarver.

Finally Johanna said, 'Ssst. Scrupilo! When do we get ours?'

This time he didn't even look at her; all his heads faced rigidly toward the Queen. 'Last, of course. You and I killed the nest, and saved Woodcarver herself.' His bodies were almost shaking with the intensity of their brace. *He's scared witless.* And suddenly Johanna guessed why. Apparently Woodcarver had no problem maintaining her mind with one outside member nearby. But the reverse would not be true. Sending one of yourself into another pack meant losing some consciousness and placing trust in that other pack. Looking at it that way . . . well, it reminded Johanna of the historical novels she used to play. On Nyjora during the Dark Age, ladies traditionally gave their sword to their queen when granted audience, and then knelt. It was a way to swear loyalty. Same thing here, except that looking at Scrupilo, Johanna realized that even as a matter of form, the ceremony might be damn frightening.

Three more medals bestowed, and then Woodcarver gobbled the chords that were Scrupilo's name. The Commander of Cannoneers went absolutely rigid, made faint whistling noises through his mouths. 'Johanna Olsndot,' said Woodcarver, then more Tinish, something about coming forward.

Johanna stood up, but not one of Scrupilo moved.

The Queen made a human laugh. She was holding two polished brooches. 'I'll explain all in Samnorsk later, Johanna. Just come forward with one of Scrupilo. Scrupilo?'

Suddenly they were the center of attention, with thousands of eyes watching. There was no more *arking* or background chatter. Johanna hadn't felt so exposed since she played First Colonist in her school's Landing Play. She leaned down so that her head was close to one of Scrupilo's. 'Come *on*, guy. We're the big heroes.'

The eyes that looked back at her were wide. 'I can't.' The words were almost inaudible. For all his jaunty cannoneer muffs and standoffish manner, Scrupilo was terrified. But for him it wasn't stage fright. 'I can't tear me apart so soon. I *can't.*'

There was murmured gobbling in the ranks behind them, Scrupilo's own cannoneers. By all the Powers, would they hold this against him? Welcome to the middle ages. *Stupid people. Even cut to pieces, Scrupilo had saved their behinds, and now—*

She put her hands on two of his shoulders. 'We did it before, you and I. Remember?'

The heads nodded. 'Some. That one part of me alone . . . could never have done it.'

'Right. And neither could I. But together we killed a wolf-nest.'

Scrupilo stared at her a second, eyes wavering, 'Yes, we really did.' He came to his feet, frisked his heads so the cannoneer muffs flapped. 'Yes!' And he moved his white-headed one closer to her.

Johanna straightened. She and White Head walked out into the open space. Four meters. Six. She kept the fingertips of one hand lightly on his neck. When they were about twelve meters from the rest of Scrupilo, White Head's pace faltered. He looked sideways up at Johanna, then continued more slowly.

Johanna didn't remember much of the ceremony, so much of her attention was on White Head. Woodcarver said something long and unintelligible. Somehow they both ended up with intricately carven decorations on their collars, and were headed back toward the rest of Scrupilo. *Then* she was aware of the crowd once more. They stretched as far as she could see under the forest canopy – and every one of them seemed to be cheering, Scrup's cannoneers loudest of all.

Midnight. Here at the bottom of the valley there were three or four hours of the dayaround when the sun dipped behind the high north wall. It didn't much feel like night, or even twilight. The smoke from the fires to the north seemed to be getting worse. She could smell it now.

Johanna walked back from the cannoneers section toward the center of camp, and Woodcarver's tent. It was quiet; she could hear little creatures scritching in the root bushes. The celebrating might have gone on longer, except that everyone knew that in another few hours they would be preparing for the climb up the valley's north wall. So now there was only occasional laughter, an occasional pack walking about. Johanna walked barefoot, her shoes slung over her shoulders. Even in the dry weather, the moss was wonderfully soft between her toes. Above her the forest canopy was shifting green and patches of hazy sky. She could almost forget what had gone before, and what lay ahead.

The guards around Woodcarver's tent didn't challenge her, just called softly ahead. After all, there weren't that many humans running around. The Queen stuck out a head. 'Come inside, Johanna.'

Inside she was sitting in her usual circle, the puppies protected in the middle. It was quite dark, the only light being what came through the entrance. Johanna flopped down on the pillows where she usually slept. Ever since this afternoon, the big award thing, she had been planning to give Woodcarver a piece of her mind. Now . . . well the party at the cannoneers had been a happy thing. It seemed kind of a shame to break the mood.

Woodcarver cocked a head at her. Simultaneously, the two puppies duplicated the gesture. 'I saw you at the party. You are a sober one. You eat most of our foods now, but none of the beer.'

Johanna shrugged. *Yes, why?* 'Kids aren't supposed to drink before they're eighteen years old.' That was the custom, and her parents had agreed with it. Johanna had turned fourteen a couple of months ago; Dataset had reminded her of the exact hour. She wondered. If none of this had happened, if she were still back at the High Lab or Straumli Realm: Would she be sneaking out with friends to try such forbidden things? Probably. Yet here, where she was entirely on her own, where she was currently a big hero, she hadn't tried a drop . . . Maybe it was because Mom and Dad *weren't* here, and following their wishes seemed to keep them closer. She felt tears coming to her eyes.

'Hmm.' Woodcarver didn't seem to notice. 'That's what Pilgrim said was the reason.' She tapped at her puppies and smiled. 'I guess it makes sense. These two don't get beer till they're older – though I know they got some second-hand partying from *me* tonight.' There was a hint of beer breath in the tent.

Johanna wiped roughly at her face. She really did not want to talk about being a teenager just now. 'You know, that was kind of a mean trick you pulled on Scrupilo this afternoon.'

'I – Yes. I talked to him about it beforehand. He didn't want it, but I thought he was just being . . . is stiff-necked the word? If I had known how upset he was, well—'

'He practically fell apart out there in front of everybody. If I understand how things work, that would have been his disgrace, right?'

'. . . Yes. Exchanging honor for loyalty in front of peers, it's an important thing. At least the way I run things; I'm sure Pilgrim or Dataset can say a dozen other ways to lead. Look Johanna, I needed that Exchange, and I needed you and Scrupilo to be there.'

'Yeah, I know. "We two saved the day." '

'Silence!' Her voice was suddenly edged, and Johanna remembered that this was a medieval queen. 'We are two hundred miles north of my borders, almost to the heart of the Flenser Domain. In a few days we will meet the enemy, and many more of us will die for we-know-not-quite-what.'

The bottom dropped out of Johanna's stomach. If she couldn't get back to the ship, couldn't finish what Mom and Dad had started . . . '*Please*, Woodcarver! It *is* worth it!'

'I know that. Pilgrim knows it. The majority of my council agrees, though grudgingly. But we of the council have talked with Dataset. We've seen your worlds and what your science can do. On the other hand, most of my people here,' she waved a head at the camp beyond the tent, 'are here on faith, and out of loyalty to me. For *them*, the situation is deadly and the goal is vague.' She paused, though her two pups continued gesturing forcefully for a second. 'Now I don't know how you would persuade your kind to take such risks. Dataset talks of military conscription.'

'That was Nyjora, long ago.'

'Never mind. The point is, my troops are here out of loyalty, mostly to me personally. For six hundred years, I have protected my people well; their memories and legends are clear on it. More than once, I was the only one who saw a peril, and it was my advice that saved all those who heeded it. *That* is what keeps most of the soldiers, most of the cannoneers going. Each of them is free to turn back. So. What should they think when our first "combat" is to fall like ignorant . . . tourists . . . onto a nest of wolves? Without the great good luck of you and part of Scrupilo being at the right place and alert, I would have been killed. Pilgrim would have been killed. Perhaps a third of the soldiers would have died.'

'If not us, perhaps someone else,' Johanna said in a small voice.

'Perhaps. I don't think anyone else came close to firing on the nest. You see the effect on my people? "If bad luck in the forest can kill our Queen and destroy our marvelous weapons, what will it be like when we face a *thinking* enemy?" That was the question in many minds. Unless I could answer it, we'd never make it out of this valley – at least not going northward.'

'So you gave the medals. Loyalty for honor.'

'Yes. You missed the sense of it, not understanding Tinish. I made a big thing of how well they had done. I gave silverwood accolades to packs who showed any competence in the ambush. That helped some. I repeated my reasons for this expedition – the wonders that Dataset describes and how much we will lose if Steel gets his way. But they've heard that argument before, and it points to far away things they can scarcely imagine. The *new* thing I showed them today was you and Scrupilo.'

'*Us?*'

'I praised you beyond the skies. Singletons often do brave things. Sometimes they are halfway clever, or talk as though they are. But alone, Scrupilo's fragment wouldn't be much more than a good knife fighter. He knew about using the cannon, but he didn't have the paws or mouths to do anything with it. And by himself, he would never have figured out where to shoot it. You, on the other hand, are a Two-Legs. In many ways you are helpless. The *only* way you can think is by yourself, but you can do it without interfering with those around you. Together you did what no pack could do in the middle of a wolf-nest attack. So I told my army what a team our two races could become, how each makes up for the age-old failings of the other. Together, we are one step closer to being the Pack of Packs. How is Scrupilo?'

Johanna smiled faintly. 'Things turned out okay. Once he was able to get out there and accept his medal,' she fingered the brooch that was pinned to her own collar; it was a beautiful thing, a landscape of Woodcarver's city, 'once he'd done that, he was totally changed. You should have seen him with the cannoneers afterwards. They did their own loyalty/honor thing, and then they drank a lot of beer. Scrupilo was telling them all about what we were doing. He even had me help demonstrate . . . You really think the army bought what you said about humans and Tines?'

'I think so. In my own language, I can be very eloquent. I've bred myself to be.' Woodcarver was silent for a moment. Her puppies scrambled across the carpet, and patted their muzzles at Johanna's hands. 'Besides . . . it may even be true. Pilgrim is sure of it. You can sleep in this same tent with me and still think. That's something that he and I can't do; in our own ways, we've each lived a long time and I think we are each at least as smart as the humans and other creatures that Dataset talks about in the Beyond. But you singleton creatures can stand next to each other, and think and build. Compared to us, I'll bet singleton races developed the sciences very fast. But now, with your help, maybe things will change fast for us too.' The two puppies retreated, and Woodcarver lowered heads to paws. 'That's what I told my people, anyway . . . You should try to get some sleep now.'

On the ground beyond the tent's entrance there were already splashes of sunlight. 'Okay.' Johanna slipped off her outer clothes. She lay down and dragged a light quilt across herself. Most of Woodcarver already looked asleep. As usual, one or two pairs of eyes were open, but their intelligence would be limited – and just now, even they looked tired. Funny, Wood-carver had worked with Dataset so much, her human voice had come to capture emotion as well as pronunciation. Just now she had sounded so tired, so sad.

Johanna reached out from under her quilt to brush the neck of Woodcarver's nearest, the blind one. 'Do *you* believe what you told every-one?' she said softly.

One of the 'sentry' heads looked at her, and a very human sigh seemed to come from all directions. Woodcarver's voice was very faint. 'Yes . . . but I am very afraid that it doesn't matter anymore. For six hundred years, I have had proper confidence in myself. But what happened on the south wall . . . should not have happened. It would not if I had followed Vendacious's advice, and come down on the New Road.'

'But we might have been seen—'

'Yes. A failure either way, don't you see? Vendacious has precise informa-tion from the highest councils of the Flenser. But he's something of a careless fool in everyday matters. I knew that, and thought I could com-pensate. But the Old Road was in far worse condition than I remembered: the wolf-nest could never have settled by it if there had been any traffic during the last few years. If Vendacious had managed his patrols properly, or if I had been managing *him* properly, we would never have been surprised. Instead we were nearly overrun . . . and my only remaining talent appears to be in fooling those who trust me into thinking I still know what I'm doing.' She opened another pair of eyes and made the smile gesture. 'Strange. I haven't said these things even to Pilgrim. Is this another "advantage" of human relations?'

Johanna patted the blind one's neck. 'Maybe.'

'Anyway, I believe what I said about things that *could* be, but I fear that my soul may not be strong enough to make them so. Perhaps I should turn things over to Pilgrim or Vendacious; that's something I must think on.' Woodcarver *shh*ed Johanna's surprised protests.

'Now sleep, please.'

32

There was a time when Ravna thought their tiny ship might fly all the way to the Bottom unnoticed. Along with everything else, that had changed. At the moment, *Out of Band II* might be the most famous starship known to the Net. A million races watched the chase. In the Middle Beyond there were vast antenna swarms beaming in their direction and listening to the stories – mostly lies – sent from the ships that pursued the *OOB*. She couldn't hear those lies directly of course, but the transmissions she received were as clear as if they were on a main trunk.

Ravna spent part of each day reading the News, trying to find hope, trying to prove to herself that she was doing the right thing. By now, she was pretty sure what was chasing them. No doubt even Pham and Blueshell would have agreed on that. *Why* they were being chased, and *what* they might find at the end was now the subject of endless speculation on the Net. As usual, whatever the truth might be was well hidden among the lies.

Crypto: 0
As received by: *OOB* shipboard ad hoc
Language path: Triskweline, SjK units
From: Hanse
   [No references prior to the fall of Relay. No probable source. This is someone
      being very cautious.]
Subject: Alliance for the Defense fraudulent?
Distribution:
   Threat of the Blight
   War Trackers Interest Group
   Homo Sapiens Interest Group
Date: 5.80 days since Fall of Sjandra Kei
Key phrases: Fools' errand, unnecessary genocide
Text of message:
   Earlier I speculated that there had been no destruction at Sjandra Kei.
Apologies. That was based on a catalog identification error. I agree with the
messages (13123 as of a few seconds ago) assuring me that the habitations of
Sjandra Kei suffered collisional damage within the last six days.
   So apparently the 'Alliance for the Defense' has taken the military action they

claimed earlier. And apparently, they are powerful enough to destroy small civilizations in the Middle Beyond. The question still remains: 'Why?' I have already posted arguments showing it unlikely that Homo sapiens is especially controllable by the Blight (though they were *stupid* enough to create that entity). Even the Alliance's own reports admit that less than half of Sjandra Kei's sophonts were of that race.

Now a large part of the Alliance fleet is chasing into the Bottom of the Beyond after a *single ship*. What conceivable damage can the Alliance do to the Blight down there? The Blight is a great threat, perhaps the most novel and threatening in well-recorded history. Nevertheless, Alliance behavior appears destructive and pointless. Now that the Alliance has revealed some of its sponsoring organizations (see messages [id numbers]), I think we know its real motives. I see connections between the Alliance and the old Aprahant Hegemony. A thousand years ago, that group undertook a similar jihad, grabbing real estate left vacant by recent Transcendences. Stopping the Hegemony was an exciting bit of action in that part of the galaxy. I think these people are back, taking advantage of the general panic attending the Blight (which is admittedly a much greater threat).

My advice: Beware of the Alliance and its claims of heroic efforts.

Crypto: 0
As received by: *OOB* shipboard ad hoc
Language path: Schirachene → Rondralip → Triskweline, SjK units
From: Harmonious Repose Communications Synod
Subject: Encounter with agents of the Perversion
Distribution:
   Threat of the Blight
Date: 6.37 days since Fall of Sjandra Kei
Key phrases: Hanse fraudulent?
Test of message:

We have no special inclination toward any of the posters on this thread. Nevertheless, it's remarkable that an entity that has not revealed its location or special interests – namely 'Hanse' – should be smearing the efforts of the Alliance for the Defense. The Alliance kept its constituents secret only during that period when its forces were being gathered, when a single stroke of the Perversion's power might destroy it entirely. Since that time, it has been quite open in its efforts.

Hanse wonders how a single starship could be worth the Alliance's attention. As Harmonious Repose was the site of the latest turn of events, we are in a position to give some explanation. The ship in question, the *Out of Band II*, is clearly designed for operations at the Bottom of the Beyond – and is even capable of limited operations within the Slow Zone. The ship presented itself as a special zonographic flight commissioned to study the recent turbulence at the

Bottom. In fact, this ship's mission is a very different one. In the aftermath of its violent departure, we have pieced together some extraordinary facts:

At least one of the ship's crew was human. Though they made great efforts to stay out of the view and used Skroderider traders as intermediaries, we have recordings. A biosequence of one individual was obtained, and it maches the patterns maintained by two out of three of the Homo sapiens archives. (It's well known that the third archive, on Sneerot Down, is in the control of Human sympathizers.) Some might say this deception was founded in fear. After all, these events happened after the destruction of Sjandra Kei. We think otherwise: The ship's initial contact with us occurred before the Sjandra Kei incident.

We have since made a careful analysis of the repair work our yards performed on this vessel. Ultradrive automation is a deep and complex thing; even the cleverest of cloaking cannot mask all the memories in it. We now know that the *Out of Band II* was from the Relay system and that it left there after the Perversion's attack. Think what this means.

The crew of the *Out of Band II* brought weapons into a habitat, killed several local sophonts, and escaped before our musicians [harmonizers? police?] were properly notified. We have good reason to wish them ill.

Yet our misfortune is a small thing compared to the unmasking of this secret mission. We are very grateful that the Alliance is willing to risk so much in following this lead.

There's more than the usual number of unsubstantiated assertions floating around on this news thread. We hope our facts will wake some people up. In particular, consider what ' "Hanse" ' may really be. The Perversion is very visible in the High Beyond, where it has great power and can speak with its own voice. Down here, it is more likely that deception and covert propaganda will be its tools. Think on this when you read postings from unidentified entities such as 'Hanse'!

Ravna gritted her teeth. The hell of it was, the facts in the posting were correct. It was the inferences that were vicious and false. And she couldn't guess if this were some shade of black propaganda or simply Saint Rihndell expressing honest conclusions (though Rihndell had never seemed so trusting of the butterflies).

One thing all the News seemed to agree on: Much more than the Alliance fleet was chasing the *OOB*. The swarm of ultradrive traces could be seen by anyone within a thousand light-years. The best guess was that three fleets pursued the *OOB*. Three! The Alliance for the Defense, still loud and boastful, even though suspected (by some) of being opportunistic genocides. Behind them, Sjandra Kei . . . and what was left of Ravna's motherland; in all the universe perhaps the only folk she could trust. And just behind them, the silent fleet. Diverse news posters claimed it was from the High Beyond. That fleet might have problems at the Bottom, but for now it was gaining. Few doubted that it was the Perversion's child. More than anything, it convinced the universe that the *OOB* or its destination was cosmically important. Just why it was important was the big question. Speculation was drifting in at the rate of five thousand messages per hour. A million different viewpoints were considering the mystery. Some of those viewpoints were so alien that they made Skroderiders and Humans look like the same species. At least five participants on this News thread were gaseous inhabitants of stellar coronas. There were one or two others that Ravna suspected were uncataloged races, beings so shy that this might be their first active use of the Net ever.

The *OOB*'s computer was a lot dumber than it had been in the Middle Beyond. She couldn't ask it to sift through the messages looking for nuance and insight. In fact, if an incoming message didn't have a Triskweline text, it was often unreadable. The ship's translator programs still worked fairly well with the major trade languages, but even there the translation was slow and full of alternative meanings and jabberwocky. It was just another sign that they were approaching the Bottom of the Beyond. Effective translation of natural languages comes awfully close to requiring a sentient translator program.

Nevertheless, with proper design, things might have been better. The automation might have degraded gracefully under the restrictions imposed by their depth. Instead, gear just stopped working; what remained was slow and error-prone. If only the refitting had been completed before the Fall of Relay. *And just how many times have I wished for that?* She hoped things were as bad aboard the pursuing ships.

So Ravna used the ship to do light culling on the Threats newsgroup. Much of what was left was inane, as from people who see 'portents in the weather'—

Crypto: 0
Syntax: 43
As received by: *OOB* shipboard ad hoc
Language path: Arbwyth → Trade 24 → Cherguelen → Triskweline, SjK units
From: Twirlip of the Mists
   [Perhaps an organization of cloud fliers in a single jovian system. Very sparse priors before this thread began. Appears to be seriously out of touch.
    Program recommendation: delete this poster from presentation.]
Subject: The Blight's goal at the Bottom
Distribution:
   Threat of the Blight
   Great Secrets of Creation
Date: 4.54 days since Fall of Sjandra Kei
Key phrases: Zone Instability and the Blight, Hexapodia as the key insight
Text of message:
   Apologies first if I am repeating obvious conclusions. My only gateway onto

the Net is very expensive, and I miss many important postings. I think that anyone following both Great Secrets of Creation and Threat of the Blight would see an important pattern. Since the events reported by Harmonious Repose information service, most agree that something important to the Perversion exists at the Bottom of the Beyond in region [. . .]. I see a possible connection here with the Great Secrets. During the last two hundred and twenty days, there have been increasing reports of zone interface instability in the region below Harmonious Repose. As the Blight threat has grown and its attacks against advanced races and other Powers continued, this instability has increased. Could there not be some connection? I urge all to consult their information on the Great Secrets (or the nearest archive maintained by that gorup). Events such as this prove once again that the universe is all ronzelle between.

Some of the postings were tantalizing—

Crypto: 0
Syntax: 43
As received by: *OOB* shipboard ad hoc
Language path: Wobblings → Baeloresk → Triskweline, Sjk units
From: Cricketsong under the High Willow
　 [Cricketsong is a synthetic race created as a jape/ experiment/instrument by the High Willow upon its Transcendence. Cricketsong has been on the Net for more than ten thousand years. Apparently it is a fanatical studier of paths to Transcendence. For eight thousand years it has been the heaviest poster on 'Where are they now' and related groups. There is no evidence that any Cricketsong settlement has itself Transcended. Cricketsong is sufficiently peculiar that there is a large news group for speculation concerning the race itself. Consensus is that Cricketsong was designed by High Willow as a probe back into the Beyond, that the race is somehow incapable of attempting its own Transcendence.]
Subject: The Blight's goal at the Bottom
Distribution:
　 Threat of the Blight
　 War Trackers Special Interest Group
　 Where are they now Special Interest Group
Date: 5.12 days since Fall of Sjandra Kei
Key phrases: On becoming Transcendent
Text of message:
　 Contrary to other postings, there are a number of reasons why a Power might install artifacts at the Bottom of the Beyond. The Abselor's message on this thread cites some: some Powers have documented curiosity about the Slow Zone and, even more, about the Unthinking Depths. In rare cases, expeditions have been dispatched (though any return from the Depths would occur long after the dispatching Power lost interest in all local questions).

However, none of these motives are likely here. To those who are familiar with Fast Burn transcendence, it is clear that the Blight is a creature seeking stasis. Its interest in the Bottom is very sudden, provoked, we think, by the revelations at Harmonious Repose. There is something at the Bottom that is critical to the Perversion's welfare.

Consider the notion of ablative dissonance (see the Where Are They Now group archive): No one knows what setup procedures the humans of Straumli Realm were using. The Fast Burn may itself have had Transcendent intelligence. What if *it* became dissatisfied with the direction of the channedring? In that case it might try to hide the jumpoff birthinghel. The Bottom would not be a place where the algorithm itself could normally execute, but avatars might still be created from it and briefly run.

Up to a point, Ravna could almost make sense of it; ablative dissonance was a commonplace of Applied Theology. But then, like one of those dreams where the secret of life is about to be revealed, the posting just drifted into nonsense.

There were postings that were neither asinine nor obscure. As usual, Sandor at the Zoo had a lot of things dead right:

Crypto: 0
As received by: *OOB* shipboard ad hoc
Language path: Triskweline, SjK units
From: Sandor Arbitration Intelligence at the Zoo [A known military corporation
   of the High Beyond. If this is a masquerade, somebody is living dangerously.]
Subject: The Blight's goal at the Bottom
Key phrases: Sudden change in Blight's tactics
Distribution:
   Threat of the Blight
   War Trackers Interest Group
   Homo Sapiens Interest Group
Date: 8.15 days since Fall of Sjandra Kei
Text of message:
   In case you don't know, Sandor Intelligence has a number of different Net feeds. We can collect messages on paths that have no intermediate nodes in common. Thus we can detect and correct tampering done en route. (There remain the lies and misunderstandings that were present to begin with, but that's something that makes the intelligence business interesting.)

   The Blight has been our top priority since its instantiation a year ago. This is not just because of the Blight's obvious strength, the destruction and the deicides it has committed. We fear that all this is the lesser part of the Threat. There have been perversions almost as powerful in the recorded past. What truly distinguishes this one is its stability. We see no evidence of internal evolution; in some ways it is *less* than a Power. It may never lose interest in controlling the High Beyond. We may be witnessing a massive and permanent change in the nature of things. Imagine: a stable necrosis, where the only sentience in the High Beyond is the Blight.

Thus, studying the Blight has been a matter of life and death for us (even though we are powerful and widely distributed). We've reached a number of conclusions. Some of these may be obvious to you, others may sound like flagrant speculation. All take on a new coloring with the events reported from Harmonious Repose:

Almost from the beginning, the Blight has been searching for something. This search has extended far beyond its aggressive physical expansion. Its automatic agents have tried to penetrate virtually every node in the Top of the Beyond; the High Network is in shambles, reduced to protocols scarcely more efficient than those known below. At the same time, the Blight has physically stolen several archives. We have evidence of very large fleets searching for off-Net archives at the Top and in the Low Transcend. At least three Powers have been murdered in this rampage.

And now, suddenly, this assault has ended. The Blight's physical expansion continues, with no end in sight, but it no longer searches the High Beyond. As near as we can tell, the change occurred about two thousand seconds before the escape of the human vessel from Harmonious Repose. Less than six hours later, we saw the beginnings of the silent fleet that so many are now speculating about. That fleet is indeed the creature of the Blight.

In other times, the destruction of Sjandra Kei and the motives of the Alliance for the Defense would all be important issues (and our organization might have interest in doing business with those affected). But all that is dwarfed by the fact of this fleet and the ship it pursues. And we disagree with the analysis from Harmonious Repose: it is obvious to us that the Blight did not know of the *Out of Band II* until its discovery at Harmonious Repose.

That ship is not a tool of the Blight, but it contains or is bound for something of enormous importance *to* the Blight. And what might that be? Here we begin frank speculation. And since we are speculating, we'll use those powerful pseudo-laws, the Principles of Mediocrity and Minimal Assumption. If the Blight has the potential for taking overall the Top in a permanent stability, then why has this not happened before? Our guess is that the Blight has been instantiated before (with such dire consequence that the event marks the beginning of recorded time), but it has its own peculiar natural enemy.

The order of events even suggests a particular scenario, one familiar from network security. Once upon a time (very long ago), there was another instance of the Blight. A successful defense was mounted, and all known copies of the Blight's recipe were destroyed. Of course, on a wide net, one can never be sure that *all* copies of a badness are gone. No doubt, the defense was distributed in enormous numbers. But even if a harboring archive were reached by such a distribution, there might be no effect if the Blight were not currently active there.

The luckless humans of Straumli Realm chanced on such an archive, no doubt a ruin long off the Net. They instantiated the Blight and incidentally – perhaps a little later – the defense program. Somehow that Blight's enemy escaped destruction. And the Blight has been searching for it ever since – *in all the wrong places*. In its weakness, the new instance of the defense retreated to depths no Power would think of penetrating, whence it could never return without outside help. Speculation on top of speculation: we can't guess the nature of this defense, except that its retreat is a discouraging sign. And now even that sacrifice has gone for naught, since the Blight has seen through the deception.

The Blight's fleet is clearly an ad hoc thing, hastily thrown together from forces that happened to be closest to the discovery. Without such haste, the quarry might have been lost to it. Thus the chase equipment is probably ill-suited to the depths, and its performance will degrade as the descent progresses. However, we estimate that it will remain stronger than any force that can reach the scene in the near future.

We may learn more after the Blight reaches the *Out of Band II's* destination. If it destroys that destination immediately, we'll know that something truly dangerous to the Blight existed there (and may exist elsewhere, at least in recipe form). If it does not, then perhaps the Blight was looking for something that will make it even more dangerous than before.

Ravna sat back, stared at the display for some time. Sandor Arbitration Intelligence was one of the sharpest posters in this newsgroup . . . But now even their predictions were just different flavors of doom. And all so damn cool they were, so analytical. She knew that Sandor was polyspecific, with branch offices scattered through the High Beyond. But they were no Power. If the Perversion could knock over Relay and kill Old One, then all of Sandor's resources wouldn't help it if the enemy decided to gobble them up. Their analysis had the tone of the pilot of a crashing ship, intent on understanding the danger, not taking time out for terror.

Oh Pham, how I wish I could talk to you like before! She curled gently in on herself, the way you can in zero gee. The sobs came softly, but without hope. They had not exchanged a hundred words in the last five days. They lived as if with guns at each others' heads. And that was the literal truth – *she* had made it so. When she and he and the Skroderiders had been together, at least the danger had been a shared burden. Now they were split apart and their enemies were slowly gaining on them. What good could Pham's godshatter be against a thousand enemy ships and the Blight behind them?

She floated for a timeless while, the sobs fading into despairing silence. And again she wondered if what she'd done could possibly be right. She had threatened Pham's life to protect Blueshell and Greenstalk and their kind. In doing so she had kept secret what might be the greatest treachery in the history of the Known Net. *Can one person make such a decision?* Pham had asked her that, and she had answered *yes* but . . .

The question toyed with her every day. And every day she tried to see some way out. She wiped her face silently. She didn't doubt what Pham had discovered.

There were some smug posters on the Net who argued that something as vast as the Blight was simply a tragic disaster, and not an evil. Evil, they argued, could only have meaning on smaller scales, in the hurt that one sophont does to another. Before RIP, the argument had seemed a frivolous playing with words. Now she saw that it was meaningful – and dead wrong. The Blight had created the Riders, a marvelous and peaceful race. Their presence on a billion worlds had been a good. And behind it all was the potential for converting the sovereign minds of friends into monsters. When she thought of Blueshell and Greenstalk, and the fear welled up and she knew the poison that was there – *even though they were good people* – then she knew she'd glimpsed evil on the Transcendent scale.

She had gotten Blueshell and Greenstalk into this mission; they had not asked for it. They were friends and allies, and she *would not* harm them because of what they could become.

Maybe it was the latest news items. Maybe it was confronting the same impossibilities for the nth time: Ravna gradually straightened, looking at those last messages. So. She believed Pham about the Skroderider threat. She also believed these two were only enemies in potential. She had thrown away everything to save them and their kind. Maybe it was a mistake, *but take what advantage there is in it. If they are to be saved because you think they are allies, then treat them as allies. Treat them as the friends they are. We are all pawns together.*

Ravna pushed gently toward her cabin's doorway.

The Skroderiders' cabin was just behind the command deck. Since the debacle at RIP, the two had not left it. As she drifted down the passage toward their door, Ravna half-expected to see Pham's handiwork lurking in the shadows. She knew he was doing his best to 'protect himself.' Yet there was nothing unusual. *What will he think of my visiting them?*

She announced herself. After a moment Blueshell appeared. His skrode was wiped clean of cosmetic stripes, and the room behind him was a jumble. He waved her in with quick jerks of his fronds.

'My lady.'

'Blueshell.' She nodded at him. Half the time she cursed herself for trusting the Riders; the other half, she was mortally embarrassed for having left them alone. 'H-how is Greenstalk?'

Surprisingly, Blueshell's fronds snapped together in a smile. 'You guessed? This is the first day with her new skrode . . . I will show you, if you'd like.'

He threaded around equipment that was scattered in a lattice across the room. It was similar to the shop equipment Pham had used to build his powered armor. And if Pham had seen it, he might have lost all self-control.

'I've worked on it every minute since . . . Pham locked us in here.'

Greenstalk was in the other room. Her stalk and fronds rose from a silver pot. There were no wheels. It looked nothing like a traditional skrode. Blueshell rolled across the ceiling and extended a front down to his mate. He rustled something at her, and after a moment she replied.

'The skrodeling is very limited, no mobility, no redundant power supplies. I copied it off a Lesser Skroderider design, a simple thing designed by Dirokimes. It's not meant for more than sitting in one place, facing in one direction. But it provides her with short-term memory support, and attention focusers . . . She is back with me.' He fussed around her, some fronds caressing hers, others pointing to the gadget he had built for her. 'She herself was not badly injured. Sometimes I wonder – whatever Pham says, maybe at the last second he could not kill her.'

He spoke nervously, as though afraid of what Ravna might say.

'The first few days I was very worried. But the surgeon is good. It gave her plenty of time to stand in strong surf. To think slowly. Since I've added on this skrodeling, she has practiced the calesthenics of memory, repeating what the surgeon or I say to her. With the skrodeling she can hold on to a new memory for almost five hundred seconds. That's usually long enough for her natural mind to commit a thought to long-term memory.'

Ravna drifted close. There were some new creases in Greenstalk's fronds. Those would be scars healing. Her visual surfaces followed Ravna's approach. The Rider knew she was here; her whole posture was friendly.

'Can she talk Trisk, Blueshell? Do you have a voder hooked up?'

'What?' Buzz. He was forgetful or nervous, Ravna couldn't tell which. 'Yes, yes. Just give me a minute . . . There was no need before. No one wanted to talk to us.' He fiddled with something on the homemade skrode.

After a moment, 'Hello, Ravna I . . . recognize you.' Her fronds rustled in time with the words.

'I know you, too. We, I am glad that you are back.'

The voder voice was faint, wistful? 'Yes. It's hard for me to tell. I do want to talk, but I'm not sure . . . am I'm making sense?'

Out of Greenstalk's sight, Blueshell flicked a long tendril, a gesture: *say yes.*

'Yes, I understand you, Greenstalk.' And Ravna resolved never again to get angry with Greenstalk about not remembering.

'Good.' Her fronds straightened and she didn't say anything more.

'See?' came Blueshell's voder voice. 'I am brightly cheerful. Even now, Greenstalk is committing this conversation to long-term memory. It goes slowly for now, but I am improving the skrodeling. I'm sure her slowness is mainly emotional shock.' He continued to brush at Greenstalk's fronds, but she didn't say anything more. Ravna wondered just how brightly cheerful he could be.

Behind the Riders were a set of display windows, customized now for the Rider outlook. 'You've been following the News?' Ravna asked.

'Yes, indeed.'

'I – I feel so helpless.' *I feel so foolish saying that to you.*

But Blueshell didn't take offense. He seemed grateful for the change of topic, preferring the gloom at a distance. 'Yes. We certainly are famous now. Three fleets chasing us down, my lady. Ha ha.'

'They don't seem to be gaining very fast.'

Frond shrug. 'Sir Pham has turned out to be a competent ship's master. I'm afraid things will change as we descend. The ship's higher automation will gradually fail. What you call "manual control" will become very important. *OOB* was designed for my race, my lady. No matter what Sir Pham thinks of us, at bottom we can fly it better than any. So bit by bit the others will gain – at least those who truly understand their own ships.'

'S-surely Pham must know this?'

'I think he must. But he is trapped in his own fears. What can he do? If not for you, my lady Ravna, he might have killed us already. Maybe when the choice comes down to dying in the next hour against trusting us, maybe then there will be a chance.'

'By then it will be too late. Look, even if he doesn't trust – even though he believes the worst of Riders – there must still be a way.' And it came to her that sometimes you don't have to change the way people think, or even whom they may hate. 'Pham wants to get to the Bottom, to recover this Counter-measure. He thinks you may be from the Blight, and after the same thing. But up to a point—' Up to a point he *can* cooperate, postpone the showdown he imagines till perhaps it won't matter.

Even as she started to say it, Blueshell was already shouting back at her. 'I'm *not* of the Blight! Greenstalk is not! The Rider race is not!' He swept around his mate, rolled across the ceiling till his fronds rattled right before Ravna's face.

'I'm sorry. It's just the potential—'

'*Nonsense!*' His voder buzzed off-scale. 'We ran into an evil few. Every race has such, people who will kill for trade. They forced Greenstalk, substituted data at her voder. Pham Nuwen would kill our billions for the sake of this fantasy.' He waved, inarticulate. Something she had never seen in a Skroderider: his fronds actually changed tone, darkened.

The motion ceased, yet he said nothing more. And then Ravna heard it, a keening that might have come from a voder. The sound was steadily growing, a howl that made all Blueshell's sound effects friendly nonsense. It was Greenstalk.

The scream reached a threshold just below pain, then broke into choppy Triskweline: '*It's true!* Oh, by all our trading, Blueshell, it's true . . .' and staticky noise came from her voder. Her fronds started shaking, random turning that must be like a human's eyes wildly staring, like a human's mouth mumbling hysteria.

Blueshell was already back by the wall, reaching to adjust her new skrode. Greenstalk's fronds brushed him away, and her voder voice continued, '*I was horrorstruck, Blueshell.* I was horrorstruck, struck by horror. And it would not stop . . .' She was silent for a moment. Blueshell stood frozen. 'I remember everything up till the last five minutes. And everything Pham says is true, dear love. Loyal as you are, and I have seen that loyalty now for two hundred years, you would be turned in an instant . . . just as I was.' Now that the dam broke, her words came quickly, mostly making sense. The horrors she could remember were graven deep, and she was finally coming out of ghastly shock. 'I was right behind you, remember, Blueshell? You were deep in your trading with the tusk-legs, so deep you did not really see. I noticed the other Riders coming toward us. No matter: a friendly meeting, so far from home. Then one touched my Skrode. I—' Greenstalk hesitated. Her fronds rattled and she began again, 'horrorstruck, horrorstruck . . .'

After a moment: 'It was like suddenly new memories in the skrode, Blueshell. New memories, new attitudes. But thousands of years deep. *And not mine.* Instantly, instantly. I never even lost consciousness. I thought just as clearly, I remembered all I had before.

'And when you resisted?' Ravna said softly.

'. . . Resisted? My Lady Ravna, *I did not resist*, I was theirs . . . No. Not theirs, for they were owned too. We were things, our intelligence in service to another's goal. Dead, and alive to see our death. I would kill you. I would kill Pham, I would kill Blueshell. You know I tried. And when I did, I wanted to succeed. You could not imagine, Ravna. You humans speak of violation. You could never know . . .' Long pause. 'That's not quite right. At the Top of the Beyond, within the Blight itself – perhaps there, *everyone* lives as I did.'

The shuddering did not subside, but her gestures were no longer aimless. The fronds were saying something in her own language, and brusthing gently against Blueshell.

'Our whole race, dear love. Just as Pham says it.'

Blueshell wilted, and Ravna felt the sort of gut-tearing she had when they learned of Sjandra Kei. That had been her worlds, her family, her life. Blueshell was hearing worse.

Ravna pushed a little closer, near enough to run her hand up the side of Greenstalk's fronds. 'Pham says it's the greater skrodes that are the cause.' Sabotage hidden billion of years deep.

'Yes, it is mainly the skrodes. The "great gift" we Riders love so . . . It is a design for control, but I fear we were remade for it, too. When they touched my skrode, I was converted instantly. Instantly, everything I cared for was meaningless. We are like smart bombs, scattered by the trillions through space that everyone thinks is safe. We will be used sparingly. We are the Blight's hidden weapon, especially in the Low Beyond.'

Blueshell twitched, and his voice came out jerkily: 'And everything Pham claims is correct.'

'No, Blueshell, not everything.' Ravna remembered that last chilling standoff with Pham Nuwen. 'He has the facts, but he weighs them wrong. As long as your skrodes are not perverted, you are the same folk that I trusted to fly me to the Bottom.'

Blueshell angled his look away from her, an angry shrug. Greenstalk's voice came instead. 'As long as the skrode has not been perverted . . . But look how easy it was done, how sudden I became the Blight's.'

'Yes, but could it happen except by direct touch? Could you be "changed" by reading the Net News?' She meant the question as ghastly sarcasm, but poor Greenstalk took it seriously:

'Not by a News item, nor by standard protocol messages. But accepting a transmission targeted on skrode utilities might do it.'

'Then we are safe here. You, because you no longer ride a greater skrode, Blueshell because—'

'Because I was never touched – but how can you know that?' His anger was still there, deep within shame, but now it was a hopeless anger, directed at something very far away.

'No, dear love, you have not been touched. I would know.'

'Yes, but why should Ravna believe *you?*'

Everything could be a lie, thought Ravna, . . . *but I believe Greenstalk. I believe we four are the only ones in all the Beyond who can hurt the Blight*. If only Pham could see it. And that brought her back to: 'You say we will start losing our lead?'

Blueshell waved an affirmative. 'As soon as we are a little lower. They should have us in a matter of weeks.'

And then it won't matter who was perverted and who was not. 'I think we should have a little chat with Pham Nuwen.' Godshatter and all.

Beforehand Ravna couldn't imagine how the confrontation would turn out. Just possibly – if he'd lost all touch with reality – Pham might try to kill them when they appeared on the command deck. More likely there would be rage and argument and threats, and they would be back to square one.

Instead . . . it was almost like the old Pham, from before Harmonious Repose. He let them enter the command deck, he made no comment when Ravna set herself carefully between himself and the Riders. He listened without interruption while Ravna explained what Greenstalk had said. 'These two are safe, Pham. And without their help we'll not make it to the Bottom.'

He nodded, looked away at the windows. Some showed natural starscape;

most were ultratrace displays, the closest thing to a picture of the enemies that were closing on the *OOB*. His calm expression broke for just an instant, and the Pham that loved her seemed to stare out, desperate: 'And you really believe all this, Rav? *How?*' Then the lid was back on, his expression distant and neutral. 'Never mind. Certainly it's true: without all of us working together we'll never make it to Tines' World. Blueshell, I accept your offer. Subject to cautious safeguards, we work together.' *Till I can safely dispose of you*, Ravna could feel the unsaid words behind his blandness. Showdown deferred.

33

They were less than eight weeks from Tines' World, both Pham and Blueshell said. If the Zone conditions remained stable. If they were not overtaken in the meantime.

Less than two months after the six already voyaged. But the days were not like before. Every one was a challenge, a standoff sometimes cloaked in civility, sometimes flaring into threats of sudden death – as when Pham retrieved Blueshell's shop equipment.

Pham was living on the command deck now; when he left it, the hatch was locked on his ID. He had destroyed, or thought he had destroyed, all other privileged links to the ship's automation. He and Blueshell were in almost constant collaboration . . . but not like before. Every step was slow, Blueshell explaining everything, allowed to demonstrate nothing. That's where the arguments came closest to deadly force, when Pham must give in to one peril or the other. For every day the pursuing fleets were a little bit closer: two bands of killers, and what was left of Sjandra Kei. Evidently some of the SjK Commercial Security fleet could still fight, wanted revenge on the Alliance. Once Ravna suggested to Pham that they contact Commercial Security, try to persuade them to attack the Blight fleet. Pham had given her a blank look. 'Not yet, maybe not ever,' he said, and turned away. In a way his answer was a relief: Such a battle would be a suicidal long shot. Ravna didn't want the last of her kinsfolk dying for her.

So the *OOB* might arrive at Tines' World before the enemy, but with what little time to spare! Some days Ravna withdrew in tears and despair. What brought her back was Jefri and Greenstalk. They both needed her, and for a few weeks more she could still help.

Mr Steel's defense plans were proceeding. The Tines were even having some success with their wideband radio. Steel reported that Woodcarver's main force was on its way north; there was more than one race against time. She spent many hours with *OOB*'s library, devising more gifts for Jefri's friends. Some things – like telescopes – were easy; but others . . . It wasn't wasted effort. Even if the Blight won, its fleet might ignore the natives, might settle for killing the *OOB* and winning back the Countermeasure.

Greenstalk was slowly improving. At first Ravna was afraid the improvement might be in her own imagination. Ravna was spending a good part of each day sitting with the Rider, trying to see progress in her responses. Greenstalk was very 'far away,' almost like a human with stroke damage and prosthesis. In fact, she seemed regressed from the articulate horror of her first conversations. Maybe her recent progress was just a mirror to Ravna's sensitivity, to the fact that Ravna was with her so much. Blueshell insisted there was progress, but with that stubborn inflexibility of his. Two weeks, three – and there was no doubt: Something was healing at the boundary between Rider and skrodeling. Greenstalk consistently made sense, consistently committed important rememberings . . . Now as often as not it was *she* helping Ravna. Greenstalk saw things that Ravna had missed: 'Sir Pham isn't the only one who is afraid of us Skroderiders. Blueshell is frightened too, and it is tearing him apart. He can't admit it even to me, but he thinks it's possible that we're infected independently of our skrodes. He desperately wants to convince Pham that this is not true – and so to convince himself.' She was silent for a long moment, one frond brushing against Ravna's arm. Sea sounds surrounded them in the cabin, but ship's automation could no longer produce surging water. 'Sigh. We must pretend the surf, dear Ravna. Somewhere it will always be, no matter what happened at Sjandra Kei, no matter what happens here.'

Blueshell was hearty gentleness around his mate, but alone with Ravna his rage showed through: 'No, no, I don't object to Sir Pham's navigation, at least not now. Perhaps we could be a little further ahead with me directly at the helm, but the fastest ships behind us would still be closing. It's the other things, My Lady. You know how untrustworthy our automation is down here. Pham is hurting it further. He's written his own security overrides. He's turning the ship's environment automation into a system of boobytraps.'

Ravna had seen evidence of this. The areas around *OOB*'s command deck and ship's workshop looked like military checkpoints. 'You know his fears. If this makes him feel safer—'

'That's not the point, My Lady. I would do anything to persuade him to accept my help. But what he's doing is deadly dangerous. Our Bottom automation is not reliable, and he's making it actively worse. If we get some sudden stress, the environment programs will likely have a bizarre crash – atmosphere dump, thermal runaway, anything.'

'I—'

'Doesn't he understand? Pham controls *nothing*.' His voder broke into a nonlinear squawk. 'He has the ability to destroy, but that is all. He needs my help. He was my friend. Doesn't he understand?'

Pham understood . . . oh, Pham understood. He and Ravna still talked. Their arguments were the hardest thing in her life. And sometimes they didn't exactly argue; sometimes it was almost like rational discussion:

'I haven't been taken over, Ravna. Not like the Blight takes over Riders, anyway. I still have charge of my soul.' He turned away from the console and flashed a wan smile in her direction, acknowledging the flaw in such self-conviction. And from things like that smile, Ravna was convinced that Pham Nuwen still lived, and sometimes spoke.

'What about the godshatter state? I see you for hours just staring at the tracking display, or mucking around in the library and the News,' scanning faster than any human could consciously read.

Pham shrugged. 'It's studying the ships that are chasing us, trying to figure out just what belongs to whom, just what capabilities each might have. I don't know the details. Self-awareness is on vacation then,' when all Pham's mind was turned into a processor for whatever programs Old One had downloaded. A few hours of fugue state might yield an instant of Power-grade thought – and even that he didn't consciously remember. 'But I know this. Whatever the godshatter is, it's a very narrow thing. It's not alive; in some ways it may not even be very smart. For everyday matters like ship piloting, there's just good old Pham Nuwen.'

'. . . there's the rest of us, Pham. Blueshell would like to help,' Ravna spoke softly. This was the place where Pham would close into icy silence – or blow up in rage. This day, he just cocked his head. 'Ravna, Ravna. I know I need him . . . And, and I'm glad I need him. That I don't have to kill him.' *Yet.* Pham's lips quivered for a second, and she thought he might start crying.

'The godshatter can't know Blueshell—'

'*Not* the godshatter. It's not making me act this way – I'm doing what any person should do when the stakes are this high.' The words were spoken without anger. Maybe there was a chance. Maybe she could reason:

'Blueshell and Greenstalk are loyal, Pham. Except at Harmonious Repose—'

Pham sighed, 'Yeah. I've thought about that a lot. They *came* to Relay from Straumli Realm. They got Vrinimi looking for the refugee ship. That smells of setup, but probably unknowing – maybe even a setup by something opposing the Blight. In any case they were innocent then, else the Blight would have known about Tines' World right from the beginning. The Blight knew nothing till RIP, till Greenstalk was converted. And I know Blueshell was loyal even then. He knew things about my armor – the remotes, for instance – that he could have warned the others about.'

Hope came as a surprise to Ravna. He really had thought things out, and – 'It's just the skrodes, Pham. They're traps waiting to be sprung. But we're isolated here, and you destroyed the one that Greenstalk—'

Pham was shaking his head. 'It's more than the skrodes. The Blight had its hand in Rider design too, at least to some degree. I can't imagine the takeover of Greenstalk's being so smooth otherwise.'

'Y-yes. A risk. A very small risk compared to—'

Pham didn't move, but something in him seemed to draw away from her, denying the support she could offer. 'A small risk? We don't know. The stakes are so *high*. I'm walking a tightrope. If I don't use Blueshell now, we'll be shot out of space by the Blighter fleet. If I let him do too much, if I trust him, then he or some part of him could betray us. All I have is the godshatter, and a bunch of memories that . . . that may be the biggest fakes of all.' These last words were nearly inaudible. He looked up at her, a look that was both cold and terribly lost. 'But I'm going to use what I have, Rav, and whatever it is I am. Somehow I'm going to get us to Tines' World. Somehow I'm going to get Old One's godshatter to whatever is there.'

It was another three weeks before Blueshell's predictions came true.

The *OOB* had seemed a sturdy beast up in the Middle Beyond; even its damaged ultradrive had failed gracefully. Now the ship was leaking bugs in all directions. Much of it had nothing to do with Pham's meddling. Without those final consistency checks, none of *OOB*'s Bottom automation was really trustworthy. But its failures were compounded by Pham's desperate security 'fixes.'

The ship's library had source code for generic Bottom automation. Pham spent several days revising it for the *OOB*. All four of them were on the command deck during the installation, Blueshell trying to help, Pham suspiciously examining every suggestion. Thirty minutes into the installation, there were muffled banging noises down the main corridor. Ravna might have ignored them, except that she'd never heard the like aboard the *OOB*.

Pham and the Riders reacted with near panic; spacers don't like unexplained bumps in the night. Blueshell raced to the hatch, floated fronds-first through the hole. 'I see nothing, Sir Pham.'

Pham was paging quickly through the diagnostic displays, mixed format things partly from the new setup. 'I've got some warning lights here, but—'

Greenstalk started to say something, but Blueshell was back and talking fast; 'I don't believe it. Anything like this should make pictures, a detailed report. Something is terribly wrong.'

Pham stared at him a second, then returned to his diagnostics. Five seconds passed. 'You're right. Status is just looping through stale reports.' He began grabbing views from cameras all over the *OOB*'s interior. Barely half of them reported, but what they showed . . .

The ship's water reservoir was a foggy, icy cavern. That was the banging sound – tonnes of water, spaced. A dozen other support services had gone bizarre, and—

—the armed checkpoint outside the workshop had slagged down. The beamers were firing continuously on low power. And for all the destruction, the diagnostics still showed green or amber or no report. Pham got a camera in the workshop itself. *The place was on fire.*

Pham jumped up from his saddle and bounced off the ceiling. For an instant she thought he might go racing off the bridge. Then he tied himself down and grimly began trying to put out the fire.

For the next few minutes the bridge was almost quiet, just Pham quietly swearing as none of the obvious things worked. 'Interlocking failures,' he mumbled the phrase a couple of times. 'The firesnuff automation is down . . . I can't dump atmosphere from the shop. My beamers have melted everything shut.'

Ship fire. Ravna had seen pictures of such disasters, but they had always seemed an improbable thing. In the midst of universal vacuum, how could a fire survive? And in zero-gee, surely a fire would choke itself even if the crew couldn't dump atmosphere. The workshop camera had a hazy view on the real thing: True, the flames ate the oxygen around them. There were sheets of construction foam that were only lightly scorched, protected for the moment by dead air. But the fire spread out, moving steadily into still-fresh air. In places, heat-driven turbulence enriched the mix, and previously burned areas blazed up.

'It's still got ventilation, Sir Pham.'

'I *know*. I can't shut it. The vents must be melted open.'

'It's as likely software.' Blueshell was silent for a second. 'Try this—' The directions were meaningless to Ravna, some low-level workaround.

But Pham nodded, and his fingers danced across the console.

In the workshop, the surface-hugging flames crept farther across the construction foam. Now they licked at the innards of the armor Pham had spent so much time on. This latest revision was only half finished. Ravna remembered he was working on reactive armor now . . . *There would be oxidizers there.* 'Pham, is the armor sealed—'

The fire was sixty meters aft and behind a dozen bulkheads. The explosion came as a distant thump, almost innocent. But in the camera view, the armor dismembered itself, and the fire blazed triumphant.

Seconds later, Pham got Blueshell's suggestion working, and the workshop's vents closed. The fire in the wrecked armor continued for another half hour, but did not spread beyond the shop.

It took two days to clean up, to estimate the damage, and to have some confidence that no new disaster was on the way. Most of the workshop was destroyed. They would have no armor on Tines' World. Pham salvaged one of the beamers that had been guarding the entrance to the shop. Disaster was scattered all across the ship, the classic random ruin of interlocking failures: They had lost fifty percent of their water. The ship's landing boat had lost its higher automation.

OOB's rocket drive was massively degraded. That was unimportant here in interstellar space, but their final velocity matching would be done at only 0.4 gees. Thank goodness the agrav worked; they would have no trouble maneuvering in steep gravitational wells – that is, landing on Tines' World.

Ravna knew how close they were to losing the ship, but she watched Pham with even greater dread. She was so afraid that he would take this as final evidence of Rider treachery, that this would drive him over the edge. Strangely, almost the opposite happened. His pain and devastation were obvious, but he didn't lash out, just doggedly went about gathering up the pieces. He was talking to Blueshell more now, not letting him modify the automation, but cautiously accepting more of his advice. Together they restored the ship to something like its pre-fire state.

She asked Pham about it. 'No change of heart,' he finally said. 'I had to balance the risks, and I messed up . . . And maybe there is no balance. Maybe the Blight will win.'

The godshatter had bet too much on Pham's doing it all himself. Now it was turning down the paranoia a little. Seven weeks out from Harmonious Repose, less than one week from whatever waited at Tines' World, Pham went into a multiday fugue. Before, he had been busy, a futile attempt to run handmade checks on all the automation they might need at Tines' World. Now – Ravna couldn't even get him to eat.

The nav display showed the three fleets as identified by the News and Pham's intuition: the Blight's agents, the Alliance for the Defense, and what was left of Sjandra Kei Commercial Security: deadly-monsters and the remains of a victim. The Alliance still proclaimed itself with regular bulletins on the News. SjK Commercial Security had posted a few terse refutations, but was mostly silent; they were unused to propaganda, or – as likely – uninterested in it. A private revenge was all that remained to Commercial Security. And the Blighter fleet? The News hadn't heard anything from them. Piecing together departures and lost ships, War Trackers Newsgroup concluded they were a wildly ad hoc assembly, whatever the Blight had controlled down here at the time of the RIP debacle. Ravna knew that the War Trackers analysis was wrong about one thing: The Blighter fleet was not silent. Thirty times over the last weeks, they had sent messages at the *OOB* . . . in skrode maintenance format. Pham had had the ship reject the messages unread – and then worried about whether the order was really followed. After all, the *OOB* was of Rider design.

But now the torment in him was submerged. Pham sat for hours, staring at the display. Soon Sjandra Kei would close with the Alliance fleet. At least one set of villains would pay. But the Blighter fleet and at least part of the Alliance would survive . . . Maybe this fugue was just godshatter getting desperate.

Three days passed; Pham snapped out of it. Except for the new thinness in his face, he seemed more normal than he had in weeks. He asked Ravna to bring the Riders up to the bridge.

Pham waved at the ultradrive traces that floated in the window. The three fleets were spread through a rough cylinder, five light-years deep and three across. The display captured only the heart of that volume, where the fastest of the pursuers had clustered. The current position of each ship was a fleck of light trailing an unending stream of fainter lights – the ultradrive trace left by that vehicle's drive. 'I've used red, blue, and green to mark my best guess as to the fleet affiliation of each trace.' The fastest ships were collected in a blob so dense that it looked white at this scale, but with colored streamers diverging behind. There were other tags, annotations he had set but which he admitted once to Ravna he didn't understand.

'The front edge of that mob – the fastest of the fast – is still gaining.'

Blueshell said hesitantly. 'We might get a little more speed if you would grant me direct control. Not much, but—'

Pham's response was civil, at least. 'No, I'm thinking of something else, something Ravna suggested a while back. It's always been a possibility and . . . I . . . think the time may have come for it.'

Ravna moved closer to the display, stared at the green traces. Their distribution was in near agreement with what the News claimed to be the remnants of Sjandra Kei Commercial Security. *All that's left of my people.* 'They've been trying to engage with the Alliance for a hundred hours now.'

Pham's glance touched hers. 'Yeah,' he said softly. 'Poor bastards. They're literally the fleet from Port Despair. If I were them, I'd—' His expression smoothed over again. 'Any idea how well-armed they are?' That was surely a rhetorical question, but it put the topic on the table.

'War Trackers thinks that Sjandra Kei had been expecting something unpleasant ever since the Alliance started talking "death to vermin." Commercial Security was providing deep space defense. Their fleet is converted freighters armed with locally designed weapons. War Trackers claims they weren't really a match for what the other side could field, *if* the Alliance was willing to take some heavy casualties. Trouble is, Sjandra Kei never expected the planet-smasher attack. So when the Alliance fleet showed up, ours moved out to meet it—'

'—and meantime the KE bombs were coming straight in to the heart of Sjandra Kei.'

Into my heart. 'Yes. The Alliance must have been running those bombs for weeks.'

Pham Nuwen laughed shortly. 'If I were shipping with the Alliance fleet, I'd be a bit nervous now. They're down in numbers, and those retread freighters seem about as fast as anything here . . . I'll bet every pilot out of Sjandra Kei is dead set on revenge.' The emotion faded. 'Hmm. There's no way they could kill all the Alliance ships or all the Blight's, much less all of both. It would be pointless to . . .

His gaze abruptly focused on her. 'So if we leave things as they are, the Sjandra Kei fleet will eventually match position with the Alliance and try to blow them out of existence.'

Ravna just nodded. 'In twelve hours or so, they say.'

'And then all that will be left is the Blight's own fleet on our tail. But if we could talk your people into fighting the right enemies . . .'

It was Ravna's nightmare scheme. All that was left of Sjandra Kei dying to save the *OOB* . . . trying to save them. There was little chance the Sjandra Kei fleet could destroy all Blighter ships. *But they're here to fight. Why not a vengeance that means something?* That was the nightmare's message. Now somehow it fit the godshatter's plans. 'There are problems. They don't know what we're doing or the purpose of the third fleet. Anything we shout back to them will be overheard.' Ultrawave was directional, but most of their pursuers were closely mingled.

Pham nodded. 'Somehow we have to talk to them, and them alone. Somehow we have to persuade them to fight.' Faint smile. 'And I think we may have just the . . . equipment . . . to do all that. Blueshell: Remember that night on the High Docks. You told us about your "rotted cargo" from Sjandra Kei?'

'Indeed, Sir Pham. We carried one third of a cipher generated by SjK Commercial Security for the razor-jaws. It's still in the ship's safe, though worthless without the other two thirds.' Gram for gram, crypto materials were about the most valuable thing shipped between the stars – and once compromised, about the most valueless. Somewhere in *Out of Band*'s cargo files there was an SjK one-time communications pad. Part of a pad.

'Worthless? Maybe not. Even one third would provide us with secure communications.'

Blueshell dithered. 'I must not mislead you. No competent customer would accept such. Certainly it provides secure communication, but the other side has no verification that *you* are who you claim.'

Pham's glance slid sideways toward Ravna. There was that smile again. 'If they'll listen, I think we can convince them . . . The hard part is, I only want one of them to hear us.' Pham explained what he had in mind. The Riders rustled faintly behind his words. After all their time together, Ravna could almost get some sense of their talk – or maybe she just understood their personalities. As usual, Blueshell was worrying about how impossible the idea was, and Greenstalk was urging him to listen.

But when Pham finished, the large Rider did not launch into objections. 'Across seventy light-years, ultrawave comm between ships is practical; we could even have live video. But you are right, the beam spread would include all the ships in the central cluster of fleets. If we could reliably identify an outlying vessel as belonging to Sjandra Kei, then what you are asking might be done; that ship could use internal fleet codes to relay to the others. But in honesty I must warn you,' continued Blueshell, brushing back Greenstalk's gentle remonstrance, 'professional communications folk would not honor your request for talk – would probably not even recognize it as such.'

'Silly.' Greenstalk finally spoke, her voder-voice gentle but clear. 'You always say things like that – except when we are talking to paying customers.'

'*Brap*. Yes. Desperate times, desperate measures. I want to try it, but I fear . . . I want there to be no accusation of Rider treachery, Sir Pham. I want you to handle this.'

Pham Nuwen smiled back. 'My thought exactly.'

'The Aniara Fleet.' That's what some of the crew of Commercial Security were calling themselves. Aniara was the ship of an old human myth, older than Nyjora, perhaps going back to the Tuvo-Norsk cooperatives in the asteroids of Earth's solar system. In the story, Aniara was a large ship launched into interstellar depths just before the death of its parent civilization. The crew watched the death agonies of the home system, and then over the following years – as their ship fell out and out into the endless dark – died themselves, their life-support systems slowly failing. The image was a haunting one, which was probably the reason it was known across millennia. With the destruction of Sjandra Kei and the escape of Commercial Security, the story seemed suddenly come true.

But we will not play it to the end. Group Captain Kjet Svensndot stared into the tracking display. This time the death of civilization had been a murder, and the murderers were almost within vengeance's reach. For days, fleet HQ had been maneuvering them to close with the Alliance. The display showed that success was very, very near. The majority of Alliance and Sjandra Kei ships were bound in a glowing ball of drive traces – which also included the third, silent fleet. From that display you might think that battle was already possible. In fact, opposing ships were passing through almost the same space – sometimes less than a billion kilometers apart – but still separated by milliseconds of time. All the vessels were on ultradrive, jumping perhaps a dozen times a second. And even here at the Bottom of the Beyond that came to a measurable fraction of a light-year on each jump. To fight an uncooperative enemy meant matching their jumps perfectly and flooding the common space with weapon drones.

Group Captain Svensndot changed the display to show ships that had exactly matched their pace with the Alliance. Almost a third of the fleet was in synch now. Another few hours and . . . 'Damnation!' He slapped his display board, sending it spinning across the deck.

His first officer retrieved the display, sent it sailing back. 'Is this a new damnation, or the usual?' Tirolle asked.

'It was the usual. Sorry.' And he really was. Tirolle and Glimfrelle had their own problems. No doubt there were still pockets of humanity in the Beyond, hidden from the Alliance. But of the Dirokimes, there might be no more than those on Commercial Security's fleet. Except for adventurous souls like Tirolle and Glimfrelle, all that was left of their kind had been in the dream terranes at Sjandra Kei.

Kjet Svensndot had been with Commercial Security for twenty-five years, back when the company had been just a small fleet of rent-a-cops. He had spent thousands of hours learning to be the very best combat pilot in the organization. Only twice had he ever been in a shootout. Some might have regretted that. Svensndot and his superiors took it as the reward for being the best. His competence had won him the best fighting equipment in Commercial Security's fleet, culminating with the ship he commanded now. The *Ølvira* was purchased with part of the enormous premium that Sjandra Kei paid out when the Alliance first started making threatening noises. *Ølvira* was not a rebuilt freighter, but a fighting machine from the keel out. The ship was equipped with the smartest processors and the smartest ultra drive that could operate Sjandra Kei's altitude in the Beyond. It needed only a three-person crew – and combat could be managed by the pilot alone with his AI associates. Its holds contained more than ten thousand seeker bombs, each smarter than the average freighter's entire drive unit. Quite a reward for twenty-five years of solid performance. They even let Svensndot name his new ship.

And now . . . Well, the true Ølvira was surely dead. Along with billions of others they had been hired to protect, she had been at Herte, in the inner system. Glow bombs leave no survivors.

And his beautiful ship with the same name, it had been a half light-year out-system, seeking enemies that weren't there. In any honest battle, Kjet Svensndot and this *Ølvira* could have done very well. Instead they were chasing down into the Bottom of the Beyond. Every fight-year took them further from the regions *Ølvira* was built for. Every light-year the processors worked a bit more slowly (or not at all). Down here the converted freighters were almost an optimum design. Clumsy and stupid, with crews of dozens, but they kept on working. Already *Ølvira* was lagging five light-years behind them. It was the freighters that would make the attack on the Alliance fleet. And once again Kjet would stand powerless while his friends died.

For the hundredth time, Svensndot glared at the trace display and contemplated mutiny. There were Alliance stragglers too – 'high performance' vehicles left behind the central pack. But his orders were to maintain position, to be a tactical coordinator for the fleet's swifter combatants. Well, he would do as he was hired . . . this one last time. But when the battle was done, when the fleet was dead, along with as many of the Alliance as they could take with them – then he would think of his own revenge. Some of that depended on Tirolle and Glimfrelle. Could he persuade them to leave the remnants of the Alliance fleet and ascend to the Middle Beyond, up where the *Ølvira* was the best of her kind? There was solid evidence about which star systems were behind the 'Alliance for the Defense.' The murderers were boasting to the News. Apparently they thought that would bring them new support. It might also bring them visitors like *Ølvira*. The bombs in her belly could destroy worlds, though not as swiftly sure as what had been used on Sjandra Kei. And even now Svensndot's mind shrank from that sort of revenge. No. They would choose their targets carefully: ships coming to form new Alliance fleets, underprotected convoys. *Ølvira* might last a long time if he always struck from ambush and never left survivors. He stared and stared at the display, and ignored the wetness that floated at the comers of his eyes. All his life he had lived by the law. Often his job had been to stop acts of revenge . . . And now revenge was all that life had left for him.

'I'm getting something peculiar, Kjet.' Glimfrelle was monitoring signals this watch. It was the sort of thing that should *have* been totally automated – and had been in *Ølvira*'s natural environment – but which was now a boring and exhausting enterprise.

'What? More Net lies?' said Tirolle.

'No. This is on the bearing of that bottom-lugger everyone is chasing. It can't be anyone else.'

Svensndot's eyebrows rose. He turned on the mystery with enormous, scarcely realized, pleasure. 'Characteristics?'

'Ship's signal processor says it's probably a narrow beam. *We* are its only likely target. The signal is strong and the bandwidth is at least enough to support flat video. If our *snarfling* digital signal processor was working right, I'd know—' 'Frelle sang a little song that was impatient humming among his kind. '—*Iiae!* It's encrypted, but at a high layer. This stuff is syntax 45 video. In fact, it claims to be using one third of a cipher the Company made a year back.' For an instant Svensndot thought 'Frelle was claiming the message itself was smart; that should be absolutely impossible here at the Bottom. The second officer must have caught his look: 'Just sloppy language, Boss. I read this out of the frame format . . .' Something flashed on his display. 'Okay, here's the story on the cipher: the Company made it and its peers to cover shipping security.' Back before the Alliance, that had been the highest crypto level in the organization. 'This is the third that never got delivered. The whole was assumed compromised, but miracle of miracles, we still have a copy.' Both 'Frelle and 'Rolle were looking at Svensndot expectantly, their eyes large and dark. Standard policy – standard *orders* – were that transmissions on compromised keys were to be ignored. If the Company's signals people had been doing a proper job, the rotted cipher wouldn't even have been aboard and the policy would have enforced itself.

'Decrypt the thing,' Svensndot said shortly. The last weeks had demonstrated that his company was a dismal failure when it came to military intelligence and signals. They might as well get some benefit from that incompetence.

'Yes sir!' Glimfrelle tapped a single key. Somewhere inside *Ølvira*'s signal processor, a long segment of 'random' noise was broken into frames and laid precisely down on the 'random' noise in the data frames incoming. There was a perceptible pause (*damn the Bottom*) and then the comm window lit with a flat video picture.

'—fourth repetition of this message.' The words were Samnorsk, and a dialect of pure *Herte i Sjandra*. The speaker was . . . for a heartstopping instant he was seing Ølvira again, alive. He exhaled slowly, trying to relax. Black-haired, slim, violet-eyed – just like Ølvira. And just like a million other women of Sjandra Kei. The resemblance was there, but so vague he would never have been taken by it before. For an instant he imagined a universe beyond their lost fleet, and goals beyond vengeance. Then he forced his attention back to business, to seeing everything he could in the images in the window.

The woman was saying, 'We'll repeat three more times. If by then you have still not responded, we will attempt a different target.' She pushed back from the camera pickup, giving them a view of the room behind her. It was low-ceilinged, deep. An ultradrive trace display dominated the background, but Svensndot paid it little attention. There were two Skroderiders in the background. One wore stripes on its skrode that meant a trade history with Sjandra Kei. The other must be a lesser Rider; its skrode was small and wheelless. The pickup turned, centered on the fourth figure. Human? Probably, but of no Nyjoran heritage. In another time his appearance would have been big news across all human civilizations in the Beyond. Now the point only registered on Svensndot's mind as another cause for suspicion.

The woman continued, 'You can see that we are human and Rider. We are the entire crew of the *Out of Band II*. We are not part of the Alliance for the Defense nor agents of the Blight . . . But we *are* the reason their fleets are down here. If you can read this, we're betting that you are of Sjandra Kei. We must talk. Please reply using the tail of the pad that is decrypting this message.' The picture jigged and the woman's face was back in the foreground. 'This is the fifth repetition of this message,' she said. 'We'll repeat two more—'

Glimfrelle cut the audio. 'If she means it, we have about one hundred seconds. What next, Captain?'

Suddenly the *Ølvira* was not an irrelevant straggler. 'We talk,' said Svensndot.

Response and counter-response took a matter of seconds. After that . . . five minutes of conversation with Ravna Bergsndot was enough to convince Kjet that what she had to say must be heard by Fleet Central. His ship would be a mere relay, but at least he had something very important to pass on.

Fleet Central refused the full video link coming from the *Out of Band*. Someone on the flagship was dead set on following standard procedures – and using compromised cipher keys stuck in their craw. Even Kjet had to settle for a combat link: The screen showed a color image with high resolution. Looking at it carefully, one realized the thing was a poor evocation . . . Kjet recognized Owner Limmende and Jan Skrits, her chief of staff, but they looked several years out of style: old video matched with the transmitted animation cues. The actual communication channel was less than four thousand bits per second; Central was taking no chances.

God only knew what they were seeing as the evocation of Pham Nuwen. The smokey-skinned human had already explained his point several times. He was having as little success as Ravna Bergsndot before him. His cool, manner had graduallly deserted him. Desperation was beginning to show on his face.'—and I'm telling you, they are *both* your enemies. Sure, Alliance for the Defense destroyed Sjandra Kei, but the Blight is responsible for the situation that made that possible.'

The half-cartoonish figure of Jan Skrits glanced at Owner Limmende. *Lord, evocations are crappy at the Bottom*, Svensndot thought to himself. When Skrits spoke, his voice didn't even match his lip movements: 'We do read Threats, Mr Nuwen. The threat of the Blight was used as an excuse to destroy our worlds. We will *not* go on random killing sprees, especially against an organization that is clearly the enemy of our enemy . . . Or are you claiming the Blight is secretly in league with the Alliance for the Defense?'

Pham gave an angry shrug. 'No. I have no idea how the Blight regards the Alliance. But you should know the evil the Blight has been up to, things on a scale far grander than this "Alliance." '

'Ah yes. That's what it says on the Net, Mr Nuwen. But those events are thousands of light-years away. They've been through multiple hops and unknown interpretations before they ever arrived in the Middle Beyond – even if the stories were true to begin with. It is not called the Net of a Million Lies for nothing.'

The stranger's face darkened. He said something loud and angry, in a language that was totally unlike anything from Nyjora. The tones jumped up and down, almost like Dirokime twittering. He calmed himself with a visible effort, but when he continued his Samnorsk was even more heavily accented than before. 'Yes. But I'm telling you. I was at the Fall of Relay. The Blight is more than the worst horrors you've heard. The murder of Sjandra Kei was its smallest side-effect. Will you help us against the Blighter fleet?'

Owner Limmende pushed her massive form back into her chair webbing. She looked at her chief of staff, and the two talked inaudibly. Kjet's gaze drifted beyond them; the flagship's command deck extended a dozen meters behind Limmende. Underofficers moved quietly about, some watching the conversation. The picture was crisp and clear, but when the figures moved it was with cartoonlike awkwardness. And some of the faces belonged to people Kjet knew had been transferred before the fall of Sjandra Kei. The processors here on the *Ølvira* were taking the narrow-band signal from Fleet Central, fleshing it out with detailed (and out of date) background and evoking the image shown. *No more evocations after this*, Svensndot promised himself, *at least while we're down here.*

Owner Limmende looked back at the camera. 'Forgive a paranoid old cop, but I think it's possible that you might be of the Blight.' Limmende raised her hand as if to ward off interruptions, but the redhead just gaped in surprise. 'If we believe you, then we must accept that there is something useful and dangerous on the star system we're all heading towards. Furthermore, we must accept that both you and the "Blighter fleet" are peculiarly qualified to take advantage of this prize. If we fight them as you ask, there will likely be few of us alive afterwards. You alone will have the prize. We fear what you might turn out to be.'

For a long moment, Pham Nuwen was silent. The wildness slowly left his face. 'You have a point. Owner Limmende. And a dilemma. Is there any way out?'

'Skrits and I have been discussing it. No matter what we do, both we and you must take big chances . . . It's only the alternatives that are more terrible. We are willing to accept your guidance in battle, *if* you will first maneuver your ship back toward us and allow us to board.'

'Give up the lead in this chase, you mean?'

Limmende nodded.

Pham's mouth opened and closed, but no words emerged. He seemed to be having trouble breathing. Ravna said, 'Then if you don't succeed, everything is lost. At least now, we have a sixty-hour lead. That might be enough to get word out about this artifact, even if the Blighter fleet survives.'

Skrits' face twisted, a cartoonish smile. 'You can't have it both ways. You want us to risk everything on your assurances. We are willing to die for this, but not to be pawns in a game of monsters.' The last words had a strange tone, the angry delivery shading away. And now there was no motion in the picture from Fleet Central except for ill-synched lip movement. Glimfrelle caught Svensndot's eye and pointed at the failure lights on his comm panel.

Skrits' voice continued, 'And Group Captain Svensndot: It's imperative that all further communications with this unknown vessel be channeled—' the image froze, and there were no more words.

Ravna: 'What happened?'

Glimfrelle made a twitter-snort. 'We're losing the link with Fleet Central. Our effective bandwidth is down to twenty bits per second, and dropping

Skrits' last transmission was scarcely a hundred bits,' *padded out to apparent legibility by the Ølvira's software.*

Kjet waved angrily at the screen. 'Cut the damn thing off.' At least he wouldn't have to put up with the evocation any further. And he didn't want to hear what he guessed was Jan Skrits' last order.

Tirolle said, 'Hei, why not leave it on? We might not notice much difference.' Glimfrelle snickered at his brother's wit, but his longfingers danced across the comm panel, and the display became a window on the stars. The two Dirokimes had a thing about bureaucrats.

Svensndot ignored them and looked at the remaining comm window. The channel to Pham and Ravna was wideband video with scarcely any interpretation; there would be no perverse subtleties if it went down. 'Sorry about that. The last few days, we've had a lot of problems with comm. Apparently, this Zone storm is the worst in centuries.' In fact, it was getting still worse: half the ultratrace displays were showing random garbage.

'You've lost contact with your command?' asked Ravna.

'For the moment . . .' He glanced at Pham. The redhead's eyes were still a bit glassy. 'Look . . . I'm even more sorry about how things have turned out, but Limmende and Skrits are bright people. You can see their point of view.'

'Strange,' interrupted Pham. 'The pictures were strange.' His tone was drifty.

'You mean our relay from Fleet Central?' Svensndot explained about the narrow bandwidth and the crummy performance of his ship's processors down here at the Bottom.

'And so their picture of us must have been equally bad . . . I wonder what they thought I was?'

'Unh . . .' *Good question.* Consider Pham Nuwen: bristly red hair, smoke-gray skin, singsong voice. If cues such as those were sent, like as not the display at Fleet Central would show something quite different from the human Kjet saw. '. . . wait a minute. That's not how evocations work. I'm sure they got a pretty clear view of you. See, a few high-resolution pics would get sent at the beginning of the session. Then those would be used as the base for the animation.'

Pham stared back lumpishly, almost as though he didn't buy it and was daring Kjet to think things through. Well damn it, the explanation was correct; there was no doubt that Limmende and Skrits had seen the redhead as a human. Yet there *was* something here that bothered Kjet . . . *Limmende and Skrits had both looked out of date.*

'Glimfrelle! Check the raw stream we got from Central. Did they send us any sync pictures?'

It took Glimfrelle only seconds. He whistled a sharp tone of surprise. 'No, Boss. And since it was all properly encrypted, our end just made do with old ad animation.' He said something to Tirolle, and the two twittered rapidly. 'Nothing seems to work down here. Maybe this is just another bug.' But Glimfrelle didn't sound very confident of his assertion.

Svensndot turned back to the picture from the *Out of Band*. 'Look. The channel to Fleet Central was fully encrypted, using one-time schemes I trust more than what we're talking with now. I can't believe it was a masquerade.' *But nausea was creeping up Kjet's guts.* This was like the first minutes of the Battle for Sjandra Kei, when he guessed how thoroughly they had been outmaneuvered, when he realized that everyone he was trying to protect would be murdered. 'Hei, we'll contact other vessels. We'll verify Central's location—'

Pham Nuwen raised an eyebrow. 'Maybe it wasn't a masquerade.' Before he could say more, one of the Riders – the one with the greater skrode – was shouting at them. It rolled across the room's apparent ceiling, pushing the humans aside to get close to the camera. 'I have a question!' The voder speech was burred, nearly unintelligible. The creature's tendrils rattled dryly against each other, as distressed as Kjet Svensndot had ever heard. 'My question: Are there Skroderiders aboard your fleet's command vessel?'

'Why do you—'

'*Answer the question!*'

'How should I know?' Kjet tried to think. 'Tirolle. You have friends on Skrits' staff. Are there any Riders aboard?'

Tirolle stuttered a few bars. '*A'a'a'a.* Yes. Emergency hires – rescues actually – right after the battle.'

'That's the best we can do, friend.'

The Skroderider trembled, unspeaking. Then its tendrils seemed to wilt 'Thank you,' it said softly. It rolled back and out of camera range.

Pham Nuwen disappeared from view. Ravna looked wildly around, 'Wait please!' she said to the camera, and Kjet was looking at the abandoned command deck of the *Out of Band*. At the limit of the pickup's hearing came sounds of mumbled conversation, voder and human. Then she was back.

'What was *that* all about?' Svensndot to Ravna.

'N-nothing any of us can help anymore . . . Captain Svensndot, it looks to me like your fleet is no longer run by the people you think.'

'Maybe.' *Probably.* 'It's something I've got to think about.'

She nodded. For a moment they looked at each other, unspeaking. So strange, so far from home and after all the heartbreak . . . to see someone so familiar. 'You were truly at Relay?' The question sounded stupid in his ears. Yet in a way she was a bridge from what he knew and trusted to the deadly weirdness of the present situation.

Ravna Bergsndot nodded. 'Yes . . . and it was like everything you've read. We even had direct contact with a Power . . . And yet it was not enough, Group Captain. The Blight destroyed it all. That part of the News is no lie.'

Tirolle pushed back from his nav station. 'Then how can anything you do down here hurt the Blight?' The words were blunt, but 'Rolle's eyes were wide and serious. In fact, he was pleading for some sense behind all the death. Dirokimes had not been the greatest part of the Sjandra Kei civilization, but they had been by far its oldest member race. A million years ago they had burst out of the Slow Zone, colonizing the three systems that humans one day would call Sjandra Kei. Long before the humans arrived, they were a race of inward dreamers. They protected their star systems with ancient automation and friendly younger races. Another half million years and their race might be gone from the Beyond, extinct or evolved into something else. It was a common pattern, something like death and old age, but gentler.

There is a common misconception about such senescent races: that their members are senescent too. In any large population, there will be variation. There will always be those who want to see the outside world and play there for a while. Humankind had gotten on very well with the likes of Glimfrelle and Tirolle.

And Bergsndot seemed to understand. 'Have any of you heard of godshatter?'

Kjet said, 'No,' then noticed that both Dirokimes had started. They whistled at each other for several seconds. 'Yes,' 'Rolle spoke at last in Samnorsk, his voice as close to awe as Kjet had ever heard. 'You know we Dirokimes have been in the Beyond for a long time. We've sent many colonies into the Transcend; some became Powers . . . And once . . . Something came back. It wasn't a Power of course. In fact, it was more like a mind-crippling Dirokime. But it knew things and did things that made great changes for us.'

'Fentrollar?' Kjet asked wonderingly, suddenly recognizing the story. It had happened one hundred thousand years before humankind arrived at Sjandra Kei, yet it was a central contradiction of the Dirokime terranes.

'Yes.' Tirolle said. 'Even now people don't agree if Fentrollar was a gift or a curse, but he founded the dream habitats and the Old Religion.'

Ravna nodded. 'That's the case most familiar to us of Sjandra Kei. Maybe it's not a happy example considering all its effects . . .' And she told them about the fall of Relay, what had happened to Old One, and what had become of Pham Nuwen. The Dirokimes side chat dwindled to zero and they were very still.

Finally Kjet said, 'So what does Nu—' he stumbled over the name, as strange as everything else about this fellow, 'Nuwen know about the thing he seeks at the Bottom? What can he do with it?'

'I-I don't know, Group Captain. Pham Nuwen himself doesn't now. A little bit at a time, the insight comes. I believe, because I was there for some of it . . . but I don't know how to make you believe.' She drew a shuddering breath. Kjet suddenly guessed what a tortured place the *Out of Band* must be. Somehow that made the story more credible. Anything that really could destroy the Blight would be unwholesomely weird. Kjet wondered how he would do, locked up with such a thing.

'My Lady Ravna,' he said, the words stilted and formal. *After all, I'm suggesting treason.* 'I, uh, I've got a number of friends in the Commercial Security fleet. I can check on the suspicions you've raised, and . . .' *say it!* 'It's possible we can give you support in spite of my HQ.'

'Thank you, sir. Thank you.'

Glimfrelle broke the silence. 'We're getting a poor signal on the *Out of Band*'s channel now.'

Kjet's eyes swept the windows. All the ultratrace displays looked like random noise. Whatever this storm was, it was bad.

'Looks like we won't be talking much longer, Ravna Bergsndot'

'Yes. We're losing signal . . . Group Captain, if none of this works, if you can't fight for us . . . Your people are all that's left of Sjandra Kei. It's been good to see you and the Dirokimes . . . after so long to see familiar faces, people I really understand. I—' as she spoke, her image square-blurred into low-frequency components.

'*Huui!*' said Glimfrelle. 'Bandwidth just dropped through the floor.' There was nothing sophisticated about their link to the *Out of Band*. Given communications problems, the ship's processors just switched to low-rate coding.

'Hello, *Out of Band*. We've got problems on this channel now. Suggest we sign off.'

The window turned gray, and printed Samnorsk flickered across it:

Yes. It is more than a communicati

Glimfrelle diddled his comm panel. 'Zip. Zero,' he said. 'No detectable signal.'

Tirolle looked up from his navigation tank. 'This is a lot more than a communications problem. Our computers haven't been able to commit on an ultradrive jump in more than twenty seconds.' They had been doing five jumps a second, and just over a light-year per hour. Now . . .

Glimfrelle leaned back from his panel. 'Hei – so welcome to the Slow Zone.'

The Slow Zone. Ravna Bergsndot looked across the deck of the *Out of Band II*. Somewhere in the dark of her mind, she had always had a vision of the Slowness as a stifling darkness lit at best by torches, the domain of cretins and mechanical calculators. In fact, things didn't look much different from before. The ceilings and walls glowed just as before. The stars still shone through the windows (only now, it might be a *very* long time before any of them moved).

It was on the *OOB*'s other displays that the change was most obvious. The ultratrace tank blinked monotonously, a red legend displaying elapsed time since the last update. Navigation windows were filled with output from the diagnostics exercising the drive processors. An audible message in Triskweline was repeating over and over, 'Warning. Transition to Slowness detected. Execute back jump at once! Warning. Transition to Slowness detected. Execute . . .'

'Turn that off!' Ravna grabbed a saddle and strapped herself down. She was actually feeling dizzy, though that could only be (a very natural) panic. 'Some bottom-lugger this is. We run right into the Slow Zone, and all it can do is spout warnings after the fact!'

Greenstalk drifted closer, 'tiptoeing' off the ceiling with her tendrils. 'Even bottom-luggers can't avoid things like this, my Lady Ravna.'

Pham said something at the ship and most of the displays cleared.

Blueshell: 'Even a huge Zone storm doesn't normally extend more than a few light-years. We were two hundred light-years above the Zone boundary. What hit us must be a monster surge, the sort of thing you only read about in archives.'

Small consolation. 'We knew something like this could happen,' Pham said. 'Things have been getting awfully rough the last few weeks.' For a change, *he* didn't seem too upset.

'Yes,' she said. 'We expected a slowing maybe, but not The Slowness.' *We are trapped.* 'Where's the nearest habitable system? Ten light-years? Fifty?' The vision of darkness had a new reality, and the starscape beyond the ship's walls was no longer a friendly, steadying thing. They were surrounded by unending nothingness, moving at some vanishing fraction of the speed of light . . . entombed; all the courage of Kjet Svensndot and his fleet, for nothing; Jefri Olsndot, forever unrescued.

Pham's hand touched her shoulder, the first touch in . . . days? 'We can still make it to the Tines' world. This is a bottom-lugger, remember? We are not trapped. Hell, the ramscoop on this buggy is better than anything I ever had in the Qeng Ho. And I thought I was the freest man in the universe back then.'

Decades of travel time, mostly in coldsleep. Such had been the world of the Qeng Ho, the world of Pham's memories. Ravna let out a shuddering breath that ended in weak laughter. For Pham, the terrible pressure was abated, at least temporarily. He could be human.

'What's so funny?' said Pham.

She shook her head. 'All of us. Never mind.' She took a couple of slow breaths. 'Okay. I think I can make rational conversation. So the Zone has surged. Something that normally takes a thousand years – even in a storm – to move a single light-year, has suddenly shifted two hundred. Hunh! There'll be people a million years from now reading about this in the archives. I'm not sure I want the honor . . . We knew there was a storm, but I never expected to be drowned,' buried beneath the sea, light-years deep.

'The sea storm analogy is not perfect,' said Blueshell. The Skroderider was still on the far side of the deck, where he had retreated after questioning the Sjandra Kei captain. He still looked upset, though he was back to sounding precise and picky. Blueshell was studying a nav display, evidently a recording from right before the surge. He dumped the picture to a display flat and rolled slowly across the ceiling toward them. Greenstalk's fronds brushed him gently as he passed.

He sailed the display flat into Ravna's hands, and continued in a lecturing tone. 'Even in a sea storm, the water's surface is never as roiled as in a big interface disturbance. The most recent News reports showed it as a fractal surface with dimension close to three . . . Like foam and spray.' Even he could not avoid the storm analogy. The starscapes hung serene beyond crystal walls, and the loudest sound was from the ship's ventilators. Yet they had been swallowed in a maelstrom. Blueshell waved a frond at the display flat. 'We could be back in the Beyond in a few hours.'

'What?'

'See. The plane of the display is determined by the positions of the supposed Sjandra Kei command vessel, the ourflying craft that we contacted directly, and ourselves.' The three formed a narrow triangle, the Limmende and Svensndot vertices close together. 'I've marked the times that contact was lost with the others. Notice: the link to Commercial Security HQ went down 150 seconds before we were hit. From the incoming signal and its requests for protocol changes, I believe that *both* we and the outflyer were enveloped at about the same time.'

Pham nodded. 'Yeah. The most distant sites losing contact last. That must mean the surge moved in from the side.'

'Exactly!' From his perch on the ceiling, Blueshell reached to tap the display. 'The three ships were like probes in the standard Zone mapping technique. Replaying the trace displays will no doubt confirm the conclusion.'

Ravna looked at the plot. The long point of the triangle – tipped by the *OOB* – pointed almost directly toward the heart of the galaxy. 'It must have been a huge, clifflike thing perpendicular to the rest of the surface.'

'A monster wave sweeping sideways!' said Greenstalk. 'And that's also why it won't last long.'

'Yes. It's the radial changes that are most often long term. This thing must have a trailing edge. We should pass through it in a few hours – and back into the Beyond.'

So there was still a race to be won . . . or lost.

The first hours were strange. 'A few hours,' had been Blueshell's estimate of when they would be back in the Beyond. They hung around the bridge, alternately watching the clock and stewing about the strange conversations just completed. Pham was building himself back to trigger tension. Any time now, they would be back in the Beyond. What to do then? If only a few ships were perverted, perhaps Svensndot could still coordinate an attack. Would that do any good? Pham played the ultratrace recordings over and over, studying every detectable ship in all the fleets. 'But when we get out, when we get out . . . I'll know what to do. Not *why* I must do it, but what.' And he couldn't explain more.

Any time now . . . There was scarcely any reason to do much about resetting equipment that would need another initialization right away.

But after eight hours: 'It really could be longer, even a day.' They had been scrounging around in some of the historical literature. 'Maybe we should do a little housekeeping.' The *Out of Band II* had been designed for both the Beyond and the Slowness, but that second environment was regarded as an unlikely, emergency one. There were special-purpose processors for the Slow Zone, but they hadn't come up automatically. With Blueshell's advice, Pham took the high-performance automation off-line; that wasn't too difficult, except for a couple of voice-actuated independents that were no longer bright enough to understand the quitting commands.

Using the new automation gave Ravna a chill that, in a subtle way, was almost as frightening as the original loss of the ultradrive. Her image of the Slowness as darkness and torchlight – that was just nightmare fantasy. On the other hand, the Slowness as the domain of cretins and mechanical calculators, there was something to that. The *OOB*'s performance had degraded steadily during their voyage to the Bottom, but now . . . Gone were the voice-driven graphics generators; they were just a bit too complex to be supported by the new *OOB*, at least in full interpretive mode. Gone were the intelligent context analyzers that made the ship's library almost as accessible as one's own memories. Eventually Ravna even turned off the art and music units; without mood and context response, they seemed so wooden . . . constant reminders that there were no brains behind them. Even the simplest things were corrupted. Take voice and gesture controls: They no longer responded consistently to sarcasm and casual slang – It took a certain *discipline* to use them effectively. (Pham actually seemed to like this. It reminded him of the Qeng Ho).

Twenty hours. Fifty. Everyone was still telling each other there was nothing to worry about. But now Blueshell said that talk of 'hours' had been unrealistic. Considering the height of the 'tsunami' (at least two hundred light-years), it would likely be several hundred light-years across – that in keeping with the scaling laws of historical precedent. There was only one trouble with this reasoning: they were beyond all precedent. For the most part, zone boundaries followed galactic mean density. There was virtually no change from year to year, just the aeons' long shrinkage that might someday – after the death of all but the smallest stars – expose the galactic core to the Beyond. At any given time, perhaps one billionth of that boundary might qualify as being in a 'storm state.' In an ordinary storm, the surface might move in or out a light-year in a decade or so. Such storms were common enough to affect the fortunes of many worlds every year.

Much rarer – perhaps once in a hundred thousand years in the whole galaxy – there would be a storm where the boundary became seriously distorted, and where surges might move at a high multiple of light speed. *These* were the transverse surges that Pham and Blueshell made their scale estimates from. The fastest moved at about a light-year per second, across a distance of less than three lights; the largest were thirty light-years high and moved at scarcely a light-year per day.

So what was known of monsters like the thing that had engulfed them? Not much. Third-hand stories in the Ship's library told of surges perhaps as big as theirs, but the quoted dimensions and propagation rates were not clear. Stories more than a hundred million years old are hard to trust; there are scarcely any intermediate languages. (And even if there were, it wouldn't have helped. The new, dumb version of the *OOB* absolutely could not do mechanical translation of natural languages. Dredging the library was pointless.)

When Ravna complained about this to Pham, he said, 'Things could be worse. What was the Ur-Partition really?'

Five billion years ago. 'No one's sure.'

Pham jerked a thumb at his library display. 'Some people think it was a "super supersurge," you know. Something so big it swallowed the races that might have recorded it. Sometimes the biggest disasters aren't noticed at all – no one's around to write horror stories.'

Great.

'I'm sorry, Ravna. Honestly, if we're in anything like most past disasters, we'll come out of it in another day or two. The best thing is to *plan* for things that way. This is like a "timeout" in the battle. Take advantage of it to have a little peace. Figure out how to get the unperverted parts of Commercial Security to help us.'

'. . . Yeah.' Depending on the shape of the surge's trailing edge the *OOB* might have lost a good part of its lead . . . *But I'll bet the Alliance fleet is completely panicked by all this*. Such opportunists would likely run for safety as soon as they're back in the Beyond.

The advice kept her busy for another twenty hours, fighting with the half-witted things that claimed to be strategy planners on the new version of the *OOB*. Even if the surge passed right this instant, it might be too late. There were players in this game for whom the surge was not a time-out: Jefri Olsndot and his Tinish allies. It had been seventy hours now since their last contact; Ravna had missed three comm sessions with them. If *she* were panicked, what must it be like for Jefri? Even if Steel could hold off his enemies, time – and trust – would be running out at Tines' world.

One hundred hours into the surge, Ravna noticed that Blueshell and Pham were doing power tests on the *OOB*'s ramscoop drive . . . Some time-outs last forever.

34

The summer hot spell broke for a time; in fact, it was almost chilly. There was still the smoke and the air was still dry, but the winds seemed less driven. Inside their cubby aboard the ship, Amdijefri weren't taking much notice of the nice weather.

'They've been slow in answering before,' said Amdi. 'She's explained how the ultrawave—'

'Ravna's never been *this* late!' Not since the winter, anyway. Jefri's tone hovered between fear and petulance. In fact, there was supposed to be a transmission in the middle of the night, technical data for them to pass on to Mr Steel. It hadn't arrived by this morning, and now Ravna had also missed their afternoon session, the time when normally they could just chat for a bit.

The two children reviewed all the comm settings. The previous fall, they had laboriously copied those and the first level diagnostics. It all looked the same now . . . except for something called 'carrier detect.' If they only had a dataset, they might have looked up what that meant.

They had even very carefully reset some of the comm parameters . . . then nervously set them back when nothing happened. Maybe they hadn't given the changes enough of a chance to work. Maybe now they had *really* messed something up.

They stayed in the command cubby all through the afternoon, their minds cycling through fear and boredom and frustration. After four hours, boredom had at least a temporary victory. Jefri was napping uneasily in his father's hammock with two of Amdi curled up in his arms.

Amdi poked idly around the room, looked at the rocket controls. No . . . not even his self-confidence was up to playing with those. Another of him jerked at the wall quilting. He could always watch the fungus grow for a while. Things were that slow.

Actually, the gray stuff had spread a lot farther than the last time he looked. Behind the quilt, it was quite thick. He sent a chain of himself squirreling back between the wall and the fabric. It was dark, but some light spilled through the gap at the ceiling. In most places the mold was scarcely an inch thick, but back here it was five or six – *wow*. Just above his exploring nose, a huge lump of it grew from the wall. This was as big as some of the ornamental moss lumps that decorated castle meeting halls. Slender gray filaments grew down from the fungus. He almost called out to Jefri, but the two of him in the hammock were so comfortable.

He brought a couple of heads close to the strangeness. The wall behind it looked a little odd, too . . . as though part of its substance had been taken by the mold. And the gray itself: like smoke – he felt the filaments with his nose. They were solid, dry. His nose tickled. Amdi froze in shocked surprise. Watching himself from behind, he saw that two of the filaments had actually passed through his member's head! And yet there was no pain, just that tickling feeling.

'What – what?' Jefri had been jostled into wakefulness as Amdi tensed around him.

'I found something really strange behind the quilts. I touched this big hunk of fungus and—'

As he spoke, Amdi gently backed away from the thing on the wall. The touch didn't hurt, but it made him more nervous than curious. He felt the filaments sliding slowly out.

'I told you, we aren't supposed to play with that stuff. It's dirty. The only good thing is, it doesn't smell.' Jefri was out of the hammock. He stepped across the cubby and lifted the quilting, Amdi's tip member lost its balance and jerked away from the fungus. There was a snapping sound, and a sharp pain in his lip.

'Geez, that thing is big!' Then, hearing Amdi's pain whistle. 'You okay?'

Amdi backed away from the wall. 'I think so.' The tip of one last filament was still stuck in his lip. It didn't hurt as much as the nettles he'd sampled a few days earlier. Amdijefri looked over the wound. What was left of the smoky spine seemd hard and brittle. Jefri's fingers gently worked it free. Then the two of them turned to wonder at the thing in the wall.

'It really has spread. Looks like it's hurt the wall, too.'

Amdi dabbed at his bloodied muzzle. 'Yeah. I see why your folks told you to stay away from it.'

'Maybe we should have Mr Steel scrub it all out.'

The two spent half an hour crawling around behind all the quilting. The grayness had spread far, but there was only the one marvelous flowering. They came back to stare at it, even sticking articles of clothing into the wisps. Neither risked fingers or noses on further contact.

Staring at the fungus on the wall was by far the most exciting thing that happened that afternoon; there was no message from the *OOB*.

The next day the hot weather was back.

Two more days passed . . . and still there was no word from Ravna.

Lord Steel paced the walls atop Starship Hill. It was near the middle of the night, and the sun hung about fifteen degrees above the northern horizon. Sweat filmed his fur; this was the warmest summer in ten years. The drywind was into its thirtieth dayaround. It was no longer a welcome break in the chill of the northland. The crops were dying in the fields. Smoke from fjord fires was visible as brownish haze both north and south of the castle. At first the reddish color had been a novelty, a change from the unending blue of sky and distance and the whitish haze of the sea fogs. Only at first. When fire struck East Streamsdell, the entire sky had been dipped in red. Ash had rained all the dayaround, and the only smell had been that of burning. Some said it was worse than the filthy air of the southern cities.

The troops on the walls backed far out of his way. This was more than courtesy, more than their fear of Steel. His troops were still not used to the cloaked ones, and the cover story Shreck was spreading did nothing to ease their minds: Lord Steel was accompanied by a singleton – in the colors of a Lord. The creature made no mind sounds. It walked incredibly close to its master.

Steel said to the singleton, 'Success is a matter of meeting a schedule. I remember you teaching me that,' *cutting it into me, in fact.*

The member looked back at him, cocked its head. 'As I remember, I said that success was a matter of adapting to changes in schedules.' The words were perfectly articulated. There were singletons that could talk that well – but even the most verbal could not carry on intelligent conversation. Shreck had had no trouble convincing the troops that Flenser science had created a race of superpacks, that the cloaked ones were individually as smart as any ordinary pack. It was a good cover for what the cloaks really were. It both inspired fear and obscured the truth.

The member stepped a little closer – nearer to Steel than anyone had been except during murders and rapes and the beatings of the past. Involuntarily, Steel licked his lips and spread out from around the threat. Yet in some ways the dark-cloaked one was like a corpse, without a trace of mind sound. Steel snapped his jaws shut and said, 'Yes. The genius is in winning, even when the schedules have fallen down the garderobe.' He looked all away from the Flenser member, scanning the red-shrouded southern horizon. 'What's the latest estimate of Woodcarver's progress?'

'She's still camped about five days southeast of here.'

'The damned incompetent. It's hard to believe she's your parent! Vendacious made things so easy for her; her soldiers and toy cannon should have been here almost a tenday past—'

'And been well-butchered, on schedule.'

'Yes! Long before our sky friends arrived. Instead, she wanders inland and then balks.'

The Flenser member shrugged in its dark cloak. Steel knew the radio was as heavy as it looked. It consoled him that the other was paying a price for his omniscience. Just think, in heat like this, to have every part of oneself muffled to the tympana. He could imagine the discomfort . . . Indoors, he could smell it.

They walked past one of the wall cannon. The barrel gleamed of layered metal. The thing had thrice the range of Woodcarver's pitiful invention. While Woodcarver had been working with Dataset and a human child's intuition, he had had the direct advice of Ravna and company. At first he'd feared their largesse, dunking it meant the Visitors were superior beyond need for care. Now . . . the more he heard of Ravna and the others, the more clearly he understood their weakness. They could not experiment with themselves, improve themselves. Inflexible, slow-changing dullards. Sometimes they showed a low cunning – Ravna's coyness about what she wanted from the first starship – but their desperation was loud in all their messages, as was their attachment to the human child.

Everything had been going so well till just a few days ago. As they walked out of earshot of the gunner pack, Steel said to the Flenser member, 'And still no word from our "rescuers."'

'Quite so.' That was the other botched schedule, the important one, which they could not control. 'Ravna has missed four sessions. Two of me is down with Amdijefri right now.' The singleton jabbed its snout toward the dome of the inner keep. The gesture was an awkward abortion. Without other muzzles and other eyes, body language was a limited thing. *We just aren't built to wander around a piece here, a piece there.* 'Another few minutes and the space folk will have missed a fifth talk session. The children are getting desperate, you know.'

The member's voice sounded sympathetic. Almost unconsciously, Lord Steel sidled a little farther out from around it. Steel remembered that tone from his own early existence. He also remembered the cutting and death that had always followed. 'I want them kept happy, Tyrathect. We're assuming communication will resume; when it does we'll need them.' Steel bared six pairs of jaws at the surrounded singleton. *'None of your old tricks.'*

The member flinched, an almost imperceptible twitch that pleased Steel more than the grovelling of ten thousand. 'Of course not. I'm just saying that you should visit them, try to help them with their fear.'

'You do it.'

'Ah . . . they don't fully trust me. I've told you before, Steel; they love you.'

'Ah! And they've seen through to your meanness, eh?' The situation made Steel proud. He had succeeded where Flenser's own methods would have failed. He had manipulated without threats or pain. It had been Steel's craziest experiment and certainly his most profitable. But '—Look, I don't have time to wetnurse anyone. It's a tiresome thing to talk to those two.' And it was very tiresome to hold his temper, to suffer Jefri's 'petting' and Amdi's pranks. In the beginning, Steel had insisted that no one else have close contact with the children. They were too important to expose to others; the most casual slipup might show them the truth and ruin them. Even now, Tyrathect was the only pack besides himself who had regular contact. But for Steel, every meeting was worse than the last an ultimate test of his self control. It was hard to think straight in a killing rage, and that's how almost every conversation with them ended for Steel. How wonderful it would be when the space folk landed. *Then* he could use the other end of the tool that was Amdijefri. *Then* there would be no need to have their trust and friendship. *Then* he would have a lever, something to torture and kill to enforce his demands.

Of course, if the aliens never landed, or if . . . 'We must do something! I will not be flotsam on the wave of the future.' Steel lashed at the scaffolding that ran along the inner side of the parapet, shredding the wood with his gleaming tines. 'We can't do anything about the aliens, so let's deal with Woodcarver. Yes!' He smiled at the Flenser member. 'Ironic, isn't it? For a hundred years, you sought her destruction. Now I can succeed. What would have been your great triumph is for me just an annoying detour, undertaken because greater projects are temporarily delayed.'

The cloaked one did not look impressed. 'There is a little matter of gifts falling out of the sky.'

'Yes, into my open jaws. And that is *my* good fortune, isn't it?' He walked on several paces, chuckling to himself. 'Yes. It's time to have Vendacious bring his trusting Queen in for the slaughter. Maybe it will interfere with other events, but . . . I know, we'll have the battle east of here.'

'The Margrum Climb?'

'Correct. Woodcarver's forces should be well concentrated coming up the defile. We'll move our cannon over there, set them behind the ridgeline at the top of the Climb. It will be easy to destroy all her people. And it's far enough from Starship Hill; even if the space folk arrive at the same time, we can keep the two projects separate.' The singleton didn't say anything, and after a moment Steel glared at him. 'Yes dear teacher, I know there is a risk. I know it splits our forces. But we've got an army sitting on our doorstep. They've arrived inconveniently late, but even Vendacious can't make them turn around and go home. And if he tries to stall things, the Queen might . . . Can you predict just what she would do?'

'. . . No. She has always had a way with the unexpected.'

'She might even see through Vendacious' fraud. So. We take a small chance, and destroy her now. You are with Farscout Rangolith?'

'Yes. Two of me.'

'Tell him to get word to Vendacious. He is to have the Queen's army coming up Margrum Climb not less than two days from now. Feel free to elaborate; you know the region better than I. We'll work out final details when both sides are in position.' It was a wonderful thing to be the effective commander of both sides in a battle! 'One more thing. It's important and Vendacious must see to it within the dayaround: I want Woodcarver's human dead.'

'What harm can she do?'

'That's a stupid question,' *especially coming from you.* 'We don't know when Ravna and Pham may reach us. Till we have them safe in our jaws, the

Johanna creature is a dangerous thing to have nearby. Tell Vendacious to make it look like an accident, but I want that Two-Legs dead.'

Flenser was everywhere. It was a form of godhood he'd dreamed of since he'd been Woodcarver's newby. While one of him talked to Steel, two others lounged about the Starship with Amdijefri, and two more padded through light forest just north of Woodcarver's encampment.

Paradise can also be an agony, and each day the torment was a little harder to bear. In the first place, this summer was as insufferably hot as any in the North. And the radio cloaks were not merely hot and heavy. They necessarily covered his members' tympana. And unlike other uncomfortable costumes, the price of taking these off *for even a moment* was mindlessness. His first trials had lasted just an hour or two. Then had come a five-day expedition with Farscout Rangolith, providing Steel with instant information and instant command of the country around Starship Hill. It had taken a couple dayarounds to recover from the sores and aches of the radio cloaks.

This latest exercise in omniscience had lasted twelve days. Wearing the cloaks all the time was impossible. Every day in a rotation, one of his members threw off its radio, was bathed, and had its cloak's liner changed. It was Flenser's hour of daily madness, when sometimes the weak-willed Tyrathect would come back to mind, vainly trying to reestablish her dominance. It didn't matter. With one of his members disconnected, the remaining pack was only four. There are foursomes of normal intelligence, but none existed in Flenser/Tyrathect. The bathing and recloaking were all done in a confused haze.

And of course, even though Flenser was 'everywhere at once,' he wasn't any smarter than before. After the first jarring experiments, he got the hang of seeing/hearing scenes that were radically different – but it was as difficult as ever to carry on multiple conversations. When he was bantering with Steel, his other members had very little to say to Amdijefri or to Rangolith's scouts.

Lord Steel was done with him. Flenser walked along the parapets with his former student, but if Steel had said anything to him it would have taken him away from his current conversation. Flenser smiled (carefully so the one with Steel would not show it). Steel thought he was talking to Farscout Rangolith just now. Oh, he would do that . . . in a few minutes. One advantage of his situation was that no one could know for sure everything Flenser was up to. If he was careful, he would eventually rule here again. It was a dangerous game, and the cloaks were themselves dangerous devices. Keep a cloak out of the sunlight for a few hours and it lost power, and the member wearing it was cut off from the pack. Worse was the problem of *static* – that was the mantis word. The second set of cloaks had killed its user, and the spacers weren't sure of the cause, except that it was some sort of 'interference problem.'

Flenser had experienced nothing so extreme. But sometimes on his farthest hikes with Rangolith, or when a cloak's power faded . . . there was an incredible shrieking in his mind, like a dozen packs crowding close, sounds that scaled between sex madness and killing frenzy. Tyrathect seemed to like times like that; she'd come bounding out of the confusion, swamping him with her soft hate. Normally she lurked around the edges of his consciousness, tweaking a word here, a motive there. After the *static*, she was much worse; on one occasion she'd held control for almost a day-around. Given a year without crises, Flenser could have studied Ty and Ra and Thect and done a proper excision. Thect, the member with the white-tipped ears, was probably the one to kill: it wasn't bright, but it was likely the capstone of the trio. With a precisely crafted replacement, Flenser might be even greater than before the massacre at Parliament Bowl. But for now, Flenser was stuck; soul surgery on one's self was an awesome challenge – even to The Master.

So. Careful. Careful. Keep the cloaks well-charged, take no long trips, and don't let any one person see all the threads of your plan. While Steel thought he was seeking Rangolith, Flenser was talking to Amdi and Jefri.

The human's face was wet with tears. 'F-four times we've missed R-ravna. *What has happened to her?*' His voice screeched up. Flenser hadn't realized there was such flexibility in the belching mechanism that humans use to make sound.

Most of Amdi clustered round the boy. He licked Jefri's cheeks. 'It could be our ultrawave. Maybe it's broken.' He looked beseechingly at Flenser. There were tears in the puppies' eyes, too. 'Tyrathect, please ask Steel again. Let us stay in the ship all the dayaround. Maybe there are messages that have come through and not been recorded.'

Flenser with Steel descended the northern stairs, crossed the parade ground. He gave a sliver of attention to the other's complaints about the sloppy maintenance around the practice stands. At least Steel was smart enough to keep the discipline scaffolds over on Hidden Island.

Flenser with Rangolith's troopers splashed through a mountain stream. Even in high summer, in the middle of a Drywind, there were still snow patches, and the streams running from under them were icy cold.

Flenser with Amdijefri edged forward, let two of Amdi rest against his sides. Both children liked physical contact, and he was the only one they had besides each other. It was all perversion of course, but Flenser had based his life on manipulating others' weakness, and – but for the pain – welcomed it. Flenser buzzed a deep purring sound through his shoulders, caressing the puppy next to him. 'I'll ask our Lord Steel the very next time I see him.'

'Thank you.' A puppy nuzzled at his cloak, then mercifully moved away; Flenser was a mass of sores beneath that cover. Perhaps Amdi realized that, or perhaps . . . more and more Flenser saw a reticence in the two. His comment to Steel had been a slip into the truth: these two really didn't trust him. That was Tyrathect's fault. On his own, Flenser would have had no trouble winning Amdijefri's love. Flenser had none of Steel's killing temper and fragile dignity. Flenser could chat for casual pleasure, all the while mixing truth with lies. One of his greatest talents was empathy; no sadist can aspire to perfection without that diagnostic ability. But just when he was doing well, when they seemed about to open to him – then Ty or Ra or Thect would pop up, twisting his expression or poisoning his choice of phrase. Perhaps he should content himself with undermining the children's respect for Steel (without, of course, ever saying anything directly against him). Flenser sighed, and patted Jefri's arm comfortingly. 'Ravna will be back. I'm sure of it.' The human sniffled a little, then reached out to pet the part of Flenser's head that was not shrouded by the cloak. They sat in companionable silence for a moment, and his attention drifted back to—

—*the forest and Rangolith's troops.* The group had been moving uphill for almost ten minutes. The others were lightly burdened and used to this sort of exercise. Flenser's two members were lagging. He hissed at the group leader.

The group leader sidled back, his squad shifting briskly out of his way. He stopped when his nearest was fifteen feet from Flenser's. The soldier's heads cocked this way and that. 'Your wishes . . . my lord?' This one was new; he had been briefed about the cloaks, but Flenser knew the fellow didn't understand the new rules. The gold and silver that glinted in the darkness of the cloaks – those colors were reserved for the Lords of the Domain. Yet there were only two of Flenser here; normally such a fragment could barely carry on a conversation, much less give reasonable orders. Just as disconcerting, Flenser knew, was his lack of mind sound. 'Zombie' was the word some of the troops used when they thought themselves alone.

Flenser pointed up the hill; the timberline was only a few yards away. 'Farscout Rangolith is on the other side. We will take a short cut,' he said weakly.

Part of the other was already looking up the hill. 'That is not good, sir.' The trooper spoke slowly. *Stupid damn duo*, his posture said. 'The bad ones will see us.'

Flenser glowered at the other, a hard thing to do properly when you are just two. 'Soldier, do you see the gold on my shoulders? Even one of me is worth *all* of you. If I say take a short cut, we do it – even if it means walking belly-deep through brimstone.' Actually, Flenser knew exactly where Vendacious had put lookouts. There was no risk in crossing the open ground here. And he was *so* tired.

The group leader still didn't know quite what Flenser was, but he saw the dark-cloaks were at least as dangerous as any full-pack lord. He backed off humbly, bellies dragging on the ground. The group turned uphill and a few minutes later were walking across open heather.

Rangolith's command post was less than a half mile away along this path—

Flenser with Steel walked into the inner keep. The stone was freshly cut, the walls thrown up with the feverish speed of all this castle's construction. Thirty feet over their heads, where vault met buttresses, there were small holes set in the stonework. Those holes would soon be filled with gunpowder – as would slots in the wall surrounding the landing field. Steel called those the Jaws of Welcome. Now he turned a head back to Flenser. 'So what does Rangolith say?'

'Sorry. He's been out on patrol. He should be here – I mean, he should be in camp – any minute.' Flenser did his best to conceal his own trips with the scouts. Such recons were not forbidden, but Steel would have demanded explanations if he knew.

Flenser with Rangolith's troops sloshed through water-soaked heather. The air over the snowmelt was delightfully chill, and the breeze pushed cool tongues partway under his wretched cloaks.

Rangolith had chosen the site for his command post well. His tents were in a slight depression at the edge of a large summer pond. A hundred yards away, a huge patch of snow covered the hill above them, fed the pond, and kept the air pleasantly cool. The tents were out of view from below, yet the site was so high in the hills that from the edge of the depression there was a clear view across three points of the compass, centered on the south. Resupply could be accomplished from the north with little chance of detection, and even if the damn fires struck the forests below, this post would be untouched.

Farscout Rangolith was lounging about his signal mirrors, oiling the aiming gears. One of his subordinates lay with snouts stuck over the lip of the hill, scanning the landscape with its telescopes. Rangolith came to attention at the sight of Flenser, but his gaze wasn't full of fear. Like most long-range scouts, he wasn't completely terrorized by castle politics. Besides, Flenser had cultivated an 'us against the prigs' relationship with the fellow. Now Rangolith growled at the group leader: 'The next time you come prancing across the open like that, your asses go on report.'

'My fault, Farscout,' put in Flenser. 'I have some important news.' They walked away from the others, down toward Rangolith's tent.

'See something interesting, did you?' Rangolith was smiling oddly. He had long ago figured out that Flenser was not a brilliant duo, but part of a pack with members back at the castle.

'When is your next session with Craddleheads?' That was the fieldname for Vendacious.

'Just past noon. He hasn't missed in four days. The Southerners seem to be on one big squat.'

'That will change.' Flenser repeated Steel's orders for Vendacious. The words came hard. The traitor within him was restive; he felt the beginnings of a major attack.

'Wow! You're going to move everything over to Margrum Climb in less than two – Never mind, that's something I'd best not know.'

Under his cloaks, Flenser bristled. *There are limits to chumminess.* Rangolith had his points, but maybe after all this was over he could be smoothed into something less . . . ad hoc.

'Is that all, my lord?'

'Yes – No.' Flenser shivered with uncharacteristic puzzlement. *The trouble with these cloaks, sometimes they made it hard to remember things. By the Great Pack, no!* It was that Tyrathect again. Steel had ordered the killing of Woodcarver's human – all things considered, a perfectly sensible move, but . . .

Flenser with Steel shook his head angrily, his teeth clicking together. 'Something the matter?' said Lord Steel. He really seemed to love the pain that the radio cloaks caused Flenser.

'Nothing, my lord. Just a touch of the *static*.' In fact there was no *static*, yet Flenser felt himself disintegrating. What had given the other such sudden power?

Flenser with Amdijefri snapped his jaws open and shut, open and shut. The children jumped back from him, eyes wide. 'It's okay,' he said grimly, even as his two bodies thrashed against each other. There really were lots of good reasons why they should keep Johanna Olsndot alive: In the long run, it assured Jefri's good will. And it could be Flenser's secret human. Perhaps he could fake the Two-Leg's death to Steel and – *No. No. No!* Flenser grabbed back control, jamming the rationalizations out of mind. *The very tricks he had used against Tyrathect she thought to turn against him. It won't work on me. I am the master of lies.*

And then her attack twisted again, became a massive bludgeoning that destroyed all thought.

With Flenser, with Rangolith, with Amdijefri – all of him was making little gibbering noises now. Lord Steel danced around him, unsure whether to laugh or be concerned. Rangolith goggled at him in frank amazement.

The two children edged back to touch him. 'Are you hurt? Are you hurt?' The human slipped those remarkable *hands* under the radio cloak and brushed softly at Flenser's bleeding fur. The world blurred in a surge of *static*. 'No. Don't do that. It might hurt him more,' came Amdi's voice. The puppies' tiny muzzles reached out, trying to help with the cloaks.

Flenser felt his being pushed downwards towards oblivion. Tyrathect's final attack was a frontal assault, without rationalizations or sly infiltration, and . . .

. . . And she looked out upon herself in astonishment. *After so many days, I am me. And in control. Enough butchering of innocents. If anyone is to die, it is Steel and Flenser.* Her head followed Steel's prancing forms, picked out the most articulate member. She gathered her legs beneath her, and prepared to leap at its throat. *Come just a little closer . . . and die.*

Tyrathect's last moment of consciousness probably didn't last longer than five seconds. Her attack on the Flenser within her was a desperate, all-out thing that left her without reserves or internal defense. Even as she tensed to leap upon Steel, she felt her soul being pulled back and down, and Flenser rising up from the darkness. She felt the member's legs spasm and collapse, the ground smash into its face . . .

. . . And Flenser was back in control. The weakling's attack had been astonishing. She really had *cared* for the ones who were to be destroyed, cared so much she was willing to sacrifice herself if it would kill Flenser. And that had been her undoing. Suicide is never something to hang pack dominance on. Her very resolve had weakened her hold on the hindmind – and given The Master his chance. He was back in control, and with a great opportunity. Tyrathect's assault had left her defenseless. The innermost mental barriers around her three members were suddenly as thin as the skin of an overripe fruit. Flenser slashed through the membrane, pawed at the flesh of her mind, spattering it across his own. The three who had been her core would still live, but never again would they have a soul separate from his.

Flenser with Steel sprawled as though unconscious, his convulsions sub-siding. Let Steel think him incapacitated. It would give him time to think of the most advantageous explanation.

Flenser with Rangolith came slowly to his feet, though the two members were still in a posture of confusion. Flenser pulled them together. No explanations were due here, but it would be best if Farscout didn't suspect soulstrife. 'The cloaks are powerful tools, dear Rangolith; sometimes a bit too powerful.'

'Yes, my lord.'

Flenser let a smile spread across his features. For a moment he was silent, savoring what he would say next. No, there was no sign of the weak-willed one. This had been her last, best try at domination – her last and biggest mistake. Flenser's smile spread further, all the way to the two with Amdijefri. It suddenly occurred to him that Johanna Olsndot would be the first person he had ordered killed since his return to Hidden Island. Johanna Olsndot would therefore be the first blood on three of his muzzles.

'There's one more item for Craddleheads, Farscout. An execution . . .' As he spoke the details, the warmth of a decision well-made spread through his members.

35

The only good thing about all the waiting had been the chance it gave the wounded. Now that Vendacious had found a way past the Flenserist defenses, everyone was anxious to break camp, but . . .

Johanna spent the last afternoon at the field hospital. The hospital was laid off in rough rectangles, each about six meters across. Some of the plots had ragged tents – those belonging to wounded who were still smart enough to care for themselves. Others were surrounded by stranded fencing; inside each of those was a single member, the survivor of what had once been an entire pack. The singletons could easily have jumped the fences, but most seemed to recognize their purpose, and stayed within.

Johanna pulled the foodcart through the area, stopping at first one patient and then another. The cart was a bit too large for her, and sometimes it got caught in the roots that grew across the forest floor. Yet this was a job that she could do better than any pack, and it was nice to find a way she could help.

In the forest around the hospital there was the sound of kherhogs being coaxed up to wagon ties, the shouts of crews securing the cannons and getting the camp gear stowed. From the maps Vendacious had shown at the meeting, it was clear the next two days would be an exhausting time – but at the end of it they would have the high ground behind unsuspecting Flenserists.

She stopped at the first little tent. The threesome inside had heard her coming and was outside now, running little circles around her cart. 'Johanna! Johanna!' it said in her own voice. This was all that was left of one of Woodcarver's minor strategists; once upon a time, it had known some Samnorsk. The pack had originally been six; three had been killed by the wolves. What was left was the 'talker' part – about as bright as a five year old, though with an odd vocabulary. 'Thank you for food. Thank you.' Its muzzles pushed at her. She patted the heads before reaching into the cart and pulling out bowls of lukewarm stew. Two of them dug in right away, but the third sat back for a moment and chatted. 'I hear, we fight soon.'

Not you anymore, but 'Yes. We are going up by the dry fall, just east of here.'

'Uh, oh.' It said. 'Uh, oh. That's *bad*. Poor seeing, no control, ambush scary.' Apparently the fragment had some memories of its own tactical work. But there was no way Johanna could explain Vendacious's reasoning to it. 'Don't worry, we will make it okay.'

'You sure? You promise?'

Johanna smiled gently at what was left of a rather nice fellow. 'Yes. I promise.'

'Ah-ah-ah . . . Okay.' Now all three had their muzzles stuck into stew bowls. This was one of the lucky ones, really. It showed plenty of interest in what went on around it. Just as important, it had childlike enthusiasms. Pilgrim said that fragments like this could grow back easily if they were just treated right long enough to bear a puppy or two.

She pushed the cart a few meters further, to the fenced square that was the symbolic corral for a singleton. There was a faint odor of shit in the air. Some of the singletons and duos were not housebroken; in any case, the camp latrines were a hundred meters away.

'Here, Blacky, Blacky?' Johanna banged an empty bowl against the side of the cart. A single head eased up from behind some root bushes; sometimes this one didn't respond even that much. Johanna got on her knees so her eyes weren't much higher than the black-faced one. 'Blacky?'

The creature pulled himself out of the bushes and slowly approached. This was all that was left of one of Scrupilo's cannoneers. She vaguely remembered the pack, a handsome sixsome all large and fast. But now even 'Blacky' wasn't whole: a falling gun had crushed his rear legs. He dragged his legless rear on a little wagon with thirty centimeter wheels . . . sort of like a Skroderider with forelegs. She pushed a bowl of stew toward him, and made the noises that Pilgrim coached her in. Blacky had refused food the last three days, but today he rolled and walked close enough that she could pet his head. After a moment he lowered his muzzle to the stew.

Johanna grinned in surprised pleasure. This hospital was a strange place. A year ago she would have been horrified by it; even now she didn't have the proper Tinish outlook on the wounded. As she continued to pet Blacky's lowered head, Johanna looked across the forest floor at the crude tents, the patients and parts of patients. It really was a hospital. The surgeons did try to save lives, even if the medical science was a horrifying process of cutting and splinting without anesthetics. In that regard, it was quite comparable to the medieval human medicine that Johanna had seen on Dataset. But with the Tines there was something more. This place was almost a spare parts warehouse. The medics were interested in the welfare of *packs*. To them, singletons were pieces that might have a use in making larger fragments workable, at least temporarily. *Injured* singletons were at the bottom of all medical priorities. 'There's not much left to save in such cases,' one medic had said to her, via Pilgrim. 'And even if there was, would you want a crippled, loose-bonded member in your self?' The fellow had been too tired to notice the absurdity of his question. His muzzles had been dripping blood; he'd been working for hours to save wounded members of whole packs.

Besides, most wounded singletons just stopped eating and died in less than a tenday. Even after a year with Tines, Johanna couldn't quite accept it. Every singleton reminded her of dear Scriber; she wanted them to have a better chance than his last remnant had. She had taken over the food cart and spent as much time with the wounded singletons as she did with any of the other patients. It had worked out well. She could get close to each patient without mindsound interference. Her help gave the brood kenners more time to study the fragments and singletons, and try to build working packs from the wreckage.

And now maybe this one wouldn't starve. She'd tell Pilgrim. He'd done miracles with some of the other matchups, and seemed to be the only pack who shared some of her feelings for damaged singletons. 'If they don't starve it often means a strength of mind. Even crippled, they could be an advantage to a pack,' he'd said to her. 'I've been crippled off and on in my travels; you can't always pick and choose when you're down to three and you're a thousand miles into an unknown land.'

Johanna set a bowl of water beside the stew. After a moment, the crippled member turned on his axle and took some shallow sips. 'Hang on, Blacky, we'll find someone for you to be.'

Chitiratte was where he was supposed to be, walking his post exactly as expected. Nevertheless, he felt a thrill of nervousness. He always kept at least one head gazing at the mantis creature, the Two-Legs. Nothing suspicious about that posture either. He was *supposed* to be doing security duty here, and that meant keeping a lookout in all directions. He shifted his crossbow nervously about from jaws to field pack and back to jaws. Just a few more minutes . . .

Chitiratte circled the hospital compound once more. It was soft duty. Even though this stretch of wood had been spared, the drywind fires had chased the bigger wildlife downstream. This close to the river, the ground was covered with softbush, and there was scarcely a thorn to be found. Pacing around the hospital was like a walk on Woodcarver's Green down south. A few hundred yards east was harder work – getting the wagons and supplies in shape for the climb.

The fragments knew that something was up. Here and there, heads stuck up from pallets and burrows. They watched the wagons being loaded, heard the familiar voices of friends. The dumbest ones felt a call to duty; he had chased three able-bodied singles back into the compound. No way such feebs could be of any help. When the army marched up Margrum Climb, the hospital would stay behind. Chitiratte wished he could too. He'd been working for the Boss long enough to guess whence his orders ultimately came; Chitiratte suspected that not many would be coming back from Margrum Climb.

He turned three pairs of eyes toward the mantis creature. This latest job was the riskiest thing he'd been a part of. If it worked out he might just demand that the Boss leave him with the hospital. *Just be careful, old fellow. Vendacious didn't get where he is by leaving loose ends.* Chitiratte had seen what happened to that easterner who nosed a little too close into the Boss's business.

Damn but the human was slow! She'd been grunting at that one single-ton for five minutes. You'd think she was having sex with these frags for all the time she spent with them. Well, she'd pay for the familiarity very soon. He started to cock his bow, then thought better of it. *Accident, accident.* It must all look like an accident.

Aha. The Two-Legs was collecting food and water bowls and stowing them on the meal cart. Chitiratte made unobtrusive haste around the hospital perimeter, positioning himself in view of the Kratzi duo – the fragment that would actually do the killing.

Kratzinissinari had been a foot trooper before losing the Nissinari parts of himself. He had no connection with the Boss or Security. But he'd been known as a crazy-headed get of bitches, a pack that was always on the edge of combat rage. Getting killed back to two members normally had a gentling influence. In this case – well, the Boss claimed that Kratzi was specially prepared, a trap ready to be sprung. All Chitiratte need do was give the signal, and the duo would tear the mantis apart. A great tragedy. Of course, Chitiratte would be there, the alert hospital warden. He would quickly put arrows through Kratzi's brains . . . but alas, not in time to save the Two-Legs.

The human dragged the meal cart awkwardly around root bushes toward Kratzi, her next patient. The duo came out of its burrow, speaking half-witted greetings that even Chitiratte could not understand. There were undertones though, a killing anger that edged its friendly mien. Of course, the mantis thing didn't notice. She stopped the cart, began filling food and water bowls, all the time grunting away at the twosome. In a moment, she would bend down to put the food on the ground . . . For half an instant, Chitiratte considered shooting the mantis himself if Kratzi were not im-mediately successful. He could claim it was a tragic miss. He really didn't like the Two-Legs. The mantis creature was a menacing thing; it was so tall and moved so weirdly. By now he knew it was fragile compared to packs, but it was scary to think of a single animal so smart as this. He shelved the temptation even faster than he had thought it. No telling what price he might pay for that, even if they believed his shot was an accident. No altruism today, thank you very much; Kratzi's jaws and claws would have to do.

One of Kratzi's heads was looking in Chitiratte's general direction. Now the mantis picked up the bowls and turned from the meal cart—

'Hei, Johanna! How is it going?'

Johanna looked up from the stew to see Peregrine Wickwrackscar walk-ing along the edge of the hospital. He was moving to get as close as possible without invading the mind sounds of the patients. The guard who had stopped there a moment before retreated before his advance and stopped a few meters further on. 'Pretty good,' she called back. 'You know the one on wheels? He actually ate some stew tonight.'

'Good. I've been thinking about him and the threesome on the other side of the hospital.'

'The wounded medic?'

'Yes. What's left of Trellelak is all female, you know. I've been listening to mind sounds and—' Pilgrim's explanation was delivered in fluent Samnorsk, but it didn't make much sense to Johanna. Brood kenning had *so* many concepts without referents in human language that even Pilgrim couldn't make it clear. The only obvious part was that since Blacky was a male, there was a chance that he and the medic threesome might have pups early enough to bind the group. The rest was talk of 'mood resonance' and 'meshing weak points with strong.' Pilgrim claimed to be an amateur at brood kenning, but it was interesting the way the docs – and even Woodcarver sometimes – deferred to him. In his travels he had been through a lot. His matchups seemed to 'take' more often than anybody's. She waved him to silence. 'Okay. We'll try it soon as I've fed everybody.'

Pilgrim cocked a head or two at the nearby hospital plots. 'Something strange is going on. Can't quite "put my finger on it," but . . . all the fragments are watching you. Even more than usual. Do you feel it?'

Johanna shrugged. 'No.' She knelt to set the water and stew bowls before the twosome patient. The pair had been vibrating with eagerness, though they had been quite polite in not interrupting. Out of the corner of her eye, she noticed the hospital guard make a strange dipping motion with its two middle heads, and—

The blows were like two great fists smashing into her chest and face. Johanna fell to the ground, and they were on her. She raised bloody arms against the slashing jaws and claws.

When Chitiratte gave the signal, both of Kratzi leaped into action – *crashing into each other*, almost incidentally knocking the mantis on her back. Their claws and teeth were tearing at empty air and each other as much as the Two-Legs. For an instant, Chitiratte was struck motionless with surprise. *She might not be dead.* Then he remembered himself and jumped over the fence, at the same time cocking and loading his bow. Maybe he could miss the first shot. Kratzi was shredding the mantis, but slow—

Suddenly, there was no possibility of shooting the twosome. A wave of snarling black and white surged over Kratzi and the mantis. Every able-bodied fragment in the hospital seemed to be running to the attack. It was instant killing rage, far wilder than anything that could come from whole packs. Chitiratte fell back in astonishment before the sight and the mind-sound of it.

Even the pilgrim seemed caught up in it; the pack raced past Chitiratte and circled the melee. The pilgrim never quite plunged in, but nipped here and there, screaming words that were lost in the general uproar.

A splash of coordinated mindsound boomed out from the mob, so loud it numbed Chitiratte twenty yards away. The mob seemed to shrink in on itself, the frenzy gone from most of its members. What had been near a single beast with two dozen bodies was suddenly a confused and bloody crowd of random members.

The pilgrim still ran around the edge, somehow keeping his mind and purpose. His huge, scarred member dived in and out of the remaining crowd, clawing at anything that still fought.

The patients dragged themselves away from the killing ground. Some that had gone in as threesomes or duos came out single. Others seemed more numerous than before. The ground that was left was soaked with blood. At least five members had died. Near the middle, a pair of prosthetic wheels lay incongruously.

The pilgrim paid it all no attention; the four of him stood around and over the bloody mound at the center.

Chitiratte smiled to himself. *Mantis splatter.* Such a tragedy.

Johanna never quite lost consciousness, but the pain and the suffocating weight of dozens of bodies left no room for thought. Now the pressure eased. Somewhere beyond the local din she could hear shouts of normal Tinish talk. She looked up and saw Pilgrim standing all around her. Scarbutt was straddling her, its muzzle centimeters away. It reached down and licked her face. Johanna smiled and tried to speak.

Vendacious had arranged to be in conference with Scrupilo and Woodcarver. Just now the 'Commander of Cannoneers' was deep into tactics, using Dataset to illustrate his scheme for Margrum Climb.

Squalls of rage sounded from down by the river.

Scrupilo looked up peevishly from the Pink Oliphaunt: 'What the muddy hell—'

The sounds continued, more than a casual brawl. Woodcarver and Vendacious exchanged worried glances even as they arched necks to see among the trees. 'A fight in the hospital?' said the Queen.

Vendacious dropped his note board and lunged out of the meeting area, shouting for the local guards to guard the Queen. As he raced across the camp, he could see that his roving guards were already converging on the hospital. Everything seemed as smooth as a program on Dataset . . . except, why so *much* noise?

The last few hundred yards, Scrupilo caught up with him and pulled ahead. The cannoneer raced into the hospital and stumbled over himself in abrupt horror. Vendacious burst into the clearing all prepared to display his own shock combined with alert resolve.

Peregrine Wickwrackscar was standing by a meal cart, Chitiratte not far behind him. The pilgrim was standing over the Two-Legs in a litter of carnage. *By the Pack of Packs, what happened?* There was too much blood by far. 'Everybody back except the doctors,' Vendacious bellowed at the soldiers who crowded at the edge of the compound. He picked his way along a path that avoided the loudest-minded patients. There were a lot of fresh wounds, and here and there speckles of blood dark on the pale tree trunks. Something had gone wrong.

Meanwhile Scrupilo had run around the edge of the hospital and was standing just a few dozen yards from the Pilgrim. Most of him was staring at the ground under Wickwrackscar. 'It's Johanna! Johanna!' For a moment it looked like the fool would jump over the fence.

'I think she's okay, Scrupilo.' Wickwrackscar said. 'She was just feeding one of the duos and it went nuts – attacked her.'

One of the doctors looked over the carnage. There were three corpses on the ground, and blood enough for more. 'I wonder what she did to provoke them.'

'Nothing, I tell you! But when she went down, half the hospital went after Whatsits here.' He waggled a nose at unidentifiable remains.

Vendacious looked at Chitiratte, at the same time saw Woodcarver arrive. 'What about it, Soldier?' he asked. *Don't screw up, Chitiratte.*

'I-it's just like the pilgrim says, my lord. I've never seen anything like it.' He sounded properly astounded by the whole affair.

Vendacious stepped a little closer to the Pilgrim. 'If you'll let me take a closer look, Pilgrim?'

Wickwrackscar hesitated. He had been snuffling around the girl, looking for wounds that might need immediate attention. Then the girl nodded weakly to him, and he backed off.

Vendacious approached, all solemn and solicitous. Inside he raged. He'd never heard of anything like this. But even if the whole damn hospital had come to her aid, she should still be dead; the Kratzi duo could have ripped her throat out in half a second. His plan had seemed fool-proof (and even now the failure would cause no lasting damage), but he was just beginning to understand what had gone wrong: For days, the human had been in contact with these patients, even Kratzi. No Tinish doctor could approach and touch them like the Two-Legs. Even some whole packs felt the effect; for fragments it must be overwhelming. In their inner soul, most of the patients considered the alien part of themselves.

He looked at the Two-Legs from three sides, mindful that the eyes of fifty packs were watching his every move. Very little of the blood was from the Two-Legs. The cuts on her neck and arms were long and shallow, aimless slashings. At the last minute, Kratzi's conditioning had failed before the notion of the human as pack member. Even now, a quick flick of a forepaw would rip the girl's throat open. He briefly considered putting her under

Security medical protection. The ploy had worked well with Scriber, but it would be very risky here. Pilgrim had been nose to nose with Johanna; he would be suspicious of any claims about 'unexpected complications.' *No. Even good plans sometimes fail. Count it as experience for the future.* He smiled at the girl and spoke in Samnorsk, 'You're quite safe now,' *for the moment and quite unfortunately.* The human's head turned to the side, looking off in the direction of Chitiratte.

Scrupilo had been pacing back and forth along the fence, so close to Chitiratte and Pilgrim that the two had been forced back. 'I won't have it!' The cannoneer said loudly. 'Our most important person attacked like this. It smells of enemy action!'

Wickwrackscar goggled at him. 'But how?'

'I don't *know!*' Scrupilo said, his voice a desperate shout. 'But she needs protection as much as nursing. Vendacious must find some place to keep her.'

The pilgrim pack was clearly impressed by the argument – and unnerved. He inclined a head at Vendacious and spoke with uncharacteristic respect, 'What do you think, Vendacious?'

Of course, Vendacious had been watching the Two-Legs. It was interesting how little humans could disguise their point of attention. Johanna had been staring at Chitiratte, now she was looking up at Vendacious, her shifty little close-set eyes narrowing. Vendacious had made a project this last year of studying human expressions, both on Johanna and in stories in Dataset. She suspected something. And she also must have understood part of Scrupilo's speech. Her back arched and raised one hand weakly. Fortunately for Vendacious, her shout came out a whisper that even he could scarcely hear. 'No . . . not like Scriber.'

Vendacious was a pack who believed in careful planning. He also knew that the best-made schemes must be altered by circumstances. He looked down at Johanna and smiled with the gentlest public sympathy. It would be risky to kill her like Scriber's frag, but – now he saw that the alternatives were far more dangerous. Thank goodness Woodcarver was stuck with her limper on the other side of the camp. He nodded at Pilgrim and drew himself together. 'I fear Scrupilo is right. Just how it might have been done, I don't know, but we can't take a chance. We'll take Johanna to my den. Tell the Queen.' He pulled cloaks from his backs and began gently to wrap the human for the last trip she would ever make. Only her eyes protested.

Johanna drifted in and out of consciousness, horrified at her inability to scream her fears. Her strongest cries were less than whispers. Her arms and legs responded with little more than twitches, even that lost in Vendacious's swaddling. *Concussion, maybe, something like that,* the explanation came from some absurdly rational corner of her mind. Everything seemed so far away, so dark . . .

Johanna woke in her cabin at Woodcarvers. What a terrible dream! That she had been so cut up, unable to move, and then thinking Vendacious was a traitor. She tried to shrug herself to a sitting position, but nothing moved. *Darn sheets are all wrapped around me.* She lay quiet for a second, still massively disoriented by the dream. 'Woodcarver?' she tried to say, but only a little moan came out. Somemember moved gently around the firepit. The room was only dimly lit, and something was wrong with it. Johanna wasn't lying in her usual place. There was a moment of puzzled lassitude as she tried to make sense of the orientation of the dark walls. Funny. The ceiling was awfully low. Everything smelled like raw meat. The side of her face *hurt*, and she tasted blood on her lips. She wasn't at Woodcarvers and that terrible dream was—

Three Tinish heads drifted in silhouette nearby. One came closer, and in the dim light she recognized the pattern of white and black on its face. *Vendacious.*

'Good,' he said. 'You are awake.'

'Where am I?' the words came out slurred and weak. The terror was back.

'The abandoned cotter's hut at the east end of the camp. I've taken it over. As a security den, you know.' His Samnorsk was quiet and fluent, spoken in one of the generic voices of Dataset. One of his jaws carried a dagger, the blade a glint in the dimness.

Johanna twisted in the tied cloaks and whispered screams. Something was wrong with her; it was like shouting on empty breath.

One of Vendacious paced the hut's upper level. Daylight splashed across its muzzle as it peered out first one and then another of the narrow slits cut in the timbers. 'Ah, it's good that you don't pretend. I could see that you somehow guessed about my . . . second career. My hobby. But screaming – even loud – won't help either. We have only a brief time to chat. I'm sure the Queen will come visiting soon . . . and I will kill you just before she arrives. So sad. Your hidden wounds were tragically severe . . .'

Johanna wasn't sure of all he said. Her vision blurred every time she moved her head. Even now she couldn't remember the details of what had happened back in the hospital compound. Somehow Vendacious *was* a traitor, but how . . . memories wriggled past the pain. 'You did murder Scriber, didn't you? *Why?*' Her voice came louder than before, and she choked on blood dribbling back down her throat.

Soft, *human*, laughter came from all around her. 'He learned the truth about me. Ironic that such an incompetent would be the only one to see through me . . . Or do you mean a larger why?' The three nearby muzzles moved closer still, and the blade in one's jaw patted the side of Johanna's cheek. 'Poor Two-Legs, I'm not sure you could ever understand. Some of it, the will to power maybe. I've read what Dataset has to say about human motivation, the "freudian" stuff. We Tines are much more complicated. I am almost entirely male, did you know that? A dangerous thing to be, all one sex. Madness lurks. Yet it was my decision. I was tired of being an indifferently good inventor, of living in Woodcarver's shadow. So many of us are her get, and she dominates most all of us. She was quite happy about my going into Security, you know. She doesn't quite have the combination of members for it. She thought that all male but one would make me controllably devious.'

His sentry member made another round of the window slits. Again there was a human chuckle. 'I've been planning a long time. It's not just Woodcarver I'm up against. The power-side of her soul is scattered all over the arctic coast; Flenser had almost a century headstart on me; Steel is new, but he has the empire Flenser built. I made myself indispensable to all of them: I'm Woodcarver's chief of security . . . and Steel's most valued spy. Played aright, I will end up with Dataset and all the others will be dead.'

His blade tapped her face again. 'Do you think you can help me?' Eyes peered close into her terror. 'I doubt it very much. If my proper plan had succeeded, you would be neatly dead now.' A sigh breathed around the room. 'But that failed, and I'm stuck with carving you up myself. Perhaps it will turn out for the best. Dataset is a torrent of information about most things, but it scarcely acknowledges the existence of torture. In some ways, your race seems so fragile, so easily killable. You die before your minds can be dismembered. Yet I know you can feel pain and terror; the trick is to apply force without quite killing.'

The three nearby members snuggled into more comfortable positions, like a human settling down for serious talk. 'And there *are* some questions you may be able to answer, things I couldn't really ask before. Steel is very confident, you know, and it's not because he has me with Woodcarver. That pack has some other advantage. Could he have his own Dataset?'

Vendacious paused. Johanna didn't answer, her silence a combination of terror and stubbornness. This was the monster that killed Scriber.

The muzzle with the knife slid between the blankets and Johanna's skin, and pain shot up Johanna's arm. She screamed. 'Ah, Dataset said a human could be hurt there. No need to answer that one, Johanna. Do you know what I think is Steel's secret? I think one of your family survived – most likely your little brother, considering what you've told us about the massacre.'

Jefri? *Alive?* For an instant she forgot the pain, almost forgot the fear. 'How . . . ?'

Vendacious gave a Tinish shrug. 'You never saw him dead. You can be sure Steel wanted a live Two-Legs, and after reading about cold sleep in Dataset, I doubt he could have revived any of the others. And he's got *something* up there. He's been eager for information from Dataset, but he's never demanded that I steal the device for him.'

Johanna closed her eyes, denying the traitor pack's existence. *Jefri lives!*

Memories rose before her; Jefri's playful joy, his childish tears, his trusting courage aboard the refugee ship . . . things she had thought forever lost to her. For a moment they seemed more real than the slashing violence of the last few minutes. But what could Jefri do to help the Flenserists? The other datasets had surely burned. *There's something more here, something that Vendacious still is missing.*

Vendacious grabbed her chin, and gave her head a little shake. 'Open your eyes; I've learned to read them, and I want to see . . . Hmm, I don't know if you believe me or not. No matter. If we have time, I will learn just what he might have done for Steel. There are other, sharper questions. Dataset is clearly the key to all. In less than half a year, I and Woodcarver and Pilgrim have learned an enormous amount about your race and civilization. I daresay we know your people better than you do. When all the violence is over, the winner will be the pack that still controls Dataset. I intend to be that pack. And I've often wondered if there are other passwords, or programs I can run that would actually watch for my safety—'

The babysitter code.

The watching heads bobbed a grin. 'Aha, so there is such a thing! Perhaps this morning's bad luck is all for the best. I might never have learned—' his voice broke into dischords. Two of Vendacious jumped up to join the one already at the window slits. Softly by her ear, the voice continued, 'It's the Pilgrim, still far away, but coming toward us . . . I don't know. You would be much better safely dead. One deep wound, all out of sight.' The knife slid further down. Johanna arched futilely back from the point. Then the blade withdrew, the point poised gently against her skin. 'Let's hear what Pilgrim has to say. No point in killing you this instant if he doesn't insist on seeing you.' He pushed a cloth into her mouth and tied it tight.

There was a moment of silence, maybe the crunch of paws in the brush right around the cabin. Then she heard a pack warble loud from beyond the timbered walls. Johanna doubted that she would ever learn to recognize packs by their voices, but . . . her mind stumbled through the sounds, trying to decode the Tinish chords that were words piled on top of one another:

> '*Johanna*
> *something* interrogative
> *screech* safe.'

Vendacious gobbled back,

> 'Hail Peregrine Wickwrackscar
> Johanna *trill*

not visible hurts
sad uncertain *squeak*.'

And the traitor murmured in her ear: 'Now he'll ask if I need medical help, and if he insists . . . our chat will have an early end.'

But the only reply Pilgrim made was a chorus of sympathetic worry. 'Damn assholes are just sitting down out there,' came Vendacious's irritated whisper.

The silence stretched on a moment, and then Peregrine's human voice, the Joker from Dataset, said in clear Samnorsk. 'Don't do anything foolish, Vendacious, old man.'

Vendacious made a sound of polite surprise – and tensed around her. His knife jabbed a centimeter deep between Johanna's ribs, a thorn of pain. She could feel the blade trembling, could feel his member's breath on her bloody skin.

Pilgrim's voice continued, confident and knowing: 'I mean we know what you're up to. Your pack at the hospital has gone completely to pieces, confessed what little he knew to Woodcarver. Do you think your lies can get by *her*? If Johanna is dead, you'll be bloody shreds.' He hummed an ominous tune from Dataset. 'I know her well, the Queen. She seems such a gracious pack . . . but where do you think Flenser got his gruesome creativity? Kill Johanna and you'll find just how far her genius in that exceeds Flenser's.'

The knife pulled back. One more of Vendacious leaped to the window slits, and the two by Johanna loosened their grip. He stroked the blade gently across her skin. Thinking? *Is Woodcarver really that fearsome?* The four at the windows were looking in all directions; no doubt Vendacious was counting guard packs and planning furiously. When he finally replied, it was in Samnorsk: 'The threat would be more credible if it were not at second hand.'

Pilgrim chuckled. 'True. But we guessed what would happen if she approached. You're a cautious fellow; you'd have killed Johanna instantly, and been full of lying explanation before you even heard what the Queen knows. But seeing a poor pilgrim amble over . . . I know you think me a fool, only one step better than Scriber Jaqueramaphan.' Peregrine stumbled on the name, and for an instant lost his flippant tone. 'Anyway, now you know the situation. If you doubt, send your guards beyond the brush; look at what the Queen has surrounding you. Johanna dead only kills you. Speaking of which, I assume this conversation has some point?

'Yes. She lives.' Vendacious slipped the gag from Johanna's mouth. She turned her head, choking. There were tears running down the sides of her face. 'Pilgrim, oh Pilgrim!' The words were scarcely more than a whisper. She drew a painful breath, concentrated on making noise. Bright spots danced before her eyes. 'Hei, Pilgrim!'

'Hei Johanna. Has he hurt you?'

'Some, I—'

'That's enough. She's alive, Pilgrim, but that's easily corrected.' Vendacious didn't jam the gag back in her mouth. Johanna could see him rubbing heads nervously as he paced round and round the ledge. He trilled something about 'stalemated game.'

Peregrine replied, 'Speak Samnorsk, Vendacious. I want Johanna to understand – and you can't talk quite as slick as in pack talk.'

'Whatever.' The traitor's voice was unconcerned, but his members kept up their nervous pacing. 'The Queen must realize we have a standoff here. Certainly I'll kill Johanna if I'm not treated properly. But even then, Woodcarver could not afford to hurt me. Do you realize the trap Steel has set on Margrum Climb? I'm the only one who knows how to avoid it.'

'Big deal. I never wanted to go up Margrum anyway.'

'Yes, but you don't count, Pilgrim. You're a mongrel patchwork. Woodcarver will understand how dangerous this situation is. Steel's forces are everything I said they weren't, and I've been sending them every secret I could write down from my investigations of Dataset.'

'My brother is alive, Pilgrim,' Johanna said.

'Oh . . . You're kind of a record setter for treason aren't you, Vendacious? Everything to us was a lie, while Steel learned all the truth about us. You figure that means we daren't kill you now?'

Laughter, and Vendacious's pacing stopped. *He sees control coming back to him.* 'More, you need my full-membered cooperation. See, I exaggerated the number of enemy agents in Woodcarver's troops, but I do have a few – and maybe Steel has planted others I don't know about. If you even arrest me, word will get back to the Flenser armies. Much of what I know will be useless – and you'll face an immediate, overwhelming attack. You see? The Queen *needs* me.'

'And how do we know this is not more lies?'

'That is a problem, isn't it? Matched only by how I can be guaranteed safety once I've saved the expedition. No doubt it's beyond your mongrel mind. Woodcarver and I must have a talk, someplace mutually safe and unseen. Carry *that* message back to her. She can't have this traitor's hides, but if she cooperates she may be able to save her own!'

There was silence from outside, punctuated by the squeaking of animals in the nearer trees. Finally, surprisingly, Pilgrim laughed. 'Mongrel mind, eh? Well, you have me in one thing, Vendacious. I've been all the world round, and I remember back half a thousand years – but of all the villains and traitors and geniuses, you take the record for bald impudence!'

Vendacious gave a Tinish chord, untranslatable but as a sign of smug pleasure. 'I'm honored.'

'Very well, I'll take your points back to the Queen. I hope the two of you are clever enough to work something out . . . One thing more: the Queen requires that Johanna come with me.'

'The Queen requires? That sounds more like your mongrel sentiment to me.'

'Perhaps. But it will prove you are serious in your confidence. View it as *my* price for cooperation.'

Vendacious turned all his heads toward Johanna, silently regarding. Then he scanned out all the windows one last time. 'Very well, you may have her.' Two jumped down to the cabin's hatch while another pair pulled her toward it. His voice was soft and near her ear. 'Damn Pilgrim. Alive, you're just going to cause me trouble with the Queen.' His knife slid across her field of view. 'Don't oppose me with her. I am going to survive this affair still powerful.'

He lifted back the hatch and daylight spilled blindingly across her face. She squinted; there was a sweep of branches and the side of the hut. Vendacious pushed and pulled her cot onto the forest floor, and the same time gobbling at his guards to keep their positions. He and Peregrine chatted politely, agreeing on when the pilgrim would return.

One by one, Vendacious trotted back through the cabin's hatch. Pilgrim advanced and grabbed the handles at the front of the cot. One of his pups reached out from his jacket to nuzzled her face. 'You okay?'

'I'm not sure. I got bashed in the head . . . and it seems kind of hard to breathe.'

He loosened the blankets from around her chest as the rest of him dragged the cot away from the hut. The forest shade was peaceful and deep, and . . . Vendacious's guards were stationed here and there about the area. How many were really in on the treason? Two hours ago, Johanna had looked to them for protection. Now their every glance sent a shiver through her. She rolled back to the center of the cot, dizzy again, and stared up into the branches and leaves and patches of smoke-stained sky. Things like Straumli tree squigglies chased each other back and forth, cluttering in seeming debate.

Funny. Almost a year ago Pilgrim and Scriber were dragging me around, and I was even worse hurt, and terrified of everything – including them. And now . . . she had never been so glad to see another person. Even Scarbutt was a reassuring strength walking beside her.

The waves of terror slowly subsided. What was left was an anger as intense, though more reasoning, than the year before. She *knew* what had happened here; the players were not strangers, the betrayal was not random murder. After all Vendacious's treachery, after all his murders, and his planning to kill them all . . . he was going to go *free!* Pilgrim and Woodcarver were just going to *overlook* that. 'He killed Scriber, Pilgrim. He killed Scriber . . .' *He cut Scriber to pieces, then chased down what was left and killed that right out of our arms.* 'And Woodcarver is going to let him go free? How can she do it? How can you do it?' The tears were coming again.

'Sh, sh.' Two of Pilgrim's heads came into view. They looked down at her, then swiveled around almost nervously. She reached out, touching the short plush fur. Pilgrim was shivering! One of him dipped close; his voice didn't sound jaunty at all. 'I don't know what the Queen will do, Johanna. She doesn't know about any of this.'

'Wha—'

'Sh.' And his voice became scarcely a buzzing through her hand. 'His people can still see us. He could still figure things out . . . Only you and I know, Johanna. I don't think anyone else suspects.'

'But the pack that confessed . . . ?'

'Bluff, all bluff. I've done some crazy things in my life but next to following Scriber down to your starship, this takes the prize . . . After Vendacious took you away, I began to think. You weren't that badly injured. It was all too much like what happened to Jaqueramaphan, but I had no proof.'

'And you haven't told anyone?'

'No. Foolish as poor Scriber, aren't I?' His heads looked in all directions 'If I was right, he'd be silly not to kill you immediately. I was so afraid I was already too late . . .'

You would have been, if Vendacious weren't quite the monster I know he is.

'Anyway, I learned the truth just like poor Scriber – almost by accident. But if we can get another seventy meters away, we won't die like him. And everything I claimed to Vendacious will be *true*.'

She patted his nearest shoulder and looked back. The tiny cabin and its ring of guards disappeared behind the forest brush.

. . . and Jefri *lives!*

Crypto: 0
  [95 encrypted packets have been discarded]
As received by: *Ølvira* shipboard ad hoc
Language path: Tredeschk → Triskweline, SjK units
From: Zonograph Eidolon
  [Co-op (or religious order) in the Middle Beyond maintained by subscription of
    several thousand Low Beyond civilizations, in particular those threatened by
    immersion]
Subject: Surge Bulletin Update and Ping
Distribution:
  Zonograph Eidolon Subscribers
  Zonometric Interest Group
  Threats Interest Group, subgroup: navigational Ping participants
Date: 1087892301 seconds since Calibration Event 239011, Eidolon Frame
[66.91 days since Fall of Sjandra Kei]

Key phrases: galactic scale event, superluminal, charitable emergency
  announcement
Text of message:
  (Please include accurate local time in any ping responses.)

  If you receive this, you know that the monster surge has receded. The new zone surface appears to be a stable froth of low dimensionality (between 2.1 and 2.3). At least five civilizations are trapped in the new configuration. Thirty virgin solar systems have achieved the Beyond. (Subscribers may find specifics in the encrypted data that follow this bulletin.)

  The change corresponds to what is seen in a normal period of two years across the whole galaxy's Slow Zone surface. Yet this surge happened in less than two hundred hours and on less than one thousandth of that surface.

  Even these numbers do not show the scale of the event. (The following can only be estimates, since so many sites were destroyed, and no instruments were calibrated for this size event.) At its maximum, the surge reached 1000 light-years above Zone Surface Standard. Surge rates of more than thirty million times lightspeed [about one light-year per second] were sustained for periods of more than 100 seconds. Reports from subscribers show more than ten billion sophont deaths directly attributable to the Surge (local network failures, failures leading to environment collapse, medical collapse, vehicle crashes, security failures). Posted economic damage is much greater.

  The important question now is what can we expect in aftersurges. Our predictions are based on instrumented sites and zonometric surveys, combined with historical data from our archives. Except for long-term trends, predicting zone changes has never been a science, but we have served our subscribers well in advising of aftersurges and in identifying available new worlds. Unfortunately, the present situation makes all previous work almost useless. We have precise documentation going back ten million years. Faster than light surges happen about every twenty thousand years (usually with speed under 7.0c). Nothing like this monster is on file. The surge just seen is the kind described at third-hand in old and glutted databases: Sculptor had one this size fifty million years ago. The [Perseus Arm] in our galaxy probably suffered something like this half a billion years ago.

  This uncertainty makes our Mission nearly impossible, and is an important reason for this public message to the Zonometry newsgroup and others: Everyone interested in zonometry and navigation must pool resources on this problem. Ideas, archive access, algorithms – all these things could help. We pledge significant contributions to non-subscribers, and one-for-one trades to those with important information. Note: We are also addressing this message to the Swndwp oracle, and direct beaming it to points in the Transcend thought to be inhabited. Surely an event such as this must be of interest even there? We appeal to the Powers Above: Let us send you what we know. Give us some hint if you have ideas about this event.

  To demonstrate our good faith, here are the estimates we have currently.

These are based on naïve scale-up of well-documented surges in this region. Details are in the non-crypted appendix to this sending. Over the next year there will be five or six aftersurges, of diminishing speed and range. During this time at least two more civilizations (see risk list) will likely be permanently immersed. Zone storm conditions will prevail even when aftersurges are not in progress. Navigation in the volume [coordinate specification] will be extremely dangerous during this period; we recommend that shipping in the volume be suspended. The time line is probably too short to admit feasible rescue plans for the civilizations at risk. Our long-range prediction (probably the least uncertain of all): The million-year-scale secular shrinkage will not be affected at all. The next hundred thousand years will however show a retardation in the shrinkage of the Slow Zone boundary in this portion of the galaxy.

Finally, a philosophical note. We of Zonographic Eidolon watch the zone boundary and the orbits of border stars. For the most part, the zone changes are very slow: 700 meters per second in the case of the long-term secular shrinkage. Yet these changes together with orbital motion affect billions of lives each year. Just as the glaciers and droughts of a pretechnical world must affect a people, so must we accept these long-term changes. Storms and surgesare obvious tragedies, near-instant death for some civilizations. Yet these are as far beyond our control as the slower movements. Over the last few weeks, some newsgroups have been full of tales of war and battle fleets, of billions dying in the clash of species. To all such – and those living more peaceably around them – we say: Look out on the universe. It does not care, and even with all our science there are some disasters that we can not avert. All evil and good is petty before Nature. Personally, we take comfort from this, that there is a universe to admire that cannot be twisted to villainy or good, but which simply *is*.

Crypto: 0
As received by: *Ølvira* shipboard ad hoc
Language path: Arbwyth → Trade 24 → Cherguelin → Triskweline, SjK units
From: Twirlip of the Mists
   [Who knows what this is, though probably not a propaganda voice. Very
      sparse priors.]
Subject: The cause of the recent Great Surge
Distribution:
   Threat of the Blight
   Great Secrets of Creation
   Zonometric Interest Group
Date: 66.47 days since Fall of Sjandra Kei
Key phrases: Zone Instability and the Blight, Hexapodia as the key insight
Test of message:
   Apologies if I am repeating obvious conclusions. My only gateway onto the Net is very expensive, and I miss many important postings. The Great Surge now in progress appears by all accounts to be an event of cosmic scope and rarity.

Furthermore, the other posters put its epicenter less than 6,000 light-years from recent warfare related to the Blight. Can this be mere coincidence? As has long been theorized [citations from various sources, three unknown to Ølvira; the theories cited are of long standing and nondisprovable], the Zones themselves may be an artifact, perhaps created by something beyond Transcendence for the protection of lesser forms or [hypothetical] sentient gas clouds in galactic cores.

Now for the first time in Net history we have a Transcendent form, the Blight, that can effectively dominate the Beyond. Many on the Net [cites Hanse and Sandor at the Zoo] believe that it is searching for an artifact near the Bottom. Is it no wonder that this could upset the Natural Balance and provoke the recent Event?

Please write to me and tell me what you think. I don't get much mail.

Crypto: 0
As received by: *Ølvira* shipboard ad hoc
Language path: Baeloresk → Triskweline, SjK units
From: Alliance for the Defense
    [Claimed union of five empires below Straumli Realm. No references prior to the Fall of the Straumli Realm. Numerous counterclaims (including from *Out of Band II*) that this Alliance is a front for the old Aprahant Hegemony. Cf, *Butterfly Terror.*]
Subject: Courageous Mission Accomplished
Distribution:
    Threat of the Blight
    War Trackers Interest Group
    Homo Sapiens Interest Group
Date: 67.07 days since Fall of Sjandra Kei
Key phrases: Action, not talk
Text of message:
    Subsequent to our action against the human nest at [Sjandra Kei] a part of our fleet pursued human and other Blight-controlled forces toward the Bottom of the Beyond. Evidently, the Perversion hoped to protect these forces by putting them in an environment too dangerous to challenge. That thinking did not count on the courage of Alliance commanders and crews. We can now report the substantial destruction of those escaping forces.

    The first major operation of your Alliance has been an enormous success. With the extermination of their most important supporters, Blight encroachment on the Middle Beyond has been brought to a standstill. Yet much remains to be done:

    The Alliance Fleet is returning to the Middle Beyond. We've suffered some casualties and need substantial reprovisioning. We know that there are still scattered pockets of humanity in the Beyond, and we've identified secondary races that are aiding humanity. The defense of the Middle Beyond must be the goal of every sophont of good will. Elements of your Alliance Fleet will soon visit systems in the volume [parameter specification]. We ask for your aid and support against what is left of this terrible enemy.

Death to vermin.

36

Kjet Svensndot was alone on *Ølvira*'s bridge when the Surge passed. They had long since done all the preparations that were meaningful, and the ship had no realistic means of propulsion in the Slowness that surrounded it. Yet the Group Captain spent much of his time up here, trying to program some sort of responsiveness into the automation that remained. Half-assed programming was a time-filler that, like knitting, must date to the beginning of the human experience.

Of course, the actual transition out of Slowness would have been totally unnoticed if not for all the alarms he and the Dirokimes had installed. As it was, the noise and lights blew him out of a half-drowse into hair-raised wakefulness. He punched the ship's comm: 'Glimfrelle! Tirolle! Get your tails up here.'

By the time the brothers reached the command deck, preliminary nav displays had been computed and a jump sequence was awaiting confirmation. The two were grinning from ear to ear as they bounced in and strapped themselves down at action posts. For a few moments there was little chitchat, only an occasional whistle of pleasure from the Dirokimes. They had rehearsed this over and over during the last hundred plus hours, and with the poor automation there was a lot for them to do. Gradually the view from the deck's windows sharpened. Where at first there had only been vague blurs, the ultrawave sensors were posting individual traces with steadily improving information on range and rates. The communication window showed the queue of fleet comm messages getting longer and longer.

Tirolle looked up from his work 'Hei, Boss, these jump figures look okay – at least as a first cut.'

'Good. Commit and allow autocommit.' In the hours after the Surge, they had decided that their initial priority should be to continue with the pursuit. What they did then . . . they had talked long on that, and Group Captain Svensndot had thought even longer. Nothing was routine any more.

'Yes, *sir!*' The Dirokime's longfingers danced across the controls, and 'Rolle added some verbal control. 'Bingo!'

Status showed five jumps completed, ten. Kjet stared out the true-view window for a few seconds. No change, no change . . . then he noticed that one of the brightest stars in the field had moved, was sliding imperceptibly across the sky. Like a juggler getting her pace, *Ølvira* was coming up to speed.

'Hei, hei!' Glimfrelle leaned over to see his brother's work. 'We're making 1.2 light-years per hour. That's better than before the Surge.'

'Good. Comm and Surveillance?' Where was everybody *else* and what were they up to?

'Yup. Yup. I'm on it.' Glimfrelle bent his slender frame back to the console. For some seconds, he was almost silent. Svensndot began paging through the mail. There was nothing yet from Owner Limmende. Twenty-five years Kjet had worked for Limmende and SjK Commercial Security. Could he mutiny? And if he did, would any follow?

'Okay. Here's the situation, Boss.' Glimfrelle shifted the main window to show his interpretation of the ship's reports. 'It's like we guessed, maybe a little more extreme.' They had realized almost from the beginning that the surge was bigger than anything in recorded history; that's not what the Dirokime meant by 'extreme.' He swept his shortfingers down, making a hazy blue line across the window. 'We guessed that the leading edge of the Surge moved normal to this line. That would account for it taking Boss Limmende out four hundred seconds before it hit the *Out of Band*, and hitting us ten seconds after that . . . Now if the trailing edge were similar to ordinary surges' – upgraded a million times – 'then we, and then the rest of the pursuing fleets should come out well before *Out of Band*.' He pointed at a single glowing dot that represented the *Ølvira*. Around and just ahead of it dozens of points of light were popping into existence as the ship's detectors reported seeing the initiation of ultradrive jumps. It was like a cold fire sweeping away from them into the darkness. Eventually Limmende and the heart of the anonymous fleet would all be back in business. 'Our pickup log shows that's about what happened. Most all the pursuing fleets will be out of the surge before the *Out of Band*.'

'Hm. So it'll lose part of its lead.'

'Yup. But if it's going where we think—' a G-star eighty light-years ahead of the fugitive. '—it'll still get there before they kill it.' He paused, pointed at a haze that was spreading sideways from the growing knot of light. 'Not everybody is still chasing.'

'Yeah . . .' Svensndot had been reading the News even as he listened to 'Frelle's summary. '. . . according to the Net, that's the Alliance for the Defense departing the battle field, victorious.'

'Say *what?*' Tirolle twisted abruptly in his harness. His large, dark eyes held none of their usual humor.

'You heard me.' Kjet put the item where the brothers could see it. The two read rapidly, 'Frelle mumbling phrases aloud, '. . . *courage* of Alliance commanders . . . *substantial* destruction of escaping forces . . .'

Glimfrelle shuddered, all flippancy departed. 'They don't even mention the Surge. Everything they say is a cowardly lie!' his voice shifted up to its normal speaking range and he continued in his own language. Kjet could understand parts of it. The Dirokimes that left their dream habitats were normally lighthearted folk, full of whimsy and gentle sarcasm. Glimfrelle sounded almost that way now, except for the high edges to his whistling and the insults more colorful than Svensndot had ever heard from them: '. . . get from a verminous cow-pie . . . killers of innocent dreams . . .' even in Samnorsk the words were strong, but in Dirokime 'verminous cow-pie' was drenched in explicit imagery that almost brought the smell of such a thing into the room. Glimfrelle's voice went higher and higher, then beyond the human register. Abruptly he collapsed, shuddering and moaning low. Dirokimes could cry, though Svensndot had never seen such a thing before. Glimfrelle rocked in his brother's arms.

Tirolle looked over Glimfrelle's shoulder at Kjet. 'Where does revenge take us now, Group Captain?'

For a moment, Kjet looked back silently. 'I'll let you know, Lieutenant.' He looked at the displays. *Listen and watch a little longer, and maybe we'll know.* 'Meantime, get us nearer the center of pursuit,' he said gently.

'Aye, sir.' Tirolle patted his brother's back gently and returned to his console.

During the next five hours, Ølvira's crew watched the Alliance fleet race helter-skelter for the higher spaces. It could not even be called a retreat, more a panicked dissolution. Great opportunists, they had not hesitated to kill by treachery, and to give chase when they thought there might be treasure at the end. Now that they were confronted with the possibility of being trapped in the Slowness, of dying between the stars, they raced for their separate safety. Their bulletins to the newsgroups were full of bravado, but their maneuver couldn't be disguised. Former neutrals pointed to the discrepancy; more and more it was accepted that the Alliance was built around the Aprahanti Hegemony and perhaps had other motives than altruistic opposition to the Blight. There was nervous speculation about who might next receive Alliance attention.

Major transceivers still targeted the fleets. They might as well have been on a network trunk. The news traffic was a vast waterfall, totally beyond Ølvira's present ability to receive. Nevertheless, Svensndot kept an eye on it. Somewhere there might be some clue, some insight . . . The majority of War Trackers and Threats seemed to have little interest in the Alliance or the death of Sjandra Kei, per se. Most were terrified of the Blight that was still spreading through the Top of the Beyond. None of the Highest had successfully resisted, and there were rumors that two more interfering Powers had been destroyed. There were some (secret mouths of the Blight?) who welcomed the new stability at the Top, even one based on permanent parasitization.

In fact, the chase down here at the Bottom, the flight of the *Out of Band*

and its pursuers, seemed the only place where the Blight was not completely triumphant. No wonder they were the subject of 10,000 messages an hour.

The geometry of emergence was enormously favorable to *Ølvira*. They had been on the outskirts of the action, but now they had hours headstart on the main fleets. Glimfrelle and Tirolle were busier than they had ever been in their lives, monitoring the fleets' emergence and establishing *Ølvira*'s identity with the other vessels of Commercial Security. Until Scrits and Limmende emerged from the Slowness, Kjet Svensndot was the ranking officer of the organization. Furthermore, he was personally known to most of the commanders. Kjet had never been the admiral type; his Group Captaincy had been a reward for piloting skills, in a Sjandra Kei at peace. He had always been content to defer to his employers. But now . . .

The Group Captain used his ranking status. The Alliance vessels were not pursued. ('Wait till we can all act together,' ordered Svensndot.) Possible game plans bounced back and forth across the emerging fleet, including schemes that assumed HQ was destroyed. With certain commanders, Kjet hinted that this last might be the case, that Limmende's flag ship was in enemy hands, and that the Alliance was somehow just a side effect of that true enemy. Very soon Kjet would be committed to the 'treason' he planned.

The Limmende flag ships and the core of the Blighter fleet came out of the Slowness almost simultaneously. Comm alarms went off across *Ølvira*'s deck as priority mail arrived and passed through the ship's crypto. 'Source: Limmende at HQ. Star Breaker Priority,' said the ship's voice.

Glimfrelle put the message on the main window, and Svensndot felt a chill certainty spread up his neck.

. . . All units are to pursue fleeing vessels. These are the enemy, the killers of our people. WARNING: Masquerades suspected. Destroy any vessels countermanding these orders. Order of Battle and validation codes follow . . .

Order of Battle was simple, even by Commercial Security standards. Limmende wanted them to split up and be gone, staying only long enough to destroy 'masqueraders.' Kjet said to Glimfrelle, 'How about the validation codes?'

The Dirokime seemed his usual self again: 'They're clean. We wouldn't be receiving the message at all unless the sender had today's one-time pad . . . We're beginning to receive queries from the others, Boss. Audio and video channels. They want to know what to do.'

If he hadn't prepared the ground during the last few hours, Kjet's mutiny wouldn't have had a chance. If Commercial Security had been a real military organization, the Limmende order might have been obeyed without question. As it was, the other commanders pondered the questions that Svensndot had raised: At these ranges, video communication was easy and the fleet had one-time ciphers large enough to support enormous amounts of it. Yet 'Limmende' had chosen printed mail for her priority message. It made perfect military sense given that the encryption was correct, but it was also what Svensndot had predicted: The supposed HQ was not quite willing to show its face down here where perfect visual masquerades were not possible. Their commands would be by mail, or evocations that any sharp observer might suspect.

Such a slender thread of reason Kjet and his friends were hanging from.

Kjet eyed the knot of light that represented the Blighter fleet. *It* was suffering from no indecision. None of *its* vessels were straggling back toward safer heights. Whatever commanded there had discipline beyond most human militaries. It would sacrifice everything in its single-minded pursuit of one small starship. *What next, Group Captain?*

Just ahead of that cold smear of light, a single tiny gleam appeared. 'The *Out of Band*!' said Glimfrelle. 'Sixty-five light-years out now.'

'I'm getting encrypted video from them, Boss. The same half-crocked xor pad as before.' He put the signal on the main window without waiting for Kjet's direction.

It was Ravna Bergsndot. The background was a jumble of motion and shouting, the strange human and a Skroderider arguing. Bergsndot was facing away from the pickup and doing her share of shouting. Things looked even worse than Kjet's recollection of the first moments of his ship's emergence.

'It doesn't *matter* just now, I tell you! Let him be. We've got to contact—' she must have seen the signal Glimfrelle was sending back to her. 'They're here! By the Powers, Pham, please—' She waved her hand angrily and turned to the camera. 'Group Captain. We're—'

'I know. We've been out of the surge for hours. We're near the center of the pursuit now.'

She caught her breath. Even with a hundred hours of planning, events were moving too fast for her. *And for me too.* 'That's something,' she said after an instant. 'Everything we said before holds, Group Captain. We need your help. That's the Blight that's coming behind us. Please!'

Svensndot noticed a telltale by the window. Sassy Glimfrelle was retransmitting this to all the fleet they could trust. *Good.* He had talked about the situation with the others these last hours, but it meant something more to see Ravna Bergsndot on the comm, to see someone from Straumli who still survived and needed their help. *You can spend the rest of your life chasing revenge in the Middle Beyond, but all you kill will be the vultures. What's chasing Ravna Bergsndot may be the first cause.*

The Butterflies were long gone, still singing their courage across the Net. Less than one percent of Commercial Security had followed 'Limmende's' order to chase after them. Those were not the problem: it was the ten percent that stayed behind and arrayed themselves with the Blight's forces that bothered Kjet Svensndot. Some of those ships might not be subverted, might simply be loyal to orders they believed. It would be very hard to fire on them.

And there would be fighting, no doubt of that. Maneuvering for conflict while under ultradrive was difficult – if the other side attempted to evade. But the Blight's fleet was unwavering in its pursuit of the *Out of Band*. Slowly, slowly the two fleets were coming to occupy the same volume. At present they were scattered across cubic light-years, but with every jump the Group Captain's Aniara fleet was more finely tuned to the stutter of their quarries' drives. Some ships were actually within a few hundred million kilometers of the enemy – or where the enemy had been or would be. Targeting tactics were set. First fire was only a few hundred seconds away.

'With the Aprahanti gone, we have numerical superiority. A normal enemy would back off now—'

'But of course, that is one thing the Blight fleet is *not*.' It was the red-haired guy who was doing the talking now. It was a good thing Glimfrelle hadn't relayed *his* face to the rest of Svensndot's fleet. The guy acted edgy and alien most of the time. Just now he seemed intent on bashing every idea Svensndot advanced. 'The Blight doesn't care what its losses are as long as it arrives with the upper hand.'

Svensndot shrugged. 'Look, we'll do our best. First fire is one hundred and fifty seconds off. If they don't have any secret advantage, we may win this one.' He looked sharply at the other. 'Or is that your point? Could the Blight—' Stories were still coming down about the Blight's progress across the Top of the Beyond. Without a doubt it was a transhuman intelligence. An unarmed man might be outnumbered by a pack of dogs, yet still defeat them. So might the Blight . . . ?

Pham Nuwen shook his head. 'No, no, no. The Blight's tactics down here will probably be *inferior* to yours. Its great advantage is at the Top, where it can control its slaves like fingers on a hand. Its creatures down here are like badly-synched waldos.' Nuwen frowned at something off camera. 'No, what we have to fear is its strategic cleverness.' His voice suddenly had a detached quality that was more unsettling than the earlier impatience. It wasn't the calm of someone facing up to a threat; it was more the calm of the demented. 'One hundred seconds to contact . . . Group Captain, we have a chance, if you concentrate your forces on the right points.' Ravna floated down from the top of the picture, put one hand on the red-head's shoulder. Godshatter, she said he was, their secret edge against the enemy. Godshatter, a Power's dying message; garbage or treasure, who really knew?

Damn. If the other guys are badly-synched waldos, what does following Pham Nuwen make us? But he motioned Tirolle to mark the targets that Nuwen was saying. Ninety seconds. Decision time. Kjet pointed at the red marks

Tirolle had scattered through the enemy fleet. 'Anything special about those targets, 'Rolle?'

The Dirokime whistled for a moment. Correlations popped up agonizingly slowly on the windows before him. 'The ships he's targetting aren't the biggest or the fastest. It's gonna take extra time to position on them.' Command vessels? 'One other thing. Some of 'em show high real velocities, not natural residuals at all.' Ships with ram drives? Planet busters?

'Hm.' Svensndot looked at the display just a second more. Thirty seconds and Jo Haugen's ship *Lynsnar* would be in contact, but not with one of Nuwen's targets. 'Get on the comm, Glimfrelle. Tell *Lynsnar* to back off, retarget.' Retarget everything.

The lights that were Aniara fleet slid slowly around the core of the Blighter fleet, searching for their new targets. Twenty minutes passed, and not a few arguments with the other captains. Commercial Security was not built for military combat. What had made Kjet Svensndot's appeal successful was also the cause of constant questioning and counter-suggestions. And then there were the threats that came from Owner Limmende's channel: kill the mutineers, death to all those disloyal to the company. The encryption was valid but the tone was totally alien to the mild, profit-oriented Giske Limmende. Everyone could now see that disbelieving Limmende was one correct decision, anyway.

Johanna Haugen was the first to achieve synch with the new targets. Glimfrelle opened the main window on the *Lynsnar*'s data stream: The view was almost natural, a night sky of slowly shifting stars. The target was less than thirty million kilometers from *Lynsnar*, but about a millisecond out of synch. Haugen was arriving just before or just after the other had jumped.

'Drones away,' Haugen's voice said. Now they had a true view of *Lynsnar* from a few meters away, from a camera aboard one of the first drones launched. The ship was barely visible, a darkness obscuring the stars beyond – a great fish in the depths of an endless sea. A fish that was now giving spawn. The picture flickered, *Lynsnar* disappearing and reappearing as the drone lost synch momentarily. A swarm of blue lights spilled from the ship's hold. Weapon drones. The swarm hung by *Lynsnar*, calibrating itself orienting on the enemy.

The light faded from around *Lynsnar* as the drones moved fractionally out of synch in space and time. Tirolle opened a window on a hundred-million klick sphere centered at *Lynsnar*. The target vessel was a red dot that flickered around the sphere like a maddened insect. *Lynsnar* was stalking prey at eight thousand times the speed of light. Sometimes the target disappeared for a second, synch almost lost; other times *Lynsnar* and the target merged for an instant as the two craft spent a tenth of a second at less than a million kilometers remove. What could not be accurately displayed was the disposition of the drones. The spawn diffused on a myriad trajectories, their sensors extended for sign of the enemy ship.

'What about the target, is it swarming back? Do you need backup?' said Svensndot. Tirolle gave a Dirokime shrug. What they were watching was three light-years away. No way he could know.

But Jo Haugen replied, 'I don't think my bogie is swarming. I've lost only five drones, no more'n you'd expect from near misses. We'll see—' She paused, but *Lynsnar*'s trace and signal remained strong. Kjet looked out the other windows. Five of Aniara were already engaged and three had completed swarm deploy. Nuwen looked on silently from *Out of Band*. The godshatter had had its way, and now Kjet and his people were committed.

And now good news and bad came in very fast:

'Got him!' from Jo Haugen. The red dot in *Lynsnar*'s swarm was no more. It had passed within a few thousand kilometers of one of the drones. In the milliseconds necessary to compute a new jump, the drone had discovered its presence and detonated. Even that would not have been fatal if the target had jumped before the blast front hit it; there had been several near misses in earlier seconds. This time the jump did not reach commit in time. A mini-star was born, one whose light would be years in reaching the rest of the battle volume.

Glimfrelle gave a rasping whistle, an untranslatable curse. 'We just lost *Ablsndot* and *Holder*, Boss. Their target must have counter-swarmed.'

'Send in *Gliwing* and *Trance*.' Something in the back of his head curled up in a knot of horror. These were his friends who were dying. Kjet had seen death before, but never like this. In police action no one took lethal chances except in a rescue. And yet . . . he turned from the field summary to order more ships on a target that had acquired defending vessels. Tirolle was moving in others on his own. Ganging up a few nonessential targets might lose in the long run, but in the short term . . . the enemy was being hurt. For the first time since the fall of Sjandra Kei, Commercial Security was hurting someone back.

Haugen: 'Powers, that guy was moving! Secondary drone got EM spectrum on the kill. Target was going 15,000 kps true speed.' A rocket bomb ramping up? Damn. They should be postponing those till *after* they controlled the battlefield.

Tirolle: 'More kills, far side of battle volume. The enemy is repositioning. Somehow they've guessed which we're after—'

Glimfrelle: *Triumph whistle*. 'Get 'em, get 'em – oops. Boss, I think Limmende has figured we're coordinating things—'

A new window had opened over Tirolle's post. It showed the five million kilometers around *Ølvira*. Two other ships were there now: the window identified them as Limmende's flag and one of the vessels that had not responded to Svensndot's recruiting.

There was an instant of stillness on *Ølvira*'s command deck. The voices of triumph and panic coming from the rest of the fleet seemed suddenly far away. Svensndot and his crew looked at death close up. 'Tirolle! How long till swarm—'

'They're on us already – just missed a drone by ten milliseconds.'

'Tirolle! Finish running current engagements. Glimfrelle, tell *Lynsnar* and *Trance* to chain command if we lose contact.' Those ships had already spent their drones, and Jo Haugen was known to all the other captains.

Then the thought was gone, and he was busy coordinating *Ølvira*'s own battle swarm. The local tactics window showed the cloud dissipating, taking on colors coded by whether they were lagging or leading relative to *Ølvira*.

Their two attackers had matched pseudospeeds perfectly. Ten times per second all three ships jumped a tiny fraction of a light-year. Like rocks skipping across the surface of a pond, they appeared in real space in perfectly measured hops – and the distance between them at every emergence was less than five million kilometers. The only thing that separated them now were millisecond differences in jump times and the fact the light itself could not pass between them in the brief time they spent at each jump point.

Three actinic flashes lit the deck, casting shadows back from Svensndot and the Dirokimes. It was second-hand light, the display's emergency signal of nearby detonation. *Run like hell* was the message any rational person should take from that awful light. It would be easy enough to break synch . . . and lose tactical control of Aniara fleet. Tirolle and Glimfrelle bent their heads away from the local window, shying from the glare of nearby death. Their whistling voices scarcely broke cadence, and the commands from *Ølvira* to the others continued. There were dozens of other battles going on out there. Just now *Ølvira* was the only source of precision and control available to their side. Every second they remained on station meant protection and advantage to Aniara. Breaking off would mean minutes of chaos till *Lynsnar* or *Trance* could pick up control.

Nearly two thirds of Pham Nuwen's targets were destroyed now. The price had been high, half of Svensndot's friends. The enemy had lost much to protect those targets, yet much of its fleet survived.

An unseen hand smashed *Ølvira*, driving Svensndot hard against his combat harness. The lights went out, even the glow from the windows. Then dim red light came from the floor. The Dirokimes were silhouetted by one small monitor. 'Rolle whistled softly, 'We're out of the game, Boss, least while it counts. I didn't know you could get misses that near.'

Maybe it wasn't a miss. Kjet scrambled out of his harness and boosted across the room to float head-down over the tiny monitor. *Maybe we're already dead.* Somewhere very close by a drone had detonated, the wave front reaching *Ølvira* before she jumped. The concussion had been the outer part of the ship's hull exploding as it absorbed the soft-x-ray component of the enemy ordnance. He stared at the red letters marching slowly across the damage display. Most likely, the electronics was permanently dead; chances were they had all received a fatal dose of gamma. The smell of burnt insulation floated across the room on the ventilator's breeze.

'*Iiya!* Look at that. Five nanoseconds more and we wouldn't have been clipped at all. We actually jumped *after* the front hit!' And somehow the electronics had survived long enough to complete the jump. The gamma flux through the command deck had been 200 rem, nothing that would slow them down over the next few hours, and easily managed by a ship's surgeon. As for the surgeon and all the rest of the *Ølvira*'s automation . . .

Tirolle typed several long queries at the box; there was no voice recognition left. Several seconds passed before a response marched across the screen. 'Central automation suspended. Display management suspended. Drive computation suspended.' Tirolle dug an elbow at his brother. 'Hei, 'Frelle, it looks like '*Vira* managed a clean disconnect. We can bring most of this back!'

Dirokimes were known for being drifty optimists, but in this case Tirolle wasn't far from the truth. Their encounter with the drone bomb had been a one-in-a-billion thing, the tiniest fraction of an exposure. Over the next hour and a half the Dirokimes ran reboots off the monitor's hardened processor, bringing up first one utility and then another. Some things were beyond recovery: parsing intelligence was gone from the comm automation, and the ultradrive spines on one side of the craft were partially melted. (Absurdly, the burning smell had been a vagrant diagnostic, something that should have been disabled along with all the rest of *Ølvira*'s automation.) They were far behind the Blighter fleet.

. . . and there *was* still a Blighter fleet. The knot of enemy fights was smaller than before, but on the same unwavering trajectory. The battle was long over. What was left of Commercial Security was scattered across four light-years of abandoned battlefield; they had started the battle with numerical superiority. If they'd fought properly, they might have won. Instead they'd destroyed the vessels with significant real velocities – and knocked out only about half the others. Some of the largest vessels survived. These outnumbered the corresponding Aniara survivors by more than four to one. The Blight could have easily destroyed all that remained of Commercial Security. But that would have meant a detour from the pursuit, and that pursuit was the one constant in the enemy's behavior.

Tirolle and Glimfrelle spent hours reestablishing communications and trying to discover who had died and who might be rescued. Five ships had lost all drive capability but still had surviving crew. Some ships had been hit at known locations, and Svensndot dispatched vessels with drone swarms to find the wrecks. Ship-to-ship warfare was a sanitary, intellectual exercise for most of the survivors, but the rubble and the destruction were as real as in any ground war, only spread over a trillion times more space.

*

345

Finally the time for miracle rescues and sad discoveries was passed. The SjK commanders gathered on a common channel to decide a common future. It might better have been a wake – for Sjandra Kei and Aniara fleet. Partway through the meeting a new window appeared, a view onto the bridge of the *Out of Band*. Ravna Bergsndot watched the proceedings silently. The erstwhile 'godshatter' was nowhere in evidence.

'What more to do?' said Johanna Haugen. 'The damn Butterflies are long gone.'

'Are we sure we have rescued everyone?' asked Jan Trenglets. Svensndot bit back an angry reply. The commander of *Trance* had become a recording loop on that issue. He had lost too many friends in the battle; all the rest of his life Jan Trenglets would live with nightmares of ships slowly dying in the deep night.

'We've accounted for everything, even to vapor,' Haugen spoke as gently as the words allowed. 'The question is where to go now.'

Ravna made a small throat-clearing sound. 'Gentlemen and ladies, if—'

Trenglets looked up at her transceived image. All his hurt transformed into a blaze of anger. 'We're not *your* gentlemen, slut! You're not some princess we happily die for. You deserve our deadly fire now, nothing more.'

The woman shrank from Trenglets' rage. 'I—'

'*You* put us into this suicidal battle,' shouted Trenglets. 'You made us attack secondary targets. And then you did nothing to help. The Blight is locked on you like a dumshark on a squid. If you had just altered your course the tiniest fraction, you could have thrown the Blighters off our path.'

'I doubt that would have helped, sir,' said Ravna. 'The Blight seems most interested in where we're bound.' The solar system a few dozen light-years beyond the *Out of Band*. The fugitives would arrive there just over two days before their pursuers.

Jo Haugen shrugged. 'You must realize what your friend's crazy battle plan has done. If we had attacked rationally, the enemy would be a fraction of its present size. If it chose to continue, we might have been able to protect you at this, this Tines' world.' She seemed to taste the strange name, wondering at its meaning. 'Now . . . no way am I going to chase them there. What's left of the enemy could wipe us out.' She glanced at Svensndot's viewpoint. Kjet forced himself to look back. No matter who might blame the *Out of Band*, it had been Group Captain Kjet Svensndot's word that had persuaded the fleet to fight as they did. Aniara's sacrifice had been ill-spent, and he wondered that Haugen and Trenglets and the others talked to him at all now. 'Suggest we continue the business meeting later. Rendezvous in one thousand seconds, Kjet.'

'I'll be ready.'

'Good.' Jo cut the link without saying anything more to Ravna Bergsndot. Seconds later, Trenglets and the other commanders were gone. It was just Svensndot and the two Dirokimes – and Ravna Bergsndot looking out her window from the *Out of Band*.

Finally, Bergsndot said, 'When I was a little girl on Herte, sometimes we would play kidnappers and Commercial Security. I always dreamed of being rescued from fates worse than death by your company.'

Kjet smiled bleakly, 'Well, you got the rescue attempt,' and you're not even a currently subscribed customer. 'This was far the biggest gun fight we've ever been in.'

'I'm sorry, Kje – Group Captain.'

He looked into her dark features. A lass from Sjandra Kei, down to the violet eyes. No way this could be a simulation, not here. He had bet everything that she was not; he still believed she was not. Yet – 'What does your friend say about all this?' Pham Nuwen had not been seen since his so-impressive godshatter act at the beginning of the battle.

Ravna's glance shifted to something off-camera. 'He's not saying much, Group Captain. He's wandering around even more upset than your Captain Trenglets. Pham remembers being absolutely convinced he was demanding the right thing, but now he can't figure out why it was right.'

'Hmm.' A little late for second thoughts. 'What are you going to do now? Haugen is right, you know. It would be useless suicide for us to follow the Blighters to your destination. I daresay it's useless suicide for you, too. You'll arrive maybe fifty-five hours before them. What can you do in that time?'

Ravna Bergsndot looked back at him, and her expression slowly collapsed into sobbing grief. 'I don't know. I . . . don't know.' She shook her head, her face hidden behind her hands and a sweep of black hair. Finally she looked up and brushed back her hair. Her voice was calm but very quiet.

'I . . . don't know. But we are going ahead. It's what we came for. Things could still work out . . . You know there's something down there, something the Blight wants desperately. Maybe fifty-five hours is enough to figure out what it is and tell the Net. And . . . and we'll still have Pham's godshatter.'

Your worst enemy? Quite possibly this Pham Nuwen was a construct of the Powers. He certainly *looked* like something built from a second-hand description of humanity. But how can you tell godshatter from simple nuttery?

She shrugged, as if acknowledging the doubts – and accepting them. 'So what will you and Commercial Security do?'

'There is no Commercial Security anymore. Virtually all our customers got shot out from under us. Now we've killed our company's owner – or at least destroyed her ship and those supporting her. We are Aniara Fleet now. 'It was the official name chosen at the fleet conference just ended. There was a certain grim pleasure in embracing it, the ghost from before Sjandra Kei and before Nyjora, from the earliest times of the human race. For they were truly cast away now, from their worlds and their customers and their former leaders. One hundred ships bound for . . . 'We talked it over. A few still wanted to follow you to Tines' world. Some of the crews want to return to the Middle Beyond, spend the rest of their lives killing Butterflies. The majority want to start the races of Sjandra Kei over again, some place where we won't be noticed, some place where no one cares if we live.'

And the one thing everyone agreed on was that Aniara must be split no further, must make no further sacrifices outside of itself. Once that was clear, it was easy to decide what to do. In the wake of the Great Surge, this part of the Bottom was an incredible froth of Slowness and Beyond. It would be centuries before the zonographic vessels from above had reasonable maps of the new interface. Hidden away in the folds and interstices were worlds fresh from the Slowness, worlds where Sjandra Kei could be born again. *Ny Sjandra Kei?*

He looked across the bridge at Tirolle and Glimfrelle. They were busy bringing the main navigation processors out of suspension. That wasn't absolutely necessary for the rendezvous with *Lynsnar*, but things would be a lot more convenient if both ships could maneuver. The brothers seemed oblivious to Kjet's conversation with Ravna. And maybe they weren't paying attention. In a way, the Aniara decision meant more to them than to the humans of the fleet: No one doubted that millions of humans survived in the Beyond (and who knew how many human worlds might still exist in the Slowness, distant cousins of Nyjora, distant children of Old Earth). But this side of the Transcend, the Dirokimes of Aniara were the only ones that existed. The dream habitats of Sjandra Kei were gone, and with them the race. There were at least a thousand Dirokimes left aboard Aniara, pairs of sisters and brothers scattered across a hundred vessels. These were the most adventurous of their race's latter days, and now they were faced with their greatest challenge. The two on *Ølvira* had already been scouting among the survivors, looking for friends and dreaming a new reality.

Ravna listened solemnly to his explanations. 'Group Captain, zonography is a tedious thing . . . and your ships are near their limits. In this froth you might search for years and not find a new home.'

'We're taking precautions. We're abandoning all our ships except the ones with ramscoop and coldsleep capability. We'll operate in coordinated nets; no one should be lost for more than a few years.' He shrugged. 'And if we never find what we seek—' *if we die between the stars as our life support finally fails* '—well then, we will have still lived true to our name.' *Aniara.* 'I think we have a chance.' More than can be said for you.

Ravna nodded slowly. 'Yes, well. It . . . helps me to know that.'

They talked a few minutes more, Tirolle and Glimfrelle joining in. They had been at the center of something vast, but as usual with the affairs of the

Powers, no one knew quite what had happened, nor the result of the strivings.

'Rendezvous *Lynsnar* two hundred seconds,' said the ship's voice.

Ravna heard it, nodded. She raised her hand. 'Fare you well, Kjet Svensndot and Tirolle and Glimfrelle.'

The Dirokimes whistled back the common farewell, and Svensndot raised his hand. The window on Ravna Bergsndot closed.

. . . Kjet Svensndot remembered her face all the rest of his life, though in later years it seemed more and more to be the same as Ølvira's.

PART THREE

37

'Tines' world. I can *see* it, Pham!'

The main window showed a true view upon the system: a sun less than two hundred million kilometers away, daylight across the command deck. The positions of identified planets were marked with blinking red arrows. But one of those – just twenty million kilometers off – was labeled 'terrestrial.' Coming off an interstellar jump, you couldn't get positioning much better than that.

Pham didn't reply, just glared out the window as if there were something wrong with what they were seeing. Something had broken in him after the battle with the Blight. He'd been so sure of his godshatter – and so bewildered by the consequences. Afterwards he had retreated more than ever. Now he seemed to think that if they moved fast enough, the surviving enemy could do them no harm. More than ever he was suspicious of Blueshell and Greenstalk, as if somehow they were greater threats than the ships that still pursued.

'*Damn*,' Pham said finally. 'Look at the relative velocity.' Seventy kilometers per second.

Position matching was no problem, but 'Matching velocities will cost us time, Sir Pham.'

Pham's stare turned on Blueshell. 'We talked this out with the locals three weeks ago, remember? You managed the burn.'

'And you checked my work, Sir Pham. This must be another nav system bug . . . though I didn't expect anything was wrong in simple ballistics.' A sign inverted, seventy kicks per second closing velocity instead of zero. Blueshell drifted toward the secondary console.

'Maybe,' said Pham. 'Just now, I want you off the deck, Blueshell.'

'But I can help! We should be contacting Jefri, and rematching velocities, and—'

'*Get off the deck, Blueshell.* I don't have time to watch you anymore.' Pham dived across the intervening space and was met by Ravna, just short of the Rider.

She floated between the two, talking fast. 'It's okay, Pham. He'll go.' She brushed her hand across one of Blueshell's wildly vibrating fronds. After a second, Blueshell wilted. 'I'll go. I'll go.' She kept an encouraging touch on him – and kept herself between him and Pham as the Skroderider made a dejected exit.

When the Rider was gone, she turned to Pham. 'Couldn't it have been a nav bug, Pham?'

The other didn't seem to hear the question. The instant the hatch had closed, he had returned to the command console. *OOB*'s latest estimate put the Blight's arrival less than fifty-three hours away. And now they must waste time redoing a velocity match supposedly accomplished three weeks earlier. 'Somebody, something, screwed us over . . .' Pham was muttering, even as he finished with the control sequence. 'Maybe it was a bug. This next damn burn is going to be as manual as it can be.' Acceleration alarms echoed down the core of the *OOB*. Pham flipped through monitor windows, searching for loose items that might be big enough to be danger- ous. 'You tie down too.' He reached out to override the five minute timer.

Ravna dived back across the deck, unfolding the free-fall saddle into a seat and strapping in. She heard Pham speaking on the general announce channel, warning of the timer override. Then the impulse drive cut in, a lazy pressure back into the webbing. Four tenths of a gee – all the poor *OOB* could still manage.

When Pham said manual, he meant it. The main window appeared to be bore-centered now. The view didn't drift at the whim of the pilot, and there were no helpful legends and schematics. As much as possible, they were seeing true view along *OOB*'s main axis. Peripheral windows were held in fixed geometry with main. Pham's eyes flickered from one to another as his hands played over the command board. As near as could be, he was flying by his own senses and trusting no one else.

But Pham still had use for the ultradrive. They were twenty million klicks off target, a submicroscopic jump. Pham Nuwen fiddled with the drive parameters, trying to make an accurate jump smaller than the standard interval. Every few seconds the sunlight would shift a fraction, coming first over Ravna's left shoulder and then her right. It made reestablishing comm with Jefri nearly impossible.

Suddenly the window below their feet was filled by a world, huge and gibbous, blue and swirling white. The Tines' world was as Jefri Olsndot advertised, a normal terrestrial planet. After the months aspace and the loss of Sjandra Kei, the sight caught Ravna short. Ocean, the world was mostly ocean, but near the terminator there were the darker shades of land. A single tiny moon was visible beyond the limb.

Pham sucked in his breath. 'It's about ten thousand kilometers off. Perfect. Except we're closing at seventy klicks per second.' Even as she watched, the world seemed to grow, falling toward them. Pham watched it for a few seconds more. 'Don't worry, we're going to miss, fly right past the, um, north limb.'

The globe swelled below them, eclipsing the moon. She had always loved the appearance of Herte at Sjandra Kei. But that world had smaller oceans and was criss-crossed with Dirokime Paths. This place was as beautiful as Relay, and seemed truly untouched. The small polar cap was in sunlight, and she could follow the coastline that came south from it toward the terminator. *I'm seeing the northwest coast. Jefri's right down there!* Ravna reached for her keyboard, asking the ship to attempt both ultrawave comm and a radio link.

'Ultrawave contact,' she said after a second.

'What does it say?'

'It's garbled. Probably just a ping response,' acknowledgment to *OOB*'s signal, the most that had been possible since the surge. Jefri was housed very near the ship these days; sometimes she had gotten responses almost immediately, even during his night time. It would be good to talk to him again even if . . .

Tines' World filled half the windows now, its limb a barely curving horizon. Sky colors stood before them, fading to the black of space. Icecap and icebergs showed detail within detail against the sea. She could see cloud shadows. She followed the coast southwards, islands and peninsulas so closely fit that she could not be sure of one from the other. Blackish mountains and black-striped glaciers. Green and brown valleys. She tried to remember the geography they had learned from Jefri. *Hidden Island?* But there were so many islands.

'I have radio contact from the planet's surface,' came the ship's voice. Simultaneously a blinking arrow pointed at a spot just in from the coast. 'Do you want the audio in real time?'

'Yes. Yes!' said Ravna, then punched at her keyboard when the ship did not respond immediately.

'Hei, Ravna. Oh, Ravna!' The little boy's voice bounced excitement around the deck. He sounded just as she had imagined.

Ravna keyed in a request for two-way. They were less than five thousand klicks from Jefri now, even if they were sweeping by at seventy kilometers per second. Plenty close enough for a radio conversation. 'Hei, Jefri!' she said. 'We're here at last, but we need—' *We need all the cooperation your four-legged friends can give us. How to say that quickly and effectively?*

But the boy on the ground already had an agenda:'—need help *now*, Ravna! The Woodcarvers are attacking *now*.'

There was a thumping, as if the transmitter was bouncing around. Another voice spoke, high-pitched and weirdly inarticulate. 'This Steel, Ravna. Jefri right. Woodcarver—' the almost human voice dissolved into a hissing gobble. After a moment she heard Jefri's voice: ' "Ambush," the word is "ambush." '

'Yes . . . Woodcarver has done big, big ambush. They all around now. We die in hours if you not help.'

353

Woodcarver had never wanted to be a warrior. But ruling for half a thousand years requires a range of skills, and she had learned about making war. Some of that – such as trusting to staff – she had temporarily *un*learned these last few days. There had indeed been an ambush on Margrum Climb, but not the one that Lord Steel had planned.

She looked across the tented field at Vendacious. That pack was half-hidden by noise baffles, but she could see he wasn't so jaunty as before. Being put to the question will loosen anyone's control . . . Vendacious knew his survival now depended on her keeping a promise. Yet . . . it was awful to think that Vendacious would live after he had killed and betrayed so many. She realized that two of herself were keening rage, lips curled back from clenched teeth. Her puppies huddled back from threats unseen. The tented area stank of sweat and the mindnoise of too many people in too small a space. It took a real effort of will to calm herself. She licked the puppies, and daydreamed peaceful thoughts for a moment.

Yes, she would keep her promises to him. And maybe it would be worth the price. Vendacious had only speculations about Steel's inner secrets, but he had learned far more about Steel's tactical situation than the other side could have guessed. Vendacious had known just where the Flenserists were hiding and in what numbers. Steel's folk had been overconfident about their super guns and their secret traitor. When Woodcarver's troops surprised them, victory had been easy – and now the Queen had some of the marvelous guns.

From behind the hills, those cannons were still pounding away, eating through the stocks of ammunition the captured gunners had revealed. Vendacious the traitor had cost her much, but Vendacious the prisoner might yet bring her victory.

'Woodcarver?' It was Scrupilo. She waved him closer. Her chief gunner edged out of the sun, sitting down an intimate twenty-five feet away. Battle conditions had blown away all notions of decorum.

Scrupilo's mind noise was an anxious jumble. He looked by parts exhausted and exhilarated and discouraged. 'It's safe to advance up the castle hill, your majesty,' he said. 'Answering fire is almost extinguished. Parts of the castle walls have been breached. There is an end to castles here, my queen. Even our own poor cannons would make it so.'

She bobbed agreement. Scrupilo spent most of his time with Dataset in learning to *make* – cannons in particular. Woodcarver spent her time learning what those inventions ultimately created. By now she knew far more than even Johanna about the social effects of weapons, from the most primitive to ones so strange that they seemed not weapons at all. A thousand million times, castle technologies had fallen to things like cannon; why should her world be different?

'We'll move up then—'

From beyond the shade of the tent there was a faint whistle, a rare, incoming round. She folded the puppies within herself, and paused a moment. Twenty yards away, Vendacious shrank down in a great cower. But when it came, the explosion was a muffled thump above them on the hill. *It might even have been one of our own.* 'Now our troops must take advantage of the destruction. I want Steel to know that the old games of ransom and torture will only win him worse.' *We'll most likely win the starship and the child.* The question was, would either be alive when they got them? She hoped Johanna would never know the threats and the risks she planned for the next few hours.

'Yes, majesty.' But Scrupilo made no move to depart, and suddenly seemed more bedraggled and worried than ever. 'Woodcarver, I fear . . .'

'What? We have the tide. We must rush to sail on it.'

'Yes, majesty . . . But while we move forward, there are serious dangers coming up on our flanks and rear. The enemy's far scouts and the fires.'

Scrupilo was right. The Flenserists who operated behind her lines were deadly. There weren't many of them; the enemy troops at Margrum Climb had been mostly killed or dispersed. The few that ate at Woodcarver's flanks were equipped with ordinary crossbows and axes . . . but they were extraordinarily well-coordinated. And their tactics were brilliant; she saw the snouts and tines of Flenser himself in that brilliance. Somehow her evil child lived. Like a plague of years past, he was slipping back upon the world. Given time, those guerrilla packs would seriously hurt Woodcarver's ability to supply her forces. Given time. Two of her stood and looked Scrupilo in the eyes, emphasizing the point: 'All the more reason to move now, my friend. We are the ones far from home. We are the ones with limited numbers and food. If we don't win soon, then we will be cut up a bit at a time.' *Flensed.*

Scrupilo stood up, nodding submission. 'That's what Peregrine says, too. And Johanna wants to chase right through the castle walls . . . But there's something else, your majesty. Even if we must lunge all forward: I worked for a ten of tendays, using every clue I could understand from Dataset, to make our cannon. Majesty, *I know* how hard it is to do such. Yet the guns we captured on Margrum have three times the range and one quarter the weight. *How could they do it?*' There were chords of anger and humiliation in his voice. 'The traitor,' Scrupilo jerked a snout in the direction of Vendacious, 'thinks they may have Johanna's brother, but Johanna says they have nothing like Dataset. Majesty, Steel has some advantage we don't yet know.'

Even the executions were not helping. Day by day, Steel felt his rage growing. Alone on the parapet, he whipped back and forth upon himself, barely conscious of anything but his anger. Not since he had been under

355

Flenser's knife had the anger been such a radiant thing. *Get back control before he cuts you more*, the voice of some early Steel seemed to say.

He hung on the thought, pulled himself together. He stared down a bloody drool and tasted ashes. Three of his shoulders were streaked with tooth cuts – he'd been hurting himself, another habit Flenser had cured him of long ago. *Hurt outwards, never toward yourself.* Steel licked mechanically at the gashes and walked closer to the parapet's edge:

At the horizon, gray-black haze obscured the sea and the islands. The last few days, the summer winds had been a hot breath, tasting of smoke. Now the winds were like fire themselves, whipping past the castle, carrying ash and smoke. All last dayaround the far side of Bitter Gorge had been a haze of fire, today he could see the hillsides: they were black and brown, crowned with smoke that swept toward the sea's horizon. There were often brush and forest fires in the High Summer. But this year, as if nature was a godly pack of war, the fires had been everywhere. The wretched guns had done it. And this year he couldn't retreat to the cool of Hidden Island and leave the coastlings to suffer.

Steel ignored his smarting shoulders and paced the stones more thoughtfully, almost analytical for a change. The creature Vendacious had not stayed bought; he had turned traitor to his treason. Steel had anticipated that Vendacious might be discovered; he had other spies who should have reported such a thing. But there had been no sign . . . until the disaster at Margrum Climb. Now the twist of Vendacious's knife had turned all his plans on their heads. Woodcarver would be here very soon, and not as a victim.

Who would have guessed that he would really need the Spacers to rescue him from Woodcarver? He had worked so hard to confront the Southerners before Ravna arrived. But now he did need that help from the sky – and it was more than five hours away. Steel almost slipped back into rage state at the thought. In the end, would all the cozening of Amdijefri be for nothing? *Oh, when this is over, how much will I enjoy killing those two.* More than any of the others, they deserved death. They had caused so much inconvenience. They had consistently required his kindliest behavior, as though *they* ruled *him.* They had showered him with more insolence than ten thousand normal subjects.

From the castle yard there was the sound of laboring packs, straining winches, the screech and groan of rock being moved about. The professional core of Flenser's Empire survived. Given a few more hours, the breaches in the walls would be repaired and new guns would be brought in from the north. *And the grand scheme can still succeed. As long as I am together, no matter what else is lost, it can succeed.*

Almost lost in the racket, he heard the click of claws on the inward steps. Steel drew back, turned all heads toward the sound. Shreck? But Shreck would have announced himself first. Then he relaxed; there was only one set of claw sounds. It was a singleton coming up the stairs.

Flenser's member cleared the steps and bowed to Steel, an incomplete gesture without other members to mirror it. The member's radio cloak shone clean and dark. The army was in awe of those cloaks, and of the singletons and duos who seemed smarter than the brightest pack. Even Steel's lieutenants who understood what the cloaks really were – even Shreck – were cautious and tentative around them. And now Steel needed the Flenser Fragment more than anyone, more than *anything* except Starfolk gullibility. 'What news?'

'Leave to sit?' Was the sardonic Flenser smile behind that request?

'Granted,' snapped Steel.

The singleton eased itself onto the stones. But Steel saw when the other winced; the Fragment had been dispersed across the Domain for almost twenty days now. Except for brief periods, he had been wrapped in the radio cloaks that whole time. Dark and golden torture. Steel had seen this member without its cloak, when it was bathed. Its pelt was rubbed raw at shoulder and haunch, where the weight of the radio was greatest. Bleeding sores had opened at the center of the bald spots. Alone without its cloak, the mindless singleton had blabbered its pain. Steel enjoyed those sessions, even if this one was not especially verbal. It was almost as if he, Steel, were now the One who Teaches with a Knife, and Flenser were his pupil.

The singleton was silent for a moment. Steel could hear its ill-concealed panting. 'The last dayaround has gone well, my lord.'

'Not here! We've lost almost all our cannon. We're trapped inside these walls.' And the starfolk may arrive too late.

'I mean out there.' The singleton poked its nose toward the open spaces beyond the parapet. 'Your scouts are well-trained, my lord, and have some bright commanders. Right now, I am spread round Woodcarver's rear and flanks.' The singleton made its part of a laughing gesture. '"Rear and flanks." Funny. To me Woodcarver's entire army is like a single enemy pack. Our Attack Infantries are like tines on my own paws. We are cutting the Queen deep, my lord. I set the fire in Bitter Gorge. Only I could see exactly where it was spreading, exactly how to kill with it. In another four dayarounds there will be nothing left of the Queen's supplies. She will be ours.'

'Too long, if we're dead this afternoon.'

'Yes.' The singleton cocked its head at Steel. *He's laughing at me.* Just like all those times under Flenser's knife when a problem would be posed and death was the penalty for failure. 'But Ravna and company should be back here in five hours, no?' Steel nodded. 'Well, I guarantee you that will be hours ahead of Woodcarver's main assault. You have Amdijefri's confidence. It seems you need only advance and compress your previous schedule. If Ravna is sufficiently desperate—'

'The starfolk are desperate. I know that.' Ravna might mask her precise motives, but her desperation was clear. 'And if you can slow Woodcarver—' Steel settled all of himself down to concentrate on the scheming at hand. He was half-conscious of his fears retreating. Planning was always a comfort 'The problem is that we have to do two things now, and perfectly coordinated. Before, it was simply a matter of *feigning* a siege and tricking the starship into our castle's Jaws.' He turned a head in the direction of the courtyard. The stone dome over the landed starship had been in place since midspring. It showed some artillery damage now, the marble facing chipped away, but it hadn't taken direct hits. Beside it lay the field of the Jaws: large enough to accept the rescue ship, but surrounded by pillars of stone, the teeth of the Jaws. With the proper use of gunpowder, the teeth would fall on the rescuers. That would be a last resort, if they didn't kill and capture the humans as they came out to meet dear Jefri. That scheme had been lovingly honed over many tendays, aided by Amdijefri's admissions about human psychology and his knowledge of how spaceships normally land. But now: '—Now we really need their help. What I ask them must do double duty, to fool them and to destroy Woodcarver.'

'Hard to do all at once,' agreed the Cloak. 'Why not play it in two steps, the first more or less undeceitful: Have them destroy Woodcarver, *then* worry about taking them over?'

Steel clicked a tine thoughtfully on stone. 'Yes. Trouble is, if they see too much . . . They can't possibly be as naïve as Jefri. He says that humankind has a history that includes castles and warfare. If they fly around too much, they'll see things that Jefri never saw, or never understood . . . Maybe I could get them to land inside the castle and mount weapons on the walls. We'll have them hostage the moment that they stand between our Jaws. *Damn.* That would take some clever work with Amdijefri.' The bliss of abstract planning foundered for a moment on rage. 'It's getting harder and harder for me to deal with those two.'

'They're both wholly puppies, for Pack's sake.' The Fragment paused a second. 'Of course, Amdiranifani may have more raw intelligence than any pack I've ever seen. You think he may even be smart enough to see past his *childishness*,' he used the Samnorsk word, 'and see the deception?'

'No, not that. I have their necks in my jaws, and they still don't see it. You're right, Tyrathect; they do love me.' *And how I hate them for it.* 'When I'm around him, the mantis thing is all over me, close enough to cut my throat or poke out my eyes, but hugging and petting. And expecting me to love him back. Yes, they believe everything I say, but the price is accepting unending insolence.'

'Be cool, dear student. The heart of manipulation is to empathize without being touched.' The Fragment stopped, as always, just short of the brink. But this time, Steel felt himself hissing at the words even before he was consciously aware of his reaction.

'Don't . . . lecture . . . *me!* You are *not* Flenser. You are a fragment. Shit! You are a fragment of a fragment now. A word and you will be cut up, dead in a thousand pieces.' He tried to suppress the trembling that spread through his members. *Why haven't I killed him before now? I hate Flenser more than anything in the world, and it would be so easy.* Yet the fragment was always so indispensable, somehow the only thing between Steel and failure. And he *was* under Steel's control.

And the singleton was doing a very good terrified cower. 'Sit up, you! Give me your counsel and not your lectures, and you will live . . . Whatever the reason, it's impossible for me to carry on the charade with these puppies. Perhaps for a few minutes at a time I can do it, or if there are other packs to keep them away from me, but none of this unending loving. Another hour of that and I – I know I'll start killing them. So. I want you to talk with Amdijefri. Explain the "situation." Explain—'

'But—' The singleton was looking at him in astonishment.

'I'll be watching; I'm not giving up those two to your possession. Just handle the close diplomacy.'

The Fragment drooped, the pain in its shoulders undisguised. 'If that is your wish, my lord.'

Steel showed all his teeth. 'It is indeed. Just remember, I'll be present for everything important, especially direct radio communication.' He waved the singleton off the parapet. 'Now go and cuddle up to the children; learn something of self-control yourself.'

After the Cloak was gone, he called Shreck up to the parapet. The next few hours were spent touring the defenses and planning with his staff. Steel was very surprised how much clearing up the puppy problem improved his quality of mind. His advisors seemed to pick up on it, relaxed to the point of offering substantive suggestions. Where the breaches in the walls could not be repaired, they would build deadfalls. The cannon from the northern shops would arrive before the end of the dayaround, and one of Shreck's people had worked out an alternate plan for food and water resupply. Reports from the far scouts showed steady progress, a withering of the enemy's rear; they would lose most of their ammunition before they reached Starship Hill. Even now there was scarcely any shot falling on the hill.

As the sun rose in the south, Steel was back on the parapets, scheming on just what to say to the Starfolk.

This was almost like earlier days, when plans went well and success was wondrous yet achievable. And yet . . . at the back of his mind all the hours since talking with the singleton, there had been the little claws of fear. Steel had the appearance of ruling. The Flenser Fragment gave the appearance of following. But even though it was spread across miles, the pack seemed more together than ever before. Oh, in earlier times, the Fragment often pretended equilibrium, but its internal tension always showed. Lately it seemed self-satisfied, almost . . . smug. The Flenser Fragment was

359

responsible for the Domain's forces south of Starship Hill, and after today –
after Steel had *forced* the responsibility upon him – the Cloaks would be
with Amdijefri every day. Never mind that the motivation had come from
within Steel. Never mind that the Fragment was in an obvious state of
agonized exhaustion. In its full genius, the Great One could have charmed a
forest wolf into thinking Flenser its queen. *And do I really know what he's
saying to the packs beyond my hearing? Could my spies be feeding me lies about
him?*

Now that he had a moment away from immediate concerns, these little
claws dug deeper. *I need him, yes. But the margin for error is smaller now.*
After a moment, he grated a happy chord, accepting the risk. If necessary,
he would use what he had learned with the second set of cloaks, something
he had artfully concealed from Flenser Tyrathect. If necessary, the Fragment
would find that death can be *radio* swift.

Even as he flew the velocity match, Pham was working the ultradrive. This
would save them hours of fly back time, but it was a chancy game, one the
ship had never been designed for. *OOB* bounced all around the solar
system. One really lucky jump was all they needed, and one really unlucky
jump, *into* the planet, would kill them – a good reason why this game was
not normally played.

After hours of hacking the flight automation, of playing ultradrive
roulette, poor Pham's hands were faintly trembling. Whenever Tines'
world came back into view – often no more than a far point of blue light –
he would glare for a second at it. Ravna could see the doubts rising within
him: His memories told him he should be good with low-tech automation,
yet some of the *OOB* primitives were almost impenetrable. Or maybe his
memories of competence, of the Qeng Ho, were cheap fakes.

'The Blighter fleet. How long?' asked Pham.

Greenstalk was watching the nav window from the Riders' cabin. It was
the fifth time the question had been asked in the last hour, yet her voice
came back calm and patient. Maybe the repeated questions even seemed a
natural thing. 'Range forty-nine light-years. Estimated time of arrival forty-
eight hours. Seven more ships have dropped out.' Ravna could subtract: one
hundred and fifty-two were still coming.

Blueshell's voder sounded over his mate's, 'During the last two hundred
seconds, they have made slightly better time than before, but I think that is
local variance in Bottom conditions. Sir Pham, you are doing well, but I
know my ship. We could get a little more time if only you'd allow me
control. Please—'

'Shut up.' Pham's voice was sharp, but the words were almost automatic.
It was a conversation – or the abortion of one – that occurred almost as
often as Pham's demand for status info on the Blighter fleet.

In the early weeks of their journey, she had assumed that godshatter was somehow superhuman. Instead it was parts and pieces, automation loaded in a great panic. Maybe it was working right, or maybe it had run amok and was tearing Pham apart with its errors.

The old cycle of fear and doubt was suddenly broken by soft blue light. Tines' World! At last, a wondrously accurate jump, almost as good as the shocker of five hours before: Twenty thousand kilometers away hung a vast narrow crescent, the edge of planetary daylight. The rest was a dark blot against the stars, except where the auroral ring hung a faint green glow around the south pole. Jefri Olsndot was on the other side of the world from them, in the arctic day. They wouldn't have radio communication until they arrived – and she hadn't figured out how to recalibrate the ultrawave for shortrange transmission.

She turned back from the view. Pham still stared upward into the sky behind her. '. . . Pham, what good is forty-eight hours? Will we just destroy the Countermeasure?' *What of Jefri and Mr Steel's people?*

'Maybe. But there are other possibilities. There must be.' That last softly. 'I've been chased before. I've been in bigger jams before.' His eyes avoided hers.

38

Jefri hadn't seen the sky for more than an hour in the last two days. He and Amdi were safe enough in the great stone dome that sheltered the refugee ship, but there was no way to see outside. *If it weren't for Amdi, I couldn't have stood it a minute.* In some ways it was worse even than his first days on Hidden Island. The ones who killed Mom and Dad and Johanna were just a few kilometers away. They had captured some of Mr Steel's guns and the last few days the explosions had gone on for hours, a booming that shook the ground beneath them and sometimes even smashed at the walls of the dome.

Their food was brought in to them, and when they weren't sitting in the ship's command cabin, the two wandered outside the ship to the rooms with the sleeping children. Jefri had kept up with the simple maintenance procedures he remembered, but looking through the chill transp of the cold sleep coffins, he was terribly afraid. Some of them weren't breathing very much. The inside temperature seemed too high. And he and Amdi didn't know how to help.

Nothing had changed here, but now there was joy. Ravna's long silence had ended. Amdijefri and Mr Steel had actually talked to her in *voice!* Three more hours and her ship would be here! Even the bombardment had ended, almost as if Woodcarver realized that her time was near to ending.

Three more hours. Left to himself, Jefri would have spent the time in a state of wall-climbing anxiety. After all, he was nine years old now, a grown-up with grown-up problems. But then there was Amdi. The pack was much smarter than Jefri in some ways, but he was such a little kid – about five years old, as near as Amdijefri could figure it. Except when he was into heavy thinking, he could not stay still. After the call from Ravna, Jefri wanted to sit down for serious worrying, but Amdi began chasing himself around the pylons. He shouted back and forth in Jefri's voice and Ravna's, and bumped into the boy accidentally on purpose. Jefri hopped up and glared at the careening puppies. *Just a little kid.* And suddenly, happy and so sad all at once: *Is this how Johanna saw me?* And so he had responsibilities now too. Like being patient. As one of Amdi came rushing past his knees, Jefri swept down to grab the wriggling form. He raised it to shoulder level as the rest of the pack converged gleefully, pounding on him from all directions.

They fell to the dry moss and wrestled for a few seconds. 'Let's explore, let's explore!'

'We have to be here for Ravna and Mr Steel.'

'Don't worry. We'll remember when.'

'Okay.' Where was there really to go?

The two walked through the torchlit dimness to the clerestory that ringed the inner edge of the dome. As far as Jefri could see, they were alone. That was not unusual. Mr Steel was very worried that Woodcarver spies might get into the ship. Even his own soldiers rarely came here.

Amdijefri had investigated the inside wall before. Behind the quilts, the stone felt cool and damp. There were some holes to the outside – for ventilation – but they were almost ten meters up, where the wall was already curving inwards toward the apex of the dome. The stone was rough cut, not yet polished. Mr Steel's workers had been in a frantic hurry to complete the protection before Woodcarver's army arrived. Nothing was polished, and the quilts were undecorated.

Ahead and behind him, Amdi was sniffing at the cracks and fresh mortar. The one in Jefri's arms gave a concerted wiggle. 'Ha! Up ahead. I knew that mortar was coming loose,' the pack said. Jefri let all of his friend rush forward to a nook in the wall. It didn't look any different than before, but Amdi was scratching with five pairs of paws.

'Even if you can get it loose, what good does it do you?' Jefri had seen these blocks as they were lowered into place. They were almost fifty centimeters across, laid in alternating rows. Getting past one would just bring them to more stone.

'Heh heh, I don't know. I've been saving this up till we had some time to kill . . . Yech. This mortar burns my lips.' More scratching, and the pack passed back a fragment as big as Jefri's head. There really was a hole between the blocks, and it was big enough for Amdi. One of him darted into the tiny cave.

'Satisfied?' Jefri plunked himself down by the hole and tried to look in.

'Guess what!' Amdi's shrill voice came from a member right by his ear. 'There's a tunnel back here, not just another layer of stone!' A member wriggled past Jefri and disappeared into the dark. Secret tunnels? That was too much like a Nyjoran fairy tale. 'These are big enough for a full-grown member, Jefri. You could get through these on hands 'n' knees.' Two more of Amdi disappeared into the hole.

The tunnel he had discovered might be large enough for a human child, but the entrance hole was a tight fit even for the puppies. Jefri had nothing to do but stare into the darkness. The parts of Amdi that remained at the entrance talked about what he had found. '—Goes on for a long, long way. I've doubled back a couple of times. The top of me is about five meters up, way over your head. This is kooky. I'm getting all strung out.' Amdi sounded even sillier than his normal playfulness. Two more of him went into the hole. This was developing into serious adventure – that Jefri could have no part of.

'Don't go too far; it might be dangerous.'

One of the pair that remained looked up at him. 'Don't worry. Don't worry. The tunnel isn't an accident. It feels like it was cut as grooves in the stones when they were laid. This is some special escape route Mister Steel made. I'm all right. I'm all right. Ha ha, hoohooo.' One more disappeared into the hole. After a moment the last remaining one ran in, but stayed near enough to the entrance so Amdi could still talk to Jefri. The pack was having a high old time, singing and screeching to itself. Jefri knew exactly what the other was up to; it was another of the games he could never play. In this posture, Amdi's thoughts would be the weirdest rippling things. *Darn.* Now that he was playing within stone, it must be even neater than before, since he was totally cut off from all thoughts except from member to adjacent member.

The stupid singing went on a little longer, and then Amdi spoke in an almost reasonable tone. 'Hei, this tunnel actually splits off in places. The front of me has come to a fork. One side is heading down . . . Wish I had enough members to go both ways!'

'Well, you don't!'

'Hei ho, I'll take the upper tunnel today.' A few seconds of silence. 'There's a little door here! Like a member-size room door. Not locked.' Amdi relayed the sounds of stone scritching against stone. 'Ha! I can see light! Up just a few more meters, it opens onto a window. Hear the wind.' He relayed wind sound and the keening of the sea birds that soared up from Hidden Island. It sounded wonderful. 'Oh oh, this is stretching things, but I wanna look out . . . Jefri, I can see the sun! I'm outdoors, sitting way up on the side of the dome. I can see all round to the south. Boy, it's smoky down there.'

'What about the hillside?' Jefri asked the nearest member; its white-splotched pelt was barely visible through the entrance hole. At least Amdi was staying in touch.

'A little browner than last tenday. I don't see any soldiers out there.' Jefri heard the relayed sound of a cannon firing. 'Yipes. There's shooting though . . . It hit just on this side of the crest. Someone's out there, just below my line of sight.' Woodcarver, come at last. Jefri shivered, angry that he couldn't see, frightened of what might be seen. He often had nightmares about what Woodcarver must truly be, how she had done it to Mom and Dad and Johanna. Images never fully formed . . . yet almost memories. *Mister Steel will get Woodcarver.*

'Uh-oh. Old Tyrathect is coming across the castle yard this way.' Thumping sounds came from the hole as Amdi blundered back down. No point in letting Tyrathect know that there was a tunnel hidden in the wall. He'd probably just order them to stay away from it. One, two, three, four – half of Amdi popped out of the wall. The four wandered around a little dazedly. Jefri couldn't tell if it was because of their stretched-out experience or if they were temporarily split from the other half of the pack. 'Act natural. Act natural.'

Then the other four arrived, and Amdi began to settle down. He led Jefri away from the wall at a fast trot. 'Let's get the commset. We'll pretend we've been trying to raise Ravna with it.' Amdi knew well that the starship couldn't be back for another thirty minutes or so. In fact, he had been the one who verified the decelaration math for Mister Steel. Nevertheless, he chased up the ship's steps and dragged down the radio. The two were already plugging the antenna into a signal booster when the public doors on the west side of the dome were unlatched. Silhouetted against the daylight were parts of a guard pack and a single member of Tyrathect. The guard retired, sliding the doors shut, and the Cloak walked slowly across the moss towards them.

Amdi rushed over and chattered about their attempts to use the radio. It was a little forced, Jefri thought. The puppies were still confused by their trip through the walls.

The singleton looked at the powdering of mortar dust on Amdi's pelt. 'You've been climbing in the walls, haven't you?'

'What?' Amdi looked himself over, noticed the dust. Usually he was more clever. 'Yes,' he said shamefacedly. He brushed the powder away. 'You won't tell, will you?'

Fat chance he'll help us, thought Jefri. Mr Tyrathect had learned Samnorsk better than Mr Steel, and besides Steel was the only one who had much time to talk with them. But even before the radio cloaks, he'd been a short-tempered, bossy sort. Jefri had had baby-sitters like him. Tyrathect was nice up to a point, and then would get sarcastic or say something mean. Lately that had improved, but Jefri still didn't like him much.

But Mr Tyrathect didn't say anything right away. He sat down slowly, as if his rump hurt. '. . . No, I won't tell.'

Jefri exchanged a surprised glance with one of Amdi. 'What is the tunnel for?' he asked timidly.

'All castles have hidden tunnels, especially in my . . . in the domain of Mr Steel. You want ways to escape, ways to spy on your enemies.' The singleton shook its head. 'Never mind. Is your radio properly receiving, Amdijefri?'

Amdi cocked a head at the comm's display. 'I think so, but there's nothing yet to receive. See, Ravna's ship had to decelerate and um, I could show you the arithmetic . . . ?' But Mr Tyrathect was obviously not interested in playing with chalk boards. '. . . well, depending on their luck with the ultradrive, we should have radio contact with them real soon.'

But the little window on the comm showed no incoming signal. They watched it for several minutes. Mr Tyrathect lowered his muzzle and seemed to sleep. Every few seconds his body twitched. Jefri wondered what the rest of him was doing.

Then the comm window was glowing green. There was a garble of sound as it tried to sort signal from background noise. '. . . over you in five minutes,' came Ravna's voice. 'Jefri? Are you listening?'

'Yes! We're here.'

'Let me talk to Mr Steel, please.'

Mr Tyrathect stepped nearer to the comm. 'He is not here now, Ravna.'

'Who is this?'

Tyrathect's laugh was a giggle; he had never heard any other kind. 'I?' He made the Tinish chord that sounded like 'Tyrathect' to Jefri. 'Or do you mean a taken name, like Steel? I don't know the exact word. You may call me . . . Mr Skinner.' Tyrathect laughed again. 'For now, I can speak for Steel.'

'Jefri, are you all right?'

'Yes, yes. Listen to Mr Skinner.' What a strange name.

The sounds from the comm became muffled. There was a male voice arguing. Then Ravna was back, her voice kind of tight, like Mom when she was mad. 'Jefri . . . what's the volume of a ball ten centimeters across?'

Amdi had been fidgeting impatiently through the conversation. All through the last year he had been hearing stories of humans from Jefri, and dreaming what Ravna might really be like. Now he had a chance to show off. He jumped for the comm, and grinned at Jefri. 'That's easy, Ravna.' His voice was perfect Jefri – and completely fluent. 'It's 523.598 cubic centimeters . . . or do you want more digits?'

Muffled conversation. '. . . No, that's fine. Okay, Mr Skinner. We have pictures from our earlier pass and a general radio fix. Where exactly are you?'

'Under the castle dome at the top of Starship Hill. It's right at the coast by a—'

A man's voice cut in. Pham? He had a funny accent. 'I got it on the map. We still can't see you direct. Too much haze.'

'That's smoke,' said the Cloak. 'The enemy is almost upon us from the south. We need your help immediately—' The singleton lowered its head from the commset. Its eyes closed and opened a couple of times. Thinking? 'Hmm, yes. Without your help, we and Jefri and this ship are lost. Please land within the castle courtyard. You know we've specially reinforced it for your arrival. Once down we can use your weapons to—'

'No way.' The guy replied immediately. 'Just separate the friendlies from the bad guys and let us take care of things.'

Tyrathect's voice took on a wheedling tone, like a little kid complaining. *He really has been studying us.* 'No, no, didn't mean to be impolite. Certainly, do it your own way. About the enemy force: everyone close to the castle on the south side of the hill are enemy. A single pass with your ship's . . . um, torch . . . would send them running.'

'I can't fly that torch inside an atmosphere. Did your Pop really land with the main jet, Jefri? No agrav?'

'Yes, sir. All we had was the jet.'

'He was a lucky genius.'

Ravna: 'Maybe we could just float across, a few thousand meters up. That might scare them away.'

Tyrathect began, 'Yes, that might—'

The public doors on the north side of the dome slid open. Mr Steel stood silhouetted against the daylight beyond. 'Let me talk to them,' he said.

The goal of all their voyaging lay just twenty kilometers below *OOB*. They were so *close*, yet those twenty thousand meters might be as hard to bridge as the twenty thousand light-years they had come so far.

They floated on agrav directly over 'Starship Hill.' *OOB*'s multispectral wasn't working very well, but where smoke did not obscure, the ship's optics could count the needles on the trees below. Ravna could see the forces of 'Woodcarver' ranged across the slopes south of the castle. There were other troops, and apparently cannon, hidden in the forests that lined the fjord south of that. Given a little more time they would be able to locate them too. Time was the one thing they did not have.

Time and trust.

'Forty-eight hours, Pham. Then the fleet will be here, all around us.' Maybe, *maybe* godshatter could work a miracle; they'd never know stewing about it up here. *Try:* 'You've got to trust somebody, Pham.'

Pham glared back at her, and for an instant she feared he might go completely to pieces. 'You'd hand yourself over to that Steel? Medieval villains are just as smart as any you've seen in the Beyond, Rav. They could teach the Butterflies a thing or two. An arrow in the head will kill you as sure as an antimatter bomb.'

More fake memories? But Pham was right on this: She thought about the just-concluded conversation. The second pack – Steel – had been a bit too insistent. He had been good to Jefri, but he was clearly desperate. And she believed him when he said that a high fly-by wouldn't scare the Wood-carvers off. They needed to come down near the ground with firepower. Just now, about all the firepower they had was Pham's beam gun. 'Okay, then! Do what you and Steel talked about. Fly the lander past Woodcarver's lines, laser blast them.'

'God damn it, you know I can't fly that. The landing boat is like nothing either of us know, and without the automation I—'

Softly: 'Without the automation, you need Blueshell, Pham.' There was horror on Pham's face. She reached out to him. He was silent for a long moment, not seeming to notice.

'Yeah.' His voice was low, strangled. Then: 'Blueshell! Get up here.'

OOB's lander had more than enough room for the Skroderider and Pham Nuwen. The craft had been built specifically for Rider use. With higher automation working, it would have been easy for Pham – for even a child – to fly. Now the craft could not provide stable flight, and the 'manual' controls were something that gave even Blueshell a hard time. *Damn automation. Damn optimization.* For most of his adult life Pham had lived in the Slowness. All those decades, he had managed spacecraft and weapons that could have reduced the feudal empire below to slag. Yet now, with equipment that should have been enormously more powerful, he couldn't even fly a damn landing boat.

Across the crew compartment, Blueshell was at the pilot's position. His fronds stretched across a web of supports and controls. He had turned off all display automation; only the main window was alive, a natural view from the boat's bow camera. *OOB* floated some hundred meters ahead, drifting up and out of view as their craft slid backwards and down.

Blueshell's fidgety nervousness – furtiveness, it seemed to Pham – had disappeared as he got into piloting the craft. His voder voice became terse and preoccupied, and the edges of his fronds writhed across the controls, an exercise that would have been impossible to Pham even if he had a lifetime of experience with the gear. 'Thank you, Sir Pham . . . I'll prove you can trust. . .' The nose lurched downwards and they were staring almost straight into the fjord-carven coastline twenty kilometers below. They fell free for half a minute while the Rider's fronds writhed on their supports. Hot piloting? No: 'Sorry, sorry.' Acceleration, and Pham sank into his restraints under a grav load that wobbled between a tenth gee and an intolerable crush. The landscape rotated and they had a brief glimpse of *OOB*, now like a tiny moth above them.

'Is it necessary to kill, Sir Pham? Perhaps simply our appearance over the battle . . .'

Nuwen gritted his teeth. 'Just get us down.' The Steel creature had been adamant that they fry the entire hillside. Despite all Pham's suspicions, the pack might be right on that. They were up against a crew of murderers that had not hesitated to ambush a starship; the Woodcarvers needed a real demonstration.

Their boat fluttered down the kilometers. Steel's fortifications were clearly visible even in the natural view: the rough polygon that guarded the refugee ship, the much larger structure that rambled across an island several kilometers westward. *I wonder if this is how my Father's castle looked to the Qeng Ho landers?* Those walls were high and unsloping. Clearly the Tines had had no idea of gunpowder till Ravna had clued them to it.

The valley south of the castle was a blot of dark smoke smoothly streaming toward the sea. Even without data enhancement, he could see hot spots, fringes of orange edging the black.

'You're at two thousand meters,' came Ravna's voice. 'Jefri says he can see you.'

'Patch me through to them.'

'I will try, Sir Pham.' Blueshell fiddled, his lack of attention spinning the boat through a complete loop. Pham had seen falling leaves with more control.

A child's piping voice: 'A-are you okay? Don't *crash*!'

And then the Steel pack's hybrid of Ravna and the kid: 'South to go! South to go! Use fire gun. Burn them quick.'

Blueshell had them down in the smoke already. For seconds they were flying blind. A break in the smoke showed the hillside less than two hundred meters off, coming up fast. Before Pham could curse at Blueshell, the Rider had turned them around and floated the boat into clearer air. Then he pitched over so they might see directly down.

After thirty weeks of talk and planning, Pham had his first glimpse of the Tines. Even from here, it was obvious they were different from any sophonts Pham had encountered: Clusters of four or five or six members hung together so close they seemed a single spiderlike being. And each pack stood separated from the others by ten or fifteen meters.

A cannon flashed in the murk. The pack crewing it moved like a single, coordinated hand to rock the barrel back and ram another charge down the muzzle.

'But if these are the enemy, Sir Pham, where did they get the guns?'

'They stole 'em.' *But muzzle loaders?* He didn't have time to pursue the thought.

'You're right over them, Pham! I can see you in and out of the smoke. You're drifting south at fifteen meters per second, losing altitude.' It was the kid, speaking with his usual incredible precision.

'Kill them! Kill them!'

Pham wriggled out of his restraints and crawled back to the hatch where they had mounted his beam gun. It was about the only thing salvaged from the workshop fire, but by God this *was* something he could operate.

'Keep us steady, Blueshell. Bounce me around and I'll fry you as likely as anything!' He pushed open the hatch, and gagged on spicy smoke. Then Blueshell's agravs wafted them into a clear space and Pham lined the beamer down the ranks of packfolk.

Originally Woodcarver had demanded Johanna stay at the base camp. Johanna's response had been explosive. Even now the girl was a little surprised at herself. Not since the first days on Tines' World had she come so close to attacking a pack. No way was anyone going to keep her from finding out about Jefri. In the end they had compromised: Johanna would accept Pilgrim as her guard. She could follow the army into the field, as long as she obeyed his direction.

Johanna looked up through the drifting smoke. *Damn.* Pilgrim was always such a carefree joker. By his own telling, he had gotten himself killed over and over again through the years. And now he wouldn't even let her go up to Scrupilo's cannons. The two of them paced across a terrace in the hillside. The brush fire had swept through here hours before, and the spicy smell of moss ash was thick around them. And with that smell came the bright memory of horror, of a year ago, right here . . .

Trusted guard packs paced their course twenty meters on either side. This area was supposedly safe from infiltration, and there had been no artillery fire from the Flenserists for hours. But Peregrine absolutely refused to let her get any closer.

It's nothing like last year. Then all had been sunny blue skies and clean air – and her parents' murder. Now she and Pilgrim had returned, and the blue sky was yellow-gray and the sweeps of mossy hillside were black. And now the packs around her were fighting *with* her. And now there was a chance . . .

'Lemme closer, damn it! Woodcarver will have the Oliphaunt no matter what happens to me.'

Peregrine shook himself, a Tinish negative. One of his puppies reached out from a jacket pouch to catch at her sleeve. 'A little longer,' Pilgrim said for the tenth time. 'Wait for Woodcarver's messenger. Then we can—'

'I want to be up there! I'm the only one who knows the ship!' *Jefri, Jefri. If only Vendacious was right about you . . .*

She was twisting about to slap at Scarbutt when it happened: A glare of heat on her back, and the smoke flashed bright. Again. Again. And then the impact of rapid thunder marching across the sky.

Pilgrim shuddered against her. 'That's not gunfire!' he shouted. 'Two of me are almost blinded. C'mon.' He surrounded her, almost knocking her off her feet as he pushed/dragged her down the hill.

For a second Johanna went along, more dazed than cooperative. Somehow they had lost their escort.

From up the hill the shouts of battle had stopped. The sharp thunder had silenced all. Where the smoke thinned she could see one of Scrupilo's cannons, the barrel extending from a puddle of melted steel. The cannoneer had been blown to bits. Not gunfire. Johanna spasmed out of Pilgrim's grip. *Not gunfire.*

'Spacers! Pilgrim, that must be a drive torch.'

Peregrine grabbed her, continuing down the hill. 'Not a drive torch! That I've heard. This is quieter – and somebody's *aiming* it.'

There had been a long stutter of separate blasts. How many of Woodcarver's people had just died? 'They must think we're attacking the ship, Pilgrim. If we don't do something, they'll wipe out everyone.'

His jaws eased their grip on her sleeves and pants. 'What can we do? Hanging around here will just get us killed.'

Johanna stared into the sky. No sign of fliers, but there was so much smoke. The sun was a dull bloody ball. If only the rescuers knew they were killing her friends. If only they could see . . . She dug her feet into the ground. 'If I can get where they can see me . . . Let go of me, Pilgrim! I'm going uphill, out of the smoke.'

He'd stopped moving but his grip was fiercely tight. Four adult faces and two puppy ones looked up at her, and indecision was in every look. 'Please, Pilgrim. It's the only way.' Packs were straggling down, some bleeding, some in fragments.

His frightened eyes stared at her an instant longer. Then he let go and touched her hand with a nose. 'I guess this hill will always be the death of me. First Scriber, now you – you're all crazy.' The old Pilgrim smile flickered across his members. 'Okay. Let's try it!' The two without puppies went up the hillside, scouting for the safest route.

Johanna and the rest of him followed. They were moving across a sloping terrace. The summer drought had drained the chill swamp water she remembered from the landing, and the blackened moss was firm under her. The going should have been easy, but Peregrine wound through the deepest hummocks, hunkering down every few seconds to look in all directions. They reached the end of the terrace and began climbing. There were places so steep she had to grab the epaulet stirrups on two of Peregrine and let him hoist her up. They passed the nearest cannon, what was left of it. Johanna had never seen such things except in stories, but the splash of metal and the carbonized flesh could only mean some kind of beam weapon. Running across the hill were similar craters, destruction punched into the already burned land.

Johanna leaned against a smooth rounding of rock. 'Just pull over this one and we're on the next terrace,' Pilgrim's voice came in her ear. 'Hurry, I hear shouting.' He leaned two of himself down, tilting his epaulets toward her hands. She grabbed them, pushing off with her feet. For a moment she and the pack teetered over a four-meter fall, and then she was lying on brownish, unburned moss. Pilgrim clustered around her, hiding her. She peeked out between his legs. The outermost walls of Steel's castle were visible from here. Tinish archers stood boldly on the ramparts, taking advantage of the chaos among Woodcarver's troops. In fact, the Queen's force had not lost many packs in the air attack, but even the unwounded were milling around. The Queen's soldiers were no cowards – Johanna knew that by now – but they had just been confronted by force beyond all defense.

Overhead the smoke faded into blue. The battlefield ahead of her lay under clear sky. In the years before the High Lab, Johanna and her mother had often gone on nature trips over Bigby Marsh at Straum. With the sensors on their camper packs they'd had no trouble watching the skygg-wings there: even if this flier's automation was not specifically looking for a human on the ground, it should notice her. 'Do you see anything?'

The four adult heads angled back and forth in coordinated pairs. 'No. The flier must be very far away or behind the smoke.'

Nuts. Johanna came off her knees, trotted toward the castle walls. They must be watching there!

'Woodcarver's not going to like this.'

Two of the Queen's soldiers were already running toward them, attracted by their purposeful movement or the sight of Johanna. Pilgrim waved them back.

Alone on an open field less than two hundred meters from the castle wall. Even with normal vision, how could they be overlooked? In fact, they were noticed: There was a soft hissing, and a meter-long arrow thunked into the turf on their left. Scarbutt grabbed her shoulder, pulling her to a crouch. The puppies shifted his shields into position: Pilgrim made a barricade of himself on the castle side and started back out of range. Back into the smoke.

'No! Run parallel! I want to be seen.'

'Okay, okay.' Soft sounds of death whispered down. Johanna kept one hand on his shoulder as they ran across the field. She felt Scarbutt falter. The arrow had caught him in the thick of his shoulder, centimeters from a tympanum. 'I'm okay! Stay down, stay down.'

The front line of Woodcarver's force was rallying toward them now, a dozen packs racing across the terrace. Pilgrim bounced up and down, shouting with a voice that punched like physical force. Something about staying back and danger from the sky. It didn't stop their advance. 'They want you away from the arrows.'

And suddenly they noticed that the fire from the castle had stopped.

Pilgrim scanned the sky. 'It's back! Coming from the east, maybe a kilometer out.'

She looked in the direction he was pointing. It was a lumpy thing, probably space-based though it had no ultradrive spines. It bobbled and staggered. There was no sign of jets. Some kind of agrav? Nonhumans? The droughts skittered through her mind, alongside the joy.

Pale light flickered from a mast on its belly and dirt geysered around the troops who were racing to protect her. Again the stuttering thunder, only now the light was marching right across her friends toward her.

Amdijefri was on the battlements. Steel hid his glares from the two. There simply was no help for it; Ravna had demanded Jefri be by the radio to guide the strike. The human was not completely stupid. It shouldn't make any difference. *An army looks like an army whether it is foe or friend.* Very soon the army beyond these walls would cease to exist.

'How did the first run go?' Ravna's voice came clearly from the comm set. But it wasn't Jefri who answered: all eight of Amdiranifani was poking around the battlements, some of him sitting on the crenellations practicing stereo vision, others eyeing Steel and the radio. Telling him to stay back had no effect. Now Amdi answered the question with Jefri's voice. 'Okay. I counted fifteen pulses. Only ten hit anything. I bet I could shoot better than that.'

'Damn it, that's the best I can do with this [unknown words].' The voice was not Ravna's. Steel heard the irritation in it. *Everybody can find something to hate in these pups.* The thought warmed him.

'Please,' said Steel. 'Fire again. Again.' He looked over the stonework. The air attack had taken out a band of enemy by the edge of the near terrace. It was spectacular destruction, like enormous cannon blows, or the separate landing of twenty starships. And all from a little craft that fluttered like a falling leaf. The enemy front line was dissolving in panic. Up and down the ramparts, his own troops danced about their stations. Things had been bleak since their cannon were knocked out; they needed something to cheer about. 'The archers, Shreck! Shoot upon the survivors.' Then, continuing in Samnorsk: 'The front ranks are still coming. They are – they are—' *Damn, what's the word for 'confident'?* 'They will kill us without more help.'

The human child looked at Steel in puzzlement. If he called that a lie, then . . . A moment later Ravna said. 'I don't know. They're well back from your walls, at least all that I can see. I don't want to butcher . . .' Rapid fire conversation with the human in the flier, perhaps not even in Samnorsk. The gunner did not sound pleased. 'Pham will pull back a few kilometers,' she said. 'We can come back instantly if your enemy advances.'

'Sssst!' Shreck's Hightalk hiss was like a physical jab. Steel wheeled, glaring. *How dare* – But his lieutenant was wide-eyed, pointing toward the center of the battlefield. Of course Steel had had a pair of eyes on that direction, but he hadn't been paying attention: *The other Two-Legs!*

The mantis figure dropped behind an accompanying pack, mercifully before Amdijefri noticed. Thank the Pack of Packs that puppies are nearsighted. Steel swept forward, surrounding some of Amdi, shouting at the others to get off the parapet. Both of Tyrathect ran in close, physically grabbing for the disobedient wretches. 'Get below!' Steel screamed in Tinish. For a second all was confusion, as his own mind sounds mixed with the puppies'. Amdi tumbled away from him, thoroughly distracted by the noise and the rough pushing. And then in Samnorsk, Steel said, 'There are more cannons out there. Get below before you're hurt!'

Jefri started for the parapet. 'But I don't see—' And fortunately there *was* nothing special to see. Now. The other Two-Legs was still crouched behind one of Woodcarver's packs. Shreck took the human child in paw and jaw. He and one of Tyrathect hustled the protesting children down the stairs. As they departed, Tyrathect was already embellishing on Steel's story, reporting on the troops it could see from below the crest of the hill.

'Blow up the lesser powder dump,' Steel hissed at the departing Shreck. That dump was nearly empty, but its destruction might persuade the spacers where words could not.

After they were gone, Steel stood for an instant, silent and shivering. He had never seen disaster so narrowly avoided. Along the ramparts, his archers were showering arrows upon the enemy pack and the Two-Legs. *Damn.* They were almost out of range.

In the castle yard, Shreck detonated the lesser dump. The explosion was a satisfying one, much louder than an artillery hit; one of the inner towers was blown apart. Flying rock showered the yard, the smallest pieces reaching all the way to where Steel stood on the ramparts.

Ravna's voice was shouting in swift Samnorsk, too fast for Steel to understand. Now all the planning, all the hopes, all balanced on a knife edge. He must bet everything: Steel leaned a shoulder close to the comm and said, 'Sorry. Things go fast here. Many more Woodcarver come up under smoke. Can you kill all on hillside?' Could the mantises see through smoke? That was part of the gamble.

The gunner's voice came back, 'I can try. Watch this.'

A third voice, thready and narrow even by human standards: 'It will be fifty seconds more, Sir Steel. We've having trouble turning.'

Good. Concentrate on your flying and your killing. Don't look at your victims too carefully. The archers had driven the human back, part way under the cover of smoke. Other packs were rushing out to protect her. By the time the Visitors circled back, there would be lots of targets, the human lost among them.

Two of him caught sight of the spacer floating down through the haze. The Visitors would have no clear view of what they were shooting at. Pale light flickered from beneath the craft. A scythe swept across the hillside toward Woodcarver's troops.

Pham was bounced around his perch as Blueshell turned the boat back to the target. They weren't moving fast; the airstream couldn't have been more than thirty meters per second. But every second was full of the damnedest jerks and tumbles. At one point Pham's grip on the gun mount was all that kept him indoors. *Forty some hours from now, the deadliest thing in the universe is going to arrive, and I'm taking potshots at dogs.*

How to take out the hillside? Steel's whiney voice still echoed in his ears. And Ravna wasn't sure what *OOB* was seeing beneath all the smoke. *We might do better without automation than with this bastard mix.* At least his beamer had a manual control. Pham embraced the barrel with one arm while he reached with the other. At wide dispersion the beam was useless against armor, but could burst eyes and set skin and hair afire – and the beam width would be dozens of meters across at ground level.

'Fifteen seconds, Sir Pham,' Blueshell's voice came in his ear.

They were low this time. Gaps in the smoke flickered past like stop-action art. Most of the ground was burned-over black, but there were precipices of naked rock and even sooty patches of snow trapped in crannies and shadowed pits . . . Here and there was a pile of doggy bodies, an occasional gun tube.

'There's a crowd of them ahead, Sir Pham. Running near the castle.'

Pham leaned down and looked forward. The mob was about four hundred meters ahead. They were running parallel to the castle walls, through a field that was a spinehide of arrowshafts. He pressed the firing stud, swept the beam out from below the boat. There was plenty of water under that dried cover; it exploded in steam as the beam passed over it . . . But further out, the wide dispersion wasn't doing much. It would be another few seconds before he'd have a good shot at the hapless packs.

Time for the little suspicions. So how come the enemy had muzzle-loading cannon? *Those* they must have made themselves – in a world with no evidence of firearms. Steel was the classic medieval manipulator; Pham had spotted the type from a thousand light-years out. They were doing the critter's dirty work, that was obvious. *Shut up. Deal with Steel later.*

Slanting in on the packs, Pham fired again, sweeping through living flesh this time. He fired ahead of them and on the castle side; maybe they wouldn't all die. He stuck his head further into the slipstream, trying for a better view. Ahead of the packs was a hundred meters of open field, a single pack of four and – *a human figure, black-haired and slim, jumping and waving.*

Pham smashed the barrel up against the hull, safing it at the same time. The back flash was a surge of heat that crisped his eyebrows. 'Blueshell! Get us down! Get us down!'

39

'A bad understanding. She was lied to.'

Ravna tried to read something behind the voice. Steel's Samnorsk was as creaky as ever, the tones childish and whiney. He sounded no different than before. But his story was stretched very thin by what had just happened . . . He was either a galactic master of impudence – or his story was actually true.

'The human must have been hurt, then lied to by Woodcarver. This explains a lot, Ravna. Without her, Woodcarver could not attack. Without her, all may be safe.'

Pham's voice came to Ravna on a private channel. 'The girl *was* unconscious during part of the ambush, Rav. But she practically scratched my eyes out when I suggested she might be wrong about Steel and Woodcarver. And the pack with her is a lot more convincing than Steel.'

Ravna looked questioningly across the deck at Greenstalk. Pham didn't know she was here. *Tough.* Greenstalk was an island of sanity amidst the madness – and she knew the *OOB* infinitely better than Ravna.

Steel spoke into her hesitation: 'See now, nothing has changed, except for the better. One more human lives. How can you doubt us? Speak to Jefri; he understands. We have done the best for the children in . . .' a gobbling noise, and (another?) voice said, 'coldsleep.'

'Certainly we must speak to him again, Steel. He's our best proof of your good intentions.'

'Okay. In a few minutes, Ravna. But see, he is also my good protection against tricks from you. I know how powerful you Visitors are. I . . . fear you. We need to—' gobbling consultation '—accommodate each other in our fears.'

'Um. We'll work something out. Just let us speak to Jefri now.'

'Yes.'

Ravna switched channels. 'What do you think, Pham?'

'There's no question in my mind. This Johanna is not a naïve kid like Jefri. We've always known Steel was a tough critter. We just had some other facts wrong. The landing site is in the middle of his territory. He's the killer.' Pham's voice became quieter, almost a whisper. 'Hell of it is, this may not change anything. Steel does have the ship. I've got to get in there.'

'It will be another ambush.'

'. . . I know. But does it matter? If we can get me time with the Countermeasure, it could be – it will be – worth it.' What matter a suicide mission within a suicide mission?

'I'm not sure, Pham. If we give him everything, he'll kill us before we ever get near the ship.'

'He'll try. Look, just keep him talking. Maybe we can get a directional on his radio, blow the bastard away.' He did not sound optimistic.

Tyrathect didn't take them back to the ship, or to their rooms. They descended stairs within the outer walls, part of Amdi first, then Jefri with the rest of Amdi, then the singleton from Tyrathect.

Amdi was still complaining. 'I don't understand, I don't understand. We can help.'

Jefri: 'I didn't see any enemy cannons.'

The singleton was full of explanations, though it sounded even more preoccupied than usual. 'I saw them from one of my other members, out in the valley. We're pulling in all our soldiers. We must make a stand, or none of us will be alive to be rescued. For now, this is the best place for you to be.'

'How do you know?' said Jefri. 'Can you talk to Steel right now?'

'Yes, one of me is still up there with him.'

'Well, tell him we have to help. We can talk better Samnorsk even than you.'

'I'll tell him right now,' was the Cloak's quick reply.

There were no more window slots cut in the walls. The only light came from wick torches set every ten meters along the tunnel. The air was cool and musty; wetness glistened on unquilted stone. The tiny doors were not of polished wood. Instead there were bars, and darkness beyond. *Where are we going?* Jefri was suddenly reminded of the dungeons in stories, the treachery that befell the Greater Two and the Countess of the Lake. Amdi didn't seem to feel it. For all his mischievous nature, Puppies was basically trusting; he had always depended on Mr Steel. But Jefri's parents had never acted quite like this, even during the escape from High Lab. Mr Steel suddenly seemed so different, as if he couldn't be bothered pretending to be nice anymore. And Jefri had never really trusted the sullen Tyrathect; now that one was acting downright sneaky.

There had been no new threat on the hillside.

Fear and stubbornness and suspicion all came together: Jefri spun around, confronting the Cloak. 'We're not going any farther. This isn't where we're supposed to go. We want to talk to Ravna and Mr Steel.' A sudden, liberating realization: 'And you're not big enough to stop us!'

The singleton backed up abruptly, then sat down. It lowered its head, blinked. 'So you don't trust me? You are right not to. There is no one here but yourselves that you can trust.' Its gaze drifted from Jefri to the range of Amdi, and then down the hall. 'Steel doesn't know I've brought you here.'

The confession was so quick, so easily made. Jefri swallowed hard. 'You brought us down here to k-kill us.' All of Amdi was staring at him and Tyrathect, every eye wide with shock.

The singleton bobbed its head in part of a smile. 'You think I am traitor?

After all this time, some healthy suspicion. I am proud of you.' Mr Tyrathect continued smoothly, 'You are surrounded by traitors, Amdijefri. But I am not one of them. I am here to help you.'

'I know that.' Amdi reached forward to touch a muzzle to the singleton's. 'You're no traitor. You're the only person besides Jefri that I can touch. We've always wanted to like you, but—'

'Ah, but you should be suspicious. You will all die if you aren't.' Tyrathect looked over the puppies, at the frowning Jefri. 'Your sister is alive Jefri. She's out there now, and Steel has known all along. He killed your parents; he did almost everything he said Woodcarver did.' Amdi backed away, shaking himself in frightened negations. 'You don't believe me? That's funny. Once upon a time I was such a good liar; I could talk the fish right into my mouths. But now, when only the truth will work, I can't convince you . . . Listen:'

Suddenly it was Steel's human-speaking voice that came from the singleton, Steel talking with Ravna about Johanna being alive, excusing the attack he had just ordered on her.

Johanna. Jefri rushed forward, fell on his knees before the Cloak. Almost without thought, he grabbed the singleton by the throat, shaking it. Teeth snapped at his hands as the other tried to shake free. Amdi rushed forward, pulled hard on his sleeves. After a moment, Jefri let go. Centimeters away from his face, the singleton peered back at him, the torchlight glinting in its dark eyes. Amdi was saying: 'Human voices are easy to fake—'

The fragment was disdainful. 'Of course. And I'm not claiming that was a direct relay. What you heard is several minutes old. Here's what Steel and I are planning this very second.' His Samnorsk abruptly stopped, and the hallway was filled with the gobbling chords of Pack talk. Even after a year, Jefri could only extract vague sense from the conversation. It did sound like two packs. One of them wanted the other to do something, bring Amdijefri – that chord was clear – up.

Amdiranifani went suddenly still, every member straining at the relayed sounds. 'Stop it!' he shrilled. And the hallway was as quiet as a tomb. 'Mr Steel, oh Mr Steel.' All of Amdi huddled against Jefri. 'He's talking about hurting you if Ravna doesn't obey. He wants to kill the Visitors when they land.' The wide eyes were ringed with tears. 'I don't understand.'

Jefri jabbed a hand at the Cloak. 'Maybe he's faking that, too.'

'I don't know. I could never fake two packs that well . . .' The tiny bodies shuddered against Jefri, and there was the sound of human weeping, the eerily familiar sound of a small child desolated . . . 'What are we going to do, Jefri?'

But Jefri was silent, remembering and finally understanding, the first few minutes after Steel's troops had rescued – captured? – him. Memories suppressed by later kindness crept out from the corners of his mind. *Mom, Dad, Johanna. But Johanna still lived, just beyond these walls . . .*

'Jefri?'

'I don't know either. H-hide maybe?'

For a moment they just stared at each other. Finally the fragment spoke. 'You can do better than hide. You already know about the passages through these walls. If you know the entrance points – and I do – you can get to almost anywhere you want. You can even get outside.'

Johanna.

Amdi's crying stopped. Three of him watched Tyrathect front, aft, and sideways. The rest still clung to Jefri. 'We still don't trust *you*, Tyrathect,' said Jefri.

'Good, good. I am a pack of various parts. Perhaps not entirely trustable.'

'Show us all the holes.' Let us decide.

'There won't be time—'

'Okay, but start showing us. And while you do, keep relaying what Mr Steel is saying.'

The singleton bobbed its head, and the multiple streams of Pack talk resumed. The Cloak got painfully to its feet and led the two children down a side tunnel, one where the wick torches were mostly burned out. The loudest sound down here was the soft dripping of water. The place was less than a year old, yet – except for the jagged edges of the cut stone – it seemed ancient.

Puppies was crying again. Jefri stroked the back of the one that clung to his shoulder, 'Please Amdi, translate for me.'

After a moment Amdi's voice came hesitantly in his ear. 'M-Mr Steel is asking again where we are. Tyrathect says we're trapped by a ceiling fall in the inner wing.' In fact, they had heard the masonry shift a few minutes before, but it sounded far away. 'Mr Steel just sent the rest of Tyrathect to get Mr Shreck and dig us out. Mr Steel sounds so . . . different.'

'Maybe it's not really him,' Jefri whispered back.

Long silence. 'No. It's him. He just seems so angry, and he's using strange words.'

'Big words?'

'No. Scary ones. About cutting and killing . . . Ravna and you and me. He . . . he doesn't like us, Jefri.'

The singleton stopped. They were beyond the last wall torch, and it was too dark to see anything but shadowy forms. He was pointed at a spot on the wall. Amdi reached forward and pushed at the rock. All the while Mr Tyrathect continued talking, reporting from outside.

'Okay,' said Amdi, 'that opens. And it's big enough for you, Jefri. I think—'

Tyrathect's human voice said, 'The Spacers are back. I can see their little boat . . . I got away just in time. Steel is getting suspicious. A few more seconds and he will be searching everywhere.'

Amdi looked into the dark hole. 'I say we go,' he said softly, sadly.

'Yeah.' Jefri reached down to touch one of Amdi's shoulders. The member led him to a hole cut in sharp-edged stone. If he scrunched his shoulders there would be enough room to crawl in. One of Amdi entered just ahead of him. The rest would follow. 'I hope it doesn't get any narrower than this.'

Tyrathect: 'It shouldn't. All these passages are designed for packs in light armor. The important thing: keep to upward curving passages. Keep moving and you'll eventually get outside. Pham's flying craft is less than, uh, five hundred meters from the walls.'

Jefri couldn't even look over his shoulder to talk to the Cloak. 'What if Mr Steel chases us into the walls?'

There was a brief silence. 'He probably won't do that, if he doesn't now where you entered. It would take too long to find you. But,' the voice was suddenly gentler, 'but there are openings on the top of the walls. In case enemy soldiers tried to sneak in from the outside, there has to be some way to kill them in the tunnels. He could pour oil down the tunnels.'

The possibility did not frighten Jefri. At the moment it just sounded bizarre. 'We've got to hurry then.'

Jefri scrabbled forward as the rest of Amdi crawled in behind him. He was already several meters deep in stone when he heard Amdi's voice back at the entrance, the last one to enter: 'Will you be okay, Mr Tyrathect?'

Or is this all another lie? thought Jefri.

The other's voice had its usual, cynical tone. 'I expect to land on my feet. Please do remember that I helped you.'

And then the hatch was shut and they scrambled forward, into the dark.

Negotiations, shit. It was obvious to Pham that Steel's idea of 'mutually safe meeting' was a cover for mayhem. Even Ravna wasn't fooled by the pack's new proposals. At least it meant that Steel was ad libbing now – that he was beyond all the scripts and schemes. The trouble was, he still wasn't giving them any openings. Pham would have cheerfully died for a few undisturbed hours with the Countermeasure, but Steel's setup would have them dead before they ever saw the inside of the refugee ship.

'Keep moving around, Blueshell. I want Steel to have us weighing on his mind, without being a good target.'

The Rider waved a frond in agreement and the boat bounced briefly up from the moss, drifted a hundred meters parallel to the castle walls, and descended again. They were in the no-man's land between the forces of Woodcarver and Steel.

Johanna Olsndot twisted around to look at him. The boat was a very crowded place now, Blueshell stretched across the Riderish controls at the bow, Pham and Johanna jammed into the seats behind him – and a pack called Pilgrim in every empty space in between. 'Even if you can locate the commset, don't fire. Jefri could be close by.' For twenty minutes Steel had been promising the momentary reappearance of Jefri Olsndot.

Pham eyed her smudged face. 'Yeah, we won't fire unless we can see exactly what we'll hit.' The girl nodded briefly. She couldn't have been more than fourteen, but she was a good trooper. Half the people he had known in Qeng Ho would have been in limp hysterics after this pickup. And of the rest, few could have given a better status report than Johanna and her friend.

He glanced at the pack. It would take a while to get used to these critters. At first he'd thought that two of the dogs were sprouting extra heads – then he noticed the small ones were just puppies carried in jacket pockets. The 'Pilgrim' was all over the boat; just what part of him should he talk to? He picked the head that was looking in his direction. 'Any theories how to deal with Steel?'

The pack's Samnorsk was better than Pham's. 'Steel and Flenser are as tricky as anything I've seen in Johanna's dataset. And Flenser is cool.'

'Flenser? Hadn't realized there was a person with that name . . . There was a "Mr Skinner" we talked to. Some kind of assistant to Steel.'

'Hmm. He's tricky enough to play flunky . . . wish we could drop back and chat with Woodcarver about this.' The request was artfully contained in his intonation. Pham wondered briefly what percentage of Packfolk were so flexible. They might be one hell of a trading race if they ever reached space.

'Sorry, we don't have time for that. In fact, if we can't get in right away, we've lost everything. I just hope Steel doesn't guess that.'

The heads subtly rearranged themselves. The biggest member, the one with a broken arrow shaft sticking up from its jacket, moved closer to the girl. 'Well, if Steel is in charge, there's a chance. He's very smart, but we think he runs amok when things get tough. Your finding Johanna has probably put him to chasing his tails. Keep him off balance, and you can expect some big mistakes.'

Johanna spoke abruptly, 'He might kill Jefri.'

Or blow up the starship. 'Ravna, any luck with Steel?'

Her voice came back over the comm: 'No. The threats are a bit more transparent now, and his Samnorsk is getting harder to understand. He's trying to bring cannon in from north of the Castle; I don't think he knows how much I can see . . . He still hasn't brought Jefri back to the radio.'

The girl paled, but she didn't say anything. Her hand stole up to grasp one of Pilgrim's paws.

Blueshell had been very quiet all through the rescue, first because he had his fronds full with flying, then because the girl and the Pack had so much to say. Pham had noticed that part of Pilgrim had been politely nosing around the Rider. Blueshell hadn't seemed upset by the attention; his race had plenty of experience with others.

But now the Rider made a *brap* for attention. 'Sir Pham, there is action in front of the castle.'

Pilgrim was on it at almost the same instant, one head helping another look through a telescope. 'Yes. That's the main sally port that's coming open. But why would Steel send packs out now? Woodcarver will chew them up.' The enemy was indeed fielding infantry. The packs spewed out the wide hole in a headlong dash, much like troops of Pham's recollection. But once they cleared the entrance they broke off into clumps of four to six dogs each and spread across the castle perimeter.

Pham leaned forward, trying to see as far along the walls as possible. 'Maybe not. These guys aren't advancing. They're staying in range of the archers on the walls.'

'Yeah. But we still have cannons.' Pilgrim's perfect imitation of humanity broke for a second, and a Tinish chord filled the cockpit. 'Something is really strange. It's like they're trying to keep someone from getting *out*.'

'Are there other entrances?'

'Probably. And lots of little tunnels, just one member wide.'

'Ravna?'

'Steel's not talking at all now. He said something about traitors infiltrating the castle. Now all I'm getting is Tinish gobble.' From embrasure to embrasure along the battlements, Pham could see enemy soldiers moving above those on the ground. Something had upset the rats' nest.

Johanna Olsndot was a vision of horrified concentration, her free hand gathered into a fist, her lips faintly trembling. 'All this time I thought he was dead. If they kill him now, I . . .' Her voice suddenly scaled up: 'What are they doing?' Cast iron kettles had been dragged to the top of the walls.

Pham could guess. Siege fighting on Canberra had involved similar things. He looked at the girl, and kept his mouth shut. *There's nothing we can do.*

The Pilgrim pack was not so kind – or not so patronizing: 'It's oil, Johanna. They want to kill someone in the walls. But if he can get out . . . Blueshell, I've read about loudspeakers. Can I use one? If Jefri is in the walls, Woodcarver can safely scrape Steel's troops off the field and battlements.'

Pham opened his mouth to object, but the Rider had already opened a channel. Pilgrim's Tinish voice echoed across the hillside. Along the castle walls heads turned. To them, the voice must have sounded like a god's. The chords and trills continued a moment longer, then ceased.

Ravna's voice was on the line an instant later, 'Whatever you did just now, it pushed Steel over the edge. I can barely understand him; He seems to be describing how he'll torture Jefri if we don't pull the Woodcarvers back.'

Pham grunted. 'Okay then. Get us in the air, Blueshell.' It felt good to kiss subtlety goodbye.

Blueshell wobbled the boat aloft. They moved forward, scarcely faster than a man can run. Behind them more of Woodcarver's troops were coming over the military crest of the hill. Those fellows had been pulled well back after Pham's strafing run: things might be decided before they got to the castle . . . But Woodcarver's reach was still long and deadly: splashes of smoke and fire appeared along the battlements, followed by sharp popping noises. Killing Jefri Olsndot was going to be a very expensive proposition for Steel.

'Can you use the beamer to clear Steel's troops away from the wall?' asked Johanna.

Pham started to nod, then noticed what was happening by the castle. 'See the oil.' Dark pools were growing between the enemy packs and the walls they guarded. Until they knew where the kid was coming out, it would be best not to start fires.

Pilgrim: 'Oops.' Then he was shouting something more on the loud-speakers. Woodcarver's artillery ceased.

'Okay,' said Pham, 'for now, all eyes on the castle wall. Circle the perimeter, Blueshell. If we can see the kid before Steel's guys, we may have a chance.'

Ravna: 'They're spread evenly around every side except the North, Pham. I don't think Steel has any idea where the boy is.'

When you challenge Heaven, the stakes are high. *And I could have won. If he had not betrayed me. I could have won.* But now the masks were down, and the enemy's brute physical power was all that counted. Steel brought himself down from the hysterical blackout of the last few minutes. *If I can not have Heaven, at least I can still take them to Hell.* Kill Amdijefri, destroy the ship the Visitors wanted so . . . most of all, destroy his traitorous teacher.

'My lord?' It was Shreck.

Steel turned a head in Shreck's direction. The time for hysteria was past. 'How goes the flooding?' he said mildly. He wouldn't ask about Tyrathect again.

'All but complete. The oil is pooling beyond the castle walls.' The two packs crouched as one of Woodcarver's bombs exploded just beyond the battlement. Her troops were already halfway back across the field – and Steel's archers were preoccupied with flooding the tunnels and watching the exits. 'We may have flushed out the traitors, my lord. Just before Wood-carver resumed fire, we heard something by the southeast wall. But I fear the Spacers will see whatever we do there.' His heads bobbed spastically.

Strange to see Shreck coming apart, Steel thought vaguely. Shreck's was the loyalty of clockwork, but now his orderly world was failing and there was nothing left to support him. The madness he was born from was all that was left.

If Shreck was close to breaking, then the siege of Starship Hill was nearly at an end. *Just a little longer, that is all I ask now.* Steel forced a confident expression upon his members. 'I understand. You have done well, Shreck. We may still win. I know how these mantises think. If you can kill the child, especially before their eyes, it will break their spirit – just as puppies can be broken by the right terrors.'

'Yes, sir.' There was dull incredulity in Shreck's eyes, but this would hold him, a plausible excuse to continue the charade.

'Light the oil beyond the walls. Move the troops in front of where you think Amdijefri will exit. The Visitors must see this if it is to have proper effect. And —' *and blow up the refugee ship!* The words almost slipped out, but he caught himself in time. The explosives built into the Jaws and the Starship dome would bring down everything interior to the outerwalls and would kill most of the packs within. Ordering Shreck to do that would make Steel's real goal all too clear.'—And move quickly before Wood-carver's troops can close. This is the Movement's last hope, Shreck.'

The pack bowed its way back down the steps. Steel maintained an expansive posture, boldly looking across the battlefield until the other was out of sight. Then he reached across the battlements and slammed the radio into the stone walkway. This one didn't break, and now the Ravna mantis's voice came querulously from it. Steel bounded down the stairs. 'You get nothing,' he shrieked back at her in Tines' talk. 'Everything you want will die!'

And then he was down the stairs and running across the courtyard. He ducked out of sight, into the hallway that circled the Jaws of Welcome. He could blow those easily, but very likely the main dome and the ship within would survive. No, he must go to the heart. Kill the ship and all the sleeping mantises. He stepped into a secret room, picked up two crossbows – and the extra *radio* cloak he had prepared. Inside that cloak was a small bomb. He had tested the idea with the second set of *radios*; the wearer had died instantly.

Down another set of stairs, into a supply corridor. The sounds of battle were lost behind him. His own tines' clatter was the loudest noise. Around him loomed bits of gunpowder, food supplies, fresh timber. The fuses and set charges were only fifty yards further on. And Steel slowed to a walk, curled his paws so the metal on them made no noise. Listening. Looking in every direction. Somehow he knew the other would be here. The Flenser Fragment. Flenser had haunted him from the beginning of his existence, had haunted him even after Flenser had mostly died. But not until this clear treason had Steel been able to free his hate. Most likely the Master thought to escape with the children, but there was a chance that Flenser schemed to win *everything*. There was a chance that he had returned. Steel knew his own death would come soon. And yet there might still be triumph. If, by his own jaws and claws, he could kill the Master . . . *Please, please be here, dear Master. Be here thinking you can trick me one more time.*

A wish granted. He heard faint mind sounds. Close. Heads rose from behind the bins above him. Two of the Fragment showed themselves in the corridor ahead.

'Student.'

'Master.' Steel smiled. All five of the others were here; the Fragment had smuggled himself all back. *But gone were the radio cloaks.* The members stood naked, their pelts covered with oozing sores. The radio bomb would be useless. Perhaps it didn't matter; Steel had seen corpses that looked healthier than these. Out of sight he raised his bows. 'I have come to kill you.'

The death's heads shrugged. 'You have come to try.'

Jaws on claws, Steel would have had no trouble killing the other. But the Fragment had positioned three of himself above, by cargo bins that looked strangely off-balance. A straight forward rush could be fatal. But if he could get good bow shots . . . Steel eased forward, to just short of where the cargo bins would fall. 'Do you really expect to live, Fragment? I am not your only enemy.' He waved a nose back up the corridor. 'There are thousands out there who hunger for your death.'

The other bobbed its heads in a ghastly smile. New blood oozed from the wounds that were opened. 'Dear Steel, you never seem to understand. *You* have made it possible for me to survive. Don't you see? I have saved the children. Even now, I am preventing you from harming the starship. In the end this will win me a conditional surrender. I will be weak for a few years, but I will survive.'

The old Flenser glittered through the pain of the wounds. The old opportunism.

'But you are a *fragment.* Three-fifths of you is—'

'The little school teacher?' Flenser lowered his heads, blinked shyly. 'She was stronger than I expected. For a while she ruled this pack, but bit by bit I forced my way back. In the end, even without the others, I am whole.'

Flenser whole once more. Steel edged back, almost in retreat. Yet there was something strange here. Yes, the Flenser was at peace with himself, self-satisfied. But now that Steel could see the pack all together, he saw something in its body language that . . . Insight came then, and with it a flash of intense pride. *For once in my life, I understand better than the Master.* 'Whole, you say? Think. We both know how souls do battle within, the little rationalizations, the great unknowings. You think you've killed the other, but whence comes your recent confidence? What you're doing is exactly what Tyrathect would do now. All thought is yours now, but the foundation is her soul. And whatever you *think*, it's the little school teacher who won!'

The Fragment hesitated, understanding. Its inattention lasted only a fraction of a second, but Steel was ready: he leaped into the open, loosing his arrows, lunging across the open space for the other's throats.

40

Any time before now, the climb through the walls would have been fun. Even though it was pitch dark, Amdi was in front and behind him, and his noses gave him a good feel for the way. Any time before now, there would have been the thrill of discovery, of giggling at Amdi's strung-out mental state.

But now Amdi's confusion was simply scary. He kept bumping into Jefri's heels. 'I'm going as fast as I can.' The fabric of Jefri's pants' knees was already torn apart on the rough stone. He hustled faster, the stabbing beat of rock on knees barely penetrating his consciousness. He bumped into the puppy ahead of him. The puppy had stopped, seemed to be twisting sideways. 'There's a fork. I say we . . . what should I say, Jefri?'

Jefri rolled back, knocking his head on top of the wormhole. For most of a year it had been Amdi's confidence, his cheeky cleverness, that had kept him going. Now . . . Suddenly he was aware of the tonnes of rock that were pressing in from all directions. If the tunnel narrowed just a few centimeters, they would be stuck here forever.

'Jefri?'

'I—' *Think!* 'Which side seems to be going up?'

'Just a second.' The lead member ran off a little ways down one fork.

'Don't go too far!' Jefri shouted.

'Don't worry. I . . . he'll know to get back.' Then he heard patter of return, and the lead member was touching its nose to his cheek. 'The one on the right goes up.'

They hadn't gone more than fifteen meters before Amdi started hearing things. 'People chasing us?' asked Jefri.

'No. I mean, I'm not sure. Stop. Listen . . . Hear that? Gluppy, syrupy.' *Oil.*

No more stopping. Jefri moved faster than ever up the tunnel. His head bumped into the ceiling and he stumbled to his elbows, recovered without thinking and raced on. A trickle of blood dripped down his cheek.

Even he could hear the oil now.

The sides of the tunnel closed down on his shoulders. Ahead of him, Amdi said, 'Dead end – or we're at an exit!' Scritching sounds. 'I can't move it.' The puppy turned around and wiggled back between Jefri's legs. 'Push at the top, Jefri. If it's like the one I found in the dome, it opens at the top.'

The darn tunnel got narrow right before the door. Jefri hunched his shoulders and squeezed forward. He pushed at the top of the door. It moved, maybe a centimeter. He crawled forward a little further, squished so tightly between the walls that he couldn't even take a deep breath. Now he pushed as hard as he could. The stone turned all the way and light spilled onto his face. It wasn't full daylight; they were still hidden from the outside behind angles of stone – but it was the happiest sight Jefri had ever seen. Half a meter more and he would be out – only now he was jammed.

He twisted forward a fraction, and things only seemed to get worse. Behind him, Amdi was piling up. 'Jefri! My rear paws are in the oil. It's filled the tunnel all up behind us.'

Panic. For a second Jefri couldn't think of anything. So close, so close. He could see color now, the bloody smears on his hands. 'Back up! I'll take off my jacket and try again.'

Backing up was itself almost impossible, so thoroughly wedged had he become. Finally he'd done it. He turned on his side, shrugged out of the jacket.

'Jefri! Two of me under . . . oil. Can't breathe.' The puppies jammed up around him, their pelts slick with oil. *Slick!*

'Jus' second!' Jefri wiped the fur, smeared his shoulders with the oil. He extended his arms straight past his head and used his heels to push back into the narrowness. Behind him, what was left of Amdi was making whistling noises. Jam. *Push. Push.* A centimeter, another. And then he was out to his armpits and it was easy.

He dropped to the ground and reached back to grab the nearest part of Amdi. The pup wriggled out of his hands. It blubbered something not Tinish and not human. Jefri could see the dark shadows of several members pulling at something out of sight. A second later, a cold, wet blob of fur rolled out of the darkness into his arms. A second more, and out came another. Jefri lowered the two to the ground and wiped goo away from their muzzles. One rolled onto its legs and began to shake itself. The other started choking and coughing.

Meanwhile the rest of Amdi dropped out of the hole. All eight were covered with some amount of oil. They straggled drunkenly into a heap, wiping at each another's tympana. Their buzzing and croaking made no sense.

Jefri turned from his friend and walked toward the light. They were hidden by a turn in the stone . . . fortunately. From around the corner he could hear the marshalling calls of Steel's troopers. He crept to the edge and peered around. For an instant he thought he and Amdi were back inside the castle yard; there were so many troopers. But then he saw the unbounded sweep of the hillside and the smoke rising out of the valley.

What next? He glanced back at Amdi, who was still frantically grooming his tympana. The chords and hums were sounding more rational now, and all of Amdi was moving. He turned back to the hillside. For an instant he almost felt like rushing out to the troops. They had been his protectors for so long.

One of Amdi bumped against his legs, and looked out for himself. 'Wow. There's a regular lake of oil between us and Mr Steel's soldiers. I—'

The booming sound was loud, but not like a gunpowder blast. It lasted almost a second, then became a background roar. Two more of Amdi stretched necks around the corner. The lake had become a roaring sea of flame.

Blueshell had maneuvered the boat within two hundred meters of the castle wall, opposite the point where the packs had bunched up. Now the lander floated just a man's height off the moss. 'Just our being here is driving the packs away,' said Pilgrim.

Pham glanced over his shoulder. Woodcarver's troops had regained the field, were racing toward the castle walls. Another sixty seconds, max, and they would be in contact with Steel's packs.

There was a loud *brap* from Blueshell's voder, and Pham looked forward. 'By the Fleet,' he said softly. Packs on the ramparts had fired some kind of flamethrowers into the pools of oil below the castle walls. Blueshell flew in a little closer. Long pools of oil lay parallel to the walls. The enemy's packs on the outside were all but cut off from their castle now. Except for one thirty-meter-wide gap, the section they had been guarding was high fire.

The boat bobbed a little higher, tilting and sliding in the fire-driven whirl of air. In most places the oil lapped the sloped base of the walls. Those walls were more intricate than the castles of Canberra – in many places it looked like there were little mazes or caves built into the base. *Looks damn stupid in a defensive structure.*

'*Jefri!*' screamed Johanna, and pointed toward the middle of the unburning section. Pham had a glimpse of something withdrawing behind the stonework.

'I saw him too.' Blueshell tilted the boat over and slid downwards, toward the wall. Johanna's hand closed on Pham's arm, pushing and shaking. He could barely hear her voice over the Pilgrim's shouting. 'Please, please, please,' she was saying.

For a moment it looked like they would make it: Steel's troops were well back from them and – though there were ponds of oil below them – they were not yet alight. Even the air seemed quieter than before. For all that, Blueshell managed to lose control. A gentle tipping went uncorrected, and the boat slid sideways into the ground. It was a slow collision, but Pham heard one of the landing pods cracking. Blueshell played with the controls and the other side of the craft settled to earth. The beamer was stuck muzzle first into the earth.

Pham's gaze snapped up at the Skroderider. He'd known it would come to this.

Ravna: 'What happened? Can you get up?'

Blueshell dithered with the controls a moment longer, then gave a Riderish shrug. 'Yes. But it will take too long—' He was undoing his restraints, unclamping his skrode from the deck. The hatch in front of him slid open, and the noise of battle and fire came loud.

'What in hell do you think you're doing, Blueshell!'

The Rider's fronds angled attention at Pham. 'To rescue the boy. This will all be afire in a moment.'

'And this boat could fry if we leave it here. You're not going anywhere, Blueshell.' He leaned forward, far enough to grab the other by his lower fronds.

Johanna was looking wildly from one to the other in an uncomprehending panic. 'No! Please—' And Ravna was shouting at him too. Pham tensed, all his attention on the Rider.

Blueshell rocked toward him in the cramped space and pushed his fronds close to Pham's face. The voder voice frayed into nonlinearity: 'And what will you do if I disobey? I go, Sir Pham. I prove I am not the thrall of some Power. Can you prove as much?'

He paused, and for a moment Rider and human stared at each other from centimeters apart. But Pham did not grab him.

Brap. Blueshell's fronds withdrew. He rolled back onto the lip of the hatch. The skrode's third axle reached the ground, and he descended in a controlled teeter. Still Pham had not moved. *I am not some Power's program.*

'Pham?' The girl was looking up at him, and tugging at his sleeve. Nuwen shook the nightmare away and saw again. The Pilgrim pack was already out of the boat. Short swords were held in the mouths of the four adults; steel claws gleamed on their forepaws.

'Okay.' He flipped open a panel, withdrew the pistol he'd hidden there. Since Blueshell had crashed the damn boat, there was no choice but to make the best of it.

The realization was a cool breath of freedom. He pulled free of the crash restraints and clambered down. Pilgrim stood all around him. The two with puppies were un-limbering some kind of shields. Even with all his mouths full, the critter's voice was as clear as ever: 'Maybe we can find a way closer in—' between the flames. There were no more arrows from the ramparts. The air above the fire was just too hot for the archers.

Pham and Johanna followed Pilgrim as he skirted pools of black goo. 'Stay as far from the oil as you can.'

The packs of Mr Steel were rounding the flames. Pham couldn't tell if they were charging the lander or simply fleeing the friendlies that chased them. And maybe it didn't matter. He dropped to one knee and sprayed the oncoming packs with his handgun. It was nothing like the beamer, especially at this range, but it was not to be ignored: the front dogs tumbled. Others bounded over them. They reached the far edge of the oil. Only a few ventured into the goo – they knew what it could become. Others shifted out of Pham's sight, behind the landing boat.

Was there a dry approach? Pham ran along the edge of the oil. There had to be a gap in the 'moat,' or surely the fire would have spread. Ahead of him the flames towered ten meters into the air, the heat a physical battering on his skin. Above the top of the glow, tarry smoke swept back over the field, turning the sunlight into reddish murk. 'Can't see a thing,' came Ravna's voice in his ear, despairing.

'There's still a chance, Rav.' If he could hold them off long enough for Woodcarver's troops . . .

Steel's packs had found a safe path inwards and were coming closer. Something zipped past him – an arrow. He dropped to the ground and sprayed the enemy packs at full rate. If they had known how fast he was getting to empty they might have kept coming, but after a few seconds of ripping carnage, the advance halted. The enemy sweep broke apart and the dogthings were running away, taking their chances with Woodcarver's packs.

Pham turned, looking back at the castle. Johanna and Pilgrim stood ten meters nearer the walls. She was standing, pulling against the pack's grasp. Pham followed her gaze . . . There was the Skroderider. Blueshell had paid no attention to the packs that ran around the edge of the fire. He rolled steadily inwards, oily tracks marking his progress. The Rider had drawn in all his externals, and pulled his cargo scarf close to his central stalk. He was driving blind through the superheated air, deeper and deeper into the narrowing gap between flames.

He was less than fifteen meters from the walls. Abruptly two fronds extended out from his trunk, into the heat. *There.* Through the heat shimmer, Pham could see the kid, walking uncertainly out from the cover of stone. Small shapes sat on the boy's shoulders and walked beside him. Pham ran up the slope. He could move faster over this terrain than any Rider. Maybe there was time.

A single burst of flame arched down from the castle, into the pond of oil between him and the Rider at the wall. What had been a narrow channel of safety was gone, and the flames spread unbroken before him.

'There's still lots of clear space,' Amdi said. He reached a few meters out from their hiding place to reconnoiter around the corners. '*The flier is down!* Some . . . strange thing . . . is coming our way. Blueshell or Greenstalk?'

There were lots of Steel's packs out there too, but not close – probably because of the flier. That was a weird one, with none of the symmetry of Straumer aircraft. It looked all tilted over, almost as if it had crashed. A tall human raced across their field of view, firing at Steel's troops. Jefri looked further out, and his hand tightened almost unconsciously on the nearest puppy. Coming toward them was a wheeled vehicle, like something out of a Nyjoran historical. The sides were painted with jagged stripes. A thick pole grew up from the top.

The two children stepped a little ways out from their protection. The spacer saw them! It slewed about, spraying oil and moss from under its wheels. Two frail somethings reached out from its bluish trunk. Its voice was squeaky Samnorsk. 'Quickly, Sir Jefri. We have little time.' Behind the creature, beyond the pond of oil, Jefri could see . . . *Johanna*.

And then the pond exploded, the fire on both sides sprouting across all escape routes. Still the Spacer was waving its tendrils, urging them onto the flat of its hull. Jefri grasped at the few handholds available. The puppies jumped up after him, clinging to his shirt and pants. Up close, Jefri could see that the stalk was the person: the skin was smudged and dry, but it was soft and it moved.

Two of Amdi were still on the ground, ranging out on either side of the cart for a better view of the fire. '*Wah!*' shrieked Amdi by his ear. Even so close, he could scarcely be heard over the thunder of the fire. 'We can never get through that, Jefri. Our only chance is to stay here.'

The Spacer's voice came from a little plate at the base of its stalk. 'No. If you stay here, you *will* die. The fire is spreading.' Jefri had huddled as much behind the Rider's stalk as possible, and still he could feel the heat. Much more and the oil in Amdi's fur might catch fire.

The Rider's tendrils lifted the colored cloth that lay on its hull. 'Pull this over you.' It waggled a tendril at the rest of Amdi. '*All* of you.'

The two on the ground were crouched behind the creature's front wheels. 'Too hot, too hot,' came Amdi's voice. But the two jumped up and buried themselves under the peculiar tarpaulin.

'Cover yourself, all the way!' Jefri felt the Rider pulling the cover over them. The cart was already rolling back, toward the flames. Pain burned through every gap in the tarp. The boy reached frantically, first with one hand and then the other, trying to get the cloth over his legs. Their course was a wild bouncing ride, and Jefri could barely keep hold. Around him he felt Amdi straining with his free jaws to keep the tarpaulin in place. The sound of fire was a roaring beast, and the tarp itself was searing hot against his skin. Every new jolt bounced him up from the hull, threatening to break his grip. For a time, panic obliterated thought. It was not till much later that he remembered the tiny sounds that came from the voder plate, and understood what those sounds must mean.

Pham ran toward the new flames. Agony. He raised his arms across his face and felt the skin on his hands blistering. He backed away.

'This way, this way!' Pilgrim's voice came from behind him, guiding him out. He ran back, stumbling. The pack was in a shallow gully. It had shifted its shields around to face the new stretch of fire. Two of the pack moved out of his way as he dived behind them.

Both Johanna and the pack were slapping at his head.

'Your hair's on fire!' the girl shouted. In seconds they had the fire out.

The Pilgrim looked a big singed, too. Its shoulder pouches were tucked safely shut; for the first time, no inquisitive puppy eyes peeked out.

'I still can't see anything, Pham.' It was Ravna from high above. 'What's going on?'

Quick glance behind him. 'We're okay,' he gasped. 'Woodcarver's packs are tearing up Steel's. But Blueshell—' He peered between in the shields. It was like looking into a kiln. Right by the castle wall there might be a breathing space. A slim hope, but—

'Something is moving in there.' Pilgrim had tucked one head briefly around the shield. He withdrew it now, licking his nose from both sides.

Pham looked again through the crack. The fire had internal shadows, places of not-so-bright that wavered . . . moved? 'I see it too.' He felt Johanna stick her head close to his, peering frantically. 'It's Blueshell, Rav . . . *By the Fleet*.' This last said too softly to carry over the fire sound. There was no sign of Jefri Olsndot, but 'Blueshell's rolling through the middle of the fire, Rav.'

The skrode wheeled out of the deeper oil. Slowly, steadily making its way. And now Pham could see fire within fire, Blueshell's trunk flaring in rivulets of flame. His fronds were no longer gathered into himself. They extended, writhing with their own fire. 'He's still coming, driving straight out.'

The skrode cleared the wall of fire, rolled with jerky abandon down the slope. Blueshell didn't turn toward them, but just before he reached the landing boat, all six wheels grated to a fast stop.

Pham stood and raced back toward the Skroderider. Pilgrim was already unlimbering his shields and turning to follow him. Johanna Olsndot stood for a second, sad and slight and alone, her gaze stuck hopelessly on the fire and smoke on the castle side. One of the Pilgrim grabbed her sleeve, drawing her back from the fire.

Pham was at the Rider now. He stared silently for a second.

'. . . Blueshell's dead, Rav, no way you could doubt if you could see.' The fronds were burnt away, leaving stubs along the stalk. The stalk itself had burst.

Ravna's voice in his ear was shuddery. 'He drove *through* that even while he was burning?'

'Can't be. He must have been dead after the first few meters. This must all have been on autopilot.' Pham tried to forget the agonized reaching of fronds he had seen back in the fire. He blanked out for a moment, staring at the fire-split flesh.

The skrode itself radiated heat. Pilgrim sniffed around it, shying away abruptly when a nose came too close. Abruptly he reached out a steel-tined paw and pulled hard on the scarf that covered the hull.

Johanna screamed, rushing forward faster than Pilgrim or Pham. The forms beneath the scarf were unmoving but unburned. She grabbed her brother by the shoulders, pulling him to the ground. Pham knelt down beside her. *Is the kid breathing?* He was distantly aware of Ravna shouting in his ear, and Pilgrim plucking tiny dogthings off the metal.

Seconds later the boy started coughing. His arms windmilled against his sister. 'Amdi, Amdi!' His eyes opened, widened. 'Sis!' And then again. 'Amdi?'

'I don't know,' said the Pilgrim, standing close to the seven – no, *eight* – grease-covered forms. 'There are some mind sounds but not coherent.' He nosed at three of puppies, doing something that might have been rescue breathing.

After a moment the little boy began crying, a sound lost in the fire sounds. He crawled across to the puppies, his face right next to one of Pilgrim's. Johanna was right behind him, holding his shoulders, looking first to Pilgrim and then at the still creatures.

Pham came to his knees and looked back at the castle. The fire was a little lower now. He stared a long time at the blackened stump that had been Blueshell. Wondering and remembering. Wondering if all the suspicion had been for naught. Wondering what mix of courage and autopilot had been behind the rescue.

Remembering all the months he had spent with Blueshell, the liking and then the hate – *Oh, Blueshell, my friend.*

The fires slowly ebbed. Pham paced the edge of receding heat. He felt the godshatter coming finally back upon him. For once he welcomed it, welcomed the drive and the mania, the blunting of irrelevant feeling. He looked at Pilgrim and Johanna and Jefri and the recovering puppy pack. It was all a meaningless diversion. No, not quite meaningless: It had had an effect, of slowing down progress on what *was* deadly important.

He glanced upwards. There were gaps in the sooty clouds, places where he could see the reddish haze of high-level ash and occasional splotches of blue. The castle's ramparts appeared abandoned, and the battle around the walls had died. 'What news?' he said impatiently at the sky.

Ravna: 'I still can't see much around you, Pham. Large numbers of Tines – probably the enemy – are retreating northwards. Looks like a fast, coordinated retreat. Nothing like the "fight-to-the-last" that we were seeing before. There are no fires within the castle – or evidence of remaining packs either.'

Decision. Pham turned back toward the others. He struggled to turn sharp commands into reasonable-sounding requests. 'Pilgrim! Pilgrim! I need Woodcarver's help. We have to get inside the castle.'

Pilgrim didn't need any special persuasion, though he was full of questions. 'You're going to fly over the walls?' he asked as he bounded toward him.

Pham was already jogging toward the boat. He boosted Pilgrim aboard, then clambered up. No, he wasn't going to try to fly the damn thing. 'No, just use the loudspeaker to get your boss to find a way in.'

Seconds later, packtalk was echoing across the hillside. *Just minutes more. Just miutes more and I will be facing the Countermeasure.* And though he had no conscious notion what might come of that, he felt the godshatter bubbling up for one final takeover, one final act of Old One's will. 'Where is the Blighter fleet, Rav?'

Her answer came back immediately. She had watched the battle below, and the hammer coming down from above. 'Forty-eight light-years out.' Mumbled conversation off-mike. 'They've speeded up a little. They'll be in-system in forty-six hours . . . I'm sorry, Pham.'

Crypto: 0
As received by: *OOB* shipboard ad hoc
Language path: Triskweline, SjK units
Apparently From: Sandor Arbitration Intelligence
   [Not the usual originator, but verified by intermediate sites. Originator may be
   a branch office or a back-up site.]
Subject: Our final message?
Distribution:
   Threat of the Blight
   War Trackers Interest Group
   Where Are They Now, Extinctions Log
Date: 72.78 days since the Fall of Sjandra Kei
Key phrases: vast new attack, the Fall of Sandor Arbitration
Text of message:
   As best we can tell, all of our High Beyond sites have been absorbed by the
Blight. If you can, please ignore all messages from those sites.
   Until four hours ago, our organization comprised twenty civilizations at the
Top. What is left of us doesn't know what to say or what to do. Things are so
slow and murky and dull now; we were not meant to live this low. We intend to
disband after this transmission.
   For those who can continue, we want to say what happened. The new attack
was an abrupt thing. Our last recollections from Above are of the Blight
suddenly *reaching* in all directions, sacrificing all its immediate security to
acquire as much processing power as possible. We don't know if we had simply
underestimated its power, or if the Blight itself is now desperate – and taking
desperate risks.
   Up to 3000 seconds ago we were still under heavy assault along our
organization's internal networks. That has ceased. Temporarily? Or is this the
limit of the attack? We don't know, but if you hear from us again, you will know
that the Blight has us.
   Farewell.

Crypto: 0
As received by: *OOB* shipboard ad hoc
Language path: Optima → Acquileron → Triskweline, SjK units
From: Society for Rational Investigation
   [Probably a single system in the Middle Beyond, 7500 light-years antispinward
   of Sjandra Kei]
Subject: The Big Picture
Key Phrases: The Blight, Nature's Beauty, Unprecedented Opportunities
Summary: Life goes on
Distribution:
   Threat of the Blight
   Society for Rational Network Management
   War Trackers Interest Group
Date: 72.80 days since the Fall of Sjandra Kei
Text of message:

It's always amusing to see people who think themselves the center of the universe. Take the recent spread of the Blight [references follow for readers not on those threads and newsgroups]. The Blight is an unprecedent change in a limited portion of the Top of the Beyond-far away from most of my readers. I'm sure it's the ultimate catastrophe for many, and I certainly feel sympathy for such, but a little humor too, that these people somehow think their disaster is the end of everything. Life goes on, folks.

At the same time, it's clear that many readers are not paying proper attention to these events – certainly not seeing what is truly significant about them. In the last year, we have witnessed the apparent murders of several Powers and the establishment of a new ecosystem in a portion of the High Beyond. Though far away, these events are without precedent.

Often before, I have called this the Net of a Million Lies. Well, people, we now have an opportunity to view things while the truth is still manifest. With luck we may solve some fundamental mysteries about the Zones and the Powers.

I urge readers to watch events below the Blight from as many angles as possible. In particular, we should take advantage of the remaining relay at Debley Down to coordinate observations on both sides of the Blight-affected region. This will be expensive and tedious, since only Middle and Low Beyond sites are available in the affected region, but it will be well worth it.

General topics to follow:

The nature of the Blight's Net communications: The creature is part Power and part High Beyond, and infinitely interesting.

The nature of the recent Great Surge in the Low Beyond beneath the Blight: This is another event without clear precedent. Now is the time to study it . . .

The nature of the Blighter fleet now closing on an off-net site in the Low Beyond: This fleet has been of great interest to War Trackers over the last weeks, but mainly for asinine reasons (who cares about Sjandra Kei and the Aprahant Hegemony; local politics is for locals). The real question should be obvious to all but the brain damaged: *Why* has the Blight made this great effort so far from its natural zone?

If there are any ships still in the vicinity of the Blight's fleet, I urge them to keep War Trackers posted. Failing that, local civilizations should be reimbursed for forwarding ultrawave traces.

This is all very expensive, but worth it, the observation of the aeon. And the expense will not continue long. The Blight's fleet should arrive at the target star momentarily. Will it stop and retrieve? Or will we see how a Power destroys the systems which oppose it? Either way, we are blessed with opportunity.

41

Ravna walked across the field toward the waiting packs. The thick smoke had been blown away, but its smell was still heavy in the air. The hillside was burned-over desolation. From above, Steel's castle had looked like the center of a great, black nipple, hectares of natural and pack-made destruction capping the hill.

The soldiers silently made way for her. More than one cast an uneasy glance at the starship grounded behind her. She walked slowly past them, toward the ones who waited. Eerie the way they sat, like picnickers but all uneasy about each other's presence. This must be the equivalent of a close staff conference for them. Ravna walked toward the pack at the center, the one sitting on silken mats. Intricate wooden filigree hung around the necks of the adults, but some of those looked sick, old. And there were two puppies sitting out front of it. They stepped precisely forward as Ravna crossed the last stretch of open ground.

'Er, you're the Woodcarver?' she asked.

A woman's voice, incredibly human, came from one of the larger members. 'Yes, Ravna. I'm Woodcarver. But it's Peregrine you want. He's up in the castle, with the children.'

'Oh.'

'We have a wagon. We can take you inwards right away.' One of them pointed at a vehicle being drawn up the hillside. 'But you could have landed much closer, could you not?'

Ravna shook her head. 'No. Not . . . anymore.' This was the best landing that she and Greenstalk could make.

The heads cocked at her, all a coordinated gesture. 'I thought you were in a terrible hurry. Peregrine says there is a fleet of spacers coming hot on your trail.'

For an instant Ravna didn't say anything. So Pham had told them of the Blight? But she was glad he had. She shook her head, trying to clear it of the numbness. 'Y-yes. We are in a great hurry.' The dataset on her wrist was linked to the *OOB*. Its tiny display showed the steady approach of the Blight's fleet.

All the heads twisted, a gesture that Ravna couldn't interpret. 'And you despair. I fear I understand.'

How can you? And if you can, how can you forgive us? But all that Ravna said aloud was, 'I'm sorry.'

The queen mounted her wagon and they rolled across the hillside toward the castle walls. Ravna looked back once. Down slope, the *OOB* lay like a great, dying moth. Its topside drive spines arched a hundred meters into the air. They glistened a wet, metallic green. Their landing had not quite been a crash. Even now, agrav cancelled some of the craft's weight. But the drive spines on the ground side were crumpled. Beyond the ship, the hillside fell steeply away to the water and the islands. The westering sun cast hazy shadows across the islands and on the castle beyond the straits. A fantasy scene of castles and starships.

The display on her wrist serenely counted down the seconds.

'Steel put gunpowder bombs all around the dome.' Woodcarver swept a couple of noses, pointing upwards. Ravna followed her gesture. The arches were more like a Princess cathedral than military architecture: pink marble challenging the sky. And if it all came down, it would surely wreck the spacecraft parked beneath.

Woodcarver said that Pham was in there now. They rolled indoors, through dark, cool rooms. Ravna glimpsed row after row of coldsleep boxes. *How many might still be revivable? Will we ever find out?* The shadows were deep. 'You're sure that Steel's troops are gone?'

Woodcarver hesitated, her heads staring in different directions. So far, pack expresions were impossible for Ravna to read. 'Reasonably sure. Anybody still in the castle would need to be behind lots of stone, or my search parties would have found them. More important, we have what's left of Steel.' The Queen seemed to read Ravna's questioning expression perfectly. 'You didn't know? Apparently, Lord Steel came down here to blow all the bombs. It would have been suicide, but that pack was always a crazy one. Someone stopped him. There was blood all over. Two of him are dead. We found the rest wandering around, a whimpering mess . . . Whoever did Steel in is also behind the rapid retreat. That someone is doing his best to avoid any confrontation. He won't be back soon, though I fear I'll have to face dear Flenser eventually.'

Under the circumstances, Ravna figured that was one problem that would never materialize. Her dataset showed forty-five fours till the Blight's arrival.

Jefri and Johanna were by their starship, under the main dome. They sat on the steps of the landing ramp, holding hands. When the wide doors opened and Woodcarver's wagon drove through, the girl stood and waved.

396

Then they saw Ravna. The boy walked first quickly then more slowly across the wide floor. 'Jefri Olsndot?' Ravna called softly. He had a tentative, dignified posture that seemed much too old for a nine year old. Poor Jefri had lost much, and lived with so little for so long. She stepped down from the wagon and walked toward him.

The boy advanced out of the shadows. He was surrounded by a near mob of small-size pack members. One of them hung on his shoulder; others tumbled around his feet without ever seeming to get in his way; still others followed his path both in front and behind. Jefri stopped well back from her. 'Ravna?'

She nodded.

'Could you step a little closer? The queen's mind sound is too close.' The voice was still the boy's, *but his lips hadn't moved.* She walked the few meters that still separated them. Puppies and boy advanced hesitantly. Up close she could see the rips in his clothing, and what looked like wound dressings on his shoulders and elbows and knees. His face looked recently washed, but his hair was a sticky mess. He looked up at her solemnly, then raised his arms to hug her. 'Thank you for coming.' His voice was muffled against her, but he wasn't crying. 'Yes, thank you, thank poor Mr Blueshell.' His voice again, sad but unmuffled, coming from the pack of pupppies all around them.

Johanna Olsndot had advanced to stand just behind them. *Only fourteen she is?* Ravna reached a hand toward her. 'From what I hear, you were a rescue force all by yourself.'

Woodcarver's voice came from the wagon. 'Johanna was that. She changed our world.'

Ravna gestured up the ship's ramp, at the glow of the interior lighting. 'Pham's up there?'

The girl started to nod, was preempted by the pack of puppies. 'Yes, he is. He and the Pilgrim are up there.' The pups disentangled themselves and started up the steps, one remaining behind to tug Ravna toward the ramp. She started after them, with Jefri close beside her.

'Who *is* this pack?' she said abruptly to Jefri, pointing to the puppies.

The boy stopped in surprise. 'Amdi of course.'

'I'm sorry,' Jefri's voice came from the puppies. 'I've talked to you so much, I forget you don't know—' There was a chorus of tones and chords that ended in a human giggle. She looked down at the bobbing heads, and was certain the little devil was quite aware of his misrepresentations. Suddenly a mystery was solved. 'Pleased to meet you,' she said, angered and charmed at the same time. 'Now—'

'Right, there are much more important things now.' The pack continued to hop up stairs. 'Amdi' seemed to alternate between shy sadness and manic activity. 'I don't know what they're up to. They kicked us out as soon as we showed them around.'

Ravna followed the pack, Jefri close behind. It didn't *sound* like anything was going on. The interior of the dome was like a tomb, echoing with the talk of the few packs who guarded it. But here, halfway up the steps, even those sounds were muted, and there was nothing coming through the hatch at the top. 'Pham?'

'He's up there.' It was Johanna, at the base of the stairs. She and Woodcarver were looking up at them. She hesitated. 'I'm not sure if he's okay. After the battle, he – he seemed strange.'

Woodcarver's heads weaved about, as if she were trying to get a good look at them through the glare of the hatch lights. 'The acoustics in this ship of yours are awful. How can humans stand it?'

Amdi: 'Ah, it's not so bad. Jefri and I spent lots of time up here. I got used to it.' Two of his heads were pushing at the hatch. 'I don't know why Pham and Pilgrim kicked us out; we could have stayed in the other room and been real quiet.'

Ravna stepped carefully between the pack's lead puppies and pounded on the hull metal. It wasn't hard-latched; now she could hear the ship's ventilation. 'Pham, what progress?'

There was a rustling sound and the click of claws. The hatch slid partway back. Bright, flickering light spilled down the ramp. A single doggy head appeared. Ravna could see white all around its eyes. Did that mean anything? 'Hi,' it said. 'Uh, look. Things are a bit tense just now. Pham – I don't think Pham should be bothered.'

Ravna slipped her hand past the gap. 'I'm not here to bother him. But I am coming in.' *How long we've fought for this moment. How many billions have died along the way. And now some talking dog tells me things are a bit tense.*

The Pilgrim looked down at her hand. 'Okay.' He slid the hatch far enough open to let her through. The pups were quick around her heels, but they recoiled before the Pilgrim's glance. Ravna didn't notice . . .

The 'ship' was scarcely more than a freight container, a cargo hull. The cargo this time – the coldsleep boxes – had been removed, leaving a mostly level floor, dotted with hundreds of fittings.

All this she scarcely noticed. It was the light, the *thing*, that held her eyes. It grew out from the walls and gathered almost too bright to bear at the center of the hold. Its shape changed and changed again, its colors shifting from red to violet to green. Pham sat crosslegged by the apparition, within it. Half his hair was burned away. His hands and arms were shivering, and he mumbled in some language she didn't recognize. Godshatter. Two times it had been the companion to disaster. A dying Power's madness . . . and now it was the only hope. *Oh Pham.*

Ravna took a step toward him, felt jaws close on her sleeve. 'Please, he mustn't be disturbed.' The one that was holding her arm was a big dog, battle scarred. The rest of the pack – Pilgrim – all faced inwards on Pham. The savage stared at her, somehow saw the anger rising in her face. Then the pack said, 'Look ma'am, your Pham's in some sort of fugue state, all the normal personality traded for computation.'

Huh? This Pilgrim had the jargon, but probably not much else. Pham must have been talking to him. She made a shushing gesture. 'Yes, yes. I understand.' She stared into the light. The changing shape, so hard to look at, was something like the graphics you can generate on most displays, the silly cross-sections of high-dimensional froths. It glowed in purest mono-chrome, but shifted through the colors. Much of the light must be coherent: interference speckles crawled on every solid surface. In places the inter-ference banded up, stripes of dark and light that slid across the hull as the colour changed.

She walked slowly closer, staring at Pham and . . . the Countermeasure. For what else could it be? The scum in the walls, now grown out to meet godshatter. This was not simply data, a message to be relayed. This was a Transcendent machine. Ravna had read of such things: devices made in the Transcend for use at the Bottom of the Beyond. There would be nothing sentient about it, nothing that violated the constraints of the Lower Zones – yet it would make the best possible use of nature here, to do whatever its builder had desired: *Its builder? The Blight? An enemy of the Blight?*

She stepped closer. The thing was deep in Pham's chest, but there was no blood, no torn flesh. She might have thought it all trick holography except that she could see him shudder at its writhing. The fractal arms were feathered by long teeth, twisting at him. She gasped, almost called his name. But Pham wasn't resisting. He seemed deeper into godshatter than ever before, and more at peace. The hope and fear came suddenly out of hiding: hope that maybe, even now, godshatter could do something about the Blight; and fear, that Pham would die in the process.

The artifact's twisting evolution slowed. The light hung at the pale edge of blue. Pham's eyes opened. His head turned toward her. 'The Riders' Myth is real, Ravna.' His voice was distant. She heard the whisper of a laugh. 'The Riders should know, I guess. They learned the last time. There are Things that don't like the Blight. Things my Old One only guessed at . . .'

Powers beyond the Powers? Ravna sank to the floor. The display on her wrist glowed up at her. Less than forty-five hours left.

Pham saw her downward glance, 'I know. Nothing has slowed the fleet. It's a pitiful thing so far down here . . . but more than powerful enough to destroy this world, this solar system. And that's what the Blight wants now. The Blight knows I can destroy it . . . just as it was destroyed before.'

Ravna was vaguely aware that Pilgrim had crawled in close on all sides. Every face was fixed on the blue froth and the human enmeshed within. 'How, Pham?' Ravna whispered.

Silence. Then, 'All the zone turbulence . . . that was Countermeasure trying to act, but without coordination. Now I'm guiding it. I've begun . . . the reverse surge. It's drawing on local energy sources. Can't you feel it?'

Reverse surge? What was Pham talking about? She glanced again at her wrist – and gasped. Enemy speed had jumped to twenty light-years per hour, as fast as might be expected in the Middle Beyond. What had been almost two days of grace was barely two hours . . . Now the display said twenty-five light-years per hour. Thirty.

Someone was pounding on the hatch.

Scrupilo was delinquent. He should be supervising the move up the hillside. He knew that, and really felt quite guilty – but he persevered in his dereliction. Like an addict chewing *krima* leaves, some things are too delicious to give up.

Scrupilo dawdled behind, carrying Dataset carefully between him so that its floppy pink ears would not drag on the ground. In fact, guarding Dataset was certainly more important than hassling his troopers. In any case, he was more or less close enough to give advice. And his lieutenants were more clever than he at everyday work.

During the last few hours, the coastal winds had taken the smoke clouds inland, and the air was clean and salty. On this part of the hill, not everything was burned. There were even some flowers and fluffy seed pods. Bob-tailed birds sailed up the rising air from the sea valley, their cries a happy music, as if promising that the world would soon be as before.

Scrupilo knew it could not be. He turned all his heads to look down the hillside, at Ravna Bergsndot's starship. He estimated the surviving drive spines as one hundred meters long. The hull itself was more than one hundred and twenty. He hunkered down around Dataset, and popped open its cushioned Oliphaunt face. Dataset knew lots about spacecraft. Actually, this ship was not a human design, but the overall shape was fairly ordinary; he knew that from his previous readings. Twenty to thirty thousand tonnes, equipped with antigravity floats and faster-than-light drive. All very ordinary for the Beyond . . . But to see it *here*, through the eyes of his very own members! Scrupilo couldn't keep his gaze from the thing. Three of him worked with Dataset while the other two stared at the irridescent green hull. The troopers and guncarts around him faded to insignificance. For all its mass, the ship seemed to rest gently on the hillside. *How long will it be before we can build such?* Centuries without outside help, the histories in Dataset claimed. *What I wouldn't give for a dayaround aboard her!*

Yet this ship was being *chased* by something mightier. Scrupilo shivered in the summer sun. He had often enough heard Pilgrim's story of the first landing, and he had seen the human's beam weapon. He had read much in Dataset about planet wrecker-bombs and the other weapons of the Beyond. While he worked on Woodcarver's cannon – the best weapons he could bring to be – he had dreamed and wondered. Until he saw the starship floating above, he had never quite felt the reality in his innermost hearts. Now he did. So a *fleet* of killers chased close behind Ravna Bergsndot. The hours of the world might be few indeed. He tabbed quickly through Dataset's search paths, looking for articles about space piloting. *If there be only hours, at least learn what there is time to learn.*

So Scrupilo was lost in the sound and vision of Dataset. He had three windows open, each on a different aspect of the piloting experience.

Loud shouts from the hillside. He looked up with one head, more irritated than anything else. It wasn't a battle alarm they were calling, just a general unease. Strange, the afternoon air seemed pleasantly cool. Two of him looked high, but there was no haze. 'Scrupilo! Look, Look!'

His gunners were dancing in panic. They were pointing at the sky . . . at the sun. He folded the pink covers over Dataset's face, at the same time looking sunward with shaded view. The sun was still high in the south, dazzling bright. Yet the air was cool, and the birds were making the cooing sounds of low-sun nesting. And suddenly he realized that he was looking straight at the sun's disk, had been for five seconds – without pain or even watering of his eyes. And there was still no haze that he could see. An inner chill spread across his mind.

The sunlight was fading. He could see black dots on the surface. *Sunspots.* He had seen them often enough with Scriber's telescopes. But that had been through heavy filters. *Something stood between him and the sun, something that sucked away its light and warmth.*

The packs on the hillside moaned. It was a frightened sound Scrupilo had never heard in battle, the sound of someone confronted by unknowable terror.

Blue faded from the sky. The air was suddenly cold as deep dark night. And the sun's color was a gray luminescence, like a faded moon. Less. Scrupilo hunkered bellies to ground. Some of him was whistling deep in the throat. *Weapons, weapons. But Dataset never spoke of this.*

The stars were the brightest light on the hillside.

'Pham, Pham. They'll be here in an hour. What have you done?' A miracle, but of ill?

Pham Nuwen swayed in Countermeasure's bright embrace. His voice was almost normal, the godshatter receding. 'What have I done? N-not much. And more than any Power. Even Old One only guessed, Ravna. The thing the Straumers brought here is the Rider Myth. We – I, it – just moved the Zone boundary back. A local change, but intense. We're in the equivalent of the High Beyond now, maybe even the Low Transcend. That's why the Blighter fleet can move so fast.'

'But—'

Pilgrim was back from the hatch. He interrupted Ravna's incoherent panic with a matter-of-fact, 'The sun just went out.' His heads bobbed in an expression she couldn't fathom.

Pham answered, 'That's temporary. Something has to power this maneuver.'

'W-why, Pham?' Even if the Blight was sure to win, why *help* it?

The man's face went blank, Pham Nuwen almost disappearing behind the other programs at work in his mind. Then, 'I'm . . . focusing Countermeasure. I see now, Countermeasure, what it is . . . It was designed by something beyond the Powers. Maybe there are Cloud People, maybe this is signalling them. Or maybe what it's just done is like an insect bite, something that will cause a much greater reaction. The Bottom of the Beyond has just receded, like the waterline before a tsunami.' The Countermeasure glared red-orange, its arcs and barbs embracing Pham more tightly than before. 'A-and now that we have bootstrapped to a decent Zone . . . things can really happen. Oh, the ghost of Old One is amused. Seeing beyond the Powers was almost worth dying for.'

The fleet stats flowed across Ravna's wrist. The Blight was coming on even faster than before. 'Five minutes, Pham.' Even though they were still thirty light-years out.

Laughter. 'Oh, the Blight knows, too. I see this is what it feared all along. This *is* what killed it those aeons ago. It's racing forward now, but it's too late.' The glow brightened, the mask of light that was Pham's face seemed to relax. 'Something very . . . far . . . away has heard me, Rav. It's coming.'

'What? What's coming?'

'The Surge. So big. It makes what hit us before seem a gentle wave. This is the one nobody believes, because no one's left to record it. The Bottom will be blown out beyond the fleet.'

Sudden understanding. Sudden wild hope. '. . . And they'll be trapped out there, won't they?' So Kjet Svensndot had not fought in vain, and Pham's advice had not been nonsense: Now there wasn't a single ramscoop in the Blighter fleet.

'Yes. They're thirty light-years out. We killed all the speed-capable ones. They'll be a thousand years getting here . . .' The artifact abruptly contracted, and Pham moaned. 'Not much time. We're at maximum recession. When the surge comes, it will—' Again a sound of pain. 'I can see it! By the Powers, Ravna, it will sweep high and last long.'

'How high, Pham?' Ravna said softly. She thought of all the civilizations above them. There were the Butterflies, and the treacherous types who had supported the pogrom at Sjandra Kei . . . And there were trillions who lived in peace and made their own way toward the heights.

'A thousand light-years? Ten thousand? I'm not sure. The ghosts in Countermeasure – Arne and Sjana thought it might rise so high it would punch into the Transcend, encyst the Blight right where it sits . . . That must be what happened Before.'

Arne and Sjana?

The Countermeasure's writhing had slowed. Its light flickered bright and then out. Bright and then out. She heard Pham's breath gasp with every darkness. Countermeasure, a savior that was going to kill a million civilizations. And was killing the man who had triggered it.

Almost unthinking, she dodged past the thing, reaching for Pham. But razors on razors blocked her, raking her arms.

Pham was looking up at her. He was trying to say something more.

Then the light went out for a final time. From the darkness all around came a hissing sound and a growing, bitter smell that Ravna would never forget.

For Pham Nuwen there was no pain. The last minutes of his life were beyond any description that might be rendered in the Slowness or even in the Beyond.

So try metaphor and simile: It was like . . . it was like . . . Pham stood with Old One on a vast and empty beach. Ravna and Tines were tiny creatures at their feet. Planets and stars were the grains of sand. And the sea had drawn briefly back, letting the brightness of thought reach here where before had been darkness. The Transcendence would be brief. At the horizon, the drawn-back sea was building, a dark wall higher than any mountain, rushing back upon them. He looked up at the enormity of it. Pham and godshatter and Countermeasure would not survive that submergence, not even separately. They had triggered catastrophe beyond mind, a vast section of the Galaxy plunged into Slowness, as deep as Old Earth itself, and as permanent.

Arne and Sjana and Straumers and Old One were avenged . . . and Countermeasure was complete.

And as for Pham Nuwen? A tool made, and used, and now to be discarded. A man who never was.

The surge was upon him then, plunging depths. Down from the Transcendent light. Outside, the Tines' world sun would be shining bright once more, but inside Pham's mind everything was closing down, senses returning to what eyes can see and ears can hear. He felt Countermeasure slough toward nonexistence, its task done without ever a conscious thought. Old One's ghost hung on for a little longer, huddling and retreating as thought's potential ebbed. But it let Pham's awareness be. For once it did not push him aside. For once it was gentle, brushing at the surface of Pham's mind, as a human might pet a loyal dog.

More a brave wolf you are, Pham Nuwen. There were only seconds left before they were fully in the depths, where the merged bodies of Countermeasure and Pham Nuwen would die forever and all thought cease. Memories shifted. The ghost of Old One stepped aside, revealing certainties it had hidden all along. *Yes, I built you from several bodies in the junkyard by*

Relay. But there was only one mind and one set of memories that I could revive. A strong, brave wolf – so strong I could never control you without first casting you into doubt . . .

Somewhere barriers slipped aside, the final failing of Old One's control, or a final gift. It did not matter which now, for whatever the ghost said, the truth was obvious to Pham Nuwen and he would not be denied:

Canberra, Cindi, the centuries avoyaging with Qeng Ho, the final flight of the *Wild Goose*. It was all real.

He looked up at Ravna. She had done so much. She had put up with so much. And even disbelieving, she had loved. *It's okay. It's okay.* He tried to reach out to her, to tell her. *Oh, Ravna, I am real!*

Then the full weight of the depths was upon him, and he knew no more.

There was more pounding on the door. She heard Pilgrim walk to the hatch. A crack of light shone in. Ravna heard Jefri's piping voice: 'The sun is back! The sun is back! . . . Hei, why is it so dark in here?'

Pilgrim: 'The artifact – the thing Pham was helping – its light went out.'

'Geez, you mean you left off the main lights?' The hatch slid all the way open, and the boy's head, along with several puppies', was silhouetted against the torchlight beyond. He scrambled over the lip of the hatch. The girl was right behind him. 'The control is right over here . . . see?'

And soft white light shone on the curving walls. All was ordinary and human, except . . . Jefri stood very still, his eyes wide, his hand over his mouth. He turned to hold onto his sister. 'What is it? What is it?' his voice said from the opened hatch.

Now Ravna wished she could not see. She dropped back to her knees. 'Pham?' she said softly, knowing there would be no answer. What was left of Pham Nuwen lay amid the Countermeasure. The artifact didn't glow any more. Its tortuous boundaries were blunted and dark. More than anything it looked like rotted wood . . . but wood that embraced and impaled the man who lay with it. There was no blood, and no charring. Where the artifact had pierced Pham there was an ashy stain, and the flesh and the thing seemed to merge.

Pilgrim was close around her, his noses almost touching the still form. The bitter smell still hung in the air. It was the smell of death, but not the simple rotting of flesh; what had died here was flesh and something else.

She glanced at her wrist. The display had simplified to a few alphanumeric lines. No ultradrives could be detected. *OOB* status showed problems with attitude control. They were deep in the Slow Zone, out of reach of all help, out of reach of the Blight's fleet. She looked into Pham's face. 'You did it, Pham. You really did it.' She said the words softly, to herself.

The arches and loops of Countermeasure were a fragile, brittle thing now. The body of Pham Nuwen was part of that. How could they break those arches without breaking . . . ? Pilgrim and Johanna gently urged Ravna out of the cargo hold. She didn't remember much of the next few minutes, of them bringing out the body. Blueshell and Pham, both gone beyond all retrieval.

They left her after a while. There was no lack of compassion, but disaster and strangeness and emergency were in too abundant a supply. There were the wounded. There was the possibility of counterattack. There was great confusion, and a desperate need for order. It made scarcely any impression on her. She was at the end of her long desperate run, at the end of all her energy.

Ravna must have sat by the ramp for much of the afternoon, so deep in loss as not to think, scarcely aware of the seasong that Greenstalk shared with her through the dataset. Eventually she realized that she was not alone. Besides Greenstalk's comfort . . . sometime earlier, the little boy had returned. He sat beside her, and around them all the puppies, all silent.

Epilogs

Peace had come to what had once been Flenser's Domain. At least there was no sign of belligerent forces. Whoever had pulled them back had done it very cleverly. As the days passed, local peasantry showed themselves. Where the people weren't simply dazed, they seemed glad to be rid of the old regime. Life picked up in the farmlands, peasants doing their best to recover from the worst fire season of recent memory, compounded by the most fighting the region had ever known.

The queen had sent messengers south to report on the victory, but she seemed in no rush to return to her city. Her troops helped with some of the farm work, and did their best not to be a burden on the locals. But they also scouted through the castle on Starship Hill, and the huge old castle on Hidden Island. Down there were all the horrors that had been whispered about over the years. But still there was no sign of the forces that had escaped. The locals were eager with their own stories, and most were ominously credible: That before Flenser had undertaken his attempt upon the Republic, he had created redoubts further north. There had been reserves there – though some thought that Steel had long since used them. Peasants from the northern valley had seen the Flenserist troops retreating. Some said they had seen Flenser himself – or at least a pack wearing the colors of a lord. Even the locals did not believe all the stories, the ones about Flenser being here and there, singletons separated by kilometers, coordinating the pull out.

Ravna and the queen had reason to believe the story, but not the foolhardiness to check it out. Woodcarver's expeditionary force was not a large one, and the forests and valleys stretched on for more than one hundred kilometers to where the Icefangs curved west to meet the sea. That territory was unknown to Woodcarver. If Flenser had been preparing it for decades – as was that pack's normal method of operation – there would be deadly surprises, even for a large army hunting just a few dozens of partisans. Let Flenser be, and hope that his redoubts had been gutted by Lord Steel.

Woodcarver worried that this would be the great peril of the next century.

But things were resolved much sooner than that. It was Flenser who sought them out, and not with a counterattack: About twenty days after the battle, at the end of a day when the sun dipped just behind the northern hills, there was the sound of signal horns. Ravna and Johanna were wakened and shortly found themselves on the castle's parapet, peering into something like a sunset, all orange and gold silhouetting the hills beyond the northern fjord. Woodcarver's aides were gazing from many eyes at the ridgeline. A few had telescopes.

Ravna shared her binocs with Johanna. 'Someone's up there.' Stark against the sky glow, a pack carried a long banner with separate poles for each member.

Woodcarver was using two telescopes, probably more effective than Ravna's gear; considering the pack's eye separation. 'Yes, I see it. That's a truce flag, by the way. And I think I know who's carrying it.' She yammered something at Peregrine. 'It's been a long time since I've talked to that one.'

Johanna was still looking through the binoculars. Finally she said, 'He . . . made Steel, didn't he?'

'Yes, dear.'

The girl lowered the binocs. 'I . . . think I'll pass up meeting him.' Her voice was distant.

They met on the hillside north of the castle just eight hours later. Woodcarver's troops had spent the intervening time scouting the valley. It was only partly a matter of protecting against treachery from the other side: one very special pack of the enemy would be coming, and there were plenty of locals who would like that one dead.

Woodcarver walked to where the hill fell off precipitously toward forest. Ravna and Pilgrim followed behind her at a Tinishly close ten meters. Woodcarver wasn't saying much about this meeting, but Pilgrim had turned out to be a very talkative sort. 'This is just the way I came originally, a year ago when the first ship landed. You can see how some of the trees were burned by the torch. Good thing it wasn't as dry that summer as this.'

The forest was dense, but they were looking down over the treetops. Even in the dryness there was a sweet, resinous smell in the air. To their left was a tiny waterfall and a path that led to the valley floor – the path their truce visitor had agreed to take. Farmland, Peregrine called the valley bottom. It was undisciplined chaos to Ravna's eyes. The Tines grew different crops together in the same fields, and she saw no fences, not even to hold back livestock. Here and there were wooden lodges with steep roofs and outward curving walls; what you might expect in a region with snowy winters.

'Quite a mob down there,' said Pilgrim.

It didn't look crowded to her: little clumps, each a pack, each well-separated from the others. They clustered around the lodge buildings. More were scattered across the fields. Woodcarver packs were stationed along the little road that crossed the valley.

She felt Pilgrim tense next to her. A head extended past her waist, pointing. 'That must be him. All alone, as promised. And—' part of him was looking through a telescope, 'now that's a surprise.'

A single pack trekked slowly down the road, past Woodcarver's guards. It was pulling a small cart – containing one of its own members, apparently. A cripple?

The peasants in the fields drifted toward the edge of the field, paralleling the lone pack's course. She heard the gobble of Tinish talk. When they wanted to be loud, they could be very, very loud. The troopers moved to chase back any local who got too close to the road.

'I thought they were grateful to us?' This was the closest thing to violence she had seen since the battle of Starship Hill.

'They are. Most of those are shouting death to Flenser.'

Flenser, Skinner, the pack who had rescued Jefri Olsndot. 'They can hate one pack so much?'

'Love and hate and fear, all together. More than a century they've been under his knife. And now he is here, half-crippled, and without his troops. Yet they are still afraid. There are enough cotters down there to overwhelm our guard, but they're not pushing hard. This was Flenser's Domain, and he treated it like a good farmer might treat his yard. Worse, he treated the people and the land like some grand experiment. From reading Dataset, I see he is a monster ahead of his time. There are some out there who might still kill for the Master, and no one is sure who they are . . .' He paused a second, just watching.

'And you know the greatest reason for fear? That he would come here alone, so far from any help we can conceive.'

So. Ravna shifted Pham's pistol forward on her belt. It was a bulky, blatant thing . . . and she was glad to have it. She glanced westward towards Hiddden Island. *OOB* was safely grounded against the battlements on the castle there. Unless Greenstalk could do some basic reprogramming, it would not fly again. And Greenstalk was not optimistic. But she and Ravna had mounted the beam gun in one of its cargo bays, and that remote was dead simple. Flenser might have his surprises, but so did Ravna.

The fivesome disappeared beneath the steepness.

'It will be a while yet,' said Pilgrim. One of his pups stood on his shoulders and leaned against Ravna's arm. She grinned: her private information feed. She picked it up and placed in on her shoulder. The rest of Peregrine sat his rumps on the ground and watched expectantly.

Ravna looked at the others of the Queen's party. Woodcarver had posted crossbow packs to her right and left. Flenser would sit directly before her and a little downslope. Ravna thought she could see nervousness in Woodcarver. The members kept licking their lips, the narrow pink tongues slipping in and out with snake-like quickness. The Queen had arranged herself as if for a group portrait, the taller members behind and the two little ones sitting erect in front. Most of her gaze seem focused on the break in the verge, where the path from below reached the terrace they sat upon.

Finally Ravna heard the scritching of claws on stone. One head appeared over the drop off, and then more. Flenser walked out onto the moss, two of his members pulling the wheeled cart. The one in the cart sat erect, its hindquarters covered by a blanket. Except for its white-tipped ears, it seemed unremarkable.

The pack's heads peered in every direction. One stayed disconcertingly focused on Ravna as the pack proceeded up the slope toward the Queen. Skinner – Flenser – was the one who had worn the radio cloaks. None were worn now. Through gaps in its jackets Ravna could see scabby splotches where the fur had been rubbed away.

'Mangy fellow, isn't he?' came the little voice in Ravna's ear. 'But cool too. Catch his insolent look.' The queen hadn't moved. She seemed frozen, every member staring at the oncoming pack. Some of her noses were trembling.

Four of Flenser tipped the cart forward, helping the white-tipped one slide to the ground. Now Ravna could see that under the blanket, its hindquarters were unnaturally twisted and still. The five settled themselves rumps together. Their necks arched up and out, almost like the limbs of a single creature. The pack gobbled something that sounded to Ravna like strangling songbirds.

Pilgrim's translation came immediately from the puppy on Ravna's shoulder. The pup spoke in a new voice, a traditional villain voice from children's stories, a dry and sardonic voice. 'Greetings . . . Parent. It has been many years.'

Woodcarver said nothing for a moment. Then she gobbled something back, and Pilgrim translated: 'You recognize me?'

One of Flenser's heads jabbed out toward Woodcarver. 'Not the members of course, but your soul is obvious.'

Again, silence from the queen. Peregrine, annotating: 'My poor Woodcarver. I never thought she would be this flummoxed.' Abruptly he spoke loud, addressing Flenser in Samnorsk. 'Well, you are not so obvious to me, O former traveling companion. I remember you as Tyrathect, the timid teacher from the Long Lakes.'

Several of the heads turned toward Peregrine and Ravna. The creature replied in pretty good Samnorsk, but with a childish voice. 'Greetings, Peregrine. And greetings, Ravna Bergsndot? Yes. Flenser Tyrathect I am.' The heads angled downwards, eyes blinking slowly.

'Sly bugger,' Peregrine muttered.

'Is Amdijefri safe?' the Flenser suddenly asked.

'What?' said Ravna, not recognizing the name at first. Then, 'Yes, they are fine.'

'Good.' Now all the heads turned back to the queen, and the creature continued in Pack talk; 'Like a dutiful creation, I have come to make peace with my Parent, dear Woodcarver.'

'Does he really talk like that?' Ravna hissed at the puppy on her shoulder.

'Hei, would I exaggerate?'

Woodcarver gobbled back, and Pilgrim picked up the translation, now in the queen's human voice: 'Peace. I doubt it, Flenser. More likely you want breathing space to build again, to try to kill us all again.'

'I wish to build again, that is true. But I have changed. The "timid teacher" has made me a little . . . softer. Something you could never do, Parent.'

'What?' Pilgrim managed to inject a tone of injured surprise into the word.

'Woodcarver, have you never thought on it? You are the most brilliant pack to live in this part of the world, perhaps the most brilliant of all time. And the packs you made, they are mostly brilliant, too. But have you not wondered on the most successful of them? You created too brilliantly. You ignored inbreeding and [things that I can't translate easily], and you got . . . me. With all the . . . quirks that have so pained you over the last century.'

'I-I have thought on that mistake, and done better since.'

'Yes, as with Vendacious? [Oh, look at my Queen's faces. He really hurt her there.] Never mind, never mind. Vendacious may well have been a different sort of error. The point is, you made *me*. Before, I thought that your greatest act of genius. Now . . . I'm not so sure. I want to make amends. To live in peace.' One of the heads jabbed at Ravna, another at the *OOB* down by Hidden Island. 'And there are other things in the universe to point our genius at.'

'I hear the arrogance of old. Why should I trust you now?'

'I helped to save the children. I saved the ship.'

'And you were always the world's greatest opportunist.'

Flenser's flanking heads shifted back. '[That's a kind of dismissing shrug.] You have the advantage, Parent, but some of my power is left in the north. Make peace, or you will have more decades of maneuvering and war.'

Woodcarver's response was a piercing shriek. '[And that's a sign of irritation, in case you didn't guess.] Impudence! I can kill you here and now, and have a century of certain peace.'

'I've bet that you won't harm me. You gave me safe passage, separately and in the whole. And one of the strongest things in your soul is your hate for lies.'

The back members of Woodcarver's pack hunkered down, and the little ones at the front took several quick steps toward the Flenser. 'It's been many decades since we last met, Flenser! If *you* can change, might not I?'

For an instant every one of Flenser's members was frozen. Then part of him came slowly to its feet, and slowly, slowly edged toward Woodcarver. The crossbow packs on either side of the meeting ground raised their weapons, tracking him. Flenser stopped six or seven meters from Wood-carver. His heads weaved from side to side, all attention on the queen. Finally, a wondering voice, almost abashed: 'Yes, you might. Woodcarver, after all the centuries . . . you've given up yourself? These new ones are . . .'

'Not all mine. Quite right.' For some reason, Pilgrim was chuckling in Ravna's ear.

'Oh. Well . . .' The Flenser backed to its previous position, 'I still want peace.'

'[Woodcarver looks surprised.] You sound changed, too. How many of you are really of Flenser?'

A long pause. 'Two.'

'. . . Very well. Depending on the terms, there will be peace.'

Maps were brought out. Woodcarver demanded the location of Flenser's main troops. She wanted them disarmed, with two or three of her packs assigned to each unit, reporting by heliograph. Flenser would give up the radio cloaks, and submit to observation. Hidden Island and Starship Hill would be ceded to Woodcarver. The two sketched new borders, and wrangled on the oversight the queen would have in his remaining lands.

The sun reached its noon point in the southern sky. In the fields below, the peasants had long since given up their angry vigil. The only tensely watchful people left were the queen's crossbow packs.

Finally Flenser stepped back from his end of the maps. 'Yes, yes, your folk can watch all my work. No more . . . ghastly experiments. I will be a gentle gatherer of knowledge [is this sarcasm?], like yourself.'

Woodcarver's heads bobbed in rippling synchrony. 'Perhaps so; with the Two-Legs on my side, I'm willing to chance it.'

Flenser rose again from his seated posture. He turned to help his crippled member back on the cart. Then he paused. 'Ah, one last thing, dear Woodcarver. A detail. I killed two of Steel when he tried to destroy Jefri's starship. [Squashed them like bugs, actually. Now we know how Flenser hurt himself.] Do you have the rest of him?'

'Yes.' Ravna had seen what was left of Steel. She and Johanna had visited most of the wounded; it should be possible to adapt *OOB* first aid for the Tines. But in the case of Steel, there had been a bit of vengeful curiosity; that creature had been responsible for so much unnecessary death. What was left of Steel didn't really need medical attention: There were some bloody scratches (self-inflicted, Johanna guessed) and one twisted leg. But the pack was a pitiable, almost an unnerving thing. It had cowered at the back of its pen, all shivering in terror, heads shifting this way and that. Every so often the creature's jaws would snap open and shut, or one member would make an aborted run at the fence. A pack of three was not of human intelligence, but this one could talk. When it saw Ravna and Johanna, its eyes went wide, the whites showing all around, and it rattled barely intelligible Samnorsk at them. The speech was a nightmare mix of threats and pleas that they 'not cut, not cut!' Poor Johanna started crying then. She had spent most of a year hating the pack these were from, yet – 'They seem to be victims, too. It's b-bad to be three, but no one will ever let them be more.' 'Well,' continued Flenser, 'I would like custody of what remains, I—'

'Never! That one was almost as smart as you, even if crazy enough to defeat. You're not going to build him back.'

Flenser came together, all eyes staring at the queen. His 'voice' was soft: 'Please, Woodcarver. This is a small matter, but I will throw over every-thing,' he jabbed at the maps, 'rather than be denied in it.'

'[Uh-oh.]' The crossbow packs were suddenly at the ready. Woodcarver came partly around the maps, close enough to Flenser that their mind noise must collide. She brought all her heads together in a concerted glare. 'If it is so unimportant, why risk everything for it?'

Flenser bumped around for an instant, his members actually staring at one another. It was a gesture Ravna had not seen till now. 'That is *my* affair! I mean . . . Steel was my greatest creation. In a way, I am proud of him. But . . . I am also responsible for him. Don't you feel the same about Vendacious?'

'I've got my plans for Vendacious.' The response was grudging. '[In fact, Vendacious is still whole; I fear the Queen made too many promises to do much with him now.]'

'I want to make up to Steel the harm I made him. You understand.'

'I understand. I've seen Steel and I understand your methods: the knives, the fear, the pain. You're not going to get another chance at it!'

It sounded to Ravna like faint music, something from far beyond the valley, an alien blending of chords. But it was Flenser answering back. Pilgrim's translating voice held no hint of sarcasm: 'No knives, no cutting. I keep my name because it is for others to rename me when they finally accept that . . . in her way, Tyrathect *won*. Give me this chance, Woodcarver. I am begging.'

The two packs stared at each other for more than ten seconds. Ravna looked from one to the other, trying to divine their expressions. No one said anything. There was not even Pilgrim's voice in her ear to speculate on whether this was a lie or the baring of a new soul.

It was Woodcarver who decided. 'Very well. You may have him.'

Peregrine Wickwrackscar was *flying*. A pilgrim with legends that went back almost a thousand years – and not one of them could come near to this! He would have burst into song except that it would pain his passengers. They were already unhappy enough with his rough piloting; even though they thought it was simply his inexperience.

Peregrine stepped across clouds, flew among and through them, danced with an occasional thunderstorm. How many hours of his life had he stared up at the clouds, gauging their depths – and now he was in them, exploring the caves within caves within caves, the cathedrals of light.

Between scattered clouds, the Great Western Ocean stretched forever. By the sun and the flier's instruments, he knew that they had nearly reached the equator, and were already some eight thousand kilometers southwest of Woodcarver's Domain. There were islands out here, the *OOB*'s pictures from space said so, and so did the Pilgrim's own memories. But it had been long since he ventured here, and he had not expected to see the island kingdoms in the lifetime of his current members.

Now suddenly he was going back. Flying back!

The *OOB*'s landing boat was a wonderful thing, and not nearly as strange as it had seemed in the midst of battle. True, they had not yet figured out how to program it for automatic flight. Perhaps they never would. In the meantime, this little flier worked with electronics that were barely more than glorified moving parts. The agrav itself required constant adjustment, and the controls were scattered across the bow periphery – conveniently placed for the fronds of a Skroderider, or the members of a pack. With the Spacers' help and *OOB*'s documentation, it had taken Pilgrim only a few days to get the hang of flying the thing. It was all a matter of spreading one's mind across all the various tasks. The learning had been happy hours, a little bit scary, floating nearly out of control, once in a screwball configuration that accelerated endlessly upward. But in the end, the machine was like an extension of his jaws and paws.

Since they descended from the purpling heights and began playing in the cloud tops, Ravna had been looking more and more uncomfortable. After a particularly stomachs-lurching bump and drop, she said, 'Will you be able to land okay? Maybe we should have postponed this till—' *unh!* '—you can fly better.'

'Oh yes, oh yes. We'll be past this, um, weather front real soon.' He dived beneath the clouds and swerved a few tens of kilometers eastwards. The weather was clear here, and it was actually more on a line with their destination. Secretly chastened, he resolved to do no more joy-riding . . . on the inbound leg, anyway.

His second passenger spoke up then, only the second time in the two-hour flight. 'I liked it,' said Greenstalk. Her voder voice charmed Pilgrim: mostly narrow-band, but with little frets high up, from the squarewaves. 'It was . . . it was like riding just beneath the surf, feeling your fronds moving with the sea.'

Peregrine had tried hard to know the Skroderider. The creature was the only nonhuman alien in the world, and harder to know than the Two-Legs. She seemed to dream most of the time, and forgot all but things that happened again and again to her. It was her primitive skrode that accounted for part of that, Ravna told him. Remembering the run that Greenstalk's mate had made through the flames, Pilgrim believed. Out among the stars, there were things even stranger than Two-Legs – it made Pilgrim's imagination ache.

On the horizon he saw a dark ring and another beyond. 'We'll have you in real surf very soon.'

Ravna: 'These are the islands?'

Peregrine looked over the map displays as he took a shot on the sun. 'Yes, indeed,' though it didn't really matter. The Western Ocean was over twelve thousand kilometers across, and all through the tropics it was dotted with atolls and island chains. This group was just a bit more isolated than others; the nearest Islander settlement was almost two thousand kilometers away.

They were over the nearest island. Pilgrim took a swing around it, admiring the tropic ferns that clung to the coral. At this tide, their bony roots were exposed. Not any flat land here at all; he flew on to the next, a larger one with a pretty glade just within the ringwall. He floated the boat down in a smooth glide that touched the ground without even the tiniest bump.

Ravna Bergsndot looked at him with something like suspicion. *Oh oh.* 'Hei, I'm getting better, don't you think?' he said weakly.

An uninhabited little island surrounded by endless sea. The original memories were blurred now; it had been his Rum member who had been a native of the island kingdoms. Yet what he remembered all fit: the high sun, the intoxicating humidity of the air, the heat soaking through his paws. Paradise. The Rum aspect that still lived within him was most joyous of all. The years seemed to melt away; part of him had come home.

They helped Greenstalk down to the ground. Ravna claimed the skrode was an inferior imitation, its new wheels an ad hoc addition. Still, Pilgrim was impressed: the four balloon tyres each had a separate axle. The Rider was able to make it almost to the crest of the coral without any help from Ravna or himself. But near the top, where the tropic ferns were thickest and their roots grew across every path, there he and Ravna had to help a bit, lifting and pulling.

Then they were on the other side and could see the ocean.

Now part of Pilgrim ran ahead, partly to find the easiest descent, partly to get close to the water and smell the salt and the rotting floatweed. The tide was nearly out now, and a million little pools – some no more than stony-walled puddles – lay exposed to the sun. Three of him ran from pool to pool, eying the creatures that lay within. The strangest things in the world they had seemed to him when he first came to the islands. Creatures with shells, slugs of all dimensions and colors, animal-plants that would become tropic ferns if they ever got trapped far enough inland.

'Where would you like to sit?' he asked the Skroderider. 'If we go all the way out to the surf right now, you'll be a meter underwater at high tide.'

The Rider didn't reply. But all her fronds were angled towards the water now. The wheels on her skrode slipped and spun with a strange lack of coordination. 'Let's take her closer,' Ravna said after a moment.

They reached a fairly level stretch of coral, pocked with holes and gullies not more than a few centimeters deep. 'I'll go for a swim, find a good place,' Peregrine said. All of him ran down to where the coral broke the water; going for a swim was not something you did by parts. *Heh heh*. Fact was, damn few mainland packs could swim and think at the same time. Most mainlanders thought that there was a craziness in water. Now Peregrine knew it was simply the great difference in sound speed between air and water. Thinking with all tympana immersed must be a little like using the radio cloaks: it took discipline and practice to do it, and some were never able to learn. But the Island folk had always been great swimmers, using it for meditation. Ravna even thought the Packs might be descended from packs of whales!

Peregrine came to the edge of the coral and looked down. Suddenly the surf did not seem a completely friendly thing. He would soon find out if Rum's spirit and his own memories of swimming were up to the real thing. He pulled off his jackets.

All at once. It's best done all at once. He gathered himself and plopped awkwardly into the water. Confusion, heads out and in. *Keep all under.* He paddled about, holding all his heads down. Every few seconds, he'd poke a single nose into the air and refresh that member. *I still can do it!* The six of him slipped through swarms of squidlets, dived separately through arching green fronds. The hiss of the sea was all around, like the mindsound of a vast sleeping pack.

After a few minutes he'd found a nice level spot, sand all about and shielded from the worst fury of the sea. He paddled back to where the sea crashed against stony coral . . . and almost broke some legs scrambling out. It was just impossible to exist all at once, and for a few moments it was every member for itself. 'Hei, over here!' He shouted to Greenstalk and Ravna. He sat licking at coral cuts as they crossed the white rock. 'Found a place, more peaceful than this—' He waved at the crash and spray.

Greenstalk rolled a little closer to the edge, then hesitated. Her fronds turned back and forth along the curving sweep of the shore. *Does she need help?* Pilgrim started forward, but Ravna just sat down beside the Rider and leaned against the wheeled platform. After a moment, Pilgrim joined them. They sat for a time, human looking out to the sea, Rider looking he wasn't sure quite where, and pack looking in most all directions . . . There was peace here, even with (or because of?) the booming surf and the haze of spray. He felt his hearts slowing, and just lazed in the sunlight. On every pelt the drying sea water was leaving a glittery powder of salt. Grooming himself tasted good at first, but . . . *yeah*, too much dry salt was one of the *bad* memories. Greenstalk's fronds settled lightly across him, too fine and narrow to provide much shade, but a light and gentle comfort.

They sat for a long while – long enough so that later some of Pilgrim's noses were blistered, and even darkskinned Ravna was sunburned.

The Rider was humming now, a sort of song that after long minutes came to be speech. 'It is a good sea, a good edge. It is what I need now. To sit and think at my own pace for a while.'

And Ravna said, 'How long? We will miss you.' That was not just politeness. Everyone would miss her. Even with her mind adrift, Greenstalk was the expert on *OOB*'s surviving automation.

'Long by your measure, I fear. A few decades . . .' She watched (?) the waves a few minutes more. 'I am eager to get down there. Ha ha. Almost like a human in that . . . Ravna, you know my memories are muddled now. I had two hundred years with Blueshell. Sometimes he was petty and a little spiteful, but he was a great trader. We had many wonderful times. And at the end even you could see his courage.'

Ravna nodded.

'We found a terrible secret on this last journey. I think that hurt him as much as the final . . . burning. I am grateful to you for protecting us. Now I want to think, to let the surf and the time work with my memories and sort them out. Maybe if this poor imitation skrode is up to it, I'll even make a chronicle of our quest.'

She touched Peregrine on two of his heads. 'One thing, Sir Pilgrim. You trust much to give me freedom of your seas . . . But you should know, Blueshell and I were pregnant. I have a mist of our common eggs within me. Leave me here and there will be new Riders by this island in future years. Please do not take that as betrayal. I want to remember Blueshell with children – but modestly; our kind has shared ten million worlds and never been bad neighbors . . . except in a way that Ravna can tell you, that cannot happen here.'

In the end, Greenstalk was not at all interested in the protected stretch of water that Peregrine had discovered. She wanted – of all the places here – the one where the ocean crashed most ferociously. It took them more than an hour to find a path down to that violent place, and another half hour to get Rider and skrode safely into the water. Peregrine didn't even try to swim here. The coral rock came in close from all sides, slimy green in patches, razor jagged in others. Five minutes in that meat grinder and he might be too weak to get out. Strange that there was so much green in the water here. It was all but opaque with sea grasses and swarms of foam midges.

Ravna was a little better off; at the water's greatest height, she could still keep feet to ground – at least most of the time. She stood in the foam, bracing herself with feet and an arm, and helped the skrodeling over the lip of rock. Once in, the mechanical crashed firmly to the bottom beside the human.

Ravna looked up at Pilgrim, made an 'okay' gesture. Then she huddled down for a moment, holding to the skrode to keep her place. The surf crashed over the two, obscuring all but Greenstalk's standing fronds. When the foam moved back, he could see that the lower fronds draped across the human's back, and hear a voder buzzing that wasn't quite intelligible against all the other noise.

The human stood and slogged through the waist deep-water toward the rocks Peregrine occupied. Peregrine grabbed onto himself, reached down to give Ravna some paws. She scrambled up the slime green and coral white.

He followed the limping Two-Legs toward the crest of tropical ferns. They stopped under the shade, and she sat down, leaned back into the mat of a fern's trunk net. Cut and bruised, she looked almost as hurt as Johanna ever had.

'You okay?'

'Yeah.' She ran her hands back through disheveled hair. Then she looked at him and laughed. 'We both look like casualties.'

Um, yes. Sometime soon he needed a fresh-water bath. He looked around and out. From the crest of the atoll ring they had a view of Greenstalk's niche. Ravna was looking down there too, minor injuries forgotten.

'How can she like that spot?' Peregrine said wonderingly. 'Imagine being smashed and smashed and smashed.'

There was a smile on Ravna's face, but she kept her two eyes on the surf. 'There are strange things in the universe, Pilgrim; I'm glad there are some you have not read about yet. Where the surf meets the shore – lots of neat things can happen there. You saw all the life that floated in that madness. Just as plants love the sun, there are creatures that can use the energy differences down at that edge. There they have the sun and the surge and the richness of the suspension . . . Still, we should keep watch a little longer.' Between each insurge of the waves, they could still see Greenstalk's fronds. He already knew that those limbs weren't strong, but he was beginning to realize that they must be very tough. 'She'll be okay, though that cheap skrode may not last long. Poor Greenstalk may end up without any automation at all . . . she and her children, the lowest of all Riders.'

Ravna turned to look at the pack. There was still that smile on her face. Wondering, yet pleased? 'You know the secret Greenstalk spoke of?'

'Woodcarver told me what you told her.'

'I'm glad – surprised – she was willing to let Greenstalk come here. Medieval minds – sorry, most any minds – would want to kill before taking even the faintest risk with something like this.

'Then why *did* you tell the queen?' About the skrode's perversion.

'It's your world. I was tired of playing god with the Secret. And Greenstalk agreed. Even if the queen had refused, Greenstalk could have used a cold box on the *OOB*.' And likely slept forever. 'But Woodcarver didn't refuse. Somehow she understood what I was saying: it's the true skrodes that can be perverted, but Greenstalk no longer has one of those. In a decade, this island's shore will be populated with hundreds of young Riders, but they would never colonize beyond this archipelago without permission of the locals. The risk is vanishing . . . but I was still surprised Woodcarver took it.'

Peregrine settled down around Ravna, only one pair of eyes still watching the Rider's fronds down in the foam. *Best to give some explanation.* He cocked a head at Ravna. 'Oh, we are medieval, Ravna – even if changing fast, now. We admired Blueshell's courage in the fire. Such deserves reward. And medieval types are used to courting treachery. So what if the risk is of cosmic size? To us, here, it is no more deadly for that. We poor primitives live with deadly risk all the time.'

'Ha!' Her smile spread at his flippant tone.

Peregrine chuckled, heads bobbing. His explanation was the truth, but not all the truth, or even the most important part. He remembered back to the day before, when he and Woodcarver had decided what to do with Greenstalk's request. Woodcarver had been afraid at first, statecraftly cautious before an evil secret billions of years old. Even leaving such a being in cold sleep was a risk. The statecraftly . . . the *medieval* . . . thing to do, would be to grant the request, leave the Rider ashore on this distant island . . . and then sneak back a day or two later and kill it.

Peregrine had settled down by his queen, closer than any but mates and relations could ever do without losing their train of thought. 'You showed more honor to Vendacious,' he had said. Scriber's murderer still walked the earth, complete, scarcely punished at all.

Woodcarver snapped at the empty air; Peregrine knew that sparing Vendacious hurt her too. '. . . Yes. And these Skroderiders have shown us nothing but courage and honesty. I will not harm Greenstalk. Yet I am afraid. With her, there's a risk that goes beyond the stars.'

Peregrine laughed. It might be pilgrim madness but – 'And that's to be expected, my queen. Great risks for great gains. I like being around the humans; I like touching another creature and being able to think at the same time.' He darted forward to nuzzle the nearest of Woodcarver, and then retreated to a more rational distance. 'Even without their starships and their datasets, they would make our world over. Have you noticed . . . how easy it is for us to learn what they know? Even now, Ravna can't seem to accept our fluency. Even now, she doesn't understand how thoroughly we have studied Dataset. And their ship is easy, my queen. I don't mean I understand the physics behind it – few even among star folk do. But the equipment is easy to learn, even with the failures it has suffered. I suspect Ravna will never be able to fly the agrav boat as well as I.'

'Hmmf. But you can reach all the controls at once.'

'That's only part of it. I think we Tines are more flexibly minded than the poor Two-Legs. Can you imagine what it will be like when we make more radio cloaks, when we make our own flying machines?'

Woodcarver smiled, a little sadly now. 'Pilgrim, you dream. This is the Slow Zone. The agrav will wear out in a few years. Whatever we make will be far short of what you play with now.'

'So? Look at human history. It took less than two centuries for Nyjora to regain spaceflights after their dark age. And we have better records than their archaeologists. We and the humans are a wonderful team; they have freed us to be everything we can be.' A century till their own spaceships, perhaps another century to start building sub-light-speed starships. And someday they would get out of the Slow Zone. *I wonder if packs can be bigger than eight up in the Transcend.*

The younger parts of Woodcarver were up, pacing around the rest. The Queen was intrigued. 'So you think, like Steel seemed to, that we are some kind of special race, something with a happy destiny in the Beyond? Interesting, except for one thing: These humans are all we know from Out There. How do they compare with other races there? Dataset can't fully answer that.'

Ah, and *there*, Woodcarver, is why Greenstalk is so important. We do need experience of more than one other race. Apparently the Riders are among the most common throughout the Beyond. We need them to talk to. We need to discover if they are as much fun, as *useful*, as the Two-Legs. Even if the risk was ten times what it seems, I would still want to grant this Rider her wish.'

'. . . Yes. If we are to be all we can be, we need to know more. We need to take a few risks.' She stopped her pacing; all her eyes turned toward Peregrine in a gesture of surprise. Abruptly she laughed.

'What?'

'Something we've thought before, dear Peregrine, but now I see how true it is. You're being a little bit clever and scheming here. A good statesman and planner for the future.'

'But still for a pilgrimly goal.'

'To be sure . . . And I, now I don't care so completely about the planning and the safety. *We will visit the stars someday.*' Her puppies waggled a joyous salute. 'I've a little of the pilgrim in me now too.'

She went down all on her bellies and crept across the floor toward him. Consciousness slowly dissolved into a haze of loving lust. The last thing Peregrine remembered her saying was, 'How wonderful the luck: that I had grown old and *had* to be new, and that you were just the change we need.'

Peregrine's attention drifted back to the present, and Ravna. The human was still grinning at him. She reached a hand across to brush one of his heads. 'Medieval minds indeed.'

They sat in the fern shade for another couple of hours and watched the tide come in. The sun fell through midafternoon – even then it was as high in the sky as any noontime sun could be at Woodcarver's. In some ways, the quality of the light and the motion of the sun were the strangest things about the scene. The sun was so high, and came down *so* straight, with none of the long sliding glide of afternoon in the arctic. He had almost forgotten what it was like in the land of Short Twilight.

Now the surf was thirty yards inland of where they had put the Rider. The crescent moon was following the sun toward the horizon; the water wouldn't rise any further. Ravna stood, shaded her eyes against the lowering sun. 'Time for us to go, I think.'

'You think she'll be safe?'

Ravna nodded. 'This was long enough for Greenstalk to notice any poisons, and most predators. Besides, she's armed.'

Human and Tines picked their way to the crest of the atoll, past the tallest of the ferns. Peregrine kept one pair of eyes on the sea behind them. The surf was well past Greenstalk now. Her location was still swept by deep waves, but it was beyond the spume and spray. His last sight of her was in the trough behind a crasher: the smoothness of the sea was broken for an instant by two of her tallest fronds, the tips gently swaying.

Summer took gentle leave of the land around Hidden Island. There was some rain, and no more brush fires. There would even be a harvest, war and drought notwithstanding. Each dayaround the sun hid deeper behind the northern hills, a time of twilight that broadened with the weeks till true night held at midnight. And there were stars.

It was something of an accident that so many things came together on the last night of summer. Ravna took the kids out skygazing on the fields by Starship Castle.

No urban haze here, nor even near-space industry. Nothing to fog the view of heaven except a subtle pinkness in the north that might have been vagrant twilight – or aurora. The four of them settled on the frosty moss and looked around. Ravna took a deep breath. There was no hint of ash left in the air, just a clean chill, a promise of winter.

'The snow will be deep as your shoulders, Ravna,' said Jefri, enthusiastic about the possibility. 'You'll love it.' The pale blotch that was his face seemed to be looking back and forth across the sky.

'It can be bad,' said Johanna Olsndot. She hadn't objected to coming up here tonight, but Ravna knew that she would rather have stayed down on Hidden Island to worry about the doings of tomorrow.

Jefri picked up on her unease – no, that was Amdi talking now; they would never cure those two of pretending to be each other. 'Don't worry, Johanna. We'll help you.'

For a moment no one said anything. Ravna looked down the hill. It was too dark to see the six hundred meter drop, too dark to see where fjord and islands lay below. But the torchlight on the ramparts of Hidden Island marked its location. Down there in Steel's old inner court – where Woodcarver now ruled – were all the working coldboxes from the ship. One hundred and fifty-one children slept there, the last survivors of the Straumer's flight. Johanna claimed that most could be revived, with best chance of success if it were done soon. The queen had been enthusiastic about the idea. Large sections of the castle had been set aside, refurbished for human needs. Hidden Island was well sheltered – if not from winter snow, at least from the worst winds. If they could be revived, the children would have no trouble living there. Ravna had come to love Jefri and Johanna and Amdi – but could she handle one hundred and fifty-one *more*? Woodcarver seemed to have no misgivings. She had plans for a school where Tines would learn of humans and the children would learn of this world . . . Watching jefri and Amdi, Ravna was beginning to see what might become of this. Those two were closer than any children she had ever known, and in sum more competent. And that was not just the puppies' math genius; they were competent in other ways.

Humans and Packs *fit*, and old Woodcarver was clever enough to take advantage of it. Ravna liked the queen, and liked Pilgrim even more, but in the end the Packs would be the great beneficiaries. Woodcarver clearly understood the disabilities of her pack race. Tinish records went back at least ten thousand years. For all their recorded history they had been trapped in cultures not much less advanced than now. A race of sharp intelligence yet they had a single overwhelming disadvantage: they could not cooperate at close range without losing that intelligence. Their civilizations were made of isolated minds, forced introverts who could never progress beyond certain limits. The eagerness of Pilgrim and Scrupilo and the others for human contact was evidence of this. *In the long run, we can move the Tines out of this cul-de-sac.*

Amdi and Jefri were giggling about something, the Pack sending runners out almost to the limit of consciousness. These last weeks, Ravna had come to learn that pell-mell activity was the norm for Amdi, that his initial slowness had been part of his hurt over Steel. How . . . perverse – or how wonderful? – . . . that a monster like Steel could be the object of such love.

Jefri shouted, 'You watch in all directions, let me know where to look.' Silence. Then Jefri's voice again: 'There!'

'*What* are you doing?' Johanna asked with sisterly belligerence.

'Watching for meteors,' one of the two said. 'Yes, I watch in all directions and jab Jefri – *there!* – where to look when one comes by.'

Ravna didn't see anything, but the boy had twisted around abruptly at his friend's signal.

'Neat, neat,' came Jefri's voice. 'That was about forty kilometers up, speed—' the two's voice murmured unintelligibly for a second. Even with the pack's wide vision, how could they know how high it was?

Ravna sat back in the hollow formed by the hummocky moss. It was a good parka the locals had made for her; she barely felt the chill in the ground. Overhead, the stars. Time to think, get some peace before all the things that would begin tomorrow. *Den Mother to one hundred and fifty-some kids . . . and I thought I was a librarian.*

Back home she had loved the night sky; at one glance she could see the other stars of Sjandra Kei, sometimes the other worlds. The places of her home had been in her sky. For a moment the evening chill seemed part of a winter that would never go away. Lynne and her folks and Sjandra Kei. Her whole life till three years ago. It was all gone now. *Don't think on it.* Somewhere out there was what was left of Aniara fleet, and what was left of her people. Kjet Svensndot. Tirolle and Glimfrelle. She had only known them for a few hours, but they were of Sjandra Kei – and they have saved more than they would ever know. They would still live. SjK Commercial Security had some ramscoops in its fleet. They could find a world, not here, but nearer the battle site.

Ravna tilted her head back, wondering at the sky. *Where?* Maybe not even above the horizon now. From here the galactic disk was a glow that climbed across the sky almost at right angles to the ecliptic. There was no sense of its true shape or their exact position in it; the greater picture was lost to nearby splendors, the bright knots of open clusters, frozen jewels against the fainter light. But down near the southern horizon, far from the galactic way, there were two splotchy clouds of light. The Magellanics! Suddenly the geometry clicked, and the universe above was not completely unknown. Aniara fleet would be—

'I – I wonder if we can see Straumli Realm from here,' said Johanna. For more than a year she had had to play the adult. Come tomorrow, that role would be forever. But her voice just now was wistful, childlike.

Ravna opened her mouth, about to say how unlikely that must be.

'Maybe we can, maybe we can.' It was Amdi. The pack had pulled itself together, snuggled companionably among the humans. The warmth was welcome. 'See, I've been reading Dataset about where things are, and trying to figure how it matches what we see.' A pair of noses were silhouetted against the sky for an instant, like a human waving his hands exuberantly at the heavens. 'The brightest things we see are just kind of local dazzle. They aren't good guide posts.' He pointed at a couple of open clusters, claimed they matched stuff he'd found in the Dataset. Amdi had also noticed the Magellanic galaxies, and figured out far more than Ravna. 'So anyway, Straumli Realm was' – *was! you got it kid* – 'in the High Beyond, but near the galactic disk. So, see that big square of stars?' Noses jabbed. 'We call that the Great Square. Anyway, just left of the upper corner and go six thousand light-years, and you'd be at Straumli Realm.'

Jefri came to his knees and stared silently for a second. 'But so far away, is there anything to see?'

'Not the Straumli stars, but just forty light-years from Straum there's a blue-white giant—'

'Yeah,' whispered Johanna. 'Storlys. It was so bright you could see shadows at night.'

'Well that's the fourth brightest star up from the corner; see, they almost make a straight line. I can see it, so I know you can.'

Johanna and Jefri were silent for a long time, just staring up at that patch of sky. Ravna's lips compressed in anger. These were good kids; they had been through hell. And their parents had fought to prevent that hell; they had escaped the Blight with the means of its destruction. But . . . how many million races had lived in the Beyond, had probed the Transcend and made bargains with devils? How many more had destroyed themselves there? Ah, but that had not been enough for Straumli Realm. They had gone into the Transcend and wakened Something that could take over a galaxy.

'Do you think anybody's left there?' said Jefri. 'Do you think we're *all* that's left?'

His sister put an arm around him. 'Maybe . . . maybe not Straumli Realm. But the rest of the universe – look, it's still there.' Weak laughter. 'Daddy and Mom, Ravna and Pham. They stopped the Blight.' She waved a hand against the sky. 'They saved most all of it.'

'Yes,' said Ravna. 'We're saved and safe, Jefri. To begin again.' And as far as it went, that comfort was probably true. The ship's zone probes were still working. Of course, a single measure point is of no use for precise zonography, but she could tell that they were deep in the new volume of the Slowness, the volume created by Pham's Revenge. And – much more significant – the *OOB* detected no variation in zonal intensity. Gone was the continuous trembling of the months before. This new status had the feeling of mountain roots, to be moved only by the passage of the ages.

Fifty degrees along the galactic river was another unremarkable space of sky. She didn't point it out to the kids, but what was of interest there was *much* nearer, just under thirty light-years out: the Blighter Fleet. Flies trapped in amber. At normal jump rates for the Low Beyond, they had been just hours away when Pham created the Great Surge. And now . . . ? If they had been bottom-luggers, ships with ramscoops, they could close the gap in less than fifty years. But Aniara Fleet had made their sacrifice; they had followed Pham's godshattered advice. And though they didn't know it, they had broken the Blight fleet. There wasn't a single Slow Zone capable vessel in the approaching fleet. Perhaps they had some in-system capability – a few thousand klicks per second. But no more, not Down Here, where new construction was not a matter of waving a magic wand. The Blight's extermination force would sweep past Tines' World in . . . a few thousand years. Time enough.

Ravna leaned back against one of Amdi's shoulders. He nestled comfortably around her neck. The puppies had *grown* these last two months; apparently Steel had kept them on some sort of stunting drugs. Her gaze lost itself in the dark and glow: far upon far that were all the Zones above her. And where are the boundaries now? How awesome was Pham's Revenge. Maybe she should call it Old One's Revenge. No, it was far more even than that. 'Old One' was just a recent victim of the Blight. Old One was no more than midwife to this revenge. The first cause must be as old as the original Blight and more powerful than the Powers.

But whatever caused it, the Surge had done more than revenge. Ravna had studied the ship's measurement of zone intensity. It could only be an estimate, but she knew they were trapped between one thousand and thirty thousand light-years deep in the new Slowness. Powers only knew how far the Surge had pushed the Slowness . . . And maybe even some of the Powers were destroyed by it. This was like some vision of planetary Armageddon – the type of thing that primitive civilizations had nightmares about – but blown up to a galactic scale. A huge hunk of the Milky Way galaxy had been gobbled up by the Slowness, all in a single afternoon. Not just the Blighter Fleet were flies trapped in amber. Why, the whole vault of heaven – excepting the Magellanics faint *and far* away – might now be a tomb of Slowness. Many must still be alive out there, but how many millions of starships had been trapped between the stars? How many automated systems had failed, killing the civilizations that depended on them? Heaven was truly silent now. In some ways the Revenge was a worse thing that the Blight itself.

And what of the Blight – not the fleet that chased the *OOB*, but the Blight itself? That was a creature of the Top and the Transcend. At a very far remove, it covered much of the sky they could see this night. Could Pham's Revenge have really toppled it? If there was a point to all the sacrifice, then surely so. A surge so great that it pushed the Slowness up thousands of light-years, through the Low and Mid Beyond, past the great civilizations at the Top . . . and into the Transcend. *No wonder it was so eager to stop us.* A Power immersed in the Slowness would be a Power no more, would likely be a living thing no more. *If, if, if.* If Pham's Surge could climb so high.

And that is something I will never know.

Crypto: 0
As received by:
Language path: Optima
From: Society for Rational Investigation
Subject: Ping
Key phrases: Help me!
Summary: Has there been a network partition, or what?

Distribution:
    Threat of the Blight
    Society for Rational Network Management
    War Trackers Interest Group
Date: 0.412 Msec since loss of contacts
Text of message:
    I have still not recovered contact with any network site known to be spinward of me. Apparently, I am right at the very edge of a catastrophe.

    If you receive this ping, please respond! Am I in danger?

    For your information, I have no trouble reaching sites that are antispinward. I understand an effort is being made to hop messages the long way around the galaxy. At least that would give us an idea how big the loss is. Nothing has come back as yet – not surprising, I guess, considering the great number of hops and the expense.

    In the meantime, I am sending out pings such as this. I am expending enormous resources to do this, let me tell you – but it is that important. I've beamed direct at all the hub sites that are in range to the spinward of me. No replies.

    More ominous: I have tried to transmit 'over the top', that is by using known sites in the Transcend that are above the catastrophe. Most such would not normally respond. Powers being what they are. But I received *no* replies. A silence like the Depths is there. It appears that a portion of the Transcend itself has been engulfed.

    Again: If you receive this message, please respond!

The End

A DEEPNESS
IN THE SKY

To Poul Anderson,

In learning to write science fiction, I have had many great models, but Poul Anderson's work has meant more to me than any other. Beyond that, Poul has provided me and the world with an enormous treasure of wonderful, entertaining stories – and he continues to do so.

On a personal note, I will always be grateful to Poul and Karen Anderson for the hospitality that they showed a certain young science fiction writer back in the 1960s.

– V.V.

Author's Note

This novel takes place thousands of years from now. The connection with our languages and writing systems is tenuous. But, for what it's worth, the initial sound in 'Qeng Ho' is the same as the initial sound in the English word 'checker.' (Trixia Bonsol would understand the problem!)

1 second — 1s

10s

1 minute — 10^2s

10^3s–ONE KILOSECOND

1 hour — 10^4s

1 day — 10^5s

1 week — 10^6s–ONE MEGASECOND

1 month

10^7s

1 year — 10^8s

1 decade — 10^9s–ONE GIGASECOND

1 century — 10^{10}s

(logarithmic scale)

ONE HOUR – approximately four kiloseconds

ONE DAY – approximately ninety kiloseconds

TWO WEEKS – slightly more than one megasecond

ONE YEAR – approximately thirty megaseconds

THIRTY YEARS – approximately one gigasecond

Prologue

The manhunt extended across more than one hundred light-years and eight centuries. It had always been a secret search, unacknowledged even among some of the participants. In the early years, it had simply been encrypted queries hidden in radio broadcasts. Decades and centuries passed. There were clues, interviews with The Man's fellow-travelers, pointers in a half-dozen contradictory directions: The Man was alone now and heading still farther away; The Man had died before the search ever began; The Man had a war fleet and was coming back upon them.

With time, there was some consistency to the most credible stories. The evidence was solid enough that certain ships changed schedules and burned decades of time to look for more clues. Fortunes were lost because of the detours and delays, but the losses were to a few of the largest trading Families, and went unacknowledged. They were rich enough, and this search was important enough, that it scarcely mattered. For the search had narrowed: The Man was traveling alone, a vague blur of multiple identities, a chain of one-shot jobs on minor trading vessels, but always moving back and back into this end of Human Space. The hunt narrowed from a hundred light-years, to fifty, to twenty – and a half-dozen star systems.

And finally, the manhunt came down to a single world at the coreward end of Human Space. Now Sammy could justify a fleet specially for the end of the hunt. The crew and even most of the owners would not know the mission's true purpose, but he had a good chance of finally ending the search.

Sammy himself went groundside on Triland. For once, it made sense for a Fleet Captain to do the detail work: Sammy was the only one in the fleet who had actually met The Man in person. And given the present popularity of his fleet here, he could cut through whatever bureaucratic nonsense might come up. Those were good reasons . . . but Sammy would be down here in any case. *I have waited so long, and in a little while we'll have him.*

'Why should I help you find anyone! I'm not your mother!' The little man had backed into his inner office space. Behind him, a door was cracked five centimeters wide. Sammy caught a glimpse of a child peeking out fearfully at them. The little man shut the door firmly. He glared at the Forestry constables who had preceded Sammy into the building. 'I'll tell you one more time: My place of business is the net. If you didn't find what you want there, then it's not available from me.'

''Scuse me.' Sammy tapped the nearest constable on the shoulder. ''Scuse me.' He slipped through the ranks of his protectors.

The proprietor could see that someone tall was coming through. He reached toward his desk. *Lordy*. If he trashed the databases he had distributed across the net, they'd get nothing out of him.

But the fellow's gesture froze. He stared in shock at Sammy's face. 'Admiral?'

'Um, "Fleet Captain," if you please.'

'Yes, yes! We've been watching you on the news every day now. Please! Sit down. You're the source of the inquiry?'

The change in manner was like a flower opening to the sunlight. Apparently the Qeng Ho was just as popular with the city folk as it was with the Forestry Department. In a matter of seconds, the proprietor – the 'private investigator,' as he called himself – had pulled up records and started search programs. '. . . Hmm. You don't have a name, or a good physical description, just a probable arrival date. Okay, now Forestry claims your fellow must have become someone named "Bidwel Ducanh."' His gaze slid sideways to the silent constables, and he smiled. 'They're very good at reaching nonsense conclusions from insufficient information. In this case . . .' He did something with his search programs. 'Bidwel Ducanh. Yeah, now that I search for it, I remember hearing about that fellow. Sixty or a hundred years ago he made some kind of a name for himself.' A figure that had come from nowhere, with a moderate amount of money and an uncanny flare for self-advertisement. In a period of thirty years, he had gathered the support of several major corporations and even the favor of the Forestry Department. 'Ducanh claimed to be a city-person, but he was no freedom fighter. He wanted to spend money on some crazy, long-term scheme. What was it? He wanted to . . .' The private investigator looked up from his reading to stare a moment at Sammy. 'He wanted to finance an expedition to the OnOff star!'

Sammy just nodded.

'Damn! If he had been successful, Triland would have an expedition partway there right now.' The investigator was silent for a moment, seeming to contemplate the lost opportunity. He looked back at his records. 'And you know, he almost succeeded. A world like ours would have to bankrupt itself to go interstellar. But sixty years ago, a single Qeng Ho starship visited Triland. Course, they didn't want to break their schedule, but some of Ducanh's supporters were hoping they'd help out. Ducanh wouldn't have anything to do with the idea, wouldn't even talk to the Qeng Ho. After that, Bidwel Ducanh pretty much lost his credibility . . . He faded from sight.'

All this was in Triland's Forestry Department records. Sammy said, 'Yes.

We're interested in where this individual is now.' There had been no interstellar vessel in Triland's solar system for sixty years. *He is here!*

'Ah, so you figure he may have some extra information, something that would be useful even after what's happened the last three years?'

Sammy resisted an impulse to violence. A little more patience now, what more could it cost after the centuries of waiting? 'Yes,' he said, benignly judicious, 'it would be good to cover all the angles, don't you think?'

'Right. You've come to the right place. I know city things that the Forestry people never bother to track. I really want to help.' He was watching some kind of scanning analysis, so this was not completely wasted time. 'These alien radio messages are going to change our world, and I want my children to—'

The investigator frowned. 'Huh! You just missed this Bidwel character, Fleet Captain. See, he's been dead for ten years.'

Sammy didn't say anything, but his mild manner must have slipped; the little man flinched when he looked up at him. 'I-I'm sorry, sir. Perhaps he left some effects, a will.'

It can't be. Not when I'm so close. But it was a possibility that Sammy had always known. It was the commonplace in a universe of tiny lifetimes and interstellar distances. 'I suppose we are interested in any data the man left behind.' The words came out dully. *At least we have closure* – that would be the concluding line from some smarmy intelligence analyst.

The investigator tapped and muttered at his devices. The Forestry Department had reluctantly identified him as one of the best of the city class, so well distributed that they could not simply confiscate his equipment to take him over. He was genuinely trying to be helpful . . . 'There may be a will, Fleet Captain, but it's not on the Grandville net.'

'Some other city, then?' The fact that the Forestry Department had partitioned the urban networks was a very bad sign for Triland's future.

'. . . Not exactly. See, Ducanh died at one of Saint Xupere's Pauper Cemeteria, the one in Lowcinder. It looks like the monks have held on to his effects. I'm sure they would give them up in return for a decent-sized donation.' His eyes returned to the constables and his expression hardened. Maybe he recognized the oldest one, the Commissioner of Urban Security. No doubt they could shake down the monks with no need for any contribution.

Sammy rose and thanked the private investigator; his words sounded wooden even to himself. As he walked back toward the door and his escort, the investigator came quickly around his desk and followed him. Sammy realized with abrupt embarrassment that the fellow hadn't been paid. He turned back, feeling a sudden liking for the guy. He admired someone who would demand his pay in the face of unfriendly cops. 'Here,' Sammy started to say, 'this is what I can—'

But the fellow held up his hands. 'No, not necessary. But there is a favor I would like from you. See, I have a big family, the brightest kids you've ever seen. This joint expedition isn't going to leave Triland for another five or ten years, right? Can you make sure that my kids, even one of them—?'

Sammy cocked his head. Favors connected with mission success came very dear. 'I'm sorry, sir,' he said as gently as he could. 'Your children will have to compete with everyone else. Have them study hard in college. Have them target the specialties that are announced. That will give them the best chance.'

'Yes, Fleet Captain! That is exactly the favor that I am asking. Would you see to it—' He swallowed and looked fiercely at Sammy, ignoring the others. '—would you see to it that they are allowed to undertake college studies?'

'Certainly.' A little grease on academic entrance requirements didn't bother Sammy at all. Then he realized what the other was really saying. 'Sir, I'll make sure of it.'

'Thank you. Thank you!' He touched his business card into Sammy's hand. 'There's my name and stats. I'll keep it up-to-date. Please remember.'

'Yes, uh, Mr Bonsol, I'll remember.' It was a classic Qeng Ho deal.

The city dropped away beneath the Forestry Department flyer. Grandville had only about half a million inhabitants, but they were crammed into a snarled slum, the air above them shimmering with summer heat. The First Settlers' forest lands spread away for thousands of kilometers around it, virgin terraform wilderness.

They boosted high into clean indigo air, arcing southward. Sammy ignored the Triland 'Urban Security' boss sitting right beside him; just now he had neither the need nor the desire to be diplomatic. He punched a connection to his Deputy Fleet Captain. Kira Lisolet's autoreport streamed across his vision. Sum Dotran had agreed to the schedule change: all the fleet would be going to the OnOff star.

'Sammy!' Kira's voice cut across the automatic report. 'How did it go?' Kira Lisolet was the only other person in the fleet who knew the true purpose of this mission, the manhunt.

'I—' *We lost him, Kira.* But Sammy couldn't say the words. 'See for yourself, Kira. The last two thousand seconds of my pov. I'm headed back to Lowcinder now . . . one last loose end to tie down.'

There was a pause. Lisolet was fast with an indexed scan. After a moment he heard her curse to herself. 'Okay . . . but do tie that last loose end, Sammy. There were times before when we were sure we'd lost him.'

'Never like this, Kira.'

'I said, you make absolutely sure.' There was steel in the woman's voice. Her people owned a big hunk of the fleet. She owned one ship herself. In fact, she was the only operational owner on the mission. Most times, that

434

was not a problem. Kira Pen Lisolet was a reasonable person on almost all issues. This was one of the exceptions.

'I'll make sure, Kira. You know that.' Sammy was suddenly conscious of the Triland Security boss at his elbow – and he remembered what he had accidentally discovered a few moments earlier. 'How are things topside?'

Her response was light, a kind of apology. 'Great. I got the shipyard waivers. The deals with the industrial moons and the asteroid mines look solid. We're continuing with detailed planning. I still think we can be equipped and specialist-crewed in three hundred Msec. You know how much the Trilanders want a cut of this mission.' He heard the smile in her voice. Their link was encrypted, but she knew that his end was emphatically not secure. Triland was a customer and soon to be a mission partner, but they should know just where they stood.

'Very good. Add something to the list, if it's not already there: "Per our desire for the best specialist crew possible, we *require* that the Forestry Department's university programs be open to all those who pass our tests, not just the heirs of First Settlers."'

'Of course . . .' A second passed, just enough time for a double take. 'Lord, how could we miss something like that?' *We missed it because some fools are very hard to underestimate.*

A thousand seconds later, Lowcinder was rising toward them. This was almost thirty degrees south latitude. The frozen desolation that spread around it looked like the pre-Arrival pictures of equatorial Triland, five hundred years ago, before the First Settlers began tweaking the greenhouse gases and building the exquisite structure that is a terraform ecology.

Lowcinder itself was near the center of an extravagant black stain, the product of centuries of 'nucleonically clean' rocket fuels. This was Triland's largest groundside spaceport, yet the city's recent growth was as grim and slumlike as all the others on the planet.

Their flyer switched to fans and trundled across the city, slowly descending. The sun was very low, and the streets were mostly in twilight. But every kilometer the streets seemed narrower. Custom composites gave way to cubes that might have once been cargo containers. Sammy watched grimly. The First Settlers had worked for centuries to create a beautiful world; now it was exploding out from under them. It was a common problem in terraformed worlds. There were at least five reasonably painless methods of accommodating the terraform's final success. But if the First Settlers and their 'Forestry Department' were not willing to adopt any of them . . . well, there might not be a civilization here to welcome his fleet's return. Sometime soon, he must have a heart-to-heart chat with members of the ruling class.

His thoughts were brought back to the present as the flyer dumped down between blocky tenements. Sammy and his Forestry goons walked through half-frozen slush. Piles of clothing – donations? – lay jumbled in boxes on the steps of the building they approached. The goons detoured around them. Then they were up the steps and indoors.

The cemeterium's manager called himself Brother Song, and he looked old unto death. 'Bidwel Ducanh?' His gaze slid nervously away from Sammy. Brother Song did not recognize Sammy's face, but he knew the Forestry Department. 'Bidwel Ducanh died ten years ago.'

He was lying. *He was lying.*

Sammy took a deep breath and looked around the dingy room. Suddenly he felt as dangerous as some fleet scuttlebutt made him out to be. *God forgive me, but I will do anything to get the truth from this man.* He looked back at Brother Song and attempted a friendly smile. It must not have come out quite right; the old man stepped back a pace. 'A cemeterium is a place for people to die, is that right, Brother Song?'

'It is a place for all to live to the natural fullness of their time. We use all the money that people bring, to help all the people who come.' In the perverse Triland situation, Brother Song's primitivism made a terrible kind of sense. He helped the sickest of the poorest as well as he could.

Sammy held up his hand. 'I will donate one hundred years of budget to each of your order's cemeteria . . . if you take me to Bidwel Ducanh.'

'I—' Brother Song took another step backward, and sat down heavily. Somehow he knew that Sammy could make good on his offer. Maybe . . . But then the old man looked up at Sammy and there was a desperate stubbornness in his stare. 'No. Bidwel Ducanh died ten years ago.'

Sammy walked across the room and grasped the arms of the old man's chair. He brought his face down close to the other's. 'You know these people I've brought with me. Do you doubt that if I give the word, they will take your cemeterium apart, piece by piece? Do you doubt that if we don't find what I seek here, we'll do the same to every cemeterium of your order, all over this world?'

It was clear that Brother Song did not doubt. He knew the Forestry Department. Yet for a moment Sammy was afraid that Song would stand up even to that. *And I will then do what I must do.* Abruptly, the old man seemed to crumple in on himself, weeping silently.

Sammy stood back from his chair. Some seconds passed. The old man stopped crying and struggled to his feet. He didn't look at Sammy or gesture; he simply shuffled out of the room.

Sammy and his entourage followed. They walked single-file down a long corridor. There was horror here. It wasn't in the dim and broken lighting or the water-stained ceiling panels or the filthy floor. Along the corridor, people sat on sofas or wheeled chairs. They sat, and stared . . . at nothing. At first, Sammy thought they were wearing head-up-displays that their vision was far away, maybe in some consensual imagery. After all, a few of them were talking, a few of them were making constant, complicated gestures. Then he noticed that the signs on the walls were *painted* there. The plain, peeling wall material was simply all there was to see. And the withered people sitting in the hall had eyes that were naked and vacant.

Sammy walked close behind Brother Song. The monk was talking to himself, but the words made sense. He was talking about The Man: 'Bidwel Ducanh was not a kindly man. He was not someone you could like, even at the beginning . . . especially at the beginning. He said he had been rich, but he brought us nothing. The first thirty years, when I was young, he worked harder than any of us. There was no job too dirty, no job too hard. But he had ill to say of everyone. He mocked everyone. He would sit by a patient through the last night of life, and then afterwards sneer.' Brother Song was speaking in the past tense, but after a few seconds Sammy realized that he was not trying to convince Sammy of anything. Song was not even talking to himself. It was as if he were speaking a wake for someone he knew would be dead very soon. 'And then as the years passed, like all the rest of us, he could help less and less. He talked about his enemies, how they would kill him if they ever found him. He laughed when we promised to hide him. In the end, only his meanness survived – and that without speech.'

Brother Song stopped before a large door. The sign above it was brave and floral: TO THE SUNROOM.

'Ducanh will be the one watching the sunset.' But the monk did not open the door. He stood with his head bowed, not quite blocking the way.

Sammy started to walk around him, then stopped, and said, 'The payment I mentioned: It will be deposited to your order's account.' The old man didn't look up at him. He spat on Sammy's jacket and then walked back down the hall, pushing past the constables.

Sammy turned and pulled at the door's mechanical latch.

'Sir?' It was the Commissioner of Urban Security. The cop-bureaucrat stepped close and spoke softly. 'Um. We didn't want this escort job, sir. This should have been your own people.'

Huh? 'I agree, Commissioner. So why didn't you let me bring them?'

'It wasn't my decision. I think they figured that constables would be more discreet.' The cop looked away. 'Look, Fleet Captain. We know you Qeng Ho carry grudges a long time.'

Sammy nodded, although that truth applied more to customer civilizations than to individuals.

The cop finally looked him in the eye. 'Okay. We've cooperated. We made sure that nothing about your search could leak back to your . . . target. But we won't do this guy for you. We'll look the other way; we won't stop you. But I won't do him.'

'Ah.' Sammy tried to imagine just where in the moral pantheon this fellow would fit. 'Well, Commissioner, staying out of my way is all that is required. I can take care of this myself.'

The cop gave a jerky nod. He stepped back, and didn't follow when Sammy opened, the door 'to the sunroom.'

The air was chill and stale, an improvement over the rank humidity of the hallway. Sammy walked down a dark stairway. He was still indoors, but not by much. This had been an exterior entrance once, leading down to street level. Plastic sheeting walled it in now, creating some kind of sheltered patio.

What if he's like the wretches in the hallway? They reminded him of people who lived beyond the capabilities of medical support. Or the victims of a mad experimentory. Their minds had died in pieces. That was a finish he had never seriously considered, but now . . .

Sammy reached the bottom of the stairs. Around the corner was the promise of daylight. He wiped the back of his hand across his mouth and stood quietly for a long moment.

Do it. Sammy walked forward, into a large room. It looked like part of the parking lot, but tented with semiopaque plastic sheets. There was no heating, and drafts thuttered past breaks in the plastic. A few heavily bundled forms were scattered in chairs across the open space. They sat facing in no particular direction; some were looking into the gray stone of the exterior wall.

All that barely registered on Sammy. At the far end of the room, a column of sunlight fell low and slanting through a break in the roof. A single person had contrived to sit in the middle of that light.

Sammy walked slowly across the room, his eyes never leaving the figure that sat in the red and gold light of sunset. The face had a racial similarity to the high Qeng Ho Families, but it was not the face that Sammy remembered. No matter. The Man would have changed his face long ago. Besides, Sammy had a DNA counter in his jacket, and a copy of The Man's true DNA code.

He was bundled in blankets and wore a heavy knit cap. He didn't move but he seemed to be watching something, watching the sunset. *It's him.* The conviction came without rational thought, an emotional wave breaking over him. *Maybe incomplete, but this is him.*

Sammy took a loose chair and sat down facing the figure in the light. A hundred seconds passed. Two hundred. The last rays of sunset were fading. The Man's stare was blank, but he reacted to the coolness on his face. His head moved, vaguely searching, and he seemed to notice his visitor. Sammy turned so his face was lit by the sunset sky. Something came into the other's eyes, puzzlement, memories swimming up from the depths. Abruptly, The Man's hands came out of his blankets and jerked clawlike at Sammy's face.

'*You!*'

'Yes, sir. Me.' The search of eight centuries was over.

The Man shifted uncomfortably in his wheeled chair, rearranging his blankets. He was silent for some seconds, and when he finally spoke, his words were halting. 'I knew your . . . kind would still be looking for me. I financed this damn Xupere cult, but I always knew . . . it might not be enough.' He shifted again on the chair. There was a glitter in his eyes that Sammy had never seen in the old days. 'Don't tell me. Each Family pitched in a little. Maybe every Qeng Ho ship has one crewmember who keeps a lookout for me.'

He had no concept of the search that had finally found him. 'We mean you no harm, sir.'

The Man gave a rasp of a laugh, not arguing, but certainly disbelieving. 'It's my bad luck that you would be the agent they assigned to Triland. You're smart enough to find me. They should have done better by you, Sammy. You should be a Fleet Captain and more, not some assassin errand boy.' He shifted again, reached down as if to scratch his butt. What was it? Hemorrhoids? Cancer? *Lordy, I bet he's sitting on a handgun. He's been ready all these years, and now it's tangled up in the blankets.*

Sammy leaned forward earnestly. The Man was stringing him along. Fine. It might be the only way he would talk at all. 'So we were finally lucky, sir. Myself, I guessed you might come here, because of the OnOff star.'

The surreptitious probing of blankets paused for a moment. A sneer flickered across the old man's face. 'It's only fifty light-years away, Sammy. The nearest astrophysical enigma to Human Space. And you ball-less Qeng Ho wonders have never visited it. Holy profit is all your kind ever cared about.' He waved his right hand forgivingly, while his left dug deeper into the blankets. 'But then, the whole human race is just as bad. Eight thousand years of telescope observations and two botched fly-throughs, that's all the wonder rated . . . I thought maybe this close, I could put together a manned mission. Maybe I would find something there, an edge. *Then, when I came back—*' The strange glitter was back in his eyes. He had dreamed his impossible dream so long, it had consumed him. And Sammy realized that The Man was not a fragment of himself. He was simply mad.

But debts owed to a madman are still real debts.

Sammy leaned a little closer. 'You could have done it. I understand that a starship passed through here when "Bidwel Ducanh" was at the height of his influence.'

'That was Qeng Ho. Fuck the Qeng Ho! I have washed my hands of you.' His left arm was no longer probing. Apparently, he had found his handgun.

Sammy reached out and lightly touched the blankets that hid The Man's left arm. It wasn't a forcible restraint, but an acknowledgment . . . and a request for a moment's more time. 'Pham. There's reason to go to OnOff now. Even by Qeng Ho standards.'

'Huh?' Sammy couldn't tell if it was the touch, or his words, or the name that had been unspoken for so long – but something briefly held the old man still and listening.

'Three years ago, while we were still backing into here, the Trilanders picked up emissions from near the OnOff star. It was spark-gap radio, like a fallen civilization might invent if it had totally lost its technological history. We've run out our own antenna arrays, and done our own analysis. The emissions are like manual Morse code, except human hands and human reflexes would never have quite this rhythm.'

The old man's mouth opened and shut but for a moment no words came. 'Impossible,' he finally said, very faintly.

Sammy felt himself smile. 'It's strange to hear that word from you, sir.'

More silence. The Man's head bowed. Then: 'The jackpot. I missed it by just sixty years. And you, by hunting me down here . . . now you'll get it all.' His arm was still hidden, but he had slumped forward in his chair, defeated by his inner vision of defeat.

'Sir, a few of us' – more than a few – 'have searched for you. You made yourself very hard to find, and there are all the old reasons for keeping the search secret. But we never wished you harm. We wanted to find you to—'
To make amends? To beg forgiveness? Sammy couldn't say the words, and they weren't quite true. After all, The Man had been *wrong*. So speak to the present: 'We would be honored if you would come with us, to the OnOff star.'

'Never. I am not Qeng Ho.'

Sammy always kept close track of his ships' status. And just now . . . Well, it was worth a try: 'I didn't come to Triland aboard a singleton, sir. I have a fleet.'

The other's chin came up a fraction. 'A fleet?' The interest was an old reflex, not quite dead.

'They're in near moorage, but right now they should be visible from Lowcinder. Would you like to see?'

The old man only shrugged, but both his hands were in the open now, resting in his lap.

'Let me show you.' There was a doorway hacked in the plastic just a few meters away. Sammy got up and moved slowly to push the wheeled chair. The old man made no objection.

Outside, it was cold, probably below freezing. Sunset colors hung above the rooftops ahead of him, but the only evidence of daytime warmth was the icy slush that splashed over his shoes. He pushed the chair along, heading across the parking lot toward a spot that would give them some view toward the west. The old man looked around vaguely. *I wonder how long it's been since he was outside.*

'You ever thought, Sammy, there could be other folks come to this tea party?'

440

'Sir?' The two of them were alone in the parking lot.

'There are human colony worlds closer to the OnOff star than we are.'

That tea party. 'Yes, sir. We're updating our eavesdropping on them.' Three beautiful worlds in a triple star system, and back from barbarism in recent centuries. 'They call themselves "Emergents" now. We've never visited them, sir. Our best guess is they're some kind of tyranny, high-tech but very closed, very inward-looking.'

The old man grunted. 'I don't care how inward-looking the bastards are. This is something that could . . . wake the dead. Take guns and rockets and nukes, Sammy. Lots and lots of nukes.'

'Yes, sir.'

Sammy maneuvered the old man's wheeled chair to the edge of the parking lot. In his huds, he could see his ships climbing slowly up the sky, still hidden from the naked eye by the nearest tenement. 'Another four hundred seconds sir, and you'll see them come out past the roof just about there.' He pointed at the spot.

The old man didn't say anything, but he was looking generally upward. There was conventional air traffic, and the shuttles at the Lowcinder spaceport. The evening was still in bright twilight, but the naked eye could pick out half a dozen satellites. In the west, a tiny red light blinked a pattern that meant it was an icon in Sammy's huds, not a visible object. It was his marker for the OnOff star. Sammy stared at the point for a moment. Even at night, away from Lowcinder's light, OnOff would not quite be visible. But with a small telescope it looked like a normal G star . . . still. In just a few more years, it would be invisible to all but the telescope arrays. *When my fleet arrives there, it will have been dark for two centuries . . . and it will almost be ready for its next rebirth.*

Sammy dropped to one knee beside the chair, ignoring the soaking chill of the slush. 'Let me tell you about my ships, sir.' And he spoke of tonnages and design specs and owners – well, most of the owners; there were some who should be left for another time, when the old man did not have a gun at hand. And all the while, he watched the other's face. The old man understood what he was saying, that was clear. His cursing was a low monotone, a new obscenity for each name that Sammy spoke. Except for the last one–

'Lisolet? That sounds Strentmannian.'

'Yes, sir. My Deputy Fleet Captain is Strentmannian.'

'Ah.' He nodded. 'They . . . they were good people.'

Sammy smiled to himself. Pre-Flight should be ten years long for this mission. That would be long enough to bring The Man back physically. It might be long enough to soften his madness. Sammy patted the chair's frame, near the other's shoulder. *This time, we will not desert you.*

'Here comes the first of my ships, sir.' Sammy pointed again. A second later, a bright star rose past the edge of the tenement's roof. It swung stately out into twilight, a dazzling evening star. Six seconds passed, and the second ship came into sight. Six seconds more, and the third. And another. And another. And another. And then a gap, and finally one brighter than all the rest. His starships were in low-orbit moorage, four thousand kilometers out. At that distance they were just points of light, tiny gemstones hung half a degree apart on an invisible straight line across the sky. It was no more spectacular than a low-orbit moorage of in-system freighters, or some local construction job . . . unless you knew how far those points of light had come, and how far they might ultimately voyage. Sammy heard the old man give a soft sigh of wonder. *He* knew.

The two watched the seven points of light slide slowly across the sky. Sammy broke the silence. 'See the bright one, at the end?' The pendent gem of the constellation. 'It's the equal of any starship ever made. It's my flagship, sir . . . the *Pham Nuwen*.'

PART ONE

One Hundred Sixty
Years Later—

I

The Qeng Ho fleet was first to arrive at the OnOff star. That might not matter. For the last fifty years of their voyage, they had watched the torch-plumes of the Emergent fleet as it decelerated toward the same destination.

They were strangers, meeting far from either side's home territory. That was nothing new to the traders of the Qeng Ho – though normally the meetings were not so unwelcome, and there was the possibility of trade. Here, well, there was treasure but it did not belong to either side. It lay frozen, waiting to be looted or exploited or developed, depending on one's nature. So far from friends, so far from a social context . . . so far from witnesses. This was a situation where treachery might be rewarded, and both sides knew it. Qeng Ho and Emergents, the two expeditions, had danced around each other for days, probing for intent and firepower. Agreements were drawn and redrawn, plans were made for joint landings. Yet the Traders had learned precious little of true Emergent intent. And so the Emergents' invitation to dinner was greeted with relief by some and with a silent grinding of teeth by others.

Trixia Bonsol leaned her shoulder against his, cocked her head so that only he could hear: 'So, Ezr. The food tastes okay. Maybe they're not trying to poison us.'

'It's bland enough,' he murmured back, and tried not to be distracted by her touch. Trixia Bonsol was planet-born, one of the specialist crew. Like most of the Trilanders, she had a streak of overtrustfulness in her makeup; she liked to tease Ezr about his 'Trader paranoia.'

Ezr's gaze flicked across the tables. Fleet Captain Park had brought one hundred to the banquet, but very few armsmen. The Qeng Ho were seated among nearly as many Emergents. He and Trixia were far from the captain's table. Ezr Vinh, apprentice Trader, and Trixia Bonsol, linguistics postdoc. He assumed the Emergents down here were equally low-ranking.

The best Qeng Ho estimate was that the Emergents were strict author-itarians, but Ezr saw no overt marks of rank. Some of the strangers were talkative, and their Nese was easily understandable, scarcely different from the broadcast standard. The pale, heavyset fellow on his left had maintained nonstop chitchat throughout the meal. Ritser Brughel seemed to be a Programmer-at-Arms, though he hadn't recognized the term when Ezr used it. He was full of the schemes they could use in coming years.

'Tas been done often enough afore, dontcha know? Get 'em when they don't know technology – or haven't yet rebuilt it,' said Brughel, con-centrating most of his efforts away from Ezr, on old Pham Trinli. Brughel seemed to think that apparent age conferred some special authority, not realizing that any older guy down among the juniors must truly be a loser. Ezr didn't mind the being ignored; it gave him an opportunity to observe without distraction. Pham Trinli seemed to enjoy the attention. As one Programmer-at-Arms to another, Trinli tried to top everything the pale, blond fellow said, in the process yielding confidences that made Ezr squirm.

One thing about these Emergents, they were technically competent. They had ramships that traveled fast between the stars; that put them at the top in technical savvy. And this didn't seem to be decadent knowledge. Their signal and computer abilities were as good as the Qeng Ho's – and that, Vinh knew, made Captain Park's security people more nervous than mere Emergent secrecy. The Qeng Ho had culled the golden ages of a hundred civilizations. In other circumstances, the Emergents' competence would have been cause for honest mercantile glee.

Competent, and hardworking too. Ezr looked beyond the tables. Not to ogle, but this place was impressive. The 'living quarters' on ramscoop ships were generally laughable. Such ships must have substantial shielding and moderate strength of construction. Even at fractional lightspeed, an inter-stellar voyage took years, and crew and passengers spent most of that time as corpsicles. Yet the Emergents had thawed many of their people before living space was in place. They had built this habitat and spun it up in less than eight days – even while final orbit corrections were being done. The structure was more than two hundred meters across, a partial ring, and it was all made from materials that had been lugged across twenty light-years.

Inside, there was the beginning of opulence. The overall effect was classicist in some low degree, like early Solar habitats before life-support systems were well understood. The Emergents were masters of fabric and ceramics, though Ezr guessed that bio-arts were nonexistent. The drapes and furniture contrived to disguise the curvature in the floor. The ventilator breeze was soundless and just strong enough to give the impression of limitless airy space. There were no windows, not even spin-corrected views. Where the walls were visible, they were covered with intricate manual artwork (oil paintings?). Their bright colors gleamed even in the half-light.

He knew Trixia wanted a closer look at those. Even more than language, she claimed that native art showed the inner heart of a culture.

Vinh looked back at Trixia, gave her a smile. She would see through it, but maybe it fooled the Emergents. Ezr would have given anything to possess the apparent cordiality of Captain Park, up there at the head table, carrying on such an affable conversation with the Emergents' Tomas Nau. You'd think the two were old school buddies. Vinh settled back, listening not for sense but for attitude.

Not all the Emergents were smiling, talkative types. The redhead at the front table, just a few places down from Tomas Nau: She'd been introduced, but Vinh couldn't remember the name. Except for the glint of a silver necklace, the woman was plainly – severely – dressed. She was slender, of indeterminate age. Her red hair might have been a style for the evening, but her unpigmented skin would have been harder to fake. She was exotically beautiful, except for the awkwardness in her bearing, the hard set of her mouth. Her gaze ranged up and down the tables, yet she might as well have been alone. Vinh noticed that their hosts hadn't placed any guest beside her. Trixia often teased Vinh that he was a great womanizer if only in his head. Well, this weird-looking lady would have figured more in Ezr Vinh's nightmares than in any happy fantasy.

Over at the front table, Tomas Nau had come to his feet. The servers stepped back from the tables. A hush fell upon the seated Emergents and all but the most self-absorbed Traders.

'Time for some toasts to friendship between the stars,' Ezr muttered. Bonsol elbowed him, her attention pointedly directed at the front table. He felt her stifle a laugh when the Emergent leader actually began with:

'Friends, we are all a long way from home.' He swept his arm in a gesture that seemed to take in the spaces beyond the walls of the banquet room. 'We've both made potentially serious mistakes. We knew this star system is bizarre.' Imagine a star so drastically variable that it nearly turns itself off for 215 years out of every 250. 'Over the millennia, astrophysicists of more than one civilization tried to convince their rulers to send an expedition here ways.' He stopped, smiled. 'Of course, till our era, tas expensively far beyond the Human Realm. Yet now it is the simultaneous object of two human expeditions.' There were smiles all around, and the thought *What wretched luck*. 'Of course, there is a reason that made the coincidence likely. Years aback there was no driving need for such an expedition. Now we all have a reason: The race you call the Spiders. Only the third non-human intelligence ever found.' And in a planetary system as bleak as this, such life was unlikely to have arisen naturally. The Spiders themselves must be the descendants of starfaring nonhumans – something Humankind had never encountered. It could be the greatest treasure the Qeng Ho had ever found, all the more so because the present Spider civilization had only recently

445

rediscovered radio. They should be as safe and tractable as any fallen human civilization.

Nau gave a self-deprecating chuckle and glanced at Captain Park. 'Till recently, I had not realized how perfectly our strengths and weaknesses, our mistakes and insights, complemented each other. You came from much farther away, but in very fast ships already built. We came from nearer, but took the time to bring much more. We both figured most things correctly.' Telescope arrays had watched the OnOff star for as long as Humankind had been in space. It had been known for centuries that an Earth-sized planet with life-signature chemistry orbited the star. If OnOff had been a normal star, the planet might have been quite pleasant, not the frozen snowball it was most of the time. There were no other planetary bodies in the OnOff system, and ancient astronomers had confirmed the moonlessness of the single world in the system. No other terrestrial planets, no gas giants, no asteroids . . . and no cometary cloud. The space around the OnOff star was swept clean. Such would not be surprising near a catastrophic variable, and certainly the OnOff star might have been explosive in the past – but then how did the one world survive? It was one of the mysteries about the place.

All that was known, and planned for. Captain Park's fleet had spent its brief time here in a frantic survey of the system, and in dredging a few kilotonnes of volatiles from the frozen world. In fact, they had found four rocks in the system – asteroids, you might call them, if you were in a generous mood. They were strange things, the largest about two kilometers long. They were solid diamond. The Trilander scientists nearly had fistfights trying to explain that.

But you can't eat diamonds, not raw anyway. Without the usual mix of native volatiles and ores, fleet life would be very uncomfortable indeed. The damn Emergents were both late and lucky. Apparently, they had fewer science and academic specialists, slower starships . . . but lots and lots of hardware.

The Emergent boss gave a benign smile and continued: 'There really is only one place in all the OnOff system where volatiles exist in any quantity – and that is on the Spider world itself.' He looked back and forth across his audience, his gaze lingering on the visitors. 'I know it's something that some of you had hoped to postpone till after the Spiders were active again . . . But there are limits to the value of lurking, and my fleet includes heavy lifters. Director Reynolt' – aha, that was the redhead's name! – 'agrees with your scientists that the locals never did progress beyond their primitive radios. All the "Spiders" are frozen deep underground and will remain so till the OnOff star relights.' In about a year. The cause of OnOff's cycle was a mystery, but the transition from dark to bright repeated with a period that had drifted little in eight thousand years.

Next to him at the front table, S. J. Park was smiling, too, probably with as much sincerity as Tomas Nau, Fleet Captain Park had not been popular with the Triland Forestry Department; that was partly because he cut their pre-Flight time to the bone, even when there had been no evidence of a second fleet. Park had all but fried his ramjets in a delayed deceleration, coming in just ahead of the Emergents. He had a valid claim to first arrival, and precious little else: the diamond rocks, a small cache of volatiles. Until their first landings, they hadn't even known what the aliens really looked like. Those landings, poking around monuments, stealing a little from garbage dumps had revealed a lot – which now must be bargained away.

'It's time to begin working together,' Nau continued. 'I don't know how much you all have heard about our discussions of the last two days. Surely there have been rumors. You'll have details very soon, but Captain Park, your Trading Committee, and I thought that now is a good occasion to show our united purpose. We are planning a joint landing of considerable size. The main goal will be to raise at least a million tonnes of water and similar quantities of metallic ores. We have heavy lifters that can accomplish this with relative ease. As secondary goals, we'll leave some unobtrusive sensors and undertake a small amount of cultural sampling. These results and resources will be split equally between our two expeditions. In space, our two groups will use the local rocks to create a cover for our habitats, hopefully within a few light-seconds of the Spiders.' Nau glanced again at Captain Park. So some things were still under discussion.

Nau raised his glass. 'So a toast. To an end of mistakes, and to our common undertaking. May there be a greater focus in the future.'

'Hey, my dear, *I'm* supposed to be the paranoid one, remember? I thought you'd be beating me up for my nasty Trader suspicions.'

Trixia smiled a little weakly but didn't answer right away. She'd been unusually quiet all the way back from the Emergent banquet. They were back in her quarters in the Traders' temp. Here she was normally her most outspoken and delightful self. 'Their habitat was certainly nice,' she finally said.

'Compared to our temp it is.' Ezr patted the plastic wall. 'For something made from parts they shipped in, it was a great job.' The Qeng Ho temp was scarcely more than a giant, partitioned balloon. The gym and meeting rooms were good-sized, but the place was not exactly elegant. The Traders saved elegance for larger structures they could make with local materials. Trixia had just two connected rooms, a bit over one hundred cubic meters total. The walls were plain, but Trixia had worked hard on the consensus imagery: her parents and sisters, a panorama from some great Triland forest. Much of her desk area was filled with historical flats from Old Earth before the Space Age. There were pictures from the first London and the first Berlin, pictures of horses and aeroplanes and commissars. In fact, those cultures were bland compared with the extremes played out in the histories of later worlds. But in the Dawn Age, everything was being discovered for the first time. There had never been a time of higher dreams or greater naïveté. That time was Ezr's specialty, to the horror of his parents and the puzzlement of most of his friends. And yet Trixia understood. The Dawn Age was only a hobby for her, maybe, but she loved to talk about the old, old first times. He knew he would never find another like her.

'Look, Trixia, what's got you down? Surely there's nothing suspicious about the Emergents having nice quarters. Most of the evening you were your usual softheaded self' – she didn't rise to the insult – 'but then something happened. What did you notice?' He pushed off the ceiling to float closer to where she was seated against a wall divan.

'It . . . it was several little things, and—' She reached out to catch his hand. 'You know I have an ear for languages.' Another quick smile. 'Their dialect of Nese is so close to your broadcast standard that it's clear they've bootstrapped off the Qeng Ho Net.'

'Sure. That all fits with their claims. They're a young culture, crawling back from a bad fall.' *Will I end up having to defend them?* The Emergent offer had been reasonable, almost generous. It was the sort of thing that made any good Trader a little cautious. But Trixia had seen something *else* to worry about.

'Yes, but having a common language makes a lot of things difficult to disguise. I heard a dozen authoritarian turns of speech – and they didn't seem to be fossil usages. The Emergents are accustomed to owning people, Ezr.'

'You mean slaves? This is a high-tech civilization, Trixia. Technical people don't make good slaves. Without their wholehearted cooperation, things fall apart.'

She squeezed his hand abruptly, not angry, not playful, but intense in a way he'd never seen with her before. 'Yes, yes. But we don't know all their kinks. We do know they play rough. I had a whole evening of listening to that reddish blond fellow sitting beside you, and the pair that were on my right. The word "trade" does not come easily to them. Exploitation is the only relationship they can imagine with the Spiders.'

'Hmm.' Trixia was like this. Things that slipped past him could make such a difference to her. Sometimes they seemed trivial even after she explained them. But sometimes her explanation was like a bright light revealing things he had never guessed. '. . . I don't know, Trixia. You know we Qeng Ho can sound pretty, um, arrogant when the customers are out of earshot.'

Trixia looked away from him for a second, stared out at strange quaint rooms that had been her family's home on Triland. 'Qeng Ho arrogance turned my world upside down, Ezr. Your Captain Park busted open the school system, opened up the Forestry . . . And it was just a side effect.'

'We didn't force anyone—'

'I know. You didn't force anyone. The Forestry wanted a stake in this mission, and delivering certain products was your price of admission.' She was smiling oddly. 'I'm not complaining, Ezr. Without Qeng Ho arrogance I would never have been allowed into the Forestry's screening program. I wouldn't have my doctorate, and I wouldn't be here. You Qeng Ho *are* gougers, but you are also one of the nicer things that has happened to my world.'

Ezr had been in coldsleep till the last year at Triland. The Customer details weren't that clear to him, and before tonight Trixia had not been especially talkative about them. Hmm. Only one marriage proposal per Msec; he had promised her no more, but . . . He opened his mouth to say—

'Wait, you! I'm not done. The reason for saying all this now is that I have to convince you: There is arrogance and arrogance, and I can tell the difference. The people at that dinner sounded more like tyrants than traders.'

'What about the servers? Did they look like downtrodden serfs?'

'. . . No . . . more like employees. I know that doesn't fit. But we aren't seeing all the Emergents' people. Maybe the victims are elsewhere. But either through confidence or blindness, Tomas Nau left their pain posted all over the walls.' She glared at his questioning look. 'The paintings, damn it!'

Trixia had made a slow stroll of leaving the banquet hall, admiring each painting in turn. They were beautiful landscapes, either of groundside locations or very large habitats. Every one was surreal in lighting and geometry, but precise down to the detail of individual threads of grass. 'Normal, happy people didn't make those pictures.'

Ezr shrugged. 'It looked to me like they were all done by the same person. They're so good, I'll bet they're reproductions of classics, like Deng's Canberran castlescapes.' A manic-depressive contemplating his barren future. 'Great artists are often crazy and unhappy.'

'Spoken like a true Trader!'

He put his other hand across hers. 'Trixia, I'm not trying to argue with you. Until this banquet, I was the untrusting one.'

'And you still are, aren't you?' The question was intense, with no sign of playful intent.

'Yes,' though not as much as Trixia, and not for the same reasons. 'It's just a little too reasonable of the Emergents to share half the haul from their heavy lifters.' There must have been some hard bargaining behind that. In theory, the academic brainpower that the Qeng Ho had brought was worth as much as a few heavy lifters, but the equation was subtle and difficult to argue. 'I'm just trying to understand what you saw, and what I missed . . . Okay, suppose things are as dangerous as you see them. Don't you think Captain Park and the Committee are on to that?'

'So what do they think now? Watching your fleet officers on the return taxi, I got the feeling people are pretty mellow about the Emergents now.'

'They're just happy we got a deal. I don't know what the people on the Trading Committee think.'

'You could find out, Ezr. If this banquet has fooled them, you could demand some backbone. I know, I know: You're an apprentice; there are rules and customs and blah blah blah. But your Family *owns* this expedition!'

Ezr hunched forward. 'Just a part of it.' This was also the first time she'd ever made anything of the fact. Until now both of them – Ezr, at least – had been afraid of acknowledging that difference in status. They shared the deep-down fear that each might simply be taking advantage of the other. Ezr Vinh's parents and his two aunts owned about one-third of the expedition: two ramscoops and three landing craft. As a whole, the Vinh.23 Family owned thirty ships scattered across a dozen enterprises. The voyage to Triland had been a side investment, meriting only a token Family member. A century or three down the line he would be back with his family. By then, Ezr Vinh would be ten or fifteen years older. He looked forward to that reunion, to showing his parents that their boy had made good. In the meantime, he was years short of being able to throw his weight around. 'Trixia, there's a difference between owning and managing, especially in my case. If my parents were on this expedition, yes, they would have a lot of clout. But they've been "There and Back Again." I am far more an apprentice than an owner.' And he had the humiliations to prove it. One thing about a proper Qeng Ho expedition, there wasn't much nepotism; sometimes just the opposite.

Trixia was silent for a long moment, her eyes searching back and forth across Ezr's face. What next? Vinh remembered well Aunt Filipa's grim advice about women who attach themselves to rich young Traders, who draw them in and then think to run their lives – and worse, run the Family's proper business. Ezr was nineteen, Trixia Bonsol twenty-five. She might think she could simply make demands. *Oh Trixia, please no.*

Finally she smiled, a gentler, smaller smile than usual. 'Okay, Ezr. Do what you must . . . but a favor? Think on what I've said.' She turned, reaching up to touch his face and gently stroke it. Her kiss was soft, tentative.

2

The Brat was waiting in ambush outside Ezr's quarters.

'Hey, Ezr, I watched you last night.' That almost stopped him. *She's talking about the banquet.* The Trading Committee had piped it back to the fleet.

'Sure, Qiwi, you saw me on the vid. Now you're seeing me in person.' He opened his door, stepped inside. Somehow the Brat stuck so close behind that now she was inside too. 'So what are you doing here?'

Qiwi was a genius at taking questions the way she wanted them: 'We got the same scut-work shift starting in two thousand seconds. I thought we could go down to the bactry together, trade gossip.'

Vinh dived into the back room, this time shutting her out. He changed into work fatigues. Of course, the Brat was still waiting when he emerged.

He sighed. 'I don't have any gossip.' *Damned if I'll repeat what Trixia said.*

Qiwi grinned triumphantly. 'Well, *I* do. C'mon.' She opened the room's outer door and gave him an elegant zero-gee bow out into the public corridor. 'I wanna compare notes with you about what you saw, but really, I bet I got a lot more. The Committee had three povs, including at the entrance – better views than you had.' She bounced down the hall with him, explaining how often she had reviewed the videos, and telling of all the people she had gossiped with since.

Vinh had first met Qiwi Lin Lisolet back in pre-Flight, in Trilander space. She'd been an eight-year-old bundle of raw obnoxiousness. And for some reason she'd chosen him as the target of her attention. After a meal or training session, she'd rush up behind him and slug him in the shoulder – and the angrier he got, the more she seemed to like it. One good punch returned would have changed her whole outlook. But you can't slug an eight-year-old. She was nine years short of the mandatory crew minimum. The place for children was before voyages and after – not in crews, especially crews bound for desolate space. But Qiwi's mother owned twenty percent of the expedition . . . The Lisolet.17 Family was truly matriarchal, originally from Strentmann, far away across Qeng Ho space. They were strange in both appearance and custom. A lot of rules must have been broken, but little Qiwi had ended up on the crew. She had spent more years of the voyage awake than any but the Watch crew. A large part of her childhood had passed between the stars, with just a few adults around, often not even her own parents. Just thinking of that was enough to cool a lot of Vinh's irritation. The poor little girl. And not so little anymore. Qiwi must be fourteen years old. And now her physical attacks had been mostly replaced by verbal ones – a good thing considering the Strentmannian high-grav physique.

Now the two were descending through the main axis of the temp. 'Hey Raji, how's business?' Qiwi waved and grinned at every second passerby. In the Msecs before the Emergents' arrival, Captain Park had unfrozen almost half of the fleet crew, enough to manage all vehicles and weapons, with hot backups. Fifteen hundred people wouldn't be more than a large party in his parents' temp. Here, it was a crowd, even if many were away on shipboard during duty time. With this many people, you really noticed that the quarters were temporary, new partitions being inflated for this crew and that. The main axis was nothing but the meeting corners of four very large balloons. The surfaces rippled occasionally when four or five people had to slip by at once.

'I don't trust the Emergents, Ezr. After all the generous talk, they'll slit our throats.'

Vinh gave an irritated grunt. 'So how come you're smiling so much?'

They floated past a clear section of fabric – a real window, not wallpaper. Beyond was the temp's park. It was barely more than a large bonsai, actually, but probably held more open space and living things than were in all the Emergents' sterile habitat. Qiwi's head twisted around and for a short moment she was quiet. Living plants and animals were about the only things that could do that to her. Her father was Fleet Life-Support Officer – and a bonsai artist known across all of near Qeng Ho space.

Then she seemed to startle back to the present. Her smile returned, supercilious. 'Because we're the Qeng Ho, if we only stop to remember the fact! We've got thousands of years of sneakiness on these newcomers. "Emergents" my big toe! They're where they are now from listening to the public part of the Qeng Ho Net. Without the Net, they'd still be squatting in their own ruins.'

The passage narrowed, curving down into a cusp. Behind and above them, the sounds of crew were muted by the swell of wall fabric. This was the innermost bladder of the temp. Besides the spar and power pile, it was the only part that was absolutely necessary: the bactry pit.

The duty here was scut work, about as low as things could get, cleaning the bacterial filters below the hydro ponds. Down here, the plants didn't smell so nice. In fact, robust good health was signaled by a perfectly rotting stench. Most of the work could be done by machines, but there were judgment calls that eluded the best automation, and that no one had ever bothered to make remotes for. In a way, it was a responsible position. Make a dumb mistake and a bacterial strain might get across the membrane into the upper tanks. The food would taste like vomit, and the smell could pass into the ventilator system. But even the most terrible error probably wouldn't kill anyone – there were still the bactries on the ramscoops, all kept in isolation from one another.

So this was a place to learn, ideal by the standards of harsh teachers: It was tricky; it was physically uncomfortable; and a mistake could cause embarrassment that would be very hard to live down.

Qiwi signed up for extra duty here. She claimed to love the place. 'My papa says you gotta start with the smallest living things, before you can handle the big ones.' She was a walking encyclopedia about bacteria, the entwined metabolic pathways, the sewage-like bouquets that corresponded to different combinations, the characteristics of the strains that would be damaged by any human contact (the blessed ones whose stink they need never smell).

Ezr came close to making two mistakes in the first Ksec. He caught them, of course, but Qiwi noticed. Normally she would have ragged him endlessly about the errors. But today Qiwi was caught up in scheming about the Emergents. 'You know why we didn't bring any heavy lifters?'

Their two largest landers could hoist a thousand tonnes from surface to orbit. Given time, they would have had all the volatiles and ore they needed. Of course, time was what the Emergent arrival had taken from them. Ezr shrugged, and kept his eyes on the sample he was drawing. 'I know the rumors.'

'Ha. You don't need rumors. You'd know the truth with a little arithmetic. Fleet Captain Park guessed we might have company. He brought the minimum of landers and habs. And he brought lots and lots of guns and nukes.'

'Maybe.' *Certainly.*

'The trouble is, the damn Emergents are so close, they brought a whole lot more – and still arrived on our heels.'

Ezr made no reply, but that didn't matter.

'Anyway. I've been tracking gossip. We've got to be really, really careful.' And she was off into military tactics and speculations about the Emergents' weapons systems. Qiwi's mother was Deputy Fleet Captain, but she was an armsman, too. A *Strentmannian* armsman. Most of the Brat's time in transit had been spent on math and trajectories and engineering. The bactry and the bonsai were her father's influence. She could oscillate between blood-thirsty armsman, wily trader, and bonsai artist – all in the space of a few seconds. How had her parents ever thought to marry? And what a lonely, messed-up kid they produced. 'So we could beat the Emergents in a straight-out fight,' said Qiwi. 'And they know that. That's why they're being so nice. The thing to do is play along with them; we need their heavy lifters. Afterwards, if they live up to the agreement, they may be rich but we'll be much richer. Those jokers couldn't sell air to a tankless temp. *If things stay square, we'll come out of this operation with effective control.'*

Ezr finished a sequence and took another sample. 'Well,' he said, 'Trixia thinks they don't see this as a trade interaction at all.'

'Um.' Funny how Qiwi insulted almost everything about Vinh – except Trixia. Mostly she just seemed to ignore Trixia. Qiwi was uncharacteristically silent. For almost a second. 'I think your friend has it right. Look, Vinh, I shouldn't be telling you this, but there's quite a split on the Trading Committee.' Unless her own mother had blabbed, this had to be fantasy. 'My guess is, there are some idiots on the Committee who think this is purely a business negotiation, each side bringing their best to a common effort – and as usual, our side being the cleverest negotiator. They don't understand that if we get murdered, it doesn't matter that the other side has a net loss. We've got to play this tough, be ready for an ambush.'

In her own bloodthirsty way, Qiwi sounded like Trixia. 'Mama hasn't said so straight out, but they may be deadlocked.' She looked at him sideways, a child pretending to conspiracy. 'You're an owner, Ezr. You could talk to—'

'Qiwi!'

'Yeah, yeah, yeah. I didn't say anything. I didn't say anything!'

She let him be for a hundred seconds or so, then started on her schemes for making profit off the Emergents, 'if we live through the next few Msecs.' If the Spider world and the OnOff star hadn't existed, the Emergents would have been the find of the century in this end of Qeng Ho space. From watching their fleet operations, it was clear that they had some special cleverness with automation and systems planning. At the same time, their starships were less than half as fast as the Qeng Ho's, and their bioscience was just bad. Qiwi had a hundred plans for turning all that to profit.

Ezr let the words wash over him, barely heard. Another time, he might have lost himself in concentration on the work at hand. No chance on this shift. Plans that spanned two centuries were all coming down to a few critical Ksecs now, and for the first time he wondered about his fleet's management. Trixia was an outsider, but brilliant and with a different viewpoint from lifelong Traders. The Brat was smart, but normally her opinions were worthless. This time . . . maybe 'Mama' *had* put her up to this. Kira Pen Lisolet's outlook had been formed very far away, about as far as you could get and still be in the Qeng Ho realm; maybe she thought a teenage apprentice could affect things just because he was from an owner's Family. Damn . . .

The shift passed without further insight. He'd be off in fifteen hundred seconds. If he skipped lunch, he had time to change clothes . . . time to ask for an appointment with Captain Park. In the two years subjective that he'd been with the expedition, he had never presumed on his Family connections. *And what good can I really do now? Could I really break a stalemate?* He dithered around that worry through the end of the shift. He was still dithering as he chucked his bactry coveralls . . . and . . . called the Captain's Audience Secretary.

Qiwi's grin was as insolent as ever. 'Tell 'em straight, Vinh. This has to be an armsman operation.'

He waved her silent, then noticed that his call hadn't gone through. Blocked? For an instant, Ezr felt a pang of relief, then saw he was preempted by an incoming order . . . from Captain Park's office. 'To appear at 5.20.00 at the Fleet Captain's planning room . . .' What was the ancient curse about getting one's wish? Ezr Vinh's thoughts were distinctly muddled as he climbed to the temp's taxi locks.

Qiwi Lin Lisolet was no longer in evidence; what a wise little girl.

The meeting was not with some staff officer. Ezr showed up at the Fleet Captain's planning room on the QHS *Pham Nuwen*, and there was the

454

Fleet Captain . . . and the expedition's Trading Committee. They did not look happy. Vinh got only a quick glimpse before coming to attention at the bracing pole. Out of the corner of his eyes he did a quick count. Yes, every one of them was here. They hung around the room's conference table, and their gaze did not seem friendly.

Park acknowledged Ezr's brace with a brusque wave of his hand. 'At ease, Apprentice.' Three hundred years ago, when Ezr had been five, Captain Park had visited the Vinh Family temp in Canberra space. His parents had treated the fellow royally, even though he wasn't a senior ship's master. But Ezr remembered more the parkland gifts from what seemed a genuinely friendly fellow.

At their next encounter, Vinh was a seventeen-year-old would-be apprentice and Park was outfitting a fleet to Triland. What a difference. They had spoken perhaps a hundred words since, and then only at formal expedition occasions. Ezr had been just as glad for the anonymity; what he wouldn't give for a return to it now.

Captain Park looked as though he had swallowed something sour. He glanced around at the members of the Trading Committee, and Vinh suddenly wondered just whom he was angry at. 'Young V – Apprentice Vinh. We have an . . . unusual . . . situation here. You know the delicacy of our situation now that the Emergents have arrived.' The Captain didn't seem to be looking for an acknowledgment, and Ezr's 'yessir' died before it reached his lips. 'At this point we have several courses of action possible.' Again a glance at the Committee members.

And Ezr realized that Qiwi Lisolet hadn't been spouting complete nonsense. A Fleet Captain had absolute authority in tactical situations, and normally a veto vote on strategic issues. But for major changes in expedition goals, he was at the mercy of his Trading Committee. And something had gone wrong with the process. Not an ordinary tie; Fleet Captains had a deciding vote in cases such as that. No, this must be a deadlock verging on a mutiny of the management class. It was a situation the teachers always mumbled about in school, but if it ever happened, then just maybe a junior owner would become a factor in the decision process. Sort of a sacrificial goat.

'First possibility,' continued Park, oblivious of the unhappy conclusions rattling around in Vinh's head. 'We play the game the Emergents propose. Joint operations. Joint control of all vehicles in this upcoming groundside mission.'

Ezr took in the appearance of the Committee members. Kira Pen Lisolet sat next to the Fleet Captain. She was dressed in the Lisolet-green uniform her Family affected. The woman was almost as small as Qiwi, her features sober and attentive. But there was an impression of raw physical strength. The Strentmannian body type was extreme even by Qeng Ho standards of diversity. Some Traders prided themselves on their masked demeanor. Not

Kira Pen Lisolet. Kira Lisolet loathed Park's first 'possibility' as much as Qiwi claimed.

Ezr's attention slid to another familiar face. Sum Dotran. Management committees were an elite. There were a few active owners, but the majority were professional planners, working their way up to a stake that would allow them to own their ships. And there was a minority of very old men. Most of the old guys were consummate experts, truly preferring management over any form of ownership. Sum Dotran was such. At one time he had worked for the Vinh Family. Ezr guessed that he opposed Park's first 'possibility,' too.

'Second possibility: Separate control structures, no jointly crewed landers. As soon as practicable, we reveal ourselves directly to the Spiders' – and let the Lord of Trade sort the greater winners from the lesser. Once there were three players, the advantage to simple treachery should be diminished. In a few years their relationship with the Emergents could become a relatively normal, competitive one. Of course, the Emergents might regard unilateral contact as a kind of betrayal in itself. Too bad. It seemed to Vinh that at least half the Committee supported this path – *but not Sum Dotran*. The old man jerked his head slightly at Vinh, making the message obvious.

'Third possibility: We pack up our temps and head back to Triland.'

Vinh's stunned look must have been obvious. Sum Dotran elaborated. 'Young Vinh, what the Captain means is that we are outnumbered and possibly outgunned. None of us trust these Emergents, and if they turn on us, there would be no recourse. It's just too risky to—'

Kira Pen Lisolet slapped the table. 'I object! This meeting was absurd to begin with. And worse, now we see Sum Dotran is simply using it to force his own views.' So much for the theory that Qiwi had been operating at her mother's direction.

'You are both out of order!' Captain Park paused a moment, staring at the Committee. Then, 'Fourth possibility: We undertake a preemptive attack against the Emergent fleet, and secure the system for ourselves.'

'Attempt to secure it,' corrected Dotran.

'I *object*!' Kira Pen Lisolet again. She waved to bring up consensual imagery. 'A preemptive attack is the only sure course.'

Lisolet's imagery was not a starscape or a telescopic view of the Spider world. It was not the org or timeline charts that often consumed the attention of planners. No, these were vaguely like planetary nav diagrams, showing the position and velocity vectors of the two fleets in relation to each other, the Spider's world, and the OnOff star. Traces graphed future positions in the pertinent coordinate systems. The diamond rocks were labeled, too. There were other markers, tactical military symbols, the notation for gigatonnes and rocket bombs and electronic countermeasures.

Ezr stared at the displays and tried to remember his military-science classes. The rumors about Captain Park's secret cargo were true. The Qeng

Ho expedition had teeth – longer, sharper teeth than any normal trading fleet. And the Qeng Ho armsmen had had some time for preparation; clearly they had used it, even if the OnOff system was barren beyond belief, with no good place to hide ambushes or reserves.

The Emergents, on the other hand: The military symbols clustered around their ships were hazy assessment probabilities. The Emergents' automation was strange, possibly superior to the Qeng Ho's. The Emergents had brought twice the gross tonnage, and the best guesses were that they carried proportionately more weapons.

Ezr's attention came back to the meeting table. Who besides Kira Lisolet favored a sneak attack? Ezr had spent much of his childhood studying the Strategies, but the great treacheries were things he'd always been taught were the domain of insanity and evil, not something a self-respecting Qeng Ho need ever or should ever undertake. To see a Trading Committee considering murder, that was a sight that would . . . stay with him awhile.

The silence grew unnaturally long. Were they waiting for him to say something? Finally Captain Park said, 'You've probably guessed we have an impasse here, Apprentice Vinh. You have no vote, no experience, and no detailed knowledge of the situation. Without meaning to offend *you*, I must say that I am embarrassed to have you at this meeting at all. But you are the only crewmember owner for two of our ships. If you have any advice to give with regard to our options, we would be . . . happy . . . to hear it.'

Apprentice Ezr Vinh might be a small playing piece, but he was the center of attention just now, and what did he have to say for himself? A million questions swirled up in his mind. At school they had practiced quick decisions, but even there he had been given more backgrounding than this. Of course, these people weren't much interested in real analysis from him. The thought nettled, almost broke him out of his frozen panic. 'F-four possibilities, Fleet Captain? Are there a-any lesser ones that didn't make it to this briefing?'

'None that had any support from myself or the Committee.'

'Um. You have spoken with the Emergents more than anyone. What do you think of their leader, this Tomas Nau?' It was just the sort of question he and Trixia had wondered about. Ezr never imagined that he would be asking the Fleet Captain himself.

Park's lips tightened, and for an instant Ezr thought he would blow up. Then he nodded. 'He's bright. His technical background appears weak compared to a Qeng Ho Fleet Captain's. He's a deep student of the Strategies, though not necessarily the same ones we know . . . The rest is guess and intuition, though I think most Committee members agree: I would not trust Tomas Nau with any mercantile agreement. I think he would commit a great treachery if it would make him even a small profit. He is very smooth, a consummate liar who puts not the faintest value on return business.' All in all, that was about the most damning statement a

Qeng Ho could make about another living being. Ezr suddenly guessed that Captain Park must be one of the supporters of sneak attack. He looked at Sum Dotran and then back to Park. The two he would trust the most were off the end of the map, in opposite directions! *Lord, don't you people know I'm just an apprentice!*

Ezr stepped on the internal whine. He hesitated for seconds, truly thinking on the issue. Then, 'Given your assessment, sir, I certainly oppose the first possibility, joint operations. But . . . I also oppose the idea of a sneak attack since—'

'Excellent decision, my boy,' interrupted Sum Dotran.

'—since that is something we Qeng Ho have little practice in, no matter how much we've studied it.'

That left two possibilities: cut and run – or stay, cooperate minimally with the Emergents, and tip off the Spiders at the first opportunity. Even if objectively justified, retreat would mark their expedition an abject failure. Considering their fuel state, it would also be extraordinarily slow.

Just over a million kilometers away was the greatest mystery-possible-treasure known to this part of Human Space. They had come across fifty light-years to get this tantalizingly close. Great risks, great treasure. 'Sir, it would be giving up too much to leave now. But we must all be like armsmen now, until things are clearly safe.' After all, the Qeng Ho had its own warrior legends: Pham Nuwen had won his share of battles. 'I-I recommend that we stay.'

Silence. Ezr thought he saw relief on most faces. Deputy Fleet Captain Lisolet just looked grim. Sum Dotran was not so reserved: 'My boy, *please*. Reconsider. Your Family has two starships at risk here. It is no disgrace to fall back before the likely loss of all. Instead, it is wisdom. The Emergents are simply too dangerous to—'

Park drifted up from his place at the table, his beefy hand reaching out. The hand descended gently on Sum Dotran's shoulder, and Park's voice was soft. 'I'm sorry, Sum. You did all you could. You even got us to listen to a junior owner. Now it's time . . . for all of us . . . to agree and proceed.'

Dotran's face contorted in a look of frustration or fear. He held it for a moment of quivering concentration, then let his breath whistle out of his mouth. He suddenly seemed very old and tired. 'Quite so, Captain.'

Park slipped back to his place at the table and gave Ezr an impassive look. 'Thank you for your advice, Apprentice Vinh. I expect you to honor the confidentiality of this meeting.'

'Yessir.' Ezr braced.

'Dismissed.'

The door opened behind him. Ezr pushed off the bracing pole. As he glided through the doorway, Captain Park was already talking to the Committee. 'Kira, think about putting ordnance on all the pinnaces.

Perhaps we can tip the Emergents that cooperating vessels will be very dangerous to hijack. I—'

The door slid shut over the rest. Ezr was overcome with relief and the shakes all at the same time. Maybe forty years ahead of his time, he had actually participated in a fleet decision. It had not been fun.

3

The Spider world – Arachna, some were calling it now – was twelve thousand kilometers in diameter, with 0.95-gee surface gravity. The planet had a stony, undifferentiated interior, but the surface was swaddled with enough volatiles for oceans and a friendly atmosphere. Only one thing prevented this from being an Earth-like Eden of a world: the absence of sunlight.

It was more than two hundred years since the OnOff star, this world's sun, had entered its 'Off' state. For more than two hundred years, its light upon Arachna had been scarcely brighter than that from the far stars.

Ezr's landing craft arced down across what would be a major archipelago during warmer times. The main event was on the other side of the world, where the heavy-lifter crews were carving and raising a few million tonnes of seamount and frozen ocean. No matter; Ezr had seen large-scale engineering before. This smaller landing could be the history maker . . .

The consensus imagery on the passenger deck was a natural view. The lands streaming silently past below were shades of gray, patches of white sometimes faintly glistening. Maybe it was just a trick of the imagination, but Ezr thought he could see faint shadows cast by OnOff. They conjured a topography of crags and mountain peaks, whiteness sliding off into dark pits. He thought he could see concentric arcs outlining some of the farther peaks: pressure ridges where the ocean froze around the rock?

'Hey, at least put an altimeter grid on it.' Benny Wen's voice came from over his shoulder, and a faint reddish mesh overlaid the landscape. The grid pretty much matched his intuition about shadows and snow.

Ezr waved away the red tracery. 'When the star is On, there's millions of Spiders down there. You'd think there'd be some sign of civilization.'

Benny snickered. 'What do you expect to see with a natural view? Most of what is sticking up is mountaintops. And farther down is covered by meters of oxy-nitrogen snow.' A full terrestrial atmosphere froze down to about ten meters of airsnow – if it was evenly distributed. Many of the most likely city sites – harbors, river joins – were under dozens of meters of the cold stuff. All their previous landings had been relatively high up, in what were probably mining towns or primitive settlements. It wasn't until just before the Emergents arrived that their current destination had been properly understood.

The dark lands marched on below. There were even things like glacier streams. Ezr wondered how they had time to form. Maybe they were air-ice glaciers?

'Lord of All Trade, will you look at that!' Benny pointed off to the left: a reddish glow near the horizon. Benny did a zoom. The light was still small, sliding quickly out of their field of view. It really did look like a fire, though it changed shape rather slowly. Something was blocking the view now, and Ezr had the brief impression of opacity rising skyward from the light. 'I've got a better view from high orbit,' came a voice from farther down the aisle, Crewleader Diem. He did not forward the picture. 'It's a volcano. It just lit off.'

Ezr followed the image as it fell behind their point of view. The rising darkness, that must be a geyser of lava – or perhaps just air and water – spewing into the spaces above it. 'That's a first,' said Ezr. The planet's core was cold and dead, though there were several magma melts in what passed for a mantle. 'Everyone seems so sure that the Spiders are all in corpsicle state; what if some of them are actually keeping warm near things like that?'

'Not likely. We've done really detailed IR surveys. We could spot any settlements around a hot spot. Besides, the Spiders just invented *radio* before this latest dark. They're in no position to be crawling around out-of-doors just yet.'

This conclusion was based on a few Msecs of recon and some plausible life-chemistry assumptions. 'I guess.' He watched the reddish glow until it slipped beyond the horizon. Then there were more exciting things directly below and ahead. Their landing ellipse carried them smoothly downward, still weightless. This was a full-sized world, but there would be no flying around in atmosphere. They were moving at eight thousand meters per second, just a couple of thousand meters above the ground. He had an impression of mountains climbing toward them, reaching out. Ridgeline after ridgeline whipped past, nearer and nearer. Behind him, Benny was making little uncomfortable noises, his usual chitchat temporarily interrupted. Ezr gasped as the last ridgeline flashed by them, so close he wondered it didn't clip the lander's dorsum. *Talk about the transfer ellipse to hell.*

Then the main jet flared ahead of them.

It took them almost 30Ksec to climb down from the point that Jimmy Diem had selected for the lander. The inconvenience was not frivolous. Their perch was partway up a mountainside but quite free of ice and airsnow. Their goal was at the bottom of a narrow valley. By rights, the valley floor should have been under a hundred meters of airsnow. By some unexpected fluke of topography and climate, there was less than half a meter. And almost hidden beneath the overhang of the valley walls was the largest collection of intact buildings they had found so far. Chances were good that this was an entrance to one of the Spiders' largest hibernation caves, and perhaps a city during OnOff's warm time. Whatever was learned here should be important. Under the joint agreement, it was all being piped back to the Emergents . . .

Ezr hadn't heard anything about the outcome of the Trading Committee meeting. Diem seemed to be doing everything possible to disguise this visit from the locals, just as the Emergents should expect. Their landing point would be covered with an avalanche shortly after they departed. Even their footprints were to be carefully erased (though that should scarcely be necessary).

By coincidence OnOff was hanging near the zenith when they reached the valley floor. In the 'sunny season' this would be high noon. Now, well, the OnOff star looked like some dim reddish moon, half a degree across. The surface was mottled, like oil on a drop of water. Without display amplification, OnOff's light was just bright enough to show their surroundings.

The landing party walked down some kind of central avenue, five suited figures and one come-along walking machine. Tiny puffs of vapor sputtered around their boots when they walked through drifts of airsnow and the volatiles came in contact with the less well insulated fabric of their coveralls. When they stopped for long, it was important not to be in deep snow, else they were quickly surrounded by sublimation mist. Every ten meters, they set down a seismo sensor or a thumper. When they got the whole pattern in place, they would have a good picture of any nearby caverns. More important for this landing, they would have a good idea what lay inside these buildings. Their big goal: written materials, pictures. Finding a children's illustrated reader would mean certain promotion for Diem.

Shades of reddish grays on black. Ezr reveled in the unenhanced imagery. It was beautiful, eerie. This was a place where the Spiders had *lived*. On either side of their path, the shadows climbed up the walls of Spider buildings. Most were only two or three stories, but even in the dim red light, even with their outline blurred by the snows and the darkness, they could not have been confused with something built by humans. The smallest doorways were generously wide, yet most were less than 150 centimeters high. The windows (carefully shuttered; this place had been abandoned in the methodical way of owners who intended to return) were similarly wide and low.

The windows were like hundreds of slitted eyes looking down on the party of five and their come-along walker. Vinh wondered what would happen if a light came on behind those windows, a crack of light showing between the shutters. His imagination ran with the possibility for a moment. What if their feelings of smug superiority were in error? These were *aliens*. It was very unlikely life could have originated on a world so bizarre as this; once upon a time they must have had interstellar flight. Qeng Ho's trading territory was four hundred light-years across; they had maintained a continuous technological presence for thousands of years. The Qeng Ho had radio traces of nonhuman civilizations that were thousands – in most cases, millions – of light-years away, forever beyond direct contact or even conversation. The Spiders were only the third nonhuman intelligent race ever physically encountered: three in the eight thousand years of human space travel. One of those had been extinct for millions of years; the other had not achieved machine technology, much less spaceflight.

The five humans, walking between the shadowy buildings with slitted windows, were as close to making human history as Vinh could imagine. Armstrong on Luna, Pham Nuwen at Brisgo Gap – and now Vinh and Wen and Patil and Do and Diem pacing down this street of Spiders.

There was a pause in the background radio traffic, and for a moment the loudest sounds were the creak of his coveralls and his own breathing. Then the tiny voices resumed, directing them across an open space, toward the far end of the valley. Apparently, the analysts thought that narrow cleft might be the entrance to caves, where the local Spiders were presumedly holed up.

'That's odd,' came an anonymous voice from on high. 'Seismo heard something – is hearing something – from the building next on your right.'

Vinh's head snapped up and he peered into the gloom. Maybe not a light, but a *sound*.

'The walker?' – Diem.

'Maybe it's just the building settling?' – Benny.

'No, no. This was impulsive, like a click. Now we're getting a regular beat, some damping. Frequency analysis . . . sounds like mechanical equipment, moving parts and such . . . Okay, it's mainly stopped, just some residual ringing. Crewleader Diem, we've got a very good position on this racket. It was on the far corner, four meters up from street level. Here's a guide marker.'

Vinh and the others moved forward thirty meters, following the marker glyph that floated in their head-up displays. It was almost funny, the furtiveness of their movements now, even though they would be in plain sight of anyone in the building.

The marker took them around the corner.

'The building doesn't look special,' said Diem. Like the others, this appeared to be mortarless stonework, the higher floors slightly outset from the lower. 'Wait, I see where you're pointing. There's some kind of . . . a ceramic box bolted to the second overhang. Vinh, you're closest. Climb up there and take a look.'

Ezr started toward the building, then noticed that someone had helpfully killed the marker. 'Where?' All he could see were shadows and the grays of stonework.

'Vinh,' Diem's voice carried more than its usual snap. 'Wake up, huh?'

'Sorry.' Ezr felt himself blushing; he got into this sort of trouble far too often. He enabled multispec imagery, and his view burst into color, a composite of what the suit was seeing across several spectral regions. Where there had been a pit of shadow, he now saw the box Diem was talking about. It was mounted a couple of meters above his head. 'Just a second; I'll get closer.' He walked over to the wall. Like most of the buildings, this one was festooned with wide, stony slats. The analysts thought they were steps. They suited Vinh's purpose, though he used them more like a ladder than like stairs. In a few seconds he was right next to the gadget.

And it was a machine; there were rivets on the sides, like something out of a medieval romance. He pulled a sensor baton from his coveralls and held it near the box. 'Do you want me to touch it?'

Diem didn't reply. This was really a question for those higher up. Vinh heard several voices conferring. 'Pan around a little. Aren't there markings on the side of that box?' Trixia! He knew she would be one of the watchers, but it was a very pleasant surprise to hear her voice. 'Yes, ma'am,' he said, and swept the baton back and forth across the box. There was something along the sides; he couldn't tell whether it was writing or an artifact of overly tricky multi-scan algorithms. If it was writing, this would be a minor coup.

'Okay, you can fasten the baton to the box now' – another voice, the acoustics fellow. Ezr did as he was told.

Some seconds passed. The Spider stairs were so steep he had to lean back against the risers. Airsnow haze streamed out from the steps, and downward; he could feel his jacket heaters compensating for the chill of the steps' edges.

Then, 'That's interesting. This thing is a sensor right out of the dark ages.'

'Electrical? Is it reporting to a remote site?' Vinh started. The last words were spoken by a woman with an Emergent accent.

'Ah, Director Reynolt, hello. No, that's the extraordinary thing about this device. It is self-contained. The "power source" appears to be an array of metal springs. A mechanical clock mechanism – are you familiar with the idea? – provides both timing and motive power. Actually, I suppose this is about the only unsophisticated method that would work over long periods of cold.'

'So what all is it observing?' That was Diem, and a good question. Vinh's imagination took off again. Maybe the Spiders were a lot more clever than anyone thought. Maybe his own hooded figure would show up in *their* recon reports. For that matter, what if this box was hooked up to some kind of weapon?

'We don't see any camera equipment, Crewleader. We have a pretty good image of the box's interior now. A gear mechanism drags a stripchart under four recording styluses.' The terms were straight out of a Fallen Civ text. 'My guess is, every day or so it advances the strip a little and notes the temperature, pressure . . . and two other scalars I'm not sure of yet.' Every day for more than two hundred years. Human primitives would have had a hard time making a moving-parts mechanism that could work so long, much less do it at low temperatures. 'It was our good luck to be walking by when it went off.'

There followed a technical dispute about just how sophisticated such recorders might be. Diem had Benny and the others ping the area with picosecond light flashes. Nothing glinted back; no lensed optics were in a line of sight.

Meanwhile, Vinh remained leaning against the stair ramp. The cold was beginning to seep past his jacket and through his full-pressure coveralls. The gear was not designed for extended contact with such a heat sink. He shifted about awkwardly on the narrow steps. In a one-gee field, this sort of acrobatics got old fast . . . But his new position gave him a view around the corner of the building. And on this side, some of the covering panels had fallen from the windows. Vinh leaned precariously out from the stairs, trying to make sense of what he saw within the room. Everything was covered with a patina of airsnow. Waist-high racks or cabinets were set in long rows. Above them were a metal framework and still more cabinets. Spider stairs connected one level to the other. Of course, to a Spider those cabinets would not be 'waist-high.' Hmm. There were loose objects piled on top, each a collection of flat plates hinged at one end. Some were folded all together, others were carelessly spread out, like vanity fans.

His sudden understanding was like an electric shock, and he spoke on the public frequency without thinking. 'Excuse me, Crewleader Diem?'

The conversation with those above came to a surprised halt.

'What is it, Vinh?' said Diem.

'Take a look through my pov. I think we've found a library.'

Somebody up above yelped with pleasure. It really sounded like Trixia.

Thumper analysis would have brought them to the library eventually, but Ezr's find was a significant shortcut.

There was a large door in back; getting the walker in was easy. The walker contained a high-speed scanning manipulator. It took a while for it to adapt to the strange shape of these 'books,' but now the robot was moving at breakneck speed down the shelves – one or two centimeters per second – two of Diem's crew feeding a steady stream of books into its maw. There was a polite argument audible from on high. This landing was part of the joint plan, all on a negotiated schedule that was to end in just under 100Ksec. In that time they might not be done with this library, much less with the other buildings and the cave entrance. The Emergents didn't want to make an exception for this one landing. Instead, they suggested bringing one of their larger vehicles right to the valley floor and scooping up artifacts en masse.

'And still a lurking strategy can be maintained,' came a male Emergent voice. 'We can blow out the valley walls, make it look like massive rockfalls destroyed the village at the bottom.'

'Hey, these fellows really have the light touch,' Benny Wen's voice came into his ear on their private channel. Ezr didn't reply. The Emergent suggestion wasn't exactly irrational, just . . . foreign. The Qeng Ho *traded*. The more sadistic of them might enjoy pauperizing the competition, but almost all wanted customers who would look forward to the next fleecing. Simply wrecking or stealing was . . . gross. And why do it when they could come back again to probe around?

High above, the Emergent proposal was politely rejected and a follow-on mission to this glorious valley was put at the head of the list for future joint adventures.

Diem sent Benny and Ezr Vinh to scout out the shelves. This library might hold one hundred thousand volumes, only a few hundred gigabytes, but that was far too much for the time remaining. Ultimately, they might have to pick and choose, hopefully finding the holy grail of such an operation – a children's illustrated reader.

As the Ksecs passed, Diem rotated his crewmembers between feeding the scanner, bringing books down from the upper stories to be read, and returning books to their original places.

By the time Vinh's meal break came, the OnOff star had swung down from its position near the zenith. Now it hung just above the crags at the far end of the valley and cast shadows from the buildings down the length of the street. He found a snow-free patch of ground, dropped an insulating blanket on it, and took the weight off his feet. Oh, that felt good. Diem had given him fifteen hundred seconds for this break. He fiddled with his feeder, and munched slowly on a couple of fruit bars. He could hear Trixia, but she was very busy. There was still no 'children's illustrated reader,' but they had found the next best thing, a bunch of physics and chemistry texts. Trixia seemed to think that this was a technical library of some sort. Right now they were debating about speeding up the scan. Trixia thought she had a correct graphemic analysis on the writing, and so now they could switch to smarter reading.

Ezr had known from the moment he'd met Trixia that she was smart. But she was just a Customer specializing in linguistics, a field that Qeng Ho academics excelled in. What could she really contribute? Now . . . well, he could hear the conversation above. Trixia was constantly deferred to by the other language specialists. Maybe that was not so surprising. The entire Trilander civilization had competed for the limited number of berths on the expedition. Out of five hundred million people, if you chose the best in some specialty . . . those chosen would be pretty damn good indeed. Vinh's pride in knowing her faltered for an instant: in fact, it was *he* who was overreaching his station in life by wanting her. Yes, Ezr was a major heir of the Vinh.23 Family, but he himself . . . wasn't all that bright. Worse, he seemed to spend all his time dreaming about other places and other times.

This discouraging line of thought turned in a familiar direction: Maybe here he would prove that he wasn't so impractical. The Spiders might be a long time from their original civilization. Their present era could be a lot like the Dawn Age. Maybe he would have some insight that would make the fleet's treasure – and earn him Trixia Bonsol. His mind slid off into happy possibilities, never quite descending to gritty detail . . .

Vinh glanced at his chron. Aha, he still had five hundred seconds! He stood, looked through the lengthening shadows to where the avenue climbed into the side of the mountain. All day, they had concentrated so much on mission priorities that they'd never really gotten to sightsee. In fact, they had stopped just short of a widening in the road, almost a plaza.

During the bright time, there had been plenty of vegetation. The hills were covered with the twisted remains of things that might have been trees. Down here, nature had been carefully trimmed; at regular intervals along the avenue there was the organic rubble of some ornamental plant. A dozen such mounds edged the plaza.

Four hundred seconds. He had time. He walked quickly to the edge of the plaza, then started round it. In the middle of the circle was a little hill, the snow covering odd shapes. When he reached the far side he was looking into the light. The work in the library had heated the place up so much that a fog of temporary, local atmosphere seeped out of the building. It flowed across the street, condensing and settling back to the ground. The light of OnOff shone through it in reddish shafts. Leaving the color aside, it might almost have been ground fog on the main floor of his parents' temp on a summer night. And the valley walls might have been temp partitions. For an instant Vinh was overcome by the image, that a place so alien could suddenly seem familiar, so peaceful.

His attention came back to the center of the plaza. This side was almost free of snow. There were odd shapes ahead, half-hidden by the darkness. Scarcely thinking, he walked toward them. The ground was clear of snow, and it crunched like frozen moss. He stopped, sucked in a breath. The dark things at the center – they were statues. Of Spiders! A few more seconds and he'd report the find, but for the moment he wondered at the scene alone and in silence. Of course, they already knew the natives' approximate form; there had been some crude pictures found by the earlier landings. But – Vinh stepped up the image scan – these were lifelike statues, molded in exquisite detail out of some dark metal. There were three of the creatures, life-sized he guessed. The word 'spider' is common language, the sort of term that dissolves to near uselessness in the light of specific examination. In the temps of Ezr's childhood there had been several types of critter called 'spiders.' Some had six legs, some eight, some ten or twelve. Some were fat and hairy. Some were slender, black, and venomous. These creatures looked a lot like the slender, ten-legged kind. But either they were wearing clothes, or they were spinier than their tiny namesakes. Their legs were wrapped around each other, all reaching for something hidden beneath them. Making war, making love, what? Even Vinh's imagination floundered.

What had it been like here, when last the sun shone bright?

4

It is an edged cliché that the world is most pleasant in the years of a Waning Sun. It is true that the weather is not so driven, that everywhere there is a sense of slowing down, and most places experience a few years where the summers do not burn and the winters are not yet overly fierce. It is the classic time of romance. It's a time that seductively beckons higher creatures to relax, postpone. It's the last chance to prepare for the end of the world.

By blind good fortune, Sherkaner Underhill chose the most beautiful days in the years of the Waning for his first trip to Lands Command. He soon realized his good luck was doubled: The winding coastal roads had not been designed for automobiles, and Sherkaner was not nearly so skilled an automobilist as he had thought. More than once he came careening into a hairpin turn with the auto's drive belt improperly applied, and nothing but steering and brakes to keep him from flying into the misty blue of the Great Sea (though no doubt he'd fall short, to the forest below, but still with deadly effect).

Sherkaner loved it. Inside of a few hours he had gotten the hang of operating the machine. Now when he tipped up on two wheels it was almost on purpose. It was a beautiful drive. The locals called this route the Pride of Accord, and the Royal Family had never dared complain. This was the height of a summer. The forest was fully thirty years old, about as old as trees could ever get. They reached straight and high and green, and grew right up to the edge of the highway. The scent of flowers and forest resin drifted cool past his perch on the auto.

He didn't see many other civilian autos. There were plenty of osprechs pulling carts, some trucks, and an inconvenient number of army convoys. The reactions he got from the civilians were a wonderful mix: irritated, amused, envious. Even more than around Princeton, he saw wenches who looked pregnant and guys with dozens of baby welts on their backs. Some of their waves seemed envious of more than Sherk's automobile. *And sometimes I'm a little envious of them.* For a while, he played with the thought, not trying to rationalize it. Instinct was such a fascinating thing, especially when you saw it from the inside.

The miles passed by. While his body and senses reveled in the drive, the back of Sherkaner's mind was ticking away: grad school, how to sell Lands

Command on his scheme, the truly multitudinous ways this automobile could be improved. He pulled into a little forest town late the first afternoon. NIGH'T'DEEPNESS, the antique sign said; Sherkaner wasn't sure if that was a place name or a simple description.

He stopped at the local blacksmith's. The smith had the same odd smile as some of the people on the road. 'Nice auto-mobile you have there, mister.' Actually it *was* a very nice and expensive automobile, a brand-new Relmeitch. It was totally beyond the means of the average college student Sherkaner had won it at an off-campus casino two days earlier. That had been a chancy thing. Sherkaner's aspect was well known at all the gambling houses around Princeton. The owners' guild had told him they'd break every one of his arms if they ever caught him gambling in the city again. Still, he'd been ready to leave Princeton anyway – and he really wanted to experiment with automobiles. The smith sidled around the automobile, pretending to admire the silver trim and the three rotating power cylinders. 'So. Kinda far from home, ain'tcha? Whatcha going to do when it stops working?'

'Buy some kerosene?'

'Aha, we got that. Some farm machinery needs it. No, I mean, what about when your contraption breaks? They all do, you know. They're kinda fragile things, not like draft animals.'

Sherkaner grinned. He could see the shells of several autos in the forest behind the smith's. This was the right place. 'That could be a problem. But you see, I have some ideas. It's leather and metal work that might interest you.' He sketched out two of the ideas he'd had that afternoon, things that should be easy to do. The smith was agreeable; always happy to do business with madmen. But Sherkaner had to pay him up front; fortunately, Bank of Princeton currency was acceptable.

Afterward, Underhill drove through the little town, looking for an inn. At first glance this was a peaceful, timeless place to live. There was a traditionalist church of the Dark, as plain and weathered as it should be in these years. The newspapers on sale by the post office were three days old. The headlines might be large and red, shrieking of war and invasion, but even when a convoy for Lands Command rumbled through, it got no special attention.

It turned out Nigh't'Deepness was too small for inns. The owner of the post office gave him directions to a couple of bed-and-breakfast homes. As the sun slid down toward the ocean, Sherkaner tooled around the country-side, lost and exploring. The forest was beautiful, but it didn't leave much room for farming. The locals made some of their living by outside trade, but they worked hard on their mountain garden . . . and they had at most three years of good growing seasons before the frosts would become deadly. The local harvest yards looked full, and there was a steady stream of carts shuttling back and forth into the hills. The parish deepness was up that way about fifteen miles. It wasn't a large deepness, but it served most of the outback folk. If these people didn't save enough now, they would surely starve in the first, hard years of the Great Dark; even in a modern civilization, there was precious little charity for able-bodied persons who didn't provide for those years.

Sunset caught him on a promontory overlooking the ocean. The ground dipped away on three sides, on the south into a little, tree-covered valley. On the crest beyond the dell was a house that looked like the one the postmaster had described. But Sherk still wasn't in a hurry. This was the most beautiful view of the day. He watched the plaids shade into limited colors, the sun's trace fading from the far horizon.

Then he turned his automobile and started down the steep dirt road into the dell. The canopy of the forest closed in above him . . . and he was into the trickiest driving of the day, even though he was moving slower than a cobber could walk. The auto dipped and slid in foot-deep ruts. Gravity and luck were the main things that kept him from getting stuck. By the time he reached the creek bed at the bottom, Sherkaner was seriously wondering if he would be leaving his shining new machine down here. He stared ahead and to the sides. The road was not abandoned; those cart ruts were fresh.

The slow evening breeze brought the stench of offal and rotting garbage. A dump? Strange to think of such a thing in the wilderness. There were piles of indeterminate refuse. But there was also a ramshackle house half-hidden by the trees. Its walls were bent, as if the timbers had never been cured. Its roof sagged. Holes were stuffed with wattle-bush. The ground cover between the road and the house had been chewed down. Maybe that accounted for the offal: a couple of osprechs were hobbled near the creek, just upstream of the house.

Sherkaner stopped. The ruts of the road disappeared into the creek just twenty feet ahead. For a moment he just stared, overwhelmed. These must be genuine backwoods folk, as alien as anything city-bred Sherkaner Underhill had ever seen. He started to get out of the auto. The viewpoints they would have! The things he might learn. Then it occurred to him that if their viewpoint was alien *enough*, these strangers might be less than pleased by his presence.

Besides . . . Sherkaner eased back onto his perch and took careful hold of the steering wheel, throttle, and brakes. Not just the osprechs were watching him. He looked out in all directions, his eyes fully adapted to the twilight. There were two of them. They lurked in the shadows on either side of him. Not animals, not people. *Children?* Maybe five and ten years old. The smaller one still had its baby eyes. Yet their gaze was animal, predatory. They edged closer to the auto.

Sherkaner revved his engine and bolted forward. Just before he reached the little creek, he noticed a third form – a larger one – hiding in the trees above the water. Children they might be, but this was a serious game of lurk-and-pounce. Sherkaner twisted the wheel hard right, bouncing out of the ruts. He was off the road – or was he? There were faint, scraped-down grooves ahead: the real fording point!

He entered the stream, the water spraying high in both directions. The big one in the trees pounced. One long arm scratched down the side of the auto, but the creature landed to the side of Sherkaner's path. And then Underhill had reached the far bank, and was rocketing upslope. A real ambush would end in a cul-de-sac here. But the road continued on and somehow his hurtling progress did not carry him off to the side. There was a final scary moment as he emerged from the forest canopy. The road steepened and his Relmeitch tipped back for a second, rotating on its rear tires. Sherkaner threw himself forward from his perch, and the auto slammed down, and scooted up over the hillcrest.

He ended up under stars and twilit sky, parked beside the home he had seen from the far side of the dell.

He killed the engine and sat for a moment, catching his breath and listening to the blood pounding in his chest. It was that quiet. He watched behind him; no one pursued. And thinking back . . . it was strange. The last he had seen, the big one was climbing slowly out of the creek. The other two had turned away, as if uninterested.

He was by the house he had seen from the other side. Lights came on in the front. A door opened, and an old lady came out on the porch. 'Who's there?' The voice was sturdy.

'Lady Enclearre?' Sherk's voice came out in kind of a squeak. 'The postmaster gave me your address. He said you had an overnight room to rent.'

She came round to the driver's side and looked him over. 'That I do. But you're too late for dinner. You'll have to settle for cold sucks.'

'Ah. That's all right, quite all right.'

'Okay. Bring yourself on in.' She chuckled and waved a little hand toward the valley Sherkaner had just escaped. 'You sure did come the long way, sonny.'

Despite her words, Lady Enclearre fed Sherkaner a good meal. Afterward they sat in her front parlor and chatted. The place was clean, but worn. The sagging floor was unrepaired, the paint peeling here and there. It was a house at the end of its time. But the pale glimmer lamps revealed a bookcase set between the screened windows. There were about a hundred titles, mostly children's primers. The old lady (and she was really old, born two generations earlier than Sherk) was a retired parish teacher. Her husband hadn't made it through the last Dark, but she had grown children – old cobbers themselves now – living all through these hills.

Lady Enclearre was like no city schoolteacher. 'Oh, I've been around. When I was younger 'n you, I sailed the western sea.' *A sailor!* Sherkaner listened with undisguised awe to her stories of hurricanes and grizzards and iceberg eruptions. Not many people were crazy enough to be sailors, even in the Waning Years, Lady Enclearre had been lucky to live long enough to have children. Maybe that was why, during the next generation, she settled down to schoolteaching and helping her husband raise the cobblies. Each year, she had studied the texts for the next grade, staying one year ahead of the parish children, all the way to adulthood.

In this Brightness, she had taught the new generation. When they were grown, she was truly getting on in years. A lot of cobbers make it into a third generation; few live the length of it. Lady Enclearre was much too frail to prepare for the coming Dark by herself. But she had her church and the help of her own children; she would have her chance to see a fourth Bright Time. Meanwhile she kept up with her gossip, and her reading. She was even interested in the war – but as an avid spectator. 'Give those bleeding Tiefers a tunnel up their rear, I say. I have two grandnieces at the Front, and I'm very proud of them.'

As Sherkaner listened, he stared out through Lady Enclearre's broad, fine-screened windows. The stars were so bright up here in the mountains, a thousand different colors, dimly lighting the forest's broad leaves and the hills beyond. Tiny woodsfairies *tick*ed incessantly at the screens, and from the trees all around, he could hear their stridling song.

Abruptly a drum started beating. It was loud, the vibrations coming through the tips of his feet and chest as much as through his ears. A second banging started, drifting in and out of synch with the first.

Lady Enclearre stopped talking. She listened sourly to the racket. 'This could go on for hours, I'm afraid.'

'Your neighbors?' Sherkaner gestured toward the north, the little valley. It was interesting that, except for her one comment about his coming the 'long way round,' she hadn't said a thing about those strange people in the dell.

. . . And maybe she wouldn't now. Lady Enclearre scrunched down on her perch, silent for the first significant period since he'd arrived. Then: 'You know the story of the Lazy Woodsfairies?'

'Sure.'

'I made it a big part of the catechism, 'specially for the five- and six-year-olds. They relate to the attercops cuz they look like little people. We studied how they grow wings, and I'd tell them about the ones that do not prepare for the Dark, the ones who play on and on till it's too late. I could make it a scary story.' She hissed angrily into her eating hands. 'We're dirt poor hereabouts. That's why I left for the sea, and also why I eventually came back, to try and help out. Some years, all the pay I got for my teaching was in farmers' co-op notes. But I want you to know, young fellow, we're good people . . . Except, here and there, there are cobbers who *choose* to be vermin. Just a few, and mostly farther up in the hills.'

Sherkaner described the ambush at the bottom of the dell.

Lady Enclearre nodded. 'I figured it was something like that. You came up here like your rear end was on fire. You were lucky you got out with your auto, but you weren't in great danger. I mean, if you held still for them, they might kick you to death, but basically they're too lazy to be much of a threat.'

Wow. Real perverts. Sherkaner tried not to look too interested. 'So the noise is—?'

Enclearre waved dismissively. 'Music, maybe. I figure they got a load of drugged fizzspit a while back. But that's just a symptom – even if it does keep me awake at night. No. You know what really makes them vermin? They don't plan for the Dark . . . and they damn their own children. That pair down in the dell, they're hill folk who couldn't stomach farming. Off and on they've done smithing, going from farm to farm and working only when they couldn't steal. Life is easy in the middle years of the sun. And all the time they're fornicating away, making a steady dribble of little ones . . .

'You're young, Mister Underhill, maybe a bit sheltered. I don't know if you realize how tedious it is to get a woman pregnant before the Waning Years. One or two little welts are all that ever come – and any decent lady will pinch them off. But the vermin down in the dell, they're whacking each other all the time. The guy is always carrying around one or two welts on his back. Thank goodness, those almost always die. But once in a while they grow into the baby stage. A few make it to childhood, but by then they've been treated like animals for *years*. Most are sullen cretins.'

Sherkaner remembered the predatory stares. Those little ones were so different from what he remembered of childhood. 'But surely some escape? Some grow into adults?'

'A few do. Those are the dangerous ones, the ones who see what they've missed. Off and on, things have been nasty here. I used to raise mini-tarants – you know, for companionship and to make a little money. Every one of them ended up stolen, or a sucked-out carcass on my front steps.' She was silent for a time, remembering pain.

'Shiny things catch the cretins' fancy. For a while, there was a gang of them that figured out how to break into my place. They'd steal candysucks mostly. Then one day they stole all the pictures in the house, even in my books. I locked the indoors good after that. Somehow they broke in a third time – and took the rest of my books! I was still teaching then. I needed those books! The parish constable rousted the vermin over that, but of course she didn't find the books. I had to buy new teacher texts for the last two years of school.' She waved at the top rows of her bookshelves, at worn copies of a dozen texts. The ones on the lower shelves looked like primers too, for all the way back to babyhood; but they were crisp and new and untouched. Strange.

The double drumbeat had lost its synchrony, dribbled slowly back into silence. 'So yes, Mister Underhill, some of the out-of-phase cobblies live to be adults. They might almost pass for current-generation cobbers. In a sense, they are the next generation of vermin. Things will get ugly in a couple of years. Like the Lazy Woodsfairies, these people will begin to feel the cold. Very few will get into the parish deepness. The rest will be out in the hills. There are caves everywhere, little better than animal deepnesses. That's where our poorest farmers spend the Dark. That's where the out-of-phase vermin are really deadly.'

The old lady noticed his look. She gave him a jagged little grin. 'I doubt I'll see another Brightness of the sun. That's okay. My children will have this land. There's a view; they might build a little inn here. But if I survive the Dark, I'll build a little cabin here and put up a big sign proclaiming me the oldest cobber living in the parish . . . And I'll look down into the dell. I hope it's washed clean. If the vermin are back, most likely it'll be because they murdered some poor farmer family and took their deepness.'

After that, Lady Enclearre turned the conversation to other things, asking about life in Princeton and Sherk's own childhood. She said that now she had revealed her parish's dark secrets, he should reveal what he was up to driving an automobile down to Lands Command.

'Well, I was thinking about enlisting.' Actually, Sherkaner intended that the Command enlist in *his* schemes rather than the other way around. It was an attitude that had driven the University Professoriate nuts.

'Hmm-hmm. 'Tis a long way to come when you could enlist in a minute back in Princeton. I noticed the luggage end of your auto is almost as big as a farmer's cart.' She waggled her eating hands in curiosity.

Sherkaner just smiled back. 'My friends warned me to carry lots of spare parts if I wanted to tour the Pride of Accord by automobile.'

'Shu, I'll bet.' She stood up with some difficulty, supporting herself on both midhands and feet. 'Well, this old lady needs her sleep, even on a nice summer's evening in such good company. Breakfast will be around sunup.'

She took him to his room, insisting on climbing the stairs, to show him how to open the windows and fold out the sleeping perch. It was an airy little room, its wallpaper peeling with age. At one time, it must have been for her children.

'. . . and the privy is on the outside rear of the house. No city luxury here, Mister Underhill.'

'It will be fine, my lady.'

'Good night then.'

She was already starting down the stairs when he thought of one more question. There was always one more question. He stuck his head out the bedroom door. 'You have so many books now, Lady Enclearre. Did the parish finally buy you the rest?'

She stopped her careful progress down the stairs, and gave a little laugh. 'Yes, years later. And that's a story too. It was the new parish priest, even if the dear cobber won't admit it; he must have used his own money. But one day, there was this postal shipment on my doorstep, direct from the publishers in Princeton, new copies of the teachers' books for every grade.' She waved a hand. 'The silly fellow. But all the books will go to the deepness with me. I'll see they get to whoever teaches the next generation of parish children.' And she continued down the stairs.

Sherkaner settled onto the sleeping perch, scrunched around until its knobby stuffing felt comfortable. He was very tired, but sleep did not come. The room's tiny windows overlooked the dell. Starlight reflected the color of burned wood from a tiny thread of smoke. The smoke had its own far-red light, but there were no flecks of living fire in it. *I guess even perverts sleep.*

From the trees all around came the sound of the woods-fairies, tiny critters mating and hoarding. Sherkaner wished he had some time for entomology. The critters' buzzing scaled up and down. When he was little there had been the story of the Lazy Woodsfairies, but he also remembered the silly poems they used to put to the fairies' music. 'So high, so low, so many things to know.' The funny little song seemed to hide behind the stridling sound.

The words and the endless song lulled him finally into sleep.

5

Sherkaner made it to Lands Command in two more days. It might have taken longer, except that his redesign of the auto's drive belt made it safer to run the downhill curves fast. It might have taken less time, except that three times he had mechanical failures, one a cracked cylinder. It had been an evasion rather than a lie to tell Lady Enclearre that his cargo was spare parts. In fact, he had taken a few, the things he figured he couldn't build himself at a backcountry smith's.

It was late afternoon when he came round the last bend and caught his first glimpse of the long valley that housed Lands Command. It cut for miles, straight back into the mountains, the valley walls so high that parts of the floor were already in twilight. The far end was blued with distance; Royal Falls descended in slow-motion majesty from the peaks above. This was about as close as tourists ever got. The Royal Family held tight to this land and the deepness beneath the mountain, had held it since they were nothing more than an upstart dukedom forty Darks ago.

Sherkaner ate a good meal at the last little inn, fueled up his auto, and headed into the Royal reservation. The letter from his cousin got him through the outer checkpoints. The swingpole barricades were raised, bored troopers in drab green uniforms waved him through. There were barracks, parade grounds, and – sunk behind massive berms – ammo dumps. But

Lands Command had never been an ordinary military installation. During the early days of the Accord, it had been mostly a playground for the Royals. Then, generation after generation, the affairs of government had become more settled and rational and unromantic. Lands Command fulfilled its name, became the hidey-hole for the Accord's supreme headquarters. Finally, it became something more: the site of the Accord's most advanced military research.

That was what most interested Sherkaner Underhill. He didn't slow down to gawk; the police-soldiers had been very definite that he proceed directly to his official destination. But there was nothing to prevent him from looking in all directions, swaying slightly on his perch as he did so. The only identification on the buildings was discreet little numerical signs, but some were pretty obvious. Wireless telegraphy: a long barracks sprouting the weirdest radio masts. Heh, if things were orderly and efficient, the building beside it would be the crypto academy. On the other side of the road lay a field of asphalt wider and smoother than any road. It was no surprise that two low-wing monoplanes sat on the far end. Sherkaner would have given a lot to see what was behind them, under tarpaulins. Farther on, a huge digger snout stuck steeply out of the lawn in front of one building. The digger's impossible angle gave an impression of speed and violence to what was the slowest conceivable way of getting from here to there.

He was nearing the end of the valley. Royal Falls towered above. A rainbow of a thousand colors floated in its spray. He passed what was probably a library, drove around a parking circle featuring the royal colors and the usual Reaching-for-Accord thing. The stone buildings around the circle were a special part of the mystique of Lands Command. By some fluke of shade and shelter, they survived each New Sun with little damage; not even their contents burned.

BUILDING 5007, the sign said. Office of Materials Research, it said on the directions the sentry had handed him. A good omen that it was right at the center of everything. He parked between two other autos that were already pulled over at the side of the street. Better not be conspicuous.

As he climbed the steps, he could see that the sun was setting almost directly down the path he had come. It was already below the highest cliffs. At the center of the traffic circle, the statues Reaching for Accord cast long shadows across the lawn. Somehow he suspected that the average military base was not quite this beautiful.

The sergeant held Sherkaner's letter with obvious distaste. 'So who is this Captain Underhill—'

'Oh, no relation, Sergeant. He—'

'—and why should his wishes count for squat with us?'

'Ah, if you will read on further, you'll see that he is adjutant to Colonel A. G. Castleworth, Royal Perch QM.'

The sergeant mumbled something that sounded like 'Dumb-ass gate security.' He settled his considerable bulk into a resigned crouch. 'Very well, Mr Underhill, just what is your proposed contribution to the war effort?' Something about the fellow was skewed. Then Sherkaner noticed that the sergeant wore medical casts on all his left legs. He was talking to a veteran of real combat.

This was going to be a hard sell. Even with a sympathetic audience, Sherkaner knew he didn't cut a very imposing figure: young, too thin to be handsome, sort of a gawky know-it-all. He had been hoping to get to an engineering officer. 'Well, Sergeant, for at least the last three generations, you military people have been trying to get some advantage by working longer into the Dark. First it was just for a few hundred days, long enough to lay unexpected mines or strengthen fortifications. Then it was a year, two, long enough to move large numbers of troops into position for attack at the next New Sun.'

The sergeant – HRUNKNER UNNERBY, his name tag said – just stared.

'It's common knowledge that both sides on the Eastern Front have massive tunneling efforts going, that we may end up with huge battles fought up to ten years into the coming Dark.'

Unnerby was struck by a happy thought and his scowl deepened. 'If that's what you think, you should be talking to the Diggers. This is Materials Research here, Mr Underhill.'

'Oh, I know that. But without materials research we have no chance of penetrating through to the really cold times. And also . . . my plans don't have anything to do with digging.' He said the last in a kind of rush.

'Then what?'

'I-I propose that we select appropriate Tiefstadt targets, wake ourselves in the Deepest Dark, walk overland to the targets, and destroy them.' Now, that piled all the impossibilities into one concise statement. He held up forestalling hands. 'I've thought about each of the difficulties, Sergeant. I have solutions, or a start on solutions—'

Unnerby's voice was almost soft as he interrupted. 'In the Deepest Dark, you say? And you are a researcher at Kingschool in Princeton?' That's how Sherkaner's cousin had put it in the letter.

'Yes, in math and—'

'Shut up. Do you have any idea how many millions the Crown spends on military research at places like Kingschool? Do you have any idea how closely we watch the serious work that they do? God, how I hate you Westerling snots. The most you have to worry about is preparing for the Dark, and you're barely up to that. If you had any stiffness in your shell, you'd be enlisting. There are people *dying* now in the East, cobber. There are thousands more who will die unprepared for the Dark, more who will die in the tunnels, and many more who may die when the New Sun lights and there is nothing to eat. And here you sit, spouting fantasy what-ifs.'

Unnerby paused, seemed to tuck his temper away. 'Ah, but I'll tell you a funny story before I boot your ass back to Princeton. You see, I'm a bit unbalanced.' He waggled his left legs. 'An argument with a shredder. Until I get well, I help filter the crank notions that people like you keep sending our way. Fortunately, most of the crap comes in the mail. About once in ten days, some cobber warns us about the low-temperature allotrope of tin—

Oops, maybe I am talking to an engineer!

'—and that we shouldn't ought to use it in solder. At least they have their facts right; they're just wasting our time. But then there are the ones who have just read about radium and figure we ought to make super digger heads out of the stuff. We have a little contest among ourselves about who gets the biggest idiots. Well, Mr Underhill, I think you've made me a winner. You figure on waking yourself in the middle of the Dark, and then traveling overland in temperatures lower than you'll find in any commercial lab and in vacuum harder than even we can create.' Unnerby paused, taken aback at having given away a morsel of classified information? Then Sherkaner realized that the sergeant was looking at something in Sherkaner's blind spot.

'Lieutenant Smith! Good afternoon, ma'am.' The sergeant almost came to attention.

'Good afternoon, Hrunkner.' The speaker moved into view. She was . . . beautiful. Her legs were slender, hard, curving, and every motion had an understated grace. Her uniform was a black that Sherkaner didn't recognize. The only insignia were her deep-red rank pips and name tag. Victory Smith. She looked impossibly young. Born out-of-phase? Maybe so, and the noncom's exaggerated show of respect was a kind of taunt.

Lieutenant Smith turned her attention on Sherkaner. Her aspect seemed friendly in a distant, almost amused way. 'So, Mr Underhill, you are a researcher in the Kingschool Mathematics Department.'

'Well, more a graduate student actually . . .' Her silent gaze seemed to call for a more forthcoming answer. 'Um, math is really just the specialization listed on my official program. I've done a lot of course work in the Medical School and in Mechanical Engineering.' He half-expected Unnerby to make some rude comment, but the sergeant was suddenly very quiet.

'Then you understand the nature of the Deepest Dark, the ultralow temperatures, the hard vacuum.'

'Yes, ma'am. And I've given these problems considerable thought.' *Almost half a year, but better not say that.* 'I have lots of ideas, some preliminary designs. Some of the solutions are biological and there's not much to show you yet. But I did bring prototypes for some of the mechanical aspects of the project. They're out in my automobile.'

'Ah, yes. Parked between the cars of Generals Greenval and Downing. Perhaps we should take a look – and move your auto to a safer place.'

The full realization was years away, but in that moment Sherkaner

Underhill had his first glimmering. Of all the people at Lands Command – of all the people in the wide world – he could not have found a more appropriate listener than Lieutenant Victory Smith.

6

In the last years of a Waning Sun there are storms, often fierce ones. But these are not the steaming, explosive agony of the storms of a New Sun. The winds and blizzards of the coming Dark are more as though the world is someone mortally stabbed, flailing weakly as life's blood leaks out. For the warmth of the world is its lifeblood, and as that soaks into the Dark, the dying world is less and less able to protest.

There comes a time when a hundred stars can be seen in the same sky as the noonday sun. And then a thousand stars, and finally the sun gets no dimmer . . . and the Dark has truly arrived. The larger plants have long since died, the powder of their spores is hidden deep beneath the snows. The lower animals have passed the same way. Scum mottles the lee of snowbanks, and an occasional glow flows around exposed carcasses: the spirits of the dead, classical observers wrote; a last bacterial scavenging, scientists of later eras discovered. Yet there are still living people on the surface. Some are the massacred, prevented by stronger tribes (or stronger nations) from entering deep sanctuary. Others are the victims of floods or earthquakes, whose ancestral deepnesses have been destroyed. In olden times, there was only one way to learn what the Dark might really be: stranded topside, you might attain tenuous immortality by writing what you saw and saving the story so securely that it survived the fires of the New Sun. And occasionally one of these topsiders survived more than a year or two into the Dark, either by extraordinary circumstance or by clever planning and the desire to see into the heart of the Dark. One philosopher survived so long that his last scrawl was taken for insanity or metaphor by those who found his words cut into stone above their deepness: 'and the dry air is turning to frost.'

On one thing the propagandists of both Crown and Tiefstadt agreed. This Dark would be different from all that had gone before. This Dark was the first to be directly assaulted by science in the service of war. While their millions of citizens retreated to the still pools of a thousand deepnesses, the armies of both sides continued to fight. Often the fighting was in open trenches, warmed by steamer fires. But the great differences were underground, in the digging of tunnels that swept deep beneath the front lines of either side. Where these intersected, fierce battles of machine guns and poison gas were fought. Where intersection did not occur, the tunnels continued through the chalky rock of the Eastern Front, yard by yard, days on days, long after all fighting on the surface had ended.

Five years after the Dark began, only a technical elite, perhaps ten thousand on the Crown side, still prosecuted the campaign below the East. Even at their depths, the temperatures were far below freezing. Fresh air was circulated through the occupied tunnels, by foram-burning fans. The last of the air holes would ice over soon.

'We haven't heard any Tiefstadter activity for nearly ten days. Digger Command hasn't stopped congratulating itself.' General Greenval popped an aromatique into his maw and crunched loudly; the chief of Accord Intelligence had never been known for great diplomacy, and he had become perceptibly more crotchety over the last days. He was an old cobber, and though the conditions at Lands Command might be the most benign left anywhere in the world, even they were entering an extreme phase. In the bunkers next to the Royal Deepness, perhaps fifty people were still conscious. Every hour, the air seemed to become a little more stale. Greenval had given up his stately library more than a year ago. Now his office consisted of a twenty-by-ten-by-four-foot slot in the dead space above the dormitory. The walls of the little room were covered with maps, the table with reams of teletype reports from landlines. Wireless communication had reached final failure some seventy days earlier. During the year before that the Crown's radiomen had experimented with more and more powerful transmitters, and there had been some hope that they would have wireless right up to the end. But no, all that was left was telegraphy and line-of-sight radio. Greenval looked at his visitor, certainly the last to Lands Command for more than two hundred years. 'So, Colonel Smith, you just got back from the East. Why don't I hear any huzzahs from yourself? We've outlasted the enemy.'

Victory Smith's attention had been caught by the General's periscope. It was the reason Greenval had stuck his cubbyhole up here – a last view upon the world. Royal Falls had stilled more than two years ago. She could see all the way up the valley. A dark land, covered now with an eldritch frost that formed endlessly on rock and ice alike. Carbon dioxide, leaching out of the atmosphere. *But Sherkaner will see a world far colder than this.*

'Colonel?'

Smith stepped back from the periscope. 'Sorry, sir . . . I admire the Diggers with all my heart.' *At least the troops who are actually doing the digging.* She had been in their field deepnesses. 'But it's been days since they could reach any enemy positions. Less than half will be in fighting form after the Dark. I'm afraid that Digger Command guessed the stand-down point wrong.'

'Yeah,' grumpily. 'Digger Command makes the record book for longest sustained operations, but the Tiefers gained by quitting just when they did.' He sighed and said something that might have gotten him cashiered in other circumstances, but when you're five years past the end of the world, there aren't a lot of people to hear. 'You know, the Tiefers aren't such a bad sort. Take the long view and you'll see nastier types in some of our own allies, waiting for Crown and Tiefstadt to beat each other into a bloody pulp. That's the place where we should be doing our planning, for the next baddies that are going to come after us. We're going to win this war, but if we have to win it with the tunnels and the Diggers, we'll still be fighting for years into the New Sun.'

He gave his aromatique an emphatic crunch and jabbed a forehand at Smith. 'Your project is our only chance to bring this to a clean end.'

Smith's reply was abrupt. 'And the chances would have been still better if you had let me stay with the Team.'

Greenval seemed to ignore the complaint. 'Victory, you've been with this project for seven years now. Do you really think it can work?'

Maybe it was the stale air, making them all daft. Indecision was totally alien to the public image of Strut Greenval. She had known him for nine years. Among his closest confidants, Greenval was an open-minded person – up to the point where final decisions had to be made. Then he was the man without doubt, facing down ranks of generals and even the King's political advisors. Never had she heard such a sad, lost question coming from him. Now she saw an old, old man who in a few hours would surrender to the Dark, perhaps for the last time. The realization was like leaning against a familiar railing and feeling it begin to give way. 'S-sir, we have selected our targets well. If they are destroyed, Tiefstadt's surrender should follow almost immediately. Underhill's Team is in a lake less than two miles from the targets.' And that was an enormous achievement in itself. The lake was near Tiefstadt's most important supply center, a hundred miles deep in Tiefer territory.

'Unnerby and Underhill and the others need only walk a short distance, sir. We tested their suits and the exotherms for much longer periods in conditions almost as—'

Greenval smiled weakly. 'Yes, I know. I jammed the numbers down the craw of the General Staff often enough. But now we're really going to do it. Think what that means. Over the last few generations, we military types have done our little desecrations around the edges of the Dark. But Unnerby's team will see the center of the Deepest Dark. What can that really be like? Yes, we think we know: the frozen air, the vacuum. But that's all guesses. I'm not religious, Colonel Smith, but . . . I wonder at what they may find.'

Religious or not, all the ancient superstitions of snow-trolls and earth-angels seemed to hover just behind the general's words. Even the most rational quailed before the thought of a Dark so intense that in a sense the world did not exist. With an effort, Victory ignored the emotions that

Greenval's words conjured. 'Yes, sir, there could be surprises. And I'd rate this scheme as a likely failure, except for one thing: Sherkaner Underhill.'

'Our pet screwball.'

'Yes, a screwball of a most extraordinary sort. I've known him for seven years – ever since that afternoon he showed up with a car full of half-made prototypes and a head full of crazy schemes. Lucky for us I was having a slow afternoon. I had time to listen and be amused. The average academic type comes up with maybe twenty ideas in a lifetime. Underhill has twenty an hour; it's almost like a palsy with him. But I've known people almost as extreme in Intelligence school. The difference is that Underhill's ideas are feasible about one percent of the time – and he can tell the good ones from the bad with some accuracy. Maybe someone else would have thought of using swamp sludge to breed the exotherms. Certainly someone else could have had his ideas about airsuits. But he has the ideas and he brings them together, and they work.

'But that's only part of it. Without Sherkaner, we could not have come close to implementing all we have in these last seven years. He has the magic ability to rope bright people into his schemes.' She remembered Hrunkner Unnerby's angry contempt that first afternoon, how it had changed over a period of days until Hrunkner's engineering imagination was totally swept up by the ideas Sherkaner was spewing at him. 'In a sense, Underhill has no patience for details, but that doesn't matter. He generates an entourage which *does*. He's just . . . remarkable.'

This was all old news to both of them; Greenval had argued similarly to his own bosses over the years. But it was the best reassurance Victory could give the old cobber now. Greenval smiled and his look was strange. 'So why didn't you marry him, Colonel?'

Smith hadn't meant that to come up, but hell, they were alone, and at the end of the world: 'I intend to, sir. But there's a war on, and you know I'm . . . not much for tradition; we'll marry after the Dark.' It had taken Victory Smith just one afternoon to realize that Underhill was the strangest person she had ever met. It had taken her another couple of days to realize he was a genius who could be used like a dynamo, could be used to literally change the course of a world war. Within fifty days she had had Strut Greenval convinced of the same, and Underhill was tucked away in his own lab, with labs growing up around him to handle the peripheral needs of the project. Between her own missions, Victory had schemed on how she might claim the Underhill phenomenon – that was how she thought of him, how the Intelligence Staff thought of him – as her permanent advantage. Marriage was the obvious move. A traditional Marriage-in-the-Waning would have suited her career path. It all would have been perfect, except for Sherkaner Underhill himself. Sherk was a person with his own plans. Ultimately he had become her best friend, as much someone to scheme with as to scheme about. Sherk had plans for after the Dark, things that Victory had never repeated to anyone. Her few other friends – even Hrunkner Unnerby – liked her despite her being out-of-phase. Sherkaner Underhill actually liked the idea of out-of-phase children. It was the first time in her life that Victory had met with more than mere acceptance. So for now they fought a war. If they both survived, there was another world of plans and a life together, after the Dark.

And Strut Greenval was clever enough to figure out a lot of this. Abruptly, she glared at her boss. 'You already knew, didn't you? That's why you wouldn't let me stay with the Team. You figure it's a suicide mission, and my judgment would be warped . . . Well it is dangerous, but you don't understand Sherkaner Underhill; self-sacrifice is not on his agenda. By our standards he's rather a coward. He's not especially taken by most of the things you and I hold dear. He's risking his life out of simple curiosity – but he's very, very careful when it comes to his own safety. I think the Team will succeed *and* survive. The odds would only have been improved if you'd let me stay with them! Sir.'

Her last words were punctuated by the dramatic dimming of the room's single lamp. 'Hah,' said Greenval, 'we've been without fuel oil for twelve hours, did you know that, Colonel? Now the lead acid batteries have about run down. In a couple of minutes Captain Diredr will be here with the Last Word from maintenance: "Begging your pardon, sir, but the last pools will freeze momentarily. Engineering begs that you join them for final shut-down."' He mimicked his aide's high-pitched voice.

Greenval stood, leaned across the desk. His doubts were hidden once more, and the old snap was back in his manner. 'In that time, I want to clear up a few things about your orders and your future. Yes, I brought you back because I don't want to risk you on this mission. Your Sergeant Unnerby and I have had some long talks. We've had nine years to put you through almost limitless risk, and to watch how your mind works when thousands of lives depend on the right answers. It's time to take you off the front lines of special operations. You are one of the youngest colonels in modern times; after this Dark, you'll be the youngest general.'

'Only if the Underhill mission succeeds.'

'Don't interrupt. However the Underhill affair goes, the King's advisors know how good you are. Whether or not I survive this Dark, you'll be sitting in my job within a few years of the starting of the New Sun – and your days of personal risk-taking must be over. If your Mr Underhill survives, marry him, breed him, I couldn't care less. But never ever again are you to put yourself at risk.' He waved his pointed hand at her head, a mock threat with an edge. 'If you do, I swear I'll come back from the grave and crack your thick shell.'

There was the sound of footsteps in the narrow hallway. Hands scratched at the heavy curtain that was the room's only door. It was Captain Diredr.

'Excuse me, General. Engineering is absolutely insistent, sir. We have thirty minutes of electrical power, at the outside. They are begging, sir—'

Greenval spat that last aromatique into a stained cuspidor. 'Very good, Captain. We are coming down instanter.' He sidled around the Colonel, and pulled back the curtain. When Smith hesitated to go before him, he waved her through the doorway. 'In this case, senior means last, my dear. I've never liked this business of cheating on the Dark, but if we have to do it, *I'm* the one who gets to turn out the lights!'

7

By rights Pham Trinli should not have been on the Fleet Captain's bridge, certainly not during a serious operation. The old man sat at one of the duplicate comm posts, but he really didn't do anything with it. Trinli was Programmer-at-Arms 3rd, though no one had ever seen him behave productively, even at that low rank. He seemed to come and go at his own pleasure, and spent most of his time down in the employees' dayroom. Fleet Captain Park was known to be a little irrational when it came to 'respect for age.' Apparently, as long as Pham Trinli did no harm, he could stay on the payroll.

Just now, Trinli sat half-turned away from his post. He listened dyspeptically to the quiet conversations, the flow of check and response. He looked past the techs and armsmen at the common displays.

The landings of Qeng Ho and Emergent vessels had been a dance of caution. Mistrust for the Emergents extended from top to bottom among Captain Park's people. Thus there were no combined crews, and the comm nets were fully duplicated. Captain Park had positioned his capital vessels in three groups, each responsible for a third of the planetary operations. Every Emergent ship, every lander, every free-flying crewman was monitored for evidence of treachery.

The bridge's consensus imagery showed most of this. Relayed from the 'eastern' cluster, Trinli could see a trio of Emergent heavy lifters coming off the frozen surface of the ocean, towing between them a quarter-million-tonne block of ice. That was the sixth lift in this op. The surface was brightly lit by the rocket glare. Trinli could see a hole hundreds of meters deep. Steaming froth masked the gouge in the seafloor. Soundings showed there were plenty of heavy metals in this section of continental shelf, and they were mining it with the same brute force that they employed when they carved the ice.

Nothing really suspicious there, though things may change when it comes time to divvy up the loot.

He studied at the comm status windows. Both sides had agreed to broadcast intership communications in the clear; a number of Emergent specialists were in constant conference comm with corresponding Qeng Ho officers; the other side was sucking in everything they could about Diem's discoveries in the dry valley. Interesting how the Emergents suggested simply grabbing the native artifacts. Very unQeng-Ho-like. *More like something I might do.*

Park had dumped most of his fleet's microsats into near-planetary space just before the Emergents arrived. There were tens of thousands of the fist-sized gadgets out there now. Subtly maneuvering, they came between the Emergents' vehicles far more often than simple chance would predict. And they reported back to the electronic intelligence window here on the bridge. They reported that there was far too much line-of-sight talk between the Emergent vessels. It might be innocent automation. More likely it was cover for encrypted military coordination, sly preparation on the part of the enemy. (And Pham Trinli had never thought of the Emergents as anything but an enemy.)

Park's staff recognized the signs, of course. In their prissy way, these Qeng Ho armsmen were very sharp. Trinli watched three of them argue about the broadcast patterns that washed across the fleet from Emergent emitters. One of the junior armsmen thought they might be seeing a mix of physical-layer and software probing – all in an orchestrated tangle. But if that were true, it was more sophisticated than the Qeng Ho's own best e-measures . . . and that was unbelievable. The senior armsman just frowned at the junior, as if the suggestion were a king-sized headache. *Even the ones who have been in combat don't get the point.* For a moment, Trinli's expression got even more sour.

A voice sounded privately in his ear. 'What do you think, Pham?'

Trinli sighed. He mumbled back into his comm, his lips barely moving, 'It stinks, Sammy. You know that.'

'I'd feel better if you were at an alternate control center.' The *Pham Nuwen*'s 'bridge' had this official location, but in fact there were control centers distributed throughout the ship's livable spaces. More than half the staff visible on the bridge were really elsewhere. In theory, it made the starship a tougher kill. In theory.

'I can do better than that. I've hacked one of the taxis for remote command.' The old man floated off his saddle. He drifted silently behind the ranks of the bridge technicians, past the view on the heavy lifters, the view of Diem's crew preparing to lift off from the dry valley, the images of oh-so-intent Emergent faces . . . past the ominous e-measures displays. No one really noticed his passage, except that as he slid through the bridge entranceway, Sammy Park glanced at him. Trinli gave the Fleet Captain a little nod.

Spineless wretches, nearly every one. Only Sammy and Kira Pen Lisolet had understood the need to strike first. And they had not persuaded a single member of the Trading Committee. Even after meeting the Emergents face-to-face, the committee couldn't recognize the other side's certain treachery. Instead, they asked a Vinh to decide for them. A *Vinh!*

Trinli coasted down empty corridors, slowed to a stop by the taxi lock, and popped the hatch on the one he had specially prepared. *I could ask Lisolet to mutiny.* The Deputy Fleet Captain had her own command, the QHS *Invisible Hand.* A mutiny was physically possible, and once she started shooting, Sammy and the others would surely have to join her.

He slipped into the taxi, started the lock pumps. *No, I wash my hands of all of them.* Somewhere at the back of his skull, a little headache was growing. Tension didn't usually affect him this way. He shook his head. Okay, the truth was, he wasn't asking Lisolet to mutiny, because she was one of those very rare people who had honor. So, he would do the best with what he had. Sammy *had* brought weapons. Trinli grinned, anticipating the time ahead. *Even if the other side strikes first, I wager we're the last men standing.* As his taxi drifted out from the Qeng Ho flagship, Trinli studied the threat updates, planning. What would the other side try? If they waited long enough, he might yet figure out Sammy's weapons locks . . . and be his own one-man mutiny.

There were plenty of signs of the treachery abuilding, but even Pham Trinli missed the most blatant. You had to guess the method of attack to recognize that one.

Ezr Vinh was quite ignorant of military developments overhead. The Ksecs spent on the surface had been hard, fascinating work, work that didn't leave much time to pursue suspicions. In all his life, he had spent only a few dozen Msecs walking around on the surface of planets. Despite exercise and Qeng Ho medicine, he was feeling the strain. The first Ksecs had seemed relatively easy, but how every muscle ached. Fortunately, he wasn't the only wimp. The whole crew seemed to be dragging. Final cleanup was an eternity of careful checking that they had left no garbage, that any signs of their presence would be lost in the effects of OnOff's relighting. Crewleader Diem twisted his ankle on the climb back to the lander. Without the freight winch on the lander, the rest of the climb would have been impossible. When they finally got aboard, even stripping off and stowing their thermal jackets was a pain.

'Lord.' Benny collapsed on the rack next to Vinh. There were groans from all along the aisle as the lander boosted them skyward. Still, Vinh felt a quiet glow of satisfaction; the fleet had learned far more from their one landing than anyone expected. Theirs was a righteous fatigue.

There was little chitchat among Diem's crewmembers now. The sound of the lander's torch was an almost subsonic drone that seemed to originate in their bones and grow outward. Vinh could still hear public conversations from on high, but Trixia was out of it. No one was talking to Diem's people now. Correction: Qiwi was trying to talk to him, but Ezr was just too tired to humor the Brat.

Over the curve of the world, the heavy lifting was behind schedule. Clean nukes had broken up several million tonnes of frozen ocean, but steam above the extraction site was complicating the remainder of the job. The Emergent, Brughel, was complaining that they had lost contact with one of their lifters.

'I think it's your angle of view, sir,' came the voice of a Qeng Ho tech. 'We can see all of them. Three are still at the surface; one is heavily obscured by the local haze, but it looks well positioned. Three more are in ascent, clean lifts, well separated . . . One moment . . .' Seconds passed. On a more 'distant' channel, a voice was talking about some sort of medical problem; apparently someone had committed a zero-gee barf. Then the flight controller was back: 'That's strange. We've lost our view of the East Coast operation.'

Brughel, his voice sharpening: 'Surely you have secondaries?'

The Qeng Ho tech did not reply.

A third voice: 'We just got an EM pulse. I thought you people were done with your surface blasting?'

'We are!' Brughel was indignant.

'Well we just got three more pulses. I – Yessir!'

EM pulses? Vinh struggled to sit up, but the acceleration was too much, and suddenly his head hurt even more than ever. *Say something more, damn it!* But the fellow who just said 'yessir' – a Qeng Ho armsman by the sound of him – was off the air, or more likely had changed mode and encrypted himself.

The Emergent's voice was clipped and angry: 'I want to talk to someone in authority. *Now.* We know targeting lasers when they shine on us! Turn them off or we'll all regret it.'

Ezr's head-up display went clear, and he was looking at the lander's bulkheads. The wallpaper backup flickered on, but the video was some random emergency-procedures sequence.

'Shit!' It was Jimmy Diem. At the front of the cabin, the crewleader was pounding on a command console. Somewhere behind Vinh there was the sound of vomiting. It was like one of those nightmares where everything goes nuts at once.

At that instant, the lander reached end-of-burn. In the space of three seconds, the terrible pressure eased off Vinh's chest and there was the comforting familiarity of zero gee. He pulled on his couch release and coasted forward to Diem.

From the ceiling it was easy to stand with his head by Diem's and see the emergency displays, without getting in the crewleader's way. 'We're really shooting at them?' *Lord, but my head hurts!* When he tried to read Diem's command console, the glyphs swam before his eyes.

Diem turned his head a fraction to look at Ezr. Agony was clear in his face; he could barely move. 'I don't know what we're doing. I've lost consensual imaging. Tie yourself down . . .' He leaned forward as though to focus on the display. 'The fleet net has gone hard crypto, and we're stuck at the least secure level,' which meant that they would get little information beyond direct commands from Park's armsmen.

The ceiling gave Vinh a solid whack on the butt, and he started to slide toward the back of the cabin. The lander was turning, some kind of emergency override – the autopilot had given no warning. Most likely, fleet command was prepping them for another burn. He tied down behind Diem, just as the lander's main torch lit off at about a tenth of a gee. 'They're moving us to a lower orbit . . . but I don't see anything coming to rendezvous,' said Diem. He poked awkwardly at the password field beneath the display. 'Okay, I'm doing my own snooping . . . I hope Park isn't too pissed . . .'

Behind them, there was the sound of more vomiting. Diem started to turn his head, winced. 'You're the mobile one, Vinh. Take care of that.'

Ezr slid down the aisle's ladderline, letting the one-tenth-gee load do the moving for him. Qeng Ho lived their lives under varying accelerations. Medicine and good breeding made orientation sickness a rare thing among them. But Tsufe Do and Pham Patil had both upchucked, and Benny Wen was curled up as far as his ties would permit. He held the sides of his head and swayed in apparent agony. 'The pressure, the pressure . . .'

Vinh eased next to Patil and Do, gently vac'd the goo that was dribbling down their coveralls. Tsufe looked up at him, embarrassment in her eyes. 'Never barfed in my life.'

'It's not you,' said Vinh, and tried to think past the pain that squeezed harder and harder. *Stupid, stupid, stupid. How could it take so long to understand?* It was not the Qeng Ho that was attacking the Emergents; somehow it was quite the reverse.

Suddenly he could see outside again. 'I got local consensus,' Diem's voice came in his earphones. The crewleader's words came in short, tortured bursts. 'Five high-gee bombs from Emergent positions . . . Target: Park's flag . . .'

Vinh leaned across the row of couches and looked out. The missiles' jets were pointing away from the lander's viewpoint; the five were faint stars moving faster and faster across the sky, closing on the QHS *Pham Nuwen*. Yet their paths were not smooth arcs. There were sharp bends and wobbles.

'We must be lasing at them. They're jinking.'

One of the tiny lights vanished. 'We got one! We—'

Four points of light blazed in the sky. The brightness grew and grew, a thousand times brighter than the faded disk of the sun.

Then the view was gone again. The cabin lights died, winked back on, died again. The bottommost emergency system came online. There was a faint network of reddish lines, outlining equipment bays, airlock, the emergency console. The system was rad-hardened but very simpleminded and low-powered. There wasn't even backup video.

'What about Park's flagship, Crewleader?' asked. Vinh. Four close-set detonations, so terribly bright – the corners of a regular tetrahedron, clasping its victim. The view was gone but it would burn in his memory forever. '*Jimmy!*' Vinh screamed at the front of the cabin. 'What about the *Pham Nuwen?*' The red emergency lights seemed to sway around him; the shouting brought him close to blacking out.

Then Diem's voice came hoarse and loud. 'I . . . I think it's g-gone.' Fried, vaped, none of the masking words were easy anymore. 'I don't have anything now, but the four nukes . . . Lord, they were right on top of him!'

Several other voices interrupted, but they were even weaker than Jimmy Diem's. As Vinh started back up the line toward him, the one-tenth-gee burn ended. Without light or brains, what was the lander but a dark coffin? For the first time in his life, Ezr Vinh felt the groundsider's disorienting terror; zero gee could mean they had reached designated orbit, or that they were falling in a ballistic arc that intersected the planet's surface . . .

Vinh clamped down on his terror and coasted forward. They could use the emergency console. They could listen for word. They could use the local autopilot to fly to the surviving Qeng Ho forces. The pain in his head grew beyond anything Ezr Vinh had ever known. The little red emergency lights seemed to get dimmer and dimmer. He felt his consciousness squeezing down, and the panic rose and choked him. There was nothing he could do.

And just before things all went away, fate showed him one kindness, a memory: Trixia Bonsol had not been aboard the *Pham Nuwen*.

8

For more than two hundred years, the clock mechanism beneath the frozen lake had faithfully advanced itself, exhausting the tension of spring coil after spring coil. The mechanism ticked reliably down through the last spring . . . and jammed on a fleck of airsnow in the final trigger. There it might have hung until the coming of the new sun, if not for certain other unforeseen events: On the seventh day of the two-hundred-and-ninth year, a series of sharp earthquakes spread outward from the frozen sea, jolting loose the final trigger. A piston slid a froth of organic sludge into a tank of frozen air. Nothing happened for several minutes. Then a glow spread through the organics, temperatures rose past the vapor points of oxygen and nitrogen, and even carbon dioxide. The exhalation of a trillion budding exotherms melted the ice above the little vehicle. The ascent to the surface had begun.

*

Coming awake from the Dark was not like waking from an ordinary sleep. A thousand poets had written about the moment and – in recent eras – ten thousand academics had studied it. This was the second time that Sherkaner Underhill had experienced it (but the first time didn't really count, since that memory was mixed with the vague memories of babyhood, of clinging to his father's back in the pools of the Mountroyal Deepness).

Coming awake from the Dark was done in pieces. Vision, touch, hearing. Memory, recognition, thought. Did they happen first one and then another and another? Or did they happen all at once, but with the parts not communicating? Where did 'mind' begin from all the pieces? The questions would rattle around in Sherkaner's imagination for all of his life, the basis for his ultimate quest . . . But in those moments of fragmented consciousness, they coexisted with things that seemed much more important: bringing self together; remembering who he was, why he was here, and what had to be done right now to survive. The instincts of a million years were in the driver's perch.

Time passed and thought coalesced and Sherkaner Underhill looked out his vessel's cracked window into the darkness. There was motion – roiling steam? No, more like a veil of crystals swirling in the dim light they floated on.

Someone was bumping his right shoulders, calling his name again and again. Sherkaner pieced together memories. 'Yes, Sergeant, I'm away . . . I mean, awake.'

'Excellent.' Unnerby's voice was tinny. 'Are you injured? You know the drill.'

Sherkaner dutifully wiggled his legs. They all hurt; that was a good start. Midhands, forehands, eating hands. 'Not sure I can feel my right mid and fore. Maybe they're stuck together.'

'Yeah. Probably still frozen.'

'How are Gil and Amber?'

'I'm talking to them on the other cables. You're the last one to get his head together, but they've got bigger hunks of body still frozen.'

'Gimme the cable head.' Unnerby passed him the sound-conducting gear, and Sherkaner talked directly to the other Team members. The body can tolerate a lot of differential thawing, but if the process doesn't complete, rot sets in. The problem here was that the bags of exotherm and fuel had shifted around as the boat melted its way to the surface. Sherkaner reset the bags and started sludge and air flowing through them. The green glow within their tiny hull brightened, and Sherkaner took advantage of the light to check for punctures in their breathing tubes. The exotherms were essential for heat, but if the Team had to compete with them for oxygen the Team would be the dead loser.

A half hour passed, the warmth enveloping them, freeing their limbs. The only frost damage was at the tips of Gil Haven's midhands. That was a better safety record than most deepnesses. A broad smile spread across Sherkaner's aspect. They had made it, wakened *themselves* in the Deep of the Dark.

The four rested a while longer, monitoring the airflow, exercising Sherkaner's scheme for controlling the exotherms. Unnerby and Amberdon Nizhnimor went through the detailed checklist, passing suspicious and broken items across to Sherkaner. Nizhnimor, Haven, and Unnerby were very bright people, a chemist and two engineers. But they were also combat professionals. Sherkaner found fascinating the change that came over them when they moved out of the lab and into the field. Unnerby especially was such a layering: hardbitten soldier atop imaginative engineer, hiding a traditional, straitlaced morality. Sherkaner had known the sergeant for seven years now. The fellow's initial contempt for Underhill schemes was long past; they had been close friends. But when their Team finally moved to the Eastern Front, his manner had become distant. He had begun to address Underhill as 'sir,' and sometimes his respectfulness was edged with impatience.

He'd asked Victory about that. It had been the last time they were alone together, in a cold burrow-barracks beneath the last operating aerodrome on the Eastern Front. She had laughed at the question. 'Ah, dear soft one, what do you expect? Hrunk will have operational command once the Team leaves friendly territory. *You* are the civilian advisor with no military training, who must somehow be tucked into the chain of command. He needs your instant obedience, but also your imagination and flexibility.' She laughed softly; only a curtain separated their conversation from the main hall of the narrow barracks. 'If you were an ordinary recruit, Unnerby would have fried your shell half a dozen times by now. The poor cobber is so afraid that when seconds count, your genius will be caught on something completely irrelevant – astronomy, whatever.'

'Um.' Actually, he had wondered how the stars might look without the atmosphere to dim their colors. 'I see what you mean. Put that way, I'm surprised he let Greenval put me on the Team.'

'Are you kidding? Hrunk demanded you be on it. He knows there'll be surprises that only you can figure out. As I said; he's a cobber with a problem.'

It wasn't often that Sherkaner Underhill felt taken aback, but this was one of those times. 'Well, I'll be good.'

'Yes, I know you will. I just wanted you to know what Hrunk is up against . . . Hey, you can look on it as a behavioral mystery: How can such radically crazy people cooperate and survive where no one has ever lived before?' Maybe she meant it as a joke, but it *was* an interesting question.

Without doubt, their vehicle was the strangest in all history: part submarine, part portable deepness, part sludge bucket. Now the fifteen-foot shell rested in a shallow pool of glowing green and tepid-red. The water was in a vacuum boil, gases swirling up from it, chilling into tiny crystals, and falling back. Unnerby pushed open the hatch, and the team formed a chain, handing equipment and exotherm tanks from one to the next to the next, until the ground just beyond the pool was piled with the gear they would carry.

They strung audio cable between themselves, Underhill to Unnerby to Haven to Nizhnimor. Sherkaner had been hoping for portable radios almost until the end, but such gear was still too bulky and no one was sure how it would operate under these conditions. So they each could talk to just one other team member. Still, they needed safety lines in any case, so the cable was no extra inconvenience.

Sherkaner led the way back to the lakeshore, with Unnerby behind him, and Nizhnimor and Haven pulling the sled. Away from their submarine, the darkness closed in. There were still glimmers of heat-red light, where exotherms had sprayed across the ground; the sub had burned tons of fuel in melting its way to the surface. The rest of the mission must be powered by just the exotherms they could carry and what fuels they could find beneath the snow.

More than anything else, the exotherms were the trick that made this walk in the Dark possible. Before the invention of the microscope, the 'great thinkers' claimed that what separated the higher animals from the rest of life was their ability to survive as individuals through the Great Dark. Plants and simpler animals died; it was only their encysted eggs that survived. Nowadays, it was known that many single-celled animals survived freezing just fine, and without having to retreat to deepnesses. Even stranger, and this had been discovered by biologists at Kingschool while Sherkaner was an undergraduate, there were forms of Lesser Bacteria that lived in volcanoes and stayed active right through the Dark. Sherkaner had been very taken by these microscopic creatures. The professors assumed that such creatures must suspend or sporulate when a volcano went cold, but he wondered if there might be varieties that could live through freezes by making their own heat. After all, even in the Dark, there was still plenty of oxygen – and in most places there was a layer of organic ruin beneath the airsnow. If there were some catalyst for starting oxidation at super-low temperatures, maybe the little bugs could just 'burn' vegetation between volcanic surges. Such bacteria would be the best adapted of all to live after Dark.

In retrospect, it was mainly Sherkaner's ignorance that permitted him to entertain the idea. The two life strategies required entirely different chemistries. The external oxidation effect was very weak, and in warm environments nonexistent. In many situations, the trick was a serious disability to the little bugs; the two metabolisms were generally poisonous to each other. In the Dark, they would gain a very slight advantage if they were near a periodic volcanic hot spot. It would never have been noticed if

Sherkaner hadn't gone looking for it. He had turned an undergraduate biology lab into a frozen swamp and gotten himself (temporarily) kicked out of school, but there they were: his exotherms.

After seven years of selective breeding by the Materials Research Department, the bacteria had a pure, high-velocity oxidizing metabolism. So when Sherkaner slopped exotherm sludge into the airsnow, there was a burst of vapor, and then a tiny glow that faded as the still-liquid droplet sank and cooled. A second would pass and if you looked very carefully (and if the exotherms in that droplet had been lucky) you would see a faint light from *beneath* the snow, feeding across the surface of whatever buried organics there might be.

The glow was sprouting brighter now on his left. The airsnow shivered and slumped and some kind of steam curled out of it. Sherkaner tugged on the cable to Unnerby, guiding the team toward denser fuel. However clever the idea, using exotherms was still a form of firemaking. Airsnow was everywhere, but the combustibles were hidden. It was only the work of trillions of Lesser Bacteria that made it possible to find and use the fuel. For a while, even Materials Research had been intimidated by their creation. Like the mat algae on the Southern Banks, these tiny creatures were in a sense social. They moved and reproduced as fast as any mat that crawled the Banks. What if this excursion set the world on fire? But in fact the high-velocity metabolism was bacterial suicide. Underhill and company had at most fifteen hours before the last of their exotherms would all die.

Soon they were off the lake, and walking across a level field that had been the Base Commander's bowling green in the Waning Years. Fuel was plentiful here; at one point the exotherms got into a fallen mound of vegetation, the remains of a traumtree. The pile glowed more and more warmly, until a brilliant emerald light exploded through the snow. For a few moments, the field and the buildings beyond were clearly visible. Then the green light faded, and there was just the heat-red glow.

They had come perhaps one hundred yards from the sub. If there were no obstacles, they had more than four thousand yards to go. The team settled into a painful routine: walk a few dozen yards, stop and spread exotherms. While Nizhnimor and Haven rested, Unnerby and Underhill would look about for where the exotherms had found the richest fuel. From those spots, they would top off everyone's sludge panniers. Sometimes, there wasn't much fuel to be found (walking across a wide cement slab), and about all they had to shovel was airsnow. They needed that, too; they needed to breathe. But without fuel for the exotherms, the cold quickly became numbing, spreading in from the joints in the suits and up from their footpads. Then success depended on Sherkaner successfully guessing where to go next.

Actually, Sherkaner found that pretty easy. He'd gotten his bearings by the light of the burning tree, and by now the patterns of airsnow that concealed vegetation were obvious. Things were okay; he wasn't refreezing. The pain at the tips of his hands and feet was sharp, and every joint seemed to be a ring of fire, the pain of pressure-swelling, cold, and suit-chafe. Interesting problem, pain. So helpful, so obnoxious. Even the likes of Hrunkner Unnerby couldn't entirely ignore it; he could hear Unnerby's hoarse breath over the cable.

Stop, refill the panniers, top off the air, and then on again. Over and over. Gil Haven's frostbite seemed to be getting worse. They stopped, tried to rearrange the cobber's suit. Unnerby swapped places with Haven, to help Nizhnimor with the sled. 'No problem, it's only the midhands,' said Gil. But his labored breathing sounded much worse than Unnerby's.

Even so, they were still doing better than Sherk had expected. They trudged on through the Dark, and their routine soon became almost automatic. All that was left was the pain . . . and the wonder. Sherkaner looked out through the tiny portholes of his helmet. Beyond the swirl of mist and the exotherms' glow . . . there were gentle hills. It was not totally dark. Sometimes when his head was angled just right, he caught a glimpse of a reddish disk low in the western sky. He was seeing the sun of the Deepest Dark.

And through the tiny roof porthole, Sherkaner could see the stars. *We are here at last.* The first to ever look upon the Deepest Dark. It was a world that some ancient philosophers had denied existence – for how can something *be*, that can never be observed? But now it was seen. It did exist, centuries of cold and stillness . . . and stars everywhere. Even through the heavy glass of the porthole, even with only his topside eyes, he could see colors there that had never been seen in the stars before. If he would just stop for a while and angle all his eyes to watch, what more might he see? Most theorists figured the auroral patches would be gone without sunlight to drive them; others thought the aurora was somehow powered by the volcanoes that lived beneath them. There might be other lights here besides the stars . . .

A jerk on the cable brought him back to earth. 'Keep moving, gotta keep moving.' Gil's voice was gasping. No doubt he was relaying from Unnerby. Underhill started to apologize, then realized that it was Amberdon Nizhnimor, back by the sled, who had paused.

'What is it?' Sherkaner asked.

'. . . Amber saw . . . light in the east . . . Keep moving.'

East. To the right. The glass on that side of his helmet was fogged. He had a vague impression of a near ridgeline. Their operation was within four miles of the coast. Over that ridge they'd have a clear view of the horizon. Either the light was quite close or very far away. Yes! There was a light, a pale glow that spread sideways and up. Aurora? Sherkaner clamped down on his curiosity, kept putting one foot in front of another. But God below, how he wished he could climb that ridge and look across the frozen sea!

Sherkaner was a good little trouper right up to the next sludge stop. He was shoveling a glowing mix of exotherms, fuel, and airsnow into Haven's panniers when it happened. Five tiny lights raced into the western sky, leaving little corners here and there like some kind of slow lightning. One of the five faded to nothing, but the others drew quickly together and – light *blazed*, so bright that Underhill's upward vision blurred in pain. But out to the sides, he could still see. The brightness grew and grew, a thousand times brighter than the faded disk of the sun. Multiple shadows showed stark around them. Still brighter and brighter grew the four lights, till Sherkaner could feel the heat soaking through the shell-cover of his suit. The airsnow all across the field burst upward in misty white-out brilliance. The warmth increased a moment more, almost scalding now – and then faded, leaving his back with the warm feeling you have when you walk into the shade on a Middle Years summer day.

The mists swirled around them, making the first perceptible wind they had experienced since leaving the sub. Suddenly it was very cold, the mists sucking warmth from their suits; only their boots were designed for immersion. The light was fading now, the air and water cooling to crystal and falling back to earth. Underhill risked focusing his upward eyes: The fierce points of light had spread into glowing disks, fading even as he watched. Where they overlapped, he saw a wavering and a folding, aurora-like; so they were localized in range as well as angle. Four, close set – the corners of a regular tetrahedron? So beautiful . . . But what was the range? Was this some kind of ball lightning, just a few hundred yards above the field?

In another few minutes they would be too faint to see. But there were other lights, now, bright flashes beyond the eastern ridgeline. In the west, pinpricks of light slid faster and faster toward the zenith. A shimmering veil of light spread behind them.

The four Team members stood motionless. For an instant, Unnerby's soldier persona was blown away, and all that was left was awe. He stumbled away from the sled, and laid one hand on Sherkaner's back. His voice came faintly across the poor connection: 'What is it, Sherkaner?'

'Don't know.' He could feel Unnerby's arm trembling. 'But someday we'll understand . . . Let's keep moving, Sergeant.'

Like spring-driven marionettes suddenly kicked into motion, the Team finished loading up, and continued on their path. The show continued overhead, and though there was nothing like the four searing suns, the lights were more beautiful and extensive than any aurora ever known. Two moving stars slid faster and faster across the sky. The ghostly curtains of their passing spread all the way down to the west. Now high in the eastern sky, they flared incandescent, miniature versions of the first burning lights. As they dimmed and spread, legs of light crept down from their point of vanishment, brightening wherever they passed through the earlier glows.

The most spectacular movements were past now, but the slow wraithlike movement of light continued. If it was hundreds of miles up, like a true aurora, there was some immense energy source here. If it was just above their heads, maybe they were seeing the Deep Dark analogue of summer lightning. Either way, the show was worth all the risks of this adventure.

At last they reached the edge of Tiefer cantonment. The strange aurora was still visible as they started down the entrance ramp.

There had never been much question about the targets. They were the ones Underhill had originally imagined, the ones that Victory Smith came up with that first afternoon at Lands Command. If somehow they could reach the Deepest Dark, four soldiers and some explosives could do various damage to fuel dumps, to the shallow deepnesses of surface troops, perhaps even to Tiefstadt's general staff. Even these targets could not justify the research investment that Underhill was demanding.

Yet there was an obvious choke point. Just as the modern military machine endeavored to gain advantage at the beginning of the Dark by fighting longer to outmaneuver a sleeping enemy, so at the beginning of the New Sun, the first armies that were effectively back in the field would win a decisive advantage.

Both sides had built large stockpiles for that time, but with a strategy quite different from that of the Waning Years and the beginning of the Dark. As far as science could determine, the New Sun grew to its immense brightness in a space of days, perhaps of hours. For a few days it was a searing monster, more than a hundred times brighter than during the Middle and Waning Years. It was that explosion of brightness – not the cold of the Dark – that destroyed all but the sturdiest structures of each generation.

This ramp led to a Tiefer outreach depot. There were others along the front, but this was the rear-echelon depot that would support their maneuver force. Without it, the best of the Tiefer troops would be compelled to stay out of combat. Tiefer forward elements at the point of the Crown's advance would have no backup. Lands Command figured that destroying the depot would force a favorable armistice, or a string of easy victories for the Crown's armies. Four soldiers and some subtle vandalism might just be enough to do it.

. . . If they didn't freeze trying to get down this ramp. There were wisps of airsnow on the steps, and an occasional shred of brush that had grown between the flags, but that was all. Now when they stopped, it was to pass forward pails of sludge from the sled that Nizhnimor and Unnerby were pulling. The darkness closed in tight around them, lit only by an occasional gleam of spilled exotherm. Intelligence reports claimed the ramp extended less than two hundred yards . . .

Up ahead glowed an oval of light. The end of the tunnel. The Team staggered off the ramp onto a field that had been open once, but that was now shielded from the sky by silvery sunblinds. A forest of tent poles stretched off all around them. In places the fall of airsnow had torn the structure, but most of it was intact. In the dim, slatted patches of light, they could see the forms of steam locomotives, rail layers, machine-gun cars, and armored automobiles. Even in the dimness, there was a glint of silver paint in the airsnow. When the New Sun lit, this gear would be ready. While ice steamed and melted, and flowed torrents down the channels that webbed this field, Tiefer combateers would come out of the nearby deepnesses and run for the safety of their vehicles. The waters would be diverted into holding tanks, and the cooling sprays started. There would be a few hours of frantic checking of inventories and mechanical status, a few hours more to repair the failures of two centuries of Dark and the hours of new heat. And then they would be off on whichever rail path their commanders thought led to victory. This was the culmination of generations of scientific research into the nature of the Dark and the New Sun. Intelligence estimated that in many ways it was more advanced than the Crown's own quartermaster science.

Hrunkner gathered them together, so they could all hear him. 'I'll bet they'll have forward guards out here within an hour of First Sunlight, but now it's just ours for the taking. . . . Okay, we top off our panniers and split up per plan. Gil, are you up to this?'

Gil Haven had weaved his way down the steps like a drunkard with broken feet. It looked to Sherkaner that his suit failure had extended back to his walking feet. But he straightened at Unnerby's words, and his voice seemed almost normal. 'Sergeant, I didn't come all this way to sit an' watch you cobbers. I can handle my part.'

And so they had come to the point of it all. They disconnected their audio cables, and each gathered up his appointed explosives and dye-black. They had practiced this often enough. If they double-timed between each action point, if they didn't fall into a drainage ditch and break some legs, if the maps they had memorized were accurate, there would be time to do it all and still not freeze. They moved off in four directions. The explosives they set beneath the sunblinds were scarcely more than hand grenades. They made silent flashes as they went off – and collapsed strategic sections of the canopy. The dye-black mortars followed, completely unimpressive, but working just as all the Materials Research work had predicted they would. The length and breadth of the outreach depot lay in mottled black, awaiting the kiss of the New Sun.

Three hours later they were almost a mile north of the depot. Unnerby had pushed them hard after they left the depot, pushed them to accomplish a final, ancillary goal: survival.

They had almost made it. Almost Gil Haven was delirious and strangely frantic when they finished at the depot. He tried to leave the depot on his own. 'Gotta find a place to dig.' He said the words again and again, struggling against Nizhnimor and Unnerby as they tied him back into the row of safety lines.

'That's where we're going now, Gil. Hang on.' Unnerby released Haven to Amber, and for a moment Hrunkner and Sherk could hear only each other.

'He's got more spirit than before,' said Sherkaner. Haven was bouncing around like a cobber on wooden legs.

'I don't think he can feel the pain anymore.' Hrunk's reply was faint but clear. 'That's not what worries me. I think he's sliding into Wanderdeep.'

Rapture of the Dark. It was the mad panic that took cobbers when the inner core of their minds realized that they were trapped outside. The animal mind took over, driving the victim to find some place, any place, that might serve as a deepness.

'Damn.' The word was muffled, chopped as Unnerby broke contact and tried to get them all moving. They were only hours from probable safety. And yet . . . watching Gil Haven struggle woke primeval reflexes in all of them. Instinct was such a marvelous thing – but if they gave in to it now, it would surely lead them to death.

After two hours, they had barely reached the hills beyond the depot. Twice, Gil had broken free, each time more frantic, to run toward the false promise of the steep defiles alongside their path. Each time, Amber had dragged him back, tried to reason with him. But Gil didn't know where he was anymore, and his thrashing had torn his suit in several places. Parts of him were stiff and frozen.

The end had come when they reached the first of the hard climbs. They had to leave the sled behind; the rest of the way would be with just the air and exotherms they could carry in their panniers. A third time, Gil ripped free of the safety line. He fled with a strange, bounding stagger. Nizhnimor took off after him. Amber was a large woman, and until now she'd had little trouble handling Gil Haven. This time was different. Gil had reached the final desperation of Wanderdeep. As she pulled him back from the edge, he turned on her, stabbing with the points of his hands. Amber staggered back, releasing him. Hrunk and Sherkaner were right behind her, but it was too late. Haven's arms flailed in all directions and he tumbled off the path into the shadows below.

The three of them stood in stupefied paralysis for a moment; then Amber began, to sidle over the edge, her legs feeling down through the airsnow for some purchase on the rocks beneath. Unnerby and Underhill grabbed her, pulled her back.

'No, let me go! Frozen he has a chance. We just have to carry him with us.'

Underhill leaned over the drop-off, took a long look below. Gil had hit naked rocks on his way down. The body lay still. If he wasn't already dead, desiccation and partial freezing would kill him before they could even get the body back to the path.

Hrunkner must have seen it too. 'He's gone, Amber,' he said gently. Then his sergeant's voice returned. 'And we still have a mission.'

After a moment, Amber's free hands curled in assent, but Sherk could not hear that she said a word. She climbed back to the path and helped to refasten their safety lines and audio.

The three of them continued up the climb, moving faster now.

They had only a few quarts of living exotherms by the time they reached their goal. Before the Dark, these hills had been a lush traumtree forest, part of a Tiefer nobleman's estate, a game preserve. Behind them was a cleft in the rocks, the entrance to a natural deepness. In any wilderness with big game, there would have to be animal deepnesses. In settled lands, such were normally taken over and expanded for the use of people – or they fell into disuse. Sherkaner couldn't imagine how Accord Intelligence knew about this one unless some Tiefers on this estate were Accord agents. But this was no prepped safe-hole; it looked as wild and real as anything in Far Brunlargo.

Nizhnimor was the only real hunter on the Team. She and Unnerby cut through three spitsilk barriers and climbed all the way down. Sherkaner hung above them, feeding warmth and light downward. 'I see five pools . . . two adult tarants. Give us a little more light.'

Sherkaner swung lower, putting most of his weight on the spitsilk. The light in his lowest hands shone all the way to the back of the cave. Now he could see two of the pools. They were almost clear of airsnow. The ice was typical of a hibernating pool – clear of all bubbles. Beneath the ice, he had a glimpse of the creature, its frozen eyes gleaming in the light. God, it was big! Even so, it must be a male; it was covered with dozens of baby welts.

'The other pools are all food stash. Fresh kills like you'd expect.' In the first year of the New Sun, such a tarant pair would stay in their deepness, sucking off the fluids of their stash, the babies growing to a size where they could learn to hunt when the fires and storms gentled. Tarants were pure carnivores and not nearly as bright as thracts, but they looked very much like real people. Killing them and stealing their food was necessary, but it seemed more like deepness-murder than hunting.

The work took another hour, and used almost all the remaining exotherms. They climbed back to the surface one last time, to reanchor the spitsilk barrier as best they could. Underhill was numb in several shoulder joints, and he couldn't feel the tips of his left hands. Their suits had been through a lot the last few hours, been punctured and patched. Some of the wrist joints in Amber's suit had burned away, victims of too much contact with airsnow and exotherms. They'd been forced to let the limbs freeze. She would likely lose some hands. Nevertheless, all three of them stood a moment more.

Finally Amber said, 'This counts as triumph, doesn't it?'

Unnerby's voice was strong. 'Yes. And you know damn well that Gil would agree.'

They reached together in a somber clasp, almost a perfect replay of Gokna's Reaching for Accord; there was even a Missing Companion.

Amberdon Nizhnimor retreated through the cleft in the rocks. Green-glowing mist spurted from the spitsilk as she passed through; down below, she would mix the exotherms into pools. The water would be cold slush, but they could burrow in it. If they opened their suits wide, hopefully they could get a uniform freeze. Against this last great peril, there was little more they could do.

'Take a last look, Sherkaner. Your handiwork.' The certainty was gone from Unnerby's voice. Amber Nizhnimor was a soldier; Unnerby had done his duty by her. Now he seemed to be out of combat mode, and so tired that he barely held his belly clear of the airsnow.

Underhill looked out. They were standing a couple of hundred feet above the level of the Tiefer depot. The aurora had faded; the moving points of light, the sky flashes – all were long gone. In that faded light, the depot was a field of splotchy black amid the starlit gray. But the black wasn't shadow. It was the powdered dye they had blasted all across the installation.

'Such a small thing,' said Unnerby, 'a few hundred pounds of dye-black. You really think it'll work?'

'Oh yes. The first hours of the New Sun are something out of hell. That powder black will make their gear hotter than any design tolerance. You know what happens in that kind of a flash.' In fact, Sergeant Unnerby had managed those tests himself. A hundred times the light of a middle-Brightness sun shining on dye-black on metal: In minutes, metal contact points were spot-welded, bearings to sleeves, pistons to cylinders, wheels to rails. The enemy troops would have to retreat underground, their most important outreach depot on the front effectively a loss.

'This is the first and last time your trick will ever work, Sherkaner. A few barriers, a few mines, and we would have been stopped dead.'

'Sure. But other things will change, too. This is the last Dark that Spiderkind will ever sleep through. Next time, it won't be just four cobbers in airsuits. All civilization will stay awake. We're going to colonize the Dark, Hrunkner.'

Unnerby laughed, obviously disbelieving. He waved Underhill toward the cleft in the rock, and the deepness below. Tired as he was, the sergeant would be the last one down, the setter-of-final-barriers.

Sherkaner had one last glimpse of the gray lands, and the curtains of impossible aurora hanging above. *So high, so low, so many things to know.*

9

Ezr Vinh's childhood had generally been a protected and safe one. Only one time had his life been in real jeopardy, and that had been a criminally silly accident.

Even by Qeng Ho standards, the Vinh.23 Family was a very extended one. There were branches of the Family that hadn't touched hands for thousands of years. Vinh.23.4 and Vinh.23.4.1 had been halfway across Human Space for much of that time, making their own fortunes, evolving their own mores. Perhaps it would have been a better thing not to attempt a synch after all that time – except that blessed chance had brought so many of all three branches together at Old Kielle, and all at the same time. So they tarried some years, built temps that most sessile civilizations would call palace-habitats, and tried to figure out what had become of their common background. Vinh.23.4.1 was a consensual demarchy. That didn't affect their trading relations, but Aunt Filipa had been scandalized. 'No one's going to vote *my* property rights away,' little Ezr remembered her saying. Vinh.23.4 seemed much closer to the branches Ezr's parents knew, though their dialect of Nese was almost unintelligible. The 23.4 Family hadn't bothered to track the broadcast standards faithfully. But the standards – even more than the blacklists – were important things. On a picnic, one checked the children's suits, and one's automation double-checked them; but one didn't expect that 'atmosphere-seconds' meant something different for your cousins' air than for your own. Ezr had climbed around a small rock that orbited the picnic asteroid; he was charmed by the way he could make his own little world move under his hands and feet, rather than the other way around. But when his air ran out, his playmates had already found their own worlds in the rock cloud. The picnic monitor ignored his suit's cries for help until the child within was nearly flatlined.

Ezr only remembered waking in a new, specially made nursery. He had been treated like a king for uncounted Ksecs afterward.

So Ezr Vinh had always come out of coldsleep in a happy mood. He suffered the usual disorientation, the usual physical discomfort, but childhood memories assured him that wherever he was things would be good.

At first, this time was no different, except perhaps gentler than usual. He was lying in near zero gee, snug in a warm bed. He had the impression of space, a high ceiling. There was a painting on the wall beyond the bed . . . so meticulously rendered; it might have been a photo. *Trixia loathed those pictures*. The thought popped up, fixed some context on this waking. Trixia. Triland. The mission to the OnOff star. And this was not the first waking there. There had been some very bad times, the Emergent ambush. How had they won over that? The very last memories before this sleep, what were they? *Floating through darkness in a crippled lander. Park's flagship destroyed. Trixia . . .*

'I think that brought him out of it, Podmaster.' A woman's voice.

Almost unwillingly, he turned his head toward the voice. Anne Reynolt sat at his bedside, and next to her was Tomas Nau.

'Ah, Apprentice Vinh. I am pleased to see you back among the living.' Nau's smile was concerned and solemn.

It took Ezr a couple of tries to gargle up something intelligible: 'Wha's . . . What's happening? Where am I?'

'You're aboard my principal residence. It's about eight days since your fleet attempted to destroy mine.'

'Guh?' *We attacked you?*

Nau cocked his head quizzically at Vinh's incoherence. 'I wanted to be here when we woke you. Director Reynolt will fill you in on the details, but I just wanted to assure you of my support. I'm appointing you Fleet Manager of what's left of the Qeng Ho expedition.' He stood, patted Vinh gently on the shoulder. Vinh's gaze followed the Emergent out of the room. *Fleet Manager?*

Reynolt brought Vinh a book of windows with more hard facts than he could easily absorb. They could not all be lies. . . . Fourteen hundred Qeng Ho had died, almost half the fleet's complement Four of the seven Qeng Ho starships had been destroyed. The ramscoops on the rest were disabled. Most of the smaller vehicles had been destroyed or seriously damaged. Nau's people were busy cleaning up the orbital flotsam of the firefights. They quite intended to continue the 'joint operation.' The volatiles and ores that had been lifted from Arachna would support habitats the Emergents were building at the L1 point of the sun/planet system.

And she let him see the crew lists. The *Pham Nuwen* had been lost with all hands. Captain Park and several members of the Trading Committee were dead. Most people on the surviving ships still lived, but the senior ones were being held in coldsleep.

The killing headache of his last few moments on the lander was gone. Ezr had been cured of the 'unfortunate contagion,' Reynolt said. But only an engineered disease could have such a convenient and universal time of onset. The Emergent lies were scarcely more than an excuse for civility. They had planned the ambush from the beginning, and down to the last second.

At least Anne Reynolt did not smile when she spoke the lies. In fact, she rarely smiled at all. Director of Human Resources Reynolt. Funny that not even Trixia had picked up on what that title might imply. At first, Ezr thought Reynolt was fighting a proper sense of shame: she hardly ever looked him directly in the eye. But gradually he realized that looking at his face was no more interesting to her than studying a bulkhead. She didn't see him as a person; she didn't care a jot for the dead.

Ezr read the reports quietly, not sneering, not crying out when he saw that Sum Dotran was gone. *Trixia's name was nowhere on the list of the dead.* Finally he came to the lists of the waking survivors and their present disposition. Almost three hundred were aboard the Qeng Ho temp, also moved to the L1 point. Ezr scanned the names, memorizing: junior people, and virtually no Trilanders or academics. No Trixia Bonsol. He paged further . . . another list. *Trixia!* Her name was there, and she was even listed under 'Linguistics Department.'

Ezr looked up from the book of windows, tried to sound casual. 'What, um, what's the meaning of this glyph beside some of the names?' *Beside Trixia's name.*

' "Focused." '

'And what does that mean?' There was an edge, unwanted, in his voice.

'They're still under medical treatment. Not everyone recovered as easily as you.' Her stare was hard and impassive.

The next day, Nau showed up again.

'Time to introduce you to your new subordinates,' he said. They coasted through a long, straight corridor to a vehicular airlock. This habitat wasn't the banquet place. There was the faintest drift of gravity, as though it were set on a small asteroid. The taxi beyond the airlock was larger than any the Qeng Ho had brought. It was luxurious in a baroque, primitive way. There were low tables and a bar that served in all directions. Wide, natural-looking windows surrounded them. Nau gave him a moment to look out:

The taxi was rising through the strutwork of a grounded habitat. The thing was incomplete but it looked as big as a Qeng Ho legation temp. Now they were above the strutwork. The ground curved away into a jumble of gray leviathans. These were the diamond mountains, all collected together. The blocks were strangely uncratered, but as somberly dull as common asteroids. Here and there the frail sunlight picked out where the surface graphite had been nicked away, and there was a rainbow glitter. Nestled between two of the mountains he saw pale fields of snow, a blocky tumble of freshly cut rock and ice; these must be the fragments of ocean and seamount they'd lifted from Arachna. The taxi rose farther. Around the corner of the mountains, the forms of starships climbed into view. The ships were more than six hundred meters long, but dwarfed by the rockpile. They were moored tightly together, the way salvage is bundled in a junkyard; Ezr counted quickly, estimated what he could not see directly. 'So you've brought everything here – to L1? You really intend a lurking strategy?'

Nau gave a nod. 'I'm afraid so. It's best to be frank about this. Our fighting has put us all near the edge. We have sufficient resources to return home, but empty-handed. Instead, if we can just cooperate . . . well, from here at L1 we can watch the Spiders. If they are indeed entering the Information Age, we can eventually use their resources to refit. In either case, we may get much of what we came for.'

Hm. An extended lurk, waiting for your customers to mature. It was a strategy the Qeng Ho had followed on a few occasions. Sometimes it even worked. 'It will be difficult.' From behind Ezr, a voice said, 'For you perhaps. But Emergents live well, little man. Best you learn that now.' It was a voice that Vinh recognized, the voice that had protested of Qeng Ho ambush even as the killing began. Ritser Brughel. Ezr turned. The big, blond fellow was grinning at him. No subtle nuance here. 'And we also play to win. The Spiders will learn that too.' Not too long ago, Ezr Vinh had spent an evening sitting next to this fellow, listening to him lecture Pham Trinli. The blond was a boor and a bully, but it hadn't mattered then. Vinh's gaze flickered across the carpeted walls to Anne Reynolt. She was watching the conversation intently. Physically, she and Brughel could have been sister and brother. There was even a tinge of red in the guy's blond hair. But there the similarity ended. Obnoxious as he was, Brughel's emotions were clear things, and intense. The only affect that Vinh had seen in Anne Reynolt was impatience. She watched the present conversation as one might watch insects in garden soil.

'But don't worry, Peddler boy. Your quarters are properly inconspicuous.' Brughel pointed out the forward window. There was a greenish speck, barely showing a disk. It was the Qeng Ho temp. 'We have it parked in an eight-day orbit of the main jumble.'

Tomas Nau raised his hand politely, almost as if asking for the floor, and Brughel shut up. 'We have only a moment, Mr Vinh. I know that Anne Reynolt has given you an overview, but I want to make sure you understand your new responsibilities.' He did something with his cuff, and the image of the Qeng Ho temp swelled. Vinh swallowed; funny, it was just an ordinary field temp, barely one hundred meters on a side. His eyes searched the lumpy, quilted hull. He had lived in there less than 2Msec, cursed its squat economies a thousand times. But now, it was the closest thing to home that still existed; inside were many of Ezr's surviving friends. A field temp is so easy to destroy. Yet all the cells looked fully inflated and there was no patchwork. Captain Park had set this one far from his ships, and Nau had spared it. '. . . so your new position is an important one. As my Fleet Manager, you have responsibilities comparable to the late Captain Park's. You will have my consistent support; I will make sure that my people understand this.' A glance at Ritser Brughel. 'But please remember: Our success – even our survival – now depends on our cooperation.'

IO

When it came to personnel management, Ezr knew he was a little slow.
What Nau was up to should have been instantly obvious. Vinh had even
studied such things in school. When they reached the temp, Nau gave an
unctuous little speech, introducing Vinh as the new 'Qeng Ho Fleet
Manager.' Nau made a special point of the fact that Ezr Vinh was the
most senior member of a ship-owning Family present. The two Vinh
starships had survived the recent ambush relatively undamaged. If there
was any legitimate master for the Qeng Ho ships, it was Ezr Vinh. And if
everyone cooperated with legitimate authority, there would yet be wealth
for all. Then Ezr was pushed forward to mumble a few words about how
glad he was to be back among friends, and how he hoped for their help.

In the days that followed, he came to understand the wedge that Nau had
slipped between duty and loyalty. Ezr was home and yet he was not. Every
day, he saw familiar faces. Benny Wen and Jimmy Diem had both survived.
Ezr had known Benny since they were six years old; now he was like a
stranger, a cooperative stranger.

And then one day, more by luck than planning, Ezr ran into Benny near
the temp's taxi locks. Ezr was alone. More and more, his Emergent
assistants did not dog his moves. They trusted him? They had him bugged?
They couldn't imagine him doing harm? All the possibilities were obnoxious, but it was good to be free of them.

Benny was with a small crew of Qeng Ho right under the outermost
balloon wall. Being near the locks, there was no exterior quilting here; every
so often the lights of a passing taxi sent a moving glow across the fabric.
Benny's crew was spread out across the wall, working at the nodes of the
approach automation. Their Emergent gang boss was at the far end of the
open space.

Ezr glided out of the radial tunnel, saw Benny Wen, and bounced easily
across the wall toward him.

Wen looked up from his work and nodded courteously. 'Fleet Manager.'
The formality was familiar now – and still as painful as a kick in the face.

'Hi, Benny. H-how are things going?'

Wen looked briefly down the length of the volume at the Emergent gang
boss. That guy really stuck out, his work clothes gray and stark against the
rampant individualism of most Qeng Ho. He was talking loudly to three of
the work crew, but at this distance his words were muffled by the balloon
fabric. Benny looked back at Ezr and shrugged. 'Oh, just fine. You know
what we're doing here?'

'Replacing the comm inputs.' One of the Emergents' first moves had been to confiscate all head-up displays. The huds and their associated input electronics were the classic tools of freedom.

Wen laughed softly, his eyes still on the gang boss. 'Right the first time, Ezr old pal. You see, our new . . . employers . . . have a problem. They need our ships. They need our equipment. But none of that will work without the automation. And how can they trust that?' All effective machinery had embedded controllers. And of course the controllers were networked, with the invisible glue of their fleet's local net that made everything work consistently.

The software for that system had been developed over millennia, refined by the Qeng Ho over centuries. Destroy it and the fleet would be barely more than scrap metal. But how could any conqueror trust what all those centuries had built in? In most such situations, the losers' gear was simply destroyed. But as Tomas Nau admitted, no one could afford to lose any more resources.

'Their own work gangs are going through every node, you know. Not just here, but on all our surviving ships. Bit by bit they are rehosting them.'

'There's no way they can replace everything.' *I hope.* The worst tyrannies were the ones where a government required its own logic on every embedded node.

'You'd be surprised what they are replacing. I've seen them work. Their computer techs are . . . strange. They've dug up stuff in the system that I never suspected.' Benny shrugged. 'But you're right, they aren't touching the lowest-level embedded stuff. It's mainly the I/O logic that gets jerked. In return, we get brand-new interfaces.' Benny's face twisted in a little smile. He pulled a black plastic oblong from his belt. Some kind of keyboard. 'This is the only thing we'll be using for a while.'

'Lord, that looks ancient.'

'Simple, not ancient. I think these are just backups the Emergents had floating around.' Benny sent another look in the direction of the gang boss. 'The important thing is, the comm gear in these boxes is known to the Emergents. Tamper with it, and there'll be alarms up the local net. In principle they can filter everything we do.' Benny looked down at the box, hefted it. Benny was just another apprentice, like Ezr. He wasn't much sharper about technical things than Ezr, but he always had a nose for clever deals. 'Strange. What I've seen of Emergent technology looks pretty dull. Yet these guys really intend to dredge and monitor everything. There's *something* about their automation that we don't understand.' He was almost talking to himself.

On the wall behind him a light grew and grew, shifted slowly sideways. A taxi was approaching the docking bay. The light slid around the curve of the wall, and a second later there was a muted *kchunk*. Shallow ripples chased out across the fabric from the docking cylinder. The lock pumps kicked in. Here, their whine was louder than at the dock entrance itself. Ezr hesitated.

The noise was enough to mask their conversation from the gang boss. *Sure, and any surveillance bugs could hear through the racket better than our own ears.* So when he spoke, it was not a conspiratorial murmur, but loud against the racket of the pumps. 'Benny, lots has happened. I just want you to know I haven't changed. I'm not—' *I'm not a traitor, damn it!*

For a moment, Benny's expression was opaque . . . and then he suddenly smiled. 'I know, Ezr. I know.'

Benny led him along the wall in the general direction of the rest of his work crew. 'Let me show you the other things that we are up to.' Ezr followed as the other pointed to this and that, described the changes the Emergents were making in the dock protocols. And suddenly he understood a little more of the game. *The enemy needs us, expects to be working us for years. There's lots we can say to each other. They won't kill us for exchanging information to get their jobs done. They won't kill us for speculating about what's going on..*

The whine of the pumps died. Somewhere beyond the plastic of the docking cylinder, people and cargo would be debarking.

Wen swung close to the open hatch of a utility duct. 'They're bringing in lots of their own people, I hear.'

'Yes, four hundred soon, maybe more.' This temp was just some balloons, inflated a few Msecs earlier, upon the fleet's arrival. But it was large enough for all the crews that had been packed as corpsicles for the fifty-light-year transit from Triland. That had been three thousand people. Now it held only three hundred.

Benny raised an eyebrow. 'I thought they had their own temp, and better than this.'

'I—' The gang boss was almost within earshot. *But this isn't conspiracy. Lord of Trade, we have to be able to talk about our jobs.* 'I think they lost more than they're letting on.' *I think we came within centimeters of winning, even though we were ambushed, even though they had knocked us down with their war disease.*

Benny nodded, and Ezr guessed that he already knew. But did he know this: 'That will still leave a lot of space. Tomas Nau is thinking of bringing more of us out of coldsleep, maybe some officers.' Sure, the senior people would be more of a risk to the Emergents, but if Nau really wanted effective cooperation . . . Unfortunately, the Podmaster was much less forthcoming about the 'Focused.' *Trixia.*

'Oh?' Benny's voice was noncommittal, but his gaze was suddenly sharp. He looked away. 'That would make a big difference, especially to some of us . . . like the little lady I have working in this duct.' He stuck his head partway through the hatch and shouted. 'Hey, Qiwi, are you done in there yet?'

The Brat? Ezr had only seen her two or three times since the ambush, enough to know she wasn't injured and not a hostage. But more than most, she had spent time outside of the temp and with the Emergents. Maybe she just seemed too young to be a threat. A moment passed; a tiny figure in a screwball harlequin outfit slipped out of the duct.

'Yeah, yeah, I'm all done. I strung the tamperproof all—' She saw Ezr. 'Hi, Ezr!' For once, the little girl did not swarm on him. She just nodded and kind of smiled. Maybe she was growing up. If so, this was the hard way to do it. 'I strung it all the way past the locks, no problem. You gotta wonder why these guys don't just use encryption, though.' She was smiling, but there were dark shadows around her eyes. It was a face Ezr would expect in someone older. Qiwi stood in the relaxed crouch of zero gee, with one checkered boot slipped under a wall stop. But she held her arms close at her sides, her hands clasping her elbows. The expansive, grabbing and punching little monster of before the ambush was gone. Qiwi's father was one of the still-infected, like Trixia. Like Trixia, he might never come back. And Kira Pen Lisolet was a senior armsman.

The little girl continued talking about the setup inside the duct. She was well qualified. Other children might have toys and games and playmates; Qiwi's home had been a near-empty ramship, out between the stars. That long alone-time had left her on the verge of being several kinds of specialist.

She had several ideas for how they might save time with the cable-pulling the Emergents required. Benny was nodding, taking notes.

Then Qiwi was on a different topic. 'I hear we're gonna have new people in the temp.'

'Yes—'

'Who? Who?'

'Emergents. Then some of our own people, I think.'

Her smile blazed for an instant, and then she forced her enthusiasm down with a visible effort. 'I-I was over at Hammerfest. Podmaster Nau wanted me to check out the cold-sleep gear before they move it to *Far Treasure*. I . . . I saw Mama, Ezr. I could see her face through the transp. I could see her slow-breathe.'

Benny said, 'Don't worry, kid. We'll . . . Things will be okay for both your mom and pop.'

'I know: That's what Podmaster Nau told me, too.'

He could see the hope in her eyes. So Nau was making vague promises to her, becoming poor Qiwi's lifeline. And some of the promises might even be true. Maybe they would finally cure her father of their damn war disease. But armsmen like Kira Pen Lisolet would be terribly dangerous to any tyrant. Short of a counterambush, Kira Lisolet might sleep for a long, long time . . . *Short of a counterambush*. His glance flickered across to Benny. His friend's stare was completely blank, a return to the earlier opacity. And suddenly Ezr knew that there really was a conspiracy. In a few Msecs at most, some among the Qeng Ho would act.

I can help; I know I can. The official coordination of all Emergent orders passed through Ezr Vinh. If he were on the inside . . . But he was also the most closely watched of all, even if Tomas Nau had no real respect for him. For a moment, fury rose in Ezr. Benny knew he wasn't a traitor – but there was no way he could help without giving the conspiracy away.

The Qeng Ho temp had escaped the ambush without a scratch. There had not even been pulse damage; before they maimed the local net, the Emergents had a great time mining the databases there.

What was left worked well enough for routine ops. Every few days, a few more people were added to the temp's population. Most were Emergents, but some were low-rank Qeng Ho released from coldsleep detention. Emergents and Qeng Ho, they all looked like refugees from disaster. There was no disguising the damage the Emergents had suffered, the equipment they had lost *And maybe Trixia is dead.* The 'Focused' were kept in the Emergents' new habitat, Hammerfest. But no one had seen any of them.

Meantime, conditions in the Qeng Ho temp slowly got worse. They were at less than one-third the temp's design population, yet systems were failing. Part of it was the maimed automation. Part of it – and this was a subtle effect – was that people weren't doing their jobs properly. Between the damaged automation and the Emergents' clumsiness with life-systems, the other side hadn't caught on. Fortunately for the conspirators, Qiwi spent most of her time off the temp. Ezr knew she could have detected the scam instantly. Ezr's contribution to the conspiracy was silence, simply not noticing what was going on. He moved from petty emergency to petty emergency, doing the obvious – and wondering what his friends were really up to.

The temp was actually beginning to stink. Ezr and his Emergent as-sistants took a trip down to the bactry pools at the innermost core of the temp, the place where Apprentice Vinh had spent so many Ksecs . . . before. He would give anything to be an apprentice forever down here, if only it would bring back Captain Park and the others.

The stench in the bactry was worse than Ezr had known outside of a failed school exercise. The walls behind the bio-weirs were covered with soft black goo. It swayed like old flesh in the breeze of the ventilators. Ciret and Marli retched, one barfing inside his respirator. Marli gasped out, 'Pus! I'm not putting up with this. We'll be just outside when you're done.'

They splashed and spattered their way out, and the door sealed. And Ezr was alone with the smells. He stood for a moment, suddenly realizing that if he ever wanted to be completely alone, this was the place!

As he started to survey the contamination, a figure in goo-spattered waterproofs and a respirator drifted out from the filth. It raised one hand for silence, and passed a signals unit across Vinh's body. 'Mmph. You're clean,' came a muffled voice. 'Or maybe they just trust you.'

It was Jimmy Diem. Ezr almost hugged him, bactry shit and all. Against all odds, the conspiracy had found a way to talk to him. But there was no happy relief in Diem's voice. His eyes were invisible behind goggles, but tension coiled in his posture. 'Why are you toadying, Vinh?'

'I'm *not*! I'm just playing for time.'

'That's what . . . some of us think. But Nau has laid so many perks on you, and you're the guy we have to clear every little thing with. Do you really think you own what's left of us?'

That was the line that Nau pushed even now. '*No!* Maybe they think they've bought me, but . . . Lord of Trade, sir, wasn't I a solid crewmember?'

A muffled chuckle, and some of the tension seemed to leave Diem's shoulders. 'Yeah. You were a daydreamer who could never quite keep his eye on the ball' – words from familiar critiques, but spoken almost fondly – 'but you're not stupid and you never traded on your Family connections . . . Okay, Apprentice, welcome aboard.'

It was the most joyful promotion Ezr Vinh had ever received. He stifled a hundred questions that percolated up; most had answers that he shouldn't be told. But still, just one, about Trixia—

Diem was already talking. 'I've got some code schemes for you to memorize, but we may have to meet face-to-face again. So the stink will get better, but it's going to continue to be a problem; you'll have plenty of excuse to visit. A couple of general things for now: We need to get outdoors.'

Vinh thought of the *Far Treasure* and the Qeng Ho armsmen in coldsleep there. Or maybe there were weapons caches in secret places aboard the surviving Qeng Ho ships. 'Hm. There are several outside repair projects where we're the experts.'

'I know. The main thing is to get the right people on the crews, and in the right job slots. We'll get you some names.'

'Right.'

'Another thing: We need to know about the "Focused ones." Where exactly are they being held? Can they be moved fast?'

'I'm trying to learn about them,' *more than you may know, Crewleader.* 'Reynolt says they're alive, that they've stopped the progression of the disease.' *The mindrot.* That chilling term was not from Reynolt, but the slip of tongue he'd heard from an ordinary Emergent. 'I'm trying to get permission to see—'

'Yeah. Trixia Bonsol, right?' Goo-sticky fingers patted Vinh's arm sympathetically. 'Hmm. You've got a solid motive to keep after them on this. Be a good boy in every other way, but push *hard* on this. You know, like it's the big favor that will keep you in line, if only they'll grant it . . . Okay. Get yourself out of here.'

Diem faded into the shrouds of odiferous glop. Vinh smeared out the fingerprint traces on his sleeve. As he turned back to the hatch, he was scarcely conscious of the smell anymore. He was working with his friends again. And they had a chance.

Just as the remains of the Qeng Ho expedition had its mock 'Fleet Manager,' Ezr Vinh, so Tomas Nau also appointed a 'Fleet Management Committee' to advise and aid in its operation. It was typical of Nau's strategy, coopting innocent people into apparent treason. Their once-per-Msec meetings would have been torture for Vinh, except for one thing: Jimmy Diem was one of the committee members.

Ezr watched the ten troop into his conference room. Nau had furnished the room with polished wood and high-quality windows; everyone in the temp knew about the cushy treatment given the Fleet Manager and his committee. Except for Qiwi, all ten realized how they were being used. Most of them realized that it would be years, if ever, before Tomas Nau released all the surviving Qeng Ho from coldsleep detention. Some, like Jimmy, guessed that in fact the senior officers might occasionally be brought out, secretly, for interrogations and brief service. It was an unending villainy that would give the Emergents the permanent upper hand.

So, there were no traitors here. They were a discouraging sight nevertheless: five apprentices, three junior officers, a fourteen-year-old, and one doddering incompetent. Okay, to be honest, Pham Trinli didn't dodder, not physically; for an old man, he was in pretty good shape. Most likely, he'd always been a goofball. It was a testament to his record that he was not being held in coldsleep. Trinli was the only Qeng Ho military man left awake.

And all this rather makes me the Clown of Clowns. Fleet Manager Vinh called the meeting to order. You'd think that being fraudulent toadies would at least make these meetings quick. But no, they often dragged on for many Ksecs, dribbling off into pickle-headed assignments for individual members. *I hope you enjoy eavesdropping on this, Nau scum.*

The first order of business was the putrefaction in the bactry. That was under control. The widespread stench should be flushed by their next meeting time. There remained some out-of-control gene lines in the bactry itself (*good!*) but they posed no danger to the temp. Vinh avoided looking at Jimmy Diem as he listened to the report. He'd met Diem in the bactry three times now. The conversations had been brief and one-sided. The things Vinh was most curious to know were just what he absolutely must not know: How many Qeng Ho were in on Diem's operation? Who? Was there any concrete plan to smash the Emergents, to rescue the hostages?

The second item was more contentious. The Emergents wanted their own time units used in all fleet work. 'I don't understand,' Vinh said to the unhappy looks. 'The Emergent second is the same as ours – and for local operations, the rest is just calendar frippery. Our software deals with Customer calendars all the time.' Certainly, there was little problem in casual conversation. The Balacrean day wasn't far off the 100Ksec shift 'day' the Qeng Ho used. And their year was close enough to 30Msec that most of the year-stem words caused no confusion.

'Sure, we can handle weird calendars, but that's in front-end applications.' Arlo Dinh had been an apprentice programmer; now he was in charge of software mods. 'Our new, um, employers are using Qeng Ho internal tools. "There will be side effects."' Arlo intoned the mantra ominously.

'Okay, okay. I'll take—' Ezr paused, experiencing a burst of administrative insight. 'Arlo, why don't *you* take this up with Reynolt? Explain the problems to her.'

Ezr looked down at his agenda, avoiding Arlo's annoyed gaze. 'Next item. We're getting more new tenants. The Pod-master says to expect at least another three hundred Emergents, and after that another fifty Qeng Ho. It looks like life-support can tolerate this. What about our other systems? Gonle?'

When their ranks had been real, Gonle Fong had been a junior quartermaster on the *Invisible Hand*. Fong's mind still hadn't caught up with the changes. She was of indeterminate age, and if not for the ambush she might have lived out her life a junior quartermaster. Maybe she was one of those people whose career paths had stopped at just the right place, where their abilities precisely matched what was asked of them. But now . . .

Fong nodded at his question. 'Yeah, I have some numbers to show you.' She plinked away at the Emergent keyboard in front of her, made some mistakes, tried to correct. On the window across the room, various error messages reported on her flailings. 'How do you turn those off?' Fong muttered, swearing to herself. She made another typo and her rage became very public. 'Goddamn it to hell, I can't stand these fucking things!' She grabbed the keyboard and smashed it down onto the polished wood table. The wood veneer cracked, but the keyboard was unharmed. She smashed it again; the error display across the room shimmered in iridescent protest and vanished. Fong half rose from her seat and waved the oddly bent keyboard in Ezr's face. 'Those Emergent fuckers have taken away all the I/O that works. I can't use voice, I can't use head-up displays. All we have are windows and these mother-damned things!' She threw the keyboard at the table. It bounced up, spinning into the ceiling.

There was a chorus of agreement, though not quite so manic. 'You can't do everything through a keyboard. We need huds . . . We're crippled even when the underlying systems are okay.'

Ezr held up his hands, waiting for the mutiny to die down. 'You all know the reason for this. The Emergents simply don't trust our systems; they feel they need to control the periphery.'

'Sure! They want spies on every interaction. I wouldn't trust captured automation either. But this is impossible! I'll use their I/O, but make 'em give us head-up displays and eye-pointers and—'

'I'll tell you, there are some people who are just going on using their old gear,' said Gonle Fong.

'*Stop!*' This was the part of being a toady that hurt the most. Ezr did his best to glare at Fong. 'Understand what you are saying, Miss Fong. Yes. This is a major inconvenience, but Podmaster Nau regards disobedience on this point as treason. It's something the Emergents see as a direct threat.' *So keep your old I/O gear but understand the risk.* He didn't say that out loud.

Fong was hunched down over the table. She looked up at him and nodded grimly.

'Look,' Ezr continued, 'I've asked Nau and Reynolt for other devices. We may get a few. But remember, we're stuck light-years from the nearest industrial civilization. Any new gadgets have to be made with just what the Emergents have here at L1.' Ezr doubted that very much would be forthcoming. 'It is deadly important for you to make the I/O ban clear to your people. For their own safety.'

He looked from face to face. Almost everyone glared back at him. But Vinh saw their secret sense of relief. When they went back to their friends, the committee members would have Ezr Vinh to point at as the spineless fellow who was ramrodding the Emergent demands – and their own unpopular position would be a little easier.

Ezr sat silent a moment more, feeling impotent. *Please let this be what Crewleader Diem wants of me.* But Jimmy's eyes were as blank and hard as the others. Outside of the bactry, he played his role well. Finally, Ezr leaned forward and said quietly to Fong, 'You were going to tell me about the newcomers. What are the problems?'

Fong grunted, remembering what they'd been discussing before she blew up. But surprisingly, she said, 'Ah, forget the numbers. The short answer is, we can handle more people. Hell, if we could control our automation properly we could house three thousand in this balloon. As for the people themselves?' She shrugged, but without any great anger. 'They're typical Chumps. The sort I've seen in a lot of tyrannies. They call themselves "managers," but they're peons. The fact is, behind some bluster they're kind of nervous about *us*.' A sneaky smile spread across her heavy features. 'We got people who know how to handle Customers like these. Some of us are making friends. There's lots they're not supposed to talk about – like how bad this "mindrot" crap really is. But I'll tell you, if their big bosses don't come clean soon, we'll find out for ourselves.'

Ezr didn't smile back. *Are you listening, Podmaster Nau? Whatever your desires, soon we will know the truth.* And what they discovered, Jimmy Diem could use. Coming in to this meeting, Ezr had been totally wrapped up in one item, the last on the agenda. Now he was beginning to see that everything fit together. And maybe he wasn't doing such a bad job after all.

That last agenda item was the upcoming explosion of the sun. And Jimmy had a fool – surely an unknowing fool – to front for them on this: Pham Trinli. The armsman made a big show of moving to the front of the table. 'Yes, yes,' he said. 'I've got the pictures here. Just a second.' A dozen engineering graphics appeared on the windows around the room. Trinli launched himself to the podium, and lectured them on Lagrange stability points. Funny, the man actually had a voice and style that bespoke command, but the ideas that came out were tendentious commonplaces.

Vinh let him ramble for a hundred seconds. Then, 'I believe your agenda item is "Preparations for Relight," Mr. Trinli. What is it the Emergents are asking us to do?'

The old man fixed Ezr with a stare as intimidating as any crewleader's: 'That's *Armsman* Trinli, if you please, Fleet Manager.' The stare continued a second longer. 'Very well, to the heart of the matter. Here we have some five billion tonnes of diamond.' A red pointer lit on the window behind him, pointing at the slowly turning pile of rocks, all the loose material that Captain Park had found in this solar system. The ice and ore that had been lifted from Arachna were smaller mountains wedged in the corners and creases of the asteroidal blocks. 'The rocks are in a classic contact jumble. At the present time, our fleets are moored to this jumble or in orbit around it. Now, as I was trying to explain a few seconds ago, the Emergents want us to emplace and manage a system of electric jets on the core blocks of the jumble.'

Diem: 'Before the Relight?'

'Indeed.'

'They want to maintain contact stability during the Relight?'

'That's exactly right.'

Uneasy looks passed around the table. Stationkeeping was a common and ancient practice. If done properly, an orbit about L1 cost very little fuel. They would be less than a million and a half kilometers from Arachna, and almost directly between the planet and its sun. In the coming bright years, they would be effectively hidden in its glare. But the Emergents didn't think small; they already had built various structures, including their 'Hammerfest,' down on the rockpile. So now they wanted the stationkeeping jets in place before Relight. OnOff would shine at fifty to one hundred sols before it settled down. The Chumps wanted to use the stationkeeping jets to keep the big rocks from shifting around during that time. It was dangerous foolishness, but the Emergents were boss. *And this will give Jimmy access to the out-of-doors.*

'Actually, I don't think there will be serious problems.' Qiwi Lisolet rose from her seat. She coasted over to Pham Trinli's maps, preempting whatever more Trinli had to say. 'I did a number of exercises like this while we were in transit. My mother wants me to be an engineer and she thought stationkeeping might be an important part of this mission.' Qiwi sounded more adultly serious than usual. This was also the first time he'd seen her dressed in Lisolet-greens. She floated in front of the windows for a moment, reading the details. Her ladylike dignity faltered. 'Lord, they are asking a lot! That rockpile is so loose. Even if we get the math right, there's no way we can know all the stresses inside the pile. And if the volatiles get into sunlight, there'll be a whole new problem.' She whistled, and her smile was one of childlike relish. 'We may have to move the jets during the Relight. I—'

Pham Trinli glowered at the girl. No doubt she had just trashed a thousand seconds of his presentation. 'Yes, it will be quite a job. We have only a hundred electric jets for the whole thing. We'll need crews down on the jumble the whole time.'

'No, no, that's not true. About the jets; I mean. We have lots more ejets over on the *Brisgo Gap*. This job isn't more than a hundred times bigger than ones I practiced—' Qiwi was wholly caught up in her enthusiasm, and for once it wasn't Ezr Vinh who was on the other side of her arguing.

Not everyone accepted the situation quietly. The junior officers, including Diem, demanded that the rockpile be dispersed during the Relight, the volatiles piled on the shadow-side of the biggest diamond. Nau be damned, this was just too risky. Trinli bristled, shouted back that he had already made these points to the Emergents.

Ezr slapped the table, then again, louder. 'Order please. This is the job we've been assigned. The best way we can help our people is by behaving responsibly with what we've got. I think we can get added help from the Emergents on this, but we have to approach them properly.'

The argument rolled on around him. *How many of them are in on the conspiracy*, he wondered. Surely not Qiwi? After some seconds of further argument, they were left where they began: with no choice but to truckle. Jimmy Diem shifted back, and sighed. 'All right, we do as we're told. But at least we know they need us. Let's put the squeeze on Nau, get him to release some senior specialists.'

There was mumbled agreement. Vinh's gaze-locked with Jimmy's, and then he looked away. Maybe they could get some hostages released for this; more likely not. But suddenly Ezr knew when the conspiracy would strike.

II

The OnOff star might better have been called 'old faithful.' Its catastrophic variability had first been noticed by the Dawn Age astronomers of Old Earth. In less than eight hundred seconds, a star catalogued as 'singleton brown dwarf [peculiar]' had gone from magnitude 26 to magnitude 4. Over a span of thirty-five years the object had faded back to virtual invisibility – and generated dozens of graduate research degrees in the process. Since then the star had been watched carefully, and the mystery had become grander. The initial spike varied by as much as thirty percent, but as a whole the light curve was incredibly regular. On, off, on, off . . . a cycle some 250 years long, with onset predictable to within one second.

In the millennia since the Dawn, human civilizations had spread steadily outward from Earth's solar system. The observations of OnOff became ever more accurate, and from smaller and smaller distances.

And finally, humans stood within the OnOff system, and watched the seconds tick down toward a new Relighting.

Tomas Nau gave a little speech, ending with: 'It will be an interesting show.' They were using the temp's largest meeting room to watch the Relight. Just now it was crowded, sagging in the microgravity at the rockpile's surface. Over in Hammerfest, Emergent specialists were over-seeing the operation. There were also skeleton crews aboard the starships. But Ezr knew that most of the Qeng Ho and all of the off-duty Emergents were here. The two sides were almost sociable, almost friendly. It was forty days since the ambush. Rumors were that Emergent security would ease up significantly after the Relight.

Ezr had latched on to a spot near the ceiling. Without huds, the only view was through the room's wallpaper. Hanging from here, he could see the three most interesting windows – at least when other people weren't coasting across his line of sight. One was a full-disk view of the OnOff star. Another window looked out from one of the microsats in low orbit around the OnOff star. Even from five hundred kilometers, the star's surface did not look threatening. The view might have been from an aircraft flying over a glowing cloud deck. If it weren't for the surface gravity, humans could almost have landed on it. The 'clouds' slid slowly past the microsat's view, glimmers of glowing red showing up between them. It was the sullen red of a brown dwarf, a black-body redness. There was no sign of the cataclysm that was due to arrive in another . . . six hundred seconds.

Nau and his senior flight technician came up to join Ezr. Brughel was nowhere to be seen. You could always tell when Nau wanted mellow feelings – just check for the absence of Ritser Brughel. The Podmaster grabbed a spot next to Vinh. He was smiling like some Customer politician. 'Well, Fleet Manager, are you still nervous about this operation?'

Vinh nodded. 'You know my committee's recommendation. For this Relight, we should have moved the volatiles behind a single rock and taken it further out. We should be in the outer system for this.' The ships of both fleets and all the habitats were moored to one side of the largest diamond rock. They would be shielded from the Relight, but if things started shifting . . .

Nau's technician shook his head. 'We've got too much on the ground here. Besides, we're running on empty; we'd have to use a lot of our volatiles to go flying around the system.' The tech, Jau Xin, looked almost as young as Ezr. Xin was pleasant enough, but did not have quite the edge of competence that Ezr was used to in senior Qeng Ho. 'I've been very impressed by your engineers.' Xin nodded at the other windows. 'They're much better than we would be at handling the rockpile. It's hard to see how they could be this sharp without zip . . .' His voice trailed off. There were still secrets; that might change sooner than the Emergents expected.

Nau smoothly filled the pause in Xin's speech. 'Your people are good, Ezr. Really, I think that's why they complained about this plan so much; they aim for perfection.' He looked out the window on the OnOff star. 'Think of all the history that comes together here.'

Around and below them, the crowd was clustered into groups of Emergents and Qeng Ho, but discussion was going on in all directions. The window on the far wall looked out onto the exposed surface of the rockpile. Jimmy Diem's work crew was spreading a silvery canopy over the tops of icy boulders. Nau frowned.

'That's to cover the water ice and airsnow, sir,' said Vinh. 'The tops are in line of sight of OnOff. The curtains should cut down on boil-off.'

'Ah.' Nau nodded.

There were more than a dozen figures out there on the surface. Some were tethered, others maneuvered free. Surface gravity was virtually nonexistent. They sailed the ties over the tops of the icy mountains with the ease of a lifetime of outside operations – and millennia of Qeng Ho experience beyond that. He watched the figures, trying to guess who was who. But they wore thermal jackets over their coveralls, and all Vinh could see were identical forms dancing above the dark landscape. Ezr didn't know the details of what the conspiracy planned, but Jimmy had set him certain errands and Ezr had his guesses. They might never have an opportunity this good again: They had access to the ejets aboard the *Brisgo Gap*. They had almost unlimited access to the outside, in places free of Emergent observers. In the seconds following the Relighting, some chaos was to be expected – and with Qeng Ho in charge of the stationkeeping operation, they could fine-tune that chaos to support the conspiracy. *But all I can do is stand here with Tomas Nau . . . and be a good actor.*

Ezr smiled at the Podmaster.

Qiwi Lisolet flounced out of the airlock in a rage. 'Damn! Damn and fuck damn and—' She swore up and down as she ripped off her thermal jacket and pants. Somewhere in the back of her mind she made a note to spend more time with Gonle Fong. Surely there must be more offensive things she could say when things got this messed up. She threw the thermals into a locker and dived down the axis tunnel without taking off her coveralls and hood.

Lord of Trade, how could they do this to her? She'd been kicked indoors to stand around with her finger up her nose, while the work *she* should be doing was taken over by Jimmy Diem!

Pham Trinli floated thirty meters above the insulation canopy they were tying across the iceberg. Trinli was official head of stationkeeping operations, though he made sure that any orders he gave were blustery generalities. It was Jimmy Diem who made most things happen. And surprisingly, it was little Qiwi Lisolet who had the best ideas about where to place the electric thrusters and how to run the stationkeeping programs. If they had followed all her recommendations, the Relight might go without a hitch.

And that would not be a good thing at all.

Pham Trinli was a member of the 'great conspiracy.' A very minor member, and not to be trusted with any critical part of the plan. All that was fine with Pham Trinli. He tipped around so that now his back was to the moonlike glow of the OnOff star, and the rockpile hung almost over his head. In the deep shadows of the rockpile, there was a further jumble: the lashed-down ships and temps and volatiles refineries, hiding against the light that would soon storm out of the sky. One of the habitats, Hammerfest, was a rooted design; it would have had a certain bizarre grace if not for all the gear around it. The Trader temp just looked like a big balloon tied to the surface. Inside it were all the waking Qeng Ho and a big hunk of the Emergent population.

Beyond the habitats, partly hidden by the shoulder of Diamond One, were the moored ramscoops. A grim sight indeed. Starships should not be tied together like that and never so close to a jumble of loose rocks. A memory floated up: piles of dead whales rotting in a sexual embrace. This was no way to run a shipyard. But then this was more a junkyard than anything else. The Emergents had paid dearly for their ambush. After Sammy's flagship was destroyed, Pham had drifted for most of a day in a wrecked taxi – but plugged into all the remaining battle automation. Presumably Podmaster Nau never figured out who was coordinating the battle. If he had, Pham would have ended up dead, or in frozen sleep with the other surviving armsmen on the *Far Treasure*.

Even ambushed, the Qeng Ho had come close to victory. *We would have won if the damn Emergent mindrot hadn't wiped us all.* It was enough to teach a body caution. An expensive victory had been turned into something close to mutual suicide: There were perhaps two starships that were still capable of ramscoop flight; a couple more might be repaired by scavenging the other wrecks. From the looks of the volatiles distillery, it would be a long time before they had enough hydrogen to boost even one vehicle up to ram speed.

Less than five hundred seconds till Relight. Pham drifted slowly upward toward the rocks, until the junkyard was blocked from view by the insulation canopy. Across the surface of the rockpile, his people – Diem and Do and Patil, now that they had sent Qiwi indoors – were supposedly doing final checks on the ejet arrays. Jimmy Diem's voice came calmly over the work-crew channel, but Pham knew that was a recording. Behind the canopy, Diem and others had disappeared around the far side of the rockpile. All three were armed now; it was amazing what you could do with an electric jet, especially a Qeng Ho model.

And so Pham Trinli was left behind. No doubt, Jimmy was just as happy to be rid of him. He was trusted, but only for simple parts of the plan, such as maintaining the appearance of a functioning work crew. Trinli moved in and out of view of Hammerfest and the temp, responding to the cues in Jimmy Diem's soundtrack.

Three hundred seconds to Relight. Trinli drifted under the canopy. From here you could see jagged ice and carefully settled airsnow. The shadowed pile dwindled off beyond the canopy, finally met the bare surface of the diamond mountain.

Diamond. Where Pham Trinli had been a child, diamonds were an ultimate form of wealth. A single gram of gem-grade diamond could finance the murder of a prince. To the average Qeng Ho, diamond was simply another allotrope of carbon, cheaply made in tonne lots. But even the Qeng Ho had been a little intimidated by these boulders. Asteroids like this didn't exist outside of theory. And although these rocks weren't single gems, there was a vast, crystalline order to them. The cores of gas giants, planets blown away in some long-ago detonation? They were just another mystery of the OnOff system.

Since work began on the rockpile, Trinli had studied the terrain, but not for the same reasons as Qiwi Lisolet, or even Jimmy Diem. There was a cleft where the ice and airsnow filled the space between Diamond One and Diamond Two. That was significant to Qiwi and Jimmy, but only in connection with rockpile maintenance. For Pham Trinli . . . with a little digging, that cleft was a path from their main work site to Hammerfest, a path that was out of sight of ships and habitats. He hadn't mentioned it to Diem; the conspirators' plan was for Hammerfest to be taken after they grabbed the *Far Treasure*.

Trinli crawled along the V-shaped cleft, closer and closer to the Emergent habitat. It would have surprised Diem and the others to know it, but Pham Trinli was not a born spacer. And sometimes when he climbed around like this, he got the vertigo that afflicted Chump groundlings. If he let his imagination go . . . he wasn't crawling hand-by-hand along a narrow ditch, but instead he was rock-climbing up a mountain chimney, a chimney that bent farther and farther back on him, till he must surely fall.

Trinli paused a second, holding his place with one hand while his whole body quivered with the need for crampons and ropes, and pitons driven solid into the walls around him. *Lord.* It had been a long time since his groundsider orientation had come back this strongly. He moved forward. Forward. Not up.

By his count of arm paces, he was just outside Hammerfest now, near its communications array. Odds were very high some camera could image him if he popped out. Of course, the odds were fairly good that no one and no program would be monitoring such a view in time to change things. Nevertheless, Trinli stayed hunkered down. If necessary, he would move closer, but for now he just wanted to snoop. He lay back in the cleft, his feet against the ice and his back against the diamond wall. He reeled out his little antenna probe. The Emergents had played smiling tyrant since the ambush. The one thing they made ugly threats about was possession of non-approved I/O devices. Pham knew that Diem and the core of the conspiracy had Qeng Ho huds, and had used black crypto across the local net. Most of the planning had been done right under the Emergents' noses. Some communication avoided automation altogether; many of these youngsters knew a variation on the old dots-and-dashes game, blinkertalk.

As a peripheral member of the conspiracy, Pham Trinli knew its secrets only because he was filthy with forbidden electronics. This little antenna reel would have been a sign of sneaky intent even in peaceful times.

The thread he spun out was transparent to almost anything that might shine on it here. At the tip, a tiny sensor sniffed at the electromagnetic spectrum. His main goal was a comm array on the Emergent habitat that had a line of sight on the Qeng Ho temp. Trinli moved his arms like a fisherman repositioning his cast. The slender thread had a stiffness that was very effective in a micrograv environment. *There.* The sensor hung in the beam between Hammerfest and the temp. Pham eased a directional element over the edge of the cleft, aimed it at an unused port on the Qeng Ho temp. From there he was hooked directly into the fleet's local net, and around all the Emergent security. This was exactly what Nau and the others were so afraid of and the reason for their death-penalty threats. Jimmy Diem wisely had not taken chances like this. Pham Trinli had some advantages. He knew the old, *old* tricks that were hidden in Qeng Ho gear . . . Even so, he would not have risked it if Jimmy and his conspirators hadn't bet so much on their takeover scheme.

Maybe he should have talked to Jimmy Diem straight out. There were too many critical things they didn't know about the Emergents. What made some of their automation so good? In the firelights at the ambush, they'd been clearly inferior in high-level tactics, but their target queuing had been better than any system Pham Trinli had ever fought.

Trinli had the ugly feeling that comes when you've been maneuvered into a corner. The conspirators figured that this might be both their best and last chance to knock over the Emergents. Maybe. But the whole thing was just too pat, too perfect.

So make the best of it.

Pham looked at the display windows inside his hood. He was intercepting Emergent telemetry and some of the video they were transmitting to the temp. Some of that he could decrypt. The Emergent bastards just trusted their line-of-sight link a little bit too much. It was time to do some real snooping.

'Fifty seconds to Relight.' The voice had been counting off in a flat monotone for the last two hundred seconds. In the auditorium, almost everyone was watching the windows in silence.

'Forty seconds to Relight.'

Ezr took a quick look around the room. The flight tech, Xin, was looking from display to display. He was visibly nervous. Tomas Nau was watching the view that came from low above OnOff's surface. His intentness seemed to hold more curiosity than fear or suspicion.

Qiwi Lisolet glared at the window that showed the insulation canopy and Jimmy Diem's work crew. Her look had been dark and scowly ever since she flew into the auditorium. Ezr could guess what had happened . . . and he was relieved. Jimmy had used an innocent fourteen-year-old as camouflage for the plot. But Jimmy had never been an absolute hardass. He had taken a chance to get the girl out of harm's way. *But I bet Qiwi won't forgive him, even when she knows the truth.*

'Wave front to arrive in ten seconds.'

Still no change in the view from the microsat. Only a mild red glow peeked between the sliding clouds. Either 'old faithful' had played a cosmic joke on them, or this was an absolute knife-edge of an effect.

'Relight.'

In the full-disk view, a point of brilliance burned in the exact center of the disk, spread outward, and in less than two seconds filled the disk. The low-altitude view had vanished sometime during that spread. The light got brighter and brighter and *brighter*. A soft, awed sigh spread around the room. The light cast shadows on the opposite wall before the wallpaper damped its output.

'Five seconds after Relight.' The voice must be automatic. 'We're up to seven kilowatts per square meter.' This was a different tech, speaking in a flat Trilander accent. *Not an Emergent?* The question flickered past Ezr's attention, swamped for the moment by the rest of the action.

'Ten seconds after Relight.' At the side of the room was a smaller window, a view of the Spider world. It had been dark and dim as ever, but now the light was coming back from it and the planetary disk glowed with its own brightness as ice and air woke to a sun that was already five times as bright as Sol standard. And still brightening:

'Twenty kilowatts per square meter.' A strip graph was playing out below the image of the new sun, comparing its output with the historical record. This Relight looked as powerful as any before.

'Neutron flux is still below detectable limits.'

Nau and Vinh exchanged relieved looks, for once sincere on both sides. *That* was the sort of danger that couldn't be detected from interstellar distances, and one of the olden-times fly-throughs had failed at about this point. At least they wouldn't fry in radiation that no one had seen from afar.

'Thirty seconds after Relight.'

'Fifty kilowatts per square meter.'

Outside, the mountainside that shielded them from the sun was beginning to *glow*.

Pham Trinli had the public audio channel playing. Even without it Relight would have been obvious. But for the moment he held those events in a small part of his mind and concentrated on what was going over the private links out of Hammerfest. It was at moments like this, when technicians were overwhelmed by externalities, that security was most likely to slip. If Diem was on schedule, he and his crew were now at the mooring point of the *Far Treasure*.

Trinli's eyes flickered across the half-dozen displays that now filled most of his hood's view space. His fleet net programs were doing a good job with the telemetry. *Ha.* You can't beat old trapdoors. Now that they needed lots of computing power, the Emergents were using more and more Qeng Ho automation, and Trinli's snooping was correspondingly more effective.

The signal strength faded. Alignment drift? Trinli cleared several display windows and looked at the world around him. The OnOff star was hidden behind the mountains, but its light glared off the hills that stuck up into its view. Where ice or airsnow was exposed, vapor steamed out. For the moment Jimmy's silver canopy was holding, but the fabric slowly swayed and flapped. There was an almost bluish color to the sky now, the mists of thousands of tonnes of water and air boiling up, turning the rockpile into a comet.

And screwing up his line of sight on Hammerfest. Trinli wiggled his antenna. Losing the link couldn't have been the mists alone. Something had shifted. *There.* He was picking up Hammerfest's traffic again. After a second his crypto re-synchronized and he was back in business. But now he kept an eye on the storm around him. The new sun was even more of a show than they had expected.

Trinli's network feelers were inside Hammerfest now. Every program had its exceptional circumstances, the situations that the designers assumed were outside the scope of their responsibility. There were loopholes that the present extremities had shaken open . . .

Strange. There seemed to be dozens of users logged into system internals. And there were big sections of the Emergent system that he didn't recognize, that weren't built on the common foundations. But the Emergents were supposed to be ordinary Chumps, recently returned to high technology with the help of the Qeng Ho broadcast net. There was just too much strange stuff here. He dipped into the voice traffic. The Emergent Nese was understandable but clipped and full of jargon. '. . . Diem . . . around front of rocks . . . according to plan.'

According to plan?

Trinli scanned related data streams, saw graphics that showed just what weapons Jimmy's crew would carry, that showed the entrance he intended to use to sneak aboard the *Far Treasure*. There were tables of names . . . of the conspirators. Pham Trinli was listed as a minor accomplice. More tables. *Jimmy Diem's black crypto*. The first version was only partially accurate; later files converged on precisely what Jimmy and the others were using. Somehow, they had been watching closely enough to see through all the tricks. There had been no traitors, just an inhuman attention to detail.

Pham jerked down his equipment and crawled a little farther. He popped up, pointing his directional at a slanted overhang of Hammerfest's roof. From here the angle should be right. He could bounce a beam down at *Far Treasure's* moorage point.

'Jimmy, Jimmy! Can you hear me?' It was Qeng Ho encrypted, but if any enemy heard, both ends of the link would be nailed.

All Jimmy Diem had ever wanted was to be a crewleader good enough to make management track. Then he and Tsufe could get married, all perfectly timed for when the voyage to the OnOff star began to pay off. Of course, that had been before the Emergents arrived and before the ambush. Now? Now he was leading a conspiracy, betting everything on a few moments of hellish risk. Well, at least they were finally acting . . .

In less than forty seconds, they had run four thousand meters, all the way around the sunside of the jumble. That would have been a good piece of free space rappelling even if the sun had not been blowing up, even if they hadn't been wrapped in silver foil. They'd almost lost Pham Patil. A fast rappel depended on knowing exactly where to put your next ground spike, exactly how much force the piton could take when you accelerated out from the surface along your cable. But their surveys of the pile had all been done for placing the stationkeeping jets. There just hadn't been an excuse to test the rappel points. Patil had been swinging out at nearly half a gee when his ground spike slipped free. He'd have floated out forever if Tsufe and Jimmy hadn't been securely tied down. A few seconds more and the direct sunlight would have fried them right through their makeshift shields.

But it worked! They were on the opposite side of the star-ships from where the bastards would expect visitors. While everyone's eyes had been on the sun, and blinded by that, they had gotten in position.

They hunkered down just short of the *Treasure's* mooring point. The ship towered six hundred meters above them, so close that all they could see was part of the throat and the forward primer tanks. But from all their careful spying, they knew this was the least damaged of all the Qeng Ho ships. And inside was equipment – and more important, *people* – who could take back freedom.

All was in shadow, but now the coma of gases had spread high. Reflected fight softened the dark. Jimmy and the others shed their silver covers and thermal outerwear. It felt suddenly chill wearing just full-pressure coveralls and hood. They slipped from hiding place to hiding place, dragging their tools and improvised guns, and trying to keep it all out of the light from the glowing sky. *It can't get any brighter, can it?* But his time display said that less than one hundred seconds had passed since Relight. They were perhaps another hundred seconds short of maximum brightness.

The three floated up the moorage pilings, the maw of *Treasure's* throat growing huge above them. One nice thing about sneaking aboard something as massive as a ramscoop, there wasn't much worry that their movement would bob the vehicle around. There would be a maintenance crew aboard the *Treasure*. But would they expect armed visitors in the middle of all this? They had thought and thought on those risks, and there was no way to make them better. But if they took the ship, they would have one of the best remaining pieces of equipment, real weapons, and the surviving Qeng Ho armsmen. They would have a chance of ending the nightmare.

Now there was sunlight coming through the raw face of the diamond rock! Jimmy paused for an instant to stare, bug-eyed. Even this high up, there were at least three hundred meters of solid diamond between them and the naked light of OnOff. Yet that was not enough. Scattered off a million fracture planes, bounced and diminished and diffused and diffracted, some of OnOff's light made it through. The light was a glitter of rainbows, a thousand tiny sun-disks glowing from everywhere across the face of the rock. And every second it grew brighter, until he could see structure within the mountain, could see fracture and cleavage planes that extended hundreds of meters into diamond. And still the light got brighter.

So much for slipping by in the dark. Jimmy shut down his imagination and dashed upward. From the ground, the rim hatch was a tiny pucker at the edge of the ramscoop's maw, but as he ascended it became larger and larger, and centered over his head. He waved Do and Patil to either side of the hatch. The Emergents had reprogrammed the hatch, of course, but they hadn't replaced the physical mechanism as they had aboard the temp. Tsufe had snooped the passcode with binoculars, and their own gloves would be accepted as matching keys. How many guards would they face? *We can take them. I know we can.* He reached up to tap on the hatch control, and—

Someone pinged him.

'Jimmy, Jimmy! Can you hear me?' The voice was tiny in his ear. A telltale claimed it was the decryption of a laser burst from the roof of the Emergent hab. But the voice was Pham Trinli's.

Jimmy froze. Worst case: the enemy was toying with him. Best case:

Pham Trinli had guessed they were going after the *Far Treasure* and now was screwing up worse than anyone could have imagined. *Ignore the fool, and if you live, beat the crap out of him.* Jimmy glanced at the sky above Hammerfest. The coma was pale violet, slowly roiling in the light of OnOff. In space, a laser link is very hard to detect. But this was no longer ordinary space. It was more like a cometary surface at close passage. If the Emergents knew where to look they could probably *see* Trinli's link.

Jimmy's reply was a millisecond compression flung back in the direction of the other's beam. 'Turn that off, you old shit. Now!'

'Soon. First: They know about the plan. They saw through your black crypto.' It was Trinli, and yet different. And Trinli had never been told about the crypto. 'This is a setup, Jimmy. But they don't know everything. Back off. Whatever they've got planned inside the *Treasure* will only make things worse.'

Lord. For a moment, Jimmy just froze. Thoughts of failure and death had haunted his every sleep since the ambush. To get this far, they had taken a thousand deadly risks. He had accepted that they might be discovered. But never had he thought it would happen like this. What the old fool had found might be important; it might be worthless. And backing down now would be nearly a worst-case outcome. *It's just too late.*

Jimmy forced his mouth to open, his lips to speak. 'I said, close down the link!' He turned back to the *Treasure*'s hull and tapped the Emergent passcode on the hatch. A second passed – and then the clamshells parted. Do and Patil dove upward into the dimness of the airlock. Diem paused just a second, slapped a small gadget onto the hull beside the door, and followed them up.

12

Pham Trinli shut down the link. He flipped and climbed rapidly back along the cleft. *So we were suckered.* Tomas Nau was too clever by half, and he had some strange kind of edge. Trinli had seen a hundred ops, some smaller than this, some that lasted for centuries. But he had never seen the sort of precise fanatical attention to detail that he had seen in those snoop logs the Emergents kept on the black crypto. Nau had either magic software or teams of monomaniacs. In the back of his mind, the planner in him was wondering what it could be and how Pham Trinli might someday take advantage of it.

For now, survival was the only issue. If Diem would only back off from the *Treasure*, the trap Nau planned might not close or might not be so deadly.

The sheer diamond face on his left was sparkling now, the largest gemstone of all time shining sunlight all round him. Ahead, the light was almost as brilliant, a dazzling nimbus where icy peaks stood in OnOff's light. The silver sun-shield was billowing high, tied down in only three places.

Abruptly, Pham's hands and knees were kicked out from under him. He spun out from the path, caught himself by one hand. And through that hand he could hear the mountains groan. Mist spewed out from the cleft all along its length – and the diamond mountain moved. It was less than a centimeter per second, stately, but it moved. Pham could see light all along the opening. He had seen the crew's rock maps. Diamonds One and Two abutted each other along a common plane. The Emergent engineers had used the valley above as a convenient placement anchor for part of the ice and snow from Arachna. All very sensible . . . and not well enough modeled. Some of the volatiles had slipped between the two mountains. The light reflecting back and forth between One and Two had found that ice and air. Now the boil-off was pushing Diamonds One and Two apart. What had been hundreds of meters of shielding was now a jagged break, a million mirrors. The light shining through was a rainbow from hell.

'One hundred forty-five kilowatts per square meter.'

'That's the top of the spike,' someone said. OnOff was shining more than a hundred times as bright as standard solar. It was following the track of its previous lightings, though this was brighter than most. OnOff would stay this bright for another ten thousand seconds, then drop back steeply to just over two solars, where it would stay for some years.

There was no triumphant shouting. The last few hundred seconds, the crowd in the temp had been almost silent. At first, Qiwi had been totally involved with her own anger at being kicked indoors. But she had quieted as one and then another of the silver canopy's ties had broken, and the ice had been touched by direct sunlight. 'I told Jimmy that wouldn't hold.' But she didn't sound angry anymore. The light show was beautiful, but the damage was far more than they had planned. Outgassing streamers were visible on all sides – and there was no way their pitiful electric jets could counter that. It would be Msecs before they got the rockpile gentled down again.

Then, at four hundred seconds into the Relight, the canopy tore free. It lifted slowly, twisting in the violet sky. There was no sign of the crewfolk who should have been sheltering under it. Worried murmuring grew. Nau did something with his cuff, and his voice was suddenly loud enough to be heard across the room. 'Don't worry. They had several hundred seconds to see the canopy was going, plenty of time to move down into the shadow.'

Qiwi nodded, but she said quietly to Ezr. 'If they didn't fall off. I don't know why they were up there in the first place.' If they had fallen off, drifted out into the sunlight . . . Even with thermal jackets, they'd just cook.

He felt a small hand slip into his. *Does the Brat even know she did that?* But after a second he squeezed her hand gently. Qiwi was staring out at the main work site. 'I should be out there.' It was the same thing Qiwi had been saying since she came indoors, but now her tone was quite different.

Then the outside views jittered, as if something had hit all the cameras at once. The light leaking through the naked face of Diamond Two brightened into a jagged line. And now there was *sound*, a moan that grew louder and louder, its pitch scaling first up and then down.

'Podmaster!' The voice was loud and insistent, not the robotlike reporting of the Emergent techs. It was Ritser Brughel. 'Diamond Two is shifting, lifting off—' And now it was obvious. The whole mountain was tilting. Billions of tonnes, loose.

And the moaning sound that still filled the auditorium must be the moorage webbing, twisting beneath the temp.

'We're not in its way, sir.' Ezr could see that now. The immensity was moving slowly, slowly, but its slide was away from the temp and Hammerfest and the moored star-ships. The view outside had slowly rotated, now was turning back. Everyone in the auditorium was scrambling for tie-downs.

Hammerfest was built into Diamond One. The big rock looked unchanged, unmoved. The starships beyond . . . They were minnows beside the bulk of the Diamonds, but each ship was over six hundred meters long, a million tonnes unfueled. And the ships were swaying slowly at the end of their mooring points on Diamond One. It was a dance of leviathans, and a dance that would totally wreck them if it continued.

'Podmaster!' Brughel again. 'I'm getting audio from the crewleader, Diem.'

'Well put him on!'

It was dark above the airlock. The lights did not come on, and there was no atmosphere. Diem and the others floated up the tunnel from the lock, their hood lights flickering this way and that. They looked out from the tunnels into empty rooms, into rooms with partitions blasted away, gutted fifty meters deep. This was supposed to be the *undamaged* ship. A coldness grew inside Diem. The enemy had come in after the battle and sucked it dry, left a dead hulk.

Behind him, Tsufe said, 'Jimmy, the *Treasure* is moving.'

'Yeah, I've got a solid contact with the wall here. Sounds like it's twisting on its mooring point.'

Diem reached out from the ladderline and pressed his hood against the wall. Yes. If there had been atmosphere, the place would be full of the sounds of ringing destruction. So the Relight was causing more shifting than anyone had guessed. A day ago that knowledge would have terrorized. Now . . . 'I don't think it matters, Tsufe. Come on.' He led Do and Patil still faster up the ladderline. So Pham Trinli had been right, and the plan was doomed. But one way or another, he was going to discover what had been done to them. And just maybe he could get the truth out to the others.

The interior locks had been ripped out and vacuum extended to every room. They floated up past what should have been repair bays and workshops, past deep holes that should have held the ram's startup injectors.

High abaft, in the shielded heart of the *Far Treasure* that was where the sickbay had been, that was where there should be coldsleep tanks. Now . . . Jimmy and the others moved sideways through the shielding. When their hands touched the walls, they could hear the creaking of the hull, feel its slow motion. So far, the close-tethered starships had not collided – though Jimmy wasn't sure if they could really know that. The ships were so large, so massive, if they collided at a few centimeters per second the hulls would just slide into each other with scarcely a jolt.

They had reached the entrance to the sickbay. Where the Emergents claimed to hold the surviving armsmen.

More emptiness? Another lie?

Jimmy slipped through the door. Their head lamps flickered around the room.

Tsufe Do cried out.

Not empty. Bodies. He swept his light about, and everywhere . . . the coldsleep boxes had been removed, but the room was . . . filled with corpses. Diem pulled the lamp from his head and stuck it to an open patch of wall. Their shadows still danced and twisted, but now he could see it all.

'Th-they're all dead, aren't they?' Pham Patil's voice was dreamy, the question simply an expression of horror.

Diem moved among the dead. They were neatly stacked. Hundreds, but in a small volume. He recognized some armsmen. Qiwi's mom. Only a few showed violent decompression damage. *When did the rest die?* Some of the faces were peaceful, but others – He stopped, frozen by a pair of glittering dead eyes that stared out at him. The face was emaciated; there were frozen bruises across the forehead. This one had lived some time after the ambush. And Jimmy recognized the face.

Tsufe came across the room, her shadow skittering across the horror. 'That's one of the Trilanders, isn't it?'

'Yeah. One of the geologists, I think.' One of the academics supposedly being held on Hammerfest. Diem moved back toward the light he had set on the wall. How many were here? The bodies stretched off into the dimness beyond where once there had been walls. *Did they kill everyone?* Nausea clawed its way up his throat.

Patil had floated motionless since that first inane question. But Tsufe was shaking, her voice going from dullness to a giddy wavering. 'We thought they had so many hostages. And all the time they had nothing but deaders.'

She laughed, high-pitched. 'But it didn't matter, did it? We believed, and that served them as well as the truth.'

'Maybe not.' And suddenly the nausea was gone. The trap had been sprung. No doubt, he and Tsufe and Patil would die very soon. But if they lived even seconds, perhaps the monsters could be unmasked. He pulled an audio box from his coveralls, found a clean piece of wall to make contact. *Another banned I/O device. Death is the penalty for possession. Yeah. Yeah.* But now he could talk the length of the *Treasure*, to the broadcaster he had left at the rim airlock. The nearside of the temp would be bathed in his message. Embedded utilities would detect it. Surely some would respond to its priority, would squirt the message to where Qeng Ho would hear it

And Jimmy began talking. 'Qeng Ho! Listen! I'm aboard the *Far Treasure*. It's gutted. They've killed everyone we thought was here . . .'

Ezr – everyone in the temp's auditorium – waited a silent second as Ritser Brughel set up the connection. Then Jimmy began talking:

'Qeng Ho! Listen! I'm—'

'Crewleader!' Tomas Nau interrupted. 'Are you all right? We can't see you outside.'

Jimmy laughed. 'That's because I'm aboard the *Far Treasure*.'

The look on Nau's face was puzzled. 'I don't understand. The *Treasure*'s crew hasn't reported—'

'Of course they haven't.' Ezr could almost hear the smile behind Jimmy's words. 'You see, *Far Treasure* is a Qeng Ho vessel and now we've taken it back!'

Shock and joy spread across the faces Ezr could see. So that was the plan! A working starship, perhaps with its original weapons. The main Emergent sickbay, the armsmen and senior crew who survived the ambush. *We have a chance now!*

Tomas Nau seemed to realize the same. His puzzled expression changed to an angry, frightened scowl. 'Brughel?' He said to the air.

'Podmaster, I think he's telling the truth. He's on the *Treasure*'s maintenance channel, and I can't raise anyone else there.'

The power graph in the main window hovered just under 145kW/m^2. The light reflected between One and Two was beginning to boil snow and ice in the shadows. Thousand- and hundred-thousand-tonne boulders of ore and ice were shifting in the clefts between the great diamonds. The motion was almost imperceptible, a few centimeters per second. But some of the boulders were now floating free. However slow-moving, they could destroy whatever human work they collided with.

Nau stared out the window for a couple of seconds. When he spoke his voice seemed more intense than commanding: 'Look, Diem. It can't work. The Relight is causing a lot more damage than anyone could have known—'

A harsh laugh came from the other end of the connection. 'Anyone? Not really. We retuned the stationkeeping network to shake things up a bit. Whatever instabilities there were, we gave them an extra nudge.'

Qiwi's hand tightened on Ezr's. The girl's eyes were wide with surprise. And Ezr felt a little sick. The stationkeeping grid couldn't have done much one way or another, but why make things *worse*?

Around them, people with full-press coveralls and hoods were zipping up; others were diving out the doors of the auditorium. A huge ore boulder floated just a hundred meters off. It was rising slowly, its top dazzling in direct sunlight. It would just miss the top of the temp.

'But, but—' For a moment the glib Podmaster seemed speechless. 'Your own people could die! And we've taken the weapons off the *Treasure*. It's our hospital ship, for God's sake!'

There was no answer for a moment, just the sound of mumbled argument. Ezr noticed that the Emergent flight technician, Xin, hadn't said a word. He watched his Podmaster with a wide-eyed, stricken look.

Then Jimmy was back on the link: '*Damn* you. So you gutted the weapons systems. But it doesn't matter, little man. We've prepared four kilos of S7. You never guessed we had access to explosives, did you? Lots of things were in with those electric jets that you never guessed.'

'No, no.' Nau was shaking his head almost aimlessly.

'As you say, Podmaster, this is your hospital ship. There are your own people here besides our armsmen in coldsleep. Even without the ship's guns, I'd say we have some negotiating leverage.'

Nau glanced beseechingly at Ezr and Qiwi. 'A truce. Until we've settled the rockpile.'

'No!' shouted Jimmy. 'You'll wriggle out soon as events don't have you by the throat.'

'Damn it, man, it's your own people aboard the *Treasure*.'

'If they were out of coldsleep, they'd agree with me, Podmaster. It's showdown time. We've got twenty-three of *your* people in the sickbay plus the five in your maintenance crew. We know how to play the hostage game, too. I want you and Brughel over here. You can use your taxis, all nice and safe. You have one thousand seconds.'

Nau had always seemed a very calculating type to Ezr Vinh. And already, he seemed recovered from his shock. Nau raised his chin dramatically and glared at the sound of Jimmy's voice. 'And if we don't?'

'We lose, but so do you. To start with, your people here die. Then we'll use the S7 to blow the *Treasure* free of its moorings. We'll ram it into your damn Hammerfest.'

Qiwi had listened with pale, wide-eyed shock. Now suddenly she was bawling. She launched herself toward the sound of Jimmy's voice. 'No! No! Jimmy! Please don't!'

For a few seconds every eye was on Qiwi. Even the frantic closing of hoods and gloves ceased, and there was only the loud moaning of the temp's mooring web as it twisted slowly about. Qiwi's mother was aboard the *Far Treasure;* her father was on Hammerfest with all the mindrot victims. In coldsleep or 'Focus,' most of the survivors of the Qeng Ho expedition were in one place or the other. Trixia. *This is too much, Jimmy. Slow down!* But the words died in Ezr's throat. He had trusted everything to Jimmy. If this deadly talk convinced Ezr Vinh, maybe it would convince Tomas Nau.

When Jimmy spoke again, he ignored Qiwi's cry, 'You have only nine hundred seventy-five seconds, Podmaster. I advise you and Brughel to get your butts over here.'

That would have been hard to do even if Nau had bolted out of the temp. He turned to Xin and the two argued in low voices.

'Yes, I can get you there. It's dangerous, but the loose stuff is moving at less than a meter per second. We can avoid it.'

Nau nodded. 'Then let's go. I want—' He fastened his full-press jacket and hood, and his voice became inaudible.

The crowd of Qeng Ho and Emergents melted away from the two as they headed toward the exit.

From the speaker link, there was a loud thump, cut off abruptly. In the auditorium someone shouted, pointing at the main window. Something flickered from the side of the *Far Treasure,* something small and moving fast. A fragment of hull.

Nau had stopped at the auditorium doors. He looked back at the *Far Treasure.* 'System status says the *Far Treasure* has been breached,' said Brughel. 'Multiple explosions in aft radial deck fifteen.'

That was coldsleep storage and sickbay. Ezr couldn't move, couldn't look away. The hull of the *Treasure* puckered out in two more places. Pale light flickered briefly from the holes. It was insignificant compared to the storm of the Relight. To an untrained eye, the *Treasure* might have looked un-damaged. The hull holes were only a couple of meters across. But S7 was the Qeng Ho's most powerful chemical explosive, and it looked as if all four kilograms had gone up. Radial deck fifteen was behind four bulkheads, twenty meters below the outer hull. Extending inward, the blast had most likely crushed the *Far Treasure's* ramscoop throat. One more starship had died.

Qiwi floated motionless in the middle of the room, beyond the reach of comforting hands.

13

Ksecs passed, busier than any time in Ezr's life. The horror of Jimmy's failure hung in the back of his mind. There wasn't room for it to leak out.

They were all too busy simply trying to save what they could from the human and natural catastrophes.

The next day, Tomas Nau addressed the survivors on the temp and at Hammerfest. The Tomas Nau that looked out of the window at them was visibly tired and lacked his usual smoothness.

'Ladies and gentlemen, congratulations. We've survived the second harshest Relight in the recorded history of OnOff. We did this despite the most terrible treachery.' He moved closer to the pov, as if looking at the exhausted Emergents and Qeng Ho huddled in the auditorium. 'Damage survey and reclamation attempts will be our most important jobs over the next Msecs . . . but I must be frank with you. The initial battle between the Qeng Ho and Emergent fleets was immensely destructive of the Qeng Ho; I regret to say that was nearly as bad for the Emergent side. We tried to disguise some of that damage. We had plenty of equipment spares, medical facilities, and the raw materials we brought up from Arachna. We would have had the expertise of hundreds of senior Qeng Ho available once the security issues were resolved. Nevertheless, we were operating near the edge of safety. After the events of yesterday, all safety margins have vanished. At this moment we do not have a single functioning ramscoop – and it's not clear if we will be able to scavenge one from the wreckage.'

Only two of the starships had collided. But apparently the *Far Treasure* had been the most functional – and after Jimmy's action, its drive and most of its life-support system were junk.

'Many of you have risked your lives over the last Ksecs trying to save some of the volatiles. That part of the disaster appears to be no one's fault. None of us had counted on the violence of this Relighting, or the effect that ice trapped between the diamonds might have. As you know, we've recaptured most of the large blocks. Only three remain loose.' Benny Wen and Jau Xin were working together to try to bring back those and several smaller ones. They were only thirty kilometers away, but the big ones massed one hundred thousand tonnes each – and all they had for hauling equipment were taxis and one crippled lifter.

'OnOff's flux is down to two point five kilowatts per square meter. Our vehicles can operate in that light. Properly suited crew can work briefly in it. But the airsnow that drifted out is lost and we fear that much of the water ice is gone too.'

Nau spread his hands, and sighed. 'This is like so many of the histories you Qeng Ho have told us of. We fought and fought, and in the end we've nearly made ourselves extinct. With what we have, we can't go home – to either of our homes. We can only guess how long we can survive on what we salvage here. Five years? One hundred years? The old truths still hold: without a sustaining civilization, no isolated collection of ships and humans can rebuild the core of technology.'

A wan smile came briefly to his face. 'And yet there is hope. In a way, these disasters have forced us to concentrate all our attention on what our missions were initially dedicated to. It is no longer a matter of academic curiosity, or even Qeng Ho selling to Customers – now our very survival depends on the sophonts of Arachna. They are on the verge of the Information Age. From everything we can tell, they will attain a competent industrial ecology during the current bright time. If we can last a few more decades, the Spiders will have the industry that we need. Our two missions will have succeeded, even if at far greater human cost than any of us ever imagined.

'Can we last three to five more decades? Maybe. We can scavenge, we can conserve . . . The real question is, can we cooperate? So far, our history here is not good. Whether in offense or defense, all our hands are drenched in blood. You all know about Jimmy Diem. There were at least three involved in his conspiracy. There may be more – but a security pogrom would just diminish our overall chances for survival. So I appeal to all of you among the Qeng Ho who may have been part of this plot, even peripherally: Remember what Jimmy Diem and Tsufe Do and Pham Patil did and tried to do. They were willing to destroy all the ships and crush Hammerfest. Instead, their own explosives destroyed them, destroyed the Qeng Ho that we were holding in coldsleep, and destroyed a sickbay full of Emergents and Qeng Ho.

'So. This will be our Exile. An Exile we have brought upon ourselves. I will continue to do my best to lead, but without your help we will surely fail. We must bury what differences and hatred there may be. We Emergents know much about you Qeng Ho; we have listened to your public network for hundreds of years. Your information made a critical difference to us as we regained technology.' That tired smile again. 'I know you did it to make more good Customers; we are grateful nevertheless. But what we Emergents have become is not what you expect. I believe we bring something new and wonderful and powerful to the human universe: Focus. It is something that will be strange to you at first. I beg you to give time a chance here. Learn our ways, as we have yours.

'With everyone's willing support, we can survive. In the end, we can prosper.'

Nau's face vanished from the display, leaving a view out on the rear-ranged surface of the rockpile. Around the room, Qeng Ho looked at one another, talked quietly. Traders had enormous pride, especially when they compared themselves with Customers. To them, even the grandest Customer civilizations, even Namqem and Canberra, were like brilliant flowers, doomed by their beauty and fixed position to fade and wither. This was the first time that Ezr had seen shame on the faces of so many Qeng Ho. *I worked with Jimmy. I helped him.* Even the ones who didn't must have gloried in Jimmy's first words from the *Far Treasure.*

How could something go so wrong?

Ciret and Marli came for him. 'Some questions related to the investigation.' The Emergent guards took him inward and up, but not to the taxi dock. Nau was in Vinh's own 'Fleet Manager's' office. The Podmaster sat with Ritser Brughel and Anne Reynolt.

'Have a seat . . . Fleet Manager,' Nau said quietly, waving at Ezr's place at the middle of the table.

Vinh approached it slowly, sat down. It was hard to look Tomas Nau in the eye. The others . . . Anne Reynolt seemed as impatient and irritable as ever. There was no trouble avoiding her gaze, since she never looked directly into his eyes anyway. Ritser Brughel seemed as tired as the Pod-master, but he had an odd smile that flickered on and off. The man was staring hard at him; Vinh suddenly realized that Brughel was brimming with unspoken triumph. All the deaths – on both sides – were nothing to this sadist.

'Fleet Manager.' Nau's quiet voice brought Vinh's head around. 'About J. Y. Diem's conspiracy—'

'I knew, Podmaster.' The words were somewhere between defiance and confession. 'I—'

Nau held up a hand. 'I know. But you were a minor participant. We've identified several others. The old man, Pham Trinli. He provided them with protective coloration – and almost died for his trouble.'

Brughel chuckled. 'Yeah, he got half poached. Bet he's whimpering even yet.'

Nau turned to look at Brughel. He didn't say anything, just stared. After a second, Ritser nodded and his demeanor became a sullen imitation of Nau's.

The Podmaster turned back to Vinh. 'None of us can afford rage or triumph in this. Now we need everyone, even Pham Trinli.' He looked at Vinh meaningfully, and Ezr fully met his gaze.

'Yes, sir. I understand.'

'We'll debrief you later about the plot, Fleet Manager. We do want to identify all those who need special watching. For now, there are much more important things than raking over the past.'

'Even after this, you want me to be Fleet Manager?' He had hated that job so much. Now he hated it even more, for entirely different reasons.

But the Podmaster nodded. 'You were the proper person before, and you still are. Furthermore, we need continuity. If you visibly and wholeheartedly accept my leadership, the community as a whole has a better chance.'

'Yes, sir.' Sometimes it was possible to atone for guilt. That was more than Jimmy and Tsufe and Pham Patil could ever do.

'Good. As I understand it, our physical situation has stabilized. There are no ongoing emergencies. What about Xin and Wen? Are they going to be able to rescue those ice blocks they're chasing? Getting them more fuel is a priority.'

'We have the distillery online, sir. We'll begin feeding it in a few Ksecs.' And could refuel the taxis. 'I'm hoping we'll have the last ice blocks grounded and in the shade within forty Ksec.'

Nau glanced at Anne Reynolt.

'The estimate is reasonable, Podmaster. All other problems are under control.'

'Then we have time for the important, human issues. Mr Vinh, we'll be putting out several announcements later today. I want you to understand them. Both you and Qiwi Lin Lisolet will be thanked for your help in tracking down what is left of the conspiracy.'

'But—'

'Yes, I know that there's an element of fabrication there, But Qiwi was never in on the conspiracy, and she has given us solid help.' Nau paused. 'The poor girl was ripped apart by this. There's a lot of rage in her. For her sake, and for the sake of the whole community, I want you to play along with the story. I need it emphasized that there are plenty of Qeng Ho who are not irrational, who have pledged to work with me.'

He paused. 'And now the most important thing. You heard my speech, the part about learning Emergent ways?'

'About . . . Focus?' About what they had really done to Trixia.

Behind Nau, the sadistic smirk flickered once again across Ritser Brughel's face.

'That's the main thing,' said Nau. 'Perhaps we should have been open about it, but the training period wasn't complete. Focus can make the difference between life and death in the present circumstances. Ezr, I want Anne to take you over to Hammerfest and explain it all to you. You'll be the first. I want you to understand, to make your peace with it. When you have, I want you to explain Focus to your people, and do it so they can accept it, so what is left of our missions can survive.'

And so the secret Vinh had pushed to know, the secret that had driven every dream for Msecs, was now to be revealed to him. Ezr followed Reynolt up the central corridor to the taxi lock. Every meter was a battle for him. Focus. The infection they could not cure. The mindrot. There had been rumors, nightmares, and now he would know.

Reynolt waved him into the taxi. 'Sit over there, Vinh.' In a paradoxical way, he preferred dealing with Anne Reynolt. She didn't disguise her contempt, and she had none of the sadistic triumph that oozed from Ritser Brughel.

The taxi sealed up and pushed off. The Qeng Ho temp was still tied down to the rockpile. The sunlight was still too bright to allow it to be released. The purple sky had faded back to black, but there were a half-dozen comet tails streaking the stars – sundry blocks of ice that now floated some kilometers away. Wen and Xin were out there somewhere.

Hammerfest was less than five hundred meters from the temp, an easy free jump if Reynolt had wished it. Instead they floated across the space in shirtsleeve comfort. If you hadn't seen it all before the Relight you might not guess the disaster that had happened. The monster rocks had long since stopped moving. Loose ice and snow had been redistributed across the shadow, larger chunks and smaller and smaller and smaller, a fractal pile. Only now there was less ice, and much less airsnow. Now the shadowed side of the jumble was lit as by a bright moon – the light reflected from Arachna. The taxi passed fifty meters above crews working to reemplace the electric jets. Last time he had checked, Qiwi Lisolet was down there, more or less running the operation.

Reynolt had strapped down across from him. 'The successfully Focused are all on Hammerfest. You can talk to almost anyone you please.'

Hammerfest looked like an elegant personal estate. It was the luxurious heart of the Emergent operation. That had been some comfort to Ezr. He'd told himself that Trixia and the others would be treated decently there. They might be held like the hostages of Qeng Ho history, like the One Hundred at Far Pyorya. But no sensible Trader would ever build a habitat rooted in a rubble pile. The taxi coasted over towers of eerie beauty, a fey castle spiring up from the crystal plane. In a short time, he would know what the castle hid . . . Reynolt's phrasing finally took hold of his attention. 'Successfully Focused?'

Reynolt shrugged. 'Focus is mindrot on a leash. We lost thirty percent in the initial conversions; we may lose more in the coming years. We had moved the sickest ones over to the *Far Treasure*.'

'But what—'

'Be quiet and let me tell you.' Her attention flicked to something beyond Vinh's shoulder, and she was quiet for several seconds. 'You remember becoming sick at the time of the ambush. You've guessed that was a disease of our design; its incubation time was an important part of our planning. What you don't know is that the microbe's military use is of secondary importance.' The mindrot was viral. Its original, natural, form had killed millions in the Emergents' home solar system, had crashed their civilization . . . and set the stage for the present era of expansion. For the original strains of the bug had a novel property: They were a treasure house of neurotoxins.

'In the centuries since the Plague Time, the Emergency has gentled the mindrot and turned it to the service of civilization. Its present form needs special help to break through the blood-brain barrier, and spreads throughout the brain in a nearly harmless way, infecting about ninety percent of the glial cells. And now we can control the release of neuroactives.'

The taxi slowed and turned precisely to match Hammerfest's lock. Arachna slid across the sky, a full 'moon' nearly a half-degree across. The planet gleamed white and featureless, cloud decks hiding its furious rebirth.

Ezr scarcely noticed. His imagination was trapped in the vision that lurked behind Anne Reynolt's dry jargon: the Emergents' pet virus, penetrating the brain, breeding by the tens of billions, dripping poison into a still-living brain. He remembered the killing pressure in his head as their lander had climbed up from Arachna. That had been the disease banging on the portals of his mind. Ezr Vinh and all the others on the Qeng Ho temp had fought off that assault – or maybe their brains were still infected, and the disease was quiescent. But Trixia Bonsol and the people with the 'Focus' glyph by their names had been given special treatment. Instead of a cure, Reynolt's people had grown the disease in the victims' brains like mold in the flesh of a fruit. If there had been even the slightest gravity in the taxi, Ezr would have vomited. 'But *why*?'

Reynolt ignored him. She opened the lock hatch and led him into Hammerfest. When she spoke again, there was something close to enthusiasm in her flat tones. 'Focusing ennobles. It is the key to Emergent success, and a much more subtle thing than you imagine. It's not just that we've created a pyschoactive microbe. This is one whose growth within the brain can be controlled with millimeter precision – and once in place, the ensemble can be guided in its actions with the same precision.'

Vinh's response was so blank that it penetrated even Reynolt's attention. 'Don't you see? We can improve the attention-focusing aspects of consciousness: we can take humans and turn them into analytical engines.' She spelled it out in wretched detail. On the Emergent worlds, the Focusing process was spread over the last years of a specialist's schooling, intensifying the graduate-school experience to produce genius. For Trixia and the others, the process had been necessarily more abrupt. For many days, Reynolt and her technicians had tweaked the virus, triggering genetic expression that precisely released the chemicals of thought – all guided by Emergent medical computers that gathered feedback from conventional brain diagnostics . . .

'And now the training is complete. The survivors are ready to pursue their researches as they never could have before.'

Reynolt led him through rooms with plush furniture and carpeted walls. They followed corridors that became narrower and narrower until they were in tunnels barely one meter across. It was a capillary architecture he had seen in histories . . . pictures from the heart of an urban tyranny. And finally they stood before a simple door. Like the others behind them, it bore a number and speciality. This one said: F042 EXPLORATORY LINGUISTICS.

Reynolt paused. 'One last thing. Podmaster Nau believes you may be upset by what you see here. I know outlanders behave in extreme ways when they first encounter Focus.' She cocked her head as though debating Ezr Vinh's rationality. 'So. The Podmaster has asked me to emphasize: Focus is normally reversible, at least to a great extent.' She shrugged, as though delivering a rote speech.

'Open the door.' Ezr's voice cracked on the words.

The roomlet was tiny, lit dimly by the glow from a dozen active windows. The light formed a halo around the head of the person within: short hair, slender form in simple fatigues.

'Trixia?' he said softly. He reached across the room to touch her shoulder. She didn't turn her head. Vinh swallowed his terror and pulled himself around to look into her face. 'Trixia?'

For an instant she seemed to look directly into his eyes. Then she twisted away from his touch and tried to peer around him, at the windows. 'You're blocking my view. I can't see!' Her tone was nervous, edging into panic.

Ezr ducked his head, turned to see what was so important in the windows. The walls around Trixia were filled with structure and generation diagrams. One whole section appeared to be vocabulary options. There were Nese words in n-to-one match with fragments of unpronounceable nonsense. It was a typical language-analysis environment, though with more active windows than a reasonable person would use. Trixia's gaze flickered from point to point, her fingers tapping choices. Occasionally she would mutter a command. Her face was filled with a look of total concentration. It was not an alien look, and not by itself horrifying; he had seen it before, when she was totally fascinated by some language problem.

Once he moved out of her way, he was gone from her mind. She was more . . . focused . . . than he had ever seen her before.

And Ezr Vinh began to understand.

He watched her for some seconds, watched the patterns expand in the windows, watched choices made, structures change. Finally, he asked in a quiet, almost disinterested voice, 'So how is it going, Trixia?'

'Fine.' The answer was immediate, the tone exactly that of the old Trixia in a distracted mood. 'The books from the Spider library, they're marvelous. I have a handle on their graphemics now. No one's ever seen anything like this, ever done anything like this. The Spiders don't see the way we do; visual fusion is entirely different with them. If it hadn't been for the physics books, I'd never have imagined the notion of split graphemes.' Her voice was distant, a little excited. She didn't turn to look at him as she spoke, and her fingers continued to tap. Now that his eyes had adjusted to the dim light, he could see small, frightening things. Her fatigues were fresh but there were syrupy stains down the front. Her hair, even cut short, looked tangled and greasy. A fleck of something – food? snot? – clung to the curve of her face just above her lips.

Can she even bathe herself? Vinh glanced downward, at the doorway. The place wasn't big enough for three, but Reynolt had stuck her head and shoulders through the opening. She floated easily on her elbows. She was staring up at Ezr and Trixia with intense interest. 'Dr Bonsol has done well, even better than our own linguists, and they've been Focused since graduate school. Because of her, we'll have a reading knowledge of their language even before the Spiders come back to life.'

Ezr touched Trixia's shoulder again. Again, she twitched away. It wasn't a gesture of anger or fear, it was as if she were shrugging off a pesky fly. 'Do you remember me, Trixia?' No answer, but he was sure she did – it simply wasn't important enough to comment on. She was an ensorcelled princess, and only the evil witches might waken her. But this ensorcellment might never have happened if he had listened more to the princess's fears, if he had agreed with Sum Dotran. 'I'm so sorry, Trixia.'

Reynolt said, 'Enough for this visit, Fleet Manager.' She gestured him out of the roomlet.

Vinh slid back. Trixia's eyes never left her work. Something like that intentness had originally attracted him to her. She was a Trilander, one of the few who had shipped on the Qeng Ho expedition without close friends or even a little family. Trixia had dreamed of learning the truly alien, learning things no human had ever known. She had held the dream as fiercely as the most daring Qeng Ho. And now she had what she had sacrificed for . . . and nothing else.

Halfway through the door, he stopped and looked across the room at the back of her head. 'Are you happy?' he said in a small voice, not really expecting an answer.

She didn't turn, but her fingers ceased their tapping. Where his face and touch had made no impression, the *words* of a silly question stopped her. Somewhere in that beloved head, the question filtered past layers of Focus, was considered briefly. 'Yes, very.' And the sound of her tapping resumed.

Vinh had no recollection of the trip back to the temp, and after that, little more than confused fragments of memory. He saw Benny Wen in the docking area.

Benny wanted to talk. 'We're back earlier that I'd ever guessed. You can't imagine how slick Xin's pilots are.' His voice dropped. 'One of them was Ai Sun. You know, from the *Invisible Hand*. She was in Navigation. *One of our own people, Ezr*. But it's like she's dead inside, just like his other pilots and the Emergent programmers. Xin said she was Focused. He said you could explain. Ezr, you know my pop is over on Hammerfest. What—'

And that was all Ezr remembered. Maybe he screamed at Benny, maybe he just pushed past him. *Explain Focus to your people, and do it so they can accept it, so what is left of our missions can survive.*

When reason returned . . .

Vinh was alone in the temp's central park, without any recollection of having wandered there. The park spread out around him, the leafy treetops reaching across to touch him from five sides. There was an old saying:

Without a bactry, a habitat cannot support its tenants; without a park, the tenants lose their souls. Even on ramships deep between the stars, there was still the Captain's bonsai. In the larger temps, the thousand-year habitats at Canberra and Namqem, the park was the largest space within the structure, kilometer on kilometer of nature. But even the smallest park had all the millennia of Qeng Ho ingenuity behind its design. This one gave the impression of forest depth, of creatures great and small waiting just behind the nearest trees. Keeping the balance of life in a park this small was probably the most difficult project in the temp.

The park was in deepening twilight, darkest in the direction of down. To his right the last glimmer of skylike blue shone beyond the trees. Vinh reached out, pulled himself hand over hand to the ground. It was a short trip; all together, the park was less than twelve meters across. Vinh hugged himself into the deep moss by a tree trunk and listened to the sounds of the cooling forest evening. A bat flickered against the sky, and somewhere a nest of butterflies muttered musically to itself. The bat was likely fake. A park this small could not stock large animals or scamperers, but the butterflies would be real.

For a blessed space of time, all thought fled . . .

. . . and returned with knives resharpened. Jimmy was dead. And Tsufe, and Pham Patil. In dying, they had killed hundreds of others, including the people who might know what to do now. *Yet I still live.*

Even half a day ago, knowing what had happened to Trixia would have put him in a rage beyond reason. Now that rage choked on his shame. Ezr Vinh had had a hand in the deaths aboard the *Far Treasure.* If Jimmy had been a little more 'successful,' all those on Hammerfest might be dead too. Was being foolish, and supporting foolish, violent people – was that as evil as committing a treacherous ambush? *No, no, no!* And yet, in the end, Jimmy had killed a good fraction of those who had survived the ambush. *And I must make amends. Now I must somehow explain Focus to my people, and do it so they can accept it, so what is left of our mission can survive.*

Ezr choked on a sob. He was supposed to convince others to accept what he would have died to prevent. In all his schooling, all his reading, all his nineteen years of life, he had never imagined there could be anything so difficult.

A tiny light swung through the middle distance. Branches shuffled aside. Someone had entered the park, was bumbling nearer the central glade. The light flashed briefly in Vinh's face, then went out.

'Aha. I figured you might go to ground.' It was Pham Trinli. The old man grabbed a low-growing branch and settled on the moss near Vinh. 'Brace up, young fellow. Diem's heart was in the right place. I helped him out as best I could, but he was a careless hothead – remember how he sounded? I never thought he was that foolish, and now a lot of people got killed. Well, shit happens.'

Vinh turned toward the sound of the words; the other's face was a grayish blob in the twilight. For a moment, Vinh teetered on the edge of violence. It would feel so *good* to pulp that face. Instead, he settled a little deeper in the dark and let his breath steady. 'Yeah. It happens.' *And maybe some will happen to you.* Surely Nau had the park bugged.

'Courage. I like that.' In the darkness, Vinh couldn't tell whether the other was smiling or if the fatuous compliment was meant seriously. Trinli slid a little closer and his voice dropped to a whisper. 'Don't take it so hard. Sometimes you have to go along to get along. And I think I can manipulate that Nau fellow. The speech he gave – did you notice? After all the death Jimmy caused, Nau was *accommodating*. I swear, he cribbed his talk from something in our own history.'

So even in hell, there are clowns. Pham Trinli, the aging martinet, whose idea of subtle conspiracy was a whispered chat in a temp's central park. Trinli was so totally clueless. Worse, he had so many things *backwards* . . .

They sat in the near-total darkness for some seconds, and Pham Trinli remained mercifully silent. The guy's stupidity was like a load of rock dumped into the pool of Vinh's despair. It stirred things up. The absurdities gave him something to hit on besides himself. Nau's speech . . . *accommodating?* In a sense. Nau was the injured party in this. But they were all injured parties. Cooperation was the only way out now. He thought back over Nau's words. *Huh.* Some of the phrases really were borrowed, from Pham Nuwen's speech at Brisgo Gap. Brisgo Gap was a shining high point in the history of the Qeng Ho, where the Traders had saved a high civilization and billions of lives. As much as something so large could be tied to a single point in space-time, Brisgo Gap was the origin of the modern Qeng Ho. The similarities with the present situation were about nil . . . except that there, too, people from all over had cooperated, had prevailed in the face of terrible treachery.

Pham Nuwen's speech had been 'cast across Human Space many times during the last two thousand years. It wasn't surprising Tomas Nau would know it. So he'd spliced in a phrase here and there, sought a common background . . . except that Tomas Nau's notion of 'cooperation' meant accepting Focus and what had been done to Trixia Bonsol. Vinh realized that some part of his mind had felt the similarities, had been moved by them. But seeing the cribbing laid out cold made things different. It was all so pat, and it ended with Ezr Vinh having to accept . . . Focus.

Shame and guilt lay so heavily on the last two days. Now Ezr wondered. Jimmy Diem had never been a *friend* of Ezr's. The other had been a few years older, and since they first met, Diem had been his crewleader, his most constant disciplinarian. Ezr tried to think back on Jimmy, think of him from the outside. Ezr Vinh was no prize himself, but he had grown up near the pinnacle of Vinh.23. His aunts and uncles and cousins included some of the most successful Traders in this end of Human Space. Ezr had listened to them and played with them since his nursery days . . . and Jimmy Diem was just not in their league. Jimmy was hardworking, but he didn't have that much imagination. His goals had been modest, which was fortunate since even working as hard as he did, Jimmy was scarcely able to manage a single work crew. *Huh. I never thought about him that way.* It was a sad surprise that suddenly made Jimmy the hardnosed crew-leader much more likable, someone who could have been a friend.

And just as suddenly, he realized how much Jimmy must have hated playing the game of high-stakes threats with Tomas Nau. He didn't have the scheming talent for such things, and in the end he had simply miscalculated. All the guy really wanted to do was marry Tsufe Do and get into middle management. *It doesn't make sense.* Vinh was suddenly aware of the darkness around him, the sounds of butterflies sleeping in the trees. The damp of the moss was chill through his shirt and pants. He tried to remember exactly what he'd heard over the auditorium speakers. The voice was Jimmy's, no doubt. The accent was precisely his Diem-family Nese. But the tone, the choice of words, those had been so confident, so arrogant, so . . . almost *joyful.* Jimmy Diem could never have faked that enthusiasm. And Jimmy would never have felt such enthusiasm, either.

And that left only one conclusion. Faking Jimmy's voice and accent would have been difficult, but somehow they had done it. And so what else had been a lie? *Jimmy didn't kill anyone.* The senior Qeng Ho had been murdered before Jimmy and Tsufe and Pham Patil ever went aboard the *Far Treasure.* Tomas Nau had committed murders on top of murders to claim his moral high ground. *Explain Focus to your people, and do it so they can accept it, so what is left of our missions can survive.*

Vinh stared up into the last light in the sky. Stars glinted here and there between the branches, a fake heaven from a sky light-years away. He heard Pham Trinli shift. He patted Ezr awkwardly on the shoulder, and his lanky form floated off the ground. 'Good, you're not bawling anymore. I figured you just needed a little backbone. Just remember, you gotta go along to get along. Nau is basically a softy; we can handle him.'

Ezr was trembling, a growl of rage climbing up his throat. He caught the growl, made it a sobbing sound, made his trembling anger an exhausted quavering. 'Y-yes. We've got to go along.'

'Good man.' Trinli patted him on the shoulder again, then turned to find his way back through the treetops. Ezr remembered Ritser Brughel's description of Trinli after the Relight. The old man was immune to Tomas Nau's moral manipulation. But that didn't matter, because Trinli was also a self-deceiving coward. *You gotta go along to get along.*

One Jimmy Diem was worth any number of Pham Trinlis.

Tomas Nau had maneuvered them all so cleverly. He had stolen the minds of Trixia and hundreds of others. He had murdered all those who might have made a difference. And he had *used* those murders to make the rest of them into his willing tools.

Ezr stared up at the false stars, at the tree branches that curved like claws across the sky. *Maybe it's possible to push someone too far, to break him so he can't be a tool anymore.* Staring up at the dark claws all around him, Vinh felt his mind spin off in separate directions. One part watched passively, marveling that such disintegration could happen to Ezr Vinh. Another part drew in on itself, drowned in pools of sorrow; Sum Dotran would never return, nor S. J. Park, and any promise of reversing Trixia's Focus must surely be a lie. But there was a third fragment, cool and analytical and murderous:

For both Qeng Ho and Emergents, the Exile would last for decades. Much of that time would be spent off-Watch, in coldsleep . . . but they still had years stretching before them. And Tomas Nau needed all the survivors. For now, the Qeng Ho were beaten down, raped, and – so Tomas Nau must be led to think – deceived. The cool one within him, the one who could kill, looked out upon that future with grim intent. This was not the life that Ezr Vinh had ever dreamed would be his. There would be no friends he could safely confide in. There would be enemies and fools all around. He watched Trinli's fight vanish at the entrance to the park. Fools like Pham Trinli could be used. As long as it didn't implicate competent Qeng Ho, Trinli was a sacrifice piece in the game. Tomas Nau had set him a role for life, and his greatest reward might be nothing more than revenge. (But maybe a chance, the original watcher tried to say, maybe a chance that Reynolt wasn't lying about Trixia and the reversability of Focus.)

The cool one took a last long look down the years of patient work that lay ahead . . . and then for the moment, it retired. Surely there were cameras watching. Better not to seem too calm after all that had happened. Vinh curled in upon himself and surrendered to the one who could weep.

PART TWO

14

Only the most literal-minded would dispute the saying 'New sun, new world.' It's true, the core of the planet is surely unchanged by the New Sun, and the continental outlines are mostly the same. But the steam-storms of the first year of the sun scour back the dry wreckage of all previous surface life. Forests and jungles, prairies and swamps, all must start again. Of Spiderkind's surface works, only stone buildings in protected valleys may survive.

Spore-borne life spreads quickly, torn apart in the storms to sprout again and again. In the first years, higher animals may poke their snouts from deepnesses, may try to gain advantage with an early taking of territory, but it is a deadly business. The 'birth of the new world' is so violent that the metaphor is strained.

. . . And yet, after the third or fourth year, there are occasional breaks in the storms. Avalanches and steam surges become rare, and plants can survive from year to year. In the winter season, when the winds have gentled and there is a gap between the storms, there are times when one can look out at the land and imagine this phase of the sun as an exuberance of life.

Pride of Accord was once more complete, a grander highway than ever it had been before. Victory Smith had the sports car up past sixty miles per hour on the straightaway, slowing to just under thirty when they entered a switchback. From his perch in the back, Hrunkner Unnerby had heart-stopping views of each new precipice. He held on to his perch with every hand and foot Except for that terrorized embrace, he was sure the last turn would have flung him out the side of the auto.

'Are you sure you wouldn't rather have me drive, ma'am?' He asked.

Smith laughed. 'And me sit back where you are? No way. I know how scary it is to watch from the back perch.'

Sherkaner Underhill tilted his head out the side window. 'Um, I never realized how exciting this ride was for passengers.'

'Okay, I get the message.' Smith slowed, drove more cautiously than any of them might have done alone. In fact, road conditions were excellent. The storm had been blown away by a hot, compressional wind, leaving the concrete surface dry and clear. In another hour, they would be back in the soup. Their mountain route scraped just under ragged, fast-moving clouds, and the lands to the south were dark with the haze of rain. The view was about as open as it ever got along Pride of Accord. The forest was just two years old, hard-barked cones sprouting tear-away leaves. Most of the treelets were scarcely a yard tall, though here and there a sproutling or a softbush might reach six or ten feet. The green stretched for miles, interrupted here and there by the brown of avalanches or the spray of waterfalls. In this phase of the sun, the Westermost Forest was like God's own lawn and from almost every point on the Pride, the travelers could see down to the ocean.

Hrunkner relaxed the grip on his perch a fraction. Behind them, he could see Smith's security detail appear around the last switchback. For most of the trip, the escort had had no trouble staying close. For one thing, the storm and rain had kept Victory to very low speeds. Now they were scrambling, and Hrunkner wouldn't blame them if they were steamed. Unfortunately, their commanding officer was about the only person they could complain to, and that was Victory Smith. Smith wore the uniform of a major in the Accord Quartermaster Corps. The branch wasn't quite a lie, since Intelligence was construed as a branch of Quartermaster whenever convenient. But Smith was no major. Unnerby had been out of the service for four years, but he still had his old drinking buddies . . . and he knew just how the Great War had finally been won: if Victory Smith was not the new chief of Accord Intelligence, Unnerby would be enormously surprised.

There had been other surprises though – at least they'd been surprises until he thought things through. Two days ago, Smith had called, inviting him back to the Service. Today, when she showed up at his shop in Princeton, he'd half expected the discreet security – but Sherkaner Underhill's presence had been totally unexpected. Not so surprising was the pleasure he'd felt in seeing the two again. Hrunkner Unnerby had achieved no fame for his role in truncating the Great War; it would be at least ten years before the records of their walk in the Dark were unsealed. But his share of the bounty for that mission had been twenty times his life's savings. Finally, an excuse to quit the Service, a chance to do something constructive with his engineering background.

In the first years of a New Sun, there were enormous works to be done, under conditions that could be as dangerous as combat. In some cases real combat was involved. Even in a modern civilization, this phase of the sun was one where treachery – from theft to murder to squatting – was common. Hrunkner Unnerby had done very well, so perhaps the biggest surprise was how easy it had been for Victory Smith to persuade him to accept a thirty-day enlistment. 'Just long enough to learn what we're up to and decide whether you'd like to come back to longer service.'

Hence this trip to Lands Command. So far, it was a welcome vacation, a meeting with old friends (and it's not often a sergeant got chauffeured by a general officer). Sherkaner Underhill was as much the unhinged genius as ever, though the nerve damage he'd suffered in their ad hoc deepness made him seem older than he was. Smith was more open and cheerful than he had ever seen her. Fifteen miles out of Princeton, beyond the temporary rowhouses and just into the foothills of the Westermost Range, the two let him in on their personal secret:

'You're what?' Unnerby had said, almost slipping off his perch. Hot rain was slamming down all around them; maybe he hadn't heard right.

'You heard me, Hrunkner. The General and I are wife and husband.' Underhill was grinning like an idiot.

Victory Smith raised a pointed hand. 'One correction. Don't call me General.'

Unnerby was usually better at masking astonishment; even Underhill could see this had taken him by surprise, and his grin got even broader. 'Surely you had guessed there was something going on between us before the Big Dark.'

'Well . . .' *Yes*, though nothing could come of it, what with Sherkaner about to head off for his very uncertain walk in the Dark. Hrunkner had always felt sorry for the two because of that.

In fact, they did make a great team. Sherkaner Underhill had more bright ideas than any dozen people the Sergeant had ever known; but most of his ideas were grossly impractical, at least in terms of what could be accomplished in one person's lifetime. On the other hand, Victory Smith had an eye for workable results. Why, if she hadn't been around at just the right time that afternoon long ago, Unnerby would have booted poor Underhill all the way back to Princeton – and his mad scheme for winning the Great War would have been lost. So, yes. Except for the timing, he wasn't surprised. And if Victory Smith was now the Director of Accord Intelligence, the country itself stood to win big. An ugly thought wormed its way to his mouth, and then seemed to pop out of its own volition: 'But children? Not now of course.'

'Yup. The General's pregnant. I'll be carrying two baby welts on my back in less than half a year.'

Hrunkner realized he was sucking on his eating hands in embarrassment. He gargled something unintelligible. They drove for half a minute in silence, the hot rain hissing back across the windshields. *How could they do this to their own children?*

Finally, the General said quietly, 'Do you have a problem with this, Hrunkner?'

Unnerby wanted to swallow his hands all over again. He had known Victory Smith since the day she came into Lands Command, a spanking new junior lieutenant, a lady with an unplaced name and an undisguisable youthfulness. You saw almost everything in the military, and everybody guessed straightaway. The junior lieutenant was truly new; she was born out-of-phase. Yet somehow she'd been educated well enough to get into officer school. The rumor was that Victory Smith was the get of a rich East Coast pervert, the fellow's family had finally disowned him, and the daughter who shouldn't exist. Unnerby remembered the slurs and worse that had followed her everywhere for the first quarter year or so. In fact his first glimmer that she was destined for greatness was the way she stood up to the ostracism, her intelligence and courage in facing the shame of her time of birth.

Finally he got his voice. 'Uk. Yes, ma'am. I know. I meant no disrespect. I was brought up to believe a certain way,' *about how decent people should live*. Decent people conceived their children in the Waning years, and gave birth with the new sun.

The General didn't reply, but Underhill gave him a backhanded pat. 'That's okay, Sergeant. You should have seen my cousin's reaction. But just wait; things change. When we have time, I'll explain why the old rules don't really make sense anymore.' And that was the most disquieting thing about Sherkaner Underhill: he probably could explain away their behavior – and remain blissfully remote from the rage it would cause in others.

But the embarrassing moment had passed. If these two could put up with Hrunkner's straitlaced nature, he would do his best to ignore their . . . quirks. Heaven knew he had put up with worse during the war. Besides, Victory Smith was the sort who seemed to create her own propriety – and once created, it was as deep as any Unnerby had known.

As for Underhill . . . his attention was already elsewhere. His nervous tremor made him look old, but the mind was as sharp – or as flaky – as ever. It flitted from idea to idea, never quite coming to rest the way a normal person's would. The rain had stopped and the wind became hot and dry. As they entered the steep country, Unnerby took a quick look at his watch and began counting how much craziness the other might come up with in the next few minutes. (1) Pointing out at the hard-armored first growth of the forest, Underhill speculated what Spiderkind might have been like if it regrew from spores after every Dark instead of emerging full-grown and with children. (2) A crack in the cloud cover appeared ahead, fortunately several miles to the side of their path. For a few minutes, the searing whiteness of once-reflected sunlight shone down upon them, clouds so bright they had to shade that side of the car. Somewhere uphill of them, direct sunlight was frying the mountainside. And Sherkaner Underhill wondered if maybe someone could build 'heat farms' on the mountaintops, using temperature differentials to generate electricity for the towns below. (3) Something green scuttled across the road, narrowly avoiding their wheels. Sherkaner had a take on that, too, something about evolution and the automobile. (And Victory commented that such evolution could work both ways.) (4) Ah, but Underhill had an idea for much safer, faster transport than autos or even aircraft. 'Ten minutes from Princeton to

Lands Command, twenty minutes across the continent. See, you dig these tunnels along minimum-time arcs, evacuate the air from them, and just let gravity do the work.' By Unnerby's watch, there was a five-second pause. Then: 'Oops, little problem there. The minimum-time solution for Princeton to Lands Command would go down kinda deep . . . like six hundred miles. I probably couldn't convince even the General to finance it.'

'You are right about that!' And the two were off in an extended argument about less-than-optimal tunnel arcs and trade-offs against air travel. The deep tunnel idea was really dumb, it turned out.

Unnerby lost track after a while. For one thing, Sherkaner was very curious about Unnerby's construction business. The fellow was a good listener, and his questions gave Unnerby ideas he might never have had otherwise. Some of those might actually make money. Lots of money. Hmm.

Smith noticed: 'Hey, I need this sergeant to be poor and in need of a generous enlistment bonus. Don't lead him astray!'

'Sorry, dear.' But Underhill did not seem apologetic. 'It's been a long time, Hrunkner. I wish we'd seen more of you these last years. You remember back then, my big, ah—'

'Screwball idea of the moment?'

'Yes, exactly!'

'I remember just before we buttoned up in that Tiefer animal deepness, you were mumbling about this being the last Dark that civilization would ever sleep through. In the hospital afterwards, you were still going on about it. You should be a science-fiction writer, Sherkaner.'

Underhill waved a hand airily, as if acknowledging a compliment. 'Actually, it's been done in fiction. But truly, Hrunk, ours is the first era where we can make it happen.'

Hrunkner shrugged. He had walked in the Great Dark; it still made him queasy. 'I'm sure there will be lots more Deep Dark expeditions, larger and better equipped than ours. It's an exciting idea, and I'm sure the Gen – Major Smith also has all sorts of plans. I could even imagine significant battles in the middle of the Dark.'

'This is a new age, Hrunk. Look at what science is doing all around us.'

They rounded the last curve of dry roadway and plowed into a solid wall of hot rain, the storm they had seen from the north. Smith was not caught by surprise. They had their windows rolled almost all the way up, and the auto was doing only twenty miles per hour when they were enveloped. Still, the driving conditions were suddenly ghastly, the windows fogging almost too fast for the car's blowers, the rain so thick that even with the deep-red rain lights they could barely see the edge of the roadway. The rain that spattered past the chinks in the windows was hot as a baby's spit. Behind them, two pairs of deep-reds loomed in the darkness, Smith's security people pulling closer.

It took a forcible effort to bring his attention back from the storm outside and remember what Underhill had been saying. 'I know about the "Age of Science," Sherk. That's been my edge in the construction business. By the last Waning we had radio, aircraft, telephones, sound recording. Even during the build-back since the New Sun, that progress has continued. Your auto is an incredible improvement over that Relmeitch you had before the Dark – and that was an expensive vehicle for its time.' And someday, Unnerby wanted to learn just how Sherkaner had obtained it on a grad student's stipend. 'Without a doubt, this is the most exciting era I could ever hope to live in. Aircraft will soon break the sound barrier. The Crown is building a national highway system. You wouldn't be behind that, would you, Major?'

Victory smiled. 'No need. There are plenty of people in Quartermaster who are. And the highway system would happen without any government help at all. But this way, we retain control.'

'So. Big things are happening. In thirty years – by the next Dark – I wouldn't be surprised if there is worldwide air traffic, picturing telephones, maybe even rocket-borne relays that orbit the world the way the world orbits the sun. If we can avoid another war, I'm going to have the time of my life. But your idea that our entire civilization will sustain itself right through the Dark – pardon me, old Corporal, but I don't think you've worked out the numbers. To do that we'd essentially have to re-create the sun. Do you have any idea of the energy involved? I remember what it took to support our diggers after Dark during the War. We used more fuel in those operations than in all the rest of the War put together.'

Ha! For once, Sherkaner Underhill didn't have a ready reply. Then he realized that Sherk was waiting for the General to speak. After a moment, Victory Smith raised a hand. 'Until now everything has been very sociable, Sergeant. I know, you've learned some things that enemies might make use of – clearly you've guessed my present job.'

'Yes. And congratulations, ma'am. Next to Strut Greenval, you're the best that ever had that job.'

'Why . . . thank you, Hrunkner. But my point is that Sherkaner's idle talk has moved us to the heart of why I asked you to take a thirty-day recruitment. What you're going to hear now is explicitly Strategic Secret.'

'Yes, ma'am.' He hadn't expected the mission brief to sneak up on him like this. Outside, the storm roared louder. Smith was pushing along at barely twenty miles per hour even on the straightaway. During the early years of a New Sun, even overcast days were dangerously bright, but this storm was so deep that the sky had darkened down to a murky twilight. The wind picked at the auto, trying to pry it off the road. The inside of the cab was like a steam bath.

Smith waved for Sherkaner to continue. Underhill leaned back in his perch and raised his voice to be heard over the growing storm. 'As it happens, I have "worked out the numbers." After the War, I peddled my ideas around a number of Victory's colleagues. That nearly ruined her promotion. Those cobbers can do the numbers almost as well as you. But things have changed.'

'Correction,' said Smith. 'Things *may* change.' The wind slid them toward a drop-off that Unnerby could barely see. Smith downshifted, forced the auto back toward the middle of the road.

'You see,' continued Underhill, undistracted, 'there really are power sources that could support civilization through the Dark. You said we'd have to create our own sun. That's close, even if no one knows how the sun works. But there's theoretical and practical evidence of the power of the atom.'

A few minutes earlier, Unnerby would have laughed. Even now, he couldn't keep the scorn out of his voice. 'Radioactivity? You're going to keep us warm with tons of refined radium?' Maybe the great secret was that the Crown's high command was reading *Amazing Science*.

Such incredulity rolled off Underhill's back as smoothly as ever. 'There are several possibilities. If they are pursued with imagination, I have no doubt that I will have the numbers on my side by the time of the next Waning.'

And the General said, 'Just so you understand, Sergeant. I *do* have doubts. But this is something we can't afford to overlook. Even if the scheme doesn't work, the *failure* could be a weapon a thousand times deadlier than anything in the Great War.'

'Deadlier than poison gas in a deepness?' Suddenly the storm outside didn't seem as dark as what Victory Smith was saying.

He realized that for an instant all her attention was upon him. 'Yes, Sergeant, worse than that. Our largest cities could be destroyed in a matter of hours.'

Underhill almost bounced off his perch. 'Worst case! Worst case! That's all you military types ever think about. Look, Unnerby. If we work at this over the next thirty years, we'll likely have power sources that can keep buried cities – not deepnesses, but waking cities – going right through the Dark. We can keep roadways clear of ice and airsnow – and by the middle years of the Dark, they'll stay that way. Surface transport could be much easier than it is during much of the Bright Times.' He waved at the hissing rain beyond the sports car's windows.

'Yeah, and I suppose air transport will be likewise simplified,' *with all the air lying frozen on the ground.* But Unnerby's sarcasm sounded faint even to himself. *Yes, with a power source, maybe we could do it.*

Unnerby's change of heart must have shown; Underhill smiled. 'You do see! Fifty years from now we'll look back at these times and wonder why it wasn't obvious. The Dark is actually a more benign phase than most any other time.'

'Yeah.' He shivered. Some would call it sacrilege, but – 'Yeah, it would be something marvelous. You haven't convinced me it can be done.'

'If it can be done at all, it will be very hard,' said Smith. 'We have about thirty years left before the next Dark. We've got some physicists who think that – in theory – atomic power can work. But God Below, it wasn't till 58//10 that they even knew about atoms! I've sold the High Command on this; considering the investment, I'll surely be out of a job if it fizzles. But you know – sorry, Sherkaner – I rather hope it doesn't work at all.'

Funny that she would support the traditional view on this.

Sherkaner: 'It will be like finding a new world!'

'No! It will be like recolonizing the present one. Sherk, let's consider the "best case" scenario that you claim we narrow-minded military types always ignore. Let's say the scientists get things figured out. Say that in ten years, or by 60//20 at the outside, we start building atomic power plants for your hypothetical "cities-in-the-Dark." Even if the rest of the world hasn't discovered atomic power on its own, this sort of construction cannot be kept secret. So even if there is no other reason for war, there will be an arms race. And it will be a lot worse than anything in the Great War.'

Unnerby: 'Ugh. Yes. The first to colonize the Dark would own the world.'

'Yes,' said Smith. 'I'm not sure I'd trust the Crown to respect property in a situation like that. But I *know* the world would wake up enslaved or dead if some group like the Kindred conquered the Dark instead.'

It was the sort of self-generated nightmare that had driven Unnerby out of the military. 'I hope this doesn't sound disloyal, but have you considered killing this idea?' He waved ironically at Underhill. 'You could think about other things, right?'

'You *have* lost the military view, haven't you? But yes, I have considered suppressing this research. Just maybe – if dear Sherkaner keeps his mouth shut – that would be enough. If no one gets an early start on this business, there's no way anybody will be ready to take over the Dark this time around. And maybe we're generations away from putting this theory into practice – that's what some of the physicists think.'

'Well, I'll tell you,' said Underhill, 'this will be a matter of engineering soon enough. Even if we don't touch it, atomic power will be a big deal in fifteen or twenty years. Only it will be too late for power plants and sealed cities. It will be too late to conquer the Dark. All atomic power will be good for is weapons. You were talking about radium, Hrunkner. Just think what large amounts of such a substance could do as a war poison. And that's just the most obvious thing. Basically, whatever we do, civilization will be at risk. At least if we try for it all, there could be a wonderful payoff, civilization all through the Dark.'

Smith waved unhappy agreement; Unnerby had the feeling that he was witnessing a much-repeated discussion. Victory Smith had bought into

Underhill's scheme – and sold it to the High Command. The next thirty years were going to be even more exciting than Hrunkner Unnerby had thought.

They reached the mountain village very late in the day, the last three hours of the trip covering just twenty miles through the storm. The weather broke a couple of miles short of the little town.

Five years into the New Sun, Nigh't' Deepness was mostly rebuilt. The stone foundations had survived the initial flash and the high-speed floods. As after every Dark going back many generations, the villagers had used the armored sprouts of the forest's first growth to build the ground floors of their homes and businesses and elementary schools. Perhaps by the year 60// 10 they would have better timber and would install a second floor and – at the church – perhaps a third. For now, all was low and green, the short conical logs giving the exterior walls a scaled appearance.

Underhill insisted they pass up the kerosene service station on the main road. 'I know a better place,' he said, and directed Smith to drive back along the old roadway.

They had rolled down the windows. The rain had stopped. A dry, almost cool wind swept over them. There was a break in the cloud cover and for a few minutes they could see sunlight on clouds. But the light was not the murky furnace of earlier in the day. The sun must be near setting. The tumbled clouds were bright with red and orange and alpha plaid – and beyond that the blue and ultra of clear sky. Brilliance splashed the street and buildings and foothills beyond. God the surrealist.

Sure enough, at the end of the gravel path was a low barn and a single kerosene pumping station. 'This is the "better place," Sherk?' asked Unnerby.

'Well . . . more interesting anyway,' The other opened the door and hopped off his perch. 'Let's see if this cobber remembers me.' He walked back and forth by the car, getting the kinks out. After the long drive, his tremor was more pronounced than usual.

Smith and Unnerby got out, and after a moment the proprietor, a heavyset fellow wearing a tool pannier, came out of the barn. He was followed by a pair of children.

'Fill it up, old cobber?' the fellow said.

Underhill grinned at him, not bothering to correct the misestimate of his age. 'Sure thing.' He followed the other over to the pump. The sky was even brighter now, blue and sunset reds shining down. 'Remember me, do you? I used to come through in a big red Relmeitch, right before the Dark. You were a blacksmith then.'

The other stopped, took a long stare at Underhill. 'The Relmeitch I remember.' His two five-year-olds danced behind him, watching the curious visitor.

'Funny how things change, isn't it?'

The proprietor didn't know just what Underhill was talking about, but after a few moments the two were gossiping like old pals. Yes, the proprietor liked automobiles, clearly the wave of the future and no more blacksmithing for him. Sherkaner complimented him on some job he had done for him long ago, and said it was a shame that there was a kerosene filling station on the main road now. He bet it wasn't nearly as good at repair work as here, and had the former blacksmith considered how street advertising was being done up in Princeton these days? Smith's security pulled into the open space beyond the road, and the proprietor scarcely noticed. Funny how Underhill could get along with almost anyone, tuning down his manias to whatever the traffic would bear.

Meantime, Smith was across the road, talking to the captain who was running her security detail. She came back after Sherk had paid for the kerosene. 'Damn. Lands Command says there's a worse storm due in about midnight. First time I take my own car, and all hell breaks loose.' Smith sounded angry, which usually meant she was irritated with herself. They got aboard the auto. She poked at the ignition motor twice. Three times. The engine caught. 'We'll bivouac here overnight.' She sat for a moment, almost indecisive. Or maybe she was watching the sky to the south. 'I know where there's some Crown land west of town.'

Smith tooled down gravel roads, then muddy trails. Unnerby almost thought she was lost except she never hesitated or backtracked. Behind them came the security vehicles, about as inconspicuous as a parade of osprechs. The mud path petered out on a promontory overlooking the ocean. Steep slopes fell away on three sides. Someday, the forest would be tall here again, but now even the millions of armored sproutlings could not hide the naked rock of the dropoff.

Smith stopped at the dead end, and leaned back on her perch. 'Sorry. I . . . made a wrong turn.' She waved at the first of the security vehicles pulling up behind her.

Unnerby stared out at the ocean and the sky above. Sometimes wrong turnings were the best kind. 'That's okay. God, what a view.' The breaks in the clouds were like deep canyons. The light coming down them flared red and near-red, reflections of sunset. A billion rubies glinted in the water droplets on the foliage around them. He scrambled out the back of the auto, and walked a little way through the sprouts toward the end of the promontory. The forest mat squelched deep and wet beneath his feet. After a moment Sherkaner followed him.

The breeze coming off the ocean was moist and cool. You didn't have to be the Met Department to know a storm was coming. He looked out over the water. They were standing less than three miles from the breakers, about as close as it was safe to be in this phase of the sun. From here you could see the turbulence and hear the grinding. Three icebergs were stranded, towering, in the surf. But there were hundreds more, stretching off to the horizon. It was the eternal battle, the fire from the New Sun against the ice of the good earth. Neither could finally win. It would be twenty years before the last of the shallows ice had surfaced and melted. By then, the sun would be waning. Even Sherkaner seemed subdued by the scene.

Victory Smith had left the auto, but instead of following them, she walked back, along the south edge of the promontory. *The poor General. She can't decide if this trip is business or pleasure.* Unnerby was just as happy they wouldn't get down to Lands Command in one whack.

They walked back to Smith. On this side of the promontory, the ground dropped into a little valley. On the high ground beyond there was some kind of building, perhaps a small inn. Smith was standing where the bedrock edge of the drop-off was nicked, and the slope was not deadly steep. Once, the road might have continued down into the little valley and up the other side.

Sherkaner stopped by his wife's side and draped his left arms over her shoulders; after a moment she slipped two of her arms over his, never saying a word. Unnerby walked to the edge and dipped his head over the drop-off. There were traces of road cut, all the way to the bottom. But the storms and floods of the Early Bright had gouged new cliffs. The valley itself was charming, untouched and clean. 'Heh, heh. No way we're going to drive down there, ma'am. The road is washed clean away.'

Victory Smith was silent for a moment. 'Yes. Washed clean. That's for the best . . .'

Sherk said, 'You know, we could probably walk across, and up the other side.' He jabbed a hand at the inn on the hill-crest beyond the valley. 'We could see if Lady Encl—'

Victory gave him a sharp, rippling hug. 'No. That place couldn't put up more than the three of us, anyway. We'll camp with my security team.'

After a moment, Sherk gave a little laugh. '. . . Fine by me. I'm curious to see a modern motorized bivouac.' They followed Smith back to the trail. By the time they reached the vehicles, Sherkaner was in full form, some scheme for lightweight tents that could survive even the storms of the First Bright.

15

Tomas Nau stood at his bedroom window, looking out. In fact, his rooms were fifty meters deep in Diamond One, but the view out his window was from the loftiest spire of Hammerfest. His estate had grown since the Relighting. Cut diamond slabs made adequate walls, and the surviving special craftsmen would spend their lives polishing and faceting, carving friezes as intricate as anything Nau had owned at home.

The grounds around Hammerfest had been planed smooth, tiled with metals from the ore dump on Diamond Two. He tried to keep the rockpile oriented so only Hammerfest's flag spire actually spiked into the sunlight. The last year or so, that caution wasn't really necessary, but staying in the shade meant that water ice could be used for shielding and some gluework. Arachna hung halfway up the sky, a brilliant blue-and-white disk almost half a degree across. Its light was bright and soft across the castle grounds. It was all quite a contrast to the first Msecs here, the hell of the Relight. Nau had worked five years to create the present view, the peace, the beauty.

Five years. And how many years more would they be stuck here? Thirty to forty was the specialists' best estimate; however long it took the Spiders to create an industrial ecology. It was funny how things had worked out. This really was an Exile, though quite unlike what he had planned back on Balacrea. That original mission had been a different kind of calculated risk: a couple of centuries away from the increasingly deadly politics of the home regime, an opportunity to breed his resources away from poachers – and the outside, golden chance that they might learn the secrets of a starfaring nonhuman race. He hadn't counted on the Qeng Ho arriving first.

Qeng Ho knowledge was the core of Balacrea's Emergent civilization. Tomas Nau had studied the Qeng Ho all his life, yet till he met them he had not understood how weirdly different the Peddlers were. Their fleet had been softheaded and naive. Infecting them with timed-expression mindrot had been trivial, arranging the ambush almost as easy. But once under attack, the Peddlers had fought like devils, clever devils with a hundred surprises they must have prepared in advance. Their flagship had been destroyed in the first hundred seconds of the battle – yet that seemed only to make them more deadly killers. When finally the mindrot shut the Peddlers down, both sides were wrecked. And after the battle had come Nau's second great misestimate of the Peddlers. Mindrot could kill Qeng Ho, but many of them could not be scrubbed or Focused. The field interrogations had gone very badly, though in the end he had turned that debacle into the means of unifying the survivors.

So Hammerfest's attic and Focus clinic and splendid furnishings – those were cut from the ruined starships. Here and there within the ruins, high technology still functioned. All the rest must come from the raw materials of the rockpile – and the eventual civilization of the Spiders.

Thirty or forty years. They could make it. There should be enough coldsleep coffins to serve the survivors. The main thing now was to study the Spiders, learn their languages, their history and culture. To span the decades, the work was split into a tree of Watches, a few Msecs on duty, a year or two off and in coldsleep. Some, the translators and scientists, would be spending a lot of time on Watch. Others – the pilots and tactics people – would be mainly unused in the early years, then live full time toward the end of the mission. Nau had explained it all in meetings with his own people and the Qeng Ho. And what he had promised was mostly true. The Qeng Ho had great expertise in such operations; with luck, the average person would get through the Exile with only ten to twelve years of lifetime spent. Along the way, he would plunder the Peddlers' fleet library; he would learn everything the Qeng Ho had ever learned.

Nau rested his hand against the surface of the window. It was as warm as the carpet on the walls. Plague's name, this Qeng Ho wallpaper was good. Even looking off to the side, there was no distortion. He chuckled softly. In the end, running the Peddler side of the Exile might be the easiest thing. *They* had some experience with the duty schedule that Nau proposed.

But for himself . . . Nau allowed a moment of self-pity. Someone trustable and competent must stay on Watch till final recovery. There was only one such person, and his name was Tomas Nau. On his own, Ritser Brughel would foolishly kill resources that could not be spared – or do his best to kill Nau himself. On her own, Anne Reynolt could be trusted for years, but if something unexpected came up . . . Well, the Qeng Ho seemed thoroughly subdued, and after the interrogations, Nau was relatively sure that no big secrets remained. But if the Qeng Ho did again conspire, Anne Reynolt would be lost.

So Tomas Nau might be a hundred years old before he saw triumph here. That was middle-aged by Balacrean standards. Nau sighed. So be it. Qeng Ho medicine would more than make up for the time lost. And then—

The room shivered, a nearly inaudible groaning sound. Where Nau's hand touched the wall, the vibration crept in along his bones. It was the third rock quake in the last 40Ksec.

On the far side of the room, the Peddler girl stirred in their bed. 'Wha—?' Qiwi Lin Lisolet emerged from sleep, her motion lifting her out of the bed. She had been working for nearly three days straight, trying yet again to find a stable configuration for the rockpile. Lisolet's gaze wobbled about. She probably didn't even know what had wakened her. Her eyes fixed on Nau standing by the window, and a sympathetic smile spread across her face. 'Oh, Tomas, you're losing more sleep worrying about us?'

She reached out her arms, a comforting. Nau smiled shyly and nodded. Hell, what she said was even approximately true. He floated across the room, stopped himself with one hand against the wall behind her head. She wrapped her arms around him and they floated, slowly sinking, toward the bed below. He slid his arms toward her waist, felt her strong legs bend around his. 'You're doing everything you can, Tomas. Don't try to do more. Things will be all right.' Her hands brushed gently against the hair at the back of his neck, and he felt the trembling in her. It was Qiwi Lisolet who worried, who would work herself to death if she thought it would add one percent to their overall chances of survival. They drifted silent for long seconds, till gravity drew them down to the froth of lace that was their bed.

Nau let his hands roam her flanks; he felt the worry slowly subside in her. Lots had gone wrong with this mission, but Qiwi Lin Lisolet could be counted as a small triumph. She had been fourteen – precocious, naive, willful – when Nau took down the Qeng Ho fleet. The girl was properly infected with mindrot. She could have been Focused; for a while he had considered making her his body toy. *Thank the Plague I didn't.*

During the first couple of years, the girl had spent much of her time in this room, crying. Diem's 'murder' of her mother had made her the first wholehearted turncoat. Nau had spent Msecs comforting her. At first that had been simply an exercise in the persuasive arts, with the possible side effect that Qiwi might improve his credibility with the other Peddlers. But as time passed, Nau came to see that the girl was more dangerous and more useful than he had guessed. Qiwi had lived much of her childhood on-Watch during the voyage from Triland. She had used the time with almost Focused intensity, learning construction engineering, life-support technology, and trading practices. It was weird; why was one child given such special treatment? Like so many of the Qeng Ho factions, the Lisolet Family had its own secrets, its own interior culture. During the interrogations, he had squeezed the probable explanation out of the girl's mother. The Lisolets used the time between the stars to mold those girl children who were intended for ruling positions in the Family. If things had gone according to Kira Pen Lisolet's plans, the girl would have been ready for further instruction here in-system, totally dominated by her loyalty toward her mother.

As things turned out, this made the girl ideal for Tomas Nau's purposes. She was young and talented, and desperately in need of someone in whom to invest her loyalty. He could run her Watch after Watch without coldsleep, just as he had to run himself. She would be a good companion for the time ahead – and one who was a constant test of his plans. Qiwi was smart and in many ways her personality was still very independent. Even now, with the evidence of what really happened to her mother and the others safely blown away, slipups could happen. Using Qiwi was a thrill ride, a constant test of his nerve. But at least he understood the danger now, and had taken precautions.

'Tomas—' She turned to face him directly. 'Do you think I'll *ever* get the rockpile stabilized?'

Indeed, that was a proper thing for her to worry about. Ritser Brughel – or even a younger Tomas Nau – would not have realized that the correct response was not a threat or even disapproval. 'Yes, you'll think of something. We'll think of something. Take a few days' vacation, okay? Old Trinli is off coldsleep this Watch. Let him balance the rockpile for a while.'

Qiwi's laughter made her sound even younger than she looked. 'Oh, yes. Pham Trinli!' He was the only one of Diem's conspirators she had more contempt than anger for. 'Remember the last time he ran the balance? He talks loud, but he started out so timid. Before he knew it, the rockpile was three meters per second off L1 track. Then he over-reacted and—' She started laughing again. The strangest things made this Peddler girl laugh. It was one of the puzzles about her that still intrigued him.

Lisolet was silent for a moment, and when she finally spoke, she surprised the Podmaster. 'Yeah . . . maybe you're right. If it's just four days, I can set things up so even Trinli can't do too much damage. I do need to step back, think about things. Maybe we can water-weld the blocks after all . . . Besides, Papa is awake on this Watch. I'd like to be with him a little more.' She looked at him questioningly, implicitly asking for release from duty.

Hunh. Sometimes the manipulation didn't work out as expected. He'd have bet three zipheads she wouldn't take him up on the offer. *I could still turn her back.* He could agree with just enough reluctance to make her ashamed. No. It wasn't worth it, not this time. *And if one does not forbid, then be wholeheartedly generous in giving permission.* He gathered her close. 'Yes! Even you have to learn to relax.'

She sighed, smiled with a hint of mischievousness. 'Oh, yes, but I've already learned that.' She reached down, and neither of them spoke for some time. Qiwi Lisolet was still a clumsy teenager, but she was learning. And Tomas Nau had years to teach her. Kira Pen Lisolet had not had nearly so much time, and had been a resisting adult. Nau smiled, remembering. Oh yes. In different ways, both mother and daughter had served him well.

Ali Lin had not been born into the Lisolet Family. He had been Kira Pen Lisolet's external acquisition. Ali was one in a trillion, a genius when it came to parks and living things. And he was Qiwi's father. Both Kira and Qiwi had loved him very much, even if he could never be what Kira was and what Qiwi would one day be.

Ali Lin was important to the Emergents, probably as important as any of the Focused. He was one of the few who had a lab outside the attic warrens of Hammerfest. He was one of the few who did not have Anne Reynolt or one of the lesser managers constantly watching out for him.

Now he and Qiwi sat in the treetops of the Qeng Ho park, playing a slow, patient game with the bugs. She had been here 10Ksec, and Papa some time more. He had her doing DNA diffs on the new strains of garbage spiders he'd been breeding. Even now, he seemed to trust her with that work, only checking her results every Ksec or so. The rest of the time he was lost in his examination of the leaves and a sort of daydreaming contemplation of how he might do the projects that Anne Reynolt had set for him.

Qiwi looked down past her feet, at the floor of the park. The trees were flowering amandors, bred for microgravity over thousands of years by people like Ali Lin. The leaves twisted down and down, bushing out so that their eyrie was almost invisible from the shadowed 'below.' Even without gravity, the blue sky and the turn of the branches gave a subtle orientation to the park. The largest real animals were the butterflies and the bees. She could hear the bees, see an occasional erratic bullet of their flight. The butterflies were everywhere. The micro-gee varieties oriented on the false sunlight, so their flight provided the visitor with one more psychological cue about up and down. Right now the park was empty of other humans, officially closed for maintenance. That was something of a fib, but Tomas Nau had not called her on it. In fact, the park had just become too popular. The Emergents loved it at least as much as the Qeng Ho. The place was so popular that Qiwi could detect the beginnings of system failure; the little garbage spiders weren't quite keeping up anymore.

She looked at her father's abstracted features and smiled. This really was maintenance time, of a sort. 'Here's the latest set of diffs; is this what you're looking for, Papa?'

'Hmm?' The other didn't look up from his work. Then abruptly he seemed to hear. 'Really? Let's see, Qiwi.'

She slid the list across to him. 'See? Here and here. This is the pattern match we were looking for. The imaginal disks will change just the way you wanted.' Papa wanted a higher metabolism, without losing the population bounds. In this park, the insects did not have bacterial predators; the contest for life went on within their genomes.

Ali took the list from her hands. He smiled gently, almost looking at her, almost noticing her. 'Good, you got the multiplier trick just right.'

Hearing such words was about as close as Qiwi Lin Lisolet could come to recapturing the past. Age nine to fourteen had been Qiwi's Lisoletish learning time. It had been a lonely time, but Mom had been right about it. Qiwi had come a long way toward growing up, learning to be alone in the great dark. She had learned about the life-support systems that were her father's specialty, learned the celestial mechanics that made all her mother's constructions possible, and most of all she had learned how much she loved to be around others during their waking times. Both her parents had spent several of those years out of coldsleep, sharing maintenance duty with her and the Watch techs.

Now Mama was dead and Papa was Focused, his soul concentrated down upon one thing: the biological management of ecosystems. But within that Focus, he and she could still communicate. In the years since the ambush, they had been together for Msecs of common Watch. Qiwi had continued to learn from him. And sometimes, when they were deep within the complexity of species stability, sometimes it was like before, in childhood, when Papa would get so trapped in his passion for living things that he seemed to forget his daughter was really a person, and they were both swallowed up by wonders greater than themselves.

Qiwi studied the diffs – but mostly she was watching her father. She knew he was very close to finishing the garbage-spider project, his part of it anyway. Long experience told her that there would be a few moments after that when Ali Lin would be approachable, when his Focus cast about for something new to bind on. Qiwi smiled to herself. *And I have the project.* It was almost what Reynolt and Tomas wanted from Papa, so diverting him would be possible if she played it just right.

There. Ali Lin sighed, gazing contentedly on the branches and leaves around them. Qiwi had maybe fifty seconds. She slipped downward from her branch, holding her position with the tip of her foot. She snagged the bonsai bubble she had smuggled in, and returned to her father. 'Remember these, Papa? Really, really small parks?'

Papa didn't ignore her words. He turned toward her as quickly as a normal person, and his eyes widened when he caught sight of the clear plastic sphere. 'Yes! Except for light, a completely closed ecology.'

Qiwi floated the empty bubble into his hands. Bonsai bubbles were a commonplace in the confines of a ramscoop under way. They existed in all levels of sophistication, from lumps of moss up to things almost as complex as this temp's park. And – 'This is a little smaller than the problems we've been working on. I'm not sure your solutions would work here.'

Appeals to pride had often worked on the old Ali, almost as often as appeals to love. Now you had to catch Papa at just the right instant. He squinted at the bubble, seemed to feel the dimensions with his hands. 'No, no! I can do it. My new tricks are very powerful . . . Would you like a little lake, maybe lipid bound to lie flat?'

Qiwi nodded.

'And those garbage spiders, I can make them smaller and give them colored wings.'

'Yes.' Reynolt would let him spend more effort on the garbage bugs. They were important for more than just the central park. So much had been destroyed in the fighting. Ali's work would allow small-scale life-support modules all through the surviving structures. It was something that would normally take a Qeng Ho specialist team and deep searches of the fleet's databases – but Papa was both Focused and a genius. He could do such design work all by himself, and in just a few Msecs.

Papa just needed a push in the right conceptual direction, something that old prune, Anne Reynolt, could rarely provide. So—

Ali Lin was suddenly grinning from ear to ear. 'I bet I can top the Namqem High Treasures. Look, the filtration webs will carry straight across. The shrubs will be standard, maybe a little modified to support your insect diffs.'

'Yes, yes,' said Qiwi. They had a real conversation, several hundred seconds; before her father lapsed into the fierce concentration that would make the 'simple changes' actually doable. The hardest part would be at the bacterial and mitochondrial level, and that was totally beyond Qiwi. She smiled at her father, almost reached out to touch his shoulder. Mama would be proud of them. Papa's methods might even be new – they certainly weren't in any of the obvious places in the historical dbs. Qiwi had guessed that they might allow some *very* nice microparks, but this was more than she had hoped for.

The High Treasure bonsais were no bigger than this, thirty centimeters across. Some of them had lived for two hundred years, complete animal/plant ecosystems – even supporting fake evolution. The method was proprietary and not even the Qeng Ho had been able to purchase all of it. Creating such things with only mission resources would be a miracle. If Papa could do better than that . . . *hmm.* Most people, even Tomas, seemed to think that Qiwi had been brought up to be an armsman, following her mother's military career. They didn't understand. The Lisolets were *Qeng Ho.* Fighting came a far second. Sure, she had learned a little about combat. Sure, Mama intended she spend a decade or two learning what to do When All Else Fails. But Trading was what everything came back to. Trading and making a profit. So they had been taken over by the Emergents. But Tomas was a decent person – and he had the hardest job she could imagine. She was doing everything she could to support him, to make what was left of their expeditions survive. Tomas couldn't help that his culture was all screwed up.

And in the end it wouldn't matter that Tomas didn't understand. Qiwi smiled at the empty plastic sphere, imagining what it would be like filled with her father's creation: In civilized places, a top bonsai might sell for the price of an entire starship. Here? Well, Qiwi might make these on the side. After all, it was a frivolity, something that Tomas probably couldn't justify to himself. Tomas had banned hoarding and favor-trading. *Uh-oh. Maybe I'll have to work around him for a while.* It was much easier to get permission afterward. In the end, she figured the Qeng Ho would change Tomas's people far more than the reverse.

She was just starting a new diffs sequence when there was a ripping sound from below, the source hidden by the lower foliage. For a second, Qiwi didn't recognize the sound. *The floor access hatch.* That was for construction only. Opening it would tear the moss layer. Damn.

Qiwi swung out from their little nest, and moved quietly downward, careful not to crack branches or cast a shadow on the bottom moss. Breaking in while the park was officially closed was only an annoyance – heck, it was the sort of thing she would do if she felt like it. But that floor hatch was not supposed to be opened. It spoiled the park's illusion, and it damaged the turf. What sort of jackass would do something like that – especially considering how seriously Emergents took official rules and regulations?

Qiwi hovered just above the bottommost canopy of leaves. In a second the intruder would be in view, but she could already hear him. It was Ritser Brughel. The Vice-Podmaster proceeded across the moss, cursing and whacking at something in the bushes. The guy was a real sewer-mouth. Qiwi was an avid student of such language, and she had listened to him before. Brughel might be the number-two boss man of the Emergent expedition – but he was also a one-man proof that Emergent leaders could be bums. Tomas seemed to realize the fellow was a bad actor; he'd put the Vice Pod-master's quarters off the rockpile, on the old *Invisible Hand.* And Brughel's Watch schedule was the same as much of the regular crew. While poor Tomas aged year after year to keep the mission safe, Brughel was out of coldsleep only 10Msec in every 40. So Qiwi didn't know him very well – but what she knew she loathed. *If this jerk could be trusted to pull his own weight, Tomas wouldn't be burning his lifetime away for us.* She listened in silence for a moment more. *Neat stuff.* But there was an undercurrent to it she didn't hear in most folk's obscenities, like the fellow meant what he was saying literally.

Qiwi pushed loudly between the branches, holding herself so that she stood half a meter in the air – about eye-to-eye with the Emergent. 'The park is closed for maintenance, Podmaster.'

Brughel gave a tiny flinch of surprise. For a second he was silent, his pale pink skin darkening in the most comical way. 'You insolent little . . . so what are *you* doing here?'

'I'm doing the maintenance.' Well, that was at least cousin to the truth. Now counterattack: 'And what are you doing here?'

Brughel's face got even darker. He pulled himself upward, his head ten centimeters above Qiwi's. Now his feet floated on air, too. 'Scum have no business questioning me.' He was carrying that silly steel baton. It was a plain metal dowel incised here and there with dark-stained dings. He braced himself with one hand and swung the baton through a glittering arc that splintered the sapling beside Qiwi's head.

Now Qiwi was getting angry, too. She grabbed one of the lower branches, hoisted herself so that she and Brughel were eye-to-eye once more. 'That's vandalism, not an explanation.' She knew that Tomas had the park monitored – and vandalism was at least the crime for Emergents that it was for Qeng Ho.

The Podmaster was so angry that he had trouble talking. 'You're the vandals. This park was beautiful, more than I thought scum could ever make. But now you're sabotaging it. I was in here yesterday – you've infected it with vermin.' He swung the metal dowel again, the blow dislodging a garbage web that was hidden in the branches. The web creatures floated off in all directions, silken glides streaming behind them. Brughel poked at the web, shaking beetle casings and dead leaves and miscellaneous detritus into a cloud around them. 'See? What else are you poisoning?' He leaned close, looking down at her from above.

For a moment Qiwi just stared, uncomprehending. He couldn't possibly mean what he was saying. How could anyone be so ignorant? *But remember, he's a Chump.* She pulled herself high enough to look down at Brughel, and shouted into his face. 'It's a zero-gee park, for God's sake! What do you think keeps the air clean of floating crap? The garbage bugs have always been here . . . though maybe they're a little overworked just now.' She hadn't meant it quite the way it came out, but now she looked the Podmaster up and down as though she had one particularly large piece of garbage in mind.

They were above the lower leaf canopies now. From the corner of her eye, Qiwi could see Papa. The sky was limitless blue, guarded by an occasional branch. She could feel the fake sunlight hot on the back of her head. If they played a few more rounds of one-up-one-up, they'd be banging their heads on plastic. Qiwi started laughing.

And now Brughel was silent, just staring at her. He slapped his steel baton into his palm again and again. There were rumors about those dark stains in the metal; it was obvious what Ritser Brughel wanted people to think they were. But the guy just didn't carry himself like a fighter. And when he swung that baton, it was as though he had never considered the possibility that there might be targets that could fight back. Just now, his only hold-on was the toe of one boot hooked between branches. Qiwi braced herself unobtrusively and smiled her most insolent smile.

Brughel was motionless for a second. His gaze flicked to either side of her. And then without another word he pushed off, floundered for a moment, found a branch, and dived for the bottom-level hatch.

Qiwi floated silent, the strangest feelings chasing up her body, down her arms. For a moment she couldn't identify them. But the park . . . how wonderful it was with Ritser Brughel gone! She could hear the little buzzing sounds and the butterflies, where a moment before all her attention had tunneled down on the Podmaster's anger. And now she recognized the tingling in her arms, and the racing of her heart: rage and fear.

Qiwi Lin Lisolet had teased and enraged her share of people. It had been almost her hobby in pre-Flight. Mama said it was mind-hidden anger at the thought of being alone between the stars. Maybe. But it had also been fun. This was different.

She turned back toward her father's nest in the trees. And plenty of people had been angry with her over the years. Back in innocent times, Ezr Vinh used to get near apoplectic. *Poor Ezr, I wish* . . . But this today had been different. She had seen the difference in Ritser Brughel's eyes. The man had really wanted to kill her, had teetered on the edge of trying. And probably the only thing that stopped him was the thought that Tomas would know. But if Brughel could ever get her alone, unseen by the security monitors . . .

Qiwi's hands were shaking by the time she reached Ali Lin. Papa. She wanted so much to be held, to have him soothe the shaking. Ali Lin wasn't even looking at her. Papa had been Focused for several years now, but Qiwi could remember the times before so well. Before . . . Papa would have rushed out of the trees at the first sound of argument below. He would have put himself between Qiwi and Brughel, steel club or no. Now . . . Qiwi didn't remember much of the last few moments except for Ritser Brughel. But there were fragments: Ali had sat unmoved among his displays and analytics. He had heard the argument, even glanced their way when the shouting became loud and close. His look had been impatient, a 'don't-distract-me' dismissal.

Qiwi reached out a still-shaking hand to touch his shoulder. He shrugged the way you might shoo off a pesky bug. In some ways Papa still lived, but in others he seemed more dead than Mama. Tomas said that Focus could be reversed. But Tomas needed Papa and the other Focused the way they were now. Besides, Tomas had been raised an Emergent. They used Focus to make people into property. They were *proud* of doing so. Qiwi knew that there were plenty of Qeng Ho survivors who considered all the talk of 'reversal of Focus' to be a lie. So far, not a single Focused person had been reversed. *Tomas wouldn't lie about something so important.*

And maybe if she and Papa did well enough, she could get him back the sooner. For this wasn't a death that went on forever. She slipped into her seat beside him and resumed looking at the new diffs. The processors had given her the beginning of results while she was off trading insults with Ritser Brughel.

Papa would be pleased.

Nau still met with the Fleet Management Committee every Msec or so. Of course, just who attended changed substantially from Watch to Watch. Ezr Vinh was present today; it would be very interesting to see the boy's reaction to the surprise he had planned. And Ritser Brughel was attending, so he had asked Qiwi to stay away. Nau smiled to himself. *Damn, I never guessed how thoroughly she could humiliate the man.*

Nau had combined the committee with his own Emergent staff meetings and called them 'Watch-manager' meetings. The point was always that whatever their old differences, they were all in this together how and survival could only come through cooperation. The meetings were not as meaningful as Nau's private consults with Anne Reynolt or his work with Ritser and the security people. *Those* often occurred between the regular Watches. Still, it wasn't a lie to say that important work was done at these per-Msec meetings. Nau flicked his hand at the agenda. 'So. Our last item: Anne Reynolt's expedition to the sun. Anne?'

Anne didn't smile as she corrected him. 'The astrophysicists' report, Podmaster. But first, I have a complaint. We need at least one unFocused specialist in this area. You know how hard it is to judge technical results . . .'

Nau sighed. She had been after him about this in private, too. 'Anne, we don't have the resources. We have just three surviving specialists in this area.' And they were all zip-heads.

'I still need a reviewer with common sense.' She shrugged. 'Very well. Per your direction, we have run two of the astrophysicists on a continuous Watch since before the Relight. Keep in mind, they've had five years to think about this report.' Reynolt waved at the air, and they were looking out on a modified Qeng Ho taxi. Auxiliary fuel tanks were strapped on every side, and the front was a forest of sensor gear. A silver shield-sail was propped on a rickety framework from one side of the craft. 'Right before the Relight, Doctors Li and Wen flew this vehicle into low orbit around OnOff.' A second window showed the descent path, and a final orbit scarcely five hundred kilometers above the surface of the OnOff star. 'By keeping the sail properly oriented, they safely flew at that altitude for more than a day.'

Actually it was Jau Xin's pilot-zipheads who had done the flying. Nau nodded at Xin. 'That was good work, Pilot Manager.'

Xin grinned. 'Thank you, sir. Something to tell my children about.'

Reynolt ignored the comment. She popped up multiple windows, showing low-altitude views in various spectral regimes. 'We've had a hard time with the analysis right from the beginning.'

They could hear the recorded voices of the two zipheads now. Li was Emergent-bred, but the other voice spoke in a Qeng Ho dialect. That must be Wen: 'We've always known OnOff has the mass and density of a normal G star. Now we can make high-resolution maps of the interior temperatures and dens—' Dr Li butted in with the typical urgency of a ziphead, '—but we need more microsats . . . Resources be damned. We need two hundred at least, right through the time of Relighting.'

Reynolt paused the audio. 'We got them one hundred microsats.' More windows popped up, Li and Wen back at Hammerfest after the Relight, arguing and arguing. Reynolt's reports were often like this, a barrage of pictures and tables and sound bites.

Wen was talking again. He sounded tired. 'Even in Off-state, the central densities were typical of a G star, yet there was no collapse. The surface turbulence is barely ten thousand kilometers deep. How? How? How?'

Li: 'And after Relight, the deep internal structure looks still the same.'

'We can't know for sure; we can't get close.'

'No, it looks perfectly typical now. We have models . . .'

Wen's voice changed again. He was speaking faster, in a tone of frustration, almost pain. 'All this data, and we have just the same mysteries as before. I've spent five years now studying reaction paths, and I'm as clueless as the Dawn Age astronomers. There *has* to be something going on in the extended core, or else there would be a collapse.'

The other ziphead sounded petulant. 'Obviously, even in Off state the star is still radiating, but radiating something that converts to low-interaction.'

'But what? What? And if there could be such a thing, why don't the higher layers collapse?'

'Cuz the conversion is at the base of the photosphere, and that *is* collapsed! Ryop, I'm using your own modeling software to show this!'

'No. Post hoc nonsense, no better than ages past.'

'But I've got *data*!'

'So? Your adiabats are—'

Reynolt cut the audio. 'They went on like this for many days. Most of it is a private jargon, the sort of things a close-bound Focused pair often invents.'

Nau straightened in his chair. 'If they can only talk to each other, we have no access. Did you lose them?'

'No. At least not in the usual way. Dr Wen became so frustrated that he began to consider random externalities. In a normal person that might lead to creativity but—'

Brughel laughed, genuinely amused. 'So your astronomer laddie lost sight of the ball, eh, Reynolt?'

Reynolt didn't even look at Brughel. 'Be silent,' she said. Nau noticed the Peddlers' startlement at her words. Ritser was second-in-command, the obvious sadist among the rulers – and here she had abruptly put him down. *I wonder when the Peddlers will figure it out.* A scowl passed briefly across Brughel's features. Then his grin broadened. He settled back in his chair and flicked an amused glance in Nau's direction. Anne continued without missing a beat: 'Wen backed off from the problem, setting it in a wider and wider context. At first, there was some relevance.'

Wen's voice resumed, the same rushed monotone as before. 'OnOff's galactic orbit. A clue.' The presumptive graph of OnOff's galactic orbit – assuming no close stellar encounters – flashed in a window. Anne was dredging from the fellow's notebooks. The plot extended back over half a billion years. It was the typical flower-petal figure of a halo-population star: Once every two hundred million years, OnOff penetrated the hidden heart of the galaxy. From there, it swung out and out till the stars spread thin and the intergalactic dark began. Tomas Nau was no astronomer, but he knew that halo-pop stars don't have usable planetary systems, and as a result aren't often visited. But surely that was the least of the strangeness of OnOff.

Somehow the Qeng Ho ziphead had become totally fixated on the star's galactic orbit. 'This thing – it can't be a star – has seen the Heart of All. Again and again and again—' Reynolt skipped through what must have been a long, trapped loop in poor Wen's thinking. The ziphead's voice was momentarily calmer: 'Clues. There are lots of clues, really. Forget the physics; just consider the light curve. For two hundred and fifteen years out of two hundred and fifty, it radiates less perceptible energy than a brown dwarf.' The windows accompanying Wen's thoughts flickered from idea to idea, pictures of brown dwarfs, the much more rapid oscillations that the physicists had extrapolated for OnOff's distant past. 'Things are happening that we can't see. Relight, a light curve vaguely like a periodic Q-nova, settling over a few Msecs to a spectrum that might almost be an explainable star riding a fusion core. And then the light slowly fades back to zero . . . or changes into something else we cannot see. It's not a star at all! It's magic. A magic machine that now is broken. I'll bet it was a fast square-wave generator once. That's it! Magic from the heart of the galaxy, broken now so that we can't understand it.'

The audio abruptly ended, and Wen's kaleidoscope of windows was fixed in mid-frenzy. 'Dr Wen has been thoroughly trapped in this cycle of ideas for ten Msec,' said Reynolt.

Nau already knew where this was going, but he put on a concerned look anyway. 'What are we left with?'

'Dr Li is doing okay. He was slipping into his own contrarian cycle till we separated him from Wen. But now – well, he's fixated on the Qeng Ho system identification software. He has an enormously complex model that matches all the observations.' More pictures, Li's theory of a new family of subatomic particles. 'Dr Li is spreading into the cognitive territory that Hunte Wen monopolized, but he's getting very different results.'

Li's voice: 'Yes. Yes! My model predicts stars like this must be common very near the galaxy's hole. Very very rarely, they interact, a strongly coupled explosion. The result gets kicked high out of the core.' Of course, Li's trajectory was identical to Wen's after the presumed explosion. 'I can fit all the parameters. We can't see blinking stars in the dust of the core; they're not bright and they're very high-rate. But once in a billion years we get this asymmetrical destruction, and an ejection.' Pictures of the hypothetical explosion of OnOff's hypothetical destroyer. Pictures of OnOff's original solar system blown away – all except a tiny protected shadow on the far side of OnOff from the destroyer.

Ezr Vinh leaned forward. 'Lord, he's explained just about everything.'

'Yes,' said Nau. 'Even the singleton nature of the planetary system.' He turned away from the jumble of windows, and looked at Anne. 'So what do you think?'

Reynolt shrugged. 'Who knows? That's why we need an unFocused specialist, Podmaster. Dr Li is spreading his net wider and wider. That can be a symptom of a classic, explain-everything trap. And his particle theory is large; it may be a Shannon tautology.' She paused. Anne Reynolt was totally incapable of showmanship. Nau had arranged his questions so her bombshell came out last: 'That particle theory is in his central specialty, however. And it has consequences, perhaps a faster ramscoop drive.'

No one said anything for several seconds. The Qeng Ho had been diddling their drives for thousands of years, since before Pham Nuwen even. They had stolen insights from hundreds of civilizations. In the last thousand years, they'd made less than a one-percent improvement. 'Well, well, well.' Tomas Nau knew how good it felt to gamble big . . . and win. Even the Peddlers were grinning like idiots. He let the good feeling pass back and forth around the room. It was very *very* good news, even if the payoff was at the end of the Exile. 'This does make our astrophysicists a precious commodity. Can you do anything about Wen?'

'Hunte Wen is not recoverable, I'm afraid.' She opened a window on medical imagery. To a Qeng Ho physician it might have looked like a simple brain diagnostic. To Anne Reynolt, it was a strategy map. 'See, the connectivity here and here is associated with his work on OnOff; I've demonstrated that by detuning some of it. If we try to back him out of his fixation, we'll wipe his work of the last five years – as well as cross connections into much of his general expertise. Remember. Focus surgery is mainly grope and peek, with resolution not much better than a millimeter.'

'So we'd end up with a vegetable?'

'No. If we back out and undo the Focus, he'll have the personality and most of the memories of before. He just won't be much of a physicist anymore.'

'Hmm,' said Nau, considering. So they couldn't just deFocus the Peddler and have the outside expert Reynolt needed. *And I'll be damned if I'll risk deFocusing the third fellow.* Yet there was a very tidy solution, that still made good use of all three men. 'Okay, Anne. Here is what I propose. Bring the other physicist online, but on a low duty cycle. Keep Dr Li in the freezer while the new fellow reviews Li's results. This won't be as good as an unFocused review, but if you do it cleverly the results should be pretty unbiased.'

Another shrug. Reynolt had no false modesty, but she also didn't realize how very good she was.

'As for Hunte Wen,' Nau continued. 'He's done his best for us, and we can't ask for more.' Literally so, according to Anne. 'I want you to deFocus him.'

Ezr Vinh was staring, openmouthed. The other Peddlers looked almost as shocked. There was a small risk here; Hunte Wen would not be the best proof that Focus could be reversed. On the other hand, he was obviously a hardship case. *Show your concern:* 'We've run Dr Wen for more than five years straight, and I see he is already middle-aged. Use whatever medical consumables it takes to give him the best health possible.'

It was the final agenda item, and the meeting didn't continue for long after that. Nau watched as everyone floated out, jabbering to one another their enthusiasm about Li's discovery and Wen's manumission. Ezr Vinh left last, but he wasn't talking to anyone. The boy had a glassy look about him. *Yes, Mr Vinh. Be good, and maybe someday I'll free the one you care about.*

16

Things got very quiet during the Tween Watch. Most Watches were multiples of an Msec, with overlap so people could brief the new Watch on current problems. The Tween was no secret, but Nau officially treated it as a glitch in the scheduling program, a four-day gap that appeared between Watches every so often. In fact, it was like the missing seventh floor, or that mythical magic day that comes between Oneday and Twoday.

'Say, wouldn't it be great to have Tween Watches back home?' Brughel joked as he led Nau and Kal Omo into the corpsicle stacks. 'I did security at Frenk for five years – it sure would have been easier if I could have declared time out every so often, and rearranged the game to suit my needs.' His voice sounded loud in the hold, the echoes coming back from several directions. In fact, they were the only ones awake aboard the *Suivire*. Down on Hammerfest, there was Reynolt and a contingent of waking zipheads. A skeleton crew of Emergents and Peddlers – including Qiwi Lisolet – were working the stabilization jets on the rockpile. But, zipheads aside, only nine people knew the hardest secrets. And here between Watches, they could do all that was necessary to protect the pod.

The interior walls of the *Suivire*'s coldsleep hold had been knocked out, and dozens of additional coffins installed. All of Watch A slept here, almost seven hundred people. Watch trees B and Misc were on the *Brisgo Gap*, while C and D were aboard the *Common Good*. But it was A's Watch that began after this Tween time.

A red light appeared on the wall; the hold's stand-alone data system was ready to talk. Nau put on his huds, and suddenly the caskets were labeled by name and affiliation. Everything looked green. *Thank goodness.* Nau turned to his podsergeant. Kal Omo's name, status, and vital signs floated in the air beside his face; the data system took its duties very literally. 'Anne's medical people will be here in a few thousand seconds, Kal. Don't let them in till Ritser and I are finished.'

'Yes, sir.' There was a faint smile on the man's face as he turned and coasted out the door. Kal Omo had been through this before; he'd helped create the hoax aboard the *Far Treasure*. He knew what to expect.

And then he and Ritser Brughel were alone. 'Okay, have you found any more bad apples, Ritser?'

Ritser was grinning; he had some surprise planned. They drifted past racks of coffins, the room light shining up from beneath their feet. The coffins had been through hell, yet they still worked reliably – the Qeng Ho ones, anyway. The Peddlers were clever; they broadcast technology throughout Human Space – yet their own goods were better than what they shouted free to the stars. *But now we have a fleet library . . . and people to make sense of it.*

'I've been running my snoops hard, Podmaster. Watch A is pretty clean, though—' He paused and stopped his coast with a hand against the rack. The slender railings flexed along the length of the rack; this really was an ad hoc setup. '—though I don't know why you put up with seditious deadwood like this.' He tapped one of the coffins with his pod-master's baton.

The Peddler coffins had wide, curved windows, and an internal light. Even without the display label, Nau would have recognized Pham Trinli. Somehow, the guy looked younger when his face was inanimate.

Ritser must have taken his silence for indecision. 'He knew about Diem's plot.'

Nau shrugged. 'Of course. So did Vinh. So did a few others. And now they're known quantities.'

'But—'

'Remember, Ritser, we agreed. We can't afford any more casual wetwork.' His biggest mistake of this whole adventure had been in the field interrogations after the ambush. Nau had followed the disaster-management strategies of the Plague Time, the hard strategies that were shrouded from the view of ordinary citizens. But the First Podmasters had been in a very different situation; they'd had plenty of human resources. In this situation . . . well, for the Qeng Ho who could be Focused, interrogation was no problem. But the others were amazingly tough. Worst of all, they didn't respond to threats in a rational way. Ritser had gotten a little crazy, and Tomas hadn't been far behind. They had killed the last of the senior Peddlers before they really understood the other side's psychology. All in all, it had been quite a debacle, but it had also been a maturing experience. Tomas had learned how to deal with the survivors.

Ritser smiled. 'Okay. At least he's good for comic relief. The way he tries to suck up to you and me – and pompous at the same time!' He waved at the racked corpsicles. 'Sure. Wake 'em all per schedule. We've had to explain too many "accidents" as it is.' He turned back toward Nau. He still wore a smile, but the bottom light made it look like the grimace it really was. 'The real problem isn't with Watch A. Podmaster, in the last four days, I've discovered clear subversion elsewhere.'

Nau stared at him with an expression of mild surprise. This was what he'd been waiting for. 'Qiwi Lisolet?'

'Yes! Wait, I know you saw the face-off I had with her the other day. The pus-sucker deserves to die for that – but that's not my complaint to you. I have solid evidence she's breaking Your Law. And she is in league with others.'

Nau actually was a bit surprised by this. 'In what way?'

'You know I caught her in the Peddlers' park with her father. She had shut the park down on her own whim. That's what made me so angry. But afterwards . . . I put my snoops on her. Random monitoring might not have noticed it for several more Watches: the little slut is diverting the pod's resources. She's stolen output from the volatiles distillery. She's embezzled time from the factory. She's diverted her father's Focus to help her with private ventures.'

Pestilence. This was more than Qiwi had told him about. 'So . . . what is she doing with these resources?'

'These resources and others, Podmaster. She has a variety of plans. And she is not alone . . . intends to barter these stolen goods for her own advancement.'

For a moment, Nau couldn't think of what to say. Of course, bartering community resources was a crime. During most of the Plague Years, more people had been executed for barter and hoarding than had died of the Plague itself. But in modern times . . . well, barter could never be totally eliminated. On Balacrea, it was periodically the excuse for major exterminations – but only that, an excuse. 'Ritser.' Nau spoke carefully, lying: 'I knew about all these activities. Certainly they are against the letter of My Law. But consider. We are twenty light-years from home. We are dealing with the Qeng Ho. They really *are* peddlers. I know it is hard to accept, but their whole existence revolves around cheating the community. We cannot hope to suppress that in an instant—'

'*No!*' Brughel pushed off the rack he had been holding, grabbed the railing next to Tomas. 'They are all scum, but it is only Lisolet and a few aggravant conspirators – and I can tell you just who they are – who are violating Your Law!'

Nau could imagine how all this happened. Qiwi Lin Lisolet had never obeyed rules, even among the Qeng Ho. Her crazy mother had set her up to be manipulated, but even so the girl was beyond direct control. More that anything, she loved to play. Qiwi had once said to him, 'It's always easier to get forgiveness than to get permission.' As much as anything, that simple claim showed the gulf that separated Qiwi's worldview from the First Podmasters'.

It took an effort of will not to retreat before Brughel's advance. *What's gotten into him?* He looked straight into the other's eyes, ignoring the baton in Ritser's twitching hand. 'I'm sure you could identify them. That's your job, VicePodmaster. And part of my job is to interpret My Law. You know that Qiwi never shook off the mindrot; if necessary, she can be easily . . . curbed. I want you to keep me informed of these possible infractions, but for now I choose to wink at them.'

'You choose to wink at them? You *choose*? I—' Brughel was wordless for a second. When he continued, his voice was more controlled, a metered rage. 'Yes, we're twenty light-years from home. We're twenty light-years from your family. And your uncle doesn't rule anymore.' The word of Alan Nau's assassination had arrived while their expedition was still three years out of the OnOff system. 'At home maybe you could break any rule, protect lawbreakers simply because they were a good lay.' He slapped his baton gently against his palm. 'Out here, and right now, you're very alone.'

Lethal force between Podmasters was beyond any law. That was a principle dating back to the Plague Years – but it was also a basic truth of nature. If Brughel were to smash his skull now, Kal Omo would follow the Vice-Podmaster. But Nau just spoke quietly. 'You are even more alone, my friend. How many of the Focused are imprinted on you?'

'I – I have Xin's pilots, I have the snoops. I could make Reynolt redirect whatever else I need.'

Ritser was teetering at the edge of an abyss that Tomas hadn't noticed before, but at least he was calming down. 'I think you understand Anne better than that, Ritser.'

And abruptly the killing flame in Brughel was quenched. 'Yeah, you're right. You're right.' He seemed to crumple. 'Sir . . . it's just that this mission has turned out so different from what I imagined. We had the resources to live like High Podmasters here. We had the prospect of finding a treasure world. Now most of our zipheads are dead. We don't have the equipment for a safe return. We're stuck here for decades . . .'

Ritser seemed on the verge of tears. The passage from threat to weakness was fascinating. Tomas spoke quietly, his tone comforting. 'I understand, Ritser. We are in a more extreme situation than anyone has been in since the Plagues. If this is painful to one as strong as you, I am very afraid for ordinary crew of the mission.' All true, though most of the crew had much less remarkable personalities than Ritser Brughel. Like Ritser, they were caught in a decades-long cul-de-sac in which family and children-raising were not an option. That was a dangerous problem, one that he must not overlook. But most of the ordinary folk would have no-trouble continuing relationships, finding new ones; there were almost a thousand unFocused people here. Ritser's drives would be harder to satisfy. Ritser used people up, and now there were scarcely any left for him.

'But there is still the prospect of treasure – perhaps all that we hoped for. Taking the Qeng Ho nearly cost us our lives, but now we are learning their secrets. And you were at the last Watch-manager meeting: we've discovered physics that is new even to the Qeng Ho. The best is yet to come, Ritser. The Spiders are primitive now, but life could scarcely have originated here; this solar system is just too extreme. We aren't the first species that has come snooping. Imagine, Ritser: a nonhuman, starfaring civilization. Its secrets are down there, somewhere in the ruins of their past.'

He guided his Vice-Podmaster around the far end of the coffin racks, and they started back along the second aisle. The head-up display reported green everywhere, though as usual the Emergent coffins were showing high wear. Sigh. In a few years, they might not have enough usable coffins to maintain a comfortable Watch schedule. By itself, a star fleet could not build another fleet, or even keep itself indefinitely provisioned with high-tech supplies. It was an old, old problem: to build the most advanced technological products you need an entire civilization – a civilization with all its webs of expertise and layers of capital industry. There were no shortcuts; Humankind had often imagined, but never created, a general assembler.

Ritser seemed calmer now, his desperate anger replaced by thought. '. . . Okay. We sacrifice a lot, but in the end we go home winners. I can gut it out as well as any. But still . . . why should it take so pus long? We should land squat on some Spider kingdom and take over—'

'They've just reinvented electronics, Ritser. We need more—'

The Vice-Podmaster shook his head impatiently. 'Yes, yes. Of course. We need a solid industrial base. I probably know that better than you; I was Podmaster at the Lorbita Shipyards. Nothing short of a major rebuild is going to save our ass. But there's still no reason for hiding here at L1. If we take over some Spider nation – maybe just pretend to ally with it – we could speed things up.'

'True, but the real problem is maintaining control. For that, timing is everything. You know I was in on the conquest of Gaspr. The early postconquest, actually; if I'd been with the first fleet, I'd own millions now.' Nau didn't keep the envy from his voice; it was a vision that Brughel would understand. Gaspr had been a jackpot. 'Lord, what that first fleet did. It was just two ships, Ritser! Imagine. They had only five hundred zipheads – fewer than we have. But they sat and lurked and when Gaspr reattained the Information Age, they controlled every data system on the planet. The treasure just fell into their hands!' Nau shook his head, dismissing the vision. 'Yes. We could try to take the Spiders now. It might speed things up. But it would be largely bluff on our part, against aliens that we don't understand. If we miscalculated, if we got into a guerrilla war, we could piss away everything very quickly . . . We'd probably "win," but a thirty-year wait might become five hundred. There's precedent for that sort of failure, Ritser, though it doesn't come from our Plague Time. Do you know the story of Canberra?'

Brughel shrugged. Canberra might be the most powerful civilization in Human Space, but it was too far away to interest him. Like many Emergents, Brughel's interest in the wider universe was minimal.

'Three thousand years ago, Canberra was medieval. Like Gaspr, the original colony had bombed itself into total savagery, except that the Canberrans weren't even halfway back. A small Qeng Ho fleet voyaged there; through some crazy mistake, they thought the Canberrans still had a profitable civilization. That was the Peddlers' first big mistake. The second was in hanging around; they tried to trade with the Canberrans as they were. The Qeng Ho had all the power, they could make the primitive societies of Canberra do whatever they wanted.'

Brughel grunted. 'I see where this is going. But the locals sound a lot more primitive than what we have here.'

'Yes, but they were human. And the Qeng Ho had much better resources. Anyway, they made their alliances. They pushed the local technology as hard as they could. They set out to conquer the world. And actually, they succeeded. But every step ground them down. The original crew lived their old age in stone castles. They didn't even have coldsleep anymore. The hybrid civilization of Peddlers and locals eventually became very advanced and powerful – but that was too late for the originals.'

The Podmaster and his Vice were almost back to the main entrance. Brughel floated ahead, turning slowly so that he touched the wall like a deck, feetfirst. He looked up at the approaching Nau with an intent expression.

Nau touched down, let the grabfelt in his boots stop his rebound. 'Think about what I've said, Ritser. Our Exile here is really necessary, and the payoff is as great as you ever imagined. In the meantime, let's work on what's bothering you. A Podmaster should not have to suffer.'

The look on the younger man's face was surprised and grateful. 'Th-thank you, sir. A little help now and then is all I need.' They talked a few moments more, setting up the necessary compromises.

Coming back from the *Suivire*, Tomas had some time to think. From his taxi, the rockpile was a glittering jumble ahead of him, the sky around it speckled with the irregular shapes of the temps and warehouses and starships that orbited the pile. Here at Tween Watch he saw no evidence of human movement. Even Qiwi's crews were out of sight, probably on the shade side of the pile. Far beyond the diamond mountains, Arachna floated in glorious isolation. Its great ocean showed patches of cloudlessness today. The tropical convergence zone was clear against the blue. More and more, the Spider world was looking like archetype Mother Earth, the one-in-a-thousand world where humans could land and thrive. It would continue to look like paradise for another thirty years or so – till once more its sun guttered out. *And by then we will own it.*

Just now, he had made that ultimate success a little more likely. He had solved a mystery and defused an unnecessary risk. Tomas's mouth twisted in an unhappy smile. Ritser was quite wrong to think that being Alan Nau's first nephew was *easy*. True, Alan Nau had favored Tomas. It was clear from the beginning that Tomas would continue the Nau dominance of the Emergency. That was part of the problem, for it made Tomas a great threat to the elder Nau. Succession – even within Podmaster families – was most often by assassination. Yet Alan Nau had been clever. He did want his nephew to carry on the line – but only after Alan had lived and ruled as long as natural life would sustain him. Giving Tomas Nau command of the expedition to the OnOff star was a piece of statecraft that saved both ruler and heir apparent. Tomas Nau would be off the world stage for more than two centuries. When he returned, it could well be with the resources to continue the Nau family's rule.

Tomas had often wondered if Ritser Brughel might be a subtle kind of sabotage. Back home, the fellow had seemed a good choice for Vice-Podmaster. He was young, and he'd done a solid job cleaning up the Lorbita Shipyards. He was of Frenkisch stock; his parents had been two of the first supporters of Alan Nau's invasion. As much as possible, the Emergency tried to transform each new conquest with the same stresses that the Plague Time had wrought upon Balacrea: the megadeaths, the mindrot, the establishment of the Podmaster class. Young Ritser had adapted to every demand of the new order.

But since they began this Exile, he'd been a pus-be-damned screwup: careless, slovenly, almost insolent. Part of that was his assigned role as Heavy, but Ritser wasn't acting. He had become closed and uncooperative. There was the obvious conclusion: The Nau family's enemies were clever, long-planning people. Maybe, somehow, they had slipped a ringer past Uncle Alan's security.

Today, the mystery and the suspicions had collided. *And I find not sabotage, nor even incompetence.* His VicePodmaster simply had certain frustrated needs, and had been too proud to talk about them. Back in civilization, satisfying those needs would have been easy; such was a normal, if unpublicized, part of every Podmaster's birthright. Here in the wilderness, all but shipwrecked . . . here Ritser faced some real hardship.

The taxi ghosted over the topmost spires of Hammerfest, and settled into the shadows below.

Satisfying Brughel would be difficult; the younger man would have to show some real restraint. Tomas was already reviewing the crew and ziphead rosters. *Yes, I can make this work.* And it would be worth it. Ritser Brughel was the only other Podmaster within twenty light-years. The Podmaster class was often deadly within itself, but there was a bond among them. Every one of them knew the hidden, hard strategies. Every one of them understood the true virtues of the Emergency. Ritser was young, still growing into himself. If the proper relationship could be established, other problems would be more tractable.

And their ultimate success might be even greater than what he told Ritser. It could be greater than Uncle Alan had imagined. It was a vision that might have eluded Tomas himself, if not for this firsthand meeting with the Peddlers.

Uncle Alan had had a respect for far threats; he had continued the

Balacrean traditions of emission security. But even Uncle Alan never seemed to realize that they were playing tyrant over a laughably tiny pond: Balacrea, Frenk, Gaspr. Nau had just told Ritser Brughel about the founding of Canberra. There were better examples he could have used, but Canberra was a favorite of Tomas Nau's. While his peers studied Emergency history to death, and added trivial nuances to the strategies, Tomas Nau studied the histories of Human Space. Even a disaster like the Plague Time was a commonplace in the larger scheme of things. The conquerors in the histories dwarfed the Balacrean stage. So Tomas Nau was familiar with a thousand faraway Strategists, from Alexander of Macedon to Tarf Lu . . . to Pham Nuwen. Of them all, Pham Nuwen was Nau's central model, the greatest of the Qeng Ho.

In a sense, Nuwen created the modern Qeng Ho. The Peddler broadcasts described Nuwen's life in some detail, but they were sugar-coated. There were other versions, contradictory whispers between the stars. Every aspect of his life was worth study. Pham Nuwen had been born on Canberra just before the Qeng Ho landing. The child Nuwen had come into the Qeng Ho from outside . . . and transformed it. For a few centuries he drove the Peddlers to empire, the greatest empire known. He had been an Alexander to all Human Space. And – as with Alexander – his empire had not lasted.

The man had been a genius of conquest and organization. He simply did not have all the necessary tools.

Nau took a last look at the sky-blue beauty of Arachna as it slipped behind Hammerfest's towers. He had a dream now. So far, it was a dream he admitted only to himself. In a few years he would conquer a nonhuman race, a race that had once flown between the stars. In a few years he would plumb the deepest secrets of the Qeng Ho fleet automation. With all that, he might be the equal of Pham Nuwen. With all that, he might make a star empire. But Tomas Nau's dream went further, for he already had a tool of empire that Pham Nuwen and Tarf Lu and all the others had lacked. *Focus.*

The fulfillment of his dream was half a lifetime away, on the other side of the Exile and deadliness he might not yet imagine. Sometimes he wondered if he was crazy to think he could get there. Ah, but the dream burned so bright in his mind:

With Focus, Tomas Nau might hold what he could grasp. Tomas Nau's Emergency would become a single empire across all Human Space. And it would be the one that lasted.

17

Officially, of course, Benny Wen's booze parlor did not exist. Benny had grabbed some empty utility space between the inner balloons. Working in their free time, he and his father had gradually populated it with furniture, a zero-pool game, video wallpaper. You could still see the utility piping on the walls, but even that was covered with colored tape.

When his tree had the Watch, Pham Trinli spent most of his free time loafing here. And there had been more free time since he botched the L1 stabilization and Qiwi Lisolet took over.

The aroma of hops and barley hit Pham the moment he got past the door. A cluster of beery droplets drifted close by his ear, then zigged into the cleaning vent by the door.

'Hey, Pham, where the hell have you been? Grab a seat.' His usual cronies were mostly sitting on the ceiling side of the game room. Pham gave them a wave and glided across the room to take a seat on the outer wall. It meant he was facing sideways from the others, but there wasn't that much room here.

Trud Silipan waved across the room at where Benny floated by the bar. 'Where's the beer and frids, Benny boy? Hey, and add on a big one for the military genius here!'

Everyone laughed, though Pham's response was more an indignant snort. He'd worked hard to be the bluff blowhard. Want to hear a tale of derring-do? Just listen to Pham Trinli for more than a hundred seconds. Of course, if you had any real-world experience yourself, you'd see the stories were mostly fraud – and where they were not, the heroic parts belonged to somebody else. He looked around the room. As usual, more than half the clientele were Follower-class Emergents, but most of the groups contained one or two Qeng Ho. It was more than six years since Relight, since the 'Diem atrocity.' For many of them, that was almost two years of lifetime. The surviving Qeng Ho had learned and adapted. They weren't exactly assimilated, but like Pham Trinli, they had become an integral part of the Exile.

Hunte Wen drifted across the room from the bar. He towed a net full of drink bulbs, and the snack food that was the most he and Benny risked importing to the parlor. Talk lulled for a moment as he passed the goods around, picked up favor scrip in return.

Pham snagged a bulb of the brew. The container was new plastic. Benny had some kind of in with the crews that ran surface operations on the rockpile. The little volatiles plant gulped in airsnow and water ice and ground diamond . . . and out came raw stocks, including the plastics for drinking bulbs, furniture, the zero-gee pool game. Even the parlor's chief attraction was the product of the rockpile – touched by the magic of the temp's bactry.

This bulb had a colored drawing on the side: DIAMOND AND ICE BREWERY, it said, and there was a picture of the rockpile being dissolved into suds. The picture was an intricate thing, evidently from a hand-drawn original. Pham stared at the clever drawing for a moment. He swallowed his wondering questions. In any case, others would ask them . . . in their own way.

There was a flurry of laughter as Trud and his friends noticed the pictures. 'Hey, Hunte, did you do this?'

The elder Wen smiled shyly and nodded.

'Hey, it's kinda cute. Not like what a Focused artist could do, of course.'

'I thought you were some kind of physicist, before you got your freedom?'

'An astrophysicist. I – I don't remember much of that anymore. I'm trying new things.'

The Emergents chatted with Wen for several minutes. Most were friendly, and – except for Trud Silipan – seemed genuinely sympathetic. Pham had vague recollections of Hunte Wen before the ambush, impressions of an outspoken, good-natured academic. Well, the good nature remained. The fellow smiled a lot, but a bit too apologetically. His personality was like a ceramic vessel, once shattered, now painstakingly reassembled, functional but fragile.

Wen picked up the last of the payment scrip and drifted back across the room. He stopped halfway to the bar. He drifted close to the wallpaper, and looked out upon the rockpile and the sun. He seemed to have forgotten all of them, was caught once more by the mysteries of the OnOff star. Trud Silipan chuckled and leaned across the table toward Trinli. 'Driftier than hell, isn't he? Most de-zips aren't that bad.'

Benny Wen came from the bar and drew his father out of sight. Benny had been one of the firebreathers. He was probably the most obvious of Diem's conspirators to survive.

Talk returned to the important issues of the day. Jau Xin wanted to find someone in Watch tree A who was willing to trade into B; his lady was stuck on the other Watch. It was the sort of swap that had to be cleared by the Podmasters, but if everyone was willing . . . Someone else pointed out that some Qeng Ho woman down in Quartermaster was brokering such deals, in return for other favors. 'Damn Peddlers put a price on everything,' Silipan muttered.

And Trinli regaled them with a story – true actually, but with enough absurdities that they would know it false – about a Long Watch mission he allegedly commanded. 'Fifty years we spent with only four Watch groups. In the end I had to break the rules, allow children In Flight. But by that time, we had a market advantage—'

Pham was coming down on the punch line when Trud Silipan jabbed him in the ribs. 'Hsst! My Qeng Ho Lord, your nemesis has arrived.' That got a round of chuckles. Pham glared at Silipan, then turned to look.

Qiwi Lin Lisolet had just sailed through the parlor's doorway. She twisted in midair, and touched down by Benny Wen. There was a lull in the room noise and her voice carried to Trinli's group up by the ceiling.

'Benny! Have you got those swap forms? Gonle can cover—' Her words faded as the two moved to the far side of the bar and other conversations resumed. Qiwi was clearly in full haggle, twisting Benny's arm about some new deal.

'Is it true she's *still* in charge of stabilizing the rockpile? I thought that was your job, Pham.'

Jau Xin grimaced. 'Give it a rest, Trud.'

Pham raised a hand, the image of an irritated old man trying to look important. 'I told you before, I got promoted. Lisolet handles the field details, and I supervise the whole operation for Podmaster Nau.' He looked in Qiwi's direction, tried to put just the right truculence into his gaze. *I wonder what she's up to now.* The child was amazing.

From the corner of his eye, Pham saw Silipan shrug apologetically at Jau Xin. They all figured Pham was a fraud, but he was well liked. His tales might be tall, but they were very entertaining. The trouble with Trud Silipan was he didn't know when to stop goading. Now the fellow was probably trying to think of some way to make amends.

'Yes,' said Silipan, 'there aren't many of us who report directly to the Podmaster. And I'll tell you something about Qiwi Lin Lisolet.' He looked around to see just who else was in the parlor. 'You know I manage the zipheads for Reynolt – well, we provide support for Ritser Brughel's snoops. I talked to the boys over there. Our Miss Lisolet is on their hot list. She's involved in more scams than you can imagine.' He gestured at the furniture. 'Where do you think this plastic comes from? Now that she's got Pham's old job, she's down on the rockpile all the time. She's diverting production to people like Benny.'

One of the others waggled a Diamonds and Ice drink bulb at Silipan. 'You seem to be enjoying your share, Trud.'

'You know that's not the point. Look. These are community resources that she and the likes of Benny Wen are messing with.' There were solemn nods from around the table. 'Whatever accidental good it does, it's still theft from the common weal.' His eyes went hard. 'In the Plague Time there weren't many greater sins.'

'Yes, but the Podmasters know about it. It's not doing any great harm.'

Silipan nodded. 'True. They are tolerating it for now.' His smile turned sly. 'For maybe as long as she's sleeping with Podmaster Nau.' That was another rumor that had been going around.

'Look, Pham. You're Qeng Ho. But basically you're a military man. That's an honorable profession, and it sets you high, no matter what your origin. You see, there are moral levels to society.' Silipan was clearly lecturing from the received wisdom. 'At the top are the Podmasters, statesmen I guess you'd call them. Below that are the military leaders, and underneath the leaders are the staff planners, the technicians, and the armsmen. Underneath that . . . are vermin of different categories: fallen members of the useful categories, persons with a chance of fitting back in the system. And below them are the factory workers and farmers. And at the very bottom – combining the worst aspects of all the scum – are the peddlers.' Silipan smiled at Pham. Evidently he felt he was being flattering, that he had set Pham Trinli among the naturally noble. 'Traders are the eaters of dead and dying, too cowardly to steal by force.'

Even Trinli's cover persona should choke on this analysis. Pham blustered, 'I'll have you know the Qeng Ho has been in its present form for thousands of years, Silipan. That's hardly the mark of failure.'

Silipan smiled with cordial sympathy. 'I know it's hard to accept this, Trinli. You're a good man, and it's right to be loyal. But I think you're coming to understand. The peddlers will always be with us, whether they're selling unlicensed food in an alley or lurking between the stars. The stargoing ones call themselves a civilization, but they're just the rabble that hangs around the edges of true civilizations.'

Pham grunted. 'I don't think I've ever been flattered and insulted so much all at the same time.'

They all laughed, and Trud Silipan seemed to think his lecture had somehow cheered Trinli. Pham finished his little story without further interruption. Talk drifted on to speculation about Arachna's spider creatures. Ordinarily, Pham would soak up these stories with well-concealed enthusiasm. Today, his lack of attention was not an act. His gaze drifted back to the parlor's bar table. Benny and Qiwi were half out of sight now, arguing about some deal. Mixed in with all the Emergent insanity, Trud Silipan did have a few things right. Over the last couple of years, an underground had bloomed here. It wasn't the violent subversion of Jimmy Diem's conspiracy. In the minds of the Qeng Ho participants it wasn't a conspiracy at all, merely getting on with business. Benny and his father and dozens of others were routinely bending and even violating Podmaster dicta. So far Nau hadn't retaliated; so far, the Qeng Ho underground had improved the situation for almost everyone. Pham had seen this sort of thing happen once or twice before – when Qeng Ho couldn't trade as free human beings, and couldn't run, and couldn't fight.

Little Qiwi Lin Lisolet was at the center of it all. Pham's gaze rested on her wonderingly. For a moment, he forgot to glower. Qiwi had lost so much. By some standards of honor, she had sold out. Yet here she was, awake Watch on Watch, in a position to do deals in all directions. Pham bit back the fond smile he felt growing on his lips, and frowned at her. If Trud Silipan or Jau Xin ever knew how he really felt about Qiwi Lisolet, they would think him stark raving mad. If someone as clever as Tomas Nau ever understood, he might put two and two together – and that would be the end of Pham Trinli.

When Pham looked at Qiwi Lin Lisolet, he saw – more than he ever had before in his life – *himself*. True, Qiwi was female, and sexism was one of

Trinli's peculiarities that was not an act. But the similarities between them went deeper than gender. Qiwi had been – what, eight years old? – when she had started on this voyage. She had lived almost half her childhood in the dark between the stars, alone but for the fleet's maintenance Watches. And now she was plunged into a totally different culture. And still she survived, and faced up to every new challenge. And she was winning.

Pham's mind turned inward. He wasn't listening to his drinking buddies anymore. He wasn't even watching Qiwi Lin Lisolet. He was remembering a time more than three thousand years ago, across three centuries of his own lifetime.

Canberra. Pham had been thirteen, the youngest son of Tran Nuwen, King and Lord of all the Northland. Pham had grown up with swords and poison and intrigue, living in stone castles by a cold, cold sea. No doubt he would have ended up murdered – or king of all – if life had continued in the medieval way. But when he was thirteen everything changed. A world that had only legends of aircraft and radio was confronted by interstellar traders, the Qeng Ho. Pham still remembered the scorch their pinnaces had made of the Great Swamp south of the castle. In a single year, Canberra's feudal politics was turned on its head.

The Qeng Ho had invested three ships in the expedition to Canberra. They had seriously miscalculated, thinking the locals would be at a much higher level of technology by the time of their arrival. But even Tran Nuwen's realm couldn't resupply them. Two of the ships stayed behind. Young Pham left with the third – a crazy hostage deal his father thought he was putting over on the star folk.

Pham's last day on Canberra was cold and foggy. The trip from the castle walls down to the fen took most of the morning. It was the first time he had been allowed to see the visitors' great ships close up, and little Pham Nuwen was on a crest of joy. There might never be a moment in Pham's life when he had so many things wrong and backwards: The starships that loomed out of the mists were simply landing pinnaces. The tall, strange captain who greeted Pham's father was in fact a second officer. Three subordinate steps behind him walked a young woman, her face twisted with barely concealed discomfort – a concubine? a handmaiden? The real captain, it turned out.

Pham's father the King gave a hand signal. The boy's tutor and his dour servants marched him across the mud, toward the star folk. The hands on his shoulders were holding tight, but Pham didn't notice. He looked up, wondering, his eyes devouring the 'starships,' trying to follow the sweeping curves of glistening maybe-metal. In a painting or a small piece of jewelry he had seen such perfection – but this was dream incarnate.

They might have gotten him aboard the pinnace before he really understood the betrayal, if it hadn't been for Cindi. Cindi Ducanh, lesser daughter of Tran's cousin. Her family was important enough to live at court, but not important enough to matter. Cindi was fifteen, the strangest, wildest person Pham had ever known, so strange that he didn't even have a word for what she was – though 'friend' would have sufficed.

Suddenly she was there, standing between them and the star folk. '*No!* It's not right. It does no good. Don't—' She held her hands up, as if to stop them. From the side, Pham could hear a woman shouting. It was Cindi's mother, screaming at her daughter.

It was such a silly, stupid, hopeless gesture. Pham's party didn't even slow down. His tutor swung his quarterstaff in a low arc across Cindi's legs. She went down.

Pham turned, tried to reach out to her, but now hard hands lifted him, trapped his arms and legs. His last glimpse of Cindi was her struggling up from the mud, still looking in his direction, oblivious, of the axemen running toward her. Pham Nuwen never learned how much it had cost the one person who had stood up to protect him. Centuries later, he had returned to Canberra, rich enough to buy the planet even in its newly civilized state. He had probed the old libraries, the fragmented digital records of the Qeng Ho who had stayed behind. There had been nothing about the aftermath of Cindi's action, nothing certain in the birth records of Cindi's family forward from her time. She and what she had done and what it had cost were simply insignificant in the eyes of time.

Pham was swept up, carried quickly forward. He had a brief vision of his brothers and sisters, young men and women with cold, hard faces. Today, one very small threat was being removed. The servants stopped briefly before Pham's father the King. The old man – forty years old, actually – stared down at him briefly. Tran had always been a distant force of nature, capricious behind ranks of tutors and contesting heirs and courtiers. His lips were drawn down in a thin line. For an instant something like sympathy might have lived in the hard eyes. He touched the side of Pham's face. 'Be strong, boy. You bear my name.'

Tran turned, spoke pidgin words to the star man. And Pham was in alien hands.

Like Qiwi Lin Lisolet, Pham Nuwen had been cast out into the great darkness. And like Qiwi, Pham did not belong.

He remembered those first years more clearly than any other time in his life. No doubt the crew intended to pop him into cold storage and dump him at the next stop. What can you make of a kid who thinks there's one world and it's flat, who has spent his whole life learning to whack about with a sword?

Pham Nuwen had had his own agenda. The coldsleep coffins scared the devil out of him. The *Reprise* had scarcely left Canberra orbit when little Pham disappeared from his appointed cabin. He had always been small for his age, and by now he understood about remote surveillance. He kept the crew of the *Reprise* busy for more than four days searching for him. In the end, of course, Pham lost – and some very angry Qeng Ho dragged him before the ship's master.

By now he knew that was the 'handmaiden' he had seen in the fen. Even knowing, it was still hard to believe. One weak woman, commanding a starship and a crew of a thousand (though soon almost all of those were off-Watch, in coldsleep). Hmm. Maybe she had been the owner's concubine, but had poisoned him and now ruled in his place. That was a credible scenario, but it made her an exceptionally dangerous person. In fact, Sura had been a junior captain, the leader of the faction that voted against staying at Canberra. Those who stayed called them 'the cautious cowards.' And now they were heading home, into certain bankruptcy.

Pham remembered the look on her face when they finally caught him and brought him to the bridge. She had scowled down at the little prince, a boy still dressed in the velvet of Canberran nobility.

'You've delayed the start of the Watches, young fellow.'

The language was barely intelligible to Pham. The boy pushed down the panic and the loneliness and glared right back at her. 'Madam. I am your hostage, not your slave, not your victim.'

'Damn, what did he say?' Sura Vinh looked around at her lieutenants. 'Look, son. It's a sixty-year flight. We've got to put you away.'

That last comment got through the language barrier, but it sounded too much like what the stable boss said when he was going to behead a horse. '*No!* You'll not put me in a coffin.'

And Sura Vinh understood that, too.

One of the others spoke abruptly to Shipmaster Vinh. Probably something like 'It doesn't matter what he wants, ma'am.'

Pham tensed himself for another futile wrestling match. But Sura just stared at him for a second and then ordered everyone else out of her office. The two of them talked pidgin for some Ksecs. Pham knew court intrigue and strategy, and none of it seemed to apply here. Before they were done, the little boy was crying inconsolably and Sura had her arm across his shoulders. 'It will be years,' she said. 'You understand that?'

'. . . Y-yes.'

'You'll arrive an old man if you don't let us put you in coldsleep.' That last was still an unfortunate word.

'*No, no, no!* I'll die first.' Pham Nuwen was beyond logic.

Sura was silent for a moment. Years later, she told Pham *her* side of the encounter: 'Yeah, I could have heaved you in the freezer. It would have been prudent and ethical – and it would have saved me a world of problems. I will never understand why Deng's fleet committee forced me to accept you; they were petty and pissed, but this was too much.

'So there you were, a little kid sold out by his own father. I'd be damned if I'd treat you the way he and the committee did. Besides, if you spent the flight on ice, you'd still be a zero when we got to Namqem, helpless in a tech civilization. So why not let you stay out of coldsleep and try to teach you the basics? I figured you'd see how long the years looked in a ship between the stars. In a few years, the coldsleep coffins might not seem quite so terrible to you.'

It hadn't been simple. Ship security had to be reprogrammed for the presence of an irresponsible human. No uncrewed Tween Watches could be allowed. But the programming was done, and several of the Watch slanders volunteered to extend their time out of coldsleep.

The *Reprise* reached ramcruise, 0.3 lightspeed, and sailed endlessly across the depths.

And Pham Nuwen had all the time in the universe. Several crewfolk – Sura for the first few Watches – did their best to tutor him. At first, he would have none of it . . . but the time stretched long. He learned to speak Sura's language. He learned generalities about Qeng Ho.

'We trade between the stars,' said Sura. The two were sitting alone on the ramscoop's bridge. The windows showed a symbolic map of the five star systems that the Qeng Ho circuited.

'Qeng Ho is an empire,' the boy said, looking out at the stars and trying to imagine how those territories compared with his father's kingdom.

Sura laughed. 'No, not an empire. No government can maintain itself across light-years. Hell, most governments don't last more than a few centuries. Politics may come and go, but trade goes on forever.'

Little Pham Nuwen frowned. Even now, Sura's words were sometimes nonsense. 'No. It has to be an empire.'

Sura didn't argue. A few days later, she went off-Watch, dead in one of the strange, cold coffins. Pham almost begged her not to kill herself, and for Msecs afterward he grieved on wounds he hadn't imagined before. Now there were other strangers, and unending days of silence. Eventually he learned to read Nese.

And two years later, Sura returned from the dead. The boy still refused to go off-Watch, but from that point on he welcomed everything they wanted to teach him. He knew there was power beyond any Canberran lordship here, and now he understood that he might be master of it. In two years, he made up for what a child of civilization might learn in five. He had a competency in math; he could use the top- and second-level Qeng Ho program interfaces.

Sura looked almost the same as before her coldsleep, except that in some strange way, she seemed younger now. One day he caught her staring at him.

'So what's the problem?' Pham asked.

Sura grinned. 'I never saw a kid on a long flight. You're what now, fifteen Canberra years old? Bret tells me you've learned a lot.'

'Yes. I'm going to be Qeng Ho.'

'Hmm.' She smiled, but it was not the patronizing, sympathy-filled smile that Pham remembered. She was truly pleased, and she didn't disbelieve his claim. 'You've got an awful lot to learn.'

'I've got an awful lot of time to do it.'

Sura Vinh stayed on Watch four straight years that time. Bret Trinli stayed for the first of those years, extending his own Watch. The three of them trekked through every accessible cubic meter of the *Reprise:* the sickbay and coffins, the control deck, the fuel tanks. The *Reprise* had burned almost two million tonnes of hydrogen to reach ramcruise speeds. In effect, she was a vast, nearly empty hulk now. 'And without lots of support at the destination, this ship will never fly again.'

'You could refuel, even if there were only gas giants at the destination. Even I could manage the programs for that.'

'Yeah, and that's what we did at Canberra. But without an overhaul, we can't go far and we can't do zip once we get there.' Sura paused, cursed under her breath. 'Those damn fools. Why did they stay behind?' Sura seemed caught between her contempt for the shipmasters who had stayed to conquer Canberra, and her own guilt at having deserted them.

Bret Trinli broke the silence. 'Don't feel so bad for them. They're taking a big chance, but if they win, they'll have the Customers we were all expecting there.'

'I know – and we're guaranteed to arrive at Namqem with nothing. Bet we'll lose the *Reprise*.' She shook herself, visibly pushing back the worries that always seemed to gnaw her. 'Okay, in the meantime we're going to create one more trained crewmember.' She nailed Pham with a mock-glare. 'What specialty do we need the most, Bret?'

Trinli rolled his eyes. 'You mean that can bring us the most income? Obviously: Programmer-Archeologist.'

The question was, could a feral child like Pham Nuwen ever become one? By now, the boy could use almost all the standard interfaces. He even thought of himself as a programmer, and potentially a ship's master. With the standard interfaces, one could fly the *Reprise*, execute planetary orbit insertion, monitor the coldsleep coffins—

'And if anything goes wrong, you're dead, dead, dead' was how Sura finished Pham's litany of prowess. 'Boy, you have to learn something. It's something that children in civilization often are confused about, too. We've had computers and programs since the beginning of civilization, even before spaceflight. But there's only so much they can do; they can't think their way out of an unexpected jam or do anything really creative.'

'But – I know that's not true. I play games with the machines. If I set the skill ratings high, I never win.'

'That's just computers doing simple things, very fast. There is only one important way that computers are anything like wise. They contain thousands of years of programs, and can run most of them. In a sense, they remember every slick trick that Humankind has ever devised.'

Bret Trinli sniffed. 'Along with all the nonsense.'

Sura shrugged. 'Of course. Look. What's our crew size – when we're in-system and everybody is up?'

'One thousand and twenty-three,' said Pham. He had long since learned every physical characteristic of the *Reprise* and this voyage.

'Okay. Now, suppose you're light-years from nowhere—'

Trinli: 'You don't have to suppose that, it's the pure truth.'

'—and something goes wrong. It takes perhaps ten thousand human specialties to build a starship, and that's on top of an enormous capital industry base. There's no way a ship's crew can know everything it takes to analyze a star's spectrum, and make a vaccine against some wild change in the bactry, and understand every deficiency disease we may meet—'

'Yes!' said Pham. 'That's why we have the programs and the computers.'

'That's why we can't survive without them. Over thousands of years; the machine memories have been filled with programs that can help. But like Bret says, many of those programs are lies, all of them are buggy, and only the top-level ones are precisely appropriate for our needs.' She paused, looked at Pham significantly. 'It takes a smart and highly trained human being to look at what is available, to choose and modify the right programs, and then to interpret the results properly.'

Pham was silent for a moment, thinking back to all the times the machines had not done what he really wanted. It wasn't always Pham's fault. The programs that tried to translate Canberran to Nese were crap. 'So . . . you want me to learn to program something better.'

Sura grinned, and there was a barely suppressed chuckle from Bret. 'We'll be satisfied if you become a good programmer, and then learn to use the stuff that already exists.'

Pham Nuwen spent years learning to program/explore. Programming went back to the beginning of time. It was a little like the midden out back of his father's castle. Where the creek had worn that away, ten meters down, there were the crumpled hulks of machines – flying machines, the peasants said – from the great days of Canberra's original colonial era. But the castle midden was clean and fresh compared to what lay within the *Reprise*'s local net. There were programs here that had been written five thousand years ago, before Humankind ever left Earth. The wonder of it – the horror of it, Sura said – was that unlike the useless wrecks of Canberra's past, these programs still worked! And via a million million circuitous threads of inheritance, many of the oldest programs still ran in the bowels of the Qeng Ho system. Take the Traders' method of timekeeping. The frame corrections were incredibly complex – and down at the very bottom of it was a little program that ran a counter. Second by second, the Qeng Ho counted from the instant that a human had first set foot on Old Earth's moon. But if you looked at it still more closely . . . the starting instant was actually about fifteen million seconds later, the 0-second of one of Humankind's first computer operating systems.

So behind all the top-level interfaces was layer under layer of support. Some of that software had been designed for wildly different situations. Every so often, the inconsistencies caused fatal accidents. Despite the romance of spaceflight, the most common accidents were simply caused by ancient, misused programs finally getting their revenge.

'We should rewrite it all,' said Pham.

'It's been done,' said Sura, not looking up. She was preparing to go off-Watch, and had spent the last four days trying to root a problem out of the coldsleep automation.

'It's been tried,' corrected Bret, just back from the freezers. 'But even the top levels of fleet system code are enormous. You and a thousand of your friends would have to work for a century or so to reproduce it.' Trinli grinned evilly. 'And guess what – even if you did, by the time you finished, you'd have your own set of inconsistencies. And you still wouldn't be consistent with all the applications that might be needed now and then.'

Sura gave up on her debugging for the moment. 'The word for all this is "mature programming environment." Basically, when hardware perform-ance has been pushed to its final limit, and programmmers have had several centuries to code, you reach a point where there is far more signicant code than can be rationalized. The best you can do is understand the overall layering, and know how to search for the oddball tool that may come in handy – take the situation I have here.' She waved at the dependency chart she had been working on. 'We are low on working fluid for the coffins. Like a million other things, there was none for sale on dear old Canberra. Well, the obvious thing is to move the coffins near the aft hull, and cool by direct radiation. We don't have the proper equipment to support this – so lately, I've been doing my share of archeology. It seems that five hundred years ago, a similar thing happened after an insystem war at Torma. They hacked together a temperature maintenance package that is precisely what we need.'

'*Almost* precisely.' Bret was grinning again. 'With some minor revisions.'

'Yes, which I've almost completed.' She glanced at Pham, saw the look on his face. 'Aha. I thought you'd rather die than use a coffin.'

Pham smiled shyly, remembering the little boy of six years before. 'No, I'll use it. Someday.'

That day was another five years of Pham's lifetime away. They were busy years. Both Bret and Sura were off-Watch, and Pham never felt close to their replacements. The foursome played musical instruments – manually, just like minstrels at court! They'd do it for Ksecs on end; there seemed be some strange mental/social high they got from playing together. Pham was vaguely affected by music, but these people worked so hard for such ordinary results. Pham did not have the patience even to begin down that path. He drifted off. Being alone was something he was very good at. There was so much to learn.

The more he studied, the more he understood what Sura Vinh had meant about 'mature programming environments.' By comparison with the crew members he knew, Pham had become an excellent programmer. 'Flaming genius' was how he'd heard Sura describe him when she hadn't known he was nearby. He could code *anything* – but life is short, and most significant systems were terribly large. So Pham learned to hack about with the leviathans of the past. He could interface weapons code from Eldritch Faerie with patched conic planners from before the conquest of space. Just as important, he knew how and where to look for possibly appropriate applications hidden in the ship's network.

. . . And he learned something about mature programming environments that Sura had never quite said. When systems depended on underlying systems, and those depended on things still older . . . it became impossible to know all the systems could do. Deep in the interior of fleet automation there could be – there must be – a maze of trapdoors. Most of the authors were thousands of years dead, their hidden accesses probably lost forever. Other traps had been set by companies or governments that hoped to survive the passage of time. Sura and Bret and maybe a few of the others knew things about the *Reprise*'s systems that gave them special powers.

The medieval prince in Pham Nuwen was entranced by this insight. *If only one could be at the ground floor of some universally popular system . . .* If the new layer was used everywhere, then the owner of those trapdoors would be like a king forever after, throughout the entire universe of use.

Eleven years had passed since a certain frightened thirteen-year-old had been taken from Canberra.

Sura had just returned from coldsleep. It was a return that Pham had awaited with increasing desire . . . since just after she departed. There was so much he wanted to tell her, so much to ask her and show her. Yet when the time finally came, he couldn't bring himself to stay at the coldsleep hold and greet her.

She found him in an equipment bay on the aft hull, a tiny niche with a real window on the stars. It was a place that Pham had appropriated several years earlier.

There was a tap on the light plastic cover. He slipped it aside.

'Hello, Pham.' Sura had a strange smile on her face. *She* looked strange. So young. In fact, she simply hadn't aged. And now Pham Nuwen had lived twenty-four years. He waved her into the tiny room. She floated close past him, and turned. Her eyes were solemn above the smile. 'You've grown up, friend.'

Pham started to shake his head. 'Yes. But I – you are still ahead of me.'

'Maybe. In some ways. But you're twice the programmer I will ever be. I saw the solutions you worked out for Ceng this last Watch.'

They sat, and she asked him about Ceng's problems and his solutions. All the glib speeches and bravado he'd spent the last year planning were swept from his mind, his conversation reduced to awkward starts and stops. Sura didn't seem to notice. *Damn. How does a Qeng Ho man take a woman?* On Canberra, he had grown up believing in chivalry and sacrifice . . . and had gradually learned that the true method was very different: a gentleman simply grabbed what he wanted, assuming a more powerful gentleman did not already own it. Pham's own personal experience was limited and surely untypical: poor Cindi had grabbed *him*. At the beginning of the last Watch, he had tried the true Canberra method on one of the female crew. Xina Rao had broken his wrist and made a formal complaint. It was something Sura would surely hear about sooner or later.

The thought blew away Pham's tenuous hold on the conversation. He stared at Sura in embarrassed silence, then blurted out the announcement he had been holding secret for some special moment. 'I . . . I'm going to go off-Watch, Sura. I'll finally start coldsleep.'

She nodded solemnly, as if she had never guessed.

'You know what really did it for me, Sura? The dustmote that broke me? It was three years ago. You were off-Watch,' *and I realized how long it would be until next I saw you.* 'I was trying to make that second-level celestial mech stuff work. You really have to understand some math to do that. For a while, I was stumped. For the hell of it, I moved up here, just started staring at the sky. I've done that before. Every year, my sun is dimmer; it's scary.'

'I'll bet,' said Sura, 'but I didn't know you could see directly aft, even from here.' She slid near the forty-centimeter port, and killed the lights.

'Yes you can,' said Pham, 'at least when your eyes adjust.' The room was dark as pitch now. This was a *real* window, not some enhancing display device. He moved close behind her. 'See, there's the four bright stars of the Pikeman. Now Canberra's star just makes his pole one tong longer.' *Silly. She doesn't know the Canberran sky.* He babbled on, a mindless cover for what he was feeling. 'But even that is not what got me; my sun is another star, so what? The thing is, the constellations: the Pikeman, the Wild Goose, the Plow. I can still recognize them, but even their shapes have changed. I know, I should have expected that. I'd been doing the math behind much harder things. But . . . it struck me. In eleven years, we have moved so far that the whole sky has changed. It gave me a gut feeling of how far we've come, how very far we still have to go.'

He gestured in the dark, and his palm slapped lightly on the smooth swell of her rear. His voice died in a little squeak, and for a measurable instant his hand sat motionless on her pants, his fingers touching her bare flesh just above the hip line. Somehow he hadn't noticed before; her blouse wasn't even tucked in. His hand swept around her waist and upward across the smooth curve of her belly, kept moving till he touched the undersides of her breasts. The move was a grab, modified and tentative perhaps, but a definite grab.

Sura's reaction was almost as swift as Xina Rao's had been. She twisted beneath him, her breast centering in the palm of his other hand. Before Pham could get out of her way, her arm was behind his neck, levering him down . . . for a long, hard kiss. He felt multiple shocks where his lips touched hers, where his hand rested, where her leg slid up between his.

And now she was pulling his shirt from his pants, forcing their bodies into a single long touch. She leaned her head back from his lips and laughed softly. 'Lord! I've been wanting to get my hands on you ever since you were fifteen years old.'

But why didn't you? I was in your power. It was the last coherent thought he had for some time. In the dark, there loomed more wonderful questions. How to get leverage, how to join the smooth endpoints of softness and hard. They bounced randomly from wall to wall, and poor Pham might never have found his way if not for his partner and guide.

Afterward she brought up the lights, and showed him how to do it in his sleeping hammock. And then again, with the lights out once more. After a long while, they floated exhausted in the dark. Peace and joy, and his arms were so full with her. Starlight was a magical faintness, that after enough time seemed almost bright. Bright enough to glint on Sura's eyes, to show the white of her teeth. She was smiling. 'You're right about the stars,' she said. 'It is a bit humbling to see the sweep of the stars, to know how little we count.'

Pham squeezed her gently, but was for the moment so satisfied he could actually think about what she said. '. . . Yes, it's scary. But at the same time, I look out and realize that with starships and coldsleep, we are outside and beyond them. We can make what we want of the universe.'

The white of Sura's smile broadened. 'Ah, Pham, maybe you haven't changed. I remember the first days of little Pham, when you could barely spit out an intelligible sentence. You kept insisting the Qeng Ho was an empire, and I kept saying we were simply traders, could never be anything more.'

'I remember, but still I don't understand. Qeng Ho has been around for how long?'

'That name for "trading fleet"? Maybe two thousand years.'

'That's longer than most empires.'

'Sure, and part of the reason is, we're not an empire. It's our function that makes us seem everlasting. The Qeng Ho of two thousand years ago had a different language, had no common culture with now. I'm sure that things like it exist off and on through all Human Space. It's a process, not a government.'

'Just a bunch of guys who happen to be doing similar things?'

'You got it.'

Pham was silent for a while. She just didn't understand. 'Okay. That is the way things are now. But don't you see the power that this gives you? You hold a high technology across hundreds of light-years of space and thousands of years of time.'

'No. That's like saying the sea surf could rule a world: It's everywhere, it's powerful, and it seems to be coordinated.'

'You could have a network, like the fleet network you used at Canberra.'

'Lightspeed, Pham, remember? Nothing goes faster. I've no idea what traders are doing on the other side of Human Space – and at best that information would be centuries out of date. The most you've seen is networking across the *Reprise;* you've studied how a small fleet network is run. I doubt you can imagine the sort of net it takes to support a planetary civilization. You'll see at Namqem. Every time we visit a place like that, we lose some crew. Life with a planetary network, where you can interact with millions of people with millisecond latencies – that is something you are still blind to. I'll bet when we get to Namqem, you'll leave, too.'

'I'll never—'

But Sura was turning in his embrace, her breasts sliding across his chest, her hand sweeping down his belly, reaching. Pham's denial was lost in his body's electric response.

After that, Pham moved into Sura's cruise quarters. They spent so much time together that the other Watch standers teased him for 'kidnapping our captain.' In fact, the time with Sura Vinh was unending joy to Pham, but it was not just lust fulfilled. They talked and talked and argued and argued . . . and set the course of the rest of their lives.

And sometimes he thought of Cindi. Both she and Sura had come after him, lifting him to new awareness. They had both taught him things, argued with him, and bedeviled him. But they were as different as summer from winter, as different as a pond from an ocean. Cindi had stood up for him at the risk of her life, stood alone against all the King's men. In his wildest dreams, Pham could not imagine Sura Vinh committing her life against such odds. No, Sura was infinitely thoughtful and cautious. It was she who had analyzed the risks of remaining at Canberra, and concluded that success was unlikely – and persuaded enough others about those risks to wangle a ship from the fleet committee and escape Canberra space. Sura Vinh planned for the long haul, saw problems where no one else could see. She avoided risks – or confronted them with overwhelming force of her own. In Pham's confused moral pantheon, she was much less than Cindi . . . and much more.

Sura never bought his notion of a Qeng Ho star kingdom. But she didn't simply deny him; she showered him with books, with economics and histories that had eluded his decade-long reading schedule. A reasonable person would have accepted her point; there had been so many 'common sense' things that Pham Nuwen had been wrong about before. But Pham still had his old stubbornness. Maybe it was Sura who wore blinders, 'We could build an interstellar net. It would just be . . . slow.'

Sura laughed. 'Yeah! Slow. Like a three-way handshake would take a thousand years!'

'Well, obviously the protocols would be different. And the usage, too. But it could change the random trading function into something much more, ah, profitable.' He had almost said *powerful*, but he knew that would just get him zinged about his 'medieval' mind-set. 'We could keep a floating database of Customers.'

Sura shook her head, 'But out of date by decades to millennia.'

'We could maintain human language standards. Our network programming standards would outlive any Customer government. Our trading culture could last forever.'

'But Qeng Ho is just one fish in a random sea of traders. . . . Oh.' Pham could see that he was finally getting through. 'So the "culture" of our broadcasts would give participants a trading edge. So there would be a reinforcement effect.'

'Yes, yes! And we could crypto-partition the broadcasts to protect against nearby competition.' Pham smiled slyly. The next point was something that little Pham, and probably Pham's father the King of all Northland, could never have conceived. 'In fact, we could even have some broadcasts in the clear. The language standards material, for instance, and the low end of our tech libraries. I've been reading the Customer histories. All the way back to Old Earth, the only constant is the churn, the rise of civilization, the fall, as often as not the local extinction of Humankind. Over time, Qeng Ho broadcasts could damp those swings.'

Sura was nodding, a far look settling into her eyes. 'Yes. If we did it right, we'd end up with Customer cultures that spoke *our* language, were molded to our trading needs, and used *our* programming environment—' Her gaze snapped up to his face. 'You still have empire on the brain, don't you?'

Pham just smiled.

Sura had a million objections, but she had caught the spirit of the idea, recast it into her experience, and now her entire imagination was working alongside his. As the days passed, her objections became more like suggestions, and their arguments more a kind of wondrous scheming.

'You're crazy, Pham . . . but that doesn't matter. Maybe it takes a crazy medievalist to be so ambitious. It's like . . . it's like we're creating a civilization out of whole cloth. We can set up our own myths, our own conventions. We'll be in at the ground floor of everything.'

'And we'll outlast any competition.'

'Lord,' Sura said softly. (It would be some time before they invented the

'Lord of All Trade' and the pantheon of lesser gods.) 'And you know, Namqem is the ideal place to start. They're about as advanced as a civilization can ever get, but they're getting a little cynical and decadent. They have propaganda techs as good as any in human histories. What you're suggesting is strange, but it's trivial compared to ad campaigns on a planetary net. If my cousins are still in Namqem space, I bet they'd bankroll the operation.' She laughed, joyous and almost childlike, and Pham realized how badly the fear of bankruptcy and disgrace had bent her down. 'Hell, we're gonna turn a *profit*!'

The rest of their Watch was a nonstop orgy of imagination and invention and lust. Pham came up with a combination of beamed and broadcast interstellar radio, schedules that could keep fleets and families in synch across centuries. Sura accepted most of the protocol design, wonder and obvious delight in her eyes. As for the human engineering, Pham's scheme of hereditary lords, and military fleets – Sura laughed at those, and Pham did not argue the judgment. After all, in people-things he was still scarcely more than a thirteen-year-old medieval.

In fact, Sura Vinh was far more awed than patronizing. Pham remembered their last conversation before he took his first turn in a coldsleep coffin. Sura had been calibrating the radiative coolers, checking the hypothermia drugs. 'We'll come out almost together, Pham, me a hundred Ksec before you. I'll be here to help.' She smiled and he could feel her gaze gently searching in him. 'Don't worry.'

Pham made some flippant remark, but of course she saw the uneasiness in him. She spoke of other things as he slipped into the coffin, a running monologue of their plans and daydreams, what they would begin when they finally reached Namqem. And, then it was time, and she hesitated. She leaned down and kissed him lightly on the lips. Her smile turned faintly teasing, but she was mocking herself as much as him: 'Sleep well, sweet prince.'

And then she was gone, and the drugs were taking effect. It didn't feel cold at all. His last thoughts were a strange floating back across his past. During Pham's childhood on Canberra, his father had been a faraway figure. His own brothers had been lethal threats to his existence. Cindi, he had lost Cindi before he ever really understood. But for Sura Vinh . . . he had the feeling of a grown child for a loving parent, the feeling of a man for his woman, the feeling of a human being for a dear friend.

In some fundamental sense, Sura Vinh had been all those things. For much of her long life, Sura Vinh had seemed to be his friend. And even though she was ultimately his betrayer – still, there at the beginning, Sura Vinh had been a woman good and true.

Someone was shaking him gently, waving a hand in his face. 'Hey, Trinli! Pham! Are you still with us?' It was Jau Xin, and he looked genuinely concerned.

'Ungh, yes, yes. I'm fine.'

'You sure?' Xin watched him for several seconds, then drifted back to his seat. 'I had an uncle who went all glassy-eyed like you just did. T'as a stroke, and he—'

'Yeah, well I'm fine. Never better.' Pham put the bluster back in his voice. 'I was just thinking, that's all.'

The claim provoked diversionary laughter all round the table. 'Thinking. A bad habit, Pham, old boy!' After a few moments, their concern faded. Pham listened attentively now, occasionally injecting loud opinions.

In fact, invasive daydreaming had been a feature of his personality since at least his leaving the Canberra. He'd get totally wrapped up in memories or planning, and lose himself the way some people did in immersion videos. He'd screwed up at least one deal because of it. From the corner of his eye, he could see that Qiwi was gone. Yes, the girl's childhood had been much like his, and maybe that accounted for her imagination and drive now. In fact, he had often wondered if the Strentmannians' crazy childrearing was based on stories of Pharn's time on the *Reprise*. At least when he had reached his destination, things got better. Poor Qiwi had found only death and deception here. But she still kept going . . .

'We're getting good translations now.' Trud Silipan was back on the Spiders. 'I'm in charge of Reynolt's translator zipheads.' Trud was more like an attendant than a manager, but no one pointed that out. 'I tell you, any day now we'll start getting information about what the Spiders' original civilization was like.'

'I don't know, Trud. Everyone says this must be a fallen colony. But if the Spiders are elsewhere in space, how come we don't hear their radio?'

Pham: 'Look. We've been over this before. Arachna must be a colony world. This system is just too hostile for life to start naturally.'

And someone else: 'Maybe the creatures don't have a Qeng Ho.' Chuckles went round the table.

'No, there'd still be plenty of radio noise. We'd hear them.'

'Maybe the rest of them are really far away, like the Perseus Mumbling—'

'Or maybe they're so advanced they don't use radio. We only noticed these guys because they're starting over.' It was an old, old argument, part of a mystery that extended back to the Age of Failed Dreams. More than anything else it was what had drawn the human expeditions to Arachna. It was certainly what had drawn Pham.

And indeed, Pham had already found Something New, something so powerful that the origin of the Spiders was now a peripheral issue for him. Pham had found Focus. With Focus, the Emergents could convert their brightest people into dedicated machines of thought. A dud like Trud Silipan could get effective translations at the touch of a key. A monster like Tomas Nau could have eyes unresting. Focus gave the Emergents a power that no one had ever had before, subtlety that surpassed any machine and patience that surpassed any human. That was one of the Failed Dreams – but they had achieved it.

Watching Silipan pontificate, Pham realized that the next stage in his plan had finally arrived. The low-level Emergents had accepted Pham Trinli. Nau tolerated, even humored him, thinking he might be an unknowing window on the Qeng Ho military mind. It was time to learn a lot more about Focus. Learn from Silipan, from Reynolt . . . someday learn the technical side of the thing.

Pham had tried to build a true civilization across all of Human Space. For a few brief centuries it had seemed he might succeed. In the end, he had been betrayed. But Pham had long ago realized that the betrayal had been just the overt failure. What Sura and the others did to him at Brisgo Gap had been inevitable. An interstellar empire covers so much space, so much time. The goodness and justice of such a thing is not enough. You need an edge.

Pham Nuwen raised his bulb of Diamonds and Ice and drank an unnoticed toast, to the lessons of the past and the promise of the future. This time he would do things right.

18

Ezr Vinh's first two years after the ambush were spread across nearly eight years of objective time. Almost like a good Qeng Ho captain, Tomas Nau was pacing their duty time to match local developments. Qiwi and her crews were out of coldsleep more than any, but even they were slowing down.

Anne Reynolt kept her astrophysicists busy, too. OnOff continued to settle along the light curve that had been seen in previous centuries; to a lay observer, it looked like a normal, hydrogen-eating sun, complete with sunspots. At first, she held the other academics to a lower duty cycle, awaiting the resumption of Spider activity.

Military radio transmissions were heard from Arachna less than one day after the Relight, even while steam-storms churned the surface. Apparently, the Off phase of the sun had interrupted some local war. Within a year or two, there were dozens of transmission sites on two continents. Every two centuries these creatures had to rebuild their surface structures almost from the foundations up, but apparently they were very good at it. When gaps showed in the cloud cover, the spacers caught sight of new roads, towns.

By the fourth year there were two thousand transmission points, the classical fixed-station model. Now Trixia Bonsol and the other linguists went to a heavier duty cycle. For the first time they had continuous audio to study.

When their Watches matched – and they often did now – Ezr visited Trixia Bonsol every day. At first, Trixia was more remote than ever. She didn't seem to hear him; the Spider talk flooded her workroom. The sounds were a squeaking shrillness that changed from day to day as Trixia and the other Focused linguists determined where in the acoustic spectrum the sense of Spider talk was hidden, and devised convenient representations, both auditory and visual, for its study. Eventually, Trixia had a usable data representation.

And then the translations really began. Reynolt's Focused translators grabbed everything they could get, producing thousands of words of semi-intelligible text per day. Trixia was the best. That was obvious from the beginning. It was her work with the physics texts that had been the original breakthrough, and it was she who melded that written language with the language spoken in two-thirds of the radio broadcasts. Even compared to the Qeng Ho linguists, Trixia Bonsol excelled; how proud she would be if only she could know. 'She's indispensable.' Reynolt passed sentence with her typical flat affect, free of both praise and sadism, a statement of fact. Trixia Bonsol would get no early out, as Hunte Wen had.

Vinh tried to read everything the translators produced. At first it was typical of raw field linguistics, where each sentence consisted of dozens of pointers to alternative meanings, alternative parsings. After a few Msecs, the translations were almost readable. There were living beings down there on Arachna, and these were their words.

Some of the Focused linguists never got beyond the annotated-style translations. They were caught in the lower levels of meaning and fought any attempt to capture the spirit of the aliens. Maybe that was enough. For one thing, they learned that the Spiders had no knowledge of any previous civilization:

'We're seeing no mention of a golden age of technology.'

Nau looked at Reynolt skeptically. 'That's suspicious in itself. Even on Old Earth, there were at least myths of a lost past.' And if ever there were an origin world, it was Old Earth.

Reynolt shrugged. 'I'm telling you that any mention of past technical civilizations is below the plausible background level. For instance, as far as we can tell, archeology is considered an insignificant academic pursuit' – not the world-creating frenzy of the typical fallen colony.

'Well, Plague take it,' said Ritser Brughel. 'If there's nothing for these guys to dig up, our payoff is just about crap.'

Pity you didn't think of that before you came, thought Ezr.

Nau looked sour and surprised, but he disagreed with Brughel:

'We've still got Dr Li's results.' His glance flickered across the Qeng Ho at the foot of the table, and Ezr was sure that something else passed through the Emergent's mind: *We've still got a Qeng Ho fleet library, and Peddlers to explore it for us.*

Trixia let Ezr touch her now, sometimes to comb her hair, sometimes just to pat her shoulder. Maybe he had spent so much time in her workroom that she thought of him as a piece of furniture, as safe as any other voice-activated machine. Trixia normally worked with a head-up display now; sometimes that gave the comforting illusion that she was actually looking at him. She would even answer his questions, as long as they stayed within the scope of her Focus and did not interrupt her conversations with her equipment and the other translators.

Much of the time, Trixia sat in the semidarkness, listening and speaking her translations at the same time. Several of the translators worked in that mode, scarcely more than automatons. Trixia was different, Vinh liked to think: like the others, she analyzed and reanalyzed, but not to insert a dozen extra interpretations beneath every syntactic structure. Trixia's translations seemed to reach for the meaning as it was in the minds of the speakers, in minds for which the Spider world was a normal, familiar place. Trixia Bonsol's translations were . . . art.

Art was not what Anne Reynolt was looking for. At first she had only little things to complain about. The translators chose an alternative ortho-graphy for their output; they represented the x^* and q^* glyphs with digraphs. It made their translations look very quaint. Fortunately, Trixia wasn't the first to use the bizarre scheme. Unfortunately, she originated far too much of the questionable novelty.

One terrible day, Reynolt threatened to bar Ezr from Trixia's workroom – that is, from Trixia's life. 'Whatever you're doing, Vinh, it's messing her up. She's giving me figurative translations. Look at these names: "Sherkaner Underhill," "Jaybert Landers." She's throwing away complications that all the translators agree on. In other places she's making up nonsense syllables.'

'She's doing just what she should be doing, Reynolt. You've been working with automatons too long.' One thing about Reynolt: Though she was crass even by Emergent standards, she never seemed vindictive. She could even be argued with. But if she barred him from seeing Trixia . . .

Reynolt stared at him for a moment. 'You're no linguist.'

'I'm Qeng Ho; To make our way, we've had to understand the heart of thousands of human cultures, and a couple of nonhuman ones. You people have mucked around this small end of Human Space, with languages based on our broadcasts. There are languages that are enormously different.'

'Yes. That's why her grotesque simplifications are not acceptable.'

'No! You need people who truly understand the other side's minds, who can show the rest of us what is important about the aliens' differences. So Trixia's Spider names look silly. But this "Accord" group is a young culture. Their names are still mostly meaningful in their daily language.'

'Not all of them, and not the given names. In fact real Spider talk merges given names and surnames, that interphonation trick.'

'I'm telling you, what Trixia is doing is fine. I'll bet the given names are from older and related languages. Notice how they almost make sense, some of them.'

'Yes, and that's the worst of all. Some of this looks like bits of Ladille or Aminese. These Ladille units – "hours," "inches," "minutes" – they just make for awkward reading.'

Ezr had his own problems with the crazy Ladille units, but he wasn't going to admit that to Reynolt. 'I'm sure Trixia sees things that relate to her central translation the way Aminese and Ladille relate to the Nese you and I speak.'

Reynolt was silent for a long moment, vacantly staring. Sometimes that meant that the discussion was over, and she had just not bothered to dismiss him. Other times it meant that she was trying very hard to understand. 'So you're saying that she's achieving a higher level of translation, giving us insight by trading on our own self-awareness.'

It was a typical Reynolt analysis, awkward and precise. 'Yes! That's it. You still want the translations with all the pointers and exceptions and caveats, since our understanding is still evolving. But the heart of good trading is having a gut feel for the other side's needs and expectations.'

Reynolt had bought the explanation. In any case, Nau liked the simplifications, even the Ladille quaintness. As time passed, the other translators adopted more and more of Trixia's conventions. Ezr doubted if any of the unFocused Emergents were really competent to judge the translations. And despite his own confident talk, Ezr wondered more and more: Trixia's meta-trans of the Spiders was too much like the Dawn Age history he had pushed at her just before the ambush. That might seem alien to Nau and Brughel and Reynolt, but it was Ezr's specialty and he saw too many suspicious coincidences.

Trixia consistently ignored the physical nature of the Spiders. Maybe this was just as well, considering the loathing that some humans felt for spiders. But the creatures *were* radically nonhuman in appearance, more alien in form and life cycle than any intelligence yet encountered by Humankind. Some of their limbs had the function of human jaws, and they had nothing exactly like hands and fingers, instead using their large number of legs to manipulate objects. These differences were all but invisible in Trixia's translations. There was an occasional reference to 'a pointed hand' (perhaps the stiletto shape that a foreleg could fold into) or to midhands and forehands – but that was all. In school, Ezr had seen translations that were this soft, but those had been done by experts with decades of face-to-face experience with the Customer culture.

Children's radio programming – at least that's what Trixia thought it was – had been invented on the Spider world. She translated the show's title as

'The Children's Hour of Science,' and currently it was their best source of insight about the Spiders. The radio show was an ideal combination of science language – which the humans had made good progress on – and the colloquial language of everyday culture. No one knew if it was really aimed at schooling children or simply entertaining them. Conceivably, it was remedial education for military conscripts. Yet Trixia's title caught on, and that colored everything that followed with innocence and cuteness. Trixia's Arachna seemed like something from a Dawn Age fairy tale. Sometimes when Ezr had spent a long day with her, when she had not spoken a word to him, when her Focus was so narrow that it denied all humanity . . . sometimes he wondered if these translations might be the Trixia of old, trapped in the most effective slavery of all time, and still reaching out for hope. The Spider world was the only place her Focus allowed her to gaze upon. Maybe she was distorting what she heard, creating a dream of happiness in the only way that was left to her.

19

It was in the midphase of the sun, and Princeton had recovered much of its beauty. In the cooler times ahead, there would be much more construction, the open theaters, the Palace of the Waning Years, the University's arboreta. But by 60//19, the street plan of generations past was fully in place, the central business section was complete, and the University held classes all the year round.

In other ways, the year 60//19 was different from 59//19, and very different from the tenth year of all generations before that. The world had entered the Age of Science. An airfield covered the river lowlands that had been farm paddies in past eras. Radio masts grew from the city's highest hills; at night, their far-red marker lights could be seen for miles.

By 60//19 most of the Accord's cities were similarly changed, as were the great cities of Tiefstadt and the Kindred, and to a lesser degree the cities of poorer nations. But even by the standards of the new age, Princeton was a very special place. There were things happening here that didn't show on the visible landscape, yet were the seeds of greater revolution.

Hrunkner Unnerby flew in to Princeton one rainy spring morning. An airport taxi drove him from the riverfront up through the center of town. Unnerby had grown up in Princeton and his old construction company had been here. He arrived before most shops' opening time; street cleaners scuttled this way and that around his taxi. A cool drizzle left the shops and the trees with glints of a thousand colors. Hrunkner liked the old downtown, where many of the stone foundations had survived more than three or four generations. Even the new concrete and the brick upper stories followed designs from before the time of any living person.

Out of the downtown, they climbed through new housing. This was a former Royal property that the government had sold to finance the Great War – the conflict the new generation was already calling simply the War with the Tiefers. Some parts of the new district were instant slums; others – the higher viewpoints – were elegant estates. The taxi trundled back and forth along the switchbacks, rising slowly toward the highest spot in the new tract. The top was obscured by dripping ferns, but here and there he glimpsed outbuildings. Gates opened silently and without apparent attendants. Hunh. There was a bloody palace up ahead.

Sherkaner Underhill stood by the parking circle at the end, looking quite out of place beside the grand entrance. The rain was just a comfortable mist, but Underhill popped open an umbrella as he walked out to greet Unnerby.

'Welcome, Sergeant! Welcome! All the years I've been after you to visit my little hillhouse, and finally you're here.'

Hrunkner shrugged.

'I have so much to show you . . . starting with two small but important items.' He tipped back the umbrella. After a moment, two tiny heads peeked up from the fur on his back. The two were babies, holding tight to their father. They could be no older than normal children in the early Bright, just old enough to be cute. 'The little girl is Rhapsa and the boy is Hrunkner.'

Unnerby stepped forward, trying to seem casual. *They probably named the child Hrunkner out of friendship. God in deepest earth.* 'Very pleased to meet you.' In the best of times, Unnerby had no way with children – training new hires was the closest he'd ever come to raising them. Hopefully, that would excuse his unease.

The babies seemed to sense his distaste, and retreated shyly from sight.

'Never mind,' said Sherkaner, in that oblivious way of his. 'They'll come out and play once we're indoors.'

Sherkaner led him inside, talking all the way about how much he had to show him, how good it was that Hrunkner was finally visiting. The years had changed Underhill, physically at least. Gone was the painful leanness; he had been through several molts. The fur on his back was deep and paternal, strange to see on anyone in this phase of the sun. The tremor in his head and forebody was a little worse than Unnerby remembered.

They walked through a foyer big enough for a hotel, and down a wide spiral of steps that looked out upon wing after wing of Sherkaner's 'little hillhouse.' There were plenty of other people here, servants perhaps, though they didn't wear the livery that the super-rich usually demanded. In fact, the place had the utilitarian feel of corporate or government property. Unnerby interrupted the other's nonstop chatter with, 'This is all a front, isn't it,

Underhill? The King never sold this hill at all, just transferred it.' To the Intelligence Service.

'No, really. I do own the ground; I bought it myself. But, um, I do a lot of consulting, and Victory – I mean Accord Intelligence – decided that security was best served by setting up the labs right here. I have some things to show you.'

'Yeah. Well, that's the point of my visit, Sherk. I don't think you're working on the right things. You've pushed the Crown into going all out for – I assume we can talk freely here?'

'Yes, yes, of course.'

Ordinarily, Unnerby wouldn't have accepted such a casual assertion, but he was beginning to realize how thoroughly secure the building was. There was plenty of Sherkaner design, the logarithmic spiral of the main rooms for instance, but there was also Victory's touch, the – guards, he now realized – lurking everywhere, the crisply clean nature of the carpets and walls. This place was probably as safe as Unnerby's labs inside Lands Command. 'Okay. You've pushed the Crown into going all out for atomic power. I'm managing more men and equipment than a billionaire, including several people almost as smart as you are.' In fact, though Hrunkner Unnerby was still a sergeant, his job was about as far from that rank as one could get. His life these days was beyond his wildest contractor's dream.

'Good, good. Victory has a lot of faith in you, you know.' He led his guest into a large and peculiar room. There were bookcases and a desk, all overflowing with reports, randomly piled books, and notepaper. But the bookcases were fastened to a cobblie jungle gym, and children's books were mixed with the arcana. His two babies hopped from his back and scuttled up the gym. Now they peered down upon them from the ceiling. Sherkaner pushed books and magazines off a lower perch and waved for Unnerby to seat himself. Thank God he didn't try to change the subject.

'Yeah, but you haven't seen my reports.'

'Yes, I have. Victory sends them to me, though I haven't had time to read them.'

'Well, maybe you should!' *Deep Secret reports are sent to him and he doesn't have time to read them – and he's the cobber who started it all.* 'Look, Sherkaner, I'm telling you it's not working out. In principle, atomic power can do everything we need. In practice – well, we've made some really deadly poisons. There are things like radium but a lot easier to produce in bulk. We've also got one isotope of uranium that's very hard to isolate, but I think if we do, we can make a hell of a bomb: we can give you the energy to keep a city warm through the Dark, but all in less than a second!'

'Excellent! That's a start.'

'That excellent start may be as far as it gets. I've had three labs taken over by the bomb cobbers. Trouble is, this is peacetime; this technology is going to leak out, first to mining interests, then to foreign states. Can you imagine what will happen once the Kindred and the Old Tiefers and God knows who else starts making these things?'

That seemed to penetrate Underhill's durable armor of inattention. '. . . Yes, that will be very bad. I haven't read your reports, but Victory is up here often. Technology gives us wonders and terrible dangers. We can't have one without the other. But I'm convinced we won't survive unless we play with these things. You're seeing just one part of it all. Look, I know Victory can get you more money. Accord Intelligence has a good credit rating. They can go beyond the tithe for a decade without having to show a profit. We'll get you more labs, whatever you want—'

'Sherkaner, have you heard of "forcing the learning curve"?'

'Well, uh—' Clearly he had.

'Right now, if I had all the wealth in the world, I could give you a city heating unit, maybe. It would suffer catastrophic failure every few years, and even when it was working "properly," its transfer fluid – superheated steam, say – would be so radioactive that your city's residents would all be dead before the Dark was even ten years old. Beyond a certain point, throwing more money and technicians at a problem just doesn't help.'

Sherkaner didn't answer immediately. Unnerby had the feeling that his attention was roaming around the top of the jungle gym, watching his two babies. This room was a truly bizarre combination of wealth, the old Underhill intellectual chaos, and the new Underhill paternity. Where the floor wasn't piled with books and knickknacks, he could see plush carpet. The wall covering was one of those superexpensive delusional patterns. The windows were quartz-paned, extending all the way to the high ceiling. They were cranked open now. The smell of ferns in the cool morning floated in past wrought-iron trellises. There were electric lamps by Underhill's desks and by the legholds of the bookcases, but they were all turned off now.

The only light was the green and near-red that filtered through the ferns. That was more than enough to read the titles on the nearest books. There were psychology, math, electronics, an occasional astronomy text – and lots of children's storybooks. The books were stacked in low piles, filling most of the space between toys and equipment. And it wasn't always clear which were Underhill's toys and which were the children's. Some of the stuff looked like travel souvenirs, perhaps from Victory's military postings: a Tiefer leg polisher, dried flowers that might have been an Islander garland. And over in the corner: it looked like a Mark 7 artillery rocket, for God's sake. The warhead hatch had been removed, and there was a dollhouse installed in place of the customary high explosives.

Finally Underhill said, 'You're right, money alone won't make progress. It takes time to make the machines that make the machines, and so on. But we still have another twenty-five years or so, and the General tells me you are a genius at managing something this large.'

Hrunkner felt an old pride in hearing that, more pride than for all the medals he had collected in the Great War; but if it hadn't been for Smith and Underhill, he never would have discovered he had such talents. He replied grumpily, careful not to give away how much such praise meant to him: 'Thank you so much. But what I'm telling you is that none of that is enough. If you want this done in less than twenty years, I need something more.'

'Yes, what?'

'You, damn it! Your insight! Since the first year of the project, you've been hidden away up here in Princeton, doing God knows what.'

'Oh . . . Look Hrunkner, I'm sorry. The atomic power stuff just isn't very interesting to me anymore.'

Knowing Underhill for all these years, Unnerby should not have been surprised by the comment. Nevertheless, it made him want to chew on his hands. Here was a fellow who abandoned fields of endeavor before others even knew they existed. If he were simply a crank, there'd be no problem. As it was, sometimes Unnerby would have cheerfully killed the cobber.

'Yes,' continued Underhill, 'you need more bright people. I'm working on that, you know; I have some things I want to show you. But even so,' he said, obliviously pouring fuel on the fire, 'my intuition is that atomic power will turn out to be relatively easy, compared to the other challenges.'

'Such. As. What?'

Sherkaner laughed. 'Such as raising children, for example.' He pointed at the antique pendulum clock on the side wall. 'I thought the other cobblies would be here by now; maybe I should show you the institute first.' He got off his perch, began waving in that silly way parents do to small children. 'Come down, come down. Rhapsa, stay off the clock!' Too late: the baby had scuttled off the gym, made a flying leap onto the pendulum, and slid all the way to the floor. 'I've got so much junk here, I'm afraid something will fall on the babies and squash them.' The two ran across the floor, hopped into their appointed places in their father's fur. They were scarcely bigger than woodsfairies.

Underhill had gotten his institute declared a division of Kingschool. The hillhouse contained a number of classrooms, each occupying an arc of the outside perimeter. And it wasn't Crown funds that paid for most of it, at least according to Underhill. Much of the research was simply proprietary, paid for by companies that had been very impressed by Underhill. 'I could have hired away some of Kingschool's best, but we made a deal. Their people continue to teach and do research downtown, but they get time up here, with a percentage of our overhead getting fed back to Kingschool. And up here, what counts is results.'

'No classes?'

When Sherkaner shrugged, the two little ones bobbed up and down on his back and made excited little *meeping*, sounds that probably meant, 'Do it again, Daddy!'

'Yes, we have classes . . . sort of. The main thing is, people get to talk to other people, across many specialties. Students take a risk because things are so unstructured. I've got a few who are having a good time, but who aren't bright enough for this to work for them.'

Most of the classrooms had two or three persons at the blackboards, and a crowd, watching from low perches. It was hard to tell who was the prof and who the student. In some cases, Hrunkner couldn't even guess the field being discussed. They stopped for a moment by one door. A current-generation cobblie was lecturing a bunch of old cobbers. The blackboard scratching looked like a combination of celestial mechanics and electro-magnetics. Sherkaner stopped, waved a smile at the people in the room. 'You remember the aurora we saw in Dark? I have a fellow here who thinks that maybe it was caused by objects in space, things that are exceptionally dark.'

'They weren't dark when we saw them.'

'Yes! Maybe they actually have something to do with the start of the New Sun. I have my doubts. Jaybert doesn't know much celestial mechanics yet. He *does* know E&M. He's working on a wireless device that can radiate at wave-lengths of just a few inches.'

'Huh? That sounds more like super far-red than radio.'

'It's not something we could ever see, but it's going to be neat. He wants to use it as an echo finder for his space rocks.'

They walked farther down the hall. He noticed that Underhill was suddenly silent no doubt to give him time to think on the idea. Hrunkner Unnerby was a very practical fellow; he suspected that was the reason he was essential to some of General Smith's wilder projects. But even he could be brought up short by an idea that was spectacular enough. He had only the vaguest notion how such short wavelengths would behave, though they should be highly directional. The power needed for echo detection would vary as the inverse fourth power of the range – they'd have effective ground uses for it before they ever had enough juice to go looking for rocks in outer space. Hmm. The military angle could be more important than anything this Jaybert was planning . . . 'Has anyone *built* this high-frequency transmitter?'

His interest must have shown; Underhill was smiling more and more. 'Yes, and that's Jaybert's real work of genius, something he calls a cavity oscillator. I've got a little antenna on the roof; it looks more like a telescope mirror than a radio mast. Victory installed a row of relays down the Westermost Range to Lands Command. I can talk to her as reliably as over the telephone cable. I'm using it as a test bed for one class's crypto schemes. We'll end up with the most secure, high-volume wireless you can imagine.'

Even if Jaybert's stargazing never works out. Sherkaner Underhill was as crazy as ever, and Unnerby was beginning to see what he was getting at, why he refused to drop everything and work on atomic power. 'You really think this school is going to produce the geniuses we need at Lands Command?'

'It's going to find them, anyway – and I think we're bringing out the best in what we find. I've never had more fun in my life. But you have to be flexible, Hrunk. The essence of real creativity is a certain playfulness, a flitting from idea to idea without getting bogged down by fixated demands. Of course, you don't always get what you thought you were asking for. From this era on, I think invention will be the parent of necessity – and not the other way around.'

That was easy for Sherkaner Underhill to say. He didn't have to engineer the science into reality.

Underhill had stopped at an empty classroom; he peeked in at the blackboards. More gobbledegook. 'You remember the cam-and-gear devices that Lands Command used in the War, to figure ballistic tables? We're making things like that with vacuum tubes and magnet cores. They're a million times faster than the cam gadgets, and we can input the numbers as symbol strings instead of vernier settings. Your physicists will love it.' He chuckled. 'You'll see, Hrunk. Except for the fact that the inventions are first-patented by our sponsors, you and Victory will have more than enough to keep you happy . . .'

They continued up the long spiral stair. It opened finally onto an atrium near the top of the hill. There were higher hills around Princeton, but the view from here was spectacular enough, even in a cool drizzle. Unnerby could see a trimotor coming in at the airport. Tracts of late-phase development on the other side of the valley were the colors of wet granite and just-laid asphalt. Unnerby knew the company on that job. They had faith in the rumors that there would be power available to live long into the next Dark. What would Princeton be like if that were so? A city under the stars and hard vacuum, yet not asleep, and its deepnesses empty. The biggest risks would be late in the Waning Years, when people must decide whether to stock up for a conventional Dark, or gamble on what Hrunkner Unnerby's engineers thought they could do. His nightmares were not of failure, but of partial success.

'Daddy, Daddy!' Two five-year-olds careered into sight behind them. They were followed by two more cobblies, but these looked almost big enough to be in-phase. For more than ten years, Hrunkner Unnerby had done his best to overlook his boss's perversions: General Victory Smith was the best Intelligence chief he could imagine, probably even better than Strut Greenval. It shouldn't matter what her personal habits were. It had certainly never bothered him that she was born out-of-phase herself; that was something a person had no control over. But that she would start a family at the beginning of a New Sun, that she would damn her own children as she had been damned . . . *And they aren't even all the same age.* The two babies had hopped off Underhill's back. They scuttled across the grass and up the legs of their two oldest siblings. It was almost as if Smith and Underhill had deliberately set out to smear offal in the eyes of society's regard. This visit, so long avoided, was turning out to be just as bad as he'd feared.

The two oldest, both boys, hoisted the babies up, pretended for a moment to carry them like real fathers. They had no back fur, of course, and the babies slipped and slid down their carapaces. They grabbed hold of their brothers' jackets and scrambled back up, their baby laughter loud.

Underhill introduced the four to the sergeant. They all trooped across the soggy grass to the protection of an awning. This was the biggest play area that Unnerby had ever seen outside a schoolyard, but it was also very strange. A proper school went through discrete grades, targeting the current age of the pupils. The equipment in Underhill's play garden spanned a number of years. There were vertical gymnets, such as only a two-year-old could easily use. There were sandboxes, several huge dollhouses, and low play tables with picture books and games.

'Junior is the reason we didn't meet you and Mr Unnerby downstairs, Dad.' The twelve-year-old flicked a pointed hand in the direction of one of the five-year-olds – Victory Junior? 'She wanted you up here, so we could show Mr Unnerby all our toys.'

Five-year-olds are not very good at hiding their feelings. Victory Junior still had her baby eyes. Even though baby eyes could turn a few degrees, there were only two of them; she had to face almost directly toward whatever she wanted to observe. In a way that could never be true of an adult, it was easy to see where Junior's attention was. Her two big eyes looked first at Underhill and Unnerby, then glanced toward her older brother. 'Snitch!' she hissed at him. 'You wanted them up here, too.' She flicked her eating hands at him, and sidled close to Underhill. 'I'm sorry, Daddy. I wanted to show my dollhouse, and Brent and Gokna still had their lessons to finish.'

Underhill lifted his forearms to enclose her in a hug. 'Well, we were going to come up here anyway.' And to Unnerby: 'I'm afraid the General has made rather a big thing of you, Hrunkner.'

'Yeah, you're an Engineer!' said the other five-year-old – Gokna?

Whatever Junior's desires, Brent and Jirlib got to show off first. Their actual educational state was hard to estimate. The two had some kind of study curriculum, but were otherwise allowed to look into whatever they wished. Jirlib – the boy who had tattled on Junior – collected things. He seemed more deeply into fossils than any child Unnerby had ever seen. Jirlib had books from the Kingschool library that would have challenged adult students. He had a collection of diamond foraminiafera from trips with his parents down to Lands Command. And almost as much as his father, he was full of crazy theories. 'We're not the first, you know. A hundred million years ago, just under the diamond strata, there are the Distorts of Khelm.

Most scientists think they were dumb animals, but they weren't. They had a magic civilization, and I'm going to figure out how it worked.' Actually, that was not new craziness, but Unnerby was a little surprised that Sherkaner let his children read Khelm's crank paleontology.

Brent, the other twelve-year-old, was more like the stereotype of an out-of-phase child: withdrawn, a little bit sullen, perhaps retarded. He didn't seem to know what to do with his hands and feet, and though he had plenty of eyes, he favored his foreview as though he were still much younger. Brent didn't seem to have any special interests except for what he called 'Daddy's tests.' He had bags of buildertoys, shiny metal dowels and connector hubs. Three or four of the tables were covered by elaborate dowel and connector structures. By clever variation of the number of dowels per hub, someone had constructed various curved surfaces for the child. 'I've thought a lot about Daddy's tests. I'm getting better and better.' He began fiddling with a large torus, breaking up the carefully built framework.

'Tests?' Unnerby waved a glare at Sherkaner. 'What are you doing with these children?'

Underhill didn't seem to hear the anger in his voice. 'Aren't children wonderful – I mean, when they aren't a pain in the ass. Watching a baby grow up, you can see the mechanisms of thought grow into place, stage by stage.' He slipped a hand gently across his back, petting the two babies, who had returned to safe haven. 'In some ways, these two are less intelligent than a jungle tarant. There are patterns of thought that just don't exist in babies. When I play with them, I can almost feel the barriers. But as the years pass, the minds grow; methods are added.' Underhill walked along the play tables as he spoke. One of the five-year-olds – Gokna – danced half a pace in front of him, mimicking his gestures, even to the tremor. He stopped at a table covered with beautiful blown-glass bottles, a dozen shapes and tints. Several were filled with fruitwater and ice, as if for some bizarre lawn party. 'But even the five-year-olds have mental blinders. They have good language skills, but they're still missing basic-concepts—'

'And it's not just that we don't understand sex!' said Gokna.

For once, Underhill looked a little embarrassed. 'She's heard this speech too many times, I fear. And by now her brothers have told her what to say when we play question games.'

Gokna pulled on his leg. 'Sit down and play. I want to show Mr Unnerby what we do.'

'Okay. We can do that – where is your sister?' His voice was suddenly sharp and loud. 'Viki! You get down from there! It's not safe for you.'

Victory Junior was on the babies' gymnet, scuttling back and forth just below the awning. 'Oh, it is safe, Daddy. Now that you're here!'

'No it's not! You come down right now.'

Junior's descent was accompanied by much loud grumbling, but within a few minutes she was showing off in another way.

One by one, they showed him all their projects. The two oldest had parts in a national radio program, explaining science for young people. Apparently Sherkaner was producing the show, for reasons that remained murky.

Hrunkner put up with it all, smiling and laughing and pretending. And each one was a wonderful child. With the exception of Brent, each was brighter and more open than almost any Unnerby remembered. All that made it even worse when he imagined what life would be like for them once they had to face the outside world.

Victory Junior had a dollhouse, a huge thing that extended back a little way into the ferns. When her turn came, she hooked two hands under one of Hrunkner's forearms and almost dragged him over to the open face of her house.

'See,' she said, pointing to a hole in the toy basement. It looked suspiciously like the entrance to a termite nest. 'My house even has its own deepness. And a pantry, and a dining hall, and seven bedrooms . . .' Each room had to be displayed to her guest, and all the furniture explained. She opened a bedroom wall, and there was a flurry of activity within. 'And I even have little people to live in my house. See the attercops.' In fact, the scale of Viki's house was almost perfect for the little creatures, at least in this phase of the sun. Eventually, their middle legs would become colored wings. They would be woodsfairies, and they wouldn't fit at all. But for the moment, they did look like little people, scurrying to and fro between the inner rooms.

'They like me a lot. They can go back to the trees whenever they want, but I put little pieces of food in the rooms and they come every day to visit.' She pulled at little brass handles and a part of one floor came out like a drawer from a cabinet. Inside was an intricate maze built of flimsy wood partitions. 'I even experiment with them, like Daddy plays with us, except a lot simpler.' Her baby eyes were both looking down so she couldn't see Unnerby's reaction. 'I put honeydrip near this exit, then let them in at the other end. Then I time how long it takes . . . Oh, you are lost, aren't you, little one? You've been here two hours now. I'm sorry.' She reached an eating hand undaintily into the box and gently moved the attercop to a ledge by the ferns. 'Heh, heh,' a very Sherkanish chuckle, 'some of them are a lot dumber than others – or maybe it's luck. Now, how do I count her time, when she never got through the maze at all?'

'I . . . don't know.'

She turned to face him, her beautiful eyes looking up at him. 'Mommy says my little brother is named after you. Hrunkner?'

'Yes. I guess that's right.'

'Mommy says that you are the best engineer in the world. She says you can make even Daddy's crazy ideas come true. Mommy wants you to like us.'

There was something about a child's gaze. It was so *directed*. There was no way the target could pretend that he wasn't the one regarded. All the embarrassment and pain of the visit seemed to come together in that one moment. 'I like you,' he said.

Victory Junior look at him for a moment more, and then her gaze slid away. 'Okay.'

They had lunch with the cobblies up in the atrium. The cloud cover was burning off, and things were getting hot, at least for a Princeton spring day in the nineteenth year. Even under the awning it was warm enough to start sweat from every joint. The children didn't seem to mind. They were still taken by the stranger who had given their baby brother his name. Except for Viki, they were as raucous as ever, and Unnerby did his best to respond.

As they were finishing, the children's tutors showed up. They looked like students from the institute. The children would never have to go to a real school. Would that make it any easier for them in the end?

The children wanted Unnerby to stay for their lessons, but Sherkaner would have none of it. 'Concentrate on studying,' he said.

And so – hopefully – the hardest part of the visit was past. Except for the babies, Underhill and Unnerby were alone back in his study in the cool ground floor of the institute. They talked for a while about Unnerby's specific needs. Even if Sherkaner was unwilling to help directly, he really did have some bright cobbers up here. 'I'd like you to talk to some of my theory people. And I want you to see our computing-machinery experts. It seems to me that some of your grunt problems would be solved if you just had fast methods for solving differential equations.'

Underhill stretched out on the perch behind his desk. His aspect was suddenly quizzical. 'Hrunk . . . socializing aside, we accomplished more today than a dozen phone calls could have done. I know the institute is a place you'd love. Not that you'd fit in! We have plenty of technicians, but our theory people think they can boss them around. You're in a different class. You're the type that can boss the thinkers around and use what ideas they have to reach your engineering goals.'

Hrunkner smiled weakly. 'I thought invention was to be the parent of necessity?'

'Hmf. It mainly is. That's why we need people like you, who can bend the pieces together. You'll see what I mean this afternoon. These are people you'd love to take advantage of, and vice versa . . . I just wish you had come up a lot earlier.'

Unnerby started to make some weak excuse, stopped. He just couldn't pretend anymore. Besides, Sherkaner was so much easier to face than the General. 'You know why I didn't come before, Sherk. In fact, I wouldn't be here now if General Smith hadn't given me explicit orders. I'd follow her through Hell, you know that. But she wants more. She wants acceptance of your perversions. I – You two have such beautiful children, Sherk. How could you do such a thing to them?'

He expected the other to laugh the question off, or perhaps to react with the icy hostility that Smith showed at any hint of such criticism. Instead, Underhill sat silently for a moment, playing with an antique children's puzzle. The little wood pieces clicked back and forth in the quiet of the study. 'You agree the children are healthy and happy?'

'Yes, though Brent seems . . . slow.'

'You don't think I regard them as experimental animals?'

Unnerby thought back to Victory Junior and her dollhouse maze. Why when he was her age, he used to fry attercops with a magnifying glass. 'Um, you experiment with everything, Sherk; that's just the way you are. I think you love your children as much as any good father. And that's why it's all the harder for me to imagine how you could bring them into the world out of phase. So what if only one was mentally damaged? I notice they didn't talk of having any contemporary playmates. You can't find any who aren't monstrous, can you?'

From Sherkaner's aspect, he could tell his question had struck home. 'Sherk. Your poor children will live their whole lives in a society that sees them as a crime against nature.'

'We're working on these things, Hrunkner. Jirlib told you about "The Children's Hour of Science," didn't he?'

'I wondered what that was all about. So he and Brent are really on a radio show? Those two could almost pass for inphase, but in the long run somebody will guess and—'

'Of course. If not, Victory Junior is eager to be on the show. Eventually, I *want* the audience to understand. The program is going to cover all sorts of science topics, but there will be a continuing thread about biology and evolution and how the Dark has caused us to live our fives in certain ways. With the rise of technology, whatever social reason there is for rigid birthing times is irrelevant.'

'You'll never convince the Church of the Dark.'

'That's okay. I'm hoping to convince the millions of open-minded people like Hrunkner Unnerby.'

Unnerby couldn't think what to say. The other's argument was all so glib. Didn't Underhill understand? All decent societies agreed on basic issues, things that meant the healthy survival of their people. Things might be changing, but it was self-serving nonsense to throw the rules overboard. Even if they lived in the Dark, there would still be a need for decent cycles of life . . . The silence stretched out. There was just the clicking of Sherk's little puzzle blocks.

Finally, Sherkaner spoke. 'The General likes you very much, Hrunk. You were her dearest cobber-in-arms – but more, you were decent to her when she was a new lieutenant and it looked like her career would end on the trash pile.'

'She's the best. She couldn't help when she was born.'

'. . . Granted. But that's also why she's been making your life so hard lately. She thought that you, of all people, would accept what she and I are doing.'

'I know, Sherk, but I *can't*. You saw me today. I did my best, but your cobblies saw through me. Junior did anyway.'

'Heh, heh. She did indeed. It's not just her name; Little Victory is smart like her mother. But – as you say – she's going to have to face much worse . . . Look, Hrunk. I'm going to have a little chat with the General. She should accept what she can get, learn a little tolerance – even if it is tolerance for your intolerance.'

'I – that would help, Sherk. Thanks.'

'In the meantime, we'll need you up here more often. But you can come on your own terms. The children would like to see you, but at whatever distance you prefer.'

'Okay. I do like them. I'm just afraid I can't be what they want.'

'Ha. Then finding the right distance will be their little experiment.' He smiled. 'They can be pretty flexible if they look at you that way.'

20

In pre-Flight, Pham Trinli had been a distant curiosity to Ezr Vinh. What little he had seen of the guy seemed sullen, lazy, and probably incompetent. He was 'somebody's relative'; it was the only explanation for how he had made the crew. It was only since the ambush that Trinli's boorish, loud-mouth behavior had made its impact on Ezr. Occasionally he was amusing; much more often he was loathsome. Trinli's Watch time overlapped Ezr's by sixty percent. When he went over to Hammerfest, there was Pham Trinli trading dirty stories with Reynolt's techs. When he visited Benny's booze parlor, there was Trinli with a gang of Emergents, loud and pompous as ever. It had been years – really since Jimmy Diem died – since anyone would think his behavior traitorous. Qeng Ho and Emergents had to get along, and there were plenty of Traders in Trinli's circle.

Today Ezr's loathing for the man had changed to something darker. It was the once-per-Msec Watch-manager meeting, chaired as always by Tomas Nau. This was not the empty propaganda of Ezr's fake 'Fleet Management Committee.' The expertise of both sides was needed if they were to survive here. And though there was never a question of who was boss, Nau actually heeded much of the advice given at these meetings. Ritser Brughel was currently off-Watch, so this meeting would proceed without pathological overtones. With the exception of Pham Trinli, the managers were people who really could make things work.

All had gone smoothly through the first Ksec. Kal Omo's programmers had sanitized a batch of head-up displays for Qeng Ho use. The new interface was limited, but better than nothing. Anne Reynolt had a new Focused roster. The full schedule was still a secret, but it looked like Trixia might get more time off. Gonle Fong proposed some Watch changes. Ezr knew these were secret payoffs for various deals she had on the side, but Nau blandly accepted them. The underground economy she and Benny had masterminded was surely known to Tomas Nau . . . but the years had passed and he had consistently ignored it. *And he has consistently benefited by it.* Ezr Vinh would never have thought that free trading could add much efficiency in such a small and closed society as this little camp at L1, but it clearly had improved life. Most people had their favored Watch companions. Many had Qiwi Lisolet's little bonsai bubbles in their rooms. Equipment allocation was about as slick as it could be. Maybe it just showed how screwed up the original Emergent allocation system had been. Ezr still clung to the secret belief that Tomas Nau was the deepest villain he had ever known, a mass murderer, who murdered simply to advance a lie. But he was so clever, so outwardly conciliatory. Tomas Nau was more than smart enough to allow this underground trade that helped him to proceed.

'Very well, last item.' He smiled down the length of the table. 'As usual, the most interesting and difficult item. Qiwi?'

Qiwi Lisolet rose smoothly, stopped herself with a hand on the low ceiling. Gravity existed on Hammerfest, but it was barely good enough to keep the drinking bulbs on the table. 'Interesting? I guess.' She made a face. 'But it's also a very irritating problem.' Qiwi opened a deep pocket and pulled out a bundle of head-up displays – all tagged with 'cleared-for-Peddler-use' seals. 'Let's try out Kal Omo's toys.' She passed them out to the various Watch managers. Ezr took one, smiled back at her shy grin. Qiwi was still child-short, but she was as compact and nearly as tall as an average Strentmannian adult. She was no longer a little girl, or even the devastated orphan of the Relighting. Qiwi had lived Watch-on-Watch in the years after the Relight; she had aged a full year for every year that passed. Since OnOff's light had faded to a more manageable level, she'd had some time off-Watch, but Ezr could see tiny creases beginning at the corners of her eyes. *She's what now? Older than I am.* The old playfulness sometimes showed even still, but she never teased Ezr anymore. And he knew the stories about Qiwi and Tomas Nau were true. Poor, damned Qiwi.

But Qiwi Lin Lisolet had become something more than Ezr ever expected. Now Qiwi balanced mountains.

She waited until they all were wearing their huds. Then: 'You know I manage our halo-orbit around L1.' Above the middle of the table, the rockpile suddenly materialized. A tiny Hammerfest stuck out of the jumble on Ezr's side; a taxi was just mooring on the high tower. The image was crisp, cutting precisely across the wall and people behind it. But when he turned his head quickly from the rockpile to Qiwi and back, the pile blurred slightly. The placement automation couldn't quite keep up with the motion, and the visual-fraud failed. No doubt, Kal Omo's programmers had been forced to replace some of the optimizations. Still, what was left was close to Qeng Ho quality, the images separately coordinated in the field of each head-up display.

Dozens of tiny red lights appeared across the surface of the rockpile. 'Those are the electric-jet emplacements' – and then even more yellow spots of light— 'and that is the sensor grid.' She laughed, as light and playful as he remembered. 'Altogether it looks like a finite element solution grid, doesn't it? But then, that's just what it is, though the grid points are real machines collecting data. Anyway, my people and I have two problems. Either one of them is fairly easy: We need to keep the jumble in orbit around L1.' The jumble shrank to a stylized symbol, tracing an ever-changing Lis-sajous figure around the glyph *L1*. On one side hung Arachna; far away but on the same line was the OnOff star. 'We have it set so we're always near the sun's limb as seen by the Spiders. It will be many years before they have the technology to detect us here . . . But the other goal of the stabilization is to keep Hammerfest and the remaining blocks of ocean ice and airsnow all in the shadow.' Back to the original view of the jumble, but now the volatiles were marked in blue and green. Every year that precious resource shrank, consumed by the humans and by evaporation into space. 'Unfortunately these two goals are somewhat inconsistent. The rubble pile is *loose*. Sometimes our L1 station-keeping causes torques and the rocks slide.'

'The rubble quakes,' said Jau Xin.

'Yes. Down here at Hammerfest, you feel them all the time. Without constant supervision, the problem would be worse.' The surface of the meeting table became a model of the juncture of Diamonds One and Two. Qiwi motioned across the blocks and a forty-centimeter swath of surface turned pink. 'That's a shift that almost got away from us. But we can't afford the human resources to—'

Pham Trinli had sat through all this in silence, his eyes squinted down in a look of angry concentration. As Nau's original choice to manage the stabilization, Trinli had a long history of humiliation on this subject. Finally he exploded. 'Crap. I thought you were going to spend some of the water, melt it into a glue you could inject between the Diamonds.'

'We did that. It helps some, but—'

'But you still can't keep things settled, can you?' Trinli turned to Nau, and half rose from his chair. 'Podmaster, I've told you before that I'm best for the job. The Lisolet girl knows how to run a dynamics program, and she

works as hard as anyone – but she doesn't have any depth of experience.'
Depth of experience? How many years of hands-on does she need, old man?

But Nau just smiled at Trinli. No matter how absurd the idiot's contentions, Nau always invited him back. For a long time, Ezr had suspected it was some sadistic humor on the Podmaster's part.

'Well, then perhaps I should give you the job, Armsman. But consider, even now it would mean at least one-third time on-Watch.' Nau's tone was courteous, but Trinli caught the dare in it. Ezr could just see the anger growing in the old man.

'One-third?' said Trinli. 'I could do it on a one-fifth Watch, even if the other crewmembers were novices. No matter how cleverly the jets are emplaced, success comes down to the quality of the guidance network. Miss Lisolet doesn't understand all the features of the localizer devices she is using.'

'Explain,' said Anne Reynolt. 'A localizer is a localizer. We've been using both ours and yours in this project.' Localizers were a basic tool of any technical civilization. The tiny devices chirped their impulse codes at one another, using time of flight and distributed algorithms to accurately locate each participating device. Several thousand of them formed the positioning grid on the rubble pile. Together they were a kind of low-level network, providing information on the orientation, position, and relative velocity of the electric jets and the rubble.

'Not so.' Trinli smiled patronizingly. 'Ours work with yours well enough, but at the price of degrading their natural performance. Here's what the units look like.' The old man fiddled with his hand pad. 'Miss Lisolet, these interfaces are worthless.'

'Allow me,' said Nau. He spoke into the air, 'here are the two types of localizers we're using.'

The landscape vanished, and two pieces of vacuum-rated electronics appeared on the table. No matter how often Ezr saw this sort of demonstration, it was hard to get used to. In a practiced presentation, with a predetermined display sequence, it was easy to use voice recognition to guide things. What Nau had just done was subtly beyond any Qeng Ho interface. Somewhere up in Hammerfest's attic, one or more of his ziphead slaves was listening to every word spoken here, giving context to Nau's words and mapping them through to the fleet's automation or other ziphead specialists. And here were the resulting images, as quick as if Nau's own mind contained the fleet's entire database.

Of course, Pham Trinli was oblivious to the magic. 'Right.' He leaned closer to the equipment. 'Except that these are really more than the localizers themselves.'

Qiwi: 'I don't understand. We need a power supply, the sensor probes.'

Trinli grinned at her, triumph dripping in his smile. 'That's what you think – and perhaps it was true in the early years when ol' OnOff was frying everything. But now—' He reached closer and his finger disappeared into the side of the smaller package. 'Can you show the localizer core, Podmaster?'

Nau nodded. 'Right.' And the image of the Qeng Ho package was cut away, component layer by component layer. In the end, all that was left was a tiny blackened fleck, not more than a millimeter across.

Sitting next to him, Ezr caught an instant of tension in Tomas Nau. The other was suddenly, intensely interested. The moment passed before Ezr was even sure it existed. 'My, that is small. Let's take a closer look.'

The dustmote image swelled until it was a meter across and almost forty centimeters high. The head-up display automation painted appropriate reflections and shadows.

'Thanks.' Trinli stood so they could all see him over the top of the lens-shaped gadget. 'This is the basic Qeng Ho localizer – normally embedded in protective barriers, and so on. But see, in a benign environment – even outside in the shade – it is quite self-sufficient.'

'Power?' said Reynolt.

Trinli waved his hand dismissively. 'Just pulse them with microwaves, maybe a dozen times a second. I don't know the details, but I've seen them used in much larger numbers on some projects. I'm sure that would give finer control. As for sensors, these puppies have several simple things built in – temperature, light levels, sonics.'

Jau Xin: 'But how could Qiwi and the rest be ignorant of all this?'

Ezr could see where it was all going, but there wasn't a thing he could do about it.

Trinli shrugged magnanimously. He still did not realize how far his ego had taken him. 'As I've been saying all along: Qiwi Lin Lisolet is young and inexperienced. Coarse-grain localizers are good enough for most projects. Besides, the advanced characteristics are most useful in military work, and I wager that the texts she studies are deliberately vague on those issues. I, on the other hand, have worked as both an engineer and an armsman. Though it's not permitted normally, the localizers are an excellent oversight facility.'

'Certainly,' Nau said, looking thoughtful. 'Localizers and attached sensors are the heart of proper security.' And these dustmotes already had sensors and independence built in. They weren't an embedded component of a system; they could be the system itself.

'What do you think, Qiwi? Would a slew of these make things simpler for you?'

'Maybe. This is all news to me; I never thought a tech book would lie to me.' She thought a moment. 'But yes, if we had lots more localizers and the processing power scales properly fitted, then we could probably cut back on the human supervision.'

'Very well. I want you to get the details from Armsman Trinli, and install an extended network.'

'I'll be glad to take over the job, Podmaster,' said Trinli.

But Nau was no fool. He shook his head. 'No, you're much more valuable in your overall supervisory role. In fact, I want you and Anne to chat about this. When he comes on Watch, Ritser will be interested, too. There should be a number of public safety applications for these gadgets.'

So Pham Trinli had handed the Emergents even better manacles and chains. For an instant something like chagrined understanding flickered across the old man's face.

Ezr did his best not to talk to anyone for the rest of the day. He had never imagined that he could hate a stupid clown so much. Pham Trinli was no mass murderer, and his devious nature was written large across his every foolish move. But his stupidity had betrayed a secret the enemy had never guessed, a secret that Ezr himself had never known, a secret that others must have taken to their deaths rather than give to Tomas Nau and Ritser Brughel.

Before, he had thought that Nau kept Trinli around for laughs. Now Ezr knew better. And not since that long-ago night in the temp park had Ezr felt so coldly murderous. If there ever came a time when Pham Trinli could have a fatal accident . . .

After second mess, Ezr stayed in his quarters. His behavior shouldn't be suspicious. The live-music people took over Benny's every day about this time, and jamming was one Qeng Ho custom that Ezr had never enjoyed, even as a listener. Besides, there was plenty of work to catch up on. Some of it didn't even require that he talk to others. He slipped on the new head-up display, and looked at the Fleet Library.

In some sense, the survival of the Fleet Library was Captain Park's greatest failure. Every fleet had elaborate precautions for destroying critical parts of their local library if capture was imminent. Such schemes couldn't be complete. Libraries existed in a distributed form across the ships of their fleet. Pieces would be cached in a thousand nodes depending on the usage of the moment. Individual chips – those damnable localizers – contained extensive maintenance and operations manuals. Yet major databases should have been zeroed in very short order. What was left would have some usefulness, but the capital insights, the terabytes of hard experimental data would be gone – or left only as hardware instantiations, understandable only by painstaking reverse engineering. Somehow that destruction had not happened, even when it was obvious that the Emergent ambush would overwhelm all the ships of Park's fleet. Or maybe Park had acted and there had been off-net nodes or backups that – contrary to all policy – had contained full copies of the library.

Tomas Nau knew a treasure when he saw it. Anne Reynolt's slaves were dissecting the thing with the inhuman precision of the Focused. Sooner or later, they would know every Trader secret. But that would take years;

zipheads didn't know where to start. So Nau was using various unFocused staff to wander about the library and report on the big picture. Ezr had spent Msecs at it so far. It was a dicey job, because he had to produce some good results . . . and at the same time he tried subtly to guide their research away from things that might be immediately useful. He knew he might slip up, and eventually Nau would sense the lack of cooperation. The monster was subtle; more than once Ezr wondered who was using whom.

But today . . . Pham Trinli had just given away so much.

Ezr forced calmness on himself. *Just look at the library. Write some silly report.* That would count as duty time and he wouldn't have to freak out in any visible way. He played with the hand control that came with the new, 'sanitized' head-up display. At least it recognized the simpler command chords: the huds seamlessly replaced his natural vision of his cabin with a view of the library's entry layer. As he looked around, the automation tracked his head motion and the images slid past almost as smoothly as if the documents were real objects floating in his room. But . . . he fiddled with the control. Damn. Almost no customization was possible. They had gutted the interface, or changed it to some Emergent standard. This wasn't much better than ordinary wallpaper!

He reached up to pull the thing from his face, to crumple it. *Calm down.* He was still too ticked by Trinli's screwup. Besides, this really was an improvement over wall displays. He smiled for a moment, remembering Gonle Fong's obscenity-spattered fit about keyboards.

So what to look at today? Something that would seem natural to Nau, but couldn't give them any more than they already had. Ah, yes, Trinli's super localizers. They'd be sitting in an out-of-the-way niche in some secure section. He followed a couple of threads, the obvious directions. This was a view of the library that no mere apprentice would have. Nau had obtained – in ways that Ezr imagined, and still gave him nightmares – top-level passwords and security parameters. Now Ezr had the same view that Captain Park himself could have had.

No luck. The pointers showed the localizers clearly. Their small size was not really a secret, but even their incidentals manifest did not show them as carrying sensors. The on-chip manuals were just as innocent of strange features. *Hunh.* So Trinli was claiming there were trapdoors in the manuals that were invisible even in a captain's view of the library?

The anger that had been churning his guts was momentarily forgotten. Ezr stared out at the data lands ranged around him, feeling suddenly relieved. Tomas Nau would see nothing strange in this situation. Except for Ezr Vinh, there might not be a single surviving Trader who would realize how absurd Trinli's story must be.

But Ezr Vinh had grown up in the heart of a great trading Family. As a child he had sat at the dinner table, listening to discussions of fleet strategies as they were really practiced. A Captain's level of access to his fleet library did not normally admit of further hidden features. Things – as always – could be lost; legacy applications were often so old that the search engines couldn't find relevance. But short of sabotage or a customizing, nonstandard Captain, there should be no isolated secrets. In the long run, such measures were simply too painful for the system maintainers.

Ezr would have laughed, except he suspected that these sanitized huds were reporting every sound he made back to Brughel's zipheads. Yet this was the first happy thought of the day. *Trinli was bullshitting us!* The old fraud bluffed about a lot of things, but he was usually careful with Tomas Nau. When it came time to give Reynolt the details, Trinli would scrounge in the chip manuals . . . and come up empty-handed. Somehow Ezr couldn't feel much sympathy for him; for once the old bastard would get what he deserved.

21

Qiwi Lin Lisolet spent a lot of time out-of-doors. Maybe with the localizer gimmick Old Trinli was promising, that would change. Qiwi floated low across the old Diamond One/Two contact edge. Now it was in sunlight, the volatiles of the earlier years moved or boiled away. Where it was undisturbed, the surface of the diamond was gray and dull and smooth, almost opalescent. The sunlight eventually burned the top millimeter or so into graphite, kind of a micro-regolith, disguising the glitter below. Every ten meters along the edge there was a rainbow glint, where a sensor was set. The ejet emplacements extended off on either side. Even this close, you could scarcely see the activity, but Qiwi knew her gear: the electric jets sputtered in millisecond bursts, guided by the programs that listened to her sensors. And even that wasn't delicate enough. Qiwi spent more than two thirds of her duty time floating around the rockpile, adjusting the ejets – and still the rock quakes were dangerously large. With a finer sensor net and the programs that Trinli was claiming, it should be easy to design better firing regimes. Then there would be millions of quakes, but so small no one would notice. And then she wouldn't have to be here so much of the time. Qiwi wondered what it would be like to be on a low-duty cycle Watch schedule like most people. It would save medical resources, but it would also leave poor Tomas even more alone.

Her mind slid around the worry. *There are things you can cure and things you can't; be grateful for what Trinli's localizers will make right.* She floated up from the cleft, and checked with the rest of her maintenance crew.

'Just the usual problems,' Floria Peres's voice sounded in her ear. Floria was coasting over the 'upper slopes' of Diamond Three. That was above the rockpile's current zero-surface. They lost a few jets there every year. 'Three loosened mountings . . . we caught them in time.'

'Very good. I'll put Arn and Dima on it. I think we're done early.' She smiled to herself. Plenty of time for the more interesting projects. She switched her comm away from her crew's public sequency. 'Hey, Floria. You're in charge of the distillery this Watch, true?'

'Sure.' There was a chuckle in the other's voice. 'I try to get that job every time; working for you is just one of the unavoidable chores that come along with it.'

'Well, I have some things for you. Maybe we can deal?'

'Oh, maybe.' Floria was on a mere ten-percent duty cycle; even so, this was a dance they had been through before. Besides, she was Qeng Ho. 'Meet me down at the distillery in a couple of thousand seconds. We can have tea.'

The volatiles distillery sat at the end of its slow trek across the dark side of the rockpile. Its towers and retorts glistened with frost in the Arachna-light; in other places, it glowed with dull red heat where fractionation and recombination occurred. What came out was the simple stock materials for their factory and the organic sludges for the bactries. The core of the L1 distillery was from the Qeng Ho fleet. The Emergents had brought along similar equipment, but it had been lost in the fighting. *Thank goodness it was ours that survived.* The repairs and new construction had forced them to scavenge from all the ships. If the distillery core had been Emergent technology, they'd've been lucky to have anything working now.

Qiwi tied down her taxi a few meters from the distillery. She unloaded her thermal-wrapped cargo, and pulled herself along the guide ropes toward the entrance. Around her lay the sweeping drifts of their remaining hoard of volatiles: airsnow and ocean ice from the surface of Arachna. Those had come a long way, and cost a lot. Much of the original mass, especially the airsnow, had been lost in the Relight and chance illuminations since. The remainder had been pushed and balanced into the safest shadows, had been melted in a vain attempt to glue the rockpile together, had been used to breathe and eat and live. Tomas had plans to hollow out portions of Diamond One as a really secure capture cave. Maybe that wouldn't be necessary. As the sun slowly dimmed, it should be easier to save what was left. Meantime, the distillery made its slow progress – less than ten meters per year – through the drifts of ice and air. Behind, it left starglint on raw diamond, and a track of anchor holes.

Floria's control cubby was at the base of the distillery's rearmost towers. As part of the original Qeng Ho module, it had been nothing more than a pressurized hutch to eat and nap in. Over the years of the Exile, its various occupants had added to it. Coming in on it from ground level . . . Qiwi paused a moment. Most of her life was spent either in close-in rooms and tunnels, or in open emptiness. Floria's latest changes made this something in between. She could imagine what Ezr would say of this: It really did look

618

like a little cabin, almost like the fairy-tale pictures of how a farmer might live in the snow-covered foothills of an ancient land, close to a glistening forest.

Qiwi climbed past the outriggers and anchor cables – the edge of the magic forest – and knocked on the cabin door.

Trading was always fun. She had tried so many times to explain that to Tomas. The poor fellow had a good heart, but he came from a culture that just could not understand.

Qiwi brought partial payment for Floria's most recent output: Inside the thermal wrap was a twenty-centimeter bonsai, something Papa had worked Msecs to build. Micro-dwarf ferns grew out into multiple canopies. Floria held the bonsai bubble close to the room's overhead light and looked up through the green. 'The midges!' – submillimeter bugs. 'They have colored wings!'

Qiwi had followed her friend's reaction with carefully pretended neutrality, but now she couldn't help herself, and she laughed. 'I wondered if you would notice.' The bonsai was smaller than Papa's usual, but it might be the most beautiful yet, better than anything Qiwi had ever seen in the library. She reached into the thermal wrap and brought out the other part of the payment. 'And this is from Gonle, personally. It's a clasp stand for the bonsai.'

'It's . . . wood.' Floria had been charmed by the bonsai. Her reaction to the wood plate was more like amazement. She reached out to slide her fingers across the polished grain.

'We can make it by the tonne lot now, kind of a reverse dry rot. Of course, since Gonle grows it in vats, it looks a little strange.' The stripes and whorls were biowaves caught in the grain of the wood. 'We'd need more space and time to get real rings.' Or maybe not; Papa thought he might be able to trick the biowaves into faking growth rings.

'Doesn't matter.' Floria's voice was abstracted. 'Gonle has won her bet . . . or your father has won it for her. Imagine. Real wood in quantity, not just twigs in a bonsai bubble, or brush in the temp's park.' She looked at Qiwi's grinning face. 'And I bet she figures this more than pays for past deals.'

'Well . . . we hoped it would soften you up.' They sat down, and Floria brought out the tea she had promised, from Gonle Fong's agris and before that from the mounds of volatiles and diamond that surrounded the distillery. The two of them worked through the list that Benny and Gonle had put together. The list was not just their orders, but the result of the brokering that went on day after day up in Benny's parlor. There were items here that were mainly for Emergent use. Lord, there were items in here that Tomas could have simply demanded, and that Ritser Brughel would certainly have demanded.

Floria's objections were a catalogue of technical problems, things she would need before she could undertake what was asked of the distillery. She would get all she could out of these deals, but in fact what was being asked of her was technically difficult. Once, in pre-Flight when Qiwi couldn't have been more than seven years old, Papa had taken her to a distillery at Triland. 'This is what feeds the bactries, Qiwi, just as the bactries support the parks. Each layer is more wonderful than the one below it, but making even the lowliest distillery is a kind of art.' Ali loved his high end of the job above all others, but he still respected those others. Floria Peres was a talented chemist, and the dead goo she made was a marvelous creation.

Four thousand seconds later, they had agreed on a web of perks and favors for the rest of Floria's Watch. They sat for a time, sipping a new batch of tea and idly discussing what they might try after the current goals were accomplished, Qiwi told her Trinli's claims about the localizers.

'That's good news, if the old fart isn't lying. Maybe now you won't have to live at such a high duty cycle.' Floria looked across at Qiwi, and there was a strange, sad expression in her eyes. 'You were a little girl, and now you're older than I am. You shouldn't have to burn your life out, child, just to keep a bunch of rocks lined up.'

'It – It's not that bad. It needs to be done, even if we don't have the best medical support.' *Besides, Tomas is always on Watch and he needs my help.* 'And there are advantages to being up most of the time. I get into almost everything. I know where there are deals to be made, goodies to be scrounged. It makes me a better Trader.'

'Hmm.' Floria looked away, and then abruptly back. 'This isn't trading! It's a silly game!' Her voice softened. 'I'm sorry, Qiwi. You can't really know . . . but I know what trade is really like. I've been to Kielle. I've been to Canberra. This,' she waved her hand, as if to encompass all of L1 – 'this is just pretend. You know why I always ask for this distillery job? I've made this control cubby into something like a home, where *I* can pretend. I can pretend I'm alone and far away. I don't have to live in the temp with Emergents who pretend they are decent human beings.'

'But many of them are, Floria!'

Peres shook her head, and her voice rose. 'Maybe. And maybe that's the most terrible part of it. Emergents like Rita Liao and Jau Xin. Just folks, eh? And every day they use other human beings like less than animals, like – like *machine parts*. Even worse, that's their living. Isn't Liao a "programmer manager" and Xin a "pilot manager"? The greatest evil in the universe, and they lap it up and then sit down with us in Benny's parlor, *and we accept them!*' Her voice scaled up to just short of a shriek, and she was abruptly silent. She closed her eyes tight and tears floated gently downward through the air.

Qiwi reached out to touch Floria's hand, not knowing if the other might simply strike her. This was a pain she saw in various people. Some she could reach. Others, like Ezr Vinh, held it so rigidly secret that all she felt was a hint of hidden, pulsing rage.

Floria was silent, hunched over on herself. But after a moment she grasped Qiwi's hand in both her own and bowed her head toward it, weeping. Her words were choked, almost unintelligible. '. . . don't blame you . . . I really don't. I know 'bout your father.' She gasped on silent sobs, and after a moment her words came more clearly. 'I know you love this Tomas Nau. That's okay. He couldn't manage without you, but we'd probably all be dead then, too.'

Qiwi put her other arm around the woman's shoulders. 'But I don't love him.' The words popped out, surprising her. And Floria looked up, surprised too.

'I mean, I respect him. He saved me when things were worst, after Jimmy killed my mother. But—' Strange to be talking to Floria like this, saying words that before she had said only inside herself. Tomas needed her. He was a good man raised in a terrible, evil system. The proof of his goodness was that he had come as far as he had, that he understood the evil and worked to end it. Qiwi doubted that she could have done as much; she would have been more like Rita and Jau, dumbly accepting, grateful to have evaded the net of Focus. Tomas Nau really wanted to change things. But love him? For all his humor, love, wisdom, there was a . . . remoteness . . . to Tomas. She hoped he never realized she felt that about him. *And I hope subversive Floria has disabled Ritser's bugs.*

Qiwi pushed the thoughts away. For a moment she and Floria just stared at each other, surprised to see the other's heart exposed. *Hmm.* She gave Floria a little pat on the shoulder: 'I've known you for more than a year of shared Watch, and this is the first time there's been any hint you felt this way: . . .'

Floria released Qiwi's hand, and wiped at the tears that still stood in her eyes. Her voice was almost under control. 'Yeah. Before, I could always keep a lid on it. "Lie low," I told myself, "and be a proper little conquered Peddler." We're naturally good at that, don't you think? Maybe it comes from having the long view. But now . . . You know I had a sister in-fleet?'

'No.' *I'm sorry.* There had been so many Qeng Ho in the fleet before the fighting, and little Qiwi had known so few.

'Luan was a wild card, not too bright, but good with people . . . the sort a wise Fleet Captain throws in the mix.' A smile came close to surfacing, then drowned in bleak remembrance. 'I have a doctorate in chemical engineering, but they Focused Luan and left me free. It should have been *me*, but they took her instead.'

Floria's face twisted with guilt that should not have been. Maybe Floria was immune to permanent infection by the mindrot, like many of the Qeng Ho. Or maybe not. Tomas needed at least as many free as Focused, else the system would die the death of details. Qiwi opened her mouth to explain, but Floria wasn't listening.

'I lived with that. And I kept track of Luan. They Focused her on their *art*. Watch-on-Watch, she and her gang carved out those friezes on Hammerfest. You probably saw her a hundred times.'

Yes, that is surely true. The carving gangs were the lowest of the Focused jobs. It wasn't the high creation of Ali Lin or the translators. The patterns of the Emergent 'legend art' left nothing to creativity. The workers beetled down the diamond corridors, centimeter by centimeter, scooping tiny bits from the walls according to the master pattern. Ritser's original plan had been that the project burn up all the 'waste human resources,' working them without medical care unto death.

'But they don't work Watch-on-Watch anymore, Floria.' That had been one of Qiwi's earliest triumphs over Ritser Brughel. The carving was made lighter work, and medical resources were made available to all who remained awake. The carvers would live through the Exile, to the manumissions that Tomas had promised.

Floria nodded. 'Right and even though our Watches were almost disjoint, I still kept track of Luan. I used to hang around the corridors, pretending to be passing through whenever other people came along. I even talked to her about that damn filthy art she loved; it was the only thing she could talk about, "The Defeat of the Frenkisch Orc"' Floria all but spat the title. Her anger faded, and she seemed to wilt. 'Even so, I still could see her and maybe, if I was a good little Peddler, she would be free someday. But now . . .' She turned to look at Qiwi and her voice once more lost its steadiness. '. . . now she's gone, not even on the roster. They claim her coffin failed. They claim she died in coldsleep. The lying, treacherous, *bastards . . .*'

Qeng Ho coldsleep boxes were so safe that the failure rate was a kind of statistical guess, at least under proper use and for spans of less than 4Gsec. Emergent equipment was flakier, and since the fighting, nobody's gear was absolutely trustable. Luan's death was most likely a terrible accident, just another echo of the madness that had nearly killed them all. *And how can I convince poor Floria of this?* 'I guess we can't be certain of anything we are told, Floria. The Emergents have an evil system. But . . . I was on one hundred percent Watch for a long time. I'm on fifty percent even now. I've been into almost everything. And you know, in all that time, I haven't caught Tomas in a lie.'

'Okay,' grudgingly.

'And why would anyone want to kill Luan?'

'I didn't say "kill." And maybe your Tomas doesn't know. See, I wasn't the only one who hung around the diamond carvers. Twice, I saw Ritser Brughel. Once he had all the women together, and was behind them, just watching. The other time . . . the other time it was just him and Luan.'

'Oh.' The word came out very small.

'I don't have evidence. What I saw was nothing more than a gesture, a posture, a look on a man's face. And so I was silent, and now Luan is gone.'

Floria's paranoia suddenly seemed quite plausible. Ritser Brughel *was* a monster, a monster barely held in check by the Podmaster system. The memory of their confrontation had never left Qiwi, the *slap slap slap* of his steel baton in his hands as he raged at her. At the time, Qiwi had felt angry triumph at putting him down. Since, she'd realized how scared she should have been. Without Tomas, she surely would have died then . . . or worse. Ritser knew what would happen if he was caught.

Faking a death, even committing an unsanctioned execution, was tricky. The Podmasters had their own peculiar record-keeping requirements. Unless Ritser was very clever, there would be clues. 'Listen, Floria. There are ways I can check on this. You could be right about Luan, but one way or another we'll find out the truth. And if you're right – well, there's no way Tomas can put up with such abuse. He needs all the Qeng Ho cooperating, or none of us have a chance.'

Floria looked at her solemnly, then reached round to give her a fierce hug. Qiwi could feel the shivers that passed through her body, but she wasn't crying. After a long moment, Floria said, 'Thank you. Thank you. This last Msec, I've been so frightened . . . so ashamed.'

'Ashamed?'

'I love Luan, but Focus made her a stranger. I should have screamed bloody murder when I heard she was gone. Hell, I should have complained when I saw Brughel with her. But I was afraid for myself. Now . . .' Floria loosened her grip and regarded Qiwi with a shaky smile. 'Now, maybe I've endangered someone else, too. But at least you have a chance . . . and you know, it's possible that she's alive even now, Qiwi. If we can find her soon enough.'

Qiwi raised her palm. 'Maybe, maybe. Let's see what I can discover.'

'Yes.' They finished their tea, discussed everything Floria could remember about her sister and what she had seen. She was doing her best now to seem calm, but relief and nervousness made her words come a bit too fast, made her gestures a bit too broad.

Qiwi helped her set the bonsai bubble and its wood stand in brackets beneath the room's main light. 'I can get you lots more wood. Gonle really, really wants you to program for meta-crylates. You might want to panel your home with polished wood, like old-time captains did their inner cabins.'

Floria looked around her little space, and played along. 'I could indeed. Tell her, maybe we can do a deal.'

And then Qiwi was standing at the lock's inner door, and pulling down her coverall hood. For a moment, the fear was back in Floria's face. 'Be careful, Qiwi.'

'I will.'

Qiwi took her taxi through the rest of its stops, inspecting the rockpile, posting problems and changes to the ziphead net. Meantime, her mind raced down scary corridors. It was just as well she had this time to think. If Floria was right, then even with Tomas on her side, this could be very dangerous. Ritser was just into too many things. If he was sabotaging the coldsleep or falsifying death records, then big parts of Tomas's net had been subverted.

Does Ritser suspect that I know? Qiwi glided down across the canyon that separated Diamond Three from Diamond Four. Arachna's blue light shone from directly behind her, illuminating the caves that were the rough interface between the blocks. There was sublimation from some of the water glue. It was too fine to show on the sensor grid, but when she hovered with her face just centimeters from the surface she could see it. Even as she called in the problem, another part of her mind was turning on the deadlier question: Floria was clever enough to sweep her little cabin, even the outside. And Qiwi was very careful with her suit. Tomas had given her permission to disable all its bugs, both official and covert. On the net it was a different story. If Ritser was doing what Floria thought, then very likely he was monitoring even pod communications. It would be tricky to discover anything without tipping him off.

So be very, very careful. She needed an excuse for anything she did now. *Ah.* The personnel studies that she and Ezr had been assigned. Coasting up from her inspection of the rockpile, it would be reasonable for her to work on that. She put in a low-priority call to Ezr asking for a conference, then downloaded a large block of the Watch and personnel database. The records on Luan would be in there, but they were now cached locally, and her processors were covered by Tomas's own security.

She brought up the bio on Luan Peres. Yes, reported dead in coldsleep. Qiwi flicker-read down through the text. There was lots of jargon, conjecture about how the unit had failed. Qiwi had had years to practice with coldsleep gear, if only as a front-end technician. She could more or less follow the discussion, though it seemed like the florid overkill of a rambling ziphead, what you might get if you *asked* a Focused person to invent a credible failure.

The taxi floated out of the rockpile's shadow and the sunlight washed away the quiet blues of Arachna-light. The rockpile sunside was naked rock, graphite on diamond. Qiwi dimmed the view and turned back to the report on Luan. It was almost a clean report. It might have fooled her if she hadn't been suspicious or if she hadn't known all the requirements of Emergent doc. Where were the third and fourth crosschecks on the autopsy? Reynolt always wanted her zips to do that; the woman lost what little flexibility she had when it came to ziphead fatalities.

The report was bogus. Tomas would understand that the moment she pointed it out to him.

A chime sounded in her ear. 'Ezr, hello.' Damn. Her call to him had just been a cover, an excuse to download a big block and look at Luan's records. But here he was. For a moment, he seemed to be sitting next to her in the taxi. Then the image flickered as her huds figured out they couldn't manage the illusion, and settled for putting him in a fixed position pseudo-display. Behind him were the blue-green walls of the Hammerfest attic. He was visiting Trixia, of course.

The picture was more than good enough to show the impatience in his face. 'I decided to get right back to you. You know I go off-Watch in sixty Ksec.'

'Yes, sorry to bother you. I've been looking over the personnel stats. For that planning committee stuff you and I are stuck with? Anyway, I came up with a question.' Her mind raced ahead of her words, searching madly for some issue that would justify this call. Funny how the least attempt at deception always seemed to make life more complicated. She stumbled along for a few sentences, finally came up with a really stupid question about specialist mixing.

Ezr was looking at her a little strangely now. He shrugged. 'You're asking about the end of the Exile, Qiwi. Who knows what we'll need when the Spiders are ready for contact. I thought we were going to bring all specialties out of cold-sleep then, and run flat out.'

'Of course, that's the plan, but there are details—' Qiwi weaseled her way toward credibility. The main thing was just to end the conversation. '—so I'll think about this some more. Let's have a real meeting after you get back on from coldsleep.'

Ezr grimaced. 'That will be a while. I'm off for fifty Msec.' Most of two years.

'What?' That was more than four times as long as his usual off-Watch.

'You know, new faces and all that.' There were branches of his Watch tree that had not had much time. Tomas and the manager committee – Qiwi and Ezr included! – had thought everyone should get hands-on time and exposure to the usual training courses.

'You're starting a little early.' And 50Msec was longer than she expected.

'Yeah. Well, you have to start someplace.' He looked away from the video pov. At Trixia? When he looked back, his tone was less impatient but somehow more urgent. 'Look, Qiwi. I'm going to be on ice for a big fifty, and even afterwards I'll be on a low duty cycle for a while.' He raised a hand as if to forestall objections. 'I'm not complaining! I participated in the decisions myself . . . But Trixia will be on-Watch all that time. That's longer than she has ever been alone. There'll be nobody to stand up for her.'

Qiwi wished she could reach out and comfort him. 'No one will harm her, Ezr.'

'Yeah, I know. She's too *valuable* to harm. Just like your father.' Something flickered in his eyes, but it wasn't the usual anger. Poor Ezr was begging her. 'They'll keep her body working, they'll keep her moderately clean. But I don't want her hassled any more than she already is. Keep an eye on her, Qiwi. You have real power, at least over small fish like Trud Silipan.'

It was the first time Ezr had really asked her for help.

'I'll watch out for her, Ezr,' Qiwi said softly. 'I promise.'

After he rang off, Qiwi sat unmoving for several seconds. Strange that a phone call that was an accident and a scam should have such an impact. But Ezr had always had that effect on her. When she was thirteen, Ezr Vinh had seemed the most wonderful man in the universe – and the only way she could get his attention was by goading him. Such teenage crushes should vape away, right? Occasionally she wondered if the Diem massacre had somehow stunted her soul, trapped her affections as they were in the last innocent days before all the death . . . Whatever the reason, it felt good that she could do something for him.

Maybe paranoia was contagious. Luan Peres dead. Now Ezr gone for even longer than they had planned. *I wonder who actually specified that Watch change?* Qiwi looked back through her cache. The schedule change was nominally from the Watch-manager committee . . . with Ritser Brughel doing the actual sign-off. That happened often enough; one Podmaster or the other had to sign for all such changes.

Qiwi's taxi continued its slow coast upward. From this distance, the rockpile was a craggy jumble, Diamond Two in sunlight, the glare obscuring all but the brightest stars. It might have been a wilderness scene except, for the regular form of the Qeng Ho temp gleaming off to the side. With augmented vision, Qiwi could see the dozens of warehouses of the L1 system. Down in the shade of the rockpile were Hammerfest and the distillery, and the arsenal at L1-A. In the spaces around orbited the temp, the warehouses, the junked and semi-junked starships that had brought them all here. Qiwi used them as a kind of soft auxiliary to the electric jets. It was a well-tended dynamical system, even though it did look like chaos compared to the close mooring of the early Exile.

Qiwi took in the configuration with practiced eyes, even as her mind considered the much more treacherous problems of political intrigue. Ritser Brughel's private domain, the old QHS *Invisible Hand*, was outward from the pile, less than two thousand meters from her taxi; she would pass less than fifteen hundred meters from its throat. *Hmm.* So, what if Ritser had kidnapped Luan Peres? That would be his boldest move ever against Tomas. *And maybe it's not the only thing.* If Ritser could get away with this, there might be other deaths. *Ezr.*

Qiwi took a deep breath. *Just take one problem at a time. So: Suppose Floria is right and Luan still lives, a toy in Ritser's private space?* There were limits to how fast Tomas could act against another Podmaster. If she complained, and there was any delay at all, Luan might die for real – and all the evidence could just . . . disappear.

Qiwi turned in her seat, got a naked-eye view of the *Hand*. She was less than seventeen hundred meters out now. It might be days before she could wangle a configuration this slick. The starship's stubby form was so close that she could see the emergency repair welds, and the blistering where X-ray fire had struck the ramscoop's projection flange. Qiwi knew the architecture of the *Invisible Hand* about as well as anyone at L1; she had lived on that ship through years of the voyage here, had used it as her hands-on example of every ship topic in her schooling. She knew its blind spots . . . More important, she had Podmaster-level access. It was just one of the many things that Tomas trusted her with. Until now she had never used it so, um, provocatively, but—

Qiwi's hands were moving even before she finished rationalizing her scheme. She keyed in her personal crypto link to Tomas, and spoke quickly, outlining what she had learned and what she suspected – and what she planned to do. She squirted the message off, delivery contingent on a deadman condition. Now Tomas would know no matter what, and she would have something to threaten Ritser with if he caught her.

Sixteen hundred meters from the *Invisible Hand*. Qiwi pulled down her coverall hood, and cycled the taxi's atmosphere. Her intuition and her huds agreed on the jump path she must follow, the trajectory that would take her down the *Hand*'s throat, in the ship's blind spot all the way. She popped the taxi's hatch, waited till her acrobatic instinct said *go* – and leaped into the emptiness.

Qiwi finger-walked down the *Hand*'s empty freight hold. Using a combination of Tomas's authority and her own special knowledge of the ship's architecture, she had reached the level of the living quarters without tripping any audible alarms. Every few meters, Qiwi put her ear to the wall, and simply listened. She was so close to on-Watch country that she could hear other people. Things sounded very ordinary, no sudden movement, no anxious talk . . . Hmm. *That* sounded like someone crying.

Qiwi moved faster, feeling something like the giddy anger of her long-ago confrontation with Ritser Brughel – only now she had more sense, and was correspondingly more afraid. During their common Watches since that time in the park, she had often felt Ritser's eyes upon her. She had always expected that there would be another confrontaion. As much as it was to honor her mother's memory, Qiwi's fanatical gym work – all the martial arts – was intended as insurance against Ritser and his steel baton. *Lot of good it will do, if he pots me with a wire gun.* But Ritser was such an idiot, he'd never kill her like that; he'd want to gloat. Today, if it came to it, she'd have time to threaten him with the message she'd left Tomas. She pushed down her fear, and moved closer to the sound of weeping.

Qiwi hovered over an access hatch. Suddenly her shoulders and arms were tense. Strange, random thoughts skittered through her mind. *I will remember. I will remember.* Freaky craziness.

Beyond this point, her only invisibility would be in her Podmaster passkey. Very likely that would not be enough. *But I just need a few seconds.* Qiwi checked her recorder and data link one last time . . . and slipped through the hatch, into a crew corridor.

Lord. For a moment, Qiwi just stared in astonishment. The corridor was the size that she remembered. Ten meters farther on, it curved right, toward the Captain's living quarters. But Ritser had pasted wallpaper on all four walls, and the pictures were a kind of swirling pink. The air stank of animal musk. This was a different universe from the *Invisible Hand* that she had known. She grasped wildly at her courage, and moved slowly up the hallway. Now there was music ahead, at least the *thump thump thump* of percussion. Somebody was singing . . . sharp, barking screams, in time with the beat.

Like they had a life of their own, her shoulders cramped tight, aching to bounce off the wall and race back the way she had come. *Do I need any more proof?* Yes. Just a look at the data system with a local override. That would mean more than any number of hysterical stories about Ritser's choice of video and music.

Door by door, she moved up the corridor. These had been staff officer quarters, but used by the Watch crew on the voyage from Triland. She had lived in the second room from the end for three years – and she really didn't want to know what that looked like now. The Captain's planning room was just beyond the bend. She flicked her passkey at the lock, and the door slid open. Inside . . . this was no planning room. It looked like a cross between a gym and a bedroom. And the walls were again covered with video wallpaper. Qiwi pulled herself over a strange, gauntleted rack and settled down, out of sight of the doorway. She touched her huds, asked for a local override connection to the ship's net. There was a pause as her location and authorization were checked, and then she was looking at names and dates and pictures. *Yes!* Ol' Ritser was running his own small-scale coldsleep business right here on the *Invisible Hand.* Luan Peres was listed . . . and *here* she was listed as living, on-Watch!

That's enough; time to get out of this madhouse. But Qiwi hesitated an instant longer. There were so many names here, familiar names and faces from long ago. Little death glyphs sat by each picture. She had been a child when she last saw these people, but not like this . . . these faces were variously sullen, sleeping, terribly bruised or burned. The living, the dead, the beaten, the fiercely resisting. *This is from before Jimmy Diem.* She knew there had been interrogations, a period of many Ksecs between the fighting and the resumption of Watches, but . . . Qiwi felt a numb horror spreading up from the pit of her stomach. She paged through the names. Kira Pen Lisolet. Mama. A bruised face, the eyes staring steadily back at her. *What did Ritser do to you? How could Tomas not know?* She wasn't really conscious of following the data links from that picture, but suddenly her huds were running an immersion video. The room was the same, but filled with the sights and sounds of long ago. As if from the other side of the rack, there came the sound of panting and moaning. Qiwi slid to the side and the vision tracked with near perfection. Around the corner of the rack, she came face-to-face with . . . Tomas Nau. A younger Tomas Nau. Out of sight, beyond the edge of the rack, he seemed to be thrusting from his hips. The look on his face was the sort of ecstatic pleasure that Qiwi had seen in his face so many times, the look he had when they could finally be alone and he could come in her. But this Tomas of years ago held a tiny, red-splattered knife. He leaned forward, out of sight, leaned down on someone whose moans changed to a shrill scream. Qiwi pulled herself over the edge of the rack and looked straight down at the true past, at the woman Nau was cutting.

'*Mama!*' The past didn't notice her cry; Nau continued his business. Qiwi doubled up on herself, spewing vomit across the rack and beyond. She couldn't see them anymore, but the sounds of the past continued, as if they were happening just on the other side of the rack. Even as her stomach emptied, she tore the huds from her face, threw them wildly away. She choked and gagged; gibbering horror was in charge of her reflexes.

The light changed as the room's door opened. There were voices. Voices in the present 'Yeah, she's in here, Marli.'

'Phew. What a mess.' Sounds of the two men quartering the room, coming closer to Qiwi's hiding place. Mindlessly she retreated, floated down beneath the nightmare equipment, and braced herself against the floor.

A face coasted across her position.

'Got h—'

Qiwi exploded upward, the blade of her hand just missing the other's neck. She slammed into the wall partition behind him. Pain lanced back along her arm.

She felt the prick of stunner darts. She turned, tried to bounce toward her attacker, but her legs were already dead. The two waited cautiously a second. Then the shooter, Marli, grinned and snagged her slowly-turning body. She couldn't move. She could barely breathe. But there was some sensation. She felt Marli draw her back to him, run his hand across her breasts. 'She's safe; don't worry, Tung.' Marli laughed. 'Or maybe you should worry. Look at that hole she put in the wall. Another four centimeters and you'd be breathing out the back of your neck!'

'Pus.' Tung's voice was sullen.

'You got her? Good.' It was Tomas's voice, from the door. Marli abruptly released his hold on her breasts. He coasted her around the equipment, into the open.

Qiwi couldn't turn her head. She saw whatever happened to be before her eyes. Tomas, calm as ever. *Calm as ever.* He glanced at her in passing, nodded to Marli. Qiwi tried to scream, but no sound came: *Tomas will kill me, like all the others . . . But if he doesn't? If he doesn't, then nothing in God's universe can save him.*

Tomas turned. Ritser Brughel was behind him, disheveled and half-naked. 'Ritser, this is inexcusable. The whole point of giving her access codes is to make capture predictable and easy. You knew she was coming, and you left yourself wide open.'

Brughel's voice was whiny. 'Plague take it. She's never twigged this soon after her last scrub. And I had less than three hundred seconds from your first warning till she arrived here. That's *never* happened before.'

Tomas glared at his Vice-Podmaster. 'The second was just bad luck – something you should count on. The first . . .' He looked back at Qiwi, and his anger turned to thoughtfulness. 'Something unexpected triggered her this time. Have Kal review just who she's been talking to.'

He gestured to Marli and Tung. 'Put her in a box and take her down to Hammerfest. Tell Anne I want the usual.'

'What cutoff time on the memories, sir?'

'I'll talk to Anne about that myself. We've got some records to look at.'

Qiwi got a glimpse of the corridor, of hands dragging her along. *How many times has this happened before?* No matter how hard she strained, she couldn't move a muscle. Inside she was screaming. *This time I will remember. I* will *remember!*

22

Pham followed Trud Silipan up the central tower of Hammerfest, toward the Attic. In a sense, this was the moment he had been angling for through Msecs of casual shmoozing – an excuse to get inside the Focus system, to see more than the results. No doubt he could have gotten here earlier – in fact, Silipan had offered more than once to show him around. Over the Watches they had known each other, Pham had made enough silly assertions about Focus, had bet Silipan and Xin enough scrip about his opinions; a plausible visit was inevitable. But there was plenty of time and Pham had never had quite the cover he'd wanted. *Don't fool yourself. Popping the localizers on Tomas Nau has put you in more danger than anything so far.*

'Now, finally, you're going to see behind the scenes, Pham old boy. After this, I hope you'll shut up about some of your crazy theories.' Silipan was grinning; clearly, he'd been looking forward to this moment himself.

They drifted upward, past narrow tunnels that forked and forked. The place was a warren.

Pham pulled himself even with the coasting Silipan. 'What's to know? So you Emergents can make people into automatic devices. So what? Even a ziphead can't multiply numbers faster than once or twice a second. Machines can do it trillions of times faster. So with zipheads, you get the pleasure of bossing people around — and for what? The slowest, crappiest automation since Humankind learned to write.'

'Yeah, yeah. You've been saying that for years. But you're still wrong.' He stuck out a foot, catching a stop with the toe of his shoe. 'Keep your voice down inside the group-room, okay?' They were facing a real door, not one of the little crawl hatches of lower down. Silipan waved it open and they drifted through. Pham's first impression was of body odor and packed humanity.

'They do get pretty ripe, don't they? They're healthy, though. I see to that.' He spoke with a technician's pride.

There was rack on rack of micro-gee seating, packed in a three-dimensional lattice that would have been impossible in any real gravity. Most of the seats were occupied. There were men and women of all ages, dressed in grays, most using what looked to be premium Qeng Ho head-up display devices. This wasn't what he had been expecting. 'I thought you kept them isolated,' in little cells such as Ezr Vinh had described in more than one tearful session in the booze parlor.

'Some we do. It depends on the application.' He waved at the room attendants, two men dressed like hospital orderlies. 'This is a lot cheaper. Two guys can handle all the potty calls, and the usual fights.'

'Fights?'

' "Professional disagreements." ' Silipan chuckled. 'Snits, really. They're only dangerous if they upset the mindrot's balance.'

They floated diagonally upward between the close-packed rows. Some of the huds flickered transparently and he could see the zipheads' eyes moving. But no one seemed to notice Pham and Trud; their vision was elsewhere.

There was low-pitched mumbling from all directions, the combined voices of all the zipheads in the room. There were a lot of people talking, all in short bursts of words — Nese, but still nonsense. The global effect was an almost hypnotic chant.

The zipheads typed ceaselessly on chording keyboards. Silipan pointed to their hands with special pride. 'See, not one in five has any joint damage; we can't afford to lose people. We have so few, and Reynolt can't completely control the mindrot. But it's been most of a year since we had a simple medical fatality — and that was almost unavoidable. Somehow the zip got a punctured colon right *after* a clean checkup. He was an isolated specialty. His performance fell off, but we didn't know there was a problem till the smell got completely rank.' So the slave had died from the inside out, too dedicated to cry his pain, too neglected for anyone to notice. Trud Silipan was only caring in the mean.

They reached the top, looked back down the lattice of mumbling humanity. 'Now in one way you're right, Mr Armsman Trinli. If these people were doing arithmetic or string sorting, this operation would be a joke. The smallest processor in a finger ring can do that sort of thing a billion times faster than any human. But you hear the zipheads talking?'

'Yeah, but it doesn't make any sense.'

'It's internal jargon; they get into that pretty fast when we work them in teams. But the point is, they're not doing low-level machine functions. They're *using* our computer resources. See, for us Emergents, the zipheads are the next system layer above software. They can apply human intelligence, but with the persistence and patience of a machine. And that's also why unFocused specialists – especially techs like me – are important. Focus is useless unless there are normal people to direct it and to find the proper balance of hardware and software and Focus. Done right, the combination is totally beyond what you Qeng Ho ever achieved.'

Pham had long ago understood that, but denying the point provoked steadily more detailed explanations from Emergents like Trud Silipan. 'So what is this group actually doing?'

'Let's see.' He motioned for Pham to put on his huds. 'Ah, see? We have them partitioned into three groups. The top third is rote-layer processing, zipheads that can be easily retargeted. They're great for routine tasks, like direct queries. The middle third is programming. As a Programmer-at-Arms, this should interest you.' He popped up some dependency charts. They were squirrelly nonsense, immense blocks with no evolutionary coherence. 'This is a rewrite of your own weapons targeting code.'

'Crap. I could never maintain something like that.'

'No, *you* couldn't. But a Programmer-Manager – someone like Rita Liao – can, as long as she has a team of ziphead programmers. She's having them rearrange and optimize the code. They've done what ordinary humans could do if they could concentrate endlessly. Together with good development software, these zips have produced a code that is about half the size of your original – and five times as fast on the same hardware. They also combed out hundreds of bugs.'

Pham didn't say anything for a moment. He just paged through the maze of the dependency charts. Pham had hacked for years at the weapons programs. Sure there were bugs, as there were in any large system. But the weapons code had been the object of thousands of years of work, of constant effort to optimize and remove flaws . . . He cleared his huds and looked across the ranked slaves. *Such a terrible price to pay . . . for such wonderful results.*

Silipan chuckled. 'Can't fool me, Trinli. I can tell you're impressed.'

'Yeah, well if it works I am. So what's the third group doing?'

But Silipan was already heading back to the entrance. 'Oh, them.' He waved negligently at the zipheads on his right. 'Reynolt's ongoing project. We're going through the corpus of your fleet system code, looking for trapdoors, that sort of thing.'

It was the wild-goose chase that preoccupied the most paranoid system administrators, but after what he'd just seen . . . suddenly Pham didn't feel quite so secure. *How long do I have before they notice some of my long-ago mods?*

They left the grouproom and started back down the central tower. 'See, Pham, you – all you Qeng Ho – grew up wearing blinders. You just *know* certain things are impossible. I see the clichés in your literature: "Garbage input means garbage output"; "The trouble with automation is that it does exactly what you ask it"; "Automation can never be truly creative." Humankind has accepted such claims for thousands of years. But we Emergents have disproved them! With ziphead support, I can get correct performance from ambiguous inputs. I can get effective natural language translation. I can get human-quality judgment as part of the automation!'

They coasted downward at several meters per second; upward traffic was sparse just now. The light at the bottom of the tower glowed brighter. 'Yeah, so what about creativity?' This was something Trud loved to pontificate on.

'Even that, Pham. Well, not all forms of creativity. Like I said, there is a real need for managers such as Rita and myself, and the Podmasters above us. But you know about really creative people, the artists who end up in your history books? As often as not, they're some poor dweeb who doesn't have a life. He or she is just totally fixated on learning everything about some single topic. A sane person couldn't justify losing friends and family to concentrate so hard. Of course, the payoff is that the dweeb may find things or make things that are totally unexpected. See, in that way a little of Focus has always been part of the human race. We Emergents have simply institutionalized this sacrifice so the whole community can benefit in a concentrated, organized way.'

Silipan reached out, lightly touching the walls on both sides, slowing his descent. He dropped behind for a moment before Pham started braking too.

'How long till your appointment with Anne Reynolt?' Silipan asked.

'Just over a Ksec.'

'Okay, I'll keep this short. Can't keep the boss lady waiting.' He laughed. Silipan seemed to have an especially low regard for Anne Reynolt. If she were incompetent, a lot of things would be simpler for Pham . . .

They passed through a pressure door, into what might have been a sickbay. There were a few coldsleep coffins; they looked like medical temporaries. Visible behind the equipment was another door, this one bearing a Podmaster special seal. Trud gave a nervous glance in that direction, and did not look back again.

'So. Here's where it all happens, Pham. The real magic of Focus.' He dragged Pham across the room, away from the half-hidden door. A technician was working by the limp form of a ziphead, maneuvering the 'patient's head into one of the large toroids that dominated the room. Those might be diagnostic imagers, though they were even clunkier-looking than most Emergent hardware.

'You already know the basic principles, right, Pham?'

'Sure.' Those had been carefully explained in the first Watch after Jimmy's murder. 'You've got this special virus, the mindrot; you infected us all.'

'Right, right. But that was a military operation. In most cases the rot didn't get past the blood/brain barrier. But when it does . . . You know about glial cells? You've got lots more of those in your brain than neurons, actually. Anyway, the rot uses the glials as a kind of broth, infects almost all of them. After four days or so—'

'—You have a ziphead?'

'No. You have the raw material for a ziphead; many of you Qeng Ho ended up in that state – unFocused, perfectly healthy, but with the infection permanently established. In such people, every neuron in the brain is adjacent to infection cells. And each rotted cell has a menu of neuro-actives it can secrete. Now, this guy—' He turned to the tech, who was still working on the comatose ziphead. 'Bil, what *is* this one in for?'

Bil Phuong shrugged. 'He's been fighting. Al had to stun him. There's no chance of mindrot runaway, but Reynolt wants his basal-five retrained on the sequence from . . .'

The two traded jargon. Pham glanced with careful disinterest at the ziphead. Egil Manrhi. Egil had been the punning-est armsman in pre-Flight. But now . . . now he was probably a better analyst than he had ever been before.

Trud was nodding at Phuong: 'Huh. I don't see why messing with basal-five will do any good. But then she is the boss, isn't she?' He grinned at the other. 'Hey, let me do this one, okay? I want to show Pham.'

'Just so you sign for it.' Phuong moved out of their way, looking faintly bored. Silipan slid down beside the gray-painted toroid. Pham noticed that the gadget had separate power cables, each a centimeter wide.

'Is this some kind of an imager, Trud? It looks like obsolete junk.'

'Ha. Not exactly. Help me get this guy's head in the cradle. Don't let him touch the sides . . .' An alarm tone sounded. 'And for God's sake, give Bil that ring you're wearing. If you're standing in the wrong place, the magnets in this baby would tear your finger off.'

Even in low gee, it was awkward to maneuver the comatose Egil Manrhi.

It was a tight fit, and the rockpile's gravity was just strong enough to drag Egil's head onto the lower side of the hole.

Trud moved back from his handiwork, and smiled. 'All set. Now you're going to see what it's all about, Pham, my boy.' He spoke commands and some kind of medical image floated in the air between them, presumably a view inside Egil's head. Pham could recognize gross anatomical features, but this was far from anything he had studied. 'You're right about the imaging, Pham. This is standard MRI, as old as time. But it's good enough. See, the basal-five harmony is generated here.' A pointer moved along a complex curve near the surface of the brain.

'Now here's the cute thing, what makes mindrot more than a neuro-pathic curiosity.' A galaxy of tiny glowing dots appeared in the three-dimensional image. They glowed in every color, though most were pink. There were clusters and strands of tiny dots, many of them flickering in time with one another. 'You're seeing infected glial cells, at least the relevant groups.'

'The colors?'

'Those show current drug secretion by type . . . Now, what I want to do . . .' More commands, and Pham had his first look at the toroid's user manual. '. . . is change the output and firing frequency along this path.' His little marker arrow swept along one of the threads of light. He grinned at Pham. '*This* is how our gear is more than an imager. See, the mindrot virus expresses certain para and dia-magnetic proteins, and *these* respond vari-ously to magnetic fields to trigger the production of specific neuroactives. So while you Qeng Ho and all the rest of humanity use MRI solely as an *observing* tool, we Emergents can use it actively, to make changes.' He tapped his keyboard; Pham heard a creaking sound as the superconducting cables spread apart from each other. Egil twitched a couple of times. Trud reached out to steady him. 'Damn. Can't get millimeter resolution with him thrashing,'

'I don't see any change in the brain map.'

'You won't till I turn off active mode. You can't image and modify at the same time.' He paused, watching the step-by-step in the manual. 'Almost done . . . There! Okay, let's see the changes.' There was a new picture. And now the glowing thread of fights was mostly blue, and frantically blinking. 'It'll take a few seconds to settle in.' He continued to watch the model as he talked. 'See, Pham. This is what I'm really good at. I don't know what you could compare me to in your culture. I'm a little like a programmer, but I don't code. I'm a little like a neurologist, except *I* get results. I guess I'm most like a hardware technician. I keep the gear going for all the higher-ups who take the credit.'

Trud frowned. '. . . Hunh? Pus.' He looked across the room at where the other Emergent was working. 'Bil, this guy's leptin-dop ratio is still low.'

'You turned off the field?'

'Of course. Basal-five should have retrained by now.'

Bil didn't come over, but apparently he was looking at the patient's brain model.

The line of blue glitter was still a jumble of random change. Trud continued, 'It's just a loose end, but I don't know what's causing it. Can you take care of it?' He hooked a thumb in Pham's direction, indicating he had other, more important business.

Bil said, dubiously, 'You did sign for it?'

'Yes, yes. Just take care of it, huh?'

'Yeah, okay.'

'Thanks.' Silipan gestured Pham away from the MRI gear; the brain image vanished. 'That Reynolt. Her jobs are the trickiest, not by the book. Then, when you do it the right way, you're likely to end up in a heap of trouble.'

Pham followed him out the door and down a side tunnel that cut through the crystal of Diamond One. The walls were a chiseled mosaic, the same style of precise artwork that had mystified Pham long ago, at the 'welcoming banquet.' Not all the zipheads were high-tech specialists: they passed a dozen slave artists clustered around the circumference of the tunnel, hunched close over magnifying glasses and needlelike tools. Pham had been along here before, several Watches earlier. Then, the frieze had been only roughly outlined, a mountain landscape with some sort of military force moving toward a nebulous goal. Even that had been a guess, based on the title: 'The Defeat of the Frenkisch Orc.' Now the figures were mostly complete, sturdy heroic fighters that glittered rainbows. Their goal was some kind of monster. The creature wasn't that novel, a typical Cthulhonic horror, tearing humans with its long claws and eating the pieces. Emergents made a big thing of their conquest of Frenk. Somehow, Pham doubted that the mutations they had warred against had been so spectacular. He slowed, and Silipan took his stare for admiration.

'The carvers make only fifty centimeters' progress every Msec. But the art brings some of the warmth of our past.'

Warmth? 'Reynolt wants things pretty?' It was a random question.

'Ha. Reynolt couldn't care less. Podmaster Braghel ordered this, per my recommendation.'

'But I thought Podmasters were sovereign in their domains.' Pham hadn't seen much of Reynolt on prior Watches, but he had seen her humiliate Ritser Brughel in meetings with Nau.

Trud continued on for several meters, not speaking. His face quirked in a silly smile, a look he sometimes got during their bull sessions at Benny's. This time though, the smile broke into laughter. 'Podmaster? Anne Reynolt? Pham, watching you boggle has already made my day – but this tops all.' He coasted for several seconds more, still chuckling. Then he saw the glower on Pham Trinli's face. 'I'm sorry, Pham. You Peddlers are clever

636

in so many ways, but you're like children when it comes to the basics of culture . . . I got you cleared to see the Focus clinic; I guess it can't hurt to spell some other things out. No, Anne Reynolt is not a Podmaster, though most likely she was a powerful one, once upon a time. Reynolt is just another ziphead.'

Pham let his glower fade to blank astonishment – which also happened to be his true reaction. 'But . . . she's running a big part of the show. She gives you orders.'

Silipan shrugged. His smile had changed to something sour. 'Yeah. She gives me orders. It's a rare thing, but it can happen. I'd almost rather work for Podmaster Brughel and Kal Omo except that they play so . . . rough.' His voice trailed off nervously.

Pham caught up. 'I think I see,' he lied. 'When a specialist gets Focused, he fixates on his specialty. So an artist becomes one of your mosaic carvers, a physicist becomes like Hunte Wen, and a manager becomes, uh, I don't know, the manager from Hell.'

Trud shook his head. 'It doesn't work like that. See, technical specialties Focus well. We got a seventy-percent success rate even with you Qeng Ho. But people skills – counseling, politics, personnel management – normally, those don't survive Focusing at all. You've seen enough zipheads by now; the one thing they have in common is flat affect. They can no more imagine what's going on in a normal person's head than a rock can. We're lucky to have as many good translators as we do; that's never been tried on this scale before.

'No. Anne Reynolt is something very, very rare. Rumor is, she was a High Podmaster in the Xevalle clique. Most of those got killed or mind-scrubbed, but the story is Reynolt had really pissed the Nauly clique. For laughs they Focused her; maybe they thought to use her as body comfort. But that's not how it turned out. My guess is, she was already close to being a monomaniac. It was one chance in a billion, but Reynolt's management abilities survived – even some of her people skills survived.'

Up ahead, Pham could see the end of the tunnel. Light shone on an unadorned hatch. Trud came to a stop and turned to face Pham. 'She's a freak, but she is also Podmaster Nau's most valued property. In principle, she doubles his reach . . .' He grimaced. 'It doesn't make it any easier to take orders from her, I'll tell you that. Personally, I think the Podmaster overrates her. She's a miraculous freak, but so what? It's like a dog that writes poetry – no one notices that it's doggerel.'

'You don't seem to care if she knows your opinion.'

Now Trud was smiling again. 'Of course not. That's the one plus of my situation. She's almost impossible to fool on things directly related to my job – but outside of that she's like any other ziphead. Why, I've played some pus-funny j—' He stopped. 'Ah, never mind. Tell her what Podmaster Nau asked you to and you'll be okay.' He winked, then started back up the corridor, away from Reynolt's office.

'Watch her close. You'll see what I mean.'

If Pham had known about Anne Reynolt, he might have postponed the whole localizer scam. But now he was sitting in her office, and there weren't many options. In a way it felt good to be winging it. Ever since Jimmy died, every one of Pham's moves had been so considered, so damned cautious.

At first, the woman didn't even acknowledge his presence. Pham sat uninvited on the chair across from her desk and looked around the room. It was nothing like Nau's office. These walls were naked, rough diamond. There were no pictures, not even the abominations that passed for Emergent art. Reynolt's desk was an agglomeration of empty storage crates and network gear.

And Reynolt herself? Pham stared at her face more intently than he might have dared otherwise. He'd been in her presence maybe 20Ksec total and those encounters had been in meetings, with Reynolt generally at the far end of the table. She always dressed plainly, except for that silver necklace tucked down into her blouse. With her red hair and pale skin, the woman might have been Ritser Brughel's sister. The physical type was rare in this end of Human Space, arising most often from local mutation. Anne might have been thirty years old – or a couple of centuries, with really good medical support. In a crazy, exotic way she was lovely. Physically lovely. *So you were a Podmaster*.

Reynolt's gaze flickered up, and impaled him for an instant. 'Okay. You're here to tell me the details of these localizers.'

Pham nodded. Strange. After that momentary glance, her gaze shifted away from his eyes. She was watching his lips, his throat, only briefly his eyes. There was no sympathy, no communication, but Pham had the chill feeling that she was seeing through all his masks.

'Good. What is their standard sensorium?'

He grumbled through the answers, claiming ignorance of details.

Reynolt didn't seem to take offense. Her questions were delivered in a uniformly calm, mildly contemptuous tone. Then: 'This isn't enough to work with. I need the manuals.'

'Sure. That's what I'm here for. The full manuals are on the localizer chips, encrypted beneath what ordinary techs are allowed to see.'

Again that long, scattered stare: 'We've looked. We don't see them.'

This was the dangerous part. At best, Nau and Brughel would be taking a very close look at Trinli's buffoon persona. At worst . . . if they realized he was giving away secrets that even top armsmen wouldn't know, he'd be in serious trouble. Pham pointed to a head-up display on Reynolt's desk. 'Allow me,' he said.

Reynolt didn't react to his flippancy, but she did put on the huds and accepted consensual imaging. Pham continued, 'I remember the passcode. It's long, though' – and the full version was keyed to his own body, but he didn't say that. He tried several incorrect codes, and acted irritable and nervous when they failed. A normal human, even Tomas Nau, would have expressed impatience – or laughed.

Reynolt didn't say anything. She just sat there. But then, suddenly, 'I have no patience for this. Do not pretend incompetence.'

She knew. In all the time since Triland, no one had ever seen this far behind his cover. He'd hoped for more time; once they started using the localizers he could write some new cover for himself. *Damn.* Then he remembered what Silipan had said. Anne Reynolt knew *something.* Most likely, she had simply concluded that Trinli was a reluctant informant.

'Sorry,' Pham mumbled He typed in the correct sequence.

A simple acknowledgment came back from the fleet library, chip doc subsection. The glyphs floated silver on the air between them. The secret inventory data, the component specifications.

'Good enough,' said Reynolt. She did something with her control, and her office seemed to vanish. The two of them floated through the inventory information, and then they were standing within the localizers' specifications.

'As you said, temperature, sonics, light levels . . . multi-spectrum. But this is more elaborate than you described at the meeting.'

'I said it was good. These are just the details.'

Reynolt spoke quickly, reviewing capability after capability. Now she sounded almost excited. This was far beyond the corresponding Emergent products. 'A naked localizer, with a good sensorium and independent operation.' And she was seeing only the part that Pham wanted her to see.

'You do have to pulse it power.'

'Just as well. That way we can limit its use till we thoroughly understand it.'

She flicked away the image, and they were sitting in her office again, the lights sparkling cool off the rough walls. Pham could feel himself beginning to sweat.

She wasn't even looking at him anymore. 'The inventory showed several million localizers in addition to those embedded in fleet hardware.'

'Sure. Inactive, they pack into just a few liters.'

Calm observation: 'You were fools not to use them for security.'

Pham glowered at her. 'We armsmen knew what they could do. In a military situation—'

But those were not the details in Anne Reynolt's Focus. She waved him silent. 'It looks like we have more than enough for our purposes.'

The beautiful janissary looked back into Pham's face. For an instant, her gaze stabbed directly into his eyes.

'You've made possible a new era of control, Armsman.'

Pham looked into the clear blue eyes and nodded; he hoped she didn't understand the full truth that she spoke. And now Pham realized how central she was to all his plans. Anne Reynolt managed almost all the zipheads. Anne Reynolt was Tomas Nau's direct control over operations. Anne Reynolt understood the things about the Emergents that a successful revolutionary must understand. And Anne Reynolt was a ziphead. She might figure out what he was up to – or she might be the key to destroying Nau and Brughel.

Things never got completely quiet in an ad hoc habitat. The Traders' temp was only a hundred meters across; the crew, bouncing around in it, created stresses that could not be completely damped. And thermal stress made an occasional loud snapping sound. But just now was in the middle of most of the crew's sleep period; Pham Nuwen's little cabin was about as quiet as it ever got. He floated in the darkened cabin, pretending to drowse. His secret life was about to become very busy. The Emergents didn't know it, but they'd just been snared by a trap that went deeper than most any Qeng Ho Fleet Captain knew about. It was one of two or three scams that Pham Nuwen had set up long ago. Sura and a few others had known about them, but even after Brisgo Gap, the knowledge hadn't seeped into the general Qeng Ho armamentarium. Pham had always wondered about that; Sura could be subtle.

How long would it take Reynolt and Brughel to retrain their people to use the localizers? There were more than enough of the gadgets to run the L1 stab operations, and also snoop all living spaces. At third meal, some of the comm people had told of spikes in the temp's cable spine. Ten times a second, a microwave pulse spread through the temp – enough wireless power to keep the localizers well fed. Just before the beginning of the sleep period, he'd noticed the first of the dustmotes come wafting through the ventilator. Right now, Brughel and Reynolt were probably calibrating the system. Brughel and Nau would be congratulating themselves on the quality of the sound and video. With good luck, they would eventually phase out their own clunky spy devices; even if he wasn't so lucky . . . well, in a few Msecs he would have the ability to subvert the reports from them.

Something scarcely heavier than a dustmote settled on his cheek. He made as if to wipe his face, and in the act settled the mote just beside his eyelid. A few moments later he poked another deep within the channel of his right ear. It was ironic, considering how much effort the Emergents had gone to, disabling untrusted I/O devices.

The localizers did everything that Pham had told Tomas Nau. Just as such devices had done through all of human history, these located one another in geometrical space – a simple exercise, nothing more than a time-of-flight computation. The Qeng Ho versions were smaller than most, could be powered by wireless across short distances, and had a simple set of sensors. They made great spy devices, just what Podmaster Nau needed. Localizers were by their nature a type of computer network, in fact a type of distributed processor. Each little dustmote had a small amount of computing ability – and they communicated with one another. A few hundred thousand of them dusted across the Traders' temp was more computing power than all the gear that Nau and Brughel had brought aboard. Of course, all localizers – even the Emergent clunkers – had such computational potential. The real secret of the Qeng Ho version was that no added interface was necessary, for output or input. If you knew the secret, you could access the Qeng Ho localizers directly, let the localizers sense your body position, interpret the proper codings, and respond with built-in effectors. It *didn't matter* that the Emergents had removed all front-end interfaces from the temp. Now a Qeng Ho interface was all around them, for anyone who knew the secrets.

Access took special knowledge and some concentration. It was not something that could happen by accident or under coercion. Pham relaxed in the hammock, partly to pretend to finally fall asleep, partly to get in the mood for his coming work. He needed a particular pattern of heartbeats, a particular cadence of breathing. *Do I even remember it anymore, after all this time?* The sharp moment of panic took him aback. One mote by his eye, another in his ear; that should be enough to provide alignment for the other localizers that must be floating in the room. That should be enough.

But the proper mood still eluded him. He kept thinking back to Anne Reynolt and to what Silipan had shown him. The Focused would see through his schemes; it was just a matter of time. Focus was a miracle. Pham Nuwen could have made the Qeng Ho a true empire – despite. Sura's treachery – if only he'd had Focused tools. Yes, the price was high. Pham remembered the rows of zombies up in Hammerfest's Attic. He could see a dozen ways to make the system gentler, but in the end, to use Focused tools, there would have to be some sacrifice.

Was final success, a true Qeng Ho empire, worth that price? Could he pay it?

Yes and yes!

At this rate he'd never achieve access state. He backed off, began the whole relax cycle again. He let his imagination slide into memories. What had it been like in the beginning times? Sura Vinh had delivered the *Reprise* and a still very naive Pham Nuwen to the megalopolis moons of Namqem. . .

He had remained at Namqem for fifteen years. They were the happiest years of Pham Nuwen's life. Sura's cousins were in-system, too – and they fell in love with the schemes that Sura and her young barbarian proposed: a method of interstellar synchronization, the trading of technical tricks where their own buying and selling would not be affected, the prospect of a cohesive interstellar trading culture. (Pham learned not to talk about his goals beyond that.) Sura's cousins were back from some very profitable adventures, but they could see the limits of isolated trading. Left to themselves, they would make fortunes, even keep them for a time . . . but in the end they would be lost in time and the interstellar dark. They had a gut appreciation for many of Pham's goals.

In some ways, his time with Sura at Namqem was like their first days on the *Reprise*. But this went on and on, the imaginings and the teaming ever richer. And there were wonders that his hard head with all its grandiose plans had never considered: children. He had never imagined how different a family could be from the one of his birth. Ratko, Butra, and Qo were their first little ones. He lived with them, taught them, played blinkertalk and evercatch with them, showed them the wonders of the Namqem world park. Pham loved them far more than himself, and almost as much as he loved Sura. He almost abandoned the Grand Schedule to stay with them. But there would be other times, and Sura forgave him. When he returned, thirty years later, Sura awaited, with news of other parts of the Plan well under way. But by then their first three children were themselves avoyaging, playing their own part in founding the new Qeng Ho.

Pham ended up with a fleet of three starships. There were setbacks and disasters. Treachery. Zamle Eng leaving him for dead in Kielle's comet cloud. Twenty years he was fleet-less at Kielle, making himself a trillionaire from scratch, just to escape the place.

Sura flew with him on several missions, and they raised new families on half a dozen worlds. A century passed. Three. The mission protocols they had devised on the old *Reprise* served them well, and across the years there were reunions with children and children's children. Some were greater friends than Ratko or Butra or Qo, but he never loved them quite so much. Pham could see the new structure emerging. Now it was simply trade, sometimes leavened with family ties. It would be much more.

The hardest thing was the realization that they needed someone at the center, at least in the early centuries. More and more Sura stayed behind, coordinating what Pham and others undertook.

And yet they still had children. Sura had new sons and daughters while Pham was light-years away. He joked with her about the miracle, though in truth he was hurt at the thought she had other lovers. Sura had smiled gently and shook her head. 'No, Pham, any child I call my own is also of you.' Her smile turned mischievous. 'Over the years, you have stuffed me with enough of yourself to birth an army. I can't use that gift all at once, but use it I will.'

'No clones.' Pham's word came out sharper than he intended.

'Lord, no.' She looked away. 'I . . . one of you is all I can handle.' Maybe she was just as superstitious as he was. Or maybe not: 'No, I'm using you in natural zygotes. I'm not always the other donor, or the only other donor. Namqem medics are very good at this kind of thing.' She turned back, and saw the look on his face. 'I swear, Pham, every one of your children has a family. Every one is loved . . . We need them, Pham. We need families and Great Families. The Plan needs them.' She jabbed at him playfully, trying to jolly the disapproval from his face. 'Hey, Pham! Isn't this the wet dream of every conquering barbarian lord? Well, I'll tell you, you've outfathered the greatest of them.'

Yes. Thousands of children by dozens of partners, raised without personal cost to the father. His own father had unsuccessfully attempted something much smaller with his campaign of regicide and concubinage in the North Coast states. Pham was getting it all without the murder, without the violence. And yet . . . how long had Sura been doing this? How many children, and by how many 'donors'? He could imagine her now, planning bloodlines, slotting the right talents into the founding of each new Family, dispersing them throughout the new Qeng Ho. He felt the strangest double vision as he turned the situation around in his mind. As Sura said, it was a barbarian wet dream . . . but it was also a little like being raped.

'I would have told you at the beginning, Pham. But I was afraid you would object. And this is so important.' In the end, Pham did not object. It *would* advance their Plan. But it hurt to think of all the children he would never know.

Voyaging at 0.3c, Pham Nuwen traveled far. Everywhere there were Traders, though beyond thirty light-years, they rarely called themselves 'Qeng Ho.' It didn't matter. They could understand the Plan. The ones he met spread the ideas still farther. Wherever they went – and farther, since some were convinced simply by the radio messages Pham sent across the dark – the spirit of the Qeng Ho was spread.

Pham returned to Namqem again and again, bending the Grand Schedule almost to its breaking point. Sura was aging. She was two or three centuries old now. Her body was at the limit of what medical science could make young and supple. Even some of their children were old, living too long in port amid their voyaging. And sometimes in Sura's eyes, Pham glimpsed unknowable experience.

Each time he returned to Namqem, he tossed the question up at her. Finally, one night after love almost as good as they had ever had, he came close to bawling. 'This wasn't how it was supposed to be, Sura! The Plan was for both of us. Come away with me. At least, go avoyaging.' *And we can meet again and again, however long we live.*

Sura leaned back from him and slipped her hand behind his neck. Her smile was crooked and sad. 'I know. We thought we could both be flyabouts. Strange that that's the biggest mistake we had in all our original scheming. But, be honest. You know that one of us has to stay in some central place, has to deal with the Plan almost in one long Watch.' There were a trillion little details involved in conquering the universe, and they couldn't be handled while you were in coldsleep.

'Yes, in the early centuries. But not for . . . not for your whole life!'

Sura shook her head, her hand brushing gently at his neck. 'I'm afraid we were wrong.' She saw the look on his face, the anguish, and she drew him down to her. 'My poor barbarian prince.' He could hear the fond, mocking smile in her words. 'You are my unique treasure. And do you know why? You're a flaming genius. You're driven. But the reason I've always loved you is something more. Inside your head, you are such a contradiction. Little Pham grew up in a rundown suburb of Hell. You saw betrayal and you were betrayed. You understand violent evil as well as the most bloody-handed villain. And yet, little Pham also bought into all the myths of chivalry and honor and quest. Somehow in your head, both live at once, and you've spent your life trying to make the universe fit your contradictions. You will come very close to achieving that goal, close enough for me or any reasonable person – but maybe not close enough to satisfy yourself. So. I must stay if our Plan is to succeed. And you must go for the same reason. Unfortunately you know that, don't you, Pham?'

Pham looked out the real windows that surrounded Sura's penthouse. They were at the top of an office spire sticking high out of Namqem's largest megalopolis moon. Tarelsk office real estate prices were in a frenzy that was downright absurd considering the power of network communication. The last time this tower had been on the open market, the annual rental on the penthouse floor could have *bought* a starship. For the last seventy years, Qeng Ho Families – mostly his and Sura's descendants – had owned the spire and huge swaths of the surrounding office territory. It was the smallest part of their holdings, a nod to fashion.

Just now, it was early evening. The crescent of Namqem hung low in the sky; the lights of the Tarelsk business district rivaled the mother world's glow. The Vinh & Mamso shipyards would rise in another Ksec or so. Vinh & Mamso were probably the largest yards in Human Space. Yet even that was a small part of their Families' wealth. And beyond that – stretching ever more tenuously to the limits of Human Space, but growing still – was the cooperative wealth of the Qeng Ho. He and Sura had founded the greatest trading culture in the history of all time. That was how Sura saw it. That was all she ever saw. It was all she ever wanted. Sura didn't mind that she wouldn't live in the era of their final success . . . because she thought it would never come.

So Pham stilled the tears that waited behind his eyes. He slipped his arms gently around Sura, and kissed her neck. 'Yes, I know,' he finally said.

Pham postponed his departure from Namqem for two years, five. He stayed so long that the Grand Schedule itself was broken. There would be appointments missed. Any more delay and the Plan itself might fail. And when he finally left Sura, something died inside him. Their partnership survived, even their love, in some abstract way. But a chasm of time had opened between them and he knew they could never bridge it again.

By the time he had lived one hundred years, Pham Nuwen had seen more than thirty solar systems, a hundred cultures. There were Traders who had seen more, but not many. Certainly Sura, huddled in planning mode back on Namqem, never saw what Pham did. Sura had only books and histories, reports from far away.

For sessile civilizations, even space-faring ones, nothing lasted forever. It was something of a miracle that the human race had survived long enough to escape Earth. There were so many ways that an intelligent race could make itself extinct. Deadlocks and runaways, plagues, atmosphere catastrophes, impact events – those were the simplest dangers. Humankind had lived long enough to understand some of the threats. Yet, even with the greatest care, a technological civilization carried the seeds of its own destruction. Sooner or later, it ossified and politics carried it into a fall. Pham Nuwen had been born on Canberra in the depths of a dark age. He knew now that the disaster had been mild by some standards – after all, the human race had survived on Canberra even though it lost its high technology. There were worlds that Pham visited multiple times during his first hundred years. Sometimes, it was centuries between the visits. He saw the Utopia that had been Neumars fade into over-populated dictatorship, the ocean cities becoming slums for billions. Seventy years later, he came back to a world with a population of one million, a world of small villages, of savages with painted faces and hand-axes and songs of heartbreak. The Voyage would have been a bust, if not for the chants of Vilnios. But Neumars was lucky compared to the dead worlds. Old Earth had been recolonized from scratch four times since the diaspora began.

There had to be a better way, and every new world Pham saw made him more sure that he knew that better way. *Empire.* A government so large that the failure of an entire solar system would be a manageable disaster. The Qeng Ho trading culture was a start. It would become the Qeng Ho trading empire . . . and someday a true, governing empire. For the Qeng Ho were in a unique position. At its peak, a Customer civilization possessed extraordinary science – and sometimes made marginal improvements over the best that had ever existed before. Most often, these improvements died when the civilization died. The Qeng Ho, however – they went on forever, patiently gathering the best that could be found. To Sura, that was the Qeng Ho's greatest trading edge.

To Pham Nuwen, it was more. *Why should we trade back all that we learn? Some, yes. That is largely how we make our living. But let us take the glittering peaks of all human progress – and hold them for the good of all.*

That was how the 'Qeng Ho' localizers had come to be. Pham had been aground on Trygve Ytre, as far from Namqem as he had ever voyaged. The people were hot even from the same ur-stock as the humans of familiar parts of Human Space.

Trygve's sun was one of those dim little M stars, the vermin of the colonizable galaxy. There were dozens of such stars for every one that was like Old Earth's sun – and most had planets. They were dangerous places to settle, the stellar ecosphere so narrow that a civilization without technology could not exist. In the early millennia of Humankind's conquest of space, that fact had been ignored, and a number of such worlds had been colonized. Ever optimistic, these humans, thinking their technology would last forever. And then at the first Fall, millions of people were left on a world of ice – or a world of fire, if the planet was on the inner side of their star's ecosphere.

Trygve Ytre was a slightly safer variant, and a common situation: The star was accompanied by a giant planet, Trygve, which orbited a bit outside of the primary's ecosphere. The giant planet had just two moons, one of them Earth-sized. Both were inhabited in the era when Pham visited. But the larger, Ytre, was the gem. Tidal and direct heating from Trygve supplemented the sun's meager output. Ytre had land and air and liquid oceans. The humans of Trygve Ytre had survived at least one collapse of their civilization.

What they had now was a technology as high as Humankind ever attained. Pham's little fleet of starships was welcomed, found decent shipyards in the asteroid belt that lay a billion kilometers out from the sun. Pham left crews aboard the ships, and took local transport inward, to Trygve and Ytre. This was no Namqem, but these people had seen other Traders. They had also seen Pham's ramscoops and his preliminary trading list . . . and most of what Pham had did not measure up to Ytre's native magics.

Nuwen stayed on Ytre for a time, some *weeks* the locals called the unit, the 600Ksec or so that it took giant Ytre to orbit Trygve. Trygve itself orbited the sun in just over 6Msec. So the Ytreisch calendar worked out neatly to ten weeks.

Though the world teetered between fire and ice, much of Ytre was habitable. 'We have a more climate-stable world than Old Earth itself,' the locals bragged. 'Ytre is deep within Trygve's gravity well, with no significant perturbers. The tidal heating has been mellow across a geologic time.' And even the dangers were no big surprise. The M3 sun was just over one degree across. A foolish person could look directly at the reddish disk, see the whorling of gasses, see sunspots vast and dark. A few seconds of such sungazing could cause serious retinal burns, since of course the star was far brighter in the near-IR than in visible light. The recommended eye protectors looked like clear plastic, but Pham was very careful to wear them.

His hosts – a group of local companies – put him up at their expense. He spent his official time trying to learn more of their language and trying to discover something his fleet had brought that might be worth something to his customers. They were trying just as hard. It was something like industrial espionage in reverse. The locals' electronics was a little better than Pham had ever seen, though there were program improvements the Qeng Ho might suggest. Their medical automation was significantly backward; that would be his foot in the door, a place to haggle from.

Pham and his staff categorized all the things they might bring from this encounter. It would pay for the voyage and more. But Pham heard rumors. His hosts represented a number of – 'cartels' was the nearest translation that Pham could make of the word. They hid things from one another. The rumor was of a new type of localizer, smaller than any made elsewhere, and needing no internal power supply. Any improvement in localizers was a profitable item; the gadgets were the positional glue that made embedded systems so powerful. But these 'super' localizers were alleged to contain sensors and effectors. If it was anything more than rumor, it would have political and military consequences on Ytre itself – destabilizing consequences.

By now, Pham Nuwen knew how to collect information in a technical society, even one where he wasn't a fluent speaker, even one where he was being watched. In four weeks he knew which cartel might have the maybe-existent invention. He knew the name of its magnate: Gunnar Larson. The Larson cartel had not mentioned the invention in their trading negotiations. It was not on the table – and Pham didn't want to hint about it when others were present. He arranged a face-to-face meeting with Larson. It was the sort of thing that would have made sense even to Pham's aunts and uncles back on medieval Canberra, though the technical subterfuge behind the meeting would have been unintelligible to them.

Six weeks after his landfall on Ytre, Pham Nuwen walked alone through the most exclusive open street in Dirby. Scattered clouds were reminders of the recent rain. They showed pink and gray in the bright twilight. The sun had just set in the deep heart of Trygve. Near the limb of the giant planet, an arch of gold and red was the memory of the sun's passing into eclipse. The disk of the giant stood across ten degrees of sky. Silent blue lightning flickered in its polar latitudes.

The air was cool and moist, the breeze carrying some natural perfume. Pham kept up his pace, pulling the leash tight every time his snarlihunds wanted to investigate something off the promenade. His cover demanded that he take things slowly, enjoy the view, wave in a courtly way to the similarly dressed people who passed by. After all, what else would a rich, retired resident be doing out in the open but admiring the lights and showing off his hunds? That's what his contact had claimed anyway. 'Security on Huskestrade isn't really tight. But if you don't have an excuse to be there, the police may stop you. Take some prize snarlihunds. That's legitimate reason to be on the promenade.'

Pham's gaze took in the palaces that showed here and there through the foliage along the promenade. Dirby seemed like a peaceful place. There was security here . . . but if enough people wanted to pull things down, it could be done in a single night of fire and riot. The cartels played a hard commercial game, but their civilization was coasting through the highest, happiest of its good times . . . Maybe 'cartels' wasn't even the right word. Gunnar Larson and some of the other magnates put on airs of deep, ancient wisdom. Larson was a boss man all right, but the word for his rank meant something more than that. Pham knew the term 'philosopher king.' But Larson was a businessman. Maybe his title meant 'philosopher-magnate.' *Hmm.*

Pham reached the Larson estate. He turned down a private offway that was almost as broad as the promenade. The output of his head-up display faded; after a few more paces, he had only a natural view. Pham was annoyed but not surprised. He walked on as if he owned the place, even let the hunds take a crap behind a two-meter stand of flowers. *Let the philosopher-magnate understand my deep respect for all the mystery.*

'Please follow, sir.' A voice came quietly from behind him. Pham suppressed a start, turned and nodded casually to the speaker. In the reddish twilight he couldn't see any weapons. High in the sky and two million kilometers away, a chain of blue lightning flickered bright on the face of Trygve. He got a good look at his guide, and three others who had been hidden by the dark. They wore corporate robes, but he couldn't miss the military bearing, or the huds they wore across their eyes.

He let them take the hunds. That was just as well. The four creatures were big and carnivore-looking mean. They might be overbred into gentleness, but it would take more than one twilight walk to make Pham a hund lover.

Pham and the remaining guards walked more than one hundred meters. He had a glimpse of delicately turned branches, moss that sat just so at joints of the roots. The higher the social position, the more these fellows went for rustic nature – and the more perfect every detail had to be. No doubt this 'forest path' had been manicured for a century to capture untrammeled wildness.

The path opened onto a hillside garden, sitting above a stream and a pond. The reddish arch of Trygve was enough for him to make out the tables, the small human form that rose to greet him.

'Magnate Larson.' Pham gave the little half bow he had seen between equals. Larson reciprocated, and somehow Pham knew the other fellow was grinning.

'Fleet Captain Nuwen . . . Please take a seat.'

There were cultures where trade couldn't begin until everyone is bored unto death by irrelevant chitchat. Pham wasn't expecting that here. He was due back in his hotel in 20Ksec – and it would be well for both of them if the other cartelists didn't realize where Pham had been. Yet Gunnar Larson seemed in no hurry. Occasional Trygve lightning showed him: typical Ytre stock, but very old, the blondish hair thinning, the pale pink skin wrinkled. They sat in the flashing twilight for more than 2Ksec. The old man chatting about Pham's history and the past of Trygve Ytre. *Hell, maybe he's getting back at me for dumping in his flowers.* Or maybe it was something Ytreisch inscrutable. On the bright side, the fellow spoke excellent Aminese and Pham wasn't backward in that language either.

Larson's estate, was strangely quiet. Dirby city contained almost a million people, and though none of the buildings were monstrously tall, there was urbanization to within a thousand meters of the high-class Huskestrade section. Yet sitting here, the loudest sounds were Gunnar Larson's inane chitchat – and the splashing of the little waterfall just down the hillside. Pham's eyes were well adjusted now. He could see the reflection of Trygve's arching light in the pond. He could see ripples when some large, shelled creature breached the surface. *I'm actually coming to like the cycle of light on Ytre.* Three weeks ago Pham would have never thought that time could come. The nights and days were long beyond any rhythm Pham could sustain, but the midday eclipses gave some respite. And after a while you began to forget that almost every color was a shade of red. There was a comfortable safeness about this world; these people had kept a prosperous peace for almost a thousand years. So maybe there was wisdom here . . .

Abruptly, without breaking the cadence of triviality, Larson said, 'So you think to learn the secret of Larson localizers?'

Pham knew his startled expression didn't go beyond his eyes.

'First I would like to learn if such things exist. The rumors are very spectacular . . . and very vague.'

The old man's teeth glinted in a smile. 'Oh, they exist.' He gestured around them. 'They give me eyes everywhere. They make this darkness into day.'

'I see.' The old man wasn't wearing a head-up. Could he guess at the sardonic expression on Pham's face?

Larson laughed softly. 'Oh yes.' He touched his temple just behind the orbit of his eye. 'There's one resting right here. The others align on it and precisely stimulate my optic nerve. It takes a lot of practice on both sides. But if you have enough Larson localizers, they can handle the load. They can synthesize views from whatever direction I choose.' He made an obscure motion with his hands. 'Your facial expressions are as clear as day to me, Pham Nuwen. And from the localizers that have dusted your hands and neck, I can even look inside. I can hear your heart beat, your lungs breathe. With a little concentration' – he cocked his head – 'I can estimate blood flow within regions of your brain . . . You are sincerely surprised, young man.'

Pham's lips tightened in anger at himself. The other had spent more than a Ksec calibrating him. If this had been in an office, away from this garden and this quiet darkness, he would have been much more on his guard. Pham shrugged. 'Your localizers are far and away the most interesting thing about the current stage of Ytreisch civilization. I'm very interested in acquiring some samples – even more interested in the program base, and the factory specification.'

'To what end?'

'That should be obvious and irrelevant. The important thing is what I can give you in trade. Your medical science is poorer than at Namqem or Kielle.'

Larson seemed to nod. 'It's worse than we had here before the Fall. We've never recovered all the old secrets.'

'You called me "young man,"' said Pham, 'but what is your own age, sir? Ninety? One hundred?' Pham and his staff had looked carefully at the Ytreisch net, gauging the locals' medical science.

'Ninety-one of your thirty-Msec years,' said Larson.

'Well, sir, I have lived a hundred and twenty-seven years. That doesn't count coldsleep, of course.' *And I look like a young man.*

Larson was silent for a long moment, and Pham was sure that he had scored a point. Maybe these 'philosopher-magnates' weren't so inscrutable.

'Yes, I would like to be young again. And millions would spend millions for the same. What can your medicine give?'

'A century or two, looking about as you see me. Two or three centuries after that, visibly aging.'

'Ah. That's even a bit better than we achieved before the Fall. But the very old will look as bad and suffer as much as the old always have. There are intrinsic limits to how far the human body can be pushed.'

Pham was politely silent, but he smiled inside. Medicine was the hook, all right. Pham would get their localizers in return for decent medical science. Both sides would benefit enormously. Magnate Larson would live a few extra centuries. If he was lucky, the current cycle of his civilization would outlive him. But a thousand years from now, when Larson was dust, when his civilization had fallen as the planetbound inevitably did – a thousand years from now, Pham and the Qeng Ho would still be flying between the stars. And they would still have the Larson localizers.

Larson was making a strange, soft sound. After a moment, Pham realized it was coughing laughter. 'Ah, forgive me. You may be a hundred and twenty-seven years old, but you are still a young man in your mind. You hide behind the dark and an expressionless face – don't be offended. You haven't trained at the right disguises. With my localizers I see your pulse and the blood flow in your brain . . . You think that someday you'll dance on my grave, no?'

'I—' *Damn.* An expert, using the very best invasive probes, couldn't see that much about another's attitude. Larson was just guessing – or the localizers were even more a treasure than Pham had thought. Pham's awe and caution were tinged with anger. The other was mocking him. Well then, truly: 'In a sense, yes. If you accept the trade I'm hoping for, you will live just as many years as I. But I am Qeng Ho. I sleep decades between the stars. You Customer civilizations are ephemera to us.' *There. That should raise* your *blood pressure.*

'Fleet Captain, you remind me a little of Fred down there in the pool. Again, no real insult intended. Fred is a *luksterfiske.*' He must be talking about the creature that Pham had noticed diving near the waterfall. 'Fred is curious about lots of things. He's been hopping around since you arrived, trying to figure you out. Can you see, right now he's sitting at the edge of the pond? Two armored tentacles are tickling the grass about three meters from your feet.'

Pham felt a shock of surprise. He had thought those were *vines.* He followed the slender limbs back to the water . . . yes, there were four eye stalks, four unblinking eyes. They glittered yellow in the waning light of Trygve's sky arch. 'Fred has lived a long time. Archeologists have found his breeding documents, a little experiment with native wildlife just before the Fall. He was some rich man's pet, about as smart as a hund. But Fred is very old. He lived through the Fall. He was something of a legend in these parts. You are right, Fleet Captain; if you live long enough you see much. In the Middle Ages, Dirby was first a ruin, then the beginning of a great kingdom – its lords mined the secrets of the earlier age, to their own great profit. For a time, this hillside was the senate of those rulers. During the Renaissance, this was a slum and the lake at the bottom of the hill an open sewer. Even the name "Huskestrade" – the epitome of high-class modern Dirby addresses – once meant something like "Street of the Outhouses."

'But Fred survived it all. He was the legend of the sewers, his existence disbelieved by sensible folk until three centuries ago. Now he lives with full honor – in the cleanest water.' There was fondness in the old man's voice. 'So Fred has lived long, and he's seen much. He's still intellectually alive, as much as a *luksterfiske* can be. Witness his beady eyes upon us. But Fred knows far less of the world and his own history than I do from reading history.'

'Not a valid analogy. Fred is a dumb animal.'

'True. You are a bright human and you fly between the stars. You live a few hundred years, but those years are spread across a span as great as Fred's. What more do you really see? Civilizations rise and fall, but all technical civilizations know the greatest secrets now. They know which social mechanisms normally work, and which ones quickly fail. They know the means to postpone disaster and evade the most foolish catastrophes. They know that even so, each civilization must inevitably fall. The electronics that you want from me may not exist anywhere else in Human Space – but I'm sure that equipment that good has been invented by humans before, and will be again. Similarly for the medical technology you correctly assume we want from you. Humankind as a whole is in a steady state, even if our domain is slowly expanding. Yes, compared to you I am like a bug in the forest, alive for one day. But I see as much as you; I live as much as you. I can study my histories and the radio accounts that float between the stars. I can see all the variety of triumph and barbarism that you Qeng Ho do.'

'We gather the best. With us it never dies.'

'I wonder. There was another trading fleet that came to Trygve Ytre when I was a young man. They were totally unlike you. Different language, different culture. Interstellar traders are simply a niche, not a culture.' Sura argued that, too. Here, in this ancient garden, the quiet words seemed to weigh more heavily than when Sura Vinh spoke them; Gunnar Larson's voice was almost hypnotic. 'Those earlier traders did not have your airs, Fleet Captain. They hoped to make their fortune, to ultimately go some-where else and set up a planetary civilization.'

'Then they would no longer be Traders.'

'True; perhaps they would be something more. You've been in many planetary systems. Your manifest says you've spent a number of years at Namqem, long enough to appreciate a planetary civilization. We have hundreds of millions of people living within a few light-seconds of each other. The local net that spans Trygve Ytre gives almost every citizen a view on Human Space that you can only have when you come to port . . . More than anything, your trading life between the stars is a Ruritania of the Mind.'

Pham didn't recognize the reference, but he got the other's point. 'Magnate Larson, I wonder that you want to live long. You have everything figured out – a universe free of progress, where all things die and no good is accumulated.' Pham's words were partly sarcasm, partly honest puzzlement. Gunnar Larson had opened windows, and the view was bleak.

Barely audible, a sigh. 'You don't read very much, do you, son?' Strange. Pham did not think the other was probing anymore. There was something like sad amusement in the question.

'I read enough.' Sura herself complained that Pham spent too much time with manuals. But Pham had started late, and had spent his whole life trying to catch up. So what if his education was a little skewed?

'You ask me the real point of it all. Each of us must take his own path on that, Fleet Captain. Different paths have their own advantages, their own perils. But for your own, human, sake . . . you should consider: Each civilization has its time. Each science has its limits. And each of us must die, living less than half a thousand years. If you truly understand those limits . . . then you are ready to grow up, to know what counts.' He was silent for a while. 'Yes . . . just listen to the peace. It's a gift to be able to do that. Too much time is spent in frenzied rushing. Listen to the breeze in the *lestras*. Watch Fred try to figure us out. Listen to the laughter of your children and your grandchildren. Enjoy the time you have, however it is given to you, and for however long.'

Larson leaned back in his chair. He seemed to be staring out at the starless darkness that was the center of Trygve's disk. The arch of light from the eclipsed sun was dim and uniform all around the disk. The lightning had long since vanished; Pham guessed that seeing it was some function of viewing angle and the orientation of Trygve's thunderheads. 'An example, Fleet Captain. Sit and feel and see: sometimes, at mid-eclipse, there is an especial beauty. Watch the middle of Trygve's disk.' Seconds passed. Pham stared upward. Trygve's lower latitudes were normally so dark . . . but now: There was faint red, first so dim that Pham thought it might just be a figment of suggestibility. The light brightened slowly, a deep, deep red, like sword steel still too cold for the hammer. There were bands of dark crossing it.

'The light is from the depths of Trygve itself. You know we get some direct warming from the planet. Sometimes, when the cloud canyons are oriented just right and the upper storms are gone, we have a very deep view – and we can see its glow with the naked eye.' The light came a little brighter. Pham glanced around the garden. Everything was in shades of red, but he could see more now than he had glimpsed in the lightning. The tall, stranded trees above the pond – they were part of the waterfall, guiding the water in extra swirls and pools. Clouds of flying things moved between the tree branches, and for a few moments they sang. Fred had climbed all the way out of the pond. He sat on multiple leg paddles and his shorter tentacles twitched upward, toward the light in the sky.

They watched in silence. Pham had observed Trygve with multispec on the way in from the asteroids. He wasn't seeing anything now that was news to him. The whole show was just a happenstance of geometry and tuning. And yet . . . being tied to a single place, on a course that was determined beyond human control, he could see how Customers might be impressed when the universe chose to reveal something. It was ridiculous, but he could feel some of the awe himself.

And then Trygve's heart was dark again and the singing in the trees died away; the whole show had lasted less than one hundred seconds.

It was Larson who broke the silence. 'I'm sure we can do business, my young-old man. In a measure I shouldn't reveal, we do want your medical technology. But still, I would be grateful for your answer to my original question. What will you do with the Larson localizers? Among the unsuspecting, they are an espionage miracle. Abused, they lead to ubiquit-ous law enforcement, and a quick end to civilization. Who will you sell them to?'

For some reason, Pham answered him frankly. As the eastern limb of Trygve slowly brightened, Pham explained his vision of empire, the empire of all Humankind. It was something that he had never told a mere Customer. It was something he told only certain Qeng Ho, the ones who seemed the brightest and the most flexible. Even then, most could not accept the whole plan. Most were like Sura, rejecting Pham's real goal, but more than willing to profit from a genuine Qeng Ho culture . . . 'So, we may keep the localizers to ourselves. It will cost us trade, but there is an *edge* we need over the Customer civilizations. The common language, the synchronized voyage plans, our public databases – all those things will give our Qeng Ho a cohesive culture. But tricks like these localizers will take us a step beyond that. In the end, we will not be random occupiers of the "trading niche"; we will be the surviving culture of Humankind.'

Larson was silent for a long moment. 'It's a marvelous dream you have, son,' Larson said. The obscure amusement was gone from his voice. 'A League of Humankind, breaking the wheel of time. I'm sorry, I cannot believe we'll ever reach the summit of your dream. But the foothills, the lower slopes of it . . . those are something marvelous, and perhaps attainable. The bright times could be brighter and they could last longer . . .'

Larson was an extraordinary person, Customer or no. But for whatever reason, he had the same blinders as Sura Vinh. Pham slumped back onto the soft wooden bench. After a moment, Larson continued. 'You're disappointed. You respected me enough to hope for more. You see rightly about many things, Fleet Captain. You see marvelously clear for someone from . . . Ruritania.' His voice seemed to smile gently. 'You know, my family's lineage is two thousand years deep. That's a blink of the Trader's eye – but only because Traders spend most of their time in sleep. And beyond the wisdom we have gathered directly, I and those before me have read of other places and times, a hundred worlds, a thousand civilizations. There are things about your ideas that could work. There are things about your ideas that are more plausibly hopeful than anything since the Age of Failed Dreams. I think I have insights that could be helpful . . .'

They talked through the rest of the eclipse, as the eastern limb of Trygve brightened, and the sun's disk formed out of the planet's depths and climbed toward open sky. The sky brightened into blue. And still they talked. Now it was Gunnar Larson who had the most to say. He was trying to be clear, and Pham was recording what the old man said. But maybe Aminese was not such a perfect mutual language as he thought; there was a lot of it that Pham never understood.

Along the way, they hit a deal for Pham's entire medical manifest, and for the Larson localizers. There were other items – a breeding sample of the mid-eclipse song creatures – but overall the trading was very easy. There was so much benefit going in both directions . . . and Pham was overwhelmed by the other things that Gunnar Larson had to say, the advice that might be worthless but that had the stench of wisdom.

*

Pham's voyage to Trygve Ytre was one of the more profitable of his trading career, but it was that dark-red conversation with the Ytreisch mystic that stuck the deepest in Pham Nuwen's memory. Afterward, he was certain Larson had used some kind of psychoactive drugs on him; Pham could never have been so suggestible otherwise. But . . . maybe it didn't matter. Gunnar Larson had had good ideas – the ones Pham could understand, anyway. That garden and the sense of peace that surrounded it – those were powerful, impressive things. Coming back from Trygve Ytre, Pham understood the peace that came from a living garden, and he understood the power of the mere *appearance* of wisdom. The two insights could be combined. Biologicals had always been a critical trade item . . . but now they would be more. The new Qeng Ho would have an ethic of living things at its heart. Every vehicle that could support a park should have one. The Qeng Ho would gather the best of living things as fanatically as they did the best of technology. That part of the old man's advice had been very clear. Qeng Ho would have a reputation for understanding living things, for a timeless attachment to nature.

Thus were the park and bonsai traditions born. The parks were a major overhead, but in the millennia since Trygve Ytre, they had become the deepest and most loved of all the Qeng Ho traditions.

And Trygve Ytre and Gunnar Larson? Larson was millennia dead, of course. The civilization at Ytre had barely outlived the man. There had been an era of ubiquitous law enforcement, and some kind of distributed terror. Most likely, Larson's own localizers had precipitated the end. All the wisdom, all the inscrutability, hadn't helped his world much.

Pham shifted in his sleep hammock. Thinking about Ytre and Larson always left him uneasy. It was wasted time . . . except tonight. Tonight he needed the mood of the time after that meeting. He needed something of the kinesthetic memory of dealing with the localizers. There must be dozens in this room by now. What was the pattern of motion and body state that would trigger them to talk back to him? Pham pulled the hammock wrap fully over his hands. Inside, his fingers played at a phantom keyboard. Surely that was too obvious. Until he had rapport, nothing like keystrokes should have an effect. Pham sighed, changed breathing and pulse yet again . . . and recaptured the awe of his first practice sessions with the Larson localizers.

A pale blue light, bluer than blue, blinked once near the edge of his vision. Pham opened his eyes a slit. The room was midnight dark. The light from the sleep panel was too faint to reveal colors. Nothing moved except the slow drifting of his hammock in the ventilator's breeze. The blue light had been from elsewhere. From inside his optic nerve. Pham closed his eyes, repeated the breathing exercise. The blue, blinking light appeared once more. It was the effect of a localizer array's synthesized beam, guiding off the two he had set by his temple and in his ear. As communication went, it was very crude, no more impressive than the random sparkles that most people ignore all the time. The system was programmed to be very cautious about revealing itself. This time he kept his eyes closed, and didn't change the level of his breath or the calmness of his pulse. He curled two fingers toward his palm. A second passed. The light blinked again, responding. Pham coughed, waited, moved his right arm just so. The blue light blinked: One, Two, Three . . . it was a pulse train, counting binary for him. He echoed back to it, using the codes that he had set up long ago.

He was past the challenge/response module. *He was in!* The lights that flickered behind his eyes were almost random stimuli. It would take Ksecs to train the localizer net to the precision that this sort of display could have. The optic nerve was simply too large, too complex for instantly clear video. No matter. The net was reliably talking to him now. The old customizations were coming out of hiding. The localizers had established his physical parameters; he could talk to them in any number of ways from now on. He had almost 3Msec remaining in his current Watch. That should be time enough to do the absolutely necessary, to invade the fleet net and establish a new cover story. What would it be? Something shameful, yes. Some shameful reason for 'Pham Trinli' to play the buffoon all these years. A story that Nau and Brughel could relate to and think to use as a lever against him. What?

Pham felt a smile steal across his face. *Zamle Eng, may your slave-trading soul rot in Hell. You caused me so much grief. Maybe you can do me some posthumous good.*

23

'The Children's Hour of Science.' What an innocent name. Ezr returned from his long off-Watch to find that it had become his personal nightmare. *Qiwi promised; how could she let this happen?* But every live show was more of a circus than the last.

And today's might be the worst yet. With good luck it might also be the last.

Ezr drifted into Benny's about a thousand seconds before show time. Till the last moment, he'd intended to watch it from his room, but masochism had won another round. He settled into the crowd and listened silently to the chatter.

Benny's booze parlor had become the central institution of their existence at L1. The parlor was sixteen years old now. Benny himself was on a twenty-five-percent duty cycle; he and his father shared the running of the place with Gonle Fong and others. The old wallpaper had blistered in places, and in some places the illusion of three-dimensional view was lost. Everything here was unofficial, either appropriated from other sites in the L1 cloud, or made from diamonds and ice and airsnow. Ali Lin had even come up with a fungal matrix that allowed the growing of incredible wood, complete with grain and something like growth rings. Sometime during Ezr's long absence, the bar and the walls had all been paneled in dark, polished wood. It was a comfortable place, almost what free Qeng Ho might make . . .

The parlor's tables were carved with the names of people you might not have seen for years, people on Watch shifts that didn't overlap your own. The picture above the bar was a continuously updated copy of Nau's Watch Chart. As with most things, the Emergents used standard Qeng Ho notation. A single glance at the chart and you could see how many Msecs – objective time or personal – it would be before you ever met any particular person.

During Ezr's off-Watch, Benny had added to the Watch Chart. Now it showed the current Spider date, in Trixia's notation: 60//21. The twenty-first year of the current Spider 'generation,' which was the sixtieth sun-cycle since the founding of some dynasty or other. There was an old Qeng Ho saying, 'You know you've stayed too long when you start using the locals' calendar.' 60//21. Twenty-one years since the Relight, since Jimmy and the others had died. After the generation and year number, there were the day number and the time in Ladille 'hours' and 'minutes,' a base-sixty system that the translators had never bothered to rationalize. And now everyone who came to the bar could read those times as easily as they could read a Qeng Ho chron. They knew to the second when Trixia's show would begin.

Trixia's show. Ezr ground his teeth hard together. A public slave show, and the worst of it was that no one seemed to care. *Bit by bit, we are becoming Emergents.*

Jau Xin and Rita Liao and half a dozen other couples – two of them Qeng Ho – were clustered around their usual tables, babbling about what might happen today. Ezr sat at the periphery of the group, fascinated and repelled. Nowadays, even some of the Emergents were his friends. Jau Xin, for instance. Xin and Liao had much of the Emergent moral blindness, but they also had touching, human problems. And sometimes, when no one else might notice, Ezr saw something in Xin's eyes. Jau was bright, academically inclined. Except for his good luck in the Emergent lottery, his university days would have ended in Focus. Most Emergents could double-think their way around such things; sometimes Jau could not.

'—so afraid this will be the last show,' Rita Liao looked genuinely distraught.

'Don't gloom on it, Rita. We don't even know if this is a serious problem.'

'That's for sure.' Gonle Fong drifted in headfirst, from above. She distributed flasks of Diamonds and Ice all around. 'I think the zipheads—'

She glanced apologetically at Ezr. '—I think the translators have finally lost it. The ads for this show just don't make any sense.'

'No, no. They're really quite clear.' It was one of the Emergents, with a fairly good explanation of what the 'out-of-phase perversion' was all about. The problem wasn't with the translators; the problem was with the human ability to accept the bizarre.

'The Children's Hour of Science' had been one of the first voice broadcasts that Trixia and the others had translated. Just mapping audio to the previously translated written forms had been a triumph. The early shows – fifteen objective years ago – had been printed translations. They'd been discussed in Benny's parlor, but with the same abstract interest as the latest ziphead theories about the OnOff star. As the years passed, the show had become popular for itself. *Fine.* But sometime in the last 50Msec, Qiwi Lin had worked a deal with Trud Silipan. Every nine or ten days, Trixia and the other translators were put on exhibit, a live show. So far this Watch, Ezr hadn't spoken more than ten words to Qiwi. *She promised to look after Trixia. What do you say to someone who breaks such a promise?* Even now, he didn't believe Qiwi was a traitor. But she was in bed with Tomas Nau. Maybe she used that 'position' to protect Qeng Ho interests. Maybe. In the end, it all seemed to benefit Nau.

Ezr had seen four 'performances' now. More than any normal human translator, far more than any machine system, each ziphead put emotion and body language into the interpretation.

'Rappaport Digby' was the zipheads' name for the show's host. (*Where do they get those crazy names?* People still asked that. Ezr knew the names came mostly from Trixia. That was one of the few things he and Trixia could really talk about, his knowledge of the First Classicism. Sometimes she asked him for new words. In fact, *Ezr* had suggested the 'Digby' name, years ago. The word fit something she saw in the background of this particular Spider.) Ezr knew the translator who played Rappaport Digby. Outside of the show, Zinmin Broute was a typical ziphead, irritable, fixated, uncommunicative. But now, when he appeared as the Spider Rappaport Digby, he was kindly and garrulous, a patient explainer to children . . . It was like seeing a zombie briefly animated by someone else's soul.

Each new Watch saw the Spider children a little differently. After all, most Watches were only a twenty-five-percent duty cycle; the Spider children lived four years for every one that most spacers lived. Rita and some of the others took to visualizing human children to go with the voices. The pictures were scattered across the parlor's wallpaper. Pictures of imaginary human children, with the names Trixia had chosen. 'Jirlib' was short, with tousled dark hair and a mischievous smile. 'Brent' was larger, not as cocky-looking as his brother. Benny had told him how Ritser Brughel once replaced the smiling faces with pictures of real Spiders: low-slung, skeletal, armored – images from the statuary Ezr had seen in his landing on Arachna, supplemented with low-res pics from the snoopersats.

Brughel's vandalism hadn't mattered; he didn't understand what was behind the popularity of 'The Children's Hour.' Tomas Nau obviously *did* understand, and was perfectly content that the customers at Benny's booze parlor could sublimate the greatest personnel problem his little kingdom faced. Even more than the Qeng Ho expedition, the Emergents had expected to live in luxury. They had expected that there would be ever-expanding resources, that marriages planned at home could result in children and families here in the OnOff system . . .

Now all that was postponed. *Our own out-of-phase taboo.* Couples like Xin and Liao had only their dreams for the future – and the children's words and children's thoughts that came from the translation of 'The Children's Hour.'

Even before the live shows, the humans noticed that all the children were the same age. Year by Arachnan year they aged, but when new children came on the show, they were the same age as those replaced. The earliest translations had been lessons about magnetism and static electricity, all free of mathematics. Later the lessons introduced analysis and quantitative methods.

About two years ago, there had been a subtle change, remarked on in the ziphead's written reports – and instantly, instinctively noticed by Jau Xin and Rita Liao: 'Jirlib' and 'Brent' had appeared on the show. They were introduced as any other children, but Trixia's translations made them seem *younger* than the others. Showmaster Digby never remarked on the difference, and the math and science in the show continued to become more sophisticated.

'Victory Junior' and 'Gokna' were the latest additions to the cast, new on this Watch. Ezr had seen Trixia play them. Her voice had hopped with childish impatience; sometimes she had bubbled with laughter. Rita's pictures showed these two Spiders as laughing seven-year-olds. It was all too pat. Why should the average age of children on the show be declining? Benny claimed the explanation was obvious. 'The Children's Hour' must be under new management. The ubiquitous Sherkaner Underhill was credited with writing the lessons now. And Underhill was apparently the father of all the new children.

By the time Ezr had returned from coldsleep, the show was packing the parlor to capacity. Ezr saw four performances, each a private horror for him. And then, surcease. 'The Children's Hour' had not been broadcast for twenty days now. Instead, there had been a stern announcement: 'After numerous listener allegations, the owners of this broadcasting station have determined that the family of Sherkaner Underhill practices the out-of-phase perversion. Pending resolution of this situation, broadcasts of "The Children's Hour of Science" are suspended.' Broute had read the announcement with a voice quite unlike that of Rappaport Digby. The new voice was cold and distant, and full of indignation.

For once, the alienness of Arachna penetrated all the glib wishful thinking. So Spider tradition only allowed new children at the beginning of a New Sun. Generations were strictly separated, each marching through life as a same-aged group. The humans had only guesses for why this should be the case, but apparently 'The Children's Hour' had been a cover for a major violation of the taboo. The show missed one scheduled broadcast, two. In Benny's booze parlor, things were sad and empty; Rita began to talk of taking down the silly pictures. And Ezr began to hope that maybe this was the end of the circus.

But that was too much to hope. Four days ago, the gloom had abruptly lifted, even if the mystery remained. Broadcasts from radio stations all across the 'Goknan Accord' announced that a spokesman for the Church of the Dark would meet in debate with Sherkaner Underhill about the 'propriety' of his radio show. Trud Silipan had promised that the zipheads would be ready, able to translate this new show format.

Now Benny's show-time clock was counting down the seconds to this special edition of 'The Children's Hour.'

In his usual place on the other side of the parlor, Trud Silipan seemed to ignore the suspense. He and Pham Trinli were talking in low tones. The two were constant drinking buddies, planning great deals that never seemed to go anywhere. *Funny, I used to think Trinli was a loud buffoon.* Pham's 'magic localizer' claims had not been a bluff; Ezr had noticed the dustmotes. Nau and Brughel had begun using the gadgets. Somehow, Pham Trinli had known a secret about the localizers that had been missing from the innermost sections of the fleet library. Ezr Vinh might be the only one to realize it, but Pham Trinli was not totally a buffoon. More and more, Ezr guessed that the old man was in no part a fool. There were secrets hidden all through the fleet library; there had to be in anything that old and that large. But for a secret that important to be known by this man . . . Pham Trinli must go back a *long* way.

'Hey, Trud!' shouted Rita, pointing at the clock. 'Where are your zipheads?' The parlor's wallpaper still looked out on the forests of some Balacrean nature preserve.

Trud Silipan rose from his table and floated down before the crowd: 'It's okay, folks. I just got word. Princeton Radio has started the "Children's Hour" intro. Director Reynolt will bring out the zipheads in a moment. They're still synching with the word stream.'

Liao's irritation melted away. 'Great! Good going, Trud.'

Silipan gave a bow, accepting kudos for what was a zero contribution on his part. 'So, in a few moments we should know what strange things this Underhill creature has been doing with his children . . .' He cocked his head, listening to his private data feed. 'And here they are!'

The dripping, blue-green forest landscape disappeared. The bar side of the room suddenly seemed to extend into one of the meeting rooms down on Hammerfest. Anne Reynolt slid in from the right, her form distorted by the perspective angle; that part of the wallpaper just couldn't handle 3-D. Behind Reynolt came a couple of technicians and five zipheads . . . Focused persons. One of those was Trixia.

This was where Ezr wanted to start screaming – or run off to some dark place and pretend the world didn't exist. Normally the Emergents hid their zipheads deep within their systems, as if they felt some remnant shame. Normally the Emergents liked to get results from computer and head-up displays, all graphics and hygienically filtered data. Benny had told him that in the beginning Qiwi's freak show had just been the zipheads' voices piped into the parlor. Then Trud told everyone about the translators' byplay, and the show went visual. Surely the zipheads couldn't intuit body language from a Spider audio. That didn't seem to matter; the byplay might be nonsense, but it was what the ghouls around him wanted.

Trixia was dressed in loose fatigues. Her hair floated out, partly tangled. Ezr had combed it sleek less than 40Ksec earlier. She shrugged off her handlers and grabbed the edge of a table. She was looking this way and that, and mumbling to herself. She wiped her face on the sleeve of her fatigue blouse and pulled herself down to a chair restraint. The others followed her, looking as abstracted as Trixia. Most were wearing huds. Ezr knew the sort of thing they were seeing and hearing, the midlevel transduction of the Spider language. That was Trixia's entire world.

'We're synched, Director,' one of the techs said to Reynolt.

The Emergent Director for Human Resources floated down the rank of slaves, moving the fidgeting zipheads about for reasons that Ezr couldn't guess. After all this time, Ezr knew the woman had a special talent. She was a stone-eyed bitch, but she knew how to get results from zipheads.

'Okay, start 'em running—' She moved up, out of the way. Zinmin Broute had risen against his seat, and was already speaking in his ponderous announcer's voice. 'My name is Rappaport Digby, and this is "The Children's Hour of Science." . . .'

Daddy took them all to the radio station that day. Jirlib and Brent were up on the top deck of the car, acting very serious and grown-up – and they looked near enough to inphase that they didn't attract attention. Rhapsa and Little Hrunk were still tiny enough to perch in Daddy's fur; it might be another year before they rejected being called the babies of the family.

Gokna and Victory Junior sat in the back, each on her separate perch. Victory stared out through the smoky glass at the streets of Princeton. This all made her feel a little like royalty. She tilted her head slyly in her sister's direction; maybe Gokna was her handmaiden.

Gokna sniffed imperiously. They were alike enough that she was certainly thinking the same thing – with herself as Great Ruler. 'Daddy, if you're doing the show today, why are we even along?'

Daddy laughed. 'Oh, you never know. The Church of the Dark thinks they own the Right. But I wonder if their debater even knows any out-of-phase children. Underneath all the indignation, she might be likable. In person, she might not be able to breathe fire on little ones just because they aren't the right age.'

That was possible. Victory thought of Uncle Hrunk, who hated the idea of their family . . . and loved them at the same time.

The car drove through crowded streets, up the crosstown avenue that led to the radio hills. Princeton Station was the oldest in the city – Daddy said it began broadcasting before the last Dark, when it was a military radio station. In this generation, the owners had built on the original foundations. They could have had their studios in town, but they made a big thing of their great tradition. So the drive to the station was exciting, wrapping round and round a hill that was the tallest ever, much taller than even the one they lived on. Outside, there was still morning frost on the ground. Victory pushed over onto Gokna's perch and the two swayed out for a better look. This was the middle of winter, and they were almost to the Middle Years of the Sun, but this was only the second time they had seen frost. Gokna jabbed a hand out toward the east. 'Look, we're high enough now – you can see the Craggies!'

'And there's *snow* on them!' The two squealed the words together. But the distant glint was really the color of morning frost. It might be a couple more years before firstsnow came to the Princeton area, even in midwinter. What would it be like to walk in show? What would it be like to fall in a drift of it? For a moment, the two pondered the questions, forgetting the other events of the day – the radio debate that had preoccupied everyone, even the General, for the last ten days.

At first, all of the cobblies and especially Jirlib had been afraid of this debate. 'It's the end of the show,' their elder brother said. 'Now the public knows about us.' The General had come up from Lands Command especially to tell them there was nothing to worry about, that Daddy would take care of the complaints. But she didn't say they would get their radio show back again. General Victory Smith was used to briefing troops and staff. She didn't quite have the knack for reassuring children. Secretly, Gokna and Victory thought that maybe this flap about the radio show made Mom more nervous than any of the wartime adventures that lurked in her past.

Daddy was the only one who wasn't caught in the gloom. 'This is what I've been waiting for all along,' he told Mom when she came up from Lands Command. 'It's more than time to go public. This debate will bring lots of things out into the open.' Those were the same ideas that Mom spoke of, but from Daddy they sounded joyous. The last ten days, he had been playing with them even more than usual. 'You're my special experts for this debate, so I can spend all my time with you and still be the dutiful worker.' He had sidled dolefully from side to side, pretending to work at an invisible job. The babies had loved it, and even Jirlib and Brent seemed to accept their father's optimism. The General had departed for the south the night before; as usual, she had lots more to worry about than family problems.

The top of Radio Hill was above the tree line. Low furze covered the ground by the parking circle. The children got out, marveling at the chill that was still in the air. Little Victory felt an odd burning all along her breathing passages, as if . . . as if *frost* was forming there. Was that possible?

'Come along children. Gokna, don't gawk.' Daddy and his older sons herded them up the broad old steps of the station. The stone was flame-pitted and unpolished, like the owners wanted people to think they represented some ancient tradition.

The walls inside were hung with photo-impressions, portraits of the owners and the inventors of radio (the same people, in this case). All of them except Rhapsa and Hrunk had been here before. Jirlib and Brent had been doing the radio show for two years, taking over from the in-phase children when Daddy bought the show's franchise. Both boys sounded older than they really were, and Jirlib was smart as most adults. Nobody had seemed to suspect their true age. Daddy had been a little irritated by that. 'I want people to guess on their own – but they're too foolish to imagine the truth!' So finally, Gokna and Victory Junior had been added to the show. That had been fun, pretending to be years older, playing up to the dumb scripts they used on the show. And Mr Digby had been nice, even if he was no real scientist.

Still, both Gokna and Junior had very young-sounding voices. Eventually, someone had overcome their faith in the goodness of all radio broadcasts, and realized that serious perversion was being flaunted across the public's maw. But Princeton Radio was privately owned, and more important it owned its patch of spectrum and had interference easements on nearby bands. The owners were Generation 58 cobbers who were still counting their money. Unless the Church of the Dark could make an effective listener boycott, Princeton Radio was going to keep 'The Children's Hour.' Hence this debate.

'Ah, Dr Underhill, such a *pleasure!*' Madame Subtrime came sweeping out of her cubicle. The station manager was all legs and pointy hands, with a body scarcely bigger than her head. Gokna and Viki got plenty of laughs imitating her. 'You won't believe the interest this debate has generated. We are forwarding to the East Coast and copies will be on the shortwave. I tell you without exaggeration, we have listeners from just *all* over!'

I tell you without exaggeration . . . Hidden from the manager, Gokna waggled her mouth parts in time with the words. Viki kept her own aspect prim, and pretended not to notice.

Daddy tipped his head to the manager. 'I'm glad to be so popular, Madame.'

'Oh, yes, indeed! We've got sponsors killing each other for the slots in this time. Simply *killing* each other!' She smiled down at the children. 'I've arranged that you can watch from our engineer's loft.'

They all knew where that was, but they followed obediently along, listening to her unending gush. None of them really knew what Madame Subtrime thought of them. Jirlib claimed that she was no fool, that under all the words lurked a cold counter of cash. 'She knows to the tenth-penny how much she can earn for the old cobbers by outraging the public.' Maybe, but Viki liked her even so, and even forgave her shrill and foolish talk. Too many people were so stuck on their beliefs that nothing would bend them.

'Didi's on duty this hour. You know her.' Madame Subtrime stopped at the entrance to the engineer's loft. For the first time she seemed to notice the babies peeking out of Sherkaner Underhill's fur. 'My, you do have all ages, don't you? I . . . will they be safe with your children? I don't know who else could take care of them.'

'Quite all right Madame. I intend to introduce Rhapsa and Little Hrunk to the representative of the Church.'

Madame Subtrime froze. For a full second, all the fidgety legs and hands were simultaneously motionless. It was the first time Viki had seen her really, *really* taken aback. Then her body relaxed into a slow, broad smile. 'Dr Underhill! Has anyone ever told you you're a genius?'

Daddy grinned back. 'Never with such good reason . . . Jirlib, make sure everyone stays in the room with Didi. If I want you to come out, you'll know it.'

The cobblies climbed into the engineering loft. Didire Ultmot was slouched on her usual perch overlooking the controls. A thick glass wall separated the room from the soundstage itself. It was soundproof, and darned hard to see through, too. The children edged close to the glass. There was someone already perched on the stage.

Didire waved a hand at them. 'That's the Church's rep out there. The cobber came an hour early.' Didi was her usual, faintly impatient, self. She was a very good-looking twenty-one-year-old. Didi wasn't as smart as some of Daddy's students, but she was bright. She was Princeton Radio's chief technician. At fourteen she had been a primetime operator, and. knew as much about electrical engineering as Jirlib. In fact, she wanted to become an electrical engineer. All that had come across the first time Jirlib and Brent met her, back when they started on the show. Viki remembered the strange way Jirlib had acted when he told them about that meeting; he seemed almost in awe of the Didire creature. She was nineteen then, and Jirlib was twelve . . . but big for his age. It took her two shows to realize that Jirlib was out-of-phase. She had taken the surprise as an intentional, personal insult. Poor Jirlib walked around like his legs were broken for a few days. He got over it – after all, there would be worse rejections in the future.

Didire more or less got over it, too. As long as Jirlib kept his distance, she was civil. And sometimes, when she forgot herself, Didi was more fun than any current-generation person that Viki knew. When they weren't onstage, she would let Viki and Gokna sit by her perch and watch her tweak the dozens of controls. Didire was very proud of her control panel. In fact – except that the frame was furniture wood and not sheet metal – it looked almost as scientific as some of the gear at Hill House.

'So what's this church cobber like?' asked Gokna. She and Viki had pressed their main eyes flat against the glass wall. The glass was so thick that lots of colors could not penetrate. The stranger perched onstage could have been dead for all the far-red you could see of her.

Didi shrugged. 'Name's "Honored Pedure." She talks funny. I think she's a Tiefer. And that cleric's shawl she's wearing? It's not just our crummy view from the control room: that shawl really is *dark*, across all colors but the farthest reds.'

Hmm. Expensive. Mom had a dress uniform like that, only most people never saw her in it.

A wicked smile grew across Didi's aspect. 'I bet she pukes when she sees the babies in your father's fur.'

No such luck. But when Snerkaner Underhill came in a few seconds later, the Honored Pedure stiffened under her shapeless cowl. A second later, Rappaport Digby trotted onto the stage and grabbed an earphone. Digby had been with 'The Children's Hour' from the beginning, long before Jirlib and Brent had started on the show. He was an old coot and Brent claimed he was really one of the station owners. Viki didn't believe it not after the way Didi sassed him.

'Okay, everybody.' Didi's voice came amplified now. Daddy and the Honored Pedure straightened, each hearing the words from the speaker on their side. 'We're coming up on fifteen seconds. Will you be ready, Master Digby, or should I play some dead air?'

Digby's snout was stuck in a wad of written notes. 'Laugh if you like, Miss Ultmot, but air time is money. One way or another, I will—'

'Three, two, one—' Didi cut her speaker and stabbed a long, pointed hand in Digby's direction.

The cobber picked up his cue as if he'd been waiting in patient alertness. His words had the usual smooth dignity, the trademark that had introduced the show for more than fifteen years: 'My name is Rappaport Digby, and this is "The Children's Hour of Science." . . .'

When Zinmin Broute spoke in translation, his motions were no longer fitful and compulsive. He looked directly forward and smiled or frowned with emotions that seemed very real. And maybe they were real – for some armored spider creature down on the surface of Arachna. Occasionally there was some hesitation, a glitch in the intermediate conversions. Even more rarely, Broute would turn away, perhaps when some important cue appeared off-center in his head-up. But unless you knew what to look for, the fellow seemed to be speaking as fluently as any human announcer reading from notes written in his birth language.

Broute as Digby began with a little self-congratulatory history of the radio program, then described the shadow that had fallen upon it in recent days. 'Out of phase,' 'perversion of birth.' Broute rattled off the words as if he'd known them all his life. 'This afternoon, we are back on the air as promised. The charges made in recent days are grave. Ladies and gentlemen, these charges of themselves are true.'

The silence was a dramatic three beat, and then: 'So my friends, you may wonder what gave us the courage – or the impudence – to return. For the answer to that, I ask you to listen to this afternoon's edition of "The Children's Hour." Whether we continue in the future will largely depend on your reactions to what you hear today . . .'

Silipan snorted. 'What a money-grubbing hypocrite.' Xin and the others waved at him to shut up. Trud sailed over to sit beside Ezr. This had happened before; he seemed to think that because Ezr sat at the edge, somehow he wanted to hear Silipan's analysis.

Beyond the wallpaper, Broute was introducing the debaters. Silipan anchored a comp to his knee and flipped it open. It was a clumsy Emergent thing, but it had ziphead support and that made it more effective than anything Humankind had created before. He punched the Explain key and a tiny voice gave him background: 'Officially, the Honored Pedure represents the traditional Church. In fact—' The voice coming from Trud's comp paused, presumably while hardware searched databases. '—Pedure is a foreigner to the Goknan Accord. She's probably an agent of the Kindred government.'

Xin looked around at them, momentarily losing track of Broute-Digby. 'Pus, these people take their fundamentalism seriously. Does Underhill know about this?'

The voice from Trud's hand comp replied. 'It's possible. "Sherkaner Underhill" is strongly correlated with Accord's security communications . . . To date, we haven't seen any military message traffic discussing this debate, but the Spider civilization is not yet well automated. There could be things we're missing.'

Trud spoke to the device: 'I have a lowest-pri background task for you. What would the Kindred want from this debate?' He glanced up at Jau and shrugged. 'Dunno if we'll get any answer. Things are pretty busy.'

Broute was almost done with his introductions. Honored Pedure was to be played by a Xopi Reung. Xopi was a thin little Emergent. Ezr knew her name only from studying rosters and talking to Anne Reynolt. *I wonder if anyone else here knows the woman's name?* thought Ezr. Certainly not Jau and Rita. Trud would, just as a livestock herder in primitive times would know his property. Xopi Reung was young; she had been brought out of the freezer to replace what Silipan called 'a senility failure.' Reung had been on-Watch for about 40Msec. She was responsible for most of the progress in learning other Spider languages, in particular 'Tiefic.' And she was already the second-best translator of 'Standard Accord' speech. Someday, she might very well be better than Trixia. In a sane world, Xopi Reung would have been a premier academic, famous across her solar system. But Xopi Reung had been selected in the Podmaster Lottery. While Xin and Liao and Silipan led fully conscious lives, Xopi Reung was part of the automation in the walls, unseen except for the occasional peculiar circumstance.

Xopi Reung spoke: 'Thank you, Master Digby. The Radio of Princeton secures itself proud by giving us this time to talk.' Daring Broute's introduction Reung's attention had flickered all around, birdlike. Perhaps her huds were out of adjustment, or maybe she preferred to scatter important cues all about her visual field. But when she started talking, something feral came into her eyes.

'Not a very good translation,' someone complained.

'She's new, remember,' said Trud.

'Or maybe this Pedure really does talk funny. You said she's a foreigner.'

Reung-as-Pedure leaned out over the table. Her voice came silky and low. 'Twenty days ago, we all discovered a corruption afester in what millions of people had been taking for years into their homes, into their husbands' and children's ears.' She continued for several moments, speaking awkward sentences that seemed very self-righteous. Then: 'So it is fitting that the Radio of Princeton should now give us opportunity to cleanse the community's air.' She paused, 'I – I—' It was as though she couldn't think of the right words. For an instant she seemed the ziphead again, fidgeting, her head cocked. Then abruptly she slammed her palm against the surface of the table. She pulled herself down to her chair and shut up.

'I told you, that one's not much of a translator.'

24

By leaning hands and forelegs on the wall, Viki and Gokna could keep their main eyes against the glass. It was an awkward pose, and the two skittered back and forth along the base of the window.

'Thank you, Master Digby. The Radio of Princeton secures itself proud by—' blah blah blah.

'She talks funny,' said Gokna.

'I already told you that. She's a foreigner.' Didire spoke abstractedly. She

667

was busy with some arcane adjustment of her equipment. She didn't seem to be paying much attention to what was actually being said on the soundstage. Brent was watching the show with stolid fascination, while Jirlib alternated between the window and standing as close as he could to Didi. He was well cured of giving her technical advice, but he still liked to stand close. Sometimes he would ask an appropriately naive question. When Didi wasn't busy, that usually got her talking to him.

Gokna grinned at Viki. 'No. I meant "Honored Pedure" talks like a bad joke.'

'Hm.' Viki wasn't so sure. Pedure's clothing was strange, of course. She hadn't seen cleric shawls outside of books. It was a shapeless cloak that came down on every side, obscuring all but Pedure's head and maw. But she had an impression of strength under cover. Viki knew what most people thought of children such as herself. Pedure was just a full-time advocate of that view, right? But her speech had a certain menace . . . 'Do you think she really believes what she's saying?'

'Sure she believes it. That's what makes her so funny. See how Daddy's smiling?' Sherkaner Underhill was perched on the other side of the sound-stage, quietly petting his babies. He hadn't said a word yet, but there was a faint smile twitching across him. Two pairs of baby eyes peered fearfully out from his fur. Rhapsa and Hrunk couldn't understand everything that was going on, but they looked frightened.

Gokna noticed, too. 'Poor babies. They're the only ones she can scare. Watch! I'm gonna Give Ten to the Honored Pedure.' She turned away from the window and ran to the side wall – and then up the rack of audio tapes. The girls were seven years old, much too big for acrobatics. *Oops.* The rack was freestanding. It swayed out from the wall, tapes and assorted junk sliding to the edge of each shelf. Gokna reached the top before anyone but Viki realized what was happening. And from there she leaped out, grabbing the top molding of the soundstage window. The rest of her body swung down against the glass with a solid *splat* sound. For an instant, she was a perfect Ten splayed out across the window. On the far side of the glass, Pedure stared in stupefied shock. The two girls shrieked with laughter. It wasn't often you could give such a perfect Ten, flaring your underwear in the target's face.

'*Quit it!*' Didi's voice was a flat hiss. Her hands flickered across the controls. 'This is the last time you little crappers get into my control room! Jirlib, get over there! Shut your sisters down or drag them out, but no more crapping nonsense.'

'Yes, yes! I'm so sorry.' Jirlib really did sound sorry. He rushed over and plucked Gokna from the glass wall. A second later Brent followed him, grabbing Victory.

Jirlib didn't seem angry, just upset. He held Gokna very close to his head. 'You must be quiet. For once you must be serious.' It occurred to Viki that maybe he was just upset because Didi was so angry with him. But it really didn't matter. All the laughter had leaked out of Gokna. She touched an eating hand to her brother's maw, and said softly, 'Yes. I'll be good for the rest of the show. I promise.'

Behind them, Viki could see Didi talking – probably to the phone in Digby's ear. Viki couldn't hear the words, but the guy was nodding agreement. He had eased Pedure back to her seat, and now segued into his introduction of Daddy. All the action on this side of the glass had accounted for virtually nothing out there. Someday she and Gokna were going to get themselves into real trouble, but it looked like that adventure was still somewhere in the future.

Xopi sat down amid general confusion. Usually the zip-heads tried to keep these shows in approximate real time. Silipan claimed that was only partly his specification – the ziphead translators really liked to stay in synch with the word stream. In some sense, they really did like to act. Today they just weren't very successful at it.

Finally, Broute got himself together and gave a relatively smooth introduction to Sherkaner Underhill.

Sherkaner Underhill. Trixia Bonsol translated him. Who else could it have been? Trixia had been the first to crack the spoken language of the Spiders. Jau had told Ezr that in the early days of the live show, she had handled all the parts, children's voices, old people, phone-in questions. After other zipheads acquired fluency and there was a consensus of style, still Trixia had taken the hard parts.

Sherkaner Underhill: That might be the first Spider they ever had a name for. Underhill showed up in an incredible range of radio broadcasts. At first, it seemed that he had invented two-thirds of the industrial revolution. That misconception had faded: 'Underhill' was a common name, and where this 'Sherkaner Underhill' was referenced, it was always one of his students who actually did the work. So the guy must be a bureaucrat, the founder of the Princeton Institute, where most of his students seemed to be. But ever since the Spiders invented microwave relays, the snoopersats had been sucking on an increasing stream of easily decrypted national secrets. The 'Sherkaner Underhill' ID showed up on almost twenty percent of all the high-security traffic that flowed across the Goknan Accord. Clearly, they were dealing with some kind of institutional name. Clearly . . . until they learned that 'Sherkaner Underhill' had children, and they were on this radio show. Even though they hadn't figured it all out, there was some real political significance to 'The Children's Hour.' No doubt, Tomas Nau was watching this show over on Hammerfest. *I wonder if Qiwi is with him.*

Trixia spoke: 'Thank you, Master Digby. I am very happy to be here this afternoon. It's time there be an open discussion of these issues. In fact, I hope that young people – both in-phase and out-of-phase – are listening. I know my children are.'

The look Trixia sent Xopi's way was relaxed and confident. Yet there was a faint tremor in her voice. Ezr stared at her face. How old was Trixia now? The full ziphead Watch schedules were classified – probably because so many were being run at one hundred percent. It should take a lifetime to learn all Trixia had learned. At least after the early years, every Watch he stood, there she was. She looked ten years older than the Trixia before Focus. And when she played Underhill, she seemed even older.

Trixia was still talking: 'But I want to correct one thing that Lady Pedure said. There was no secret plot to keep the age of these children a secret. My two oldest – they're fourteen, now – have been on the show for some time. It's quite natural that they should participate, and from the letters they got, I know that they were very popular with both current-generation children and their parents.'

Xopi looked down the table at Trixia: 'And of course, that is simply because they kept quiet their true age. On the radio, you can't tell such small a difference. On the radio, some . . . obscenities . . . go unnoticed.'

Trixia laughed. 'Indeed they do. But I want our listeners to think on this. Most of them are fond of Jirlib and Brent and Gokna and Viki. Meeting my children "blind" on the radio showed our listeners a truth they might have missed otherwise: the oophase are as decent as anyone else. But again, I hid nothing. Eventually . . . well, eventually the facts of the matter were so obvious that no one could ignore them.'

'So blatant, you mean. Your second clutch of oophases is scarce seven years old. *That* obscenity even radio can not disguise. And when we met here in the studio, I see you have two *newborns* suckling in your fur. Tell me, sir, is there any limit to how much evil you will do?'

'Lady Pedure, what evil, what harm? Our audience has listened to one or another of my children for more than two years. They know Jirlib and Brent and Viki and Gokna as real and likable people. You see Little Hrunk and Rhapsa looking at you from my shoulders—' Trixia paused as if to give the other time for a look. 'I know it pains you to see babies so far from the Waning Years. But in a year or two they will be old enough to talk, and I fully intend to have "The Children's Hour" include all the ages of my children. From program to program, our audience will see that these little cobblies are just as worthy as ones born at the end of the Waning Years.'

'Absurdity! Your scheme only wins if you sneak up on decent people a small step at a time, getting them to accept this waiver of morality and then that, until . . .'

'Until what?' Trixia asked, smiling benignly.

'Until – until—' Behind her semiclear huds, Ezr could see that Xopi was staring wildly. 'Until decent people will kiss upon those ill-timed maggots you carry on your back!' She was out of her chair, waving her arms in Trixia's direction.

Trixia was still smiling. 'In a word, my dear Pedure, "Yes." Even you see that there can be acceptance. But out-of-phase children are not maggots. They do not need a First Darkness to give them their souls. They are creatures who can become lovable Spiders in their own right. As the years pass, "The Children's Hour" will make this obvious to everyone, perhaps even to you.'

Xopi sat down. She looked very much like a debater who has been bested and is casting about for some different line of attack. 'I see appeal to decency has no strength with you, Master Underhill. And there may be weak people in the audience who move to perversion by your gradual approach. Everyone has immoral inclinations, in that we agree. But we also have quite moral ones, innate. Tradition guides us between the two . . . but I can see that tradition has small weight with such as you. You are a scientist, not so?'

'Hm, yes.'

'And one of the four Darkstriders?'

'. . . Yes.'

'Our audience may not realize so distinguished a person lurks behind "The Children's Hour." You are one of four who has actually seen the Deepest Dark. Nothing holds mystery for you.' Trixia started to respond, but Xopi as Pedure rolled right over her words. 'I daresay this explains much of your flaw. You are blind about the striving of previous generations, the slow learning of what is deadly and what is safe in Spiderly affairs. There are reasons for moral law, sir! Without moral law, diligent hoarders will be robbed by the indolent at the end of the Waning Years. Without moral law, innocents in their deepnesses will be massacred by the first-getting-awake. We all want many things, but some of those are bottomly destructive of all desires.'

'This last is true, Lady Pedure. What is your point?'

'The point is that there are *reasons* for rules, in especial for the rules against oophaseness. As a Darkstrider you make trivial of things, but even you must know the Dark is the great cleanser. I've listened to your children. Today before air time, I watched them in the engineer's control room. There is a scandal within your secret, but not surprising. At least one of your children – the one named Brent? – is a cretin, is he not?'

Xopi stopped talking, but Trixia didn't respond. Her gaze was steady; she wasn't scrambling to keep up with the intermediate-layer data reps. And suddenly, Ezr felt the strangest change in perspective, like a change in imagined-down, but enormously more intense. It wasn't caused by the translators' words or even the emotion in their words. It was the . . . silence. For the first time, Ezr knew a Spider as a person, a person who could be hurt.

The silence stretched on for several more seconds. 'Ha,' said Silipan. 'That's pretty good confirmation on a lot of guesses. The Spiders breed in large clutches, and then Mother Nature kills off the weak ones during the Dark. Slick.'

Liao grimaced. 'Yeah, I guess.' Her hand reached to her husband's shoulder.

Zinmin Broute abruptly broke the silence. 'Master Underhill, are you going to reply to the Honored Pedure's question?'

'Yes.' The quaver in Trixia's voice was more pronounced than before. 'Brent is no cretin. He's not verbal and he learns differently than other children.' Her voice picked up enthusiasm, and there was a shadow of a smile. 'Intelligence is such a remarkable thing. In Brent I see—'

Xopi cut her off. '—In Brent *I* see the classical birth wreck of the oophase child. My friends, I know the strength of the Church suffers now in this generation. There is so much change, and the old ways are so much thought tyrannical. In previous times, a child such as Brent could only happen in backwoods townships, where barbarism and perversion have always been. In previous times, such was easy to explain: "The parents evaded the Dark, like not even animals would do. They brought poor Brent into the world to live some years of crippled life, and rightly should they be loathed for their cruelty." But in our times, it is an intellectual such as Underhill' – a nod in the direction of Trixia – 'who makes this sin. He makes you laugh upon tradition, and I must fight him with his own reasons. Look upon this child, Master Underhill. How many more have you borne like him?'

Trixia: 'All my cobblies—'

'Ah, yes. No doubt there have been other failures. You have six that we know of. How many more are there? Do you kill the clear failures? If the world follows your perversion, civilization will die before even the next Dark comes, smothered in hordes of ill-conceived and crippled cobblies.' Pedure went on in this vein at some length. In fact, her complaints were very concrete: birth deformities, overpopulation, forced killings, riots in deepnesses at the beginning of the Dark – all would follow if there were a popular move toward out-of-phase births. Xopi rattled on until she was visibly out of breath.

Broute turned to Trixia as Underhill: 'And your reply?'

Trixia: 'Ah, it is nice to be able to reply.' Trixia was smiling again, her tone almost as light as at the beginning of the program. If Underhill had been unhinged by the attack on his son, maybe Pedure's long speech had given him time to recover. 'First, all my children are living. There are only six. That should not be surprising. It's hard to conceive children out-of-phase. I'm sure everyone knows this. It is also very hard to nurture the out-of-phase baby welts long enough for them to grow eyes. Nature does indeed prefer that cobblies be created right before the Dark.'

Xopi leaned forward, speaking loudly. 'Take careful note, friends! Underhill just now admits that he commits crime against nature!'

'Not at all. Evolution has caused us to survive and thrive within Nature. But times change—'

Xopi sounded sarcastic: 'So times change? Science made you a Darkstrider, and now you are greater than Nature?'

Trixia laughed. 'Oh, I'm still very much a part of Nature. But even before technology – did you know that ten million years ago, the length of the sun's cycle was less than one year?'

'Fantasy. How could creatures live—'

'How indeed?' Trixia was smiling more broadly, and her tone was one of triumph. 'But the record of fossil edgings is very clear. Ten million years ago, the cycle was much shorter and the variation in brightness much less intense. There was no need for deepnesses and hibernation. As the cycle of light and dark became longer and more extreme, all surviving creatures adapted. I imagine it was a harsh process. Many great changes were necessary. And now—'

Xopi made a cutting gesture. Did she make those up or were they somehow implied by the Spider broadcast? 'If not fantasy, it's still not proved. Sir, I will not argue evolution with you. There are decent people who believe it, but it is speculation – no basis for death-and-life decisions.'

'Ha! Point for Daddy!' From their perches atop Brent and Jirlib, the two girls exchanged quiet editorial comments. Where Didire couldn't see, they were also making maw-gestures at the Honored Pedure. After that first Ten, there had been no obvious reaction, but it felt good to show the cobber how they felt about her.

'Don't worry, Brent. Daddy's going to get this Pedure.'

Brent had been even more quiet than usual. 'I knew this was going to happen. Things were hard enough. Now Dad has to explain about me, too.'

In fact, Daddy had almost lost it when Pedure called Brent a cretin. Viki had never seen him look quite so lost. But he was taking back lost ground now. Viki had thought Pedure would be a know-nothing, but she seemed familiar with some of what Daddy was throwing at her. It didn't matter. Honored Pedure wasn't that knowledgeable; besides, Daddy was *right*.

And he was on a real pounce now: 'Strange that tradition should not show more interest in the earliest past, Lady Pedure. But no matter. The changes that science is making in this current generation will be so great that I might better use them to illustrate. Nature enforced certain strategies – and the cycle of generations is one of them, I agree. Without that enforcement, we likely would not exist. But think of the waste, my lady. All our children are in one stage of life in each year. Once past that stage, the tools of their schooling must lie idle until the next generation. There is no need for such waste anymore. With science—'

Honored Pedure gave a whistling laugh, full of sarcasm and surprise. 'So you admit it there! You plot that oophase be a way of life, not your isolated sin.'

'Of course!' Daddy bounced up. 'I want people to know that we live in an era that is different. I want people to be free to have children in every season of the sun.'

'Yes. You intend to invade the rest of us. Tell me, Underhill, do you already have secret schools for the oophase? Are there hundreds or thousands like your six, just waiting for our acceptance?'

'Uh, no. So far we have not found playmates for my children.'

Over the years, all of them had wanted playmates. Mother had searched for them, so far without success. Gokna and Viki had concluded that other oophases must be very well hidden . . . or very rare. Sometimes, Viki wondered if maybe they really were damned; it was so hard to find any others.

Honored Pedure leaned back on her perch, smiling in an almost friendly way. 'That last is comfort to me, Master Underhill. Even in our times, most folk are decent, and your perversions are rare. Nevertheless, "The Children's Hour" continues to be popular, even though the in-phase are now more than twenty years old. Your show is a lure that didn't exist beforetimes. And our view exchange is therefore terribly important.'

'Yes, indeed. I think so, too.'

Honored Pedure cocked her head. What rotten luck. The cobber realized that Daddy meant it. If she got Daddy to speculating . . . things could be very sticky. Pedure's next question was spoken in a casual tone of honest curiosity. 'It seems to me, Master Underhill, that you understand moral law. Do you consider it, maybe, to be something like the law of creative art – to be broken by the greatest thinkers, such as yourself?'

'Greatest thinkers, fooey.' But the question had clearly caught Daddy's imagination, drawing him away from persuasive rhetoric. 'You know, Pedure, I never looked at moral rules like that before. What an interesting idea! You suggest that they could be ignored by those who have some innate – what? Talent for goodness? Surely not . . . Though I confess to being an illiterate when it comes to moral argument. I like to play and I like to think. The Darkstriding was a great lark, as much as it was important to the war effort. Science will create wonderful change in the near future of Spider-kind. I'm having enormous fun with these things, and I want the public – including those who *are* experts at moral thought – to understand the consequences of the change.'

Honored Pedure said, 'Indeed.' The sarcasm was there only if you were listening as suspiciously as Little Victory was. 'And you intend somehow for science to replace the Dark as the great cleanser and the great mystery?'

Daddy made dismissing gestures with his eating hands. He seemed to have forgotten that he was on the radio. 'Science will make the Dark of the

674

Sun as innocuous and knowable as the night that comes at the end of every day.'

In the control room, Didi gave a little yip of surprise. It was the first time Viki had ever heard the engineer react to the broadcasts she was supervising. Out on the soundstage, Rappaport Digby sat up as straight as if someone had stuck a spear up his rear. Daddy didn't seem to notice, and Honored Pedure's response was as casual as if they were discussing the possibility of rain: 'We'll live and work right through the Dark as if it was just one long night?'

'Yes! What do you think all the talk of nuclear power means?'

'So then we all will be Darkstriders, and there will be no Dark, no mystery, no Deepness for the mind of Spiderkind to rest within. Science will take all.'

'Piffle. On this one small world, there will be no more real darkness. But there will always be the Dark. Go out tonight, Lady Pedure. Look up. We are surrounded by the Dark and always will be. And just as our Dark ends with the passage of time in a New Sun, so the greater Dark ends at the shores of a million million stars. Think! If our sun's cycle was once less than a year, then even earlier our sun might have been middling bright all the time. I have students who are sure most of the stars are just like our sun, only much much younger, and many with worlds like ours. You want a deepness that endures, a deepness that Spiderkind can depend on? Pedure, there is a deepness in the sky, and it extends forever.' And Daddy was off on his space-travel thing. Even graduate students glazed over when Daddy started on this; only a hard core of crazies specialized in astronomy. It was all so upside down and inside out. For most people, the idea that lights as steady as stars could be like the sun was a leap of faith greater than most religions asked for.

Digby and Honored Pedure watched open-mawed as Daddy built the theory up in more and more elaboration. Digby had always liked the science part of the show, and this had him all but hypnotized. Pedure on the other hand . . . her shock faded quickly: Either she had heard this before, or it was tending away from the path she wanted to follow.

The clock on the control-room wall was ticking down toward the orgy of commercial messages that always ended the show. It looked like Daddy was going to get the last word . . . except that Viki was sure Honored Pedure was watching that clock more intensely than anything in the studio, waiting for some precisely chosen strategic instant.

And then the cleric grabbed her mike close, and spoke loudly enough to break into Sherkaner's flow of thought. 'So interesting, but colonizing the space between the stars is surely beyond the time of this current generation.'

Daddy waved dismissively. 'Perhaps yes, but—'

Honored Pedure continued, her voice academic and interested, 'So the great change during our time is simply the conquest of the next coming Dark, that which ends this cycle of the sun?'

'Correct. We – all who hear this radio broadcast – will have no need of deepnesses. That is the promise of nuclear power. All the great cities will have sufficient power to stay warm for more than two centuries – all the way through the upcoming Dark. So—'

'I see, and so very large building projects must happen to enclose the cities?'

'Yes, and farms. And we'll need to provide—'

'And this then is also the reason you want an added generation of adults. This is why you push oophase births.'

'Oh, not directly. It is simply a feature of the new situ—'

'So the Goknan Accord will enter the coming Dark in fact with hundreds of millions of Darkstriders. What of the rest of the world?'

Daddy seemed to realize that he was headed for trouble. 'Um, but other technologically advanced countries may do the same. The poorer countries will have their conventional deepnesses, and their awakening will come later.'

Now Pedure's voice had steel in it, a trap that was finally sprung: ' "Their awakening will come later." During the Great War, four Darkstriders brought down the most powerful nation of the world. In the next Dark, you will be Darkstriders by the millions. This seems not different from a preparation for the greatest deepness massacres in history.'

'No, it's not like that at all. We wouldn't—'

'I'm sorry, lady and sir, our time has run out.'

'But—'

Digby rumbled on over Daddy's objections. 'I'd like to thank you both for being with us today and—' blah blah blah.

On the soundstage, Pedure stood up the moment Digby finished his spiel. The microphones were off now and Viki couldn't hear the words. The cleric was evidently exchanging pleasantries with the announcer. On the other side of the stage, Daddy looked very nonplussed. As Honored Pedure swept past him, Daddy stood and followed her offstage, talking animatedly. Pedure's only expression was a haughty little smile.

Behind Viki, Didi Ultmot was pushing levers, tuning the most important part of the broadcast, the commercials. Finally, she turned away from the controls. There was something a little dazed about her aspect. '. . . You know, your dad has some really . . . weird . . . ideas.'

There was a sequence of chords that might have been music, and the words, 'Sharpened hands are happy hands. Brim the tinfall with mirthly bands—'

Spider commercials were sometimes the high point of Princeton Radio programs. Molt refresh, eye polish, leggings – many of the products made some sense, even if the selling points did not. Other products were just nonsense words, especially if it was a previously unknown product, and second-string translators.

Today, it was the second-stringers. Reung, Broute, and Trixia sat fidgeting, cut off from the signal stream. Their handlers were already moving in to clear them from the stage. Today the crowd in Benny's parlor pretty much ignored the commercials, too:

'Not as much fun as when the kids are on, but—'

'Did you get the angle on spaceflight? I wonder what this does to the Schedule? If—'

Ezr wasn't paying attention. His gaze stayed on the wall, and all the chitchat was just distant buzzing. Trixia looked worse than usual. The flicker of her gaze seemed desperate to Ezr. He often thought that, and a dozen times Anne Reynolt had claimed the behavior was nothing but eagerness to get back to work.

'Ezr?' A hand brushed gently against his sleeve. It was Qiwi. Sometime during the program she had slipped into the parlor. She had done this before, sitting silently, watching the show. Now she had the gall to act like a friend. 'Ezr, I—'

'Save it.' Ezr turned away from her.

And so he was looking directly at Trixia when it happened: The handlers had moved Broute out of the room. As they led Xopi Reung past her, Trixia shrieked and lunged from her chair, her fist smashing into the younger woman's face. Xopi twisted away, jerking out of her handler's grip. She stared dazedly at the blood streaming from her nose, then wiped her face with her hand. The other tech grabbed the screaming Trixia before she could do more damage. Somehow Trixia's words made it onto the general audio channel: 'Pedure bad! Die! Die!'

'Oh, boy.' Next to Ezr, Trud Silipan bounced off his seat and pushed his way toward the entrance to Benny's parlor. 'Reynolt is going to have a fit about this. I gotta get back to Hammerfest.'

'I'm coming, too.' Ezr brushed past Qiwi and dived for the door. Benny's parlor was silent for a shocked moment, then everyone was talking—

—but by that time, Ezr was nearly out of earshot, and chasing Silipan. They moved quickly to the main corridor, heading for the taxi tubes. At the locks, Silipan tapped something on the scheduler, then turned. 'What do you two want?'

Ezr looked over his shoulder, saw that Pham Trinli had followed them out of Benny's. Ezr said, 'I have to come, Trud. I have to see Trixia.'

Trinli sounded worried too. 'Is this going to screw our deal, Silipan? We need to make sure that—'

'Oh, pus. Yeah, we gotta think how this may affect things. Okay. Come along.' He glanced at Ezr. 'But you. There's nothing you can do to help.'

'I'm coming, Trud.' Ezr found himself less than ten centimeters from the other, with his fists raised.

'Okay, okay! Just stay out of the way.' A moment later, the taxi lock blinked green and they were aboard and accelerating out from the temp. The rockpile was a sunlit jumble just to one side of Arachna's blue disk. 'Pest, this would happen when we were on the far side. Taxi!'

'Sir?'

'Best time to Hammerfest.' Normally, they had to baby the taxi hardware – but apparently the automation recognized Trud's voice and tone.

'Yessir.' The taxi pushed off at nearly a tenth of a gee. Silipan and the others grabbed for restraints, and tied down. Ahead of them the rockpile grew and grew. 'This really sucks, you know that? Reynolt is going to say I was absent from my post.'

'Well, weren't you?' Trinli had settled down right beside Silipan.

'Of course, but it shouldn't matter. Hell, one handler should have been enough for the whole pus-be-damned translator crew. But now, *I'm* going to be the one who looks bad.'

'But is Trixia all right?'

'Why did Bonsol blow up like that?' said Trinli.

'It beats me. You know they bicker and fight, especially some of the ones in the same specialty. But this came from nowhere.' Silipan abruptly stopped talking. For a long moment he stared into his huds. Then, 'It'll be okay. It'll be okay. I bet there was still some audio feed from the ground. You know, a live mike, a failure of their show management. Maybe Underhill took a swipe at the other Spider. That might make Bonsol's action "valid translation." . . . Damn!'

Now the guy was really worried, grasping at random explanations. Trinli seemed too dense to notice. He grinned and slapped Silipan lightly on the shoulder. 'Don't worry about it. You know Qiwi Lisolet is in on the deal. That means that Podmaster Nau wants the zips to be more widely used, too. We'll just say you were aboard the temp to help me with the details.'

The taxi turned end for end, braking for its landing. The rockpile and Arachna tumbled across the sky.

25

They didn't see the Honored Pedure on the way out of the radio station. Daddy was a little subdued, but he smiled and laughed when the cobblies told him how much they liked his performance. He didn't even, scold Gokna for Giving Ten. Brent got to sit up front with Daddy on the way back to Hill House.

Gokna and Victory didn't talk much in the car. They both knew that everybody was fooling everybody.

When they got home, it was still two hours until dinner. The kitchen staff claimed that General Smith had returned from Lands Command and that she would be at dinner. Gokna and Viki exchanged looks. *I wonder what Mother will say to Daddy*. The juiciest parts wouldn't be at dinner. *Hmm. So what to do with the rest of the afternoon?* The sisters split up, separately recon'd the spiraled halls of Hill House. There were rooms – lots of rooms – that were always locked. Some of them were ones that they had never even been able to steal keys for. The General had her own offices here, even if the most important stuff was down at Lands Command.

Viki poked into Daddy's ground-floor den and the tech-level cafeteria, but only briefly. She'd bet Gokna that Daddy would not be hiding, but now she realized that today 'not hiding' did not preclude 'difficult to find.' She roamed through the labs, found the typical signs of his passage, graduate students in various states of puzzlement and sudden, surprised enlightenment. ('Underhill Dazzle' was what the students called it: If you came away puzzled, chances were that Daddy had said something worthwhile. If you were instantly enlightened, it probably meant Daddy had fooled both himself and you with a facile misinsight.)'

The new signals lab was near the top of the house, under a roof full of experimental antennas. She caught Jaybert Landers coming down the steps from there. The cobber wasn't showing any symptoms of Underhill Dazzle. Too bad.

'Hello, Jaybert. Have you seen my—'

'Yeah, they're both up in the lab.' He jerked a hand over his shoulder.

Aha! But Viki didn't immediately sidle past him. If the General was already here, maybe she should get some far intelligence. 'So what's happening, Jaybert?'

Of course, Jaybert took the question to be about his work. 'Damnedest thing. I put my new antenna on the Lands Command link just this morning. At first the alignment was fine, but then I started getting these fifteen-second patches where it looks like there are two stations on the line-of-sight. I wanted to ask your father—' Viki followed him a few steps down the stairs, making agreeable-sounds to the other's unintelligible talk about amplifier stages and transient alignment failures. No doubt Jaybert had been very pleased to get Daddy's quick attention, and no doubt Daddy had been delighted for an excuse to hole up in the signals lab. And then Mother showed up . . .

Viki left Jaybert down by his office-cubby, and climbed back up the stairs, this time circling around to the lab's utility entrance. There was a column of light at the end of the corridor. Ha! The door was partway open. She could hear the General's voice. Viki slipped down the hallway to the door.

'—just don't understand, Sherkaner. You are a brilliant person. How can you behave like such an idiot?'

Victory Junior hesitated, almost backed out of the darkened hall. She had never heard Mom sound quite so angry. It . . . hurt. On the other hand,

Gokna would give anything to hear Viki's report-of-action. Viki moved silently forward, turned her head sideways to peek through the narrow gap. The lab was pretty much as she remembered it, full of oscilloscopes and high-speed recorders. The covers were off some of Jaybert's gear, but apparently Mom had arrived before the two got into any serious electronic dismemberment. Mother was standing in front of Daddy, blocking his best eyes from seeing Viki. *And I bet I'm near the center of Mom's blind spot.*

'. . . Was I really that bad?' Daddy was saying.

'Yes!'

Sherkaner Underhill seemed to wilt under the General's glare. 'I don't know. The cobber got me off guard. The comment about little Brent. I knew that was coming. You and I had talked about that. Even Brent and I talked about it. And even so, it knocked my legs out. I got confused.'

Mom jerked her hand, dismissing the comment. 'That was no problem, Sherk. You gave a good response. Your hurt came across in a caring, paternal way. And yet a few minutes later she sucked you in—'

'Except for the astronomy, I only said things we had planned for the show over the next year.'

'But you said them all at once!'

'. . . I know. Pedure started talking like a bright curious person. Like Hrunk or people here at Hill House. She raised some interesting questions and I got carried away. And you know? Even now . . . this Pedure is smart and flexible. Given time, I think I could have won her over.'

The General's laugh was sharp and unhappy. 'God Below, you are a fool! Sherk, I . . .' Mom reached out to touch Daddy. 'I'm sorry. Funny, I don't chew out my own staffers the way I do you.'

Daddy made a kindly sound, like when he was talking to Rhapsa or Little Hrunk. 'You know the reason for that dear. You love me as much as yourself. And I know how much you chew on yourself.'

'Inside. Only silently, and inside.' They were quiet for a moment and Little Victory wished that she had lost her recon game with Gokna. But when Mother spoke again, her voice was more normal. 'We both screwed up on this.' She keyed open her travel case and picked out some papers. 'Over the next year, "The Children's Hour" was to introduce the virtue and the possibility of life in the Dark, on schedule with the first construction contracts. Someday, we knew there would be military consequences, but we didn't expect anything at this stage.'

'Military consequences now?'

'Deadly maneuvering, anyway. You know this Pedure cobber is from Tiefstadt.'

'Sure. Her accent is unmistakable.'

'Her cover is good, partly because it's mainly true. Honored Pedure is Cleric Three in the Church of the Dark. But she's also midlevel intelligence with Action of God.'

'The Kindred.'

'Indeed. We've had friendly relations with the Tiefers since the war, but the Kindred are beginning to change that. They already have several minor states in their effective control. They're a legitimate sect of the Church, but—'

Far down the corridor behind Little Victory, someone turned on a hall light. Mom raised a hand and stood very still. *Oops.* Maybe she had noticed a faint silhouette, familiar grooves and armored fluting. Without turning, Smith extended a long arm in the direction of the eavesdropper. 'Junior! Shut the door and get yourself back to your room.'

Little Victory's voice was small and abashed. 'Yes, Mother.'

As she slid the utility door closed, she heard one last comment: 'Damn. I spend fifty million a year on signal security, and my own daughter is running intercepts on me—'

Just now, the clinic under Hammerfest was a crowded place. On Pham's previous visits, there had been Trud, sometimes another technician, and one or two 'patients.' Today – well, a hand grenade would have caused more turmoil among the Focused, but not by much. Both the MRI units were occupied. One of the handlers was prepping Xopi Reung for MRI; the woman moaned, thrashing against his efforts. Over in a corner, Dietr Li – the physicist? – was strapped down, mumbling to himself.

Reynolt had one foot hooked over a ceiling stay, so that she hung down close to the MRI without getting in the way of the techs. She didn't look around as they came in. 'Okay, induction complete. Keep the arms restrained.' The tech slid his patient out into the middle of the room. It was Trixia Bonsol; she looked around, obviously not recognizing anyone, and then her face collapsed into hopeless sobbing.

'You've deFocused her!' Vinh shouted, pushing past Trud and Trinli. Pham anchored and grabbed, all in one motion, and Vinh's forward motion reversed, bouncing him lightly against the wall.

Reynolt looked in Vinh's direction. 'Be silent or get out,' she said. She jerked a hand at Bil Phuong. 'Insert Dr Reung. I want—' The rest was jargon. A normal bureaucrat would certainly have kicked them out. Anne Reynolt really didn't care, as long as they didn't get in her way.

Silipan drifted back to Pham and Vinh. He looked subdued and grim. 'Yeah. Shut up, Vinh.' He glanced at the MRI's display. 'Bonsol's still Focused. We've just detuned her linguistics ability. It'll make her easier to . . . treat.' He glanced at Bonsol uncertainly. The woman had bent in on herself as far as the restraints would permit. Her weeping continued, hopeless and inconsolable.

Vinh struggled briefly in Pham's grasp, and then he was still except for a tremor that only Pham could feel. For a second it looked like he might start bawling. Then the boy twisted, turned his face away from Bonsol, and screwed his eyes shut.

Tomas Nau's voice came loud in the room. 'Anne? I've lost three analysis threads since this outage began. Do you know—'

Reynolt's tone was almost the same she had used with Vinh: 'Give me a Ksec. I have at least five cases of runaway rot.'

'Lordy . . . keep me posted, Anne.'

Reynolt was already talking to someone else. 'Hom! What's the story on Dr Li?'

'He's rational, ma'am; I've been listening to him. Something happened during the radio show, and—'

Reynolt sailed across the room to Dieter Li, somehow missing techs, zipheads, and equipment. 'That's bizarre. There shouldn't have been live crosstalk between physics and the radio show.'

The tech tapped a card attached to Li's blouse. 'His log says he heard the translation.'

Pham noticed Silipan swallow hard. Could this be one of his screwups? Damn. If the man was disgraced, Pham would lose his pipeline into the Focus operation.

But Reynolt still hadn't noticed her AWOL technician. She leaned close to Dietr Li, listened for a moment to his mumbling. 'You're right. He's stuck on what the Spider said about OnOff. I doubt he's suffering from real runaway. Just keep watching him; let me know if he starts looping.'

More voices from the walls, and these sounded Focused: '. . . Attic lab twenty percent inchoate . . . probable cause: cross-specialty reactions to audio stream ID2738 "Children's Hour" . . . Instabilities are undamped . . .'

'I hear you, Attic. Prep for fast shutdown.' Reynolt returned to Trixia Bonsol. She stared at the weeping woman, her look an eerie combination of intense interest and total detachment. Abruptly she turned, her gaze skewering Trud Silipan. 'You! Get over here.'

Trud bounced across the room to his boss's side. 'Yes, ma'am! Yes, ma'am!' For once there was no hidden impudence. Vengeance might be unthinkable to Reynolt, but her judgments were ones that Nau and Braghel would enforce. 'I was checking out the effectiveness of the translations, ma'am, how well laypersons' – namely the patrons of Benny's booze parlor – 'would understand her.'

The excuses were lost on Reynolt. 'Get an offline team. I want Dr Bonsol's log checked out.' She leaned closer to Trixia, her gaze probing. The translator's weeping had stopped. Her body was curled in a quivering tetany. 'I'm not sure if we can save this one.'

Ezr Vinh twisted in Pham's grip, and for a moment it seemed he might start shouting again. Then he gave Pham a strange look and remained silent. Pham loosened his grip and gave him a gentle pat on the shoulder.

The two of them stayed silent, watching. 'Patients' came and went. Several more were detuned. Xopi Reung came out of the MRI much like Trixia Bonsol. Over the last few Watches, Pham had had plenty of opportunity to watch Silipan work, and pump him about procedures. He'd even got a look at a beginning textbook on Focus. This was the first time he'd had a solid look at how Reynolt and the other technicians worked.

But something really deadly had happened here. Mindrot runaway. In attacking the problem, Reynolt came as close to emotion as Pham had ever seen her. Some parts of the mystery were solved right away. Trud's query right at the beginning of the debate had triggered a search across many specialities. That was the reason so many zipheads had been listening to the debate. Their analysis had proceeded very normally for several hundred seconds, but then as the results were posted, there was a surge in communication between the translators. Normally, that was consultative, tuning the words that they spoke aloud. This time, it was deadly nonsense. First Trixia and then most of the other translators began to drift, their brain chemistry indicating an uncontrolled excursion of the rot. Real damage had been done even before Trixia attacked Xopi Reung, but that had marked the beginning of the massive runaway. Whatever was being communicated within the ziphead net provoked a cascade of similar flareups. Before the emergency was fully appreciated, about twenty percent of all the zipheads were affected, the virus in their brains producing out of bounds, flooding them with psychoactives and frankly toxic chemicals.

The nav zipheads were not affected. Brughel's snoops were moderately affected. Pham watched everything Reynolt did, trying to absorb every detail, every clue. *If I can make something like this happen to the L1 support network, if Brughel's people could be disabled . . .*

Anne Reynolt seemed to be everywhere. Every technician deferred to her. It was she who saved most of Ritser's zips; she who managed the reboot of limited Attic operations. And it came to Pham that without Anne Reynolt, there might not have been any recovery. Back in the Emergents' home solar system, ziphead crashes might be occasional inconveniences. There were universities to generate replacements, hundreds of clinics for Focusing newly created specialists. Here, twenty light-years from the Emergent civilization, it was a different story. Here, little failures could grow unbounded . . . and without some supernally competent manager, without Anne Reynolt, Tomas Nau's operation could collapse.

Xopi Reung flat-lined shortly after they brought her out of the MRI. Reynolt broke off from managing the Attic reboot, spent frantic moments with the translator. Here, she had no success. A hundred seconds later, the runaway infection had poisoned Reung's brain stem . . . and the rest didn't matter. Reynolt looked at the still body for a second more, frowning. Then she waved for the techs to float the body out.

*

Pham watched as Trixia Bonsol was moved out of the clinic. She was still alive; Reynolt herself was at the front of Bonsol's carrier.

Trud Silipan followed her toward the door. Suddenly he seemed to remember the two visitors. He turned and made a come-along gesture. 'Okay, Trinli. End of show.'

Silipan's face was grim and pale. The exact cause of the runaway was still unknown; it was some obscure interaction between the zipheads. Trud's use of the ziphead net – his query at the beginning of the debate – should have been an innocuous use of the resources. But Trud was at the pointy end of some very bad luck. Even if his query hadn't triggered the debacle, it was connected to it. In a Qeng Ho operation, Silipan's query would have just been another clue. Unfortunately, the Emergents had some very post hoc methods for defining sin.

'Are you going to be okay, Trud?'

Silipan gave a frightened little shrug and chivied them out of the clinic. 'Get on back to the temp – and don't let Vinh come after his ziphead.' Then he turned and followed Reynolt.

Pham and Vinh hiked up from the depths of Hammerfest, alone except for the certain presence of Brughel's snoops. The Vinh boy was quiet. In a way, today had been the biggest kick in the face he had suffered in years, maybe since Jimmy Diem's death. For an n-times-removed descendant, Ezr Vinh had a face that was entirely too familiar. He reminded Pham of Ratko Vinh when Ratko was young; he had a lot of Sura's face. That was not a pleasant thought. *Maybe my subconscious is trying to tell me something . . . Yes.* Not just in the clinic, but all this Watch. Every so often the kid would look at him . . . and the look was more of calculation than contempt. Pham thought back, trying to remember just how his Trinh character had behaved. Certainly it was a risk to be so interested in Focus. But he had Trud's scams as a cover for that. No, even while they were standing in the clinic and Pham's mind had been totally concentrated on Reynolt and the Bonsol mystery – even then he was sure he hadn't looked anything but mildly dazed, an old charlatan worried that this debacle would mess up the deals he and Trud had planned. Yet somehow this Vinh had seen through him. How? And what to do about it?

They came out of the main vertical corridor, and started down the ramp to the taxi locks. The Focused murals were everywhere, ceilings, walls, floors. In places, the diamond walls had been planed thin. Blue light – the light of full Arachna – came softly through the crystal, darker or lighter depending on the depth of the carving. Because Arachna was always in full phase from L1 and the rockpile was kept in a fixed phase relative to the sun, the light had been steady for years. There might have been a time when Pham Nuwen would have fallen in love with that art, but now he knew how it had been made. Watch after Watch, he and Trud Silipan would come down this ramp and see workers, carving. Nau and Brughel had pissed away the lifetimes of non-academic zipheads to make this art. Pham guessed that at least two had died of old age. The survivors were gone now, too, perhaps finishing the carvings on lesser corridors. *After I take over, things will be different.* Focus was such a terrible thing. It must never be used except for the most critical needs.

They passed a side corridor paneled in tank-grown wood. The grain swirled smoothly, following the curve of the corridor that led downward to Tomas Nau's private quarters.

And there was Qiwi Lin Lisolet. Maybe she had heard them coming. More likely she had seen their departure from the clinic. Either way, she had been waiting long enough that she stood with feet on the floor, as if in normal planetary gravity.

'Ezr, please. Can we talk, just for a moment? I never meant these shows to hurt—'

Vinh had been drifting ahead of Pham, silently pulling himself along. His head snapped up when he saw Qiwi. For an instant it seemed he might float on by her. Then she spoke. Vinh pushed hard against the wall, diving fast and directly toward her. The action was as bluntly hostile as swinging a fist at another's face.

'Here now!' Pham blustered, and forced himself to hang back in seeming impotence. He'd already waylaid the fellow once today, and this time the scene would be quite clear to the snoops. Besides, Pham had watched Qiwi work outside. She was in better condition than anyone at L1, and a natural acrobat. Maybe it would do Vinh some good to learn he couldn't off-load his anger on her.

But Qiwi didn't defend, didn't even flinch. Vinh twisted, delivering a powerful, openhanded slap that sent them spinning apart. 'Yes, we'll talk!' Vinh's voice was ragged. He bounced after her and he slapped her again. And again Qiwi didn't defend, didn't even raise her hands to shield her face.

And Pham Nuwen pushed forward before he'd really thought. Something in the back of his mind was laughing at him for risking years of masquerade just to protect one innocent. But that same something also cheered.

Pham's dive turned into an apparently uncontrolled spin, one that just accidentally slammed his shoulder into Vinh's gut and smashed the younger man into the wall. Out of sight of any camera, Pham gave his opponent a piece of elbow. An instant after the impact, the back of Vinh's head smacked against the wall. If they had still been down in the carved diamond corridors, that might have caused serious injury. As it was, when Vinh came off the wall, his arms were flailing weakly. Little droplets of blood sprouted up from the back of his head.

'Pick on someone your own size, Vinh! Cowardly, scummy piece of vermin. You Great Family Traders are all alike.' Pham's rage was real – but it was also rage against himself, for risking his cover.

The wits slowly percolated back into Vinn's eyes. He glanced at Qiwi, four meters down the hallway. The girl looked back, her expression a strange combination of shock and determination. And then Vinh looked at Pham, and the old man felt a chill. Maybe Brughel's cameras hadn't caught all the details of the fight, but the kid knew how calculated Pham's assault had been. For an instant the two stared at each other, and then Vinh shrugged free of his grasp and scooted back down the ramp toward the taxi locks. It was the scuttling retreat of a shamed and beaten man. But Pham had seen the look in his eyes; something would have to be done about Ezr Vinh.

Qiwi started after Vinh, but dragged herself to a stop before she had gone ten meters. She floated in the T of the corridors, staring off in the direction Vinh had gone.

Pham came near. He knew he had to get out of here. No doubt several cameras were watching him now, and he was just no good at staying in character around Qiwi. So what to say that would get him safely gone? 'Don't worry, kid. Vinh is just not worth it. He won't bother you again; I guarantee it.'

After a moment, the girl turned to face him. Lord, she looked so much like her mother; Nau had been running her nearly Watch-on-Watch. There were tears in her eyes. He couldn't see any cuts or blood, but bruises were beginning to show on her dark skin. 'I really didn't meant to hurt him. God, I don't know what I'll do if Trixia d-dies.' Qiwi brushed back her close-cut black hair. Grown-up or not, she looked as lost as during the first days after the Diem 'atrocity.' She was so alone she would confide in a windbag like Pham Trinli. 'When . . . when I was little, I admired Ezr Vinh more than anyone in the universe, except my parents.' She glanced at Pham; her smile was tremulous and hurt. 'I wanted so much for him to think well of me. And then the Emergents attacked us, and then Jimmy Diem killed my mother and all the others . . . We are all in a very small lifeboat. We can't have any more killing.' She gave her head a sharp little shake. 'Did you know that Tomas has not used coldsleep since the Diem massacre? He's lived every second of all these years. Tomas is so serious, so hardworking. He believes in Focus, but he's open to new ways of doing things.' She was telling him what she had wanted to tell Ezr. 'Benny's parlor wouldn't exist without Tomas. None of the trading and bonsai would exist. Little by little we are making the Emergents understand our ways. Someday, Tomas will be able to release my father and Trixia and all the Focused. Someday—'

Pham wanted to reach out and comfort her. Pham Nuwen might be the only living person besides the murderers who knew what had really happened to Jimmy Diem, and who knew what Nau and Brughel were doing with Qiwi Lin Lisolet. He should give her a gruff brush-off and leave, but somehow he couldn't do that. Instead he hung in place, looking embarrassed and confused. *Yes. Someday. Someday, child, you will be avenged.*

26

Ritser Brughel's quarters and command post were aboard the *Invisible Hand*. He often wondered how the Peddlers had come up with such a perfect name, in two words expressing the essence of Security. In any case, the *Hand* was the most nearly undamaged of all the hulls, Qeng Ho or Emergent. The flight-crew quarters were sound. The main drive could probably sustain a one-gee thrust for several days. Since the takeover, the *Hand*'s comm and ECM had been refurbished to Focused standards. Here on the *Invisible Hand*, he was something of a god.

Unfortunately, physical isolation was no protection against a mindrot runaway. Runaway was triggered by emotional imbalance in the Focused mind. That meant it could propagate across communications networks, though normally that only happened between closely cooperating zipheads. Back in civilization, runaway was a constant, low-level concern, just another reason for having hot swaps available. Here in the godforsaken nowhere, it was a deadly threat. Ritser had been aware of the runaway almost as quickly as Reynolt – but he couldn't afford to shut down his zips. As usual, Reynolt gave him second-class service, but he managed. They split the snoops into small groups, and ran each separately from the others. The resulting intelligence was fragmented; their logs would require lots of later analysis. But they had missed nothing big . . . and eventually they would catch up with all the details.

In the first 20Ksec, Ritser lost three snoops to the runaway. He had Omo flush them and keep the others running. He went down to Hammerfest, had a long meeting with Tomas Nau. It looked like Reynolt was going to lose at least six people, including a big hunk of her translation department. The Senior Podmaster was properly impressed with Brughel's lower casualties. 'Keep your people online, Ritser. Anne thinks the translators chose sides in that damn Spider debate, that the runaway rot was an escalation of a normal ziphead disagreement. Maybe so, but the debate was well removed from center of the translators' Focus. Once things stabilize, I want you to go over every second of your records, comb it for suspicious events.'

After another 60Ksec, Brughel and Nau agreed that the crisis was past, at least for the Security zips. Podsergeant Omo put the snoops back into consultation with Reynolt's people, but via a buffered link. He began a detailed scan of the immediate past. The debacle had indeed blown away Ritser's operation, albeit very briefly. For about one thousand seconds, they had totally lost emission security. Closer investigation showed that nothing had been beamed toward any outside system; their long-term secrecy was intact. Locally, the translators had screamed something past the controllers, but the Spiders had not noticed; not surprising, since the chaotic transmissions would have seemed like transient noise.

In the end, Ritser was forced to conclude that the runaway was simply very bad luck. But amid the trivia there were some very interesting tidbits:

Normally Ritser stayed up on the *Hand*'s bridge, where he could maintain a command perspective on the L1 rubble pile and Arachna far beyond. But with Ciret and Marli helping out on Hammerfest, there were just Tan and Kal Omo to run nearly one hundred Security snoops. So today he was mucking around in the guts of the operation with Omo and Tan.

'Vinh has tripped three flags this Watch, Podmaster. Two times during the runaway, as matter of fact.'

As he floated in over Omo, Ritser glanced down at the zip-heads on Watch. About a third were asleep in their saddles. The rest were immersed in data streams, reviewing the logs, correlating their results with Reynolt's Focused on Hammerfest. 'Okay, so what do you have on him?'

'This is camera analysis of Reynolt's lab and a corridor near Podmaster Nau's residence.' The scenes flickered by quickly, highlighted where the snoops had seen exceptionable body language.

'Nothing overt?'

Omo's hatchetlike face spread in a humorless smile. 'Plenty that would be actionable back home, but not under the current RoE.'

'I'll bet.' Podmaster Nau's Rules of Enforcement would have been reason for his instant removal anywhere in the Emergency. For more than twenty years, the Senior Podmaster had let the Peddler swine get away with their excesses, perverting law-abiding Followers in the process. It had driven Ritser to distraction at first. Now . . . Now he could understand. Tomas was right about so many things. They had no margin for further destruction. And letting people talk yielded a lot of information, secrets they could use when the noose was retightened. 'So what's different about this time?'

'Analysts Seven and Eight both correlate on the last two events.' Seven and Eight were the zipheads at the end of the first row. As children they might have had names, but that was long ago and before they entered the Police Academy. Frivolous names and 'Doctor' titles might be used in civilian work, but not in a serious police shop. 'Vinh is intent on something that goes beyond his normal anxiety. Look at this head tracking.'

It didn't mean anything to Ritser, but then his job was to lead, not to understand forensic details. Omo continued, 'He's watching Trinli with great suspicion. It happens again in the corridor by the taxi locks.'

Brughel riffled through the video index of Vinh's visit to Hammerfest. 'Okay. He fought Trinli. He harassed Trud Silipan. Lordy—' Brughel

couldn't help laughing. '—he *assaulted* Tomas Nau's private w
you say the security flags are for eye contact and body language?'

Omo shrugged. 'The overt behavior fits with the guy's known p⸜
sir. And it doesn't come under the RoE.'

So Qiwi Lisolet got slapped around, right on Tomas's doorstep. Ritser found himself grinning at the irony. All these years, Tomas had fooled the little slut. The periodic mindscrubs had come to be a bright spot in Ritser's life, especially since he saw her reaction to a certain video. Still, he couldn't deny his envy. He, Ritser Brughel, couldn't have maintained a masquerade, even with mindscrubs. Ritser's own women just didn't last. A couple of times a year, he had go back to Tomas and wheedle more playthings out of him. Ritser had used up the most attractive expendables. Sometimes he had a bit of luck, as with Floria Peres. She would have noticed Qiwi's mindscrub for sure; chemical engineer or no, she had to be taken down. But there were limits to such good fortune . . . and the Exile stretched out years more ahead of him. The thought was dark and familiar, and he resolutely pushed it away.

'Okay. So your point is, Seven and Eight figure that Vinh is hiding something that wasn't in his consciousness before – at least not at this level of intensity.'

Back in civilization, there'd have been no problem. They'd just bring the perp in and cut the answers out of him. Here . . . well, they'd had their chance to do some cutting; they had learned disappointingly little. Too many of the Qeng Ho had effective blocks, and too many couldn't be properly infected with mindrot.

He cycled through the highlighted incidents. 'Hmm. Do you suppose he's figured out that Trinli is really Zamle Eng?' The Peddlers were crazy; they tolerated almost any corruption, but had blood hatred for one of their own simply because he traded in flesh. Ritser's lip turned in disgust. *Pus. How far we've fallen. Blackmail was a fitting weapon between Podmasters, but simple terror should suffice for people like Pham Trinli.* He scanned once more through Omo's evidence. It was really frail. 'Sometimes I wonder, maybe we have the trigger threshold set too low on our snoops.'

That was something that Omo had suggested before. The podsergeant was too clever to gloat, however. 'It's possible, sir. On the other hand, if there weren't questions left for managers to decide, there would be no need for real people.' The vision of one Podmaster ruling a universe of Focused was fantasy fiction. 'You know what I wish, Podmaster Brughel?'

'What?'

'I wish we could bring those run-alone Qeng Ho localizers aboard Hammerfest. There's something perverse about having *worse* security in our own space than we do in the Qeng Ho temp. If these incidents had happened aboard the temp, we would have had Vinh's blood pressure, his heart rate – hell, if the localizers are on the subject's scalp, we'd have EEG.

between the Peddlers' signal processors and our zipheads, we could practically read the subject's bloody mind.'

'Yeah I know.' The Qeng Ho localizers were an almost magical improvement over previous standards of law enforcement. There were hundreds of thousands of the millimeter-size devices all through the Peddler temp – probably hundreds in the open areas of Hammerfest since Nau had relaxed the frat rules. All they had to do was re-program Hammerfest's utility system for pulsed microwave, and the localizers' reach would be instantly extended. They could say goodbye to camera patches and similar clumsy gear. 'I'll bring this up again with Podmaster Nau.' Anne's programmers had been studying the Peddler localizers for more than two years', futilely searching for hidden gotchas.

In the meantime . . . 'Well, Ezr Vinh is back aboard the temp now, with all the localizer coverage you could dream of.' He grinned at Omo. 'Divert a couple more zipheads onto him. Let's see how much an intense analysis can show.'

Ezr got through the emergency without cracking up again. Regular reports emerged from Hammerfest. The mindrot runaway had been stopped. Xopi Reung and eight other Focused persons had died. Three more were 'seriously damaged.' *But Trixia was marked as 'returned to service, undamaged.'*

The speculations swept back and forth across Benny's parlor. Rita was sure the runaway was a near-random crash. 'We used to get them every couple of years in my shop on Balacrea; only one time did we nail the cause. It's the price you pay for close-coupling.' But she and Jau Xin were afraid the runaway would eliminate even delayed audio translations of 'The Children's Hour.' Gonle Fong said that didn't matter, that Sherkaner Underhill had lost his strange debate with Pedure and so there wouldn't be any more broadcasts to translate. Trud Silipan was gone from the discussion; he was still over on Hammerfest maybe working for a change. Pham Trinli made up for that spouting Silipan's theory that Trixia had been acting out a real fight – and that had precipitated the runaway. Ezr listened to it all, numb and silent.

His next duty was in 40Ksec; Ezr went back to his quarters early. It would be a while before he could face Benny's again. So many things had happened, and they were all shameful or hurting or lethally mysterious. He floated in the semidarkness of his room, skewered on Hell's rotisserie. He'd think impotently on one problem for a time . . . and then escape to something that soon was equally terrible, and then escape again . . . finally returning to the first horror.

Qiwi. That was his shame. He had struck her twice. Hard. *If Pham Trinli had not interfered, would I have gone on beating her?* There was a horror opening up before him that he had never imagined. Sure, he had always been afraid that someday he would blunder, or even be a coward, but . . . today he had seen something in himself, something basically indecent. Qiwi had helped to put Trixia on exhibit. Sure. But she wasn't the only one involved. And yes, Qiwi did benefit under Tomas Nau . . . but Lord, she'd been only a child when all this began. *So why did I go after her?* Because she had once seemed to care? Because she wouldn't fight back? That was what the implacable voice in the back of his mind insisted. At bottom, maybe Ezr Vinh was not just incompetent or weak, maybe he was simply filth. Ezr's mind danced round and round that conclusion, closing ever tighter, until he escaped out sideways to—

Pham Trinli. That was the mystery. Trinli had acted twice yesterday, both times saving Ezr from being an even greater fool and villain. There was a crust of blood across the back of his head, where Trinli's 'clumsy' body block had smashed him into the wall. Ezr had seen Trinli in the temp's gym. The old man made a thing of exercise, but his body wasn't in especially good shape. His reaction time was nothing spectacular. But somehow he knew how to move, how to make accidents happen. And thinking back, Ezr remembered times before when Pham Trinli had been in the right place . . . The temp park right after the massacre. *What had the old man actually said?* It hadn't revealed anything to the cameras, it hadn't even tweaked Ezr's own attention – but *something* he said had wakened the certainty that Jimmy Diem had been murdered, that Jimmy was innocent of all Nau claimed. Everything Pham did was loud and self-serving and incompetent, yet . . . Ezr thought back and forth over all the details, the things he might be seeing that others would miss. Maybe he was seeing mirages in his desperation. When problems go beyond hope of solution, insanity comes creeping. And yesterday, something had broken inside him . . .

Trixia. That was the pain and the rage and the fear. Yesterday Trixia had come very close to death, her body as tortured and twisted as Xopi Reung's. Maybe even worse . . . He remembered the look on her face when she came out of the MRI programmer. Trud said her linguistics ability had been temporarily detuned. Maybe that was the cause for her desperation, losing the one thing that still had meaning for her. And maybe he lied, as he suspected Reynolt and Nau and Brughel lied about many things. Maybe Trixia *had* been briefly deFocused and looked about her, and seen how she had aged, and realized that they had taken her life. *And I may never know. I will continue to watch her year after year, impotent and raging and . . . silent.* There had to be someone to strike against, to punish . . .

And so the rotisserie cycled back to Qiwi.

Two Ksec passed, four. Enough time to return again and again to problems that were beyond solution. This sort of thing had happened a few terrible times before. Sometimes he'd spend the whole night on the rotisserie. Sometimes he got so tired, he'd just fall asleep – and that would stop it. Tonight, the nth time thinking on Pham Trinli, Ezr got angry at the process. So what if he was crazy? If all he had were mirages of salvation, well then, *grab them*! Vinh got up and put on his huds. Awkward seconds were spent getting through the library access routines. He still wasn't used to the crummy Emergent I/O interface, and they had yet to enable decent customization. But then the windows around him lit up with text from the latest report he was doing for Nau.

So, what did he know about Pham Trinli? In particular, what did he know that had escaped the notice of Nau and Brughel? The fellow had an uncanny ability in hand-to-hand fighting – mugging, more accurately. And he cloaked the ability from the Emergents; he was playing a game with them . . . And after today, he must know that *Vinh* knew this.

Maybe Trinli was simply an aging criminal doing his best to blend in and survive. But then what about the localizers? Trinli had revealed their secret to Tomas Nau, and that secret had increased Nau's power a hundredfold. The tiny flecks of automation were everywhere. There on his knuckle – that might be a glint of sweat, but it also might be a localizer. The little glints and flecks could be reporting the position of his arms, some of his fingers, the angle of his head. Nau's snoops could know it all.

Those capabilities were simply not documented in the fleet library, even with top-level passwords. So Pham Trinli knew secrets that went deep in the Qeng Ho past. And very likely what he had revealed to Tomas Nau was just a cover for . . . *what*?

Ezr pounded on that question for a few moments, got nowhere. Think about the man. Pham Trinli. He was an old thug. He knew important secrets *above* the level of Qeng Ho fleet secrets. Most likely, he had been in at the founding of the modern Qeng Ho, when Pham Nuwen and Sura Vinh and the Council of the Gap had done their work. So Trinli was enormously old in objective years. That was not impossible, nor even excessively rare. Long trading missions could take a Trader across a thousand years of objective time. His parents had had one or two friends who had actually walked on Old Earth. Yet it was highly unlikely any of them had access to the founding layers of Qeng Ho automation.

No, if Trinli was what Ezr's insane reasoning implied, then he would likely be a figure visible in the histories. Who?

Vinh's fingers tapped at the keyboard. His ongoing assignment was a good cover for the questions he wanted to ask. Nau had an insatiable interest in everything Qeng Ho. Vinh was to write him summaries, and propose research tracks for the zipheads. However mellow and diplomatic he might seem, Ezr had long ago realized that Nau was even crazier than Brughel. Nau studied in order to someday rule.

Be careful. The places he really wanted to look must be fully covered by the needs of his report writing. On top of it all, he must keep up a random pattern of truly irrelevant references. Let the snoops try to find his intent in those!

He needed a list: Qeng Ho males, alive at the beginning of the modern Qeng Ho, who were not known to be dead at the time Captain Park's expedition left Triland. The list shrank substantially when he also eliminated those known to be far from this corner of Human Space. It shrank again when he required that they be present at Brisgo Gap. The conjunction of five booleans, the work of a spoken command or a column of keystrokes – but Ezr could not afford such simplicity. Each boolean was part of other searches, in support of things he really needed for the report. The results were scattered across pages of analysis, a name here, a name there. The orrery floating by the ceiling showed less than 15Ksec remaining before the walls of his quarters would begin to glow dawnlight . . . but he had his list. Did it mean anything? A handful of names, some pale and improbable. The booleans themselves were very hazy. The Qeng Ho interstellar net was an enormous thing, in a sense the largest structure in the histories of Humankind. But it was all out of date, by years or centuries. And even the Qeng Ho sometimes lied among themselves, especially where the distances were short and confusion could give commercial advantage. A handful of names. How many and who? Even scanning the fist was painstakingly slow, else the hidden watchers would surely notice. Some names he recognized: Tran Vinh.21, that was Sura Vinh's g'grandson and the male-side founder of Ezr's own branch of the Vinh Family; King Xen.03, Sura's chief armsman at Brisgo Gap. Xen could not have been Trinli. He was just over 120 centimeters tall, and nearly as wide. Other names belonged to people who had never been famous. Jung, Trap, Park . . . *Park?*

Vinh couldn't help the surprise. If Brughel's zipheads reviewed the records, they would surely notice. The damn localizers could probably pick up on pulse, maybe even blood pressure. *If they can see the surprise, make it a big thing.* 'Lord of All Trade,' Vinh whispered, bringing the picture and bio material up on all his windows. It really did look like their own S. J. Park, Fleet Captain of the mission to the OnOff star. He remembered the man from his own childhood; that Park hadn't seemed so very old . . . In fact, some of this biodata seemed vague. And the DNA record did not match the latter-day Park. Hmm. That might be enough to deflect Nau and Reynolt; they didn't have Ezr's firsthand experience with backstairs Family affairs. But the S. J. Park at Brisgo Gap – two thousand years ago – had been a ship's captain. He'd ended up with Ratko Vinh. There had been some weird scandal involving a failed marriage contract. After that there was nothing.

Vinh followed a couple of obvious leads on Park – then gave up, the way you might when you learned something surprising but not universe-breaking. The other names on the list . . . it took him another Ksec to get through them, and none looked familiar. His mind kept returning to S.J. Park, and he almost panicked. *How well can the enemy read me?* He looked at some pictures of Trixia, surrendered to the familiar pain; he did that often enough just before finally going to bed. Behind his tears, his mind raced. If Ezr was right about Park, he went way, *way* back. No wonder his parents had treated Park as more than a young contract captain. Lord, he could have been on Pham Nuwen's voyage to the far side. After Brisgo Gap, when Nuwen was about as rich as he'd ever been, he'd departed with a grand fleet, heading for the far side of Human Space. That was typical of Nuwen's gestures. The far side was at least four hundred light-years away. The merchanting details of its environment were ancient history by the time they arrived on this side. And his proposed path would take him through some of the oldest regions of Human Space. For centuries after the departure, the Qeng Ho Net continued to report the progress of the Prince of Canberra, of his fleets growing and sometimes shrinking. Then the stories faltered, often lacked valid authentication. Nuwen probably never got more than partway to his goal. As a child, Ezr and his friends had often played at being the Lost Prince. There were so many ways it might have ended, some adventurous and gruesome, some – the most likely – involving old age and a string of business failures, ships lost to bankruptcy across dozens of light-years. And so the fleet had never returned.

But parts of it might have. A person here or there, perhaps losing heart with a voyage that would take them forever far from their own time. Who knew just which individuals returned? *Very likely, S. J. Park had known.* Very likely S. J. Park had known precisely who Pham Trinli was – and had worked to protect that identity. Who from the era of Brisgo Gap could be so important, so well known . . . ? S. J. Park had been loyal to someone from that era. Who?

And then Ezr remembered hearing that Captain Park had personally chosen the name of his flagship. The *Pham Nuwen*.

Pham Trinli. Pham Nuwen. The Lost Prince of Canberra.

And I have finally gone totally crazy. There were library checks that would shoot down this conclusion in a second. Yes, and that would disprove nothing; if he were right, the library itself would be a subtle lie. *Yeah, sure.* This was the sort of desperate hallucination he must guard against. If you raise your desires high enough, certainty can grow out of the background noise. *But at least it got me off the rotisserie!*

It was awfully late. He stared at the pictures of Trixia for a while longer, lost in sad memories. Inside, he calmed down. There would be other false alarms, but he had years ahead of him, a lifetime of patient looking. He would find a crack in the dungeon somewhere, and when it happened he wouldn't have to wonder if it was a trick of his imagination.

Sleep came, and dreams filled with all the usual distress and the new shame, and now mixed with his latest insanity. Eventually there was something like peace, floating in the dark of his cabin. Mindless.

And then another dream, so real that he didn't doubt it until it was over. Little lights were shining in his eyes, but only when he kept his eyes closed. Awake and sitting, the room was dark as ever. Lying down, eyes asleep, then the sparkles started again.

The lights were talking to him, a game of blinkertalk. When he was very young he had played a lot of that, flitting from rock to rock across the out-of-doors. Tonight, a single pattern repeated and repeated, and in Vinh's dream state the meaning formed almost effortlessly:

'NOD UR HEAD IF U UNDRSTND ME . . . NOD—'

Vinh made a wordless groan of surprise – and the pattern changed:

'SHUT UP SHUT UP SHUT UP . . .' for a long time. And then it changed again. 'NOD UR HEAD IF U UNDRSTND ME . . .'

That was easy too. Vinh moved his head a fraction of a centimeter.

'OK. PRETEND TO BE ASLEEP. CLOSE UR HAND. BLINK ON PALM.'

After all the years, conspiracy was suddenly so easy. Just pretend your palm was a keyboard and type at your fellow-conspirators. Of course! His hands were under the covers, so no one else could see! He would have laughed out loud at the cleverness, except that would be out of character. It was so obvious now who had come to save them. He closed his right hand and tapped: 'HI O WISE PRINCE. WHT TOOK U SO DAM LONG?'

For a long time there were no more little flashes. Ezr's mind drifted slowly toward deeper sleep.

Then: 'U NU BFR TNITE? DAM ME.' Another long pause. 'I VRY SORRY. I THOT U BROKN.'

Vinh nodded to himself, a little proud. And maybe someday Qiwi would forgive him, and Trixia would return to life, and . . .

'OK,' Ezr tapped at the Prince. 'HOW MNY PEOPLE WE GOT?'

'SECRET. ONLY I KNO. EACH CAN TALK BUT NO ONE KNOS ANYONE ELSE.' Pause. 'TILL U TONITE.'

Aha. Almost the perfect conspiracy. The members could cooperate, but no one but the Prince could betray anyone else. Things would be so much easier now.

'WELL IM VRY TIRED NOW. WANNA SLEEP. WE CAN TALK MORE LATR.'

Pause. Was his request so strange? Nights are for sleeping. 'OK. LATR.'

As consciousness drifted finally away, Vinh shrugged deeper into his hammock and smiled to himself. He was not alone. And all along, the secret had been as close as his hand. Amazing!

The next morning, Vinh woke up rested and strangely happy. Huh. What had he done to deserve this?

He floated into the shower bag and sudsed up. Yesterday had been so dark, so shameful. Bitter reality seeped back into him, but strangely slow . . . Yeah, there had been a dream. *That* was not unusual, but most of his dreams hurt so much to remember. Vinh turned the shower to dry and hung for a moment in the swirling jets of air. What had it been about this one?

Yes! It was another of those miracle escape dreams, but this time things hadn't turned bad at the end. Nau and Brughel had not leaped out of hiding at the last moment.

So what had been the secret weapon this time? Oh, the usual illogic of dreams, some kind of magic that turned his own hands into a comm link with the chief conspirator. Pham Trinli? Ezr chuckled at the thought. Some dreams are more absurd than others; strange how he still felt comforted by this one.

He shrugged into his clothes and set off down the temp's corridors, his progress the typical zero-gee push, pull, bounce at the turns, swing to avoid those moving more slowly or going in the other direction. *Pham Nuwen. Pham Trinli.* There must be a billion people with that given name, and a hundred flagships named *Pham Nuwen*. Recollection of his library search of the night before gradually percolated back to mind, the crazy ideas he'd been thinking just before he went to bed.

But the truth about Captain Park had been no dream. By the time he arrived at the dayroom, he was moving more slowly.

Ezr drifted headfirst into the dayroom, said hello to Hunte Wen by the door. The atmosphere was relatively relaxed. He quickly discovered that Reynolt had brought her surviving Focused back online; there had been no more flareups. On the far ceiling, Pham Trinli was pontificating about what had caused the runaway and why the danger was past. This was the Pham Trinli he had dealt with several Ksecs of each wake period on every overlapping Watch since the ambush. Suddenly the dream and the library session before it were reduced to the proper and completely absurd perspective.

Trinli must have heard him talking to Hunte. The old fraud turned, and for a moment looked back down the room at Vinh. He didn't say anything, didn't nod, and even if an Emergent spy were looking right down Vinh's line of sight, it would have not likely mattered. But to Ezr Vinh, the moment seemed to last forever. In that moment, the buffoon that had been Pham Trinli was gone. There was no bluster in that face, but there was lonely, quiet authority and an acknowledgment of their strange conversation of the night before. Somehow it had not been a dream. The communication had not been magical. And this old man truly was the Lost Prince of Canberra.

'But it's firstsnow. Don't you want to see it?' Victory's voice took on a whine, a tone that worked with virtually no one except this one older brother.

'You've played in snow before.'

Sure, when Daddy took them on trips to the far north. 'But Brent! This is firstsnow at Princeton. The radio says it's all over the Craggies.'

Brent was absorbed in his dowel and hub frameworks, endless shiny surfaces that got more and more complicated. By himself, he never would have considered sneaking out of the house. He continued working at his designs for several seconds, ignoring her. In fact, that was how Brent treated the unexpected. He was quite good with his hands, but ideas came slowly to him. Beyond that he was very shy – surly, grown-ups often said. His head didn't move, but Viki could tell he was looking at her. His hands never slowed as they weaved back and forth across the surface of the model, sometimes building, sometimes wrecking. Finally, he said, 'We aren't supposed to go out 'less we tell Dad.'

'Pfui. You know he sleeps in. This morning is the coldest yet, but we'll miss it if we don't go now. Hey, I'll leave a note for him.'

Her sister Gokna would have argued the point back and forth, finally exceeding Viki herself in clever rationalizations. Her brother Jirlib would have gotten angry at her manipulation. But Brent didn't argue, returning instead to his finicky modeling for a few minutes, part of him watching her, part of him studying the dowel and connector pattern that emerged from beneath his hands, and part of him looking out across Princeton at the tinge of frost on the near ridges. Of all her brothers and sisters, he was the one who wouldn't really want to go. On the other hand, he was the only one she could find this morning, and he was even more grown-up-looking than Jirlib.

After a few moments more, he said, 'Well, okay, if that's what you want.' Victory grinned to herself; as if the outcome were ever in doubt. Getting past Captain Downing would be harder – but not by much.

It was early morning. The sunlight hadn't reached the streets below Hill House. Victory savored each breath, the faint stinging she felt at the sides of her chest as she tasted the frosty air. The hot blossoms and woodsfairies were still wound tight in the tree branches; they might not even come out today. But there were other things about, things she had only read about before now. In the frost of the coldest hollows, crystal worms edged slowly out. These brave little pioneers wouldn't last long – Viki remembered the radio show she had done about them last year. These little ones would keep dying except where the cold was good enough to last all day long. And even then, things would have to get much colder before the rooted variety showed up.

Viki skipped briskly through the morning chill, easily keeping up with the slower, longer strides of her big brother. This early there was hardly anyone about. Except for the sound of distant contruction work, she could almost imagine that they were all alone, that the city was deserted. Imagine what it would be like in coming years, when the cold stayed, and they could only go out as Daddy had done in the war with the Tiefers. All the way to the bottom of the hill, Viki built on the idea, turning every aspect of the chilly morning into the fantastical. Brent listened, occasionally offering a suggestion that would have surprised most of Daddy's grown-up friends. Brent was not so dumb, and he did have an imagination.

The Craggies were thirty miles away, beyond the King's high castle, beyond the far side of Princeton. No way could they walk there. But today lots of people wanted to travel to the near mountains. Firstsnow meant a fair-sized festival in every land, though of course it happened at various and unpredictable times. Viki knew that if the early snow had been predicted, Dad would have been up early, and Mom might have flown in from Lands Command. The outing would have been a major family affair – but not the least bit adventurous.

A sort of adventure began at the bottom of the hill. Brent was sixteen years old now and he was big for his age. He could pass for in-phase. He had been out on his own often enough before. He said he knew where the express buses made their stops. Today, there were no buses, and scarcely any traffic. Had everyone already gone to the mountains?

Brent marched from one bus stop to another, gradually becoming more agitated. Viki tagged along silently, for once not making any suggestions; Brent got put down often enough that he rarely asserted any sort of knowledge. It hurt when he finally spoke up – even to a little sister – and then turned out to be wrong. After the third false start, Brent hunkered down close to the ground. For a moment, Viki thought maybe he was just going to wait for a bus to come along – a thoroughly unpleasant possibility to Viki. They'd been out for more than an hour and they hadn't even seen a local jitney. Maybe she would have to stick her pointy little hands into the problem . . . But after a minute, Brent stood up and started across the street. 'I bet the Big Dig people didn't get the day off. That's only a mile south of here. There are always buses from there.'

Ha. That was just what Viki had been about to suggest. Blessed be patience.

The street was still in morning shadow. This was the deepest part of the winter season at Princeton. Here and there the frost in the darker nooks was so deep that it might have been snow itself. But the section they were walking through now was not gardened. The only plants were unruly weeds and free crawlers. On sweaty, hot days between storms, the place would have been alive with midges and drinkers.

On either side of the street were multistory warehouses. Things weren't so quiet and deserted here. The ground buzzed and thrummed with the sound of unseen diggers. Freight trucks moved in and out of the area. Every few hundred yards, a plot of land was barricaded off from all but the construction crews. Viki tugged at Brent's arms, urging him to crawl under the barricades. 'Hey, it's our dad who's the reason for all this. We deserve to see!' Brent would never accept such a rationalization, but his little sister was already past the no-trespassing signs. He had to come along just to protect her.

They crept past tall bundles of reinforcement steel, and piles of masonry. There was something powerful and alien about this place. In the house on the hill, everything was so safe, so orderly. Here . . . well, she could see endless opportunities for the careless to lacerate a foot, cut an eye. Heck, if you tipped over one of those standing slabs, it would squash you flat. All the possibilities were crystal clear in her mind . . . and exciting. They carefully made their way to the lip of a caisson, avoiding the eyes of the workman and the various interesting opportunities for fatal accidents.

The railing was two strands of twine. *If you don't want to die, don't fall off!* Viki and her brother hunkered close to the ground and stuck their heads over the abyss. For a moment, it was too dark to see. The heated air that drifted up carried the smell of burning oil and hot metal. It was a caress and a slap in the head all at once. And the sounds: workers shouting, metal grinding against metal, engines, and a strange hissing. Viki dipped her head, letting all her eyes adjust to the gloom. There was light, but nothing like day or night. She had seen small electric-arc lamps in Daddy's labs. These ones were huge: pencils of light glowing mostly in the ultra and far ultra – colors you never see bright except in the disk of the sun. The color splashed off the hooded workers, spread speckling glints up and down the shaft . . . There were other less spectacular lights, steadier ones, electric lamps that shone local splotches of tamed color here and there. Still twelve years before the Dark, and they were building a whole city down there. She could see avenues of stone, huge tunnels leading off from the walls of the shaft. And in the tunnels she glimpsed darker holes . . . ramps to smaller diggings? Buildings and homes and gardens would come later, but already the caves were mostly dug. Looking down, Viki felt an attraction that was new to her, the natural, protective attraction of a deepness. But what these workers were doing was a thousand times grander than any ordinary deepness. If all you wanted to do was sleep frozen through the Dark, you needed just enough space for your sleeping pool and a startup cache. Such already existed in the city deepness beneath the old town center – and had existed there for almost twenty generations. This new construction was to *live* in, awake. In some places, where air seal and insulation could be assured, it was built right at ground level. In other areas, it was dug down hundreds of feet, an eerie reverse of the buildings that made Princeton's skyline.

Viki stared and stared, lost in the dream. Until now, it had all been a story at a distance. Little Victory read about it, heard her parents talk about it, heard it on the radio. She knew that as much as anything, it was the reason why so many people hated her family. That, and being oophase, were the reasons they weren't supposed to go out alone. Dad might talk and talk about evolution in action and how important it was for small children to be allowed to take chances, how if that didn't happen then genius could not develop in the survivors. The trouble was, he didn't mean it. Every time Viki tried to take on something a little risky, Dad got all paternal and the project became a padded security blanket.

Viki realized she was chuckling low in her chest.

'What?' said Brent.

'Nothing. I was just thinking that today we are getting to see what things are really like – Daddy or no.'

Brent's aspect shifted into embarrassment. Of all her brothers and sisters, he was the one who took rules the most literally and felt the worst about bending them. 'I think we should leave now. There are workers on the surface, getting closer. Besides, how long does the snow last?'

Grumble. Viki backed out and followed her brother through the maze of wonderfully massive things that filled the construction yard. At the moment, even the prospect of snowdrifts was not an irresistible attraction.

The first real surprise of the day came when they finally reached an in-use express stop: Standing a little apart from the crowd were Jirlib and Gokna. No wonder she hadn't been able to find them this morning. They had snuck off without her! Viki sidled across the plaza toward them, trying to look not the least perturbed. Gokna was grinning her usual one-upness. Jirlib had the grace to look embarrassed. Along with Brent he was the oldest, and should have had the sense to prevent this outing. The four of them drifted a few yards away from the stares and stuck their heads together.

Buzz, mumble. Miss One-Upness: 'What took you so long? Had trouble sneaking past Downing's Detainers?' Viki: 'I didn't think *you* would even dare try. We've done lots already this morning.' Miss One-Upness: 'Like what?' Viki: 'Like we checked out the New Underground.' Miss One-Upness: 'Well—'

Jirlib: 'Shut up the both of you. Neither of you should be out here.'

'But we're radio celebrities, Jirlib.' Gokna preened. 'People love us.'

Jirlib moved a little closer and lowered his voice. 'Quit it. For every three who like "The Children's Hour," there are three that it worries – and four more are trads who still hate your guts.'

The children's radio hour had been more fun than anything Viki had ever done, but it hadn't been the same since Honored Pedure. Now that their age was public, it was like they had to prove something. They had even found some other oophases – but so far none were right for the show. Viki and Gokna hadn't gotten friendly with other cobblies, even the pair that had been their age. They were strange, unfriendly children – almost the stereotype of oophase. Daddy said it was their upbringing, the years in hiding. That was the scariest thing of all, something she only talked about with Gokna, and then only in whispers in the middle of the night. What if the Church was right? Maybe she and Gokna just imagined they had souls.

For a moment, the four of them stood silently, taking Jirlib's point. Then Brent asked, 'So why are you out here, Jirlib?' From anyone else it would have been a challenge, but verbal fighting was outside Brent's scope. The question was simple curiosity, an honest request for enlightenment.

As such, it poked deeper than any gibe. 'Um, yeah. I'm on my way downtown. The Royal Museum has an exhibit about the Distorts of Khelm . . . *I'm* not a problem. I look quite old enough to be in-phase.' That last was true. Jirlib wasn't as big as Brent, but he already had the beginning of paternal fur showing through the slits of his jacket. But Viki wasn't going to let him off that easily. She jabbed a hand in Gokna's direction: 'So what is this? Your pet tarant?'

Little Miss One-Upness smiled sweetly. Jirlib's whole aspect was a glare. 'You two are walking disaster areas, you know that?' Exactly how had Gokna fooled Jirlib into taking her along? The question sparked real professional interest in Viki. She and Gokna were by far the best manipulators in the whole family. That was why they got along so badly with each other.

'We at least have a valid academic reason for our trip,' said Gokna. 'What's your excuse?'

Viki waved her eating hands in her sister's face. 'We're going to see the snow. That's a learning experience.'

'Hah! You just want to roll in it.'

'Shut up.' Jirlib raised his head, took in the various bystanders back at the express stop. 'We should all go home.' Gokna shifted into persuasion mode: 'But Jirlib, that would be worse. It's a long walk back. Let's take the bus to the museum – see, it's coming right now.' The timing was perfect. An express had just turned onto the uphill thoroughfare. Its near-red lights marked it as part of the downtown loop. 'By the time we get done there, the snow fanatics should be back in town and there'll be an express running all the way back home.'

'Hey, I didn't come down here to see some fake alien magic! I want to see the snow.'

Gokna shrugged. 'Too bad, Viki. You can always stick your head in an icebox when we get home.'

'I—' Viki saw that Jirlib had reached the end of his patience, and she didn't have any real counterargument. A word from him to Brent, and Viki would find herself carried willy-nilly back to the house. '—uh; what a fine day to go to the museum.'

Jirlib gave a sour smile. 'Yeah, and when we arrive we'll probably find Rhapsa and Little Hrunk already there, having sweet-talked security into driving them down direct.' That started Viki and Gokna laughing. The two littlest ones were more than babies now, but they still hung around Dad nearly all the day. The image of them outsmarting Mother's security team was a bit much.

The four of them maneuvered back to the edge of the crowd, and were the last to board the express . . . Oh well. Four really was safer than two, and the Royal Museum was in a safe part of town. Even if Dad caught on, the children's evident planning and caution would excuse them. And for all the rest of her life there would be the snow.

Public expresses were nothing like the cars and airplanes that Viki was used to. Here everyone was packed close. Rope netting – almost like babies' gymnets – hung in sheets spaced every five feet down the length of the bus. Passengers spread arms and legs ignominiously through the webwork and hung vertically from the ropes. It made it possible to pack more people on board, but it felt pretty silly. Only the driver had a proper perch.

This bus wouldn't have been crowded – except that the other passengers gave the children a wide berth. *Well, they can all shrivel. I don't care.* She stopped watching the other passengers, and studied the cross streets streaming past.

With all the work going on underground, there were places where street repairs had been neglected. Every bump and pothole set the rope netting asway – kind of fun. Then things smoothed out. They were entering the poshest section of the new downtown. She recognized some of the insignias on the towers above them, corporations like Under Power and Regency Radionics. Some of the largest companies in the Accord wouldn't even exist if it weren't for her father. It made her proud to see all the people going in and out of those buildings. Dad was important in a good way to many people.

Brent swayed out from the rope netting, his head coming close to hers. 'You know, I think we're being followed.'

Jirlib heard the quiet words too, and stiffened on the ropes. 'Huh? Where?'

'Those two Roadmasters. They were parked near the bus stop.'

For a second, Viki felt a little thrill of fear – and then relief. She laughed. 'I bet we didn't fool anyone this morning. Dad let us go, and Captain Downing's people are following along the way they always like to do.'

Brent said, 'These cars don't look like any of the usual ones.'

28

The Royal Museum was at the City Center express stop. Viki and her siblings were deposited on the very steps of the place.

For a moment Viki and Gokna were speechless, staring upward at the curving stone arch. They had done a show about this place, but they had never been here. The Royal Museum was only three stories tall, dwarfed by the buildings of modern times. But the smaller building was something more than all the skyscrapers. Except for fortifications, the museum was the oldest intact surface structure in Princeton. In fact, it had been the Royals' principal museum for the last five cycles of the sun. There had been some rebuilding, and some extensions, but one of the traditions of the place was that it should remain true to King Longarms's vision. The outside sloped in a curving arch, almost like an inverted section of aircraft wing. The wind-run-arch was the invention of architects two generations before the scientific era. The ancient buildings at Lands Command were nothing compared with this; they had the protection of deep valley walls. For a moment, Viki tried to imagine what it must be like here in the days right after the sun came to life: the building hunkered low beneath winds blasting at near sound-speed, the sun blazing hell-bright in all the colors from ultra to farthest red. So why did King Longarms build right on the surface? To dare the Dark and the Sun, of course. To rise-above the deep little hidey-holes and *rule*.

'Hey you two! Are you asleep, or what?' Jirlib's voice-jabbed at them. He and Brent were looking back from the entrance. The girls scrambled up the steps, and for once didn't have any smart reply.

Jirlib continued on, mumbling to himself about daydreaming twits. Brent dropped behind the other three, but followed close.

They passed into the shade of the entryway, and the sounds of the city faded behind. A ceremonial guard of two King's troopers perched silently in ambush niches on either side of the entrance. Up ahead was the real guardian – the ticket clerk. The ancient walls behind his stand were hung with announcements of the current exhibits. Jirlib was grumbling no more. He jittered around a twelve-color 'artist's conception' of a Distort of Khelm. And now Viki could see how such foolishness had made it into the Royal Museum. It wasn't just the Distorts. This season's museum theme was 'Crank Science in All Its Aspects.' The posters advertised exhibits on deepness-witching, autocombustion, videomancy, and – ta-da! – the Distorts of Khelm. But Jirlib seemed oblivious of the company his hobby was keeping. It was enough for him that a museum finally honored it.

The current-theme exhibits were in the new wing. Here the ceilings were high, and mirrored pipes showered sunlight in misty cones upon the marble floors. The four of them were almost alone, and the place had an eerie quality of sound about it, not quite echoing, but magnifying. When they weren't talking, even the tick of their feet seemed loud. It worked better than any 'Quiet Please' signs. Viki was awed by all the incredible quackery. Daddy thought such things were amusing – 'like religion but not so deadly.' Unfortunately, Jirlib had eyes only for his own quackery. Never mind that Gokna was engrossed by the autocombustion exhibit to the point of active scheming. Never mind that Viki wanted to see the glowing picture tubes in the videomancy hall. Jirlib was going straight to the Distorts exhibit, and he and Brent made sure their sisters stayed right with them.

Ah, well. In truth, Viki had always been intrigued by the Distorts. Jirlib had been stuck on them for as long as she could remember; here, finally, they would get to see the real thing.

The entrance to the hall was a floor-to-ceiling exhibit of diamond foraminifera. How many tons of fuel sludge had been sifted to find such perfect specimens? The different types were carefully labeled according to the best scientific theories, but the tiny crystal skeletons had been artfully positioned in their trays behind magnifying lenses: in the piped sunlight, the forams glittered in crystal constellations like jeweled tiaras and bracelets and backdrapes. It reduced Jirlib's collection to insignificance. On a central table, a bank of microscopes gave the interested visitor a closer look. Viki stared through the lenses. She had seen this sort of thing often enough before, but these forams were undamaged and the variety was boggling. Most were six-way symmetric, yet there were many that had the little hooks and wands that the living creatures must have used to move around in their microscopic environment. Not a single diamond skeleton creature lived in the world anymore, and none had for more than fifty million years. But in some sedimentary rock, the diamond foram layer was hundreds of feet thick; out east, it was a cheaper fuel than coal. The largest of the critters was barely flea-sized, but there had been a time when they were the most common animal in the world. Then, about fifty million years ago – poof. All that was left was their skeletons. Uncle Hrunkner said that was something to think about when Daddy's ideas went over the top.

'C'mon, c'mon.' Jirlib could spend hours at a time with his own foram collection. But today, he gave the ranked glitter of the King's Own Exhibit barely thirty seconds, the signs on the far doors proclaimed the Distorts of Khelm. The four of them ticktoed to the darkened entrance, scarcely whispering to one another now. In the hall beyond, a single cone of piped sunlight shone down on the central tables. The walls were drowned in shadow, lit here and there by lamps of the extreme colors.

The four eased quietly into the room. Gokna gave a little squeak of surprise. There were figures in the dark . . . and they were taller than the average adult was long. They wavered on three spindly legs and their forelegs and arms rose almost like the branches of a Reaching Frondeur. It was everything Chundra Khelm had ever claimed for his Distorts – and in the dark, it promised more detail to anyone who would come closer.

Viki read the words that glowed beneath the figures, and smiled to herself. 'Hot stuff, huh?' she said to her sister.

'Yeah – I never imagined—' Then she read the description, too. 'Oh, more crapping fakes.'

'Not a fake,' said Jirlib, 'an admitted reconstruction.' But she could hear the disappointment in his voice. They walked slowly down the darkened hall, peering at ambiguous glimmers. And for a few minutes, the shapes were a tantalizing mystery that floated just beyond their grasp. There were all fifty of the racial types that Khelm described. But these were crude models, probably from some masquerade supplier. Jirlib seemed to wilt as he walked from display to display, and read the writeup under each. The descriptions were expansive: 'The elder races that preceded ours . . . the creatures who haunted the Arachnans of ancient times . . . Darkest deepnesses may still contain their spawn, waiting to take back their world.' This last sign was beside a reconstruction that looked a lot like a monster tarant, poised to bite off the viewer's head. It was all tripe, and even Viki's little brother and sister would have known it. Chundra Khelm admitted that his 'lost site' was beneath foram strata. If the Distorts were anything, they had been extinct at least fifty million years – extinct millions of years before even the earliest proto-Arachnan ever lived.

'I think they're just making fun of it, Jirl,' said Viki. For once she didn't tease about it. She didn't like it when outsiders mocked her family, even unknowingly.

Jirlib shrugged agreement. 'Yeah, you're right. The farther we walk, the funnier they get. Ha. Ha.' He stopped by the last display. 'They even admit it! Here's the last description: "If you have reached here, you understand how foolish are the claims of Chundra Khelm. But what are the Distorts then? Fakery from a conveniently misplaced digging site? Or some rare natural feature of metamorphic rock? You be the judge . . ."' His voice trailed off as his attention shifted to the brightly lit pile of rocks in the center of the room, hidden from earlier view by a partition.

Jirlib did a rolling hop, bounding to the bright-lit exhibit. He was practically jittering with excitement as he peered down into the pile. Each rock was separately displayed. Each rock was clearly visible in all the colors of the sunlight. They looked like nothing more than unpolished marble. Jirlib sighed, but in awe. 'These are real Distorts, the best that anyone besides Chundra Khelm has ever found.'

If they had been polished, some of the rocks would have been kind of pretty. There were swirls that were more the color of elemental carbon than marble. If you used your imagination, they looked a little bit like regular shapes that had been stretched and twisted. They still didn't look like anything that had ever been alive. On the far side of the pile was one rock that had been carefully sliced into tenth-inch sheets, so thin that the sunlight glowed right through. The stack of one hundred slices was mounted on a steel frame, with a gap between each slice. If you got really close and moved your head up and down, you had sort of a three-dimensional view of how the pattern was spread through the rock. There was a glittering swirl of diamond dust, almost like forams, but all smudged out. And around the diamond, a sort of webbery of dark-filled cracks. It was beautiful. Jirlib just stood there, his head pressed closed to the steel frame, tilting back and forth to see the light through all the slices. 'This was alive once. I know it, I know it,' he said. 'A million times bigger than any foram, but based on the same principles. If we could just see what it was like before it got all smeared apart.' It was the old, Khelmic refrain – but this thing *was* real. Even Gokna seemed to be entranced by it; it was going to be a little while before Viki got a closer look. She walked slowly around the central pile, looked at some of the microscopic views, read the rest of the explanations. Leave aside the laughs, the junk statues – this was supposed to be the best example of Distorts around. In a way, that should discourage poor Jirlib as much as anything. Even if these had once been living things, there was certainly no evidence of intelligence. If the Distorts were what Jirlib really wanted, their creations should have been awesome. So where were their machines, their cities?

Sigh. Viki quietly moved away from Gokna and Jirlib. She was in plain sight behind them, but they were so caught by the translucent distort that neither seemed to notice her. Maybe she could sneak into the next hall, the videomancy thing. Then she saw Brent. *He* was not distracted by the exhibit. Her brother had hunkered down behind a table in one of the darkest corners of the room – and right next to the exit she was heading for. She might not have noticed him except that his eye surfaces gleamed in the extreme-color lamps. From where he sat, Brent could lurk on both entrances and still see everything they were doing at the central tables.

Viki gave him a wave that was also a grin and drifted toward the exit. Brent didn't move or call her back. Maybe he was in an ambush mood, or just daydreaming about his buildertoys. As long as she stayed in sight, maybe he wouldn't squawk. She moved through the high-arched exit, into the videomancy hall.

The exhibit began with paintings and mosaics, generations old. The idea behind videomancy went back long before modern times, to the superstition that if you could only picture your enemies perfectly, you would have power over them. The notion had inspired a lot of art, the invention of new dyes and mixing formulas. Even now, the best pictures were only a shadow of what the Spider eye could see. Modern videomancy claimed that science could produce the perfect picture, and the ancient dreams would be realized. Daddy thought the whole thing was hilarious.

Viki walked between tall racks of glowing video tubes. A hundred still landscapes, fuzzy and blurred . . . but the most advanced tubes showed colors you never saw except in extreme lamps and sunlight. Every year, the video tubes got better. People were talking about picture radio even. That idea fascinated Little Victory – forget the mind-control quackery.

From somewhere beyond the far end of the hall there were voices, frolicsome jabber that sounded like Rhapsa and Little Hrunk. Viki froze in startlement. A few seconds passed . . . and two babies came bounding through the far entrance. Viki remembered Jirlib's sarcastic prediction that Rhapsa and Hrunk would show up, too. For an instant she thought he'd been right. But no, two strangers followed them into the hall, and the children were younger than her little sister and brother.

Viki squeaked something excited and raced down the hall toward the children. The adults – the parents? – froze for an instant, then swept up their children and turned in retreat.

'Wait! Wait, please! I just want to talk.' Viki forced her legs down to a casual walking gait and lifted her hands in a friendly smile. Behind her, Viki could see that Gokna and Jirlib had left the Distort display, and were staring after her with expressions of stark surprise.

The parents stopped, came slowly back. Both Gokna and Viki were clearly out-of-phase. That seemed to encourage the strangers more than anything.

They talked for a few minutes, politely formal. Trenchet Suabisme was a planner at New World Construction; her husband was a surveyor there. 'Today seemed like a good day to come to the museum, what with most of the day-off people up in the mountains playing in the snow. Was that your plan, too?'

'Oh, yes,' said Gokna – and for her and Jirlib maybe that was so. 'But we are so glad to meet you, a-and your children. What are their names?' It was so weird to meet strangers who seemed more familiar than anyone but family. Trenchet and Alendon seemed to feel it too. Their children squirmed around loudly in their arms, refusing to retreat to Alendon's back. After a few minutes, their parents set them back on the floor. The babies took two big hops each and ended up in the arms of Gokna and Viki. They scrambled around, chattering nonsense, their nearsighted baby eyes turning this way and that with excited curiosity. The one climbing all over Viki – Alequere, she was – couldn't be much over two years old. Somehow, neither Rhapsa nor Little Hrunk had ever seemed so cute. Of course, when *they* had been two, Viki had been only seven and still out to get all the attention she could for herself. These children were nothing like the surly oophases they had met before now.

The most embarrassing thing was the adults' reaction when they learned exactly who Viki and her siblings were. Trenchet Suabisme was silent for a shocked second, 'I-I guess we should have known. Who else could you be? . . . You know, when I was in my teens, I used to listen to your radio program. You seemed so awfully young, the only Outies I had ever heard. I really liked your show.'

'Yeah,' said Alendon. He smiled as Alequere wormed her way into the pocket on the side of Viki's jacket. 'Knowing about you made it possible for me and Trenchet to think about having our own children. It's been hard; we lost our first baby welts. But once they get eyes, they're cute as can be.'

The baby made happy squeaking noises as it scrambled around in Viki's jacket. Her head finally emerged, waving eating hands. Viki stretched back to tickle the little hands. It made Viki proud to know that some had listened and gotten Daddy's message, but – 'It's sad you still have to avoid the crowds. I wish there were more like you and your children.'

Surprisingly, Trenchet chuckled. 'Times are changing. More and more, people expect to be awake right through the Dark; they're beginning to see that some rules have to change. We'll need grown children around to help finish the construction. We know two other couples in New World who are trying to have children out-of-phase.' She patted her husband's shoulders. 'We won't be alone forever.'

The enthusiasm flowed across to Viki. Alequere and the other cobblie – Birbop? – were as nice as Rhapsa and Little Hrunk, but they were *different*, too. Now finally they might know lots of other children. For Viki it was like opening a window, and seeing all the sunlight's colors.

They walked slowly down the videomancy hall, Gokna and Trenchet Suabisme discussing various possibilities. Gokna was all for having the house on the hill turned into a meeting place for oophase families. Somehow, Viki suspected that would not fly with either Dad or the General, though for different reasons. But overall . . . something could be worked out; it made strategic sense. Viki followed the others, not paying much attention. She was having a very interesting time jiggling little Alequere. Playing with the cobblie was far more fun than seeing the snow could have been.

Then behind all the chatting, she heard the distant ticking of many feet on marble. Four people? Five? They'd be coming through the same doorway that Viki had, just a few minutes before. Whoever it was would have an interesting surprise – the sight of six oophases, from babies to near-adults.

Four of the newcomers were current-generation adults, big as any of Mother's security people. They didn't pause or even act surprised when they saw all the children. Their clothes were the same nondescript commercial jackets that Viki was used to back in the house on the hill. The leader was a sharp, last-generation cobber with the look of a senior noncom. Viki should have felt relief; these must be the people Brent had seen following them. But she didn't recognize them—

The leader held them all in her gaze, then gestured familiarly at Trenchet Suabisme. 'We can take it from here. General Smith wants all the children back inside the security perimeter.'

'W-what? I don't understand?' Suabisme lifted her hands in confusion.

The five strangers walked steadily forward, the leader nodding pleasantly. But her explanations were nonsense: 'Two guards just aren't enough for all the children. After you left, we got a tip there might be problems.' Two of the security types stepped smoothly between the children and the Suabisme adults. Viki felt herself pushed un-gently toward Jirlib and Gokna. Mother's people had never behaved like this. 'Sorry, this is an emergency—'

Several things happened at once, totally confused and nonsensical. Both Trenchet and Alendon were shouting, panic mixed with anger. The two biggest strangers were pushing them back from the children. One was reaching into his pannier.

'Hey, we've missed one!' *Brent.*

Very high up, something was moving. The videomancy exhibit consisted of towering racks of display tubes. With inexorable grace, the nearest came toppling down, its pictures flickering out in showers of sparks and the sound of crumpling metal. She had a glimpse of Brent sailing off the top, just ahead of the destruction.

The floor smashed up at her when the display rack hit. Everywhere was the bang of imploding video tubes, the buzz of uncontrolled high voltage. The rack had come down between her and the Suabismes – and right on top of two of the strangers. She had a glimpse of colored blood oozing across the marble. Two motionless forehands extended from under the rack; just beyond their grasp lay a snub-barreled shotgun.

Then time resumed. Viki was grabbed roughly round her midsection and hauled away from the wreckage. On the other side of her abductor, she could hear Gokna and Jirlib shouting. There was a dull crunch. Gokna shrieked and Jirlib went silent.

'Teamleader, what about—'

'Never mind! We bagged all six. Move it. Move it!'

As she was carried from the hall, Viki got one glance back. But the strangers were leaving their two dead pals – and she couldn't see beyond the fallen rack to where the Suabismes would be.

29

It was an afternoon that Hrunkner Unnerby would never forget. In all the years he had known Victory Smith, it was the first time he'd seen her come close to losing control. Just past noon the frantic call came over the microwave communications link, Sherkaner Underhill breaking through all military priorities with word of the kidnappings. General Smith dumped Sherkaner from the line and pulled her staff into emergency session. Suddenly Hrunkner Unnerby went from being a projects director to something like . . . like a sergeant. Hrunkner got her tri-prop on the flight line.

He and lower staff checked background security. He wasn't going to let his General take chances. Emergencies like this were just the things that enemies like to create, and when you're thinking that nothing matters but that emergency, *then* they strike at their true targets.

The tri-prop took less than two hours to make it from Lands Command to Princeton. But the aircraft was no flying command center; such things were beyond current budgets. So the General had two hours with only a low-speed wireless link. That was two hours away from the command and control hub at Lands Command or its near equal at Princeton. Two hours to listen to fragmentary reports and try to coordinate a response. Two hours for grief and anger and uncertainty to gnaw. It was midafternoon when they landed, then another half hour before they reached Hill House.

Their car had scarcely stopped when Sherkaner Underhill was pulling the doors open, urging them out. He caught Unnerby by the arm, and spoke around him to the General. 'Thanks for bringing Hrunkner. I need you both.' And he walked them across the foyer, drawing them down to his den on the ground floor.

Over the years, Unnerby had observed Sherkaner in various tricky situations: talking his way into Lands Command in the middle of the Tiefer War, guiding an expedition right through the vacuum of the Deepest Dark, debating trads. Sherk didn't always win, but he was always so full of surprise and imagination. Everything was a grand experiment and a wonderful adventure. Even when he failed, he saw how the failure would make for more interesting experiments. But today . . . today Sherkaner had met despair. He reached out to Smith, the tremor in his head and arms more pronounced than ever. 'There has to be a way to find them. There has to be. I have computers, and the microwave link to Lands Command.' All the resources that had served him so well in the past. 'I can get them back safely. I know I can.'

Smith was very still for a moment. Then she moved close to him, laid an arm across Sherk's shoulders, caressing his fur. Her voice was soft and stern, almost like a soldier bracing another about lost comrades. 'No, dear. You can only do so much.' Outside, the afternoon was moving into overcast. A thin whistle of wind came through the half-opened windows, and the ferns scraped back and forth on the quartz panes. A dark green gloom was all that filtered down through the clouds and the shrubbery.

The General stood with her head close to Sherkaner's, the two just staring at each other. Unnerby could almost feel the fear and the shame echoing back and forth between the two. Then, abruptly, Sherkaner collapsed toward her, his arms wrapping her. The soft hiss of Sherkaner's weeping joined the wind as the only sounds in the room. After a moment, Smith raised one of her back hands, gently motioning for Hrunkner to leave.

Unnerby nodded back at her. The deep carpet was littered with toys –

Sherkaner's and the children's – but he was careful where he stepped and managed a silent exit.

The twilight quickly became night, as much a product of the gathering storm as the setting of the sun. Unnerby didn't see much of the weather, since the house command post had only tiny, beetling windows. Smith showed up there almost half an hour after Unnerby. She acknowledged her subordinates' attention, then slid onto the perch next to Hrunkner. He waggled hands at her questioningly. She shrugged. 'Sherk will be okay, Sergeant. He's up with his graduate students, doing what he can. Now where are we?'

Unnerby pushed a stack of interviews across the table toward her. 'Captain Downing and his team are still here, if you want to talk to them yourself, but all of us' – all the staff that had come up from Lands Command – 'think they're clean. The children were just too clever.' The children had made fools of an efficient security setup. Of course, they had lived with the setup for a long time, knew Security's habits, were friends of the team members. And till now, the external threat had been a matter of theory and occasional rumor. It all worked in the cobblies' favor when they decided to go for a jaunt . . . But that security team was a creation of General Victory Smith's own staff. The team members were smart people, loyal people; they were hurting as much as Sherkaner Underhill.

Smith pushed the reports back at him. 'Okay. Get Daram and his team back in the loop. Keep them busy. What's new with the search reports?' She waved the other staffers close, and she herself became very busy.

The house command post had good maps, a real situation table. With the microwave link; it could double for the command center at Lands Command. Unfortunately, it had no special advantage for comm into Princeton. It would be several hours before that problem was cured. There was a steady stream of runners moving in and out of the room. Many were fresh from Lands Command, and not part of the day's debacle. That was a good thing, their presence leavening the fatigued despair that showed in the aspects of some. There were leads. There was progress . . . both heartening and ominous.

The chief of counter-Kindred operations showed up an hour later. Rachner Thract was very new to his job, a young cobber and a Tiefer immigrant. It was strange to see someone with such a combination in that post. He seemed bright enough, but more bookish than deadly. Maybe that was okay; God knew they needed people who really understood the Kindred. How could traditional values go so wrong? In the Great War, the Kindred had been minor schismatics within the Tiefer empire, and secret supporters of the Accord. But Victory Smith thought they would be the next great threat – or maybe she just followed her general suspicion of trads.

Thract laid his rain cape on the coatrack and undid the pannier he carried. He set the documents down in front of his boss. 'The Kindred are up to their shoulders in this one, General.'

'Why am I not surprised?' said Smith. Unnerby knew how tired she must be, but she seemed fresh, almost the usual Victory Smith. Almost. She was as calm, as courteous as at any staff meeting. Her questions were as clever as always. But Unnerby saw a difference, a faint distraction. It didn't come across as anxiety; it was more like the General's mind was somewhere else, contemplating. 'Nevertheless, Kindred involvement was only a low probability this morning. What has changed, Rachner?'

'Two interviews and two autopsies. The cobbers who were killed had been through plenty of physical training, and it doesn't look like athletics; there were old nicks in their chitin, even a patched bullet hole.'

Victory shrugged. 'It's been clear this was a professional job. We know there are domestic threats, trad fringe groups. They might hire competent operators.'

'They might, but this was the Kindred, not the local trads.'

'There's hard evidence?' asked Unnerby, relieved and a little ashamed by the feeling.

'Um.' Thract seemed to consider the questioner as much as the question. The cobber couldn't quite decide where Unnerby – a civilian addressed as 'Sergeant' – might fit in the chain of command. *Get used to it, sonny.* 'The Kindred make a big thing of their religious roots; but before now, they've been careful about interfering with us domestically. Covert funding of local trad groups was about their limit. But . . . they blew it today. These were Kindred professionals. They went to great trouble to be untraceable, but they didn't count on our forensic labs. Actually, it's a test one of your husband's students invented. See, the ratio of pollen types in the breathing passages of both corpses is foreign; I can even tell you which Kindred base they launched from. These two hadn't been in-country for more than fifteen days.'

Smith nodded. 'If it had been longer, the pollen would be gone?'

'Right, captured by their immune system and flushed, the techs say. But even so, we still would have figured most of this out. You see, the other side had a lot more bad luck today than we did. They left behind two living witnesses . . .' Thract hesitated, obviously remembering that this was *not* an ordinary ops meeting, that for Smith the usual definition of operational success might count as catastrophic failure.

The General didn't seem to notice. 'Yes, the couple. The ones who brought their children to the museum.'

'Yes, ma'am. And they are half the reason why this thing blew up in the enemy's face. Colonel Underville' – the domestic ops chief – 'has had people talking to them all afternoon; they are desperately anxious to help. You've already heard what she got from them right away, how one of your sons brought down an exhibit and killed two of the kidnappers.'

'And that all the children were taken alive.'

'Right. But Underville has learned more. We're almost sure now . . . The kidnappers intended to steal all your children. When they saw the Suabismes' little ones, they assumed those were yours. There just aren't that many oophases in the world, even now. They naturally assumed the Suabismes were *our* security people.'

God in the good cold earth. Unnerby gazed out the narrow windows. There was a little more light than before, but now it was the actinic ultras of security lamps. The wind was steadily picking up, driving sparkling droplets across the windows, and bending the ferns back and forth. There was supposed to be a lightning storm tonight.

So the Kindred screwed up because they had too high an opinion of Accord security. Naturally, they assumed that *someone* would be with the children.

'We got a lot from the two civilians, General: the story these fellows used when they walked in, some turns of phrase after things blew up . . . The kidnappers didn't intend to leave any witnesses. The Suabismes are the luckiest people in Princeton tonight even if they don't see it that way. The two that your son killed were pushing the Suabismes away from the children. One of them had unholstered an automatic shotgun, and all its safeties were off. Colonel Underville figures the original mission was to grab all your children and leave no witnesses. In fact, dead civilians and lots of blood was fine with their scenario, since it would all be blamed on our trad factions.'

'In that case, why not leave a couple of dead children, too? That would also have made the getaway easier.' Victory's question was calm, but it had a distanced quality about it.

'We don't know, ma'am. But Colonel Underville thinks they're still in-country, maybe even in Princeton.'

'Oh?' Skepticism seemed to war with hope. 'I know Belga clamped down awfully fast – and the other side had its problems, too. Okay. This will be your first big in-country operation, Rachner, but I want it done arm-in-arm with Domestic Intelligence. And you'll have to involve the city and commercial police.' The classic anonymity of Accord Intelligence was going to get badly bent in the next few days. 'Try to be nice to the city and commercial people. We don't have a state of war. They can cause the Crown a world of trouble.'

'Yes, ma'am. Colonel Underville and I are running patrols with the city police. When the phones are set up, we'll have some kind of joint command post with them here at Hill House.'

'Very good . . . I think you were ahead of me all the time, Rachner.'

Thract gave a little smile as he came to his feet. 'We'll get your cobblies back, Chief.'

Smith started to reply, then noticed two small heads peeping around the doorjamb. 'I know you will, Rachner. Thank you.'

Thract stepped back from the table, and a brief stillness spread through the room. The two youngest of Underhill's children – maybe all who were left alive – walked shyly into the room, followed by the head of their guard team and three troopers. Captain Downing carried a furled umbrella, but it was clear that Rhapsa and Little Hrunk had not taken advantage of it. Their jackets were soaked and drops of rain stood on their glassy black chitin.

Victory had no smile for the children. Her gaze took in their soaked clothes and the umbrella. 'Were you running around?'

Rhapsa answered, more subdued than Hrunkrier had ever heard the little hellion. 'No, Mother. We were with Daddy, but now he is busy. We stayed right by Captain Downing, between him and the others . . .' She stopped, tilted her head shyly at her guard.

The young captain snapped to attention, but he had the terrible look of a soldier who has just seen combat and defeat. 'Sorry, ma'am. I decided not to use the umbrella. I wanted to be able to see in all directions.'

'Quite right, Daram. And . . . it's right that you brought them here.' She stopped, just staring at her children for a quiet second. Rhapsa and Little Hrunk were motionless, staring back. Then, as if some central switch had been tripped, the two swarmed across the room, their voices raised in a wordless keen. For a moment they were all arms and legs, scrambling up Smith, hugging her like a father. Now that the dam of their reserve was broken, their crying was loud – and the questions, too. Was there any news about Gokna and Viki and Jirlib and Brent? What would happen now? And they didn't want to be by themselves.

After a few moments things settled down. Smith tilted her head at the children, and Unnerby wondered what was going through her mind. She still had two children. Whatever the bad luck or incompetence of this day, it was two other young children who were stolen instead of these. She raised a hand in Unnerby's direction. 'Hrunkner. I have a request. Find the Suabismes. Ask them . . . offer them my hospitality. If they would like to wait this out here at Hill House . . . I would be honored.'

They were high up, in some kind of vertical ventilator shaft.

'No, it's not a ventilator shaft!' said Gokna. 'Real ones have all sorts of extra piping and utility cabling.'

There was no rumble of ventilator fans, just the constant whistle of the wind from above. Viki concentrated on the view straight above her head. She could see a grilled window at the top, maybe fifty feet up. Daylight shone through, splashing this way and that down the metal walls of the shaft. Here at the bottom they were in twilight, but it was more than bright enough to see the sleep mats, the chemical toilet, the metal floor. Their prison got steadily warmer as the day progressed. Gokna was right. They'd done enough exploring back home to know how real utility cores looked. But what else could this be? 'Look at all the patches.' She waved at the disks that were sloppily welded here and there on the walls. 'Maybe this place was abandoned – no, maybe it's still under construction!'

'Yeah,' said Jirlib. 'All this work is fresh. They just tackwelded covers on the access holes, maybe an hour's work.' Gokna nodded, not even trying to get the last word. So much had changed since this morning. Jirlib was no longer a distant, angry umpire to their disputes. He was under more pressure than ever before, and she knew how bitterly guilty he must feel. Along with Brent, he was the eldest – and he'd let this happen. But the pain didn't show directly; Jirlib was more patient than ever before.

And when he spoke, his sisters listened. Even if you didn't count that he was just about an adult, he was by far the smartest of all of them.

'In fact, I think I know exactly where we are.' He was interrupted by the babies, stirring in their perches on his back. Jirlib's fur was just not deep enough to properly comfort, and he was already beginning to stink. Alequere and Birbop alternated between caterwauling demands for their parents and nerve-racking silence, when they pinched tight onto poor Jirlib's back. It looked like they were returning to noise mode. Viki reached out, coaxing Alequere into her arms.

'Where is that?' asked Gokna, but with no trace of argument in her voice.

'See the attercop webs?' said Jirlib, pointing upward. They were fresh, tiny patches of silk that floated in the breeze by the grill. 'Each type has its own pattern. The ones up there are local to the Princeton area, but they nest in the highest places. The top of Hill House is just barely high enough for them. So – I figure we're still in town, and we're so high up we must be visible for miles. We're either in the hill district or in that new skyscraper at City Center.'

Alequere started crying again. Viki rocked her gently back and forth. It was the sort of thing that always cheered up Little Hrunk, but . . . A miracle! Alequere's wailing quieted. Maybe she was just so beaten down that she couldn't make healthy noise. But no, after a few seconds the baby waved a weak little smile at her and twisted around so that she could see everything. She was a good little cobblie! Viki rocked the baby a few more seconds before she spoke. 'Okay. Maybe they just drove us around in circles – but City Center? We've heard a few aircraft, but where are the street noises?'

'They're all around.' It was almost the first thing Brent had said since the kidnapping. Slow and dull, that was Brent. And he was the only one of all of them who had guessed what was happening this morning. He was the one who dropped away from the others and lurked in the dark. Brent was grown-up-sized – riding that exhibit down on top of the enemy could have crippled him. When they were dragged out through the museum's freight entrance, Brent had been limp and silent. He hadn't said anything during the drive that followed, just waved when Jirlib and Gokna asked him if he was okay.

In fact, it looked like he had cracked one foreleg and injured at least one other, but he wouldn't let them look at the damage. Viki understood. Brent would feel just as ashamed as Jirlib – and even more useless. He had withdrawn into a sullen pile, and then – after the first hour in their present captivity – had begun to limp around and around, tapping and ticking at the metal. Every so often he would plunk himself down flat, like he was pretending to be dead – or was totally despairing. That was his posture just now.

'Can't you hear them?' he said again. 'Belly-listen.'

Viki hadn't played that game in years. But she and the others imitated him, sprawling absolutely flat, with no grasping arch at all. It wasn't very comfortable, and you couldn't hold on to anything while you did it. Alequere hopped out of her arms. Birbop joined his sister. The two ticked from one of the older children to another, prodding at them. After a moment, the two started giggling.

'Sh, sh,' Viki said softly. That only made the giggling louder. How long had Viki been praying for spirit to return to these two? And now she wanted them just to be quiet for a bit. She shut them out of her mind and concentrated. Hunh. It wasn't exactly sound, not for the ears in your head, anyway. But all along her underside she could feel it. There was a steady background hum . . . and other vibrations, that came and went. Ha! It was a ghost of the thrumming life you felt in the tips of your feet when you walked around downtown! And there! The unmistakable burring of heavy brakes making a fast stop.

Jirlib was chuckling. 'I guess that settles that! They thought they were so clever with that closed cargo box, but now we know.'

Viki rose to a more comfortable position and exchanged looks with Gokna. Jirlib was smarter, but when it came to sneakiness he had never been in a class with his sisters. Gokna's reply was mild, partly to be polite, partly because the appropriate tones would have sent the babies back into hiding. 'Jirl, I don't think they were really trying to hide things from us.'

Jirlib shifted his head back, almost his 'brother knows best' gesture. Then he caught her tone. 'Gokna, they could have gotten us here in a five-minute drive. Instead, we were on the the road for more than an hour. What—'

Viki said, 'I think that may have been just to evade Mother's security. These cobbers had several cars running around; they switched us twice, remember. Maybe they actually tried to get out of town, and saw that they couldn't do it.' Viki waved at their quarters. 'If they have any sense, they know we've seen way too much.' She tried to keep her voice light. Birbop and Alequere had wandered over to the still-sprawled Brent and were picking his pockets. 'We could identify them, Jirlib. We also saw the driver and the lady down in the museum loading area.'

And she told him about the automatic shotgun she'd seen on the floor at the museum. An expression of horror flickered across Jirlib. 'You don't think they're trads, just trying to embarrass Dad and the General?'

Both Gokna and Viki gestured no. Gokna said, 'I think they're soldiers, Jirl, no matter what they say.' In fact, there had been lies on top of lies. When the gang appeared at the videomancy exhibit, they'd claimed to be from Mother's security. But by time they dumped the cobblies here, they were talking like trads: The children were a horrible example for decent folk. They weren't to be harmed, but their parents would be revealed as the perverts that they were. That's what they said, but both Gokna and Viki noticed their lack of fire. Most traditionalists on the radio positively fumed; the ones Viki and Gokna had met in person got all torn up just at the sight of oophase children. These kidnappers were cool; behind the rhetoric, it was clear that the children were just cargo. Viki had noticed only two honest emotions under their professionalism. The leader was truly angry about the two that Brent had squashed . . . and every so often, there was a hint of distant regret for the children themselves.

Viki saw Jirlib flinch as the implications hit home, but he remained silent. Two shrieks of laughter interrupted his grim introspection. Alequere and Birbop weren't paying any attention to Gokna and Viki, or Jirlib. They had discovered the play twine that Brent kept hidden in his jacket. Alequere hopped back, drawing the twine out in a soaring arc. Birbop jumped to grab it, ran in a quick circle around Brent as if to trap him round the legs.

'Hey, Brent, I thought you had outgrown that stuff,' said Gokna, a forced cheeriness in her teasing.

Brent's answer was slow and a little defensive. 'I get bored when I'm away from my sticks 'n' hubs. You can play with twine anywhere.' For what it was worth, Brent was an expert at making twine patterns. When he was younger, he'd often roll onto his back and use all his arms and legs – even his eating hands – to wrap ever more complicated patterns. It was the sort of silly, intricate hobby that Brent loved.

Birbop grabbed the tip of the rope from Alequere and raced ten or fifteen feet up the wall, nimbly taking advantage of every grasp point the way only the very young can. He wiggled the rope at his sister, daring her to try to drag him down. When she did so, he jerked it back and climbed upward another five feet. He was just like Rhapsa used to be, maybe even a bit more nimble.

'Not so high, Birbop, you'll fall!' – and Viki was sounding just like Daddy now.

The walls stretched up and up above the baby. And at the top, fifty feet above them, was the tiny window. Behind herself, Viki saw Gokna start with surprise. 'Are you thinking what I am?' Viki said.

'P-probably. When she was little, Rhapsa could have climbed to the top.' Their kidnappers weren't as smart as they thought. Anyone who had looked after babies would know better. But both the male kidnappers were young, current-generation. 'But if he falls—'

If he fell, there would be no gymnet base web, not even a soft carpet. A two-year-old might weigh fifteen or twenty pounds. They loved to climb; it was as if they sensed that once they got big and heavy, they'd be stuck with climbing stairs and making only the most trivial jumps. Babies could fall a lot farther than grown-ups without serious injury, but long falls would still kill them. Two-year-olds didn't know that. A simple suggestion would send Birbop off for the window at the top. The chances were good that he would make it . . .

Normally, Viki and Gokna would jump into any wild scheme, but this was someone else's life . . . The two stared at each other for a moment. 'I – I don't know, Viki.'

And if they did nothing? The babies would likely be killed along with the rest of them. There could be terrible consequences whatever they chose. Suddenly Viki was more frightened than she had ever been before; she walked across the floor to stand under the grinning Birbop. Her arms reached up as if with a life of their own, to coax the baby back down. She forced her arms down, forced her voice into a light, teasing tone. 'Hi, Birbop! Do you think you can carry the twine all the way to that little window?'

Birbop tilted his head, turned his baby eyes upward. 'Sure.' And he was off, scuttling back and forth from weld patch to pipefitting, upward and upward. *I owe you, little one, even if you don't know it.*

On the ground, Alequere squawked outrage that Birbop should have all the attention. She jerked hard on the twine, leaving her brother dangling by three arms from a narrow ledge twenty feet up. Gokna scooped her off the floor and away from the twine, and handed her to Jirlib.

Viki tried to shake off the terror she felt; she watched the baby climb higher and higher. *And if we can get to the window, then what?* Throw out notes? But they had nothing to write with – and they didn't know just where they were or where the wind might carry a note . . . And suddenly she saw how one thing might solve two problems. 'Brent, your jacket.' She jerked her bands, waving for Gokna to help him take it off.

'Yes!' Gokna was pulling at the sleeves and pants almost before Viki finished talking. Brent stared in surprise for a second, and then he got the idea and started helping. His jacket was almost as big as Jirlib's, but without the slits down the back. The three of them stretched it flat between them and sidled this way and that, trying to track the lateral movements of the high-climbing Birbop. Maybe, even if he fell . . . It was the sort of thing that always worked in adventure stories. Somehow, standing here holding the jacket, it seemed absurd to imagine such success.

Alequere was still screeching, struggling to get out of Jirlib's grasp. Birbop laughed at her. He was quite happy to be at the center of attention, doing something he normally would have gotten whacked for. Forty feet up. He was slowing. The foot and handholds' were scarce; he was beyond the main ventilator fixtures. A couple of times he almost lost the twine as it slipped from hand to hand. He gathered himself on an impossibly narrow ledge and leaped sidewise up the remaining three feet – and one of his hands snagged the window grille. An instant later, his body was silhouetted in the light.

With only two eyes, and those in front, babies almost had to turn around to see behind themselves. Now for the first time, Birbop looked down. His triumphant laughter choked as he saw just how far he had come, so far that even his baby instincts told him he was at risk. There were reasons parents didn't let you climb as high as you wanted. Birbop's arms and legs clamped reflexively to the grillework.

And they couldn't persuade him that no one could come up to help him, and that he could get down by himself. Viki had never imagined that this would be a problem. On the occasions that Rhapsa or Little Hrunk had escaped to unholy heights, neither had any trouble getting back down.

Just when it seemed that Birbop was in a permanent state of paralysis, his sister stopped crying and began laughing at him. After that, it wasn't hard to persuade him to thread the twine through the grillework and then use it as a kind of pulley to support his descent.

Most babies came on the idea themselves, sailing downward on play twine; maybe it went back to some animal memories. Birbop started down with five limbs wrapped securely around the descending strand and three others braking the ascending strand. But after he had descended a few feet and it became clear how smoothly the play twine worked, he was holding with just three arms – and then two. He bounced off the walls with his feet, flying downward like some pouncing tarant. Below him, Viki and the others hopped around in a vain effort to keep their makeshift net under him . . . and then he was down.

And they had a loop of play twine extending from the floor to the window grille and back. It glowed and twitched as it released stretch energy.

Gokna and Viki argued about which of them would do the next step. Viki won that one; she weighed under eighty pounds, the least of any of them. She pulled and swung on it while Brent and Gokna ripped the silk lining out of his jacket. The lining was dyed with red and ultra splotches. Better yet, it was constructed of folded layers; cutting it along the stitching gave them a banner that was light as smoke, but fifteen feet on a side. Surely someone would notice.

Gokna folded the lining down to a neat square and handed it to her. 'The twine, you really think it'll hold?'

'Sure.' Maybe. The stuff was slick and stretchy, like any good play twine – and what would happen when she stretched it all the way?

What Brent said comforted her more than any wishful thinking: 'I think it will hold. I like to hang things in my designs. I took this from the mechanics lab.'

Viki took off her own jacket, grabbed the homemade flag in her eating hands, and started up. In her rear view, the others dwindled into an anxious little pattern around the 'safety net.' Lot of good that would do if someone as big as her fell. She swayed out and in, bouncing step by step up the wall. Actually, it was, easy. Even a full-grown adult wouldn't have trouble climbing a vertical with two support ropes – as long as the ropes held. As much as she watched the twine and the wall, she watched the doorway down below. Funny how she hadn't started worrying about interruptions until now. But success was so close. It would all be for nothing if one of the goons chose now to look in on them. Just a few more feet . . .

She slipped her forehands through the window grille, and hoisted herself close to the open air. There was no room to perch, and the grille bars were too close-set for even a baby to sneak through – but ah, the view! They were at the top of one of the giant new buildings, at least thirty stories up. The sky had become a tumbling overcast, and the wind swept fiercely past the window. Her view downward was partly blocked by the shoulders of the building, but Princeton spread before her like some beautiful model. She had a straight view down one street, could see buses, automobiles, people. And if they looked in her direction . . . Viki unwrapped the jacket liner and poked it through the grille. The wind almost pulled it from her grasp. She caught hold more firmly, tearing the fabric with points of her hands. The stuff was so flimsy! Gently, carefully she pulled the ends back, tied them in four separate places. Now the wind spread the colored square out from the side of the building. The fabric snapped in the wind, sometimes rising to cover the window, sometimes falling against the stonework below her view.

One last look at freedom: Out where the land met the overcast, city hills disappeared in the murk. But Viki could see enough to orient herself. There was a hill, not quite so high as the others, but with a spiraling pattern of streets and buildings: Hill House! She could see all the way home!

Viki sailed down from the window, gleeful out of all proportion. They would win yet! She and the others pulled down the sparkling twine, hid it back in Brent's jacket. They sat in the gathering dimness, wondering when their jailers would show up again, arguing about what to do when that happened. The afternoon got awfully dark and the rain started. Still, the sound of fabric snapping in the wind was a comfort.

Sometime after midnight, the storm tore the banner free and lost it in the darkness.

30

The Right of Petition to the Podmaster was a convenient tradition. It even had a basis in historical fact, though Tomas Nau was sure that centuries ago, in the middle of the Plague Times, the only petitions granted were matters of propaganda. In modern times, the manipulation of petitions had been Uncle Alan's preferred way of maintaining popularity and undermining rival factions.

It was a clever tactic, as long as you avoided Alan's mistake of allowing assassins as petitioners. In the twenty-four years since their arrival at OnOff, Tomas Nau had passed on about a dozen petitions. This one today was the first that had claimed 'time is of the essence.'

Nau looked across the table at the five petitioners. Correction: representatives of Petitioners. They claimed one hundred backers, and on just 8Ksec notice. Nau smiled, waved them to their seats. 'Pilot Manager Xin. You are senior, I believe. Please explain your Petition.'

'Yes, Podmaster.' Xin glanced at his girlfriend, Rita Liao. Both were Emergents from the home world, from families that had contributed Focused and Followers for more than three hundred years. Such were the backbone of the Emergent culture, and running them should have been easy. Alas, nothing was easy out here, twenty light-years from civilization. Xin was wordless for a second more. He stole a nervous glance at Kal Omo. Omo's returning look was very cold, and Nau suddenly wished he'd taken time to be briefed by the podsergeant. With Brughel currently off-Watch, there would be no one to blame if he had to deny the Petition.

'As you know, Podmaster, many of us are working with the ground analysis. Many more have a general interest in the Spiders we watch—'

Nau gave him a gentle smile. 'I know. You hang out at Benny's and listen to the translations.'

'Yes, sir. Um. We very much like "The Children's Hour," and some of the story translations. They help us with our analysis. And . . .' His eyes got a faraway look. 'I don't know. The Spiders have a whole world down there, even if they aren't human. Compared to us, sometimes they seem more—' *Real*, Nau was sure he was going to say. 'I mean, we've come to be fond of some of the Spider children.'

As planned. The live translations were heavily buffered now. They had never discovered precisely what caused the mindrot runaway – or even if it had been connected will the live show. Anne figured that the current risk was no more than that of their other operations. Nau reached to his right, gently touched Qiwi's hand. She smiled back. The Spider children were important. This was something he might never have understood if not for Qiwi Lisolet. Qiwi had been so good for so much. Watching her, talking to her, deceiving her – there was so much to learn. Real children would be an impossible drain on L1's resources, but *something* had to substitute. Qiwi and her schemes and her dreams had shown him the way. 'We're all fond of the cobblies, Pilot Manager. Your petition has something to do with the kidnapping?'

'Yes, sir. It's been seventy Ksec since the abduction. The "Accord" Spiders are using their best comm and intelligence gear more intensely than ever before. It's not doing *them* any good, but our zipheads are getting a lot from it. The Accord microwave links have been full of intercepted Kindred messages. Most of the Kindred encryption is algorithmic, not one-time pads. The Accord can't break any of it, but the algorithms, are easy for us. For the last forty Ksec, we – I – have been using our translators and analysts. I think I know where the children are being held. Five analysts give near certainty that—'

'Five analysts, three translators, and part of the snoop array over on the *Invisible Hand*.' Reynolt's voice was loud and implacable, overriding Xin's. 'In addition, Manager Xin has been using almost a third of the support hardware.'

Omo came on like a chorus, perhaps the first time Nau had ever seen Reynolt and Security in such concert: 'And furthermore, it couldn't happen unless the Pilot Manager and a few other privileged managers were using emergency resource codes.' Sergeant Omo's glance flickered across the petitioners. They shrank before his gaze, the Emergents more fearfully than Qeng Ho. *Abuse of the community's resources.* It was the primal sin. Nau smiled to himself. Brughel would have been still scarier, but Omo would do.

Nau raised his hand, and silence spread across the room. 'I understand, Podsergeant. I want a report from you and Director Reynolt as to any lasting damage that might result from this . . .' He wouldn't actually use the words. '. . . activity.' He was silent for a moment more, schooling his expression as if to hide the conflict of a just man trying to reconcile the desires of individuals with the long-term needs of the community. He felt Qiwi squeeze his hand. 'Pilot Manager, you understand that we can't reveal ourselves?'

Xin looked completely cowed. 'Yes, Podmaster.'

'You of all people should know how thin we are stretched here. After the fighting, we were short on Focus and staff. After the rotting runaway of a few Watches back, we are even more lacking in Focus. We have no capital equipment, few weapons, and scarcely even an in-system transport capability. We *might* be able to intimidate a Spider faction or ally ourselves with one, but the risks would be enormous. Our surest course is the one we have pursued ever since the Diem Massacre: We must wait and lurk. We are just a few years short of this world's Information Age. Eventually, we will establish human automation in the Spiders' networks. Eventually they will have a civilization that can restore our ships, and one that we can safely manage. Till then . . . till then, we dare not take any direct action.'

Nau's gaze took in each of the petitioners: Xin, Liao, Fong. Trinli sat a little apart, as if to show that he had tried to dissuade the others. Ezr Vinh was off-Watch, else he would surely be here. They were all troublemakers by Ritser Brughel's measure. Every Watch, their tiny pod here at L1 drifted further and further from the norms of an Emergent community. Part of it was their desperate circumstances, part of it was Qeng Ho assimilation. Even in defeat, the Peddler attitudes were corrosive. Yes, by civilized standards, these people were troublemakers – but they were also the people who, along with Qiwi, made the mission possible.

For a moment no one spoke. Tears leaked silently from Rita Liao's eyes. Hammerfest's microscopic gravity wasn't enough to tug them down her cheeks. Jau Xin's head bowed in submission. 'I understand, Podmaster. We withdraw the petition.'

Nau gave a gracious nod. There would be no punishment, and an important point had been made.

Then Qiwi patted his hand. She was grinning! 'So why not make this a test for what we will do later? True, we can't reveal ourselves, but look at what Jau has done. For the first time, we're really using the Spiders' own intelligence system. Their automation may be twenty years short of an Information Age, but they are pushing computers even harder than in Earth's Dawn Age. Eventually, Anne's translators will be inserting information back into their systems, why not start now? Each year we should do a little more meddling and a little more experimentation.'

Hope shone in Xin's eyes, but his words were still in retreat. 'But are they that far along? These creatures just launched their first satellite last year. They don't have pervasive localizer nets – or any localizer nets at all. Except for that pitiful link from Princeton to Lands Command, they don't even have a computer net. How can we get information back into their system?'

Yes, how?

But Qiwi was still smiling. It made her look so young, almost like the first years that he'd had her. 'You said that the Accord has intercepted Kindred comm related to the kidnapping?'

'Sure. That's how *we* know what's going on. But Accord Intelligence can't break the Kindred crypto.'

'Are they trying to break the intercepts?'

'Yes. They have several of their largest computers – big as houses – flailing away at both ends of the Princeton/Lands Command microwave link. It would take them millions of years to come on the right decryption key . . . Oh.' Xin's eyes got even wider. 'Can we do that without them twigging?'

Nau got the point at almost the same moment. He asked the air: 'Background: How are they generating test keys?'

After a second, a voice replied, 'A pseudo-random walk, modified by what their mathematicians know about the Kindred's algorithms.'

Qiwi was reading something in her huds. 'Apparently the Accord is experimenting with distributed computation across the link. That's frivolous, since there are less than ten computers on their entire net. But we have a dozen snoopersats that pass across the lines of sight of their microwave link. It would be easy to mung up what's going between their relays – that's how we were going to do our first inserts, anyway. In this case, we'll just make small changes when they are sending trial keys. It might be as few as a hundred bits, even counting the framing.'

Reynolt: 'Okay. Even if they investigate later, it would be a plausible glitch. Do it for more than one key, and I say it's too dangerous.'

'One key would be enough, if it's for the right session.'

Qiwi looked at Nau. 'Tomas, it could work. It's low-risk, and we should be experimenting with active measures any way. You know the Spiders are more and more interested in space activities. We may be forced to meddle a lot, fairly soon.' She patted his shoulder, cajoling more publicly than ever before. No matter how cheerful she seemed, Qiwi had her own emotional stake in this.

But she's right. This could be the ideal first sending for Anne's zipheads. Time to be grandly generous. Nau smiled back. 'Very well, ladies and gentlemen. You have convinced me. Anne, arrange to reveal one key. I think Manager Xin can show you the critical session. Give this operation first transient priority for the next forty Ksec – and retroactively for the last forty.' So Xin and Liao and the others were officially off the hook.

They didn't cheer, but Nau sensed enthusiasm and abject gratitude as the petitioners stood and floated out of the room.

Qiwi started to follow them, then turned quickly back and kissed Nau on the forehead. 'Thanks, Tomas.' And then she was gone with the others.

He turned to the only remaining visitor, Kal Omo. 'Keep an eye on them, Sergeant. I'm afraid things will be more complicated from now on.'

During the Great War, there had been times when Hrunkner Unnerby had gone without sleep for days at a time, under fire all the while. This single night was worse. God only knew how bad it was for the General and Sherkaner. Once the phone lines were in place, Unnerby spent most of his time in the joint command post, just down the hall from the Accord-secure room. He worked with the local cops and Underville's comm team, trying to track the rumors around town. The General had been in and out, the picture of composed intensity. But Unnerby could tell that his old boss was over the edge. She was managing too much, involving herself at low levels and high. Hell, she'd been gone now for three hours, off with one of the field teams.

Once, he went out to check on Underhill. Sherk was holed up in the signals lab, right below the top of the hill. Guilt lay like a blight on him, dimming the happy spirit of genius he used to bring to every problem. But the cobber was trying, substituting obsession for buoyant enthusiasm. He was pounding away with his computers, coopting everything he could. Whatever he was doing, it looked like nonsense to Unnerby.

'It's math, not engineering, Hrunk.'

'Yeah, number theory.' This from the scruffy-looking postdoc whose lab this was. 'We're listening for . . .' He leaned forward, apparently lost in the mysteries of his own programming. 'We're trying to break the crypto intercepts.'

Apparently he was talking about the signal fragments that had been detected coming out of the Princeton area just after the abduction. Unnerby said, 'But we don't even know if that's from the kidnappers.' *And if I were the Kindred, I'd be using one-time code words, not some keyed encryption.*

Jaybert what's-his-name just shrugged and continued with his work. Sherkaner didn't say anything either, but his aspect was desolate. This was the best he could do.

So Unnerby had fled back to the joint command post, where there was at least the illusion of progress.

Smith was back about an hour after sunrise. She looked through the negative reports quickly, a nervous edge to her movements. 'I left Belga downtown with the local cops. Damnation, her comm isn't much better than the locals'.'

Unnerby rubbed his eyes, trying vainly to put a polish there that only a good sleep could accomplish. 'I fear Colonel Underville doesn't really like all this fancy equipment.' In any other generation, Belga would have been fine. In this one – well, Belga Underville was not the only person having trouble with the grand new era.

Victory Smith slid down next to her old sergeant. 'But she has kept the press off our backs. What word from Rachner?'

'He's down in the Accord-secure center.' In fact, the young major did not confide in Unnerby.

'He's so sure this is a pure Kindred operation. I don't know. They are in on it . . . but, you know the museum clerk is a trad? And the cobber working the museum's loading dock has disappeared. Belga's discovered he's a traditionalist, too. I think the local trads are in this up to their shoulders.' Her voice was mild, almost contemplative. Later, much too much later, Hrunkner would remember back: The General's voice was mild, but she sat with every limb tensed.

Unfortunately, Hrunkner Unnerby was lost in his own world. All night long he had watched the reports, and stared out into the windy dark. All night long he had prayed to the coldest depths of the earth, prayed for Little Victory, Gokna, Brent, and Jirlib. He spoke sadly, almost to himself. 'I watched them grow into real people, cobblies that anyone could love. They do have souls.'

'What do you mean?' The sharpness in Victory's voice didn't penetrate his fatigue. He had years afterward to think back on this conversation, this single moment, to imagine the ways he might have avoided disaster. But the present did not feel the desperate gaze of the future, and he blundered on: 'It's not their fault that they were brought into the world out-of-phase.'

'It's not their fault my slippery modern ideals have killed them?' Smith's voice was a cutting hiss, something that even sorrow and fatigue could not block from Unnerby's attention. He saw that his General was trembling.

'No, I—' But it was finally, irrevocably too late.

Smith was on her feet. She flicked a single long arm across his head, whiplike. *'Get out!'*

Unnerby staggered back. His right side vision was a coruscating ray of plaid agony. In all other directions, he saw officers and noncoms caught with aspects of shocked surprise.

Smith advanced on him. 'Trad! Traitor!' Her hands jabbed with each word, killing blows just barely restrained. 'For years you've pretended to be a friend, but always sneering and hating us. Enough!' She stopped her relentless approach, and brought her arms back to her sides. And Hrunkner knew she had capped her rage, and what she said now was cold and calm and considered . . . and it hurt even more than the wound across his eyes. 'Take your moral baggage and go. Now.'

Her aspect was something he had seen once or twice before, during the Great War, when their backs were against the wall and still she had not yielded. There would be no argument, no relenting. Unnerby lowered his head, choked on words he was desperate to say. *I'm sorry. I meant no harm. I love your children.* But it was too late for words to change anything. Hrunkner turned, walked quickly past the shocked and silent staff and out the door.

When Rachner Thract heard that Smith was back in the building, he hightailed it down to the joint command post. That's where he should have been during the night, *except I'll be damned if I let my crypto get exposed to the domestic branch and the local police.* The separate operation had worked, thank goodness. He had hard information for the chief.

He ran into Hrunkner Unnerby going the other way. The old sergeant had lost his usual martinet bearing. He walked unsteadily down the hallway, and there was a long, milky welt across the right side of his head.

He waved at the sergeant. 'You okay?' But Unnerby walked on past him, ignoring Rachner as a beheaded osprech might ignore a farmer. He almost turned to follow the cobber, then remembered his own urgency and continued into the joint command post.

The place was silent as a deepness . . . or a graveyard. Clerks and analysts sat motionless. As Rachner walked across the room toward General Smith, the rattle of work resumed, sounding strangely self-conscious.

Smith was paging through one of the operation logs, just a little too fast to be getting much out of it. She waved him to the perch beside her. 'Underville sees evidence of local involvement, but we still don't have anything solid.' Her tone was casual, belying or ignoring the astounded silence of a moment before. 'Have you got anything new? Any reaction from our Kindred "friends"?'

'Lots of reaction, Chief. Even the superficial stuff is intriguing. About an hour after the kidnap story broke, the Kindred turned up the volume on their propaganda – especially the stuff aimed at the poorer nation-states. The spew is "murder after Dark" fearmongering, but more intense than usual. They're saying that the kidnapping is the desperate act of decent people, people who realize that non-trad elements have taken over the Accord . . .'

Everything was getting quiet again. Victory Smith spoke, a little sharply. 'Yes, I know what they say. This is how I'd expect them to react to the kidnappings.'

Maybe he should have begun with the big news. 'Yes, ma'am, though they did respond a bit too quickly. Our usual sources hadn't heard about this beforehand, but now – well, it's beginning to look like the kidnappings are just a symptom that the Extreme Measures faction has achieved decisive control within the Kindred. In fact, at least five of the Deepest were executed yesterday, "moderates" like Klingtram and Sangst, and – alas – incompetents like Droobi. What's left is clever and even more risk-attracted than before—'

Smith leaned back, startled. 'I – see.'

'We haven't known for more than half an hour, ma'am. I've got all the area analysts on it. We see no related military developments.'

For the first time, he seemed to have her full attention. 'That makes sense. We're years away from the point where a war would benefit them.'

'Right, Chief. Not war, not now. The Kindred grand strategy must still be to wear down the developed world as far as possible before the Dark, and then fight whoever is still awake . . . Ma'am, we also have less certain information.' Rumors, except that one of his deep-cover agents had died to get them out. 'It looks like Pedure is now the Kindred's head of external ops. You remember Pedure. We thought she was a low-level operator. Apparently she is smarter and more bloody-handed than we guessed. She's probably responsible for this coup. She may be first among the new Deepest. In any case, she's convinced them that you and, more particularly, Sherkaner Underhill are the key to the Accord's strategic successes. Assassinating you would be very difficult, and you've protected your husband almost as well. Kidnapping your children opens a—'

The General's hands tapped a staccato on the situation table. 'Keep talking, Major.'

Pretend we're talking about somebody else's cobblies. 'Chief, Sherkaner Underhill has talked often enough about his feelings on the radio, how much he values each child. What I'm getting now' – from the agent who had blown cover to get the word out – 'is that Pedure sees almost no downside to grabbing your children, and any number of advantages. At best she hoped to get all of your children out of the Accord, and then quietly play with you and your husband over a period of – years, perhaps. She figures that you could not continue in your present job with that sort of side conflict.'

Smith began, 'If they were killed one by one, pieces of them sent back to us . . .' Her voice faded. 'You're right about Pedure. She would understand how things work with Sherkaner and me. Okay, I want you and Belga to—'

One of the desk phones chattered, an in-building direct line. Victory Smith flicked a pair of long arms across the table and grabbed the handset. 'Smith.'

She listened for a moment, then whistled softly. 'They *what*? But . . . Okay, Sherkaner, I believe you. Yes, Jaybert was right to pass it on to Underville.'

She rang off, and said to Thract, 'Sherkaner's found the key. He's deciphered last night's radio intercepts. It looks like the cobblies are being held in the Plaza Spar, downtown.'

Now the phone by Thract went off. He stabbed the Public On hole, and said, 'Thract here.'

Belga Underville's voice sounded faint and off-mike: 'They have? Well, shut them up!' Then louder: 'Listen, Thract? I've got my hands full down here. Now I get a call from your techie-freaks saying the victims are being held on the top floor of the Plaza Spar. Are you cobbers for real?'

Thract: 'They're not my techs. It's important intelligence, Colonel, wherever it came from.'

'Damn, I already had a real lead. The city police spotted a silk banner snagged on the Bank of Princeton tower.' That was about half a mile from the Plaza Spar. 'It was the jacket fabric that Downing described to us.'

Smith leaned close to the mike, and said, 'Belga, was there anything attached? A note?'

There was an instant's hesitation, and Thract could imagine Belga Underville getting her temper under control. Belga didn't mind complaining to her fellows about all the 'bloody stupid technology,' but not with Smith on the line.

'No, Chief. It was pretty well shredded. Look. The techs could be right about the Plaza Spar, but that's a busy place. I'll send a team to the lower floors, pretending to be customers. But—'

'Good. No alarms; get in close.'

'Chief, I think the tower where we found the banner is a better bet. It's mostly vacant, and—'

'Fine. Go after both.'

'Yes, ma'am. The problem is the city police. They went off on their own, sirens, everything.'

Last night, Victory Smith had lectured Thract on the power of local police. But that power was economic, and political. Just now she said, 'They have? Well, shut them up! I'll take responsibility.'

She waved to Thract. 'We're going downtown.'

31

Shynkrette paced about her 'command post.' Talk about luck. This mission had been designed as a hundred-day lurk-and-pounce. Instead, they'd bagged their targets less than ten days after insertion. The whole op had been an incredible combination of happenstance and screwup. So what else was new? Promotions came from pulling success out of real-world situations, and Shynkrette had survived worse than this. Barker and Fremm getting squashed had been bad luck and inattention. Maybe the worst mistake had been leaving the witnesses – at least it was the worst mistake that could be laid on her own back. On the other hand they had six children, at least four of them the targets. The getaway from the museum had been smooth, but the airport pickup fell through. The Accord's local security was just a little too quick – maybe again because of those surviving witnesses.

This office space ringed the Plaza Spar, twenty-five stories up. It gave an excellent view of city activity, except directly below. In one sense, they were completely trapped here – who had ever hidden by sticking themselves up in the sky? In another sense – Shynkrette paused behind her team sergeant. 'What does Trivelle say, Denni?'

The sergeant lifted the phone from his head. 'Ground-floor lobby is about average busy. He has some. Business visitors. An old coot and some last-generation cobbers. They want to rent office space.'

'Okay. They can look at the third-floor suites. If they want to look at anything else, they can come back tomorrow.' Tomorrow, Deep willing, Shynkrette and her team would be long gone. They would have been gone last night, if not for the storm. Kindred Special Operations could do things with helicopters that the Accord military had never imagined . . . If good luck and competence held another day or two, her team would be back home with their prize. The Kindred book of doctrine had always been big on assassinations and decapitating strikes. With this op, the Honored Pedure was writing a new and experimental chapter. Deep, what Pedure would do with those six children. Shynkrette's mind shied away from the thought. She had been in Pedure's inner circle ever since the Great War, and her fortunes had risen accordingly. But she much preferred doing the Honored's fieldwork to being with her in the Kindred torture chambers. Things could get so easily . . . turned around . . . in the chambers. And death could be so slow there.

Shynkrette moved from quarter to quarter, scanning the streets with a reflecting magnifier . . . Damn, a police convoy, emergency lights blinking. She recognized the special gear on those trucks. This was the police 'heavy weapons' team. Their great success lay in scaring criminals into surrender. The lights – and the sirens she would surely start hearing in a minute – were all part of the intimidation. In this case, the police had made a very large mistake. Shynkrette was already running back around the ring of offices, pulling her little shotgun off her back as she ran.

'Team Sergeant! We're going upstairs.'

Denni raised his head in surprise. 'Trivelle says he hears sirens, but they don't seem to be coming this way.'

A coincidence? Maybe the police had someone else they wanted to wave their guns at? Shynkrette balanced in a rare moment of indecision. Denni held up a hand, continued, 'But he says he thinks three of the oldsters have left the sales' tour, maybe gone to the washroom.'

So much for indecision; Shynkrette waved the sergeant to his feet. 'Tell Trivelle to melt away,' *if he can*. 'We're into Alt Five.' There was always an Alternative Plan; that was a grim joke in Special Operations. They had had some warning. Very likely they could get out of the building, melt into the sea of civilians. Corporal Trivelle had less of a chance, but he knew so little it wouldn't matter. The mission would not end up an embarrassment. If they took care of one last piece of business, it might even be counted a partial success.

As they raced up the central stairs, Denni was pulling down his own shotgun and combat knife. Success in Alt 5 meant taking a few minutes for a little detour, long enough to kill the children. Long enough so it would look really messy. Pedure apparently thought that would screw someone's head on the Accord side. It sounded nuts to Shynkrette, but she didn't know all the facts. It didn't matter. At the end of the war, she had helped massacre a sleeping deepness. Nothing could be uglier than that, but the stolen hoards had financed the Kindred's resurgence.

Hell, she was probably doing these children a favor, now they would miss their date with Honored Pedure.

Through most of the morning, Brent had lain flat on the metal floor. He looked as discouraged as Viki and Gokna felt. Jirlib at least had his hands full trying to comfort the two babies. The little ones were totally and loudly unhappy now, and wouldn't have anything to do with the sisters. The last time anyone had been fed was the previous afternoon.

There wasn't even much left to conspire about. By morning twilight, it had been obvious that their rescue flag was gone. A second attempt tore loose in less than thirty minutes. After that Gokna and Viki spent three hours wrapping the play twine in intricate patterns through the pipe stubs above the room's only entrance. Brent had been a real help with that – he was so good with knots and patterns. If anyone unfriendly came through that door, they would get a mawful of unpleasantness. But if their visitors were armed, how could it be enough? At that question, Brent had retreated from their arguments, gone to splay himself out on the cold floor.

Above them, a narrow square of sunlight crept foot by foot across the high walls of their prison. It must be almost noon. 'I hear sirens,' Brent said abruptly, after an hour of silent sitting. 'Lie down close and listen.'

Gokna and Viki did. Jirlib shushed the babies, for what that was worth. 'Yeah, I hear them.'

'Those are *police* sirens, Viki. Feel the *thump, thump?*'

Gokna jumped up, was already racing for the doorway.

Viki stayed on the floor a moment longer. 'Be *quiet*, Gokna!'

And even the babies were quiet. There were other sounds: the heavy thrum of fans somewhere lower in the building, the street noise that they had heard before . . . but now the staccato sound of many feet, running up steps.

'That's close,' said Brent.

'Th-they're coming for us.'

'Yes.' Brent paused, in his usual dull way. 'And I hear others coming, quieter or farther away.'

It didn't matter. Viki ran to the doorway, hoisted herself up after Gokna. What they planned was pretty pitiful, but the worst and the best of it was that they didn't have any other choice. Earlier, Jirlib had argued that he was bigger, that he should swing down from above. Yeah, but he was only one target and someone had to keep the babies out of the line of fire. So now Gokna and Viki stood against the wall, five feet above the doorway on either side, bracing themselves against Brent's clever ropework.

Brent rose, ran to the right side of the doorway. Jirlib stood well off to the side. He held the children tight in his arms, and didn't try to quiet them anymore. But now, suddenly, they were quiet. Maybe they understood. Maybe it was something instinctive.

Through the wall, Viki could feel the running steps now. Two people. One said something low to the other. She couldn't hear the words but she recognized the leader of the kidnappers. A key rattled in the lock. On the floor to her left, Jirlib gently set the babies down behind him. They stayed quiet, totally still – and Jirlib turned back to the door, ready to pounce. Viki and Gokna crouched lower against the wall. They had twisted all the leverage they dared out of the twine. A final look passed between the two.

They had gotten the others into this mess. They had risked the life of an innocent bystander to try to get out. Now it was time for payback.

The door slid open, metal slipping across metal. Brent tensed for a leap. 'Please don't hurt me,' he said, his voice the same sullen monotone as always. Brent couldn't act to save his soul, yet in a weird way that tone sounded like someone scared into abject mindlessness.

'No one's going to hurt you. We want to move you someplace better, and get you some food. Come on out.' The boss kidnapper sounded as reasonable as always. 'Come on out,' a bit more sharply. Did she think she could bag them all without even mussing her jacket? There was quiet for a second or two . . . Viki heard a faint sigh of irritation. There was a rush of motion.

Gokna and Viki dived as hard as they could. They were only five feet up. Without the twine, they would have crushed their skulls on the floor. Instead, the elastic snapped them back, heads down, through the open doorway.

Gunfire flashed sideways, seeking Brent's voice.

Viki had a glimpse of head and arms, and some kind of gun. She smashed into the leader at the rear of her back, knocking her flat, sending her gun skittering across the floor. But the other cobber was a couple of feet behind. Gokna hit him in the hard of his shoulders, scrabbled to hold on. But the other bounced her off. A single burst of fire from his gun smashed Gokna's middle. Shards and blood spattered the wall behind her.

And then Brent was upon him.

The one under Viki bucked upward, smashing her into the top of the doorway. Things got very dark and distant after that. Somewhere she heard more gunfire, other voices.

32

Viki wasn't badly hurt, a small amount of internal bleeding that the doctors could easily control. Jirlib had taken a lot of dents and some twisted arms. Poor Brent was worse off.

When that strange Major Thract was done asking his questions, Viki and Jirlib visited Brent in the house infirmary. Daddy was already there, perched beside the bed. They had been free almost three hours; Daddy still looked stunned.

Brent lay in deep padding, a siphon of water within reach of his eating hands. He tilted his head as they came in, and waved a weak smile. 'I'm okay.' Just two split legs and a couple of buckshot holes.

Jirlib patted his shoulders.

'Where's Mother?' asked Viki.

Dad's head swayed uncertainly, 'She's in the building. She promised she'll see you this evening. It's just that so much has happened. You know this wasn't just some crazy people who did this, right?'

Viki nodded. There were more security types in the house than ever before and even some uniformed troops outside. Major Thract's people had been full of questions about the kidnappers, their mannerisms, how they acted toward each other, their choice of words. They even tried to hypnotize Viki, to squeeze out every last driblet of recollection. She could have saved them the trouble. Viki and Gokna had tried for years to hypnotize each other without any success.

Not a single kidnapper had survived the capture; Thract implied that at least one had killed herself to avoid capture.

'The General needs to figure out who is behind this, and how it changes the way the Accord looks at its enemies.'

'It was the Kindred,' Viki said flatly. She truly had no evidence beyond the military bearing of the kidnappers. But Viki read the newspapers as much as anyone, and Daddy talked enough about the risks of conquering the Dark.

Underhill shrugged at her assertion. 'Probably. The main thing for the family is that things have changed.'

'Yes.' Viki's voice cracked. '*Daddy!* Of course things have changed; how can they ever be the same?'

Jirlib lowered his head till it rested limply on Brent's perch.

Underhill seemed to shrink in on himself. 'Children, I am so sorry. I never meant for you to be hurt. I didn't mean for . . .'

'Daddy, it was Gokna 'n' me who snuck out of the house – Be quiet, Jirlib. I know you are the oldest, but we could always tweak you around.' It was true. Sometimes the sisters used their brother's ego, sometimes his intellectual interests – as with the Distort exhibit. Sometimes they simply traded on his fondness for his little sisters. And Brent had his own set of weaknesses. 'It was Gokna and me who made this possible. Without Brent doing his ambush at the museum, we'd all be dead now.'

Underhill gestured no. 'Oh, Little Victory, without you and Gokna the rescuers would have been a minute too late. You would all be dead. Gokna—'

'*But now Gokna is dead!*' Suddenly her armor of unfeeling was broken, and she was swept away. Viki shrieked without words and raced from the room. She fled down the hall to the central stairs, weaving round the uniforms and the everyday inhabitants of the house. A few arms reached out for her, but someone called out from behind, and she was let past.

Up and up Viki ran, past the labs and the classrooms, past the atrium where they always played, where they first met Hrunkner Unnerby.

At the summit was the little gabled attic that she and Gokna had demanded and pleaded and schemed for. Some like the deepest and some like the highest. Daddy always reached for the highest and his two daughters had loved to look down from their lofty perch. It wasn't the highest place in Princeton, but it had been enough.

Viki ran inside, slammed the door. For an instant, she was a little dizzy from the nonstop climb. And then . . . She froze, staring all around her. There was the attercop house, grown huge over the last five years. As the winters got colder, it had lost its original charm; you couldn't pretend the little critters were people when they started sprouting wings. Dozens of them flittered in and out of the feeders. The ultra and blue of their wings was almost like a wallboard design on the sides of the house. She and Gokna had argued endlessly over who was the mistress of that house.

They had argued about almost everything. There by the wall was the artillery-shell dollhouse that Gokna had brought up from the den. It really had been Gokna's, yet still they argued about it.

The signs of Gokna were everywhere, here. And Gokna would never be here again. They could never talk again, not even to argue. Viki almost turned and bolted back out of the room. It was as though a monstrous hole had been torn in her side, her arms and legs ripped from her body. There was nowhere left for her life to stand. Viki sank down in a pile, shivering.

Fathers and mothers were very different sorts of people. From what the children had been able to figure, some of this was true even for normal families. Dad was around all the time. He was the one who had infinite patience, the one they could usually wheedle extra favors from. But Sherkaner Underhill had his own special nature, surely not the usual: He regarded every rule of nature and culture as an obstacle to be thought about, experimented with. There was humor and cleverness in everything he did.

Mothers – their mother, anyway – was not around every minute, and could not be depended upon to buckle to every childish demand. General Victory Smith was with her children often enough, one day out of ten up in Princeton, and much more so when they went on trips down to Lands Command. She was there when real rules had to be laid down, ones that even Sherkaner Underhill might hesitate to bend. And she was there when you had really, really screwed up.

Viki didn't know how long she had been lying in a huddle when she heard steps ticking up the stairs to her room. Surely not more than half an hour; beyond the windows, it was still the middle of a cool, beautiful afternoon.

There was soft tapping at her door. 'Junior? Can we talk?' *Mother*.

Something strange stirred in Viki: welcome. Daddy could forgive, he always forgave . . . but Mother would understand how terrible she really had been.

Viki opened the door, stepped back with her head bowed. 'I thought you were busy until tonight.' Then she noticed that Victory Smith was in uniform, the black-black jacket and sleeves, the ultra and red shoulder tabs.

She had never seen the General in that uniform up here in Princeton, and even down in Lands Command it had been reserved for special times, for briefings given to certain superiors.

The General stepped quietly into the room. 'I – decided this was more important.' She motioned Little Victory to sit beside her. Viki sat, feeling calmness for the first time since this all began. Two of the General's forearms draped lightly across her shoulders. 'There have been some serious . . . mistakes made. You know that both your father and I agree about that?'

Viki nodded. 'Yes, yes!'

'We can never bring Gokna back. But we can remember her, and love her, and correct the mistakes that allowed this terrible thing to happen.'

'Yes!'

'Your father – I – thought we should keep you out of the larger problems, at least until you were grown. Up to a point, we were right perhaps. But now I see, we put you at terrible risk.'

'No! . . . Mother, don't you understand? It was me, a-and Gokna, who broke the rules. We fooled Captain Downing. We just didn't believe the things that Dad and you warned us about.'

The General's arms tapped Viki's shoulders lightly. Mother was either, surprised, or suddenly angry. Viki couldn't tell which, and for a long moment her mother was silent. Then, 'You're right. Sherkaner and I made mistakes . . . but so did you and Gokna. Neither of you meant any harm . . . but now you know that's not enough. In some games, when you make mistakes, people get killed. But think about it, Victory. Once you saw things turned bad, you behaved very well – better than many cobbers with professional training would have done. You saved the lives of the Suabisme children—'

'We risked little Birbop to—'

Smith shrugged angrily. 'Yes. You'll find a hard lesson there, daughter. I've spent most of my life trying to live with that one.' She was silent again, and something about her seemed very far away. It suddenly occurred to Viki that indeed, even Mother must make mistakes; it wasn't just courtesy that she said so. All their lives, the children had admired the General. She didn't talk about what she did, but they knew enough to guess she was more than the heroine of any dozen adventure novels. Now Viki had a glimpse of what that must really mean. She moved closer to her mother's side.

'Viki, when the crunch finally came, you and Gokna did what was right. All four of you did. There was a terrible price, but if we – you – don't learn from that, then we've really screwed up.' *Then Gokna died for nothing.*

'I'll change; I'll do anything. Tell me.'

'The outside changes aren't so big. I'll get you some tutors in military topics, maybe some physical training. But you and the younger children still have so much book learning to do. Your time will be pretty much as before.

The big change will be inside your head and in the way we treat you. Beyond the learning, there are enormous, deadly risks that you must understand. Hopefully, they'll never be the minute-to-minute deadliness of this morning – but in the long run the dangers are much greater. I'm sorry, this is a time more risky than any before.'

'And with more good possibilities, too.' Daddy always said that. What would the General say to that now?

'Yes. That is true. And that is why he and I have done what we have. But it will take more than hope and optimism to achieve what Sherkaner intends, and the years until then will be more and more dangerous. What happened today is just the beginning. It's possible that the deadliest times will come when I'm very old. And your father is a half generation older than I . . .

'I said you four did well today. More than that, you were a team. Have you ever thought that our whole family is like a team? We have a special advantage over almost anyone else: We're not all of a single generation, or even two. We're spread from Little Hrunk all the way up to your father. We're loyal to one another. And I think we're very talented.'

Viki smiled back at her mother. 'None of us is near as smart as Daddy.'

Victory laughed. 'Yes, well. Sherkaner is . . . unique.'

Viki continued, analytical: 'Actually, except for maybe Jirlib, none of us is even in a class with Daddy's students. On the other hand, me and G-Gokna, we took after you, Mom. We – I can plan with people and with things. I think Rhapsa and Little Hrunk are somewhere in between, once they settle down. And Brent, he's not stupid, but his mind works in funny ways. He doesn't get along with other people, but he's the most naturally suspicious of any of us. He's always watching out for us.'

The General smiled. 'He'll do. There's five of you left now, Viki. Seven when you count myself and Sherkaner. The team. You're right in your estimates. What you can't know is how you compare to the rest of the world. Let me tell you my coldly professional assessment: You children can be the best. We wanted to postpone starting things a few more years for you, but that has changed. If the times I fear come, I want you five to know what is going on. If necessary, I want you five to be able to act even if everyone else is in a mess.'

Victory Junior was more than old enough to understand about service oaths and chains of command. 'Everyone? I—' She pointed at the rank tabs on her mother's shoulders.

'Yes, I live by my loyalty to the Crown. I'm saying that there may come times when – in the short term – serving the Crown means doing things outside the visible chain of command.' She smiled at her daughter. 'Some of the adventure novels are right, Viki. The head of Accord Intelligence does have her own special authority . . . Oops, I have postponed my other meetings long enough. We will talk again, very soon, all of us.'

After the General was gone, Viki wandered around her little bedroom at the top of the hill. She was still in a daze, but no longer felt unrelieved horror. There was also wonder and hope. She and Gokna had always played at espionage. But Mother didn't talk of what she did, and she was so far above the military of everyday that it seemed a foolish dream to try to follow her. Business intelligence, maybe with companies like Hrunkner Unnerby had founded, that seemed more realistic. Now—

Viki played with Gokna's little dollhouse for a moment. She and Gokna would never get to argue about these plans. Mother's team had suffered its first loss. But now it knew it was a team: Jirlib and Brent, Rhapsa, Little Hrunk, Viki, Victory and Sherkaner. They would learn to do their best. *And in the end, that will be enough.*

33

For Ezr Vinh, the years passed quickly, and not just because of his quarter-time Watch cycle. The time since the ambush and the murders was almost a third of his life. These were the years his inner self had promised would be played out with unswerving patience, never giving up the struggle to destroy Tomas Nau and win back what still survived. It was a time he had thought would stretch into endless torment.

Yes. He had played with unswerving patience. And there had been pain . . . and shame. Yet his fear was most times a distant thing. And though he still didn't know the details, just knowing that he was working for Pham Nuwen gave Ezr the sure feeling that in the end they would triumph. But the biggest surprise was something that popped up again and again for uneasy introspection: In some ways, these years were more satisfying than any time since early childhood. Why was that?

Podmaster Nau made thrifty use of the remaining medical automation, and he kept critical 'functions' such as translators on-Watch much of the time. Trixia was in her forties now. Ezr saw her almost every day he was on-Watch, and the little changes in her face tore at him.

But there were other changes in Trixia, changes that made him think that his presence and the passing years were somehow bringing her back to him.

When he came early to her tiny cell in Hammerfest's Attic, she would still ignore him. But then once, he arrived one hundred seconds after the usual time. Trixia was sitting facing the door. 'You're late,' she said. Her tone was the same flat impatience that Anne Reynolt might use. All the Focused were notorious about punctilio. Still. Trixia had noticed his absence.

And he noticed that Trixia was beginning to do some of her own grooming. Her hair was brushed back, almost neatly, when he arrived for their sessions. Now, as often as not, their conversations were not completely one-sided . . . at least if he was careful about the topics.

This day, Ezr entered her cell on time, but with some smuggled cargo – two delitesse cakelets from Benny's parlor. 'For you.' He reached out, bringing one cakelet close to her. The fragrance filled the cell. Trixia stared at his hand, briefly, as if contemplating a rude gesture. Then she waved the distraction away. 'You were going to bring the Cur-plus-One translation requests.'

Sigh. But he left the confection tacked to the workspace near her hand. 'Yes, I have them.' Ezr settled in his usual spot by the door, facing her. Actually, the list wasn't long today. Focus could work miracles, but without a glue of normal common sense, the different specialist groups wandered off into private navel inspection. Ezr and the other normals read summaries of the Focused work and tried to see where each group of specialists had found something that was of interest beyond the zipheads' fixation. Those were reported upward, to Nau, and back downward, as requests for additional work.

Today, Trixia had no trouble accommodating the requests, though she muttered darkly at some of them, 'Waste of time.'

'Also, I've been talking to Rita Liao. Her programmers are very enthusiastic about the stuff you've been giving them. They've designed a suite of financial applications and network software that should run great on the Spiders' new microprocessors.'

Trixia was nodding. 'Yes, yes. I talk to them every day.' The translators got along famously with the low-code programmers and the financial/legal zipheads. Ezr suspected it was because the translators were ignorant of those fields, and vice versa.

'Rita wants to set up a groundside company to market the programs. They should beat anything local, and we want saturation.'

'Yes, yes. Prosperity Software Incorporated; I already invented a name. But it's still too early.'

He chatted it back and forth with her, trying to get a realistic time estimate to pass on to Rita Liao. Trixia was on a co-thread with the zipheads who were doing the insertion strategy, so their combined opinion was probably pretty good. Doing everything across a computer network – even with perfect knowledge and planning – depended on the sophistication of that net. It would be at least five years before a big commercial market developed in software, and a little longer before the Spiders' public networks took off. Until then, it would be next to impossible to be a major groundside player. Even now, the only manipulations they could do consistently were of the Accord's military net.

Too soon, Ezr came to the last item on his list. It might seem a small thing, but from long experience he knew it was trouble. 'New topic, Trixia

– but it's a real translation question: about the color "plaid." I notice you are still using that term in descriptions of visual scenes. The physiologist—'

'Kakto.' Trixia's eyes narrowed slightly. Where the zipheads interacted, there was normally an almost telepathic closeness – or else they hated each other's guts with the sort of freezing hostility usually seen only in academic romance novels. Norm Kakto and Trixia oscillated between these states.

'Yes. Um, anyway, Dr Kakto gave me a long lecture about the nature of vision and the electromagnetic spectrum and assured me that talking about a color "plaid" could not correspond to anything meaningful.'

Trixia's features screwed into a frown, and for a moment she looked much older than Ezr liked to see. 'It's a real word. I chose it. The context had a feel—' The frown intensified. More often than not what seemed a translation mistake turned out to be – perhaps not a literal truth, but at least a clue to some unrecognized aspect of the Spiders' reality. But the Focused translators, even Trixia, could be wrong. In her early translations, where she and the others were still feeling their way across an unknown racial landscape – there had been hundreds of facile word choices; a good portion of them had to be abandoned later.

The problem was that zipheads did not take easily to abandoning fixation.

Trixia was coming close to real upset. The signs were not extreme. She often frowned, though not this fiercely. And even when she was silent, she was endlessly active with her two-handed keyboard. But this time the analysis coming back at her spilled from her head-up display to paint across the walls. Her breath came faster as she turned the criticism back and forth in her mind and on the attached network. She didn't have any counterexplanation.

Ezr reached out, touched her shoulder. 'Follow-up question, Trixia. I talked with Kakto about this "plaid" thing for some time.' In fact, Ezr had all but badgered the man. Often that was the only way that worked with a Focused specialist: Concentrate on the ziphead's specialty and the problem at hand, and keep asking your question in different ways. Without some skill and reasonable luck, the technique would quickly bring communication to an end. Even after seven Watch years, Ezr wasn't an expert, but in this case Norm Kakto had finally been provoked into generating alternatives: 'We were wondering, perhaps the Spiders have such a surplus of visual methods that the Spider brain has to multiplex access – you know, a fraction of a second sensing in one spectral regime, a fraction of a second in another. They might sense – I don't know, some kind of rippling effect.'

In fact, Kakto had dismissed the idea as absurd, saying that even if the Spider brain time-shared on its visual senses, the perception would still seem continuous at the conscious level.

As he spoke the words, Trixia became nearly motionless, only her fingers continuing to move. Her constantly shifting gaze fixed for a long second . . . directly on Ezr's eyes. He was saying something that was nontrivial and near the center of her Focus. Then she looked away, began muttering to her voice input, and pounded even more furiously on the keys. A few seconds passed and her eyes began darting around the room, tracking phantoms that were only visible in her own head-up. Then, abruptly, 'Yes! That is the explanation. I never really thought before . . . it was just the context that made me pick the word, but—' Dates and locations spread across the walls where they could both see. Ezr tried to keep up, but his own huds were still barred from the Hammerfest net; he had to depend on Trixia's vague gestures to know the incidents she was citing.

Ezr found himself grinning. Just now Trixia came about the closest she could to normality, even if it was a kind of frenetic triumph . . . 'Look! Except for one case of pain overload, every use of "plaid" has involved clear air, low humidity, and a wide range of brightness. In those situations, the whole color . . . the *vetmoot3* . . .' She was using internal jargon now, the inscrutable stuff that flowed between the Focused translators. 'The language *mood* is changed. I needed a special word, and "plaid" is good enough.'

He listened and watched. He could almost see the insight spreading within Trixia's mind, setting up new connections, no doubt improving all later translations. Yes, it looked real. The jackboots could not complain about the color 'plaid.'

It was altogether a good session. And then Trixia did something that was a wondrous surprise. With scarcely a break in her speech, one hand left her keyboard and snatched sideways at the delitesse. She broke the cakelet free of its anchor and stared into the froth and fragrance – as if suddenly recognizing what the cakelet was and the pleasure that came from eating such things. Then she jammed the thing into her mouth, and the light frosting splashed in colorful drops across her lips. He thought for a moment that she was choking, but the sound was just a happy laugh. She chewed, and swallowed . . . and after a moment she gave the most contented sigh. It was the first time in all these years that Ezr had seen her happy about something outside her Focus.

Even her hands stopped their constant motion for a few seconds. Then, 'So. What else?'

It took a moment for the question to penetrate Ezr's daze. 'Ah, um.' In fact, that had been the last item on his list. But *joy!* The delitesse had made a miracle. 'J-just one thing more, Trixia. Something you should know.' *Maybe something you can finally understand.* 'You are not a machine. You're a human being.'

But the words had no impact. Maybe she didn't even hear them. Her fingers were tapping at her keys again, and her gaze was somewhere in huds imagery he couldn't see. Ezr waited several seconds, but whatever attention there had been seemed to have vanished. He sighed, and moved back to the cell's doorway.

Then perhaps ten or fifteen seconds after he had spoken, Trixia abruptly looked up. There was expression on her face again, but this time it was surprise. 'Really? I'm not a machine?'

'Yes. You are a real person.'

'Oh.' Disinterest again. She returned to her keyboards, muttering on the voice link to her invisible ziphead siblings. Ezr quietly slipped out. In the early years, he would have felt crushed, or at least set back, by the curt dismissal. But . . . this was just ziphead normality. And for a moment he had broken through it. Ezr crawled back through the capillary corridors. Usually these kinking, barely-shoulders-wide passages got on his nerves. Every two meters another cell doorway, right side, top, left side, bottom. What if there was ever a panic here? What if they ever needed to evacuate? But today . . . echoes came back to him, and suddenly he realized he was whistling.

Anne Reynolt intercepted him as he emerged into Hammerfest's main vertical corridor. She jabbed a finger at the carrier trailing behind him. 'I'll take that.'

Damn. He'd intended to leave the second delitesse with Trixia. He gave Reynolt the carrier. 'Things went well. You'll see in my report—'

'Indeed. I think I'll have that report right now.' Reynolt gestured down the hundred-meter drop. She grabbed a wall stop, flipped feet for head, and started downward. Ezr followed. Where they passed openings in the caisson, OnOff's light shone through a thin layer of diamond crystal. And then they were back in artificial light, deeper and deeper in the mass of Diamond One. The mosaic carving looked as fresh as the day it was done, but here and there the hand and foot traffic had laid patches of grime on the fretwork. There weren't many unskilled zipheads left, not enough to maintain Emergent perfection. They turned sideways at the bottom, still gently descending but coasting past busy offices and labs – all familiar to Ezr now. The ziphead clinic. There, Ezr had been only once. It was closely guarded, closely monitored, but not quite off-limits. Pham was a regular visitor there, Trad Silipan's great friend. But Ezr avoided the place; it was where souls were stolen.

Reynolt's office was where it had always been, at the end of the lab tunnel, behind a plain door. The 'Director of Human Resources' settled in her chair and opened the carrier she had taken from Ezr.

Vinh pretended to be unperturbed. He looked around the office. Nothing new, the same rough walls, the storage crates and seemingly loose equipment that still – after decades on-Watch – were her principal furniture. Even if he had never been told, Ezr would have long since guessed that Anne Reynolt was a ziphead. A miraculous, people-oriented ziphead, but still a ziphead.

Reynolt was obviously not surprised by the contents of the carrier. She sniffed at the delitesse with the expression of a bactry technician assessing slime ferment. 'Very aromatic. Candy and junk food are not on the allowed diet list, Mr Vinh.'

'I'm sorry. I just meant it as a treat . . . a little reward. I don't do it often.'

'True. In fact, you've never done it before.' Her gaze flickered around his face, then moved away. 'It's been thirty years, Mr Vinh. Seven years of your own life-time on-Watch. You know that zipheads do not respond to such "rewards"; their motive system is primarily within their area of Focus and secondarily attached to their owners. No . . . I think you still have your secret plans to waken love in Dr Bonsol.'

'With a dessert confection?'

Reynolt gave him a hard little smile. His sarcasm would have gone right past an ordinary ziphead. It didn't deflect Reynolt, but she recognized it. 'With the smell, perhaps. I imagine you've been into some Qeng Ho neurology courses – found something about olfactory pathways having independent access to the higher centers. Hmm?' For an instant her gaze skewered him like a bug in a collection.

That's exactly what the neuro courses said. And the delitesse was something that Trixia would not have smelled since before she was Focused. For a moment, the walls around Trixia's true self had thinned to barely more than a veil. For a moment, Ezr had touched her.

Ezr shrugged. Reynolt was so very sharp. If she ever thought to look, she was surely bright enough to see all the way through him. She was probably bright enough to see through even Pham Nuwen. The only thing that saved them was that Pham and Ezr were at the edge of her Focus. *If Ritser Brughel had a snoop even half as good, Pham and I would be dead now.*

Reynolt turned away from him, for a moment tracked phantoms in her huds. Then, 'Your misbehavior has caused no harm. In some ways, Focus is a robust state. You may think you see changes in Dr Bonsol, but consider: Over the last few years, all the best translators have begun to show synthetic affect. If it hurts performance, we'll take them down to the clinic for some tuning . . .

'However, if you actively attempt manipulation again, I will keep you out of Dr Bonsol's way.'

It was a totally effective threat, but Ezr tried to laugh. 'What, no death threats?'

'My assessment, Mr Vinh: Your knowledge of Humankind's Dawn Age civilization makes you extremely valuable. You're, an effective interface between at least four of my groups – and I know that the Podmaster uses your advice as well. But make no mistake: I can get along without you in the translation department. If you cross me again, you won't see Dr Bonsol till after the mission is complete.'

Fifteen years? Twenty?

Ezr stared at her, feeling the utter certainty in her words. What an implacable creature this woman was. Not for the first time, he wondered what she had been like before. He was not alone in that. Trud Silipan regaled the patrons at Benny's with the speculations. The Xevalle clique had once been the second most powerful in the Emergency; Trud claimed she had been high in its ranks. At one time she might have been a greater monster than Tomas Nau. At least some of them got punished; crushed by their own kind. Anne Reynolt had fallen far, from being a knowing Satan to being a Satan's tool.

. . . Whether that made her more or less than before, she was dangerous enough for Ezr Vinh.

That night, alone in the dark of his room, Ezr described the encounter to Pham Nuwen. 'I get the feeling that if Reynolt ever transferred to Brughel's operation, she'd figure out about you and me in a matter of Ksecs.'

Nuwen's chuckle was a distorted buzzing sound deep in Ezr's ear. 'That's a transfer that will never happen. She's the only thing that's holding the ziphead operation together. She had a staff of four hundred unFocused interface types before the Ambush – now she's *buzz zzzt*.'

'Say the last again.'

'I said, "Now she's depending for much of her support on untrained help."'

The buzz that was not quite a voice faded in and out of intelligibility. There were still times when Ezr had to ask for three or four repetitions. But it was a big improvement over the blinkertalk they had used in the beginning. Now, when Ezr pretended to go to sleep, he had a single millimeter-long localizer pressed deep in his ear. The result was mostly buzzing and hissing, nearly inaudible, but with enough practice you could normally guess the speech behind it. The localizers were scattered all around the room – all around the Traders' temp. They had become Brughel and Nau's primary security tool here.

'Still, maybe I shouldn't have tried the delitesse trick.'

'. . . Maybe. I wouldn't have tried anything so overt.' *But then Pham Nuwen wasn't in love with Trixia Bonsol.* 'We've talked about this before. Brughel's zipheads are more powerful than any security tool we Qeng Ho ever imagined. They're sniffing all the time, and they can read' – Ezr couldn't make out the word: 'naive'? 'innocent'?; he didn't feel like asking for clarification – 'people like you. Face it. They surely guess that you don't believe their story about the Diem Massacre. They know you're hostile. They know you're scheming – or wishing to scheme – about something. Your feelings for Bonsol give you a cover, a lesser lie to hide the greater one. Like my Zamle Eng thing.'

'Yeah.' *But I think I'll cool it for a while.* 'So you don't think Reynolt is that much of a threat?'

For a moment, all he heard was buzzing and hissing; maybe Pham wasn't saying anything. Then: 'Vinh, I think very much the opposite. In the long run, she's the deadliest threat we face.'

'But she's not in Security.'

'No, but she maintains Brughel's snoops, tweaks up their poor brains when they begin to drift. Phuong and Hom can only do the simpler cases; Trud pretends he can do everything, but he just follows her directions. And she has eight ziphead programmers going through our fleet code. Three of them are still grinding away at the localizers. Eventually, she's going to see how I've scammed them, *bzzz mumble* Lord! The power Nau has.' Pham's voice cut out, and there was just the background noise.

Ezr reached out from his blankets and stuck a finger in his ear, pushing the tiny localizer deeper. 'Say again? Are you still there?'

bzzt 'I'm here. About Reynolt: She's deadly. One way or another, she must be removed.'

'Kill her?' The words caught in Ezr's throat. For all that he hated Nau and Brughel and the whole system of Focus, he didn't hate Anne Reynolt. In her own limited way, she looked after the slaves. Whatever Anne Reynolt had been, now she was just a tool.

'I hope not! Maybe . . . if Nau would just take the bait on the localizers, if he would just start using them in Hammerfest. Then we'd be as safe over there as we are here. If that happens before her zips figure out that it's a trap . . .'

'But the whole point of the delay was to give her time to study the localizers.'

'Yeah. Nau is no fool. Don't worry. I'm tracking things. If she gets too close, I'll . . . take care of her.'

For a moment, Ezr tried to imagine what Pham might do, then forced his mind from the imaginings. Even after two thousand years, the Vinh Family still had a special place in its affection for the memory of Pham Nuwen. Ezr remembered the pictures that had been in his father's den. He remembered the stories his aunt had told him. Not all of them were in the Qeng Ho archives. That meant the stories weren't true – or else they were truly private reminiscences, what G'mama Sura and her children had really thought of Pham Nuwen. They loved him for more than founding the modern Qeng Ho, for more than being g'papa to all the Vinh Families. But some of the stories showed a hard side to the man.

Ezr opened his eyes, looked quietly around the darkened room. Vague night-gleams lit his fatigues floating in the closet sack, showed the delitesse still sitting uneaten on his desk. Reality. 'What can you really do with the localizers, Pham?'

Silence. Faraway buzzing. 'What can I do? Well, Vinh, I can't kill with them . . . not directly. But they are good for more than this crummy audio link. It takes practice; there are tricks you have to see.' Long pause. 'Hell, you need to learn 'em. There could be times when I'm out of link, and

744

they're the only things that can save your cover. We should get together in person—'

'Huh? Face-to-face? How?' Dozens, maybe hundreds of times he and Pham Nuwen had plotted as they did tonight, like prisoners tapping anonymously on dungeon walls. In public, they saw less of each other than in the early Watches. Nuwen had said that Ezr just wasn't good enough at controlling his eyes and body language, that the snoops would guess too much. Now—

'Here in the temp, Brughel and his zipheads are depending on the localizers. There are places 'tween the balloon hulls where some of their old cameras have died. If we run into each other there, they'll have nothing to contradict what I feed them through the localizers. The problem is, I'm sure the snoops rely on statistics as much as anything. Once upon a time I ran a fleet security department, like Ritser's except a bit more mellow. I had programs that highlighted suspicious behavior – who was out of sight when, unusual conversations, equipment failures. It worked pretty well, even when I couldn't catch the bad guys red-handed. Zipheads plus computers should be a thousand times better. I bet they have stat traces extending back to the beginning of L1. For them, innocuous behaviors add up and add up – and one fine day Ritser Brughel has circumstantial evidence. And we're dead.'

Lord of Trade. 'But we could get away with almost anything!' Wherever the Emergents depended on Qeng Ho localizers.

'Maybe. Once. Curb the impulse.' Even in the buzzing speech, Ezr could tell that Pham was chuckling.

'When can we meet?'

'Sometime that minimizes the effect on Ritser's merry analysts. Let's see . . . I'm going off-Watch in less than two hundred Ksec. I'll be partway through a Watch the next time you are on. I'll fix things so we can do it right after that.'

Ezr sighed. *Half a year of lifetime away.* But not as far away as some things; it would do.

34

Benny's booze parlor had begun as something sublegal, the visible evidence of a large network of black-market transactions – capital crimes by Emergent standards; in pure Qeng Ho Nese, the term 'black market' existed, but only to denote 'trade you must do in secret because it offends the local Customers.' In the small community around the rock-pile, there was no way to conduct trade or bribe in secret. During the early years, only Qiwi Lisolet's involvement had protected the parlor. Now . . . Benny Wen smiled to himself as he stacked the drinks and dinners into his weir. Now he managed here full time whenever he was on-Watch. Best of all, it was a job his father could mostly handle when Benny and Gonle were off. Hunte Wen was still a drifty, gentle soul, and he had never regained his competence in physics. But he had come to love managing the parlor. When he managed it alone, strange things could happen to the place. Sometimes they were ludicrous failures, sometimes marvelous improvements. There was the time he cadged a perfumed lacquer from the volatiles refinery. The smell was okay in small quantities, but painted on the parlor's walls, it gave off a terrible stink. For a while the largest dayroom became the social hub of the temp. There was another time – four real years later – when he redeemed a Watch's worth of favor scrip, and Qiwi's papa devised a zero-gee vine and associated ecosystem to decorate the parlor's walls and furniture. The place was transformed into a beautiful, park-like space.

The vines and flowers still remained, even though Hunte had been off-Watch for almost two years.

Benny moved up from the bar, in a long circuit through the forest of greenery. Drinks and food were delivered to tables of customers, paper favors paid in return. Benny set a Diamonds and Ice and a meal bucket in front of Trud Silipan. Silipan slipped him a promise-of-favor with the same smug look as always. He obviously figured the promise counted for nothing, that he only paid off because it was convenient.

Benny just smiled and moved on. Who was he to argue – and in a sense, Trud was right. But since the early Watches, very few favors were ever flatly repudiated. Weaseled, yes. The only favors Trud could really give involved service time with the Focused, and he constantly chiseled on his obligations, not finding quite the right specialists, not spending enough ziphead time to get the best answers. But even Trud came through often enough, as with the zero-gee vines he'd caused Ali Lin to design. For behind the farce of paper favors, everyone knew that there was Tomas Nau, who – from clever self-interest or love of Qiwi – had made it clear that the Qeng Ho underground economy had his protection.

'Hello, Benny! Up here!' Jau Xin waved to him from the upper table, the 'debating society' table. Watch on Watch, the same sort of people seemed to hang out here. There was usually some overlap between Watches – apparently enough so that even when most of the customers were different, they still sat over here if they wanted to argue about 'where it will all end.' This Watch it was Xin and of course Rita Liao, five or six other faces that were no surprise, and – aha, someone who really knew his stuff: 'Ezr! I thought it would be four hundred Ksec before you showed up here.' Damn if he didn't wish he could stay and listen.

'Hi, Benny!' Ezr's face showed the familiar grin. Funny when you didn't see a guy for a while, how the changes from times earlier were suddenly sharp. Ezr – like Benny – was still a young man. But they were no longer kids. There were the faintest creases near Ezr's eyes. And when he spoke, there was a confidence Benny had never seen when they had been on Jimmy

Diem's work crew. 'Nothing solid for me, Benny. My gut is still complaining about being unfrozen. There was a four-day change in schedule.' He pointed at the Watch-tree display on the wall by the bar. Sure enough, the update was there, hidden in a flurry of other small changes. 'Looks like Anne Reynolt has need of my presence.'

Rita Liao smiled. 'That by itself is reason for a meeting of the Debating Society.'

Benny distributed the bulbs and buckets that floated in the weir behind him. He nodded at Ezr. 'I'll get you something to soothe your just-thawed carcass.'

Ezr watched Benny Wen head back to the bar and food prep. Benny probably could find something that wouldn't upset his stomach. Who'd have thought he'd end up like this? Who'd have thought any of them would. At least Benny was still a Trader, even if on a heartbreakingly small scale. *And I'm . . . what?* A conspirator with cover so deep that sometimes it fooled even him. Ezr was sitting here with three Qeng Ho and four Emergents – and some of the Emergents were better friends than the Qeng Ho. No wonder Tomas Nau did so well. He had coopted them all, even as they thought they were following the Traders' Way. Nau had blunted their minds to the slavery that was Focus. And maybe it was for the best. Ezr's friends were protected from the deadliness of Nau and Brughel – and Nau and Brughel were dulled to the possibility that there might be Qeng Ho who still worked against them.

'So what got you out of the freezer early, Ezr?'

Vinh shrugged. 'Beats me. I'm going down to Hammerfest in a few Ksecs.' *Whatever it is, I hope it doesn't mess up my meeting with Pham.*

Trud Silipan rose up through the floor spaces, settled in an empty seat. 'It's no big thing, a snit between the translators and the hard-science zipheads. We got it resolved earlier today.'

'So why did Reynolt change Ezr's schedule?'

Silipan rolled his eyes. 'Ah, you know Reynolt. No offense, Ezr, but she thinks that since your specialty is the Dawn Age, we can't get along without you.'

Hardly, thought Ezr, remembering his last encounter with the Director of Human Resources.

Rita said, 'I'll bet tas something to do with Calorica Bay. The children are down there now, you know.' When Rita spoke of 'the children' she was talking about the Spiders from the old 'Children's Hour of Science.'

'They're not children anymore,' Xin said gently. 'Victory Junior is a young wo – young adult.'

Liao shrugged irritably. 'Rhapsa and Little Hrunk still qualify as children. They've all moved down to Calorica.'

There was an embarrassed pause. The adventures of specific Spiders were an unending drama for many – and as the years passed, it became easier to get more details. There were other families being followed by the Spider fans, but the Underhill one was still the most popular. Rita was easily the biggest fanatic, and sometimes she was just too pathetically obvious.

Trud was oblivious of the sad byplay. 'No, Calorica is a scam.'

Xin laughed. 'Hey, Trud, there really is a launch site just south of Calorica. These Spiders are launching satellites.'

'No, no. I meant to say the *cavorite* thing is a scam. That's what got Ezr rousted early.' He noticed Ezr's reaction and his smirk broadened. 'You recognize the term.'

'Yes, it's—'

Trud rolled on, not interested in classical trivia: 'It's another of the translators' screwball references, just more obscure than most. Anyway, a year ago, some Spiders were using abandoned mines in the altiplano south of Calorica, trying to find a difference between gravitational mass and inertial mass. The whole thing makes you wonder how bright these creatures really are.'

'The idea is not stupid,' said Ezr, 'until you've done. some experiments to see otherwise.' He remembered the project now. It had been mainly Tiefer scientists. Their reports had been nearly inaccessible. The human translators had never learned Tiefic in the depth that they had the Accord languages. Xopi Reung and a couple of others might have become fluent in Tiefic, but they had died in the mindrot runaway.

Trud waved off the objection. 'What's stupid is, these Spiders eventually found a *difference*. And they posted their foolishness, claimed to have discovered antigravity in the altiplano.'

Ezr glanced at Jau Xin. 'Have you heard of this?'

'I think so . . .' Jau looked thoughtful. Apparently this had been kept under wraps until now. 'Reynolt has had me in with the zipheads a couple of times. They wanted to know about any orbital anomalies in our snoopersats.' He shrugged. 'Of course there are anomalies. That's how you do subsurface density maps.'

'Well,' Trud continued, 'the Spiders who did this had about an Msec of fame before they discovered they couldn't reproduce their miraculous discovery. Their retraction came out just a few Ksecs ago.' He chuckled. 'What idiots. In a human civilization, their claim wouldn't have lasted a day.'

'The Spiders are *not* stupid,' said Rita.

'They're not incompetent, either,' said Ezr. 'Sure, most human societies would be very skeptical of such a report. But humans have had eight thousand years of experience with science. Even a fallen civ, if it were advanced enough to study such questions, would have library rains that contained the human heritage.'

'Yeah, right. "Everything the Spiders do is for the first time."'

'But it's true, Trud! We know they're first-timers. We have only one case that's really comparable – our rise upon Old Earth. And there are so many things that human first-timers got wrong.'

'In fact, we're doing them a big favor by taking over.' That from Arlo Dinh, a Qeng Ho. He made the assertion with all the moral smugness of an Emergent.

Ezr nodded reluctantly. 'Yeah, our Dawn Age ancestors had an awful lot of good luck to get out of the single-planet trap. And the Spider geniuses are no better than the old-time human ones. Look at this guy Underhill. His students have made a lot of things work, but—'

'But he's full of superstitions,' Trud put in.

'Right. He has no concept of the limits of software design, and of the limits that puts on hardware. He thinks immortality and godlike computers are just around the corner, the product of just a little more progress. He's a walking library of the Failed Dreams.'

'See! That's the real reason you're Reynolt's favorite. You know what fantasies the Spiders might believe. When the time comes to take over, that will be important.'

'When the time comes . . .' Jau Xin gave a lopsided smile. On the far wall, by the Watch Chart, Benny had a window on the Coming-Out Party Betting Pool. Guessing just when they would come out of hiding, when the Exile would end – that was the eternal topic of parlor debate. 'It's been more than thirty real years since the sun relighted. I'm outside a lot, you know, almost as much as Qiwi Lisolet and her crews. These days, the sun is dimming down. We have just a few years till it's dead again. The Spiders have themselves a deadline. I'm betting they'll be into the Information Age in less than ten years.'

'No, not far enough for us to make a smooth takeover,' said Arlo.

'Okay. But in the end, other things may force our hand. The Spiders have the beginnings of a space program. In ten years, our operations – our presence here at L1 – may be impossible to disguise.'

Trud: 'So? They get too uppity, we whack 'em.'

Jau: 'And cut our own throats, man.'

'You're both talking nonsense,' said Arlo. 'I'll bet we have fewer than ten nukes left. Seems we used all the rest on each other a while back—'

'We have directed-energy weapons.'

'Yes, if we were in close orbit. I tell you, we could *bluff* a good game, but—'

'We could drop our wrecked starships on the buggers.'

Ezr exchanged a glance with Rita Liao. This was the argument that sent her into full froth. She – and Jau and most of the people round the table – thought of the Spiders as people. That was Trixia's triumph. The Emergents, at least outside the Podmaster class, were uncomfortable with the notion of megamurder. In any case, Jau Xin was certainly right: Whether or

749

not the Emergents had the firepower, the whole object of the Lurk was to create a Customer who could put the mission back in business. Blowing them up made sense only to crazies like Ritser Brughel.

Ezr leaned back, out of the argument. He had seen Pham's name on the Watch Chart; just a few more days and they would have their first real meeting. *Take it slow and patient, no rush*. Okay. He hoped the Debating Society would move on to something more interesting, but even this nonsense was a pleasant familiar buzz. Not for the first time, Ezr realized this was almost like having family, a family that argued endlessly about problems that never seemed to change. He got along with even the Emergents, and they with him. Almost like a normal life . . . He looked through the lattice of z-vines that filled the spaces around them. The flowers actually smelled faintly – though nothing like that stink-lacquer that Hunte tried before. Ah. A clear view opened through the flowers and leaves, to Benny's station on the floor of the parlor. He started to wave to Benny. Maybe he could stomach some real food, after all. Then he saw a flash of checkered pants and fractille blouse.

Qiwi.

She and Benny were deep in negotiation. Benny pointed at the crappy section of wallpaper that stretched across the parlor's bottom wall. Qiwi nodded, consulting some sort of list. Then she seemed to feel his gaze. She turned, and waved at Ezr's group up by the ceiling. *She is so beautiful.* Ezr looked away, his face suddenly chill. Once Qiwi had been the brat who irritated him beyond measure. Once Qiwi had seemed a betrayer, abusing the zipheads. And once Ezr had hit her and hit her . . . Ezr remembered the rage, how *good* it felt to get some revenge for Jimmy Diem and Trixia Bonsol. But Qiwi was no betrayer; Qiwi was a victim more than she knew. If Pham was right about mindscrub – and he must be; the horror fit the facts too well – then Qiwi was a victim almost beyond human imagination. And in beating Qiwi, Ezr had learned something about himself. He had learned that Ezr Vinh's decency must be a shallow thing. That self-knowledge was something he could keep tucked away most of the time. Maybe he could still do good, even if at bottom he was something vile . . . But when he actually saw Qiwi, and when she saw him . . . then it was impossible to forget what he had done.

'Hi Qiwi!' Rita had noticed Qiwi's wave. 'Got a second? We want you to settle something for us.'

Qiwi grinned. 'Be right there.' She turned back to Benny. He was nodding, handing her a bunch of paper favors. Then she came bouncing up the latticework of vines. She trailed Benny's net, filled with beer refills and more snacks. In effect, she was doing some of Benny's work for him. That was Qiwi for you. She was part of the underground economy, the hustlers that made things relatively comfortable here. Like Benny, she didn't hesitate to lend a hand, to *work*. And at the same time, she had the

Podmaster's ear; she brought a softness to Nau's regime that Emergents like Jau Xin could not consciously admit. But you could see it in Jau and Rita's eyes; they were almost in awe of Qiwi Lisolet.

And she smiled at him. 'Hi, Ezr. Benny figured you might want more.' She slid the bucket into sticking contact with the table in front of him. Ezr nodded, not able to meet her gaze.

Rita was already babbling at her; maybe no one noticed his awkwardness. 'Not to ask for inside news, Qiwi, but what's the latest estimate for our Coming-Out date?'

Qiwi smiled. 'My guess? Twelve years at the outside. Spider progress with spaceflight may force our hand before that.'

'Yeah.' Rita slid a glance at Jau. 'Well, we were wondering. Suppose we can't grab everything via their computer networks. Suppose, we have to take sides, play one power block off against another. Who would we back?'

35

Diamond One was more than two thousand meters long and nearly as wide, by far the largest of all the rocks in the pile. Over the years, the crystal directly beneath Hammerfest had been carved into a labyrinth of caves. The upper levels were the labs and offices. Below that were Tomas's private rooms. Below that was the latest addition to the inverted architecture: a lens-shaped void more than two hundred meters across. The making of it had worn out most of the thermal diggers, but Qiwi had not objected; in fact, this had been partly her idea.

Their three human forms were almost lost in the scale of the place. 'So is this impressive, or is this impressive?' Qiwi asked, smiling at Tomas:

Nau was staring straight upward, his face slack with wonder. That didn't happen often. He hadn't noticed yet, but he'd lost his balance and was slowly falling over backward. 'I . . . yes. Even the huds mockup didn't do it justice.'

Qiwi laughed, and patted him back toward vertical. 'I confess. In the mockups I didn't show the lights.' Actinic arcs were buried in the anechoic grooves of the ceiling. The lamps turned the sky into a coruscating gem. By tuning their output, almost any lighting effect could be obtained, but always tinged with rainbows.

On her right, Papa was also staring, but not with rapture, and not upward. Ali Lin was on his hands. He pretty much ignored the subtle hints of gravity as he poked at the pebble-textured surface the diggers had left in the diamond floor. 'There's nothing living here, nothing at all.' His face screwed up in a frown.

'It will be the largest park you've ever done, Papa. A blank slate for you to work on.' The frown eased. *We'll work on it together, Papa. You can teach me new things.* This one should be big enough for real animals, maybe even the flying kittens. Those were more dream than memory, from the time Mama and Papa and Qiwi spent at the Trilander departure temp.

And Tomas said, 'I'm so glad you pushed me on this, Qiwi. I just wanted a little better security and you've given me something wonderful.' He sighed, smiled down at her. His hand brushed down her back to just above her hips.

'It'll be a large park, Tomas, even by Qeng Ho standards. Not the largest, but—'

'But it likely will be the *best*.' He leaned past her to pat Ali on the shoulder.

'Yes.' *Yes, it likely will be the best.* Papa had always been a premier parkbuilder. And now, for fifteen years of his lifetime he had been Focused on his specialty. Every year of that time had produced new wonders. His bonsais and microparks were already better than the finest of Namqem. Even the Focused Emergent biologists were as good as the Qeng Ho best, now that they had access to the fleet's life library.

And when the Exile is over, Papa, when you are finally free, then you will truly know what wonders you have made.

Nau's glance swept back and forth across the empty, glittering cavern. He must be imaging some of the landscapes it might sustain – savannah, cool rain forest, meadowland in mountains. Even Ali's magic couldn't create more than one ecosystem at a time here, but there were choices . . . She smiled: 'How would you like a lake?'

'What?'

'Code "wetwater," in my design library.' And Qiwi keyed her own huds to the design.

'Unh . . . you didn't tell me about this!'

Overlaid on the diamond reality of the cavern was one of Ali's forestland schemes – but now the center of the cavern was a lake that widened and widened into the distance till it reached island mountains that seemed kilometers away. A sailboat had just cast off from the arbored moorage down the hill from them.

Tomas was silent for a moment. 'Lord. That's on my uncle's estate at North Paw. I spent summers there.'

'I know. I got it from your biography.'

'It's beautiful, Qiwi, even if it is impossible.'

'Not impossible! We've got lots of water topside; this will be a good secondary storage for some of it.' She waved at the distance, where the lake spread wide. 'We dig out the far side of the cavern a little, and run the lake right out to the wall. We can scavenge enough wallpaper to make realistic far imagery.' That might not be true. The video wallpaper from the wrecked ships had suffered considerable vacuum damage. It didn't matter. Tomas

752

liked to wear huds, and they could paint the far scenery for anyone who did not participate in the imaging.

'That's not what I mean. We can't have a real lake, not in microgravity. Every little rockquake would send it crawling up the walls.'

Qiwi let her smile grow broad. 'That's the real surprise. I can do it, Tomas! We have thousands of servo valves from the wrecked starships, more than we can use for anything else. We put them at the bottom of the lake, and run them off a network of localizers. It would be easy to damp the water waves, keep the thing confined.'

Tomas laughed. 'You really like stabilizing the intrinsically unstable, don't you, Qiwi! Well . . . you did it for the rockpile, maybe you can do it here.'

She shrugged. 'Sure I can. With a restricted shoreline, I could even do it with Emergent localizers.'

Tomas turned to look at her, and now she saw no visions before his eyes. He was back in the hard sterile world of the diamond cavern. But he had seen the wonder, and she knew she had pleased him. 'It would be marvelous . . . a lot of resources, though, and a lot of work.' Work by non-zipheads, he meant. Even Tomas didn't think of the Focused as real people.

'It won't get in the way of important things. The valves are scrap. The localizers are surplus. And people owe me lots of favors.'

After a time, Nau led his woman and the ziphead back out of the cavern. Qiwi had surprised him once again, this time more spectacularly than usual. And damn. This was just another reason why they needed the localizers in Hammerfest. Reynolt's people still hadn't cleared the devices; just how complicated could that be? *Leave it for later.* Qiwi said they could get some kind of lake even with Emergent localizers.

They went back up through the lower levels, acknowledging the various salutes and waves of techs, both Emergent and former Qeng Ho. They dropped Ali Lin off in the garden park that was his workshop. Qiwi's father wasn't caged in the Attic honeycomb. In fact, his specialty demanded open spaces and living things. At least, that was how Tomas Nau presented the issue to Qiwi. It was plausible, and it meant the girl was not continually exposed to the usual face of Focused operations; that helped slow her inevitable slide toward understanding.

'You have to go over to the temp, Qiwi?'

'Yes, some errands. To see some friends.' Qiwi had her trades to accomplish, her favors to collect.

'Okay.' He swept her up in a kiss, visible the length of the office hall. No matter. 'You did well, my love!'

'Thanks.' Her smile was a dazzling thing. Over thirty years old, and Qiwi Lisolet still hung on his approval. 'See you this evening.'

She departed up the central shaft, pulling herself hand over hand faster and faster, all but rocketing past the other people in the shaft. Qiwi still practiced every day in a two-gee centrifuge, still practiced the martial killing arts. It was all that was left of her mother's influence, at least all that was visible. No doubt a lot of her driving energy was some sort of sublimated effort to please her mother.

Nau looked up, almost oblivious of the people coming down around him; they would stay out of his way. He watched her figure dwindle into the heights of the main shaft.

After Anne Reynolt, Qiwi was his most precious possession. But he had essentially inherited Reynolt; Qiwi Lin Lisolet was his personal triumph, a brilliant, unFocused person, working unstintingly for him for all these years. Owning her, manipulating her – it was a challenge that never got stale. And there was always an edge of danger. She had the strength and speed, at least, to kill with her hands. He hadn't understood that in the early years. But that was also before he had realized what a valuable thing she was.

Yes, she was his triumph, but Tomas Nau was realistic enough to know he'd been lucky, too. He had first possessed Qiwi at just the right age and context – when she was old enough to have absorbed a depth of Qeng Ho background, yet young enough to be molded by the Diem Massacre. In the first ten years of the Exile, she had seen through his lies only three times.

A little smile quirked his lips. Qiwi thought she was changing *him*, that she had shown him how well the methods of freedom worked. Well, she was right. In the early years, allowing the underground economy had been part of the game he was playing with her, a temporary weakness. But the underground economy really *worked*. Even the Qeng Ho texts claimed that free markets should be meaningless in an environment as closed and limited as this. And yet, year by year, the Peddlers had made things better – even for operations that Nau would have required anyway. So now, when she assured him that people owed her favors, that they would work really hard to make the lake park – *Pestilence, I really want that lake* – Tomas Nau didn't laugh behind his hand at her. She was right: the people – even the Emergents – would do better on that park because they owed Qiwi than they would because Tomas Nau was Podmaster with the ultimate power to space them all.

Qiwi was a tiny figure at the very top of the shaft. She turned and waved. Nau waved back, and she disappeared to the side, down one of the taxi access tunnels.

Nau stood a moment longer, staring upward with a smile on his face. Qiwi had taught him the power of managed freedom. Uncle Alan and the Nauly clique had bequeathed him the power of Focused slaves. And the OnOff star . . . ? The more they learned of the star and its planet, the more he had the awed conviction that there were miracles hiding here, maybe not the treasures they had expected, but much greater things. The biology, the physics, the star system's far galactic orbit . . . their combined implications were just beyond the analysts' comprehension, teasing at his intuition.

And in a few years, the Spiders would hand him an industrial ecology with which to exploit it all.

There had never been a place and a time in the histories of Humankind where so much opportunity had come to one man. Twenty-five years ago, a younger Tomas Nau had quailed before the uncertainties. But the years had passed, and step by step he had met the problems and mastered them. What came out of Arachna would be the power of a dynasty like none Humankind had ever seen. It would take time, perhaps another century or two, but he would scarcely be out of Qeng Ho middle age by the end of it. He could sweep the Emergent cliques aside. This end of Human Space would see the greatest empire in all the histories. The legend of Pham Nuwen would pale in the light that Tomas Nau would cast.

And Qiwi? He cast a final look upward. He hoped she would last through the end of the Exile. There were so many things she could help him with when they took the Spiders down. But the mask was fraying. Mindscrub was not perfect; Qiwi was catching on faster than in the early years. Without destroying large amounts of brain tissue, Anne could not eliminate what she called 'residual neural weighting.' And of course there were some contradictions that coldsleep amnesia could not plausibly cover. Eventually, even with the most skillful manipulation . . . How could he explain reneging on his promises of manumission? How could he explain the measures he would take against the Spiders, or the human breeding programs that would be necessary? No. Inevitably, but most regrettably, he would have to dispose of Qiwi. And yet, even then she could still serve him. Children by her would still be possible. Someday his reign would need heirs.

Qiwi pulled into Benny's parlor about two thousand seconds later. And it was Benny running things this Watch. Good. He was her favorite master of the parlor. They dickered for a moment over the new gear he wanted. 'Lord, Benny! You need more wallpaper? There are other projects that could use some, you know.' Like a certain park under Hammerfest.

Benny shrugged. 'Get the Podmaster to allow consensual imaging, and I won't need wallpaper. But the stuff just wears out. See?' He waved at the floor, where the image of Arachna was a permanent fixture. She could see a storm system that would probably reach Princeton in a few Ksecs; certainly the display drivers were still alive. But she could also see the distortions and the colored smudges.

'Okay, we still have some to strip out of the *Invisible Hand*, but it'll cost you.' Ritser Brughel would froth and shriek, even though he had no use for the wallpaper. Ritser regarded the *Hand* as his private fiefdom. She looked at Benny's handwritten list, at the other items. The finished foods were all from the temp's bactry and ags – Gonle Fong would want to handle that.

Volatiles and feedstock, aha. As usual, Benny was negotiating on the side for those, trying to short-circuit Gonle by going directly to the mining operation on the rockpile. For best friends, the two took their business competition awfully seriously.

At the edge of her vision, something moved. She glanced up. Over by the ceiling, Xin's gang was hanging out in its usual place. Ezr! An involuntary smile spread across Qiwi's face. He had turned from the others, was looking in her direction. She waved to him. Ezr's face seemed to close down, and he turned away. For a moment, a lot of old pain floated up in Qiwi's mind. Even now, when she saw him, there was always this quick, involuntary twinge of joy, like seeing a dear friend you have so much to say to. But the years had passed, and every time he turned away. She hadn't meant to harm Trixia Bonsol; she helped Tomas because he was a good man, a man who was doing his best to bring them through the Exile.

She wondered if Ezr would ever let her close enough to explain. Maybe. There were years to come. At Exile's end, when they had a whole civilization to help them and Trixia was returned to him – surely then he would forgive.

36

The space between the temp's outer skin and the habitable balloons was a buffer against blowouts. Over the years, various of Gonle Fong's farming-rackets had used the space; a pressure loss would have killed some truffles or her experiments with Canberra flowers. Even now, Fong's ags occupied only a part of the dead space. Pham met Ezr Vinh well away from the little farm plots. Here the air was still and cold, and the only light was OnOff's dim glow seeping through the outer wall.

Pham hooked his foot under a wall stop and waited quietly. Earlier in the Watch, he had made sure that these volumes were well populated with localizers. They were scattered here and there on the walls. A few always floated in the air around him, though even in bright light they would have been scarcely more than dustmotes. And so, hiding here in the twilight, Pham was a one-man command post. He could hear and see from wherever he commanded – just now, the airgap between the balloons. Someone was approaching cautiously. At the back of his eyes he had vision now, almost as good as Qeng Ho huds. It was the Vinh boy, looking nervous and stealthy.

How old was Vinh now, thirty? Not really a kid anymore. But he still had that cast to his features, that serious manner . . . just like Sura. Not a person to trust, oh no. But hopefully a person he could use.

Vinh appeared to the naked eye, coming around the curve of the inner balloon. Pham raised a hand and the boy stopped, sucked in a breath of surprise. For all his caution, Vinh had almost passed Pham by, not noticing him floating in the inward notch of the wall fabric. 'I – Hello.' Vinh was whispering.

Pham floated out from the wall, to where the light of OnOff was a little better. 'We meet at last,' he said, giving the boy a lopsided smile.

'Y-yes. Truly.' Ezr turned, looked at him for a long moment, and then gave – Lord! – a little bow. His Sura features spread into a shy smile. 'It's strange to actually see you, not Pham Trinli.'

'Hardly a visible difference.'

'Oh sir, you don't know. When you are Trinli, all the little things are different. Here, even in this light, you look different. If Nau or Reynolt saw you for even ten seconds, they would know, too.'

The kid had an overactive imagination. 'Well, the only thing they're seeing for the next two thousand seconds is the lies my localizers are feeding them. Hopefully, that's long enough to get you started—'

'Yes! You can actually see with the localizers, you can actually input commands to them?'

'With enough practice.' He showed the boy where to set localizer grains around the orbit of his eye, and how to cue the nearby localizers to cooperate. 'Don't do that in public. The synthesized beam is very narrow, but might still be noticed.'

Vinh stared as if sightless. 'Ah, it's like something is nibbling at the back of my eyes.'

'The localizers are tickling your optic nerve directly. What pops up may be very weird at first. You can learn the commands with some simple exercises, but learning to make sense of the visual tickle . . . well, I guess that's like learning to see again.' Pham guessed it was a lot like a blind man learning to use a visual prosthesis. Some people could do it, some remained blind. He didn't say that out loud. Instead, he led Ezr through some test patterns, patterns that Vinh could practice with.

Pham had thought a lot about just how much of the command interface to show the Vinh boy. But Ezr already knew enough to betray him. Short of killing him, there was no cure for that. *All the bloody clues I laid, pointing at the Zamle Eng story, and he still picked up on the truth. Pray it was only his Great Family background that made that possible.* Pham had kept him in ignorance for years now, watching for signs of counterscheming, trying to measure the boy's actual ability. What he had seen was a compulsive, unsure adolescent coming of age in a tyranny – and still retaining some sense.

When the crunch came, when Pham finally moved against Nau and Brughel, he would need someone to help pull all the strings. The boy should be taught some of the tricks . . . but there were nights Pham ground his teeth, thinking of the power he was handing to a Vinh.

Ezr learned the command set very quickly. Now he should have no trouble learning the other techniques that Pham had opened for him. Full vision would come slowly, but—

'Yes, I know you still can't see more than flashes of light. Just keep trying the test patterns. In a few Msecs, you'll be as good as I am.' *Almost as good.*

Just the assurance seemed to calm the boy. 'Okay, I'll practice and practice – all in my room, as you say. This makes me feel . . . I don't know, like I've accomplished more just now than I have in years.'

One hundred seconds of the alloted time remained. The masking that disguised them to the snoops couldn't be aborted. Never mind. Just react to the kid naturally. Platitudes. 'You did plenty in the past. Together, we've learned a lot about the Hammerfest operation.'

'Yes, but this will be different . . . What will things be like after we win, sir?'

'Afterwards?' What not to say? 'It will be . . . magnificent. We will have Qeng Ho technology and a planetary civilization very nearly capable of using it. By itself, that is the most powerful trading position any Qeng Ho has ever had. But we will have more. Given time, we'll have ram-drives that take advantage of what we've learned from OnOff's physics. And you know the DNA diversity on Arachna. That by itself is an enormous treasure, a box of surprises that could power—'

'And all the Focused will be set free.'

'Yes, yes. Of course. Don't worry, Vinh, we'll get Trixia back.' That was an expensive promise, but one Pham intended to keep. With Trixia Bonsol free, maybe Vinh would listen to reason about the rest. Maybe.

Pham realized that the boy was looking at him strangely; he had let the silence stretch into unwelcome implications. 'Okay. I think we've covered the ground. Practice the input language and the visual test patterns. For now, our time is up.' *Thank the Lord of All Trade.* 'You take off first, back the way you came. The cover story is you got almost to the taxi port, then decided to go back to the dayroom for breakfast.'

'Okay.' Vinh hesitated an instant, as if wanting to say more. Then he turned and floated back around the curve of the inner balloon.

Pham watched the timer that hung at the back of his vision. In twenty seconds, he would depart in the other direction. The localizers had fed two thousand seconds of carefully planned lies back to Brughel's snoops. Later, Pham would check it over for consistency with what was really going on throughout the rest of the temp. There would be some patching necessary, no doubt. This kind of meeting would have been easy if the enemy had been ordinary analysts. With ziphead snoops, covering your ass was a major exercise in paranoia.

Ten seconds. He stared into the dimness at where Ezr Vinh had just disappeared. Pham Nuwen had a lifetime of experience in diplomacy and deception. *So why the bloody hell wasn't I smoother with the kid?* The ghost of Sura Vinh seemed suddenly very close, and she was laughing.

*

'You know, we really need to get localizers aboard Hammerfest.' The request had become a ritual at the beginning of Ritser Brughel's security briefings. Today, maybe Ritser was in for a surprise.

'Anne's people haven't finished their evaluation.'

The Vice-Podmaster leaned forward. Over the years, Ritser had changed more than most. Nowadays, he was on-Watch almost fifty percent, but he was also making heavy use of medical support and the Hammerfest gym. He actually looked healthier than he had during the early years. And somewhere along the way, he had learned to satisfy his . . . needs . . . without producing an unending stream of dead zip-heads. He had grown to be a dependable Podmaster. 'Have you seen Reynolt's latest report, sir?'

'Yes. She's saying five more years.' Anne's search for security holes in the Peddler localizers was close to impossible. In the early years, Tomas had been more hopeful. After all, the Qeng Ho security hackers had had no ziphead support. But the quagmire of Qeng Ho software was almost eight thousand years deep. Every year, Anne's zipheads pushed back their dead-line for certainty another year or two. And now this latest report.

'Five more years, sir. She might as well be saying "never." We both know how unlikely it is that these localizers are a danger. My zipheads have been using them for twelve years on the temp and in the junked starships. My zips aren't programmer specialists, but I'll tell you, in all that time the localizers have come up as clean as anything Qeng Ho. These gadgets are so useful, sir. Nothing gets past them. *Not* using them has its own risks.'

'Such as?'

Nau saw the other's faint start of surprise; this was more encouragement than Ritser had received in some time. 'Um. Such as the things we miss because we aren't using them. Let's just look at the current briefing.' There followed a not-too-relevant discourse on all the recent security concerns: Gonle Fong's attempts to acquire automation for her black-market farms; the perverse affection people of all factions had developed for the Spiders – a desirable sublimation, but a potential problem when the time for real action finally arrived; the proper level for Anne's paranoia. 'I know you monitor her, sir, but I think she's drifting. It's not just this fixation about system trapdoors. She's become significantly more possessive of "her" zipheads.'

'It's possible I've tuned her too edgy.' Anne's suspicions about sabotaged zipheads were totally amorphous, quite unlike her usual analytical precision. 'But what does that have to do with enabling localizers in Hammerfest?'

'With localizer support in Hammerfest, my snoops could do constant, fine-grain analysis – correlate the net traffic with exactly what is happening physically. It's . . . it's a scandal that our weakest security is in the place where we need the strongest.'

'Hmm.' He looked back into Ritser's eyes. As a child, Tomas Nau had learned an important rule: Whatever else, never lie to yourself. Throughout history, self-deception had ruined great men from Helmun Dire to Pham Nuwen. Be honest: He really *really* wanted the lake that Qiwi had shown him under Hammerfest. With such a park, he would have made something of this squalor, a splendor that the Qeng Ho rarely exceeded even in civilized systems. All that was no excuse to break security – but maybe his self-denial was itself making things worse. *Take a different tack: Who appears to be pushing this?* Ritser Brughel was awfully enthusiastic about it. He must not be underestimated. Less directly, Qiwi had created this dilemma: 'What about Qiwi Lisolet, Ritser? What do your analysts say about her?'

Something glittered in Ritser's eyes. He still held a homicidal hatred for Qiwi. 'We both know how fast she can twig the truth – close surveillance is more important than ever. But at the moment she's absolutely, totally clean. She doesn't love you, but her admiration for you is nearly as strong as love. She is a masterpiece, sir.'

Qiwi was twigging about every other Watch now. But her last scrubbing was very recent – and extending the localizer coverage would keep her under an even tighter watch. Nau thought it over for a moment more, then nodded. 'Okay, Vice-Podmaster, let's bring the localizers to Hammerfest.'

Of course, the Qeng Ho localizers were already aboard Hammerfest. The dustlike motes spread on air currents, stuck to clothes and hair and even skin. They were ubiquitous throughout all inhabited spaces around the rockpile.

Ubiquitous they might be, but without power the localizers were harmless pieces of metallic glass. Now Anne's people reprogrammed Hammerfest's cable spines – and extended them into the newly dug caves beneath. Now, ten times a second, microwaves pulsed in every open space. The energy was far below biological-damage thresholds, so low that it didn't interfere with the other utilities in place. The Qeng Ho localizers didn't need much power, just enough to run their tiny sensors and communicate with their nearest neighbors. Ten Ksec after the microwave pulses were turned on, Ritser reported that the net had stabilized and was providing good data. Millions of processors, scattered across a diameter of four hundred meters. Each was scarcely more powerful than a Dawn Age computer. In principle, they were the most powerful computer net at L1.

In four days, Qiwi finished digging out the cave, and emplaced the wave servos. Her father was already brewing soil on the uplands. The water would come last, but it would come.

After the fact, Nau wondered how they had managed without the localizers all this time. Ritser Brughel had been absolutely correct. Before, their security had been all but blind in Hammerfest. Before, the Qeng Ho temp had in fact been a safer place for secure operations. Nau supervised Brughel and his snoops in a thorough, many-day sweep of all Hammerfest and then of the starships and the warehouse cloud. He even broke with tradition and ran the localizers for 100Ksec in the L1-A arsenal vault. It was like shining a spotlight into dark places. They found and closed dozens of security lapses . . . and found not a single trace of subversion. Altogether, the experience was a wonderful confidence builder, as when you check for house parasites, find none, but also see where to put poison and barriers against future infestation.

And now, Tomas Nau had greater knowledge of his own domain than any Podmaster in Emergent history. Ritser's snoops, using the localizers, could give Nau the location and emotional state – even cognitive state – of anyone in Hammerfest. After a time, he realized that there were experiments he should have undertaken long before.

Ezr Vinh. Maybe something more could be done with him. Nau studied the fellow's biography again. At the next briefing, he was ready. This was Vinh's standard meeting time. It was just the two of them, but by this time the Peddler was very used to the interaction. Vinh showed up at Nau's office to discuss his summaries for the last ten days, the progress he was seeing with the ziphead groups in their understanding of the Spider world.

Tomas let the Peddler rattle on. He listened, nodded, asked the reasonable questions . . . and watched the analysis that spread across his huds. *Lordy.* The localizers in the air, on Vinh's chair, even on his skin, reported to the *Invisible Hand*, where programs analyzed and sent the results back to Nau's huds, painting Vinh's skin with colors that showed galvanic response, skin temperature, perspiration. Standard graphics around the face showed pulse and other internals. An inset window showed what Vinh was seeing from his place across the desk, and mapped his every eye motion with red tracks. Two of Brughel's snoops were allocated to this interview, and their analysis was a flowing legend across the top of Nau's vision. *Subject is relaxed to tenth percentile of normal interview level. Subject is confident but wary, without sympathy for the Podmaster. Subject is not currently trying to suppress explicit thought.*

It was more or less what Nau would have guessed, but with a wealth of added detail, better than the best instrumented soft interrogation, since it was invisible to the subject.

'So the strategic politics are much clearer now,' concluded Vinh, blissfully unaware of the dual nature of the interview. 'Pedure and the Kindred have some real advantages in rocketry and nuclear weapons, but they've consistently lagged behind the Accord in computing and networks.'

Nau shrugged. 'The Kindred are a strict dictatorship. Haven't you told me that the Dawn Age tyrannies couldn't cope with computer networks?'

'Yes.' *Subject reacts, suppressing probable feeling of irony.* 'That's part of it. We know they're planning on a first strike sometime after the sun goes out, so that accounts for their overspending on weapons. And on the Accord side, Sherkaner Underhill is just *so* enthusiastic about automation that Pedure can't keep up. Frankly, I think we're headed for a crunch,

Podmaster.' *The subject is sincere in this statement.* 'Spider civilization only discovered the inverse square law a couple of generations ago; their mathematics lagged behind our Dawn Age accordingly. But the Kindred have made solid progress in rocketry. If they show one-tenth the curiosity of Sherkaner Underhill, they're going to detect us in less than ten years.'

'Before we can completely control their networks?'

'Yes, sir.'

That's what Jau Xin had been saying, reasoning off of his pilot zipheads. A pity. But at least the shape of the end of the Exile was becoming clear . . . Meantime:

Subject's guard is down. Nau smiled to himself. This was as good a time as any to shake up Manager Vinh. *Who knows, maybe I can actually manipulate him.* Either way, Vinh's reaction would be interesting. Nau leaned back in his chair, pretended to gaze idly at the bonsai floating over his desk. 'I've had years to study the Qeng Ho, Mr Vinh. I'm not under false illusions. You people understand the different ways of civilization better than any sessile group.'

'Yes, sir.' *Subject still calm, but the comment brings sincere agreement.*

Nau cocked his head. 'You're in the Vinh line; if any in the Qeng Ho really understand things, it should be you. You see, one of my personal heroes has always been Pham Nuwen.'

'You've . . . mentioned that before.' The words were wooden. In Nau's display, Vinh's face was transformed by color, his pulse and perspiration spiking. Somewhere over on the *Hand*, the snoops analyzed, and reported: *Subject feels substantial anger directed at the Podmaster.* 'Honestly, Mr Vinh, I'm not trying to insult your traditions. You know that Emergents hold much of the Qeng Ho culture in contempt, but Pham Nuwen is a different matter. You see . . . I know the truth about Pham Nuwen.'

The diagnostic colors were shading toward normalcy, as was Vinh's heart rate. His eye dilation and tracking were consistent with suppressed anger. Nau felt a fleeting incongruity; he would have read a tinge of fear in Vinh's reaction. *Maybe I have some things to learn from all this automation.* And now he was frankly puzzled: 'What's the matter, Mr Vinh? For once, let's be frank.' He smiled. 'I won't tell Ritser, and you won't gossip with Xin or Liao or . . . my Qiwi.'

The pulse of anger was very stark on that one, no disagreement there. The Peddler was hung up on Qiwi Lisolet, even if he couldn't admit it to himself.

The signs of anger receded. Vinh licked his lips, a gesture that might have been nervousness. But the glyphs across the top of Nau's huds said, *Subject is curious.* Vinh said, 'It's just that I don't see the similarities between Pham Nuwen's life and Emergent values. Sure, Pham Nuwen was not born a Peddler, but more than anyone he made us what we are today. Look at the Qeng Ho archives, his life—'

'Oh, I have. They're a bit scattered, don't you think?'

'Well, he was the great traveler. I doubt he ever cared much about the historians.'

'Mr Vinh, Pham Nuwen valued the regard of history as much as any of the giants. I think – I *know* – your Qeng Ho archives have been carefully gardened, probably by your own Family. But you see, someone as great as Pham Nuwen attracted other historians – from the worlds he changed, from other spacefaring cultures. Their stories also float across the ages, and I've collected all that passed through this end of Human Space. He is a man I have always tried to emulate. Your Pham Nuwen was no lickspittle trader. Pham Nuwen was a Bringer of Order, a conqueror. Sure, he used your Trader techniques, the deception and the bribery. But he never shrank from threats and raw violence when that was necessary.'

'I—' The diagnostics painted an exquisite combination of anger and surprise and doubt across Vinh's face, just the mix that Nau would have estimated.

'I can prove it, Mr Vinh.' He spoke key words into the air. 'I've just transferred some of *our* archives to your personal domain. Take a look. These are unvarnished, non-Qeng Ho views of the man. A dozen little atrocities. Read the true story of how he ended the Strentmannian Pogrom, of how he was betrayed at Brisgo Gap. Then let's talk again.'

Amazing. Nau had not intended to speak so bluntly, but the evoked effects were so interesting. They exchanged a few meaningless sentences, and the meeting was over. Red shimmered around Vinh's hands, symptoms of an invisible trembling, as he approached the door.

Nau sat quietly for a moment after the Peddler was gone. He stared off into the distance, but in fact he was reading from his huds. The snoops' report was a stream of colored glyphs against the landscape of Diamond One. He would read the report carefully . . . later. First, there were his own thoughts to get in order. The localizer diagnostics were almost magical. Without them, he knew he would have scarcely noticed Vinh's agitation. *More important, without the diagnostics I wouldn't have been able to guide the conversation, zeroing in on the topics that needled Vinh.* So yes, active manipulation did appear feasible; this wasn't simply a snoop technique. And now he knew that Ezr Vinh had some substantial portion of his self-image bound up in the Qeng Ho fairy tales. Could the boy actually be turned by a different vision of those stories? Before now, he never would have believed it. With these new tools, maybe . . .

37

'We should have another face-to-face talk.'

'. . . Okay. Look, Pham. I don't believe these lies that Nau dumped on me.'

'Yeah, well everyone gets to write their own version of the past. The main thing is, I want to give you some drill about handling that sort of ambush interview.'

'I'm sorry. For a few seconds, I thought he was on to us.' The boy's voice was faint in Pham's ear. Ezr Vinh had become quite good with their secret comm link; good enough that Pham could hear the stunned tone in his voice.

'You did okay, though. You'll do better with some feedback training.' They talked a few moments more, setting up a time and a cover story. Then the tenuous link was broken, and Pham was left to think on the day's events.

Damn. Today had been a disaster just barely avoided . . . or just temporarily avoided. Pham floated in the darkened room, but his vision flitted across the gap of kilometers, to Diamond One and Hammerfest. The localizers were everywhere there now, and they were operational – though the MRI units in the Focus clinic fried any nearby localizers almost immediately. Getting live localizers onto Hammerfest was the breakthrough he had waited years for, but – *If I hadn't meddled with the diagnostics coming off Vinh, we could have lost everything.* Pham had known how the Podmaster might use his new toys; similar, if less intense, things had been going on in the temp for years. What he hadn't guessed was that Nau would have such deadly good luck in his choice of words. For nearly ten seconds, the boy had been sure that Nau had figured out everything. Pham had damped the snoops' report on that reaction, and Vinh himself had covered for it pretty well, but . . .

I never thought that Tomas Nau would know so much about me. Over the years, the Podmaster had often claimed to be a great admirer of 'the historical giants,' and he always included Pham Nuwen on his list. It had always seemed a transparent attempt to establish a common ground with the Qeng Ho. But now, Pham wasn't sure. While Tomas Nau had been busy 'reading' Ezr Vinh, Pham had run similar diagnostics on the Podmaster. Tomas Nau really *did* admire his notion of the historical Pham Nuwen! Somehow, the monster thought he and Pham Nuwen were alike. *He called me a 'Bringer of Order.'* That rang a strange resonance. Though Pham had never thought to use the term, it was almost what he wished of himself. *But we are nothing alike. Tomas Nau kills and kills and it is for himself. All I ever wanted was an end to killing, an end to barbarism. We are different!* Pham stuffed the absurdity back in its bottle. The really amazing thing was that Nau had so much of the true story. For the last 10Ksec, Pham had watched over Vinh's shoulder as the boy read through much of it. Even now, he was trickling the whole database out of Vinh's domain and into the distributed memory of the localizer net. Over the next Msec, he would study the whole thing.

What he had seen so far was . . . interesting. Much of it was even true. But whether truth or lie, it was not the awed mythology that Sura Vinh had left in the Qeng Ho histories. It was not the lie that covered Sura's ultimate treachery. *And how will Ezr Vinh take it?* Pham had already been much too open with Vinh. Vinh was totally inflexible about Focus; he just wouldn't stop whining about the zipheads. It was strange. In his life, Pham had blithely lied to crazies and villains and Customers and even Qeng Ho . . . but playing up to Vinh's obsession left him exhausted. Vinh just didn't understand the miracle that Focus could make.

And there were things in Nau's archive that would make it very difficult for Pham to disguise his true goals from the boy.

Pham dipped back into Nau's version of history, followed one story and then another, swore at the lies that made him out to be a monster . . . winced when the story was the truth, even if his actions had been the best he could do. It was strange to see his real face again. Some of these videos had to be real. Pham could almost feel the words of those speeches flowing up his throat and out his lips. It brought back memories: the high years, when almost every destination had brought him into contact with Traders who understood what could be made of an interstellar trading culture. Radio had outpaced him and delivered his message with good effect And less than a thousand years after Little Prince Pham had been given away to the traveling merchants, his life plan was close to success. The idea of a true Qeng-Ho had spread across most of Human Space. From worlds on the Far Side that he might never know, to the tilled and refilled heart of Human Space – even on Old Earth – they had heard his message, they had seen his vision of an organization durable enough and, powerful enough to stop the wheel of fate. Yes, many of them saw nothing more than Sura had. These were the 'practical minds,' only interested in making great wealth, insuring the benefit to themselves and their Families. But Pham had thought then – *and Lord, I still want to believe now* – that the majority believed in the greater goal that Pham himself preached.

Across a thousand years of real time, Pham had left the message, the plan for a Meeting more spectacular than any meeting before, a place and a time where the new Qeng Ho would declare the Peace of Human Space, would agree to serve that cause. It had been Sura Vinh who set the place:

Namqem.

True, Namqem was well on the coreward side of Human Space, but it was near the center of heavy Qeng Ho activity. The Traders who could most certainly participate were in relatively easy reach; they would need less than one thousand years of lead time. Those were the reasons that Sura said. And all the time she smiled her old disbelieving smile, as if humoring poor Pham. But Pham had believed he would be given his chance at Namqem.

In the end, there was another reason for agreeing to meet at Namqem. Sura had traveled so little; she had always been the planner at the center of Pham's schemes. Decades and centuries had passed. Even with occasional coldsleep and the best medical technology in all Human Space, Sura Vinh was now insupportably old, five hundred years of life? six hundred? In the last century before the Meeting, her messages made her seem so very old. If they didn't have the Meeting at Namqem, maybe Sura would never see the success of what Pham had worked for. Maybe Sura would never see how Pham was right. *She was the only one I totally trusted. I set myself up for her.*

And Pham drowned in an old, old rage, remembering . . .

The mother of all meetings. In a sense, the entire method and mythology that Pham and Sura had invented had been dedicated to this single moment. So it wasn't surprising that the arrivals were timed with unprecedented precision. Instead of trickling in over a decade or two, five thousand ramscoops from more than three hundred worlds were falling inward toward the Namqem system, all to arrive within an Msec of one another.

Some had left port less than a century earlier, coming in from Canberra and Torma. There were ships from Strentmann and Kielle, from worlds with ethnicities that by now were almost different species. Some had launched from so far away that they had only heard of the Meeting by radio. There were three ships from Old Earth. Not all the Attendees were true Traders; some were government missions hoping for the solutions in Pham's message. Perhaps a third of the visitors' departure worlds would have fallen from civilization in the time it took for voyage and return.

Such a meeting could not be moved or postponed. The opening of Hell itself could not successfully deflect it. Still, decades out from port, Pham had known that Hell was cracking open for the people of Namqem.

Pham's Flag Captain was only forty years old. He had seen a dozen worlds, and he should have known better. But he had been born on Namqem. 'They've been civilized since before you first showed up out of the Dark, sir. They know how to make things work. How can this be?' He looked disbelievingly at the analysis that had arrived with Sura Vinh's latest transmission.

'Sit down, Sammy.' Pham kicked a chair out from the wall, gestured for the other to settle himself. 'I've read the reports, too. The symptoms are classic. The last decade, the rate of system deadlocks has steadily increased throughout Namqem. See here, thirty percent of business commuting between the outer moons is in locked state at any given time.' All the hardware was in working order, but the system complexity was so great that vehicles could not get the go-ahead.

Sammy Park was one of Pham's best. He understood the reasons behind all the synthetic beliefs of the new Qeng Ho – and he still embraced them. He could make a worthy successor to Pham and Sura – maybe better than Pham's oldest children, who were often as cautious as their mother. But Sammy was seriously rattled: 'Surely the governance of Namqem understands the danger? They know everything Humankind has ever learned about stability – and they have better automation than we! Surely, in another few dozen Msecs we'll hear that they've reoptimized.'

Pham shrugged, not admitting to his own disbelief. *Namqem was so good, for so long.* Aloud he said, 'Maybe. But we know they've had thirty years to work a fix.' He waved at Sura's report. 'And still the problems get worse.' He saw the look on Park's face, and softened his voice. 'Sammy, Namqem has had peace and freedom for almost four thousand years. There's not another Customer civilization in all Human Space that can say that. But that's the point. Without help, even they can't go on forever.'

Sammy's shoulders hunched down. 'They've avoided the killing disasters. They haven't had war plagues or nuclear war. The governance is still flexible and responsive. There are just these Lord-be-damned technical problems.'

'They are technical *symptoms*, Sammy, of problems I'm sure the governance understands very well.' *And can't do a thing about.* He remembered back to the cynicism of Gunnar Larson. In a way this conversation was rambling down the same dead-end street. But Pham Nuwen had had a lifetime to think of solutions. 'The flexibility of the governance is its life and its death. They've accepted optimizing pressures for centuries now. Genius and freedom and knowledge of the past have kept them safe, but finally the optimizations have taken them to the point of fragility. The megalopolis moons allowed the richest networking in Human Space, but they are also a choke point . . .'

'But we knew – I mean, they knew that. There were always safety margins.'

Namqem was a triumph of distributed automation. And every decade it became a little better. Every decade the flexibility of the governance responded to the pressures to optimize resource allocation, and the margins of safety shrank. The downward spiral was far more subtle than the Dawn Age pessimism of Karl Marx or Han Su, and only vaguely related to the insights of Mancur Olson. The governance did not attempt direct management. Free enterprise and individual planning were much more effective. But if you avoid all the classic traps of corruption and central planning and mad invention, still – 'In the end there will be failures. The governance will have to take a direct hand.' If you avoided all other threats, the complexity of your own successes would eventually get you.

'Okay, I know.' Sammy looked away, and Pham synched his huds to follow what the younger man was seeing: Tarelsk and Marest, the two largest moons. Two billion people on each. They were gleaming disks of city lights as they slid across the face of their mother world – which itself was the largest park in Human Space. When the end finally came to Namqem, it would be a steep, swift collapse. Namqem solar system was not as naturally desolate as the pure asteroidal colonies of the early days of the Space Age . . . but the megalopolis moons required high technology to sustain their billions. Large failures there could easily spread into a system-wide war. It was the sort of debacle that had sterilized more than one of Humankind's homes. Sammy watched the scene, peaceful and wondrous – and now years out-of-date. And then he said, 'I know. This is everything you've been telling people, all the years I've been with the Qeng Ho. And for centuries before. Sorry Pham. I always believed . . . I just never thought my own birthplace would die, so soon.'

'I . . . wonder.' Pham looked across the command deck of his flag vessel and, in smaller windows, the command decks of the other thirty ships in his fleet. Here in midvoyage, there were only three or four people on each bridge. It was the dullest work in the universe. But the Nuwen fleet was one of the largest coming to the Meeting. More than ten thousand Qeng Ho slept in the holds of his ships. They had departed Terneu just over a century ago, and flew in the closest formation that wouldn't interfere with their ramfields. The farthest command deck was less than four thousand light-seconds from Pham's flag. 'We're still twenty years' travel time from Namqem. That's a lot of time if we choose to spend it on-Watch. Maybe . . . this is an opportunity to prove that what I've been talking about can actually work. Namqem will likely be chaos by the time we arrive. But we are help from outside their planetary trap, and we are arriving in enough numbers to make a difference.'

They were sitting on the command deck of Sammy's ship, the *Far Regard*. This bridge was almost busy, with five of the thirty command posts occupied. Sammy looked from post to post, and finally back at Pham Nuwen. Something like hope was spreading across his face. 'Yes . . . the whole reason for the Meeting can be *illustrated*.' On the side he was running scheduling programs, already caught up in the idea. 'If we use contingency supplies, we can support almost a hundred on-Watch per ship, all the way to Namqem. That's enough to study the situation, come up with action plans. Hell, in twenty years, we should be able to coordinate with the other fleets, too.'

Sammy Park was all Flag Captain now. He stared into his calculations, twiddling the possibilities. 'Yes. The Old Earth fleet is less than a quarter light-year from us. Half of all the Attendees are less than six light-years from us now, and of course that distance is decreasing. What about Sura and the Qeng Ho already in-system?'

Sura had put down roots over the centuries, but 'Sura and company have their own resources. She'll survive.' Sura understood the wheel of fate, even if she didn't believe it could be broken. She had moved her headquarters off Tarelsk a century before; Sura's 'temp' was a hoary palace in the asteroid belt. She would guess what Pham was about to try. The wave front of her analysis was probably headed in their direction even now. Maybe there really was a Lord of All Trade. There was certainly an Invisible Hand. The Meeting at Namqem would mean more than even he had imagined.

Year on year, the fleet of fleets converged upon Namqem. Five thousand threads of light, fireflies visible across light-years – thousands of light-years to decent telescopes. Year on year, the flares of their deceleration became tighter, a fine ball of thistledown in the windows of every arriving ship.

Five thousand ships; more than a million human beings. The ships held machines that could slag worlds. The ships held libraries and computer nets . . . And all together they were not a puff of thistledown compared to the power and resources of a civilization like Namqem. How could a puff of thistledown save a falling colossus? Pham had preached his answer to that question in person and across the Qeng Ho network. Local civilizations are all isolated traps. A simple disaster could kill them, but a little outside help might lead them to safety. And for the nonsimple cases – like Namqem – where generations of clever optimization finally crushed itself, even those disasters depended on the closed-system nature of sessile civilizations. A governance had too few choices, too many debts, and in the end it would be swept away by barbarism. An outside view, a new automation, that was something the Qeng Ho could supply. That was what Pham claimed would make the difference. Now he was going to get a chance to prove his point, not just argue it. Twenty years was not too much time to get ready.

In twenty years, Namqem's once gentle decline had gone beyond inconvenience, beyond economic recession. The governance had fallen three times now, each time replaced by a regime designed to be 'more effective' – each time opening the way to more radical social and technical fixes, ideas that had failed on a hundred other worlds. And with each downward step, the plans of the approaching fleets became more precise.

People were dying now. A billion kilometers out from Namqem world, the fleets saw the beginnings of Namqem's first war. Literally saw it with their naked eyes: the explosions were in the gigatonne range, the destruction of a competing governance that had seceded with two-thirds of the outer planets' automated industry. After the detonations, only one-third of that industry remained, but it was firmly in control of the megalopolitan regimes.

Flag Captain Sammy Park reported at a meeting: 'Alqin is trying to evacuate to the planetary surface. Maresk is on the verge of starvation; the pipeline from the outer system will empty out just a few days before we arrive.'

'The stump governance on Tarelsk seems to think they're still running a going concern. Here is our analysis . . .' The new speaker's Nese was fluent; they had had twenty years now to synch their common language. This Fleet Captain was a young . . . man . . . from Old Earth. In eight thousand years, Old Earth had been depopulated four times. Without the existence of the daughter worlds, the human race would have gone extinct there long ago. What lived on Earth was strange now. None of their kind had been this far out from the center of Human Space before. But now, as fleets made their final approach into the Namqem system, the Old Earth ships were barely ten light-seconds from Pham's flag. They had participated as much as anyone in setting up what they all were calling the Rescue.

Sammy waited politely to be sure the other was finished. Chatting at many seconds' remove took a special discipline. Then he nodded. 'Tarelsk will probably be the site of the first megadeaths, though we're not sure of the precise cause.'

Pham was sitting in the same meeting room as Sammy. He took advantage of his location to butt in before the other's time slot was truly ended. 'Give us your summary on Sura's situation, Sammy.'

'Trader Vinh is still in the main asteroid belt. She is about two thousand light-seconds from our present location.' It would still be a while before Sura could participate firsthand. 'She's supplied a lot of useful background intelligence, but she's lost her temp and many of her ships.' Sura owned a number of estates in the belt; no doubt she was safe for the moment. 'She recommends we shift the venue of the Grand Meeting to Brisgo Gap.'

Seconds drifted slowly past as they waited for comment from farther out. Twenty seconds. Nothing from the Old Earth fleet; but that could be politeness. Forty seconds. The Strentmannian Fleet Captain took the floor, naturally enough a woman: 'Never heard of it. Brisgo Gap?' She held up her hand, indicating she was not giving up her speaking slot. 'Okay, I see. A density-wave feature in their asteroid belt.' She gave a sour laugh. 'I suppose that's a place that won't be subject to contention. Very well, we could pick a longitude close to Trader Vinh's holdings and all meet there . . . *after* we accomplish the Rescue.'

They had come across dozens, some of them hundreds, of light-years. And now their Grand Meeting would be in empty space. As best he could across the time delay between them, Pham had argued with Sura about this suggestion. Meeting in a nowhere place was a confession of failure. When the *Far Regard*'s speaking turn came, Pham took the floor. 'Sure, Trader Vinh is right in picking an out-of-the-way corner of the Namqem system for the Meeting. But we've had years to plan for the Rescue. We have our five thousand ships. We have action strategies for each of the megalopolis populations and for those already moved down to Namqem world. I agree with Fleet Captain Tansolet. I propose that we execute our plan before we meet at this wherever-it-is gap.'

38

There was a war on. Three separate megalopolitan populations were at risk. The resources of almost a thousand ships were dedicated to suppressing the ragtag military that had grown up in the chaos. The lander resources of two hundred ships were sent down to the surface of Namqem itself. The world had been a manicured park for several thousand years – but now it would become the home of billions. Part of one megalopolis population was already down on the surface.

More than two thousand ships were headed for Maresk. The regime there was almost nonexistent . . . but starvation was only a few Msecs away. Much of Maresk might be saved by a combination of subtlety and brute cargo-hauling power.

Tarelsk still had an active governance, but it was like no governance in the history of the Namqem system. This was something out of darker times on other worlds, when rulers mouthed words about reconciliation – and willingly killed by the millions. The Tarelsk governance was an unplumbed madness.

One of Sammy's analysts said, 'Beating them down will be almost like an armed conquest.'

'Almost?' Pham looked up from the approach plots; every crewman was wearing full-press coveralls and hoods. 'Hell, this is the real thing.' In the simplest case, the Qeng Ho rescue mission was three coordinated coups. If they succeeded, it would not be remembered that way. If they succeeded, each operation would be a little miracle, salvation that the locals could not provide for themselves. Perhaps ten times in all the histories had there been real interstellar war across more than a couple of light-years. Pham wondered what his father would have thought if he could have known what his throwaway son would one day accomplish. He turned back to the approach plots. The fastest would take 50Ksec to reach Tarelsk. 'What's the latest?'

'As expected, the Tarelsk governance isn't buying our arguments. They consider us invaders, not rescuers. And they aren't forwarding what we say to the Tarelsk population.'

'Surely the people know, though?'

'Maybe not. We've had three successful flybys.' The robots had been dropped off 4Msec before, recon darts that could make almost one-tenth lightspeed. 'We only got a millisecond look, but what we saw is consistent with what Sura's spies are telling us. We think the governance has opted for ubiquitous law enforcement.'

Pham whistled softly. Now every embedded computing system, down to a child's rattle, was a governance utility. It was the most extreme form of social control ever invented. 'So now they have to run everything.' The notion was terribly seductive to the authoritarian mind . . . The only trouble was, no despot had the resources to plan every detail in his society's behavior. Not even planet-wrecker bombs had as dire a reputation for eliminating civilizations. The rulers of Tarelsk had regressed far indeed. Pham leaned back in his seat. 'Okay. This makes things easier and riskier. We'll take the least-time course; these guys will kill everyone if they are just left to themselves. Follow drop schedule nine.' That meant wave after wave of unmanned devices. The first would be fine-targeted pulse bombs, trying to blind and numb Tarelsk's eyes and automation. Closer in, the drops would be diggers, flooding the moon's urban areas with Qeng Ho automation. If Pham's plans worked, Terelsk's automation would be confronted with another system, quite alien to, and uncontrollable by, the rulers' ubiquitous law enforcement.

Pham's fleet made a low-altitude pass by Namqem world. The maneuver kept them out of Tarelsk's direct fire for a few thousand seconds. In itself, it was a kind of first. Civilized systems didn't like large fusion rockets – much less starship drives – operating in the middle of urban areas. Heavy fines, even ostracism or confiscation were the price of such violations. For once, it was nice to give the finger to all of that. Pham's thirty were decelerating at torch max, more than one gee, and had been for Ksecs. They swept over Namqem's middle north latitudes at less than two hundred kilometers – and moving at almost two hundred kilometers per second. There was a glimpse of forests, of manicured deserts, of the temporary cities that housed the refugees from Alqin. And then they were heading out, their trajectory scarcely bent by the planetary mass. It was like something out of a children's graphic, a planet literally whipping past their viewpoint.

Just kilometers ahead of them, space was alive with hellish light, and only some of it was defensive fire. This was the real reason why high-speed flight in an urban area was insane. The space near Namqem world had once been an orderly scene of optimized usage. There had even been talk of setting up orbital towers. *That* optimization had been successfully resisted by the governance, but even so, low space was saturated with thousands of vehicles and satellites. In the best of times, microcollisions had created so much junk that garbage collection was the largest industry in near Namqem space.

That orderly commerce had ended many Msecs earlier. The Qeng Ho armada had not precipitated this chaos, but they were rushing through it with bomb flares and ramfields that stretched out and sideways for hundreds of kilometers. Pham's ramfields swept across millions of tonnes of junk and freighters and governance military vehicles . . . Their coming had been announced; perhaps there were no innocent casualties. What was left behind was as tumbled and charred as any battlefield.

Tarelsk lay directly ahead. The million lights of its great days had been put out, either by governance fiat or by Pham's pulse bombs. But the satellite was not dead. Casualties were as light as humanly possible. And in less than fifty seconds Pham's ships would cut their torches. What followed would be the riskiest time of the adventure for them personally. Without the torches, they could not run their ramfields . . . and without the ramfields even accidental pieces of high-speed junk could cause damage.

'Forty seconds to flameout.' Their torches were already tuning down, so as not to destroy Tarelsk's surface.

Pham scanned the reports from the other fleets: the landers down on Namqem world, the two thousand starships moving to save the starving at Maresk. Maresk floated like a deep-sea leviathan in the middle of a feeding frenzy. Many of the two thousand had been able to dock. The rest hung off-surface. The last of the freighters from the outer system was visible beyond Maresk's limb. That huge, slow blimp had been launched Msecs earlier, when the outermost farms were still under effective automation. The freighter was as big as a starship, but with none of a ramscoop's structural over-head. There were ten million tonnes of grain aboard it, enough to sustain Maresk a little while longer.

'Twenty seconds to flameout.'

Pham watched the view of Maresk for a couple of seconds more. Clouds of lesser craft swarmed around the Qeng Ho visitors there, but they were not fighting. The people there had not lost out to crazies as at Tarelsk. Silver glyphs tripped across the top of Pham's view, chilling fragments of ice. The message was from Sura's agents on Maresk: *Sabotage detected in harbored vehicles. Flee! Flee! Flee!* And the view of Maresk vanished from Pham's huds. For a moment he was looking out across the *Far Regard's* bridge at an unembellished view back toward Namqem world. Daylight spread serenely across two-thirds of its face. In this true view, Maresk was hidden behind the planet.

And then the fringe of Namqem's atmosphere flared with the light of a sun, a new sun that had been born somewhere beyond it. Two seconds later, there was another flash, and then another.

A moment before, the *Far Regard's* bridge crew had been totally intent on the flameout countdown and preparing for the dangers that would follow the loss of their ramfield protection. Now there was a surge of activity as they turned startled attention upon the lights that flashed across the limb of Namqem world. 'Multigigatonne detonations around Maresk.' The analyst was trying to keep his voice level. 'Our fleets near the surface – Lord – they're gone!' Gone along with the billion-plus population of the megalopolis.

Sammy Park sat frozen, staring. Pham realized he might have to take over the bridge. But then Sammy leaned forward against his harness, and his voice was loud and sharp. 'Tran, Lang, back to your stations. Look to our fleet!'

Another voice: 'Flameout . . . *now.*'

Pham felt the familiar, falling lightness as *Far Regard*'s main torch quenched to zero. His huds showed that all thirty of his fleet had flamed out within a hundred milliseconds of the planned instant. Less then four kilometers ahead floated Tarelsk, so near that it did not seem a moon or a planet so much as a landscape that stretched out and out around them. Before the coming of Humankind, Tarelsk had been just another dead and cratered moon, scarcely larger than the original Luna. But like Luna, the economics of transport had brought it greatness. By the light of Namqem world, Tarelsk was a landscape of pastels and soaring artificial mountains. And unlike old Luna, this world had never known human-made catastrophe . . . until now.

'Closing velocity fifty-five meters per second. Range thirty-five hundred meters.' By intent, they had finished their decel so close that the other side could not attack them without wounding themselves. *But this mad governance just killed a billion people.* 'Sammy! Get us *down*! Land anywhere, hard.'

'Uh—' Sammy's gaze caught his, and now he understood, too. But it was too late.

All systems died, a vanishing that left his huds clear and silent. For the first time in his life, Pham Nuwen felt a physical jolt on a starship. A million tonnes of hull and shielding absorbed and smoothed out the event, but *something* had smashed against them. Pham looked around the bridge. A crowd of voices came through the air, reports from all over but without filtering or analysis.

'Contact nuke, by God!'

One by one, a scattering of displays came online, the backup wallpaper. The view slid smoothly across the Tarelsk landscape and into the sky. The *Far Regard* was turning at several degrees per second. Some of the junior analysts were climbing out of their restraints.

Sammy shouted across the bridge. 'Pick up drill! Contact secondaries!'

On the single functioning window-wall, the Tarelsk landscape came back into view, ramps and towers and clear domes over farmland. Tarelsk was so large that it could almost survive without the outer-system agriculture. And they were headed down into that at – fifteen meters per second? Without functioning huds he couldn't see a closing velocity.

'How fast, Sammy?'

His Flag Captain shook his head. 'Don't know. That nuke hit us from the Tarelsk side, and almost on center. We can't be going more than twenty meters per second now.' But in the spinning wreck that the *Far Regard* had become, there was no way they could slow down any more.

Sammy's crew were busy to distraction, trying to contact the rest of the ship, resuming contact with the other ships of the thirty. Pham sat listening, watching. All the thirty had been nuked. The *Far Regard* was not the most or the least damaged. As the reports trickled in, their view turned and turned . . . and the landscape grew. Pham could see blast damage. The crazies had trashed some of their own farms in this attack. Almost dead ahead . . . Lord . . . it was the old office towers that he and Sura had bought in the first century.

Ship collisions came in enormous variety, from millimeter-per-second bruisings, chiefly of interest to harbor police . . . to vast, bright flashes that wreck planetoids and vaporize spacecraft. The *Far Regard*'s encounter with Tarelsk was something in between the extremes. A million tonnes of starship drove downward through pressure domes and multilevel residences, but not much faster than a human might run in a one-gee field.

A million tonnes does not stop easily. The collision went on and on and on, a screaming, twisting fury. The city levels crushed more easily than hull metal and drive core, but the ship and the city around it mingled into a single ruin.

It couldn't have lasted more than twenty seconds, but when it was over, Pham and the others hung on their harnesses in the two-tenths gravity of Tarelsk's surface. Light flickered from the buckled walls, and the displays were mostly nonsense. Pham unlatched from his harness and slid down to walk on the ceiling. Dust swirled near the ventilator grids, but his full-press coveralls were tightening. The bridge itself was sucking vacuum. On the command channel, he could hear Sammy working down through damage assessment. There had been five hundred living people aboard the *Far Regard* . . . until just moments before.

'We lost all forward stowage, Fleet Captain. It'll take Ksecs to get the bodies out. We—'

Pham climbed a wall to the hatch, and slid it open just a crack. There was a brief gale of equalizing wind. 'Our landing crews, Sammy. Are they okay?'

'Yes, sir. But—'

'Get 'em together. You can leave the others as a rescue party, but we're going out.' *And kick some ass.*

The next few Ksecs were confused. There was so much happening, and happening all at once. For all the years of planning, no one had really believed that the operation might end up as ground combat. And even the Qeng Ho armsmen were not real fighters. Pham Nuwen had seen more blood and death in medieval Canberra than most of them had seen in their whole lives.

But what they were fighting was not a real military either. The mad governance of Tarelsk had not even warned the surface boroughs of the impending collisions. Acting on their own, most people had pulled back from the highest levels, but still, millions had died in the long, slow crushing. Pham's teams worked their way downward, to the second-level supertrams. He had comm with the other landings now. The people of Tarelsk were only a few years removed from the highest technology and best education in all Human Space. *They* understood the disaster; for the most part, *they* understood what their mad governance did not. But they were helpless before the systems that this last set of rulers used against them.

In his headset, Pham could hear another ship's landing party, thirty kilometers away. They had run into ubiquitous law enforcement. 'Everything is working here, sir – against us. I lost fifteen of my people at the tram station.'

'No help for it, Dav. You have pulse bombs. Use 'em, and then flood the utility cores with our automation.'

Sammy's party was slipping farther and farther away from Pham's. They had climbed through the same rents in hull metal, but at every turning, Sammy was going the other way. At first it didn't matter. Comm through the walls was still easy, and the separation made them a more dispersed target . . . but hell, Sammy was already two klicks down-east from him. Pham's party was surrounded by locals now, and some claimed to be utility system managers, people who could show them where to try for overrides. 'Wait up, Sammy!'

The field link could support only low-rate video, so Pham couldn't see what Sammy's team was up to. But they were moving still farther away. After a moment: 'Pham! We've broken through the rubble into . . . a university campus. There's a blowout, and—' A still-pic from Sammy's group popped up in Pham's huds. There was a parklike lawn, at least several dozen locals running toward the camera—none of them wearing pressure suits. But up near the ceiling, dust and loose papers swirled. The audio feed was, full of the high-pitched whistle of a substantial leak.

A second still-pic was mostly formed, this showing Sammy's men at work with industrial patching equipment. The large crowd was coming out of nowhere, some of them children – the place must be one of those inverse towers. Sammy's voice was back on the comm. 'These are my people, Pham!'

Pham remembered that the Tarelsk side of Sammy Park's family had been academics. *Damn.* 'Don't get sidetracked, Sammy. This place has more floorspace than all the cities on an average planet. The chances are zero we came down next to—'

'Not zero . . .' His voice broke in and out of audibility. '. . . didn't tell you, seemed like a small thing. I made sure *Far Regard* would end up near the Polytech.'

Double damn.

'Look, we can save them, Pham! But more – they've been waiting for us . . . Some of Sura's people are here. Between them, they've got the core utility plans . . . and some of the new regime's software changes. Pham, they think they know where the screwballs are holed up!'

Maybe it was a good thing that Sammy had had his own agenda; as ground combateers, the Qeng Ho pretty much stank. But with the core utility plans, they had a good fix on the governance and its control net.

Ten Ksec later, Pham had a comm link with the madmen who called themselves governance: a half-dozen red-eyed, panicky people. Their leader wore a uniform that might once have been from park maintenance. They were an endpoint of civilization.

'There's nothing you can do but make things worse,' Pham told them.

'Nonsense. We have Tarelsk. We've wiped you and the gluttons at Maresk. We have more than enough resources to make Tarelsk self-sufficient. With you gone, we will bring a new order.' And then the video wavered and faded; Pham never knew if the break was deliberate or just the fractured comm system.

It didn't matter. The conversation had lasted long enough to identify the intermediate nodes. And Pham Nuwen's forces had hardware and software that was outside the heredity of Namqem. With their equipment and the help of the local population, the mad governance couldn't survive more than a few more Ksecs.

When it was gone, the hardest work of the Rescue began.

39

The Qeng Ho Grand Meeting was held 20Msec later. Namqem solar system was still a disaster area. Alqin was mostly empty, its people camped on Namqem world, but not starving. Maresk, the smallest moon, was a radioactive wreck; rebuilding it would be the work of centuries. Almost a billion people had died there. But the last food shipment had been saved, the outer system agri automation restarted, and there was enough food for the two billion survivors on Tarelsk. The automation of Namqem had been trashed, and was operating at perhaps ten percent of its pre-debacle efficiency. The people of Namqem system who had survived till now would live to rebuild. There would be no extinction, no dark age. The survivors' grandchildren would wonder at the terror of this time.

But there still was no civilized venue for the Grand Meeting. Pham and Sura stuck by the original decision. The Meeting would be out in Brisgo Gap, the most deserted place in the middle system. At least there was no destruction to look upon there, no local problems to solve. From Brisgo

Gap, Narhqem world and its three moons were just a blue-green disk and three spots of light.

Sura Vinh used the last of her asteroid resources to build the Grand Meeting temp. Pham had hoped that she would be impressed by the success that the Qeng Ho Plan had had. 'We saved the civilization, Sura. Surely you believe me now. We can be more than furtive traders.'

But Sura Vinh was so old now. At the dawn of civilization, medical science had promised immortality. In the early millennia, progress had been rapid. Two hundred years of life, even three hundred, were achieved. After that, each advance was less impressive and more costly. And so Humankind had gradually lost another of its naive dreams. Coldsleep might postpone death for thousands of years, but even with the best medical support, you couldn't expect much more than five hundred years of real lifetime. It was the ultimate limit on one man's reach. And getting near that limit took an awful toll.

Sura's powered chair was more like a mobile hospital ward than a piece of furniture. Her arms twitched up, weak even in zero gee. 'No, Pham,' she said. Her eyes were clear and green as ever, surely transplants or artificial. Her voice was more obviously synthetic, but Pham could hear the familiar smile in it. 'The Grand Meeting must decide, remember? We've never agreed on your plans. The point of coming together was to put the issue to a vote.'

That was what Sura had said ever since the earliest centuries, when she'd realized that Pham would never give up his dream. *Oh, Sura, I don't want to hurt you, but if my view must explicitly win over yours, so be it.*

The temp that Sura towed into the middle of Brisgo Gap was enormous, even by the standards of her pre-debacle holdings. The starships of all the surviving fleets could moor at it, and Sura provided security extending out more than two million kilometers beyond the Gap.

The temp's central volume was a zero-gee meeting hall. It was probably the grandest in history, large beyond all practical use. For Msecs before the Meeting itself, there was socializing, the largest single meeting of Traders there had ever been, probably the largest that would ever be. Pham took every Ksec he could from the rescue schedules to participate. Every day, he was making more contacts, interacting more than he could in a century of his life until now. Somehow he had to convert the doubters. And there were so many of them. They were basically decent, but so cautious and clever. Many of them were his own descendants. Their admiration – even their affection – seemed sincere, but he was never sure how many he had really convinced. Pham realized that he was edgier than he had ever been in combat, or even in hard trading. *Never mind*, he told himself. He had waited all his life for this. Small wonder that he should be nervous when the final test was just Msecs away.

The last Msecs before the Meeting were a frantic rearrangement of schedules. Namqem solar system still lacked decent automation. There would probably be a decade more during which outside help would be necessary to keep things from backsliding, to make sure that no more opportunists surfaced. But Pham wanted his own people at the Meeting. And Sura didn't play games with his wish. Together, they set up a scheme that would bring all Pham's people to the temp, and still not put the new governance of Namqem at risk.

And finally, Pham's time came. His one, greatest opportunity to make things work. He looked out past the veil of the entrance curtains, at the sweep of the hall. Sura had just finished her introduction of Pham and was departing the speaker's platform. Applause swept up from every direction. 'Lord—' Pham muttered.

Behind him, Sammy Park said, 'Nervous, sir?'

'Damn straight.' In fact, only once had he ever been frightened just this way . . . when as a little boy he had stepped onto a starship's bridge and confronted the Traders of the Qeng Ho for the first time. He turned to look at his Flag Captain. Sammy was smiling. Since the rescues of Tarelsk, he had seemed happier than ever before. Too bad. He might not be starfaring again, not with Pham's fleet, anyway. The people his crew had rescued, they really were his own family. And that cute little great-great-grandniece of his: Jun was a good person, but she had her own ideas about what Sammy should do with his life. Sammy stuck out his hand. 'G-good luck, sir.'

And then Pham was through the curtains. He passed Sura on his way up. There was no time to speak, no way to hear. Her frail hand brushed his cheek. He rose to the central platform through wave upon wave of applause. *Be calm.* There were still at least twenty seconds before he had to say anything. *Nineteen, eighteen* . . . The Great Hall was nearly seven hundred meters across, and built in the most ancient tradition of an auditorium. His audience was an almost complete sphere of humanity, stationed at their ease along the inner surface of the hall, and facing on the tiny speaker's platform. Pham looked this way and that, and up and down, and wherever he looked faces looked back. Correction: There was a swath of empty seats, nearly a hundred thousand, for the Qeng Ho who died in the destruction of Maresk. Sura had insisted on that layout – to honor the dead. Pham had agreed, but he knew that it was also Sura's way of reminding everyone that what Pham proposed could have a terrible price.

Pham raised his arms as he reached the platform. All across his field of view, he saw the Qeng Ho responding. After a second, their applause came even louder to his ears. Through clear huds, he could not make out faces. From this distance, he could only guess at them according to the seating pattern. There were women all across the crowd. In a few places, they were rare. In most places, they were as common as the men. In some places – the Strentmannian Qeng Ho – women were the overwhelming majority. Maybe he should have appealed more to them; since Strentmann, he had come to realize that women can have the longest view. But the prejudices of medieval Canberra still had some subtle hold on him, and Pham had never really figured out how to lead women.

He turned his palms outward, and waited as the shouting gradually faded. The words of his speech floated in silver before his eyes. He had spent years thinking on this speech, and Msecs since the Rescue, polishing every nuance, every word.

But suddenly he didn't need the little silver glyphs. Pham's eyes saw past them to the humanity all around, and his words came effortlessly forth.

'My people!'

The crowd noise died to near silence. A million faces looked up at him, across at him, down at him.

'You hear my voice now with barely a second's time lag. Here in Meeting, we hear our fellow Qeng Ho, even those from far Earth, in less than a second. For this first and maybe only time, we can see what we all are. And we can decide what we will be.

'My people, congratulations. We have come across light-centuries and rescued a great civilization from extinction. We did this despite the most terrible treachery.' He paused, gestured solemnly at the sweep of empty seats.

'Here at Namqem, we have broken the wheel of history. On a thousand worlds, Humankind has fought and fought, and even made itself extinct. The only thing that saves the race is time and distance – and until now that has also condemned humanity to repeat its failures.

'The old truths still hold: Without a sustaining civilization, no isolated collection of ships and humans can rebuild the core of technology. But at the same time: Without help from outside, no sessile civilization can persist.'

Pham paused. He felt a wan smile steal across his face. 'And so there is hope. Together, the two halves of what Humankind has become can make the whole live forever.' He looked all around, and let his huds magnify individual faces. They were listening. Would they finally agree? 'The whole can live forever . . . if we can make the Qeng Ho more than mere sellers to customers.'

Pham didn't remember much of the actual speaking of his speech; the ideas and the entreaties were such deep habits in his mind. His recollection was of the faces, the hope he saw in so many, the guarded caution he saw in so many more. In the end, he reminded them that a vote would be coming up, a final call on everything he had ever asked for. 'So. Without your help we will surely fail, destroyed by the same wheel that crushes our Customer civilizations. But if you look just a little beyond the trade of the moment, if you make this extra investment in the future, then no dream will be beyond our ultimate reach.'

*

If the hall had been under acceleration, or on a planetary surface, Pham would have stumbled coming down from the platform. As it was, Sammy Park had to snag him as he passed the entrance curtains.

Above their heads, past the curtains, the sound of applause seemed to be getting louder.

Sura had remained in the anteroom, but there were other new faces – Ratko, Butra, and Qo. His first children, now older than he was.

'Sura!'

Her chair gave a little *chuff*, and she floated across the space between them.

'Will you congratulate me on my speech?' Pham grinned, still feeling giddy. He extended his hands, gently took Sura's. She was so frail, so old. *Oh Sura! This should be our triumph.* Sura was going to lose this one. And now she was so old, she would never see it as anything but defeat. She would never see what they both had wrought.

The applause above them grew still louder. Sura glanced up. 'Yes. In every way, you have done better than I had thought. But then, you have always done better than anyone could imagine.' Her synthetic voice managed to sound sad and proud at the same time. She gestured away from the anteroom and the noise. Pham followed her out, and the sounds faded behind him. 'But you know how much of this is luck, don't you?' she continued. 'You wouldn't have had a chance if Namqem hadn't come apart just as the fleet of fleets arrived.'

Pham shrugged. 'It was good luck indeed. But it proved my point, Sura! We both know that a collapse like this can be the deadliest – and we saved them.'

What he could see of Sura's body was clothed in a quilted business suit that could not disguise the gauntness of her limbs. But her mind and will remained, sustained by the medical unit in her chair. Sura's shake of the head was as forceful and almost as natural as when she'd been a young woman. 'Saved them? You made a difference certainly, but billions still died. Be honest, Pham. It took a thousand years for us to set up this meeting. It's not the sort of thing that can be done every time some civilization goes down the toilet. And without the Maresk die-off, even your five thousand ships would not have been enough. The whole system would be at the edge of its carrying capacity, with still greater disasters in the near future.'

All that had occurred to Pham; he had argued against variants of the point for Msecs before the Meeting. 'But Namqem is the hardest rescue we could possibly face, Sura. An old civilization, entrenched a civilization exploiting every solar-system resource. We would have had a much easier time with a world threatened with bio-plague or even a totalitarian religion.'

Sura was shaking her head. Even now she ignored what Pham set before her. 'No. In most cases, you can make a difference, but more often than not it will be like Canberra – a small difference for the better, and written in Trader blood. You're right: Without the fleet of fleets, civilization would have died here in Namqem system. But some people would have survived on Namqem world; some of the asteroid-belt urbs might have survived. The old story would have been repeated, and someday there would be civilization here again, even if by external colonization. You have bridged that abyss, and billions are rightly grateful . . . but it will take years of careful management to bring this system back. Maybe we here' – her hand twitched in the direction of the Meeting Hall – 'can do that, and maybe not. But I know that we can't do it for the universe and for all time.' Sura did something, and her chair *chuff*'d to a halt.

She turned, extended her arms to touch Pham's shoulders. And suddenly Pham had the strangest feeling, almost a kinesthetic memory, of looking up into her face and feeling her hands on his shoulders. It was a memory from before they were partners, before they were lovers. A memory from their earliest time on the *Reprise:* Sura Vinh, the young woman, serious. There were times when she'd gotten so angry with little Pham Nuwen. There were times when she'd reached out to grab his shoulders, tried to hold him still long enough to make him understand what his young barbarian mind chose to ignore. 'Son, don't you see? We span all Human Space, but we can't manage whole civilizations. You'd need a race of loving slaves to do it. And we Qeng Ho will never be that.'

Pham forced himself to look back into Sura's eyes. She had argued this since the beginning, and never wavered. *I should have known it would come to this someday.* So now she would lose, and Pham could do nothing to help her. 'I'm sorry Sura. When you give your speech, you can say this to a million people. Many of them will believe. And then we'll all vote. And—' And from what he had seen in the Great Hall, and what he saw in Sura Vinh's eyes . . . for the first time, Pham *knew* that he had won.

Sura turned away, and her artificial voice was soft. 'No. I won't be giving that speech. Elections? Funny that you should be depending on them now . . . We've heard how you ended the Strentmannian Pogrom.'

The change in topic was absurd, but the comment touched a nerve. 'I was down to one ship, Sura. What would you have done?' *I saved their damn civilization, the part that wasn't monstrous.*

Sura raised her hand. 'I'm sorry . . . Pham, you are just too lucky, too good.' She seemed almost to be talking to herself now. 'For almost a thousand years, you and I have worked to make this meeting. It was always a sham, but along the way, we created a trading culture that may last as long as your optimistic dreams. And I always knew that in the end, when we were all face-to-face in a Grand Meeting, common sense would prevail.' She shook her head, and a smile quavered. 'But I never imagined that luck would give you the Namqem debacle so perfectly timed – or that you would master it like magic. Pham, if we follow your way, we'll likely have disaster

782

here in Namqem within a decade. In a few centuries, the Qeng Ho will fragment into a dozen conflicting structures that all think themselves "interstellar governances." And the dream we shared will be destroyed.

'You're right, Pham. You might win the election . . . and that's why there won't be one, at least not the kind you think.'

The words didn't register for a moment. Pham Nuwen had been exposed to treachery a hundred times. The sense for it was burned into him before he'd ever seen a starship. But . . . *Sura*? Sura was the only one he could always trust his savior, his lover, his best friend, the one he'd schemed with for a lifetime. And now—

Pham looked around the room, his mind undergoing a change-of-ground more profound than any in his life. Besides Sura, there were Sura's aides, six of them. There were also Ratko and Butra and Qo. Of his own assistants – there was only Sammy Park. Sammy stood a little off to the side; he looked sick.

Finally he looked back at Sura. 'I don't understand . . . but whatever the game, there's no way you can change the election. A million people heard me.'

Sura sighed 'They heard you, and you might have a bare majority in a fair election. But many you think supported you . . . are really with me.'

She hesitated, and Pham looked again at his three children. Ratko avoided his gaze, but Butra and Qo looked back with grim steadiness. 'We never wanted to hurt you, Papa,' Ratko said, finally looking at him. 'We love you. This whole charade of a meeting was supposed to show you that the Qeng Ho could not be what you wished. But it didn't go the way we expected—'

Ratko's words didn't matter. It was the look on his children's faces. It was the same closed stoniness of Pham's brothers and sisters, one Canberra morning. And all the love in between . . . *a charade*?

He looked back at Sura. 'So how do you propose to win? With the sudden, accidental death of half a million people? Or just the selective assassination of thirty thousand hardcore Nuwenists? It won't work, Sura. There are too many good people out there. Maybe you can win this day, but the word will remain, and sooner or later, you'll have your civil war.'

Sura shook her head. 'We're not killing anyone, Pham. And the word won't go out, at least not widely. Your speech will be remembered by those in the hall, but their recorders – most are using our information utilities. Our free hospitality, remember? Ultimately your speech will be polished into something . . . safer.'

Sura continued, 'Over the next twenty Ksec, you will be in special meeting with your opposition. Coming out of that you will announce a compromise: The Qeng Ho will put a much greater effort into our network information services, the sort of thing that can help rebuild civilizations. But you will withdraw your notion of interstellar governance, convinced by the arguments of the rest of us.'

A charade. 'You could fake that. But afterwards, you'll still have to kill a lot of people.'

'No. You will announce your new goal, an expedition to the far side of Human Space. It will be clear that this is partly out of bitterness, but you will wish us well. Your far fleet is almost ready, Pham, about twenty degrees back along the Gap. We have equipped it honestly and well. Your fleet's automation is unusually good, far more expensive than what would be profitable. You won't need a continuous Watch, and the first wake-up will be centuries from now.'

Pham looked from face to face. Something like Sura's treachery could work, but only if most of the Fleet Captains that he thought supported him were really like Ratko and Butra and Qo. And then only if they had set up proper lies with their own people. 'How . . . long have you been planning this, Sura?'

'Ever since you were a young man, Pham. Most of the years of my life. But I prayed it would never come to this.'

Pham nodded, numb. If she had planned that long, there would be no obvious mistakes. It didn't matter. 'My fleet awaits, you say?' His lips twisted around the words. 'And all the incorrigibles will surely be its crew. How many? Thirty thousand?'

'A good deal less, Pham. We've studied your hard-core supporters very carefully.'

Given the choice, who wanted to go on a one-way trip to forever? They had been very careful to keep those supporters out of this room. All but Sammy. 'Sammy?'

His Flag Captain met his eyes, but his lips were trembling. 'Sir. I'm s-sorry. Jun wants a different life for me. We – we're still Qeng Ho, but we can't ship with you.'

Pham inclined his head. 'Ah.'

Sura floated closer, and Pham realized that if he pushed off, he could probably grab the handle on her chair and ram his fist right through her scrawny quilted chest. *And break my hand for the effort.* Sura's heart had been a machine for centuries. 'Son? Pham? It was a beautiful dream, and along the way it made us what we are. But in the end it was just a dream. A failed dream.'

Pham turned away without responding. Now there were guards by the doors, waiting to escort him. He didn't look at his children. He brushed past Sammy Park without a word. From somewhere in the still, cold depths of his heart, something wished his Flag Captain well. Sammy had betrayed him, but not like the others. And no doubt Sammy believed the lies about a far fleet. He hoped that Sammy would never see through them. Who would ever pay for a fleet such as Sura described? Not crafty merchants like Sura

Vinh and her stone-faced children and the others who had plotted this day. Far cheaper, far safer to build a fleet of real coffins. *My father would have understood.* The best enemies are the ones who sleep without end.

Then Pham was in a long corridor, surrounded by guards who were also strangers. His last vision of Sura's face still hung in Pham's imagination. There had been tears in the old woman's eyes. One last fakery.

A tiny cabin, mostly dark. The kind of room a junior officer might have in a small temp. Work jackets floated in a closet bag. A lapel tag whispered, and a name floated in his eyes: *Pham Trinli.*

As always, when Pham let the anger fill him, the memories were more vivid than any huds, and the return to the present was a kind of mocking. Sura's 'far fleet' had not been a fleet of coffins. Even now, two thousand years after Sura's betrayal, Pham still could not explain that. Most likely, there had been other traitors, ones with some power and some conscience, who had insisted that Pham and those who wouldn't betray him must not be killed. The 'fleet' had been scarcely more than refitted ram barges, with space for nothing but the refugees and their coldsleep tanks. But there had been a separate trajectory for each ship of the 'fleet.' A thousand years later they were scattered across the width and height of Human Space.

They had not been killed, but Pham had learned his lesson. He had begun his slow, silent journey back. Sura was beyond mortal reach. But there was still the Qeng Ho that he and she had created, the Qeng Ho that had betrayed him. He still had his dream.

. . . And he would have died with it at Triland, if Sammy had not dug him up. Now fate and time had handed him a second chance: the promise of Focus.

Pham shook away the past, and readjusted the localizers at his temple and in his ear. There was more work than ever to be done. He should have risked more face-to-face meetings with Vinh before now. With good feedback drills, Vinh could learn to handle shocks like this crazy Nau interview, without giving everything away. Yeah that was the easy part. The hard part would be to keep him distracted from where Pham was ultimately headed.

Pham turned in his sleeping bag, let his breathing shift to a light snore. Behind his eyes, the images shifted to the action traces he was running on Reynolt and the snoops. He had fooled them again. In the long run . . . ? If there weren't any more stupid surprises, in the long run, Anne Reynolt was still the greatest threat.

40

Hrunkner Unnerby flew into Calorica Bay on the First Day of the Dark. Over the years, Unnerby had been at Calorica a number of times. Hell, he'd been here right after mid-Brightness, when the bottom of the pit was still a boiling cauldron. In the years after that, the edge of the mountains had harbored a small town of construction engineers. During the mid-Brightness, conditions were hellish even at high altitude, but the workers were very well paid; the launch facilities farther up in the altiplano were funded by a combination of royal and commercial monies, and after Hrunk installed good cooling machines, it wasn't an uncomfortable place to live. The rich people hadn't begun showing up until the Waning Years, settling as they had for each of the last five generations, in the caldera wall.

But of all Hrunk's visits, this had the strangest feel. The First Day of the Dark. It was a boundary in the mind more than anywhere else – and perhaps that made it even more important.

Unnerby had taken a commercial flight out of High Equatoria, but it was no tourister. High Equatoria might be only five hundred miles away, but it was as far as you could get from the wealth of Calorica Bay on the First Day of the Dark. Unnerby and his two assistants – bodyguards actually – waited until the other passengers had clambered forward along the aisle webway. Then they pulled down their parkas and heated leggings and the two panniers that were the whole reason for the flight. Just short of the exit hatch, Hrunkner lost his grip on the webbing and one of the panniers fell by the feet of the aircraft's steward. The all-weather covering split partway open, revealing the contents to be shale-colored powder, carefully wrapped in plastic sacks.

Hrunkner dropped from the aisle webbing and refastened the pannier. The steward laughed, bemused. 'I've heard it said High Equatoria's best export was plain mountain dirt – never expected to see anyone take it seriously.'

Unnerby shrugged his embarrassment. Sometimes that was the best cover. He reshouldered the pannier and made to button his parka.

'Ah, um.' The steward seemed about to say something more, but then stepped back and bowed them off the aircraft. The three of them rattled down the ladders to the tarmac, and suddenly it was obvious what else the fellow had been about to say. Just an hour ago, as they were leaving High Equatoria, the air had been eighty below freezing and the wind over twenty miles per hour. They had needed heated breathers just to walk from the High Eq terminal to the aircraft.

Here . . . 'By damn, this place is a furnace!' Brun Soulac, his junior security agent, set down her pannier and shrugged out of her parka.

The senior agent laughed, though she was guilty of the same foolishness. 'What do you expect, Brun! It's Calorica Bay.'

'Yeah, but this is the First Day of the Dark!'

Some of the other passengers had been similarly shortsighted. They made a grotesque parade, hopping about as they shed parkas and breathers and leggings. Even so, Unnerby noticed that whenever Brun's hands and feet were totally occupied with shedding cold-weather gear, Arla Undergate had free hands and a clear view around them. Brun was similarly alert when Arla was shucking her overclothes. By some magic, their service pistols were never visible during the exercise. They could act like idiots, but underneath the act, Arla and Brun were as good as any soldiers Unnerby had known in the Great War.

The mission to High Equatoria might have been low-tech and low-key, but the Intelligence team in the airport was efficient enough. The bags of rock flour were carted off in armored cars; even more impressive, the major in charge had not even wisecracked about the absurdity of the operation.

Inside of thirty minutes, Hrunk and his now not-so-relevant bodyguards were out on the street.

'What d'ya mean, "not relevant"?' Arla waved her arms in exaggerated wonder. 'Not relevant was shepherding that . . . stuff across the continent.' Neither of the two knew the importance of the rock flour, and they had not been shy in showing their contempt for it. They were good agents, but they didn't have the attitude Hrunk was used to. 'Now we have something important to guard.' She jerked a hand in Unnerby's direction, and there was something serious behind the good humor. 'Why didn't you make our life easy, and go with the major's people?'

Hrunkner smiled back. 'It's more than an hour before I meet the chief. Plenty of time to walk the distance. Aren't you curious, Arla? How many ordinary folks get to see Calorica on the First Day of the Dark?'

Arla and Brun glowered at that the look of noncoms confronted by stupid behavior that they could not correct. Unnerby had felt that way often enough in his life, though normally he hadn't shown his disapproval so obviously. The Kindred had demonstrated more than once their willingness to be violent on other peoples' lands. *But I've lived seventy-five years, and there are so many things to be afraid of.* He was already moving away, toward the lights at the water's edge. Unnerby's usual bodyguards, the ones who accompanied him on his foreign site visits, would have bodily restrained him. Arla and Brun were loaners, not so well briefed: After a moment, they scurried forward to pace him. But Arla was talking into her little telephone. Unnerby grinned to himself. No, these two weren't stupid. *I wonder if I'll notice the agents she's calling.*

Calorica Bay had been a wonder of the world since the earliest times. It was one of only three volcanic sites known – and the other two were under ice and ocean. The bay itself was actually the broken-down bowl of the volcano, and ocean waters drowned most of its central pit.

In the early years of a New Sun, it was a hell of hells, though no one had directly observed the place then. The steeply curving walls of the bowl concentrated the sun's light and the temperatures climbed above the melting point of lead. Apparently this provoked – or allowed – fast lava seepage, and a continuous series of explosions, leaving new crater walls by the time the sun had dimmed to mid-Brightness. Even in those years, only the most foolhardy explorers poked themselves over the altiplano rim of the bowl.

But as the sun dimmed into the Waning Years of its cycle, a different visitor appeared. As northern and southern lands found winters that were steadily harsher, now the highest reaches of the bowl were pleasant and warm. And as the world cooled, lower and lower parts of the bowl became first accessible, and then a paradise. Over the last five generations, Calorica Bay had become the most exclusive resort of the Waning Years, the place where people so rich that they didn't have to save and work to prepare for the Dark could come and enjoy themselves. At the height of the Great War, when Unnerby was pounding snow on the Eastern Front, and even later, when most of the war was tunnel fighting – even then, he remembered seeing tinted engravings showing the life of mid-Brightness leisure that the idle rich led at the bottom of Calorica's bowl.

In a way, Calorica at the beginning of the Dark was like the world that modern engineering and atomic energy were bringing to the entire race of Spiders, for all the years of the Dark. Unnerby walked toward the music and lights ahead, wondering what he would see.

The crowds swirled everywhere. There was laughter and pipe music and occasional argument. And the people were strange in so many ways that for a while Unnerby did not notice the most important things.

He let the crowd motion jostle them this way and that like particles in a suspension. He could imagine how nervous Arla and Brun felt about this mob of uncleared strangers. But they made the most of it, blending into the rowdy noise, just accidentally staying within arm's reach of Unnerby. In a matter of minutes, the three had been swept down to the water's edge. Some in the crowd waved burning sticks of incense, but there was a stronger perfume here at the bottom of the crater, a sulfurous odor that drifted on the warm breeze. Across the water, at the middle of the bay, molten rock glowed in red and near-red and yellow. Steam floated up, wraithlike, all round the center pile. This was one body of water where no one need worry about bottom ice and leviathans – though a volcanic blast would kill them all just as dead.

'Damn!' Brun slipped out of character, jostled Unnerby back from the edge of the plaza. 'Look out there in the water! There are people drowning!'

Unnerby stared a second at where she was pointing. 'Not drowning. They're . . . by the Dark, they're playing in the water!' The half-submerged figures were wearing some sort of pontoons to keep from sinking. The three of them just stared, and he noticed they were not alone in their surprise, though most of the onlookers tried to cover their shock. Why would anyone *play* at drowning? For a military goal perhaps; in warmer times, both Kindred and Accord had warships.

Thirty feet down the stone palisade, another reveler splashed into the water. Suddenly, the water's edge seemed like the edge of a deadly cliff. Unnerby backed off, away from the screams of delight or horror that came from the water. The three of them drifted across the bottom plaza toward light-bedecked trees. Here, in the open, they had a clear view of the sky and the caldera walls.

It was midafternoon, yet except for the cool-colored lights in the trees, and the heat colors from crater-center, it was as dark as any night. The sun looked down on them, a faint blotch in the sky, a reddish disk pocked with small dark marks.

The First Day of the Dark. Religions and nations set minor variations in the date. The New Sun began with an explosive blaze of light, though no one was alive to see it. But the end of the light – that was a slow waning that extended across almost the whole of the Brightness. For the last three years, the sun had been a pale thing, scarcely warming your back at high noon, dim enough to stare at with a fully open gaze. For the last year, the brighter stars had been visible all through the day. But even that was not officially the beginning of the Dark, though it was a sign that green plants couldn't grow anymore, that you'd better have your main food supplies in your deepness, and that tuber and grub farms would be all that could sustain you until it came time to retreat beneath the earth.

So in that gradual slide toward oblivion, what was it that marked the instant – the day at least – that was the first of the Dark? Unnerby stared straight at the sun. It was the color of a warm stovetop, but so dim he felt no warmth. It would get no dimmer. Now the world would simply grow colder and colder and colder with nothing more than starlight and that reddish disk to light it. From now on, the air would always be too cold to be easily breathed. In past generations, this marked the beginning of the final rush to store the necessities in one's deepness. In past generations, it marked the last chance for a father to provide for his cobblies' future. In past generations, it marked a time of high nobility and great treason and cowardice, when all those who were not quite prepared were confronted by the fact of the Dark and the cold.

Here, today – Hrunk's attention moved to those on the plaza between him and the trees. There were some – old cobbers and many from the proper current generation – who raised their arms to the sun and then lowered them to embrace the earth and the promise that the long sleep should represent.

But the air around them was mild as a summer evening in the Middle Years. And the ground was warm, as if the sun of the Middle Years had just set and left the afternoon heat to seep up at them. Most of the people around them were not acknowledging the departure of light. They were laughing, singing – and their clothes were as bright and expensive as if they'd never given any thought to the future. Maybe the rich had always been like that.

The cool-colored lights in the trees must be powered by the main fission plant that Unnerby's companies had built in the highlands above the caldera, almost five years ago. They turned the bottomland forest all aglimmer. Someone had imported lazy woodsfairies, released them by the tens of thousands. Their wings glistened blue and green and far-blue in the light, as the creatures swirled in sympathy with the crowds under the trees.

In the forest, the people danced in piles, and some of the youngest ones ran up into the trees to play with the fairies. The music became frantic as they walked to the center of the grove and started up a gentle incline that would lead to the bottom estates. By now he was used to the sight of out-of-phase people. Even though his instincts still called them a perversion, they really were necessary. He liked and respected many of them. On either side of him, Arla and Brun were unobtrusively clearing the way for him. Both his guards were oophase, about twenty years old, just a little younger than Little Victory must be now. They were good cobbers, as good as any he had ever fought alongside of. Yes, case by case, Hrunkner Unnerby had come to terms with his revulsion. But . . . *I've never seen so many oophases, all together.*

'Hey, old fellow, come dance with us!' Two young ladies and a male pounced on him. Somehow Arla and Brun got him free, all the time pretending to be jolly dancers themselves. In the darkened space beneath one tree, Unnerby got a glimpse of what looked like a fifteen-year-old's molt. It was as if all the carven images of sin and laziness had suddenly become real. Sure, the air was pleasantly warm, but it carried the stench of sulfur. Sure, the ground was pleasantly warm, but he knew that it was not sun's warmth. Instead, it was a heat in the earth itself that extended down and down, like heat from a rotting body. Any deepness dug here would be a death trap, so warm that the sleepers' flesh would rot in their shells.

Unnerby didn't know how Arla and Brun managed it, but eventually they were on the far side of the forest. Here there were still the crowds and the trees – but the mania of the bottom was muted. The dancing was sedate enough that clothes were not torn. Here, the woodsfairies felt safe enough to land on their jackets, to sit and swing the colored lace of their wings with lazy impudence. Everywhere else in the world, these creatures had lost their wings years ago. Five years ago, Unnerby had walked through Princeton streets after a heavy frost, his boot tips crunching through thousands of colored petals, the wings of sensible woodsfairies, now burrowing deep to lay their tiny eggs. The lazy variant might have a few more summer seasons of life, but they were doomed . . . or should have been.

The three walked higher and higher, up the first slopes of the crater wall. Ahead, the mansions of the Late Waning stretched in a ring of light all the way around the wall. Of course, none of these was more than ten years old, but most were built in the parasol-and-bauble style of the last generation. The buildings were new, but the money and the families were old. Almost every estate was a radial property, extending up the crater wall. The mansions of the early waning, halfway up the wall, were often dark, their open architecture unusable. Unnerby could see the glisten of snow on those higher mansions. Sherkaner's place was up there somewhere, among those rich enough to weatherize the high ground of an estate, but too cheap to rebuild down at the bottom. Sherkaner knew that even Calorica Bay could not escape the Dark of the Sun . . . it took nuclear power to do that.

Between the lights of the bottom forest and the ring of estates, there was shadow. The woodsfairies took off, their wings faintly glistening, to fly back to the bottom. The sulfur smell was faint, not as sharp as the clean chill of the air. Above them, the sky was dark but for the stars and the pale disk of the sun. That was real, the Dark. Unnerby just stared for a moment, trying to ignore the lights of the bottom. He tried to laugh. 'So which would you rather have, cobbers, some honest enemy action or another run through that mob?'

Arla Undergate's answer was serious. 'I'd opt for the mob, of course. But . . . that was very strange.'

'Scary, you mean.' Brun sounded downright uneasy.

'Yeah,' said Arla. 'But did you notice? A lot of those cobbers were scared, too. I don't know, it's like they're all – we're all – lazy woodsfairies. When you look up and *see* the Dark, when you see that the sun has died . . . you feel awfully small.'

'Yeah.' Unnerby didn't know what more to say. These two youngsters were oophase. Surely, they hadn't been submerged in trad notions all their lives. And yet they had some of the same gut misgivings as Hrunkner Unnerby. Interesting.

'C'mon. The funicular station is around here someplace.'

41

Most of the midlevel mansions were huge things, stone and heavy timber frontis-halls, extending back to natural caves in the crater wall. Hrunkner had been expecting some kind of 'Hill House South,' but in fact Underhill's place was a disappointment. It looked like a guest house for one of the real mansions, and much of the space inside was shared with security staff, doubled now that the chief was in residence. Unnerby was informed that his precious cargo had already been delivered, and that he would be called for soon. Arla and Brun collected their receipt for delivering him, and Hrunk was shown into a not-so-spacious staff lounge. He passed the afternoon reading some very old news magazines.

'Sergeant?' It was General Smith, standing in the doorway. 'Sorry for the delay.' She wore an unmarked quartermaster uniform, very much like Strut Greenval used to wear. Her figure was almost as lean and delicate as ever, though her gestures seemed a little inflexible. Hrunkner followed her back through the security section, and then up winding wooden stairs. 'We've had some good luck on this one, Sergeant, you catching Sherk and me so close to your discovery.'

'Yes, ma'am. Rachner Thract set up the itinerary.' The stairs circled round and round between jade walls. Closed doors and an occasional darkened room showed to the sides. 'Where are the children?' The question slipped thoughtlessly out of him.

Smith hesitated, certainly looking for some complaint in his words. '. . . Junior enlisted a year ago.'

That he had heard. It had been so long since he had seen Little Victory. He wondered how she would like the military: She had always seemed a tough little cobblie, but with a piece of Sherkaner's whimsy. He wondered if Rhapsa and Little Hrunk might still be around.

The stairs emerged from the crater wall. This part of the residence presumably had existed in the early part of the Waning Years. But where before there had been open courts and patios, now triple-paned quartz stood strong against the Dark. It dimmed all the far colors, but the view was naked and stark. The city lights glittered across the bottomland, circling the heat-red lake at the center. A cold fog hung in the air above the water. It glowed dimly with all the light from below. The General pulled the shades on the view as they ascended toward what must have been the original owner's high perch.

She waved him into a large, brightly lit room.

'Hrunk!' Sherkaner Underhill emerged from the overstuffed pillows that were the room's furniture. Surely these were furnishings of the original owner. Unnerby couldn't imagine either the General or Underhill choosing such ornaments.

Underhill trotted awkwardly across the room, his enthusiasm over-matching his agility. He had a large guide-bug on a leash, and the creature corrected his course, patiently bringing him toward the entrance. 'You've missed Rhapsa and Little Hrunk by a couple of days, I'm afraid. Those two aren't the cobblies you remember; they're seventeen years old now! But the General didn't approve of the atmosphere around here, and she shipped them back to Princeton.'

Behind himself, Hrunkner saw the General glower at her husband, but she made no comment. Instead she walked slowly from window to window, pulling the blinds, shutting out the Dark. At one time, this room had been an open gazebo; now there were a lot of windows. They settled themselves. Sherkaner was full of news about the children. The General sat in silence. As

Sherk launched into Jirlib and Brent's latest adventures, she said, 'I'm sure the Sergeant isn't that interested in hearing about our children.'

'Oh, but I—' Unnerby began, then saw the tenseness in the General's aspect. 'But I guess we have much else to talk about, don't we?'

Sherk hesitated, then leaned forward to stroke his guide-bug's carapace fur. The creature was large, must have weighed seventy pounds, but it looked gentle and smart. After a moment, the bug began purring. 'I wish the rest of you were as easy to please as Mobiy here. But yes, we do have a lot to talk about.' He reached under a filigreed table – the thing looked like a Treppen-dynasty original, something that had survived four passages through the deepnesses of some rich family – and pulled out one of the plastic bags that Hrunk had brought from High Equatoria. He set it on the table with a thump. Wisps of rock flour spread across the polished wood.

'I boggle, Hrunk! Your magic rock dust! What put you on to this? You make one little detour – and bag a secret that all our external intelligence had totally missed.'

'Wait, wait. You make it sound like somebody fell down on the job.' Some people might look very bad unless he set things straight. 'This was outside channels, but Rachner Thract cooperated with me one hundred percent. He loaned me the two cobbers that I came in with. More important, it was his agents at High Equatoria – you know the story?' Four of Thract's people had trekked across the altiplano, brought back that rock flour from the Kindred's inner refinery.

Smith nodded. 'Yes. Don't worry, I blame myself for missing this. We've gotten too confident with all our technical superiority.'

Sherkaner was chuckling. 'Quite so.' He poked around in the rock flour. The lights in here were bright and full-color, much better than down in airport customs. But even in good light, the powder looked like nothing more than shale-colored dust – upland equatorial shale, if one were well-trained in mineralogy. 'But I still don't see how you came upon this – even as a possibility.'

Unnerby leaned back. Actually, the pillows felt pretty good compared with third-class passenger webbing. 'Well, you remember, about five years ago, that joint Kindred-Accord expedition to the center of the altiplano? They had a couple of physicists who claimed gravity was screwball there.'

'Yes. They thought the mine shafts there would be a good place to establish a new lower boundary for the equivalence principle; instead they found big differences, which depended on the time of day. As you say, they got screwball answers, but they retracted the whole thing after they recalibrated.'

'That's the story – but when I was putting in the power plant for West Undergate, I ran into one of the Accord physicists from that expedition. Triga Deepdug is a solid engineer, even if she is a physicist; I got to know her pretty well. Anyway, she claimed that the experimental method on that first expedition was fine, and that she was squeezed out of later participation . . . So I began to wonder about that huge open-pit mining operation the Kindred started on the altiplano just a year after the expedition. That's almost centered on the physics site – and they had to build five hundred miles of rail to serve it.'

'They found copper,' said Smith. 'A good strike, and that's no lie.'

Unnerby smiled at her. 'Of course. Anything less and you would have tumbled to it right away. But still . . . the copper mine is a marginal operation. And my physicist friend knows her business. The more I thought about it, the more I thought it would be nice to see what's going on there.' He waved at the bag of rock powder. 'What you see there is from their third-level refining. The Kindredian miners had to go through several hundred tons of Equatoria shale to filter out this little packet. My guess is they filter it another hundredfold before they get their final product.'

Smith nodded. 'And I'll wager that is kept in harder vaults than the Tiefer holy gemstones.'

'Sure. Thract's team didn't come close to the final product.' Hrunkner tapped at the rock powder with the tip of one hand. 'I hope this is enough that you can prove we found something.'

'Oh, it is. It is!'

Unnerby stared at Sherk in surprise. 'You've had it hardly four hours!'

'You know me, Hrunk. This may be a vacation resort, but I've got my hobbies.' And a laboratory to pursue them, no doubt. 'Under proper lighting, your rock flour weighs almost half a percent less than otherwise . . . Congratulations, Sergeant, you've discovered antigravity.'

'I—' Triga Deepdug had been so sure, but until now Unnerby hadn't really believed. 'Okay, Mister Instant Analysis, how does it work?'

'Beats me!' Sherk was practically vibrating with glee. 'You've found something genuinely new. Why, not even the . . .' He seemed to be searching for words, then settled for: 'But it's a subtle thing. I ground a sample of the dust even finer – and you know, nothing floats off the top; you can't distill the "antigravity fraction." I think we're seeing some kind of group effect. My lab here isn't up to doing more. I'm going to fly back to Princeton with this first thing tomorrow. Besides its magic weight, there's only one strange thing I've found. These upland shales always have some diamond foram content, but in this stuff the smallest forams – the millionth-inch hexens – are enriched by a factor of a thousand. I want to look for evidence of classical fields in the dust. Maybe these foram particles mediate something. Maybe—' And Skerkaner Underhill was off into a dozen speculations, and plans for a dozen dozen tests to extract the truth from those speculations. As he talked, the years seemed to fall away from him. He still had the tremor, but all his hands had come away from his guide-bug's leash, and his voice was full of joy. It was the enthusiasm that had pushed his students and Unnerby and Victory Smith to make a new world. As he spoke, Victory rose from her perch and came over to sit close beside him. She draped her right arms across his shoulders and gave him a sharp, rippling hug.

Unnerby felt himself grinning back at Sherkaner, captured by the other's words. 'Remember all the trouble you got into on the children's radio hour? Saying "all the sky can be our deepness"? By God, Sherk, with this stuff, who needs rockets? We can hoist real ships into space. We can finally find out what caused those lights we saw in the Dark! Maybe we can even find other worlds out there.'

'Yes, but—' Sherkaner began, but suddenly weaker, almost as if getting manic enthusiasm reflected back on him made him realize all the problems that stood between dream and reality. 'But, um, we still have Honored Pedure and the Kindred to contend with.'

Hrunkner remembered his walk through the bottom forest. *And we still have to learn to live in the Dark.*

The years seemed to come back down upon Sherkaner. He reached out to pet Mobiy, and set two other hands on the animal's leash. 'Yes, there are so many problems.' He shrugged, as if acknowledging his age and the distance to his dreams. 'But I can't do anything more to save the world till I get to Princeton. This evening is my best chance in a while to see how crowds react to the Dark. What did you think of our First Day of the Dark, Hrunk?'

Down from the heights of hope, head to head with the limitations of Spiderkind. 'It was – scary, Sherk. We've given up all the rules one by one, and I saw what's left down there this afternoon. Even – even if we win against Pedure, I'm not sure what we'll be left with.'

The old grin wavered across Sherkaner's aspect. 'It's not that bad, Hrunk.' He came slowly to his feet and Mobiy guided him toward the door. 'Most folks left in Calorica are foolish old-money rich . . . you have to expect a little dissipation. But there's still something to be learned by watching them.' He waved at the General. 'I'm going to take a walk around the bottom of the ringwall, my dear. These young folks may have some interesting insights.'

Smith came off her pillows, walked around Mobiy to give her husband a little hug. 'You'll take the usual security team? No tricks?'

'Of course.' And Hrunkner had the feeling her request was deadly serious, that since twelve years ago Sherkaner and all the Underhill children were very good about accepting protection.

The jade doors closed softly behind Sherkaner, and Unnerby and the General were alone. Smith returned to her perch, and the silence stretched long. How many years had it been since he had talked to the General in person without a roomful of staff around? They exchanged electronic mail constantly. Unnerby wasn't officially on Smith's staff, but the fission-plant program was the single most important civilian part of her plan, and he

795

took her advice as his command, moving from city to city according to her schedule, doing his best to build to her specs and her deadlines – and still keep the commercial contractors happy. Almost every day, Unnerby was on the phone to her staff. Several times a year they met at staff meetings.

Since the kidnappings . . . the barrier between them had been a fortress wall. The barrier had existed before that, growing year by year as her children grew; but before Gokna's death, they could always reach over it. Now, it felt very strange to be sitting here alone with the General.

The silence stretched on, the two of them staring at each other and pretending not to. The air was stale and cold, as if the room had been shut for a long time. Hrunkner forced his attention to wander across the baroque tables and cabinets, all painted with a dozen colored varnishes. Practically every piece of woodwork looked a couple of generations old. Even the pillows and their embroidered fabric were in the overdone style of the Generation 58. Yet he could tell that Sherk really worked here. The perch on his right was by a desk littered with gadgets and papers. He recognized Underhill's shaky penmanship in one title: 'Videomancy for High Payload Steganography.'

Abruptly, the General broke the tense silence. 'You did well, Sergeant.' She stood, and walked across the room to sit closer to him, on the perch in front of Sherk's desk. 'We had totally missed what the Kindred had discovered here. And we'd still be clueless if you hadn't brought the matter up with Thract.'

'Rachner set up the operation, ma'am. He's turned out to be a good officer.'

'Yes . . . I'd appreciate it if you'd let me do any follow-up on this with him.'

'Sure.' Need to know and all that.

And then there was more silence with nothing to say. Finally, Hrunkner waved at the absurd pillow furniture, the smallest worth a sergeant's yearly salary. Except for Sherk's desk, there was not a sign of either of his friends in this place. 'You don't come here often, do you?'

'No,' she said shortly. 'Sherk wanted to see how people live after the Dark – and this is as near as we could get to it before we all do it ourselves. Besides, it seemed like a safe place to bring our youngest.' She looked at him defiantly.

How not to make an argument out of this? 'Yes, well I'm glad you sent them home to Princeton. They're . . . they're good cobblies, ma'am, but this is not a good place for them. I had the strangest feeling down there on the bottom. The people were afraid, like the old stories about folks who don't plan and then are left alone in the Dark. They don't have any goal, and now it's Dark.'

Smith sat a little lower on her perch. 'We've got millions of years of evolution to battle; sometimes that's harder to deal with than nuclear physics and the Honored Pedure. But people will get used to it.'

That was what Sherkaner Underhill would have said, all smiling and oblivious of the uneasiness around him. But Smith sounded more like a trooper in a hole, repeating the High Command's assurances about enemy weakness. Suddenly he remembered how thoroughly she had shuttered every one of the windows. 'You feel the same as I do about it, don't you?'

For a moment he thought she would blow up. Instead, she sat inscrutably silent. Finally, '. . . You're right, Sergeant. As I said, there's a lot of instinct we're running up against.' She shrugged. 'Somehow, it doesn't bother Sherkaner at all. Or rather, he knows the fear and it fascinates him, just another wonderful puzzle. Every day he goes down to the crater bottom and watches. He even mingles, bodyguards and guide-bug and all – you have to see it to believe it. He would have been down there all today if you hadn't shown up with your own kind of fascinating puzzle.'

Unnerby smiled. 'That's Sherk for you.' Maybe he was on a safe topic. 'Did you see how he lit up when we talked about my "magic rock dust"? I can't wait to see what he does with it. What happens when you give a miracle to a miracle worker?'

Smith seemed to search for words. 'We'll figure out the rock dust, that's certain. Eventually. But . . . hell, Hrunkner, you deserve to know. You've been with Sherk as long as I have. You noticed how his tremor is getting worse? The truth is, he's not aging as well as most in your generation.'

'I noticed he's frail, but look at all the results coming out of Princeton these days. He's doing more than ever.'

'Yes. Indirectly. Over the years, he's brought together a larger and larger circle of genius students. There are hundreds of them now, scattered all over the computer net.'

'. . . But all those papers by "Tom Lurksalot"? I thought that was Sherk and his students being coy.'

'That? No. That's . . . that's only his students being coy. They play anonymous games on the net; they make credit-taking into a guessing game. It's just . . . silliness.'

Silly or not, it was amazingly productive. Over the last few years, 'Tom Lurksalot' had provided breakthrough insights about everything from nucleonics to computer science to industrial standards. 'It's hard to believe. Just now, he seemed the same as always – mentally, I mean. The ideas seemed to come as fast as ever.' *A dozen weird ideas a minute, when he's on a roll.* Unnerby smiled to himself, remembering. Flightiness, thy name is Underhill.

The General sighed, and her voice was soft and distant. She might have been talking about made-up storybook characters, not her own personal tragedy. 'Sherk has had thousands of crazy ideas and hundreds of beautiful winners. But that's . . . changed. My dear Sherkaner hasn't come up with anything new in three years. He's into videomancy these days, did you know that? He has all his old flamboyance, but . . .' Smith's voice guttered into silence.

For almost forty years, Victory Smith and Sherkaner Underhill had been a team, Underhill producing an endless avalanche of ideas and Smith selecting the best and feeding them back to him. Sherk used to describe the process more colorfully, back when be thought artificial intelligence was the wave of the future: 'I'm the idea-generating component and Victory is the crap-detector; we're an intelligence greater than anything on ten legs.' These two had transformed the world.

But now . . . what if half the team had lost its genius? Sherk's brilliant whimsy had kept the General on track as much as the reverse. Without Sherk, Victory Smith was left with her own assets: courage, strength, persistence. Was that enough?

Victory didn't say anything more for a time. And Hrunkner wished that he could walk over and put his arms across her shoulders . . . but sergeants, even old sergeants, don't do that to generals.

42

The years had passed, and the danger had grown. More implacably than any human Pham had ever known, Reynolt kept searching and searching. As far as possible, he had avoided manipulating the zipheads. He had even arranged for his operations to continue while he was off-Watch; that was very risky, but it evaded the obvious correlations. It didn't help. Now Reynolt seemed to have concrete suspicions. Pham's tracers showed her searches intensifying, closing in on her suspect – most likely Pham Nuwen. There was no cure for it. However risky the operation, Anne must be eliminated. The open house for Nau's new 'office' might be the best chance Pham would get.

'North Paw' was what Tomas Nau called it. Most everybody else – certainly the Qeng Ho who did the engineering – called it simply the Lake Park. Now everyone on-Watch had their one opportunity to see the final result.

The last of the crowd was still trickling in when Nau appeared on the porch of his timbered lodge. He wore a glistening full-press jacket and green pants. 'Keep your feet on the ground, people. My Qiwi has invented a whole special etiquette for North Paw.' He was smiling, and those in the crowd laughed. Gravity on Diamond One was more of a hint than a physical law. Around the lodge, the 'ground' was cleverly textured grabfelt. So everyone did have feet on the ground, but their notion of vertical was only a vague consensus. Beside him on the porch, Qiwi was chuckling at the appearance of the hundreds of people standing before them, tilting this way and that like drunks. A black-furred kitten lay curled across the lace of her blouse.

Nau raised his hands again. 'My people, my friends. This afternoon, please enjoy and admire what you have built here. And think about it. Thirty-eight years ago we nearly destroyed ourselves in battle and in treachery. For most of you, that time is not so long ago, just ten or twelve years on-Watch. You remember after that, how I said this was a time like the Plague Years on Balacrea. We had destroyed most of the resources we brought here, we had destroyed our star-faring capabilities. To survive, I said, we must put aside the animosities, and work together no matter how different our backgrounds . . . Well, my friends, we did that. We are not out of physical danger; our destiny with the Spiders is still to be. But look around you, and you will see how we have healed ourselves. *You* all built this from the bare rock and ice and airsnow. This North Paw – Lake Park – is not large, but it is a work of highest art. Look upon it. You've made something that rivals the best that whole civilizations might create.

'I'm proud of you.' He reached out to slip his arm across Qiwi's shoulders, displacing the kitten into the crook of Qiwi's arm. Once upon a time, the relationship between Nau and Lisolet had been an ugly rumor. Now – Pham could see people smiling comfortably at the sight. 'You see this is more than a park, more than a Podmaster's sanctum. What you see here is evidence of something new in the universe, a melding of the best that Qeng Ho and Emergent have to offer. Emergent Focused persons—' Pham noticed that he still didn't talk about the slaves as bluntly as he might. '—did the detailed planning for this park. Qeng Ho trade and individual action made it reality. And I personally have learned something: On Balacrea and Frenk and Gaspr, we Podmasters rule for the community good, but we rule largely by personal direction – and often by force of law. Here, working with you former Qeng Ho, I see another way. I know that the work on my park was accomplished as payback for that silly pink scrip you've been hiding from me for so long.' He raised a hand and several bills fluttered into the air. Laughter passed around the crowd again. 'So! Think what the combination of Podmaster direction and Qeng Ho efficiency can do once we have completed our mission!'

He bowed to enthusiastic applause. Qiwi slipped in front of him, to stand at the porch railing – and the applause just got louder. The kitten, finally fed up with the noise and the jostling, jumped off Qiwi's arm and sailed into the air over the crowd. It unfurled soft wings and slowed its upward trajectory, then curved back to circle over its mistress. 'Take note,' Qiwi said to the crowd, 'Miraow *is* allowed to fly here. But she has wings!' The cat made a mock dive at her, then flew off into the forest that grew all around the inland side of Nau's lodge. 'Now I invite you to the side of the Podmaster's house for refreshments.'

Some of the visitors were already there. The rest shuffled round the pathways to trestled tables that bowed subtly downward, as if from the weight of the food that was set upon them. Pham moved along with everyone, loudly greeting anyone who would talk with him. It was important to establish his presence here in as many minds as possible. Meantime, in the back of his eyes, the view from his tiny spies built up the tactical picture of the park and the forest.

Cultures clashed at the food tables, but by now Benny's parlor had established an etiquette for going after food. In a few moments, most people had their first buckets and bottles full of refreshment, and spread back into the open. Pham walked up behind Benny and slapped him on the back. 'Benny! This stuff is good! But I thought you were supplying.'

Benny Wen swallowed, coughing. 'Of course it's good. And of course it's mine – and Gonle's.' He nodded at the former quartermaster clerk who was standing beside him. 'Actually, Qiwi's father sprouted some new stuff he found in the libraries. We've had it for about half a year now, saving it for this party.'

Pham puffed himself up: 'I did my part out-of-doors. Someone had to supervise the added drilling and the melt-water for the Podmaster's lake.'

Gonle Fong showed her mercenary smile. More than any Qeng Ho – in a way more than Qiwi herself – Fong bought into Tomas Nau's 'cooperative vision.' Gonle had done very well by doing good. 'Everybody got something out of this. My farms are openly endorsed by the Podmaster now. And I've got real automation.'

'You have something better than a keyboard how?' Pham said slyly.

'You bet. And today, I'm in charge of services.' She lifted her hand dramatically and a food tray floated docilely over to them. It rotated beneath her hand, bobbed politely as she grabbed at spiced seaweed. Then it moved to Benny and then Pham. Pham's little spies looked at the gadget from all directions. The tray maneuvered on tiny gas jets, almost silently. It was mechanically simple, but it moved with grace and intelligence. Benny noticed too. 'It's controlled by a Focused person?' he said, sounding a little sad.

'Um, yes. The Podmaster thought it worthwhile, considering the event.' Pham watched the other trays. They swept in wide circles, out from the food tables, picking out just the guests who hadn't been fed. *Clever.* The slaves were kept diplomatically offstage, and people could pretend what Nau had often declared, that Focus took civilization to a higher level. *But Nau is right! Damn him.*

Pham said something appropriately truculent to Gonle Fong, words that showed that 'old fart Trinli' was truly impressed but determined not to admit it. He walked out from the center of the crowd, apparently intent on food. *Hmm.* Ritser Brughel was off-Watch just now – another cleverness of Tomas Nau. Many people bought into some part of Nau's 'vision' nowadays, but Ritser Brughel could unnerve even the fully converted. But if

Brughel was off-Watch, and if Nau and Reynolt were diverting rote-layer zipheads to manual serving . . . this was a chance even better than he had thought. *So where is Reynolt?* The woman could be surprisingly hard to track; sometimes she dropped off Brughel's direct monitor list for Ksecs at a time. Pham pushed his attention outward. There were millions of the tiny particles scattered throughout the park. The ones stabilizing the lake and running the ventilators were mostly tasked, but that still left immense processing power. No way he could handle all the viewpoints and images. As his mind swept back and forth though the park, he was vaguely aware that he was swaying on his feet. *Aha, there!* Not a close view, but there inside Nau's lodge, he had a glimpse of Reynolt's red hair and pinkish skin. As expected, the woman wasn't participating in the festivities. She was hunched over an Emergent input pad, her eyes hidden behind stark black buds. She looked the same as ever. Tense, intense, as if on the verge of some deadly insight. *And for all I know, she is.*

Someone whacked him on the shoulder, as hard as he had struck Benny a few moments earlier. 'So Pham, my man, what do you think?'

Pham pushed away the inner visions and looked around at his assailant: Trud Silipan had dressed up for the event. His uniform was like nothing he'd seen except in some Emergent historicals: blue silk, fringed and tasseled, and somehow imitating torn, stained rags. It was the dress of the First Followers, Trud had once told him. Pham let his surprise become exaggerated. 'What do I think about what – your uniform or the view?'

'The view, the view! I'm in uniform just because this is such a milestone. You heard the Podmaster's speech. Go ahead, you take a few more moments. Take in the view of Lake Park and tell me what you think.'

Behind them, Pham's inner vision showed Ezr Vinh bearing down on them. *Damn.* 'Well—'

'Yes, what do you think, Armsman Trinli?' Vinh walked around till he stood facing them. He looked straight into Pham's eyes for an instant. 'Of all the Qeng Ho here, you are the oldest, most traveled. Of all of us, you must have the deepest experience. How does the Podmaster's North Paw compare to the great parks of the Qeng Ho?'

Vinh's words had a double meaning that went unnoticed by Trud Silipan, but Pham felt an instant of cold rage. *You're part of the reason I have to kill Anne Reynolt, you little jerk.* Nau's 'true' histories of Pham Nuwen had eaten into the boy. For at least a year now, it was clear that he understood the true story of Brisgo Gap. And he guessed what Pham really wanted with Focus. His demands for guarantees and reassurance had become more and more pointed.

The localizers painted false-color images of Ezr Vinh's face, showed his blood pressure and skin temperature. Could a good ziphead snoop look at such pictures and guess that the boy was playing some kind of game? Maybe. The boy's hate for Nau and Brughel still outweighed his feelings against Pham Nuwen; Pham could still use him. But he was one more reason why Reynolt must be removed.

The thoughts passed through Pham's mind even as his mouth twisted into a self-satisfied smirk. 'Putting it that way, my boy, you're absolutely right. Book learning can't compare to traveling the light-years and seeing the sights with your own two eyes.' He turned away from them and looked down the footpath, past the lodge, to the moorage and the lake beyond. *Pretend to be thoughtfully considering.*

He had spent Msecs invisibly prowling this construction; it should have been easy to play his proper role. But standing here, he could feel the air drifting slowly out of the trees behind him. It was moist, faintly chill, with a tarry scent that whispered of a thousand kilometers of forest stretching out behind him. Sunlight came warm through high patchy clouds. That, too, was fake. Nowadays, the real sun was not as bright as a decent moon. But the light systems embedded in the diamond sky could imitate almost any visual effect. The only clue to the fakery was the faint shimmering rainbows that arched across the farther distances . . .

Down the hill from him was the lake itself. That was Qiwi's triumph. The water was real, thirty meters deep in places. Qiwi's network of servos and localizers kept it stable, the surface flat and smooth, reflecting clouds and blue from overhead. The Podmaster's lodge overlooked a moorage that sat at the head of an inlet. The inlet spread and spread. Kilometers out – actually less than two hundred meters – two rocky islands rose from the mists, guarding the far shore.

The place was a Lord-blessed masterpiece. 'It's a *tresartnis*,' said Pham, but he made the word sound like an insult.

Silipan frowned. 'What—?'

Ezr said, 'It's parkbuilder jargon. It means—'

'Oh, yes. I've heard the word: a park or a bonsai that goes to extremes.' Trud puffed up defensively. 'Well, it is extreme; the Podmaster pushed for that. Look! An enormous microgravity park, perfectly imitating a planetary surface. It breaks a lot of aesthetic rules – yet knowing when to break the rules is the mark of a great Podmaster.'

Pham shrugged, and continued to munch on Gonle's refreshments. He turned idly and looked up into the forest. The crest of the hill matched the true wall of the cavern, a standard parkbuilder trick. The trees stood ten and twenty meters tall, moss glistening cool and dark on their long trunks. Ali Lin had grown them on wires in incubator tents on Diamond One's surface. A year ago they had been three-centimeter seedlings. Now, by Ali's magic, these trees might have been centuries old. Here and there, dead wood of 'older' forest generations lay gray within the blue and green. There were parkbuilders who could achieve such perfection from a single viewpoint. But Pham's hidden eyes looked from all directions, throughout the forest.

The Podmaster's park was such a perfection at every level. Cubic meter for cubic meter it was as perfect as the finest Namqem bonsai.

'So,' said Silipan, 'I think you see why I have reason to be proud! Podmaster Nau provided the vision, but it was my work with system automation that guided the implementation.'

Pham sensed the anger building in Ezr Vinh. No doubt he could contain it, but a good snoop would still pick it up. Pham punched Ezr lightly on the shoulder and gave the braying laugh that was a Trinli trademark. 'Did you get that, Ezr? Trud, what you mean is the Focused persons you supervise did this.' And supervise was too strong a word. Silipan was more of a custodian, but saying that would be an insult Trud could not forgive.

'Er, yes, the zipheads. Isn't that what I said?'

Rita Liao approached from the crowd around the tables. She was carrying food for two. 'Anyone seen Jau? This place is so big you can lose someone.'

'Haven't seen him,' said Pham.

'The flight tech? I think he went around the other side of the lodge' – this from an Emergent, someone whose name Pham should not know. Nau and Qiwi had arranged an intersection of Watches for this open house so that there were some near-strangers in the crowd.

'Well, pus. I should just bounce off the ceiling and take a look.' But even in the present mellow circumstances, Rita Liao was a good Emergent Follower. She kept her feet squarely on the gripping ground as she turned to scan the crowd. 'Qiwi!' she shouted. 'Have you seen my Jau?'

Qiwi detached herself from the group around Tomas Nau and shuffled up the walk toward them. 'Yes,' she said. Pham noticed Ezr Vinh backing off, heading for another group. 'Jau didn't believe the pier was real, so I suggested he go take a look.'

'It's real? The boat, too?'

'Sure. Come on down. I'll show you.' The five of them walked down the path. Silipan strutted along in his silken rags, waving at others to follow. 'See what we've done here!'

Pham sent his inner gaze ahead, studying the rocks around the pier, the bushes that leaned out over the water. This Balacrean vegetation was beautiful in a stark way that fit with the cool air. And the entrance to the utility tunnel was hidden in the cliff behind the blue-green fronds. *This may be my best chance.* Pham walked next to Qiwi, asking questions that hopefully would mark his presence later. 'You can actually sail in it?'

Qiwi smiled. 'See for yourself.'

Rita Liao made an exaggerated shivering sound. 'It's cold enough to be real. North Paw is pretty, but can't you redial for something tropical?'

'No,' said Silipan. He hurried to walk in front of them and lecture. 'It's too real for that. Ali Lin's whole point was realism and detail.' Now that Qiwi was present, he spoke of the zipheads like human beings.

The path wound back and forth, realistic switchbacks that took them down the rocky face of the harbor wall. Most of the guests were following, curious to see what this moorage could really be.

'Water looks awfully flat,' someone said.

'Yes,' said Qiwi. 'Realistic, waves are the hardest part. Some of my father's friends are working on that. If we can form the water surface on a short scale both in time and—' There was startled laughter as a trio of winged kittens zipped low and fast over their heads. The three skimmed out across the water, then climbed into the sky like strafing aircraft.

'I'll bet you they don't have *that* at the real North Paw!'

Qiwi laughed. 'True. That was my price!' She smiled up at Pham. 'Remember the kittens we had in the pre-Flight temp? When I was little—' She looked around, searching for a face in the crowd. 'When I was little, someone gave me one for a pet.'

There was still a little girl inside, who remembered other times. Pham ignored the wistfulness in her voice. His words came out bluff and patronizing. 'Flying kittens don't have real significance. If you'd wanted a solid symbol, you'd have wombed some flying pigs.'

'Pigs?' Trud stumbled, almost lost his stride. 'Oh yeah, the "noble winged pig."'

'Yes, the spirit of programming. There are winged pigs in all the grandest temps.'

'Yeah, sure . . . just get me an umbrella!' Trud shook his head, and some of those behind him were laughing. The flying pig mythos had never caught on at Balacrea.

Qiwi smiled at the byplay. 'Maybe we should – I don't think I'll ever convince the kitties to scavenge floating trash.'

In less than two hundred seconds, the crowd had ranged itself along the water's edge. Pham drifted away from Qiwi and Trud and Rita. He moved as if seeking the best vantage point. In fact, he was coming closer to the cover of the blue-green fronds. With any luck, there would be some excitement in the next few moments. Surely some fool would fall off the ground. He began a final security sweep across the localizer net . . .

Rita Liao was no fool, but when she saw where Jau Xin was, she got a little careless. 'Jau, what in Plague's Name are you doing—' She handed her food and drink to someone behind her and rushed out onto the pier. The boat there had slipped free, was sliding smoothly out into the inlet. Like the lodge and the pier, it was dark timber. But this wood was tarred near the boat's waterline, varnished and painted at the gunnels and prow. A Balacrean sail was hoisted on its single mast. Jau Xin grinned at the crowd from his seat amidships.

'Jau Xin, you come back here! That's the Podmaster's boat. You'll—' Rita started running down the pier. She realized her mistake and tried to stop herself. When her feet left the ground she was moving at just a few centimeters per second. She floated off the platform, a-spin and embarrassed, and loudly angry. If no one snagged her, she would sail over her errant husband's head, and come down in the lake a few hundred seconds later.

Time to move. His programs told him no one in the crowd was watching. His probes into Nau's security showed that no snoop was on him right now, and he had a glimpse of Reynolt still working at some drudge task back in the lodge. He blinded the localizers for an instant and stepped into the fronds. Just a little massaging of the digital record and there'd be proof he was here the whole time. He could do what was necessary and get back unnoticed. It was still as dangerous as hell, even if Brughel's snoops were not on alert. *But taking out Reynolt is necessary.*

Pham finger-walked up the cliff face, slowed by the need to stay hidden behind the bushes. Even here, the artistry of Ali Lin was evident. The cliff could have been simple raw diamond, but Ali had imported rocks from the mineral dumps on the surface of the L1 jumble. They were discolored as if etched by the seepage of a thousand years. The rock was watercolor art as great as any ever painted on paper or digital. Ali Lin had been a first-rank parkbuilder before the expedition to OnOff. Sammy Park had picked Ali for the crew for that reason. But in the years since his Focus, he had become something greater, what a human could become if all his mind was concentrated on a single love. What he and his fellows had done was subtle and deep . . . and as much as anything it proved the power that Focus gave to the culture that possessed it. *Using it is right.*

The tunnel entrance was still a few meters farther up. Pham sensed a half-dozen localizers floating there, imaging the outlines of the door.

A small fraction of his attention remained with the crowd back at the harbor. No eyes looked back in his direction. Some of the nimbler partyers had scrambled out onto the pier and formed a chain of life that reached six or seven meters into the air, an acrobatic tumble of humanity. The men and women of the chain were in a dozen different orientations, the classic zero-gee pose for such an operation. It broke the illusion of downness, and some of the Emergents looked away, groaning. Imagining the sea as flat and down was one thing. Suddenly seeing the sea as a watery cliff or a ceiling was enough to provoke nausea.

But then the tip of the chain extended a hand and grabbed Rita's ankle. The chain contracted, bringing her back to the ground. Pham tapped his palm, and the audio from the scene below came louder in his ear. Jau Xin was beginning to get embarrassed. He apologized to his wife. 'But Qiwi said it was okay. And face it, I am a space pilot.'

'A pilot *manager*, Jau. It's not the same thing.'

'Close enough. I can do some things without a ziphead to make it right.' Jau sat back down by the mast. He tweaked the sail a little. The boat moved out around the pier. It stayed level in the water. Maybe suction was keeping it fitted to the surface. But its wake rose a half meter into the air, twisting and braiding the way surface tension makes free water do. The crowd applauded – even Rita, now – and Jau swung the craft around, trying to make it back to the moorage.

Pham pulled himself even with the tunnel entrance. His remotes had already been fiddling with the hatch. *Everything* in this park was localizer-compatible, thank the Lord. The door opened silently. And when he drifted through, he had no trouble closing it behind him.

He had maybe two hundred seconds.

He pushed quickly up the narrow tunnel. Here there was no illusion. These walls were raw crystal, the naked stuff of Diamond One. Pham pushed faster. The maps that unrolled before his eyes showed what he had seen before. Tomas Nau intended the Lake Park to be his central site; after this open house, outsider visits would be strictly limited. Nau had used the last of the thermal diggers to cut these narrow tunnels. They gave him direct physical access to the critical resources of Hammerfest.

Pham's tiny spies showed him to be just thirty meters short of the new entrance to the Focus clinic. Nau and Reynolt were safely at the party. All the MRI techs were at the party or off-Watch. He would have his time in the clinic, enough time for some sabotage. Pham twisted head for feet, and extended his hands as brakes against the walls.

Sabotage? *Be honest.* It was murder. *No, it's an execution. Or a combat death upon an enemy.* Pham had killed his share in combat, and not always at the end of a ship-to-ship trajectory. *This is no different.* So what if Reynolt was a Focused automaton now, a slave to Nau? There had been a time when her evil had been self-aware. Pham had learned enough about the Xevalle clique to know that its villainy was not just the invention of those who had destroyed it. There had been a time when Anne Reynolt had been like Ritser Brughel, though doubtless more effective. In appearance, the two could have been twins: pale-skinned, reddish haired, with cold, killing eyes: Pham tried to catch the image, amplify it in his mind. Someday he would overthrow the Nau/Brughel regime. Someday Pham would invade the *Invisible Hand* and end the horror that Brughel had made there. *What I do to Anne Reynolt is no different.*

And Pham realized he was floating in front of the clinic entrance, his fingers poised to command it open. *How much time have I wasted?* The time line he kept at the edge of his vision said only two seconds.

He tapped his fingers angrily. The door slid open, and he floated through into the silent room. The clinic was brightly lit, but the vision behind his eyes was suddenly dark and vacant. He moved cautiously, like a man suddenly struck blind. The localizers from the tunnel, and what he shook out from his clothing, spread out around him, slowly giving him back his vision. He moved quickly to the MRI control table, trying to ignore the absence of vision in the corners and dead spaces. The clinic was one place where the localizers could not survive long-term. When the big magnets were pulsed on, they fried the electronics in the localizers. Trud had taken to vacuuming them out after a magnet-accelerated dustmote had cut his ear.

But Pham Nuwen had no intention of pulsing the magnets, and his little spies would stay alive and well for the time it took him to set his trap. He moved across the room, quickly cataloguing the gear. As always, the clinic was an orderly maze of pale cabinets. Here wireless was not an option. Optical cables and short laser links connected automation to magnets. Superconducting power cables snaked back into areas he couldn't see yet. *Ah.* His localizers drifted near the controller cabinet. It was set just the way Trud had left it the last time he had been here. Nowadays, Pham spent many Ksecs each Watch with Trud in the clinic. Pham Trinli had never seemed pointedly curious about the workings of the Focus gear, but Trud liked to brag and Pham was gradually learning more and more.

Focus could kill easily enough. Pham floated above the alignment coils. The inner region of the MRI was less than fifty centimeters across, not even big enough for whole-body imaging. But this gear was for the head only, and imaging was only part of the game. It was the bank of high-frequency modulators that made this different from any conventional imagers. Under program control – programs mostly maintained by Anne Reynolt, despite Trud's claims – the modulators could tweak and stimulate the Focus virus in the victim's head. Millimeter by cubic millimeter the mindrot could be orchestrated in their psychoactive secretion. Even done perfectly, the disease had to be retuned every few Msecs, or the ziphead would drift into catatonia or hyperactivity. Small errors could produce dysfunction – about a quarter of Trud's work had to be redone. Moderate errors could easily destroy memory. Large errors could provoke a massive stroke, the victim dying even faster than. Xopi Reung had.

Anne Reynolt was due for such a massive cerebral accident the next time she retuned herself.

He'd been gone from the Lake Park for almost one hundred seconds. Jau Xin was taking small groups for rides in the boat. Someone had finally fallen in the lake. *Good. That will buy more time.*

Pham pulled the hood off the controller box. There were interfaces to the superconductors. Things like that could fail, on rare occasions with no warning. Weaken the switch, tweak the management programs to recognize Reynolt when next she used the gear on herself . . .

Since he'd entered the clinic, the active localizers he'd brought with him had spread across the clinic. It was a little like light spreading farther and farther into absolute dark, revealing more and more of the room. He'd set the images at a low priority while he examined the SC switch with nearly microscopic vision.

A flicker of motion. He glimpsed a pants leg passing near one of the background views. Someone was hiding in the dead space behind the cabinets. Pham oriented on the localizers and dived for the open space above the cabinets.

A woman's voice: 'Grab a stop and freeze!'

It was Anne Reynolt. She emerged from between the cabinets, just beyond where he could reach. She was holding a pointing device as though it were some kind of weapon.

Reynolt steadied herself on the ceiling and waggled the pointer at him. 'Hand over hand, walk yourself back to the wall.'

For an instant, Pham teetered on the edge of a frontal attack. The pointer could be a bluff, but even if it were guiding a cannon, what did it matter? The game was up. The only option left was swift and overwhelming violence, here and with the localizers all across Hammerfest. *And maybe not* . . . Pham retreated as instructed.

Reynolt came out from behind the cabinets. She hooked a foot under a restraint. The pointer, in her hand did not waver. 'So. Mr Pham Trinli. It's nice to finally know.' With her free hand, she brushed her hair back from her face. Her huds were clear, and he had a good view into her eyes. There was something strange about her. Her face was as pale and cold as always, but the usual impatience and indifference was overlaid with a kind of triumph, a conscious arrogance. And . . . there was a smile, faint yet unmistakable, on her lips.

'You set me up, Anne, didn't you?' Back at Nau's lodge, he took another, longer look at what he thought had been Anne Reynolt. It was a patch of wallpaper, lying loosely on a bed. She had blinded the eyes that could get really close, and fooled him with a crude video.

She nodded. 'I didn't know tas you, but yes. It's been clear for a long time that someone was manipulating my systems. At first, I thought it was Ritser or Kal Omo, playing political games. You were an outside bet, the fellow who was too often in the middle of things. First you were an old fool, then an old slavemaster in hiding as a fool. Now I see that you are something more, Mr Trinli. Did you really think you could outsmart the Podmaster's systems forever?'

'I—' Pham's vision swept out of the room, roamed across Lake Park. The party was continuing. Tomas Nau himself and Qiwi had joined Jau Xin on the little sailboat. Pham zoomed in on Nau's face: he was not wearing huds. He was not a man overseeing an ambush. *He doesn't know!* 'I was very afraid I couldn't outsmart his systems forever – you, in particular.'

She nodded. 'I guessed whoever-it-was would target me. I'm the critical component.' She glanced briefly away from him, at the uncovered controller box. 'You knew I was re-tuning in the next Msec, didn't you?'

'Yes.' *And you need retuning more than I knew.* Hope surged in him. She was behaving like a character in an idiot adventure. She hadn't told her boss what she was up to. She probably had no backups. And now she was just floating there, talking! *Keep her talking.* 'I figured I could weaken the SC switches. When you used the device, it would jam high and—'

'—And I'd have a capillary blowout? Very crude, very fatal, Mr Trinli. But then, you're not clever enough to try real reprogramming, are you?'

'No.' *How far out of calibration is she? Hit at emotion.* 'Besides, I wanted you dead. You and Nau and Brughel are the only real monsters here. For now, you're the only one I can reach.'

Her smile widened. 'You're crazy.'

'No, *you* are. Once upon a time you were a Podmaster just like them. Your problem is you lost. Or don't you remember? The Xevalle clique?'

Her arrogant smile vanished and for a moment her gaze was the usual frowning indifference. Then she was smiling again. 'I remember very well. You're right, I was a loser – but tas a century before Xevalle, and I was fighting all the Podmasters.' She advanced slowly across the room. Her pointer never wavered from Pham's chest. 'The Emergents had invaded Frenk. I was an ancient-lit major at Arnham University . . . I learned to be other things. For fifteen years we fought them. They had technology, they had Focus. At first, we had numbers. We lost and lost, but we made them pay for every victory. Toward the end we were better-armed, but by then there were so few of us. And still we fought.'

The look in her eyes was . . . joyous. He was hearing the history of Frenk from the other side. 'You – you're the Frenkisch Orc!'

Reynolt's smile broadened and she came even nearer, her slim body straightening out of zero-gee crouch. 'Yes indeed. The Podmasters wisely decided to rewrite the histories. The "Frenkisch Orc" makes a better villain than "Anne of Arnham." Rescuing Frenks from a mutant subspecies makes a better story than massacre and Focus.'

Lord. But some automatic part of him still remembered why he was here. He slid his feet back along the wall, positioning for a kick-lunge.

Reynolt stopped her approach. She lowered her aim, to his knees. 'Don't try it, Mr Trinli. This pointer is guiding a program in the MRI controller. If you had had a moment more, you would have seen the nickel pellets I put in the magnet target area. It's an ad hoc weapon, but good enough to blow your legs off – and you would still face interrogation.'

Pham sent his vision back into the MRI gear. Yes, there were the pellets. Given a proper magnetic pulse, they would be high-velocity buckshot. But the program, if it was in the controller . . . Tiny eyes swept along the superconductor interface. He had enough localizers to talk through the optical link and wipe her pointer program. *She still doesn't know what I can do with them!* The hope was like a bright flame.

He tapped his fingers on the palms of his hands, maneuvering the devices into place. Hopefully, it would look like nervous gesturing to Reynolt. 'Interrogation? You're still loyal to Nau?'

'Of course. How could it be otherwise?'

'But you're working behind his back.'

'Only to serve him better. If this had turned out to be Ritser Brughel's work, I wanted a complete case before going to my Podmas—'

Pham lunged outward from the wall. He heard Reynolt's pointer click uselessly, and then he slammed into her. The two of them tumbled back into the MRI cabinets. Reynolt fought almost silently, slamming her knee into him, trying to bite at his throat. But he had her arms pinned, and as they sailed past the magnet box, he twisted and slammed her head against the cover plate.

Reynolt went limp. Pham caught himself on a stop, ready to smash her again.

Think. The party at North Paw was still going on, an idyll. Pham's timer showed that 250 seconds had passed since he had left the harbor. *I can still make this work!* There were necessary changes. The blow to Reynolt's head would show up on an autopsy . . . But – miracles! – her clothes showed no sign of the struggle. There would have to be some changes. He reached into the MRI target area and swept the nickel pellets into a safety bin . . . Something like his original plan could still work. Suppose she had been trying to recalibrate the controllers and had an accident?

Pham moved her body carefully into position. He held her tightly, watching for any sign of consciousness.

The monster. The Frenkisch Orc. Of course, Anne Reynolt was neither. She was a tall, slender woman – as much a human as Pham Nuwen or any of the far descendants of Earth. Now the carven legends on the Hammerfest walls had a clear translation. For years and years, Anne Reynolt had fought against Focus, her people driven back step by step, to that last redoubt in the mountains. Anne of Arnham! Now all that remained was the myth of a twisted monster . . . and the real monsters like Ritser Brughel, the descendants of the surviving Frenks, the conquered and the Focused.

But Anne of Arnham had not died. Instead, her genius had been Focused. And now it was deadly danger to Pham and all he worked for. And so she must die . . .

. . . Three hundred seconds. *Wake up.* Pham tapped out instructions. Botched. He typed them again. Once he weakened the SC connectors, this little program would be enough It was a simple thing, a coded beat of high-frequency pulses that would turn the bugs in Anne's head into little factories, flooding her brain with vasoconstrictors, creating millions of tiny aneurisms. It would be quick. It would be lethal. And Trud had claimed so many times that none of their operations were physically painful.

Unconscious, Anne's face had relaxed; she might have been asleep. There were no marks, no bruises. Even the slender silver chain around her throat, even that had survived their struggle, though it had been pulled free of her blouse. There was a 'membrance gem at the end of the chain. Pham couldn't help himself. He reached over her shoulder and squeezed the greenish stone. The pressure was enough to power a moment of imagery. The stone cleared, and Pham was looking down on a mountain hillside. His viewpoint seemed to be on the cupola of an armored flyer. Ranged around the hillside were a half-dozen other such vehicles, dragons come down from the sky to point their energy cannons at what was already ruins, and the entrance to a cave. In front of the guns stood a single figure, a red-haired young woman. Trud said that 'membrance gems were moments of great happiness or ultimate triumph. And maybe the Emergent taking the picture thought this was such a moment. The girl in the picture – and it was clearly Anne Reynolt – had lost. Whatever she guarded in the cave behind her would be taken from her. And yet, she stood straight, her eyes looking up into the viewpoint. In a moment she would be brushed aside, or blown away . . . but she had not surrendered.

Pham let the gem go, and for a long moment he stared without seeing. Then slowly, carefully, he tapped a long control sequence. This would be much trickier. He altered the drug menu, hesitated . . . seconds . . . before entering an intensity. Reynolt would lose some recent memory, hopefully thirty or forty Msec. *And then you will begin closing in on me again.*

He tapped 'execute.' The SC cables behind the cabinet creaked and spread apart from each other, delivering enormous and precise currents to the MRI magnets. A second passed. His inner vision sputtered into blindness. Reynolt spasmed in his arms. He held her close, keeping her head away from the sides of the cabinet.

Her twitching subsided after a few seconds; her breath came relaxed and slow. Pham eased himself away from her. *Move her out from the magnets.* Okay. He touched her hair, brushing it away from her face. Nothing like that red hair had existed on Canberra . . . but Anne Reynolt reminded him of someone from a certain Canberra morning.

He fled blindly from the room, down the tunnel, back to the party by the lake.

43

The open house at North Paw was the high point of the Watch, of any Watch to date. There wouldn't be anything so spectacular until the end of the Exile. Even the Qeng Ho who had made the park possible were amazed that so much could be done with such limited resources. Maybe there was something to Tomas Nau's claims about Focused systems and Qeng Ho initiative.

The party wound on for Ksecs after Jau Xin's frolic. At least three people ended up in the water. For a while there were meter-wide droplets wobbling above the lake. The Podmaster asked his guests to come back to the lodge and let the water settle itself. The favors of hundreds of people over a year had been expended on the party supplies, and the usual fools – including, most spectacularly, Pham Trinli – got very drunk.

Finally, the guests straggled out and the doors in the hillside were closed behind them. Privately, Ezr was sure this would be the last time the riffraff were invited into the Podmaster's domain. The riffraff had made the party possible, and Qiwi had obviously enjoyed every second of it, but Tomas Nau was beginning to fray toward the end of the party. The bastard was a clever one. For the price of one tedious afternoon, the Podmaster had gotten more goodwill than ever. A few decades of tyranny couldn't make Qeng Ho forget their heritage . . . but Nau had made their situation an ambiguous kind of not-tyranny. *Focus is slavery.* But Tomas Nau promised to free the zipheads at the end of the Exile. Ezr shouldn't hate the Qeng Ho for accepting the situation. Many otherwise free societies accepted part-time slavery. *In any case, Nau's promise is a lie.*

Anne Reynolt's unconscious body was found 4Ksecs after the end of the party. All the next day, there were rumors and panics: Reynolt was really brain-dead, some said, and the announcements, were simply soft lies. Ritser Brughel hadn't been in coldsleep, others claimed, and now he had staged a coup. Ezr had his own theory. *After all the years, Pham Nuwen has finally acted.*

Twenty Ksec into the workday, the ziphead support for two of the research teams fell into deadlock, a temperamental snit that Reynolt could have cleared in a few seconds. Phuong and Silipan whacked at the problem for 6Ksecs, then announced that the zipheads involved would be down for the rest of the day. No, they weren't translators – but Trixia had been working with one of them, some kind of geologist. Ezr tried to go over to Hammerfest.

'You're not on my list, buddy.' There was actually a guard at the taxi port, one of Omo's goons. 'Hammerfest is off-limits.'

'For how long?'

'Dunno. Read the announcements, will you.'

And so Ezr ended up in Benny's parlor, along with a mob and a half of other people. Ezr wedged down at the table with Jau and Rita. Pham was there, too, looking decidedly hungover.

Jau Xin had his own tale of woe: 'Reynolt was supposed to retune my pilots. Not a big deal, but our drills went like crap without it.'

'What are you complaining about? Your gear is still functioning, right? But we were trying to do an analysis of this Spider spaceflight stuff – and now our ziphead allocation is offline. Hey, I know bits of chemistry and engineering, but there's no way I can put it all to—'

Pham groaned loudly. He was holding his head with both hands. 'Quit your bitching. This all makes me wonder about Emergent "superiority."

One person gets knocked out and your house of cards comes apart. Where's the superiority in that?'

Normally Rita Liao was a gentle sort, but the look she gave Pham was venomous. 'You Qeng Ho murdered our superiority, remember? When we came here we had ten times the clinical staff we have now, enough to make our systems as good as anything back home.'

There was an embarrassed silence. Pham glared at Rita, but didn't argue further. After a moment he gave the abrupt shrug that everyone recognized: Trinli was bested, but unwilling to retreat or apologize.

A voice from the next table broke the silence. 'Hey, Trud!'

Silipan was standing halfway through the parlor doorway, looking up at them. He was still wearing the Emergent dress uniform of the day before, but now the silken rags had new stains, and they were not artistic tints.

The silence dissolved, people shouting questions, inviting Trud to come up and talk to them. Trud climbed up through the vines toward Jau Xin's table. There was no room left, so they flipped another table over to make a double-decker. Now Ezr was almost eye to eye with Silipan, even though the other's face was inverted from his. The crowd from other tables swarmed in close, anchoring themselves among the vines.

'So when are you going to break that deadlock, Trud? I've got zipheads reserved, waiting for answers.'

'Yeah, why are you over here when—'

'—There's only so much we can do with raw hardware, and—'

'Lord of Trade Almighty, give the fellow a chance!' Pham's voice boomed, loud and irritated. It was a typical Trinli turnabout, always the truculent cannon, but pointing in whatever direction might make him look good. It also, Ezr noticed, silenced the crowd.

Silipan sent Pham a grateful look. The technician's cockiness was a fragile thing today. There were dark rings under his eyes, and his hand shook slightly as he raised the drink Benny had set before him.

'How is she, Trud?' Jau asked the question in sympathetic, quiet tones. 'We heard . . . we heard, she's brain-dead.'

'No, no.' Trud shook his head and smiled weakly. 'Reynolt should make a full recovery, minus maybe a year of retrograde amnesia. Things will be a bit chaotic till we get her back online. I'm sorry about the deadlock. Why, I'd have it fixed by now' – some of the old confidence crept back into his voice – 'but I was reassigned to something more important.'

'What really happened to her?'

Benny showed up with a shrimp-tentacle dinner, his best entree. Silipan dug in hungrily, seeming to ignore the question. This was the most attentive audience Trud had ever had, literally breathless to hear his opinions. Ezr could tell the guy realized this, that he was enjoying his sudden and central importance. At the same time, Trud was almost too tired to see straight. His once perfect uniform actually stank. His fork took a wobbling course from food bucket to mouth. After a few moments, he turned a bleary-eyed look in the direction of his questioner. 'What happened? We're not sure. The last year or so, Reynolt's been slipping – still in Focus, of course, but not well tuned. Tas a subtle thing, something that only a pro could notice. I almost missed it myself. She seemed to be caught up on some subproject – you know the way zipheads can obsess. Only thing is, Reynolt does her own calibration, so there was nothing I could do. I tell you, tas making me damn uneasy. I was about to report it to the Podmaster when—'

Trud hesitated, seemed to realize that this was a brag with consequences. 'Anyway, it looks like she was trying to adjust some of the MRI control circuits. Maybe she knew that her tuning was adrift. I don't know. She had the safety hood off and was running diagnostics. It looks like there was some kind of situational flaw in the control software; we're still trying to reproduce that. Anyway, she got a control pulse right in the face. There was a little piece of her scalp in the cabinet behind the controls, where she spasmed. Fortunately, the stimulated drug production was alpha-retrox. She has a concussion and a retrox overdose . . . Like I say, it's all repairable. Another forty days and our old lovable Reynolt will be back.' He laughed weakly.

'Minus some recent memories.'

'Of course. Zipheads aren't hardware; I don't have backups.'

There was some uncomfortable mumbling around the table, but it was Rita Liao who put the idea into words: 'It's all too convenient. It's like someone wanted to shut her down.' She hesitated. Earlier in the day, it had been Rita pushing the rumors about Ritser Brughel. It showed how far these Emergents had come that they would stick their noses into what might be a Podmaster conflict. 'Has Podmaster Nau checked into the off-Watch status of the VicePodmaster?'

'And his agents?' That from a Qeng Ho behind Ezr.

Trud slapped his fork down on the table. His voice came out angry and squeaky. 'What do you think! The Podmaster is looking into the possibilities . . . very carefully.' He took a deep breath, and seemed to realize that the price of fame was too high. 'You can be absolutely sure that the Podmaster is taking this seriously. But look – the retrox flood was simply a massive overdose, unlocalized, just what you'd expect in an accident. The amnesia will be a patchy thing. Any saboteur doing that would be a fool. She could be dead and it would've looked just as much like an accident.'

For a moment everyone was silent. Trud glared back and forth at all of them.

Silipan picked up his fork, set it down again. He stared into his half-finished bucket of shrimp tentacles. 'Lord, I am so tired. I go back on duty in twenty – damn it fifteen – Ksecs.'

Rita reached out to pat his arm. 'Well, I'm glad you came over and gave us the straight story.' There was a murmur of agreement from the people all around.

'Bil and I will be running the show for some time now. It all depends on us.' Trud looked from face to face, seeking comfort. His voice boasted and quailed at the same time.

They met later that day, in the buffer space beneath the temp's outer skin. This was a meeting agreed on long before the Lake Park open house. It was a meeting Ezr had waited for with impatience and fear – the meeting where he would lay it on the line to Pham Nuwen about Focus. *I have my little speech, my little threats to make. Will they be enough?*

Ezr moved quietly past Fong's sprouting trays. The bright lights and the smell of trebyun greens faded behind him. The dark that was left was too deep for unaided eyes. Eight years ago, on his first meeting with Nuwen, there had been faint sunlight. Now the hull plastic showed only darkness.

But nowadays, Ezr had other ways to see . . . He signaled the localizer that sat on his temple. A ghostly vision rose. The colors were just shades of yellow, such as you might see if you pressed your finger firmly against the side of your eye. But the light wasn't random patterns. Ezr had worked long and hard with Pham's exercises. Now the yellow light revealed the curving walls of the balloon membranes and the outer hull. Sometimes the view was distorted. Sometimes the perspective was from beneath his feet or behind his head. But with the right commands, and lots of concentration, he could see where no unaided person could. *Pham can still see better.* There had been hints, over the years. Nuwen used the localizers like a private empire.

Pham Nuwen was up ahead, standing behind a wall brace, invisible but for the fact that there were localizers beyond him, looking back. As Ezr closed the last few meters' distance between them, his vision wavered as the other swung his tiny servants into a different constellation.

'Okay, make it quick.' Pham had stepped out to face him. The yellow pseudo-light painted his face haggard and drawn. He hadn't dropped the Trinli persona? No, this looked like the hangover Pham had shown in the parlor, but there was something deeper to it.

'You – You promised me two thousand seconds.'

'Yeah, but things have changed. Or haven't you noticed?'

'I've noticed a lot of things. I think it's time we finally really talked about them. Nau, he truly admires you . . . you know that, don't you?'

'Nau is full of lies.'

'True. But the stories he showed me, some large part of them is true. Pham, you and I have worked together through several Watches now. I've thought about things my aunt and my grand-uncles used to say about you. I'm past the hero worship. Finally, I realize how much you must . . . love . . . Focus. You've made me many promises, but they've always been so carefully framed. You want to beat Nau and take back what we lost – but more than anything, you want Focus, don't you?

The silence stretched out for five seconds. *To the direct question, what will he say?* When he finally spoke, his voice was grating: 'Focus is the key to making a civilization that lasts – across all of Human Space.'

'Focus is slavery, Pham.' Ezr spoke the words softly. 'Of course, you know that; and in your heart I think you hate it. Zamle Eng – you made him your inner cover story; I think that was your heart crying out to you.'

Pham was silent for a second, glaring at him. His mouth twisted. 'You're a fool, Ezr Vinh. You read Nau's stories and you still don't understand. I was betrayed once before by a Vinh. It won't happen again. Do you think I'll let you live if you cross me?'

Pham glided closer. Ezr's vision was abruptly snuffed out; he was cut off from all localizer input. Ezr raised his hands, palms up. 'I don't know. But I am a Vinh, Sura's direct descendant, and also yours. We are a Family of secrets within secrets; someday I would have been told the truth about Brisgo Gap. But even as a child, I heard little things, hints. The Family has not forgotten you. There's even a motto that we never say on the outside: "We owe all to Pham Nuwem be thou kind unto him." So even if you kill me, I have to talk to you.' Ezr stared into the silent dark; he didn't even know where the other was standing now. 'And after yesterday . . . I think you will listen. I think I have nothing to fear.'

'After *yesterday?*' Pham's voice was angry and near. 'My little Vinh snake, what can you possibly know about yesterday?'

Ezr stared out in the direction of the voice. There was something about Pham's voice, a hatred that went beyond reason. *What did happen with Reynolt?* Things were going terribly wrong, but all he had were the words already planned: 'You didn't kill her. I believe what Trud said. Killing her would have been easy, and could have looked just as much like an accident. And so I think I know about where Nau's stories are true and where they are lies.' Ezr reached out with both arms, and his hands fell on Pham's shoulders. He stared intently into the dark, willing vision. 'Pham! All your life you have been driven. That, and your genius, made us what we are. But you wanted more. Quite what, is never clear in the Qeng Ho histories, but I could see it in Nau's records. You had a wonderful dream, Pham. Focus might give it to you . . . but the price is too high.'

There was a moment of silence, then a sound, almost like an animal in pain. Abruptly, Ezr's arms were struck aside. Two hands grabbed him at the throat, viselike and squeezing shut. All that was left was shocked surprise, dimming toward final blackout . . .

And then the hands relaxed their pressure. All around him glowbugs flashed stark white light, dozens of tiny popping sounds. He gasped, dazed, trying to understand. Pham was blowing the capacitors in all the nearby localizers! The pinpoint flashes showed Pham Nuwen in bright and black stop action. There was a glittering madness in his eyes that Ezr had never seen.

The lights were farther away now, the destruction spreading outward from them. Ezr's voice came out a terrified croak: 'Pham. Our cover. Without the localizers—'

The last of the tiny flashes showed a twisted smile on the other's face. 'Without the localizers, we die! Die, little Vinh. I no longer care.'

Ezr heard him turn and push off. What was left was darkness and silence – and death that must be just Ksecs away. For no matter how hard Ezr tried, he found no sign of localizer support.

What do you do when your dream dies? Pham floated alone in the dark of his room, and thought about the question with something like curiosity, almost indifference. At the edge of his consciousness, he was aware of the ragged hole he had punched in the localizer net. The net was robust. That disruption was not automatically revealed to the Emergent snoops. But without careful revision, news of the failure would eventually percolate out to them. He was vaguely aware that Ezr Vinh was desperately trying to cover the burnout. Surprisingly, the boy had not made things worse, but he had not a prayer of doing the high-level cover-up. A few hundred seconds, at most, and Kal Omo would alert Brughel . . . and the charade would be over. It really didn't matter anymore.

What do you do when your dream dies?

Dreams die in every life. Everyone gets old. There is promise in the beginning when life seems so bright. The promise fades when the years get short.

But *not* Pham's dream. He had pursued it across five hundred light-years and three thousand years of objective time. It was a dream of a single Humankind, where justice would not be occasional flickering light but a steady glow across all of Human Space. He dreamed of a civilization where continents never burned, and where two-bit kings didn't give children away as hostages. When Sammy had dug him out of the cemeterium at Low-cinder, Pham was dying, but *not* the dream. The dream had been bright as ever in his mind, consuming him.

And here he had *found* the edge that could make the dream come true: Focus, an automation deep enough and smart enough to manage an interstellar civilization. It could create the 'loving slaves' whose possibility Sura had made jest of. So what if it was slavery? There were far greater injustices that Focus would banish forever.

Maybe.

He had looked away from Egil Manrhi, now scarcely more than a scanning device. He had looked away from Trixia Bonsol and all the others, locked for years in their tiny cells. But yesterday, he'd been forced to look upon Anne Reynolt, standing alone against all the power of Focus, spending her life to resist that power. The particulars had been a great surprise, to Pham, but he had been fooling himself to think that such was not part of the price for his dream. Anne was Cindi Ducanh writ large.

And today, Ezr Vinh and his little speech: *'The price is too high!'* Ezr *Vinh*! Pham might have his dream . . . if he gave up the reason for it.

Once before, a Vinh had stepped between him and final success. *Let the Vinh snake die. Let them all die. Let me die.*

Pham curled inward upon himself. He was suddenly conscious that he was weeping. Except as a deceit, he hadn't cried since . . . he didn't remember . . . perhaps since those days at the other end of his life when he first came aboard the *Reprise*.

So what do you do when your dream dies?

When your dream dies, you give it up.

And then what is left? For a long time, Pham's mind dwelled in a nothingness. And then once more, he became aware of the images flickering around him from the localizer net: down on the rockpile, the Focused slaves crammed by the hundreds in the honeycombs of Hammerfest, Anne Reynolt asleep in a cell as small as any.

They deserved better than what had happened to them. They deserved better than what Tomas Nau had planned for them. Anne deserved better.

He reached out into the net, and gently touched Ezr Vinh, motioned him aside. He gathered up the boy's efforts and began building them into an effective patch. There were details: the bruises on Vinh's neck, the need for ten thousand new localizers in the temp interspace. He could handle them, and in the longer run—

Anne Reynolt would eventually recover from what he had done to her. When that happened, the game of cat-and-mouse would resume, but this time he must protect her and all the other slaves. It would be so much harder than before. But maybe with Ezr Vinh, if they worked as a real team . . . The plans formed and re-formed in Pham's mind. It was a far cry from breaking the wheel of history, but there was a strange, rising pleasure in doing what felt wholly right.

And somewhere before he finally fell asleep, he remembered Gunnar Larson, the old man's gentle mocking, the old man's advice that Pham understand the limits of the natural world, and accept them. *So maybe he was right.* Funny. All the years in this room he had lain awake, grinding his teeth, planning his plans and dreaming what he might do with Focus. Now that he had given it up, there were still plans, still terrible dangers . . . but for the first time in many years there was also . . . peace.

That night he dreamed of Sura. And there was no pain.

PART THREE

44

There is always an angle. Gonle Fong had lived her whole life by that principle. The mission to the OnOff star had been a long shot, the sort of thing that appealed mainly to scientists. But Gonle had seen angles. Then had come the Emergent ambush, and the long shot had been turned into servitude and exile. A prison run by thugs. But even then there was an angle. For almost twenty years of her life she had played the angles and prospered – if only by the standards of this dump.

Now things were changing. Jau Xin had been gone for more than four days, at least since the beginning of her current Watch. At first the rumor was that he and Rita had been unofficially moved to Watch tree C, and that they were still in coldsleep. That screwed some of the programming deals she had planned with Rita – and it was also as unusual as hell. Then Trinli reported that two pilot zipheads were missing from the Hammerfest Attic. So. Rita might still be on ice, but Jau Xin and his zipheads were . . . elsewhere. The rumors grew from there: Jau was on an expedition to the dead sun, Jau was landing on the Spider world. Trud Silipan strutted around Benny's, smug with some inner secret that for once he was not sharing. More than anything, that proved that something very strange was going on.

Gonle had run a betting pool on the speculations, but she was suffering from sucker fever herself. She wasn't one bit disappointed when the big bosses decided to let them all in on the secret.

Tomas Nau invited a handful of the peons down to his estate for the briefing. This was the first time Gonle had been to Lake Park since the open house. Nau had made a big thing of his hospitality then. Afterward, the place had been locked tight – though to be honest, part of that might be because of what happened to Anne Reynolt during the open house.

As Gonle and the three other chosen peons shuffled down the footpath toward Nau's lodge, she passed her critical judgment on the scene. 'So they figured out how to do rain.' It was more a windblown mist, so fine it dewed her hair and eyelashes, so fine that the lack of real gravity didn't matter.

Pham Trinli gave a cynical chuckle. 'I'll bet it's partly garbage collection. In my time, I've seen plenty of these faked gravity parks, usually built by some Customer with more money than sense. If you want to have a groundside and a skyside, the clutter starts piling up. Pretty soon you have a sky full of crap.'

Walking beside him, Trud Silipan said, 'Sky looks pretty clean to me.'

Trinli looked up into the driven mist. The clouds were low and gray, moving quickly in from the lake's far shore. Some of this was real and some must be wallpaper, but the two were seamlessly meshed. Not a cheerful scene by Gonle Fong's standards, but one that was chill and clean. 'Yeah,' he said after a moment. 'I gotta hand it to you, Trud. Your Ali Lin is a genius.'

Silipan puffed up a little. 'Not just him. It's the coordination that counts. I've got a team of zipheads on this. Every year it just gets better. Someday we'll even figure out how to make natural-looking sea waves.'

Gonle looked across at Ezr Vinh and rolled her eyes. Neither of these buffoons liked to acknowledge how much everyone's cooperation – very profitable cooperation – was involved here. Even if the peons weren't welcome anymore, they still supplied a constant stream of food, finished woods, live plants, and program designs.

The mist made little swirls around the lodge, and the illusion of gravity was sorely tested as the visitors tilted this way and that on their grabber-soled shoes. Then they were in the lodge, warmed by very natural-looking burning logs in Tomas Nau's big fireplace. The Podmaster gestured them toward a conference table. There were Nau, Brughel, and Reynolt. Three other figures were silhouetted against the windows and the gray light beyond. One was Qiwi.

'Well hello, Jau,' said Ezr. 'Welcome . . . back.'

Sure enough, it was Jau and Rita. Tomas Nau brightened the room lights. The warmth and brightness were nothing more than in any civilized habitation, but somehow the cold and gloom so expensively maintained outside made this inner light a joyous security.

The Podmaster waved them to seats, then sat down himself. As usual, Nau was a picture of generous and high-minded leadership. *But he doesn't fool me for a moment*, thought Gonle. Before this mission, she had had a long career, dealing with a dozen Customer cultures, on three worlds. Customers came in all the sizes and colors of humanity. And their governments were even more varied – tyrannies, democracies, demarchies. There was always a way of doing business with them. Big boss Nau was a villain, but a smart villain who understood that he had to do business. Qiwi had seen to that, years ago. It was too bad he held the physical upper hand – *that* was not part of the standard Qeng Ho business environment. Things were dicey when you couldn't run away from the bad guys. But in the long term, even that didn't matter.

The Podmaster nodded to each of them. 'Thanks for coming in person. You should know that this meeting is being shown live on the local net, but I hope you'll tell your friends what you've seen firsthand.' He grinned. 'I'm sure it will make for good conversation at Benny's. What I have is incredibly good news, but it's also a great challenge. You see, Pilot Manager Xin has just returned from low Arachna orbit.' He paused. *I bet there's total, awesome silence in Benny's.* 'And what he discovered there is . . . interesting. Jau – please. Describe the mission.'

Xin came to his feet a little too quickly. His wife caught his hand and he stood on the floor, facing them. Gonle tried unsuccessfully to catch Rita's eye, but the woman's entire attention was on Jau. *I bet they kept her on ice until he was back; that was the only thing that would have kept her mouth shut about this.* Rita's expression was one of vast relief. Whatever this news was, it couldn't be bad.

'Yes, sir. Per your instructions, I was brought on-Watch early, to undertake a close approach of Arachna.' As he spoke, Qiwi passed around some Qeng Ho-quality huds. Gonle mouthed a buy offer at Qiwi as she passed; the other grinned and whispered 'Soon!' back at her. The big bosses still didn't let peons own these things. Maybe finally that would change, too. A second went by as the huds synched on the consensus image. The space above the table rippled and became a view of the L1 rockpile. Far away, beyond the floor, there was the disk of the Spider world.

'My pilots and I took the last functioning pinnace.' A thread of gold arced out from the rockpile; the tip accelerated to the halfway point and then began to slow. Their pov caught up with the pinnace; ahead, the disk of Arachna grew wide. The world looked almost as frozen and dead as when the humans had first arrived. There was one big difference: a faint glitter of city lights across the northern hemisphere, webbing here and there at major cities.

Pham Trinli's voice came from beyond the dark, an incredulous hoot. 'I bet you got spotted!'

'They pinged us. Show the defense radars and native satellites,' he said to the display. A cloud of blue and green dots blossomed in the space around the planet. On the ground, there were arcs of flashing light, the sweep of the Spiders' missile radars. 'It's going to be more of a problem in the future.'

Anne Reynolt's voice cut across the Pilot Manager's. 'My network people deleted all the hard evidence. The risk was well worth it.'

'Hunh! That must have been something motherloving important.'

'Oh Pham, tas. Tas.' Jau stepped to one side of the consensus image, and jabbed his hand deep into the haze of satellites, marking one blue dot with the label KINDRED GROUND RECON SATELLITE 543 followed by orbital parameters. He glanced in Pham's direction, and there was a quiet smile on his face, as if he were expecting some reaction. The numbers didn't mean anything to Gonle. She leaned to one side, looked at Trinli around the edge of the image. The old fraud looked just as mystified as any, and not at all happy with Xin's smile or Silipan's smug chuckle.

Trinli squinted into the display. 'Okay, so you matched orbits with

Recon543.' Beside him, Ezr Vinh sucked in a surprised breath. This made Trinli's frown even deeper. 'Launch date seven hundred Ksec ago, booster chemical, period synchronous, altitude . . .' His voice trailed off in a kind of gargle: 'Altitude twelve thousand damn-all kilometers! That must be a mistake.'

Jau's grinned widened. 'No mistake. That's the whole reason I went down for a close look.'

The significance finally percolated through to Gonle. In Supplies and Services, she dealt mainly with bargaining and inventory managment. But shipping was a big part of price points, and she was Qeng Ho. Arachna was a terrestroid planet, with a 90Ksec day. Synchronous altitude should have been way higher than twelve thousand klicks. Even for a nontechnical person, the satellite was a magical impossibility. 'It's stationkeeping?' she asked. 'Little rockets?'

'No. Even fusion rockets would have trouble doing that for days at a time.'

'Cavorite.' Ezr's voice was faint, awed. Where had she heard that word before?

But Jau was nodding. 'Right.' He said something to the display, and now the view was from his pinnace. 'Getting a close look was a problem, especially since I didn't want to show my main torch. Instead, I fried the satellite's cameras and then did an instantaneous match from below . . . You can begin to see it now, at the center of my target pointer. The closing speed has fallen from fifty meters a second, to an instant now where we're stopped relative to each other. It's about five meters above us now.' There was something in the pointer, something boxy and dead black, falling toward them like a yo-yo on a string. It slowed, passed a meter or two below them, and started back up. The topside was not black but an irregular pattern of dark grays. 'Okay, freeze the image. This should give you a good look. A flat architecture, probably gyro-stabilized. The polyhedral shell is for radar evasion. Except for the impossible orbit, this thing is a typical low-tech stealthed satellite . . .' The satellite slid upward again, but this time was met by grappling hooks. 'This is where we took it aboard the pinnace – and left behind a credible explosion.'

'Good flying, man.' That from Pham Trinli, acknowledging someone almost as good as himself.

'Ha. Tas even tougher than it looks. I had to run my zipheads near the edge of a nonrecoverable panic all through the rendezvous. There were just too many inconsistencies in the dynamics.'

Silipan interrupted cheerily, 'That will change. We're re-programming all the pilots for cavorite maneuvers.'

Jau killed the imagery and frowned at Silipan. 'You screw up, and we'll have no pilots.'

Gonle couldn't take much more irrelevant chitchat. 'The satellite. You have it here? How did the Spiders do this?'

She noticed Nau grinning at her. 'I think Miss Fong has identified the immediate issue. Do you remember those stories of gravity anomalies in the altiplano? The short of it is, those stories were *true*. The Kindred military discovered some kind of – call it antigravity. Apparently they've been pursuing this for ten years now. We never caught on because Accord Intelligence missed it, and our penetration of the Kindred side has always lagged. This little satellite massed eight tonnes, but almost two tonnes of that was "cavorite" cladding. The Kindred Spiders are using this remarkable substance simply to increase their rockets' throw weight. I have a little demonstration for you . . .'

He spoke to the air. 'Douse the fireplace, cut ventilation.' He paused, and the room became very quiet. Over by the wall, Qiwi closed a tall window that had drawn a taste of moistness in from the lake. The park's fake sun peeked between breaks in the clouds, and streamers of light glittered on the water. Gonle wondered vaguely if Nau's zipheads were so good that they could orchestrate his world for these moments. Probably.

The Podmaster took a small case out of his shirt. He opened it, and held something that glittered in the lowering sun. It was a small square, a tile. There were flecks of light that might have been cheap mica, except that the colors swept in coordinated iridescence. 'This is one of the cladding tiles from the satellite. There was also a layer of low-power LEDs, but we've stripped those off. Chemically, what is left is diamond fragments bound in epoxy. Watch.' He set the square down on the table and shined a hand light on it. And they all watched . . . And after a moment the little square of iridescence floated upward. At first the motion looked like a commonplace of the microgravity environment, a loose paperweight wafting on an air current. But the air in the room was still. And as the seconds passed, the tile moved faster, tumbling, falling . . . straight up. It hit the ceiling with an audible clink – and remained there.

No one said anything for several seconds.

'Ladies and gentlemen, we came to the OnOff star hoping for treasure. So far we've learned some new astrophysics, developed a slightly better ramdrive. The biologicals of the Spider world are another treasure, also enough to finance our coming. But originally, we expected more. We expected to find the remains of a starfaring race – well, after forty years, it looks like we have succeeded. Spectacularly.'

Maybe it was just as well that Nau had not scheduled this as a general meeting. Everyone was suddenly talking at once. Lord only knew what it was like over at Benny's. Ezr Vinh finally got a question on the floor. 'You think the Spiders made this stuff?'

Nau shook his head. 'No. The Kindred had to mine thousands of tonnes of low-grade ore to get this much magic.'

Trinli said, 'We've known for years that the Spiders evolved here, that they never had a higher tech.'

'Quite so. And their own archeologists have no solid evidence of visitations. But this . . . this stuff *is* an artifact, even if only we can see it as such. Anne's automation has spent several days on this. It's a coordinated processing matrix.'

'I thought you said it was refined from native ores.'

'Yes. It makes the conclusion all the more fantastic. For forty years we've thought the diamond powders of Arachna were either infalls or biological skeletons. Now it looks like they are fossil processing devices. And at least some of them reassert their mission when brought close together. Like localizers, but much much smaller, and with a special purpose . . . to manipulate physical laws in ways we don't begin to understand.'

Trinli looked as if someone had punched him in the face, as if decades of bombast had been beaten out of him. He said softly, 'Nanotech. The dream.'

'What? Yes, the Failed Dream. Till now.' The Podmaster looked up at the tile lying on the ceiling. He smiled. 'Whoever visited here, it was millions or billions of years ago. I doubt we'll ever find any camp tents or garbage middens . . . but the signs of their technology are everywhere.'

Vinh: 'We were looking for starfarers, but we were too small and all we saw were their ankles.' He tore his gaze down from the ceiling. 'Maybe even these—' He waved at the window, and Gonle realized that he was talking about the big diamonds of L1. 'Maybe even these are artifacts.'

Brughel moved forward in his chair. 'Nonsense. They are simple diamond rocks.' But there was an edge of uncertainty in the aggressive look he flashed around the table.

Nau hesitated an instant, then gave an easy chuckle, waving his thug silent. 'We're all beginning to sound like some Dawn Age fantasy. The hard facts are extraordinary, without adding superstitious mumbo-jumbo. With what we already have, this expedition may be the most important in human history.'

And the most profitable, too. Gonle shifted back on her chair, and tried to catalogue all the things they might do with the glittering material that was lying on the ceiling. *What's the best way to sell something like that? How many centuries of monopoly might be wrung out of it?*

But the Podmaster had returned to more practical matters. 'So that's the fantastic news. In the long term, it is good beyond our wildest dreams. In the short term – well, it puts a real knot in the Schedule. Qiwi?'

'Yes. As you know, the Spiders are about five years from having a mature planetary computer network, something we can reliably act through.'

Something advanced enough that we can use. Until today, that had been the biggest treasure that Gonle Fong had envisioned coming out of these years of exile. Forget about marginal advances in ramdrives or even biologicals. There was a whole industrialized world down there, with a culture guaranteed to be alien from other markets. If they controlled that, or even had a dominant bargaining position, they would rank with the legends of the Qeng Ho marketing. Gonle understood that. Surely Nau did. Qiwi did too, though right now she was talking simple idealism:

'Till now, we thought that they were also about five years away from really needing our help. We thought that any Kindred/Accord war wouldn't happen till then. Well . . . we were wrong. The Kindred don't have much of a computer net – but they do have the cavorite mines. Their cavorite satellites are stealthed for now, but that's only for temporary advantage. Very soon, their missile fleet will be upgraded. Politically, we see them moving to subvert smaller countries, egging them into confrontation with the Accord. We simply can't wait another five years to take a hand in things.'

Jau said, 'There are other reasons for advancing the deadlines. With this cavorite, it's going to be next to impossible to keep our operations a secret much longer. The Spiders are going to be out in local space very soon. Depending on how much of that' – he jerked his thumb at the glistening tile on the ceiling – 'they have, they may actually be more maneuverable than we are.'

Beside him, Rita was looking more and more upset. 'You mean there's a chance Pedure's crowd could *win*? If we have to advance the Schedule, then it's time we stopped pussyfooting. We need to come down with military force, on the side of the Accord.'

The Podmaster nodded solemnly in Liao's direction. 'I hear you, Rita. There are people down there that we've all come to respect, even to—' He waved his hand as if to push aside deeper sentiments, to concentrate on hard reality. 'But as your Podmaster, I have to look at priorities: My highest priority is the survival of you and all the humans in our little pod. Don't mistake the beauty you have all created here. The truth is, we have precious little real military power.' The setting sun had turned the lake to gold, and now the slanting rays lit the meeting room with a gentle, even warmth. 'In fact, we are almost castaways, and we are about as far from Humankind as anyone has ever been. Our second priority – and it's inextricably bound to the first – is the survival of the Spiders' advanced industrial civilization, and therefore its people and their culture. We must act very carefully. We can't act out of simple affection . . . And you know, I listen to the translations, too, I think that people like Victory Smith and Sherkaner Underhill would understand.'

'But they can help!'

'Maybe. I'd call them in an instant if we had better information and better network penetration. But if we reveal ourselves unnecessarily, we could unite them all against us – or alternatively, provoke Pedure into attacking them immediately. We must save them, and we must not sacrifice ourselves.'

Rita wavered. To Nau's right, but just in the shadows, Ritser Brughel glowered at her. The younger Podmaster had never really grasped the fact that the old, Emergent rules must change. The idea of someone giving back talk still sent him into a rage. *Thank the Lord he's not running things*. Nau was a tough nut, smooth and ruthless despite all the nice words – but you could do business with him.

No one else spoke in support of Rita's position, yet she made one more try. 'We know Sherkaner Underhill is a genius. He would understand. He could help.'

Tomas Nau sighed. 'Yes, Underhill. We owe him a lot. Without him, we'd probably be twenty years short of success, not just five. But, I'm afraid . . .' He glanced down the table at Ezr Vinh. 'You know more about Underhill and Dawn Age technology than anyone, Ezr. What do you think?'

Gonle almost laughed. Vinh had been following the conversation like a spectator at a racquet match; now the ball had hit him square between the eyes. 'Um. Yes. Underhill is remarkable. He's like von Neumann, Einstein, Minsky, Zhang – a dozen Dawn Age geniuses wrapped into one body. Either that or the guy is just a genius at picking graduate students.' Vinh smiled sadly. 'I'm sorry, Rita. For you and me, the Exile time has only been ten or fifteen years. Underhill has lived it all, second by second. By Spider standards – and pre-tech human ones – he's an old man. I'm afraid he's at the edge of senility. He's lived through all the easy technical payoffs, and now he's hit the dead ends . . . What was flexibility has become super-stitious mush. If we have to give up our Lurk advantage, I'd suggest we just contact the Accord government, play things as a straight business deal.'

Vinh might have continued, but the Podmaster said, 'Rita, we're trying for the safest outcome for everyone. I promise, if that means throwing ourselves on the Spiders' mercy – well, so be it.' His glance flickered to his right, and Gonle realized that the message was directed at Brughel as much as anyone. Nau paused a moment, but no one had anything more to say. His voice became more businesslike. 'So, the Schedule is suddenly very much advanced. Tas forced on us, but I am pleased by the challenge.' His smile flashed in the fake sunset. 'One way or another, our Exile will be over in a year. We can afford to – we must – expend resources. From now till we've saved the Spider world, almost everyone will be on-Watch.'

Wow.

'We'll start running the volatile plant at redline duty cycle.' Heads went up all around the table. 'Remember, if we still need it in a year, we will have lost. We have an awful lot of planning in front of us, people – we need to unleash every last bit of our potential. As of now, I'm dropping the last community use limits. The "underground" economy will have access to everything except the most critical security automation.'

Yes! Gonle grinned across the table at Qiwi Lisolet, saw her grinning right back. So that was what Qiwi had meant by 'soon'! Nau went on for some seconds, not so much making detailed plans as undoing this and that stupid rule that had kept operations so hobbled over the years. She could feel the enthusiasm building with every sentence. *Maybe I can start a futures market on groundside trade.*

The meeting ended on an incredible high. On the way out, Gonle gave Qiwi a hug. 'Kiddo, you did it!' she said softly.

Qiwi just grinned back, but it was a wider smile than Gonle had seen her wear in a long time.

Afterward, the four visiting peons walked back up the hillside, the last of the sunlight throwing long shadows before them. She took a last look behind her before they entered the forest. *Presumptuous, this park. But still it was beautiful, and I had something to do with it.* The last light of the sun showed from under far clouds. It might be Nauly manipulation or the random outcome of the park's automation. Either way, it seemed auspicious. Old Nau thought he manipulated everything. Gonle knew that this sudden, final liberalization was something the Podmaster might try to stuff back in the bottle later on, when imagination and sharp trading was more a risk than the alternatives. But Gonle was Qeng Ho. Over the years, she and Qiwi and Benny and dozens of others had chipped away at the Emergents' tight little tyranny, until almost every Emergent was 'corrupted' by the underground trade. Nau had learned that you win by doing business. After the Spider markets were opened up, he would see there was no advantage to stuffing freedom back in the bottle.

Tomas Nau's second meeting was later in the day, aboard the *Invisible Hand*. Here they could talk, far from innocent ears. 'I got Kal Omo's report, Podmaster. From the snoops. You fooled almost everyone.'

'Almost?'

'Well, you know Vinh – but he didn't see through everything you said. And Jau Xin looks . . . dubious.'

Nau glanced a question at Anne Reynolt.

Reynolt's reply was quick. 'Xin is one we really need, Podmaster. He's our only remaining Pilot Manager. We would have lost that pinnace if not for him. The ziphead pilots glitched when they saw the cavorite orbit. Suddenly all the rules had changed and they just couldn't deal with the situation.'

'Okay, he's a secret doubter.' There was no help for that really. Xin had been near the operational center of too many things. He probably suspected the truth behind the Diem Massacre. 'So we can't ice him, and we can't fool him, and we'll need him at the bloodiest stage of the job. Still . . . I think

Rita Liao is a sufficient lever. Ritser. Make sure Jau knows that her welfare depends on his quality of service.'

Ritser gave a little smile, and made a note.

Nau scanned Omo's report for himself. 'Yes, we did quite well. But then, telling people what they want to believe is an easy job. No one seemed to catch all the consequences of pushing the Schedule forward five years. There's no way we can pull a smooth network takeover now, and we need an intact industrial ecology on the planet – but there's no need for the whole planet to participate. Right now' – Nau glanced at the latest reports from Reynolt's zips – 'seven Spider nations have nuclear weapons. Four have substantial arsenals, and three have delivery systems.'

Reynolt shrugged. 'So we engineer a war.'

'A precisely limited one, one that leaves the world financial system intact and controlled by us.' An exercise in disaster management.

'And the Kindred?'

'We want them to survive, of course – but weak enough that we can bluff full control. We'll throw a bit more "good luck" their way.'

Reynolt was nodding. 'Yes. We can tailor things. Southland has long-range missiles but is otherwise backward; most of its population will be hibernating through the Dark. They're very frightened of what will be done to them by the advanced powers. Honored Pedure has plans for taking advantage of that. We can make sure she succeeds—' Anne went on, detailing what frauds and miscues could be implemented, which cities could be safely murdered, how to save the Accord sites that held resources the Kindred did not yet have. Most of the deaths would be delivered by their proxies, which was just as well, considering the sorry state of their own weapons systems . . . Brughel was watching her with a certain bemused awe – the way he always did when Anne talked like this. Dispassionate and calm as ever, yet she could be as bloody-minded as Brughel himself.

Anne Reynolt had been a young woman when the Emergency came to Frenk. If history were written by the losing side, her name would be legend. After the Frenkisch military had surrendered, Anne Reynolt's ragtag partisans had fought on for years – and not as a fringe nuisance. Nau had seen the Intelligence estimates: Reynolt had tripled the cost of the invasion. She had taken an inchoate popular opposition and come within a hairsbreadth of defeating the Emergency's expeditionary force. And when her cause had ultimately failed – well, enemies such as that were best disposed of quickly. But Alan Nau had noticed that this enemy was peculiar to the point of uniqueness. Focusing the higher, people-oriented skills was normally a losing proposition. The very nature of Focusing tended to leave out the broad sensibilities that were necessary to manage people. And yet . . . Reynolt was young, brilliant, with an absolute dedication to principle. Her fanatical resistance was like nothing so much as a ziphead's loyalty to its subject matter. What if she *could* be profitably Focused?

Uncle Alan's long shot had paid off. Reynolt's only academic specialty had been ancient literature, but Focus had somehow captured the more subtle skills of her accidental career: warfare, subversion, leadership. Alan had kept his discovery carefully out of sight, but he had used this very special ziphead over the following decades. Her skills had helped establish Uncle Alan as the dominant Podmaster of the Home Regime. She had been a very special gift to a very favored nephew . . .

And though he would never admit it to Ritser Brughel, sometimes when Tomas looked into Reynolt's pale blue eyes . . . he felt a superstitious chill. For a hundred years of her lifetime, Anne Reynolt had worked to undo and suppress everything that was important to her unFocused self. If she wanted to cause him harm, she could do so much. But that was the beauty of Focus; that was the reason the Emergency would prevail. With Focus you got the capabilities of the subject without the humanity. And given attentive maintenance, all the ziphead's interest and loyalty stayed squarely on its subject matter and its owner.

'Okay, get your people on it, Anne. You have one year. We'll probably need a major vessel in low orbit during the final Ksecs.'

'You know,' said Ritser, 'I think the groundside of this is working out for the best. With the Kindred, one or two guys are in charge. We'll know who to hold responsible when we give orders. With that pus-be-damned Accord—'

'True. There are too many autonomous power centers within the Accord; their nonsovereign-kingship thing is even crazier than a democracy.' Nau shrugged. 'It's the luck of the draw. We have to take what we know we can control. Without the cavorite, we'd have another five years of slack. By then, the Accord would have a mature network, and we could take over everything without anyone firing a shot – more or less the goal I'm still hoping for in public.'

Ritser leaned forward. 'And that is going to be our biggest problem. Once our people realize this is a major Spider fry and their special friends are the main course—'

'Of course. But handled properly, the final outcome should appear to be an unavoidable tragedy, one that would have been much more horrible without our efforts.'

'It will be even trickier than the Diem thing. I wish you hadn't given the Peddlers increased resource access.'

'It's unavoidable, Ritser. We need their logistical genius. But I will withhold full network processing from them. We'll bring out all your security zips, do really intense monitoring. If necessary, there can be some fatal accidents.'

He glanced at Anne. 'And speaking of accidents . . . is there any progress on your sabotage theory?' It had been almost a year since Anne's maybe-accident in the MRI clinic. A year and not a sign of enemy action. Of course, there had been precious little evidence before the event, either.

But Anne Reynolt was adamant. 'Someone is manipulating our systems, Podmaster, both the localizers and the zipheads. The evidence is spread through large patterns; it's not something I can put into words. But he's getting more aggressive . . . and I'm very close to nailing him, maybe as close as when he got me before.'

Anne had never bought the explanation that a stupid mistake had wiped her. But her Focus *had* been out of tune, even if so subtly it slipped past his own checks. *Just how paranoid should I be?* Anne had cleared Ritser of suspicion in the affair. 'He? Him?'

'You know the suspect list. Pham Trinli is still at the top of it. Over the years, he's wrung my techs dry. And he was the one who gave us the secret of the Qeng Ho localizers.'

'But you've had twenty years now to study them.'

Anne frowned. 'The ensemble behavior is extremely complex, and there are physical-layer issues. Give me another three or four years.'

He glanced at Ritser. 'Opinion?'

The junior Podmaster grinned. 'We've been over this before, sir. Trinli is useful and we have a hold on him. He's a weasel, but he's *our* weasel.'

True. Trinli stood to gain much with the Emergents, and lose even more if the Qeng Ho ever learned of his traitorous past. Watch after Watch, the old man had passed every one of Nau's tests, and in the process become ever more useful. In retrospect, the fellow was always just as sharp as he had to be. Of course, that was the strongest evidence against him. *Pus and Pest.* 'Okay. Ritser, I want you and Anne to set things up so we can pull the plug on Trinli and Vinh at an instant's notice. Jau Xin we'll have to keep alive in any case – but we have Rita to keep him in line.'

'What about Qiwi Lisolet, sir?' Ritser's face was bland, but the Podmaster knew there was a smirk hidden just below the surface.

'Ah. I'm sure Qiwi will figure things out; we may have to scrub her several times before the crisis point.' But with luck she might be of use right to the end. 'Okay. Those are our special problem cases, but almost anyone could twig the truth if we have bad luck. Surveillance and suppression readiness must be of the highest order.' He nodded to his Vice-Podmaster. 'It will be hard work, this next year. The Peddlers are a competent, dedicated crowd. We'll need them on duty till the action begins – and we'll need many of them in the aftermath. The only letup may be during the takeover itself. It's reasonable that they be simply observers then.'

'At which time, we'll feed them the story of our noble efforts to limit the genocide.' Ritser smiled, intrigued by the challenge. 'I like it.'

They set up the overall plan. Anne and her strategy zips would flesh out the details. Ritser was right; this would be trickier than the Diem wetwork. On the other hand, if they could just maintain the fraud till the takeover . . . that might be enough. Once he controlled Arachna, he could pick and choose from both Spiders and Qeng Ho, the best of both their worlds. And discard the rest. The prospect was a cool oasis at the end of his long, long journey.

45

The Dark was upon them once more. Hrunkner could almost feel the weight of traditional values on his shoulders. For the trads – and deep down, he would always be one – there was a time to be born and a time to die; reality turned in cycles. And the greatest cycle was the cycle of the sun.

Hrunkner had lived through two suns now. He was an old cobber. Last time when the Dark had come, he had been young. There had been a world war going on, and real doubt if his country could survive. And this time? There were minor wars, all over the globe. But the big one had not occurred. If it did, Hrunkner would be partly responsible. And if it didn't – well, he liked to think that he would be partly responsible for that, too.

Either way, the cycles were shattered forever. Hrunkner nodded to the corporal who held the door for him. He stepped out onto frost-covered flagstones. He wore thick boots, covers, and sleeves. The cold gnawed the tips of his hands, burned his breathing passages even behind his air warmer. The alignment of the Princeton hills kept out the heaviest snows; that and the deep river moorage were the reasons why the city had returned cycle after cycle. But this was late afternoon on a summer day – and you had to search to find the dim disk that had been the sun. The world was beyond the soft kindliness of the Waning Years, beyond even the Early Dark. It stood at the edge of the thermal collapse, when weakening storms would circle and circle, squeezing the last water from the air – opening the way to times much colder, and the final stillness.

In earlier generations, all but soldiers would be in their deeps by now. Even in his own generation, in the Great War, only the die-hard tunnel warriors still fought this far into the Dark. This time – well, there were plenty of soldiers. Hrunkner had his own military escort. And even the security cobbers around the Underhill house were in uniform nowadays. But these were not caretakers, guarding against endcycle scavengers. Princeton was *overflowing* with people. The new, Dark Time housing was jammed. The city was busier than Unnerby had ever seen it.

And the mood? Fear close to panic, wild enthusiasm, often both in the same people. Business was booming. Just two days earlier, Prosperity Software had bought a controlling interest in the Bank of Princeton. No doubt the grab had gutted Prosperity's financial reserves, and put them in a business that their software people knew nothing about. It was insane – and very much in the spirit of the times.

Hrunkner's guards had to push their way through the crowd at the Hill House entrance. Even past the property limits, there were reporters with their little four-color cameras hanging from helium balloons. They couldn't know who Hrunkner was, but they saw the guards and the direction he was heading.

'Sir, can you tell us—'

'Has Southland threatened preemption?' This one tugged on his balloon's string, dragging the camera down till it hung just over Hrunkner's eyes.

Unnerby raised his forearms in an elaborate shrug. 'How should I know? I'm just a friggin' sergeant.' In fact, he *was* still a sergeant, but the rank was meaningless. Unnerby was one of those rankless cobbers who made whole military bureaucracies hop to their tune. As a young fellow he had been aware of such. They had seemed as distant as the King himself. Now . . . now he was so busy that even a visit with a friend had to be counted by the minute, balanced against what it might cost the life-and-death schedules he must keep.

His claim stopped the reporters just long enough for his team to get past and scuttle up the steps. Even so, it might have been the wrong thing to say. Behind him, Unnerby could see the reporters clustering together. By tomorrow, his name would be on their list. Ah, for the times when everyone thought that Hill House was just a plush annex to the University. Over the years, that cover had frayed away. The press thought they knew all about Sherkaner now.

Past the armored-glass doors there were no more intruders. Things were suddenly quiet, and it was much too warm for jackets and leggings. As he shed the insulation, he saw Underhill and his guide-bug standing just around the corner, out of the reporters' sight. In the old days, Sherk would have come outside to greet him. Even at the height of his radio fame, it hadn't bothered him to come outside. But nowadays Smith's security had its way.

'So, Sherk. I came.' *I always come when you call.* For decades, every new idea had seemed crazier than the last – and changed the world still again. But things had slowly changed with Sherkaner too. The General had given him the first warning, at Calorica, five years ago. After that, there had been rumors. Sherkaner had drifted away from active research. Apparently his work on antigravity had gone nowhere, and now the Kindred were launching floater satellites, for God's sake!

'Thanks, Hrunk.' His smile was quick, nervous. 'Junior told me you would be in town and—'

'Little Victory? She's here?'

'Yes! In the building somewhere. You'll be seeing her.' Sherk led Hrunkner and his guards down the main hall, talking all the while about Little Victory and the other children, about Jirlib's researches and the youngest ones' basic training. Hrunkner tried to imagine what they looked like. It had been seventeen years since the kidnappings . . . since he had last seen the cobblies.

It was quite a caravan they made trooping down the hall, the guide-bug leading Sherkaner leading Hrunkner and the latter's security. Underhill's progress was a slow drift to the left, corrected by Mobiy's constant gentle tugging on his tether. Sherk's lateral dysbadisia was not a mental disease; like his tremor, it was a low-level nervous disorder. The luck of the Dark had made him a very late casualty of the Great War. Nowadays he looked and talked like someone a generation older.

Sherkaner stopped by an elevator; Unnerby didn't remember it from his previous visits. 'Watch this, Hrunk . . . Press nine, Mobiy.' The bug extended one of its long, furry forelegs. The tip hovered uncertainly for a second, then poked the '9' slot on the elevator door. 'They say no bug can be taught numbers. Mobiy and I, we're working on it.'

Hrunkner shed his entourage at the elevator. It was just the two of them – and Mobiy – who headed upward. Sherkaner seemed to relax, and his tremor eased. He patted Mobiy's back gently, but no longer held so tight to the tether. 'This is just between you and me, Sergeant.'

Unnerby sharpened his gaze. 'My guards are Deep Secret rated, Sherk. They've seen things that—'

Underhill raised a hand. His eyes gleamed in the ceiling lights. Those eyes seemed full of the old genius. 'This is . . . different. It's something I've wanted you to know for a long time, and now that things are so desperate—'

The elevator slowed to a stop and the doors opened. Sherkaner had taken them all the way to the top of the hill. 'I have my office up here now. This used to be Junior's, but now that she's been commissioned, she has graciously willed it to me!' The hall had once been out-of-doors; Hrunkner remembered it as a path overlooking the children's little park. Now it was walled with heavy glass, strong enough to hold pressure even after the atmosphere had snowed out.

There was the sound of electric motors, and doors slid aside. Sherkaner waved his friend into the room beyond. Tall windows looked out on the city. Little Victory had had quite a room. Now it was a Sherkaner jumble. Over in the corner was that rocket bomb/dollhouse, and a sleeping perch for Mobiy. But the room was dominated by processor boxes and super-quality displays. The pictures shown were Mountroyal landscapes, the colors wilder than Hrunk had ever seen outside of nature. And yet the pictures were surreal. There were shaded forest glens, but with plaid undertones. There were grizzards sleeting across an iceberg eruption, all in the colors of lava. It was graphical madness . . . silly videomancy. Hrunkner stopped, and waved at the colors. 'I'm impressed, but it's not very well calibrated, Sherk.'

'Oh, it's calibrated, all right – but the inner meaning hasn't been derived.' Sherk mounted a console perch, and seemed to be looking at the pictures. 'Heh. The colors *are* gross; after a while, you stop noticing . . . Hrunkner, have you ever thought that our current problems are more serious than they should be?'

'How should I know? Everything is new.' Unnerby let himself sag. 'Yeah, things are on an infernal slide. This Southland mess is every nightmare we imagined. They have nuclear weapons, maybe two hundred, and delivery systems. They've bankrupted themselves trying to keep up with the advanced nations.'

'Bankrupted themselves, just to kill the rest of us?'

Thirty-five years ago, Sherk had seen the shape of all this, at least in general outlines. Now he was asking moron questions. 'No,' said Unnerby, almost lecturing. 'At least, that's not how it started out. They tried to create an industrial/agricultural base that could stay active in the Dark. They failed. They've got enough to keep a couple of cities going, a military division or two. Right now Southland is about five years further into the cold than the rest of the world. The dry hurricanes are already building over the south pole.' Southland was a marginally livable place at best; at the middle of the Bright Time, there were a few years where farming was possible. But the continent was fabulously rich in minerals. Over the last five generations, the Southlanders had been exploited by northern mining corporations, more avariciously each cycle than the last. But in this generation, there was a sovereign state in the South, one that was very afraid of the North and the coming Dark. 'They spent so much trying to make the leap to nuclear-electrics that they don't even have all their deepnesses provisioned.'

'And the Kindred are poisoning whatever goodwill there might otherwise be.'

'Of course.' Pedure was a genius. Assassination, blackmail, clever fearmongering. Whatever was evil, Pedure was very good at. And so now the Southland government figured that it was the Accord that planned to pounce on them in the Dark. 'The news networks have it right, Sherk. The Southies might nuke us.'

Hrunkner looked beyond Sherkaner's garish displays. From here, he could see Princeton in all directions. Some of the buildings – like Hill House – would be habitable even after the air condensed. They could hold pressure, and had good power connections. Most of the city was just slightly underground. It had taken fifteen years of construction madness to do that for the cities of the Accord, but now an entire civilization could survive, awake, through the Dark. But they were so close to the surface; they would quickly die in any nuclear war. The industries Hrunkner had helped to create had done miracles . . . *So now we're more at risk than ever.* More miracles were needed. Hrunkner and millions of others were struggling with

834

those impossible demands. During the last thirty days, Unnerby had averaged only three hours' sleep a day. This detour to chat with Underhill had scuttled one planning meeting and an inspection. *Am I here out of loyalty . . . or because I hope that Sherk can save us all again?*

Underhill steepled his forearms, making a little temple in front of his head. 'Have . . . have you ever thought that maybe something else is responsible for our problems?'

'Damn it, Sherk. Like what?'

Sherkaner steadied himself on his perch, and his words came low and fast. 'Like aliens from outer space. They've been here since before the New Sun. You and I saw them in the Dark, Hrunkner. The lights in the sky, remember?'

He rattled on, his tone so unlike the Sherkaner Underhill of years past. The Underhill of old revealed his weird speculations with an arch look or a challenging laugh. But now Underhill spoke in a rush, almost as if someone would stop him . . . or contradict him? This Underhill spoke like . . . a desperate man, grasping at fantasy.

The old fellow seemed to realize that he had lost his audience. 'You don't believe me, do you, Hrunk.'

Hrunkner shrank back on his perch. What resources had already been sunk into this horrifying nonsense? Other worlds – life on other worlds – that was one of Underhill's oldest, craziest ideas. And now it was surfacing after years of justified obscurity. He knew the General; she'd be no more impressed by this than he was. The world was teetering on the edge of an abyss. There was no room to humor poor Sherkaner. Surely the General did not let this distract her. 'It's like the videomancy, isn't it, Sherk?' *All your life, you've made miracles. But now you need them faster and more desperately than ever before. And all you have left is superstition.*

'No, no, Hrunk. The videomancy was just a means, a cover so the aliens wouldn't see. Here, I'll show you!' Sherkaner's hands tapped at control holes. The pictures flickered, the color values changing. One landscape morphed from summer to winter. 'It'll be a moment. The bit rate is low, but channel setup is a very big computation.' Underhill's head tilted toward tiny displays that Hrunkner could not see. His hands tapped impatiently on the console. 'More than anyone, you deserved to know about this, Hrunk. You have done so much for us; you could have done so much more if only we'd brought you into it. But the General—'

On the display, the colors were shifting, the landscapes melting into low-resolution chaos. Several seconds passed.

And Sherkaner gave a little cry of surprise and unhappiness.

What was left of the picture was recognizable, if much lower bandwidth than the original video. This appeared to be a standard eight-color video stream. They were looking out a camera in Victory Smith's office at Lands

Command. It was a good picture, but crude compared to true vision, or even Sherk's videomancy displays.

But this picture showed something real: General Smith stared back at them from her desk. The work was piled high around her. She waved an aide out of the office, and stared out at Underhill and Unnerby.

'Sherkaner . . . you brought Hrunkner Unnerby to your office.' Her tone was tight and angry.

'Yes, I—'

'I thought we discussed this, Sherkaner. You can play with your toys as much as you please, but you are not to bother people who have real work to do.'

Hrunkner had never heard the General use such tones and such sarcasm with Underhill. However necessary it might be, he would have given anything not to witness it.

Underhill seemed about to protest. He twisted on his perch, and his arms flailed, begging. Then: 'Yes, dear.'

General Smith nodded and waved at Hrunkner. 'I'm sorry for this inconvenience, Sergeant. If you need help getting back on schedule . . .'

'Thank you, ma'am. That may be. I'll check with the airport and get back to you.'

'Fine.' The image from Lands Command vanished.

Sherkaner lowered his head until it rested on the console. His arms and legs were inward-drawn and still. The guide-bug moved closer, pushed at him questioningly.

Underhill moved toward him. 'Sherk?' he said softly. 'Are you all right?'

The other was silent for a moment. Then he raised his head. 'I'll be okay. I'm sorry, Hrunk.'

'I – um, Sherkaner, I've got to go. I have another meeting—' That wasn't quite true. He had already missed both the meeting and the inspection. What was true was that there were so many other things to attend to. With Smith's help he might be able to get out of Princeton fast enough to catch up.

Underhill climbed awkwardly down from his perch and let Mobiy guide him after the sergeant. As the heavy doors slid open, Sherkaner reached out a single forehand, gently tugging on one of his sleeves. *More insanity?*

'Don't ever give up, Hrunk. There's always a way, just like before; you'll see.'

Unnerby nodded, mumbled something apologetic, and eased out of the room. As he walked down the glass-walled hallway toward the elevator, Sherkaner stood with Mobiy at the entrance to the office. Once upon a time, Underhill would have followed all the way down to the main foyer. But he seemed to realize that something had changed between them. As the elevator doors shut behind Unnerby, he saw his old friend give a shy little wave.

Then he was gone, and the elevator was sinking downward. For a moment, Unnerby surrendered to rage and sadness. Funny how the two emotions could mix. He had heard the stories about Sherkaner, and had willed disbelief. Like Sherkaner, he had *wanted* certain things to be true and had ignored the contrary symptoms. Unlike Sherk, Hrunkner Unnerby could not ignore the hard truths of their situation. And so this ultimate crisis would have to be won or lost without Sherkaner Underhill . . .

Unnerby forced his mind away from Sherkaner. There would come a time later, hopefully a time to remember the good things instead of this afternoon. For now . . . if he could commandeer a jet out of Princeton, he might be back at Lands Command in time to chat up his deputy directors.

Around the level of the cobblies' old park, the elevator slowed. Unnerby had thought this was Sherkaner's private lift. Who might this be?

The doors slid back—

'Well! Sergeant Unnerby! May I join you?'

A young lady lieutenant, dressed in quartermaster fatigues. Victory Smith as she had been so many years ago. Her aspect had the same brightness, her movement the same graceful precision. For a moment, Unnerby could only boggle at the apparition beyond the doors.

The vision stepped into the elevator, and Unnerby involuntarily moved back, still in shock. Then the other's military bearing slipped for an instant. The lieutenant lowered her head shyly. 'Uncle Hrunk, don't you recognize me? It's Viki, all grown up.'

Of course. Unnerby gave a weak laugh. 'I – I'll never call you Little Victory again.'

Viki put a couple of arms affectionately across his shoulders. 'No. You're allowed. Somehow, I don't think I'll ever be giving you orders. Daddy said you were coming up today. . . . Have you seen him? Do you have a moment to talk with me?'

The elevator was sliding to a stop, foyer level. 'I – Yes, I did . . . Look, I'm in a bit of rush to get back to Lands Command.' After the debacle upstairs, he just didn't know what he could say to Viki.

'That's okay. I'm on minus minutes myself. Let's share the ride to the airport.' She waved a grin. 'Twice the security.'

Lieutenants might manage a security escort, but they are rarely the subject of one. Young Victory's group was about half the number of Unnerby's but, from the look of them, even more competent. Several of the guards were clearly combat veterans. The fellow on the top perch behind the driver was one of the biggest troopers Unnerby had ever seen. When they slid into the car, he'd given Unnerby an odd little salute, not a military thing at all. Huh! That was Brent!

'So. What did Daddy have to say?' The tone was light, but Hrunkner could hear the anxiety. Viki was not quite the perfect, opaque intelligence officer. It might have been a flaw, but then he had known her since she had cobblie eyes.

And that made it all the harder for Unnerby to say the truth. 'You must know, Viki. He's not himself anymore. He's all into alien monsters and videomancy. It took the General herself to shut him up.'

Young Victory was quiet, but her arms drew into an angry frown. For a moment, he thought she was angry with him. But then he heard her faint mutter, 'The old fool.' She sighed, and they rode in silence for a few seconds.

Surface traffic was sparse, mainly cobbers traveling between disconnected boroughs. The streetlights splashed pools of blue and ultra, glittered off the frost that lined the gutters and the sides of buildings. Light from within the buildings glowed through the rime, showing greenish where it caught flecks of snow moss in the ice. Crystal worms grew by the millions on the walls, their roots probing endlessly for morsels of heat. Here in Princeton, the natural world might survive almost into the heart of the Dark. The city around and beneath them was a growing, warming thing. Behind those walls, and below the ground, things were busier than ever in the history of Princeton. The newer buildings of the business district glowed from ten thousand windows, boasting power, spilling broad bands of light upon the older structures . . . And even a modest nuclear attack would kill everyone here.

Viki touched his shoulder. 'I'm sorry . . . about Daddy.'

She would know much better than he how far Sherkaner had fallen. 'How long has he been into this? I remember him speculating on space monsters, but it was never serious.'

She shrugged, obviously unhappy with the question. '. . . He started playing with videomancy after the kidnappings.'

That far back? Then he remembered Sherkaner's desperation when the poor cobber realized that all his science and logic couldn't save his children. And so the seeds of this insanity had been planted. 'Okay, Viki. Your mother is right. The important thing is that this nonsense not get in the way. Your father has the love and admiration of so many people' – *including me, still.* 'No one will believe this crap, but I'm afraid that more than a few would try to help him, maybe divert resources, do experiments he suggests. We can't afford that, not now.'

'Of course.' But Viki hesitated an instant, her hand tips straightening. If Unnerby had not known her as a child, he would have missed it. She wasn't telling him everything, and was embarrassed by the deception. Little Victory had been a great fibber, except when she felt guilty about something.

'The General is humoring him, isn't she? Even now?'

'. . . Look, nothing big. Some bandwidth, some processor time.' Processor time on what? Underhill's desktop machines, or Intelligence Service superarrays? Maybe it didn't matter; he realized now how much of Sherk's low profile was simply the General keeping her husband from interfering with critical projects. *But pray for the poor lady.* For Victory Smith, losing Underhill must be like having your right legs shot off at the hips.

'Okay.' Whatever resources Sherk might be pissing away, there was nothing Hrunkner Unnerby could do about it. Maybe the best wisdom was the old *soldier on, soldier.* He glanced at Young Victory's uniform. The name tag was on her far collar, out of sight. Would it be Victory Smith (now, *that* would catch a superior officer's attention!), or Victory Underhill, or what?

'So, Lieutenant, how is your life in the military?'

Viki smiled, surely relieved to talk about something else. 'It is a great challenge, Sergeant.' Formality slipped. 'Actually, I'm having the time of my life. Basic training was – hmm, well you know as well as I. In fact, it is sergeants like you who make it the "charming" experience it is. But I had an edge: When I went through BT, almost all the recruits were in-phase, years older than I am. Heh heh. It wasn't hard to do well by comparison. Now – well, you can see this isn't your average first posting.' She waved at the car, and the security around them. 'Brent is a senior sergeant now; we're working together. Rhapsa and Little Hrunk will go through officer school eventually, but for now they're both junior enlisted. You may see them at the airport.'

'You're all working together?' Unnerby tried to keep the surprise out of his voice.

'Yes. We're a team. When the General wants a quick inspection, and needs absolute trust – we're the four she sends.' All the surviving children except Jirlib. For a moment, the revelation just added to Unnerby's depression. He wondered what the General Staff and midrankers thought when they saw a troop of Smith's relatives poking into Deep Secret affairs. But . . . Hrunkner Unnerby had once been deep in Intelligence himself. Old Strut Greenval had also played by his own rules. The King gave certain prerogatives to the chief of Intelligence. A lot of midlevel Intelligence people thought it was simply stupid tradition, but if Victory Smith thought she needed an Inspector General team from her own family – well maybe she did.

Princeton's airport was in chaos. There were more flights, more corporate charters, more crazy construction work than ever before. Chaotic or not, General Smith was ahead of the problem; a jet had already been diverted for his use. Viki's cars were cleared to drive right out onto the military side of the field. They moved cautiously down designated lanes, under the wings of taxiing aircraft. The secondary paths were torn by construction, a craterlike pit every hundred feet. By the end of the year, all service operations were to be conducted without external exposure. Ultimately, these facilities would have to support new types of fliers, and operations in air-freezing cold.

Viki dropped him off by his jet. She hadn't said where she was bound this evening. Unnerby found that pleasing. For all the strangeness of her present situation, at least she knew how to keep her mouth properly shut.

She followed him out into the freeze. There was no wind, so he risked going without the air heater. Every breath burned. It was so cold he could see clouds of frost hanging around the exposed joints of his hands.

Maybe Viki was too young and strong to notice. She trooped across the thirty yards to his jet, talking every second. If it weren't for all the dark omens rising out of this visit, seeing Viki would have been an absolute joy. Even out-of-phase, she had turned out so beautifully, a wonderful incarnation of her mother – with Smith's hard edge softened by what Sherkaner had been at his best. Hell, maybe part of it was *because* she was out-of-phase! The thought almost made him stop in the middle of the runway. But yes, Viki had spent her whole life out of step, seeing things from a new angle. In a weird way, watching her diminished all his misgivings about the future.

Viki stepped aside as they reached the weather shelter at the base of his jet. She drew herself up and gave him a well-starched salute. Unnerby returned the gesture. And then he saw her name tag.

'What an interesting name, Lieutenant. Not a profession, not some bygone deepness. Where—?'

'Well, neither of my parents is a "smith." And no one knows which "underhill" Daddy's family might be ascended from. But, see behind you—' She pointed.

Behind him the tarmac spread away from them, hundreds of yards of flatness and construction work, all the way back to the terminal. But Viki was pointing higher, up from the river-bottom flatlands. The lights of Princeton curved around the horizon, from glittering towers to the suburban hills.

'Look about five degrees to your right-rear of the radio tower. Even from here you can see it.' She was pointing at Underhill's house. It was the brightest thing in that direction, a tower of light in all the colors that modern fluorescents could make.

'Daddy designed well. We've hardly had to make any changes in the house at all. Even after the air has frozen, his light will still be up there on the hill. You know what Daddy says: We can go down and inward – or we can stand on high places and reach out. I'm glad that's where I grew up, and I want that place to be my name.'

She lifted her name tag so it glittered in the aircraft lights. LIEUTENANT VICTORY LIGHTHILL. 'Don't worry, Sergeant. What you and Dad and Mother started is going to last a long time.'

46

Belga Underville was getting a bit tired of Lands Command. It seemed that she was down here almost ten percent of the time – and it would be a lot more if she hadn't become a heavy telecomm user. Colonel Underville had been head of Domestic Intelligence since 60//15, more than half the past Bright Time. It was a truism – at least in modern times – that the end of the Brightness was the beginning of the bloodiest wars. She had expected things to be rough, but not like this.

Underville got to the staff meeting early. She was more than a little nervous about what she intended; she had no desire to cross the chief, but that was exactly how her petition might look. Rachner Thract was already there, getting his own show in order. Grainy, ten-color reconnaissance photos were projected on the wall behind him. Apparently he'd found more Southlander launch sites – further evidence of Kindred aid for 'the potential victims of Accord treachery.' Thract nodded civilly as she and her aides sat down. There was always some friction between External Intelligence and Domestic. External played by rules that were unacceptably rough for domestic operations, yet they always found excuses for meddling. The last few years, things had been especially tense between Thract and Underville. Since Thract had screwed up in Southland, he'd been much easier to handle. *Even the end of the world can have short-term advantages*, Belga thought sourly.

Underville flipped through the agenda. God, the crackpot distractions. Or maybe not: 'What do you think about these high-altitude bogies, Rachner?' It was not meant as an argumentative question; Thract should not be in trouble when it came to air defense.

Thract's hands jerked in abrupt dismissal. 'After all the screaming, Air Defense claims only three sightings. "Sightings" my ass. Even now that we know about Kindred anti-gravity capabilities, they still can't track the cobbers properly. Now the AD Director claims the Kindred have some launch site I don't know about. You know the chief is going to stick me with finding it . . . Damn!' Underville couldn't tell if that was his one-word summary answer, or if he had just noticed something obnoxious in his notes. Either way, Thract didn't have anything more to say to her.

The others were trickling in now: Air Defense Director Dugway (seating himself on a perch far from Rachner Thract), the Director of Rocket Offense, the Director of Public Relations. The chief herself entered, followed almost immediately by the King's Own Finance Minister.

General Smith called the meeting to order, and formally welcomed the Finance Minister. On paper, Minister Nizhnimor was her only superior short of the King himself. In fact, Amberdon Nizhnimor was an old crony of Smith's.

The bogies were first on the agenda, and it went about as Thract had predicted. Air Defense had done further crunching on the three sightings. Dugway's latest computer analysis confirmed that these were Kindred satellites, either pop-up recon jobs or maybe even the tests of a maneuvering anti-gravity missile. Either way, none of them had been seen twice. And none of them had been launched from any of the known Kindred sites. The director of Air Defense was very pointed about the need for competent ground intelligence from within Kindred territory. If the enemy had mobile launchers, it was essential to learn about them. Underville half-expected Thract to explode at the implication that his people had failed once more, but the Colonel accepted AD's sarcasm and General Smith's expected orders with impassive courtesy. Thract knew that this was the least of his problems; the last item on today's agenda was his real nemesis.

Next up, Public Relations: 'I'm sorry. There's no way we can call a War Plebiscite, much less win one. People are more frightened than ever, but the time scales make a Plebiscite flatly unworkable.' Belga nodded; she didn't need some flack from Public Relations for this insight. Within itself, the King's Government was a rather autocratic affair. But for the last nineteen generations, since the Covenant of Accord, its civil power had been terrifyingly limited. The Crown retained sole title to its ancestral estates such as Lands Command, and had limited power of taxation, but had lost the exclusive right to print money, the right of eminent domain, the right to impress its subjects into military service. In peacetime, the Covenant worked. The courts ran on a fee system, and local police forces knew they couldn't get too frisky or they might encounter real firepower. In wartime, well, that's what the Plebiscite was for – to suspend the Covenant for a certain time. It had worked during the Great War, just barely. This time around, things moved so fast that just talking about a Plebiscite might precipitate a war. And a major nuclear exchange could be over in less than a day.

General Smith accepted the platitudes with considerable patience. Then it was Belga's turn. She went through the usual catalogue of domestic threats. Things were under control, more or less. There were significant minorities that loathed the modernization. Some were already out of the picture, asleep in their own deepnesses. Others had dug themselves deep redoubts, but not to sleep in; these would be a problem if things went really bad. Hrunkner Unnerby had worked more of his engineering miracles. Even the oldest towns in the Northeast had nuclear electricity now, and – just as important – weatherized living space. 'But of course not much of this is hardened. Even a light nuclear strike would kill most of these people, and the rest wouldn't have the resources for a successful hibernation.' In fact, most of those resources had been spent on creating the power plants and underground farms.

General Smith gestured at the others. 'Comments?' There were several. Public Relations suggested buying in to some of the hardened enterprises; he was already planning for after the end of the world, the bloody-minded little wimp. The chief just nodded, assigned Belga and the wimp to look into the possibility. She checked the Domestic Intelligence report off her copy of the agenda.

'Ma'am?' Belga Underville raised a hand. 'I do have one more item I'd like to bring up.'

'Certainly.'

Underville brushed her eating hands nervously across her mouth. She was committed now. Damn. If only the Finance Minister weren't here. 'I – Ma'am, in the past you have been very, um, generous in your management of subordinate operations. You give us the job, and let us do it. I have been very grateful for that. Recently though, and very likely this is without your precise knowledge, people from your inner staff have been making unscheduled visits' – midnight raids, actually – 'on domestic sites in my area of responsibility.'

General Smith nodded. 'The Lighthill team.'

'Yes, ma'am.' *Your own children, running around as though they were the King's Inspectors General.* They were full of crazy, irrational demands, shutting down good projects, removing some of her best people. More than anything, it made her suspect that the chief's crazy husband still had great influence. Belga hunkered down on her perch. She really didn't have to say more. Victory Smith knew her well enough to see she was upset.

'On these inspection visits, did Lighthill find anything significant?'

'In one case, ma'am.' One fairly serious problem that Belga was sure she would have pounced on herself inside of another ten days. Around the table, Underville could see that most of the others were simply surprised by the complaint. Two nodded faintly in her direction – she already knew about them. Thract tapped an angry tattoo on the table; he seemed about to jump into the fray. It was no surprise that he had been targeted by the chief's nepotistic crew, but *please God, grant him the cleverness to keep his maw shut.* Thract was already in such poor standing that his support would be about as much help as a steel anvil to a racing-climber.

The chief inclined her head, waited a polite moment for anyone else to comment. Then, 'Colonel Underville, I understand that this can hurt your people's morale. But we are entering very critical times, far deadlier than a declared war. I need special assistants, ones who can act very quickly and who I understand completely. The Lighthill team acts directly for me. Please tell me if you feel their behavior is out of line – but I ask you to respect their delegated authority.' Her tone seemed sincerely regretful, but the words were uncompromising; Smith was changing policy of decades' standing. Belga had the sinking feeling that the chief knew all her cobblies' depredations.

The Finance Minister had looked almost bored so far. Nizhnimor was a war hero; she had walked through the Dark with Sherkaner Underhill. You might forget that when you saw her; Amberdon Nizhnimor had spent all the decades of this generation climbing up the Other Side of the royal service, as a court politician and arbitrator. She dressed and moved like an old coot; Nizhnimor was a cartoon caricature of a Finance Minister. Big, lank, frail. Now she leaned forward. Her wheezy voice sounded as harmless as she looked. 'I fear this is all a bit outside my realm. But I do have some advice. Though we can't have a Plebiscite, we are very much at war. Internal to the government, we are moving to a war footing. Normal chains of appeal and review are in suspension. Given this extraordinary situation, it's important for you to realize that both I and – more importantly – the King have complete faith in General Smith's leadership. You all know that the chief of Intelligence has special prerogatives. This is not outmoded tradition, ladies and gentleman. This is considered, royal policy, and you must all accept it.'

Wow. So much for 'frail' finance ministers. There were sober nods from all around the table and no one had anything more to say, least of all Belga Underville. In a strange way, Belga felt better for getting so definitively squashed. Things might be on a road straight to Hell, but she didn't have to worry about who was on the driver's perch.

After a moment, General Smith returned to her agenda. '. . . We have one item left. It is also the most critical problem we're up against. Colonel Thract, will you tell us about the Southland situation?' Her tone was courteous, almost sympathetic. Nevertheless, poor Thract was in for it.

But Thract showed some hardshell. He bounced off his perch and walked briskly to the podium. 'Minister. Ma'am.' He nodded at Nizhnimor and the chief. 'We believe the situation has stabilized somewhat in the last fifteen hours.' He poked up the recon pictures that Belga had seen him studying before the meeting. Much of Southland was shrouded in a swirl of storm, but the launch sites were high in the Dry Mountains and mostly visible. Thract tapped away at his pictures, analyzing the supply situation. 'The long-range Southlander rockets are liquid fueled, very fragile things. Their parliament has seemed insanely bellicose these last few days – their "Ultimatum for Cooperative Survival," for instance – but in fact, we don't think that more than a tenth of their rockets are launch-ready. It will take three or four days for them to get all the tanks topped off.'

Belga: 'That seems awfully stupid on their part.'

Thract nodded. 'But remember, their parliamentary system makes them less decisive than either us or the Kindred. These people have been tricked into thinking that they must either fight a war now, or be murdered in their sleep. The Ultimatum may have been a mistake in timing, but it was also an attempt by some in Parliament to make the prospect of war so frightening that their colleagues would back down.'

The Director of Air Defense: 'So you figure things will stay peaceful until they complete fueling?'

'Yes. The crunch will be the Parliament meeting at Southmost in four days. That's where they review our response – if we've made one – to the Ultimatum.'

The wimp from Public Relations asked, 'Why not just accede to their demands? They aren't asking for territory. We are so strong that giving in would scarcely be a loss of prestige.'

There was a rattle of indignation from around the table. General Smith answered in terms a good deal milder than the question merited. 'Unfortunately, it's not a matter of prestige. The Southland Ultimatum requires us to weaken several of our military arms. In fact, I doubt that it would make the Southlanders any safer in their deepnesses – but it would increase our vulnerability to a Kindred first strike.'

Chezny Neudep, Director of Rocket Offense: 'Indeed. Now the Southlanders are simply Kindred puppets. Pedure and her bloodsuckers must be happy. No matter how this comes out, they win.'

'Maybe not,' said Minister Nizhnimor. 'I know many of the top Southlanders; they are not evil, or insane, or incompetent. We have come down to a matter of trust here. The King is willing to go to Southmost for this next meeting of the Southlander Parliament, and stay there for the remainder of this session. It's hard to imagine a greater expression of trust on our part – and I think the Southlanders will accept it, no matter what Pedure may wish.'

Of course, this is what Kings were for. Nevertheless, the Minister's offer was a shock; even 'Old Megadeath' Neudep seemed taken aback. 'Ma'am . . . I know it's the King's power to do such things, but I can't agree that this is a problem of trust. Certainly, there are honorable people in high positions in the South. A year ago, the Southland was nearly an ally. We had sympathizers at all levels of government. Colonel Thract told us that we had – to be blunt – *spies* in positions of power there. If not for that, I don't think General Smith ever would have encouraged the technical growth of Southland . . . But in less than a year, it seems we have lost all our advantage there. What I see now is a state thoroughly infiltrated by the Kindred. Even if the majority of Parliament is honorable, *it doesn't matter.*' Neudep shot two arms in Thract's direction. 'Your analysis, Colonel?'

Blame-assignment time. It had been part of each of the recent staff meetings, and each time Thract had been more the target.

Thract gave a little bow in Megadeath's direction. 'Sir, your assessment is generally correct, though I see little infiltration of the Southland rocket forces, per se. We had a friendly government there – and one that I would swear was carefully "instrumented" with Accord agents. The Kindred were active, but we had them stymied. Then, step by step, we lost ground. At first, it was bungled surveillance, then fatal accidents, then assassinations we weren't quick enough to block. Lately there have been trumped-up criminal prosecutions . . . Our enemy is clever.'

'So the Honored Pedure is a genius beyond our ken?' asked the Director of Air Defense. Sarcasm dripped.

Thract was silent for a moment. His eating hands twisted back and forth. At earlier meetings, this was where he would counterattack with statistics and fine new projects. Now – something seemed to break inside him. Belga Underville had counted Thract as a bureaucratic enemy ever since the chief's children were kidnapped, but now she felt embarrassed for him. When Thract finally spoke, his voice came out an anguished squeak. '*No!* Don't you know I . . . I've had friends die; I've lost others because I began mistrusting them. For a long time, I thought there must be a Kindred agent high in my own organization. I shared critical information with fewer and fewer people, not even with my own superior—' He nodded at General Smith. 'In the end, there were secrets plucked from us that only I knew and which I communicated with my own crypto equipment.'

There was silence, as the obvious consequence of these claims hardened in the minds of his audience. Thract's attention seemed to turn inward, as if he didn't care that others thought he might be the Father of All Traitors. He continued more quietly, 'As far as one person can be a paranoid and be everywhere, so I have been. I have used different comm paths, different crypto. I have used differential frauds . . . And I tell you, our enemy is something more than any single "Honored Pedure." Somehow, all of our clever science is working against us.'

'Nonsense!' said Air Defense. 'My department uses more of what you call "clever science" than anyone, and we are entirely satisfied with the results. In competent hands, computers and networks and satellite reconnaissance are incredibly powerful tools. Just look at what our deep analysis did with the unidentified radar sightings. Certainly, networks can be abused. But we are the world's leaders in these technologies. And no matter what else may be broken we have a completely robust encryption technology . . . Or do you claim the enemy can break our crypto?'

Thract swayed slightly from his place behind the podium. 'No, that was my first great suspicion, but we had penetrated to the heart of the Kindred's encryption establishment – and we were safely there until very recently. If I trust anything, it is that they can't break our encryption.' He waved at them all. 'You really don't understand, do you? I tell you, there is some force in our networks, something that is actively opposing us. No matter what we do, It knows more and It is supporting our enemies . . .'

The scene was pathetic, a kind of abject collapse. Thract was left with nothing but phantoms to explain his failures. Maybe Pedure really was clever beyond all imagination; more likely, Thract was a Father Traitor.

Belga watched the chief with half her attention. General Smith was deep in the King's trust. No doubt she could survive Thract's collapse simply by starkly disowning him.

Smith beckoned the guard sergeant by the door. 'Help Colonel Thract to the staff office. Colonel, I'll be along to talk to you in a few minutes. Consider yourself as still on duty.'

It seemed to take a second for the words to penetrate Thract's funk. He was headed out the door, but apparently not for arrest or even imminent quizzing by underlings. 'Yes, ma'am.' He straightened to a semblance of smartness and followed the sergeant out.

The room was very quiet after Thract's departure. Belga could tell that everyone was watching everyone else, and thinking very dark thoughts. Finally, General Smith said, 'My friends, the Colonel has a point. No doubt we are infested with deep-cover Kindred agents. But they are effective across much too large a range of our departments. There is some systematic flaw in our security, and yet we have no idea what it is . . . Now you see the reason for the Lighthill team.'

47

It was forty years since the OnOff star had last come to life. Ritser Brughel had not been on-Watch all that time, yet still the Exile had consumed years of his life. And now it was drawing to an end. What had been years was now a matter of days. In less than four days, he would be vice-ruler of a world.

Brughel hung over the shoulder of the ziphead operating the remote lander, and quietly watched what the tiny device was sending back. A few seconds earlier, the lander had come out of its brake and spread its meter-wide wings. Still forty kilometers up, they had ghosted over an unending carpet of lights, threaded by a glowing web work that refined itself into recursive infinity. Greater Kingston South was the ziphead name for the place. A Spider supercity. This world was cold and freezing colder, but it was no wasteland. The Spiders' megalopolises looked almost Frenkisch. This was a real civilization, crowned by forty years of sustained progress. Its capital technology was still short of Humankind's highest standards, but with ziphead guidance, that could be corrected in a decade or two. *For forty years, I have been reduced to a Master of Tens, and soon I will be Master of Tens of Millions*. And beyond that . . . if the Spider world really held clues to a Higher Technology . . . someday he and Tomas Nau would return to Frenk and Balacrea to rule there too.

In the space of three seconds, the picture fragmented into a dozen copies, and then a dozen dozen. 'What—'

'The lander just broke into submunitions, Podmaster.' Reynolt's explanation was cold, almost mocking. 'Almost two hundred mobiles – we'll get some into Southmost.' She turned from the display and almost looked him in the eyes. 'Strange that you are suddenly so interested in operational details, Podmaster.'

He felt a flicker of the old rage at her impudence, but it was a mild thing, not affecting his breathing, much less his vision. He gave a little shrug at the question. *Nowadays I can get along even with Reynolt.* Maybe Tomas Nau was right; maybe he was growing up. 'I want to see what the creatures really look like.' Know your slaves. Soon they would fry Spiders by the hundred million, but somehow he must learn to tolerate those that were spared. The spylets arced silently downward, across a frozen strait. A few were still spinning, and Ritser had a glimpse of clouds, the topside of a – hurricane? Two hundred thumbsized pellets. Over the next thousand seconds they all came down, many in deep snow, some on rocky wasteland. But there were successes, too.

Several ended up on some kind of roadway, drenched in blue streetlight. One of the views showed snow-draped ruins in the distance. Heavy, closed vehicles lumbered by. Reynolt's ziphead wiggled his spylets out onto the road. He was trying to hitch a ride. One by one, they ceased transmitting, squashed flat. Ritser glanced at an inventory window. 'This better work, Anne. We only have one more multi-lander.'

Reynolt didn't bother to reply. Ritser pulled himself down to tap her specialist on the shoulder. 'So, are you going to be able get one indoors?'

The odds were against any answer; a Focused mind in a control loop is usually unreachable. But after a moment the zip nodded. 'Probe 132 is doing well. I've got three hundred seconds left on the high-gain link. We're just a few meters this side of the weather door. This one is getting in—' The fellow hunched lower over the controls. He swayed back and forth like an addict playing a hand-eye game, which in a sense was exactly the situation. One of the pictures panned up and down as he wiggled the device into traffic.

Brughel looked back at Reynolt. 'That damn time lag. How can you expect to—'

'Running a remote like this isn't the worst. Melin' – the ziphead operator – 'has very good delayed coordination. Our main problem is operations on the Spiders' networks. We can dredge for data, but very soon we'll be interacting in tight real time. A ten-second turnaround is longer than some network timeouts.'

As she spoke, a flashing tread flew past the little camera. By some magic of ziphead intuition, Melin had flipped the gadget onto the side of the vehicle. The image spun madly for several seconds as Melin synched the rotation with the view. A door opened in the wall ahead of them, and they drove on through. Thirty seconds passed. The walls seemed to slide upward. Some kind of elevator? But if the scale information were true, the room was wider than a racquetball court.

Seconds passed, and Brughel found himself caught by the scene. For years now, everything they had gotten about the Spiders had been second-hand, from Reynolt's ziphead translators. Some large percentage of that had to be fairy-tale crap; it was just too cute. Real pictures were what he needed. Microsat optical reconnaissance produced some pictures, but the resolution was awful. For several years, Ritser had thought that when the Spiders finally invented hi-res video, he would get a good look. But the visual physiologies were just too different. Nowadays, about five percent of all Spider military comm was this extremely hi-res stuff that Trixia Bonsol called 'videomancy.' Without heavy interpretation, it was just a jumble to humans. He would have been very suspicious that it was a steganographic cover, except that the translators had proven to Kal's snoops that it was innocent video – all quite impressive if you were a Spider.

But now, in a very few seconds, he would get to see how the monsters looked from a human pov.

No motion was visible. If this was an elevator, they were going down a long way. That made sense, considering what the south pole weather was like. 'Are we going to lose signal?'

Reynolt didn't answer immediately. 'I don't know. Melin's trying to get relays into that elevator shaft. I'm more worried about it being discovered. Even if the meltdown-triggers work—'

Brughel laughed. 'Who cares? Don't you see, Reynolt? We're less than four days from grabbing it all.'

'The Accord is beginning to panic. They just sacked a senior manager. I've got meeting logs that show Victory Smith now suspects network corruption.'

'Their Intelligence boss?' The news stopped Brughel for a moment. This must have happened very recently. Still, 'They have less than four days. What can they do?'

Reynolt's gaze was the usual stone thing. 'They could partition their net, maybe stop using it altogether. That would stop us.'

'And also lose them the war against the Kindred.'

'Yes. Unless they could provide the Kindred with solid proof of "Monsters from Outer Space."'

And that was not bloody likely. The woman was obsessive. Ritser smiled at her frowning face. *Of course. That's how we made you.*

The elevator doors had opened. The camera was giving them only one frame a second now, with low resolution. Damn.

'Yes!' That was Melin, triumphant about something.

'He's got a relay in place.'

Suddenly the picture turned crisp and smooth. As the spylet crept out from the elevator doors, Melin turned its eyes to look down an incredibly steep set of stairs, more like a ladder really. Who knew what this area was, a loading garage? For now, the little camera hid in corners and looked out upon the Spiders. From the scale bar, he could see that the monsters were of the expected size. A grown one would come up to about Brughel's thigh. The creatures stretched far across the ground in a low posture, just as in the library pictures retrieved before Relight. They look very little like the mental picture that the ziphead translators evoked. Did they wear clothes? Not like humans. The monsters were swathed with things that looked like banners with buttons. Huge panniers hung from the sides of many of them. They moved in quick, sinister jerks, their bladelike forelegs cutting this way and that before them. There was a crowd here, chitinous black except for the mismatched colors of their clothing. Their heads glittered as with large flat gemstones. Spider eyes. And as for the Spider mouth – there the translators had used the proper word: *maw*. A fanged depth surround by tiny claws – was that what Bonsol & Co. called 'eating hands'? – that seemed to be in constant, writhing motion.

Massed together, the Spiders were more a nightmare than he'd imagined, the sort of things you crush and crush and crush and still more of them come at you. Ritser sucked in a breath. One comforting thought was that – if all went well – in just under four days, these particular monsters would be dead.

For the first time in forty years, a starship would fly across the OnOff system. It would be a very short hop, less than two million kilometers, scarcely a remooring by civilized standards. It was very nearly the most that any of the surviving starships could manage.

Jau Xin had supervised the flight prep of the *Invisible Hand*. The *Hand* had always been Ritser Brughel's portable fiefdom, but Jau knew it was also the only starship that had not been wholly cannibalized over the years.

In the days before their 'passengers' embarked, Jau had drained the L1 distillery of hydrogen. It was just a few thousand tonnes, a droplet in the million-tonne capacity of the ramscoop's primer tanks, but enough to slide them across the gap between L1 and the Spider world.

Jau and Pham Trinli made a final inspection of the star-ship's drive throat. It was always strange, looking at that two-meter narrowness. Here the forces of hell had burned for decades, driving the Qeng Ho vessel up to thirty-percent lightspeed. The internal surface was micrometer smooth. The only evidence of its fiery past was the fractal pattern of gold and silver that glittered in the light of their suit lamps. It was the micronet of processors behind those walls that actually guided the fields, but if the throat wall cavitated while under way, the fastest processors in the universe wouldn't save them. True to form, Trinli made a big deal of his laser-metric inspection, then was contemptuous of the results. 'There's ninety-micron swale on the port side – but what the hell. There's no new pitting. You could carve your name in the walls here, and it wouldn't make any difference on this flight. What are you planning, a couple hundred Ksecs at fractional gee?'

'Um. We'll start with a long gentle push, but the braking burn will be a thousand seconds at a little more than one gravity.' They wouldn't brake till they were low over open ocean. Anything else would light Arachna's sky brighter than the sun, and be seen by every Spider on the near side of the planet.

Trinli waved his hand in an airy gesture of dismissal. 'Don't worry about it. Many times, I've taken bigger chances with in-system flight.' They crawled out the bow side of the throat; the smooth surface widened into the beginnings of the forward field projectors. All the while, Trinli continued with his bogus stories. No. Most of the stories could be true, but abstracted from all the real adventurers the old man had ever known. Trinli did know something about ship drives. The tragedy was that they didn't have anyone who knew much more. All the Qeng Ho flight engineers had been killed in the original fighting – and the pod's last ziphead engineer had fallen to mindrot runaway.

They emerged from the bow end of the *Hand* and climbed a mooring strand back to their taxi. Trinli paused and turned. 'I envy you, Jau my boy. Take a look at your ship! Almost a million tonnes dryweight! You won't be going far, but you'll be bringing the *Hand* to the treasure and the Customers it sailed fifty light-years to find.'

Jau followed his broad gesture. Over the years, Jau had realized that Trinli's theatrics were a cover . . . but sometimes they reached out and plucked at your soul. The *Invisible Hand* looked quite starworthy, hundred meter after hundred meter of curving hull sweeping off into the distance, streamlined for speeds and environments at the limit of all human accomplishment. And beyond the stern rings – 1.5 million kilometers beyond – the disk of Arachna showed pale and dim. *A First Contact, and I will be the Pilot Manager.* Jau should have been a proud man . . .

Jau's last day before departure was busy, filled with final checks and provisioning. There would be more than a hundred zipheads and staff. Jau didn't learn just which specialties were represented, but it was obvious that the Podmasters wanted to manipulate the Spiders' networks intensively, without the ten-second time delay of L1 operations. That was reasonable. Saving the Spiders from themselves would involve some incredible frauds, perhaps the taking over of entire strategic weapons systems.

Jau was coming off his shift when Kal Omo appeared at Xin's little office just off the *Hand*'s bridge.

'One more job, Pilot Manager.' Omo's narrow face broke into a humorless grin. 'Call it overtime.'

They took a taxi down to the rockpile, but not to Hammerfest. Around the arc of Diamond One, embedded in ice and diamond, was the entrance to L1-A. Two other taxis were already moored by the arsenal's lock.

'You've studied the *Hand*'s weapon fittings, Pilot Manager?'

'Yes.' Xin had studied everything about the *Hand*, except Brughel's private quarters. 'But surely a Qeng Ho would be more familiar—'

Omo shook his head. 'This isn't appropriate work for a Peddler, not even Mr Trinli.' It took some seconds to get through the main lock security, but once inside they had a clear passage into the weapons area. Here they were confronted by the noise of fitting machines and cutters. The squat ovoids racked along the walls were marked with the weapons glyph – the ancient Qeng Ho symbol for nukes and directed-energy weapons. For years, the gossip had speculated just how much survived at L1-A. Now Jau could see for himself.

Omo led him down a crawl line past unmarked cabinets. There was no consensual imagery in L1-A. And this was one of the few places left at L1 that did not use the Qeng Ho localizers. The automation here was simple and foolproof. They passed Rei Ciret, supervising a gang of zipheads in the construction of some kind of launch rack. 'We'll be moving most of these weapons to the *Invisible Hand*, Mr Xin. Over the years we've cobbled together parts, tried to make as many deliverable devices as possible. We've done the best we could, but without depot facilities, that's not a hell of a lot.' He waved at what looked like Qeng Ho drive units mated to Emergent tactical nukes. 'Count 'em. Eighteen short-range nukes. In the cabinets we have the guts of a dozen weapon lasers.'

'I – I don't understand, Podsergeant. You're an armsman. You have your own specialists. What need is there for—'

'—For a Pilot Manager to be concerned with such things?' Again the humorless smile. 'To save the Spider civilization, it's entirely possible that we'll have to use these things, from the *Invisible Hand* in low orbit. The fitting and engagement sequences will be very important to your pilots.'

Xin nodded. He'd been over some of this. The most likely start of a planet-killer war was the current crisis at the Spiders' south pole. After they arrived, they'd be in position over that site every fifty-three hundred seconds, with near-constant coverage from smaller vehicles. Tomas Nau had already announced about the lasers. As for the nukes . . . maybe they could help with bluffing.

The podsergeant continued the tour, pointing out the limitations of each resurrected device. Most of the weapons were shaped charges, and Omo's zipheads had converted them into crude digger bombs. '. . . and we'll have most of the network zipheads on board the *Hand*. They'll supply fire-control information for your maneuvers; we may have to make substantial orbit changes depending on the targets.'

Omo talked with an ordnanceman's enthusiasm, and quickly left Jau with no place to hide. For a year, Jau had watched the preparations with increasing fear; there were details that could not be disguised from him. But for every treacherous possibility, there had always been some reasonable explanation. He had held to those 'reasonable explanations' so fiercely. They allowed him to feel a shred of decency; they made it possible for him to laugh with Rita as they planned what the future would be like with the Spiders, and with children she and he would have.

The horror must have shown on Jau's face. Omo stopped his parade of murderous revelation, and turned to looked at him. Jau asked, 'Why . . . ?'

'Why must I spell it out for you?' Omo jabbed a finger at Jau's chest, pushing him away from the crawl line and into the wall. He jabbed again. His hard face showed an angry indignation. It was the righteous indignation of Emergency authority, what Jau had grown up with on Balacrea. 'It shouldn't really be necessary, should it? But you're like too many of our pod. You've gone bad inside, become a kind of Peddler. The others we can let drift for a while longer, but when the *Hand* reaches low orbit, we need your intelligent, instant obedience.' Omo jabbed him once more. 'Do you understand now?'

'Y-yes. Yes!' *Oh Rita! We will always be part of the Emergency.*

48

More than a hundred zipheads were leaving Hammerfest's Attic. Genius that he was, Trud Silipan had scheduled the transfer as a single move. As Ezr headed for Trixia's cell, he was swimming against a current of humanity. The Focused were being herded in groups of four and five, first out of the little capillary hallways that led to their roomlets, then into the tributary halls and finally into the main corridors. The handlers were gentle, but this was a difficult maneuver.

Ezr pulled himself sideways, into a utility nook, a back-eddy in the flow. There were people drifting past that he hadn't seen in years. These were Qeng Ho and Trilander specialists, Focused right after the ambush, just like Trixia. A few of the handlers were friends of the Focused they guided. Watch on Watch they had come to visit the lost ones. At first there had been many such people. But the years passed and hope had dimmed. Maybe someday . . . they had Nau's promise of manumission. In the meantime, the zip-heads seemed beyond caring; a visit was at most an irritation to them. Only rare fools kept at it for years.

Ezr had never seen so many zipheads moving about. Corridor ventilation was not as good as in the little cells; the smell of unwashed bodies was strong. Anne kept the pod's property healthy, but that didn't mean they were clean and pretty.

Bil Phuong hung on a wall strap by a confluence of streams, directing his team handlers. Most teams had a common specialty. Vinh caught scraps of agitated conversation. Could it be that they cared about what was planned for the Spider world? . . . But no, this was impatience and distraction and technical gibberish. An older woman – one of the network protocol hackers – pushed her handler, actually spoke directly to him. 'When then?' Her voice was shrill. 'When do we get back to work?'

One of the woman's team members shouted something like 'Yeah, the stackface is stale!' and moved in on the handler from the other side. Away from their inputs, the poor things were going nuts. The entire team began screaming at the handler. The group was the nucleus of a growing clot in the stream. Suddenly, Ezr realized that something like a slave revolt could really happen – if the slaves were taken from their work! This was clearly a danger the Emergent team handler understood. He slid to the side, and yanked the stun lanyards on the two loudest zipheads. They spasmed, then went limp. Deprived of a center, the others' complaints subsided into diffuse irritability.

Bil Phuong arrived to calm the last of the combative zipheads. He spared a frown for the team handler. 'That's two more I have to retune.' The team handler wiped blood from his cheek and glared back. 'Tell it to Trud.' He grabbed the lanyards and floated the unconscious zipheads out over their fellows. The crowd moved on, and in a few seconds Vinh had a clear jump to the end of the corridor.

The translators weren't going with the *Invisible Hand*. Their section of the Attic should have been peaceful. But when Ezr arrived, he found the cell doors open and the translators clogging the capillary corridor. Ezr wormed his way past the fidgeting, shouting zipheads. There was no sign of Trixia. But a few meters up the hall he ran into Rita Liao coming from the other direction.

'Rita! Where are the handlers?'

Liao raised both hands in irritation. 'Busy elsewhere, of course! And now some idiot has opened the translators' doors!'

Trud had really outdone himself, though most likely this was only a related glitch. Ironically, the translators – who weren't supposed to go anywhere – had needed no urging to leave their cells, and now were loudly demanding directions. 'We want to go to Arachna!' 'We want to get in close!'

Where was Trixia? Ezr heard more shouting from around an upward corner. He followed the fork, and there she was, with the rest of the translators. Trixia looked badly disoriented; she just wasn't used to the world outside of her cell. But she seemed to recognize him. 'Shut up! Shut up!' she shouted, and the gabble quieted. She looked vaguely in Ezr's direction. 'Number Four, when do we go to Arachna?'

Number Four? 'Um. Soon, Trixia. But not on this trip, not on the *Invisible Hand*.'

'Why *not?* I don't like the time lag!'

'For now, your Podmaster wants you close by.' In fact, that was the official story: only lower network functions were needed in close orbit of Arachna. Pham and Ezr knew a darker explanation. Nau wanted as few people as possible on the *Hand* when it performed its real mission. 'You'll go when it's safe, Trixia. I promise.' He reached out toward her. Trixia didn't flinch away, but she held tight to a wall stop, resisting any effort to draw her back to her cell.

Ezr looked over his shoulder at Rita Liao. 'What should we do?'

'Wait one.' She touched her ear, listened. 'Phuong and Silipan will be here to stuff 'em back in their holes, just as soon as they get the others settled down on the *Hand*.'

Lord, that could take a while. In the meantime, twenty translators would be loose in the Attic maze. He gently patted Trixia's arm. 'Let's go back to your room, Trixia. Uh, look, the longer you're out here, the more you're out of touch. I'll bet you left your huds in your room. You could use them to ask fleet net your questions.' Trixia had probably left her huds behind because they were offline. But at this point, he was just trying to make reasonable noises.

Trixia bounced from wall stop to wall stop, full of indecision. Abruptly she pushed past him and flitted back to the downward fork that led to her little room. Ezr followed.

The cell reacted to Trixia's presence, the lights coming to their usual dim glow. Trixia grabbed her huds, and Ezr synched to them. Her links weren't completely down. Ezr saw the usual pictures and splashes of text; it wasn't quite live from groundside, but it was close. Trixia's eyes darted from display to display. Her fingers pounded on her old keyboard, but she seemed to have forgotten about contacting the fleet information service. Just the sight of her workspace had drawn her back to the center of her Focus. New text windows popped up. Glyphics nonsense shifted so fast across it that it must be a representation of spoken Spider talk, some radio show or – considering the current state of affairs – a military intercept. 'I just can't stand the time lag. It's not fair.' Again a long silence. She opened another text screen. The pictures beside it went through a flickering series of colors, one of the Spiders' video formats. It still didn't look like a real picture, but he recognized this pattern; he had seen it often enough in Trixia's little room. This was a Spider commercial newscast that Trixia translated daily. 'They're wrong. General Smith will go to Southmost instead of the King.' She was still tense, but now it was her usual, Focused absorption.

A few seconds later, Rita Liao stuck her head into the room. Ezr turned, saw a look of quiet amazement on her face. 'You're a magician, Ezr. How'd you get everyone calmed down?'

'I . . . I guess Trixia just trusts me.' That was an innermost hope phrased as diffident speculation.

Rita pulled her head out of the doorway to look up and down the corridor. 'Yeah. But you know, after you got her back to work? All the others just quietly returned to their rooms. These translator types have more control functionality than military zips. All you have to do is convince the alpha member, and everyone falls into line.' She grinned. 'But I guess we've seen this before, the way the translators can control the rote-layer zips. They're the keystone components, all right.'

'Trixia is a person!' *All the Focused are people, you damn slaver!*

'I know, Ezr. Sorry. Really, I understand . . . Trixia and the other translators do seem to be different. You have to be pretty special to translate natural languages. Of all – of all the Focused, the translators seem the closest to being real people . . . Look, I'll take care of buttoning things down and let Bil Phuong know things are under control.'

'Okay,' Ezr replied, his voice stiff.

Rita backed out of the room. The cell door slid shut. After a moment, he heard other doors thumping shut along the corridor.

Trixia sat hunched over her keyboard, oblivious of the opinions just rendered. Ezr watched her for some seconds, thinking about her future, thinking about how he would finally save her. Even after forty years of Lurk, the translators couldn't masquerade real-time voice comm with the Spiders. Tomas Nau would gain no advantage by having his translators down by Arachna . . . yet. Once the world was conquered, Trixia and the others would be the voice of the conqueror.

But that time will not come. Pham and Ezr's plan was proceeding down its own schedule. Except for a few old systems, a few electromechanical backups, the Qeng Ho localizers could have total control. Pham and Ezr were finally moving toward real sabotage – most important the Hammerfest wireless-power cutoff. That switch was an almost pure mechanical link, immune to all subtlety. But Pham had one more use for localizers. True grit. These last few Msecs, they had built up layers of grit near that switch, and set up similar sabotage in other old systems, and aboard the *Invisible Hand*. The last hundred seconds would involve flagrant risk. It was a trick that they could try only once, when Nau and his gang were most distracted with their own takeover.

If the sabotage worked – *when* it worked – the Qeng Ho localizers would rule. *And our time will come.*

49

Hrunkner Unnerby spent a lot of time at Lands Command; it was essentially the home base of his construction operations. Perhaps ten times a year he visited the inner sanctums of Accord Intelligence. He talked with General Smith every day by email; he saw her at staff meetings. Their meeting at Calorica – was that five years ago already – had been not cordial but at least an honest sharing of anxiety. But for seventeen years . . . for all the time since Gokna died . . . he had never been in General Smith's private office.

The General had a new aide, someone young and oophase. Hrunkner barely noticed. He stepped into the silence of the chief's den. The place was as big as he remembered, with open-storied nooks and isolated perches. For the moment he seemed to be alone. This had been Strut Greenval's office, before Smith. It had been the Intelligence chief's innermost den for two generations before that. Those previous occupants would scarcely recognize it now. There was even more comm and computer gear than in Sherk's office in Princeton. One side of the room was a full vision display, as elaborate as any videomancy. Just now it was receiving from cameras topside: Royal Falls had stilled more than two years ago. He could see all the way up the valley. The hills were stark and cooling; there was CO_2 frost in the heights. But nearby . . . the colors beyond red leaked from buildings, flared bright in the exhaust of street traffic. For a moment, Hrunk just stared, thinking what this scene must have been like just one generation earlier, five years into the last Dark. Hell, this room would have been abandoned by then. Greenval's people would have been stuck up in their little command cave, breathing stuffy air, listening for the last radio messages, wondering if Hrunk and Sherk would survive in their submarine deepness. A few more days and Greenval would have closed down his operation, and the Great War would have been frozen in its own deadly sleep.

But in this generation, we just go on and on, headed for the most terrible war of all time.

Behind him, he saw the General step silently into the room. 'Sergeant, please sit down.' Smith gestured to the perch in front of her desk.

Unnerby pulled his attention away from the view, and sat. Smith's U-shaped desk was piled with hardcopy reports and five or six small reading displays, three alight. Two showed abstract designs, similar to the pictures that Sherkaner had lost himself in. *So she does still humor him.*

The General's smile seemed stiff, forced, and so it might be sincere. 'I call you Sergeant. What a fantasy rank. But . . . thank you for coming.'

'Of course, ma'am.' *Why did she call me down here?* Maybe his wild scheme for the Northeast had a chance. Maybe – 'Have you seen my excavation proposals, General? With nuclear explosives we could dig shielded caves, and quickly. The Northeast shales would be ideal. Give me the bombs and in one hundred days I could protect most of the agri and people there.' The words just tumbled out. The expense would be enormous, out of range of the Crown or free financing. The General would have to take emergency powers, Covenant or no. And even then, it would not make a happy ending. But if – *when* – the war came, it could save millions.

Victory Smith raised one hand, gently. 'Hrunk, we don't have a hundred days. One way or another, I expect things will be settled in less than three.' She gestured to one of the little displays. 'I just got word that Honored Pedure is actually at Southmost in person, orchestrating things.'

'Well, damn her. If she lights off a Southmost attack, she'll fry too.'

'That's why we're probably safe until she leaves.'

'I've heard rumors, ma'am. Our external intelligence is in the garbage? Thract has been cashiered?' The stories just grew and grew. There were terrible suspicions of Kindred agents at the heart of Intelligence. Deepest crypto was being used on the most routine transmissions. Where the enemy had not succeeded with direct threats, they might now win simply because of the panic and confusion that were everywhere.

Smith's head jerked angrily. 'That's right. We've been outmaneuvered in the South. But we still have assets there, people who depended on me . . . people I have let down.' That last was almost inaudible, and Hrunk doubted it was addressed to him. She was silent for a moment, then straightened. 'You're something of an expert on the Southmost sub-structure, aren't you, Sergeant?'

'I designed it; supervised most of the construction.' And that had been when the South and the Accord had been as friendly as different nation-states ever got.

The General edged back and forth on her perch. Her arms trembled. 'Sergeant . . . even now, I can't stand the sight of you. I think you know that.'

Hrunk lowered his head. *I know. Oh, yes.*

'But for simple things, I trust you. And, oh, by the Deep, just now I need you! An order would be meaningless . . . but will you help me with Southmost?' The words seemed to be wrung from her.

You have to ask? Hrunkner raised his hands. 'Of course.'

Evidently, the quick response had not been expected. Smith just gobbled for a second. 'Do you understand? This will put you at risk, in personal service to me.'

'Yes, yes. I have always wanted to help.' *I've always wanted to make things right again.*

The General stared at him a moment more. Then: 'Thank you, Sergeant.' She tapped something into her desk. 'Tim Downing' – that young new aide? – 'will get you the detailed analysis later. The short of it is, there's only one reason Pedure would be down there in Southmost: The issue there is not decided. She doesn't have all the key people entrapped. Some members of the Southland Parliament have requested I come down to talk.'

'But . . . it should be the King that goes for something like this.'

'Yes. It seems that a number of traditions are being broken in this new Dark.'

'You can't go, ma'am.' Somewhere in the back of his mind, something chuckled at the violation of noncom etiquette.

'You aren't the only person with that advice . . . The last thing Strut Greenval said to me, not two hundred yards from where we're sitting now, was something similar.' She stopped, silent with memories. 'Funny. Strut had so much figured out. He knew I'd end up on his perch. He knew there would be temptations to get into the field. Those first decades of the Bright, there were a dozen times when I know I could have fixed things – even saved lives – if I'd just go out and do what was necessary myself. But Greenval's advice was more like an order, and I followed it, and lived to fight another day.' Abruptly she laughed, and her attention seemed to come back to the present. 'And now I'm a rather old lady, hunkered down in a web of deceit. And it's finally time to break Strut's rule.'

'Ma'am, General Greenval's advice is right as ever. Your place is here.'

'I . . . let this mess happen. It was my decision, my necessary decision. But if I go to Southmost now, there's a chance I can save some lives.'

'But if you fail, then you die and we certainly lose!'

'No. If I die things will be bloodier, but we'll still prevail.' She snapped her desk displays closed. 'We leave in three hours, from Courier Launch Four. Be there.'

Hrunkner almost shrieked his frustration. 'At least take special security. Young Victory and—'

'The Lighthill team?' A faint smile showed. 'Their reputation has spread, has it?'

Hrunkner couldn't help smiling back. 'Y-yes. No one knows quite what they're up to . . . but they seem to be as wacko as we ever were.' There were stories. Some good, some bad, all wild.

'You don't really hate them, do you, Hrunk?' There was wonder in her voice. Smith went on. 'They have other, more important things to do during the next seventy-five hours . . . Sherkaner and I created the present situation by conscious choice, over many years. We knew the risks. Now it's payoff time.'

It was the first she had mentioned Sherkaner since he'd entered the room. The collaboration that had brought them so far had broken, and now the General had only herself.

The question was pointless, but he had to ask. 'Have you talked to Sherk about this? What is he doing?'

Smith was silent, but her look was closed. Then, 'The best he can, Sergeant. The best he can.'

The night was clear even by the standards of Paradise. Obret Nethering walked carefully around the tower at the island's summit, checking the equipment for tonight's session. His heated leggings and jacket weren't especially bulky, but if his air warmer broke, or if the power cord that trailed behind him was severed . . . Well, it wasn't a lie when he told his assistants that they could freeze off an arm or a leg or a lung in a matter of minutes. It was five years into the Dark. He wondered if even in the Great War there had been people awake this late.

Nethering paused in his inspection; after all, he was a little ahead of schedule. He stood in the cold stillness and looked out upon his specialty – the heavens. Twenty years ago, when he was just starting at Princeton, Nethering had wanted to be a geologist. Geology was the father science, and in this generation it was more important than ever, what with all mega-excavations and heavy mining. Astronomy, on the other hand, was the domain of fringe cranks. The natural orientation of sensible people must be downward, planning for the safest deepness in which to survive the next Darkness. What was there to see in the sky? The sun certainly, the source of all life and all problems. But beyond that nothing changed. The stars were such tiny constant things, not at all like the sun or anything else one could relate to.

Then, in his sophomore year, Nethering had met old Sherkaner Under-hill, and his life was changed forever – though, in that, Nethering was not unique. There were ten thousand sophomores, yet somehow Underhill could still reach out to individuals. Or maybe it was the other way around: Underhill was such a blazing source of crazy ideas that certain students gathered round him like woodsfairies round a flame. Underhill claimed that all of math and physics had suffered because no one understood the simplicity of the world's orbit about the sun or the intrinsic motions of the stars. If there had been even *one* other planet to play mind games with – why, the calculus might have been invented ten generations ago instead of two. And this generation's mad explosion of technology might have been spread more peaceably across multiple cycles of Bright and Dark.

Of course, Underhill's claims about science weren't entirely original. Five generations ago, with the invention of the telescope, binary star astronomy had revolutionized Spiderkind's understanding of time. But Underhill brought the old ideas together in such marvelous new ways. Young Nether-ing had been drawn further and further away from safe and sane geology, until the Emptiness Above became his love. The more you realized what the stars really were, the more you realized what the universe must really be. And nowadays, all the colors could be seen in the sky if one knew where to look, and with what instruments. Here on Paradise Island, the far-red of the stars shone clearer than anywhere in the world. With the large telescopes being built nowadays, and the dry stillness of the upper air, sometimes he felt like he could see to the end of the universe.

Huh? Low above the northeast horizon, a narrow feather of aurora was spreading south. There was a permanent loop of magnetism over the North

Sea, but with the Dark five years old, auroras were very rare. Down in Paradise Town, what tourists were left must be oohing and aahing at the show. For Obret Nethering, this was just an unexpected inconvenience. He watched a second more, beginning to wonder. The light was awfully cohesive, especially at the northern end, where it narrowed almost to a point. Huh. If it did wreck tonight's session, maybe they should just fire up the far-blue scope and take a close look at it. Serendipity and all that.

Nethering turned back from the parapet and headed for the stairs. There was a loud rattle and bang that might have been a troop of one hundred combateers coming up the stairs – but was more likely Shepry Tripper and his four hiking boots. A moment passed, and his assistant bounced out onto the open. Shepry was just fifteen years old, about as far out-of-phase as a child could be. There had been a time when Nethering couldn't imagine talking to, much less working with, such an abomination. That was another thing that had changed for him at Princeton. Now – well, Shepry was still a child, ignorant of so many things. But there was something starkly strong about his enthusiasm. Nethering wondered how many years of research were wasted at the end of Waning Years because the youngest researchers were already in early middle age, starting families, and too dulled to bring intensity to their work.

'Dr Nethering! Sir!' Shepry's voice came muffled by his air warmer. The boy was gasping, losing whatever time his dash up the stairs had gained him. 'Big trouble. I've lost the radio link with North Point' – five miles away, the other end of the interferometer. 'There's blooming static all across the bands.'

So nothing would be left of his plans for tonight. 'Did you call Sam on the ground line? What—' He stopped. Shepry's words slowly sinking in: *static all across the bands.* Behind him the strange auroral 'spike' moved steadily southward. Irritation merged silently into fear. Obret Nethering knew the world was teetering on the edge of war. Everyone knew that. Civilization could be destroyed in a matter of hours if the bombs started falling. Even out-of-the-way places like Paradise Island might not be safe. *And that light?* It was fading now, the bright point vanished. A nuke burst in the magnetopatch might look like aurora, but surely not so asymmetrical and not with such a long rise time. Hmm. Or maybe some clever physics types had built something more subtle than a simple nuclear bomb. Curiosity and horror skirmished in Nethering's head.

He turned and dragged Shepry back toward the stairs. *Slow down.* How many times had he given Shepry that advice? 'Step by step, Shepry, and watch your power cord for snags. Is the radar array up tonight?'

'Y-yes.' Shepry's heavy boots clomped down the stairs just behind him. 'But the log will just be noise.'

'Maybe.' Bouncing microwaves off ionization trails was one of the minor projects that Nethering and Tripper managed. Almost all the reflections could be tied to returning satellite junk, but every year or so they'd see something they couldn't explain, a mystery from the Great Empty. He'd almost gotten a research article out of that. Then the damn reviewers – the ubiquitous T. Lurksalot – ran their own programs, and didn't buy his conclusions. Tonight there would be another use for the array. The pointed end of the strange light – what if it were a physical object?

'Shepry, are we still on the net?' Their high-rate connection was optical fiber strung across the ocean ice; he'd intended to use mainland super-computers to guide tonight's run. Now—

'I'll check.'

Nethering laughed. 'We may have something interesting to show Prince-ton!' He poked up the radar log, began scanning. Was it Nature or War that was talking to them tonight? Either way, the message was important.

50

Nowadays, flying made Hrunkner Unnerby feel very old. He remembered when piston engines spun wood propellers, and wings were fabric on wood.

And Victory Smith's aircraft was no ordinary executive jet: They were flying at nearly one hundred thousand feet, moving south at three times the speed of sound. The two engines were almost silent, just a high thready tone that seemed to bury itself in your guts. Outside, the star- and sunlight together were just bright enough so colors could be seen in the clouds below. Deck upon deck, the clouds layered the world. From this altitude, even the highest of the clouds seemed to be low, crouching things. Here and there canyons opened in the air, and they glimpsed ice and snow. In a few more minutes they would reach the Southern Straits and pass out of Accord airspace. The flight communications officer said there was a squadron of Accord fighter craft all around them, that they would be in place all the way to the embassy airfield at Southmost. The only evidence Unnerby saw for the claim was an occasional glint in the sky above them. Sigh. Like everything important nowadays, they moved too fast and too far to be seen by mere mortals.

General Smith's private craft was actually a supersonic recon bomber, the sort of thing that was becoming obsolete with the advent of satellites. 'Air Defense practically gave it to us,' Smith had remarked when they came on board. 'All this will be junk when the air begins to snow out.' There would be a whole new transportation industry then. Ballistic vehicles, maybe? Antigravity floaters? Maybe it didn't matter. If their current mission didn't work out, there might not be any industry at all, just endless fighting among the ruins.

The center of the fuselage was filled with rack on rack of computer and communications gear. Unnerby had seen the laser and microwave pods when they came aboard. The flight techs were plugged into the Accord's military net almost as securely as if they'd been back at Lands Command. There were no stewards on this flight. Unnerby and General Smith were strapped into small perches that seemed awfully hard after the first couple of hours. Still, he was probably more comfortable than the combateers hanging on nets in the back of the aircraft. A ten-squad; that was all the General had for bodyguards.

Victory Smith had been quiet and busy. Her assistant, Tim Downing, had carried all her computer gear aboard: heavy, awkward boxes that must be very powerful, very well shielded, or very obsolete. For the last three hours she had sat surrounded by half a dozen screens, their light glittering faintly off her eyes. Hrunkner wondered what she was seeing. Her military networks combined with all the open nets must give her an almost godlike view.

Unnerby's display showed the latest report on the Southmost underground construction. Some of it was lies – but he knew enough of the original designs to guess the truth. For the nth time, he forced his attention back to the reading. Strange; when he was young, back in the Great War, he could concentrate just like the General was now. But today, his mind kept flitting forward, to a situation and a catastrophe that he couldn't see any way around.

Out over the Straits now; from this altitude, the broken sea ice was an intricate mosaic of cracks.

There was a shout from one of the comm techs. 'Wow! Did you see that?'

Hrunkner hadn't seen a damn thing.

'Yes! I'm still up though. Check it out.'

'Yes, sir.'

On their perches ahead of Unnerby, the techs crouched over their displays, tapping and poking. Lights flickered around them, but Unnerby couldn't read the words on their screens – and the display format wasn't anything he'd trained on.

Behind him, he saw that Victory Smith had risen off her perch and was watching intently. Apparently her gear was not linked with the techs'. Huh. So much for the 'godlike view' he'd been imagining.

After a moment she raised a hand, signaled one of them. The fellow called back to her. 'It looks like somebody went nuclear, ma'am.'

'Hm.' said Smith. Unnerby's display hadn't even flickered.

'It was very far away, probably over the North Sea. Here, I'll set up a slave window for you.'

'And for Sergeant Unnerby, please.'

'Yes, ma'am.' The Southmost report in front of Hrunkner suddenly was replaced by a map of the North Coast. Colored contours spread concentrically about point twelve hundred kilometers northeast of Paradise Island. Yes, the old Tiefer refueling depot a useless chunk of seamount except when you wanted to project force across ice. That *was* far away, almost the other side of the world from where they were right now.

'Just one blast?' said Smith.

'Yes, very high up. A pulse attack . . . except that it wasn't more than a megaton. We're building this map off satellites and ground analysis from the North Coast and Princeton.' Legends scattered across the picture, bibliographic pointers to the network sites that contributed to the analysis. Hah. There was even an eyewitness report from Paradise Island – an academic observatory, according to the code.

'What did we lose?'

'No military losses, ma'am. Two commercial satellites are offline, but that may be temporary. This was barely a jab.'

What then? *A test? A warning?* Unnerby stared at the display.

Jau Xin had been here less than a year before, but that had been on a six-man pinnace, sneaking in and out in less than a day. Today he managed the piloting of the *Invisible Hand*, a million tonnes of starship.

This was the true arrival of the conquerors – even if those conquerors were duped into thinking they were rescuers. Next to Jau, Ritser Brughel sat in what had once been a Peddler Captain's seat. The Podmaster spouted an unending stream of trivial orders – you'd think he was trying to manage the pilots himself. They'd come in over Arachna's north pole, skirting the atmosphere, decelerating in a single strong burn, nearly a thousand seconds at better than one gee. The decel had been over open ocean, far from Spider population centers, but it must have been enormously bright to those few who saw it. Jau could see the glow reflected in the ice and snow below.

Brughel watched the icy waste rolling out before them. His features were pursed with some intense feeling. Disgust, to see so much that looked totally worthless? Triumph, to arrive on the world that he would corule? Probably both. And here on the bridge, both triumph and violent intent leaked into his tone, sometimes even his words. Tomas Nau might have to keep the fraud going back on L1, but here Ritser Brughel was shedding his restraint. Jau had seen the corridors that led to Brughel's private quarters. The walls were a constant swirl of pink, sensuous in a heavy, threatening way. No staff meetings were held down those corridors. On the way from L1, he heard Brughel brag to Podcorporal Anlang about the special treat he would bring out of the freezer to celebrate the coming victory. *No, don't think on it. You know too much already.*

The voices of Xin's pilots spoke in his ear, confirming what he already saw on his tracking display. He looked up at Brughel and spoke with the formality the other seemed to like. 'The burn is complete, sir. We're in polar orbit, altitude one hundred fifty kilometers.' Any lower and they would need snowshoes.

'We were visible across thousands of kilometers, sir.' Xin matched his words with a concerned look. He'd been playing naive idiot on the trip down from L1. It was a dangerous game, but so far it had given him some leeway: *And maybe, maybe there is some way I can avoid mass murder.*

Brughel grinned back smug superiority. 'Of course we were seen, Mr Xin. The trick is to let them see – and then corrupt how they interpret the information.' He opened the comm channel to the *Hand*'s ziphead deck. 'Mr Phuong! Have you cloaked our arrival?'

Bil Phuong's voice came back from the *Hand*'s ziphead hold. The place had been a madhouse the last time Jau looked, but Phuong sounded cool: 'We're on top of the situation, Podmaster. I've got three teams synthesizing satellite reports. L1 tells me they look good.' That would be Rita's team talking to Bil. She should be going off duty any moment now, for what Nau would probably claim was a rest break before the heavy work. Jau had known for a day that that 'lull' was when the killing would begin.

Phuong continued, 'I must warn you, sir. Eventually the Spiders will sort things out. Our disguise won't last for more than a hundred Ksec, less if someone down there is clever.'

'Thank you, Mr Phuong. That should be more than enough.' Brughel smiled blandly at Jau.

Part of their horizon-spanning view disappeared, replaced by Tomas Nau back on L1. The senior Podmaster was sitting with Ezr Vinh and Pham Trinli in the lodge in Lake Park. Sunlight sparkled on the water behind them. This would be a public two-way conversation, visible to all the Followers and Qeng Ho. Nau looked out across the *Hand*'s bridge and his gaze seemed to find Ritser Brughel.

'Congratulations, Ritser. You are well placed. Rita tells me you have already achieved a close synch with the ground nets. We have some good news of our own. The Accord Intelligence chief is visiting Southmost. Her opposite number in the Kindred is already there. Short of accidents, things should be peaceful for a while more.'

Nau sounded so sincere and well-meaning. The amazing thing was that Ritser Brughel was almost as smooth: 'Yes, sir. I'm setting up for the announcement and network takeover in—' He paused, as if checking his schedule. '—in fifty-one Ksec.'

Of course, Nau didn't reply immediately. The signal from the *Hand* had to be bounced out of radio shadow to a relay and then across five light-seconds of space to L1. Any reply would take at least another five seconds coming the other way.

Sharp on ten seconds, Nau smiled. 'Excellent. We'll set the pacing here so everybody will be fresh when the workload spikes. Good luck to all of you down there, Ritser. We're depending on you.'

There were a couple more rounds in their dance of deception; then Nau was gone. Brughel confirmed that all comm was local. 'The go codes should come down any time, Mr Phuong.' Brughel grinned. 'Another twenty Ksec, and we fry some Spiders.'

Shepry Tripper gaped at the radar display. 'It's – it's just like you said. Eighty-eight minutes, and there it is coming out of the north again!'

Shepry knew plenty of math and had worked for Nethering almost a year. He certainly understood the principles of satellite flight. But like most people, he still boggled at the notion of 'a rock that gets thrown up and never comes down.' The cobblie would chortle delight when some comsat came trucking over the horizon at the time and azimuth that the math had predicted.

What Nethering had done tonight was a prediction of a different order, and he was just as awed as his assistant – and a whole lot more frightened. They had had only two or three clear radar bearings on the narrow end of the aurora. The thing had been decelerating even though it was well outside of the atmosphere. The Air Defense site at Princeton had not been impressed by his report. Nethering had a long-term relationship with those people, but tonight they treated him like a stranger, their autoresponse thanking him for his information and assuring that the matter was being taken care of. The world network was full of rumors of a high-altitude nuke. But this had been no bomb. Departing southward, it had appeared to be in low orbit . . . and now it was coming back from the north, right on schedule.

'Do you think we'll be able to see it this time, sir? It's gonna pass almost right over us.'

'I don't know. We don't have any scope that can slew fast enough to track it overhead.' He started back toward the stairs. 'Maybe we could use the ten-inch.'

'Yeah!' Shepry raced around him—

'Button your breather! Watch the power cords!'

—and was out of sight, banging up the stairs.

But the little cobblie was right! There were fewer than two minutes until the object was directly overhead, then a couple more before it was gone again. Huh. Maybe not even time for the scope. Nethering paused, grabbed a widefield 4-ocular from his desk. Then he was running up the stairs after Tripper.

Topside, there was a faint breeze, a cold that bit like tarant fangs, even through his electric leggings. The sun would rise in about seventy minutes; dim though its light was, the best part of his observing time would be gone. For once it just didn't matter. Serendipity was up from the good cold earth this night.

There was at most a minute until the mystery came overhead. It should be well above the horizon now, gliding southward toward them. Nethering moved around the curved wall of the main dome, and stared into the north.

From the equipment closet ahead of him, he heard Shepry struggling with the ten-inch, the little scope they showed the tourists. He should be helping the child but there was really no time.

Familiar starfields extended crystal clear down to the horizon. That clarity was, for Obret Nethering, what made this little island truly paradise. There should be a fleck of reflected sunlight rising slowly across the sky. It would be very faint; the dead sun was such a pale thing. Nethering stared and stared, straining for the slightest motion-triggered gleam . . . Nothing. Maybe he should have stuck with the radar, maybe right now they were missing their one chance to get really good data. Shepry had the ten-inch out of the closet now. He was struggling to get it aligned. 'Help me, sir!'

They both had guessed wrong. Serendipity might be an angel, but she was a fickle one. Obret turned back to Shepry, a little ashamed for ignoring him. Of course, he was still watching the sky, the swath just short of the zenith where there should be a tiny speck of light. A bite of blackness flickered across the glowing pile of the Robber's Cluster. A bite of blackness. Something . . . huge.

All dignity forgotten, Nethering fell on his side, brought the 4-ocular up to his lesser eyes. But tonight it was all he had . . . He turned slowly, tracking along his guess at a skypath, praying he could recapture his target.

'Sir? What is it?'

'Shepry, look up . . . just look up.'

The cobblie was silent for a second. 'Oh!'

Obret Nethering wasn't listening. He had the *thing* in the 4-ocs field and all his attention was on keeping up with it, on seeing and remembering. And what he saw was an absence of light, a silhouette that raced across the galactic swath of star clouds. It was almost a quarter of a degree across. In the gap between star clouds it was invisible again . . . and then he saw it for another second. Nethering almost had a sense of the shape of it: a squat cylinder, downward-pointing, with a hint of complexity sticking out amidships.

Amidships.

The rest of its track crossed lonely starfields down to the southern horizon. Nethering tried in vain to follow it all the way. If it hadn't been for its crossing the Robber's Cluster, he might not have latched on to it at all. *Thank you, Serendipity!*

He lowered the 4-ocs and stood. 'We'll keep watch a few more minutes.' What other junk might be flying along with the thing?

'Oh, please, let me go below and put this on the net!' said the cobblie. 'More than ninety miles up, and so big I could see its shape. It must be half a mile long!'

'Okay. Go ahead.'

Shepry disappeared down the stairs. Three minutes passed. Four. There was a glint sliding across the southern horizon, most likely a Low-Comm S satellite. Nethering pocketed his 4-ocs and climbed slowly down the stairs. This time, Air Defense would have to listen to him. A good part of Nethering's contract money came from Accord Intelligence; he knew about the floater satellites the Kindred had recently begun launching. *This is not one of ours, and not one of the Kindred's. And all our warfare is reduced to petty squabbling by this arrival.* The world had been so close to nuclear war. And now . . . what? He remembered how old Underhill had gone on about the 'deepness in the sky.' But angels should come from the good cold earth, never from the empty sky.

Shepry met him at the bottom of the stairs. 'It's no good, sir. I can't—'

'The link to the mainland is down?'

'No. It's up. But Air Defense brushed me off just like they did on the first pass.'

'Maybe they already know.'

Shepry jerked his hands in agitation. 'Maybe. But something perved is happening on the gossips, too. The last few days, crank postings have pounded the ceiling. You know, end-of-the-world claims, snow-troll sightings. It's been kind of a laugh; I even did some counter-crapping of my own. But tonight the cranks have totally pounced.' Shepry paused, seemed to run out of jargon. Suddenly he looked very young and uncertain. 'It's . . . it's not natural, sir. I found two postings that described just what we saw. That's about what you'd expect for something that just happened over mid-ocean. But they're lost in all crazy crap.'

Hmm. Nethering walked across the room, settled down on his old perch beside the control bays. Shepry fidgeted back and forth, waiting for some judgment. *When I first came to the observatory, the controls covered three walls, instruments and levers, almost all analog.* Now most of the gear was tiny; digital, precise. Sometimes he joked with Shepry, asking him whether they should really trust anything they couldn't see the guts of. Shepry had never understood his lack of faith in computer automation. Until tonight.

'You know, Shepry, maybe we should make some phone calls.'

51

Hrunkner had been in a dry hurricane once before, during the Great War. But that had been on the ground – underground most of the time – and about all he remembered was the ceaseless wind and the fineness of the snow that swirled and piled, and penetrated every crevice and gap.

This time he was in the air, descending through forty thousand feet. In the dim sunlight, he could see the swirl of the hurricane spread across hundreds of miles, its sixty-mile-per-hour winds brought to stillness by distance. A dry hurricane could never equal the fury of a Bright Time water hurricane. Yet this kind of storm would last for years, its eye of cold widening and widening. The world's heat balance had paused on a kind of thermal plateau, water's energy of crystallization. Once past this plateau, temperatures would fall steadily toward the next, much colder level, where the air itself began to dew out.

Their jet slid down toward the walls of cloud, bucking and slewing on invisible turbulence. One of the pilots remarked that the air pressure was less now than it had been at fifty thousand feet back over the Straits. Hrunkner tilted his head up to a window, looked almost directly ahead. In the hurricane's eye, sunlight glinted off motley snow and ice. There were also lights, the hot reds of Southland industry just below the surface.

Far ahead, a ragged edge of mountains pierced the clouds and there were colors and textures he hadn't seen since he and Sherkaner took their long-ago walk in the Dark.

The Accord Embassy at Southmost had its own airport, a four-mile-by-two-mile property just outside the city core. Even this was just a fragment of the enclave that colonial interests had held in previous generations. The remnant of empire was alternately an obstacle to friendly relations and an economic boost for both nations. To Unnerby it was just an overly short, oil-smudged strip of ice. Their converted bomber made the most exciting landing of Hrunkner's career, a rolling skid past an unending blur of snow-covered warehouses.

The General's pilot was good, or very lucky. They came to a stop just a hundred feet short of snowdrifts that marked the no-more-excuses end of the runway. In minutes, beetle-shaped vehicles had driven up and were pulling them toward a hangar. Not a single person walked about in the open. Away from their path, the ground glittered with CO_2 frost.

Inside the cavernous hangar, the lights were bright and – once the doors were shut – ground crews rushed out with stairs. There were a few fancy-looking cobbers down there, waiting by the base of the stairs. Very likely the Accord ambassador and the head of the embassy guards. Since they were still on Accord ground, it was unlikely that any Southlanders would be here . . . Then he saw the parliamentary ensign on the jackets of two of the VIPs. Someone was eager beyond the bounds of clever diplomacy.

The mid-hatch was opened; a bolus of frigid air spilled into the cabin. Smith had already gathered up her gear and was climbing back to the hatch. Hrunkner remained on his perch a moment longer; He waved at one of the Intelligence techs. 'Have there been any more nukes?'

'No, sir, nothing. We've got confirmation up and down the net. It was an isolated, one-megaton burst.'

The NCO Club at Lands Command was a bit out of the ordinary. Lands Command was more than a day's drive from civilian entertainment and the post had a fat budget compared to most out-of-the-way places. The average noncom at Lands Command was likely to be a tech with at least four years of academic training, and many of the troopers here worked at the deepmost Command and Control Center, several stories beneath the club. So, there were the usual game tables and gym sets and fizzbar, but there were also a good book collection and a number of net-connected-arcade games that could also be used as study stations.

Victory Lighthill slouched in the dimness behind the fizz-bar and watched the panorama of commercial video on the far wall. Maybe the most unusual thing about the club was that she was allowed in. Lighthill was a junior lieutenant, the natural bane and antagonist of many NCOs. Yet the tradition here was that if an officer covered her rank and was invited in by a noncom, then that officer's presence was tolerated.

Tolerated, but in Lighthill's case, not really welcomed. Her team's reputation for inspection raids and its special connection with the Director of Intelligence made the average cobber uneasy about her and the team. But hey, the rest of the team were noncoms. Right now they were scattered around the club, each with a bulging departure pannier. For once, the other NCOs were talking to them, if not actually socializing. Even the ones who weren't in Intelligence knew that things were teetering on the edge – and the ever-mysterious Lighthill team must surely have inside knowledge.

'It's Smith down there at Southmost,' said a senior sergeant sitting at the bar. 'Who else could it be?' He tipped his head in the direction of one of Lighthill's corporals and waited for some reaction. Corporal Suabisme just shrugged, looking very innocent and – by trad standards – indecently young. 'I wouldn't be knowing, Sergeant. I truly wouldn't.'

The senior sergeant waved his eating hands in a sneer. 'Oh? So how come you Lighthill flunkies are all carrying departure bags? I'd say you're just waiting to hop on a plane for someplace.'

It was the sort of probing that would normally bring Viki into action, either to withdraw Suabisme or – if necessary – to shut the senior sergeant down. But in the NCO club, Lighthill had zero authority. Besides, the point of being here was to keep the team out of official sight. But after a moment, the senior sergeant seemed to realize he wasn't going to provoke any slips from the young soldier; he turned back to his buddies at the bar.

Viki let out a quiet sigh. She hunkered down until just the tops of her eyes were above the level of the fizzbar. The place was getting busy, the ping of spit in cuspidors a kind of background music. There was little talk, and even less laughter. Off-duty NCOs should be a more lively lot, but these cobbers had plenty on their minds. The center of attention was the television. The NCO cooperative had bought the latest variable-format video. In the dimness behind the bar, Viki smiled in spite of herself. If the world could survive even a few more years, such gear would be as good as the videomancy gear Daddy used.

The TV was sucking from a commercial news site. One window was a crude image from some rent-a-camera at the embassy airport at Southmost: the aircraft coasting down the embassy runway was a type that Lighthill herself had seen only twice before. Like many things, it was secret and obsolete all at the same time. The press scarcely commented on it. On the main window, an editorialist was congratulating herself on this journalistic coup, and speculating just who was aboard the daggercraft.

'. . . It's not the King himself, despite what our competitors may claim. Our coverage around the palace and at the Princeton airfields would have detected any movement of the Royal Household. So who is this now arriving at Southmost?' The announcer paused and the cameras moved closer, surrounding her forebody. The picture expanded to spill over the nearby displays. The maneuver gave the impression suddenly of intimate conversation. 'We now know that the emissary is the head of the King's Own Intelligence Service, Victory Smith.' The cameras backed off a little. 'So, to the King's Information Officers, we say: You can't hide from the press. Better to give us full access. Let the people see Smith's progress with the Southlanders.'

Another camera, from inside a hangar: Mom's daggercraft had been towed all the way into the embassy hangar, and the clamshell doors were being pulled shut. The scene looked like a diorama built from children's toys; the futuristic aircraft, the closed-body tractors chugging around the hangar's wide floor. No people were visible. *Surely they don't have to pressurize the hangar?* Even at the eye of the dry hurricane, the pressure couldn't be that low. But after a moment, soldiers popped out of a van. They pushed a stairway up to the side of the dagger. Everyone in the NCO Club became suddenly very quiet.

A soldier climbed to the aircraft's mid-hatch. It cracked open, and . . . the embassy rent-a-camera feed went dead, replaced by the King's seal.

There was startled laughter, then applause and hooting. 'Good for the General!' someone shouted. As much as anyone, these cobbers wanted to know what was happening at Southmost, but they also had a long-standing dislike for the news companies. They regarded these latest, very open discussions as a personal affront.

She looked at her team members. Most had been watching the television, but without great interest. They already knew what was going on, and – as Senior Sergeant Loudmouth had speculated – they expected to see action themselves very soon. Unfortunately, the television couldn't help them with that. At the back of the room, far from the fizzbar and the television, a few hard-core gamers hung around their arcade boxes. That included three of Lighthill's people. Brent had been there since they began to loiter. Her brother was hunched down under a custom game display, the helmet covering most of his head. To look at him, you'd never guess that the world was teetering on the edge of destruction.

Viki slipped off her perch and walked quietly back toward the arcade machines.

In all its thirty-five-year existence, this was the booze parlor's finest moment. *But, who knows, maybe after this we'll carry on, turn into a real business.* Stranger things had happened. Benny's parlor had been the social center of their strange community at L1. Very soon that community would include another race, the first high-tech alien race Humankind had ever met. The parlor might well be the centerpiece of the marvelous combination.

Benny Wen floated from table to table, directing his helpers, greeting customers. Yet still occasionally his attention was off in a fabulous future, trying to imagine what it would be like to cater to Spiders.

'The bottom wing is out of brew, Benny.' Hunte's voice came in his ear.

'Ask Gonle, Papa. She promised she'd cover whatever is needed.' He looked around, caught a glimpse of Fong down a tunnel of flowers and vines, over in the east wing of the parlor.

Benny didn't hear his father's reply. He was already talking to the party of Emergents and Qeng Ho that floated down around the just-prepped table. 'Welcome, welcome. Lara! I haven't seen you in so many Watches.' Pride at showing off the parlor and pleasure at meeting old friends mixed all together, warming him.

After a moment's chat he drifted away from the table, to the next, and the next, all the time keeping track of the overall service situation. Even with Gonle and Papa both on duty, they were just barely keeping their helpers coordinated.

'She's here, Benny.' Gonle's voice sounded in his ear.

'She came!' he replied. 'I'll meet her at the front table!' He drifted in from the tables, toward the central cavity. All six cardinal points had customer wings. The Podmaster had allowed, encouraged, them to knock out walls and consume the volume that had been meeting rooms. The parlor was now the biggest single space on the temp. Except for the Lake Park, it was the biggest single living space at L1. Today, almost three-quarters of all the Emergents and Qeng Ho were on-Watch simultaneously, the climax of the rushed preparations for the Spider Rescue. And for a short time before the final push, virtually everyone was here at Benny's. The affair was as much a reunion as it was a rescue and a new beginning.

The central core of the parlor was an icosahedron of display devices, a tent of their best remaining video wallpaper. It was primitive and warmly communal at the same time. From all directions, his customers would look inward at the shared views. Benny glided quickly across the empty space, his feet just missing a corner of the displays. In the directions outward from here, he could see the hundreds of his customers, dozens of tables nestled among the vines and flowers. He grabbled a vine and brought himself to a graceful stop at a table on the up wing, at the edge of the empty core. 'The table of honor' was how Tomas Nau had put it.

'Qiwi! Please, sit and be welcome!' He flipped over the table to float beside her.

Qiwi Lisolet smiled hesitantly back at Benny. By now she was five or six years older than he, but suddenly she seemed very young, uncertain. Qiwi was holding something close at her shoulder; it was one of the North Paw kittens, the first that Benny had ever seen outside of the Lake Park. Qiwi looked around the parlor, as if surprised to see the crowds. 'So almost everyone is here.'

'Yes we are! We're so glad you could come. You can give us the inside view of what's going on.' A goodwill ambassador from the Podmaster. And Qiwi looked the part. No pressure-coveralls for Qiwi today. She wore a lacey dress that floated in soft swirls as she moved. Even at the Lake Park open house she hadn't looked so beautiful.

Qiwi sat hesitantly at the table. Benny sat down for a moment too, a courtesy. He handed her a control wand. 'This is what Gonle gave me; sorry we don't have better.' He pointed out the display and link options. 'And this gives you voice access to all the parlor. Please use it. More than anyone here, you know what going on.'

After a moment, Qiwi took the wand. Her other hand held tight to the kitten. The creature wriggled its wings into a more comfortable position, but didn't otherwise complain. For years Qiwi had been the most popular of the Podmaster's inner circle. She wasn't really an ambassador; she was more like a princess. That was how Benny had once described her to Gonle Fong. Gonle had smirked cynically at the word, and then agreed with him. Qiwi was trusted by all, a gentle restraint on tyranny . . . And yet there were times when she seemed to be lost. Today was one of those times. Benny sat back in his seat. Let the others do some hustling for a bit. Somehow he knew that Qiwi needed his time more.

She looked up after a moment, a little of the old smile on her face. 'Yes, I can run the show. Tomas showed me how.' She loosened her grip on the kitten and patted his hand. 'Don't worry, Benny. This rescue is a tricky thing, but we'll bring it off.'

She played with the wand, and the display core of the parlor flared into announcement colors, the light splashing back onto the flowered vines. When she spoke, her voice came from a thousand microspeakers, phased so that she seemed at everyone's side. 'Hello, everybody. Welcome to the show.' Her voice was happy and confident, the Qiwi they all knew.

The display core was sorting itself into multiple views: Qiwi's face, Arachna as seen from the *Invisible Hand*, Podmaster Nau working at his lodge at North Paw, schematics of the *Hand*'s orbit and the military configuration of the various Spider nations.

'As you know, our old friend Victory Smith has just arrived in Southland.

In a few moments she'll be at their parliament, and we'll have a treat none of us have experienced before – a direct human-camera view from the ground. Finally, after all these years, we'll be seeing firsthand.' On the big center display, Qiwi's face opened into a smile. 'Think of it as a taste of things to come, the beginning of our life with the people of Arachna.

'But before we get to that point, you know we have a war to prevent, and our presence finally to reveal.' She looked down at the displays, and her voiced hesitated, as if she were suddenly struck by the enormity of what they were attempting. 'We have planned to announce ourselves in just over forty Ksec, when our low-orbit network manipulations are in place, and the *Hand*'s orbit takes it over the capitals of both Kindred and Accord. I think you know how tricky it will be. The Spiders, our hoped-for friends, are poised on more dangerous ground than most human civilizations can survive. But I know you have prepared for this day well. When the time for announcement and contact comes, I know we will succeed.

'So, watch for now. Soon we will be very busy.'

52

Oddly enough, Rachner Thract retained his rank of colonel, not that former colleagues would trust him to scrape out their latrines. General Smith had treated him gently. They couldn't *prove* he was a traitor, and apparently she was unwilling to use extreme interrogation on him. So Colonel Rachner Thract, formerly of the unnamed service, found himself with a salary and per diem worthy of full duty . . . and nothing whatsoever to do.

It had been four days since that terrible meeting at Lands Command, but Thract had seen his disgrace building for almost a year. When it finally overcame him . . . it had been such a relief, except for the unhappy detail that he survived it, a living ghost.

Old-time officers, especially Tiefers, would decapitate themselves after such ignominy. Rachner Thract was one-half Tiefer, but be hadn't cut off his head with a weighted blade. Instead, he'd numbed his brain with five straight days of fizz, chewing his way round and round the Calorica Strip. *An idiot right to the end.* Calorica was the only place in the world where it was too warm to lapse into fizz coma.

So he'd heard the reports that someone – Smith, it had to be Smith – was flying to Southmost, was trying to recover something of what Thract had lost. As the hours counted down toward Smith's arrival at Southmost, Rachner had eased off on the fizz. He sat staring at the news feeds in the public houses. Sat and prayed that somehow Victory Smith could succeed where Thract's life effort had failed. But he knew that she would fail. No one believed him, and even Rachner Thract didn't know the how and why. But he was sure: There was something backing up the Kindred. Even the

Kindred didn't know about it, but it was there, twisting every one of the Accord's technical advantages back on itself.

On the multiple screens, live from Southmost, Smith passed through the Great Doors of Parliament Hall. Even here, the rowdiest public house on the Strip, the clientele was suddenly very silent. Thract settled his head upon the bar, and felt his stare become glazed.

And then his telephone began ringing. Rachner hauled it out of his jacket. He held it by his head, stared at it with uninterested disbelief. *It must be broken.* Or someone was sending him an advertisement. Nothing important could ever come over this unsecured piece of junk.

He was about to throw it to the floor when the cobber on the next perch whacked him across the back. 'Damn military bum! Get out!' she shouted.

Thract came off his perch, not sure if he was about to follow the other's demand, or defend the honor of Smith and all the others who tried to keep the peace.

In the end, house management decided the issue; Thract found himself out on the street, cut off from the television that might have shown him what his General was attempting. And his telephone was still ringing. He stabbed ACCEPT and snarled something incoherent into the microphone.

'Colonel Thract, is that you?' The words were jerky and garbled, but the voice was vaguely familiar. 'Colonel? Is your end a secure comm?'

Thract swore loudly. 'The bleeding hell *no!*'

'Oh thank goodness!' came the almost-familiar voice. 'There's a chance then. Surely even *they* can't meddle with all the world's idle talk.'

They. The emphasis cut through Thract's fizz hangover. He brought the microphone close his maw, and his next words came out almost casually curious. 'Who is this?'

'Sorry. Obret Nethering here. *Please* don't hang up. You probably don't remember me. Fifteen years ago, I taught a short course on remote sensing. At Princeton. You sat in.'

'I, ah, remember.' In fact it had been a rather good course.

'You do? Oh good, good! So you'll know I'm not a crank. Sir, I know how busy you must be right now, but I pray you'll give me just a minute of your time. Please.'

Thract was suddenly aware of the street and the buildings around him. Calorica Strip stretched around the bottom of the volcanic bowl, perhaps the warmest place left on the surface of the world. But the Strip was just a faded memory of the time when Calorica had been a playground for the super-rich. The bars and hotels were dying. Even, the snowfalls were long ended. The snow piled up in the alley behind him was two years old, filtered with fizz barf and streaked with urine. *My high-tech command center.*

Thract hunkered down, out of the wind. 'I suppose I can give you a moment.'

'Oh, thank you! You're my last hope. All my calls to Professor Underhill come up blocked. Not surprising, now that I understand . . .' Thract could almost hear the cobber collecting his wits, trying not to blather. 'I'm an astronomer out on Paradise Island, Colonel. Last night I saw' – a spaceship as big as a city, its drives lighting the sky . . . and ignored by Air Defense and all the networks. Nethering's descriptions were short and blunt, and took just under a minute. The astronomer continued. 'I'm no crank, I tell you. This is what we saw! Surely there are hundreds of eyewitnesses, but somehow it's invisible to Air Defense. Colonel, you've got to believe me.' His tone segued into uncomfortable self-realization, an understanding that no one in his right mind could buy such a story.

'Oh, I believe you,' Rachner said softly. It was a floridly paranoid vision . . . and it explained everything.

'What did you say, Colonel? Sorry, I can't send you much hard evidence. They cut our landline about half an hour ago; I'm using a hobbyist's packet radio to reach rout—' Several syllables were jumbled into incoherence. 'So that's really all I had to tell you. Maybe this is some Deepest Secret plot on the part of Air Defense. If you can't say anything, I'll understand. But I had to try to get through. That ship was so large, and—'

For a moment, Thract thought the other had paused, overcome. But the silence continued for several seconds, and then a synthetic voice blatted from the telephone's tiny speaker: 'Message 305. Network error. Please retry your call later.'

Rachner slowly tucked the telephone back in his jacket. His maw and eating hands were numb, and it wasn't just the cold air. Once upon a time, his network intelligence cobbers had done a study on automated snooping. Given enough computing power, it was in principle possible to monitor *every* in-the-clear communication for keywords, and trigger security responses. In principle. In fact, development of the necessary computers always lagged behind the size of the contemporary public networks. But now it looked like someone had just that power.

A Deep Secret plot on the part of Air Defense? Not likely. Over the last year, Rachner Thract had watched the mysteries and the failures encroach from all directions. Even if Accord Intelligence and Pedure and all the intelligence agencies of the world had *cooperated*, they could not have produced the seamless lies that Thract had sensed. No. Whatever they faced was larger than the world, a grander evil than anything Spiderly.

And now at last he had something concrete. His mind should climb into combat alertness; instead he was filled with panicked confusion. *Damn the fizz.* If they were up against an alien force so deep, so crafty – what did it matter that Obret Nethering and now Rachner Thract knew the truth? What could they do? But Nethering had been permitted to talk for more than a minute. He'd spoken a number of keywords before the connection was chopped. The aliens might be better than Spiders – but they weren't gods.

The thought brought Thract to a halt. So they weren't gods. The word of their monster ship must be percolating across the civilized world, slowed and suppressed to one-on-one contacts between little people without access to power. *But that couldn't hide the secret more than a few hours.* And that meant . . . whatever the purpose of this vast fraud, it must be headed for consummation in the next few hours. Right now the chief was risking her life down at Southmost, trying to bail them out from a disaster that was actually a trap. *If I could get through to her, to Belga, to anybody at the top . . .*

But telephones and network mail would be worse than useless. He needed some direct contact. Thract ran a weaving course down the deserted sidewalk. There was a bus stop somewhere beyond the corner. How long until the next one came through? He still had his private helicopter, a rich cobber's toy . . . that might be too network-smart. The aliens might simply take it over and crash him. He pushed the fear away. Just now, the chopper was his only hope. From the heliport he could reach any place within two hundred miles. Who would be in that range? He skidded around the corner. Grand Boulevard extended off beneath an endless row of trichrome lights, down from the Strip and through the Calorica forest. The forest was long dead, of course. Not even its leaves were left to spore, the ground beneath being too warm. The center had been cleared flat for a heliport. From there he could fly to . . . Thract's gaze reached across the bowl. The boulevard lights dwindled to tiny sparkles. Once upon a time, they had ascended the caldera walls, to the mansions of the Waning Years. But the truly rich had abandoned their palaces. Only a few were still occupied, inaccessible from below.

But Sherkaner Underhill was up there, back from Princeton. At least that had been the word in the last situation report he had seen, the day his career had ended. He knew the stories about Underhill, that the poor cobber had lost it mentally. No matter. What Thract needed was a sidewise path into Lands Command, maybe through the chief's daughter, a path that did not pass through the net.

A minute later the city bus pulled up behind Thract. He hopped aboard, the only passenger, even though it was mid-morning. 'You're in luck.' The driver grinned. 'The next one isn't until three hours after noon.'

Twenty miles an hour, thirty. The bus rumbled down the Grand Boulevard toward the Dead Forest Heliport. *I can be on his doorstep in ten minutes.* And suddenly Rachner was aware of the fizz barf that crusted his maw and eating hands, of the stains on his uniform. He brushed at his head, but there was nothing he could do about the uniform. A madman come to see a senile old coot. Maybe it was fitting. It also might be the last chance any of them had.

A decade earlier, in friendlier times, Hrunkner Unnerby had advised the Southlanders in the design of New Southmost Under. So in a strange way, things became more familiar after they left the Accord Embassy and entered Southland territory. There were lots of elevators. The Southland had wanted a Parliament Hall that would survive a nuclear strike. He had warned them that future ordnance developments would likely make their goal impossible, but the Southlanders hadn't listened, and had wasted substantial resources that could have gone to Dark Time agriculture.

The main elevator was so large that even the reporters could get aboard, and they did so. The Southland press was a privileged class, explicitly protected by Parliament law – even on government property! The General did all right with the mob. Maybe she had learned from watching Sherkaner deal with journalists. Her combateers hulked innocuously in the background. She made a few general remarks, and then politely ignored their questions, letting the Southland police keep the reporters out of her physical way.

A thousand feet underground, their elevator started sideways on an electric polyrail. The elevator's tall windows looked out on brightly lit industrial caves. The Southlanders had done a lot here and on the Coastal Arc, but they didn't have enough underground farms to support it all.

The two Elected Representatives who had greeted her at the airfield had once been powerful in the South. But times had changed: there had been assassinations, subornations, all Pedure's usual tricks – and lately a near-magical good luck on the Kindred side. Now these two were, at least publicly, alone in their friendliness for the Accord. Now they were regarded as toadies of a foreign king. The two stood close to the General, one close enough that he could talk with her behind a screen. Hopefully, only the General and Hrunkner Unnerby could hear. *Don't count on it*, Unnerby thought to himself.

'No disrespect, ma'am, but we had hoped that your king would come in his own person.' The politico wore a finely tailored jacket and leggings – and an air of spiritual bedragglement.

The General nodded reassuringly. 'I understand, sir. I'm here to make sure the right things can be done, and done safely. Will I be allowed to address Parliament?' In the present situation, Hrunk guessed that there was no 'inner circle' to speak to – unless you counted the group that was firmly controlled by Pedure. But a parliamentary vote could make a difference, since the strategic rocket forces were still loyal to it.

'Y-yes. We have set that up. But things have gone too far.' He waved his watch hand. 'I wouldn't put it past the Other Side to cause an elevator wreck and—'

'They let us get this far. If I can talk to Parliament, I think there will be an accommodation.' General Smith smiled at the Southlander, an almost conspiratorial look.

Fifteen minutes later, the elevator had deposited them at the main esplanade. Three sides and the roof simply lifted off. *That* was an embellishment he hadn't seen before. Unnerby the engineer couldn't resist: He froze and stared up into the glaring lights and darkness, trying to see the mechanism that had such a large and silent effect.

Then the crush of police and politicians and reporters swept him off the platform . . .

. . . and they were climbing up the stairs of Parliament Hall.

At the top, Southland security finally separated them from the reporters and Smith's own combateers. They passed by five-ton timbered doors . . . into the hall itself. The hall had always been an underground affair, in earlier generations squatting just above the local deepness. Those early rulers had been more like bandits (or freedom fighters, depending on your source of propaganda) whose forces roamed the mountainous land.

Hrunkner had helped design this incarnation of Parliament Hall. It was one of the few projects he'd worked on where a major design goal was awesome appearance. It might not really be bombproof, but it looked damned spectacular.

The hall was a shallow bowl, with levels connected by gently curving stairs, each level a wide setback with rows of desks and perches. The rock walls curved in an enormous arch that carried fluorescent tubes – and a half-dozen other lighting technologies. Together those lights had almost the brightness and purity of a mid-Bright day, a light rich enough to show all the colors in the walls. Carpeting as deep and soft as father's-pelt covered the stairs and aisles and proscenium. Paintings were hung on the polished wood that faced each level, paintings done with a thousand dyes by artists who knew how to exploit every illusion. For a poor country, they had spent much on this place. But then, their parliament was their greatest pride, an invention that had ended banditry and dependence, and brought peace. Until now.

The doors swung closed behind them. The sound returned deep echoes from the dome and the far walls. In here, there would be just the Elected, their visitors, and – high above, Hrunkner could see clusters of lenses – the news cameras. Across the curves of desks, almost every perch was filled. Unnerby could feel the attention of half a thousand Elected.

Smith and Unnerby and Tim Downing started down the steps that led to the proscenium. The Elected were mostly quiet, watching. There was respect here, and hostility, and hope. Maybe Smith would have her chance to keep the peace.

For this day of triumph, Tomas Nau had set North Paw's weather to be its sunniest, the kind of warm afternoon that could extend all the summer day round. Ali Lin had grumbled, but made the necessary changes. Now Ali was weeding in the garden beneath Nau's study, his irritation forgotten. So what if the park's patterns were upset; fixing the problem would be Ali's next task.

And my task is to manage everything together, Tomas thought. Across the table from him sat Vinh and Trinli, working with the site monitoring he had assigned them. Trinli was essential to the cover story, the only Peddler that Tomas was confident would support the lies. Vinh . . . well, a credible excuse would take him offline for critical moments, but what he did see would corroborate Trinli. That would be tricky, but if there were any surprises . . . well, that was what Kal and his men were here to handle.

Ritser's presence was just a flat image, showing him sitting in the Captain's chair aboard the *Hand*. None of his words would be heard by innocent ears. 'Yes, Podmaster! We'll have the picture in a moment. We got a functioning spybot into Parliament Hall. Hey, Reynolt, your Melin got something right.'

Anne was up in the Hammerfest Attic. She was present only as a private image in Tomas's huds, and a voice in his ear. At the moment, her attention was split in at least three directions. She was running some kind of ziphead analysis, watching a Trixia Bonsol translation on the wall above her, and tracking the data stream from the *Hand*. The ziphead situation was as complicated as it had ever been. She didn't respond to Ritser's words.

'Anne? When Ritser's spy pics come, pipe them directly to Benny's. Trixia can do overlay translation, but give us some true audio, too.' Tomas had already seen some of the spybot transmissions. Let the people at Benny's see living Spiders up close and in motion. That would be a subtle help in the postconquest lies.

Anne didn't look away from her work. 'Yes, sir. I see that what you say is heard by Vinh and Trinli.'

'Quite so.'

'Very well. Just want you to know . . . our internal enemies have stepped up the pace. I'm seeing meddling all through our automation. *Watch Trinli.* I'll bet he's sitting there diddling his localizers.' Anne's gaze flicked up for an instant, catching the question in Nau's eyes. She shrugged. 'No, I'm still not sure it's him. But I'm very close. Be ready.'

A second passed. Anne's voice came again, but now publicly audible here and in the Peddlers' temp. 'Okay. Here we have live video from Parliament Hall at Southmost. This is what a human would actually see and hear.'

Nau looked to the left, where his huds showed Qiwi's pov in the temp. The main facets of Benny's display flickered. For an instant it wasn't clear what they were seeing. There was a jumble of reds and greens, actinic blues. They were looking into some kind of a pit. Stone ladders were cut into the walls. Moss or hairy pelts grew from rock. The Spiders crowded like black roaches.

Ritser Brughel glanced up from the pictures of Parliament and shook his head almost in awe. 'It's like some Frenkisch prophet's vision of Hell.'

Nau gave a silent nod of acknowledgment. With the ten-second time lag, casual chitchat was to be avoided. But Brughel was right; seeing so many together was even worse than the earlier spybot videos. The zipheads' cozy, human-esque translations gave a very unreal view of the Spiders. *I wonder how much we are missing about their minds.* He called up a separate image of the scene, this one synthesized by ziphead translators from a Spider news feed. In this picture, the steep pit became a shallow amphitheater, the ugly splashes of color were orderly mosaics worked into the carpet (which no longer looked like scraggly hair). The woodwork was everywhere glistening with polish (not stained and pitted). And the creatures themselves were somehow more sedate, their gestures almost meaningful in human body language.

In both displays, three figures appeared at the Parliament's entrance. They climbed (walked) down the stone stairs. The air was full of hissing and clicking, the true sound of these creatures.

The threesome disappeared into the bottom of the pit. A moment passed and they reappeared, climbing the far side. Ritser chuckled. 'The midsized one in front must be the spy chief, that's what Bonsol calls "Victory Smith."' One detail of the ziphead story was accurate: The creature's clothing was dead black, but it was more a pile of interlocking patches than a uniform. 'The hairy creature behind Smith, that must be the engineer, "Hrunkner Unnerby." Such quaint names for monsters.'

The three climbed out onto an arching spike of stone. A fourth Spider, already on the precarious structure, clambered to its pointed end.

Nau turned from the Spiders' hall to look at the crowd at Benny's. They were silent, watching in vast shock. Even Benny Wen's helpers were motionless, their gaze captured by the images from the Spider world.

'Introductions by the Parliamentary Speaker,' spoke a zip-head voice. 'The Parliament will come to order. I have the honor to—' Around the sensible words, Ritser's spy robot sent back the reality, the hissing clatter, the stabbing gestures with forelegs that ended in rapier points. In truth, these creatures did look like the statues the Qeng Ho had seen at Lands Command. But when they moved it was the chilling grace of predators, some gestures slow, some very very fast. Strangest of all, for all their superior vision, it wasn't easy to identify their eyes. Across the fluted ridges of the head, there were patches of smooth glassiness, bulbous here and there, with extensions that might be the cool-down points for its thermal infrared vision. The front of the Spider body was a nightmarish eating machine. The razor mandibles and clawlike helper limbs were in constant motion. But the creature's head was almost immobile on the thorax.

The Speaker left the tip of the stone needle, and General Smith climbed up, negotiating a tricky passage around the other. Smith was silent for a moment, once she reached the point. Her forelegs waved in a little spiral, as if encouraging foolish persons to get close to her maw. Hiss and clatter came from the speaker. On the 'translated' image, a legend appeared over her representation: SMILING GENTLY AT THE AUDIENCE.

'Ladies and gentlemen of the Parliament.' The voice was strong and beautiful – Trixia Bonsol's voice, Nau noticed Ezr Vinh's head jerk slightly at the sound of her. The diag traces on Vinh rose with the usual conflicted intensity. *He'll be usable, just long enough*, thought Nau.

'I come here speaking for my King, and with his full authority. I come here hoping I can offer enough to win your trust.'

'Ladies and gentlemen of the Parliament.' Rank on rank, the Elected looked back upon Victory Smith. All their attention was hers, and Hrunkner felt the power of the General's personality flowing as strongly as ever it had done. 'I come here speaking for my King, and with his full authority. I come here hoping I can offer enough to win your trust.

'We are at a point in history where we can destroy all progress that has been made – or we can make good on all the efforts of the past and achieve an unbounded paradise. These two outcomes are the two sides of our one situation. The bright outcome depends on trust for one another.'

There were scattered hoots of derision, the Kindred partisans. Unnerby wondered if all of those had tickets off Southland. Surely they must realize that any lesser payoff would leave them as dead as the country they were betraying, once the bombs started falling.

The General had told him that Pedure was down here herself. *I wonder . . .* Unnerby looked in all directions as the General spoke, his gaze most intensely upon the shadows and sergeants-at-arms. *There.* Pedure was sitting on the proscenium, not a hundred feet from Smith. After all these years, she was more confident than ever. *Wait a little longer, dear Honored Pedure. Maybe my General can surprise you.*

'I have a proposal. It is simple but it has substance – and it can be put into place very quickly.' She motioned for Tim Downing to pass the data cards to the Speaker's clerk. 'I think you know my position in the force structure of the Accord. Even the most suspicious of you will grant that, while I am here, the Accord must show the restraint it has publicly promised. I am authorized to offer a continuance of this state. You of the Southland Parliament may pick any three persons of the Accord – including myself, including the King himself – for indefinite residence at our embassy here at Southmost.' It was the most primitive peacekeeping strategy, though more generous than ever in the past, since she was offering the choice of hostages to the other side. And more than ever in history, it was practical. The Accord Embassy at Southmost was plenty big enough to house a small city, and with modern communications it would not even cripple the important activities of the hostage. If the Parliament was not totally corrupted, this might stick a bar between the legs of onrushing disaster.

The Elected were silent, even Pedure's buddies. Shocked? Facing up to the only real options they had? Listening for instructions from their boss?

Something was going on. In the shadows behind Smith, Hrunkner could see Pedure talking intensely to an aide.

When Victory Smith's speech ended, Benny's parlor rang with applause. There had been stark shock when the speech began, when everyone saw how living Spiders really looked. But the words of the speech had fit the personality of Victory Smith, and that was something most people were familiar with. The rest would take a lot of getting used to, but . . .

Rita Liao caught Benny's sleeve as he sailed by with drinks for the ceiling. 'You shouldn't have Qiwi up front all by herself, Benny. She can squeeze in here, and still talk to everyone.'

'Um, okay.' It was the Podmaster who had suggested the front-row solitude, but surely it couldn't matter when things were going so well. Benny delivered the drinks, listening to the happy speculations with half his attention.

'—between that speech and our meddling, they should be safe as temps at Triland—'

'Hey, we could be *on the ground* in less than four Msecs! After all these years—'

'Space or ground, who cares? We'll have the resources to dump the birth bans—'

Yes, the birth bans. Our own, human version of the oophase taboo. Maybe I can finally ask Gonle – Benny's mind shied away from the thought. It was tempting fate to act too soon. Nevertheless, he suddenly felt happier than he had in a long time. Benny avoided the tables by diving across the central gap, a quick detour in Qiwi's direction.

She nodded at Rita's suggestion. 'That would be nice.' Her smile was tentative, and her eyes had barely flicked away from the parlor's display screens. General Smith was climbing down from the speaker's platform.

'Qiwi! Things are working out just like the Podmaster planned. Everyone wants to congratulate you!'

Qiwi petted the kitten in her arms gently, but with a kind of intense protectiveness. She looked at him and her expression was oddly puzzled. 'Yes, it's all working out.' She rose from the table and followed Benny across the space to Rita's table.

'I have to talk to him, Corporal. *Immediately.*' Rachner drew himself up as he spoke the words, projecting fifteen years of colonelcy into his manner.

And for a moment the young corporal wilted before his glare. Then the oophase cobblie must have noticed the traces of fizz barf on Thract's maw and the bedraggled state of his uniform. He shrugged, his gaze watchful and closed. 'I'm sorry, sir, you're not on the list.'

Rachner felt his shoulders droop. 'Corporal, just ring down to him. Tell him it's Rachner, and it's a matter of . . . of life and death.' And as soon as he said the words, Thract wished he hadn't asserted this absolute truth. The cobblie stared at him for a second – debating whether to throw him out? Then something like sick pity seemed to rise in his aspect; he opened a comm line and spoke to someone inside.

A minute passed. Two. Rachner paced the visitor holding box. At least it was out of the wind; he'd frozen the tips of two hands just climbing the stairs from Underhill's helipad. But . . . an external guard, and a holding box? Somehow, he hadn't expected such security. Maybe some good had come out of his losing his job. It had wakened the others to the need for protection.

'Rachner, is that you?' The voice that came from the sentry's comm was frail and querulous. Underhill.

'Yes, sir. Please, I've got to talk to you.'

'You – you look *terrible*, Colonel. I'm sorry, I—' His voice faded. There was mumbling in the background. Someone said, 'The speech went well . . . plenty of time now.' Then he was back, and sounding much less drifty. 'Colonel, I'll be up in a few minutes.'

53

'An excellent speech. It could not have been better if we had scripted it.' In the flat video from the *Hand*, Ritser rattled on, well pleased with himself. Nau just nodded, smiling. Smith's peace proposal was strong enough to bring the Spider militaries to a pause. It would give the humans time to announce themselves, and propose cooperation. That was the official story, a risky plan that would leave the Podmasters in a second-class position. In fact, about 7Ksec from now, Anne's zipheads would initiate a sneak attack by Smith's own military. The resulting Kindred 'counterattack' would complete the planned destruction. *And we'll step in and pick up the pieces.*

Nau looked out over North Paw's afternoon brightness, but his huds were filled with a view of Trinli and Vinh, sitting in the flesh just a couple meters from him. Trinli had a faintly amused expression, but his fingers never stopped their flickering work on his assignment, monitoring the nuclear munitions in Kindred territory. Vinh? Vinh looked nervous; the diagnostic tags that hovered by his face showed that he knew something was up but hadn't quite figured out what it was. It was time to move him out of the way, a few brief errands. When he came back events would be in motion . . . and Trinli would back up the Podmaster's story.

Anne Reynolt's voice came tiny in Nau's ear. 'Sir, we have an emergency.'

'Yes, go ahead.' Nau spoke easily, not turning away from the lake. Inside, though, something froze in his guts. This was the closest he had ever heard Anne come to panicky sharpness.

'Our pet subversive has stepped up the pace. There's much less masking.

He's grabbing everything that's loose. A few thousand more seconds and he can shut us zipheads down . . . It's Trinli, sir, ninety percent probability.'

But Trinli is sitting right here, before my very eyes! And I need him to back up the post-attack lies. 'I don't know, Anne,' he said aloud. Maybe Anne was freaking. It was possible, though he had been tracking her meds and MRI tuning more closely than ever before.

Anne shrugged, didn't reply. It was the typical dismissive gesture of a ziphead. She had done her best, and he was welcome to ignore her advice and go to hell.

This was not a distraction he needed when forty years' work was coming to a cusp. *Which was exactly why an enemy might pick this moment finally to act.*

Kal Omo was standing right behind Nau, and was on the private link with Reynolt. Of the other three guards, only Rei Ciret was actually in the room. Nau sighed. 'Okay, Anne.' He gave Omo an invisible signal to get the rest of his team into the room. *We'll put these two on ice, deal with them later.*

Nau had given his targets no warning, yet – from the corner of his vision, he saw Trinli's hand flicker in a throwing gesture. Kal Omo gave a gargling scream.

Nau pulled himself under the table. Something slammed into the thick wood above him. There was a chatter of wire-gun fire, another scream.

'He's getting away!'

Nau slid across the floor and bounced up toward the ceiling on the far side of the table. Rei Ciret was in midair, flailing at Ezr Vinh. 'Sorry, sir! This one jumped me.' He pushed the bleeding body away; Vinh had bought Trinli the instant he needed to escape. 'Marli and Tung will get him!'

Indeed they were trying. The two sprayed wire-fire up the hillside, toward the forest. But Trinli was way ahead of them, flying from tree to tree. Then he was gone, and Tung and Marli were halfway to the forest in hot pursuit.

'Wait!' Nau's voice roared over the lodge speakers. A lifetime of obedience stopped their reckless pursuit. They came carefully back down the hillside, scanning for threats all the way. Shock and rage were strong in their faces.

Nau continued in a lower voice. 'Get inside. Guard the lodge.' It was the sort of basic direction a podsergeant would give, but Kal Omo was . . . Nau floated back to the meeting table, the etiquette of consensual gravity set aside for the moment. Something sharp and shiny was wedged in the edge of the table, just at the point where he had dived for cover. A similar blade had slashed across Omo's throat; its butt end protruded from the podsergeant's windpipe. Omo had stopped twitching. Blood hung all around him, drifting only slowly toward the floor. The podsergeant's wire gun was half out of its holster.

Omo was a useful man. *Do I have time to put him on ice?* Nau thought a second more on tactics and timing . . . and Kal Omo lost.

The guards hovered around the lodge's windows, but their eyes kept straying back to their podsergeant. Nau's mind raced down chains of consequences. 'Ciret, get Vinh tied down. Marli, find Ali Lin.'

Vinh moaned weakly as they shoved him onto a chair. Nau came over the table to look more closely at the man. It looked like he'd taken a wire-gun nick across the shoulder. It was bloody, but it wasn't spouting. Vinh would live . . . long enough.

'Pus, that Trinli was fast,' Tung said, blabbering with released tension. 'All these years he was just a loud old fart and then – *bam* – he scragged the podsergeant. Scragged him and then got clean away.'

'Wouldn't have been clean if this one hadn't gotten in the way.' Ciret prodded Vinh's head with the muzzle of his wire-gun. 'They were both fast.'

Too fast. Nau slipped the huds off his eyes, and stared at them for a moment. Qeng Ho huds, driven by data off the localizer net. He crumpled the huds into a wad, and dug out the fiberphone that Reynolt had insisted upon as backup. 'Anne, can you hear me? Did you see what happened?'

'Yes. Trinli was in motion the moment you signaled Kal Omo.'

'He *knew*. He could hear your side of the conversation.' Pestilence! How could Anne detect the subversion and not notice that Trinli had broken into their comm?

'. . . Yes. I only guessed a part of what he was up to.' So the localizers were Trinli's customized weapon. A trap built across millennia. *Who am I fighting?*

'Anne. I want you to cut the wireless power to all the localizers.' But localizers were the backbone of Plague knew how many critical systems. Localizers maintained the stability of the lake itself. 'Inside North Paw, leave the stabilizers on. Have your zipheads manage them directly, over the fiber.'

'Done. Things will be rough, but we can manage. What about the ground ops?'

'Get in touch with Ritser. Things are too complicated to be subtle. We have to advance the groundside time line.'

He could hear Anne punching out instructions to her people. But gone was his view of the orders and the threads of ziphead processing assigned to each project. This was like fighting blind. They could lose while they were staggering around in shock.

A hundred seconds later, Anne was back to him. 'Ritser understands. My people are helping him set up a simple attack run. We can fine-tune the results later.' She spoke with her old, calm impatience. Anne Reynolt had fought battles much harder than this, won a hundred times against overwhelming odds. If only all enemies could be so used.

'Very good. Have you spotted Trinli? I'll bet he's in the tunnels.' *If he isn't circling back for a second ambush.*

'Yes, I think so. We're hearing movement off the old geophones.' Emergent equipment.

'Good. Meantime, patch together some synthetic voice to keep the people at Benny's happy.'

'Done,' came her immediate reply. Already done.

Nau turned back to his guards and Ezr Vinh. A very small breathing space had been created. Long enough to get new orders to Ritser. Long enough to find out a little about what he was really up against.

Vinh had regained consciousness. There was a glaze of pain in his eyes – and a glitter of hatred. Nau smiled back at him. He gestured for Ciret to twist Vinh's maimed shoulder. 'I need a few answers, Ezr.'

The Peddler screamed.

Pham boosted himself faster and faster up the diamond corridor, guided by green images that smeared and wobbled . . . and dimmed toward total darkness. He coasted blind for a few seconds, still not slowing. He patted at his temples, trying to reset the localizers there. They were in place, and he knew there were thousands of localizers drifting through the length of the tunnel. Anne must have cut off the wireless power pulses, at least in this tunnel.

The woman is unbelievable! For years, Pham had avoided direct manipulation of the ziphead system. Yet somehow Anne had still noticed. The mindscrub had slowed her progress for a while, but this last year she had tightened the noose and tightened it, until . . . *We were so close to disabling the power cutoff, and now we've lost everything.* Almost everything. Ezr had died to give him one more chance.

The tunnel turned somewhere just ahead. He reached into the dark, touching the walls lightly, then harder, breaking his dive and turning himself feetfirst. The maneuver was a fraction of a second late. Feet, knees, hands, smashed into the unseen surface, about like a bad fall groundside – except that he bounced back, spinning into another wall.

He caught himself and finger-walked back to the turn. Four separate corridors branched from here. He felt for the openings, and started down the second one, but very quietly this time. *Anne hadn't known for sure until a few seconds ago.* The cache he had set in this tunnel should still be in place.

After a few meters, his hands touched a cloth bag tacked to the wall. *Ha.* Planting the cache had been a big risk, but endgame maneuvers usually are, and this one had paid off. He slipped the bag open, found the ring light inside. A glint of yellow glowed up around his hand. Pham grabbed at the rest of the gear, the light following his hands, rainbows and shadows hurtling back and forth around him. There were tiny balls in one of the packages. He bounced one of them down a side tunnel. It flew silently for a second, and then there was a thud and miscellaneous banging – a decoy for Anne's listening zipheads.

So our cover was blown, just a few Ksecs too soon. But screwups happen more often than not when plans finally meet reality. If things had gone right, he'd never have needed this pack – which was just why he'd planted it. One by one, Pham considered the contents of the pack: the respirator, the amplifying receiver, the medikit, the trick dart gun.

Nau and Company had some choices. They might gas the tunnels or dump them into vacuum – though that last would destroy a lot of valuable equipment. They might try to chase him around in here. That would be fun; Nau's goons would find just how dangerous their tunnels had become . . . Pham felt the old, old enthusiasm rising in him, the rush he always got when the crunch came, when the planning and thought became action. He tucked the gear into his pockets as the plan-of-the-moment grew sharper in his mind. *Ezr, we'll win, I promise. We'll win despite Anne . . . and for her.*

Quiet as a fog, he started up the tunnel, his ring light just bright enough for him to see the side tunnels up ahead. It was time to pay Anne a visit.

The *Invisible Hand* coasted 150 kilometers above the Spiders' world. It was so low that only a limited ground swath of Spiders might directly see them, yet when the time came it would pass precisely over the ordained targets. And whatever the lies they were telling Rita and the others at L1, aboard the *Hand* the Spider sites were called *targets*.

Jau Xin sat in the Pilot Manager's chair – once, when the Qeng Ho had owned this ship, it had been the executive officer's – and surveyed the gray curve of the horizon. He had three ziphead pilots on this, but only one was actually monitoring flight. The others were plugged into Bil Phuong's ordnance systems, plotting options. Jau tried to ignore the words he heard from the Captain's chair beside him. Ritser Brughel was enjoying this, giving his boss on Hammerfest a running account of what was happening on the ground.

Brughel paused in his perverse analysis, was mercifully silent for some seconds. Abruptly, the Vice-Podmaster swore. 'Sir! What—' Suddenly he was shouting. 'Phuong! There's shooting at North Paw. Omo is down and – pus, I've lost my huds link. Phuong!'

Xin turned in his chair, saw Brughel pounding on his console. The man's pale face was flushed. The Vice-Podmaster listened on his private channel for a moment. 'But the Podmaster survived? Okay, put Reynolt on then. Put her on!'

Apparently Anne Reyolt was not immediately available. One hundred seconds passed. Two hundred. Brughel steamed and fumed, and even his goons backed away. Jau turned to his own displays, but they flowed by him meaninglessly. *This wasn't in Tomas Nau's script.*

'Slut! Where have you been? What—' Then Brughel was silent again. He grunted occasionally, but did not interrupt what must have been a monologue. When he spoke again, he sounded more thoughtful than enraged. 'I understand. You tell the Podmaster he can count on me.'

The long-distance conversation continued through one more exchange, and Jau began to guess what was coming. Jau couldn't help himself; his gaze slid sideways, toward the Vice-Podmaster. Brughel was looking back at him. 'Pilot Manager Xin. Our present position?'

'Sir, we're southbound over the ocean, about sixteen hundred kilometers from Southmost.'

Brughel glanced over his head, taking in a more precise view coming up on his huds. 'So, and I see on this pass we'll overfly the Accord's missile fields as we progress north.'

There was a hard lump in Xin's throat. This moment had been inevitable, *but I thought I had more time.* '. . . We'll pass some hundreds of kilometers east of the fields, sir.'

Brughel gestured dismissively. 'A main torch burn would correct that . . . Phuong, you're tracking this? Yes, we're advancing things by seven Ksec. So? Maybe they will notice us, but it'll be too late to matter. Have your people generate a new ops sequence. Of course it'll mean more direct involvement. Reynolt is diverting all her loose zips to your disposal. Synch 'em up as best you can . . . Good.'

Brughel relaxed on his Qeng Ho Captain's chair, and smiled. 'The only drawback to all this is we won't have time to get Pedure out of Southmost. Pedure we had figured out; I think she would have made a good native viceroy . . . But, you know, for myself I'm not fond of any of them.' He saw that Xin was following his words with undisguised horror. 'Careful, careful, Pilot Manager. You've been too long with your Qeng Ho friends. Whatever they just tried, it *failed.* Do you have that straight? The Podmaster survived and still has his resources.' He looked beyond Jau, seeing something in his huds. 'Synch your pilots with Bil Phuong's zipheads. You'll have concrete numbers in a few seconds. Over Southmost we won't fire any of our own weapons. Instead you'll locate and trigger the short-range rockets the Kindred have offshore, the "Accord sneak attack" we already had planned. Your real job will come a few hundred seconds later. Your people will take out the Accord's missile fields.' That would involve using the small number of rockets and beam weapons that remained to the humans. But those weapons were quite sufficient against the Spiders' more primitive antimissile defenses . . . and after that, thousands of Kindred missiles would murder cities across half the planet.

'I—' Xin choked, horrorr-struck. If he didn't do this, they would murder

Rita. Brughel would kill Rita and then Jau. But if he followed orders . . . *I know too much.*

Brughel watched him intently. It was a look Jau had never seen in Ritser Brughel before . . . a cool, assessing, almost Nauly look. Brughel cocked his head, and spoke mildly. 'You have nothing to fear in following orders. Oh, maybe a mindscrub; you'll lose a little. But we *need* you, Jau. You and Rita can serve us for many years, a good life. If only you follow orders now.'

Before everything blew up, Reynolt had been in the Attic. Pham guessed she'd be there even now, camped in the grouproom with Trud and every bit of comm access she could manage, doing her best to protect and manage her people . . . and use their combined genius to do Nau's will.

Pham flitted upward through the darkness, easing through tunnels that finally narrowed to less than eighty centimeters across. These had been machine-carved over decades, beginning when Hammerfest's roots were driven into Diamond One. Sometime in the third decade of the Exile, Pham had penetrated the Emergents' architecture programs, and the tunnels – some of them – had simply been lost; other connections had been added. He was betting that not even Anne knew all the places he could go.

At every turning point, he slowed himself with easy hand presses, and flickered his light briefly. Searching, searching. Even without external power, the localizers' capacitors could drive a last, brief computation. With the amplifying receiver he could still get clues – he knew he was high in the Hammerfest tower, on the grouproom side of the structure.

But the nearby localizers were almost exhausted. He drifted around a corner, past what he'd thought was the most likely spot. The walls glittered dim rainbows, unblemished. A few more meters. *There!* A faint circle etched in the wall of diamond. He coasted up to it and gently touched a control code to the surface. There was a click. Light blazed all around the disk as it turned back, revealing a storeroom beyond. Pham slipped through the opening. There were racks of food rations and toiletries.

He came around the racks, was almost across the room, almost to its more official entrance – when someone opened that door. Pham dove to the side of the doorway, and as the visitor stepped through, he reached out and lightly plucked off his huds. It was Trud Silipan.

'Pham!' Silipan looked more surprised than frightened. 'What the devil – do you know, Anne is having a fit about you? She's gone nuts, says you've killed Kal Omo and taken over North Paw.' His words guttered to a stop as he realized that Pham's presence here was equally unlikely.

Pham grinned at Silipan, and shut the door behind him. 'Oh, the stories are all true, Trud. I've come to take back my fleet.'

'Your . . . fleet.' Trud just stared for a moment, fear and wonder playing across his face. 'Pus, Pham. What are you on? You look strange.' *A little adrenaline, a little freedom. Amazing what it can do for you.* Silipan shrank before the smile that was growing on Pham's face. 'You're crazy, man. You know you can't win. You're trapped here. Give up. Maybe we can pass this off as – as temporary insanity.'

Pham shook his head. 'I'm here to win, Trud.' He raised his little dart gun up where Silipan could see. 'And you're going to help. We're going out to the grouproom, and you're going to cut off all ziphead support—'

Silipan brushed irritably at Nuwen's gun hand. 'Impossible. There's a critical need for them, supporting the ground op.'

'Supporting Nau's Spider-extermination program? All the better to cut them off right now. It should have an interesting effect on the Podmaster's lake, too.'

Pham could almost see the Emergent balancing the risks in his mind: Pham Trinli, his old drinking buddy and fellow-braggart, now armed with a debatably effective dart gun – against all the Podmasters' lethal power. 'No way, Pham. You got yourself into this, and now you're stuck with it.'

The huds that Pham held crumpled in his right hand were making muffled, angry noises. There was a final squawk, and the door to the storeroom popped open. 'What's the matter with you, Silipan? I told you we need—' Anne Reynolt slid into the room. She seemed to take in the tableau instantly, but she had nothing to bounce out on.

And Pham was just as fast as she. His hand turned, the little dart gun fired, and Reynolt convulsed. An instant later, a strange thudding rocked her body. Pham turned back to Trud, and now his smile was broader. 'Explosive darts, don't you know? They get inside, then – *bam* – your guts are hamburger.'

Trud's complexion turned a pale shade of ash. 'Unh-unh . . .' He stared at the body of his former boss/slave, and he looked about ready to puke.

Pham tapped Silipan's chest with the little dart gun. Trud stared down, horror-frozen, into the muzzle. 'Trud, my friend, why so glum? You're a good Emergent. Reynolt was just a ziphead, a piece of furniture.' He gestured at Reynolt's body, its convulsions fading toward the limpness of fresh death. 'So let's stow this garbage out of the way, and then you can show me how to disconnect the zipheads' comm.' He grinned and moved back to snag the body. Trud was visibly trembling as he started toward the door.

The instant Silipan turned away from him, Pham's casual grip on Anne became gentle, careful. *Lord, that sounded like the real thing, not a stun dart and a noisemaker.* It had been half a lifetime since he'd used this trick; what if he'd botched it? For the first time since the action started, panic seeped through the adrenaline rush. He slipped one hand to the side of her throat . . . and found a strong, steady pulse. Anne was thoroughly stunned and nothing more.

Pham pasted the predatory smile back on his face and followed Trud into the zipheads' grouproom.

54

The news companies had had the last laugh after all. So what if Accord Security had blacked out Mom's getting off the daggercraft? Within minutes, she was on Southland territory – and the local news services were more than willing to show Victory Smith and every person in her entourage. For a few minutes, the cameras were so close that she could see the inner expression of the General's eating hands. Mom looked as calm and military as ever . . . but for a few minutes Victory Lighthill felt more like a small child than a lieutenant in the Intelligence Service. This was as bad as the morning Gokna had died. *Mom, why are you taking this risk?* But Viki knew the answer to that. The General was no longer essential to the great counterlurk that she and Daddy had created; now she could help those she had put in greatest peril.

The NCO Club was crowded with cobbers who normally would have been on sleep shift or at other amusements. It was the closest place they could come to being back on the job. And for once 'the job' was clearly the most important thing any cobber could be doing.

Victory drifted among the arcade games, discreetly signaled her people that things were cool. Finally, she hopped on a perch next to Brent. Her brother had not taken off his game helmet. His hands were in constant motion across the games console. She tapped him on a shoulder. 'Mom will be talking any second now,' she said softly.

'I know,' was all Brent said. 'Critter nine sees our op, but it still is fooled. It thinks the problem is local.'

Viki almost grabbed her brother's helmet off his head. *Damn. I might as well be deaf and blind.* Instead, she took a telephone from her jacket and poked out a number. 'Hi, Daddy? Mom has started talking.'

The speech was short. It was good. It blocked the threat from the South. *And so what?* Going down there was still too much of a risk. On the displays over the fizz bar, Viki could see the General handing her formal offer to Tim to pass out to Parliament. Maybe that end of things would work out. Maybe the trip was worth it. Several minutes passed. The cameras at Parliament Hall scanned back and forth across growing tumult. Mom had departed the platform with Uncle Hrunk. A scruffy little cobber in dark clothes approached them. *Pedure.* They were arguing . . .

And suddenly none of it mattered anymore. Brent shrugged against her. 'Bad news,' he said, still not pulling the game display off his head. 'I've lost them all. Even our old friend.'

Lighthill jumped off her game perch and signaled the team. Her gesture could have been a shrill whistle for the effect it had. Her team was on its feet, saddled up with panniers, and all headed for the door. Brent pulled up his game hat and hustled out just ahead of Lighthill.

Behind them, she saw curious glances, but most of the club's clientele were too stuck on the television to pay them much attention.

Her team had bounced down two stories before the attack alarums started screaming.

'What do you mean, we've lost ziphead support? Was the fiber cut?' Trinli had somehow found all the fibers?

'N-no, sir: At least I don't think so.' Podcorporal Marli was competent enough, but he was no Kal Omo. 'We can still ping through, but the control channels don't respond. Sir . . . it's as though somebody just took the zips offline.'

'Hm. Yes.' This could be another Trinli surprise, or maybe there was a traitor in the Attic. Either way . . . Nau looked across the room at Ezr Vinh. The Peddler's eyes were glazed with pain. There were important secrets behind those eyes, but Vinh was as tough as any that he and Ritser had interrogated to death. It would take time or some special lever to get real information out of him. Time they didn't have. He turned back to Marli. 'Can I still talk to Ritser?'

'I think so. We've got fiber to the laser station on the outside.' He tapped hesitantly at the console. Nau suppressed the impulse to rage at his clumsiness. But without ziphead support, everything was clumsy. *We might as well be Qeng Ho.*

Marli grinned suddenly. 'Our session link to the *Invisible Hand* is still active, sir! I just keyed audio to your collar mike.'

'Very good . . . Ritser! I don't know how much you've got of this, but—' Nau gave a quick rehash of the debacle, finishing with: 'I'll be out of touch for the next few hundred seconds; I'm evacuating to L1-A. The bottom-line question: Without our zipheads, can you still prosecute the ground operation?'

It would be at least ten seconds before an answer came back on that. Nau glanced at his second surviving guard. 'Ciret, get Tung and the ziphead. We're going to L1-A.'

From the arsenal vault, they would have direct power of life and death over everyone in L1 space, with no intervening automation. Nau opened the cabinet behind him and touched a control. A section of the parquet floor slid aside, revealing a tunnel hatch. The tunnel went directly through Diamond One to the arsenal vault, and it had never been automated with localizers or cut with cross tunnels. The security locks at both ends were keyed to his thumbprint. He touched the reader. The tiny access light stayed red. *How could Trinli sabotage that?* Nau forced down panic, and tried the thumb pad again. Still red. Again. The light shifted reluctantly to pass-green, and the hatch beneath the floor rotated to unlocked position. The software must be correlating on his blood pressure, concluding he was under coercion. *We could still be balked at the other end.* He keyed his thumbprint for the far lock. It took two tries, but that one finally showed pass-green, too.

Ciret and Tung were back, pushing Ali Lin ahead of them. 'You're breaking the rules,' the old man scolded them. 'We should *walk*, like this, with our feet on the floor.' Ali's face was a mix of irritation and puzzlement. Zipheads never liked to be taken off their Focused task. Very likely, weeding the Podmaster's garden had been as important in Ali's mind as the most delicate gene-splicing. Now suddenly he was being forced indoors and all the fake-gravity etiquette of his park was being ignored.

'Just stand still, and keep quiet. Ciret, unlatch Vinh. We're taking him, too.'

Ali stood still, his feet planted firmly on the tacky floor. But he did not remain silent. He stared past Nau with a typical far gaze, and just went on complaining. 'You're ruining everything, can't you see?'

Abruptly, Ritser Brughel's voice filled the room. 'Sir, the situation here is under control. The *Hand*'s zipheads are still online. We won't really need the high-latency services till after the nukes have fallen. Phuong says that short-term, we may be better off without L1. Just before they dropped out, some of Reynolt's units were getting very erratic. Here's the attack schedule. Southmost gets burned in seven hundred seconds. Soon after that, the *Hand* will be overflying the Accord's antimissile fields. We'll scrag them ourselves—'

Brughel's reply was turning into a report, the usual fate of long-distance conversation. Lin had quieted. Nau felt a coolness on his back, the sunlight fading. A cloud? He turned – and saw that for once, a ziphead's far gaze was meaningful. Tung stepped around Lin to look out the den's lake-facing windows. 'Pus,' the guard said, softly.

'Ritser! We have more problems. I'll get back to you.'

The voice from the *Invisible Hand* blathered on, but now no one was listening.

Like some undine of Balacrean myth, the waters of North Paw had slowly gathered themselves, rising and spreading from Ali Lin's carefully designed shore. 'Sunlight' wavered through the million tonnes of water that billowed over them. Even without controls, the park lake should have stayed approximately in place. But the enemy had left the lakebed servos running in rhythm . . . and the sea had quietly oscillated into catastrophe.

Nau dived for the tunnel hatch. He braced himself and pulled on the massive security cover. The wall of water touched the lodge. The building groaned and the windows shattered before a mountain of water moving implacably at something more than a meter per second.

And the wall of water became a thousand arms seeking through the breaking wall, swarming chill around his body, tearing him away from the hatch. Screams and shouts, quickly drowned, and for a moment Nau was completely submerged. The only sound was the rumbling crumbling of his lodge as it was torn to rubble. He had a last glimpse of his den, his burl-surfaced desk, the marble fireplace. Then the slow tsunami broke out the far wall and Nau was lifted up and up in the swirl.

Still submerged, lungs burning. The water was numbing cold. Nau twisted, trying to make sense of the blurs he could see. The clearest view was downward. He saw the green of the forest behind the lodge. Nau swam down, toward the air.

He broke free, sending threads of water skittering ahead of the main surface, and launching himself into the open space beyond. For a second or two, Nau floated alone, drifting just fast enough to stay ahead of the flying sea. The air was filled with a sound Nau had never imagined, an oleaginous rumble, the sound of a million tonnes of water turning, spreading, falling. The surge had hit the cavern's roof, and now the sea was coming down, and he beneath it. In the forest below, the butterflies had for once stopped their song. They huddled in massive clusters in the largest groteselms. But far away, *something* was in the air. Tiny dots hovered near the side of the towering sea. The winged kittens! They seemed not the least frightened of it – but then Qiwi claimed they were an old sky breed. He saw one splash into the side of the undine. It was gone for a moment, and then emerged, and dived in again. The damn cats might be just agile enough to survive.

He turned again and looked back through the water, into the park's sunlight. It glittered golden on rubble, on human figures trapped like flies in amber. The others were paddling his way, some weakly, some with emphatic force. Marli dove into the air. An instant later Tung breached the water wall, then Ciret with Ali Lin in his arms. *Good man!*

There was one more figure, Ezr Vinh. The Peddler came half out of the water, about ten meters from the rest of them. He was dazed and choking, but more awake than he had seemed during the interrogation. He looked down upon the treetops they were falling toward, and made a sound that might have been a laugh. 'You're trapped, Podmaster. Pham Nuwen has outsmarted you.'

'Pham *who*?'

The Peddler squinted at him, seemed to realize that he had let slip information that he had been dying to protect. Nau waved at Marli. 'Fetch him here.'

But Marli had nothing to bounce against. Vinh splashed against the water, drawing himself back within – to drown, but out of their reach.

Marli turned, firing his wire gun into the forest and propelling himself back toward the falling water. Nau could see Ezr Vinh silhouetted in the sunlight, flailing weakly, but now several meters deep in the water.

The treetops were brushing up around them. Marli looked around wildly. 'We have to get out of the way, sir!'

'Just kill him then.' Nau was already grabbing at the tree-tops. Above him, Marli fired several short bursts. The flying wire was designed to tear and mangle flesh; its range in water was almost zero. But Marli was lucky. A haze of red bloomed around the Peddler's body.

And then there was no more time. Nau pulled himself from branch to branch, diving through the open spaces beneath the forest canopy. All around was the sound of breaking tree limbs as the water pushed through the groteselms and oleenfirn, a sound that conjured fire and wetness all at once. The water wall shredded into a million fractal fingers, twisting, reeling, merging. It touched the edge of a butterfly horde, and there was an instant of piping song, louder than Nau had ever heard – and then the cluster was swallowed.

Marli boosted ahead of him, and turned. 'The water is between us and the general entrance, sir.'

Trapped, just as the Peddler said.

The four of them moved along the groundwort, parallel to the wall of the park. Above them, the roof of water came lower and lower, well past the forest crown and still descending. The sunlight was a glow from all directions, through dozens of meters of water. There had only been so much water in the lake. There would be enormous air pockets throughout the park – but they had not been lucky. Their space was a not-so-large cave, water on four sides of them.

Ali Lin had to be dragged from branch to branch. He seemed fascinated by the undine, and totally oblivious of the danger.

Maybe . . . 'Ali!' Nau said sharply.

Ali Lin turned toward him. But he wasn't frowning at the interruption; he was *smiling*. 'My park, it's ruined. But I see something better now, something no one has ever done. We can make a true micrograv lake, bubbles and droplets trading in and out for dominance. There are animals and plants I could—'

'Ali. Yes! You'll build a better park, I promise. Now, I have to know, is there any way we can get out of the park – without drowning first?'

Thank goodness the ziphead could see an upside to this. Ali's central interests had been frustrated again and again in the last few hundred seconds. Normally, ziphead loyalty was unbreakable, but if they thought you were getting between them and their specialty . . . After a moment, Ali shrugged and said, 'Of course. There's a sluiceway behind that boulder. I never welded it shut.'

Marli dived for the rock. A sluiceway here? Without his huds, Nau didn't know. But there were dozens of them opening into the park, the channels they'd used to bring the ice down from the surface.

'The zip's right, sir! And the open codes work.'

Nau and the others moved around the rock, looked into the hole that Marli had uncovered. Meantime, the walls of their cave of air – their bubble – were moving. In another thirty seconds, this would be under water too. Marli looked across at Nau, and some of the triumph leaked out of his expression. 'Sir, we'll be safe from the water in there, but—'

'But there's nowhere to go from there. Right. I know.' The channel would end in a sealed hatch, with vacuum beyond that. It was a dead end.

A slowly curling stalactite of water splashed across Nau's head, forcing him to crouch beside Marli. The lowering mound of water retreated, and for a moment their ceiling rose. *Step by step, I've lost almost everything.* Unbelievable. And suddenly Tomas knew that Ezr Vinh's blurted claim must be true. Pham Trinli was not Zamle Eng; that had been a convenient lie, tailored for Tomas Nau. All these years, his greatest hero – and therefore the deadliest possible enemy – had been within arm's reach. Trinli *was* Pham Nuwen. For the first time since childhood, Nau was gripped by paralyzing fear.

But even Pham Nuwen had had his flaws, his abiding moral weakness. *I've studied the man's career all my life, taking the good parts for my own. As much as anyone, I know his flaws. And I know how to use them.* He looked at the others, cataloguing them and their equipment: an old man that Qiwi loved, some comm gear, some weapons, and some gunmen. It would be enough.

'Ali, isn't there a fiber headpoint at the outer end of these sluices? Ali!'

The ziphead turned away from his inspection of the ceiling's undulation. 'Yes, yes. We needed careful coordination when we brought down the ice.'

He waved Marli into the sluiceway. 'It's okay. This will work fine.' One by one; they slipped through the narrow entrance. Around them, the bottom of the bubble broke free of the ground. Now there was half a meter of water covering the ground, and it was rising. Tung and Ali Lin came through in a shower of water. Ciret dived through last, and slammed the hatch shut behind them. A few dozen liters of undine came in too, now just a mess of spilled water. But on the other side of the hatch, they could hear the sea piling deep. Nau turned to Marli, who was shining his comm laser as a diffuse light. 'Let's hike up to the headpoint, Corporal. Ali Lin is going to help me make a phone call.'

Pham Nuwen had come close to winning, but Nau still had a mind and the ability to reach out and manipulate others. As they coasted up the sluiceway, he thought on just what he should say to Qiwi Lin Lisolet.

General Smith retired from the speaker's perch. The information on Tim Downing's cards had been distributed to the Elected, and now five hundred heads were thinking over the deal. Hrunkner Unnerby stood in the shadows behind the perch and wondered. Smith had made another miracle. In a just world it would surely work. So what would Pedure invent to counter this?

Smith stepped back until she was even with him. 'Come with me, Sergeant. I saw someone I've been wanting to talk to for a long time.' There would be a vote called later in the day. Before that there could well be follow-up questions for the General. There was plenty of time for political maneuver. He and Downing followed the General to the far end of the proscenium, blocking the exit. A scruffy cobber in extravagant leggings was coming toward them. Pedure. The years had not been kind to her – or maybe the stories about the attempted assassinations were true. She made to sidle around Victory Smith, but the General stepped into her path.

Smith smiled at her. 'Hello, Cobblie Killer. So nice to meet you in person.'

The other hissed. 'Yes. And if you don't move from my path, I will be very pleased to kill you.' The words were heavily accented, but the tiny knife on her hand was clear enough.

Smith stretched her arms sideways, an extravagant shrug that would catch notice all across the hall. 'In front of all these people, Honored Pedure? I don't think so. You're—'

Smith hesitated, raised a pair of hands to her head, and seemed to listen. To her telephone?

Pedure just stared, her entire aspect full of suspicion. Pedure was a small female with galled chitin, and gestures that were just a bit too quick. A totally untrustworthy picture. She must be so used to killing from afar that personal charm and facility with language were long-discarded talents. She was out of her element here, managing things directly. It made Unnerby just a shade more confident.

Something buzzed in Pedure's jacket. Her little knife disappeared and she grabbed her phone. For a moment, the two spy chiefs looked like old friends, communing with their memories.

'*No!*' Pedure spasmed; her voice was a scream. She grabbed the phone with her eating hands, all but stuffed it into her maw. 'Not here! Not now!' The fact that they were a sudden spectacle did not seem to matter to her.

General Smith turned toward Unnerby. 'Everyone's schemes just went down the toilet, Sergeant. Three ice-launched missiles are coming our way. We've got about seven minutes.' For an instant, Unnerby's gaze caught on the dome above them. It was a thousand feet underground, proof against tactical fission bombs. But he knew the Kindred fleet had progressed to much bigger things. A triple launch would most likely be a deep-penetration strike. Even so – *I helped design this place.* There were stairs nearby, access to much deeper places. He reached for one of Smith's arms. 'Please, General. Follow me.' They started back across the proscenium.

Villains and good guys, Unnerby had seen courage and cowardice among them all. Pedure . . . well, Honored Pedure was almost twitching with panic. She twisted this way and that in little hops, screaming Tiefic into her telephone. Abruptly she stopped, and turned back to Smith. Terror warred with incredulous surprise. 'The missiles. They're *yours!* You—' With a shriek, she launched herself toward Smith's back, her knife a silver extension of her longest arm.

Unnerby slipped between them before Smith could even turn. He gave Honored Pedure the hard of his shoulders, sending her flying off the stage. Around them everything was confused. Pedure's people swarmed up from the floor, and were met by Smith's combateers swinging down from the visitors' gallery. Shock spread across the hall as cobbers lifted their heads from their readers and noticed just who was fighting. Then from high at the back there was a scream. 'Look! The network news! The Accord has launched missiles on us!'

Unnerby led the combateers and his General out a side entrance. They raced down stairs toward the hidden shafts that dropped to the security core. Seven minutes to live? Maybe. But suddenly Hrunkner's heart soared free. What was left was so simple, just as it had been with Victory long ago. Life and death, a few good troops, and a few minutes to decide it all.

55

Belga Underville was senior in the Command and Control Center. That really didn't count for much; Underville was Domestic Intelligence. What happened here could change her job forever, but she was out of this chain of command, just a link to civil defense and the King's household forces. Belga watched Elno Coldhaven, the shiny new Director of External Intelligence, the acting CO of the center. Coldhaven knew the firestorm of failures that had ended the career of his predecessor. He knew that Rachner Thract was no dummy and probably no traitor. And now Elno had the same job, and the chief was out of the country. He was operating very much without a safety net. More than once in the last few days he had taken Underville aside and earnestly asked her advice. She suspected that this had been the chief's reason for having her stay down here rather than return to Princeton.

The CCC was more than a mile inside the promontory headrock of Lands Command, beneath the old Royal Deepness. A decade ago, the Center had been a huge thing, dozens of intelligence techs with the funny little CRT displays of the era. Behind them had been glassed-in meeting rooms and oversight bridges for the presiding officers. But year by year, computer systems and networks improved. Now Accord Intelligence had better eyes and ears and automation, and the CCC itself was scarcely bigger than a conference room. A quiet, strange conference room of outward-sitting perches. The air was fresh, always lightly moving; bright lighting left no shadows. There were data displays, but now the simplest ones were twelve-color-capable. And there were still technicians, but each of them managed a thousand nodes scattered across the continent and into the near-space recon system. Indirectly, each had hundreds of specialists available for interpretation. Eight technicians, four field-rank officers, a commanding officer. Those were all that need be physically present.

The center screen showed the chief being introduced to Parliament. It was the same commercial feed that the rest of the world saw – External Intelligence had decided not to try to sneak special video into Parliament Hall. One of the techs was working with freeze-frames from the video. He popped up a composite of a dozen snippets, fiddled with the lighting. A scruffy-looking character appeared on the screen, the details of her dark clothing vague. Beside Belga, General Coldhaven said softly, 'Good. That's a positive identification. Ol' Pedure herself . . . She can't very well act when her own head is on the line.'

Underville listened with half her attention. There was so much going on . . . The General's speech was even more a shock than seeing Pedure. When Smith made the hostage offer, several of the technicians looked from their work, their eating hands frozen in their maws. 'God!' she heard Elno Coldhaven mutter.

'Yeah,' Belga whispered back. 'But if they go for it, we might have a way out.'

'If they pick the King as hostage. But if they want General Smith—' If Smith had to stay down South, things would get very complicated, especially for Elno Coldhaven. Coldhaven couldn't quite conceal his stark discomfort. *So this is news to him, too.*

'We can manage,' said Kred Dugway, the Director of Air Defense. Dugway was the only other general officer present. The AD director had been one of poor Thract's biggest critics, and Elno Coldhaven's former superior. And Dugway seemed to think he was still Elno's boss.

In the video from Southland, General Smith had climbed down from the speaker's perch. She handed her formal proposal to Tim Downing. The camera followed Smith offstage. 'She's headed for Pedure!'

Dugway chuckled. 'Now, *this* will be interesting.'

'Damn.' The camera had turned back to watch Major Downing hand out copies of the General's proposal.

'Can you give me anything on the chief? Does she still have audio?'

'Sorry, sir. No.'

Attention colors lit the Air Defense displays. The technician hunched down, hissed something over his voice link. Then, 'Sir, I don't understand quite what is happening, but—'

Dugway jabbed a hand at the composite situation map of Southland. 'Those are launches!'

Yes. Even Belga recognized the coding. Crosses marked the estimated launch sites. 'A launch of three. *Not* Southland-based; those are from ice subs. They could be—' They couldn't be anything but Kindred. Accord and Kindred were the only nations with missile-launching ice-tunnelers.

And now the first target estimates had appeared on the display. The three circles were all near the south pole.

Coldhaven made a chopping gesture at the attack-management technicians. 'Go to condition Most Bright.' On the main display, the news cameras were still panning around Parliament Hall, soaking up the reactions to General Smith's speech.

One of the attack-management techs rose from her perch. 'Sir! Those missiles are ours. They're from the Seventh, the *Icedug* and *Crawlunder!*'

'Say what?' General Coldhaven's voice cut through whatever his former boss had been about to say.

'Autologs from the ships themselves. I'm trying to get through to their captains right now, sir – we're still bidding each other's crypto.'

Dugway pounced on the report. 'And until we talk to them direct, I don't believe anything. I know those commanders. Something strange is going on here.'

'We have real launches and real targets, sir.' The technician tapped the crosses and circles.

Dugway: 'You have nothing but pretty lights!'

'It's across the secure net, sir, direct from our launch-detection satellites.'

Coldhaven motioned both of them to be quiet. 'This seems a bit like the problems my predecessor ran into.'

Dugway glared at his former protégé . . . and slowly the significance seemed to sink in. 'Yes . . .'

Coldhaven grunted. 'It's not just us. There have been rumors going around on the unswitched analog radio.' There were still people who used such things; Underville had rural agents who resisted all upgrades. The surprise was that anyone at Lands Command would seriously listen to such comm. Coldhaven noticed Belga's expression. 'My wife works in the technical museum out front.' A smile flitted across his aspect. 'She says her old-time radio friends aren't cranks. And now we're seeing the impossible, too. In the past we could blame the contradictions on someone else's idiocy. Now . . .' The arrival time on the shrinking target circles was barely three minutes away. The targeting satellites all agreed on their destination now: Southmost.

Underville boggled for a moment. All Rachner's paranoia – *true*? 'So maybe the launch is a fake. Anything we see—'

'At least anything we see on the net—'

'—could be a lie.' It was a technophobe's most extravagant nightmare.

The point was finally getting through to Dugway. A faith built over twenty years was being shattered. 'But the encryption, the crosschecking . . . what can we *do*, Elno?'

Coldhaven seemed to wilt. His theory was accepted, and that left them with disaster. 'We – we can shut down. Disassociate command and comm from the net. I've seen it as a war-game option – only *that* was on the net, too!'

Belga put a hand on his shoulders. 'I say do it. We can use analog radio from the museum. And I've got people, couriers. It will be slow—' Far too slow, but at least they would discover what they were up against.

There were others a moment away across the net – Nizhnimor, the King himself – and now nothing seemed unstable. Dugway was present, but Elno Coldhaven was the CCC commanding officer. Coldhaven hesitated, but didn't defer to Dugway. He called to his chief sergeant. 'Plan Network Corrupt. I want the notice hand-carried to the museum.'

'Yes, sir!' The tech had been following the conversation, and seemed not quite as dumbfounded as his seniors. The target circles showed two minutes to impact. On the video from Parliament Hall, stark chaos reigned. For an instant, Underville was caught by the horror of the scene. The poor cobbers. Before, war had been an ominous cloud on the horizon; now the Southland Elected found themselves at ground zero with less than two minutes to live. Some sat frozen, staring upward at where megatons would burst. Others were stampeding down the carpeted stairs, searching for some way out, some way downward. And somewhere beyond their view, General Smith was facing the same fate.

By some miracle, the senior sergeant had hardcopies of Plan Network Corrupt. He handed them to his techs and started the procedures for opening the CCC's blast doors.

But the doors were already opening. Belga stiffened. *Nothing* was supposed to come in until the shift ended, or Coldhaven gave the release code. A CCC guard entered with a confused backward gait, his rifle held at an uneasy port arms. 'I saw your clearance, ma'am, but no one is allowed—'

An almost familiar voice followed him. 'Nonsense. We have clearance, and you saw that the doors opened. Please stand aside.' A young lieutenant strode into the room. The plain black uniform, the slender, deadly build. It was as if Victory Smith had not only escaped from the South but had returned as young as the first time Underville had ever seen her. After the lieutenant came a huge corporal and a team of combateers. Most of the intruders carried stubby assault rifles.

General Dugway spouted indignant rage at the young lieutenant. Dugway was a fool. More than anything, this looked like a decapitating strike – but why weren't they shooting? Elno Coldhaven edged back around his desk, his hands reaching for some unseen drawer. Belga stepped between him and the intruders and said, 'You're Smith's daughter.'

The lieutenant snapped Underville a salute. 'Yes ma'am. Victory Lighthill, and this is my team. We're authorized by General Smith to make inspections per our best judgment. With all respect, ma'am, that's what we're here for now.'

Lighthill sidled past the frothing Director of Air Defense; old Dugway was angry beyond words. Behind Belga, and mostly shielded by her body, Elno Coldhaven was tapping out command codes.

Somehow Lighthill realized what was going on. 'Please step away from your console, General Coldhaven.' Her big corporal waggled his assault rifle in Coldhaven's direction. Now Underville recognized the corporal. Smith's retarded son. Damn.

Elno Coldhaven stepped back from his desk, his hands raised slightly in the air, acknowledging that they were far beyond any 'inspection.' The two techs nearest the door sprinted past the intruders. But these combateers were *fast*. They turned, pouncing on the techs, dragging them back into the CCC.

The blast doors swung slowly shut.

And Coldhaven made one more try, the most frail of all: 'Lieutenant, there's massive corruption in our signals automation. We have to get our Command and Control off the net.'

Lighthill stepped close to the displays. There was still a picture from Parliament Hall, but no one was behind the camera: the view wandered aimlessly, finally centering on the ceiling. Across the other displays, Most Bright lights had blossomed, queries to the Command Center, launch announcements from the King's Rocket Offense forces. The world coming to an end.

Finally, Lighthill spoke. 'I know, sir. We are here to prevent you from doing that.' Her combateers had spread around the now crowded Command and Control Center. Not a single tech or officer was out of their reach now. The big corporal was pulling open a cargo pannier, setting up additional equipment . . . game displays?

Dugway finally found his voice. 'We suspected a deepcover agent. I was sure it was Rachner Thract. What fools we were. All along it was Victory Smith working for Pedure and the Kindred.'

A traitor at the heart. It explained everything, but – Belga looked at the displays, the network-massaged reports of Accord launches coming in from all directions. She said, 'What of it is really true, Lieutenant? Is it all a lie, even the attack on Southmost?'

For a moment Underville thought the lieutenant wouldn't answer. The target circles at Southmost had shrunk to points. The news camera view of Parliament Hall dome lasted a second longer. Then Belga had a fleeting impression of the rock bulging downward, of light beyond – and the display went blank. Victory Lighthill flinched, and when she finally answered Belga, her voice was soft and hard. 'No. That attack was very real.'

56

'You're sure she'll be able to see me?'

Marli looked up from his gadgets. 'Yes, sir. And I've got a clear-to-talk from her huds.'

You're on, Podmaster. The greatest performance of your life. 'Qiwi! Are you there?'

'Yes, I—' and he heard Qiwi's quick intake of breath. Heard. There was no video coming back this way; the desperation of this situation was no fake. 'Father!'

Nau cradled Ali Lin's head and shoulders in his arms. The ziphead's wounds were gouges, oozing a swamp of blood through makeshift bandages. *Pest, I hope the guy isn't dead.* But above all, this had to look real; Marli had done his best.

'Tas Vinh, Qiwi. He and Trinli jumped us, killed Kal Omo. They would have killed Ali if . . . if I hadn't let them get away.' The words tumbled out, fueled by true rage and fear and guided by the tactical necessities. The savage attack of traitors, timed for when everything was most critical, when an entire civilization stood at risk. The destruction of North Paw. 'I saw two of the kittens drown, Qiwi. I'm sorry, we couldn't get close enough to save them—' Words failed him, but artfully.

He heard small choking sounds from the other end of the connection, the sounds Qiwi made in moments of absolute horror. Damn, that could start a memory cascade. He pushed down his fear and said, 'Qiwi, we still have a chance. Have the traitors shown themselves at Benny's?' *Has Pham Nuwen gotten through to the parlor?*

'No. But we know something has gone terribly wrong. We lost the video from North Paw, and now it looks like war down on Arachna. This is a private link, but everyone saw me leave Benny's.'

'Okay. Okay. This is good, Qiwi. Whoever are in this with Vinh and Trinli are still confused. We have a chance, the two of us—'

'But surely we can trust—' Qiwi's protest trailed off, and she didn't give him any argument. Good. This soon after a scrubbing, Qiwi was most unsure of herself. 'Okay. But *I* can help. Where are you hiding? One of the sluiceways?'

'Yes, trapped behind the outer hatch. But if we can get out, we can rescue the situation. L1-A has—'

'Which sluiceway?'

'Uh.' He looked at the face of the hatch. A number was just visible in Marli's light. 'S-seven-four-five. Does that—'

'I know where it is. I'll see you in two hundred seconds. Don't worry, Tomas.'

Lord. Qiwi's recovery was awesome. Nau waited a moment, then glanced questioningly at Marli.

'The connection is down, sir.'

'Okay. Realign. See if you can punch through to Ritser Brughel.' This might be his last chance to check on the ground operation before everything was settled, one way or another.

The *Invisible Hand* was over the horizon from Southmost when the missiles arrived there. Nevertheless, Jau's displays showed flashes against the upper atmosphere. And their trailing satellites relayed a detailed analysis of the destruction. All three nukes were on target.

But Ritser Brughel was not entirely happy, 'The timing wasn't right. They didn't get the best penetration.'

Bil Phuong's voice came over the bridge-wide channel. 'Yes, sir. That depended on high-level ordnance knowledge – things that are up on L1.'

'Okay. Okay. We'll make do. Xin!'

'Yes, sir?' Jau looked up from his console.

'Are your people ready to hit the missile fields?'

'Yes, sir. The burn we just completed will put us over most of them. We'll take out a good part of the Accord's forces.'

'Pilot Manager, I want you to personally—' A tone sounded on Braghel's console. There was no video, but the Vice-Podmaster was listening to something incoming. After a moment, Brughel said, 'Yes, sir. We can make up for that. What is your situation?'

What's happening up there? What's happening to Rita? Jau forced his attention away from the long-distance conversation, and looked at his own situation board. In fact, he was pushing his zipheads to the limit. They were beyond finesse now. There was no way they could disguise this operation from the Spider networks. The Accord missile fields stretched across a swath of the northern continent, and they only approximately followed the track of the *Invisible Hand*. Jau's pilots were coordinating a dozen ordnance zipheads. The *Hand*'s patchwork of battle lasers could take out near-surface launchpads, but only if they were given a fifty-millisecond dwell time. Hitting everything would be a miracle ballet of firepower. Some of the deepest targets, offensive sites, would be hit by digger bombs. Those had already been launched, were now arcing down behind them.

Jau had done everything he could to make this work. *I didn't have any choice.* Every few seconds, the mantra floated up through his consciousness, the response to the equally persistent *I am not a butcher.*

But now . . . now there might be a safe way to evade Brughel's terrible orders. *Be honest, you're still a butcher.* But of hundreds, not millions.

Without the detailed geographic and ordnance advice from L1, any number of small errors might be made. The Southmost strike showed that. Jau's fingers drifted over his keyboard, sending last-second advice to his team. The mistake was very subtle. But it would introduce a tree of random deviations into their attack on the antimissiles. Many of those strikes would now be way off target. The Accord would have a chance against the Kindred nukes.

Rachner Thract paced back and forth in the visitor holding box. How long could it take Underhill to come out? Maybe the cobber had changed his mind, or simply forgotten what he was about. The sentry looked upset, too. He was talking on some kind of comm line, his words inaudible.

Finally, there was the whine of hidden motors. A moment later the old wood doors slid aside. A guide-bug emerged, closely followed by Sherkaner Underhill. The guard came racing around his sentry box. 'Sir, could I have a word with you? I'm getting—'

'Yes, but let me talk to the Colonel here for just a moment.' Underhill seemed to sag under the weight of his parka, and every step took him steadily to the side. The sentry fidgeted by his post, not sure what to do. The guide-bug patiently dragged Underhill back onto a more or less straight path headed for Thract.

Underhill reached the visitor holding box. 'I have a few free minutes now, Colonel. I'm very sorry about your losing your job. I want to—'

'That's not important now, sir! I have to tell you.' It was a miracle that he had gotten through to Underhill. *Now, if I can just convince him before that sentry gets up the courage to intervene.* 'Our command automation is corrupt, sir. I have proof!' Underhill was raising his arms in protest, but Rachner rumbled on. This was his last chance. 'It sounds crazy, but it explains everything: There's an—'

The world exploded around them. Colors beyond color. Pain beyond the brightest sun of Thract's imagination. For a moment the color of pain was all there was, squeezing out consciousness, fear, even startlement.

And then he was back. In agony, but at least aware. He was lying in snow and random wreckage. His eyes . . . his eyes *hurt*. The afterimages of Hell were burned all across his foreview, blocking his vision. The afterimages showed stark silhouettes against a beam of utter darkness: the sentry, Sherkaner Underhill.

Underhill! Thract came to his feet, pushed aside the flat-boards that had fallen on him. Now other pains were surfacing. His back was a single massive ache. *Getting punched through walls will do that to you.* He took a few shaky steps, but nothing seemed broken.

'Sir? Professor Underhill?' His own voice seemed to be coming from a great distance. Rachner turned his head this way and that, like a child still with its baby eyes. He had no choice; his forevision was filled with burning afterimages. Downhill, along the curve of the caldera wall, there was a row of smoking holes. But the destruction here was enormously greater. None of the Underhill outbuildings still stood, and fire was spreading across all that was flammable. Rachner took a step toward where the sentry had been standing. But now that was the edge of a steep, steaming crater. The hillside above him was blown out. Thract had seen something like this before, but that had been a terrible accident, an ammo dump struck by penetrating artillery. *What hit us? What was Underhill storing below?* Something in the back of his mind was asking the questions, but he had no answers and plenty of more immediate concerns.

There was an animal hissing sound, right at his feet. Rachner turned his head. It was Underhill's guide-bug. Its fighting hands were poised to stab, but its body lay twisted in the wreckage. The poor beast's shell must be cracked. When he tried to sidle around it, the bug shrieked more fiercely and made a ghastly effort to pull its crushed body out from the flatboards.

'Mobiy! It's okay. It's okay, Mobiy.' It was Underhill! His voice was muffled, but so were all sounds just now. As Thract slipped past the guide-bug, it pulled its broken body from the flatboards and followed him toward Underhill's voice. But the bug's hissing was no longer a threat. It was more a sobbing whimper.

Thract walked along the edge of the crater. The edge was piled deep with debris that had been thrown up. The glassy sides were already slumping, collapsing inward. And still there was no sign of Underhill.

The guide-bug pulled himself past Thract. There, right ahead of the bug: a single Spiderly arm stuck sharp and high from the mangle. The guide-bug shrilled, and started feebly digging. Rachner joined him, pulling boards out of the way, shoveling the warm splatter dirt to the side. Warm? It was hot as the Calorica bottomland. There was something especially horrifying about being buried in warm earth. Thract dug desperately faster.

Underhill was buried rear-end down, his head just a foot below the air. In seconds, they had him free down past his shoulders. The ground lurched, sliding with the rest of the crater's edge. Thract reached out, twined his arms around Underhill's – and pulled. An inch, a foot . . . the two of them fell onto the high ground just as Underhill's grave slid into the pit.

The guide-bug crawled around them, his arms never letting go of his master. Underhill patted the animal gently. Then he turned, weaving his head about in the same silly way Thract had been. There were blisters in the crystal surfaces of his eyes. Sherkaner Underhill had shaded the blast from Thract's eyes; the whole top of the old cobber's head had been directly exposed.

Underhill seemed to be looking toward the pit 'Jaybert? Nizhnimor?' He said softly, disbelievingly. He came to his feet, and started for the drop-off. Both Thract and the bug held him. At first, Underhill let them guide him back over the crest of the splatter. It was hard to tell under the heavy clothes, but at least two of his legs seemed to be cracked.

Then: 'Victory? Brent? Can you hear me? I've lost—' He turned and started back toward the pit. This time, Rachner actually had to fight him. The poor cobber was drifting in and out of delirium. *Think!* Rachner looked downslope. The helipad was tilted but the ground above had shielded it from the flying debris. His chopper still sat there, apparently undamaged. 'Ah! Professor – there's a telephone in my helicopter. Come on, we can call the General from there.' The improvisation was thin, but Underhill was drifting in and out of delirium. He swayed for a moment, almost collapsed. Then a moment of false lucidity: 'A helicopter? Yes . . . I have a use for that.'

'Okay. Let's go down there.' Thract started for the top of the stairs, but Underhill still hesitated. 'We can't leave Mobiy. Nizhnimor and the others yes. They are surely dead. But Mobiy . . .'

Mobiy is dying. But Thract didn't say that aloud. The guide-bug had stopped crawling. Its arms waved gently in Underhill's direction. 'It's an animal, sir,' Thract said softly.

Underhill chuckled, delirious. 'That's all a matter of scale, Colonel.'

So Thract took off his outer jacket and made a sling for the guide-bug. The creature seemed like about eighty pounds of very dead weight. But they were going downhill, and now Sherkaner Underhill followed without further complaint, needing only occasional help to keep on the stairs. *So what better could you be doing now, eh, Colonel?* The lurking Enemy had finally pounced. Thract looked out across the caldera at the pattern of smoking destruction. Likely it was repeated on the altiplano, trashing the King's strategic defenses. Doubtless, the High Command had been nuked. *Whatever it was I came to do, it's too late now.*

57

The taxi floated up from the L1 jumble. Below them, the mouth of S745 was open, exhausting air and ice particles. If not for Qiwi, they would still be trapped behind the sluiceway's pressure hatch. Qiwi's landing and ad hoc lock work were something that even well-managed zipheads might not have accomplished.

Nau slid Ali Lin gently into the front seat beside Qiwi. The woman turned from her controls, and her face twisted in grief. 'Papa? Papa?' She reached to feel for his pulse, and her expression eased a fraction.

'I think he'll make it, Qiwi. Look, there's medical automation at L1-A, and—'

Qiwi pulled back into her seat. 'The arsenal . . .' But her gaze stayed on her father, and the horror was shading toward thoughtfulness. Abruptly, she looked away and nodded. 'Yes.'

The taxi boosted on its little reaction jets, sending Nau and his men on a quick scramble for handholds. Qiwi was overriding the taxi's sedate automation. 'What happened, Tomas? Do we have a chance?'

'I think so. If we can get into L1-A.' He related the story of treachery, almost the truth except for Ali Lin.

Qiwi slewed the taxi smoothly into its braking approach. But her voice was near sobbing. 'It's the Diem Massacre all over again, isn't it? And if we don't stop them this time, we'll all die. And the Spiders too.'

Bingo. If Qiwi hadn't been so freshly scrubbed, this would be a very dangerous line of thought. A few days more and she'd have a hundred little inconsistencies to piece together; she'd quickly see through it all. But now, for the next few Ksecs, the analogy with Diem played in his favor. 'Yes! But this time we have a chance to stop them, Qiwi.'

The taxi descended swiftly across Diamond One. The sun was like a dim red moon, its light glistening here and there off the last of their stolen snow. Hammerfest had disappeared around the corner. Most likely, Pham Nuwen was trapped in the Attic there. The fellow was a genius, but he'd achieved only half a victory. He had cut off ziphead services, but he hadn't stopped the Arachna operation, and he hadn't reached allies.

And in this game, half a victory was worth nothing. *In a few hundred seconds, I'll have the firepower at L1-A.* Strategy would crystalize in assured destruction, and Pham Nuwen's own moral weakness would give all the game to Tomas Nau.

Ezr never lost consciousness; if he had, there would have been no waking. But for a time, all awareness was centered within himself, on the numbing cold, the tearing pain in his shoulder and down his arm.

The urge to gasp air into his lungs became overpowering. Somewhere there must be air; the park had as much breathable space as ever. But *where*? He turned in the direction where the fake sunlight was brightest. Some remnant of reason noted that the water had come out of that direction. It would be falling now. *Swim toward the brightness.* He kicked feebly and as hard as he was able, guiding with his good hand.

Water. More water. Water forever. Reddish in the sunlight.

He burst through the surface, coughing and vomiting, and *breathing* at last. The sea lay around him. It writhed and climbed, with no horizon. It was like something from a Canberra swords-and-pirates story he had watched as a child; he was a sailor trapped in a final maelstrom. He stared up and up. The water curved around and closed above his head. His seascape was a bubble, perhaps five meters across.

With orientation came something like rational thought. Ezr twisted, looked down and behind him. No sign of pursuers. But maybe it didn't matter. The water around him was stained with his own blood; he could *taste* it. The cold that had slowed the flow of blood and numbed some of the pain was also paralyzing his legs and his good arm.

Ezr stared through the water, trying to estimate how far his air bubble was from the outer surface. The water on the sun side did not seem deep, but . . . He looked down and back toward what had been the forest. Through the blur and the flow, he could see the ruins of the trees. Nowhere was this water more than a dozen meters deep. *I'm out of the main mass.* His bubble was itself part of a free droplet drifting slowly across North Paw's sky.

Drifting *downward*, by some combination of microgravity and the sea's collision with the cavern roof. Ezr watched numbly as the ground came up around him. He would hit the lake bed, just off the lodge's moorage.

When it came, the collision was dreamlike slow, less than a meter per second. But the water swept swiftly around him, spraying and streaming. He hit on his legs and butt and bounced upward, sharing space with a tumble of jiggling, spinning blobs of water. All around him was a clacking sound, a mindless mechanical applause. The stone casement of the seawall was less than a meter away. He reached out, almost stopped his spin. Then his bad shoulder touched the casement, and everything disappeared in a blaze of agony.

He was gone for only a second or two. When consciousness returned, he saw that he was about five meters above the seabed. Near him, the stones of the casement were covered with a line of moss and stain, the old sea level. And the clacking applause . . . he looked across the seabed. He could see them in their hundreds, the stabilizer servos, pursuing the same sabotage that had set the sea to marching.

Ezr climbed the rough-cut stone of the seawall. It was only a few meters to the top, to the lodge . . . to where the lodge had been. There were recognizable foundations. The stubs of wall frames still stood. But a million tonnes of water, even moving slow, had been enough to sweep the place away. Here and there, rubble swayed up, snagged in the deeper wreckage.

Ezr moved from point to point, using his good hand to climb across the ruins. The sea had settled into a deep layer that hugged the forests and climbed the far walls of the cavern. It still roiled and shifted. Ten-meter blobs of water still coasted across the sky. Much of the sea might eventually pool back in the basin, but Ali Lin's masterpiece was destroyed.

Things were getting fuzzy and dim; he didn't hurt as much as before. Somewhere out there in the drowned forest, Tomas Nau was trapped along with his merry men. Ezr remembered the triumph he had felt when he saw them sinking into the trees beneath the water. *Pham, we won.* But this wasn't the original plan. In fact, Nau had somehow seen through them, almost killed them both. Nau might not be trapped at all. If he could get out of the cavern, he could track down Pham or get to L1-A.

But the fear was far away, receding. Ribbons of sticky red water floated around him now. He bent his head to look at his arm. Marli's wire gun had shattered his elbow, opening an artery. The previous wound in his shoulder, and the torture, had created a kind of accidental tourniquet, but *I'm bleeding out.* Logically, the thought was cause for frantic alarm, but all he really wanted to do was let loose of the ground and rest awhile. *And then you die, and then maybe Tomas Nau wins.*

Ezr forced himself to keep moving. If he could stop the bleeding . . . but no way could he even take off his jacket. His mind drifted away from the impossible. Grayness crept in around the edges of his mind. *What can I do in the seconds I have left?* He picked his way across the wreckage, his vision narrowed down to the ground just centimeters from his face. If he could find Nau's den, even a comm set. *At least I could warn Pham.* There was no comm set, just endless rubble. The fine woods that Fong had grown were all kindling now, their spiral grain shattered.

A naked white arm reached from beneath a crushed armoire. Ezr's mind stumbled on the horror and the mystery. *Who did we leave behind?* Omo, yes. But this limb was naked, glistening, bloodless white. He touched the hand at the end of the arm. It twitched, slid around his fingers. Ah, not a corpse at all, just one of those full-press jackets that Nau favored. An idea floated up from the dimness, *Maybe to stop the bleeding.* He tugged on the jacket sleeve. It slid, caught, and then floated free. He lost his grip on the ground, and for a moment it was a dance between himself and the jacket. The left sleeve slit open, forking down through the fingers. He slipped his arm along its length and the jacket closed from fingers to shoulder. He pulled the fabric across his back, and fit the right side loosely around his mangled arm. Now he could bleed to death, and no one would see another drop. *Tighten the fabric.* He shrugged it snug. *Tighter,* a real tourniquet. He slid his left hand down the cover of his ruined arm, squeezing agony from the flesh beneath. But the full-press fabric responded, stiffening. Far away, he heard himself groan with pain. He lost consciousness for a moment, woke lying lightly on his head.

But now his right arm was immobilized, the full-press sleeve at maximum tension. Such a painful extreme of fashion, but it might be enough to keep him alive.

He drank from drifting water, and tried to think.

There was a querulous mewing sound behind him. The sky-kitten slid into view, settled onto his chest and good arm. He reached up, felt the trembling body. 'You in trouble too?' he asked. His words came as croaks. The kitten's great dark eyes peered back at him and it burrowed deeply at the space between his chest and left arm. Strange. Normally, a sick kitten would go off and hide; that had caused Ali lots of problems, even though the creatures were tagged. The sky-kitten was soaked, but it seemed alert. Maybe, 'You came to comfort me, Little One?'

He could feel it purring now, and the warmth of its body. He smiled; just having someone to listen made him feel more alert.

There was a thutter of wings. Two more kittens. Three. They hung above him and meowed irritably as if to say, 'What have you done with our park,' or maybe 'We want dinner.' They swirled around him, but didn't chase the little one from his arms. Then the largest, a rag-eared tom, swooped away from Ezr and settled on the highest point in the ruin. He glowered down at

Ezr, and began grooming his wings. The damn creature didn't even look wet.

The highest point left in the ruin . . . a diamond tube almost two meters across, surmounted by a metal cap. Ezr suddenly realized what he was looking at: a tunnel head in Tomas Nau's den, most likely a direct route to L1-A. He coasted up the hill to the metal-topped pillar. The tom hunkered down, reluctant to move out of Ezr's way. Even now the creatures were as possessive as ever.

The control lights on the hatch glowed pass-green.

He looked at the big tom. 'You know you're sitting on the key to everything, don't you, fellow?'

He gently disengaged the littlest kitten from his jacket, and shooed them all away from the hatch mechanism. It slid back, locked itself open. Would the little stupids try to follow? He gave them a last wave. 'Whatever you may think, you really don't want to come with me. Gun wire hurts.'

The Attic grouproom was crammed with extra seating; there was scarcely room to maneuver around the edges. And the moment Silipan turned off the zipheads' comm links, the place turned into a madhouse. Trud dived away from the reaching arms, retreated to the control area at the top of the room. 'They really *really* don't like to be taken off their work.'

It was worse than Pham had thought it would be. If the zipheads hadn't been tied down, he and Trud would have been attacked. He looked back at the Emergent. 'It had to be done. This is the core of Nau's power, and now it's denied him. We're taking over all across L1, Trud.'

Silipan's stare was glassy. There had been too many shocks. 'All over L1? That's impossible . . . You've killed us all, Pham. You've killed me.' Some alertness returned; no doubt he was imagining what Nau and Brughel would do to him.

Pham steadied him with his free hand. 'No. I intend to win. If I do, you'll survive. So will the Spiders.'

'What?' Trud bit his lip. 'Yeah, cutting off support will slow Ritser. Maybe those damned Spiders will have a chance.' His gaze became distant, then snapped back to Pham's face. 'What are you, Pham?'

Pham answered softly, pitching his voice just over the shouted demands from the zipheads. 'Just now, I'm your only hope.' He drew Silipan's confiscated huds from his jacket pocket, and handed them to the man.

Trud carefully straightened the crumpled material and slipped them over his eyes. He was silent for a moment, then: 'We have more huds. I can get you a pair.'

Pham smiled the foxy grin that Silipan had never seen till two hundred seconds ago. 'That's okay. I have something better.'

'Oh.' Trud's voice was small.

'Now I want you to do a damage assessment. Is there any way you can get work from your people here, with Nau cut off?'

Trud shrugged angrily. 'You know that's imposs—' He looked up again at Pham. 'Maybe, maybe there are some trivial things. We do offline computing. I might be able to trick the numerical control zipheads . . .'

'Good man. Calm these people down, see if any of them will help us.'

They parted. Silipan descended to the zipheads, talked soothing words, bagged the floating vomitus that the sudden upset had generated. The shouting only got louder:

'I need the tracking updates!'

'Where are the translations on the Kindred response?'

'You stupids, you've lost the comm!'

Pham slid sideways across the ceiling, looking downward through the ranks of seated zipheads, listening to the complaints. On the far wall, Anne and her other assistant floated motionless on grabfelt rests. She should be safe and out of it. *Your final battle is being fought, just a century or two after you thought all was lost.*

The vision behind Pham's eyes faded in and out. In most of the Attic, he'd been able to restart the microwave pulse power. He had perhaps one hundred thousand localizers in reach and alive. It was a bright meta-light extending his vision in disjoint fingers through the Attic, to wherever a cloud of localizers had come alive and could find a thread of links back to him.

Status, status. Pham scanned across the readouts on zip-heads in the grouproom and beyond. There were only a few still locked in their roomlets in the capillary tunnels, specialists that hadn't been needed in the current operation. Many of them had gone into convulsive tantrums when their job stream was blocked. Pham eased into the control system and opened some of the incoming communications. There were things he had to know, and it might ease the discomfort of the Focused. Trud looked up uneasily; he could tell that someone was messing with his system.

Pham reached beyond the Attic, searching for some glimmer from localizers on the rockpile's surface. There! One or two isolated images, low-rate and monochrome. He had a glimpse of a taxi coming down on naked rock, near Hammerfest. Damn, sluiceway S745. If Nau could negotiate that lockless hatch, there was no doubt where he'd go next.

For a fleeting moment Pham felt the overwhelming fear of facing an unstoppable adversary. *Ah, it's like being young again.* He had perhaps three hundred seconds before Nau got to L1-A. No point in holding anything back. Pham sent out the command to bring all reachable localizers online – even the ones without power. Their tiny capacitors held enough charge for a few dozen packets each. Used cleverly, he could get a fair amount of I/O.

Behind his eyes, pictures slowly formed, bit by bit by bit.

Pham slid around three walls, staying carefully beyond the zipheads' reach, occasionally dodging a thrown keyboard or drinking bulb. But the renewed incoming data flow was having some calming effect. The translator section was almost quiet, their talk mostly directed at one another. Pham drifted down next to Trixia Bonsol. The woman was hunched over her keyboards with fierce intentness. Pham plugged into the data stream that was coming up from the *Invisible Hand*. There should be some good news there, Ritser and company bogged down just when they were ready to commit mass murder . . .

It took him an instant to orient to the multiplex stream. There was stuff for the translators, trajectory data, launch codes. *Launch codes?* Brughel was going ahead with Nau's sucker punch! The execution was awkward; the Accord would be left with a good fraction of its weapons. Ballistics were arcing up, dozens of launches per second.

For a moment, Pham's attention was swallowed by the horror of it. Nau had conspired to kill half the people in a world. Ritser was doing his best to accomplish the murders. He stepped through the log of Trixia Bonsol's last few hundred seconds. The log had gone berserk when her job stream had been cut off, a metaphorical upchuck. There were pages of disordered nonsense, a gabble of files that showed no last-access date. His eyes caught on a passage that almost made sense:

It is an edged cliché that the world is most pleasant in the years of a Waning Sun. It's true that the weather is not so driven, that everywhere there is a sense of slowing down, and most places experience a few years where the summers do not burn and the winters are not yet overly fierce, it is the classic time of romance. It's a time that seductively beckons higher creatures to relax, postpone. It's the last chance to prepare for the end of the world.

By blind good fortune, Sherkaner Underhill chose the most beautiful days in the years of the Waning for his first trip to Lands Command . . .

It was clearly one of Trixia's translations, the sort of 'human-colored' description that irritated Ritser Brughel so much. But Underhill's 'first trip to Lands Command'? That would be before the last Dark. Strange that Tomas Nau had wanted such retrospectives.

'It's all messed up now.'

'What?' Pham's mind came back to the Attic grouproom, the irritable voices of the zipheads. It was Trixia Bonsol who had just spoken. Her eyes were distant and her fingers still twitched across her keys.

Pham sighed. 'Yeah, you got that right,' he replied. Whatever she was talking about, the comment was appropriate.

His low-rate synthesis from the unpowered net was complete: He had a view down on L1-A. If he could trigger a little more connectivity, he might reach the ejets near L1-A. No great processing power there, but those sites were on the ejet power grid . . . and more important, *Maybe we can use the electric jets themselves!* If they could target a few dozen of them on the Podmaster . . . 'Trud! Have you had any luck with the numerical people?'

58

Rachner Thract's helicopter lifted clean of the tilted landing pad, its turbine and rotor sounds healthy. By turning his head this way and that, Thract was able to keep track of the terrain. He took them eastward, along the caldera wall. The punched-hole craters marched off ahead of them, a line of destruction that disappeared over the top of the far wall. In the city below, there were emergency lights now, and ground traffic heading for the craters that had been apartments and occupied mansions.

On the perch beside him, Underhill was moving feebly, pulling at the panniers on his guide-bug's back. The animal was trying to help, but it was injured far worse than its master. 'I need to see, Rachner. Can you help me with Mobiy's pack?'

'Just a minute, sir. I want to bring us around to the heliport.'

Underhill pushed a few inches up from his perch. 'Just put it on autopilot, Colonel. Please, help me.'

Thract's helicopter contained dozens of embedded processors, themselves hooked into traffic control and information nets. Once he had been very proud of this fancy aircraft. He hadn't flown it on automatic since that last staff meeting at Lands Command. 'Sir . . . I don't trust the automatics.'

Underhill gave a gentle laugh, then broke into liquid coughing. 'It's okay, Rach. Please, I have to see what's happening. Help me with Mobiy.'

Yes! By the Dark, what did it matter now! Rachner slammed four hands into the control sockets, and wiggled on full auto. Then he turned to his passengers and quickly unzipped the bag on the top of Mobiy's broken back.

Underhill reached in and removed the gear within as if it were some King's crown jewels. Rachner turned his head for a closer look. What . . . a bloody computer game helmet, it was!

'Ah, it looks okay,' Underhill said softly. He started to settle the helmet across his eyes, then winced away. Rachner could see why; there were blisters all across the cobber's eyes. But Underhill didn't give up. He held the device just off his head, then turned on the power.

Glittering light splashed out and around his head. Rachner jerked back reflexively. The cabin of the heli was suddenly awash in a million shifting colors, bright and plaid. He remembered the rumors about Underhill's crazy hobbies, the videomancy. So it had all been true; this 'gaming helmet' must have cost a small fortune.

Underhill mumbled to himself, shifting the helmet this way and that, as if to see around the blind spots in his burned eyes. There really wasn't much to see, just an incredibly beautiful shifting of lights, the mesmerizing power of computers in the service of quackery. It seemed to satisfy Sherkaner Underhill. He stared and stared, petting his guide-bug with a free hand. 'Ah . . . I see,' he said softly.

And the helicopter's turbines suddenly began a banshee twistup, well past their redline. The power was like magic, and would burn them out in a matter of an hour or two. That's why no reasonable controls would allow such performance.

'What the devil—' The words caught in Thract's throat as the turbine windup finally reached the blades above. His aircraft suddenly became a maniac, clawing its way up and up, over the caldera ridge.

The turbines briefly idled as the helicopter soared over the top, five hundred feet, a thousand feet above the altiplano. Rachner had a glimpse of the flatlands. The single row of destruction they had seen at Calorica was actually part of a grid. Stretched out south and west of them were hundreds of steaming plumes. *The antimissile fields.* But the crappers had missed! Wave after wave of interceptor rockets were sweeping up from their silos across the altiplano. Hundreds of launches, quick and profligate as short-range rocket artillery—except that the silos were dozens of miles away. Those rocket plumes were pushing smart payloads toward long-range intercepts thousands of miles away, and scores of miles up. It was awesome beyond all the staff-meeting hype that Air Defense had ever shilled . . . and it must mean that the Kindred had just launched everything they had.

Sherkaner Underhill didn't seem to notice. He moved his head back and forth under the helmet's light show. 'There has to be some reconnect. There has to be.' His hands twitched at the game controls. Seconds passed. 'It's all messed up now,' he sobbed.

Trud left his numerical-control zipheads and rejoined Pham Trinli by the translators. 'The pure numericals I can manage, Pham. I mean I can get answers. But for control—'

Trinli just nodded, brushing the objections aside. *Trinli looks so different. I've known him years of Watch time, and now he's a different person.* The old Pham Trinli had been loud and arrogant, a bluster that you could argue and joke with. This Pham was quieter, but his actions were like knives. *Killing us all.* Trud's eyes slid unwillingly to where Anne Reynolt's body hung like meat on a hook. And even if he could conceive a scheme to betray Pham, it probably wouldn't save him. Nau and Brughel were Podmasters, and Trud knew he had passed beyond foriveness.

'—still a chance, Trud.' Pham's voice cut through his fear. 'Maybe we could open things a little further, fool the zipheads into—'

Silipan shrugged. Not that it mattered, but, 'Do that and the Podmaster will be down our throat instantly. I'm getting fifty service requests a second from Nau and Brughel.'

Pham rubbed his temples and his eyes got a faraway look. 'Yeah, I see what you're saying. Okay. What do we have? The temp—'

'The cameras at Benny's show a lot of very puzzled people. If they're lucky they'll stay where they are.' And afterward the Podmasters would have no claim of vengeance on them.

One of the zipheads – Bonsol – interrupted, the typical irrelevance of the Focused: 'There are millions of people on the ground. They will start dying in a few seconds.'

The comment actually seemed to derail Pham. Even the new Pham Trinli was still an amateur when it came to dealing with zipheads. 'Yeah,' he said, more to himself than to Silipan or the ziphead. 'But at least the Spiders have a chance. Without our zipheads, Ritser can't tighten the screws any more.' Of course, Bonsol ignored the reply, just went on tapping at her keys.

Trinli's attention snapped back to Silipan. 'Look. Nau is in a taxi, coming in on the L1-A site. There are electric stab jets all over the area. If we can get a few zipheads to work them—'

Trud felt anger sweeping up. Whatever he was, Pham Trinli was still a fool. 'Plague take you! You just don't understand Focused loyalty! We need to—'

Bonsol interrupted. 'Ritser can't tighten the screws, but we can't loosen them either.' She was laughing, almost inaudibly. 'What an intriguing thing. We have a deadlock.'

Trud motioned for Pham to move back toward the ceiling, out of range of this random ziphead commentary. 'They'll go on like that forever.'

But Pham turned back to the ziphead, abruptly giving her all his attention. 'What do you mean "we have a deadlock"?' he said quietly.

'Pus take it, Pham! What does it matter!' But Trinli jerked his hand up, commanding silence. The gesture had the peremptory confidence of a senior Podmaster – and Silipan's protests died on his lips. Inside, his fear just grew and grew. So much for miracles. If there had been any chance for keeping Nau out of L1-A, it was vanishing in this delay. And Silipan knew what was in L1-A. Oh yes. Beyond all automation and subtlety, L1-A would give the Podmaster back his absolute power. The clock at the corner of Trud's vision counted mercilessly on, the seconds of life dribbling out. And of course, the ziphead wasn't even paying attention to Pham, much less his question.

The silence stretched for ten or fifteen seconds. Then, abruptly, Bonsol's head snapped up and she stared directly into Pham's eyes – the way a ziphead almost never did, except when role-playing. 'I mean you're block-ing us and we're blocking you,' she said. 'My victory thought you were all monsters, that we couldn't trust any of you. And now we are all paying for that mistake.'

It was ziphead nonsense, just more portentous than most. But Pham pulled himself down to Bonsol's chair. His mouth was half-open as if in unutterable surprise, the look of a man whose world has suddenly been blown apart, who is falling headlong into insanity. And when he finally spoke, his words were crazy, too. 'I – mostly we're not monsters. If the deadlock were to end, can you run everything? And afterwards . . . we would be at your mercy afterwards. How can we trust you?'

Bonsol's gaze had wandered. She didn't answer, and her hands roamed her console. Silent seconds ticked by, but now a cold surmise stole up Trud's spine. *No.*

Sharp on ten seconds, Trixia Bonsol spoke again: 'If you restore full access, we can control the most important things. At least that was the plan. As for trust . . .' Bonsol's face twisted in a strange smile, mocking and wistful all at once. 'Well, you know us much better than the reverse. You must choose your own monsters.'

'Yes,' said Pham. He rubbed his temple and squinted at something invisible to Trud. He turned to Silipan, and he was smiling the same feral smile as when he had popped up in the supply closet, the smile of someone who is risking everything – and expects to win. 'Let's restore all the comm links, Trud. It's time to give Nau and Brughel the ziphead support they deserve.'

59

Nau watched Qiwi guide their taxi in; ahead and below were the snow mounds that he had piled around the L1-A lock. With only the automation aboard the taxi, Qiwi had found the sluiceway, overridden the hatch safeties, and rescued them – all in a few hundred seconds. If only she would last a few more seconds, he would have an absolute whip hand. If only she would last that few more seconds . . . He saw the looks she was giving her father. The sight of Ali was somehow pushing her toward the edge of understanding. *Pestilence! Just get us safely down, that's all I ask.* Then he could kill her.

Marli looked up from his comm gear. There was surprised relief on his face. 'Sir! I'm getting acks back from the ziphead channels. We should have full automation in a few seconds.'

'Ah.' Finally some unexpected good news. Now he could limit the destruction necessary to regain control. *Except this is Pham Nuwen you're up against, and almost anything is possible.* This could be some incredible masquerade. 'Very good, Podcorporal. But for the moment, don't use that automation.'

'Yes, sir.' Marli sounded puzzled.

Nau looked out the taxi's window. Strange to be seeing raw nature with no enhancement. The L1-A lock was about seventy meters away now, deep in shadow; There was something strange about it . . . the lip of metal was highlighted in red. *But I'm not wearing huds.*

'Qiwi—'

'I see it. Someone is—'

There was a loud snapping sound. Marli screamed. His hair was on fire. The hull by his seat was glowing red.

'Shit!' Qiwi boosted the taxi up. 'They're using *my* electric jets!' She spun the taxi even as she jinked it back and forth. Nau's stomach crawled up his gut. *Nothing is supposed to fly like this.*

The glow on the L1-A lock, the hot spot in the hull behind him – the enemy must be using all the stab jets within line of sight. Each jet by itself could only be an accidental, local danger. Somehow, Nuwen had ganged dozens of them to shine precisely on the two targets that mattered.

Marli was still screaming. Qiwi's piloting jammed Nau up into his restraints, turned him as he came back down. He had a glimpse of the podcoporal in the arms of his fellows. As least he wasn't burning anymore. The other guards' eyes were wide. 'X rays,' one of them said. The splash from those electron beams could fry them all. A long-term peril, all things considered—

Still spinning the taxi, Qiwi swung them close to the hillsides of Diamond One. The craft was precessing now, a wild triple spin. No way could the enemy keep their guns on one spot. And yet, the glow in the wall grew brighter with each rev. *Pestilence.* Somehow Nuwen had full system automation.

The nose and then the butt of the taxi smashed into the ground, splashing snow up from the surface. The hull groaned but held. And now, in the floating haze of rising volatiles, Nau could see the beams of the ejets. The ice and air in their way exploded into incandescence. Five beams, maybe ten, they shifted in and out as the taxi spun, and several were always on the glowing spot in their hull.

Around them the swirl of vapor and ice grew thicker. The glowing spot in the hull began to dim as the snows soaked and diffused the murderous beams. Qiwi damped their spin with four precise bursts of attitude control, at the same time snaking their craft over the boiling snows toward the L1-A airlock.

Peering forward, Nau saw the lock approach from dead ahead, a certain crash. But somehow Qiwi was still in control. She flipped the taxi up, slamming the docking collar into its mate on the lock. There was the sound of bending metal, and then they were stopped.

Qiwi tapped at the lock controls, then bounded out of her chair, to the forward hatch mechanism. 'It's jammed, Tomas! Help me!'

And now they were locked down, trapped like dogs in a pit shoot. Tomas rushed forward, braced himself, and pulled with Qiwi at the taxi hatch. It was jammed. Almost jammed. Together, they pulled it partway open. He reached through, spent precious seconds clearing security on the L1-A hatch. *All right!*

He looked over Qiwi's head at the hull behind them. The red spot was more like a bull's-eye now, a ring of red, a ring of orange, and glaring white in the middle. It was like standing in front of an open kiln.

The white-hot center bubbled outward, and was gone. All around them was a cascading thunderclap of departing atmosphere.

Things had been very quiet since Victory Lighthill took the Command and Control Center. The Intelligence techs had been moved away from their perches. They and the staff officers had been herded back against Underville, Coldhaven, and Dugway. *Like bugs at a slaughter-suck*, thought Belga. But it didn't matter. The situation map showed that much of the world was going down to slaughter now:

The tracks of thousands of Kindred missiles curved across the map, and more were being launched each second. There were target circles drawn across every Accord military site, every city – even the trad deepnesses.

And the strange *Accord* launchings that had showed just after Lighthill arrived – those had disappeared from the maps. Lies, no longer needed.

Victory Lighthill walked up and down the line of perches, gazing briefly over the shoulders of each of her techs. She seemed to have forgotten Underville and the others. And strangely, she seemed just as horror-struck as CCC's proper occupants. She wheeled on her brother, who seemed quite in another world, entertaining himself with his game helmet. 'Brent?'

The big corporal groaned. 'I'm sorry, I'm sorry. Calorica is still down. Sis . . . I think they hit Dad.'

'But how? There's no way they could know!'

'I dunno. Only the low-level ones are talking, and by themselves, they're never very helpful. I think it happened a while ago, just after we lost contact with the High Perch—' He paused, communing with his game? Light leaked from the edges of his helmet, flickering. Then: 'He's back! Listen!'

Lighthill brought a phone to the side of her head. 'Daddy!' Joyous as a cobblie home from school. 'Where—?' Her eating hands clasped each other in surprise and she shut up, listening to some extended speech. But she was almost bouncing with excitement, and her renegades were suddenly pounding on their consoles.

Finally: 'We copy all, Daddy. We—' She paused, watching her techs for an instant. '—we're getting control, just like you say. I think we can do it, but for God's sake, route through someplace closer. Twenty seconds is just too long. We need you now more than ever!' And then she was talking to her techs. 'Rhapsa, target only the ones we can't stop from above. Birbop, fix this damn routing—'

And on the situation map . . . the missile fields across High Equatoria had come alive. The map showed the colored traces of dozens, hundreds of antimissiles, the long-range interceptors arcing up to meet the enemy. More lies? Belga looked across the suddenly joyous aspects of Lighthill and the other intruders, and felt hope climbing into her own heart.

The first contacts were still half a minute away. Belga had seen the simulations. At least five percent of the attacking missiles would get through. The deaths would be a hundred times more than during the Great War, but at least it wasn't annihilation . . . But other things were happening on the map. Well behind the leading wave of the attack, here and there, enemy markers were *vanishing*.

Lighthill waved at the display, and for the first time since the takeover addressed Underville and the others. 'The Kindred had callback capability on some of their missiles. We're using that wherever we can. Some of the others, we can attack from above.' *From above?* As if by an invisible eraser, sweeping northward over the continent, a swath of missile markers disappeared. Lighthill turned toward Coldhaven and the other officers, and came to full attention. 'Sir, ma'am. Your people might be best at managing the amissiles. If we can coordinate—'

'Damn, yes!' chorused Dugway and Coldhaven. The techs rushed back to their places. There were precious lost moments, re-upping target lists, and then the first of the amissiles scored.

'Positive EMP!' shouted one of the AD techs. Somehow it seemed more real than all the rest.

General Coldhaven dipped a hand at Lighthill, an odd sort of reverse salute. Lighthill said quietly, 'Thank you, sir. This isn't quite what the chief planned, but I think we can make it work . . . Brent, see if you can make the situation map completely truthful.'

. . . Hundreds of new markers glittered across the board. But they weren't missiles. Belga knew the tags well enough to recognize satellites, though these looked like broken graphics. There were missing data fields and there were fields that contained nonsense strings. Moving off the north edge of the display was a strange rectangle. It pulsed with chevron modifiers. General Dugway hissed. 'That can't be true. A dozen size-chevrons. That would make it a thousand feet long.'

'Yes, sir,' said Lieutenant Lighthill. 'The standard display programs can't quite handle this. That vehicle is almost two thousand feet long.' She didn't seem to notice the look that came over Dugway. She contemplated the apparition a second longer. 'And I think it has just about outlived its usefulness.'

Ritser Brughel seemed pleased with himself. 'We've done pus good even without Reynolt's people.' The VicePodmaster came over from his Captain's chair to hover beside his Pilot Manager. 'Maybe we launched a few more nukes than precisely needed, but that balanced your botch of the amissile fields, eh?' He slapped Xin familiarly on the shoulder. Jau had the sudden realization that his single, frail treason had been detected.

'Yes, sir' was all he could think to say. Ahead, the curve of the planet glittered with a web of lights, the cities they had come to call Princeton, Valdemon, Mountroyal. Maybe the Spiders weren't the people Rita imagined, maybe that was a fraud of translation. But whatever the truth, those cities were in the last seconds of their existence.

'Sir.' Bil Phuong's voice came across bridge-wide comm. 'I've got a high-level ack from Anne's people. We'll have full automation in a matter of seconds.'

'Ha. About time.' But there was a note of relief in Ritser Brughel's voice.

Jau felt a mutter of vibration. Again. Again. Brughel's head snapped up, and he gazed off at a virtual display. 'That sounds like our battle lasers, but—'

Jau's eyes flickered across the status listings. The weapons board was clean. Core power had jagged as if charging capacitors – but now that was level, too. And, 'My pilots aren't reporting any fire, sir.'

Thutter. Thutter. They had passed over the great cities, were coasting north into the arctic, over tiny lights scattered across an immensity of dark, frozen land. Nothing there, but behind them . . . *Thutter.* The sky lit with three pale beams, diverging, fading . . . the classic look of battle lasers in upper atmosphere.

'Phuong! What the fuck is going on down there!'

'Nothing, sir! I mean—' Sounds of Phuong moving among his zipheads. 'Uh, the zips are working on valid target lists from L1.'

'Well, they're totally out of synch with *my* target list. Pull your head out, man!' Brughel cut the connection and turned back to his Pilot Manager. The Podmaster's pale face was ruddy with building anger. 'Shoot the bloody zips and get new ones!' He glared at Jau. 'So what's your problem?'

'I – maybe nothing, but we're being illuminated from below.'

'Hunh.' Brughel squinted at the electronic intelligence. 'Yeah. Ground radars. But this happens several times on every rev . . . oh.'

Xin nodded. 'This contact has lasted fifteen seconds. It's like they're tracking us.'

'That's impossible. We *own* the Spider nets.' Brughel bit his lip. 'Unless Phuong has totally screwed up the L1 comm.'

The radar tag faded for a moment . . . and then it was back, brighter, focused. 'That's a targeting lock!'

Brughel jerked as if the image had turned into a striking snake. 'Xin. Take control. Main torch if it will help. Get us out of here.'

'Yes, sir.' There weren't many missile sites in the Spiders' far north. But what there were would be nuke armed. Even a single hit could cripple the *Hand*. Jau reached to enable his pilots—

—and the rumble of auxiliary thrusters filled the bridge.

'That wasn't me, sir!'

Brughel had been looking right at him when the sound began. He nodded. 'Get through to your pilots. Get control!' He bounced up from his place beside Xin and waved to his guards toward the aft hatch. 'Phuong!'

Jau pounded frantically on his controls, shouted the command codes over and over. He saw scattered diagnostics, but no response from his pilots. The horizon had tilted slightly. The *Hand*'s auxiliaries were being run full-out, but not by Jau. Slowly, slowly, the ship seemed to be coming back to a nose-down, cruise attitude. Still no response from his pilots, but – Jau noticed the rising trace from the power core.

'Main torch burn, sir! I can't stop it—'

Brughel and his guards grabbed for hold-ons. The torch subsonics were unmistakable, vibrating out from bones and teeth. Slowly, slowly, the acceleration ramped up. Fifty milligees. One hundred. Loose junk floated faster and faster sternward, spinning and bouncing off obstacles. Three hundred milligees. A huge gentle fist pressed Jau back into his chair. One of the guards had been in open space, unable to reach a hold-down. He drifted past now, he *fell* past, crashing into the aft wall. Five hundred milligees, and still increasing. Jau twisted in his harness and looked back, up, at Brughel and the others. They were pinned aft, trapped by the acceleration that went on and on . . .

And then the torch sound faded, and Jau floated up in against his restraints. Brughel was shouting to his guards, gathering them together. Somewhere in the action he had lost his huds. 'Status, Mr Xin!'

Jau stared at his displays. The status board was still a random jumble. He looked out, forward along the *Hand*'s orbit. They had passed through a sunrise. Dim lit, the frozen ocean stretched to the horizon. But that wasn't what mattered. The horizon itself looked subtly different. *Not your classical de-orbit burn, but it will do.* Jau licked his lips. 'Sir, we'll be in the soup in one or two hundred seconds.'

For a moment, horror registered in Brughel's face. 'You get us back up, mister.'

'Yes, sir.' What else was there to say?

Brughel and his goons coasted across the bridge to the aft hatch.

Phuong: 'Sir. I have a voice transmission from L1.'

'Well, put it on.'

It was a woman's voice, Trixia Bonsol. 'Greetings to the humans aboard *Invisible Hand*. This is Lieutenant Victory Lighthill, Accord Intelligence Service. I have taken control of your spacecraft. You will be on the ground shortly. It may be some time before our forces arrive on the scene. Do not, I repeat, do not resist those forces.'

Stark, gape-mouth surprise held everyone on the bridge . . . but Bonsol said nothing more. Brughel recovered first, but his voice wavered. 'Phuong. Shut down the L1 link. All the protocol layers.'

'Sir. I-I can't. Once up, the interconnect—'

'Yes you can. Get physical. Take a club to the equipment, but get yourself *offline.*'

'Sir. Even without the local zipheads . . . I think L1 has workarounds.'

'I'll take care of that. We're coming down.'

The guard by the hatch looked up at Brughel. 'It won't open, sir.'

'*Phuong!*'

There was no answer.

Brughel jumped to the wall beside the hatch, began pounding the direct opener. He might as well have been pounding a rock. The Podmaster turned, and Jau saw that the red was gone from his face. He was dead white and his eyes were wild. He had a wire gun in his hand now, and he looked around the bridge as if in search of a target. His gaze locked on Jau. The gun twitched up.

'Sir, I think I've gotten through to one of my pilots.' It was an absolute lie, but without his huds, Brughel couldn't know.

'Ah?' The gun muzzle slipped a fraction. 'Good. Keep at it, Xin. It's your neck, too.'

Jau nodded, turned back to diddle fiercely with the dead controls.

Behind him, the search for the hatch's manual override was frantic and obscene and incompetent . . . and finally terminated by the chatter of gunfire. Tumbling wires caromed around the bridge. 'Bloody hell. That won't do it,' Brughel said. There was the sound of a cabinet opening, but Jau kept his head down, doing his best to look desperately busy. 'Here. Try this.' There was a pause, then a string of earnumbing detonations. *Lordy!* Brughel kept that kind of ordnance on a starship's bridge?

Triumphant shouts were faint behind the ringing in his ears. Then Brughel was shouting. 'Go! Go! Go!'

Jau turned his head slightly, got a sidelong look at the bridge behind him. The hatch was still closed, but now there was a ragged hole punched in it. Twisted metal and less identifiable junk floated up from it.

And now Jau Xin was all alone on the *Hand*'s bridge. He took a deep breath and tried to make sense of his displays. Ritser Brughel was right about one thing. It was Jau's neck on the line here.

The core power trace was still high. He looked out across the curving horizon. No question now. The *Hand* was down, consistent with the eighty-thousand-meter altitude on the status board. He heard the rumble of the aux thrusters. *Did I get through?* If he could orient properly and somehow fire the main torch . . . But no, they weren't turning in the right direction! The great ship was aligning on their direction of flight, rear end first. To the left and right of the aft view, parts of the starship's outer hull could be seen, angular spidery structures that were meant for the flows of interstellar plasma but never the atmosphere of a planet. Now their edges were glowing. Soft yellows and reds splashed out around them, cascading like glowing ocean spray. The sharpest edges glowed white, and sloughed away. But the aux thrusters were still firing, a pattern of tiny bursts. On off. On off. Whoever was running his pilots was making a perverse attempt to keep the *Hand* oriented. Without such precise control, the flow past the ship's irregular hull would send them into a long tumble, a million tonnes of hardware torn apart by forces it had never been designed to face.

The glow across the stern was a spreading sheet of light, clear only in a few places where the shock was not hot enough to vaporize the hull. Jau drifted back into his chair, the acceleration growing gently, inexorably. Four hundred milligees, eight hundred. But this acceleration was not caused by the ship's torch. This was a planetary atmosphere, having its way with them.

And there was another sound. Not the rumble of the aux. It was a rich, growing tone. From its throat to its outer hull, the *Hand* had become a vast organ pipe. The sound fell from chord to chord as the ship rammed deeper, slower. And as the glow of ionization trembled and faded, the *Hand*'s dying song rose in a crescendo – and was gone.

Jau stared out the aft view, at a scene that should have been impossible. The angular hull structures were smoothed and melted by their passage through the heat. But the *Hand* was a million tonnes, and the pilots had kept it precisely oriented in the flow, and most of its great mass had survived.

Nearly a standard gee pressed him against his chair, but this was almost at right angles to the earlier acceleration. This was planetary gravity. The *Hand* was a kind of aircraft now, a disaster skidding across the sky. They were forty thousand meters up, coming down at a steady hundred meters per second. Jau looked at the pale horizon, the ridges and blocks of ice that swept beneath his view. Some of those were five hundred meters high, ice pressed upward by the slow freezing of the ocean depths. He tapped at his console, got a flicker of attention from one of the pilots, a scrap of further information. They would clear that ridgeline and the three beyond it. Beyond that, near the horizon, the shadows were softer . . . a deception of distance, or maybe snow piled deep on the jagged ice.

Echoing up through the *Hand*'s corridors, Jau heard the rapid pounding of Brughel's heavy gun. There was shouting, silence, then the pounding again, farther away. *Every hatch must be sealed.* And Ritser Brughel was punching through every one. In a way, the Podmaster was right; he controlled the physical layer. He could reach the hull optics, knock out the link to LT. He could 'disconnect' whatever local zip-heads still offended . . .

Thirty thousand meters. Dim sunlight reflected off the ice, but there was no sign of artificial lights or towns. They were coming down in the middle of the Spiders' grandest ocean. The *Hand* was still making better than mach three. The sink rate was still one hundred meters per second. His intuition plus the few hints from the status board told him they would smear across the landscape at more than the speed of sound. Unless – the core power was still rising – if the main torch could be fired once more, and fired at precisely the right instant . . . a miracle touch might do it. The *Hand* was so big that its belly and throat might be used as a cushion, shredded across kilometers of crash path, leaving the bridge and the occupied quarters intact. Pham Trinli's silly bragging had included such an adventure.

One thing was certain. Even if Jau were given full control at this instant, and all his pilots' skills, there was no way he could accomplish such a landing.

They had cleared the last line of ridges. The aux thrusters burned briefly, a one-degree yaw, guiding them as if with special knowledge of conditions ahead.

Ritser Brughel's time for killing had shrunk down to a few seconds. Rita would be safe. Jau watched the tumbled land rise toward him. And with it came the strangest feeling of terror, and triumph, and freedom. 'You're too late, Ritser. You're just too late.'

60

Belga Underville had rarely seen joy or fear so strong, and never attached to the same events by the same people. Coldhaven's techs should have been cheering as wave after wave of their long-range interceptors scored against the Kindred ballistics, and hundreds of other enemy missiles blew themselves up or otherwise aborted. The success rate was already nearing ninety-nine percent. Which left thirty live nuclear warheads arcing into Accord territory. It was the difference between annihilation and mere isolated disaster . . . and the technicians chewed on their eating hands as they struggled to stop those last, straggling threats.

Coldhaven walked down his row of techs. One of Lighthill's people, an oophase corporal, was by his side. The General was hanging on Rhapsa Lighthill's every word, making sure his techs got the benefit of all the new intelligence that was flooding across their displays. Belga hung back. There was nothing she could do but get in the way. Victory Lighthill was deep in some weird conversation with the aliens, every few sentences punctuated by long delays, time for side conversations with her brother and Coldhaven's people. She paused, waiting, and gave Belga a shy smile.

Belga gave her a little wave back. The cobblie wasn't quite the same as her mother – except, perhaps, where it mattered.

Then Lighthill's phone came alive again – some relatively near collaborator? 'Yes, good. We'll get people out there. Five hours maybe . . . Daddy, we're back on track. Critter Number Five is playing fair. You were right about that one. Daddy? . . . Brent, we've lost him again! That shouldn't happen now . . . Daddy?'

*

Rachner's helicopter had stopped its zigzag, evasive course, though not before Thract became thoroughly lost. Now the heli flew low and fast across the altiplano, as if fearless of hostile observation from above. A passenger on his own pilot's perch, Thract watched the sky show with an almost hypnotized wonder, only partly aware of Sherkaner Underhill's delirious mumbling, and the strange lights coming from his game helmet.

The sheets of amissile launches were long gone, but all across the horizon the evidence of their mission was lighting the sky. *At least we fought back.*

The timbre of the rotor noise changed, bringing Thract back from his terrible, far vision. The heli was sliding down through the dark. Shading his eyes against the sky lights, Thract could see that they were headed for a landing on a random stretch of naked stone, hills and ice all around.

They touched down, roughly, and the turbines idled till the rotors were spinning slow enough to see. It was almost quiet in the cabin. The guide-bug stirred, pushed insistently at the door beside Underhill.

'Don't let him out, sir. If we lose him here, he might stay lost.'

Underhill's head bobbed uncertainly. He set down the game helmet; its lights flickered and died. He patted his guide-bug, and pulled shut the closures of his jacket. 'It's okay, Colonel. It's all over now. You see, we won.'

The cobber sounded as delirious as ever. But Thract was beginning to realize: delirious or not, Underhill had saved the world. 'What happened, sir?' He said softly. 'Alien monsters controlled our nets . . . and you controlled the monsters?'

The old, familiar chuckle. 'Something like that. The problem was, they aren't all monsters. Some of them are both clever and good . . . and we almost squashed each other with our separate plans. That was terribly expensive to fix.' He was silent for a second, his head wavering. 'It will be okay, but . . . just now I can't see much.' The cobber had taken a full head of the aliens' killer beam. The blisters on Underhill's eyes were spreading, a pervasive, creamy haze. 'Maybe you can take a moment and tell me what you see.' The cobber jerked a hand skyward.

Rachner pushed his best side close to the south-facing window. The shoulder of the mountain cut off part of the view, but there were still one hundred degrees of horizon. 'Hundreds of nukes, sir, glowing lights in the sky. I think those are our interceptors, way far off.'

'Ha. Poor Nizhnimor and Hrunk . . . when we walked in the Dark, we saw something similar. Though it was much colder then.' The guide-bug had the trick of the door. It popped it open a crack, and a slow draft of coldest air licked into the cabin.

'Sir—' Rachner started to complain about the draft.

'It's okay. You won't be here long. What else do you see?'

'Lights spreading out from the hits. I guess that's ionization in the magnetopatches. And—' Rach's voice caught in his throat. There were other things, and these he recognized. 'I see reentry traces, sir. Dozens, of them. They're passing overhead, and to our east.' Rach had seen similar things in Air Defense tests. When the warheads finally came down through the atmosphere, they left trails that glowed in a dozen colors. Even in the tests, they'd been horrible things, the stabbing hands of a spirit tarant, pouncing from the sky. A dozen traces, more coming. Thousands of missiles had been stopped, but what remained could destroy cities.

'Don't worry.' Underhill's voice came softly from Thract's blind side. 'My alien friends have taken care of those. Those warheads are dead carcasses now, a few tonnes of radioactive junk. Not much fun if one drops directly on your head, but otherwise no threat.'

Rachner turned, followed the tracks anxiously across the sky. *My alien friends have taken care of those.* 'What are the monsters really like, Sherkaner? Can we trust them?'

'Heh. Trust them? What a thing for an Intelligence officer to ask. My General never trusted them, any of them. I've studied the *humans* for almost twenty years, Rachner. They've been traveling in space for hundreds of generations. They've seen so much, they've done so much . . . The poor crappers think they know what is impossible. They're free to fly between the stars, and their imagination is trapped in a cage they can't even see.'

The glowing streaks had passed across the sky. Most had faded to far-red or invisibility. Two converged toward a point on the horizon, probably the High Equatoria launch site. Thract held his breath, waiting.

Behind him, Underhill said something like, 'Ah, dear victory,' and then was very quiet.

Thract strained to watch the north. If the warheads were still live, the detonations would be visible even from over the horizon. Ten seconds. Thirty. There was silence and cold. And to the north, there was only the light of the stars. 'You're right, sir. What's left is just falling junk. I—' Rachner turned, suddenly conscious of just how cold the heli's cabin had become.

Underhill was gone.

Thract lunged across the cabin to the half-open door. 'Sir! *Sherkaner!*' He started down the outside steps, turning his head this way and that, trying to catch a glimpse of the other. The air was still, but so cold that it cut. Without a heated breather, he'd have burned lungs in a matter of minutes.

There! A dozen yards from the heli, in the shade of both stars and sky glow, two far-red blotches. Underhill limped slowly behind Mobiy. The guide-bug tugged him gently along, at every step probing the hillside with its long arms. It was the instinctive behavior of an animal in hopeless cold, trying to the last to find an effective deepness. Here, in a random nowhere, the critter didn't stand a chance. In less than an hour he and his master would be dead, their tissues desiccated.

Thract scrambled down the steps, shouting at Underhill. And above him, the heli's blades began to spin up. Thract cringed beneath the frigid wash.

As the turbines ramped up and the blades began to provide real lift, he turned and pulled himself back into the cabin. He pounded on the autopilot, poking at every disconnect.

It didn't matter. The turbines hit takeoff power and the heli lifted. He had one last glimpse of the shadows hiding Sherkaner Underhill. Then the craft tilted eastward and the scene was lost behind him.

61

Blowouts in small volumes were normally fatal. Quickly fatal. It was one of his guards who unintentionally saved Tomas Nau. Just as the hull melted through, Tung released his harness and dived up toward the hatch. The blowout clawed at all of them, but Tung was loose and closest to the hole. He rammed headfirst into the wall melt, sucked through to his hips.

Somehow Qiwi had kept her place by the jammed taxi hatch. Now she had the L1-A hatch open, too. She turned back, grabbed her father, and boosted him into the lock beyond. The action was a single smooth motion, almost a dance. Nau had scarcely begun to react when she turned a second time, hooked a foot into a wall loop, and reached out to snag his sleeve with the tips of her fingers. She pulled gently, and as he came closer, grabbed him by main force and shoved him through to safety.

Safe. And I was as good as dead just five seconds ago. The hiss of escaping air was loud. The damaged docking collar could blow in a second.

Qiwi dropped back from hatchway. 'I'll get Marli and Ciret.'

'Yes!' Nau came back to the opening, and cursed himself for losing his wire gun in the chaos. He looked into the taxi. One guard was clearly dead: Tung's legs weren't even twitching. Marli was probably dead too, certainly out of it, though Qiwi was struggling to get both him and Ciret free. In a second she would have them out, as quick and effectively as she had saved himself and Ali Lin. Qiwi was just too dangerous, and this was his last sure opportunity to get her out of the picture.

Nau pushed on the L1-A hatch. It turned smoothly, pressed by the air currents, and slammed shut with an ear-numbing crash. His fingers danced across the access control, tapping out the code for an emergency jettison. From the other side of the wall there was the explosive *whump* of exhausting gas, the banging of metal on metal. Nau imagined the airless taxi, floating out from the lock. *Let Pham Nuwen take his target practice on the dead.*

The lock's pressure rose quickly to normal. Nau popped the inner hatch and took Ali Lin through, into the corridor beyond. The old man mumbled, semiconscious. At least his bleeding had stopped. *Don't die on me, damn it.* Ali was worthless meat right now, but in the long run he was a treasure. Things would be expensive enough without losing him.

He coasted Ali gently up the long corridor. The walls around him were green plastic. This had been the security vault aboard *Common Good*. Its irregular shape had made sense there; nowadays its value lay in its monolithic construction and its shielding, several meters of composites with the melting point of tungsten. All the firepower Pham Nuwen possessed couldn't get him in here.

Till a few days ago, the vault had held most of the surviving heavy weapons in the OnOff system. Now it was almost empty, stripped to support the mission of the *Invisible Hand*. No matter. Nau had been very careful that enough nukes remained. If necessary, he could play the old, old game of total disaster management.

So what can be salvaged? He had only the vaguest idea how much Pham Nuwen controlled. For an instant, Nau quailed. All his life he had studied such men, and now he was pitted against one. *But in winning, I will be all the more.* There were a dozen things to be done, and only seconds to do them. Nau let Ali loose, free to slowly fall in the rockpile's microgravity. A comm set and local huds were tacked to grabfelt by the door. He snatched them up and spoke brief commands. The automation here was primitive, but it would do. Now he could see out from the vault. The Peddlers' temp was above his horizon, and there was no taxi traffic, there were no suited figures approaching around the rockpile's surface.

He dove across the open space, unshipped a small torpedo. The flag at the corner of his view told him that his call to Hammerfest had made it through. The ring pattern disappeared, and Pham's voice came in his ear.

'Nau?'

'Right the first time, sir.' Nau floated the nuke across to the launch tube that Kal Omo had installed just thirty-five days ago. It had seemed a maniac precaution then. Now it was his last chance.

'It's time that you surrendered, Podmaster. My forces control all of L1 space. We—'

Pham's voice held quiet certainty, with none of the bluster of Old Pham Trinli. Nau could imagine ordinary people gripped by that voice, led. But Tomas Nau was a pro himself. He had no trouble interrupting: 'On the contrary, sir. I hold the only power that is worth noting.' He touched the panel by the launch tube. There was a thump as compressed air blew out the top end and cleared the snow. 'I've programmed and loaded a tactical nuclear weapon. The target is the Peddlers' temp. The weapon is ad hoc, but I'm sure it's sufficient.'

'You can't do that, Podmaster. Three hundred of your own people are over there.'

Nau laughed gently. 'Oh, I *can* do it. I lose a lot, but I still have some people in coldsleep. I – are you really Pham Nuwen?' The question slipped out, almost uncalculated.

There was a pause, and when Nuwen spoke, he sounded distracted, 'Yes.'

And you're handling everything yourself, aren't you? It made sense. An ordinary conspiracy would have been detected years ago. It had been just Pham Nuwen and Ezr Vinh, right from the beginning. Like a single man pulling his wagon across a continent, Nuwen had persevered, had almost conquered. 'It's an honor to meet you, sir. I've studied you for many years.' As he spoke, Nau popped up a view of the torpedo's diagnostics. He was looking straight down the launch rail; the tube was clear. 'Perhaps your only mistake is that you have not fully understood the Podmaster ethos. You see, we Podmasters grew out of disaster. That is our inner strength, our edge. If I destroy the temp, it will be an enormous setback for the L1 operation. But my personal situation will *improve*. I will still have the rockpile. I will still have many of the zipheads. I will still have the *Invisible Hand*.' He turned away from the launch tube. He looked across the equipment bays, at the remaining torpedoes; he might have to knock out the Hammerfest Attic, too. *That* had not been part of even the most extreme disaster plans. Maybe there was some way to do it that would leave some of the zipheads alive. Another part of his mind waited curiously for what Pham Nuwen would say. Would he cave in like an ordinary person, or did he have the true heart of a Podmaster? That question was the essence of Pham Nuwen's moral weakness.

Abruptly, there was a clattering sound that echoed through the vault. Ali Lin had fallen beyond his view, into the downward end. But the sound came again and again, a million metal plates crashing together. *Maybe the inward entrance?* That was at the lowest point in the vault. Nau moved silently toward the edge of the drop-off.

Pham Nuwen's voice was faint against the racket: 'You're wrong, Podmaster. You don't have the—' Nau cut the audio with a swipe of his hand and moved slowly forward. He did a manual traverse of the vault's fixed cameras. Nothing. The primitive automation was a salvation and a pest. Okay. Weapons. Was there anything smaller than a nuke around here? The database wasn't set up for such trivia. He let the catalogue listings stream by his huds, and he moved close to wall, still out of sight from below. The clanking and banging continued. *Ah, that was the lake-bed servos, their noise channeled down the tunnel!* Quite a fanfare for a secret break-in.

The ambusher, such as he was, floated up into sight.

'Ah, Mr Vinh. I thought you were well drowned.'

In fact, Vinh looked semiconscious, his face pasty pale. There was no sign of his wire-gun wounds. *No, he stole one of my jackets.* The full-press was trim and perfectly creased, but the right arm was subtly twisted, lumpy. Vinh held Ali gently against his left shoulder. He looked back at Nau, and hatred seemed to bring him more alertness.

But the downward end of the vault was empty of further intruders. And Nau's catalogue search had completed: there were three wire guns in the cabinet immediately behind him! Nau breathed a sigh of relief and smiled at the Peddler. 'You did well, Mr Vinh.' A few seconds' difference and Vinh would have been here first, setting a real ambush. Instead . . . the fellow appeared to be unarmed, one-armed, weak as a kitten. And Tomas Nau stood between him and the wire guns. 'I don't have time to talk, I'm afraid. Stand aside from Ali, please.' He spoke mildly, but didn't take his eyes off the two. His left hand moved up to open the gun cabinet. Maybe the calm style would work on Vinh, and he would have a clean kill.

'Tomas!'

Qiwi stood above them, at the entrance to the vault's open space.

For an instant, Nau just stared. She had a nosebleed. Her lacy dress was torn and splattered. But she was alive. *The jettison must have jammed along with the taxi hatch.* With the taxi still in place, lock security would not reset – and somehow she had clawed her way back in.

'We were trapped, Tomas. Somehow the lock was defective.'

'Oh, yes!' The anguish in Nau's voice was completely sincere. 'It slammed shut and I heard venting. I – I was so sure you were dead.'

Qiwi came down from the ceiling, guiding the body of Rei Ciret onto a grabfelt rest. The guard might be alive, but he was clearly of no use just now. 'I – I'm sorry, Tomas. I wasn't able to save Marli.' She came across the room to hug him, but there was something tentative about the gesture. 'Who are you talking to?' Then she saw Vinh and Ali. '*Ezr?*'

For once, some good luck: Vinh was perfect, his full-press jacket stained like a butcher's smock, with Ali's blood. From behind Vinh came the banging of the ruined park. The Peddler's voice was gasping and harsh. 'We've taken over L1, Qiwi. Except for a few of Nau's thugs, we haven't hurt anyone' – this while her own father lay bleeding in his arms! 'Nau is using you like he always does. Only this time, he's going to kill us all. Look around! He's going to nuke the temp.'

'I—' But Qiwi did look around, and Nau didn't like what he saw in her eyes.

'Qiwi,' said Nau, 'look at me. We're up against the same group that was behind Jimmy Diem.'

'You murdered Jimmy!' shouted Vinh.

Qiwi wiped her bloody nose on the fine white fabric of her sleeve. For a moment she looked very young and lost, as lost as when he'd first taken her. She caught her foot on a wall stop and turned toward him, considering. Somehow, he had to make time, just a handful of seconds:

'Qiwi, think who's saying these things.' Nau gestured in the direction of Vinh and Ali Lin. It was a terrible risk he was taking, a desperate manipulation. But it was working! She actually turned a bit, her gaze shifting away from him. He slipped his hand into the cabinet, feeling for the butt of a wire gun.

*

'Qiwi, think who's saying these things.' Nau gestured in the direction of Ezr and Ali Lin. Poor Qiwi actually turned to look. Behind her, Ezr saw a smile flicker across Tomas Nau's face.

'You know Ezr. He tried to kill your father back at North Paw; he thought he could get at me through Ali. If he had a knife, he would be cutting into your father right now. You know what a sadist Ezr Vinh is. You remember the beating he gave you; you remember how I held you afterwards.'

The words were for Qiwi, but they hit Ezr like battering rams, horrid truths mixed with deadly lies.

Qiwi was motionless for a moment. But now her fists were clenched; her shoulders seemed to hunch down with some terrible tension. And Ezr thought, *Nau is going to win, and I'm the reason.* He pushed back the grayness that seemed to close on him from all sides and made one last try: 'Not for me, Qiwi. For all the others. For your mother. Please. Nau has lied to you for forty years. Whenever you learn the truth, he scrubs your mind. Over and over again. And you can never remember.'

Recognition and stark horror spread across Qiwi's face. 'This time I *will* remember.' She turned as Nau pulled something from the cabinet behind them. Her elbow jabbed into his chest. There was a sound like snapping branches; Nau bounced back against the cabinet and floated outward, into the vault's open space. A wire gun floated after him. Nau lunged for the weapon, but it was centimeters beyond his reach and he had only thin air to brace upon.

Qiwi stood out from the wall, stretched, and snagged the wire gun. She pointed the muzzle at the Podmaster's head.

Nau was slowly tumbling; he twisted about to track on Qiwi. He opened his mouth, the mouth that had a persuasive lie for every occasion. 'Qiwi, you can't—' he began, and then he must have seen the look on Qiwi's face. Nau's arrogance, the smooth cool arrogance that Ezr had watched for half a lifetime, was suddenly melted away. Nau's voice became a whisper. 'No, *no.*'

Qiwi's head and shoulders trembled, but her words were stony hard. 'I remember.' She shifted her aim away from Nau's face, to below his waist . . . and fired a long burst. Nau's scream became a shriek that ended as the wire-fire spun him around and struck his head.

62

Things were very dark, and then there was light. She floated upward toward it. *Who am I?* The answer came quickly, on a crest of terror. *Anne Reynolt.*

Memories. The retreat into the mountains. The final days of hide-and-seek, the Balacrean invaders finding her every cave. The traitor, unmasked too late. The last of her people ambushed from the air. Standing on a mountain hillside, circled by Balacrean armor. The stench of burnt flesh was strong even in the chill morning air, but the enemy had stopped shooting. They had captured her alive.

'Anne?' The voice was soft, solicitous. The voice of a torturer, building the mood toward greater horror. 'Anne?'

She opened her eyes. Balacrean torture gear bulked large around her, just at the limits of her peripheral vision. It was all the horror she expected, except that they were in free fall. *For fifteen years, they've owned our cities. Why take me into space?*

Her interrogator drifted into view. Black hair, typical Balacrean skin tone, a young-old face. This must be a senior Podmaster. But he wore a strange fractille jacket, like no Podmaster Anne had ever seen. There was a look of false anxiety pasted on his face. *A fool; he's overacting.* He floated a bouquet of soft white flowers into her lap, as though making a gift. They smelled of warm summers passed. *There must be some way, to die. There must be some way to die.* Her arms were tied down, of course. But if he came close enough, she still had her teeth. Maybe, if he was enough of a fool—

He reached out, gently touched her shoulder. Anne twisted hard around, caught a bite from the Podmaster's groping hand. He pulled back, leaving a trail of tiny red drops floating in the air between them. But he wasn't enough of a fool to kill her on the spot. Instead, he glared across the ranked equipment at someone out of sight. 'Trud! What the devil have you done to her?'

She heard a whiny voice that was somehow familiar. 'Pham, I warned you this was a difficult procedure. Without her guidance, we can't be sure—' The speaker came into view. He was a small and nervous-looking fellow in a Balacrean tech's uniform. His eyes widened as he saw the blood in the air. The look he gave Anne was satisfyingly – and inexplicably – full of fear. 'Al and I can do only so much. We should have waited till we get Bil back . . . Look, maybe it's just temporary memory loss.'

The older fellow flared into anger, but he seemed afraid, too. 'I wanted a deFocus, not a god-damned mindscrub!'

The little man, Trud . . . *Trud Silipan*, retreated. 'Don't worry. I'm sure she'll come around. We didn't touch the memory structures, I swear.' He shot another fearful glance her way. 'Maybe . . . I don't know, maybe the deFocus worked fine and we're seeing some kind of autorepression.' He came a little closer, still beyond her hands and teeth, and gave her a sickly smile. 'Boss? You remember me, Trud Silipan? We've worked together for years of Watch time, and before that back on Balacrea, under Alan Nau. Don't you remember?'

Anne stared at the round face, the weak smile. Alan Nau. Tomas Nau. Oh . . . dear . . . *God.* She had wakened to a nightmare that had never ended. The torture pits, and then the Focus, and then a lifetime of *being* the enemy.

Silipan's face had blurred, but his voice was suddenly cheerful. 'See, Pham! She's crying. She does remember!'

Yes. Everything.

But now Pham Nuwen's voice sounded even angrier. 'Get out, Trud. Just get out.'

'It's easy to verify. We can—'

'Get out!'

She didn't hear Silipan after that. The world had collapsed into pain, sobbing grief that took away her breath and senses.

She felt an arm across her shoulders, and this time she knew it wasn't the touch of a torturer. *Who am I?* That had been the easy question. The real question, *What am I?*, had eluded her a few seconds more, but now the memories were flooding in, the monstrous evil she had been since that day in the mountains above Arnham.

She shuddered from Pham's arm, only to encounter the straps that held her down.

'Sorry,' he muttered, and she heard the shackles fall away. And now it didn't matter. She curled up into a ball, barely aware of his comfort. He was talking to her, simple things, repeated over and over in different ways. 'It's all right now, Anne. Tomas Nau is dead. He's been dead for four days. You're free. We're all free . . .'

After a while, he was quiet, only the touch of his arm on her shoulders announcing his presence. Her tearing sobs wound down. There was no terror now. The worst had happened, over and over, and what was left was dead and empty.

Time passed.

She felt her body slowly relax, unbend. She forced open her tight-shut eyes, forced herself to turn and face Pham. Her face *hurt* with the crying, and how she wished she could be hurt a million times more. 'You . . . damn you for bringing me back. Let me die now.'

Pham looked back at her quietly, his eyes wide and attentive. Gone was the bluster she had always guessed was a fake. In its place, intelligence . . . awe? No, that couldn't be. He reached down beside her and laid the white andelirs back in her lap. The damn things were warm, furry. Beautiful. He seemed to consider her demand, but then he shook his head. 'You can't go yet, Anne. There are more than two thousand Focused persons left here. You can free them, Anne.' He gestured to the Focusing gear behind her head. 'I got the feeling that Al Hom was playing roulette when he worked on you.'

I can free them. The thought was the first lightness in all the years since that morning in the mountains. It must have leaked out into her expression, because a hopeful smile appeared on Pham's lips. Anne felt her eyes narrow down. She knew as much about Focus as any Balacrean. She knew all the tricks of reFocusing, of redirecting loyalty. 'Pham Trinli – Pham Whoever-

You-Really-Are – I've watched you for many years. Almost from the beginning, I thought you were working against Tomas. But I could also see how much you loved the idea of Focus. You lusted after that power, didn't you?'

The smile left his face. He nodded slowly. 'I saw . . . I saw it could give me what I had spent a lifetime fighting for. And in the end, I saw the price was too high.' He shrugged, and looked down, as if ashamed.

Anne stared into that face, thinking. Once upon a time, not even Tomas Nau could deceive her. When Anne was Focused, the edges of her mind had been sharp as razors, unencumbered by distraction and wishful thinking – and knowing Tomas's true intent was no more use to her than a hatchet knowing it is for murdering. Now, she wasn't sure. This man could be lying, but what he asked of her was what she yearned to do more than anything else in the world. And then, having paid back as best she could, then she could die. She returned his shrug with one of her own. 'Tomas Nau lied to you about deFocus.'

'He lied about many things.'

'I can do better than Trud Silipan and Bil Phuong, but still there will be failures.' The greatest horror of all: There would be some who would damn her for bringing them back.

Pham reached across the flowers and took her hand. 'Okay. But you will do your best.'

She looked down at his hand. Blood still oozed from the gash she had opened on the side of his palm. Somehow the man was lying, but if he let her deFocus the others . . . *Play along.* 'You're running things now?'

Pham chuckled. 'I have some say. Certain Spiders have a bigger say. It's complicated, and it's still in chaos. Four hundred Ksec ago, Tomas Nau was still running things.' His smile widened with enthusiasm. 'But a hundred Msec from now, two hundred Msec, I think you are going to see a renaissance. We'll have our ships repaired. Hell, we may have new ones. I've never seen an opportunity like this.'

Just play along. 'And what do you want of me?' *How long till I am reFocused as your tool?*

'I – I just want you to be free, Anne.' He looked away. 'I know what you were before, Anne. I've seen the story of what you did on Frenk, your final capture. You remind me of someone I knew when I was a child. She also stood up against impossible odds, and she also was crushed.' His face half-turned back to her. 'There were times I've feared you more than Tomas Nau. But ever since I've known you were the Frenkisch Orc, I've prayed you could have another day.'

He was such a very good liar. Too bad for him that his lie was so bald-faced, so pandering. She felt an overwhelming urge to push it over the edge: 'So in a few years we'll have functioning starships again?'

'Yes, and probably better-equipped than we came with. You know the physics we've discovered here. And it looks like there are other things—'

'And you will control those ships?'

'Several of them.' He was still nodding, blundering his deception forward.

'And you just want to help. Me, the Frenkisch Orc. Well, sir, you are uniquely qualified. Lend me those ships. Come with me to Balacrea and Frenk and Gaspr. Help me free *all* the Focused.'

It was amusing to see Pham's smile freeze as he boggled on her words. 'You want to take down a starfaring empire, an empire with Focus, with just a handful of ships? That's . . .' Words for such insanity failed to come, and he just stared at her for a moment. Then, amazingly, his smile was back. 'That's marvelous! Anne, give me time to prepare, time to make alliances here. Give me a dozen of your years. We may not win. But I swear, we'll make the attempt.'

Whatever she asked he simply agreed to. It had to be a lie. Yet if true, it was the only promise that could make her want to live. She stared into Pham's eyes, trying to see behind the lie. Maybe the inevitable destruction of deFocus had taken her sharpness, for however deeply she looked, she only saw awed enthusiasm. *He's a genius. And lie or truth, now he has me for twelve years.* For just a moment she relaxed into belief. For just a moment she fantasized that this man was not a liar. *The Frenkisch Orc might yet free them all.* The strangest thrill flowed out from her heart, tingling through her body. It took her a moment to recognize something that had been lost to her for so very long: joy.

63

Pham sent Ezr Vinh groundside to negotiate.

'Why me, Pham?' This was the most extraordinary trade situation in the history of Humankind. It was also a war waiting to happen. 'You should—'

Nuwen held up his hand, interrupting. 'There are reasons for sending you. You know the Spiders better than any of our other unFocused people, certainly better than me.'

'I could be staff. I could help you.'

'No, I'll be on *your* staff.' He paused, and Ezr saw a glint of worry. 'You're right, son, this is tricky. In the short run they hold the whip hand, and they have plenty of reason to hate us. We think the Lighthill faction still has the ear of the King, but—'

There were other factions in the Accord regime. Some of them thought Focused translators were a negotiable commodity.

'That's why it's even more important you go, Pham.'

'It's not our choice. You see, they've asked for you specifically.'

'What?'

'Yeah. I guess over the years, working with Trixia, they think they've got you figured out.' He grinned. 'They want to see you close up.'

That almost made sense. 'Okay.' He thought a moment. 'But they're not getting Trixia. I go down with some other translator.' He glared at Pham. 'She's the star; Underville's crew would love to get their hands on her.'

'Hm. Maybe someone down there is thinking the same way. The King asked for Zinmin to accompany you.' He noticed the expression on Ezr's face. 'There's more?'

'I – yes. I want Trixia deFocused. Soon.'

'Of course. I've given you my word. I've given Anne the same promise.'

Ezr stared at him for a moment. *And you've changed inside; given up that dream.* After all that had happened, Ezr didn't doubt But suddenly he couldn't wait anymore. 'Move her to the front of the queue, Pham. I don't care that you need her translations. Move her up. I want her deFocused by the time I get back.'

Pham raised an eyebrow. 'An ultimatum?'

'No. Yes!'

The older man sighed. 'You got it. We'll start on Trixia immediately. I – I confess. We've been holding back on the translators. We need them so much.' He pursed his lips. 'Don't expect perfection, Ezr. This is just another place where Nau lied to us. Some of the deFocused are almost as sharp as Anne. Some—'

'I *know*.' Some came back vegetables, the mindrot in an explosive runaway, triggered by the deFocus process. 'But sooner or later we have to try. Sooner or later you have to give up using them.' He bounced up and left Pham's office. More talk would have just torn them both.

The transport to Arachna was a humble thing, Jau Xin's pinnace with ad hoc software revised specially by Qiwi. Humankind had the high ground and the remnants of high technology – and precious little in the way of physical resources or automation. As their zipheads were deFocused, the Emergent software became useless junk – and it would be some time before the Qeng Ho automation could be adapted to the hybrid jumble that remained at L1. They were trapped in a nearly empty solar system, with the only industrial ecology down on Arachna. They might drop a few rocks on the planet, or even a few nukes, but Humankind was nearly toothless. The Spiders were powerless, too, but that would change. They knew about the invaders now, and they knew what could be done with technology. They had large parts of the *Invisible Hand* intact. Sometime soon, the Spiders would be out here in force. Pham thought they had maybe a year to turn things around, to establish some basis of trust. Qiwi said that if *she* were a Spider, she could do it in far less than a year.

The temp's axial corridor was filled from end to end when Ezr and

Zinmin entered the taxi lock. Almost every unFocused human at L1 was here.

Pham and Anne were there. They floated close, a pair that Ezr Vinh would never have guessed in years past. 'We've started the deFocus prep,' Anne said. She didn't have to say who she was talking about. 'We'll do our best, Ezr.'

Qiwi wished him luck, as solemn as he had ever seen her. She seemed uncertain for a moment, then abruptly shook his hand, another thing she had never done before. 'Come back safe, Ezr.'

Somehow Rita Liao had put herself right before the hatch, blocking his way. Ezr reached out to comfort her. 'I'll bring Jau back, Rita.' *I'll do my best* was what he thought, not having the courage to show his doubts.

Rita's eyes were bloodshot. She looked even more distracted than when they had talked a few Ksecs before. 'I know, Ezr. I know. The Spiders are good people. They'll know Jau didn't want to harm them.' She had spent much of her lifetime enamored with the life on Arachna, but her faith in the translations seemed to be slipping away. 'But, but if they won't let you have him . . . Please. Give him . . .' She pushed a clear little box into his hand. It had a thumb lock, presumably keyed to Jau Xin. He saw a 'membrance gem inside. She broke off and melted back into the crowd.

64

It was 200Ksec to Lands Command. On the ground, the Spiders drove them up that long valley road. Eerie memories floated through Ezr's mind. Many of the buildings here were new, but *I was here before it all began.* It had been so unknowable then. Now there was the superficial gloss of information on everything. Zinmin Broute bounced from window to window and boggled with enthusiasm, naming everything he saw. They passed the library he had raided with Benny Wen. The Museum of the Dark Time. And the statues at the head of King's Way, that was Gokna's Reaching for Accord. Zinmin could tell you about every one of the twisted figures.

But today they were not lurkers stealing through someone else's sleep. Today the lights were very bright, and when they finally moved underground, it was as stark and alien as Ritser Brughel's Spiderish nightmares. The stairs were steep as ladders, and ordinary rooms were so low-ceilinged that Ezr and Zinmin had to crouch to move from place to place. Despite ancient drugs and millennia of gengineering, the full pull of planetary gravity was a constant, debilitating distraction. They were housed in what Zinmin claimed were royalty-class apartments, rooms with hairy floors and ceilings high enough to stand in. The negotiations began the next day.

*

The Spiders they had known in the translations were mostly absent. Belga Underville, Elno Coldhaven – those were names that Ezr recognized, but they had always been at a distance. They had not been part of Sherkaner Underhill's counterlurk. They must be consulting Victory Lighthill, though. As often as not during the negotiations, Underville would withdraw and there would be hissing conversations with persons unseen.

After the first couple of days, Ezr realized that some of those persons were *very* far away: Trixia. Back in their rooms, Ezr called L1. Of course, the link went through Spider control. Ezr didn't care. 'You told me that Trixia was in deFocus.'

The pause seemed much longer than ten seconds. Suddenly Ezr couldn't wait for the excuses and the evasions. 'Listen, damn you! The promise was that she would be in deFocus. Sooner or later you have to stop using her!'

Then Pham's voice came back. 'I know, Ezr. The problem is, the Spiders have insisted that she be available, still Focused. It's a dealbreaker if we refuse . . . and Trixia refuses to cooperate with us in deFocus. We'd have to force it on her.'

'I don't care. I don't care! They don't own her any more than Tomas Nau.' He choked on the fear, and almost started bawling. Across the room, Zinmin Broute looked as happy as any ziphead Ezr had ever seen. He was sitting cross-legged on the hairy carpet, paging through some kind of Spider picture book. *We're using him, too. We have to, just for a short while more.*

'Ezr, it's only for a short time. This is breaking Anne up, too, but it's the only sure insight the Spiders have on us. They almost trust the Focused. Everything we say, every assertion, they are talking over with the zips. We don't have a chance of getting the *Hand* people back without that trust. We don't have a chance of undoing Nau's work without that.'

Rita and Jau. The thumb-locked box sat at the top of Ezr's kit. Strange. The Spiders had not insisted on getting into it or his other things. Ezr crumpled. 'Okay. But, after this meeting, no one *owns* anyone. The deal dies – I kill the deal – otherwise.' He cut the connection before any answer could come back. After all, it didn't matter what the other replied.

Almost every day, they took the tortuous climb down to the same ghastly conference room. Zinmin claimed that this was the chief of Intelligence's private office, a 'bright and open-storied room, with nooks and isolated perches.' Well, there were nooks, dark fluting chimneys with hidden lairs at the top. And the video along the walls was a constant nonsense. He and Zinmin had to cross cold stone to sit on piled furs. Four or five Spiders were usually present, and almost always Underville or Coldhaven.

But the negotiations were actually going well. With the Focused to back up his story, the Spiders seemed to believe what Ezr had to say. They seemed to understand how good things could become with only a little cooperation. Certainly, the Spiders could have a presence at the rockpile.

Technology would be transferred downward without restriction, in return for human access to the ground. In time, the rockpile and the temps would be moved into high Arachna orbit and there would be joint construction of a shipyard.

Sitting with the Spiders for Ksecs each day was a wearing experience. The human mind was not designed to warm to such creatures. They seemed not to have eyes, just the crystal carapaces that saw better than any human Vision. You could never tell what they were looking at. Their eating hands were in constant motion, with meanings that Ezr was only beginning to understand. And when they gestured with their principal arms, the movement was abrupt and aggressive, like a creature on the attack. The air had a bitter, stale smell, which was strongest when extra spiders crowded around. *And next time, we bring our own toilets.* Ezr was getting bowlegged trying to accommodate himself to the local facilities.

Zinmin did most of the interactive translations. But Trixia and the others were there, and sometimes when the greatest precision was desired, it was her voice that would speak Underville's or Coldhaven's words: Underville the implacable cop, Coldhaven the sleek young general officer. Trixia's voice, others' souls.

At night, there were dreams, often more unpleasant than the reality he faced in the day. The worst were the ones he could understand. Trixia appeared to him, her voice and thoughts slipping back and forth between the young woman he once knew and the alien minds that owned her now. Sometimes her face would morph into a glassy carapace as she spoke, and when he asked about the change she would say he was imagining things. It was a Trixia who would remain forever Focused, ensorcelled, lost. Qiwi was in many of the dreams, sometimes the bratling, sometimes as she had been when she killed Tomas Nau. They would talk, and often she would give him advice. In the dreams it always made sense – and when he woke he could never remember the details.

One by one, the issues were resolved. They had gone from genocide to commerce in less than one million seconds. From L1, Pham Nuwen's voice was filled with pleasure at the progress. 'These guys negotiate like Traders, not governments.'

'We're giving up plenty, Pham. Since when have Customers had a site presence like we'll be giving the Spiders?'

The usual long pause. But Pham's tone was still bright: 'Even that may work out, son. I'll wager some of these Spiders may eventually want to be partners.' Qeng Ho.

'. . . One other thing,' Pham continued. 'Get through the POW negotiations' – the single remaining agenda item – 'and we'll be able to take Trixia off the case. Lighthill got that as a promise from the Underville faction.'

*

The last day of negotiation started like the others. Zinmin and Ezr were guided down a – 'spiral staircase' was what Zinmin called it. In human terms, it was a vertical shaft cut straight downward through the rock. An endless draft of warm air swept up past them. The shaft was almost two meters across, the walls set with five-centimeter ledges. Their guards had no trouble; they could reach from one side of the shaft to the other, supporting themselves on all sides. As they descended, the Spiders slowly turned round and round with the spiral. Every ten meters or so, there was an offset, a 'landing' for them to catch their breath. Ezr was both grateful for and uneasy about the harness/leash outfit the guards insisted he wear.

'These stairs are really just to intimidate us, aren't they, Zinmin?' He'd asked the question on earlier climbs, but Zinmin Broute had not deigned to answer.

The Focused translator was even more unsteady than Ezr on the narrow ledges, especially since he tried to imitate the splayed stance that made sense only for Spiders. Today he responded to the question. 'Yes . . . No. This is the main staircase down to the Royal Deepness. Very old. Traditional. An honor—' He slipped, swung out over the chasm, for a moment suspended by his rope and harness from the guard above them. Ezr hugged the damp wall, was almost knocked loose himself as Broute regained his footing.

They reached the final landing. The ceiling was low even by Spider standards, just over a meter high. Surrounded by their guards, they stooped and hobbled toward wide, wide doors. Beyond, the lighting was faint and blue. The Spiders could see across such a wide range. You'd think their preferred lighting would be sun-spectrum broad. But as often as not they went in for faint glimmers – or lights beyond where a human could see.

There was a familiar hiss from the dimness ahead of them.

'Come in. Sit down,' Zinmin Broute said, but the thought was from the Spider within the room. Ezr and Zinmin crossed the stone flags to their 'perches.' He could see the other now, a large female on a slightly higher perch. Her smell was strong in the closed air. 'General Underville,' Ezr said politely.

The POW issue should have been simple compared with the problems already solved. But he noticed that this time they were alone with Underville. There were no comm links to the outside here; at least none were offered. They were alone, almost in the dark, and Zinmin Broute's phrasing drifted into threatening turns of phrase. Frightening . . . yet somewhere out of the depths of Ezr Vinh's Trader childhood, insights drifted up. This was deliberately intimidating. Underville had promised Lighthill that the translators would be free *after* the POW negotiations were complete. She had been beaten down on so many things; this was her last stab at saving face.

He opened his pack and put on a pair of huds. According to the Spiders, all the humans aboard the *Hand* had survived its forced landing. The starship's wreckage was strewn across twenty thousand meters of ocean ice, the occupied crew decks virtually the only intact pieces of the vehicle. That anyone had survived was a miracle of Pham's advice to the ziphead pilots. Once on the ground, however, there had been numerous fatalities. Against all sanity, Brughel and his goons started a firefight with the arriving Spider troops. The goons had all died. With the agility of a true Podmaster, Brughel had abandoned them at the last moment, and attempted to hide among the surviving crew. The Spiders claimed there had been no fatalities after that initial shootout.

'The zipheads you can have back,' said Underville via Zinmin. 'We know that they are not responsible, and some of them made our victory possible.' Zinmin's tone was irritable. 'The rest are criminals. They killed hundreds. They attempted to kill millions.'

'No, only a small minority were in on that. The rest resisted – or were simply lied to about the operation.'

Ezr went down the crew list, explaining the roles of the different members. There had been twenty poor souls in coldsleep, Ritser's special toys. Clearly, *they* were victims, but Underville didn't want to give up the equipment. One by one, Ezr got Underville's permission for release, contingent on access to specialists who could explain the ruins that her agency now owned. Finally, they were down to the toughest cases. 'Jau Xin. Pilot Manager.'

'Jau Xin, the trigger man!' said the general. Ezr had pumped up the amplification in his huds. His view was not as dim as before. All through the conversation, Underville had sat very still, the only movement being the ceaseless play of her feeding hands. It was a posture that Zinmin represented as face-forward alertness. 'Jau Xin was charged with initiating the actual attacks.'

'General, we've looked at the records. Your interviews with Jau's Focused pilots are probably even more complete. It's clear to us that Jau Xin sabotaged much of the Emergent attack. I know Jau, ma'am. I know his wife. Both wish your people well.' The ziphead analysts, Trixia among them, thought that such family references might mean something. Maybe. But Belga Underville might be much more the classical 'national interest' type.

Zinmin Broute tapped away on his tiny console, putting Ezr's words into an intermediate language and then guiding the audio output. Ghostly hissing came from Broute's soundbox, Ezr's thoughts as a Spider might speak them.

Underville was silent for a moment, then gave forth a shrill squeak. Ezr knew that counted as a disdainful snort.

But this interview could ultimately be shown to other Spiders. *I'm not letting you off the hook, Underville.* Ezr reached into his pack and held up Rita's tiny box.

'And what is that?' said Underville. There was no hint of curiosity in Broute-as-Underville's voice.

'A gift to Jau Xin from his wife. A remembrance, in case you still refuse to free him.'

Underville was sitting almost two meters away, but even now Ezr didn't realize just how far a Spider's forearms could reach. Four spearlike black arms flashed out at him, plucking the box from his grasp. Underville's arms flickered back, held the box close to first one part and then another of her glassy carapace. Her stiletto hands made little scritching noises as she pried at the box's top and thumb lock.

'It's keyed to Jau Xin. If you force it open, the contents will be destroyed.'

'So be it then.' But the Spider stopped pressing the pointed tips of her limbs into the box. She held it a moment more, then gave a screeching hiss, and flung it back at Ezr's chest.

The ugly screeching continued as Zinmin Broute began translating. 'Damn your cobblie eyes!' Broute's voice was tight and angry. 'Take back this gift for a murderer. Take back Xin and the other staff.'

'Thank you, General. Thank you.' Ezr scrambled to recover Rita's gift.

The Spider's voice tumbled into silence, then resumed more quietly, sounding somehow like drops of water spatting off hot metal. 'And I suppose you think to rescue Ritser Brughel also?'

'Not to rescue him, ma'am. Over the years, Ritser Brughel has probably killed more of our people than ever he did of yours. He has much to answer for.'

'Indeed. But there is no way we will give that one up to you.' Now Broute's voice was smug, and Ezr guessed this was one point where there were no divisions on the Spider side.

And maybe that was for the best. Ezr shrugged. 'Very well. It is for you to punish him.'

The Spider had become very still, even unto her eating hands. 'Punish? You misunderstand. This silly negotiation has left us with only a single functioning human. Any punishment will necessarily be incidental. We're learning much from dissecting the human corpses, but we desperately need a living experimental subject. What are your physical limitations? How do you creatures respond to extremes of pain and fear? We want to test with stimuli we don't see in your databases. I intend that Ritser Brughel live a long, long time.'

Ritser Brughel is about as weird a human type as you can find. But somehow that might not be the wisest thing to say here and now. Instead, Ezr simply nodded. And for the first time he saw how Ritser might find a fate to match his crimes. The Podmaster's nightmare of Spiders would be the rest of his life.

65

Ezr Vinh returned a hero to L1. It was possible that no owner or fleet partner had every been greeted with the enthusiasm he saw at the rockpile. He brought with him the first of the released prisoners, including Jau Xin. He also brought with him the first of their new partners: The first Spiders to fly in space.

Ezr scarcely noticed. He smiled, he talked, and when he saw Rita and Jau together he felt a distant pleasure.

Last out of the pinnace was Floria Peres. She had been one of the coldsleep victims in Ritser's hidden cache, saved up unused until the very end. Even after 200Ksec, the woman had a terrible, lost look about her. As Ezr guided her out into the open, a silence came upon the crowd in the corridor. Qiwi glided forward. She had asked to help the victims, but when she came to a stop just short of Floria, Qiwi's eyes got very wide and her lips trembled. The two stared at each other for a moment. Then Qiwi offered Floria her hand, and the crowd opened behind them.

Ezr watched them depart, but his mind's eye was elsewhere: Anne Reynolt had begun Trixia's deFocus a Ksec after he left Arachna. During the 200Ksec of transit back to the rockpile, Pham had reported regularly on her progress. This time there was no backing out. Trixia was beyond the prep stage. First, the mindrot had been rendered quiescent, and then Trixia had been put into an artificial coma. From there, the rot's pattern of drug release was slowly altered. 'Anne has done this hundreds of times now, Ezr,' said Pham. 'She says this is going well. She should be out of the clinic just a few Ksecs after you get back here.'

No more delays. Trixia would finally be free.

Two days later, the word came. *Trixia is ready.*

Ezr visited Qiwi before he went to the deFocus clinic. Qiwi was working with her father, remaking the lake park. Most of the trees had died, but Ali Lin thought he could bring them back. Even deFocused, Ali had wonderful ideas for the park. But now the man could love his daughter, too. *Trixia will be like this, as free as before the nightmare.*

Qiwi was talking to the Spiders when Ezr came down the path through the ruined forest. Kittens circled high above them, curiosity battling with arachnophobia.

'We want to do something new with the lake, some kind of free form, with its own special ecology.' The Spiders stood a little taller than Qiwi. In microgravity, they were no longer low, wide creatures. The natural tension in their limbs produced a Spider version of zero-gee crouch; their arms and legs extended long beneath them, making them tall and slender. The smallest one – probably Rhapsa Lighthill – was talking now. The hissing voice was almost musical compared to Belga Underville's voice.

'We'll watch, but I doubt if many will want to live here. We want to experiment with our own temps.' Broute Zinmin was translating, his tone happy and conversational. As of now, he might be the last of the Focused translators.

Qiwi grinned at the Spider. 'Yeah, I'm so curious about what you'll finally do. I—' She looked up, saw Ezr.

'Qiwi, can I talk to you?'

She was already moving toward him. 'A moment, Rhapsa, please?'

'Sure.' The Spiders tiptoed away, Zinmin continuing to spout questions at Ali Lin.

Ezr and Qiwi faced each other across thirty centimeters. 'Qiwi. They deFocused Trixia about two thousand seconds ago.'

The girl smiled, a bright gesture. There was still a childlike intensity about her. Somehow through it all, Qiwi had remained an open human being. And now she was at the center of their dealings with the Spiders, the engineer they sought over all others. Now he could truly see how bright her wits extended, from dynamics to bioscience to very sharp trading. Qiwi was very much like the spirit of the Qeng Ho.

'Is – is she going to be okay?' Qiwi's eyes were large, and her hands were tightly clasped in front of her.

'Yes! A little disorientation, Anne says, but her mind and personality are intact, and . . . and I can go see her later today.'

'Oh, Ezr! I'm so happy for her.' Qiwi's hands let go of each other, and reached out to his shoulders. Suddenly her face was very close and lips brushed across his cheek.

'I wanted to see you before I talked to her—'

'Yes?'

'I – I just wanted to thank you for saving my life, for saving us all.' *I want to thank you for giving me back my soul.* 'If Trixia and I can ever do anything to help you . . .'

And she was back at arm's length, and her smile seemed a little odd. 'You're welcome, Ezr. But . . . no thanks needed. I'm glad you have a happy ending.'

Ezr let go, and was already turning toward the guide ropes Ali had installed for his reconstruction work. 'It's more a happy beginning, Qiwi. All these years have been dead time, and now finally . . . Hey, I'll talk to you later!' He waved and pulled himself faster and faster, back toward the cavern's entrance.

Reynolt had converted the Attic grouproom into a recovery ward. Where zipheads had spent Watch after Watch Focused in Podmaster service, now they were being freed.

Anne stopped him in the corridor just outside the grouproom. 'Before you go in, keep in mind—'

Vinh was already edging around her. He stopped. 'You said she was coming out okay.'

'Yes. Total affect is normal. General cognition is as good as before; she has even retained her specialized knowledge. We're doing almost three thousand deFocus operations, more manumissions than any team in Emergent history. We're getting very good.' She frowned, but it was not the impatient gesture of her old Focus. This was a frown of pain. 'I – I wish we could redo the first ones. I think I could do better now.'

Ezr could see the pain, and he felt shame for his sudden joy: *So the delay has been for the best.* Trixia had had the benefit of all the earlier experience. Maybe she would have been okay anyway. After all, Reynolt had come through all right. But either way, things had worked out. And just beyond Reynolt, down the cool green corridor, was Trixia Bonsol, the princess now finally wakened. He slipped past Reynolt, flew down through the blueness.

Behind him Anne called, 'But, Ezr . . . Look, Pham wants to talk to you when you get done.'

'Okay. Okay.' But he wasn't really listening now. And then he was into the grouproom. Part of it was still open, and ten or fifteen of the chairs were even occupied, people sitting in little circles, talking. Heads turned in his direction, eyes filled with curiosity that would have been impossible before. Some of the faces were fearful. Many had the sad, lost look of Hunte Wen after he was deFocused. The Emergents among them had no one to go back to. They woke to freedom, but a lifetime and light-years from everything they had known.

Ezr smiled embarrassment and slipped past them. *Things have turned out right for Trixia and me, but these lost ones must be helped.*

The far side of the room had been partitioned into cubicles. Ezr flitted past the opened doors, stopped at the closed ones just long enough to read the patient labels. And finally . . . TRIXIA BONSOL. His headlong rush suddenly ended, and he realized he was wearing work clothes and his hair floated all spiky. Like some ziphead, he had ignored everything except his focus.

He brushed his hair down as best he could . . . and tapped on the light plastic of the privacy hatch.

'Come in.'

. . . 'Hi, Trixia.'

She floated in a hammock not much different from an ordinary bed. Medical instrumentation was a fine haze around her head. It didn't matter, Ezr had been expecting it. Anne had begun instrumenting the patients, using the data to guide the deFocusing, and afterward to monitor for stroke and infection.

It made it hard to hug someone as thoroughly as Ezr Vinh wanted. He floated near, looking into Trixia's face, lost in it. Trixia looked back – not around him, not impatient that he was blocking her data – but directly into his eyes. A faint, tremulous smile hovered on her lips.

'Ezr.'

And then she was in his arms, her hands reaching up to him. Her lips were soft and warm. He held her for a moment, gently encircling her within her hammock. Then he backed his head away, angling carefully around the medical gear. 'So many times I thought we'd never make it back. Do you remember all the times' – years of life time, literally – 'that I sat with you in your damn little cell?'

'Yes. You suffered far more than I. For me, it was a kind of dream, and time was a slippery thing. Everything outside of Focus was a blur. I could hear your words but they never seemed to matter.' Her hand came up to the side of his neck, gently stroking, a gesture from their real time together.

Ezr smiled. *We're talking. Really. Finally.* 'And now you're back, and we can live again. I have so many plans. I've had years to think on them, what we might do if Nau could be destroyed and you could be saved. After all the death, the mission is turning out to be a greater treasure than we ever imagined.' Great risks, great treasure. But the risks had been taken, the sacrifices made, and now – 'With our share of the mission bounty we . . . we can do anything. We could set up our own Great Family!' Vinh.23.7, Vinh-Bonsol, Bonsol.1, it didn't matter; it would be theirs.

Trixia was still smiling, but there was the beginning of tears in her eyes. She shook her head. 'Ezr, I don't—'

Vinh rushed on. 'Trixia, I know what you're going to say. If you don't want a Family – that's okay too.' In the years under Tomas Nau, there had been plenty of time to think things through, to see what sacrifices were really not sacrifices at all. He took a deep breath and said, 'Trixia, even if you want to go back to Triland . . . I'm willing to go there, to leave the Qeng Ho.' The Family wouldn't like it; he was no longer a junior heir. This expedition would make the Vinh.23 Family fabulously richer, but . . . he knew that Ezr Vinh had scarcely been responsible for that. 'You can be whatever you want, and we can still be together.'

He leaned closer, but this time she pushed him gently back. 'No, Ezr, that's not it. You and I, we're years older. I – it's been a long, long time since we were together.'

Ezr's voice came out high-pitched. 'It's been years for me! But for you? You said Focus is like a dream, where time didn't matter.'

'Not exactly. For some things, for the things at the center of my Focus, I probably remember the time better than you.'

'But—' She raised her hand, and he was silent.

'I had it easier than you. I was Focused, and something more, though I never consciously realized it and – thank goodness – neither did Brughel or

Tomas Nau. I had a world to escape to, a world that I could build out of my translations.'

Despite himself: 'I wondered. There was so much that seemed to be Dawn Age fantasy. So . . . that was fiction, not the real Spiders?'

'No. It was as close as we could come to the Spider viewpoint in a human mind. And if you read carefully, you get hints of where it can't be literally true . . . I think you guessed, Ezr. Arachna was my escape. As a translator, everything about being a Spider was within my Focus. Knowing what it was to be a free Spider consumed us. And when dear Sherkaner understood, even at the beginning when he thought we were machines, it was suddenly a world that accepted us, too.'

That was what had undone Nau, and saved them all, but – 'But now you are back, Trixia. This isn't the nightmare anymore. We can be together, better than we ever thought!'

She was shaking her head again. 'Don't you see, Ezr? We both have changed, and I have changed even more than you, even though I was—' She thought a second. '—even though I spent the years "ensorcelled." See? I do remember what you used to say to me. But Ezr, it's not the same anymore. I and the Spiders, we have a future—'

He tried to keep his voice in an even, persuasive tone, but what came out sounded half-panicked even to his own ears. *Dear Lord of Trade, I can't lose her now!* 'I know. You're still identifying with the Spiders. We're the aliens to you.'

She touched his shoulder. 'A little. During the first stages of the deFocus, it was like waking *into* a nightmare. I know how humans look to Arachnans. Pale, soft, grublike. There are pests and food animals like that. But we aren't as gruesome to them as the reverse.' She looked up at him and her smile was momentarily wider. 'The way you have to turn your head to see is endearing. You don't realize it, but any Arachnan with paternal fur on his back, and most females too, are enthralled when they talk to you close up.'

Like the dreams he had had groundside. In Trixia's mind, she was still part Spider. 'Trixia, look. I'll come and see you every day. Things will change. You'll get over this.'

'Oh, Ezr, Ezr.' Her tears floated into the air between them, but she was crying for him and not for herself or for the two of them. 'This *is* what I want to be, a translator, a bridge between you all and my new Family.'

A bridge. *She's not out of Focus.* Somehow Pham and Anne had frozen her partway between Focus and freedom. The realization was like a fist in the belly . . . nausea, followed by rage.

He caught Anne in her new office. 'Finish the job, Anne! The mindrot is still running Trixia.'

Reynolt's face seemed even paler than usual. He suddenly guessed that she'd been waiting for him. 'You know there's no way we can destroy the virus, Ezr. Tune them down, make them dormant, yes, but . . .' Her voice was tentative, utterly unlike the Anne Reynolt of times past.

'You know what I mean, Anne. *She's still in Focus.* She's still fixed on the Spiders, on her Focused mission.'

Anne was silent. She knew.

'Bring her all the way back, Anne.'

Reynolt's mouth twisted, as if stifling physical pain. 'The structures are so deep. She'd lose knowledge she's gained, probably her born language talent. She'd be like Hunte Wen.'

'But she would be *free*! She could learn new things, just like Hunte has.'

'I – I understand. Till yesterday, I thought we could bring it off. We were down to triggering the last restructuring – but Ezr, Trixia doesn't want us to take it any further!'

That was just too much, and suddenly Ezr was shouting. 'By damn, what do you expect? She's Focused!' He brought his voice down, but the words had the intensity of deadly threat. 'I know. You and Pham still need slaves, especially ones like Trixia. You never meant to free her.'

Reynolt's eyes grew wide and her features flushed bright red. It was something he had never seen in her, though Ritser Brughel had always turned that shade when he climbed into a towering rage. Her mouth opened and shut but no words came out.

There was a solid *thump* on the office wall, someone arriving in a hell of a hurry. An instant later, Pham came through the door. 'Anne, please. Let me handle this.' His voice was gentle. After a moment, Anne sucked in a breath. She nodded, seemed to be coughing. She came around her desk without saying anything, but Ezr noticed how fiercely she grasped Pham's hand.

Pham shut the door quietly behind her. When he turned back to Ezr, his expression was not gentle. He jerked a finger at the seat in front of Reynolt's desk. 'Tie down, mister.'

There was something about his voice that froze Ezr's rage, and forced him to sit down.

Pham settled himself by the other side of the desk. For a moment, he just stared at the younger man. It was strange. Pham Nuwen had always had a presence, but suddenly it felt like before this, he had never really turned it on. Finally, Pham said, 'A couple of years ago you gave me some straight talk. You forced me to see that I was wrong and that I must change.'

Ezr stared back coldly. 'Looks like I failed.' *You're in the slave business anyway.*

'You're wrong, son. You succeeded. Not many people have turned me around. Even Sura couldn't do it.' A strange sadness seemed to flicker across him, and he was silent for a moment. Then, 'You've done Anne a great disservice, Ezr. I think someday you'll want to apologize to her for it.'

'Not likely! You two have things so neatly rationalized. DeFocusing is just too expensive for you.'

'Um. You're right, it's expensive. It's been a near calamity. Under the Emergent system, the zipheads were supporting virtually all of our automation, their work mixed seamlessly with the real machines'. Worse, all the maintenance programming in the fleet has been done by Focused persons; we're left with millions of lines of incoherent junk. It will be some time before we have our old systems working well . . . But you know that Anne is the Frenkisch Orc, the "monster" in all the diamond friezes.'

'Y-yes.'

'Then you know that she would die to give the Focused freedom. It was her one nonnegotiable demand of me when she came back from Focus. It is her life's meaning.' He stopped, looked away from Ezr. 'You know the most evil thing about Focus? It's not that it's effective slavery, though Lord knows that puts it worse than most any other villainy. No, the greatest evil is that the rescuers become a type of killer themselves, and the original victims are mutilated a second time. Even Anne didn't fully understand that, now it's tearing her apart.'

'So because they want to be slaves, we leave them that way?'

'No! But a Focused person is a still a human being, not too different from certain rare types that have always existed. If they can live on their own, if they can clearly express their wishes – well at that point, you have to listen . . . Until about half a day ago, we thought everything was going to be okay with Trixia Bonsol. Anne had prevented the rot from doing a random runaway. Trixia wasn't going to be one of the psychotics or one of the vegetables. She was free of Emergent loyalty fixation. She could be talked to, evaluated, comforted. But she absolutely refuses to give up any more deep structure. Understanding the Spiders is the center of her life, and she wants it to stay that way.'

They sat in silence for a moment. The most terrible thing was, Pham might not be lying. He might not even be rationalizing. Maybe they were just talking about one of life's tragedies. In that case, Tomas Nau's evil would ride Ezr for the rest of his life. *Lord, this is hard.* And even though Reynolt's office was brightly lit, it reminded him of that dark time in the temp's park, right after Jimmy was murdered. Pham had been there too, and giving comfort that Ezr couldn't understand. Ezr wiped his face with the back of his hand. 'Okay. So Trixia is free. Then she's also free to change in the future.'

'Yes, of course. Human nature will always be beyond analysis.'

'I waited half my life for her. As long as it takes, I'll wait for her.'

Pham sighed. 'I'm just afraid you might do that.'

'Huh?'

'You're one of the more dedicated types I've met. And you have a talent for people. More than most, it was you who kept the Qeng Ho going in the face of Nau's thuggery.'

'No! I could never stand up to the man. All I could do was nibble around the edges, try to make things a little less hellish. And it still got people killed. I had no backbone, no admin ability; I was just an idiot that Nau could use to keep better people in line.'

Pham was shaking his head. 'You were the only person I trusted for conspiracy, Ezr.' He stopped abruptly, grinned. 'Of course, part of that was you were the only one clever enough to figure out who I was. You didn't bend, and you didn't break. You even jerked my chain . . . You know how far I go back.'

Ezr looked up. 'Of course. So?'

'I've seen a lot of hotshots.' A lopsided grin. 'Sura and I founded many of the Great Families in this end of Qeng Ho space. But you measure up, Ezr Vinh. I'm proud we are related.'

'Hmm.' Ezr didn't quite think that Pham would lie about something like this, but what he was saying was just too – extravagant – to be true.

But the other wasn't finished. 'There's a downside to your virtues, though. You had the patience to play a role for hundreds of Msecs. You stuck to your goals when lots of other people had started whole new lives. Now you're talking about waiting for Trixia however long *that* may take. And I believe you really would wait . . . forever. Ezr, have you ever thought, you don't always need the mindrot to get Focused? Some people can get fixated all by themselves. I should know! Their will is so strong – or their mind is so rigid – that they can exclude everything outside of the central fixation. That's what you needed during the years under Nau and Brughel. It was the thing that saved you, and helped carry the rest of the Qeng Ho along. But think now, recognize the problem. Don't throw your life away.'

Ezr swallowed. He remembered the Emergents' claims that society had always depended on people who 'didn't have a life.' But, 'Trixia Bonsol *is* a worthwhile goal, Pham.'

'Agreed. But you're talking about a very high price, waiting the rest of your life for something that may never happen.' He stopped, cocked his head to one side. 'It's a shame you *aren't* Focused with the Emergent bug; that might be easier to undo! You're so fixated on Trixia that you can't see what's going on around you, can't see the people that you are hurting, or the person who could love you.'

'Huh. Who?'

'Think, Ezr. Who engineered the rockpile stability system? Who persuaded Nau to loosen the leash? Who made Benny's parlor and Gonle's farms possible? And did it in spite of repeated mindscrubs? Who saved your butt when the crunch finally came?'

'Oh.' The word came out small and embarrassed. 'Qiwi . . . Qiwi is a good person.'

Real anger showed in Pham's face, the first time he'd seen that since the fall of Tomas Nau. 'Wake up, damn you!'

'I mean she's smart, and brave, and—'

'Yes, yes, yes! Fact is, she's a flaming genius in almost every department. I've only seen a couple like her in all my life.'

'I—'

'Ezr, I don't believe you're a moral idiot or I wouldn't be talking to you now, and I certainly wouldn't be telling you about Qiwi. But *wake up*! You should have seen it years ago – but you were too fixed on Trixia and your own guilt trips. And now Qiwi is waiting for you, but without much hope since she's so honorable she respects what you want for Trixia. Think about what she has been like, since we got rid of Nau.'

'. . . She's been into everything . . . I guess I see her every day.' He took a deep breath. This *was* like deFocus – seeing what you saw before, in a totally new way. It was true, he depended on Qiwi even more than he did Pham or Anne. But Qiwi had her own burdens. He remembered the look on her face when she greeted Floria Peres. He remembered her smile when she said she was happy for his happy ending. It was strange to feel shame for something you'd been totally unaware of a moment before. 'I'm so sorry . . . I just . . . never thought.'

Pham eased back. 'That's what I hoped, Ezr. You and I, we have this little problem: We're long on high principles and short on simple human understanding. It's something we have to work on. I praised you a second ago, and it wasn't a lie. But, truly, Qiwi is the wonder.'

For a moment, Ezr couldn't say anything. Someone was rearranging the furniture inside his soul. Trixia, the dream of half a lifetime, was *slipping away* . . . 'I've got to think.'

'Do so. But talk to Qiwi about it, okay? You're both hiding behind walls. You'd be amazed what can come from just talking straight out.'

Another idea that was like a new sun. *Just talk to Qiwi about it.* 'I will . . . I will!'

66

Time passed, but Arachna still had a long way to cool. The last dry hurricanes still blew fitfully through the mid-latitudes, edging ever nearer to the world's equator.

Their flyer had no wings, no jets or rockets. It came down along a ballistic arc, and slowed to a gentle touchdown on the naked rock of the altiplano.

Two space-suited figures emerged, one tall and slim, the other low, with limbs spreading in all directions.

Major Victory Lighthill tapped at the ground with the tips of her hands. 'Our bad luck that there is no snow cover here. No footprints to track.' She waved at the rocky hillside a few dozen yards away. There was snow there, caught in crevices, lying in the windshade of the moment. It glimmered ghostly reddish in the sunlight 'And where there is snow, the wind is always blowing it around. Can you feel the wind?'

Trixia Bonsol leaned into the breeze. She could hear it singing beyond her hood. She laughed. 'More than you. I've got to stand up in it with only two legs.'

They walked toward a hillside. Trixia had her net-link audio turned way down. This was a place and a time she wanted to experience firsthand, without interruptions. Yet the buzz of sound and the displays at the upper corners of her vision kept her in tenuous contact with what was going on in space, and at Princeton. In the real world beyond her hood display, the light was barely brighter than Trilander moonlight, and the only movement was the low scudding of the frost dust beneath the wind. 'And this is our best guess where Sherkaner left the helicopter?'

'It was, but there's no sign of him here. The log files are all jumbled. Daddy was controlling Rachner's aircraft through the net. Maybe he was going someplace special. More likely he was heading for random nowhere.' Trixia was not hearing Little Victory's true voice. Those sounds were downshifted and processed in Trixia's hood. The result was not a human speech and certainly not Spider sound, but Trixia could understand it as easily as Nese, and listening left her eyes and hands free for other things.

'But . . .' Trixia waved her arm at the tumbled land ahead of them. 'Sherkaner sounded rational to me, even at the end when everything was coming apart.' She spoke in the same intermediate language she listened to. The suit processor took care of the routine shifting of sounds to what Viki could hear.

'Wanderdeep can be like that,' said Victory. 'He had just lost Mom. Nizhnimor and Jaybert and the counterlurk center had just been blown out from under him.'

At the bottom of her view, Trixia saw the twitch in Viki's forearms. That was the equivalent of pursed lips, of a person confronting pain. In her years of Focus, she had always imagined herself talking to them head to head, on the same level. In free fall, that was more or less how things worked. But on the ground . . . well, human bodies extended upward, and Spider bodies sideways. If she didn't keep a downward view, she missed out on 'facial' expressions – and even worse, she might walk into her best friends.

'Thanks for coming with me, Trixia.' The cues in the intermediate language showed that Viki's voice was tremulous. 'I've been here and at Southmost before, officially, and with my brothers and sister. We promised each other we'd leave it alone for a while, but . . . I can't . . . and I can't face it alone either.'

Trixia waggled her hand in a way that meant comfort, understanding. 'I've wanted to come here ever since I came out of Focus. I feel like I'm a person finally, and being with you I feel I have a family.'

One of Viki's free arms reached up to rub Trixia's elbow. 'You were always a person to me. I can remember when Gokna died, when the General told us about you. Daddy showed us the logs, all the way back to when you first contacted him. Back then, he still thought you translators were some kind of A1. But you seemed to be a person to me, and I could tell you liked Dad very much.'

Trixia gestured a smile. 'Dear Sherk was so sure of impossible things like A1. For me, Focus was like a dream. My mission was to understand you Spiders perfectly, and the emotions just came along with it. It was the side effect Tomas Nau never expected.' Personhood as a Spider had come slowly, growing with each advance in language knowledge. The radio debate had been the turning point, where Trixia and Zinmin Broute and the others had actually transformed and taken sides in the perfection of their craft. *I'm so sorry, Xopi. We were Focused and suddenly you were the enemy. When we scrambled your MRI codes, we didn't really know we'd murdered you. Any of us could have been the Pedure translator, any of us could have been in your place.* And that had been when Trixia first reached down across the comm links and revealed herself to Sherkaner Underhill.

The smooth rock was broken now, rising into the hillside. Here there were patches of snow, and clefts shadowed from sun- and starlight. Victory and Trixia scrambled over the lower rocks of the hill, and peered into the shadows. This wasn't a serious search; it was more an act of reverence. Air and orbit surveys had been completed many days before.

'Do – do you think we'll ever find him, Victory?' During most of her years of Focus, Sherkaner Underhill had been the center of Trixia Bonsol's universe. She'd been scarcely aware of Anne Reynolt or Ezr's hundreds of faithful visits, but Sherkaner Underhill had been real. She remembered the old cobber who needed a guide-bug to keep from walking in circles. How could he be gone?

Victory was silent for a moment. She was several meters up the hillside, poking around beneath an overhang. Like all of her race, she was more than humanly good at rock climbing. 'Yes, eventually. We know he's not on the surface. Maybe . . . I think Mobiy must have lucked out, found a hole more than a few yards deep. But even that wouldn't be a viable deepness; Dad's body would dry to death in a short time.' She pulled out from under the rock. 'It's funny. When the Plan was coming apart, I thought it was Mom we had lost and Dad we could save. But now . . . you know the humans just made new sonograms of the bottom of Southmost? The Kindred nukes crushed Parliament Hall and the upper layers. Below that there are millions of tons of fractured bedrock – but there is open space, what's left of the Southlanders' superdeepness. If Mother and Hrunk made it alive to one of those . . .'

Trixia frowned; she had seen the news. 'But the report says it's too dangerous to dig, that it would just crush the open spaces.' And when the

New Sun came, those millions of tons of rock would surely collapse upon the deepness.

'Ah, but we have time to plan. We'll improve on the humans' digging technology. Maybe we can come in from miles out and tunnel really deep, maintaining the balance with cavorite. Someday before the next New Sun, we'll know what's in those superdeeps. And if Mother and Hrunk are down there, we'll rescue them.'

They walked northward, around the hillock. Even if this were the hill where Sherkaner left Thract, they were well away from where Rachner could have landed. Still, Victory peeped into every shadow.

Trixia couldn't keep up. She straightened and looked away from the hillside. The sky above the southern horizon glowed, as if over a city. And it almost was. The old missile fields were gone, but now the world had a better use for the altiplano. Cavorite mines. Companies from all over the waking world had descended on it. From orbit, you could see the open pit mines stretching from the original Kindred operation, a thousand miles across the wasteland. A million Spiders worked there now. Even if they never figured out how to synthesize the magic substance, cavorite would revolutionize local spaceflight, partly making up for the lack of other bodies in this solar system.

Victory seemed to notice that Trixia's pace had faltered. The Spider found a rounded knob of rock, shaded from the wind, and settled on it. Trixia sat down beside her, pleased that they could be on the same level. Across the plains to the south, they could see hundreds of hillocks, any one of which might mark Sherkaner's final rest. But in the sky glow beyond the horizon, tiny dots of light drifted slowly upward, antigrav freighters hauling mass into space. In all human histories, antigravity had been one of the Failed Dreams. And here it was.

Viki didn't speak for a time. A human who didn't know the Spiders might think she was asleep. But Trixia could see the telltale movements of eating hands, and she heard untranslated keening. Every so often Viki would be like this; every so often she had to shed the image that she projected to her team and Belga Underville and the aliens from space. Little Victory had done very well, at least as well as her mother could have done, Trixia was sure. She had managed the final triumph of her parents' Great Lurk. In her own huds, Trixia could see a dozen calls pending for Major Lighthill. An hour or two alone, that was all Victory could spare these days. Outside of Brent, Trixia was probably the only person who knew the doubts that lived inside Victory Lighthill.

OnOff climbed into the sky, turning the shadows across the tumbled lands. This was the warmest High Equatoria would be for the next two hundred years, yet the best that OnOff could do was raise a soft haze of sublimation.

'I hope for the best, Trixia. The General and Dad, they were so very clever. They can't both be dead. But they – and I – had to do so many hard things. People who trusted us died.'

'It was a war, Victory. Against Pedure, against the Emergents.' That was what Trixia told herself now, when she thought about Xopi Reung.

'Yeah. And the ones who survived are doing well. Even Rachner Thract. He's never coming back to the King's Service. He feels betrayed. He *was* betrayed. But he's up there with Jirlib and Didi now' – she jerked a hand in the direction of L1 – 'becoming a kind of Spiderish Qeng Ho.' She was quiet, then abruptly slapped at the rock of her perch. Trixia could hear that her real voice was angry, defensive. 'Damn it, Mother was a good general! I could never have done what she did; there's too much of Daddy in me. And in the early years it worked; his genius and hers multiplied together. But it got harder and harder to disguise the counterlurk. Videomancy was a great cover, it let us have independent hardware and a covert data stream right under the humans' snouts. But if there were even *one* slip, if the humans ever guessed, they could kill us all. That corroded Mom's heart.'

Her eating hands fluttered aimlessly and there was a choked hissing sound. Victory was weeping. 'I just hope she told Hrunkner. He was the most loyal friend we ever had. He loved us even though he thought we were a perversion. But Mother just could not accept that. She wanted too much from Uncle Hrunk, and when he couldn't change she—'

Trixia slid her arm across the other's midback. It was the closest a human could come to giving a multi-arm hug.

'You know how much Daddy wanted to tell Hrunk about the counterlurk. That last time in Princeton, Daddy and I thought we could manage it, that Mother would go along. But no. The General was so . . . unforgiving. In the end . . . well, she wanted Hrunk along on her trip to Southmost. If she trusted him with that, surely she would tell him the rest. Wouldn't she? She'd tell him that it was not all in vain.'

Epilogue

SEVEN YEARS, LATER –

The Spiders' world had a moon; the L1 rockpile had been coaxed into a synchronous orbit on Princeton's longitude. By the standards of most habitable worlds, it was a pitiful moon, barely visible from the ground. Forty thousand kilometers out, the lump of diamonds and ice glinted dimly in the light of the stars and the sun. Yet it reminded half the world that the universe was not what they had thought.

Fore and aft of the rockpile stretched a string of tiny stars, beads that grew brighter year by year: the Spiders' temps and factories. In the early years, they were the most primitive structures ever to fly in space, cheap and overbuilt and overcrowed, hoisted on cavorite wings. But the Spiders learned fast and well . . .

There had been state dinners in the Arachnan Grand Temp before. The King himself had ascended to orbit for the departure of the fleet to Triland. That had been four starships, refurbished by the new capital industries of his empire and the entire world. And that fleet had carried not just Qeng Ho and Trilanders and former Emergents. Two hundred Spiders had been aboard, led by Jiriib Lighthill and Rachner Thract. They carried first implementations of the improved ramdrives and coldsleep equipment. More important, they carried the keys for the encrypted knowledge beamed earlier across the light-years to Triland and Canberra.

For that departure, nearly ten thousand Spiders had come into space, the King on one of the first all-Arachnan ferries, and that 'dinner' had stretched across more than 300Ksec. Since that time, there had been more Spiders in near Arachna space than humans.

To Pham Nuwen, that was only fitting. Customer civilizations should dominate the territory around their planets. Hell, to the Qeng Ho, it was the locals' most important function – to be havens where ships could be rebuilt and refurnished, to be the markets that made trekking across interstellar distances a profitable thing.

For this second departure, the Grand Temp was almost as crowded as at the Triland Farewell, but the actual dinner was much smaller, ten or fifteen people. Pham knew that Ezr and Qiwi and Trixia and Vila had engineered this affair to be small enough that people could talk and be heard. This might be the last time so many of the surviving players might ever see each other in one place.

The ballroom of the Arachnan Grand Temp was something new in the universe. The Spiders had been in space only 200Msec now, scarcely seven of their years. The ballroom was their first attempt at grandeur in free fall. They weren't up to the bioengineering of Qeng Ho parks. In fact, most Spiders hadn't yet realized that for starfarers, a living park is the greatest symbol of power and ability in space. Instead, the King's designers had borrowed from Qeng Ho inorganic construction and tried to adapt their own architectural traditions to free fall. Doubtless, within another century they would regard the effort as laughable. Or maybe the mistakes would become part of tradition:

The outer wall was a tesselation of hundreds of transparent plates, held in a grid of titanium. Some were diamond, some were quartz, some were almost opaque to Pham's eyes. The Spiders still preferred direct views. Video wallpaper and human display technologies didn't come close to matching the range of their vision. The polyhedral surface swept outward to form a bubble fifty meters across. At its base the Spider designers had built a terraced mound, rising to the dining tables at the top. The slope was gentle by Arachna standards, with broad sweeping stairs. To human eyes, the mound was a cliff-walled pinnacle and the stairs were strange, broad ladders. But the overall effect was – for humans or Spiders – that wherever you were sitting around the dining table, you could look out on half the sky. The Grand Temp was a long structure, tidally stabilized, and the ballroom was on the Arachna-facing end. To someone looking straight up, the Spiders' world filled much of the view. To someone looking off to the side, the rockpile and human temps were an orderly jumble, every year longer than before. In the other direction, you could see the Royal Shipyards. At this distance, the Yards were an undistinguished cluster of lights, flickering now and then with tiny flashes. The Spiders were building the tools to build the tools. In another year or so they would lay the spine for their first ramscoop vessel.

Anne and Pham arrived at precisely the appointed time. Small this banquet might be, but the hosts had specified formality. They floated up past tier after tier of the mound, touching the stairs here and there to guide themselves to the circular table at the top. The hosts were already present, Trixia and Viki, Qiwi and Ezr, as were all the other guests, both Arachnan and human. Anne and Pham were last to arrive, the guests of Farewell.

After they were settled, Spider attendants came out from the base of the mound, carrying a mix of Spider and human dishes. The two races could actually eat together, even if each found the other's food mostly grotesque.

They ate the welcoming appetizers in the Spider-traditional silence. Then Trixia Bonsol rose from her place among the Spiders and made a set speech as stately as anything at Jirlib's Farewell. Pham groaned to himself. Except for Belga Underville, all here were close friends. He knew they were scarcely more formal than himself. Yet there was a sadness in this occasion and it seemed greater than even a normal leavetaking should be. He sneaked a look around the table. So solemn, the humans in free-fall formal dress that went back at least a thousand years. But it was not like they had to follow diplomatic niceties here. Underville was probably the prickliest creature here, but even she wasn't big on formalities. Now if someone didn't speak up, they might go the whole dinner without really talking.

So when Trixia finished and sat down, Pham gently dumped a half-liter of wine into the air above his place at the table. The dark red liquid wobbled back and forth upon itself, an embarrassing spill that would be even more embarrassing depending on who it splashed onto. Pham stuck his finger into the hobbling wetness, and wiggled it just so. The blob stretched out, braided itself with its own surface tension. He definitely had their attention now, the Spiders even more than the humans. Pham waved off an attendant who floated close with a vacuum napkin. He grinned at his audience. 'Neat trick, isn't it?'

Qiwi leaned forward, to look across at him. 'It'll be a neater trick if you can land that thing clean.' She was also grinning. 'I should know; my daughter plays with her food, too.'

'Yes. Well, I'll keep it in one piece as long as I can.' His hand formed the spinning braid back into a wobbling sphere. So far he hadn't even stained the lace on his cuffs. Qiwi was watching with intent, professional interest. This was the sort of trick she had once done with billion-tonne rocks. He didn't doubt that little Kira Vinh-Lisolet played with her food; Qiwi probably encouraged the little devil.

He left the red bauble floating above his place, and waved for the attendants to bring the next course. 'I'll show you some other tricks later; just watch me.'

Victory Lighthill rose a little from her perch. Her mouth hands modulated her voice into a sad chirping. 'Tricks . . . long sad gone . . . drexip.' At least that's what Pham thought she said. Even after all this time – even with the downshifter gadget to make all the phonemes audible – Spidertalk was harder than any human language he knew of. Sitting next to Lighthill, Trixia smiled and gave her own translation. 'We will miss your tricks, Magician.' Her voice held the same sadness that he recognized in the Spider's sounds. *Damn. They make this sound like a wake.*

So Pham smiled brightly and pretended to miss the point. 'Yes. In less than a megasecond, Anne and I will be gone.' Along with a thousand others, Emergents, exFocused, even some Qeng Ho. Three starships and a thousand crew. 'When we return, perhaps two centuries will have passed. But hey! There are often longer partings among the Qeng Ho. I know there are ships a-building in your yards.' He waved at the flickering in the far sky behind Victory Lighthill. 'Many of you will be 'faring, too. Very likely some of us will meet again – and when we do we'll have new stories to exchange, just like Qeng Ho and people from starfaring worlds always have.'

Ezr Vinh was nodding. 'Yes, there will be future times, even if we don't know quite how we will meet, or where. But for many of us this will be the last meeting.' Ezr didn't quite meet his eye. *At bottom, even Ezr doubts*. And Ezr had given half his mission bounty to help Pham and Anne prepare.

But Qiwi laid her hand on Ezr's shoulder. 'I say we set up some meeting marks, just like the Great Families do.' A time and a place, and a space of life span passed. She looked across at Anne and smiled. Now Qiwi was a mother as well as an engineer. Most times she seemed to be the happiest person around. But Pham still saw a shadow sometimes, perhaps when she thought of her own mother, the other Kira. Qiwi *approved* this sending to Balacrea. Hell, he was sure she would be aboard if not for Ezr, and her children, and the new world she was creating here. Ezr had learned much about managing people, even more since he was truly the Fleet Manager for all the humans. But Qiwi's genius was the framework that Ezr depended on. She was the person who could figure out just what technology the Spiders would value most. If not for the deals she had worked out, the Spiders' shipyard would still be a dream. Ezr had always thought of himself as a failed younger son. *I wonder if he and Qiwi really understand what they are creating*. They had children, and so had Jau and Rita, and many others. Gonle and Benny had built a nursery for all the new little ones, a place where kids and cobblies played while their parents worked together. The human-Spider enterprise grew every year. Like Sura Vinh long ago, Qiwi and Ezr might not fare much themselves, but this end of Qeng Ho space was due for an explosion of light, a nascence that would dwarf Canberra and Namqem.

An explosion of light. Yes! 'We'll set a marker, then! The next New Sun – or maybe a few Msecs after, since I seem to remember things being a bit unpleasant right when the sun lights up.' About two centuries. *That will fit well with my other plans.*

Victory via Trixia; 'Yes, just after the next Brightness. Here in the Grand Temp – however grander it may be.' A gentle laugh. 'I'll make a note not to be asleep or light-years away.'

'Agreed.' 'Agreed!' The voices went round the table.

Belga Underville buzzed and hissed, and as usual Pham didn't understand a thing she said except that her tone was full of truculent incredulity. Fortunately, as the King's chief of Intelligence, she rated a full-time translator. Zinmin Broute sat beside her, listening to her with a faint smile. Broute actually seemed to like the old biddy. When she finished, he wiped the smile from his face and put on a good glower. 'This is rank foolishness, or human insanity I don't yet understand. You have three ships, and with them you intend to bring down the Emergent empire? But for the last seven years, you have been saying that we Spiders have nothing to fear from outside invasion, that a planetary civilization with high technology can always mount a successful defense. The Emergents must have thousands of military vessels in their home territories, yet you talk of overthrowing them. Have you been lying to us, or are you just very wishful thinkers?'

Victory Lighthill buzzed a question, put so simply and clearly that Trixia didn't have to translate. 'But, maybe . . . you get help . . . from far Qeng Ho?'

'No,' said Ezr. 'I . . . I'll tell you frankly, Qeng Ho don't like to fight. It's much easier just to let tyrannies alone. "Let them trade with themselves," as the old saying goes.'

Anne Reynolt had been quiet through all this. Now she said, 'It's okay, Ezr. You *have* helped us . . .' She turned to Belga Underville. 'Madame General, someone has to do this. The Emergents and Focus are something new. Leave them alone and they will just grow stronger – and someday they'll come to eat you.'

Incredulity was patent in the flick of Underville's longest arms. 'Yes, more contradictions. Over the last years you have persuaded us to go beyond trade in helping to arm and outfit you.' A human speaker might have cast a look in Victory Lighthill's direction; Victory had the ear of the King in this. 'But what does it serve that you commit suicide? That is how I see the odds.'

Anne smiled, but Pham could tell the questions made her tense. Belga had pounded on these questions in more official forums, and it was unlikely she would receive any satisfaction here. The questions haunted Anne as well. But Belga did not understand that, for Anne Reynolt, this mission gave better odds than she had ever had. 'Not suicide, Madame General. We have special advantages, and Pham and I know how to use them.' She put her hand on Pham's. 'I employ one of the few commanders in human histories who has succeeded at such a thing.'

Yeah, the Strentmannian thing was similar. God help me. No one said anything for a moment. The half-liter of wine had drifted upward. Pham poked his finger into its center of rotation and slid it gently back in front of where he sat. 'We have advantages more concrete than my fearless leadership. Anne knows as much as any Podmaster about how the inner system works.' And their little fleet would carry some surprising hardware, the first products of human/Spider new technology. But that wasn't the fleet's greatest strength. The crews of their three ships were mostly exFocused who understood the mechanisms of the Emergents' automation and who wanted as much as Anne to overthrow it. There were even a few of the original unFocused Emergents. As he spoke, Pham saw Jau Xin watching him intently – and Rita Liao watching Jau. They would come if they didn't have their three little ones. And even now, there was a chance. Pham still had four days to persuade them. Xin had been Pilot Manager for Nau's uncle before the voyage to Arachna. And the latest comm from Balacrea showed the Nau clique was back at the top of the heap.

Pham looked from face to face as he described the plans. Ezr and Qiwi, Trixia and Victory, certainly Jau and Rita: *They don't really think this is a wake. They understand we have a good chance, but they worry for us.* 'And we've been studying Nau's records and the transmissions that he received – that we're still receiving from Balacrea. We've spoofed them into thinking the Emergents won here. We plan on being able to get in-system before they realize that we aren't friendly. We understand a *lot* about the internal factions at the top of their society. All together—' All together, it might not be something he should undertake. But Anne was right about Focus, and Anne wanted this more than anything. And afterward, well, there was *his* great project and having Anne in on that would be worth all the risks. 'All together, we have a chance. It will be a gamble, an adventure. I wanted to call our flagship the *Wild Goose*, but Anne wouldn't let me.'

'Hah!' said Anne. 'I think *Emergents' Reward* is a much more proper name. After we win, *then* you can name it the *Wild Goose!*'

The first course of the banquet was already arriving, and Pham didn't have a chance to answer her back. Instead, he showed the others that you really can tuck a half-liter of wine back into a drinking bulb without creating any smaller droplets. He grinned to himself. Even the other Qeng Ho hadn't seen that. It was just one of the advantages of being well traveled.

The banquet lasted a number of Ksecs. They had time to talk of many things, to remember where they had been and the friends who had died in making the present day. But the greatest surprise didn't come until right at the end, when Anne pointed out something that none of the Spiders, not even Victory Lighthill, had guessed at.

Anne had relaxed as the dinner progressed. Pham knew she still was uneasy with groups of people. She could *act* almost any role, but inside there was a shyness that didn't come out except when she was being open. She had learned to trust these people; as long as the conversation stayed clear of what she must do with the Emergency, she could genuinely enjoy herself. And Anne Reynolt still had many things that her friends here needed. More than anyone, she understood the exFocused. Pham listened to her chat with Trixia Bonsol and Victory Lighthill, suggesting ways they might get even more translation services. *From the first moment I saw you, you seemed very special.* The flaming red hair, the pale, almost pink skin. Such a contrast to his own black hair and smoky complexion. On this side of Human Space, her looks were rare indeed. But then he had learned what was behind those looks, the brains, the courage . . . Following her to Balacrea would be worth it even if there were no plans for afterward.

After-dinner drinks were floated around to the humans. The Spider equivalent were little black balls to puncture and suck and spit into elaborate cuspidors.

Pham found himself toasting to the success of each group's endeavor – and the meeting they had set for two centuries later.

Ezr Vinh leaned around Qiwi to look at him. 'And after our remeeting? After you free Balacrea and Frenk? What then? When will you finally tell us about that?'

Anne smiled at Pham. 'Yes, tell them about your wild-goose chase.'

'Hmmpf.' Pham wasn't entirely pretending embarrassment. Except with Anne, he hadn't talked about this. Maybe it was because the scheme was grandiose even compared with his grandiose scheming of the past. '. . . Okay. You know why we came to Arachna: the mystery of the OnOff star and the existence of intelligent life here. We spent forty years with Tomas Nau's boot on our necks, but still we learned amazing things.'

Ezr: 'True. In one single place, Humankind has never found so many different kinds of wonderful things.'

'We humans thought we knew what was impossible. Only a few nut cases still wondered otherwise, mainly astronomers watching far enigmas. Well, OnOff was the first of those that we've seen close up. And look at what we found: a stellar physics we still don't properly understand; cavorite, which we understand even less—'

Pham broke off, noticing the look in Qiwi's eyes. She was remembering something from a nightmare. She looked away, but Pham didn't continue, and after a moment she spoke very softly. 'Tomas Nau used to talk like this. Tomas was an evil man, but—' But evil men, the most dangerous of them, often have sharp ideas. She swallowed, and continued more firmly, 'I remember when the Focused ran DNA analysis on the ocean ice we had brought up. The variety – it was greater than a thousand worlds. The analysts thought it was caused by the variety of life niches on Arachna. Tomas . . . Tomas thought instead that there was so much variety because once, very long ago, Arachna had been a crossroads.'

Ezr took Qiwi's hand. 'Not just Tomas Nau. We've all wondered about these things. There's way too much crystal carbon around – the diamond forams, the rockpile. Somebody's computers? But the forams are too small, and our L1 mountains are too big . . . and they're, all just dead stone how.'

From across the table, Jau Xin said, 'Maybe not quite. There *is* cavorite.'

Belga Underville rasped something that did not sound impressed; Victory was buzzing laughter. After a moment, Zinmin's translation came. 'So the Distorts of Khelm have a new believer, except that now our world is a junkyard and we Spiders are evolved from the gods' garbage-vermin. If this is true, where is the rest of the super-empire?'

'I . . . I don't know. Remember this was fifty to one hundred million years ago. Maybe they had a war. One of the easiest explanations for your solar system is that it was a war zone, with a sun destroyed, and all planets but one volatilized.' And that one survivor protected by some great magic. 'Or maybe the empire grew into something else, or is leaving us to develop at our own pace.' Some of the possibilities sounded very foolish when he said them out loud.

Underville's eating hands spread in a gesture that Pham recognized as a doubting smile. 'You do sound like Khelm! But see, your theory "explains" all sorts of things without helping to do anything, much less providing tests for itself.'

Gonle Fong jabbed at the air with her hand, a Spiderish gesture unconsciously adopted. 'So what's to disagree? "Arachna was a place where once all the Failed Dreams were true." Fine. It's a simple, unifying assumption. At the same time, we live in the here and now, a few hundred light-years, a few thousand years. Whatever the explanation, there is a lifetime of profit to be made just playing with what we see on Arachna now!'

Pham nodded politely. 'Yes. A good Qeng Ho attitude. But, Gonle – I was born in a civilization of castles and cannon. I've lived a long time – not counting coldsleep – and I've seen a lot. Since the Dawn Age, we humans have learned a little here, a little there – but mainly we've learned of limits. Planetary civilizations rise and fall. At the height they're wonderful things, but there is so much darkness.' Castles and cannon, and worse. 'And even the Qeng Ho – we survive and prosper, but we've found limits that we can only edge toward, like lightspeed itself. I broke myself on those limits at Brisgo Gap. When I learned about Focus, I thought it might be the way to end the darkness between civilizations. I was wrong.' He looked into Anne's eyes. 'So I gave up my dream, the dream of my whole life . . . and then I looked around. Here at Arachna, we've finally found something from *outside* all our limits. It's a tiny glimpse, shreds and dregs of brightest glory. Gonle, there are planning horizons and there are planning horizons . . . Ezr asked me what I was going to do after we bring down the Emergents, after we all meet again. Well, just this: I'm going whence Arachna came.'

Trixia's translation of his words rattled on a moment longer, and then there was absolute silence all around the table. Ezr sat transfixed. Pham had kept this between himself and Anne; considering all else that was happening, it had been an easy secret to keep. But Ezr Vinh had lived his whole life admiring the Dawn Age and the Failed Dreams, and now he saw how they might yet be attained. The boy stared for a moment, enraptured. Then critical thought came awake again. His words weren't complaints; he *wanted* Pham's plan to succeed, but—

'But what bearing will you take? And—'

'What bearing? That's the easy question, though we'll have a couple of centuries to think it over. But look, Humankind has been staring at the stars with high technology for thousands of years. At one time or another, almost every Customer civilization has mounted arrays of hundred-meter mirrors, and undertaken all the other clever ways to snoop on things far away. We see some far enigmas. Here and there across this galaxy we see ramscoops and ancient radio transmissions.'

'So if there were anything more, we would have seen it,' said Ezr, but he clearly knew what was coming. The arguments were ancient history.

'Only if it's a place we can look. But parts of the galactic core are plenty shrouded. If our supercivilization doesn't use radio, if they have something better than ramscoops . . . down by the core is the one place they might have escaped our detection.' And OnOff's eccentric orbit had at least passed through those unseen depths.

'Okay, Pham. I agree, it all fits. But you're talking about thirty thousand light-years to the core, almost that far to the umbral clouds.'

Gonle: 'That's a hundred times farther than anything the Qeng Ho have tried. Without depot civilizations in between, your ramscoops will fail in less than a thousand years. We can dream of such a mission, but it's totally beyond our ability.'

Pham grinned at them all: 'It's totally beyond our ability *now*.'

'That's what I said! It's always been beyond us.'

But the light was beginning to come on in Ezr's eyes. 'Gonle, he means that it may not be beyond us in the future.'

'*Yes!*' Pham leaned forward, wondering how many of them he could capture in this dream. 'Do a little mind experiment. Put yourself back in the Dawn Age. Back then, for a few brief centuries, people *expected* things to become radically improved in the future. With Arachna, you will bring a little bit of that spirit back. Maybe you don't believe it now. You don't see the civilization that you are building. Ezr and Qiwi, you're founding a Great Family that will outshine any in Qeng Ho history. Trixia and Victory and all the Spiders will be the greatest thing that ever happened to our business. And you're just beginning to understand the contradictions of Arachna. You're right; today, talk of 'faring toward the core is like a child wading in the surf and talking of crossing an ocean. But I'll lay you a wager: By the next Bright Time, you'll have the technology I need.'

He looked at Anne beside him. She smiled back, a grin that was both happy and a little mocking. 'Anne and I and those on our fleet of three intend to take down the Emergent system. If we succeed there – *when* we succeed – what's left will still be a high-tech civilization. We'll make a larger fleet, at least a fleet of twenty. And Anne will let me rename her flagship the *Wild Goose*. And we will return here and outfit to go . . . a-searching.' And would Anne really come with him then? She said she would. Would tearing down the Emergents' tyranny lift the *geas* that drove her? Maybe not. Winning would leave whole worlds like the deFocus ward in Hammerfest's Attic. Maybe she would find it impossible to leave the people she had rescued. What then? *I don't know.* Once upon a time, he was very good at being alone. Now, *how strangely I have changed.*

Anne's smile was gentle now. She squeezed his hand and nodded at the pact he had just described. Pham glanced from face to face: Qiwi looked stunned. Ezr looked like someone who desperately wanted to believe, but had more than a life-full of other endeavors to distract him. As for the Spiders, their aspects ranged from Underville's truculent 'show me' to—

Throughout his speech, Victory Lighthill had sat still and silent, even her eating hands motionless. Now she spoke, a burring warble, soft and sad and wondering, that needed Trixia to translate the words: 'Daddy would have loved this plan.'

'Yes.' Pham's voice caught. Underhill had been a genius and a dreamer, straight out of the Dawn Age. Pham had long since read Trixia's 'video-mancy diaries,' the story of Underhill's counterlurk. The cobber had dug deep into the Emergents' automation, sometimes so deep that the Focused Anne Reynolt had noticed the tampering and thought it evidence of human conspiracy. At the end, Underhill knew what Focus was; he knew the humans didn't have AI or any technology enormously beyond his own. Sherkaner Underhill must have been very disappointed to learn the limits of progress.

Beside him, Anne started to nod, hesitated. And that was when she surprised them all, herself included, but the Spiders most of all. She cocked her head, and a slow smile started across her face. 'And what makes you think he didn't survive? He had as much information as any of us – and a good bit more imagination. What makes you think this isn't *his* plan, too?'

'Anne, I've read the diaries. If he were alive, he'd be here.'

She shook her head. 'I wonder. Wanderdeep is something we humans aren't built to understand, and Sherkaner thought sure that Smith was dead. But Sherkaner Underhill confounded both humans and Spiders more than once. He took Spiderness in unthought directions – he saw the deepness in the sky. I think he's down there somewhere, and he intends to outlast all the mysteries.'

'It could be . . . it could be.' The words, ultimately Trixia's or Victory's, Pham could not tell, were spoken in soft awe. 'We don't really know where he landed on the altiplano. If it was something he had scouted out before, he would have a chance.'

Pham looked outward, at Arachna. The planet spread across thirty degrees, a vast, black pearl. Traceries of gold and silver gleamed all across the continent into the southern hemisphere, and across the faint luster of the eastern sea. And yet, there were still large areas of unrelieved dark, protected lands that would remain still and cold until the end of the Dark. Pham felt a sudden thrill of understanding. *Yes.* Somewhere down there the old Spider might still sleep, waiting for his lady lost . . . and beginning on his greatest Lurk of all.

So high, so low, so many things to know.

The End

ACKNOWLEDGMENTS
A Fire Upon The Deep

I am grateful for the advice and help of: Jeff Allen, Robert Cademy, John Carroll, Howard L. Davidson, Michael Gannis, Gordon Garb, Corky Hansen, Dianne L. Hansen, Sharon Jarvis, Judy Lazar, and Joan D. Vinge.

I am very grateful to James R. Frenkel for the wonderful job of editing he has done with this book.

Thanks to Poul Anderson for the quote that I use as the motto of the Qeng Ho.

During the summer of 1988 I visited Norway. Many things I saw there influenced the writing of this story. I am very grateful to: Johannes Berg and Heidi Lyshol and the Aniara Society for showing me Oslo and for wonderful hospitality; the organizers of the Arctic '88 distributed systems course at the University of Tromsøy, in particular Dag Johansen. As for Tromsøy, and the surrounding lands: I had not dreamed that so pleasant and beautiful a place could exist in the arctic.

Science fiction has imagined many alien creatures; this is one of the genre's great charms. I don't know what in particular inspired me to make the Riders in this novel, but I do know that Robert Abernathy wrote about a similar race in his short story, 'Junior' (*Galaxy*, January 1956). 'Junior' is a beautiful commentary on the spirit of life.

V.V.

ACKNOWLEDGMENTS
A Deepness In The Sky

I am grateful for the advice and help of: Robert Cademy, John Carroll, Howard L. Davidson, Bob Fleming, Leonard Foner, Michael Gannis, Jay R. Hill, Eric Hughes, Sharon Jarvis, Yoji Kondo, Cherie Kushner, Tim May, Keith Mayers, Mary Q. Smith, and Joan D. Vinge.

I am very grateful to James Frenkel for the wonderful job of editing he has done with this book and for his timely insight on problems with the earlier drafts.